ALSO BY E L JAMES

MW01092899

FREED

E L James

Bloom books

Copyright © 2012, 2021 by Fifty Shades Ltd
Cover and internal design © 2021 by Sourcebooks
Cover design by Erika Mitchell and Brittany Vibbert/Sourcebooks
Cover photographs © Erika Mitchell
Heart photography by Andrew Melzer/Sourcebooks

Sourcebooks and the colophon are registered trademarks of Sourcebooks. Bloom Books is a trademark of Sourcebooks.

All rights reserved. No part of this book may be reproduced in any form or by any electronic or mechanical means including information storage and retrieval systems—except in the case of brief quotations embodied in critical articles or reviews—without permission in writing from its publisher, Sourcebooks.

The characters and events portrayed in this book are fictitious or are used fictitiously. Any similarity to real persons, living or dead, is purely coincidental and not intended by the author.

Portions of this book, including significant portions of the dialogue and e-mail exchanges, have previously appeared in the author's prior works.

All brand names and product names used in this book are trademarks, registered trademarks, or trade names of their respective holders. Sourcebooks is not associated with any product or vendor in this book.

Published by Bloom Books, an imprint of Sourcebooks
P.O. Box 4410, Naperville, Illinois 60567-4410
(630) 961-3900
sourcebooks.com

Library of Congress Cataloging-in-Publication Data is on file with the publisher.

Printed and bound in the United States of America.
WOZ 10 9 8 7 6 5 4 3 2 1

For Eva and Sue.
Thank you, thank you, thank you
for all that you do.

And for Catherine.
We are a woman down.

SUNDAY, JUNE 19, 2011

We lie in postcoital bliss beneath pink paper lanterns, meadow flowers, and fairy lights that twinkle in the rafters. As my breathing slows, I hold Anastasia close. She's sprawled all over me, her cheek against my chest, her hand resting on my racing heart. The darkness is absent, driven out by my dream catcher…my fiancée. My love. My light.

Could I be happier than I am right now?

I commit the scene to memory: the boathouse, the soothing rhythm of the lapping waters, the flora, the lights. Closing my eyes, I memorize the feel of the woman in my arms, her weight on top of me, the slow rise and fall of her back as she breathes, her legs entwined with mine. The scent of her hair fills my nostrils soothing all my corners and jagged edges. This is my happy place. Dr. Flynn would be proud. This beautiful woman has consented to be mine. In every way. Again.

"Can we marry tomorrow?" I whisper near her ear.

"Hmm." The sound in her throat reverberates with a soft strum across my skin.

"Is that a yes?"

"Hmm."

"A no?"

"Hmm."

I grin. She's spent. "Miss Steele, are you incoherent?" I sense her answering smile and my joy erupts in a laugh, as I tighten my arms around her and kiss her hair. "Vegas, tomorrow, it is then." She raises her head, eyes half closed in the soft light from the lanterns—she looks sleepy yet sated.

"I don't think my parents would be very happy with that." She lowers her head and I skim my fingertips across her naked back, enjoying the warmth of her sleek skin.

"What do you want, Anastasia? Vegas? A big wedding with all the trimmings? Tell me."

"Not big. Just friends and family."

"Okay. Where?"

She shrugs, and I'm guessing she hasn't thought about it.

"Could we do it here?" I ask.

"Your folks' place? Would they mind?"

I laugh. Grace would leap at the chance. "My mother would be in seventh heaven."

"Okay, here. I'm sure my mom and dad would prefer that."

So would I.

For once we're in agreement. No arguing.

Is this a first?

Gently, I stroke her hair, that's a little mussed from our spent passion. "So, we've established where, now the when."

"Surely you should ask your mother?"

"Hmm. She can have a month, that's it. I want you too much to wait any longer."

"Christian, you have me. You've had me for a while. But okay, a month it is." She plants a tender kiss on my chest and I'm grateful that the darkness remains quiet. Her presence is keeping it at bay.

"We'd better head back. I don't want Mia interrupting us like she did that time."

Ana laughs. "Ah, yes. That was close. My first punishment fuck." She grazes my jaw with her fingertips and I roll over, taking her with me, and pressing her into the deep-pile rug on the floor.

"Don't remind me. Not one of my finest moments."

Her lips lift in a coy smile, her eyes sparkling with humor. "As punishment fucks go, it was okay. And I won back my panties."

"You did. Fair and square." Chuckling at the recollection, I kiss her quickly and rise. "Come, put your panties on and let's get back to what's left of the party."

I ZIP UP HER emerald dress and drape my jacket over her shoulders. "Ready?" She laces her fingers with mine and we walk to the top of the stairs of the boathouse. Pausing, she looks back at our floral haven as if *she's* memorizing the setting. "What about all the lights and these flowers?"

"It's okay. The florist is returning tomorrow to dismantle this bower. They've done a great job. And the flowers will go to a local seniors' home."

She squeezes my hand. "You're a good man, Christian Grey."

I hope I'm good enough for you.

MY FAMILY IS IN the den, abusing the karaoke machine. Kate and Mia are up dancing, and singing "We Are Family," with my parents as their audience. I think they're all a little tipsy. Elliot is slumped on the couch, sipping his beer and mouthing the lyrics.

Kate spots Ana and beckons her toward the mic. "OMG!" squeals Mia, drowning out the song. "Look at that rock!" She grabs Ana's hand and whistles. "Christian Grey, you delivered."

Ana gives her a shy smile while Kate and my mother gather round to inspect her ring, making the appropriate admiring noises. Inside I feel ten feet tall.

Yeah. She likes it. They like it.

You did good, Grey.

"Christian, could I talk to you?" Carrick asks as he stands up, his expression grim.

Now?

His stare is unwavering as he directs me out of the room.

"Um. Sure." I glance at Grace, but she's studiously avoiding my gaze.

Has she told him about Elena?

Fuck. I hope not.

I follow him to his study, and he ushers me in, closing the door behind him.

"Your mother told me," he says with no preamble whatsoever.

I glance at the clock—it's 12:28. It's too late in the day for this talk…in every sense. "Dad, I'm tired—"

"No. You are not avoiding this conversation." His voice is stern and his eyes narrow to pinpricks as he peers at me over his glasses. He's mad. Really mad.

"Dad—"

"Quiet, son. You need to listen." He sits on the edge of his desk, removes his glasses, and begins to clean them with the lint cloth he pulls from his pocket. I stand before him, as I often have, feeling like I did when I was fourteen years old and I'd just been expelled from school—again. Resigned, I take a deep breath and, sighing as loudly as I can, place my hands on my hips and wait for the onslaught.

"To say I'm disappointed is an understatement. What Elena did was criminal—"

"Dad—"

"No, Christian. You don't get to speak right now." He glares at me. "She deserves to be locked up."

Dad!

He pauses and slides his glasses back into place. "But I think it's your deception that disappoints me the most. Every time you left this house with some lie that you were studying with your friends—friends we never got to meet—you were fucking that woman."

Christ!

"How am I to believe anything you've ever said to us?" he continues.

Oh, for fuck's sake. This is a complete overreaction. "Can I speak now?"

"No. You can't. Of course, I blame myself. I thought I'd given you some semblance of a moral compass. And now I'm wondering if I've taught you anything at all."

"Are you asking a rhetorical question?"

He ignores me. "She was a married woman and you had no respect for that, and you're shortly to become a married man—"

"This has nothing to do with Anastasia!"

"Don't you dare shout at me," he says, with such quiet venom that I'm silenced immediately. I don't think I've ever seen or heard him this angry. It's sobering. "It has everything to do with her. You are about to make a huge commitment to a young woman." His tone softens. "It's a surprise to all of us. And I'm happy for you. But we are talking about the sanctity of marriage. And if you have no respect for that, then you have no business being married."

"Dad—"

"And if you're that cavalier about the sacred vows that you will soon be affirming, you seriously need to consider a prenuptial agreement."

What? I raise my hands to stop him. He's gone too far. I'm an adult, for heaven's sake. "Don't bring Ana into this. She's not some grubby gold-digger."

"This is not about her." He stands and steps toward me. "It's about you. You living up to your responsibilities. You being a trustworthy and decent human being. You being husband material!"

"For fuck's sake, Dad, I was fifteen years old!" I shout, and we're nose to nose, glowering at each other.

Why is he reacting so badly to this? I know I've always been a huge disappointment to him, but he's never spelled it out so plainly.

He shuts his eyes and pinches the bridge of his nose, and I realize that in my moments of stress I do the same. This habit comes from him, but in my case the apple has fallen far, far from the tree.

"You're right. You were a vulnerable child. But what you fail to see is that what she did was wrong, and clearly you still can't see it because you've continued to associate with her, not only as a family friend, but in business. Both of you have been lying to us for all these years. And that's what hurts the most." His voice drops. "She was your mother's friend. We thought she was a good friend. She's the opposite. You *will* cut all financial ties with her."

Fuck off, Carrick.

I want to tell him that Elena was a force for good, and that I wouldn't have continued my association with her if I thought anything else. But I know this will fall on deaf ears. He didn't want to listen when I was fourteen and struggling in school, and it appears he doesn't want to listen now.

"Have you quite finished?" The words hiss with bitterness through my gritted teeth.

"Think about what I've said."

I turn to go. I've heard enough.

"Think about the prenup. It will save you a great deal of grief in the future."

Ignoring him, I stalk out of his office and slam the door.

Fuck him!

Grace is standing in the hallway.

"Why did you tell him?" I spit at her, but Carrick has followed me out of the study so she doesn't answer. Her frosty glare is directed at him.

I'm going to fetch Ana. We're going home.

My mood savage, I follow the sound of caterwauling into the den and find Elliot and Ana at the mic strangling "Ain't No Mountain High Enough." If I wasn't so angry I'd laugh. Elliot's tuneless rumbling can't really be classed as singing, and he's drowning out Ana's sweet voice. Fortunately, the song is nearly over so I'm spared the worst of it.

"I think Marvin Gaye and Tammi Terrell are spinning in their graves," I observe dryly when they finish.

"I thought that was a pretty good rendition." Elliot bows theatrically to Mia and Kate, who are laughing and applauding with exaggerated gusto. They're definitely all inebriated. Ana giggles, looking flushed and lovely.

"We're going home," I tell her.

Her face falls. "I told your mother we'd stay."

"You did? Just now?"

"Yes. She brought down a change of clothes for us. I was looking forward to sleeping in your bedroom."

"Darling, I was really hoping you'd stay." It's a plea from my mother, who stands in the doorway, Carrick behind her. "Kate and Elliot are, too. I like having all my chicks under one roof." She reaches out and clasps my hand. "And we thought we'd lost you this week."

Muttering an expletive beneath my breath, I keep my temper in check. My siblings seem to be completely oblivious to the drama that is unfolding in front of them. I expect this cluelessness from Elliot but not from Mia.

"Stay, son. Please." My father's eyes bore into me, but he appears genial enough. It's not like he's just told me that I'm a complete and utter disappointment.

Again.

I ignore him and respond to my mother. "Okay." But it's only because Ana's giving me such an imploring look, and I know that if I leave in my present mood it will be a blight on what has been a wonderful day.

Ana wraps her arms around me. "Thank you," she whispers. I smile down at her and the dark cloud that hangs over me begins to dissipate.

"Come on, Dad." Mia thrusts the mic into his hand and drags him in front of the screen. "Last song!" she says.

"Bed." It's not a request to Ana. I've had enough of my family for one night. She nods in agreement and I knit her fingers with mine. "Good night, all. Thanks for the party, Mother."

Grace hugs me. "You know we love you. We only want the best for you. I am so happy with your news. And so happy that you're here."

"Yeah, Mom. Thanks." I give her a swift peck on the cheek. "We're tired. We're going to bed. Good night."

"Good night, Ana. Thank you," she says and gives her a swift hug. I tug Ana's hand to leave as Mia puts on "Wild Thing" for Carrick to sing.

That I do not want to see.

SWITCHING ON THE LIGHT, I close my bedroom door and pull Ana into my arms, seeking her warmth and trying to put Carrick's blistering rebuke out of my mind.

"Hey, are you okay?" she murmurs. "You're brooding."

"I'm just mad at my dad. But that's nothing new. He still treats me like I'm an adolescent."

Ana hugs me tighter. "Your father loves you."

"Well, tonight he's very disappointed in me. Again. But I don't want to discuss that right now." I kiss the top of her head and she tilts her face up, focusing on me, compassion and understanding shining in her eyes, and I know neither of us wants to raise the specter of Elena…*Mrs. Robinson.*

I'm reminded of earlier this evening, when Grace, in all her avenging glory, threw Elena out of the house. I wonder what my mother would have said, back in the day, if she'd caught me with a girl in my room. Suddenly I'm energized by the same teenage thrill I had when Ana and I snuck up here last weekend during the masquerade ball.

"I've got a girl in my room." I grin.

"What are you going to do with her?" Ana's answering smile is seductive.

"Hmm. All the things I wanted to do with girls when I was an adolescent." But couldn't. Because I couldn't bear to be touched. "Unless you're too tired." I trace the soft curve of her cheek with my knuckle.

"Christian. I'm exhausted. But thrilled, too."

Oh, baby. I kiss her quickly and take pity on her. "Maybe we should just sleep. It's been a long day. Come. I'll put you to bed. Turn around."

She complies and I reach for the zipper on her dress.

WHILE MY FIANCÉE SLUMBERS beside me, I text Taylor and ask him to bring us a change of clothes from Escala in the morning. Scooting down beside Ana, I focus on her profile, marveling that she's asleep already…and that she's agreed to be mine.

Will I ever be good enough for her?

Am I husband material?

My father seems to doubt it.

I sigh and lie on my back, staring up at the ceiling.

I'm going to prove him wrong.

He's always been strict with me. More so than with Elliot or Mia.

Fucker. He knows I'm a bad seed. As I replay his earlier tirade in my head, I drift until sleep claims me.

> *Arms up, Christian.* Daddy has a serious face. He is teaching diving into the pool. *That's right. Now curl your toes around the edge of the pool. Good. Arch your back. That's right. Now push off.* I fall. And fall. And fall. Splash. Into the cool, clear water. Into the blue. Into the calm. Into the quiet. But my water wings push me back to the air. And I look for Daddy. *Look, Daddy, look.* But Elliot jumps on him. And they fall on the ground. Daddy tickles Elliot. Elliot laughs. And laughs. And laughs. And Daddy kisses his tummy. Daddy doesn't do that to me. I don't like it. I'm in the water. I want to be up there. With them. With Daddy. And I'm standing in the trees. Watching Daddy and Mia. She shrieks with joy as he tickles her. And he laughs. And she wriggles free and jumps on him. He swings her around and catches her. And

I stand in the trees alone. Watching. Wanting. The air smells good. Of apples.

"Good morning, Mr. Grey," Ana whispers as I open my eyes. The morning sun glimmers through the windows and I'm curled around her like a vine. The knot of homesickness and heartache—evoked by a dream, surely—unravels at the sight of her. I'm smitten and aroused, my body rising to greet her.

"Good morning, Miss Steele." She looks impossibly beautiful in spite of the fact that she's wearing Mia's *I ♥ Paris* T-shirt. She cups my face, her eyes sparkling and her hair wild and glossy in the morning light. She runs a thumb along my chin, tickling the stubble.

"I was watching you sleep."

"Were you now?"

"And looking at my beautiful engagement ring." She stretches out her hand and wiggles her fingers. The diamond captures the light and throws tiny rainbows across my old movie and kickboxing posters on the walls.

"Ooh!" she coos. "It's a sign."

A good sign, Grey. Hopefully.

"I'm never going to take it off."

"Good!" I move so that I'm covering her. "Watching me for how long?" I run my nose down hers and press my lips to hers.

"Oh, no." She pushes at my shoulders and my stab of disappointment is real, but she rolls me onto my back and straddles my hips. Sitting up, she sweeps her T-shirt off in one swift move, and throws it to the floor. "I was thinking about giving you a wake-up call."

"Oh?" My cock and I rejoice.

Before I can steel myself against her touch, she leans down and places a soft kiss on my chest, her hair tumbling around us both, creating a chestnut haven. Bright blue eyes peek at me.

"Starting here." She kisses me again.

I inhale sharply.

"Then moving down to here." She runs her tongue in a wayward line down my sternum.

Yes.

The darkness stays quiet, subdued by the goddess on top of me or by my bursting libido. I don't know which.

"You taste mighty fine, Mr. Grey," she breathes against my skin.

"I'm glad to hear it." The words are hoarse in my throat.

She licks and nips me along the base of my rib cage as her breasts graze over my lower belly.

Ah!

Once, twice, three times.

"Ana!" I clutch her knees as my breathing accelerates, and squeeze. But she squirms on top of my groin, so I let go, and she rises up, leaving me waiting and wanting. I think she's going to take me. She's ready.

I'm ready.

Fuck, I'm so ready.

But she moves down my body, kissing my stomach and my belly, her tongue slipping into my navel, then grazing through my happy trail. She nips me once more and I feel the bite right through my cock.

"Ah!"

"There you are," she whispers and she stares greedily at my eager dick and then peeps up at me with a coquettish grin. Slowly, her eyes on mine, she takes me in her mouth.

Sweet Jesus.

Her head bobs up and down, her teeth sheathed behind her lips, as she pulls me farther into her mouth each time. My fingers find her hair and sweep it out of the way so I can enjoy an uninterrupted view of my future wife with her lips around my cock. I tighten my buttocks, pushing up my hips, seeking more depth, and she takes it, clamping her mouth around me.

Harder.

Harder still.

Ah. Ana. You fucking goddess.

She picks up the rhythm. And, closing my eyes, I fist my hand in her hair.

She is so good at this.

"Yes," I hiss through my teeth and I lose myself in the rise and fall of her exquisite mouth. I'm going to come.

All of a sudden, she stops.

Damn. No! I open my eyes and watch her move above me, then sink oh-so-slowly onto my bursting dick. I groan, relishing every precious inch. Her hair tumbles to her naked breasts and, reaching up, I caress each one, running my thumbs across her hardening nipples, over and over and over.

She lets out a lengthy moan, thrusting her tits into my hands.

Oh, baby.

Then she pitches forward, kissing me, her tongue invading my mouth, and I taste and savor my saltiness in her sweet mouth.

Ana.

I move my hands to her hips and ease her up off me and then pull her down, thrusting up at the same time.

She cries out, grabbing on to my wrists.

And I do it again.

And again.

"Christian," she calls to the ceiling in a quiet plea as she matches my tempo and we move together. In time. As one. Until she falls apart on top of me, taking me with her and triggering my own release.

I NUZZLE HER HAIR and thrum my fingers down her back.

She takes my breath away.

This is still new. Ana in charge. Ana initiating. I like it.

"Now that's my idea of Sunday worship," I whisper.

"Christian!" She whips her head to mine, eyes round with disapproval.

I laugh out loud.

Will this ever get old? Shocking Miss Steele?

I hug her hard and roll us both over so she's beneath me.

"Good morning, Miss Steele. It's always a treat to wake up to you."

She strokes my cheek. "And you, Mr. Grey." Her tone is soft. "Do we have to get up? I like being here in your room."

"No." I glance at my watch on the nightstand. It's 9:15. "My parents will be at Mass." I shift to her side.

"I didn't know they were churchgoers."

I grimace. "Yes. They are. Catholic."

"Are you?"

"No, Anastasia."

God and I went our separate ways a long time ago.

"Are you?" I ask, recalling that Welch could find no religious affiliations during her background check.

She shakes her head. "No. Neither of my parents practice a faith. But I would like to go to church today. I need to thank…someone for bringing you back alive from the helicopter accident."

I sigh, visualizing a bolt of lightning burning me to a cinder if I step onto the hallowed grounds of a church, but for her, I'll go.

"Okay. I'll see what we can do." I kiss her quickly. "Come, shower with me."

THERE'S A SMALL LEATHER duffel outside my bedroom door—Taylor has delivered clean clothes. I scoop up the bag and shut the door. Ana is wrapped in a towel, beads of water glistening on her shoulders. Her attention is focused on my bulletin board, paused at the photograph of the crack whore. She turns her head toward me, a question on her beautiful face…a question I don't want to answer. "You still have it," she says.

Yeah. I still have the photo. What of it?

As her question hangs in the air between us, her eyes grow luminous in the morning sunshine, drinking me in, begging me to say something. But I can't. This is not somewhere I want to go. For a moment, I'm reminded of the gut punch I felt when Carrick handed me the photograph so many years ago.

Hell. Don't go there, Grey.

"Taylor brought a change of clothes for us," I whisper as I sling the duffel onto the bed. There's an impossibly long silence before she responds.

"Okay," she says, and she walks toward the bed and unzips the bag.

I'VE EATEN MY FILL. My parents have returned from Mass and my mother has cooked her traditional brunch: a delicious, coronary-inducing plate of bacon, sausage, hash browns, eggs, and English muffins. Grace is a little quiet, and I suspect that she might have a hangover.

Throughout the morning I have avoided my father.

I haven't forgiven him for last night.

Ana, Elliot, and Kate are in a heated debate—about bacon, of all things—and arguing over who should have the last sausage. I half listen with amusement while I read an article about the failure rate of local banks in the Sunday edition of *The Seattle Times.*

Mia shrieks and reclaims her place at the table, holding her laptop. "Look at this. There's a gossipy item on the *Seattle Nooz* website about you being engaged, Christian."

"Already?" Mom says, surprised.

Don't these assholes have anything better to do?

Mia reads the column out loud. "'Word has reached us here at the *Nooz* that Seattle's most eligible bachelor, *the* Christian Grey, has finally been snapped up, and wedding bells are in the air.'"

I glance at Ana, who pales as she stares, doe-eyed, from Mia to me.

"'But who is the lucky, lucky lady?'" Mia continues. "'The *Nooz* is on the hunt. Bet she's reading one helluva prenup.'" Mia starts giggling.

I glare at her. *Shut the fuck up, Mia.*

She stops and presses her lips together. Ignoring her, and all the anxious looks exchanged at the table, I turn my attention to Ana, who blanches even more.

"No," I mouth, trying to reassure her.

"Christian," Dad says.

"I'm not discussing this again," I snarl at him. He opens his mouth to say something. "No prenup!" I snap with such vehemence that he closes his mouth.

Shut up, Carrick!

Picking up the paper, I find myself rereading the same sentence in the banking article over and over while I fume.

"Christian," Ana murmurs. "I'll sign anything you and Mr. Grey want."

I look up and she's beseeching me, a sheen of unshed tears reflecting in her eyes.

Ana. Stop.

"No!" I exclaim, imploring her to drop this subject.

"It's to protect you."

"Christian, Ana—I think you should discuss this in private," Grace chastises us and scowls at Carrick and Mia.

"Ana, this is not about you," Dad mumbles. "And please call me Carrick."

Don't try and make it up to her now. I seethe, inwardly, and suddenly there's a burst of activity. Kate and Mia get up to clear the table and Elliot quickly stabs the last remaining sausage with his fork.

"I definitely prefer sausage," he roars with forced levity.

Ana is staring at her hands. She looks crestfallen.

Jesus. Dad. Look what you've done.

I reach over and grasp both her hands in mine, and whisper so only she can hear me, "Stop it. Ignore my dad. He's really pissed about Elena. That stuff was all aimed at me. I wish my mom had kept her mouth shut."

"He has a point, Christian. You're very wealthy, and I'm bringing nothing to our marriage but my student loans."

Baby, I'll have you any way I can get you. You know this!

"Anastasia, if you leave me, you might as well take everything. You left me once before. I know how that feels."

"That was different," she mumbles. And she frowns once more. "But, you might want to leave me."

Now she's being ridiculous.

"Christian, you know I might do something exceptionally stupid—and you..." She stops.

Ana, I think that's highly unlikely. "Stop. Stop now. This subject is closed. We're not discussing it anymore. No prenup. Not now—not ever."

I scramble through my thoughts, trying to find safer ground, and inspiration hits me. Turning to Grace, who's wringing her hands and looking anxiously at me, I ask, "Mom, can we have the wedding here?"

Her expression shifts from alarm to joy and gratitude. "Darling. That would be wonderful." And she adds as an afterthought, "You don't want a church wedding?"

I give her a sideways look and she capitulates immediately.

"We'd love to host your wedding. Wouldn't we, Cary?"

"Yes. Yes, of course." My father smiles benignly at both Ana and me, but I can't look at him.

"Have you a date in mind?" Grace asks.

"Four weeks."

"Christian. That's not enough time!"

"It's plenty of time."

"I need at least eight!"

"Mom. Please."

"Six?" she pleads.

"That would be wonderful. Thank you, Mrs. Grey," Ana pipes up, and shoots a warning glance at me, daring me to contradict her.

"Six it is," I state. "Thanks, Mom."

ANA IS QUIET ON the drive back to Seattle. She's probably thinking about my outburst at Carrick this morning. Our argument from last night still rankles—his disapproval a burr chafing at my skin. Deep down, I'm worried that he's right; maybe I'm not husband material.

Damn, I'm going to prove him wrong.

I'm not the adolescent he thinks I am.

I stare at the road ahead, deflated. My girl is beside me, we have a date for our wedding, and I should feel on top of the world, but I'm picking over the remains of my father's angry tirade about Elena and the prenup. On the plus side, I think he knows he fucked up. He tried to make it up to me when we parted earlier but his fumbling, inadequate attempt to make amends still smarts.

Christian, I've always done everything in my power to protect you. And I failed. I should have been there for you.

But I didn't want to hear him. He should have said this last night. He did not.

I shake my head. I want out of this funk.

"Hey, I have an idea." I reach over and squeeze Ana's knee.

PERHAPS MY LUCK IS turning—there's a parking space outside St. James Cathedral. Ana peers through the trees at the majestic building that dominates a whole block on Ninth Avenue, then turns to me, a question in her eyes.

"Church," I offer, by way of explanation.

"This is big for a church, Christian."

"True."

She smiles. "It's perfect."

Hand in hand, we head through one of the front doors into the antechamber, then proceed onward into the nave. Out of instinct I reach toward the stoup for Holy Water to bless myself, but I stop just in time, knowing that if a bolt of lightning is going to strike, it will be now. I catch Ana's openmouthed surprise, but look away to admire the impressive ceiling as I wait for God's judgment.

No. No thunderbolt today.

"Old habits," I mutter, feeling a little embarrassed, but relieved that I've not been rendered into a pile of ashes on the grand threshold. Ana turns her attention to the magnificent interior: the lofty ornate ceilings, the rust-colored marble columns, the intricate stained glass. Sunlight streams in a steady beam through the oculus in the transept's dome, as if God were smiling down on the place. There's a whispered hush that fills the nave, enveloping us in a spiritual calm that's disturbed only by the occasional echoing cough from one of the few visitors. It's quiet, a refuge from the hustle and bustle of Seattle. I'd forgotten just how tranquil and beautiful it is in here, but then I've not been inside for years. I'd always loved the pomp and ceremony of a Catholic Mass. The ritual. The responses. The smell of burning incense. Grace made sure her three children were well versed in all things Catholic, and there was a time when I would have done anything to please my new mother.

But puberty arrived and all that went to shit. My relationship with God never recovered, and it changed the relationship with my family, especially my father. We were always at odds with each other from the time I hit thirteen. I brush off the memory. It's painful.

Now standing in the hushed splendor of the nave, I'm overwhelmed by a familiar sense of peace. "Come. I want to show you something." We walk down the side aisle, the sound of Ana's heels ringing over the flagstones, until we reach a small chapel. Its golden walls and dark floor are the perfect setting for the exquisite statue of Our Lady, surrounded by flickering candles.

Ana gasps when she sees her.

Without a doubt this is still one of the most beautiful shrines I've ever seen. The Virgin, eyes cast down at the floor in modesty, holds her child aloft. Her gold-and-blue robes shimmer in the light from the burning candles.

It's stunning.

"My mother used to bring us here sometimes for Mass. This was my favorite place. The Shrine of the Blessed Virgin Mary," I whisper.

Ana stands and soaks up the scene, the statue, the walls, the dark ceiling covered in gold stars. "Is this what inspired your collection? Your Madonnas?" she asks, and there's wonder in her voice.

"Yes."

"Motherhood," she murmurs, and she peeks up at me.

I shrug. "I've seen it done well and done badly."

"Your birth mom?" she asks.

I nod, and her eyes grow impossibly large, revealing some deep emotion that I don't want to acknowledge.

I look away. It's too raw.

I place a fifty-dollar bill in the offertory box and hand her a candle. Ana clasps my hand briefly in gratitude, then lights the wick from one of the tapers and places her candle in an iron sconce on the wall. It flickers brightly among its companions. "Thank you," she says quietly to Mary, and wraps an arm around my middle, placing her head on my shoulder. Together we stand in quiet contemplation in this most exquisite of sanctuaries in the heart of the city.

The peace, the beauty, and being with Ana restores my good humor. To hell with work this afternoon. It's Sunday. I want some fun with my girl. "Shall we go to the game?" I ask.

"Game?"

"The Phillies are playing the M's at Safeco Field. GEH has a suite there."

"Sure. Sounds like fun. Let's go." Ana beams.

Hand in hand, we head back to the R8.

Monday, June 20, 2011

This morning has been extremely aggravating, and I'm ready to rip someone limb from limb. There were hordes of reporters, including a couple of TV crews, camped outside Escala and Seattle Independent Publishing.

Have they nothing better to do?

It was easy to avoid them at home because we arrived and left through the underground garage. At SIP it's another issue. I'm confounded and appalled that these vultures have managed to track Ana down so quickly.

How?

We dodged them by skirting the SIP building and going to the rear loading doors. But now Ana's trapped inside her office and I'm ambivalent about that. At least she's safe there, but I'm sure she's not going to tolerate confinement for long.

My heart sinks. Of course the Seattle media are curious about my fiancée. It's part of the Christian Grey *bonus*. I just hope to God this attention doesn't drive her away.

Sawyer pulls up outside Grey House, where another couple of hacks are lurking, but with Taylor beside me I storm past them, ignoring their shouted questions.

What a fucking start to the morning!

Still aggravated, I wait for the elevator. I have a to-do list longer than my dick and I have to deal with the fallout from the weekend: missed calls from my dad, my mom, and Elena Lincoln.

Why the hell she's calling me I don't know. We're done. I made that clear on Saturday night.

I'd rather be at home with my girl.

In the elevator I check my phone. There's an e-mail from Ana.

From: Anastasia Steele
Subject: Showing A Fiancée A Good Time
Date: June 20 2011 09:25
To: Christian Grey

My dearest husband-to-be
I feel it would be remiss of me not to thank you for
a) surviving a helicopter crash
b) an exemplary hearts-and-flowers proposal
c) a wonderful weekend
d) a return to the Red Room
e) a very pretty rock, which everyone has noticed!
f) my wake-up call this morning (especially this! ;))
Ax

Anastasia Steele
Acting-Editor, Fiction, SIP

PS: Do you have a strategy for dealing with the press?

From: Christian Grey
Subject: Showing a man a good time
Date: June 20 2011 09:36
To: Anastasia Steele

My darling Ana
You are entirely welcome.
Thank you for a wonderful weekend.
I love you.
I'll come back to you about a strategy for the f****** press.

Christian Grey
CEO, Grey Enterprises Holdings, Inc.

PS: I think wake-up calls are underrated.
PPS: F****** BLACKBERRY!!!!!!!!!!

How many times do I have to tell you, woman!

Amused and mollified by our e-mail exchange, I charge out of the elevator. Andrea is at her desk in my outer office. "Good morning, Mr. Grey," she says. "I…um…I'm glad you're still with us."

"Thank you, Andrea. I appreciate that. And thank you for all your help on Friday night. It was invaluable."

She flushes, embarrassed, I think, by my gratitude. "Where's the new girl?" I ask.

"Sarah? She's on an errand. Coffee?"

"Please. Black. Strong. I have a great deal to do."

She gets to her feet.

"If my father, mother, or Mrs. Lincoln call, take a message. Refer all press inquiries to Sam. But if the FAA, Eurocopter, or Welch call, put them through."

"Yes, sir."

"And, of course, Anastasia Steele."

Andrea's face softens with one of her rare smiles. "Congratulations, Mr. Grey."

"You know?"

"Everyone knows, sir."

I laugh. "Thank you, Andrea."

"I'll get your coffee."

"Great, thanks."

At my desk, I wake my iMac. There's another e-mail from Ana.

From: Anastasia Steele
Subject: The Limitations of Language
Date: June 20 2011 09:38
To: Christian Grey

. **, **** *******!

*** ***** ** ***********.

* **** ***, ***.

Ax

I laugh out loud even though I have no idea what she's written. Andrea enters with my coffee and sits down so we can run through the day's schedule ahead of my first call.

I'VE BEEN ON THE phone for what feels like three solid hours. When I finally hang up, stand, and stretch, it's 1:15. *Charlie Tango* is being recovered today and should be back at Boeing Field tonight. The Federal Aviation Administration has handed the inquiry into the emergency landing over to the National Transportation Safety Board.

The Eurocopter engineer who was one of the first on-site says it's incredibly fortunate that I put the fire out with the extinguishers. It will help to speed up theirs and the NTSB's investigation. I'm hoping to have their initial report tomorrow.

Welch has informed me that as a precaution, he's secured all of last week's CCTV footage from the helipad in Portland, and from in and around *Charlie Tango*'s private hangar at Boeing Field. A shiver skates up my spine. Welch thinks it might be sabotage, and I have to admit the possibility has been at the back of my mind since *both* engines caught fire.

Sabotage.

But why?

I've asked him to have his team comb through all the recordings and see if they find anything suspicious.

After much wheedling from Sam, my VP for publicity, I've agreed to a brief press conference later this afternoon. Sam's nagging voice rings in my head. *"You need to get in front of this, Christian. Your miraculous escape is still all over the news cycle. They have aerial footage of the recovery operation."*

Frankly, I think Sam just loves the drama. I hope that a press briefing will stop them from hounding Ana and me.

Andrea buzzes my phone.

"What?"

"Dr. Grey is on the line again."

"Fuck," I whisper under my breath. I guess I can't avoid her forever. "Okay, put her through." Leaning against my desk, I wait for her dulcet tones.

"Christian. I know you're busy, but two things."

"Yes, Mother."

"I've found a wedding planner I want to use. Her name is Alondra Gutierrez. She organized this year's Coping Together Ball. I think you and Ana should meet her."

I roll my eyes. "Sure."

"Good. I'll arrange a meeting later this week. Secondly, your father really wants to talk to you."

"I spoke to my father at length on the night I announced my

engagement. We were also celebrating my twenty-eighth year in the world and, as you know, I'm always reluctant to mark these milestones." I'm on a roll. "And I'd just survived a hair-raising crash-landing." My voice is rising. "Dad really rained on my parade. I think he said enough then. I don't want to talk to him now."

He's a pompous prick.

"Christian. Stop sulking. Talk to your dad."

Sulking! I'm fucking pissed, Grace.

My mother's silence stretches between us, laced with her censure.

I sigh. "Okay, I'll think about it." The other line on my phone flashes. "I've got to go."

"Very well, darling. I'll let you know about the meeting with Alondra."

"Good-bye, Mom."

My phone buzzes again. "Mr. Grey, I have Anastasia Steele for you."

My rancor disappears. "Great. Thanks, Andrea."

"Christian?" Her voice is small, and uneven. She sounds scared.

My breath catches in my throat. "Ana, is everything all right?"

"Um…I went out for some fresh air. I thought they'd be gone. And, well…"

"The reporters and photographers?"

"Yes."

Fuckers.

"I didn't comment on anything. I just turned around and ran back into the building."

Damn. I should have sent Sawyer to watch over her, and I'm grateful once more that Taylor persuaded me to keep him on after the Leila Williams incident. "Ana, it's going to be fine. I was going to call you. I've just agreed to give a press conference later this afternoon about *Charlie Tango.* They'll ask about our engagement. I'll give them the barest of details. Hopefully that will be enough to satisfy them."

"Good."

I chance my luck. "Would you like me to send Sawyer to watch over you?"

"Yes," she says immediately.

Whoa. That was easy. She must be more shaken than I thought. "Are you sure you're okay? You're not normally so amenable."

"I have my moments, Mr. Grey. They usually occur after I've been pursued by the media through the streets of Seattle. It was quite the workout. I was breathless when I got back to the office." She's making light of the situation.

"Really, Miss Steele? You have such great stamina, normally."

"Why, Mr. Grey, what on earth are you referring to?" I hear the smile in her voice.

"I think you know," I whisper.

Her breath hitches and the sound travels straight to my groin.

"Are you flirting with me?" she asks.

"I hope so."

"Will you test my stamina later?" Her voice is low and sultry.

Oh, Ana. Desire streaks through my body like lightning.

"Nothing would give me greater pleasure."

"I'm so glad to hear that, Christian Grey."

She's far too good at this game. "I'm so happy you called me," I say. "Made my day."

"I aim to please." She giggles. "I must call your personal trainer, so I can keep up with you!"

I laugh. "Bastille will be delighted."

She's silent for a moment. "Thank you for making me feel better."

"Isn't that what I'm supposed to do?"

"It is. And you do it well."

I bask in her loving words. *Ana, you make me feel whole.*

There's a knock on my door, and I know it's either Andrea or Sarah with my lunch.

"I've got to go."

"Thank you, Christian," she says.

"For what?"

"Being you. Oh, one more thing. The news of you buying SIP is still embargoed, isn't it?"

"Yes, for another three weeks."

"Okay. I'll try and remember that."

"Do. Laters, baby."

"Okay. Laters, Christian."

ANDREA AND SARAH HAVE gone all out today. I have my favorite sandwich—turkey club with a pickle on the side—a sprinkling of salad, and some potato chips, all served on a tray with GEH linen, a cut crystal highball glass with sparkling water, and a matching vase sporting a perky pink rose.

"Thanks," I mutter, bemused, as they both fuss setting up the tray.

"Pleasure, Mr. Grey," Andrea says with a smile that is becoming less rare. They both seem strangely distracted and a little skittish today. *What are they up to?*

While I tuck into lunch I check my messages. There's another one from Elena.

Shit.

ELENA
Call me. Please.

ELENA
Call me. I'm going crazy.

ELENA
I don't know what to say. I've been thinking about what happened all weekend. And I don't know why things got so out of control. I'm sorry. Call me.

ELENA
Please answer my calls.

I have to deal with her. My parents want me to cut ties with Mrs. Lincoln, and frankly I don't know how we come back from all that we spewed at each other on Saturday evening.

I said some pretty awful things.

So did she.

It's time to end it.

I told Ana I would gift Elena the company.

I scroll through my contacts and find the number of my personal lawyer. Ironically, it was Elena who first put us in touch. Debra Kingston is a commercial lawyer who also happens to enjoy the same lifestyle that I do. She's drafted all my D/s contracts and NDAs, and handled my dealings with Mrs. Lincoln and our joint business.

I press call.

"Christian, good afternoon. Long time no speak. I understand congratulations are in order."

"Thanks, Debra."

Jesus! She knows, too.

"What can I do for you?"

"I want to gift the salon business to Elena Lincoln."

"Excuse me?" Her voice rings with disbelief.

"You heard me right. I want to gift the business to Elena. I'd like you to draw up a contract. Everything. Loans. Property. Assets. All of it. It's all hers."

"Are you sure?"

"Yes."

"You're cutting ties?"

"I am. I want nothing to do with it. No liabilities."

"Christian, as your lawyer I have to ask, are you sure you want to do this? This is an incredibly generous gift. You stand to lose hundreds of thousands of dollars."

"Debra, I'm well aware of that."

She huffs into the phone. "Okay, if you insist. I'll send over a draft in the next couple of days."

"Thank you. And I want to conduct all correspondence with her through you."

"You two have really fallen out."

I am not going to discuss my private life with Debra. Well, not this aspect of my private life.

"I get it," she adds. "Keeping the ball and chain happy?"

What. The. Hell?

"Debra, just do the fucking contract."

Her response is tight-lipped. "Very well, Christian. And I'll let Mrs. Lincoln know."

"Good. Thank you."

That should get Elena off my back.

I hang up.

Whoa. I've done it.

And it feels good. A relief. I've just kissed good-bye to a small fortune by GEH standards, but I owe her that much. Without her there would be no GEH.

"I've been thinking about our recent conversation, Christian."

"Yes, Ma'am?"

"You, leaving Harvard. I'll lend you $100,000 to start your business."

"You'd do that?"

"Christian, I have every faith in you. You are destined to be a master of the universe. It will be a loan and you can pay me back."

"Elena… I…"

"You can thank me by showing me what you learned earlier today. You top. I'll bottom. Don't mark me."

I shake my head; so began my training as a Dominant. My success as a businessman is tied to my lifestyle choice. I smirk at the pun and then frown. I can't believe I've never consciously made the connection before.

Shit. I can't cower behind my desk. I owe her a call.

Showtime, Grey.

Reluctantly, I press her contact on my phone.

She answers on the first ring. "Christian, why haven't you called me?"

"I'm calling you now."

"What the hell is wrong with your mother and your…fiancée?" she sneers over that final word.

"Elena, this is a courtesy call. I'm gifting you the business. I've been in touch with Debra Kingston; she's drawing up the paperwork. It's over. We can't do this anymore."

"What? What are you talking about?"

"I mean it. I no longer have the energy for your bullshit. I asked you to leave Ana alone and you ignored my request. We reap what we sow, Mrs. Lincoln. It's over. Don't call me."

"Chris—" I hear the alarm in her voice as I hang up.

My phone buzzes immediately, her name flashing on my screen. I switch it off and look over my to-do list.

I have about an hour before the press conference, so to take my mind off Elena, I pick up my office phone and call my brother.

"Hey, hotshot. Having second thoughts?"

"Fuck off, Elliot."

"*She's* having second thoughts?" He snickers.

"Could you silence your inner asshole for two minutes?"

"That long? Dubious."

"I'm buying a house."

"Whoa. For you and the future Mrs. Grey? That was quick. You knocked her up?"

"No!" *For fuck's sake.*

He cackles on his end of the phone. "Don't tell me. It's in Denny-Blaine or Laurelhurst?"

Ah, the tech millionaires' suburbs of choice.

"No."

"Medina?"

I laugh. "That's far too near Mom and Dad. It's on the water just north of Broadview."

"You're kidding."

"No. I want to watch the sun sink into the Sound, not rise above a lake."

Elliot laughs. "Man. Who knew you were such a romantic?"

I scoff. I certainly didn't. "It needs gutting."

"It does?" That has Elliot's interest. "You want me to recommend someone?"

"No, dude. I want you to do it. I want something sustainable and environmentally friendly. You know, all the shit you champion at family meals."

"Oh. Wow." He sounds surprised. "Can I see the place?"

"Yes, of course. I've not gone to contract yet, but we're going ahead with surveys over the next week or so."

"Sure. This is rad. But you'll need an architect. I can only do so much."

“What was the name of the woman who oversaw the renovations in Aspen?”

“Um…Gia Matteo. She’s cool. She’s now at some fancy downtown firm.”

“She did a great job at the house in Aspen. And I seem to remember she had an impressive and imaginative portfolio. Do you recommend her?”

“Yeah. Um… Sure.”

“You sound hesitant.”

“Well, you know. She’s the kind of woman who doesn’t take no for an answer.”

“What do you mean?”

“She’s…ambitious. Hungry. Driven to get what she wants.”

“I’ve got no problem with that.”

“Neither have I,” says Elliot. “In fact, I rather like a predatory female.”

“You do?” *Well, Kavanagh fits that bill.*

“She and I…” Elliot trails off.

I can’t help my eye roll. My brother suffers from sexual incontinence. “Will that be awkward?”

“No. Of course not. She knows her shit.”

“I’ll call her. And take a look at her updated portfolio.” I scribble down her name.

“Cool. Let me know when we can scout the place.”

“Will do. Laters.”

“Dude.”

I hang up, wondering how many women he’s fucked. I shake my head. Does he know that Katherine Kavanagh has designs on him? Could he not see that over the weekend? I hope he doesn’t end up with her. She is possibly the most annoying woman I know.

Sam has e-mailed the statement for the press conference, which is in half an hour. I review it and make some changes; as usual, his prose is overwrought and pretentious. Sometimes I don’t know why I hired him.

Twenty minutes later he’s knocking on my door.

“Christian. Are you ready?”

"SO, MR. GREY, ARE you suggesting that this could be sabotage?" the journalist from *The Seattle Times* asks.

"I'm not saying that at all. We are keeping an open mind and waiting for the accident report."

"Congratulations on your engagement, Mr. Grey. How did you meet Anastasia Steele?" I think this woman is from *Seattle Metropolitan.*

"I'm not answering any specific questions about my private life. I'll just reiterate, I'm thrilled she's consented to be my wife."

"That's the last question, thank you, ladies and gentlemen." Sam comes to my rescue and ushers me out of the GEH conference room.

Thank God that's over.

"You did well," Sam says, as if I need his approval. "I'm sure the press are going to want a picture of you and Anastasia together. I don't think they'll stop hounding you until they have one."

"I'll think about it. Right now I just want to go back to my office."

Sam smirks. "Of course, Christian. I'll send you a compilation of the conference press coverage when we get it."

"Thanks." *Why is he smirking?*

I step into the elevator and I'm delighted to find that I have it to myself. I check my phone. There are missed calls from Elena.

For heaven's sake, Mrs. Lincoln. We're done.

There's also an e-mail from Ana.

From: Anastasia Steele
Subject: The News!
Date: June 20 2011 16:55
To: Christian Grey

Mr. Grey
You give good press conference.
Why does that not surprise me?
You looked hot.
Loved your tie.
Ax

PS: Sabotage?

My hand strays to my tie. *That Brioni tie. My favorite.*

I looked hot. These words give me more pleasure than they should. I like to look hot for Ana, and her e-mail gives me an idea.

From: Christian Grey
Subject: I'll Show You Hot
Date: June 20 2011 17:08
To: Anastasia Steele

My darling wife-to-be
Maybe I can use the tie this evening, when I test your stamina.

Christian Grey
Impatient CEO, Grey Enterprises Holdings, Inc.

PS: The sabotage is just conjecture. Don't worry about it. This is not a request.

THE ELEVATOR DOORS OPEN.

"Happy birthday, Mr. Grey!" There's a cacophony of voices. Andrea is standing by the doors, holding a large frosted cake with *Happy Birthday and Congratulations, Mr. Grey* written in blue icing across the top. There's a solitary gold candle burning on top.

What the fuck.

This has never happened.

Ever.

The throng—which includes Ros, Barney, Fred, Marco, Vanessa, and all the VPs of their departments—breaks into a rousing chorus of "Happy Birthday." I fix a smile on my face to hide my surprise and, when they finish, blow out the candle. They all cheer and start applauding, as if I've done something worthy of celebration.

Sarah offers me a champagne flute.

There are shouts of "Speech. Speech."

"Well, this is a surprise." I turn to Andrea, who gives me a slight shrug. "But thank you."

Ros pipes up, "We're all grateful you're still here, Christian, especially me, because it means I'm still here, too." There's a smattering of polite laughter and applause. "So we wanted to express our gratitude in some way. All of us." She extends an arm to our colleagues. "We also want to wish you a happy birthday and congratulations on your good news. Let's raise a glass." She does. "To Christian Grey."

My name echoes through the office.

I raise my glass to salute her and take a large swig.

There's more applause.

I really don't understand what has gotten into my staff. Why now? What gives?

"Was this your idea?" I ask Andrea when she hands me a slice of cake.

"No, sir. It was Ros's."

"But you got all this together."

"Sarah and I did, sir."

"Well, thank you. I appreciate it."

"You're welcome, Mr. Grey."

Ros gives me a warm smile and tips her glass toward me, and I remember I owe her a pair of navy Manolos.

IT TAKES ME THIRTY-FIVE minutes to extricate myself from the little gathering in my office. I'm touched, and I'm surprised that I'm touched. I must be going soft in my old age. But as ever, I'm anxious to return home…anxious to see Ana.

She comes dashing out of the rear entrance to SIP and my heart flips to see her. Sawyer is by her side; he opens the Audi door and she slides in beside me while Sawyer climbs in front with Taylor.

"Hi." Her smile is dazzling.

"Hi." Taking her hand, I kiss her knuckles. "How was your day?"

TUESDAY, JUNE 21, 2011

Elena's eyes are like flint. Cold. Hard. She's in my face. Angry. *I was the best thing that ever happened to you. Look at you now. One of the richest, most successful entrepreneurs in the United States. Controlled, driven, you need nothing. You are master of your universe.* Now she's on her knees. In front of me. Bowed. Naked. Her forehead pressed to the basement floor. Her hair a shining coronet of lightning against the dark wooden boards. Her hand is stretched out. Splayed. Tipped with scarlet nails. She's begging. *Keep your head on the floor.* My voice echoes off the concrete walls. She wants me to stop. She's had enough. My grip tightens on the crop. *Enough, Grey.* I wrap my fingers around my cock, hard from her mouth, covered in crimson smears from her lipstick. My palm moves up and down. Faster. Faster. Faster. *Yes.* I come and come. With a loud guttural cry. Painting her back with my cum. I stand over her. Panting. Heady. Sated. There's a crash. The door flies open. His frame fills the doorway. He roars, and the blood-curdling sound fills the room. *No.* Elena screams. *Fuck. No. No. No.* He's here. He knows. Elena stands between me and him. *No,* she cries, and he hits her so hard she falls to the floor. She screams. And screams. *Leave him. Leave him.* I'm in shock. And he hits me. A right hook to my chin. I fall. And fall. My head spins. I'm faint. *No. Stop the screaming. Stop.* It goes on. And on. I'm under the kitchen table. My hands on my ears. But they don't shut out the noise. He's here. I hear his boots. Big boots. With buckles. She's screaming. And screaming. What did he do? Where is she? I smell his stench before I see him and he peers under the table, a lit cigarette in his hand. *There you are, you little shit.*

I wake instantly, gasping for air and doused in a sheen of sweat with fear streaking through my veins.

Where am I?

My eyes adjust to the light. I'm at home. Escala. The coming dawn casts a faint rosy glow over Ana's sleeping form, and relief rushes through me like a cool autumn breeze.

Thank fuck.

She's here. With me.

I blow out a long, steadying breath as I try to clear my head.

What the hell was that about?

I rarely dream about Elena, much less about *that* horrific moment in our shared history. I shudder as I lie staring at the ceiling, and I know I'm too wired to get back to sleep. I contemplate waking Ana—wanting to lose myself in her once more—but I know that's not fair. Last night she more than proved her stamina; she has to work later today and she needs her sleep. Besides, I'm ill at ease, my skin's crawling, and the nightmare has left a sour taste in my mouth. It must be the severing of my friendship and business relationship with Elena that's haunting my psyche. After all, Mrs. Lincoln has been my lodestar for over a decade.

Shit.

It had to be done.

It's over. *All of that is over.*

Sitting up I run my hand through my hair, careful not to disturb Ana. It's early—5:05—and right now, I need a glass of water.

I swivel out of bed and find I'm standing on my tie, discarded after last night's diverting shenanigans. A delicious memory of Ana invades my senses, her hands bound above her head, her body rigid, her head tipped back in ecstasy as she clutches the pale gray slats of the headboard, while I lavish my attention on her clitoris with my tongue. It's a much more pleasing recollection than the remnants of my nightmare. I pick up my tie, fold it, and place it on the nightstand.

It's unusual for me to have nightmares when Ana is sleeping beside me. I hope it's a one-off. I'm grateful that I have an appointment with Flynn later today so I can dissect this new development with him.

Pulling on my PJ pants, I grab my phone and exit the bedroom. Perhaps some Chopin or Bach will soothe me.

As I sit down at the piano, I check my messages, and there's one from Welch, left at midnight, that catches my eye.

WELCH
Sabotage suspected. Initial report first thing this morning.

Fuck. My scalp tingles as the blood drains from my head.

My fears have been confirmed. Someone wants me dead.

Who?

My mind rolls through the few business associates I've outplayed over the years.

Woods? Stevens? Carver? Who else? Waring?

Would they stoop to this?

They all made money; lots of money. They just lost their companies. I can't believe this could be connected to my commercial activities.

Perhaps it's personal?

There's only one person who looms large in that regard and it's Linc. But Elena's ex-husband already took his revenge on her, and that was years ago. Why would he act now?

Perhaps it's someone else. A disgruntled employee? An ex? I can't think of anyone who would do this. Apart from Leila, they're all doing well.

I need to process this.

Ana! Shit!

If they're coming after me, they could hurt her. Fear steals through me like a ghost, leaving goose bumps in its wake. I have to protect Ana at all costs. I text Welch.

Meet this morning.
8 am Grey House

WELCH
Copy

I text Andrea so she can clear any meetings I may have, then e-mail Taylor.

From: Christian Grey
Subject: Sabotage
Date: June 21 2011 05:18
To: J B Taylor

Welch has informed me that *Charlie Tango* may have been sabotaged. The initial report will be with us later this morning. We're meeting at Grey House at 8 am.
Reinstate Reynolds and Ryan if they're still available. I want Ana accompanied at all times. Sawyer can stay with her today.
Thanks.

Christian Grey
CEO, Grey Enterprises Holdings, Inc.

I need to release all my pent-up nervous energy and decide on a workout. Sneaking into my closet, I change quickly and quietly, not wanting to wake Ana.

While I run on the treadmill, I watch the markets on TV, listen to the Foo Fighters, and wonder who the hell wants to kill me.

ANA SMELLS OF SLEEP and sex and a fragrant orchard in the fall. For a moment I'm transported to a happier time, when I'm hassle free, and it's just me and my girl. "Hey, baby, wake up." I nuzzle her ear.

She opens her eyes, and her face, already soft from sleep, glows like a golden dawn. "Good morning," she says, and runs her thumb across my lips, then gives me a chaste kiss.

"Sleep well?" I ask.

"Hmm…you smell so good. You look so good."

I grin. It's just a well-tailored suit. "I have to go into the office early."

She sits up. "Already?" She glances at the radio alarm. It's 7:08.

"Something's come up. Sawyer will stick close today and keep the press at bay. You okay with that?"

She nods.

Good. I don't want to frighten her with the news about *Charlie Tango.*

"I'll see you later." I kiss her forehead and leave before I'm tempted to stay.

THE REPORT IS BRIEF.

FAA Accident and Incident Reporting System (AIRS)

GENERAL INFORMATION
Data Source: ACCIDENT AND INCIDENT DATABASE
Report Number: 20110453923
Local Date: 17-JUN-11
City: CASTLE ROCK State: WA
Airport Name: PORTLAND HELIPORT
Event Type: INCIDENT
Mid Air Collision: NOT A MIDAIR

AIRCRAFT INFORMATION
Aircraft Damage: SUBSTANTIAL
Aircraft Make: EURCPT Aircraft Model: EC-135
Aircraft Series: EC-135-P2
Airframe Hrs: 1470
Operator: GEH INC
Type of Operation: AIR TAXI/COMMUTER
Registration Nbr: N124CT
Total Aboard: 2 Fatalities: 0 Injuries: 0
Aircraft Weight Class: UNDER 12501 LBS
Number of Engines: 2
Engine Make: TURBOM Engine Model: ARRIUS 2B2

ENVIRONMENTAL/OPERATIONS INFO
Primary Fight Conditions: VISUAL FLIGHT RULES
Secondary Flight Conditions: WEATHER NOT A FACTOR
Flight Plan Filed: YES

PILOT IN COMMAND
Pilot Certificate: COMMERCIAL PILOT
Pilot Rating: ROTORCRAFT/HELICOPTER
Pilot Qualification: QUALIFIED
Flight Time Total Hours: 1180
Total in Make/Model: 860 Total in Last 90 Days: 28

EVENT REMARKS
ON JUNE 17, 2011, AT APPROXIMATELY 14:20 PT, AN EC-135, N124CT, OWNED AND OPERATED BY GREY ENTERPRISES HOLDINGS INC, HAD A MAJOR INCIDENT. THE AIRCRAFT WAS STABLE WHEN THE AIRCRAFT SUDDENLY PITCHED AND THE #1 ENGINE FIRE-LIGHT ILLUMINATED. THE PILOT SECURED THE #1 ENGINE WITH THE FIRE

BOTTLE AND ATTEMPTED TO RETURN TO SEA-TAC ON THE REMAINING ENGINE. #2 ENGINE FIRE-LIGHT ILLUMINATED. THE PILOT MADE AN EMERGENCY LANDING AT THE SOUTH-EAST CORNER OF SILVER LAKE. ON LANDING THE PILOT DEPLOYED THE SECOND FIRE BOTTLE AND SHUTDOWN AND EVACUATED THE AIRCRAFT. NO INJURIES WERE REPORTED. THE PILOT DEPLOYED THE ONBOARD PORTABLE FIRE EXTINGUISHER. THE AIRCRAFT MANUFACTURER IS EXAMINING THE AIRCRAFT ENGINES AND THE INITIAL ASSESSMENT IS THAT THE DAMAGE IS SUSPICIOUS AND MAY BE A RESULT OF MALICIOUS INTERFERENCE. THE NTSB WILL REQUIRE FURTHER REVIEW.

In my office, Welch, Taylor, and I pore over the report. Welch's grizzled face is craggier than ever in the harsh morning light, his expression grim. "At the moment, the NTSB only suspects sabotage, but we should proceed as if there was malicious interference. To that end, we've checked through all the CCTV footage at the helipad in Portland and found no suspicious activity." He shuffles in his chair and clears his throat. "However, there's an issue in the GEH hangar at Boeing Field."

Oh?

"Two of the cameras were inoperative, so we don't have complete coverage."

"What! How did that happen?" *What the fuck do I pay these people for?*

"We're endeavoring to find out," Welch answers, his voice deep and gravelly like an old car exhaust. "It's a major breach."

No shit, Sherlock. "Who's responsible?"

"There's a rolling shift system. So, it's down to four or five people."

"If they're found to be negligent, they're fired. All of them."

"Sir." He glances at Taylor.

"At present, we have no leads as to who's behind this," Taylor says.

"There's going to be a forensic examination of the aircraft," Welch adds. "My hope is that they'll turn something up."

"I want more than fucking hope!" I raise my voice.

"Yes, sir." Both men speak at the same time. Each of them looks contrite.

Hell. It's not their fault. *Grey. Get a grip.*

I continue in a more measured tone. "Find out who fucked up at the hangar. Fire them. And as soon as we have an idea of what occurred, I want to know. In the meantime, make sure the jet's secured and it's safe."

"Yes, sir," Taylor says.

"We're on it," Welch growls. He's pissed. He should be, this has happened on his watch. "The National Transportation Safety Board is all over this and I expect they'll brief law enforcement as their inquiries continue and, if appropriate, invite them to investigate in parallel. I'll circle back with the NTSB to confirm this."

"The police?" I ask.

"No. It'll be the FBI."

"Okay. Maybe they'll find something. Where are we with backup close protection?" I ask Taylor.

"Both Reynolds and Ryan are available and will start today."

"I want to keep Anastasia out of this. She doesn't need the worry. And I want to see the shortlist of who might be behind this. I have to say I'm at a loss."

"My team is compiling a list of potential suspects," Welch says.

"I'll do the same."

"Sir, now that this is on the FAA site, the press may pick it up and start asking questions," Taylor says.

Shit. "You're right. You can brief Sam now. I'll get him up here."

"Will do," he responds.

If this is going public, I have to tell Ana, too.

How the hell did we come to this?

Sabotage!

I do not need this shit right now.

I leave the two men discussing likely suspects and poke my head out of the door. Andrea looks up from her computer. "Mr. Grey?"

"Ask Sam and Ros to join us."

"Will do."

THERE'S A KNOCK ON my office door. It's Andrea. "Would you like more coffee?" she asks.

"Please."

On my computer screen is a list of all the acquisitions I've made since I started my company. I'm going through each one to see if I can find any potential suspects. So far I've drawn a blank; it's depressing. Deep down I'm worried about Ana—if someone wants to hurt me, she could end up as collateral damage. How could I live with myself if that was the case?

"Latte?"

"No. Black. Strong."

"Yes, sir." She closes the door and an e-mail pops up from my girl.

From: Anastasia Steele
Subject: Quiet Before/After the Storm?
Date: June 21 2011 14:18
To: Christian Grey

My dearest Mr. Grey
You are most quiet today. This concerns me.
I hope all is well in the land of high finance and business dealings.
Thank you for last night. You are quite the mouthful. ;)
Axx
PS: I see Mr. Bastille late this afternoon.

Ana! A warm flush spreads under my collar and I loosen my tie. She is quite the wanton with her choice of words. I type my response.

From: Christian Grey
Subject: Storm is here
Date: June 21 2011 14:25
To: Anastasia Steele

My darling fiancée
I must congratulate you on remembering your BlackBerry.
The storm clouds are gathering here and I will apprise you of the weather report and coming deluge when home.
In the meantime, I hope Bastille is not too hard on you. That's my job. ;)
Thank YOU for last night. Your stamina and your mouth continue to amaze me in the best of ways. ;) ;) :)

Christian Grey
Meteorologist & CEO, Grey Enterprises Holdings, Inc.

PS: I'd like to collect your remaining belongings from your apartment this week. You're never there...

From: Anastasia Steele
Subject: Weather Predictions
Date: June 21 2011 14:29
To: Christian Grey

Your e-mail has done little to assuage my concerns. I comfort myself in knowing that should it be needed, you own a shipyard and can no doubt build an ark. You are, after all, the most competent man I know.
Your loving Ana xxx
PS: Let's talk this evening about when I move in.
PPS: Is meteorology really your thing?

Her e-mail makes me smile and I run my index finger over the *x*'s.

From: Christian Grey
Subject: You Are My Thing.
Date: June 21 2011 14:32
To: Anastasia Steele

Always.

Christian Grey
Madly in Love CEO, Grey Enterprises Holdings, Inc.

IT'S 5:30 WHEN DR. FLYNN waves me into his office. "Good afternoon, Christian."

"John." I amble over to the couch, sit down, and wait for him to take his chair.

"So, big weekend for you," he says, sounding affable.

I look away. I don't know where to start.

"What is it?" he asks.

"Someone's trying to kill me."

Flynn pales—a first, I think. "The crash?" he asks.

I nod.

"I'm sorry to hear that." He frowns.

"My people are all over it. But I'm at a loss as to who it might be."

"You have no inkling?"

I shake my head.

"Well," he says, "I hope the police are involved and that you find the culprit."

"It will be the FBI. But my main concern is Ana."

John nods. "Her safety?"

"Yes. I've put additional security in place, but I don't know if it'll be enough." I swallow my rising anxiety.

"We've talked about this," he replies. "I know you loathe feeling out of control. I know you're panicked about Ana, and I understand why you feel that way. But you have the resources and you've put measures in place to keep her safe. That's all anyone can do." His gaze is level and sincere, and his words are reassuring. He smiles and adds, "You can't lock her up."

My laugh is cathartic. "I know."

"I also know you'd like to but put yourself in her shoes."

"Yeah. I know. I get it. I don't want to drive her away."

"Exactly. Good."

"That's not all I want to talk about."

"There's more?"

I let out a long sigh and recount in the briefest of terms the argument with Elena at my birthday party, and the subsequent rows with each of my parents.

"I have to say, Christian, it's never a dull moment with you." Flynn rubs his chin in response to my resigned smile. "We only have an hour—what do you want to talk about?"

"I had a nightmare last night. About Elena."

"I see."

"I've cut ties with her, as per my parents' requests. Gifted her the business."

"That's generous."

I shrug. "It is. But I'm okay with that, I think. Of course, she's still calling, but it was only twice today."

"She's been a huge influence in your life."

"She has. But it's time for me to move on."

He looks thoughtful. "Which did you find more upsetting, the argument with Elena or your parents?"

"Elena's was awkward, because Ana was in the room. We were spiteful to each other." My regret is clear in my tone, and deep down I wish we'd parted on better terms. "And Grace was so mad at me. I've never heard her curse before. But the argument with my dad was the worst. He was an asshole."

"He was angry?"

"Very." I ignore the stab of guilt in my guts at my disloyalty to Carrick.

"I wonder if he's projecting his anger at himself onto you. You can understand why he felt that way, can't you?"

No. Yes. Maybe.

Flynn continues, "Whether you agree or not, your father probably thinks Elena took advantage of a vulnerable adolescent. It was his job to protect you. He failed. That's probably how he sees it."

"She didn't take advantage. I was more than willing." My frustration echoes in my words.

I am so done with that argument.

John sighs. "We've discussed this many, many times, and I don't want to get into a debate with you about it again, but you might want to try and look at the situation from your father's point of view."

"He said I might not be husband material."

Flynn seems taken aback. "Oh. How did you feel about that?"

"Angry. Worried that he might be right." *Ashamed.*

"In what context did he say it?"

I wave my hand dismissively. "He was lecturing me about the sanctity of marriage. He said if I had no respect for that, I had no business being married."

John's brows draw together.

"Since Elena was married." I clarify for him.

"I see." Flynn purses his lips. "Christian," he says gently. "Your father may have a point."

What?

"Either you were a willing participant in a relationship with a married woman, a relationship that cost her her marriage—and much more, considering what happened to her—or you were a vulnerable adolescent who was taken advantage of. Which is it? You cannot have it both ways."

I glare at him. *What. The. Hell?*

"Marriage is a serious business," he says.

"Fuck it, John, I know that. You sound just like him!"

"Do I? That's not my intention. I'm just here to give you some perspective."

Perspective? Fuck.

I glare at him, then down at my hands, as the silence grows between us.

Perspective, my ass. "I think Carrick's wrong," I mumble eventually, and I realize that I sound like the surly teen my father still thinks I am.

"Of course he is. No matter what my views are on your relationship with Mrs. Lincoln, over the years you've demonstrated a constant commitment to her. I think it's your regret at terminating all contact with her that is wearing on your conscience."

"There's no regret!" I snap. "I've done this willingly."

"Guilt, then?"

I sigh. "Guilt? I don't feel guilty." *Do I?*

John remains impassive.

"Hence the nightmares?" I ask.

"Maybe." He taps his lip with his index finger. "You're giving up a long-standing pivotal relationship to please your parents."

"It's not for my parents. It's for Ana."

He nods. "You are rejecting everything you know for Anastasia, the woman you love. It's a huge step." He smiles once more. "In the right direction, if you ask me."

I gaze at him, not knowing what to say.

"Think about all I've said. Time's up," he says. "We can continue talking about this when I see you next."

I get up, feeling somewhat bemused. Flynn, as ever, has given me a great deal to chew on. But until we speak again, I have one outstanding question. "How's Leila?"

"Making good progress."

"Well, that's a relief."

"It is. I'll see you next week."

TAYLOR IS WAITING OUTSIDE in the Q7.

"I'm going to walk home," I inform him. I need some time to think. "I'll see you back at Escala."

He gives me a pained look.

"What?"

"Sir, I'd be much more comfortable if you rode in the car."

Oh, yes. Someone's trying to kill me.

I scowl as Taylor opens the rear door, but resigned, I climb inside.

Am I no longer master of my own universe?

My dark mood worsens.

"WHERE'S ANA?" I ASK Mrs. Jones when I enter the living room.

"Good evening, Mr. Grey. I believe she's in the shower."

"Thanks."

"Dinner in twenty minutes?" she asks as she stirs a pot on the stove. The aroma is tantalizing.

"Make it thirty." Ana in the shower has possibilities. Mrs. Jones tries to hide her smile, but I see it and ignore it. I go in search of my girl. She's not in the bathroom but the bedroom, standing at the window, wrapped in a towel and dewy from her shower.

"Hi," she says with a huge smile that vanishes as I approach. "What's wrong?"

Before I can reply, I wrap her in my arms and hold her tight, inhaling her sweet, just-showered fragrance. It soothes my soul.

"Christian. What is it?" She runs her hands up my back, pressing me close.

"I just want to hold you." I bury my face in her hair that's twisted into a chaotic topknot.

"I'm here. I'm not going anywhere." Her voice is tinged with tension. I hate it when she's anxious. I bring my hand up to cradle her head, tip it back, then press my lips to hers and kiss her, pouring my anxiety into our kiss. She responds immediately, caressing my face, opening up to me, her tongue sparring with mine.

Oh, Ana.

When she pulls away we're both winded, and I'm hard.

Fucking hard. For her.

"What's wrong?" she asks, gently cajoling me and scrutinizing my face for clues.

"Later," I murmur against her lips, and start walking her backward to the bed. She grabs at my lapels and tries to divest me of my jacket while her towel falls to the floor, leaving her naked in my arms.

Reaching up, I tug on the elastic holding her precarious bun and release her hair so that it tumbles down around her shoulders and breasts. My hands skim down her back and I cup her backside, pulling her against me. "I want you."

"I can tell." She wriggles against my erection.

Fuck. I grin and gently push her onto the bed so that she sprawls across it in all her naked glory, while I stand over her, my legs between her knees.

"That's better," I whisper, my earlier pique forgotten.

"Mr. Grey, as much as I like you in a suit, you seem to be overdressed." Gone is her anxiety—her eyes shine up at me, full of teasing desire. It's arousing.

"Well, I'll have to see what I can do about that, Miss Steele."

She bites down on her lower lip and runs her fingers down between her breasts. Her nipples are rosy, erect and ready. For my mouth.

It takes all my willpower not to rip off my clothes and bury myself in her. Instead, I grab the knot of my tie and gently tug it so it slowly unravels. Once it's loose, I toss it on the floor and undo the top button on my shirt.

Ana's mouth opens in a sexy, appreciative gasp.

Next, I shrug off my jacket and let it fall to floor, where it lands with a soft thud. I think that's my phone. But I ignore the sound and yank the hem of my shirt from my pants.

"Off or on?" I ask.

"Off. Now. Please." Ana doesn't hesitate.

I grin and ease my left cuff link from its place, then repeat the process with the right cuff.

Ana squirms on the bed.

"Keep still, baby," I whisper while I undo the lowest button on my shirt, then move my fingers up to the next, and the next, my eyes not leaving hers. When my shirt is undone, it follows the way of my jacket, and I grasp my belt. Ana's eyes widen and we drink each other in. I drag the end through the belt loop and undo the buckle, and as slow as I can I tug my belt free.

Ana angles her head slightly, watching me, and I notice the rise and fall of her breasts increases as her breathing accelerates.

I fold the belt in half and let it slide between my fingers.

Oh, Ana…what I'd like to do with this.

Her hips rise and fall, too.

I tug both ends of my belt so it snaps against itself, with a sharp crack. She doesn't flinch, but I know she hasn't signed up for this, so I drop it on the floor. She forces out a shallow breath, looking both relieved and maybe a little disappointed—I don't know. But now's not the time to think about that. I step out of my shoes and dispense with my socks, then undo the button on my pants and slide down the fly.

"Ready?" I ask.

"And waiting." Her voice is husky with lust. "But I'm enjoying the floor show."

I grin and drop my pants and boxer briefs, freeing my straining cock. Kneeling on the floor, I trail kisses up the inside of her calf, to her thigh, along the line of her pubic hair, up to her navel, to each of her breasts, until I'm hovering over her, poised and ready.

"I love you," I whisper, and ease into her, kissing her at the same time.

She groans. "Christian."

And I start to move. Slowly. Savoring her. My sweet, sweet Ana. My love.

She wraps her legs around me, her fingers diving into my hair and tugging hard.

"I love you, too," she purrs in my ear and moves with me, so we're in sync.

Together.

Us.

As one.

And when she falls apart in my arms, she takes me with her.

"Ana!"

SHE NUZZLES MY CHEST and I tense, waiting for the darkness, so she stops and raises her head. "As much as I liked your impromptu striptease and its aftermath, are you going to give me the weather report that you mentioned in your missives, and tell me what's wrong?"

I trail my fingertips up and down her back. "Can we eat first?"

She smiles. "Yes. I'm hungry. And maybe I need another shower."

I grin. "I like making you dirty." I sit up and slap her backside. "Up! I told Gail we'd be half an hour."

"You did?" Ana is scandalized.

"I did." I grin.

MRS. JONES'S THAI GREEN CURRY is delicious, as is the glass of Chablis we're enjoying with it. "So, the initial report came back from the FAA, and it will go public at some point."

"Oh?" Ana looks up from her meal.

"It appears that *Charlie Tango* was tampered with."

"Sabotage?"

"Exactly. I've upped our security arrangements until we nail who's responsible. And I think it's better if you stay here for now."

She nods, her eyes round with alarm.

"We have to be vigilant."

"Okay."

I arch a brow.

"I can do that," she adds hastily.

Good. That was easy.

But she looks stricken.

"Hey, don't worry," I murmur. "I'll do everything in my power to protect you."

"It's not me I'm worried about, it's you."

"Taylor and his people are all over this. Don't worry."

She frowns and places her fork on her plate.

"And don't stop eating."

Ana toys with her bottom lip and I reach across to clutch her hand. "Ana. It's going to be okay. Trust me. I won't let anything happen to you." I change the subject, hoping to move us to a safer topic. "How was Bastille?"

Her expression lightens, with her fond smile. "He was good. Thorough. I think I'm going to enjoy my sessions with him."

"I look forward to sparring with you."

"I thought we did that already, Christian."

I laugh. *Ah, touché, Anastasia…touché.*

Thursday, June 23, 2011

The morning sun is streaming through my office window as Ros enters, and we sit down at my small conference table. "How are you feeling?" I ask.

"Good, thanks, Christian. I think I've fully recovered from last week's crash-landing helicopter escapade."

"Your feet?"

She laughs. "Yes. Blisters are under control. You?"

"Yes, thanks. I think so. Though knowing it's sabotage is a bitch."

"Who would do such a thing?"

"I've no idea."

"Have you considered a disgruntled employee?"

"Welch's team is scrutinizing all the employee and ex-employee files to see if they can turn up any likely suspects. We've only identified Jack Hyde, the guy I fired at SIP."

"The book editor?" Ros's disbelief is obvious from her high-pitched exclamation. Her shocked expression almost makes me laugh.

"Yes."

"Seems unlikely."

"It does. Welch is trying to track him down, as it appears he's not been to his apartment since I fired him. He's following up on that."

"Woods?" she offers, as if suddenly inspired.

"He's definitely a suspect. Again, Welch is investigating."

"Whoever it is, I hope you catch the bastard."

"I hope so, too." Sooner rather than later. "What's first on your agenda this morning?"

"Kavanagh Media. We need to crack on with this deal. Have you approved the costs?"

"I know. I know. I have a couple of queries, which I'll discuss with Fred. But once I've done that, our final proposal can go. If their people approve the cost per foot, we can start on the fiber optic surveys."

"Okay. I'll hold off until you've checked with Fred."

"I'm seeing him later. I'll discuss it then. He's showing me his latest iteration of the tablet. I think we're ready for the next prototype."

"That's good news. Have you thought about the next step with Taiwan?"

"I read the reports. They're interesting. It's obvious their shipyard is thriving, and I understand why they want to expand. But what I can't get a handle on is why they're looking to the U.S. for investment."

"Uncle Sam is on our side," Ros asserts.

"True. I'm sure there will be tax advantages, but it's a big step to move some of our construction effort out of Seattle. I need to know they're solid, and that it works for GEH."

"Christian, it'll be cheaper in the long run. You know this."

"Undoubtedly, and with the price of steel climbing as it is right now, it might be the only way to keep the GEH shipyard open long term and retain jobs here."

"I think we should do a full impact assessment on what this will mean for our shipyard and the workforce."

"Yes." I respond. "That's a smart idea."

"Okay. I'll talk to Marco and get his team on it. But I don't think we can stall for too long. They'll go elsewhere."

"I get it. What's next?"

"The plant. Detroit. Bill has identified three potential brownfield sites and we're waiting for you to make a decision." She gives me a pointed look; she knows I've been procrastinating.

Why the fuck does it have to be Detroit?

I sigh. "Okay. I know Detroit is offering the best incentives. Let's do a comparative cost analysis, then talk through the pros and cons of each site. Let's try and get that done by next week."

"Okay. Good."

We move on to discuss Woods once more, and what legal recourse we're going to take, if any, for his disregard of our NDA.

"I think he's hung himself," I mutter with disdain. "The press has not been kind to him."

"I've drafted a letter and threatened legal action."

"And expressed our disappointment?"

She laughs. "Yes."

"Let's see if that shuts him up. Asshole," I mumble under my breath, but Ros frowns in disapproval at my epithet.

"He *is* an asshole," I exclaim in my defense. "And he's a suspect."

Ever the professional, Ros ignores my rudeness. "On a personal note—we're on track for your house purchase. You'll need to put the money in escrow. I'll send you the details and we can proceed with the surveys."

"I told my contractor that we'll start them next week, though I'm not sure I need them. I'll be making changes to the house."

"It can't do any harm. It would be good for your contractor to know what they're up against."

I nod. "You're right."

Her brows knit together once more. "You know, I've been thinking." She pauses.

"What?"

"Given the threat to your life, have you thought about installing a panic room in your apartment?"

I'm taken aback. "No, it's never occurred to me. I live in a penthouse. But you're right, maybe I should now."

Her smile is grim. "My work here is done."

"Not quite." From under the table I grab the Nordstrom bag that Taylor delivered earlier this morning. "These are for you. As promised."

"What?" Ros frowns, puzzled, as she takes the bag and peeks inside.

"Manolos," I say. "Your size, hopefully."

"Christian, you—" she protests.

I hold up my hands. "I gave you my word. I hope they fit."

She inclines her head and regards me with what looks like affection. It's unnerving. "Thank you," she says. "And for the record, in spite of what happened, I would fly with you again, anytime."

Wow. That is the greatest compliment.

AFTER SHE'S LEFT, I sit down at my desk and call Vanessa Conway in Procurement. I've been meaning to do this for a couple of days.

"Mr. Grey," she answers.

"Hi, Vanessa, this is a tall order, but here goes: after my helicopter went down Ros and I were rescued by a guy named Seb, who drove a semi. He's a one-man operation. I don't know if we could use him—he drives a huge rig."

"You want me to contact him?"

"I do. But you'll need to find him first. I don't have his details."

"Hmm. I'll see what I can do."

"He travels mostly between Portland and Seattle. I think."

"Okay. Leave it with me."

"Thanks, Vanessa." I hang up and wish once more that Seb had given me a card. At least he has mine, if he hasn't thrown it away. I'd like to repay him somehow.

I turn to my computer to check my e-mails. There's one from Ana.

From: Anastasia Steele
Subject: Missing you
Date: June 23 2011 11:03
To: Christian Grey

That is all.
Axx

From: Christian Grey
Subject: Missing you more
Date: June 23 2011 11:33
To: Anastasia Steele

I wish you'd change your mind and move the rest of your things to Escala this weekend.
You're with me every night as it is and what's the point in paying rent for a place that you never stay in?

Christian Grey
CEO, Grey Enterprises Holdings, Inc.

I've been subtly trying to persuade Ana to move in full-time. But as of yet, she refuses. Why is she hesitating over this? Since she arrived in Seattle, she's hardly lived in her own apartment. She's agreed to marry me...but not to this? I don't get it. It's irritating.

Move in with me, Ana.

From: Anastasia Steele
Subject: Stay With Me
Date: June 23 2011 11:39
To: Christian Grey

Nice try, Grey.
I have some wonderful memories of you in my apartment.
I told you. I want more.
I always want more.
Stay with me there.
Axx

Oh, Ana, Ana, Ana. You always want more. And I would, if we were safe.

From: Christian Grey
Subject: Your Safety
Date: June 23 2011 11:42
To: Anastasia Steele

Means more to me right now than making memories.
I can keep you safe in my Ivory Tower.
Please reconsider.

Christian Grey
CEO, Grey Enterprises Holdings, Inc.

PS: I hope you like the wedding planner.

My mother is meeting us tonight at Escala with The Wedding Planner. This is not how I would like to spend the evening. Why couldn't we just go to Vegas and get married? We'd be husband and wife by now. I might feel happier about it if Ana would stop procrastinating about moving in.

Why is she reluctant?

Does she need her apartment as a bolt hole, just in case she changes her mind?

Fuck.

Doubt is an ugly word, for an ugly feeling.

Why won't she fully commit?

Enough, Grey.

She's agreed to marry you!

To distract myself from these unsettling thoughts, I pick up the phone to call Welch for an update on the investigation into the crash, to ask if he's located Jack Hyde, and to inquire about panic rooms.

TAYLOR WILL NOT LET me walk to or from the mayor's office, so after a long lunch with the mayor, I reluctantly climb into the back of the Audi for the short drive back to Grey House. I'm not sure I appreciate him flapping around me like a mother hen. It's suffocating. I let out a long, slow breath, remembering Ana accusing me of doing precisely that.

Hell. I hope she's tolerating Sawyer's watchful eye.

On the plus side, Taylor has advised me to stop playing golf. Apparently there are too many trees surrounding the golf course where an assassin could find cover. I'm not a fan of the sport, so it's no hardship to give it up, though I believe Taylor is being a tad dramatic.

Glancing up through the panoramic sunroof, I catch a glimpse of brilliant summer blue above the steel and glass of downtown Seattle. For a moment I wish I was up there.

The freedom of walking on air.

I need to get back up there with Ana. We'd be safe in a sailplane, soaring the skies. And no longer under the ever-present vigilance of our security. The idea is extremely appealing. Only thing is, if I want to take Ana, I need a new sailplane, a model made for two. I rub my hands with glee, as this presents my kind of shopping opportunity. I fish my phone out of my pocket and start scouring the Alexander Schleicher website for their latest aircraft designs.

"THANK YOU SO MUCH, Christian, Ana. It has been wonderful to meet you, and you're going to have the most magical wedding."

"Thank you, Alondra," Grace coos. "I love your ideas." My mother claps her hands in uncharacteristic enthusiasm while I make a supreme effort to keep my smile fixed and not roll my eyes. I am on my best behavior. Ms. Gutierrez's ideas are great. I just want them done, and quickly, so we can get married.

"I'll see you out," Ana says, and leads her to the foyer.

"What do you think?" Grace asks.

"She's fine."

"Oh, Christian." Mom sounds irritated. "She's much more than fine."

"Okay. She's God's gift to wedding planning." My sarcasm bleeds into my words. Grace's lips thin and I think she's about to scold me, but Ana reenters the room.

"What did you think?" Ana asks, her gaze searching my face for answers.

"I thought she was fine. Did you like her?" That's the important question.

"Of course. I thought she was full of imaginative ideas. Dr. Gre—"

"Ana, *please*. Call me Grace."

"Grace," Ana says with an embarrassed smile. "So, we need to do a save-the-date note to all our guests?" Ana blinks rapidly, suddenly looking shell-shocked. "We don't even have a guest list," she whispers.

"That's easily done," I reassure her. Apart from the family, I think I have two guests: Ros and Dr. Flynn and their respective partners. Maybe Bastille…and Mac.

"There is one more thing," Grace says.

"What?"

"I know you don't want a Catholic ceremony, but would you consider asking Reverend Michael Walsh to officiate?"

Reverend Walsh. The name rings a bell.

"He's the chaplain at my hospital. He's such a dear friend, and I know you never saw eye to eye with any of the priests we know."

"Oh, yes. I remember him. He was always kind to me. I don't want a religious ceremony, but I'm fine with him conducting it, if that's okay with Ana."

Ana nods, a little pale; she looks overwhelmed.

"That's great. I'll talk to him tomorrow. In the meantime, I'll leave you two to get on with a list." Grace raises her cheek to me and I give her a quick peck. "Good-bye, darling," she says. "Ana, good-bye. I'll call."

"Great," Ana replies, though I think she lacks conviction. Is she not happy with the wedding planner? Is she as bewildered as I feel? I give her hand a reassuring squeeze, and together we walk my mother out to the foyer. Grace turns to me as we wait for the elevator.

"Please call your father, Christian."

I sigh. "I'll think about it."

"Stop sulking," she warns, quietly.

"Grace!" *Back off.*

Ana glances at the two of us, but wisely holds her tongue and says nothing. I'm saved by the ping of the elevator and its opening doors. I reach for Ana's hand as Grace steps inside. "Good night," she says, and the doors close.

"You're not talking to your father?" Ana asks.

I shrug. "I wouldn't go as far as to say that."

"Is this from last weekend? Your fight with him?"

I return her curious gaze, but say nothing. This is between him and me.

"Christian, he's your dad. He's only looking out for you."

I hold up my hand in the hope that she'll stop. "I don't want to discuss this." She folds her arms and raises that stubborn Steele chin. "Anastasia. Drop it."

Her eyes flash cobalt blue, but she sighs and lowers her arms, regarding me with what I think is a mixture of frustration and compassion.

Fifty Shades, baby.

"We have another issue," she says. "My dad wants to pay for the wedding."

"Does he, now?"

No way. It will cost a fortune, which he doesn't have. I'm not bankrupting my father-in-law. "I think that's out of the question."

"What? Why?" Ana's hackles are up.

"Baby, you know why." I don't want to debate this. "The answer's no."

"But—"

"No."

Her mouth forms that mulish line I know so well.

"Ana, you have carte blanche on this wedding. Whatever you

want. But not that. You know it's not fair to your father. It's 2011, not 1911."

She sighs. "I don't know what I'll say to him."

"Tell him my heart is set on providing everything for us. Tell him it's a deep-seated need that I have."

Because that's the truth.

She sighs again, resigned, I think.

"Now, shall we work on the guest list?" I ask, in the hope that starting this process will relieve her anxiety and also distract her from Ray.

"Sure," she acquiesces, and I know I've avoided a fight.

I NUZZLE HER EAR as she gasps for breath, fresh from her orgasm. Sweat beads on her forehead and her fingers still grip my hair.

"How was that, Anastasia?"

She garbles my name and I think she says "fantastic."

I grin. "Please move in with me."

"Yes. But not this weekend. Please. Christian." She's breathless. Her eyes flutter open and she implores me. "Please," she mouths.

Damn.

"Okay," I whisper. "My turn." I nip her earlobe and flip her onto her front.

Tuesday, June 28, 2011

"Leila wants to talk to you," Flynn says, and I know from the narrowing of his eyes that he's focusing on my reaction. I *think* this is a test, but I'm not sure.

"About what?" I ask, cautiously.

"I would guess that she wants to thank you."

"Should I?"

John leans back in his chair. "Talk to her? I don't think it's a good idea."

"What harm could it do?"

"Christian, she has strong feelings for you. She's displaced all that she felt for her deceased lover onto you. She thinks she's in love with you."

My scalp tingles and anxiety grips my heart.

No! How can she love me?

The thought is intolerable.

It will only ever be Ana. The sun, the moon, the stars—they rise and set with her.

"I think for Leila's sake you'll need to establish clear boundaries if you're going to engage with her," Flynn says.

Probably for my sake, too. "Can we keep all communication between Leila and me through you? She has my e-mail address, but she hasn't been in touch."

"I suspect that's because she's afraid you won't answer."

"She's right. I'll never forgive her for holding Ana at gunpoint."

"If it's any consolation, she's full of remorse."

I blow out a breath in exasperation; I'm not interested in her remorse. I want her healed and gone. "But doing well?" I ask.

"Yes. Very much so. The art therapy is working wonders; I think she wants to return to her hometown and pursue a fine-arts program."

"Has she found a school?"

"She has."

"If she stays away from Ana—and me, for that matter—I'll fund her studies."

"That's very generous of you." Flynn frowns, and I suspect he might be about to object.

"I can afford to be generous. I'm just glad she's recovering," I add quickly.

"She'll be discharged this week. She's going back to her folks."

"In Connecticut?"

He nods.

"Good." She'll be on the other side of the country.

"I've recommended a psychiatrist for her in New Haven, so she doesn't have to travel too far. She'll be well looked after." He pauses, then changes the subject. "Have the nightmares ceased?"

"For now."

"And Elena?"

"I've avoided all contact, but I signed the contracts yesterday. It's done. The Esclava group is hers now." The name Elena chose for her salons and the group has always made me smile. Even now.

"How does that make you feel?"

"I haven't really thought about it." My mind is cluttered with other concerns. "I'm just relieved it's over."

Flynn eyes me for a moment, and I think he's going to continue this line of inquiry, but he shifts. "And how are you feeling in general?"

I pause to consider his question, and the truth is, apart from the sabotage of my beloved *Charlie Tango*, and that someone wants me dead, I feel…good. I'm anxious, of course, and I'm pissed Ana won't move in to Escala yet, but I understand that she wants another night with me in her apartment, and that could happen this weekend. The panic rooms are going into the penthouse and we need to be out of there. It's a hotel, *The Grace*, or Ana's.

"I'm good."

"I can see that. I'm surprised." Flynn looks thoughtful.

"Why? What is it?" I ask.

"It's good to see you externalizing your anxiety, rather than turning it in on yourself."

I frown. "I think the threat to my life is external."

He nods. "Yes. It is. But it distracts you from giving yourself a hard time."

"I've not thought of it that way."

"Have you spoken to your father?"

"No."

Flynn remains impassive, his lips tightening slightly.

I sigh. "I'll get around to it."

He glances at the clock. "Time's up."

FRIDAY, JULY 1, 2011

There's a knock on my office door, and as Andrea enters, I look up from the selection of wedding stationery that Ana has sent me. "Yes?" I ask, surprised by her intrusion.

"Your father is here."

What? "In the office?"

"He's on his way up."

Shit!

"I'm sorry, Mr. Grey," Andrea continues. "I didn't want to leave him in the lobby." She shrugs apologetically. "He's your father."

For heaven's sake. I check the time. It's 5:15 and I'm due to leave at 5:30 for the long weekend.

"Ask him to wait."

"Yes, sir." She leaves and closes the door behind her.

What the hell.

I do not want another conversation with good old Dad. The last one went so well. But thanks to my PA, I have no choice.

Damn.

He never turns up unannounced…unlike my mother. Taking a deep breath, I stand and stretch. I roll down my shirt sleeves and don the cuff links that have been lying on my desk. Grabbing my jacket from the back of the chair, I slip it on and fasten one button. I tug at my shirt cuffs, then straighten my tie and run my hands through my hair.

Showtime, Grey.

Carrick is standing outside my door, holding his battered briefcase. "Dad." I keep my voice neutral.

His lips curl into a warm open smile that reveals twenty-four years of love and paternal pride.

Whoa. It floors me.

"Son," he says.

"Come in. Can I get you anything?" I ask, trying to keep a handle on my suddenly warring emotions.

Does he want a fight? Make peace? What?

"Andrea's already offered me something. I'm fine," he says. "I won't be long." He enters my office and takes a quick look around as I close the door. "It's a while since I've been here."

"Yes," I mutter.

"What a lovely portrait of Ana."

On the wall facing my desk, a monochrome Ana looks captivating as she stares at us, her smile sweet and shy, hinting at her amusement and belying her strength. I like to think she's laughing at me in that way she does; in that way that makes me laugh at myself. "My newly acquired portrait. Her friend from WSU, José Rodriguez, took it. He had an exhibition in Portland. You've met him at my place. The night *Charlie Tango* went down. There's a series. Seven in total. I had this one installed earlier this week. She has such a beautiful smile." I'm babbling.

Carrick's look is warm but guarded, and he runs his hand through his hair.

"Christian, I—" He stops, as if he's had a particularly painful thought.

"What?" I ask.

"I came to apologize."

And just like that all the wind is out of my sails, and I'm becalmed and lost at sea.

"What I said was wrong. I was angry. At myself." His gaze sears mine as his fingers grip the handle of the old valise that he's had for years. My throat tightens and burns as I search for something to say, and I remember how his briefcase always sat on a weathered chair in his study.

"Christian, this is the second school that has been forced to expel you for your belligerent behavior." Dad is beside himself. He's in full asshole mode. "This is totally unacceptable. Your mother and I are at our wits' end." He paces in front of his desk, his hands behind his back.

I stand before him, my knuckles raw and throbbing. My side aches from the kicking I've endured. But I don't give a fuck. Wilde deserved it. Stupid bullying prick. He likes to pick on kids smaller than he is. Poorer than he is. He's garbage, and the fucker's been expelled, too.

"Son, we are running out of options."

Dad and Mom are connected. I know they can find some other school. Fuck it, I don't need to further my education.

"We've even discussed military school."

He removes his glasses like he's in a movie and glares at me, waiting and wanting a reaction. But fuck him. Fuck military school. If that's what they want to do to get rid of me, fuck them. Bring it. I lower my eyes and stare at the stupid case he carries everywhere, ignoring the fire in my throat.

Why doesn't he take my side?

Ever.

The guy jumped me.

I stood my ground.

Fuck him.

Now the lines around his eyes are deeper and the lenses in his glasses thicker, and he's watching me, waiting for an answer to his apology in his calm and patient way.

Dad.

I nod. "Me, too," I murmur.

"Good." He clears his throat and glances once more at Ana on my wall. "She's a beautiful girl."

"She is. In every way."

His eyes soften. "Well, I won't keep you."

"Okay."

He flashes me a quick smile and before I can take another breath he's gone, the door closing behind him.

I exhale and the knot at the back of my throat tightens and pulls at my heart.

Fuck. An apology. From my dad. This is a first. I can barely believe it. I look at Ana with her secret smile, and it's as if she knew this was coming. *Christian, he's your dad. He's only looking out for you.* I hear her voice in my head and I realize I need to hear her in real time. Now.

I return to my desk and grab my phone.

Ana answers in one ring as if she's been expecting my call. "Hi." Her tone is soft and breathy, a gentle salve to my ragged soul.

"Hi," I whisper. "I've missed you."

I can almost hear her smile. "I've missed you, too, Christian."

"Ready for this evening?"

"Yes."

"Council of war?"

"Yes," she giggles.

Tonight. We sort the wedding. At her place.

ANA OPENS THE DOOR to her apartment and stands silhouetted in the kitchen light. She's wearing a floaty floral dress I've not seen before that's sheer against the light. All her lines and planes and curves are etched like a fine sculpture, outlined just for me. She's stunning.

"Hi," she says.

"Hi. Nice dress."

"This old thing?" She does a quick twirl, the skirt clinging to her legs, and I know she's worn it especially for me.

"I look forward to peeling you out of that later." I hold out the bunch of blush peonies I bought from Pike Place Market.

"Flowers?" Her face glows as she reaches for them and buries her nose in the bouquet.

"Can't I buy my fiancée flowers?"

"You may and you do. Though I believe this is the first time I've had a personal delivery."

"I think you're right. May I come in?"

She laughs, opening her arms, and I step into her embrace and hold her close. I nuzzle her hair, inhaling her intoxicating fragrance.

Home. Is. Ana.

She is my life.

"Are you okay?" She rests her palm on my cheek, her vivid blue eyes searching mine.

"I am now." I lean down for a quick kiss. Her lips brush mine, and what I mean to be a grateful, I'm-so-pleased-to-see-you kiss… becomes more. Much more. The fingers from her free hand wind around the nape of my neck and she opens up for me like an exotic flower, her mouth warm and welcoming. She sucks in a breath as my hand skirts down the soft fabric that adheres to her body and squeezes her backside. Her tongue greets mine, in every language, until we're both panting, and desire races through my veins looking for an out.

I groan and pull back, staring down into her beautiful dazed face.

"Okay, Taylor, you can go," I say.

"Thank you, sir." From behind me, Taylor steps out of the shadows of the stairwell, deposits my leather overnight bag inside the door, gives us both a nod, and heads back down the stairs.

Ana giggles. "I didn't know he was there."

"I forgot, too." I grin.

To my great disappointment, Ana releases me. "I have to put these gorgeous flowers in water." I watch as she moves over to the concrete kitchen island and I'm reminded of the last time I was here when Ana was facing an armed and deranged Leila. A shiver runs up my spine. That meeting could have gone so tragically wrong. No wonder Ana's been on about the two of us spending another night here. I'm sure she'd love to supersede the last memory she has of us in this place. Thankfully, Leila's recovered, and far across the country at her parents' place in Connecticut.

"Where's Kate?" I ask, remembering that Ana does not live alone.

"She's out with your brother." She fills a vase with water.

"So we have the place to ourselves." I shrug out of my jacket, take off my tie, and undo the top two buttons of my shirt.

"We do." Ana holds up a notebook. "And I have listed everything we need to discuss for the wedding."

"Can we take a rain check?"

"No. I know what your rain check will involve. And we need to do this, Christian. Council of war, remember?" She waves the book at me, raising that Steele chin in determination.

It's a good look on Ana.

I know she's been stressing about the wedding, though I don't know why. Ms. Gutierrez seems competent and is handling all the arrangements in an unflappable and efficient manner; our discussion should not take long.

"Don't pout," she adds, with her familiar amused smile.

I laugh. "Okay. Let's do this."

AN HOUR LATER WE'RE sitting on barstools at the kitchen counter and we've completed the application for a marriage license. Agreed on stationery. Color scheme. Menus. Cake design. And party favors.

Party favors!

"Christian, I don't think we should have a registry."

"Registry?"

"For wedding gifts."

"God, no."

"But if people want to give something, perhaps they could contribute something to your parents' charity, Coping Together?"

I stare at her, amazed and humbled at once. "That's genius."

Ana nods. "I'm glad you like the idea."

I lean forward and kiss her. "This is why I'm marrying you."

"I thought it was for my cooking."

I nod. "That, too."

She laughs, and it's a joyful sound.

"Okay, I've asked Kate to be my maid of honor," Ana says.

"Makes sense." I ignore my sinking feeling; Katherine is the most irritating woman I know. But she's Ana's best friend…so… *Suck it up, Grey.*

"I'm going to ask Mia to be my bridesmaid."

"Mia would love that, I'm sure."

"You'll need to find a best man."

"Best man?"

"Yes."

Well, it can only be Elliot. I'll have to ask him, and he'll give me shit.

"You don't really enjoy this, do you?" Ana fixes her gaze on me.

"I will enjoy being married to you."

She cocks her head to one side, and I know that she's not satisfied with my answer. I sigh. "No. I don't. I have never enjoyed being the center of attention, which is one of the reasons I'm marrying you."

Ana's brow creases and I run a knuckle down her cheek, because I haven't touched her in minutes. "You'll be the center of attention."

Ana rolls her eyes. "We'll see about that. I'm sure you'll look mighty fine in your wedding regalia, Mr. Grey."

"Do you have a dress?"

"Kate's mother is designing one for me." She looks down at her fingers and adds, "I asked my dad to pay for it."

"He's happy with that?"

She nods. "I think he's relieved he's not footing the bill for the wedding, but he's delighted he can contribute."

I grin. "Anastasia Steele, you're brilliant. I knew you'd find a compromise. You are such a good negotiator." I lean over and give her a peck on her lips.

"Hungry?" she asks.

"Yes."

"I'll cook us some steaks."

"SO, THE PANIC ROOMS, how will they work?" Ana asks as she slices into her filet mignon.

"There's one going into Taylor's office, and our bedroom closet will become one, too. Press a button and the doors will close and they'll be impenetrable. There'll be enough time for help to arrive. That's the plan, anyway."

"Oh." Ana blanches.

I clutch her hand. "It's merely a precaution. Here's hoping we never have to use them." I raise my glass of pinot noir and release her.

"I'll drink to that." She clinks my glass with hers.

"Don't look so worried. I will do everything in my power to keep you safe."

"It's not me I'm worried about, Christian. You know that. How... how is the investigation going?"

"Not fast enough, which is frustrating. But don't think about it. My team is on it." I don't want to trouble Ana with our lack of progress. "That steak was delicious." I put down my knife and fork.

"Thank you," she says, and pushes her empty plate aside.

"What shall we do now?" I ask, and I pitch my voice low, hoping my intention is clear. We have the whole apartment to ourselves, something we don't have at home.

Ana peers at me through her lashes. "I have an idea." Her voice is soft and sultry, and arousing. She skims her tongue across her top lip, and places her hand on my knee. The air is almost crackling between us with my desire.

Ana.

She leans in, giving me a wonderful view of her cleavage, and she murmurs in my ear, "It will involve getting wet."

Oh. She runs her thumb up the inside of my thigh.

Fuck.

"Yes." She leans in farther, her breath tickling my ear. "We could...wash the dishes."

What!

Tease!

Well, this is unexpected. And a challenge.

I stifle my smile, and not taking my eyes off hers, I skim my index finger over her cheek to her chin, then down her throat and her sternum to the *v* in her dress. Her lips part as her breathing deepens. I pinch the soft fabric between my thumb and forefinger and tug, pulling her toward me. "I have a better idea."

She gasps.

"A much better idea," I continue.

"What?"

"We could fuck."

"Christian Grey!"

I grin. I love shocking Ana. "Or we could make love," I add.

Smooth, Grey. Smooth.

"I like your ideas better than mine." Her voice is low and husky for real this time.

"Do you, now?"

"Mm-hmm. I'll take option one." Her eyes are smoky.

Ana, you goddess.

"Good choice. Take that dress off, now. Slowly."

She stands up so that she's between my thighs, and I think she's going to do as she's told, but she bends her head and places her hands on my thighs, then caresses the corner of my mouth with her lips. "You do it," she whispers against my skin, and every hair on my body stands to attention as desire heats my blood.

"As you wish, Miss Steele." I reach for the tie that holds her wrap dress together and gently unravel the bow so that her dress falls open.

Ana's not wearing a bra. *Deep joy.*

I run my hands up her back as she cups my face and starts to kiss me. Her lips are insistent and her tongue demanding. I groan and close my eyes as we revel in each other's kiss. Her skin is soft beneath my fingers as I draw her closer, pressing her to my chest. Her hands twist in my hair. And she tugs, forcing my head up.

Fuck.

Ana takes my bottom lip between her teeth and pulls.

Ow.

Ana!

I yank my head back and grab her wrists. "You're a little wild," I whisper, awed. She shimmies between my legs, her nipples brushing against my shirt and hardening as I watch. Her hair falls over her shoulders and shrouds her breasts while my pants grow tighter by the second.

What has gotten into her?

She's exhilarating. Provocative.

"Are you teasing me?" I ask.

"Yes. Take me."

"Oh, I will. Right here. When I'm ready."

She gasps, eyes sultry and full of invitation, and I think she must have consumed more pinot than I thought. Gently I steer her backward and release her hands as I rise off my seat. I peer down at her as she studies me from beneath her long lashes.

"How about here?" I pat the top of the stool.

She blinks a couple of times as her lips part in surprise.

"Bend over," I whisper.

Her teeth dig into her plump lip, leaving little indent marks, and I know she's doing this on purpose.

"I believe you requested option one," I remind her.

"I did."

"I won't ask you again." I unbutton my pants and slowly tug down my zipper, giving my erection some much-needed room.

Ana stares at me, looking licentious and lovely, dressed only in her pretty open frock, a pair of white panties, and her high-heeled sandals. She raises her hands, and I think she's going to take her dress off.

"Leave it on," I insist, and reaching into my pants, I ease out my cock. "Ready?" I ask, and start to move my hand up and down, pleasuring myself. Her dark gaze strays from my hand to my face, and with a knowing smile, she turns and lies right over the stool.

"Grab the legs," I urge, and she does, wrapping her fingers around the iron struts. Her hair brushes the floor and I move her dress so it hangs down her left side, leaving her glorious ass in view. "Let's get rid of these," I murmur, and run a finger across her skin above the elastic of her underwear. I kneel and slowly drag them down her legs and over her shoes. I toss them to the side and take her ass in my hands and squeeze.

"You look mighty fine from this angle, Miss Steele," I whisper and kiss her butt. She squirms appropriately and I can't help myself. I slap her hard so that she yelps and I ease one finger inside her. Her moan is loud and she strains her body, pushing against my hand.

She wants this.

She's wet.

So wet.

Ana. You never disappoint.

I kiss her ass once more and stand up while moving my finger in. Out. In. Out.

"Legs. Wider," I order as I fondle her backside. She moves her feet. "Wider."

She shuffles them to the side until I'm satisfied.

Perfect.

"Hold on, baby." I withdraw my hand and with infinite care slowly slide into her.

She gasps.

Fuck. She's heaven.

I place my hand on her back and with the other I clutch the edge of the kitchen counter. I do not want to topple us both.

"Hold on," I say once more and ease out of her, then slam into her.

"Ah!" she cries.

"Too much?"

"No. Keep going!" she whimpers.

And her wish is my command. I start to fuck her. Hard. Each stroke. Each push. Takes me away from everything, all my strife, all my worries. There's only Ana. My girl. My lover. My light.

She cries out. Once, twice, three times. Begging me for more. And I keep going, taking her with me. Taking her higher. On and on until she calls out a strangled, loud version of my name. And she comes, over and over, with the force of a spring tide.

"Ana!" I cry and join her.

I collapse over her, then drop to the floor, taking her with me and cradling her in my arms. I kiss her eyelids, her nose, her mouth, and she puts her arms around my neck.

"How was option one?" I ask.

"Hmm..." she hums with a dazed smile.

I grin. "Same for me."

"I'd like some more."

"More? Jesus, Ana."

She kisses my chest where my shirt is open, and I realize I'm still fully dressed.

"Let's try the bed this time," I whisper into her hair.

ANA MOANS. "PLEASE!" Her hands are fastened, courtesy of her robe tie, to the spindles of her bedstead. She's naked, her nipples long and hard, and pointing skyward, courtesy of my lips and tongue. I have her feet in one hand, pushed up on the bed near her behind, so her legs are akimbo and she's straining for release. Slowly I ease my index finger in and out of her while my thumb circles her clitoris.

She can't move.

"How's this?" I ask.

"Please!" She's hoarse.

"Do you like me to tease you?"

"Yes," she cries.

"Do you like teasing me?"

"Yes."

"I like it, too." I stop my thumb and still my hand, my finger still inside her.

"Christian! Don't stop!"

"Tit for tat, Anastasia." She's endeavoring to push her hips up on my hand to find her release. "Still," I whisper. "Stay still."

Her mouth is slack, eyes dark and full of lust and need and all a man could want.

"Please," she whispers, and I can tantalize her no more. I release her feet and withdraw my hand. Taking hold of her knee, I run my nose and lips down her thigh to my ultimate goal.

"Ah!" she yells when my tongue swirls over her swollen clitoris. I slide two fingers inside her, pushing once, twice, and she lets out a boisterous cry and her orgasm washes over me. I kiss her belly, her stomach, between her breasts, then I slowly sink into her as her climax dies.

"I love you, Ana," I whisper, and I start to move.

ANA SLUMBERS BESIDE ME while above me, the tie from her robe is still attached to the bed spindles. I contemplate waking her and having my wicked way with her a third time, marveling that I still want more. Will I ever have enough of Anastasia Steele? But she needs to sleep. Tomorrow we go sailing. Just the two of us and *The Grace*. She'll need her energy to help me on board. We'll be away from everyone for three whole days, enjoying our own July Fourth celebration, and my hope is that I can finally relax, at least for a few days.

My mind drifts to my dad and his surprise apology, to menus and party favors, to the crash and the unknown saboteur. I hope Reynolds and Ryan are okay outside.

They're keeping watch.

Ana's safe. We're safe.

TUESDAY, JULY 5, 2011

Sitting at my desk and staring out at the distant Sound, I can't help but notice the heartwarming glow that's emanating either from my skin or from somewhere deep inside my chest. It could be a combination of sea, sun, and wind from being aboard *The Grace* for the long weekend, or it could be because I've spent three uninterrupted days with Anastasia. Despite all the vexing issues I've dealt with over the past few weeks, I've never felt as relaxed as I did with her on board my catamaran. Ana is food for my soul.

Anastasia is fast asleep. The early morning light shimmers through the portholes skimming over her tousled hair so that it gleams, burnished and beautiful. Sitting down on the edge of the bed, I place a cup of tea on the nightstand, as The Grace *bobs gently on the water in Bowman Bay. I lean over and plant a tender kiss on her cheek.*

"Wake up, sleepy head. I'm lonely."

She groans, but her expression softens. I kiss her again and her eyes flutter open, and her face shines with a breathtaking smile. Reaching up, she caresses my cheek.

"Good morning, husband-to-be."

"Good morning, wife-to-be. I've made you tea."

She chuckles, in disbelief, I think. "You dear man," she says. "This belongs on the list of firsts!"

"I believe it does."

"And I can tell you're very pleased with yourself." Her grin mirrors mine.

"Miss Steele. I am. I make an excellent cup of tea."

She sits up, and to my disappointment pulls up the covers to conceal her naked breasts. She can't seem to stop grinning. "I'm so impressed. It's such a complicated process."

"Indeed, it is," I reply. "I had to boil the water and everything."

"And dip the tea bag. Mr. Grey, you are so competent."

I laugh and narrow my eyes. "Are you belittling my tea-making skills?"

She gasps in mock horror and clutches imaginary pearls. "I wouldn't dare," she says and, reaching over, takes the cup.

"Just checking—"

A knock on my office door brings me back to the now. Andrea pops her head around the door. "Mr. Grey, your tailor is here."

"Oh, great. Show him in."

I need a new suit for the wedding.

MARCO HANDLES THE COMPANY portfolio as well as our Mergers and Acquisitions. This morning he's taking the senior team through GEH's latest additions to our shareholdings. "We now own twenty-five percent of Blue Cee Tech, thirty-four percent of FifteenGenFour, and sixty-six percent of Lincoln Timber." I've been listening with half an ear, but my attention is momentarily piqued by that last piece of news. This is a long-term project of mine, and I'm pleased we now own a majority stake in Lincoln Timber through one of our shell companies. Linc must need the money. Interesting.

Revenge is a dish…

Enough, Grey. Concentrate.

Marco moves on to his latest list of potential acquisitions. There are two companies that he is especially keen to pursue. He's running through the pros while my mind strays to the weekend and Ana.

Ana is at the helm of The Grace *as we glide over the sparkling ocean, past Admiralty Head on Whidbey Island. Her hair is flying in the wind and glinting in the sun. Her smile could melt the hardest of hearts.*

It thawed mine.

She looks beautiful. Relaxed. Free.

"Hold her steady," I shout over the rush of the sea.

"Aye-aye, Captain. I mean, Sir." Ana bites her lip, and I know

she's teasing me, as usual. She salutes when I give her a bogus scowl, and I go back to tightening the bowline, unable to hide my smile.

Marco mentions a solar energy company that's struggling to find investment.

An enticing aroma of batter and bacon welcomes me with open arms as I enter the galley. My girl is making pancakes. She's dressed in a T-shirt and far-too-short denim shorts, and her hair is in pigtails.

"Good morning." I wrap my arms around her, pressing her back to my front, and skim my lips down her neck. She smells so good, of soap and warmth and sweet, sweet Ana.

"Good morning, Mr. Grey." She angles her head, giving me better access to her throat.

"This takes me back," I murmur against her skin, and tug one of her pigtails.

She giggles. "That seems a lifetime ago. These, however, are not cherry-popped-by-would-be-Dominant pancakes. These are Independence Day pancakes. Happy Fourth of July."

"There's no other way I'd like to celebrate than with pancakes." I kiss her beneath her earlobe. "Well, I can think of one way." I gently tug her pigtail once more. "You always get an A."

"Christian," Ros says, her tone abrupt. Seven pairs of eyes are all directed at me. *Shit.* I stare blankly back at Ros, ignoring everyone else, and tilt my head to one side.

"What do you think?" She's barely disguising her irritation, and I assume this is not the first time she's asked.

Come clean, Grey. "I'm sorry, I was miles away."

Her lips form a thin line and she glances at Marco, who gives me a warm smile and proceeds to give me an executive summary of what he's just outlined.

"Okay," I respond when he's finished. "Let's go after Geolumara. They could be a worthwhile addition to the energy division. We need to widen our footprint in green energy."

"The others?"

I shake my head. "We should consolidate. Let's concentrate on Geolumara. Send me all the details."

"Will do."

"We need a decision on the Taiwan shipyard. They are eager for a response from us." Ros looks pointedly at me.

"I read the impact assessment."

"And?"

"This is a gamble."

"It is," she acknowledges.

"But everything in life is a gamble, and at least as a joint venture we'll share the risk and it might secure the future of the shipyard here."

Ros and Marco nod.

"Let's move this forward."

"I'll get the team on that," Marco says.

"Good. I think that's it. Thank you, everyone."

They all rise, except for Ros. "Can I have a quick word?" she asks.

"Sure."

She waits until everyone leaves.

"Well?" And I wait for her to chastise me for my daydreaming.

"Woods has withdrawn his legal threats. We're all good."

"That's not what I was expecting you to say."

"I know. Honestly, Christian, it's like you're on your honeymoon already."

"Honeymoon? I haven't even thought about a honeymoon."

Shit. Something else to organize.

Ros scoffs. "You'd better get on it." She shakes her head. "I know I'd whisk Gwen away to Europe."

I'm surprised by Ros's candor—she rarely discusses her home life, although I know she has a domestic partnership with Gwen. Frequent attempts to legalize gay marriage in Washington have been thwarted. I make a mental note to talk to Senator Blandino about this when we next meet; surely she can apply some pressure to the governor and help push this agenda? "I thought Ana and I might stay somewhere near Bellevue overnight. We're both working."

"Grey, you can do better than that." Ros screws up her face in mock disgust as she starts to gather her papers together.

I laugh. "Yes, I can. And what's more, I'll have fun figuring out what to do. Europe, you say."

Ana's always wanted to see Europe. England especially.

Ros's lips twitch into a benevolent smile as she stands. "Good luck with that." Her parting words echo through the empty room, leaving me to contemplate where the hell I'm going to take the future Mrs. Grey for a honeymoon.

I hope she has a passport.

BACK IN MY OFFICE I check my computer, and there's an e-mail from Ana that she sent an hour ago.

From: Anastasia Steele
Subject: Jibbing and Jibing. Bowlines and Halyards.
Date: July 5 2011 9:54
To: Christian Grey

My darling Mr. Grey
What a spectacular weekend! The best July 4th ever. Thank you.
I am also giving you advance notice that I will be staying at my apartment with Kate on Friday. I will be packing so I can move in with you on Saturday. But, I should warn you, this will be a girls-only evening, so your presence will not be required, but much missed.
Maybe you can write your vows?
Just an idea.
Laters, baby.
Axxx

From: Christian Grey
Subject: Abandoning ship.
Date: July 5 2011 11:03
To: Anastasia Steele

My darling fiancée
Thank YOU for the most relaxed July 4th I've ever experienced.
I will miss you on Friday.
But will help you move in on Saturday.
You make my dreams come true.
I will consider my vows and maybe write a few...

I did not mean that to rhyme!

Christian Grey
CEO & poet, Grey Enterprises Holdings, Inc.

PS: Do you possess a passport?

From: Anastasia Steele
Subject: Citizen of the USA
Date: July 5 2011 11:14
To: Christian Grey

Dear Poet
I'd stick to high finance if I were you.
Though I'm glad your dreams doth come true.
I'm thrilled and honored to report.
I do possess a new passport.
Now you have me thinking why?
Are we off someplace to fly?
I'd love to travel the world with you.
Not as one, but as two.

Curious of Seattle xxx
(And not a poet, as you can tell!)

My future wife is a dreadful poet! Grinning at her response, I grab my gym bag and head out of the office, and down to the basement to face Bastille.

FRESH FROM THE GYM, I finish my chicken-salad sandwich at my desk and pick up the phone. It's time to call Elliot. I've been putting this off because I know he'll give me shit.

"Hotshot. What gives?"

"Hello, Elliot. How are you?"

He laughs. "Jesus, man, you sound bored as fuck!"

Why is this so difficult?

"I'm not bored. I'm working. And taking some time out to talk to you."

"Now you sound pissed."

"I am."

"Something I said?" He cackles over the line, and I'm tempted to hang up and try again later.

I take a deep breath. "I need to ask you something."

"About the new house?"

"No."

Game on, Grey. Ask him.

"Spit it out, man," he says when I don't respond. "This is like waiting for concrete to cure."

"Will you be my best man?"

There. It's done. And there's a deafening silence on the other end of the phone, save for his quick gasp. *Shit.* Is he going to say no?

"Elliot?"

"Sure," he says with uncharacteristic brevity. "Um…I'd be honored." He sounds stunned. Why? Surely he knew this was coming?

"Good. Thank you." My relief is clear in my voice.

He laughs, and I know my brother has recovered his dickwad humor. "Of course, this means I get to organize your goddamned bachelor party!" He whoops like a deranged gorilla.

Bachelor party? He's got to be kidding.

"Whatever, Elliot." An idea pops into my head. "Come over Friday. We can shoot some pool. Ana is spending the evening with Kate."

"Yeah, I heard. Sure thing. We can talk strippers, and where we'll leave you handcuffed at the end of a drunken night!"

I laugh, because he has no idea. "*We?*" I ask.

"I know you have no friends, you fucking recluse. I'll drum up a posse who know how to party."

Oh no.

"Let's talk Friday," I respond.

"Can't wait. By the way, have you been in touch with Gia?"

"Yes, I have. Ana and I had a look at her portfolio online. We both liked what we saw. Ms. Matteo was going with the real estate agent to check out the property so that when we meet she knows what we are talking about."

"I need to see this place, too, hotshot."

"I know. Let's do it Friday. After work."

"Rad. Sounds good."

"Okay. Laters, Elliot." An unexpected surge of warmth fills my chest. "And, um…thank you."

"What are brothers for?"

•

"So, this is your new office, hotshot." Elliot strolls through the door, as laid-back as his tone.

"Do you have to call me that, Lelliot?" I stress his nickname and wave him toward my white leather couch.

"It's what you are. Look at this place." He waves a hand in the direction of my outer office. Wearing jeans, a T-shirt, and his Aztec jacket from San Diego State, he looks like the proverbial fish out of water here.

I sit down opposite him and notice that his knee is bouncing to a crazy beat and he's avoiding eye contact.

What the hell? He's nervous.

I don't think I've ever seen him this way.

"What is it?" I ask.

He shuffles in his seat and presses his hands together. "I want to start my own construction company." He blurts out the words in a rush.

Ah! "You're looking for investment."

His vibrant blue eyes finally meet mine. "Yes," he says with a steeliness that surprises me.

"How much do you need?"

"About 100K."

I smirk at the irony. That's what I started my business with.

"It's yours."

Elliot balks. "You're not going to ask for a business plan? A pitch?"

"No. You may be an utter fucking asshole sometimes, but you work hard. I see that. You're passionate about what you do. This is your dream. And I believe in it, too. We should all be striving for sustainable living. Besides, you're my brother, and what are brothers for?"

When Elliot smiles, he lights up a room.

Feeling uncomfortable at the sudden swell of feelings for my brother, I dial Welch's number for an update on his investigation.

NIGHT SHROUDS MY STUDY at Escala. I've been poring over the documents Marcus sent me regarding Geolumara. Based in Nevada, their solar farms are already producing enough kilowattage to light up two neighboring towns. They have the expertise to bring cheaper renewable energy to other parts of the U.S. I think they have a great deal of potential. I'm excited to acquire the company and see what we can add to their business model. I e-mail Marcus to confirm my enthusiastic interest, then go find Ana.

She's in the library, curled up in her armchair, laptop on her knees and Snow Patrol playing quietly over the sound system. I assume she's working on an upcoming book, and it occurs to me that we should get her a desk and chair in here.

"Hi," I say when she looks up.

"Hi." She smiles.

"Are you reading another manuscript?"

"I'm doing the first draft of my vows."

"I see." I saunter into the room. "How's that going?"

"It's intimidating, Mr. Grey. A little like you."

"Intimidating? Moi?" I press my hand to my chest and feign surprise.

She purses her lips to hide her smile. "It's your specialty."

Settling into the armchair beside Ana's, I lean toward her, my elbows resting on my knees. "Oh. I thought I had other specialties..." Even from this distance I catch a whisper of her fragrance.

Pure Ana. It's intoxicating.

A pretty pink stains her cheeks. "Well, yes. You are blessed with other specialties. This is true." She closes her laptop, tucks her feet beneath her, and raises her chin with the air of a prim, old-fashioned schoolteacher.

I laugh. I know better. Ana has an inner freak. "As long as you promise to love, honor, and obey, I'm sure your vows will be perfect."

Ana laughs. "Christian, I am not promising to obey you."

"What?" *She thinks I'm joking?*

"No way," she says simply.

"What do you mean you're not going to obey?" My stomach feels like it's dropped twenty feet. I meant my comment to be an amusing quip, but I'm thrown by her response. Ana flicks her hair over her shoulder, and it captures the light from the table lamp, highlighting the few red and gold strands; it's beautiful, distracting me. But my attention shifts to her mouth. Her lips flatten into a stubborn line, as she folds her arms and straightens her shoulders in that way she does when she's gearing up for a fight.

Hell. She's going to argue with me?

"You can't be serious! I'll love and honor you always, Christian. But obey? I don't think so."

"Why not?" I'm perfectly serious.

"Because it's the twenty-first century!"

"And?" *How can she oppose me on this?* The conversation is not going the way I expected.

"Well, I'd hope that we could come to some consensus on issues within our marriage through discussion. You know…communicating with each other," she continues.

"I'm hoping for that, too. But if we can't, and we reach an impasse and you go off and put yourself in unnecessary danger—" All manner of horrific scenarios flit through my mind, and unease spawns exponentially in my gut.

Her face softens as she relaxes, her eyes glowing with understanding. "Christian, you always think the worst. You worry too much." She reaches out to stroke my face, her fingers soft and gentle against my skin.

"Ana. I need this," I whisper.

With a heavy sigh, she withdraws her hand and stares at me, as if she's trying to convey a message via telepathy. "Christian, I'm not religious, but our wedding vows will be sacred, and I'm not prepared to make a vow I might break."

Her response is a gut punch, echoing Carrick's words when he lectured me about Elena. *We are talking about the sanctity of marriage. And if you have no respect for that, then you have no business being married.*

I stare at her as my anxiety boils over into frustration. "Anastasia, be reasonable."

She shakes her head. "Christian. *You* be reasonable. You know you have a tendency to overreact. The answer's no."

Me? Overreact?

I glare at her, and for the first time in a long while I don't know what to say.

"You're just tense about the wedding," she says, gently. "We both are."

"I'm a hell of a lot more tense knowing you're not willing to obey. Ana, reconsider. Please." I sweep my hand through my hair and stare into her big blue eyes, but I see nothing except her determination and courage. She's not budging.

Fuck.

This is getting us nowhere, and the grasp on my temper is slipping. It's time to back away before I say something I regret. I get up and try one last attempt. "Think about it. But for now, I have some work to finish." And before she can stop me, I leave the library and head back into my study, trying to think of some way to get her to see sense.

One of us has to be in charge, for fuck's sake.

I stomp over to my desk and slump into my chair, feeling blindsided by her attitude and resentful that I'm only now finding out that she won't obey.

To hell with it.

I'll have to make her see reason.

How?

Shit.

I'm too wound up to think clearly, so I shelve my frustration and open my computer to look through my e-mails. The good news is that my new sailplane will be arriving from Germany next week. It's being shipped to my hangar at the Port of Ephrata. I allow myself a moment of excitement, a glider built for two. I want to run and tell Ana, but right now I'm mad at her.

Damn.

It's depressing. To cheer myself up I reread the specs for the new aircraft, and when I've exhausted all there is to read, I get back to my financial reports.

A tentative knock interrupts me.

"Come in."

Ana pokes her head around the door. "It's nearly midnight," she says with a winsome smile. She eases the door open and stands on the threshold dressed in one of her satin nightgowns. The soft material caresses her body, molding itself to every curve and dip, leaving nothing to my imagination. My mouth dries and my body responds, hot and heavy with longing.

"Are you coming to bed?" she whispers.

I ignore my arousal. "I have a few more things to do."

"Okay." She smiles, and I half smile in return, because I love her. But I'm not going to concede on this. She has to come to her senses. Ana turns to leave but gives me a quick provocative look over her shoulder before closing the door and leaving.

Once more I'm on my own.

Hell.

I want her.

But she won't obey and that's pissed me off. Big-time.

I turn back to the latest figures from Barney's division at GEH. They're not nearly as seductive as the delectable, and disobedient, Miss Steele.

WEDNESDAY, JULY 6, 2011

Ana is fast asleep when I crawl into bed beside her. Ever thoughtful, she's left my bedside light switched on so I won't be lost in the dark. And yet, that's exactly how I feel. *Lost.* And if I'm being honest, discouraged. Why can't she understand? It's not that big a deal, is it? *Is it?*

Watching her lovely, tranquil face and the steady rise and fall of her breasts as she sleeps, an ugly undercurrent looms beneath my ribs; it's envy. I'm lying here, bewildered and miserable, and she's sleeping like she hasn't a care in the world.

But would I want her any other way?

Of course not. I want her happy and I want to protect her. But how can I do that if she's not willing to obey me?

Deal with it, Grey.

Sighing, I lean over and brush her hair with my lips; it's the gentlest of touches, as I don't want to wake her. But I silently implore her to change her mind.

Please, Ana. Grant me this.

Switching off the light, I stare, unflinching, into the dark, and suddenly the silence in the room is deafening and oppressive. My heart rate doubles and I'm dragged down into a swamp of despair. It's overwhelming. Maybe this is a huge mistake. Our marriage is never going to work if she can't do this.

What was I thinking?

Maybe I want—no, *need*—someone more submissive.

I *need* to be in control.

Always.

Without control, there is chaos. And anger. And hurt, and fear… and pain.

Shit. What am I going to do?

This is an impossible hurdle to overcome.

Isn't it?

But living without Ana would be unbearable. I know what it's like to bathe in her light. She is warmth and life and home. She is everything. I want her by my side. I love her.

How can I get her to reconsider?

I rub my face, trying to fend off my bleak thoughts.

Get a grip, Grey. She'll come around.

I close my eyes and try to utilize Dr. Flynn's mindfulness exercises and find my happy place. Maybe a flowery bower in a boathouse…

I'm walking on air, soaring high in the sky above Ephrata. The Washington landscape is a patchwork beneath me. I wing over and marvel at the quilt of browns and blues and greens crisscrossed by roads and irrigation canals. Catching a thermal I rise above a ridge on the Beezley Hills. The sky is unencumbered, a dazzling, shimmering blue, and I'm at peace. The wind my companion. Constant. Rushing. The only sound. I am alone. Alone. Alone. I wing over again. My world turned upside down. And Ana is in front of the cockpit, her hands stretched out to the canopy, squealing with joy. And wonder. My heart is brimming. This is happiness. This is love. This is what it feels like. I bank, and suddenly I'm in a tailspin. Ana's disappeared. I stamp my feet, but the rudder's gone. I fight the control stick, but the ailerons don't respond. I have no control. All I hear is the roar of the wind and someone screaming. We're going down. Fuck. Spinning. Down. Down. Down. *Shit.* I'm going to hit the ground. *No. No!*

I wake with a start.

Fuck.

I'm wrapped around Ana, and she's threading her fingers through my hair. Her scent is soothing and it's filling the desperate emptiness that's deep in my soul. "Good morning," she says, and immediately I'm calmer. Back to earth.

"Good morning," I whisper, confused. I normally wake before Ana.

"You were having a bad dream."

"What time is it?"

"It's just after seven-thirty."

"Shit. I'm late." I give her a brief, chaste kiss and bound out of bed.

"Christian," she calls.

"I can't stop. I'm late," I mutter as I disappear into the bathroom, recalling her defiance from last night.

And I'm still pissed.

AT MY DESK, I eye the model glider that Anastasia gave me when she left. It took me a whole day to make. Unease circles my gut; maybe it's the echo of that dream or a reminder of the desolation I felt when she was gone. I touch the wing tip, holding the cool plastic between my thumb and forefinger; I never want to feel like that again.

Ever.

I shake off the feeling and take a sip of the espresso that Andrea has prepared, followed by a bite of fresh croissant. I glance at my iMac to see an e-mail has arrived from Ana.

From: Anastasia Steele
Subject: Eat!
Date: July 6 2011 9:22
To: Christian Grey

My dearest husband-to-be
It is not like you to skip breakfast. I missed you.
I hope you're not hungry. I know how disagreeable that is for you.
I hope your day is a good one.
Axxx

I'm comforted by the number of small *x*'s at the end of her message, but I glance at her portrait on my office wall, close the e-mail, and summon Andrea into my office to go through my schedule.

I'm still pissed.

AFTER LUNCH, I'M IN the elevator returning from an external meeting with Eamon Kavanagh when I check my BlackBerry. There's another e-mail from Ana.

From: Anastasia Steele
Subject: Are you okay?
Date: July 6 2011 14:27
To: Christian Grey

My dearest husband-to-be
It's not like you not to reply.
The last time you didn't reply—your helicopter went missing.
Let me know you're okay.

Ana
Worried of SIP

Shit. A twinge of guilt flares in my stomach, especially as there is a distinct lack of kisses on her note.

For fuck's sake.

I'm mad at you, Anastasia.

But I don't want her to worry. I type out a brief reply.

From: Christian Grey
Subject: Are you okay?
Date: July 6 2011 14:32
To: Anastasia Steele

I'm fine.
Busy.

Christian Grey
CEO, Grey Enterprises Holdings, Inc.

I press send and hope my response will alleviate her worries. Andrea eyes me warily when I exit the elevator into the outer office.

"Yes?" I snap.

"It's nothing, Mr. Grey. I just wanted to know if you wanted any coffee?"

"Where's Sarah?"

"She's photocopying the reports you requested."

"Good. And no thanks to coffee," I add in a softer tone. *Why am I being an asshole to my staff?* "Get me Welch on the line."

She nods and picks up the phone.

"Thanks," I mumble, and head into my office. I slouch into my chair and stare despondently out of the window. The day is bright, unlike my mood.

My phone buzzes. "Grey."

"I have Anastasia Steele on the line for you."

Shit. Is she okay?

"Put her through."

"Hi." Her voice wavers, soft and breathy. She sounds uncertain and sad, and a chill grips my heart.

"What is it? Are you okay?" I ask.

"I'm fine. It's you I'm worried about."

My relief turns to irritation. My worry is misplaced. "I'm fine, but busy."

"Let's talk when you get home."

"Okay," I reply, knowing that I'm being abrupt.

She doesn't respond, but I hear her breathing on the other end of the line. She sounds, unsettled, and the chill I felt a moment earlier is replaced by a familiar homesickness.

What is it, Ana? What do you want to say? Silence stretches between us, full of recrimination and unspoken truths.

"Christian," she says eventually.

"Anastasia, I have things to do. I have to go."

"Tonight," she whispers.

"Tonight." I hang up and scowl at the phone.

It's not too much to ask, Anastasia.

"HOME?" TAYLOR ASKS AS he takes the wheel of the Audi.

"Sure," I murmur, distracted. Part of me doesn't want to go home. I still don't have a coherent argument to persuade Ana to change her mind. And I have work to do this evening. A reading project—two weighty reports from the Environmental Sciences Department at WSU—results from the test sites in Africa and Professor Gravett's paper on the microbe responsible for nitrogen fixation in soils. Apparently, microbes are essential to soil regeneration and regeneration holds the key to carbon sequestration. Later this week, I'll be reviewing my funding to her department.

Perhaps I should take Ana out, and we can discuss her vows at dinner. Maybe I can sway her over a glass of wine. I'm reminded of our dinner to discuss the D/s contract.

Hell. That didn't go to plan.

Feeling glum, I stare through the privacy glass at the jostling tourists and commuters, and a sense of righteous indignation settles over me. I'm not asking for much, for fuck's sake. It's the only thing that I want. She can have whatever she likes. Knowing that she'll obey me will give me a sense of security. Does she not understand?

On the sidewalk a young man in shades and loud, flowery shorts is arguing with a woman in an equally loud dress. Their fight is attracting disconcerted looks from passersby.

That will be Ana and me tonight. I know it. And the thought depresses me even more.

I'll just have to tell her what it means to me. I need to keep her safe.

Yes. She'll see.

The woman turns, and in a dramatic gesture raises her arms and storms off, leaving the man alone and bewildered on the sidewalk. I think he's drunk.

Asshole.

Maybe I could fuck Ana into agreeing. That might work. The thought gives me a modicum of hope, and I settle back into my seat for the rest of the drive to Escala.

"GOOD EVENING, MR. GREY," Mrs. Jones chimes as I enter the living room. From the enticing aroma I know there's a pot of her delicious Bolognese sauce bubbling on the stove. My mouth waters.

"Hello, Gail. Smells good. Where's Ana?"

"I believe she's in the library, sir."

"Thank you."

"Dinner in half an hour?"

"Works for me. Thanks." I'll have time for a quick run on the treadmill, since I missed my workout this morning.

I head to the bedroom to change, avoiding the library.

THE BOSS BLARES IN my ears as I push my body to its limits. I run three miles in twenty minutes, and I'm a panting hot mess when I come off the treadmill. Dragging air into my lungs and using the back of my hand to wipe the sweat that's pouring off my brow, I bend over to catch my breath and stretch my hamstrings.

It feels good.

When I stand, Anastasia is leaning against the frame in the doorway, watching me, eyes wide and wary. She's wearing a pale gray sleeveless shirt and a tight gray skirt. She looks every bit the publishing executive. But young. So young. And miserable.

Shit.

"Hi," she says.

"Hi," I respond between breaths.

"You didn't say hello when you came in. Are you avoiding me?"

Ana does not beat around the bush. And in that moment, I want to banish the look of misery on her face and her wariness. "I needed to exercise," I pant. "I can say hello now." I open my arms and step toward her, knowing full well I'm soaked with sweat.

Ana laughs, grimacing, and raises her palms. "I'll take a rain check."

I bound up to her and pull her into my arms before she can retreat. She shrieks, shrinking from me, but she's laughing, too. And it's like a weight has lifted from my soul.

I love making her laugh.

"Oh, baby. I missed you." I kiss her, not caring that I'm not fit for human consumption, and to my delight, she kisses me back. Her fingers tighten around my shoulders, her fingernails digging deeper into my flesh as our tongues dance the dance they know so well.

We're both winded when we come up for air. I cradle her face and brush my thumb over her swollen lips, staring into her dazed, beautiful eyes. "Ana," I whisper, imploring her. "Change your vows. Obey. Don't argue with me. I hate it when we argue. Please."

My lips hover above hers, waiting for an answer, but she blinks several times as if she's clearing a haze, then shrugs me off and steps out of my embrace. "No. Christian. Please," she says, condensing her frustration into four syllables.

I drop my hands to my sides as her words douse me with a cold splash of reality.

"If this is a deal breaker for you, please tell me," she continues, her voice rising steadily. "Because it is for me, and I can stop trying to organize our wedding and go back to my apartment and get drunk with Kate."

"You'd leave?" My voice is barely audible; her statement has knocked my world off-kilter.

"Right now. Yes. You're behaving like a spoiled teen."

"That's not fair," I retort. "I need this."

"No, you don't. You just think you do. We're supposed to be grown-ups, for heaven's sake. We'll talk things out. Like adults do."

We gaze at each other, over the gulf between us.

She's not budging.

Fuck.

"I need a shower," I mutter, and she steps out of my way to let me pass.

WHEN I ENTER THE living room Ana is seated at the kitchen counter, where there are two places laid for dinner. Gail hovers over the stove.

"I'm not hungry," I announce. "And I have work to do."

Ana frowns, and opens her mouth as if to say something but shuts it again as I walk past her. I don't miss the look that passes between her and Mrs. Jones.

Are they conspiring?

The thought makes my blood boil, so I storm into my study and slam the door.

Shit.

The noise startles me and it's an abrupt wake-up.

I *am* behaving like a spoiled teen.

Ana's right. *Hell.*

And I'm hungry.

I hate being hungry.

A dark, twisted memory of fear and hunger from before I was Christian Grey threatens to resurface, but I dampen it down.

Don't go there, Grey.

The reports are on my desk where Taylor left them. I sit down, pick up the first one, and start to read.

A GENTLE KNOCK PULLS my attention away from the multiple crop rotations we're trying in Ghana, and my heart stutters.

Ana.

"Come in."

Gail opens the door.

My disappointment is real, my momentary excitement now a sad, deflated balloon that's lost its helium. On the plus side, she's carrying a tray with a bowl of steaming pasta.

She says nothing as she places it on my desk.

"Thank you."

"Ana's idea. She knows you love spaghetti Bolognese." Her tone is clipped, and before I can reply, she turns and leaves, taking her disapproval with her. I scowl at her departing figure. Of course it was Ana's idea. And once again I'm in awe of her thoughtfulness. Why isn't that enough? She says she loves me. So why do I want or need her obedience?

Feeling even more morose, I stare at the long shadows and golden pink hues painted across my study walls by the sun as it sinks into the horizon.

Why does she defy me?

I pick up my fork and dig into my meal, twirling the pasta into a big, solid bite of bliss. It's delicious.

ANA HAS LEFT THE lamp on for me again. She's fast asleep, and as I slide into the bed beside her my body comes alive. I hunger for her.

I contemplate my plan to fuck her into agreeing, but deep down I know she's made up her mind. She might say no, and right now I don't think I'd survive the rejection.

I turn onto my side, away from her, and switch off my light. The room is plunged into darkness, reflecting my mood; I'm more miserable now than I was this morning.

Damn. Why did I let this get so out of hand?

I close my eyes.

Mommy! Mommy! Mommy is asleep on the floor. She has been asleep for a long time. I brush her hair because she likes that. She doesn't wake up. I shake her. *Mommy!* My tummy hurts. It's hungry. He isn't here. I am thirsty. In the kitchen, I pull a chair to the sink, and I have a drink. The water splashes over my blue sweater. Mommy is still asleep. *Mommy, wake up!* She lies still. She is cold. I fetch my blankie, and I cover Mommy, and I lie down on the sticky green rug beside her. Mommy is still asleep. I have two toy cars. They race by the floor where Mommy is sleeping. I think Mommy is sick. I search for something to eat. In the icebox I find peas. They are cold. I eat them slowly. They make my tummy hurt. I sleep beside Mommy. The peas are gone. In the freezer is something. It smells funny. I lick it and my tongue is stuck to it. I eat it slowly. It tastes nasty. I drink some water. I play with my cars, and I sleep beside Mommy. Mommy is so cold, and she won't wake up. The door crashes open. I cover Mommy with my blankie. He's here. *Fuck. What the fuck happened here? Oh, the crazy fucked-up bitch. Shit. Get out of my way, you little shit.* He kicks me, and I hit my head on the floor. My head hurts. He calls somebody and he goes. He locks the door. I lay down beside Mommy. My head hurts. The lady policeman is here. No. No. No. Don't touch me. Don't touch me. Don't touch me. I stay by Mommy. No. Stay away from me. The lady policeman has my blankie, and she grabs me. I scream. Mommy! Mommy! I want my mommy. The words are gone. I can't say the words. Mommy can't hear me. I have no words.

"Christian! Christian!" Her voice is urgent, pulling me from the depths of my nightmare, and my despair. "I'm here. I'm here," she cries.

I wake and Ana's leaning over me, grasping my shoulders, shaking me, her face taut with anguish, eyes wide and brimming with tears.

"Ana." My voice is a hoarse whisper, the taste of fear tarnishing my mouth. "You're here."

"Of course I'm here."

"I had a dream."

"I know. I'm here, I'm here."

"Ana." Her name is an incantation on my lips, a talisman against the dark, choking panic coursing through my body.

"Hush, I'm here." She curls around me, her limbs cocooning mine, her warmth seeping into my soul, forcing back the shadows, forcing back the fear. She is sunshine, she is light. She is mine.

"Please, let's not fight." I wrap my arms around her.

"Okay."

"The vows. No obeying. I can do that. We'll find a way." The words rush out of my mouth in a tumble of emotion and confusion and anxiety.

"Yes. We will. We'll always find a way," Ana whispers, and her lips are on mine, silencing me, bringing me back to the now.

FRIDAY, JULY 8, 2011

Dr. Flynn rubs his chin and I don't know if he's playing for time or genuinely intrigued. "She threatened to leave?"

"Yes."

"Seriously?"

"Yes."

"So, you capitulated."

"I didn't have much choice."

"Christian, you always have a choice. Do you think Anastasia was being unreasonable?"

I meet his gaze and want to shout yes, but deep down I know Ana isn't an unreasonable person.

That's you, Grey.

Unreasonable could be your middle name. Ana's words haunt me. She said that, long ago.

Christ, my negativity is a real prick sometimes.

"How are you feeling now?" Flynn asks.

"Wary," I whisper, and my admission is a jab to the solar plexus, almost winding me.

She could leave me.

"Ah. Your feelings of insecurity and abandonment are coming to the fore again."

I remain mute, distracted by the sliver of afternoon light that brightens the cluster of mini orchids on his coffee table. *What can I say?* I don't want to admit this out loud. It makes my fears real. I loathe feeling this weak. This exposed. Ana has the power to wound me and deliver a fatal blow.

"Is it giving you second thoughts about the wedding?" John asks.

No. Maybe.

I'm afraid she'll hurt me.

Like she did before...when she left.

"No," I answer, because I don't want to lose her.

He nods, as if this is what he wants to hear. "You've relinquished a great deal for her."

"I have." I stifle my indulgent smile. "She's a good negotiator."

Flynn rubs his chin again. "Do you resent that?"

"Yes. Partly. I've given so much and she won't give me this."

"You sound like you're mad at her."

"I am."

"Have you thought about telling her that?"

"How mad I am? No."

"Why not?"

"I'm worried I'll say something I'll regret and she'll leave. She left once before."

"But you hurt her then."

"I did." The memory of her tearful face and her bitter rebuke are never far from my mind. *You are one fucked-up son of a bitch.*

I shudder, but I hide it from Flynn. Whenever I think of that time, my shame almost swallows me whole. "I don't want to hurt her again. Ever."

"That's a good goal to work toward," Flynn says. "But you need to find a healthy way to express and channel your anger. You've directed it inwardly for so long. Too long." He pauses. "But you know my views on that. I am not going to rehash that now, Christian. You're incredibly resilient and resourceful. You had the solution to this impasse all along; you capitulated. Problem solved. Life is not always going to go your way. The key is to recognize those moments. Sometimes it's better to concede the battle to win the war. Communicate and compromise—that's what marriage is all about."

I snort, remembering Ana's e-mail from a lifetime ago.

"What's so funny?"

"Nothing." I shake my head.

"Have a little faith in yourself, and in her."

"Marriage is a huge leap of faith," I mumble.

"It is. For everyone. But you're well equipped to cope. Focus on where you want to be. How you want to be. I think you have over the last few weeks. You've seemed happier."

I meet his gaze.

"This is just a small setback," he says.

I hope so.

"I'll see you next week."

IT'S DUSK, AND ELLIOT and I are standing on the terrace of the new house, admiring the view. "I can see why you bought the place." Elliot whistles his appreciation through his teeth. We're both quiet for a moment, absorbing the majesty of twilight over the Sound: the opal sky, the distant orange haze, the dark purple waters. The beauty. The calm.

"Stunning, isn't it?" I murmur.

"Yep. This is a great spot for a beautiful home."

"Which you're going to remodel." I grin and Elliot play-punches my arm.

"Glad I can help. It's gonna take some hard work, and it ain't gonna be cheap to make this place more sustainable. But, hey, you can afford it. I'll talk to Gia next week and see what she has in mind, and if it's possible."

"I'll close on this sometime before the end of July. I think Ana, you, Gia, and I should meet here once that's done."

"Do it before. Doesn't sound like the results of any survey will stop you from buying this place."

"You're right. I'll look at my schedule. When do you think you might have time?"

"For what?"

"The build, dude. The build."

"Ah. Well, if the Spokani Eden project stays on schedule, maybe early fall?" He shrugs.

"It's going well?"

"Yeah." Elliot looks pleased with himself.

He should. It's an ambitious project, and, once complete, it will be a showcase for his sustainable building methods. He shoves his Seahawks cap back on his head and claps his hands. "T.G.I.F., hotshot. Let's get back to your place and get our beer on." Rolling my eyes, I follow my big brother around the side of the house to where my car is parked in the driveway.

"I WONDER WHAT OUR women are doing?" Elliot says on the drive back to Escala.

"Packing up Ana's things, I hope." I glance at Elliot. He's got his fucking foot on my dashboard, and he's watching the passing scenery as if he doesn't give a shit.

Lord, I envy him.

"They're probably eating pizza, drinking too much wine, and talking about us," he quips.

I hope they're not talking about us!

"Or they could be watching the game." He cackles.

"Kate into baseball?"

"Yeah. She likes all sports."

Of course she does. I'm once more confounded by why she and Ana are friends. Ana doesn't seem interested in sports at all. Though we both enjoyed watching the Mariners recently. "So, do you think of Kate as your woman, then?" I ask, curious.

"Yeah. For now."

"It's not serious between you?"

He shrugs. "She's cool. We'll see. She doesn't hassle me. You know?"

"I don't know, thank God," I mutter to myself, and shake my head. This might be the longest "relationship" he's ever experienced.

"Let's stop at a bar," he says.

"No. I'm not drinking and driving."

"Dude, you're driving like Dad."

"Fuck off, asshole." I put my foot down and the R8 screeches up the on-ramp onto I-5 and we speed toward the city.

"Have you found the prick who totaled your chopper?"

I sigh. "Helicopter, Elliot. And no. It's really pissing me off."

"Man, who would want to do that?"

"I don't know. My team has turned up zilch. I'm waiting for the report from the NTSB. They're taking their sweet time. I've had to up our security. I've got two guys watching Ana and Kate's place tonight."

"No kidding! Don't blame you, man. There are some wackos out there."

I give him a look.

"What? I'm just stating the obvious. I'm glad they'll be safe," he says, and I'm beginning to think he might really care for Kavanagh. "What do you want to do for your bachelor party?" he asks as we come off I-5.

"Elliot, I don't want or need a bachelor party."

"Man, you up and marry the first girl who's given you any serious attention. Of course you need a bachelor party."

I laugh. *Dude, you have no idea.*

"I thought you'd knocked her up."

I go cold. "Fuck off, bro. I'm not that careless. Ana's far too young for kids. We have a life to live before we get into all that shit."

Elliot laughs. "You with kids. That'll loosen you up."

I ignore him. "Have you heard from Mia?"

"She's chasing cock."

"What?"

"Kate's brother. I don't think he's interested."

"I dislike the words *cock* and *Mia* in the same sentence."

"She's not a kid anymore, hotshot. You know, she's only slightly younger than Ana and Kate."

I'd rather not think about that.

"Are we playing pool or watching the game?" He wisely changes the subject.

"Whatever you want, bro, whatever you want." We pull into the underground garage at Escala while I'm still trying not to think about Mia and Ethan Kavanagh.

ELLIOT IS SNORING IN front of the TV. He works too damned hard, he plays too damned hard, but he'll sleep off his overconsumption of beer in the spare bedroom. We've had a chill evening: we watched highlights of the Mariners-Angels game (Mariners lost), he thrashed me at *Call of Duty*, but I won at pool, for a change. Tomorrow morning, I'll be at Ana's apartment to help move the rest of her belongings here. It's taken enough time. I glance at my watch, wondering what she might be doing. My phone buzzes, and it's as if she's heard my thoughts.

ANA
I'm packed. Missing you.
Sleep well. No nightmares.
This is not a request.
I'm not there to hold you.
Love you. ♥

Her words warm my heart. Flynn said our recent fight was just a small setback; I hope he's right. I text back.

Dream of me.
I hope to dream of you.
No nightmares.

ANA
Promise?

No promises.
Just hope. And dreams.
And love. For you.

ANA
You once said you don't do romance.
I'm so glad that you're wrong. I'm swooning here!
I love you, Christian.
Good night xxx.

Good night, Ana.
I like to make you swoon.
I love you. Always. x

Monday, July 11, 2011

I read through the press release that I've rewritten for Sam.

For Immediate Release

GREY ENTERPRISES HOLDINGS INC.
ACQUIRES SEATTLE INDEPENDENT PUBLISHING

Seattle, WA, July 11, 2011—Grey Enterprises Holdings, Inc., (GEH) announces the acquisition of Seattle Independent Publishing (SIP) of Seattle, WA, for $15 million.

A spokesperson for GEH stated: "GEH is thrilled to add SIP to its portfolio of local companies." CEO Christian Grey said, "I'm eager to branch into publishing and to use GEH's technological expertise to grow SIP and further develop a solid publishing platform that offers a voice to authors based in the Pacific Northwest."

Seattle Independent Publishing was founded thirty-two years ago by Jeremy Roach, who will continue as CEO. SIP has had considerable success championing local authors, including three-time *USA Today* bestseller Bee Edmonston and poet and performance artist Keon Kinger, whose latest collection, *By the Sound,* was shortlisted for the prestigious Arthur Rense Prize in 2010.

SIP will continue to function independently and will retain all thirty-two of its employees. Roach said, "This is a tremendous opportunity for all the staff and the authors at SIP, and we're very excited to see where our partnership with GEH will take us over the next decade and beyond."

All inquiries to Sam Saster
VP, Director of Publicity, Grey Enterprises Holdings, Inc.

Ana's words come back to me. *Of course I'm mad at you. I mean, what kind of responsible business executive makes decisions based on who he is currently fucking?*

I do, Ana.

But only because I'm fucking *you.*

Memories of her tied to her little white bed, slick and sticky with ice cream, me attempting to chop peppers, her calling me an ass, float into my head. I glance at my glider. Maybe that's why she doesn't want to obey, because she thinks I'm an ass.

Grey. Enough.

Doubt is an ugly, futile feeling.

This is my new mantra. Flynn said our dispute was a small setback. All relationships have them. She's moved in with me, and we're getting married in less than three weeks. What more do I want?

Damn. I wish we were married already. The wait is shredding my nerves. I don't want her to change her mind. She's been quiet this weekend. We were busy moving her stuff into the apartment, and she's been knee-deep in wedding preparations.

She's just tired.

Stop with the negative, Grey.

Focus on the matter in hand.

I pick up the phone and call Sam.

"Christian."

Sometimes it really grates on my nerves when he uses my first name. In an arctic tone I inform him, "I've sent you a revised, less wordy press release. Brevity is everything. Try and remember that."

"As you wish, Mr. Grey."

Good. Point made.

"And, Sam, delete the price and put 'undisclosed sum.'"

"Will do."

I hang up and turn to my computer. I'm hoping some e-mail banter with my fiancée will improve my disposition and hers.

From: Christian Grey
Subject: The Ultimate Consumer. Consuming.
Date: July 11 2011 08:43
To: Anastasia Steele

My darling Anastasia
I was reminiscing about the day you found out I had purchased SIP. I believe you called me an ass, when I was merely exercising my rights as a citizen of our fine country to purchase whatever I please. As the

Ultimate Consumer (again, your epithet) I am informing you that the news of my most recent acquisition is no longer embargoed and a press release will be issued today.
I'm so glad you've moved in.
I slept well last night knowing you were there.
I love you.

Christian Grey
CEO, Entrepreneur, not an ass, Grey Enterprises Holdings, Inc.

From: Anastasia Steele
Subject: Boss or Bossy
Date: July 11 2011 08:56
To: Christian Grey

My dearest husband-to-be
You were an ass (I stand by that appellation) and my boss's boss's boss. I remember that we enjoyed a thoroughly entertaining and sticky evening. Perhaps a helping of ice cream this evening? It is so warm out…
I love you back. Very much.
I'm preparing an agenda for our meeting this evening with Alondra about final preparations!
Any last-minute requests?
Are you still happy for the rehearsal dinner to take place at Escala?

Anastasia Steele
Acting Editor, Fiction, SIP

From: Christian Grey
Subject: How Many Times!
Date: July 11 2011 08:59
To: Anastasia Steele

My darling Anastasia
Let's make it a short service.
I'm impatient for you to be mine.
Yes, to Escala. Fewer prying eyes there.
Oh, and BLACKBERRY!!!
AND BEN & JERRY'S & ANA.
My favorite dessert.

Christian Grey
Bossy CEO, Grey Enterprises Holdings, Inc.

From: Anastasia Steele
Subject: Uber Bossy
Date: July 11 2011 09:02
To: Christian Grey

Oh fiddle-dee-dee Mr. Grey.
It's my favorite dessert too.
Ana x

I smile. Now she's quoting *Gone with the Wind* at me. She seems happy enough. I shake my head and summon Andrea, my disposition much improved.

Thank you, Miss Steele.

MID-MORNING, ANDREA PUTS Darius Jackson from the Port of Ephrata through.

"Good morning, Christian."

"Darius, it's good to hear your voice. Has she arrived?" Suddenly I'm ten years old again, and it's Christmas. I can barely contain my excitement.

"She has, Mr. Grey, and she's a beauty."

"Have you put her together?"

"Working on it now. I'll send you some photographs when she's complete."

"I can't wait to see her."

"I have the registration ready, and I'm wondering if you want me to take her up for a test flight, or if you'd like to do that."

"No. Take her up. Let me know how she handles."

"I'd be delighted to. When can we expect you?"

"I'll try and get up there this weekend. I'll let you know."

"Okay. I'll get back to her. I don't like to leave a lady waiting." He chuckles, hangs up, and I laugh.

Me neither, Darius, unless she's misbehaved…

I sigh. Perhaps Ana and I can go soaring this weekend.

ANA IS SUBDUED DURING dinner, picking at her risotto.

Maybe she's having second thoughts?

"What's wrong?" I ask.

"Nothing. It was just a long day."

My anxiety simmers. There's something she's not telling me. "Sawyer told me there were paparazzi outside your building," I prompt.

"We left via the loading bay. We managed to avoid them."

So, it's not the continual harassment from the fourth estate that's bugging her. *What is it?* I try a different tack. "What did you do today?"

She snorts. "I spent most of the day on the phone with authors, trying to soften the blow of the news."

I almost spit out my food. *What the hell!*

She laughs at my expression, her reaction immediately lifting my spirits.

"Yes, big business exploiting artistic endeavor," she clarifies.

"Ah."

"Roach called the senior editorial team together this morning to give us all the news of your takeover. Of course, I knew already, when everyone else was in the dark. It was strange. It set me apart…you know."

"I see." Surely that's a good thing—knowledge is power.

"Christian." Her eyes are full of misgiving, and her words pour out in a steady torrent. "My fiancé owns the company I work for. Roach stared at me a few times during the meeting and I didn't know what he was thinking. I remember he went a little crazy when he found out we were getting married. The whole meeting was odd. I felt uncomfortable and self-conscious."

Shit!

"You didn't tell me he went a little crazy." *Asshole.*

"That was a while ago, when he found out we were engaged."

"Did *he* make you feel uncomfortable?"

I'll fire him if he did.

She studies me, her face serious, as if considering my question. "A little. Maybe. Maybe not. Or maybe I'm projecting. I don't know. Anyway, he confirmed my position as editor."

"Today?"

"This afternoon."

Hmm. I've not yet removed the moratorium on hiring new staff.

Wily old bastard.

Reaching over, I grasp her hand. "Congratulations. We should celebrate. Were you worried about telling me?"

"I thought you knew and you hadn't said anything." Her voicc trails off.

I laugh. "No, I didn't. But it's great news."

She looks relieved. Is this why she's been so quiet? "Don't sweat it, Ana. To hell with what your colleagues think and what Roach thinks. I hope everyone at the company was reassured by the press release. I'm not planning any changes in the immediate future. And I'm sure your authors were delighted to hear from you."

"Some yes. Some no. There are a few who still miss Jack."

"Really? That amazes me."

"He took a gamble on a couple. They're loyal. I suspect they'll move with him when he finds another job."

He's never going to find another job if I have my way.

She tightens her fingers around mine.

"Anyway, thank you," she says.

"What for?"

"Listening." Her brow furrows once again, and I wonder if she wants to say more.

What, Ana? Tell me.

"Are you ready for the wedding planner?" she asks.

"Of course. Better finish up." I look pointedly at her food. And to my relief she scoops up a large bite of risotto and pops it into her mouth. I slowly unwind; she just wanted to tell me about her promotion and expected me to know about it.

For fuck's sake, Grey.

Relax.

"ALL THAT REMAINS IS to decide what you'll do after the wedding reception." Alondra Gutierrez has an easy smile.

"We haven't discussed that yet." Ana turns to me.

"It's in hand," I tell Ms. Gutierrez, and Ana looks surprised.

Oh, baby. I've got this.

"I'll take this up with you separately, Alondra."

"Very good, Mr. Grey. I can't wait to hear!"

"Neither can I," Ana says.

"You'll have to wait until the big day." I smile.

I hope you enjoy what I have planned.

Ana pushes out her bottom lip in the semblance of a pout, but there's humor in her expression and something else…something darker, more sensual, that speaks to my dick.

Fuck.

Alondra gathers her things, letting us know that we can still make last-minute changes as we thank her for all that she's done.

We all rise as Taylor appears at the entrance to the living room and Alondra takes her leave. We both watch her depart, and once she's out of earshot I turn to Ana.

"She's got it all in hand."

"Alondra's good at her job," she says.

"She is," I agree. "Now what do you want to do?" I add in a whisper.

Ana whips her eyes to mine and her lips part as she gazes at me. We're inches from each other. Not touching. But I feel her. All of her. The silence between us gets louder, expanding to fill the space surrounding us as we each drink the other in.

Suddenly, there's no oxygen in the vast room. There's only us, only our desire, crackling invisibly between us. I see it in the summer of her eyes. Her pupils growing wider. Darker. Reflecting my thirst. My love. Our love.

"You've been so distant." Her voice is barely audible. "All weekend."

"No. Not distant. Afraid."

"No!" she says in a quiet rush of tenderness. She closes the gap between us without moving. Reaching up, her fingertips skim over my stubble, her touch echoing through my every bone and sinew.

I close my eyes as my body responds.

Ana.

Her fingers are at my shirt, undoing the buttons. "Don't be afraid," she breathes, and places a kiss on one of my scars above my pulsing heart. I can bear no more: I cup her face and bring her lips to mine, kissing her ferociously. She's a banquet for a starving man. She tastes of love and lust and Ana.

"Let's go. Now. Vegas. Get married," I implore against her fevered lips. "We can tell everyone we couldn't wait." She moans and I kiss her again, taking all she's got to give, drowning in her desire, drowning in her love, aching for her, desperate for her.

When she pulls back we're both dragging air into our lungs, her dazed eyes on me. "If that's what you want," she says, breathless and brimming with compassion.

I crush her to me.

She'd do this for me.

She won't obey...but she'll do this.

Damn.

And I know I have to give her a wedding she deserves. Not some rushed affair in a chapel of love in Vegas. My girl deserves the best.

"Come to bed," I whisper in her ear, and she laces her fingers into my hair as I lift her into my arms.

"I thought you'd never ask," she says, and I carry her into the bedroom.

SATURDAY, JULY 16, 2011

"Wake up, sleepy head." Gently I tug Ana's earlobe with my teeth.

"Hmm…" She groans and refuses to open her eyes. I tug again. "Ah!" she gripes and her eyes flutter open.

"Good morning, Miss Steele."

"Good morning." She reaches up to stroke my face. I'm fully dressed and lying stretched out beside her.

"Sleep well?" I kiss her palm.

She gives me a sleepy nod.

"I have a surprise."

"Oh?"

"Up." I slide off the bed.

"What surprise?"

"If I told you…"

She slides her head to one side, unimpressed. She needs an answer.

"Floating above the Pacific Northwest?"

She gasps and sits up immediately. "Soaring?" she asks.

"The very same."

"We can chase the"—she glances out of the window—"rain?" She looks crestfallen.

"It's sunnier where we're going."

"Then we can chase the midday sun!"

"We can. If you get up!"

She squeals with delight and scrambles out of bed, all haste and long limbs. She stops to give me a swift chaste kiss before dashing into the bathroom.

"It should be warm," I call after her with a huge grin. I think she's pleased.

AS WE SPEED DOWN I-90 in the R8, fleeing the dreary weather, I allow myself the luxury of being in the moment. My girl is beside me,

The Killers are on the sound system, and we're going soaring, in my new sailplane. All is right in the world.

Flynn would be proud.

Of course, we're being followed by Sawyer and Reynolds, but a guy can't have everything.

"Where are we going?" Ana asks, peering through the drizzle.

"Ephrata."

From the corner of my eye I see she's perplexed. "It's about two and a half hours away. It's where I keep my sailplanes."

"You have more than one?"

"Two. Now."

"The Blaník?" she asks, and when I frown she continues, sounding a little less certain. "You mentioned it to the pilot when we went soaring in Georgia." She looks down at her fingers and starts twisting her engagement ring. "It's why I bought you the model one." Her voice drops so I have to strain to hear her.

"The only Blaník I have is that little glider. It has pride of place on my desk at work." Reaching over, I grasp her knee, briefly recalling the circumstances when she gifted the little model to me.

Don't go there, Grey.

"I trained to fly in a Blaník. Right now, I have a brand-new, state-of-the-art ASH 30. One of the first in the world. It will be my—our maiden flight in her." I flash her a quick grin.

Ana's face erupts into smile and she shakes her head fondly.

"What?" I ask.

"You."

"Me?"

"Yes. You and your toys."

"A man has to chill, Ana." I wink at her and she blushes.

"You're never going to let me live that down, are you?"

"That and the 'are you gay' question."

Ana laughs. "You enjoy expensive pursuits."

"This is not news."

She stifles her smile and shakes her head again, and I don't know if she's laughing at me or with me.

Plus ça change, Anastasia.

WE TURN INTO THE parking lot at Ephrata Municipal Airport just before eleven. The promised sun has materialized, dispersing the rain clouds and ushering in pretty white cumulus, perfect for soaring. I'm itching to see my new plane and get her airborne. "Ready?" I ask.

"Yes!" Ana's eyes shine, her excitement palpable. Like mine.

"It's so bright, we're going to need shades." From the glove box I take my aviators and hand a pair of Wayfarers to Ana, then retrieve the two Mariners caps.

"Thank you. I forgot my sunglasses."

As I climb out of the car, Sawyer arrives in the Q7 and parks beside the R8. I give him a wave and he rolls down the window. "There's a pilot's lounge if you guys want to wait in there," I say. "Follow us in."

"Mr. Grey, please." Sawyer's tone stops me. And I know he wants to check out the offices before Ana and I go inside. I step out of the way to let Reynolds and Sawyer through.

This is getting old.

I take a deep breath. I won't let his vigilance dampen my spirits—after all, it's what I pay him to do. Taking Ana's hand, I follow our security into the office, where Darius Jackson is waiting.

"Christian Grey," he calls out, and pumps my hand with a hearty shake. It's great to see him. He's a big guy, tall, but rounder than when I last saw him. "You're keeping well," he observes.

"As are you, Darius. This is my fiancée, Anastasia Steele."

"Miss Steele." Darius gives her a broad, brilliant smile.

"Ana," she corrects us both, but smiles and takes his hand.

"Darius was my flight instructor," I explain to Ana.

"You were my star pupil, Christian," he says. "He's a natural."

Ana eyes me, and I think it's pride I see etched on her beautiful face.

"Congratulations on your engagement," Darius says.

"Thanks. Is she ready?" I ask, because I find Ana's pride in me difficult to swallow, and of course I can't wait to see my new sailplane.

"Sure is. She's all lined up for you. My son Marlon is going to spot."

"Whoa! Marlon," I exclaim. Marlon, in his mid-teens now, has close-cropped hair and a smile and handshake that matches his father's. "You've gotten so tall!"

"Kids. They grow." Darius's dark eyes are brimming with paternal love.

"Thanks for helping out, Marlon."

"No worries, Mr. Grey."

Out on the tarmac, N88765CG is waiting. She is without doubt the most graceful sailplane on the planet: a Schleicher ASH 30, she's a gleaming white, with an impressive eighty-seven-foot wingspan and a large canopy. Even from this distance it's obvious she's a marvel of modern engineering.

She's yar.

Darius gives me a play-by-play account of her maiden flight, his face animated by the memory, as the three of us stroll around the glider, taking in her beauty and elegance. "She's got it all, Christian. It's like walking on air," he says, and the awe in his voice is worthy of such a sleek and cutting-edge aircraft.

"She looks mighty fine," I agree.

I open the canopy and Darius talks me through each of the controls. "And I've put more ballast in"—he glances at Ana—"as you'll need it."

"I understand."

"I'll fetch your chutes."

"Wow," Ana exclaims as she gazes into the cockpit. "It has more dials and technical doohickeys than the other glider."

I laugh. "She sure does."

"She?"

"She. But more biddable," I add with a smirk.

Ana cocks her head to one side and squints at me while trying unsuccessfully to hide her amusement. "Biddable, eh?"

I peer down my nose at her. "Easy to handle. Does as she's told…"

Darius returns and hands me the chutes before heading back into the office. I squat down on the ground with Ana's, and help her into it, tightening the straps around her thighs. "As you know, Miss Steele, I like my women biddable."

"To a point, Mr. Grey," she says as I stand. "Sometimes you like to be defied."

I grin. "Only by you." I cinch the shoulder buckles up tight.

"You love doing that, don't you?" she whispers.

"More than you could ever know."

"I think I have a clue. Maybe we should do it later."

I stop and tug her closer so that I can breathe in her scent. "Maybe we should," I murmur. "I'd like that very much."

Ana peeks up at me through her lashes. "So would I." Her words are as soft as the summer breeze and she leans up to kiss me. My breath catches in my throat as her lips touch mine and desire flashes though my body like wild fire. But before I can react, she steps back to give me some room to don my own chute.

Tease.

Eyes blazing, she watches me as I strap on my parachute. I take extra care to tighten my own straps.

"That was hot," she whispers.

Chuckling, and before I make a complete fool of myself and her, I do another circuit of my new plane. This time I'm examining her for anything that looks loose or out of place; all part of my preflight checks. Darius, who taught me to glide, would expect no less.

She's in fine, fine shape.

Like my fiancée.

Ana is still watching me as I run a hand over the tip of her wing.

"She's good," I say when I return to Ana's side. She slides on her cap and threads her ponytail through the gap at the back.

"You look mighty fine, too, Miss Steele," I whisper as I slip on my aviators.

Darius and Marlon join us, and together we push the ASH 30 onto the runway.

Once in position, I help Ana into the front seat of the cockpit and have the pleasure of strapping her in once more. "These should keep you in your place," I whisper with a wicked grin, then jump in behind her and close the canopy.

Darius attaches the tow cable and, with a thumbs-up sign, heads to the waiting single-engine Cessna Skyhawk.

"Ready?" I ask Ana.

"You bet!"

"Don't touch anything."

"Wait."

"What?"

"You've not flown this before."

I laugh. "Nope. I hadn't flown the Blaník L23 before, but we survived that."

She remains silent.

"Ana, they're all the same really. And you have your chute. Don't sweat it."

"Okay." She sounds a little uncertain.

"Honestly. It's going to be fine. Trust me."

I do a thorough check of the controls to orient myself: elevator, ailerons, the stick are all full and free. Straps good. Brakes good and now locked. Canopy locked. Flight instruments good—no cracked glass; shouldn't be, she's new.

Darius's voice crackles over the radio and I let him know that we're ready. A quick glance to the starboard side reveals Marlon standing by, holding the wing tip as Darius fires up the Skyhawk.

"Here we go! Let's chase those thermals and the midday sun," I shout above the shrill whine of the Cessna's engine.

Darius eases forward, and suddenly we're racing across the tarmac. Using the pedals at my feet and the stick in front of me, we sail into the air before the Cessna has left the runway.

She's so quick off the ground!

We climb higher and higher. The Ephrata office building is a child's toy as it disappears into the distance. Darius banks his aircraft and we sail toward the Beezley Hills, where we are sure to find some lift.

"That was so smooth," Ana says, an edge of quiet awe in her voice.

"Much smoother than the Blaník," I agree. ASH is awesome. She's so light and responsive.

We reach 3,000 feet and I radio Darius to let him know I'm releasing the cable. He's flown us into a thermal, and as he pulls away, I hold us in a wide circle, keeping the attitude constant as we rise and rise and rise. Washington falls away beneath us in all her checkered glory.

"Wow," Ana breathes.

"On the port side, you can see the Cascades."

"Port?"

"Left."

"Oh, yes."

There is still a sprinkling of snow kissing the top of the mountains, even in July.

"What's the water down there?"

"Banks Lake."

"Christian, this is beautiful."

We're at 7,000 feet, and I know we could go higher. We could go for miles and miles, and land in some field leagues and leagues away. The thought is appealing—Ana and I alone in some wilderness—but I don't think Sawyer or Reynolds or maybe even Ana would appreciate it.

"Look!" Ana calls. Below us, a substantial dust devil swirls into the air.

The lift!

I make a beeline for it and we travel higher. Fast.

"Wow!" Ana cries, with exhilaration. "No acrobatics today?" she asks.

"I'm just getting the feel of her first."

Fuck it. I love making Ana scream. I wing over and she squeals with delight as we hang above the earth, her hands stretched out, her ponytail tumbling down—the Washington plains beneath us.

"Holy shit!" she exclaims, and I pitch us upright again and Ana laughs and laughs. The sound fills my soul and makes me feel a thousand feet tall. ASH is a dream to fly; she has carried us to the top of the world, where the sun reigns above the clouds; it's tranquil, and we're surrounded by a breathtaking view. The love of my life sits before me, happy and free above the earth. And for the first time in a while a sense of peace unfurls within me. We're together, cradled in the sky, and my heart is full to overflowing.

I don't want this feeling to end.

This high. It's intoxicating.

Focus on where you want to be.

How you want to be.

I think you have for the last few weeks. You've seemed happier.

Flynn's words come back to me.

Ana is my happiness. She holds the key.

The thought is too big, too all-encompassing. I know it could swallow me whole if I let it. To distract myself, I ask Ana if she wants a try.

"No. This is your maiden voyage. You enjoy it, Christian. I'm thrilled to come along for the ride."

I smile. "I bought her for you."

"Really?"

"Yes. I have a single-seater glider made by the same German company but it's for solo flights. This sailplane is a dream. She's fantastic."

"She is." Ana looks ahead at the horizon. "We are floating on air," she says, her voice soft and dreamy.

"That we are, baby…that we are."

WE TOUCH DOWN AN hour later, a landing that's as smooth as the takeoff. I'm thrilled with the new plane. She's everything I knew she would be and more. I'd really like to take her up one day to see how far she'll take us. Perhaps later this summer.

Darius rushes toward us as I unlock the canopy.

"How was it?" he gushes when he reaches us.

"Amazing. She's one helluva plane." Adrenaline is still coursing through my body.

"Ana?" Darius turns his attention to her.

"I agree with Christian. She's amazing."

I undo my straps, clamber out, and stretch. Then lean in to unbuckle Ana's straps.

"This has been inspiring," I whisper, and give her a swift kiss as I make short work of the seat belt.

Her lips part in surprise but I turn to Darius who is still with us. "Let's put her in the hangar."

I'M BEHIND ANA AS we walk back to the cars with Sawyer and Reynolds. Her ponytail swings jauntily behind her. She's still wearing the cap, and beneath the short navy baseball jacket her ass is shielded in tight blue jeans. Her hips sway back and forth, a metronome as she walks, and the rhythm is hypnotizing. She looks so damned hot. I stride around to her side of the car and open the door. "You look great. I don't think I told you that this morning."

"I think you did," she answers with a sweet smile.

"Well, I'd like to tell you again."

"Back at you, Christian Grey." She runs her fingers over my white T-shirt, and the feeling echoes through my chest and the rest of my body.

I need to get her home.

But first. Lunch. A late lunch. I close her door and head to the driver's side.

We stop in Ephrata for pizza.

"Do you mind if we get takeout?" I ask as we enter the small restaurant.

"Eat in your car?"

"Yes."

"Your immaculate R8?"

"The very same."

"Sure." Ana looks puzzled.

"I'm anxious to get home."

"Why?"

I stare at her, quirking an eyebrow with only one thought in my mind. *Why do you think, Ana?*

"Oh," she says, and her teeth drill into her lower lip to suppress her smile, her cheeks flushing that shade of pink I love so much. "Okay. Yes. Takeout," she blurts, and I have to laugh.

"THIS IS THE BEST damn pizza," Ana says with her mouth full. I'm glad I doubled down on paper napkins.

"More?" I ask. And she holds the slice up for me to bite. As I open my mouth, she moves it away and takes another bite.

"Hey!"

She giggles. "My pizza!"

I pout. Because I'm driving and there's nothing else I can do.

"Here," she says, and this time lets me take a bite.

"You know I'll get you back."

"Uh-huh?" she taunts. "Bring it, Grey."

"Oh, I will. I will..." And I start to contemplate various scenarios, which have an immediate impact on my body. I shift in my seat. "More pizza, please."

Ana continues to feed me. And tease me. Much to her and my delight.

We should do this more often.

"All done," Ana says, and pops the pizza box in her footwell.

I feel sated. I'm with my girl, in my favorite car, Radiohead on play, and we're speeding through the majestic landscape beside the Columbia River toward the Vantage bridge. I'm overwhelmed by a sense of belonging.

Before Ana, how did I spend my weekends?

Soaring, Sailing, Fucking...

I laugh. It doesn't sound like much has changed, but that's simply not true—everything has changed, and all because of the young woman sitting next to me. I didn't know I was lonely until I met her. I didn't know I needed her, and here she is beside me. I glance at Ana, who's sucking the tip of her index finger. The sight is stirring, and I recall her earlier remark about harnesses.

"You love doing that, don't you?"

"More than you could ever know."

"I think I have a clue. Maybe we should do it later."

"Maybe we should..."

The thought drives me wild. Putting my foot down, I push the R8 to ninety. I want to get us home.

MY ANTICIPATION IS at DEFCON 1 when we finally arrive at the garage at Escala. "Home again," Ana breathes when I switch off the ignition. Her voice is husky and quiet, drawing my attention. Her eyes meet mine and we stare at each other as the atmosphere within the R8 slowly simmers.

It's here. Between us. Our desire.

It's almost a separate entity, it's so powerful.

Drawing us together.

Consuming me…us.

"Thank you," she says.

"You're most welcome."

She's looking at me through her lashes, her eyes smoky and full of sensual promise. Compelled, I can't look away. I'm under her powerful spell. Beside us, Sawyer and Reynolds pull up, park, and disembark the Q7, locking it up behind them. They head to the service elevator, and I can't tell if they're waiting for us or not. I don't know. I don't care. Ana and I ignore them, our focus only on each other. The silence in the car is heady, ringing with unspoken thoughts.

"The new glider, that was mind-blowing."

"I like blowing your mind."

A slow, seductive smile tugs at her lips. "I like that, too."

"I have a plan."

"You do?"

I nod, holding my breath as myriad images of Ana harnessed in the playroom run through my head.

"Red Room?" she asks tentatively.

I nod.

Her pupils grow wide and dark, and her breasts rise as she inhales. "Bring it."

And I am out of the car.

She's out when I reach the passenger side. "Come." I take her hand and trek briskly to the elevator. Fortunately, it's waiting for us and we dart in. I squeeze her hand as we both stand against the back wall. She sidles closer to me and her intention is clear as she raises her face to mine.

"No. Wait." I release her hand and step to the side as the elevator climbs.

"Christian," she whispers, her look scorching.

I shake my head.

I'm gonna make you wait, baby.

She presses her lips together, her displeasure obvious, but there's a flash of steel in her eyes. My girl does not back down from a challenge.

The game is on.

The doors of the elevator open and I step back, giving Ana a courtly wave. "Ladies first."

She smirks, and with head held high, sashays out of the elevator into the foyer, where she stops.

Sawyer is waiting for us.

Well, this is inconvenient.

"Mr. Grey, is there anything else you require?" He's aware that Taylor has gone to visit his daughter, and I think he's trying to fill Taylor's shoes. He looks expectantly from me to Ana, whose attention is suddenly concentrated on the floor as she tries not to laugh.

Hiding my amusement, I respond. "I'm good, thank you," then, out of devilment, add, "Ana?"

"All good." She shoots me a what-the-fuck look and it takes all my self-control not to burst out laughing in front of Sawyer. She scuttles out of the foyer.

"You and Reynolds can stand down. We're not going out this evening. Anastasia is going out tomorrow. I'll text you in the morning to let you know when." Ana has a fitting for her wedding dress in the morning.

"Very good, sir." He turns and I follow him out into the corridor. A quick glance in the living room reveals Ana is not there. Sawyer heads into Taylor's office while I go in search of Miss Steele. I find her in the bedroom, where she's unlacing her boots.

She looks up. "Mr. Grey, you are truly evil."

"I try my best. Playroom. Ten minutes." I turn on my heel and leave her, mouth open, in my…our bedroom.

THE PLAYROOM IS SOFTLY illuminated, the light glowing off the red walls. It feels, once more, like my haven. It's been a few weeks since we've been in here. *Why is that? Where does the time go?* I chuckle—I sound like my dad. I strip off my jacket, and remove my shoes and socks, enjoying the warmth of the wooden floor on the soles of my feet. From the bottom of the toy chest, I remove a leather suspension harness; it's going to be fun strapping Ana into this. I can barely contain myself. She won't be fully suspended, so I think she'll be within her limits. I lay it out on the bed, then retrieve a few other items. Putting a couple of them in the back pocket of my jeans, I leave the rest on the chest, then head next door to the en suite in the submissive's room.

I pause when I come out of the bathroom. The room is unchanged since Susannah left. Ana never really occupied this space; it has an empty, abandoned feel. The decor is still neutral. White. Cold. Susannah never wanted to decorate.

Grey, stop.

I don't want to go down that rabbit hole right now. Not when my girl should be waiting for me.

When I enter the room, Ana is barefoot by the bed, examining the harness. The sight of her halts me in my tracks. She's changed into some lacy lingerie. She's all long legs, arms, and black lace, and fine see-through panties.

Just for me.

I can see everything.

Everything.

Shrouded in lace.

My mouth dries as she steps toward me, her hair free, falling and curling under her breasts. "Mr. Grey. You're overdressed."

I could play this one of two ways. We are still finding ourselves in here. Today, the Dominant wins. "You want to play?"

"Yes."

"Yes what?"

Ana's lips part in surprise. "Sir."

"In that case, turn around."

She blinks, astonished at my tone, I think, and a furrow forms on her brow.

"Don't frown."

"Suspension?"

"Not fully, no. Your toes will be on the floor. It'll be intense."

Come on, Ana. Don't lose your nerve.

"We don't have to do this," I whisper.

Her mouth twists into that challenging smirk I know so well, and I think she's considering her options. I cock my head to the side as her eyes stray to the harness on the bed. They linger on it—she's intrigued, I can tell. I tip her chin up and brush my lips against hers. "Do you want to wear this harness or not?"

"What will you do to me?" Her words are breathy and barely audible. She's turned on. Just at the sight of it.

"Whatever I want."

She gasps and turns around immediately.

Yes!

From the top of the chest of drawers, I grab a hair tie and gather her hair in my hands and begin braiding it.

It would never do to get her luscious locks caught in any of the straps.

I make quick work of her braid and, once it's fastened, give it a tug. She steps back into my arms. "You look mighty fine, Miss Steele," I murmur into her ear. "Love the lingerie. Remember, you don't have to do anything you don't want to do. Just tell me to stop. Now, go and assume the position by the door." She gives me a most unsubmissive look, which in another lifetime would have earned her a good spanking, but she moves to the door and kneels, resting her palms on her thighs and parting her legs.

That's my girl.

She looks gorgeous. I could come just looking at her.

Steady, Grey. Get a grip.

Ignoring my arousal, I go back to the chest, pull out my iPod, and place it in the dock. I switch on the Bose system, choose a track, and press repeat.

"Sinnerman." Nina Simone. *Perfect.*

Ana is watching me.

"Eyes down," I warn, and she dutifully casts them to the floor.

I close my eyes. Every time she does as she's told it's music to my soul. I can't get her to obey outside this room, but I'm going to take full advantage in here. I amble back to her and stand directly in front of her. "Legs. Wider."

She shuffles and moves her thighs. I groan in approval, strip off my T-shirt, and toss it on the floor. Slowly I unbuckle my belt and pull it through the belt loops. Ana's fingers flex on her thighs.

Is she wondering what I'm going to do with the belt?

Those days are over, Ana.

But, for maximum effect, I drop it and it clatters to the floor. She flinches at the sound.

Shit.

Reaching down, I caress her hair. "Hey, don't sweat it, Ana."

She gazes up at me, every bit a Dom's wet dream, and I know my cock is bursting in anticipation. Taking my sweet time, I unbutton my fly and tug down the zipper while I tighten my hold on her hair. My intention is clear and she regards me with a look that could set me alight from head to foot, and I think that's a good thing, because she opens her mouth, ready for me.

"No, not yet," I whisper, and, still clutching her hair, I ease my hardened cock from my jeans and run my hand up and down the length. Her eyes do not leave mine. With my thumb, I rub the bead of dew that's emerged, into the head, and run my hand along its length once again. I want nothing more than to take her mouth. But I want to make this moment last. "Kiss me," I murmur.

Ana's breasts are rising and falling faster. Her nipples pebbling under my gaze. She's excited. She puckers her lips and presses them against my dick.

"Open up for me."

She parts her lips and I ease myself into her warm, wet, willing mouth.

Fuck.

I ease back, then push my way in once more. This time she's sheathed her teeth, so the effect is immediate as she sucks me in.

Oh, yes.

Groaning my approval, I grip her hair and move. Back. Forth. Fucking her mouth, and like the goddess she is…she takes me.

All of me.

Over and over. More and more. Deeper and deeper.

On and on. I lose myself in her wondrous mouth.

Fuck. I'm going to come. But I don't care. I release her head and put my hand on the wall to keep me upright and I let go.

I cry out as my orgasm rolls through me in a rush and consumes me while Ana moves, gripping my thighs, taking all I have to give.

"*I need you.*" Nina rasps over the sound system, as I pull out of Ana's mouth and lean against the wall to recover my equilibrium.

Ana peers up at me with a look of triumph. She wipes her mouth with the back of her hand and then licks her lips as I adjust myself and zip up my fly.

"A," I whisper, and she smiles. I give her my hand. "Up." I pull her into my arms and kiss her; pushing her against the wall and spilling all my gratitude into our kiss. She tastes of me and sweet Ana; it's a provocative, potent mix.

When I pull back she's winded, and her lips are a little swollen.

"That's better."

"Hmm…" she responds, the sound a deep, sexy noise in her throat.

I grin. "Now we're going to have some real fun." I lead her to the bed, where the harness is laid out. Now that I've come, I'm calmer, and so ready for part two. I look down at Ana, who is gazing at me expectantly. "As much as I love what you're wearing, we need to get you naked."

She hooks her finger into the waistband of my jeans. "And what about you?"

"All in good time, Miss Steele."

She pushes her lower lip out in a moue and I gently take it between my teeth. "No pouting," I whisper, and start unhooking the basque she's wearing, freeing her beautiful breasts. Slowly, I peel her out of it. Once it's off, I place it beside the harness.

"And now these." Kneeling, I slide her panties gently down her legs, ensuring that my fingertips skate across her skin. When I reach her ankles I stop, and give her time to step out of them. I place them on top of her basque. "Hello there," I address her vulva, and plant a kiss just above her clitoris.

She smirks, and I remember a time that a kiss on this part of her anatomy would make her fidget and blush.

Oh, Ana. We've come a long way.

Standing, I grab the harness. "This is like the parachute earlier today."

"Where you got the idea?"

"Yes. Well, you gave me the idea. So, step in, here." I hold the thigh straps open and Ana grabs on to my biceps and steps into one side and then the other. Once in, I hook the shoulder bindings over her shoulders and proceed to buckle all the straps. This includes the one across her chest, at her back, at her waist, and each of those around her upper arms.

I step back to admire my handiwork and my future wife.

Man, she looks hot.

Oh, Sinnerman, Nina sings.

"Feel okay?" I ask

She nods quickly, her eyes dark and full of carnal curiosity.

Oh, Ana. It gets better.

From the top of the drawers I grab the leather cuffs. I fasten them to each of her wrists and then hook their carabiners to the brass loops embedded in each of the upper arm cuffs. Ana's hands are now tethered, level with her shoulders, and effectively immobile.

"Okay?" I ask.

"Yes," she breathes.

Gently, I tug at one of the hooks embedded in the chest strap and lead Ana to the edge of the restraining system in the ceiling of the playroom. From above, I unhook the trapeze and tug it into position above Ana. From each end of the trapeze there are two short cords with carabiners at the end. I clip these to the hooks in her shoulder straps. She watches me intently as I complete the task.

She's now hooked in place. Her feet flat on the floor. For now.

"So, the exciting feature of this device is that I can do this." I step to the side and from the large brass cleat that's attached to the wall, I unwind the cords that are secured to the trapeze via the restraining system. With both hands I tug, and Ana's suddenly hoisted onto the balls of her feet. Ana gasps and totters from side to side and front and back, attempting to find her balance. I rewrap the cords around the cleat, leaving Ana dancing on the tips of her toes.

She's helpless. And completely at my mercy.

It's a thrilling thought and sight.

"What are you going to do?" she asks.

"Like I said, exactly what I want. I'm a man of my word."

"You won't leave me like this?" She looks panicked.

I grasp her chin. "No. Never. Rule number one: never leave someone who's restrained alone. Ever." I kiss her quickly. "You okay?"

She's breathing hard, excited, and I think she's daunted, but she nods. I kiss her again, this time with infinite tenderness, my lips brushing hers. "Right. You've seen enough." From my back pocket, I retrieve a blindfold and slip it over her head and cover her eyes.

"You look so fucking hot, Ana." Taking a few steps back to the drawers, I pull out the item I require and slip it into my back pocket. I circle Ana, admiring my handiwork, until I'm facing her once more. I run my thumb over her lips, then down her chin, down her sternum.

Power, Nina bellows out through the playroom.

"Are you going to obey me in here?" I whisper.

"Do you want me to?" she asks, her voice all breathy and needy.

I skim my hands over her breasts and her nipples lengthen beneath my thumbs. I tug them both. Hard.

"Ah!" she cries. "Yes. Yes," she says quickly.

"Good girl." I continue kneading her nipples between my thumbs and forefingers. She moans, tossing her head back, and teeters on her toes.

"Oh, baby, feel it. Do you want to come this way?"

"Yes. No. I don't know."

"I think not. I have another plan for you."

Her groan fills the room. I place my hands on her waist and dip my head and suck a nipple into my mouth, taunting it with my tongue and my lips. Ana cries out, and I move to its twin and lavish the same attention on it, until Ana is pulling against her restraints.

When I don't think she can take much more, I kneel at her feet and trail kisses across her belly, my tongue circling her navel and then continuing a journey south. Grabbing her thighs, I hoist her legs over my shoulders and slide her vulva toward my mouth. She tips back in the harness and lets out a guttural cry as my lips and tongue find her clitoris, swollen and ready for my attention. I go to town, dedicating myself to the small powerhouse at the apex of her thighs.

Teasing. Testing. Torturing her with my mouth.

"Christian," she gasps, and I know she's close.

I stop and set her back on her toes. I want her to come with her toes bouncing on the floor. It'll be intense. Standing, I steady her, and from my back pocket, I grab the ridged glass dildo and run it over her belly. "Feel this?"

"Yes. Yes. Cold," she breathes.

"Cold. Good. I'm going to put it inside you. And after you've come, I'm going to put me inside you."

She makes a strangled groan.

"Legs apart," I order.

Ana ignores me. "Ana!"

Tentatively she moves her feet and I run the end of the dildo up her thigh and oh-so-slowly slip it inside her.

"Argh!" she groans. "Cold!" Gently to begin with, I pump my hand, knowing that the glass wand is shaped to hit that potent, sweet, sweet spot inside her. This is not going to take long. With my other hand, I circle her waist, holding her close and kissing her throat, inhaling her rousing scent.

Ana, come apart in my arms.

She's so close. So close. My hand continues to move. Harder. Faster. Taking her higher. Her legs are stiffening and suddenly she goes rigid and screams as her climax rips though her. She bucks against her bindings as I thrust the dildo inside her, making her ride out her orgasm. When her head tips back, her mouth slack, I ease it out of her and toss it onto the bed. I unclip first one and then the other carabiner from her shoulder straps, then carry her to the bed.

I lay her out. Still harnessed. Her hands still tied. I remove the blindfold. Her eyes are closed. I unzip my jeans and swiftly remove them and my boxer briefs. Standing over her, I grab her thighs, lift them to either side of my hips, and slam into her. Then still.

She cries out and opens her eyes.

She's wet. Really wet.

And mine.

Our eyes stay on each other. Hers dazed and full of passion. And want. And need.

"Please," she whispers, and I flex my ass and start to move. Grinding into her. My fingers grip her thighs and she crosses her legs behind me. Holding me. I rock into her. Back and forth. Back and forth. And as I get closer, I release her legs, which she tightens around me, and I lean over her, my hands on either side of her shoulders, my fingers crushing the red satin sheets. "Come on, baby. Again," I shout, and my voice is almost unrecognizable to me.

Ana lets go, taking me with her. I come, long and hard, with a cry and it's her name.

Ana.

I collapse beside her. Utterly. Spent.

As my reason returns, I lean up over her and unclip the wrist restraints and then pull her into my arms. "How was that?" I murmur.

I think she says "mind-blowing" before she closes her eyes and nestles into my arms. I grin and hold her close.

Nina is still singing her heart out. I find the remote on the bed and switch her off, letting silence fall over Ana and me and the playroom. "Well done, Ana Steele. I'm in awe of you," I whisper, but she's fast asleep…in the harness. I smile and kiss the top of head.

Ana, I love you and I love your inner freak.

MONDAY, JULY 18, 2011

It's early and Bastille is his usual tyrannical self as we warm up. "Good cross. Again," he shouts, his words a staccato.

I jab and land a punch on his palm pad.

"Again. Jab. Cross."

I comply.

"Change hands. Leg back."

My right leg is back and I'm in fight stance.

"Go."

I throw my weight behind my right glove and the sound of leather slapping on leather echoes around the basement gym at Grey House.

"Good. Again. Keep going. We gotta keep you in shape, Grey. You gotta look good walking down the aisle." He cackles.

Ignoring his tone, I rain blows on his palm pads.

"Cool. Good. Enough."

I stop and catch my breath. I'm wired. Ready. Bouncing on my toes. Adrenaline flowing through my veins. I'm ready to strike. I'm on top of the fucking world.

"I think that's enough warm-up. Let's blow the corporate bullshit out of your brain."

"You're on, dude. You are going down."

He flashes me a broad, bright grin as he slides his gloves over taped hands. "That's fighting talk, Grey. You know, your girl is making fine progress. She'll keep your ass in line. She'll make one worthy opponent."

She's a worthy opponent now.

And she keeps my ass in line.

And I keep hers—

Don't think about that now!

He raises his fists. "Ready, old man?"

What? I'm ten years his junior.

"Old. I'll give you old, Bastille." I lunge at him.

FEELING REFRESHED AND READY for the day, I take my seat at my desk and fire up the iMac. Ana is waiting at the top of my inbox.

From: Anastasia Steele
Subject: Soaring, In and Out of the Red Room.
Date: July 18 2011 09:32
To: Christian Grey

My dearest Mr. Grey
It's hard to know which I prefer: sailing, soaring or the Red Room of ~~Pain~~ Pleasure. Thank you for yet another unforgettable weekend.
I love flying high in every way with you.
I am, as ever, in awe of your talents...all of them. ;)
Your soon-to-be wife xxxx

My grin in response to Ana's e-mail is out of control. But I don't care. I look up when Andrea places a cup of coffee on my desk, and she looks a little disconcerted.

"Thanks, Andrea."

"Shall I ask Ros to come up?" Andrea asks, recovering her composure.

"Please do." I clear my throat, wondering what's bothering my PA. I type a quick response to Ana.

From: Christian Grey
Subject: Physical Pursuits
Date: July 18 2011 09:58
To: Anastasia Steele

My darling Anastasia
I love soaring with you.
I love playing with you.
I love doing you.
I love you.
Always.

Christian Grey
CEO, Grey Enterprises Holdings, Inc.

PS: Which talent in particular? Inquiring minds need to know.

Ros knocks and enters my office. "Good morning, Christian," she chimes as I press send. She's unusually cheerful. Standing, I wave her to the table.

"Good morning."

"Why the frown?" she asks as she sits down.

"I don't think I've ever seen you so upbeat."

Her smile could rival the Great Sphinx at Giza. "God is good."

I raise my eyebrows. This is very un-Ros-like behavior. Taking a seat opposite her, I wait patiently for an explanation. She shuffles her papers and hands me the agenda for our meeting. It's obvious she's not going to elucidate, and I don't wish to pry. I glance down at the first item. "The Taiwan shipyard?"

"They're offering a full disclosure of their P&L, their assets and liabilities. They want to partner with a U.S. company. They'd like to pitch."

"They sound eager."

"They do," Ros confirms.

"I think we should take them up on the offer and conduct our due diligence. Then we can take it from there. Agreed?"

"I think so. We have nothing to lose at this stage."

"Okay. Let's do it."

"I'll put the paperwork in place." Ros scribbles down a note and moves to the next item on the agenda.

THERE'S AN E-MAIL FROM Ana waiting for me when I've concluded my meeting with Ros.

From: Anastasia Steele
Subject: Your Physical Pursuits
Date: July 18 2011 10:01
To: Christian Grey

Why, Mr. Grey...so rude and so modest! I think you can guess—your sexpertise knows no bounds.
I'm very much looking forward to seeing the house again this evening.
I am in a meeting that concludes at 5 p.m. I'll see you then?
Ax

I pick up my phone and dial her direct line.

"Ana Steele," she answers in her crisp, executive voice.

"Ana Steele, Christian Grey."

"Ah, my talented fiancé. How are you?"

"Very well, thank you. Taylor and I will be there at five."

"Great. Now, I need to get back to daydreaming...I mean work. I don't want my boss's boss's boss to catch me shirking my responsibilities."

"What do you think he'd do if he did?"

She gasps and the sound sends a thrill through my body. "Something unspeakable," she whispers.

"That could be arranged."

"Your twitchy palm?"

"As you know, it's perpetually twitchy. And not been used to its full potential of late."

"Stop. You're making me moist."

What!

"Moist." I clear my throat. "Miss Steele. That word should only be reserved for cakes. I like you wet."

"I like that you like me wet." Her voice is almost inaudible.

I shift in my chair. "Five p.m.," I whisper.

"How can you make three syllables sound so alluring?"

"It's a curse."

"It's a gift." Her voice is husky.

Damn, but she has an answer for everything. "See you at five, Ana. Laters, baby." I'm on top of the world. She giggles in that delightful way she does, and it takes all my willpower to hang up.

I bound out of my chair feeling effervescent. Flirting with Ana is always a joy. And so is discussing the latest prototype of the GEH solar tablet with Fred and Barney. I head out of my office, wondering if I should have studied engineering at school.

AS I'M EATING MY lunch, my phone flashes with Elliot's goofy face.

"Bro?"

"Hey, dude, we still on for later today?"

"Yes. Ana and I are looking forward to it."

"Cool." He pauses.

"What is it?" I ask. "Gia? She'll be there, too."

He scoffs. "Like that would ever be a problem. I'm talking bachelor party, hotshot. Saturday."

"Elliot—"

"Don't be an uptight asshole," he interrupts. "It's happening. Even if I have to kidnap you."

"Fuck—"

"No ifs or buts, bro. I've got the construction crew on standby with duct tape and a cargo van. Suck it up."

My sigh is as exaggerated as I can make it.

Elliot laughs. "What's the worst that can happen?"

"I don't know, Elliot. It depends what you have planned."

"It will take your mind off your woes."

Woes? "What fucking woes?"

"I dunno. Someone trying to kill you?"

Oh, yes. That. "You're so crass. Hard to believe we've been raised by the same people."

He laughs. "Laters, dude." And he hangs up.

Asshole.

But he has a point. Welch has made no further progress in uncovering *Charlie Tango*'s saboteur. I've fired the entire team responsible for her care and maintenance, and I'm still waiting for the report from the NTSB. I'm beginning to wonder if the original FAA assessment was hasty in suspecting malicious interference, or if the damage was a random act of vandalism. Both these outcomes are possible, and give me a modicum of hope, but I don't want to drop my guard yet. Ana's safety is all that I care about. I've had security ramped up around the GEH Gulfstream and she's been on two test flights since *Charlie Tango*'s demise. She'll be taking us to Europe for our honeymoon.

I'm still waiting to hear from Burgess about the yacht, but I have my fingers crossed that I'll get the one I want. I imagine Ana stretched out on deck in a bikini.

Wait. Does she own a bikini?

I don't remember including swimwear in the clothes the personal shopper at Neiman Marcus sourced for Ana. That was a lifetime ago. As my wife, Ana is going to need more clothes—for her vacation, functions, her work… I scroll through my contacts, and when Caroline Acton's name appears, I press call.

From: Christian Grey
Subject: Dedicated Follower of Fashion
Date: July 18 2011 15:22
To: Anastasia Steele

My darling Anastasia
I have made an appointment for us to meet Caroline Acton at 10:30 on Saturday morning to furnish you with a new wardrobe for our honeymoon.
No arguments.
Please.

Christian Grey
CEO, Grey Enterprises Holdings, Inc.

From: Anastasia Steele
Subject: Threads?
Date: July 18 2011 15:27
To: Christian Grey

Me? Argue?
Do I need a new wardrobe?
I don't think so. I have plenty of clothes.
See you at 5 p.m.
Ax

I frown. This is not going to be easy.

From: Christian Grey
Subject: New Threads
Date: July 18 2011 15:29
To: Anastasia Steele

Yes. You do.

Christian Grey
CEO, Grey Enterprises Holdings, Inc.

From: Anastasia Steele
Subject: Men with more money than sense…
Date: July 18 2011 15:32
To: Christian Grey

Is brevity the soul of wit?
Ana

From: Christian Grey
Subject: That's Me.
Date: July 18 2011 15:33
To: Anastasia Steele

Yes. ;)

Christian Grey
CEO, Grey Enterprises Holdings, Inc.

From: Anastasia Steele
Subject: Grrr…
Date: July 18 2011 15:34
To: Christian Grey

I am late for my meeting.
Stop being so funny.
Laters. Baby.
Axx

My phone buzzes. "Yes, Sam."

"Christian, *Star* magazine has gotten hold of some shots of Anastasia and want to run a story on her; a rags-to-riches kinda thing."

"What the fuck?"

"I know."

"What kind of shots?"

"Nothing salacious."

Thank fuck.

Wait. There shouldn't be any salacious shots of Ana. Should there?

"Tell them to fuck off. Rope Ros in. Threaten them with legal action."

Sam takes a deep breath. "They'll be published while you're away on your honeymoon. The photos are okay. If you want my advice, let them run and ignore them. It will be more of a story if you don't."

I can almost hear his *I told you so* vibe over the phone. He wanted us to do a photoshoot; maybe I should have conceded.

Hell.

"Send me what you have," I snap.

Fucking paparazzi!

A moment later his e-mail pops up in my inbox, and I read the attachment quickly. Grudgingly, I admit he might be right. It's not that bad, and the photographs of Ana are okay, if grainy. But they also have her yearbook photo. She looks cute. And young. I call him. "Let me think about this."

AT THE NEW HOUSE, we follow Gia Matteo through each room. "I love the staircase," she enthuses. "I'm not surprised you want to retain it." She beams at me as if it were my idea.

Sweetheart. I wanted to knock this house down and build something new. It's Ana who has fallen in love with the old place.

"I love the period features," Ana asserts.

Gia flashes her a smile. "Of course," she says. We follow her into the main living area. Elliot hangs back; he's uncharacteristically quiet, and I wonder if it's because he has a sexual history with Ms. Matteo—I don't know. She's vocal, with some out-of-the-box ideas, and I remember meeting her briefly when she did the renovation to my house in Aspen. She did a fantastic job on that.

"I love this room," Gia says when we enter the main living room. "It has an airy quality that I think we should embrace." She reaches over and pats my arm.

Damn.

I've spent my life subtly maneuvering myself out of anyone's reach. It's a self-defense mechanism that I've cultivated over the years to keep people out of my space and make them back the hell off. A step here, a slide to the side there, angling my shoulders left or right to avoid physical contact, I have it down to a fine art. I *hate* to be touched. No. I fear it. Except by Ana, of course. Kickboxing has helped. I can tolerate the rough and tumble of a match and a firm handshake…or the bite of a cane or lash.

Don't think about that.

But that's it.

In addition, I've developed a fuck-off-don't-touch-me glare that's proven effective.

However, not on Gia Matteo.

She's fucking touchy-feely.

It's irritating.

And not only with me. She reaches out to Elliot as he enters the main living room and gives him what can only be described as a carnal smile as she takes his arm. Elliot gapes at her cleavage, which is on show for all of us. Ana notices, and I see a frown cross her face. I wonder if what my brother says about Ms. Matteo is true. She's a woman who doesn't take no for an answer, one of those overtly sexual, tactile women who disregards all boundaries.

A bit like Elena.

The unpleasant thought pops into my head and makes me a pause. I don't remember Gia being that way when we met a couple of years ago.

Stop overthinking this, Grey.

But as we walk through the house I find myself putting as much distance as I can between her and me.

"A glass wall would be amazing at this end of the room," Gia says. "It will really open out this whole space."

Ana smiles, but keeps her counsel and takes my hand.

TAYLOR WEAVES THROUGH THE evening traffic back to Escala.

"What did you think?" I ask Ana.

"Of Gia?"

I nod.

"The Gia show," she says.

"Yeah. She has a lot of personality. But she had some great ideas, and we've seen her portfolio. It's impressive."

Ana bursts out laughing. "Yes. Her impressive portfolio was on full display."

I laugh. "I don't know what you mean."

Ana arches a brow. And I laugh again and take her hand. "Thank you for being funny," I whisper, and kiss her knuckles. "What do think? Should we find someone else?"

"She did have some good ideas." Ana sounds almost begrudging, but she smiles. "Let's see what she comes back with."

"Agreed. Shall we go out to eat? We've been cooped up enough at Escala."

"Is it safe?"

"I think so." I turn and catch Taylor's eye in the rearview mirror. "Columbia Tower, please, Taylor."

"Yes, sir."

"Mile High Club?" I suggest to Ana.

"Suits me."

I clasp her hand.

"I did like her idea for opening up the view from the back of the house," Ana says.

"Yes. Me, too, but we're in no rush."

She smiles once more. "I love your ivory tower."

"I love having you there."

Her eyes meet mine and her expression is suddenly serious. "I'm glad, because you're about to commit to having me there for a lifetime."

Whoa. I swallow.

This is huge.

A whole lifetime with Anastasia...will it be enough?

"Good point, well made, Miss Steele."

And from nowhere I'm overwhelmed with a depth of feeling that has become all too familiar, but it's still new and shiny and terrifying. I'm happier than I've ever been before—but I'm afraid, too.

It could all end.

Everything could come crashing down.

Life is ephemeral.

I know this. I've lived it.

From nowhere the image of a pale, still, young woman comes to mind. She's lying on a grubby rug in a grubbier room as a small child tries in vain to shake her awake.

Shit.

The crack whore.

No. Don't think about her!

Reaching over, I take Ana's face between my hands, memorizing every detail: the shape of her nose, her full lower lip, her stunning eyes. I want her with me for a lifetime. I close my eyes and kiss her, pouring all my fear into her.

Don't ever leave me.

Don't die.

SATURDAY, JULY 23, 2011

"What do you think Elliot has planned?" Ana is sprawled over me, her index finger making small circles through my chest hair. It's a weird sensation, one that I'm not entirely comfortable with.

Enough.

I grab her hand, threading my fingers through hers, and plant a kiss on the tip of the offending digit.

"Too much?" she whispers.

I slide her finger into my mouth, clamping my teeth gently around her knuckle and teasing the tip with my tongue.

"Ah!" she coos, as a sensuous spark ignites in her eyes, and she tips her pelvis against my thigh.

Baby.

She tugs her hand and I relax my jaw but close my lips as she eases her finger out of my mouth.

She tastes mighty fine.

Tenderly she kisses the spot on my chest that her finger traced, while I stroke her hair and revel in this quiet moment. It's early, and the only items on today's agenda are my "bachelor party," Ana's bachelorette party, and a shopping excursion with Caroline Acton.

Ana raises her head. "Do you think he'll take you to a…a…strip joint?"

A chuckle rumbles in my chest. "Strip joint?"

Ana giggles. "I don't know what they're called."

I sigh and close my eyes, envisioning the hell that Elliot probably has planned. "Knowing Elliot, it's a distinct possibility."

"I'm not sure how I feel about that," Ana replies, tartly.

I grin and, rolling over, press her into the mattress. "Why, Miss Steele, do you disapprove?" I run my nose down hers and she squirms beneath me.

"Deeply."

"Jealous?"

She makes a face.

"I'd rather be here with you," I reassure her.

"You're not really a party animal, are you?" she says.

"No. More the loner."

"I've figured this out." Her teeth graze my chin.

"Could say the same about you," I murmur.

"I'm the wallflower, nose-in-a-book type."

I skim my lips from her ear to her throat. "You're too beautiful to be a wallflower."

She groans and runs her fingernails over my shoulder blades as her body rises to welcome mine. She's still slick and wet from earlier, and I ease into her and we move together, slower and sweeter this time. Her nails dig into my back as she wraps her legs around mine and she raises her hips to meet me. Over and over. Slow and sweet. She's building.

I stop.

"Christian, don't stop. Please," she begs.

I love it when you beg, baby.

I move slowly and grip her hair at her nape with both hands, so she cannot turn her head. I gaze down at her, marveling at the intricate color of her irises. I move again. Slowly. In. Out. And then stop once more.

"Christian, please," she breathes.

"It will only ever be you, Ana. Always."

Don't be jealous.

"I love you." I start once more. She closes her eyes and tips her head back and comes around me, triggering my own orgasm. With a cry, I fall to her side to catch my breath. When I resurface, I turn over and pull her to me, kissing her hair.

I love waking up to Ana.

Closing my eyes, I imagine every Saturday could be like this. Anastasia Steele has given me a meaningful future, something I've not considered with any seriousness before. And next Saturday, I get the piece of paper that proves it.

She'll be mine.

Until death do us part.

Ana lying on the cold, hard floor flashes before my eyes.

No!

I rub my face.

Stop. Grey. Stop.

I kiss her hair, breathing in her life-affirming fragrance, and I'm calmer.

It must be about 9 a.m. I grab my phone from my nightstand to check the time. There's a text from Elliot.

> ELLIOT
> Good morning, Asshole. I'm sitting in your vast living room waiting for you to get your lazy ass out here. Stop what you're doing. Now. You dirty dog.

What the hell?

"What is it?" Ana asks, looking tousled and fuckable.

"Elliot's here."

"Outside?" Ana sounds bemused.

I ease her out of my embrace. "No. He's here."

She frowns.

"Yeah, I don't understand it, either." I get up, stalk into my closet, and drag on a pair of jeans.

Elliot is sprawled on my couch, staring at his phone. "Good morning, hotshot, about time!" he hollers. "Glad you dressed for the occasion." He eyes my naked chest and feet with amused disdain.

"What in God's name are you doing here, dude? It's nine a.m."

"Yep. Surprise! Get your ass in gear. I got the day planned."

What? "I'm supposed to take Ana shopping."

He scoffs, disgusted. "She's a grown woman. She can do her own damn shopping."

"But—"

"Dude. I'm saving you. Shopping with women is hell. Go. Put some clothes on, you pervert. And for fuck's sake have a shower. I can smell the sex from here."

"Fuck off," I reply without heat.

He really is a douche sometimes.

"You'll need hiking boots and sneakers," he calls after me.

Both?

"HOW DID YOU GET in?" I ask as we head down to the garage in the elevator.

"Taylor."

"Ah. That's why we have no security following us."

"Yep. I figured you were leaving with me, so you'd be fine. Your man Taylor was reluctant, but I persuaded him."

I nod, pleased. Being continually dogged by our close protection team has been wearing. Ana and I have been holed up at Escala for what feels like forever. Sawyer and Reynolds will keep an eye on her today, though. That's non-negotiable.

"He's been very helpful," Elliot says.

"Who?"

"Taylor." And with that he hides his sly smile and stops talking.

What does he have planned?

ELLIOT IS IN AN ebullient mood. It's catching. We're cruising in his pickup north along I-5. "Where exactly *are* we going?" I ask, over the godawful yacht-rock blasting through the cab.

"Surprise," he shouts. "Relax. It's going to be fine."

It's too late to tell him I'm not a fan of surprises, so I sit back and enjoy the cityscape as we head out of Seattle. We haven't spent any time together since we went mountain biking near Portland. That was a most interesting night…the first night I slept with Ana. The first night I slept with anyone! And Elliot fucked Ana's best friend—but then Elliot has fucked many of the women with whom he's come into contact. It's not surprising, really; he's good company. Easygoing. Good-looking, I suppose. Women flock to him, I'll give him that. He puts them at ease.

He's always been able to charm our mother. He knows how to treat Grace. I used to envy the easy way he'd spin her around the kitchen floor or hug her or give her a passing peck on her cheek.

He makes it look easy.

As yet, he shows no signs of settling down.

And if he does, I hope to God it's not with Kavanagh.

I send a quick text to Ana.

No idea what Elliot has in mind. This is not how I planned to spend the day. Enjoy your shopping experience with Caroline Acton. Missing you. x

ANA
Missing you, too. Love you. Ax

Elliot leaves I-5 for the 532.

"Camano Island?" I ask.

He winks at me, which is annoying. I check my watch, then my phone.

"Dude! What gives? She'll be fine without you, for fuck's sake. Show some dignity. I packed some snacks. I know how disagreeable you get without food."

"Snacks? Where?"

He opens the car caddy, revealing subs, chips, and Coke. Ah, all of life's pleasures…if you're Elliot.

"Nutritious," I mutter dryly.

"It's all good stuff, bro. Quit complaining. This is your bachelor party."

I laugh, because chips and Coke is not my idea of a good time. Subs, on the other hand…I smirk at my little private joke and reach for a can of Coke.

ABOUT FIVE MILES INTO Camano Island, Elliot turns right. We drive through a farm gate into an open pasture, along a track, and up to a barn, where he pulls into a parking lot.

"We're here."

"Where is here?"

"Friend's place. It's not open to the public yet. But it will be soon. We're guinea pigs."

"What?"

"Well, I figured marriage is pretty much a high-wire activity. I thought you should get some practice."

"What are you talking about?"

"We're going zip-lining." He grins and clambers out of the car.

This! This is my bachelor party? It is not what I was expecting. But hey, zip-lining could be fun.

Elliot greets our hosts, and we're directed into the barn, where a series of hooks hold the safety equipment: hard hats, harnesses, straps, and carabiners. It all looks reassuringly familiar.

"Hey, hotshot, these harnesses are damned freaky. We could get up to some kinky shit in these," Elliot blurts as he slips his on. And for once I'm at a complete loss as to what to say.

Does he know?

Are the tips of my ears red?

Shit! Has Ana talked to Kate?

Elliot looks his usual guileless self, so I assume not, because if he knew, he'd have razzed the shit of me. "You're an idiot. This is like a chute," I reply. Distraction is the best policy. "Got a new sailplane last week. You should come out to Ephrata for a day and we can take her up."

"For two?"

"Yep."

"That would be super cool."

WE'RE ON THE FIRST platform surrounded by pine trees. "To infinity and beyond!" Elliot shouts and leaps off, with all the fearlessness that I associate with his devil-may-fucking-care attitude. He whoops like a gorilla in heat as he whizzes down the line, his joy contagious. He lands surprisingly gracefully on the next platform, about one hundred feet away.

Danielle, one of our guides, radios ahead to say I'm set and clips my lifeline to the zip-line trolley. "Ready, Christian?" she asks with an overeager smile.

"As I'll ever be."

"Off you go."

Taking a deep breath, I grab the carabiner beneath the trolley with one hand, my lifeline with the other, and I jump. I fly through the fresh, lush forest, the pulley whistling above me and the summer breeze on my face. I'm on a roller coaster without a car, sailing between the Douglas firs beneath a brilliant blue sky, and it's thrilling and liberating in equal measure. I land safely on the platform beside Elliot and the other guide.

"Whaddya think?" Elliot claps me on the back.

I grin. "This is pretty fucking excellent."

Danielle is last to land on the platform. "That was our first. They get higher and faster."

"Bring it!" I exclaim.

TWO HOURS LATER, STILL buzzing from our high-wire activity, we're back on the road, Elliot behind the wheel. "Bro, as experiences go, that was right up there," I acknowledge.

"Better than sex?" Elliot cackles. "You've only just discovered it—so probably not."

"I'm a little more discerning in my tastes than you are, dude."

"I just like to spread the love around. The Big E wants what the Big E wants."

I shake my head with a snort of derision. I do not want to think about the Big E. "Can we get some real food now?"

Elliot grins. "Nope, sorry, bro. You don't want a full stomach for what we have planned next. Eat the sub."

"Next? Elliot, the zip line was great. There's more?"

"Oh, yes. Suck it up, buttercup."

Gingerly, I pick up one of the subs.

"Those are made by my own fair hand."

"Don't put me off."

"The finest bologna, tomato, and provolone cheese this side of the Rockies have gone into those sandwiches."

"I'll take your word for it."

"You need to broaden your culinary horizons."

"With bologna?"

"Whatever it takes. Unwrap that for me."

I peel off the parchment paper and hand him the dubious-looking creation. He shoves it in his mouth and starts to chow down. It's not a sight for the fainthearted, and I realize I have no choice, it's bologna or starve.

While I eat, I text Ana.

Zip-lining. That's what Elliot had planned. And bologna sandwiches. I'm living the dream.

ANA
LOL! I'm spending a great deal of your money. Not entirely consensually. Caroline Acton is a force to be reckoned with. She reminds me of you. Stay safe with whatever Elliot throws at you! Love you. And miss you. xxx

I love it when you spend my money. It will very soon be your money, too. Will report on Elliot's next "surprise." xxx

Elliot drives smoothly off I-5 onto the 2. *Where the fuck are we going?* I thought we were headed back to Seattle.

"Surprise," he responds to my questioning look.

Seems to be his word of the day.

Fifteen minutes later he pulls into the parking lot at Harvey Airfield.

"Hey, there's a steakhouse here—we could have had some real food," I grumble.

"Maybe later—we've got a class to catch."

"Class?"

"Come on, hotshot, you've not guessed it yet?" He drives past the steakhouse.

"No."

"We're taking the plunge, because you're taking the plunge."

What the hell?

Elliot puts me out of my misery. "Skydiving."

"Oh. Okay." *Fuck!*

"It'll be great. I've done a tandem jump before. It's wild."

Of course he has.

"You'll be fine."

"Yeah. Sure."

"Listen, you get married and women don't let you do this shit. Come on." Together we walk through the parking lot toward the sky-diving school, and my heart races. I like to be in control; tandem jumping means someone else is in control…and I'm strapped to them.

And they're touching me. At a great altitude.

Hell.

I've been as high up as 15,000 feet in my sailplane, and 20,000 feet in *Charlie Tango.* But then I was seated and piloting an aircraft that could fly. Leaping out of a plane? Into the sky? At height?

Never.

Shit.

But I cannot, simply cannot, wimp out in front of Elliot. I swallow my apprehension as we enter the building.

My brother has booked us an exclusive jump. After a short informative video, we sit through a briefing with Ben, our instructor, and I'm grateful that it's just Elliot and me in the class. I was coached on how to use a parachute as part of my glider training, but I've never actually done a jump. While Ben is explaining what we need to do and what to expect, it occurs to me that I haven't provided this training for Ana. She needs to do this before she goes up in ASH 30 again.

When Ben, who looks younger than me, has completed our instruction, he hands us each a waiver. Elliot signs it immediately, while I read through. My anxiety begins to climb, settling in my stomach. I am about to jump out of an aircraft from a high altitude.

Deep breath, Grey.

I realize that if something were to happen to me, Ana would be left with nothing.

To hell with that.

Once I've signed the form, on the back I write:

This is my last will and testament. In the event of my death I leave all my worldly goods to my beloved fiancée, Anastasia Steele, to be dispensed with as she sees fit.
Signed: Christian Grey Date: 07/23/2011

I take a quick photo with my phone and zap it to Ros, before handing the signed waiver back to Ben, who laughs.

"You'll be fine, Christian."

"Just preparing for all eventualities." I give him a quick, forced smile.

He laughs again. "Okay. Let's get you suited up."

We leave the building and head across the tarmac to an open-air hangar where all the safety gear is located: chutes, helmets, and harnesses.

I'm detecting a theme.

Elliot swaggers to the hangar as if he doesn't have a care in the world; it's infuriating, and right now I envy him more than ever. Ben hands us each a jumpsuit.

Literally. A. Jumpsuit.

Whoa!

"Hey, hotshot. More kinky shit!" Elliot crows as he pulls the safety harness over his attire.

I roll my eyes and turn to Ben. "I apologize for Elliot. He only speaks asshole."

"You two related?" Ben asks.

Elliot and I exchange a look. *Yes. But no. But yes.*

"Brothers," Elliot responds, looking at me, and we both break into *that* secret smile that adopted siblings share. Ben knows he's missing something, but says nothing and helps first Elliot, then me, into our harnesses.

It's decided that I will tandem-jump with Ben, and we're joined by Matt, who will tandem-jump with Elliot. Another instructor, Sandra, tags along, complete with a GoPro to film the whole escapade.

"Hi," Matt says as he shakes our hands. "Special occasion?"

"My brother's bachelor party. He's experiencing the last gasp of freedom," Elliot says.

"Congratulations," Matt says.

"Thanks," I mutter dryly. "This is a surprise."

"Good surprise?"

"Jury's out."

Matt laughs. "You'll love it. Let's go, pilot's ready."

The five of us make our way across the runway to the waiting single-engine Cessna.

Last chance to change your mind, Grey.

There are only two seats at the front of the plane, behind the pilot. But Matt and Ben sit down on the floor and motion for us to sit in front of them. We comply and they start the process of buckling us onto their harnesses. As his hands move over the straps, I realize that I'm not unnerved by the physical contact with Ben; he'll have my life in his hands.

"You flown before?" he asks, raising his voice above the sound of the engine.

"I'm a qualified commercial pilot," I respond. "Rotorcraft. And I have a couple of sailplanes."

"This'll be easy for you."

My laugh is hollow.

Yeah. No. I'm a pilot for a reason.

I'm in control.

I take a deep breath as the plane leaves the runway and begins its ascent. Snohomish Valley falls away as we climb higher and higher into the cloudless sky.

Matt and Elliot are talking crap. Ben joins in. I block them out and think of Ana.

What's she doing? Is her wardrobe complete? I think of her in my arms this morning, wrapped around me. I place my hand on my chest where her finger traced small circles.

Calm, Grey. Calm.

As we near 12,000 feet Ben hands me a leather cap complete with chin strap, and some goggles. As I put them on he runs through a quick reminder of all that I need to know. The other instructor opens the rear door; the draft is almost deafening.

Shit. This is happening.

"You got that?" Ben shouts, referring to his quick refresher.

"Yes."

Ben checks the altimeter on his right wrist. "It's time. Excited? Let's go." We shuffle toward the open door, the sound of the single engine and the wind rush even more thunderous. I glance at Elliot, who gives me a thumbs-up sign and a fuck-you grin.

"You asshole!" I yell, and he laughs. I cross my arms and clutch on to my harness like my life depends on it…because my life depends on it. Then I'm hanging, attached to a man I don't know, over fucking Washington and the Snohomish Valley. I squeeze my eyes shut, and for the first time in a billion years offer a prayer to the God that abandoned me years ago. Then I open them again.

Whoa. I can see the Cascades, Possession Sound, the San Juan Islands—and nothing but air beneath me.

"Here we go," Ben shouts, and launches us out of the aircraft.

"Ffffuuuuuccccckkkkkk!" I bellow.

And I'm flying.

Really flying, above the earth. Either I don't have time to be afraid or the adrenaline streaking through my body has blotted out the fear. It's super-exhilarating. I can see for miles, and because I'm not behind glass or plastic, it's hyper-real. I'm in the sky, cloaked in it. It's holding me up. The rushing sound of air as we dive to the ground is familiar, like an old friend. I free my hands and hold them out to feel the wind racing through my fingers. Ben holds a thumb up in front of my face and I return the compliment.

This is beyond amazing.

Scanning above, I get a glimpse of Elliot and Matt. And Sandra comes whooshing past us, the camera turned toward Ben and me. My grin is goofy.

"This is great!" I call out to Ben as we surf the sky.

I see Ben raise his wrist. We're at 5,000 feet. He tugs at his rip cord and we slow immediately as above us a multicolored canopy unfurls. The nature of the dive changes from terminal velocity to slow motion, and all is quiet as we hang in the air. My anxiety evaporates, replaced by an inner calm that surprises me. I'm on top of the world, quite literally walking on air. Ben's got this; he knows what he's doing. And from somewhere deep in my mind, the thought materializes in my head: I hope that my marriage to Ana is this thrilling and this easy.

The view is breathtaking.

I wish she were here.

Though it would give me a coronary watching her jump out of a plane.

"Want to steer?" Ben asks.

"Sure."

He hands me the risers; I tug on the left and we turn, slowly and gracefully, in a wide circle.

"Dude, you've got this," Ben calls, patting my upper arm.

We do another circle before Ben takes the risers back in order to steer us toward the landing zone. The ground is approaching at speed, and I lift my knees as instructed as Ben gently drops us to the ground. We both land on our asses, and the ground team is there to welcome us.

Ben unclips his harness from mine and I stand, feeling a little unsteady from the adrenaline rush. Behind us, Elliot and Matt land, Elliot whooping like a gorilla again—his favorite form of expressing excitement.

I pause and catch my breath.

"How was it?" Ben asks.

"Man, that was sublime. Thank you."

"Great!" He offers a fist-bump and I return it.

Elliot rushes over to join us.

"Fuck, man!" I exclaim.

"Rad, huh?"

"I was shitting bricks."

"I know! It's good to see you finally losing your fucking cool for once. It's a rare event, bro." Elliot laughs, but his grin reflects mine. "Better than sex?" he asks.

"No…but close."

FIFTEEN MINUTES LATER WE'RE back in his pickup.

"Dude, I could use a drink after that," I say, and I can't shake my shit-eating grin.

"Me, too. Well, we're going to part three of your bachelor party."

"Fuck, there's more?"

Elliot clams up. *Smug asshole.* He's not telling me. I check my phone.

ANA
Home. We shopped till we dropped. I'm going to have a bath. Then get ready to meet Kate. I haven't heard from you. You know I worry. Axxx

We were SKYDIVING!! from 12,000 feet. You were right to worry. But it was amazing!! Reminds me. You need parachute training. If I don't see you—enjoy your night out. But not too much.

ANA
Skydiving. Wow! Glad you're safe. Parachute training? Didn't we do that last weekend in the Red Room? ;)

I laugh out loud.

"What?" Elliot asks.

I shake my head. "Nothing."

Elliot drives back to Escala, though this time he lets me play some decent music from his phone. As we ride the elevator up to the penthouse he says, "You need to get changed. Something smarter."

"What have you got planned?"

He winks.

"Asshole."

"That's a given." He grins.

The doors to the elevator open, and I'm hoping to see Ana.

"My gear is in your spare bedroom. I'll see you down here in half an hour. We're leaving then."

"Okay." I'm hoping to catch Ana in the bath.

She's not in the living room, and I worry that she's left already, but I find her in the bedroom. Halting on the threshold, I watch quietly as she adds the final touches to her makeup.

Wow! Ana looks stunning. Her hair is styled in an elegant chignon. She's wearing high heels and an off-the-shoulder black dress that shimmers. She turns, and is startled when she sees me. She takes my breath away. Hanging from her ears are her second-chance earrings. "I didn't mean to spook you," I whisper. "You look lovely."

She smiles her warm, welcoming smile that's full of love; it swells my heart, and she sashays toward me. "Christian. What a lovely surprise. I wasn't expecting to see you." She raises her lips to mine, and I give her a quick kiss, then pull back. She smells of heaven and home.

"If I kiss you properly, I'm going to mess up your makeup, and peel you out of that elegant dress."

"Oh, that would never do." She giggles and does a quick twirl. Her skirt flares up slightly, revealing a little more leg. "You like?" she asks.

I lean against the doorjamb and cross my arms. "It's not too short. I approve. You look great, Ana. Who's going to be there?" I narrow my eyes, feeling at once ridiculously proud that she's mine, but also territorial—she's mine.

"Kate, Mia, some girlfriends from WSU. Should be fun. We're starting with cocktails."

"Mia?"

Ana nods.

"I haven't seen her in a while. Say hi from me. I hope there's food on your itinerary." I arch a brow in warning. "Drinking rule number one."

She laughs. "Oh, stow your twitchy palm, Christian. We're having a meal."

"Good." I don't want her getting drunk.

She glances at her watch. "I'd better go. I don't want to be late. I'm glad you're back in one piece. I'd never forgive Elliot if anything happened to you."

She offers me her lips once more and I get another swift kiss.

"You look gorgeous, Anastasia."

She picks up her evening bag from the bed. "Laters, baby," she says with a coquettish smile, and she struts past me out of the room, looking like a million dollars. I follow her out and watch her join

Sawyer and Reynolds in the foyer. I salute them, and they all file into the elevator.

I head back into my en suite for a quick shower.

TWENTY MINUTES LATER, DRESSED in a dark navy suit and crisp white shirt, I'm in my kitchen, waiting for Elliot. In the fridge, I find some pretzels.

Fuck, I'm hungry.

Elliot appears in the doorway. He's wearing a dark suit, a gray shirt, and a tie.

Shit.

"Do I need a tie?"

Where the hell are we going?

"No."

"Sure?"

"Yep."

"Why are you wearing one?"

"You get to dress like this all the time. I don't. Changes it up for me. Besides, a suit and tie is catnip to women."

What about Kavanagh?

Elliot smirks at my questioning look, and Taylor joins us.

"Ready, sir?" he asks Elliot.

TAYLOR DRIVES US SOUTH on I-5.

"Where the fuck are we going, Elliot?" I ask.

"Relax, Christian. It's all good." He looks out of the window, seemingly at ease, while I drum my fingers on my knee. I hate not being in the know.

Taylor takes the turn off for Boeing Field, and I wonder if there's some seedy strip club based around here. I glance at my watch: 6:20 p.m. He turns into Signature Flight Support and behind the terminal, sitting on the tarmac, is the GEH Gulfstream.

"What?" I exclaim to Elliot.

From his inside jacket pocket Elliot produces a passport. "You're going to need this."

We're leaving the country?

Taylor drops us at the terminal entrance, and I follow Elliot into the building, bewildered.

"Elliot!" Kavanagh's blond, surfer-dude brother strides up to my brother and shakes his hand. He scrubs up well in his pale gray suit. I note he's not wearing a tie, either.

"Ethan, great to see you," Elliot responds, and claps him on the back.

"Christian." Ethan shakes my hand.

"Hi," I respond.

"Mac!" Elliot exclaims, and Liam McConnell—who works at the GEH shipyard, and also looks after my yacht, *The Grace*—strides toward us.

Mac! We shake hands. "It's good to see you," I tell him. "I'd just like you to know that I have no idea what the hell is going on."

He laughs. "Neither do I."

We all laugh and turn to Elliot as Taylor joins us.

"You knew about this?" I ask Taylor.

"Yes, sir." His look is earnest and amused in equal measure.

I laugh and shake my head.

"Shall we go?" Elliot says.

"CANADA?" I GUESS.

"Correct," Elliot responds.

We are installed in the first four seats of my G550, sipping Cristal champagne and eating the canapés that Sara, our flight attendant, distributed as we taxied onto the runway. Taylor is at the back reading a Lee Child novel. Stephan and First Officer Beighley are at the controls.

"I'm guessing Vancouver," I say to Elliot.

"Bingo! I figured you might have less of a chance being recognized behaving badly in British Columbia."

"What the hell have you got planned?"

"Easy, tiger," Elliot responds, and raises his glass.

Once we're airborne, Sara serves beer and fresh, hot pepperoni pizza, from a local pizzeria in Georgetown. I think this is a first, pizza in my private jet—but this is Elliot's idea of heaven. Frankly, I'm so hungry, it's mine, too. Mac, who's sitting opposite, and I both wolf down our food.

"That didn't touch the sides," Mac says in his Irish brogue.

"Elliot has had me zip-lining and tandem skydiving already today."

"Holy shit! No wonder you're starving."

THE JOURNEY TIME IS less than fifty minutes. When we pull up outside the Vancouver Signature Flight Support terminal Taylor is the first off, carrying our passports for the immigration official who has come to meet the plane.

"Ready?" Elliot says, unbuckling his seat belt and standing up to stretch his legs. Taylor is at the wheel of a Suburban on the tarmac. We all pile in, and he sets off for the bright lights of downtown Vancouver. We have a cooler full of beer. My three companions dive in, but I decline.

"Man, you are not staying sober tonight," Elliot splutters in disgust and hands me a beer.

Fuck. I loathe being drunk. With a roll of my eyes, reluctantly I take the bottle. It's early. We'll be drinking more; I'll need to pace myself. I clink bottles with him, and Mac and Ethan, who are seated behind us. "Cheers, gentlemen." I take a sip and let the drink linger in my hand.

Our first stop is the bar at the Rosewood Georgia hotel. I've been before, on business, but never in the evening. Its wood-paneled walls and leather seats give it an old-world charm and tonight it's heaving with the great and the good of Vancouver. Men in suits, women elegantly dressed. It has a lively vibe. Elliot orders a round, and we sit at a reserved table and our conversation turns to Ethan's endeavors to get into Seattle University to do a master's in psychology. Since Ana moved out, he's now living with Kate, in Ana's old room. Maybe living with his sister is challenging, I wouldn't be surprised—perhaps that's why he's outpacing us on drinks. He's finished his beer first and volunteers to buy the next round.

Mac talks to us about *The Grace.* He's one of the craftsmen who built her, but it seems he's turning his hand to boat design and has some ideas to make the catamaran we custom-build even more aerodynamic.

It's weird, I never do this. It's only when Elliot drags me out, usually with his friends—of whom there are many—that I get to enjoy the company of men my own age. Elliot is a social glue, sticking us all together and never letting the conversation lag. He's such a people person. Our conversation moves, inevitably to the Mariners, then the Seahawks. We're all fans, it would seem, of both teams. By the end of the second round we've all relaxed into one another's company, and I'm enjoying myself.

"Okay. Drink up. Next stop," Elliot announces.

Taylor is waiting outside in the SUV.

Ethan is already buzzed. This could get interesting. I'm tempted to ask him about Mia but part of me doesn't want to know.

The next venue is in Yaletown, a district renowned for redeveloped old warehouses that now house hip bars and restaurants. Taylor drops us at a nightclub where dance music pulses into the street even though it's still relatively early. Inside the dark industrial interior, the bar is doing brisk business and we have a table in the VIP area. I stick with beer, while Ethan and Mac scan the room, I think to check out the local talent.

"You're not interested?" I ask Elliot.

He laughs. "Not tonight, hotshot." He side-eyes Ethan, and I wonder if he's holding back the "Big E" because Kate's brother is here.

I glance at my watch, curious to know what Ana is doing, and I'm tempted to call Sawyer. Frankly, there's only so much socializing I can tolerate, but our conversation turns to the new house.

After another two rounds Elliot has us on the move again.

Taylor is ready with the SUV, and he drives us to the next venue.

A strip club.

Shit.

"Dude, don't get uptight. This stop is in the bachelor-party rule book." Ethan claps his hands, but his smile doesn't reach his eyes. I think he's just as uncomfortable as I am.

"Do not under any circumstances buy me a lap dance," I warn Elliot. And I'm reminded of a time, not too long ago, when I was in the dark depths of a private club in Seattle.

Where anything goes.

That was a lifetime ago.

Elliot laughs. "What happens in Vancouver stays in Vancouver." He winks at me as we're led to another VIP table. This time my brother has ordered a bottle of vodka, which arrives with ceremony: sparklers and a chorus of women in short red skirts and bikini tops that barely cover their nipples, who are all cheers and enthusiastic applause. I worry for a moment that they're going to sit down with us, but once the shot glasses are lined up, they move on.

There are beautiful women everywhere. I watch one, a lithe blonde with dark eyes. She starts to remove her clothes with athletic grace, while doing various gymnastic moves and poses on the pole. I can't help thinking that if she were a man, this would be an Olympic sport.

Mac is mesmerized, and I wonder if he has a partner.

"No, I'm single. Looking," he says when I ask. His eyes return to the energetic blonde. I nod, but I'm at a loss as to what to say, because I'm in no position to offer any relationship advice. I'm still amazed that Ana has consented to be mine. In fact, she's consented to a great many things.

I smirk as my mind catapults to thoughts of the Red Room last weekend.

Yeah.

The memory has an arousing effect on my body. I take out my phone.

"No," Elliot says. "Put it away."

"My phone?"

We both laugh. And I sink a shot of vodka.

"Let's go somewhere else," I say.

"You don't like it here?"

"No."

"Jesus, you're one uptight motherfucker."

Dude, this is not my scene.

"Okay. We have one more stop. This was the traditional, customary part of your bachelor party. You know, it's the unwritten law."

"I don't think Ana would be very impressed."

Ethan claps me on the back and I freeze. "So don't tell her."

And something in his tone puts my hackles up. “Are you fucking my sister?”

Ethan jerks his head back as if I’ve hit him. Shocked, he raises both his hands. “No. No. Dude, no offense. She’s attractive and all, but she’s just a friend.”

“Good. Keep it that way.”

He laughs, nervously, I think, and downs two shots of vodka.

My work here is done.

“You going to frighten off all her would-be boyfriends?” Elliot asks.

“Maybe.”

He rolls his eyes. “Let’s get you out of here. This place is doing nothing for your mood.”

“Okay.”

We ditch the vodka and I leave an obscene cash tip on the table.

Back in the SUV, my humor is restored. Taylor’s at the wheel and we’re heading out of downtown Vancouver, in the direction of the airport.

But we don’t go back to the plane. Taylor pulls up outside a sprawling, nondescript hotel-and-casino complex that flanks the Fraser River.

“Marriage is a gamble,” Elliot says with a grin.

“Life is a gamble, dude. But this is more my scene.”

“I figured. You always beat me at cards,” he responds. “How are you still sober?”

“It’s just math, Elliot. I haven’t had that much to drink, and right now, I’m grateful.”

Elliot and Ethan head for the craps and roulette tables, while Mac favors the blackjack and I the poker table.

THERE’S A RESPECTFUL BUT expectant hush in the room. I am $118,000 up, and this is the last game I’m going to play. It’s getting late; behind me, Elliot is watching. I don’t know where Ethan and Mac are. The final hand is in play, and both players beside me fold in turn. I have two jacks, and because this is the final game and I’m on a roll, I raise, and toss $16,000 worth of chips into the pot. The opponent on my left, a woman who must be in her fifties, folds immediately. "I've got nothing," she grumbles.

My remaining opponent—who reminds me of my dad—glances at me, then back at his cards, and carefully, counting out chips, he matches my bet.

Game on, Grey.

The dealer collects the folded cards and briskly lays out the flop.

Hallelujah.

A jack and a pair of nines. I have a full house.

I stare impassively at my rival as he fidgets, checks his cards once more, his lively, dark eyes flitting to me and back to his cards. He swallows.

He's got jack shit.

"Check," my challenger says.

Showtime, Grey.

Slowly, for full effect, I tap my finger on the green baize, then gather my chips together and place $50,000 into the pot. "Raise," I state.

The dealer responds, "Fifty-thousand-dollar raise."

My opponent huffs, picks up his cards, and tosses them in disgust into the center of the table. Inside, I'm dancing. I've made $134K. Not bad for forty-five minutes of play.

"I'm done," says the lady beside me, and she nods in my direction.

"Thanks for the game. I've got to go, too." I toss a generous chip to the dealer as a tip, gather the rest of my winnings, and stand.

"Good night."

Elliot steps forward and helps me with my chips.

"You're a lucky son of a bitch," he says.

JUST BEFORE MIDNIGHT, WE board the plane.

"I'll have an Armagnac, Sara, thank you."

"Now you start drinking!" Elliot exclaims.

"We all came out on top," Mac observes. "Must be your luck rubbing off on us, Christian."

"I'll drink to that," says Ethan.

I smile, settling into the plush leather of my seat. Yes. My win is a good omen. What a great way to end a most enjoyable evening.

Sunday, July 24, 2011

As we begin our descent into Boeing Field I reach for my seat belt and chuckle to myself. I've spent most of today buckling and unbuckling.

Elliot, sitting opposite me, looks up. "What's so funny?"

"Nothing. I just wanted to say thank you. For today. It's been amazing."

Elliot glances at his watch. "Technically, it was yesterday."

"I had a blast. You've acquitted yourself well as best man. Your one remaining duty is to make a speech. Doesn't have to be a long one."

Elliot pales. "Dude. Don't remind me."

"Yeah." I make a face. "I've still got to write my vows."

"Shit. That's heavy." He's horrified. "But this time next week it'll all be over. You'll be married."

"Yeah. And on this plane."

"Cool. Where are you taking Ana?"

"Europe. But it's a surprise. She's never left the U.S."

"Wow."

"I know. I never thought that I, I would…I can't…" My voice trails off as a sudden unexpected surge of emotion sweeps over me. Is it fear, exhilaration, anxiety, or *happiness*? I don't know, but it's overwhelming.

Fuck. I'm getting married.

Elliot frowns. "Dude, why? You're a good-looking guy. You're a douche, but, hey, that's because you're a master of the universe with a big swinging dick." He shakes his head. "I never understood why you weren't interested in any of Mia's friends. They were always crushing on you. Man, I thought you were gay." He shrugs.

I smile, knowing my whole family thought I was gay. "I was just waiting for the right woman."

"I think you found her." His expression softens, but there's a wistful look in his vivid blue eyes.

"I think I have."

"Love suits you," Elliot says, and I roll my eyes at him, because it's possibly the sappiest thing he's ever said to me.

"Get a room, boys," Mac exclaims, and we touch down on the tarmac.

"I'm never going to let you forget that you're the only groom in the Pacific Northwest who remained sober at his own bachelor party."

I laugh. "Well, I'm just grateful I'm not handcuffed naked to a lamppost somewhere in Vegas."

"Dude, if I ever get married, that's exactly how I'd like to finish my bachelor party!" Elliot says.

"I'll make a mental note."

Elliot laughs. "Time to wake Ethan."

TAYLOR IS AT THE wheel of the Q7, driving Elliot and me back to Escala. Mac and Ethan, after some backslapping good-byes, have already left in a waiting cab. "Thanks for this evening, Taylor," I say as I stretch out in the back. Elliot looks like he's asleep.

"It's been a pleasure, sir." His eyes meet mine in the rearview mirror, and even in the surrounding darkness I notice the amused crinkles in the corners. I take my phone out of my jacket pocket.

No messages.

"Have you heard from Sawyer or Reynolds?"

"Yes, sir," Taylor responds. "Miss Steele and Miss Kavanagh are still out."

What? I check my watch. It's after one o'clock in the morning.

"Where is she?" I swallow my alarm and glance at a comatose Elliot.

"At a nightclub."

"Which one?"

"Trinity."

"Pioneer Square?"

"Yes, sir."

"Take me there."

Taylor's eyes flick to mine, his expression doubtful.

"You don't think it's a good idea?" I ask.

"No, sir."

Damn.

Count to ten, Grey.

I remember the one and only time I've been in a nightclub with Ana was at that bar in Portland, where she was celebrating her final exams.

She got so drunk she passed out.

In my arms.

Shit.

"Sir, Sawyer and Reynolds are with her."

This is true.

Put yourself in her shoes. Flynn's words nag me.

This is her night. With her friends.

Grey, leave her be.

"Okay, take us back to Escala."

"Yes, sir."

I hope I've made the right decision.

I ROUSE ELLIOT AS we pull into the underground garage at Escala.

"Wake up, we're here."

"I wanna go home. But if you wanna nightcap or something, I'm up for it." He can barely open his eyes.

"Taylor will take you home, Elliot."

"I'd like to see you into the apartment first, Mr. Grey," Taylor says.

"Okay." I sigh, knowing that he's still in mother-hen mode, concerned about my safety. He parks beside the elevator and climbs out of the car.

Elliot opens his eyes. "I'll stay in the car," he mutters. I reach over to shake his hand, but he grabs it, forcibly. "Fuck off with your fucking handshake," he grumbles, and tugs me into an awkward embrace, which is clumsy and male and…welcome.

"Don't crease the suit," I warn, feeling oddly touched by his gesture. He releases me.

"Good night, bro."

I slap his knee. "Thanks again. Do you need the stuff you left here?"

"I'll be back Friday night for the rehearsal dinner."

"Okay. Good night, Lelliot."

He grins and closes his eyes.

TAYLOR ACCOMPANIES ME UP to the penthouse.

"You know you don't have to do this, Taylor."

"It's my job, sir." He looks straight ahead.

"Are you armed?"

Taylor's eyes flick in my direction. "Yes, sir."

I loathe firearms; I wonder if he took the gun to Canada and, if so, how he got it through security, but I don't want to know the gory details.

Plausible deniability.

"Why don't you ask Ryan to take Elliot home? You must be exhausted."

"I'm good, Mr. Grey."

"Thank you again for your part in all the organization of today."

He turns to me with a warm smile. "It was a pleasure."

The doors to the penthouse open and I wander in. Ryan is standing, waiting for me.

"Good evening, Mr. Grey."

"Ryan, hi. All quiet tonight?"

"Yes, sir. Nothing to report. Do you need anything?"

"No. I'm fine. Good night." I leave him in the foyer and amble into the kitchen. From the fridge I pull a bottle of sparkling mineral water, unscrew the top, and start to drink directly from the bottle.

My apartment is quiet. The low hum of the fridge and the distant rumble of traffic are the only sounds I hear. The place feels empty.

Because Ana's not here.

My footsteps echo across the room as I meander to the window. The moon is high, and it shines in a clear night sky with the promise of another halcyon day, like today. Ana is near, under the same moon. She'll be home soon. *Surely.* I lean my forehead against the glass. It's cool, but not cold. As I let out a long sigh, my breath mists the pane.

Shit.

I saw her a few hours ago, and yet I'm missing her.

For fuck's sake, Grey. You've got it bad. Pull yourself together.

I've had the most fulfilling day. Carefree. Adventurous. Sociable.

Flynn would be proud. I remember when we first sailed on *The Grace*, Ana asked me if I had any friends. Well, now I can say yes. *Maybe.*

I don't understand why I'm suddenly feeling despondent; a familiar sense of loneliness is creeping into my psyche. I recognize its key ingredients: the emptiness, the longing, like I'm missing something. I've not felt it since I was a teenager.

Hell.

I haven't felt lonely for years. I've had my family, though I've kept them at a distance. And there was Elena, of course, and I've been content with my own company and the occasional company of my submissives.

But now, without Ana here, I'm lost.

Her absence is an ache—a scar on my soul.

The silence is becoming intolerable.

I would have thought after all the noise of this evening—the bars, the night club, the casino floor—I would welcome some quiet.

But no.

The silence is oppressive, and it's making me melancholy.

Fuck this.

I stalk over to the piano, lift the lid, and settle onto the stool. Taking a moment to gather my thoughts, I place my hands on the keys, enjoying the grounding feel of the ivory beneath my fingertips. I begin to play the first piece that comes to mind; the Bach-Marcello, and I'm soon lost in the morose melody that perfectly reflects my mood. The second time through the composition I'm distracted by a noise.

"Shh..."

I look up, and Ana is standing by the kitchen counter, swaying slightly. She's carrying her strappy high heels in one hand and she's wearing what looks like a plastic tiara that may have perched on the top of her head at one time, but is now looking decidedly lopsided.

A sash with the word *bride* in an elaborate serif hangs over her shimmering black dress. She has her index finger at her lips.

She is without doubt the most beautiful girl in the world.

And I'm delighted she's home.

Behind her, Sawyer and Reynolds are stony-faced. Rising from the stool, I tip my chin at them in thanks. They smile as one and leave us.

Ana turns and stumbles a little to watch them leave. "Bye!" she almost shouts, and waves them away with a wide sweep of her arm.

She's clearly intoxicated.

Turning back to face me, she rewards me with the biggest, warmest, most drunken smile and stumbles toward me. "Mr. Christian Grey!"

I catch her before she falls and fold her into my arms, and she gazes up at me with unfocused joy. Her expression feeds my soul. "Miss Anastasia Steele. How lovely to see you. Did you have fun?"

"The best!"

"Please tell me you had something to eat."

"Yes! Food has been eaten." She drops her shoes and they clatter on the floor, while she winds her arms around my neck.

"Can I fix your crown?" I try to straighten her tiara.

"You fixed my crown long ago," she slurs.

What?

"You have the most beautiful mouth." She runs her index finger shakily over my lips.

"Do I?"

"Hmm…yes. You do things to me with that mouth."

"I like doing things to you with my mouth."

"Shall we do it now?" Her unfocused gaze moves from my mouth to my eyes.

"Tempting though that sounds, I'm not sure that's a good idea right now."

She sways a little and I tighten my hold on her. "Dance with me," she mumbles, grinning up at me. She lets her hands run down my jacket lapels, and tugs me closer so I feel her down the length of my body.

"We should put you to bed."

"I wanna dance…with you," she whispers, and offers me her lips.

"Ana," I warn, tempted to carry her to bed, but I'm enjoying the feel of her in my arms and the way she's imploring me with her big blue eyes. "Okay. What would you like to dance to?" I'm feeling indulgent.

"Muuuusic."

I laugh, a little exasperated, and move us over to the kitchen counter, where I pick up the remote and press play. Moby's "Bodyrock" starts over the sound system. It's one of my favorites from my youth, but a bit frenetic for now. I skip the track and Nina Simone's "My Baby Just Cares for Me" echoes through the room.

"This?" I state in response to Ana's inebriated smile.

"Yes." She throws her head and arms back with such enthusiasm that I almost drop her.

"Shit. Ana!" I'm glad I have my arm around her waist, otherwise she'd be sprawled on the floor. She starts to stagger and I wonder if she's going to pass out, then realize she's attempting to dance.

Whoa.

I clamp my arms around her. I've never danced with someone as inebriated as Ana. She is all arms and legs and unpredictable spins.

It's an education.

I try to take both her hands and lead her around the room, in a semblance of a dance—that's more a jig—so it's not entirely successful. It's unsettling.

Suddenly she stops and clutches her head. "Oh. The room is spinning."

Oh no. "I think we should go to bed."

She looks up at me between her fingers. "Why? What are you going to do?"

Is she flirting or is this a serious question?

"Let you sleep," I reply, deadpan.

She makes a face, which I interpret as disappointment, but, taking her hand, I guide her back to the kitchen counter. From the cupboard I grab a glass and fill it with water. "Drink this." I pass it to her, and she does as she's told. "All of it."

She narrows her eyes and squints—I suspect to get me in focus. "You've done this before."

"Yes. With you. Last time you were inebriated."

She drains the glass and wipes her mouth with the back of her hand. "Are you going to fuck me?"

"No. Not tonight."

She frowns.

"Come." I guide her to our bedroom suite, switch on the bedside lights from the wall, and release her by the bed. "Do you feel sick?"

"No!" she says emphatically.

That's a relief. "Do you need to use the bathroom?"

"No!"

"Turn around," I demand.

She gives me a lopsided smile, and I remove the tiara.

"Turn around—let me unzip your dress." I drag the ridiculous sash over her head.

"You are so good to me." She lays her hand on my chest, splaying out her fingers.

"Enough. Turn around. I won't ask you again."

She grins. "There he is..."

Oh, baby.

I grasp her shoulders and gently turn her around so I can unfasten her dress. It obliges and falls immediately, pooling at her feet. She's wearing a black lacy bra, matching panties, and a white garter. I undo her bra and step forward, bringing her body flush to mine, and I drag the straps down her arms. She rubs her ass against me and moves her hand behind her to fondle my more-than-interested dick.

Ana!

I allow myself a brief moment of pure pleasure and push my hips forward as her hand fumbles the length of my hardening cock.

Yes!

I drop her bra on the floor, move her hair aside, and run my lips down her neck. "Stop," I whisper.

She continues to rub her hand over me. I groan and step back. Kneeling, I slip the garter—which I suspect came with the sash and tiara—and her panties down her legs, and kiss her behind. "Step." She does, and I remove her underwear and gather her clothes together before pulling back the duvet. "Into bed."

Now she turns around. "Join me," she says with a provocative smile. She's naked and lovely and wanton and tempting.

She's also completely drunk.

"Get into bed. I'll be back."

She sways, sits down, then flops back on the bed, and I lift her feet onto the mattress and cover her up.

"Are you going to punish me?" she slurs.

"Punish you?"

"For getting this drunk. A punishment fuck. You can do anything you want to me," she whispers, and holds out her arms.

Oh God.

A million erotic thoughts flit through my mind, and it takes all my willpower to lean over, gently plant a kiss on her forehead, and leave.

In the closet, which is still full of shopping bags from her earlier trip, I place her clothes in the laundry basket and strip out of my suit and shirt.

I drag on my PJs and a T-shirt and head into the bathroom.

While brushing my teeth I contemplate what I could do to a drunken Ana. She wants punishing? My thoughts do little to ease my erection.

"Pervert," I mouth at my reflection.

I switch off the lights and head back into the bedroom. As I suspected, Ana is out cold, her hair spilling in all directions over the pillows. She looks lovely. I climb in beside her and roll onto my side to watch her sleep.

She's going to have one helluva hangover in the morning.

Leaning over, I kiss her hair. "I love you, Anastasia," I whisper, and I lay back and stare at the ceiling. I'm surprised that I'm not furious with her. No, I found her charming, and funny.

Maybe, I'm growing up. *Finally.*

I hope so. This time next week, I'll be a married man.

Tuesday, July 26, 2011

I hang up from my call with Troy Whelan, my banker. I've set up a joint account for me and Ana that will go live once she's Mrs. Anastasia Grey. I'm not sure what she'll ever need it for—but, if something happens to me… Jeez. If something happens to her…

My phone buzzes, distracting me from a slew of dark thoughts. "Mr. Grey, I have your mother on the line," Andrea says.

I suppress a groan. "Put her through."

"Will do. Here you go, sir."

"Grace."

"Darling. How are you?"

"I'm good. What is it?"

"Always so brusque. I'm checking up on you, that's all. I talk to Ana more than you these days."

"Well, I'm good. Still here. Still getting married. Thank you for all that you've done. Is there anything specific you want?"

She sighs. "No, darling. I'm looking forward to the rehearsal dinner, and having Ana stay with us the night before the wedding. And of course her mother and her step-father, Bob, too. I'm glad we're meeting them before the big day. Are they on good terms with her dad?"

"With Ray? I think so. But I don't know, you'll need to ask Ana."

"I'll do that. I'm glad he's staying with you."

It was not my idea. "Ana is hoping that we'll bond." Frankly, Raymond Steele intimidates me.

Grace pauses. "I'm sure you will. Do you have a marriage license?"

I scoff. "Of course we do. We picked it up last week."

"Honeymoon?"

"It's all arranged."

"And your suit?"

I direct my eye roll at the phone. "It was delivered today. It fits."

"Rings?"

Rings?

Shit.

Rings!

How the hell did we forget about rings? "In hand," I mutter, and laugh, because both Ana and I have overlooked the rings.

"What's so funny?"

"Nothing, Mom. Anything else?"

"You forgot the rings?"

I sigh. *Busted.* "How did you know?"

"I'm your mother…and you called me Mom. You rarely do that." The humor and warmth in her voice is soothing.

"Perceptive, Dr. Grey."

She chuckles. "Oh, Christian, I love you so much. If you don't have rings, you'd better get some. Everything here is on track; the pavilion goes up tomorrow, and the decorators will follow."

"Thanks, Mom. Thanks for everything."

"See you Friday." She hangs up and I stare out at the Seattle skyline, grateful to all that is holy, for Dr. Grace Trevelyan-Grey.

Mom.

I call Ana.

"Anastasia Steele." She sounds distracted.

"We forgot the rings."

"Rings? Oh! Rings!"

I laugh, because her reaction is the same as mine, and I can imagine her eyes widening in shock. "I know! How could we forget?"

"My mom always says the devil is in the details," Ana agrees.

"She's not wrong. What sort of ring would you like?"

"Oh…um…"

"I thought a platinum band to match your engagement ring?"

"Christian, that would be…that…um…that would be more than mighty fine." Her voice is a whisper.

I smile. "I'll get matching ones."

She gasps. "You'll wear one, too?"

"Why wouldn't I?" I'm surprised by her question.

"I don't know. I'm thrilled that you would."

"Ana, I'm yours. I want the world to know."

"I'm very pleased to hear that."

"You should know this by now."

"I do know," she whispers. "It still gives me all the feels when you say it."

"The feels?"

She giggles. "Yes. The feels."

"Sounds painful."

"No. It's the opposite of painful."

My heart soars. Sometimes she takes my breath away. I swallow, trying to contain my elation. "I'd better get right on this."

"You better!"

"Laters, baby."

"Laters, Christian. I love you."

I let her words settle into my heart.

She loves me.

"Are you going to hang up?" she asks.

"No."

She laughs. "I have to go. I have a meeting and my boss's boss's boss…you know."

"Yeah. He can be an asshole."

"He can…but he can also be the best of men."

I'm staring at her portrait on my office wall; her shy, teasing smile is directed at me. My body and my soul stir. This has to be one of the sweetest things she's ever said to me.

"I'll see you tonight," she says, and the line goes dead before I have a chance to respond.

Anastasia Steele, you are the most disarming woman I know. I stare at her photograph, digesting her words, and I know my smile would light up a dark and soulless night.

Feeling inspired, I find the number for Astoria Fine Jewelry and press call. It's not only rings I need, but a wedding present for my future wife, too.

MY MEETING WITH WELCH is inconclusive: there is still no lead on the perpetrator, and I'm beginning to believe the sabotage is a figment of my overactive imagination. Welch's team is drilling down into all ex-employee records of the companies that GEH has acquired to see if he can find something, but we've been over this ground and I think he's grasping at straws. The only potential suspects we had were Hyde and Woods, but Hyde has been discounted, as he's been in Florida since he was fired, and there's no evidence that links Woods to the crash, yet.

"I know how exasperating this is for you, Grey," Welch says, his voice as gruff as ever. "We are keeping an extra-watchful eye on the Gulfstream."

"I'm wondering if we overreacted to the FAA report."

"No. We did not. Not where your safety is concerned. We'll just have to be patient for the NTSB report. I'm expecting it any day."

"As soon as you have it..." I let the sentence finish itself.

"Yes, sir."

"In the meantime, please liaise with Taylor. He's coming with us to oversee our security while we're on our honeymoon."

"Will do. And congratulations once again."

I nod my thanks. "Okay. That's it. Thanks for coming in."

Welch rises and we shake hands.

BACK AT MY DESK, I check my e-mails.

From: Dr. John Flynn
Subject: FW: For Christian Grey
Date: July 26 2011 14:53
To: Christian Grey

Christian
I received the attached from Leila Williams. We can discuss when I see you on Thursday.
JF

From: Leila Williams
Subject: For Christian Grey
Date: July 26 2011 06:32 EST
To: Dr. John Flynn

Dearest John
Thank you for your continued support. I cannot begin to tell

> you what it has meant for me. My parents have embraced me back into the fold. I can hardly believe how considerate they've been, given all the trouble I've caused them. My divorce from my husband should be final next month. At last I'll be able to move on with my life.
>
> My only regret is that I haven't been able to thank Mr. Grey in person. Please pass on this note to him. I would really like to deliver my thanks personally. My life could have taken such a bad turn if not for his and your intervention.
>
> Many thanks
> Leila

No fucking way. Leila is the last person in the world I want to see. But I'm glad she's in a better place and healing, and divorcing the cockroach she married. I delete the e-mail and resolve to push her from my mind.

I buzz Andrea. I need coffee. Stat.

IT'S LATE. THE SUN has sunk beneath the horizon, and I'm staring at a blank screen in my study.

Vows.

Drafting them is trickier than I thought. Everything I write will be spoken aloud in front of our nearest and dearest, and I'm trying to find the words to express to Ana how I feel about her, how excited I am to share our life together, and how honored I am that she's chosen me.

Damn it. This is hard.

My thoughts stray to earlier this evening, when Ana and I met with Gia Matteo. Gia wanted our feedback on a few ideas for the new house. Her vision is bold: I like the approach, but I'm not sure that Ana is entirely on board. When we eventually see Gia's drawn-up plans we'll be able to judge.

Fortunately, the meeting was brief. And she touched me once, that's all.

Since then, I've been attempting to write my vows while Ana's been on a call with Alondra Gutierrez. They've each been working tirelessly on this wedding.

I just hope it will be everything Ana wants. And, frankly, as long as Ana's happy, I'm happy.

But most of all, I want to keep her safe.

Life without Ana would be unbearable.

A flurry of images flash unwelcome through my brain: Ana at gunpoint in her old apartment; Ana, not Ros, seated beside me as *Charlie Tango* drops to the ground; Ana lying pale and unmoving on a squalid once-green rug—

Grey, stop. Stop.

I need to get a handle on my morbid thoughts.

Concentrate, Grey. Focus on where you want to be.

With Ana.

I want to give her the world.

I turn back to my screen, to my vows, and start to type.

ANA LOOKS UP WHEN I enter the library, and gives me a sweet but tired smile. She's been reading a manuscript.

"Hi."

"Hi," she answers, as I sit down in the armchair beside her and open my arms. She doesn't hesitate; she uncurls her long legs from beneath her and hops over to me, complete with manuscript, and crawls into my lap. Wrapping her in my arms, I kiss the top of her head and breathe in her scent. She is heaven on earth.

Ana lets out a soft, contented sigh.

She's so good to hold.

A balm to my senses.

My Ana.

We sit in a comfortable, companionable silence. I could never have imagined doing this even three months ago. *No. Two months ago.* I'm changed beyond recognition. The residue of doubt and fear I felt earlier melts away. She's safe, in my arms.

And I'm safe…with her.

Thursday, July 28, 2011

The senior management meeting has gone well; everybody is up to speed on what each division is doing, and what steps need to be taken next. I'm leaving my company in safe hands—but then, I never doubted that for a moment. However, if I'm honest, it still makes me anxious. This is the first time I've taken a vacation for more than a few days. As everyone leaves the boardroom, they shake my hand and wish me well. "I'll be here tomorrow," I remind Marcus.

"Christian, you deserve a break," he says. "Enjoy your honeymoon."

"Thank you."

Blowing out a breath, I scrape a hand through my hair. Why the hell am I so apprehensive? Ros sidles up to me when everyone else has left. "The house. It's yours."

"It's done?"

"Signed and sealed."

"Great. Thanks for orchestrating. Keys?"

"They are being biked over."

"I'll give them to my brother. He's going to oversee the renovation."

Her eyes widen. "Renovating, too? You have a great deal on your plate, Christian. I think it's about time you took a vacation."

"You know, I'm ready and looking forward to it."

"Where will you go?"

"I took your advice. Europe."

She brightens. "Gwen and I are really looking forward to Saturday."

"I'll be glad when it's over." I give her a tight smile.

"Christian!" She looks taken aback. "You've got to enjoy the day!"

"I want Ana to enjoy the day."

Ros's stance softens immediately. "You *have* got it bad."

I laugh, because she's never made such a personal comment before. "Guilty as charged."

She grins, her eyes warming. It's a good look on her.

"I'll certainly enjoy my honeymoon knowing that you're heading this place up and keeping the GEH wheels turning."

Her grin broadens. "Don't look so anxious. You'll be in Europe, not on Mars. If I need you, I'll call."

"Thanks, Ros."

"Now, excuse me while I get on with today's business." I step aside and she struts past me. And in that moment, I'm so grateful she's on my team.

"CHRISTIAN, YOU'RE LIKE A caged lion. What is it?" Flynn asks. He's sitting in his chair, regarding me with his usual professional detachment, while I pace up and down his office, treading a path into the thick pile of his rug. I come to a halt at his question and glance through the window to see Taylor waiting by the car. He's watching the street from behind mirrored aviators.

"Nerves?" I hazard a guess, and returning to the couch, I slump into it.

"That's a reasonable reaction to the fact that you're getting married in a couple of days."

"Is it?"

"Of course it is. It's perfectly natural to be nervous. You are publicly going to declare how much Anastasia means to you. It's all getting real."

Yes. It is.

"But it's just taken so long to get to this point and at the last minute we forgot the rings." I throw my hands up in frustration. "What does that say about us?"

"That you're both busy people?" he offers, his tone mollifying.

But his observation doesn't appease me. "Everyone keeps telling me to enjoy myself." My brows knit together.

Flynn looks pensive but remains mute, waiting for me to elucidate.

"I just want it done!"

"Do you? Are you sure you want to go through with this?"

What! I glare at him as if he's sprouted an additional head. "The wedding? Of course I do!"

"I thought so."

"Then why ask me if I have doubts?" I snap.

"Christian, I'm trying to unpack the source of your restlessness."

"I just want it over." I fire the words at him, exasperated. But Flynn says nothing and continues to observe me with a calm and measured expression while I wait for him to offer up some insight. When he doesn't, I know he's testing me.

Damn.

"It's taken so long. I'm not a patient man," I mutter.

"It's been a few weeks, it's not that long."

I huff out a breath as I struggle to unscramble my feelings. "I hope Ana doesn't change her mind."

"I think at this stage Ana is very unlikely to change her mind. Why would she? She loves you." He holds my gaze.

I stare at him, silent, unable to articulate what I want to say. It's frustrating.

"You just want to be married?" Flynn prompts.

"Yes! Then she's mine. And I can protect her. Properly."

"Ah." Flynn nods and lets out a soft sigh. "This isn't just nerves, Christian. Tell me."

Showtime, Grey.

I swallow, and from the depths of my soul, I confess my darkest fear. "Life would be unbearable without her." My words are almost inaudible. "I'm having awful, morbid thoughts."

He nods and taps his lip, and I realize this is what he's been waiting for me to say. "Do you want to talk about them?" he asks.

"No." If I do, I'll make them *real.*

"Why not?"

I shake my head feeling exposed—vulnerable—like I'm naked on top of a treeless hill, the wind howling around me.

John rubs his chin. "Christian, your fears are totally understandable. But they come from the place of an abused, neglected child who was abandoned by the death of his mother."

Closing my eyes, I see the crack whore dead on the floor.

Except she's Ana.

Fuck.

"You're an adult now. A pretty successful one at that," John continues. "None of us have any guarantees in life, but it's extremely unlikely that anything's going to happen to Ana, given everything you've put in place."

I open my eyes to meet Flynn's, and he still wants more.

"I fear for her more than I fear for myself," I whisper.

His expression softens. "I understand, Christian. You love her. But what you have to do is to get that fear into perspective and under control. It's irrational. And fundamentally you know this."

I let out a long breath. "I know. I know."

His forehead creases with a brief frown as he glances at his lap. "I just want to sound a word of caution." He looks up to make sure he has my full attention. "I don't want you to sabotage your happiness, Christian."

"What?"

"I know you feel you don't deserve it and it's a relatively new concept for you, but you should nurture and treasure it."

Where the hell is he going with this?

"I do," I try to reassure him. "But it makes me anxious."

"I know. Just be mindful."

I nod.

"You have the tools to overcome your anxiety. Use them. Free your rational mind."

Okay. Okay.

I'm tiring of this lecture that I've heard before. "Let's move on."

His lips thin. "Are you sure?"

"Yes."

He changes the subject. "Now, speaking of sabotage, do you have any news on the saboteur?"

"No!" The word is an expletive. I wish I had an answer. "I'm beginning to wonder if we overreacted."

"It wouldn't be the first time."

My mouth twists into a half smile. "Ana said that."

"She knows you well."

"She does. Better than anyone. Apart from you."

"You flatter me, Christian. I'm sure she knows you better than

I do. We choose what we show to different people. It's part of what makes us human. I think she's seen the worst and the best of you."

That's true. "She brings out the worst and the best in me."

"If you put your mind to it, you can concentrate on the best. Don't dwell on the negative and be mindful. Use all that you've learned here," he asserts.

"I can try."

"Don't try. Do. You're more than capable, Christian." He crosses his legs and continues. "How are you getting on with your parents?"

"Much better." And I fill him in on my latest interaction with Grace.

"That all sounds great. And your dad?"

"Nothing to report since his surprise apology."

"Good." He pauses. "Did you get the e-mail I forwarded from Leila?"

"Yes. I don't want to see her."

"That's probably wise. I'll let her know."

"Thank you."

He smiles. "You know, you may not be looking forward to your wedding, but my wife is beyond excited."

I laugh.

"We're bringing the boys. I hope you've nailed everything down."

"I think Ros, my chief operating officer, is bringing her kids, too."

"Have you discussed children with Ana?"

"Only generally. We've got years to think about that. We're both young. In fact, I forget how young Ana is sometimes."

Yes, and I'm the sulky teen.

"You're both young." He glances at the clock on the wall behind me. "I think we're done, unless there's anything else you want to talk about? I won't see you in a professional capacity for a while."

"I'm good. Thanks for listening."

"It's my job. Remember. Don't dwell on the negative. Focus on the positive."

I nod and stand.

"And a bit of advice, on a personal level," John says. "Happy wife. Happy life. Trust me on this one."

I chuckle and he grins. "It's good to see you laugh, Christian."

ANA AND I STARE at each other. We lie in my bed…our bed, nose-to-nose, each sated, neither of us sleepy. "That was nice," Ana whispers.

I narrow my eyes. "There's that word again."

She grins, and I run my fingers down her cheek. Her smile fades.

"What is it?" I ask, and she shifts her gaze downward, away from me. "Ana?"

Her eyes find mine, and fix me with an intense stare. "We've not been too hasty, have we?" she asks in a rush, her voice breathy and quiet.

All my senses are suddenly on high alert.

Where the fuck is she going with this?

"No! Why do you think so?"

"It's just that I'm so happy right now, I don't know if I could be any happier. I don't want to change anything."

I close my eyes, savoring my relief. She lays her hand on my cheek. "Are you happy?" she asks.

Opening my eyes, I regard her with all the sincerity I can muster from every fiber of my being. "Of course I'm happy. You have no idea how you've changed my life for the better. But I'll be happier once we're married."

"You're anxious. I can see it in your eyes." Her fingers graze my chin.

"I'm anxious to make you mine."

"I am yours," she murmurs, and her words force a smile.

Mine.

I continue, "And we have to endure two days of enforced socializing."

She giggles. "Yes. There's that."

"I can't wait to take you away."

"I can't wait, either. Where are we going?"

"It's a surprise."

"I like surprises."

"I like you."

"I like you, too, Christian." She leans forward and kisses the tip of my nose.

"Are you sleepy?" I ask.

"No."

Good. "Me neither. I'm not finished with you yet."

SATURDAY, JULY 30, 2011

Elliot takes a swig of Macallan. It's just after midnight, and he's sprawled out on my couch, feet up, taking up about as much space as he can. The man has no sense of decorum.

"Man, this is good scotch."

"Should be." *It's expensive.*

"What did she get you?" he asks. From my pocket I remove the turquoise Tiffany box that contains my wedding gift from Ana. Opening it up for the second time, I study the platinum cuff links, engraved with an elaborate C entwined with an A. She's never bought me anything like this, and I love them. I'll wear them tomorrow when we marry.

I hand them to Elliot and he nods in approval as he examines them. "Nice gift."

"Yes. They're perfect."

"It's late, bro." He yawns. "We should turn in. In case it's slipped your mind, you're getting hitched in the morning."

"We should." My sip of Armagnac warms the back of my mouth before sliding smoothly down my throat. "It'll be weird sleeping on my own."

Now, there's a sentence I never thought I'd utter.

"Tonight was cool," he says, ignoring me. "I dig Ana's parents. Bob doesn't say much. Come to think of it, Ana's dad doesn't, either."

"They're both taciturn." I arch an eyebrow. "Carla has a type."

Elliot laughs. "It's always the quiet ones. Like you, hotshot." He raises his glass and grins at me.

Fuck off, Elliot. I scowl at him. "Like me? I have no idea what you're alluding to, and I don't even want to think about it. They're my in-laws, for fuck's sake."

"I don't know. Ana's mom's hot. I could get into older women."

I'm not going there with Elliot!

"Dude! What about Kavanagh?"

He gives me a sheepish grin, and I think he's kidding. "Bet you're glad all the parentals hit it off." He steers us to safer ground. "And Ray is a Mariners fan, so he can't be all bad, but the jury is out on the Sounders. I'm not a fan of soccer."

I nod. It's a relief: even Raymond Steele loosened up under Grace's warm and tireless attention. And there's no animosity between him and Ana's mother, so that's good news. Ray has retired for the night. It's ironic that he's sleeping in the bedroom I had hoped would be Ana's, if she'd agreed to be my submissive.

Perhaps it's best if I keep that information to myself.

"And your Mrs. Jones did you proud," Elliot continues.

"She did. Gail is a great cook. I think she likes to stretch her culinary legs on occasion."

Elliot downs his drink and smacks his lips together in appreciation. *Uncouth, bro, uncouth.*

"That's damn fine whisky, hotshot. I'm going to turn in. You?"

"I have some business to attend to."

Elliot looks at his watch. "Now? It's late."

"I need to deal with an e-mail that came in before dinner. It won't take long." I'm not sure I can sleep, anyway.

"It's your funeral…well, wedding." He grins and bounds off the couch with his usual spontaneous energy. "Good night. Try and sleep, K?" He punches me on the arm and takes his leave.

"Good night," I call after him. "Don't forget the rings!"

He responds with the finger. In spite of myself, he makes me chuckle. Rising, I slip the Tiffany box back in my pocket.

In my study, I open the e-mail that has been preoccupying me since I received it earlier this evening. It's from Welch, and it contains the report from the NTSB on *Charlie Tango*'s accident.

From: Welch, H. C.
Subject: NTSB Report
Date: July 29 2011 18:57
To: Christian Grey
Cc: J B Taylor

Mr. Grey

Attached is the detailed report from the National Transportation Safety Board. They have been more than thorough and confirm sabotage. The fuel lines were cut, allowing aviation kerosene to leak into the engines.

The report has been forwarded to the FBI and will be used to continue the criminal investigation. Fortunately, the NTSB has kept them updated and the FBI dusted for prints last week as part of their investigation. They are in the process of eliminating the engineers and ground staff from their inquiries, but at present they're no nearer to finding a suspect.

Tomorrow I'd like to move the Gulfstream to Sea-Tac, so you'll depart from there and not Boeing Field. I'll arrange for you to be dropped off airside.

I've added four additional security officers to your wedding detail. Résumés are attached. Taylor has approved them. Two of them have been dispatched to the wedding venue to keep watch overnight.

Apologies for this arriving on the eve of your nuptials.

Leave this with us. And try to enjoy your big day.

Welch

Fuck. Our instincts were right.

But who wants to kill me? Who?

I type a quick response to Welch.

From: Christian Grey
Subject: NTSB Report
Date: July 30 2011 12:23
To: Welch, H. C.
Cc: J B Taylor

Agreed. And thanks.

Christian Grey
CEO, Grey Enterprises Holdings, Inc.

I toss back the remains of my Armagnac and decide to read the full report in bed. I'm on my own because Ana left with my parents to stay at their place tonight.

To hell with these stupid traditions.

She should be here. With me. I miss her.

At least Sawyer went with her. He'll watch over her.

As I gather up the pages of the NTSB report from my printer, my mood grows bleaker. I am done with this shit.

The report is extensive and rather dull, but in spite of my drooping eyelids, I manage to finish it. The next steps are to hand *Charlie Tango* over to the FBI, and once they've finished with her, they'll return her to Eurocopter for a full assessment. I'm hopeful she can be repaired and GEH won't have to deal with any insurance adjusters.

I switch off my side light and stare up at the ceiling.

Why is this happening the night before my wedding?

I'm shrouded in darkness, and conscious of an empty feeling creeping into my chest. I'm now able to recognize it as loneliness; my heart is missing a piece, as Ana is not beside me. Though, strictly speaking, I'm not alone. My future father-in-law is probably asleep above me, Elliot is in the spare bedroom next door, and the staff quarters are almost at capacity. But Anastasia Steele is conspicuous by her absence. I wish she were here; I'd wrap her in my arms and lose myself in her. I'm tempted to text her, but it might wake her, and she needs her sleep. *Fuck it.* Without her, I'm lost. And someone out there wants me dead, and we don't know who.

Damn. Push it from your mind, Grey.

I close my eyes.

Breathe, Grey. Breathe.

I start counting sheep.

We are soaring. Ana is in front of the cockpit, her hands stretched out to the canopy, squealing with joy and wonder. My heart is full. This is happiness. This is love. This is what it feels like. We're on top of the world. Our life stretched in a colorful patchwork of greens and browns beneath us. I bank, and suddenly I'm in a tailspin. Ana is screaming. Screaming. We're in *Charlie Tango* and we're losing height. I smell the fire. I'm fighting the controls to keep my helicopter upright. I need to find a place to land. All I hear is the roar of the engines and Ana screaming. We're going down. *Fuck.* Spinning. Down. Down. Down. *Shit.* I'm going to hit the ground. No. No! Ana is lying on a sticky green rug. I'm shaking her. She won't wake up. Ana. Ana. Ana! There's a crash. And he fills the doorway. *There you are, you little shit!* No. *No.* Ana. Ana. *Ana!*

I'm jerked awake, a fine film of sweat bathing my chest and stomach in the first blink of dawn.

It's too early.

I rub my face, bringing my breathing and terror under control, then close my eyes and turn over. Reaching out, I grab Ana's pillow and tug it toward me. I immerse myself in her scent. *Ah...*

Grandpa Theodore hands me an apple. It's bright red. And sweet. There's a light breeze on my face. It's cooling in the sunshine. We stand together in the orchard. He holds my hand. His palm is rough with calluses. Mom and Dad and Elliot are coming. They have a picnic basket. Dad lays out the blanket. And Ana sits down on the blanket. Ana. She's here. With me. With us. She laughs. And I laugh. Ana caresses my face. *Here*, she says. And she hands me Baby Mia. *Mia.* And suddenly I'm six again. *Mee-a*, I whisper. Mom looks at me. *What did you say? Mee-a. Yes. Yes.*

Darling boy. You have your words. Mia. Her name is Mia.

And Mommy starts to cry happy tears.

I open my eyes, startled by an image from my dream that I can't quite grasp.

What was I dreaming about?

The sun is higher in the sky, announcing that it's a more acceptable time to rise. I shake my head to rouse myself, and then I remember—today, I make Ana mine.

Today, at 12 p.m.

Yes!

And then I get to spend three weeks with her in Europe. I can't wait to show Ana all the sights. As I lie in bed feeling excited about what I have planned, I have an idea.

Hmm… I'm going to pack a few toys from the playroom to add to the fun.

Yes.

I bound out of bed, grab a T-shirt, and head toward the kitchen. From the corridor I hear voices. Ray is sitting at the kitchen counter, tucking into bacon, eggs, hash browns, and sausages. He's chatting with Mrs. Jones. Unlike me, he's dressed, in his wedding shirt and tuxedo pants. "Good morning," I greet him.

"Good morning, Christian. How are you feeling?"

"Good."

"Morning, Mr. Grey," Gail gushes. "Coffee?"

"Please."

"It's a mighty fine place you have here," Ray says, motioning to the ceiling with his knife.

"Thank you."

"Ana tells me you've bought a house."

"Yes. It's up the coast."

Ray nods. "She says you have a place in Aspen and New York, too."

"Um…yes. You know, property. Um. It's about diversifying my portfolio."

He nods, but gives nothing away. "A lot of places for one person to mind."

"Well, after today, there'll be two of us minding them."

His eyebrows rise high into his forehead, and a slow smile that is either admiration or incredulity spreads across his face. I hope it's admiration. "I guess you're right," he says.

I want to move the conversation off this topic. "Did you sleep well?"

"I did. That room is probably one of the fanciest I've ever stayed in. And that is some view."

"I'm glad you were comfortable."

"Here you are, Mr. Grey." Mrs. Jones places a black coffee on the counter in front of me.

"Thank you, Gail."

"What would you like for breakfast?"

"What Ray's having."

She smiles. "Coming right up, sir."

I slide onto the stool beside Ray and ask him if he's been fishing recently. His eyes light up.

EVEN I HAVE TO admit that Elliot looks good in a tux. We're in the back of the Q7, and nearing our parents' place in Bellevue. "How are you feeling?" he asks.

"I wish people would stop asking me that."

"You? Nervous? You're the coolest dude I know. What gives? Is it because you're saddling yourself to the same woman for the rest of your life? I'd be nervous, too."

I roll my eyes. "Your promiscuity knows no bounds, Elliot. One of these days someone is going to turn your world upside down. I didn't know it would happen to me. And yet here we are."

His eyes cloud, and he looks out of the window as we pull up to our parents' house. There are a number of cars queuing for the valet service, and guests in their wedding finery are following the pale pink carpet to the rear of the house. As Taylor steers us into the driveway, two guys in dark suits, with discreet earpieces and regulation aviators, step forward and open our doors. They're the additional security.

"Ready?" asks Elliot with a quick, reassuring glance at me. "If you want to back out, there's still time."

"Fuck off."

He grins and climbs out of the car.

I take a deep breath.

This is it.

Showtime, Grey.

My phone buzzes and I glance at it.

Fuck. My scalp tingles. It's a text from Elena.

> ELENA
> You're making a big mistake. I know you. But I'll be here for you when your life falls apart. And it will. I'll be here because in spite of what I said I love you. I'll always love you.

What the everlasting fuck is this?

"Christian," Elliot distracts me. "Are you coming?" He's waiting.

"Yes," I snap. I quickly delete the text and climb out of the car.

Fuck her.

"You okay?" Elliot frowns when I join him.

"Yes. Let's do this." I storm ahead, trying to bring my burst of anger under control. How dare Elena try to derail me on my wedding day! I ignore the young woman who's standing on the path, all smiles. She's carrying a clipboard, but I charge past her, leaving Elliot to check in with her, as I head through the front door. Grace is in the hall.

"Darling, you're here."

"Mother."

"You look so handsome, Christian." She puts her arms around me, gives me a swift, restrained hug, and inclines her head toward me, offering a cheek.

"Mom," I whisper, and she steps back, concern flashing in her eyes.

"Are you okay?"

I nod, not trusting myself to speak.

"Ana is upstairs—you can't see her until the wedding. She slept in your room last night. Come with me." She takes my hand and leads me down the hallway into the den.

"Is it nerves, darling? I'd hug you properly, but I don't want to get makeup on your suit," Grace says. "The aesthetician put it on with a trowel. It will take months to get it off."

I laugh, and I'm so grateful that it's Grace I got to see first. "I'm okay, Mom."

She clasps both of my hands. "Are you sure?"

"Yes." My anger has evaporated, beaten back by the woman I call Mom, and I resolve that, today of all days, I will not think about Mrs. Lincoln.

"I'm so excited for you, darling," Grace adds, beaming up at me.

"You look good, Mom. Makeup and all."

"Thank you, dear. Oh, the donations to Coping Together have been unprecedented. I can't thank you enough. It's so generous of you."

I chuckle. "That was Ana's idea. Not mine."

"Oh, that's lovely." She's trying to hide her surprise.

"I told you. She's not acquisitive."

"Of course she isn't. It's a wonderful gesture on both your parts. Are you sure you're okay?"

"Yes. I got an aggravating text from an old business associate."

Grace narrows her eyes, and I think I may have said too much, but she chooses to ignore my explanation and checks her watch. "Kickoff is in fifteen minutes. I have your boutonniere here. Now, do you want to wait here, or go out to the pavilion?"

"I think Elliot and I should go take our seats and wait."

Mom pins the white rose to my lapel and steps back to admire her handiwork.

"Oh, darling." She stops, placing her fingers over her lips, and I think she's going to cry.

Shit. Mom.

My throat tightens, but Elliot steps into the room, saving us both. "What am I, chopped liver?" he chastises Grace, with a wicked gleam in his eye.

"Oh, darling. You look so handsome, too." She recovers and cups his face and pinches his cheeks, and I feel a momentary stab of envy that they have such a touchy-feely relationship.

"Mom, you look like a queen." My brother, charming as ever, plants a kiss on her forehead. She laughs, a girlish, sweet laugh, and she pats her hair.

"You boys," she admonishes us. "You'd better get out there. The ushers will show you where to go. But first let me pin on your boutonniere, Elliot."

AS WE HEAD TO the pavilion, Taylor intercepts me.

"Sir, I've picked up Miss Steele's suitcase, and everything else has been sent on to Sea-Tac."

"Excellent. Thanks, Taylor."

His lips twitch into a smile. "Good luck, sir."

I nod my thanks and continue with Elliot toward the barnlike tent.

A STRING QUARTET IS playing "Halo" by Beyoncé while I wait for Miss Anastasia Steele. My folks have gone all-out; the pavilion looks opulent. Elliot and I are seated at the front of several rows of gold chairs, which are filling up fast. I stare at the scene in front of me, noting all the details, hoping it will distract me from my nerves. A pale pink carpet leads to an impressive, arched flowery bower pitched at the water's edge. It's made of white and pink roses, intertwined with ivy and pale pink peonies that remind me of Ana's blushing cheeks. Reverend Michael Walsh, my mother's friend and her hospital's chaplain, will officiate. He's standing in his designated place patiently waiting, like us. His dark eyes twinkle at Elliot and me. Behind the floral arch the sun skips across the shining waters of Meydenbauer Bay. It's a beautiful day to get married. One of the official photographers is stationed near Walsh, and her lens is directed at me. I look away and turn to Elliot. "You've got the rings?" I ask, probably for the tenth time.

"Yes," he hisses.

"Dude! Just checking."

I turn and survey our guests as they arrive, nodding and waving to those I know. Bastille and his wife are here; Flynn arrives with his wife, Rhian, each holding one of their small boys firmly by the hand.

Taylor and Gail are seated together. The photographer José Rodriguez and his father are here. Ros arrives with her partner, Gwen, and they usher their little girls into their seats. Eamon Kavanagh; his wife, Britt; and Ethan are here—Mia will be pleased. Mac salutes me; he's sitting with a young blond woman I've not seen before. Grandma and Grandpa Trevelyan are shown to their seats near us. Grandma waves enthusiastically at both Elliot and me. Alondra Gutierrez is in the background, directing her small team of people. There are a number of guests that I don't recognize—either friends of my folks or of Ana's parents. My mother and father and Carla and Bob make their way to the front of the gathering to take their seats. My dad breaks rank and dashes toward us. He's brimming with pride, and Elliot and I both stand to greet him.

"Dad." I hold my hand out to shake his, but he takes it and pulls me into a bearlike hug.

"Good luck, son," he enthuses. "I'm so proud of you."

"Thanks, Dad." I squeeze the words past the sudden tangled knot of emotion that's lodged in my throat.

"Elliot." Carrick hugs him, too.

The general buzz of the congregation changes to an expectant hush. Dad scuttles back to his seat behind us as the string quartet breaks into "Chasing Cars."

Of course, Snow Patrol. One of Ana's favorite bands.

She loves this song.

Mia is walking down the central aisle, dressed in a pale pink explosion of tulle. Behind her, Kate Kavanagh looks sleek and elegant in a pale pink silk gown.

Ana.

My mouth dries.

She's stunning.

She's in a fitted white lace dress, her shoulders bare but for a gossamer-thin veil. Her hair is pinned in an updo with a few tendrils framing her beautiful face. Her bridal bouquet is intricate—made of pink and white roses woven together. Ray walks by her side, his hand covering hers as she grips his arm, and it's obvious he's holding back his tears.

Oh shit. The knot tightens in my throat.

Ana's eyes meet mine, and beneath her veil her face lights up like a summer's day, her smile electrifying.

Oh, baby.

They walk up beside us and Ana passes her bouquet to Kate, who stands with Mia. Ray raises Ana's veil and kisses her cheek. "I love you, Annie," I hear him say, his voice hoarse, and, turning to me, he gives me Ana's hand. Our eyes meet, his glistening, and I have to look away because his expression may be my undoing.

"Hi," I say to my bride, because that's all I'm capable of right now.

"Hi," she replies, and squeezes my hand.

"You look lovely."

"So do you." She grins, and all my nerves melt away, as does the music, and it's just Ana and me and Reverend Michael. He clears his throat, commanding everybody's attention, and the wedding begins.

"Dearly beloved, we are gathered here today to witness the joining in matrimony of Christian Trevelyan-Grey and Anastasia Rose Steele." The good reverend smiles benevolently down at both of us, and I tighten my hold on Ana's hand.

He asks the congregation if anyone knows of any impediment to our marriage. Elena's text flits through my mind, and I'm annoyed with myself that I let it. Fortunately, Ana distracts me by glancing back at the crowd. When no one says anything, a collective sigh of relief flutters through the gathering, followed by muffled chuckles and titters. Ana peeks up at me, her eyes sparkling in amusement.

"Phew," I mouth.

Ana stifles her smile.

Reverend Michael asks us each in turn to declare that there's no legal reason why we can't be joined in marriage.

As he addresses us about the seriousness of our commitment to each other, the burning sensation returns to my throat. Ana watches him, absorbed, and I notice she's wearing elegant drop pearl earrings I've not seen before. I wonder if they are a present from her folks.

"And now I invite both of you to offer your vows to each other." He looks encouragingly at me. "Christian?"

I take a deep breath, and gazing at the love of my life, I recite my vows from memory, my words ringing out over the throng: "I, Christian Trevelyan-Grey, do take thee, Anastasia Rose Steele, to be my lawfully wedded wife. I solemnly vow that I will safeguard, and hold dear and deep in my heart, our union and you. I promise to love you faithfully, forsaking all others, through the good times and the bad, in sickness and in health, regardless of where life takes us. I will protect you, trust you, and respect you."

Tears glimmer in Ana's eyes and the tip of her nose turns a fetching pink.

"I will share your joys and sorrows, and comfort you in times of need. I promise to cherish you and uphold your hopes and dreams and keep you safe at my side. All that is mine is now yours. I give you my hand, my heart, and my love, from this moment on, for as long as we both shall live."

Ana wipes a tear from her eye, and I take a deep breath, relieved that I've remembered the words.

"Ana?" the good reverend prompts her. From beneath her sleeve she takes a small slip of pink paper and reads:

"I, Anastasia Rose Steele, do take thee, Christian Trevelyan-Grey, to be my lawfully wedded husband. I give you my solemn vow to be your faithful partner, in sickness and in health, to stand by your side in good times and in bad, to share your joy as well as your sorrow." She gazes up at me and continues her vows without reading, and I stop breathing. "I promise to love you unconditionally, to support you in your goals and dreams, to honor and respect you, to laugh with you and cry with you, to share my hopes and dreams with you, and bring you solace in times of need. And to cherish you for as long as we both shall live." She blinks back her tears, and I fight mine.

"You two will now exchange rings as a symbol of your abiding love for each other. A ring is a constant circle. It is unbroken and everlasting, a symbol of perpetual unity. So, too, will be your commitment to each other and to this marriage, from this day forth, until death do you part.

"Christian, place the ring on Anastasia's finger." Elliot hands me Ana's ring and I position it at the tip of Ana's left ring finger.

"Repeat after me," Reverend Michael says. "Anastasia, I give you this ring as a sign of our enduring faith in each other, our unity and our everlasting love."

I repeat the words, loud and clear, and slip the ring fully onto Ana's finger.

"Anastasia, place the ring on Christian's finger," Reverend Michael says. Elliot flashes a grin at Ana and passes her my ring.

"Repeat after me," the reverend continues. "Christian, I give you this ring as a sign of our enduring faith in each other, our unity and our everlasting love."

Ana's words sound out sweetly for the rest of the congregation to hear, and she slips the ring onto my finger.

Reverend Michael clasps both of our hands in his and says in a booming voice to our audience, "Love is the reason we are here. Marriage is founded on love. These two young people have pledged their everlasting love to each other. We honor them and wish them strength, courage, and trust to grow together, to learn from each other and to remain true to each other on the path that life takes them.

"Christian and Anastasia, you two have agreed to be married and to live together in matrimony. You have declared your love for each other and promised to uphold that love with your vows. With the power vested in me by the state of Washington, I now declare you husband and wife." He releases our hands and Ana beams up at me.

Wife.

Mine.

My heart soars.

"You may kiss the bride," Reverend Michael says with a huge grin.

"Finally, you're mine," I whisper, and pull her into my arms, flush against me, and plant a soft kiss on her lips. There are tiny buttons at the back of her dress and I fantasize about slowly undoing them. I ignore the cheers and applause from our guests, as my body comes alive. "You look beautiful, Ana." I caress her face. "Don't let anyone take that dress off but me, understand?" I gaze down at her, trying to convey a sensual promise. She nods, her eyes darkening with desire.

Oh, Ana.

I want to pick her up and carry her to my boyhood room and consummate our marriage. *Now.* But I'm sure I won't get away with that.

Get a grip, Grey.

"Ready to party, Mrs. Grey?" I smile at my wife.

"Ready as I'll ever be."

I bask in the warmth of her smile. Taking her hand, I extend the other to Reverend Michael.

"Thank you, Reverend. That was a lovely ceremony. And it was brief."

"I had my instructions," he says, and shakes our hands in turn. "Congratulations, both of you."

I have to release Ana as Kate drags her into a hug, and Elliot wraps his arms around me. "Man, you did it. Congratulations."

"Christian!" Mia hollers, and barrels into my arms. "I love Ana! I love you!" she gushes, and crushes me.

"Mia. Steady. I need my ribs intact."

So begins an endless round of congratulations, kisses, and hugs. I gird my loins to tolerate all the unnecessary touching I'm about to endure. It helps that I'm elated. When I turn to my mother, she's sobbing. I give her a brief hug, mindful of her makeup, while Carrick slaps me on the back. Carla and Bob are next. Ray Steele shakes my hand, squeezing harder and harder.

"Congratulations, Christian. You should know, if you hurt her, I'll kill you."

"I'd expect no less, Ray."

"I'm glad we understand each other." He grins and releases my now throbbing hand and claps me on the back. I flex my fingers and remind myself that Raymond Steele is ex-army.

SIPPING A COUPE OF vintage Grande Année Rosé, I watch my beautiful wife as she makes her way toward me. We've just completed what feels like a major photoshoot with the wedding photographers, and now I'm standing near our table in the hope of having a bite to eat—getting married has given me an appetite. Ana stops every so often to talk to our guests, welcoming them and graciously receiving their good wishes. Her light shines so bright, her smile bringing everyone she greets to life.

She's an extraordinary person. A stunning woman.

And she's mine.

When she finally reaches me, I take her hand and pull it to my lips. "Hi," I whisper. "I've missed you."

"Hi. I've missed you, too."

"You've dispensed with your veil. It was lovely."

"It was. But people kept treading on it!"

I cringe. "That must have been annoying."

"It was."

My father takes the microphone. "Good afternoon, all," he says. "Welcome to our home here in Bellevue, and to Christian and Ana's wedding. If you don't know me, I am very proud to say I am Christian's dad, Carrick. I'm hoping to speak to all of you at some point during the afternoon or evening. In the meantime, you should all have a glass of the good stuff and I'd like us all to raise our glasses to Christian and his beautiful wife, Ana. Congratulations you two. Welcome to the family, Ana. And both of you, be kind to each other. To Christian and Ana!"

My father gives me a warm, tender smile, which I feel all the way to my toes. I raise my glass to him as everyone raises their glasses and the words "Christian and Ana" hover around us all.

"Please make your way to your table. We'll be starting lunch shortly," Dad continues.

I pull out Ana's chair; she sits and I take the seat beside her. From here we have the best view of the entire pavilion. I'm thankful to be seated at last. I'm ravenous. The table looks lovely covered in white linen and floral arrangements with white and pink roses. Our parents join us, with Elliot and Kate and Mia and Bob.

Ana and my mom have opted for a buffet, but as the bridal party, we're served our appetizers while our guests find their seats. There's fresh sourdough, with some herby-looking butter, and a delicious cheese soufflé with a delicate garden salad. My wife and I tuck in.

ELLIOT IS GOING TO make a speech. He's had several glasses of champagne, so this could go either way. We've finished our entrée of king salmon en croute and I take a gulp of Bollinger and brace myself.

Elliot winks at me and rises from the table. "Good afternoon, everyone. Welcome. I've drawn the short straw—I mean, I'm honored to be Christian's best man, and his brother, and to be asked to make a speech. But forgive me—public speaking is not my thing. Growing up with Christian Grey was not my thing, either. He was a nightmare of a brother. Just ask my folks."

Fuck! Elliot? But this gets a laugh. Ana squeezes my hand.

"This man can beat the shit out of me and did, frequently. And any of you who have ever kickboxed with him will know, don't mess with him. He's badass. He's a solitary guy. When he was younger he'd rather have had his head stuck in a book than be out tearing up the town with the likes of me. You've all heard how he found school challenging, so I'll gloss over that—but somehow, by some fluke, and not because he's smart or anything, he managed to get some sort of education and even talked his way into Harvard.

"But it turned out Harvard wasn't for him, either. He wanted to throw himself into the world of commerce and high finance. So, he did...he's doing kinda okay with that." Elliot shrugs, apparently unimpressed, and again the audience laughs.

"During this whole time, not once did he show any interest in the opposite sex. None. Well, I'll leave you to deduce what we all thought."

Oh, for fuck's sake. I roll my eyes, and Elliot grins. "So, imagine our collective surprise and delight when not too long ago he shows up with this beautiful young woman, Anastasia Steele. It was obvious from the beginning that she'd captured his heart. And for some strange reason, maybe she was dropped on her head as a child"—he shrugs once more—"she fell for him."

Again, with the laughter from our guests!

"Today they tied the knot, and I just want to say, Christian, Ana, congratulations. We are rooting for you. And no, she's not pregnant!"

There's a communal gasp around all the tables.

"To our bride and groom, Ana and Christian!" He raises his glass. I want to kill him, and judging by Ray Steele's expression, so does he.

Ana's cheeks are pink, and she looks a little shocked.

"Thanks, Elliot," she says, laughing.

I throw my napkin at him and turn to Ana. "Shall we cut the cake?"

"Sure."

THE DJ IS PRIMED and ready as Ana and I make our way to the dance floor. I sweep her into my arms as everyone gathers around us, and Ana settles her arms around my neck. The sweet, soulful words of the song ring through the pavilion, and from the corner of my eye I see Carla clutch her throat in recognition. And then I've only got eyes for my wife as Corinne Bailey Rae starts to sing "Like a Star."

Everyone else fades away. And it's just the two of us gliding across the floor. "Like a star across my sky," Ana whispers. She lifts her lips to mine and I'm lost…and found.

"**MOM, THANK YOU FOR** not insisting on a Catholic wedding."

"Don't be ridiculous, Christian. I couldn't force it on you. I thought Michael did a wonderful service."

"He did." Leaning forward, I kiss my mother on her forehead. She closes her eyes, and when she opens them again they burn with a curious intensity. "You look so happy, darling. I'm so thrilled for both of you."

"Thanks, Mom."

I glance over to where Kate and Ana are in a deep conversation. Elliot is watching them. *No.* Elliot is watching Kate. He can't take his eyes off her. Perhaps he cares for her more than he's letting on.

The dance floor is full; Ray and Carla are taking a turn. They really do get on. I glance at my watch—it's 5 p.m.—time we thought about leaving. I amble over toward my wife. Kate hugs her, hard, then grins at me, and I feel slightly less antagonistic toward her.

"Hi, baby." I slip my arms around Ana and kiss her temple. "Kate," I acknowledge her.

"Hello again, Christian. I'm off to find your best man, who happens to be my best man, too." With a smile to us both, she heads over to Elliot, who is drinking with Ethan and José.

"Time to go," I whisper.

I'm done with this party. I want to be alone with my wife.

"Already?" Ana says. "This is the first party I've been to where I don't mind being the center of attention." She turns in my arms and smiles up at me.

"You deserve to be. You look stunning, Anastasia."

"So do you."

"This beautiful dress becomes you." I love how it reveals her enticing shoulders.

"This old thing?" She peers up at me, in that way that she does, all shy and bewitching through her lashes. She's irresistible. Leaning down, I kiss her.

"Let's go. I don't want to share you with all these people anymore."

"Can we leave our own wedding?"

"Baby, it's our party, and we can do whatever we want. We've cut the cake. And right now, I'd like to whisk you away and have you all to myself."

She giggles. "You have me for a lifetime, Mr. Grey."

"I'm very glad to hear that, Mrs. Grey."

"Oh, there you two are! Such lovebirds."

Oh shit. Grandma Trevelyan strikes.

"Christian, darling—one more dance with your grandma?"

"Of course, Grandmother." I swallow my sigh.

"And you, beautiful Anastasia, go and make an old man happy—dance with Theo."

"Theo, Mrs. Trevelyan?"

"Grandpa Trevelyan. And I think you can call me Grandma. Now, you two seriously need to get working on my great-grandkids. I won't last too much longer." Her smile borders on the lecherous.

Grandma! Jesus!

"Come, Grandmother," I say, hastily.

We have years before we have to think about kids.

I lead her slowly onto the dance floor, glancing apologetically back at Ana and rolling my eyes. "Laters, baby!"

Ana gives me a little wave.

"Oh, darling boy, you look so handsome in your suit. And your bride! Stunning. You'll make beautiful children together."

"One day, Grandmother. Are you enjoying the wedding?" I need to move her on to another subject.

"Your parents know how to throw a party. Of course, your mother gets that from me. Theo would rather be puttering around on the farm. But then you know that."

"I do." I have a stack of fond memories of helping Grandpa in his orchard. It's one of my favorite places. "I'll have to bring Ana to visit."

"You must. You promise, now."

"I promise."

We shuffle around the dance floor to "Just the Way You Are," a Bruno Mars track, which morphs into "Moves Like Jagger" by Maroon 5. My grandmother is loving it. I think she may have consumed a little too much Bollinger. But when the first few bars of "Sex on Fire" blast over the speakers, I decide it's time to deliver Grandma back to her table.

Ana is not here. I sit down with Grandpa Trevelyan, and he tells me how he's expecting a bumper harvest this fall. "Those apples'll be the sweetest yet!"

"I can't wait to try one," I shout, because he's a little hard of hearing.

"You happy, boy?" he asks.

"Very."

"Yeah. You look it." He pats my knee. "It's good to see. Your bride, she's a beautiful girl. You take good care of her, mind, and she'll take good care of you."

"I'm going to do just that. Right now, I'm going to find her. Good to see you, Grandpa."

"I think she went to the restroom."

I stand and Flynn approaches me, holding one of his boys, asleep on his shoulder. Rhian, his wife, holds the other—also out for the count.

"John!"

"Christian, congratulations. Lovely wedding." He shakes my hand. "You know, I'd hug you, but I'm burdened with a small child, and I think it might breach my doctor-patient ethics."

I laugh. "You're good. Thanks for coming."

"Good day, Christian," Rhian says. "Great wedding. We have to take these two rascals home."

"They were very well behaved."

"That's because we drugged them." She winks.

I gasp.

"That's a joke." John side-eyes his wife. "Tempting though that might be on occasion, we've not resorted to it yet."

She laughs. "They're exhausted from running around the yard. Your folks have so much space, here."

"Enjoy your honeymoon," Flynn says, and takes Rhian's hand.

"Thank you, good-bye."

I watch them stroll across the lawn toward the house, weighed down by their responsibilities.

Better them than me.

I spy Ana standing on the terrace by the French doors to the house and text Taylor that we'd like to leave. I stick my hands in my pants pockets and amble over the lawn toward my wife. She's pensive as she watches the dancing and the luminous dusk over distant Seattle.

I wonder what she's thinking about.

"Hi," I say as I reach her.

"Hi." She smiles.

"Let's go." I'm a little impatient to be alone with my wife.

"I have to change." She reaches for my hand, and I think she means to drag me inside, but I resist. Her brows knit together in confusion. "I thought you wanted to be the one to take this dress off," she states.

"Correct." I squeeze her hand. "But I'm not undressing you here. We wouldn't leave until…I don't know." I wave my hand, hoping that's enough of an explanation.

She blushes and releases me.

As much as I want to peel her out of that dress, we have a jet waiting for us with an allotted takeoff time. "And don't take your hair down, either," I whisper, trying and failing to keep my desire out of my tone.

"But—" She frowns.

"No buts, Anastasia. You look beautiful. And I want to be the one to undress you. Pack your going-away clothes. You'll need them." For when we arrive at our destination. "Taylor has your main suitcase."

"Okay." She gives me a sweet smile, and I leave her and go in search of my mother and Alondra to tell them we're off. It's Alondra I find first.

"Thank you." I shake her hand. "Everything went so well."

"You're so welcome, Mr. Grey. I'll round everyone up right now."

"Great. Thanks again."

A MISTY-EYED CARLA WATCHES her daughter and ex-husband exchanging an awkward hug while Ana clutches her wedding bouquet. Ana's eyes glisten.

"You'll make one hell of a wife, too," Ray murmurs, and once again tears glint in his eyes. Spying me, he shakes his head, and then my hand, warmly. "Look after my girl, Christian."

"I fully intend to, Ray. Carla." I give Ana's mom a kiss on the cheek.

Outside the French doors, our remaining guests have gathered and formed a human arch from the terrace around the side of the house and all the way to the front.

I check Ana's expression. Her smile is back. "Ready?"

"Yes."

Hand in hand, we duck beneath all the outstretched arms and dash through the arch, where we're showered with rice and good wishes and luck and love. At the end, my mom and dad are waiting.

"Thank you, Mom," I whisper as she hugs me, no longer worried about getting makeup on my suit. Dad pulls me into another hug.

"Well done, son. Have a wonderful honeymoon."

They both kiss and hug Ana, and Grace starts crying again.

Mom! Get it together.

Taylor, standing by the driver's door, moves to open the back passenger door. I shake my head, and instead I open it for Ana, who turns suddenly and tosses her wedding bouquet into the waiting crowd. Mia catches it with a loud whoop of joy that can be heard above the whistles and cheers of approval from everyone gathered to say good-bye.

I help Ana into the Audi, scooping her dress up so it doesn't catch in the door. Giving everyone a quick wave, I sprint to the other side of the car, where Taylor is holding open my door.

"Congratulations, sir," he says warmly.

"Thank you, Taylor." I slide in beside my wife.

Thank God! We're finally leaving. I thought we'd never get away.

Taylor eases the Audi down the driveway to the sound of enthusiastic cheers and rice pelting the car. Reaching for Ana's hand, I draw her knuckles to my lips and kiss each one in turn. "So far so good, Mrs. Grey?"

"So far so wonderful, Mr. Grey. Where are we going?"

"Sea-Tac."

Ana looks puzzled, so I brush my thumb across her lip.

"Trust me?"

"Implicitly," she breathes.

"How was your wedding?"

"Fantastic. Yours?"

"Amazing." And we're grinning at each other like idiots.

WE DRIVE AIRSIDE THROUGH the security gates at Sea-Tac and steer toward the GEH Gulfstream. "Don't tell me you're misusing company property again!" Ana blurts when she spots the plane. Her eyes shine and she grips my hand, radiating excitement.

"Oh, I hope so, Anastasia." I give her my most wicked grin.

Taylor stops the car at the foot of the steps to the plane, climbs out, and opens my door. I exit. "Thanks again, Taylor. We'll see you in London," I murmur, so Ana doesn't hear.

"I'm looking forward to it, sir. Safe travels."

"You, too."

"I'll grab Mrs. Grey's hand luggage," he says, and my heart warms at Ana's new honorific. I walk around to her door and open it wide. Leaning in, I lift her into my arms.

"What are you doing?" she squeals.

"Carrying you over the threshold."

She giggles, wrapping her arms around my neck, and I carry her up the plane steps, where we're met by Captain Stephan.

"Welcome aboard, sir. Mrs. Grey," he greets us, with a bold grin. I set Ana down and shake his hand. "Congratulations to you both," he continues.

"Thank you, Stephan. Anastasia, you know Stephan. He's our captain today, and this is First Officer Beighley."

"Delighted to meet you," Beighley says to Ana.

Ana looks a little shell-shocked, but she responds in kind to them both.

"All preparations complete?" I ask Beighley.

"Yes, sir," she replies with her usual confidence.

"We have the all clear," Stephan informs us. "Weather is good from here to Boston."

"Turbulence?"

"Not before Boston. There's a weather front over Shannon that might give us a rough ride."

"I see. Well, we hope to sleep through it all."

"We'll get underway, sir," Stephan says. "We'll leave you in the capable care of Natalia, your flight attendant."

Natalia?

Where's Sara?

Natalia looks vaguely familiar.

I ignore my misgivings. "Excellent," I say to Stephan, and taking Ana's hand, I guide her to one of the seats. "Sit."

She does as she's told, folding herself into the seat with surprising grace. I remove my jacket, undo the buttons on my vest, and sit down opposite her.

"Welcome aboard, sir, ma'am, and congratulations," Natalia welcomes us, poised with two crystal flutes of pink champagne.

"Thank you." I take both and offer one to Ana, while Natalia disappears into the galley.

"Here's to a happy married life, Anastasia." I raise my glass to Ana's and we clink.

"Bollinger?" she asks.

"The same." We've been drinking it for most of the afternoon.

"The first time I drank this it was out of teacups." Her eyes have a faraway look.

"I remember that day well. Your graduation."

What a day that was… I think spanking was involved. Hmm… and a discussion about soft and hard limits.

I shift in my seat.

"Where are we going?" Ana drags me back to the now.

"Shannon."

"In Ireland?" she squeaks.

"To refuel."

"Then?" Ana's eyes are out on stalks; her excitement is contagious.

I grin at her and say nothing, tantalizing her.

"Christian!"

I put her out of her misery. "London."

She gasps, looking shocked and awed at once. Then her light-up-Seattle smile is back.

"Then Paris. Then the South of France," I continue.

I think Ana is going to combust.

"I know you've always dreamed of going to Europe. I want to make your dreams come true, Anastasia."

"You are my dreams come true, Christian."

"Back at you, Mrs. Grey." Her words warm my soul, and I take another sip of champagne. "Buckle up."

Ana grins. I think she's pleased. And so am I. We're flying through the sunset to chase the dawn on the other side of the Atlantic.

ONCE WE'RE AIRBORNE, NATALIA serves us dinner. Again, I'm starving.

Why?

Getting married really takes it out of a man. Ana and I discuss our highlights of the wedding. Mine was seeing her for the first time in her beautiful dress.

"Mine was seeing you," Ana confesses. "And that you were *there*!"

"There?"

"Part of me had wondered if this was all a dream and that maybe you wouldn't show up."

"Ana, wild horses couldn't have dragged me away."

"Dessert, Mr. Grey?" Natalia asks.

I decline, and turn to study my wife. Running my finger across my bottom lip, I watch Ana, waiting for her response.

"No, thank you," she says to Natalia, gazing intently at me. Natalia leaves us.

Oh, sweet heaven. I'm going to claim my wife.

"Good," I whisper. "I'd rather planned on having you for dessert."

Ana's eyes meet mine and darken while her teeth tease her bottom lip.

Rising from the table, I offer her my hand. "Come." We head to the back of the cabin, away from the galley and the cockpit. I point to a door at the far end. "There's a bathroom here." Passing through a short corridor, we emerge into the aft cabin where the queen-size bed is ready for us.

I pull Ana into my arms. "I thought we'd spend our wedding night at thirty-five thousand feet. It's something I've never done before."

Ana inhales sharply, and the sound echoes in my groin.

"But first I have to get you out of this fabulous dress."

Her breathing deepens. She wants this, too.

"Turn around," I whisper.

She complies instantly, and I study her updo. Each hairpin has a tiny pearl on it—they're exquisite. *Like Ana.* Gently, I start to extract each one, letting every strand of her hair fall free. My fingertips graze her temple, her neck, her earlobe, but it's the lightest of touches. I want to tease and tantalize the hell out of my wife. And it's working. She's surreptitiously shifting her weight from foot to foot. She's restless. Impatient. Her breathing is louder.

She's aroused.

Just by my touch. And for me, her response is equally arousing.

"You have such beautiful hair, Ana." I breathe the words against her temple, enjoying her delicious fragrance, and a soft sigh escapes her lips. When I've removed all the pins, I ease my fingers into her hair and begin to slowly massage her scalp.

She lets free a heartfelt moan of pleasure and leans back against me. My fingers travel over the back of her head to her nape. I take a fistful of her lush hair and tug, giving me access to her throat. "You're mine." I tease her earlobe with my teeth.

She groans.

"Hush now." I sweep her hair over her shoulder and skim my finger along the lace edging of her dress. A tremor runs through her as I press my lips to her skin above the top button.

"So beautiful," I whisper, and undo it. "You have made me the happiest man alive today." Taking my sweet time, I continue unfastening each delicate button. Her dress falls open, revealing her pale pink corset with delicate hooks at the back.

My cock approves. Big-time.

"I love you so much." I skim my lips from her nape to her shoulder. Murmuring between kisses. "I. Want. You. So. Much. I. Want. To. Be. Inside. You. You. Are. Mine."

She angles her head, offering her throat to me.

"Mine," I utter against her skin, and slip her sleeves down her arms so that her bridal gown falls to her feet, in a delicate shock of silk and lace, leaving her in her corset with garters and stockings.

Sweet Jesus. Stockings. All the blood in my body heads south.

"Turn around." My voice is hoarse.

Inhaling sharply, I study my wife. She looks demure and really fucking hot all at once; her breasts forced up and full beneath her corset and her hair a tumbling riot of lush chestnut.

"You like?" she asks, and she turns a fetching pink that matches her sexy underwear.

"More than like, baby. You look sensational. Here." I offer her my hand, and she steps out of her dress.

"Keep still," I warn, locking my eyes on hers. I run a finger over the soft swell of her breasts. They quiver beneath my touch as she inhales and exhales, faster…and shallower.

I love turning my wife on.

Reluctantly, I lift my finger from her skin and spin it in the air.

Turn around for me.

She does. When she's facing the bed, I ask her to stop. Encircling her waist, I pull her back against my chest and kiss her neck. From this angle, I have a glorious top view of her straining breasts and I can't resist them. I embrace each and hold them, letting my thumbs move over their soft swell to her nipples, circling each over and over. Ana moans.

"Mine," I breathe.

"Yours," she whispers.

She pushes her ass against me and I have to fight my urge to press myself into her. As I skim my hands down the soft satin, over her stomach, her belly, to her thighs—my thumbs briefly skating over her vulva—she leans her head against me, eyes closed, and groans. My fingers find her garters and I unhook both of them at the same time. Then I move my hands to her fine ass.

"Mine," I whisper. As I caress her backside, my fingertips brush beneath her panties.

"Ah," she moans.

She's wet.

Fuck. Ana. You siren.

"Hush." I unclip her garters at the back, then lean down and pull the duvet back. "Sit down." She obliges and I kneel at her feet and tug off each of her shoes, placing them by her dress. I'm aware of her burning gaze as I slowly remove her left stocking, my thumbs skimming over her skin as I peel it off. I do the same with its twin. "This is like unwrapping my Christmas presents," I whisper, and peek up at Ana.

"A present you've had already," she says quietly.

What? Her comment takes me by surprise. "Oh, no, baby," I reassure her, if that's what she needs. "This time it's really mine."

"Christian, I've been yours since I said yes." She moves forward and holds my face between her palms. "I'm yours. I will always be yours, husband of mine."

Husband. It's the first time she's said it since the ceremony.

"Now," she says softly against my lips, "I think you're wearing too many clothes." She leans down to kiss me, but the word *husband* is ringing in my heart.

I'm hers. Really hers.

I kneel up and kiss her, grasping her head with both hands, weaving my fingers into her hair.

"Ana," I whisper. "My Ana." And I kiss her again. Properly. Pushing my tongue into her mouth and tasting her. Tasting my wife. She answers my wordless passion with her own, her tongue finding and embracing mine.

"Clothes," she says when we surface for air, and attempts to remove my vest. I release her and shuck it off while she regards me with her beautiful blue eyes that are darkening with want. "Let me, please," she pleads.

I sit back on my heels, and she leans forward and takes my tie.

That tie.

My favorite.

And she slowly undoes it and pulls it free.

I lift my chin and she unfastens my top button. She moves to my cuffs and removes each of my new cuff links in turn. I hold out my hand, and she places them in my palm. Clasping them in my fist, I kiss my hand and then slip them into my pants pocket.

"Mr. Grey, so romantic."

"For you, Mrs. Grey—hearts and flowers. Always."

She reaches for my hand, and peering up at me through her long, dark lashes, she kisses my wedding ring.

Oh God. I close my eyes and groan. "Ana."

She starts to unbutton my shirt. As she unfastens each one, she plants a soft kiss where the button once was and whispers a word. "You. Make. Me. So. Happy. I. Love. You."

It's too much. I want her.

Fuck, do I want her.

I groan and shake my shirt off, then lift her onto the bed and lay her down beneath me. My lips find hers and I hold her head, keeping her still as we share our first horizontal kiss as husband and wife.

Ana.

My pants are getting too tight. I kneel up between her legs and Ana is panting, her lips swollen from our kisses, and she's staring up at me with want.

Fuck.

"You are so beautiful, wife." I run my hands down each of her legs and grab her left foot. "You have such lovely legs. I want to kiss every inch of them. Starting here." I press my lips to her big toe and graze the pad with my teeth.

"Ah!" Ana makes a garbled sound and closes her eyes. I taste her instep and run my tongue to her heel, which I nip, then run my tongue to her ankle. I leave a path of soft wet kisses up the inside of her calf, and Ana squirms.

"Still, Mrs. Grey," I warn, and for a moment I watch her breasts rising and falling against the constraints of her corset.

It's a thing of beauty.

Enough. It needs to go.

I flip her onto her stomach, and continue my journey of kisses up her body: the backs of her legs, her thighs, her backside. And for a moment I contemplate all that I want to do to her ass.

Ana protests. "Please."

"I want you naked," I murmur, and unhook her corset, one hook at a time, at a languid pace. Once it's off, I plant a soft, wet kiss at the base of her spine, then trail my tongue up the length of her backbone.

Ana wriggles. "Christian, please."

I'm leaning over her, my constrained cock resting against her ass, and she wriggles against me. "What do you want, Mrs. Grey?" I utter the words just beneath her ear.

"You."

"And I you, my love, my life." I undo my pants, kneel up beside her, and turn her onto her back. Standing, I dispense with my pants and underwear while Ana regards me, wide-eyed and wanting. I grasp her panties and whisk them off so that she's naked in all her glory beneath me.

"Mine," I mouth.

"Please," Ana implores me.

I can't help my grin. *Oh, baby. I love it when you beg.*

Crawling onto the bed, I lay a new path of wet kisses up her other leg, getting closer and closer to the top of her thighs. My objective. The sacred apex. When I reach my goal, I push her legs wider apart. She's wet and wanting. Just how I like her. "Ah, wife of mine," I whisper, and I run my tongue over her, tasting her and pinpointing her clitoris.

Hmm… Slowly, I begin to torture her with my mouth. Round and round, my tongue teases her oh-so-sensitive bud. Ana grabs my hair and writhes underneath me, her hips moving in a rhythm I know so well. She bucks once. But I hold her still and continue my sweet torment.

"Christian," she calls, and tugs at my hair.

She's close.

"Not yet." I move up her body, dipping my tongue in her navel.

"No!" she cries out in frustration, and I grin against her belly.

All in good time, my love.

I kiss her soft stomach. "So impatient, Mrs. Grey. We have until we touch down on the Emerald Isle."

When I reach her breasts, I worship each with tender kisses, and take a nipple between my lips and tug. I watch her as I lavish my attention on it; her eyes are dark and her mouth slack. "Husband, I want you. Please."

And I want you.

I cover her body with mine, resting my weight on my elbows, and run my nose down hers. Her hands are on me.

My shoulders.

My back.

My backside.

"Mrs. Grey. Wife. We aim to please." I brush my lips over hers. "I love you."

"I love you, too." She's pushing her hips up for me.

"Eyes open. I want to see you."

Her eyes are a startling blue.

"Christian. Ah," she calls out, as I slowly claim her, inch by inch.

"Ana, oh, Ana," I breathe. Her name is a prayer.

She is heaven. My heaven.

I start to move, relishing the feel of her.

Her fingernails dig into my butt and it drives me on.

And on.

And on.

She's mine.

She's really mine.

Finally, she cries out my name and falls apart beneath me, her climax triggering mine, and I come and come inside my love. My life. My wife.

TUESDAY, AUGUST 16, 2011

It's the sound of the sea lapping against the hull of *M.Y. Fair Lady* that wakes me. The crew are on deck; I hear them, no doubt shining the brass and making their preparations for the day. We are moored in the bay outside Monte Carlo harbor. It's a blissful summer's morning in the Mediterranean, and beside me, Mrs. Anastasia Grey is fast asleep. I turn onto my side and study her, as I have done most mornings since we started our honeymoon. She is sun-kissed. Her hair is a little lighter. Her lips are parted, and she sleeps soundly.

As she should.

I smirk at the memory.

It was a late night. And she came and came and came.

She looks so serene; I envy her that.

Though I have to confess, I've relaxed a little.

There's been the occasional call from Ros and from Marco after the drama of last week's Black Monday. Marco and I avoided any substantial losses with some last-minute repositioning into defensive assets. We're both keeping a watchful eye on the markets and liaising on a strategy to survive the downturn.

But generally, no work and all play has been invigorating.

I smile fondly at Ana, and still she sleeps.

I have discovered new facets to my wife.

She adores London.

She loves afternoon tea at Brown's Hotel.

She loves pubs and the fact that Londoners spill out of them and drink pints and smoke on the sidewalks.

She loves Borough Market, especially the Scotch eggs.

She's not keen on shopping, except at Harrods.

She is not a fan of English ale, but then neither am I. It's warm.

Who drinks warm beer?

She's not keen on shaving…but she'll let me shave her.

Now, that's a memory I'll treasure.

She loves Paris.

She loves the Louvre.

She loves the Pont des Arts, and we left a padlock there to prove it.

She loves the Hall of Mirrors in Versailles.

"Mr. Grey. It is no hardship to see you from every angle in here."

She loves me…or so it would seem.

I'm tempted to wake her, but we enjoyed a late night yesterday. We saw *La Songe*, a ballet based on Shakespeare's *A Midsummer Night's Dream*, at L'Opéra de Monte-Carlo, then went to the casino, where Ana won a few hundred euros at the roulette table. She was thrilled.

Her eyes flicker open, as if I've willed her awake. She smiles. "Hi."

"Hi, Mrs. Grey, good morning. Sleep well?"

She stretches. "I had the best sleep and the best dreams."

"You are the best dream." I kiss her forehead. "Sex, or morning swim around the yacht?"

She smiles her oh-so-sexy smile. "Both," she mouths.

ANA IS BUNDLED UP in a robe fresh from her swim, sipping tea and reading one of her SIP manuscripts as we're served breakfast on deck. "I could get used to this," she says, dreamily.

"Yes. She's a fine, fine vessel." I stare at Ana and swallow the last of my espresso. Ana quirks an eyebrow, but before she can respond, our steward Rebecca sets a plate of scrambled eggs and smoked salmon in front of each of us.

"Breakfast," Rebecca says with a warm smile. "Can I get you anything else?"

"This is great." I return her smile.

"I'm good, thank you," Ana says.

"Let's go to the beach today," I suggest.

RARELY DO I GET the opportunity to read so much. But on my honeymoon I've devoured two thrillers, two books on climate change, and now I'm reading Morgenson and Rosner's tome on how greed and corruption led to the 2008 financial crisis, while Ana is dozing beneath a parasol at the Beach Plaza Monte Carlo. Stretched out on a sunbed in the afternoon sun, she's wearing a rather fetching turquoise bikini that leaves very little to the imagination.

I'm not sure I approve.

I've asked Taylor and his two French cohorts, the Ferreux twins, to keep a lookout for any photographers. The paparazzi are parasites who will stop at nothing to invade our privacy. For some bizarre reason, probably since the *Star* ran its gossip piece on Ana, the press are thirsty for pictures of us. Why, I don't know or understand—it's not like we're celebrities, and it makes me mad. I don't want my wife appearing on Page Six wearing practically nothing just because it's a slow news day.

The sun has shifted so Ana is under its full glare, and it's been a while since I applied her sunscreen. I lean over and whisper in her ear, "You'll burn."

She startles awake and grins. "Only for you."

My heart beats a little faster.

How does she do that with just three short words and a smile?

With a swift tug, I drag her bed into the shade. "Out of the Mediterranean sun, Mrs. Grey."

"Thank you for your altruism, Mr. Grey."

"My pleasure, and I'm not being altruistic at all. If you burn, I won't be able to touch you."

Ana curls her lips in a smirk.

I narrow my eyes. "But I suspect you know that, and you're laughing at me."

"Would I?" She bats her lashes, trying, and frankly failing, to look innocent.

"Yes, you would, and you do. Often." I kiss her. "It's one of the many things I love about you." I nibble at her lower lip.

"I was hoping you'd rub me down with more sunscreen."

Deep joy.

"It's a dirty job, but that's an offer I can't refuse. Sit up."

I love this. Touching her. Out here. In public.

She presents her front to me, and I squirt some sunscreen on my fingers, then slowly and thoroughly, so as not to miss a spot, massage it into her skin. Her shoulders, her neck, her arms, the tops of her breasts, her belly. "You really are very lovely. I'm a lucky man."

"Yes, you are, Mr. Grey." Her coy demeanor stirs my blood.

"Modesty becomes you, Mrs. Grey. Turn over. I want to do your back."

She lies down and I undo the strap of her bikini.

"How would you feel if I went topless, like the other women on the beach?" she asks, her voice soft and languid, like the day.

I squirt more sunscreen on my hand and rub it into her skin.

"Displeased. I'm not very happy about you wearing so little right now." I don't want some sleazy fucking pap ogling my wife through a lens while she's relaxing on the beach. They're everywhere. Like vermin.

Ana looks defiant.

I lean down and whisper in her ear. "Don't push your luck."

"Is that a challenge, Mr. Grey?"

"No. It's a statement of fact, Mrs. Grey."

This isn't a game, Ana.

Her back and legs are done. I slap her backside. "You'll do, wench."

My phone buzzes. I glance at the screen. It's Ros with her morning report.

It's early in Seattle. I hope she's okay.

"My eyes only," I warn Ana half-jokingly, and slap her ass once more before I take the call. Ana wriggles her backside provocatively, and closes her eyes while I talk to Ros.

"Hi, Ros, why so early?" I ask.

"I can't sleep, and I can get work done when the house is quiet."

"Anything wrong?"

"No. It's all good. Yesterday after we spoke, I got a call from Bill. We're being pressured by the Detroit Brownfield Redevelopment Authority. You need to make a decision."

My heart sinks.

Detroit. Damn. "Okay. Okay. Of the three sites that Bill sent through, the second was the best."

"The Schaefer Road site?" she asks.

"That's the one."

"Okay. I'll push on that. There's one more thing. Woods."

Hell. He's still on our list of suspects. "What's that asshole doing now?"

Ros ignores my epithet. "He's rattling his ex-employees."

"Poisoning the well?"

"Yes. I think they need a visit," she says.

"You should go."

"Not from me. You."

"Hmm…something to consider when I get back."

"I think so."

"I fancy a trip to New York. Take the wife."

I hear her smile. "How's the Côte d'Azur?"

My gaze lingers on my dozing wife…and her pert backside. "It's beautiful. Especially the view here."

"Great. Enjoy it. I'll get on with this."

"You do that, Ros."

"You know, I think with you gone, I'm all fired up."

I laugh. "Don't get too used to it. I'll be back."

"Believe it or not, I'm missing you."

I open my mouth to respond, but I'm stumped and don't know what to say.

"Afternoon, Christian." She hangs up, and I stare at my phone, wondering if she's okay.

Grey, she's fine. She's one of the most competent people you know.

I go back to my book.

BY MID-AFTERNOON THE TEMPERATURE is scorching. I order some drinks from the hotel waitress, as I'm parched. Ana wakens and turns her attention to me. "Thirsty?"

"Yes," she replies, sleepily.

She's lovely. "I could watch you all day. Tired?"

In the shade of the parasol, her face flushes. "I didn't get much sleep last night."

"Me neither."

I recall a vision from last night: Ana riding me hard.

My body stirs. *Shit.*

I need to cool down. *Now.* Standing, I make quick work of slipping out of my denim shorts. "Come for a swim with me." I hold out my hand, and Ana blinks, a little dazed. "Swim?" I ask again. When she doesn't answer, I scoop her into my arms. "I think you need a wake-up call."

She squeals and giggles at once. "Christian! Put me down!"

"Only in the sea, baby." Laughing, I carry her across the hellish hot sand, grateful to reach the cooler, damper shoreline. Ana wraps her arms around my neck, her eyes alight with amusement as I wade into the Mediterranean.

This has woken her up. She's clinging to me like a limpet. "You wouldn't," she says, a little breathless.

I can't help my grin. "Oh, Ana, baby, have you learned nothing in the short time we've known each other?" Leaning down, I kiss her and she grasps my head, her fingers running through my hair. Greedily, she kisses me back with a passion that catches me unawares and takes my breath away.

Ana.

I'm grateful I'm waist-deep in the water.

"I know your game," I murmur against her lips, and slowly sink into the sea, kissing her once more. The cool water, her hot, wet mouth against mine, it's arousing. She's wrapped around me, warm and wet, cloaking me in her long, lovely limbs.

This is heaven.

I consume her, our passion building while my mind empties.

It's just Ana, my beautiful girl, and me. In the sea.

I want her.

Here. Now.

"I thought you wanted to swim," she whispers, when we stop for air.

"You're very distracting." I tug her lower lip and suck. "And I'm not sure I want the good people of Monte Carlo to see my wife in the throes of passion."

She grazes my jaw with her teeth.

She wants more.

"Ana," I warn, twisting her ponytail around my wrist. I gently tug so I have access to her throat. She tastes of salt water, coconut sunscreen, sweat, and, best of all, Ana. "Shall I take you in the sea?"

"Yes." Her answer is a whisper that stokes my libido.

Fuck. Enough.

This is getting out of hand.

"Mrs. Grey, you're insatiable and so brazen. What sort of monster have I created?"

"A monster fit for you. Would you have me any other way?"

"I'll take you any way I can get you, you know that. But not right now. Not with an audience." I tilt my head to the shore.

Ana glances at the sunbathers taking an intrusive interest in what we are doing.

Enough, Grey.

Grabbing her around her waist, I boost her into the air and she lands with a satisfying splash in the sea. When she surfaces, she's laughing and spluttering with feigned indignation. "Christian!" she cries, and skates her hand across the surface of the water, splashing me.

I splash her right back, grinning because she looks so disappointed.

I'm not exposing her to an audience while we fuck!

"We have all night," I explain, delighted by her reaction. Before I change my mind and get us both arrested—though this is France, so who knows—I prepare to dive. "Laters, baby," I call, and plunge beneath the calm, clean water and swim away. A fast crawl will cool me down and expend some of this excess energy.

LATER, FEELING CALMER AND much refreshed, I stride up the beach, wondering how my wife is faring.

What the actual fuck!

Ana is topless on her sunbed.

I quicken my pace and scan the beach as I go, catching Taylor's eye from where he sits at the bar. He's sipping Perrier with our French security officers, who happen to be twin brothers. Between them, they survey our surroundings. Taylor shakes his head, and I think he's telling me that he's not spotted any photographers.

I don't fucking care. I think I'm going to have a coronary.

"What the hell do you think you're doing?" I yell, seething at Ana when I reach her.

She opens her eyes.

Was she feigning sleep? On. Her. Back?

She looks around, panicked. "I was on my front. I must have turned over in my sleep," she whispers.

I grab her bikini top off my sunbed and toss it toward her, growling, "Put this on!"

Fucking hell. I specifically asked you not to do this.

Not for my fucking health. But for your privacy!

"Christian, no one is looking."

"Trust me. They're looking. I'm sure Taylor and the security crew are enjoying the show!"

She grabs her breasts.

"Yes," I hiss. "And some sleazy fucking paparazzi could get a shot of you, too. Do you want to be all over the cover of *Star* magazine? Naked this time?"

Ana looks horrified and scrambles to put her top on.

Yeah! Why did you think I said no?

"L'addition!" I snap at the waitress. "We're going," I say to Ana.

"Now?"

"Yes. Now."

Don't argue with me, Ana.

I'm so fucking mad I don't even bother to dry myself. I drag on my shorts and T-shirt, and when the waitress returns I sign the check. Ana dresses hurriedly beside me while I signal to Taylor that we're leaving. He picks up his phone, presumably to call the *Fair Lady* and summon the tender. I gather my book and phone and put on my aviators.

What the hell was she thinking?

"Please don't be mad at me," Ana says quietly as she takes my belongings and places them in her backpack.

"Too late for that," I grumble, trying and utterly failing to bring my temper under control. "Come." I clasp her hand and wave at Taylor and the Ferreux brothers, who follow us through the hotel to the entrance.

"Where are we going?" Ana asks.

"Back to the boat."

I'm relieved to see the tender with its Jet Ski at the dock. Ana hands Taylor her backpack, and he gives her a life jacket. Taylor looks hopefully at me, but I shake my head. He blows out a quick breath of frustration, and I know he wants me to wear one, as well, but I'm too fucking angry. Ignoring him, I check that Ana's straps are cinched tightly. "You'll do," I mutter, and clamber onto the Jet Ski, then offer my hand to Ana. Once she's behind me, I kick us away from the dock and attach the kill-cord to the hem of my T-shirt. "Hold on," I growl, and she settles her arms around me, hugging me hard. I tense when she nuzzles my back, because…old memories, and also I'm mad at her. But, truth is, I love being in her arms. "Steady," I mutter, and twist the ignition, starting the engine. The motor roars to life, and slowly I twist the accelerator and we race forward toward the *Fair Lady*.

As we zip over the water my temper improves.

When the tender catches up with us, Ana tightens her hold around me, and I open the accelerator to the max and we speed ahead.

Ha! I love this!

This is fun.

Big-time fun.

Enjoy the moment, Grey.

The Mediterranean is calm and flat, so it's easy to fly over the brine. We tear past the yacht and out toward the open sea. The summer wind in my face, the spray, the speed at which we race across the water, and Ana clinging to me; it's such a thrill. I steer us in an arc toward the boat—but I want more.

"Again?" I shout at Ana. Her huge smile is all the encouragement I need, and I shoot around the *Fair Lady* and out to open sea again, in Ana's tight embrace.

I want to shout my happiness.

But…I'm still a little pissed at her.

ONE OF THE YOUNG stewards, Gerard, helps Ana off the Jet Ski and onto the *Fair Lady*'s small platform. Ana scoots up the wooden stairs and waits for me on deck. "Mr. Grey," Gerard says, and offers his arm.

I wave him away, climb off the machine, and follow Ana. She looks lovely, if a little apprehensive. Her skin glows from the fresh air and the kiss of the sun. "You've caught the sun," I say absentmindedly and undo her life vest. I hand it to Greg, another of the stewards.

"Will that be all, sir?" he asks.

"Would you like a drink?" I ask Ana.

"Do I need one?"

I frown. "Why would you say that?"

"You know why."

Yes, Ana. I'm mad at you.

"Two gin and tonics, please. And some nuts and olives."

Greg acknowledges my request with a nod. As he leaves, I realize what Ana's implying. "You think I'm going to punish you?" I ask.

"Do you want to?"

"Yes," I answer without hesitation, surprising myself.

Her eyes widen. "How?"

Oh, Ana. You sound interested. "I'll think of something. Maybe when you've had your drink." I let my eyes stray to the horizon as various erotic images float through my mind. "You want to be?"

Her eyes darken. "Depends." Her cheeks flush with telltale interest.

Oh, baby.

"On what?"

"If you want to hurt me or not."

For fuck's sake. I thought we were over this.

Her response irks me, but I lean over and kiss her forehead. "Anastasia, you're my wife, not my sub. I don't ever want to hurt you. You should know that by now." I sigh. "Just…just don't take your clothes off in public. I don't want you naked all over the tabloids. You don't want that, and I'm sure your mom and Ray don't want that, either."

Ana pales.

Yes, Ana. You'd be mortified. Ray would be furious. And he'd probably blame me!

Greg arrives with our drinks and places them on the table.

"Sit," I order, and Ana sits down in one of the director's chairs.

Dismissing the steward with a smile, I take a seat beside her, hand her a drink, and pick up my own. "Cheers, Mrs. Grey."

"Cheers, Mr. Grey." She takes a sip, watching me carefully.

What am I going to do with her?

Some kinky fuckery. I think.

It's been a while.

"Who owns this boat?" she asks, distracting me from my salacious plans.

"A British knight. Sir Somebody-or-Other. His great-grandfather started a grocery store. His daughter is married to one of the crown princes of Europe."

"Wow!" Ana mouths. "Super-rich?"

"Yes."

"Like you."

"Yes. And like you." I take an olive.

"It's odd," she says. "Going from nothing to"—she waves at the deck and the fabulous view of Monte Carlo—"to everything."

"You'll get used to it." *I have.*

"I don't think I'll ever get used to it," she answers, her voice low.

Taylor appears at my right. "Sir, you have a call." He hands me my phone.

"Grey," I snap as I rise from my seat and walk to the rail.

It's Ros.

Again?

She's following up on the meeting I had in London with the European GNSS agency about their Galileo Satellite Navigation. I'm hoping we can incorporate their service into Barney's solar tablet. I answer her queries, surprised that she didn't ask me all this earlier.

"Thanks. I'll let Marco know," she says.

"You know, you could have e-mailed me."

"I will next time. Barney's persistent. He's just sent me another e-mail about this. You know." She laughs, a little embarrassed, I think.

I chuckle in response. "He's eager. I know. That's why he works with us, thank goodness. Is that it? Because I'd really like to get back to my wife."

"You do that, Christian. Thank you. I'll try not to bother you again. Good-bye."

I turn my attention to Ana, who's sipping her gin and tonic and staring at the coastline with a faraway look. She's deep in thought.

What is she thinking about? Going topless? Punishment fucks? My wealth? Our wealth!

I hazard a guess. "You will get used to it," I say as I sit down beside her once more.

"Used to it?"

"The money."

She shoots me an unreadable look and pushes the dish of almonds and cashews toward me. "You're nuts, sir." I notice her half smile. She's trying not to laugh. At me. Again.

My plan crystalizes in my mind. "I'm nuts about you."

And that's the truth.

I take a cashew as I recall that night after her bachelorette party: Ana in bed, naked, holding out her hands to me.

"Are you going to punish me?"

"Punish you?"

"For getting this drunk. A punishment fuck. You can do anything you want to me."

The thought stirs my blood. She wants punishing. It would be rude of me not to oblige. "Drink up. We're going to bed."

She gapes at me.

"Drink," I tell her, quietly.

Ana raises her glass to her lips and drains it in one long gulp.

Wow. Without hesitating, my courageous girl has picked up the gauntlet.

She never backs down.

Game on, Grey.

Standing up, I lean over, resting my hands on the arms of her director's chair, and murmur against her ear, "I'm going to make an example of you. Come. Don't pee."

Her gasp is gratifying, and her face is a picture of shock.

I smirk, knowing where her mind has gone.

No, Ana, don't sweat it, that's not my scene.

"It's not what you think." I hold out my hand. "Trust me?"

Her lips lift in a come-hither smile. "Okay." She places her hand in mine, and together we make our way to the master cabin.

Once inside, I release Ana and lock the door. We don't want to be disturbed. Quickly, I strip out of my clothes and remove my flip-flops, which I shouldn't be wearing anyway, but the crew are too polite to tell me.

Ana is watching me, wide-eyed, unconsciously chewing her bottom lip. I grasp her chin, freeing her plump lower lip, and skim my thumb over the little indentations her teeth have left. "That's better."

From inside the armoire I retrieve my bag of toys and produce two pairs of ankle-to-wrist cuffs, the key for them, and an eye mask. Ana hasn't moved. Her eyes are darker than before.

She's turned on, Grey.

Let's blow her mind.

"These can be quite painful." I hold up a pair so that she has a better view of them. "They can bite into the skin if you pull too hard. But I really want to use them on you now. Here." I step toward her and hand her one set. "Do you want to try them first?" I keep my voice gentle, while trying to keep a grip on my libido.

I want this.

Big-time.

Ana examines the cuffs, turning the cold metal over in her hand. The sight of her handling them is erotic enough. "Where are the keys?" she asks, her voice wavering.

I open the palm of my hand, revealing the key. "This does both sets. In fact, all sets." She looks from my palm to my face, her eyes full of questions, full of curiosity…full of yearning. I caress her cheek with my index finger, trailing it down to her mouth and across her lips. Leaning in, as if to kiss her, I breathe, "Do you want to play?"

"Yes," she answers almost inaudibly.

"Good." I take a deep breath, inhaling her unique scent: Ana and a hint of her arousal.

Already!

Closing my eyes, I pour my gratitude into the gentle kiss I plant on her forehead.

Thank you for this, my love.

"We're going to need a safe word."

Ana shoots her eyes to mine.

"*Stop* won't be enough," I continue hastily, "because you will probably say that, but you won't mean it." I run my nose down hers.

Trust me, Ana.

"This is not going to hurt. It will be intense. Very intense, because I am not going to let you move. Okay?"

She inhales sharply, her breathing labored as her excitement builds.

I love turning you on, baby.

Her eyes drift down to my cock.

Yeah, baby. I'm ready and waiting.

"Okay," she whispers.

"Choose a word, Ana."

A soft furrow puckers her brow.

"A safe word," I clarify.

"Popsicle," she blurts, breathy and flustered.

"Popsicle?" I want to laugh.

"Yes."

"Interesting choice. Lift up your arms."

She does as she's told—which turns me on, too—and I raise her dress over her head, discarding it on the floor. Holding out my palm, she surrenders the handcuffs, and I place those and the other cuffs, key, and blindfold on the nightstand. I yank the quilt off the bed and let it fall to the floor.

"Turn around," I order.

She complies immediately, and I undo her bikini top, letting it fall to the floor. "Tomorrow, I will staple this to you," I mutter, and a kernel of an idea sprouts in my mind.

Love-bites.

I free her hair from its ponytail and gather it in my hand, tugging gently so she's forced to step back against me. Angling her head to one side, I glide my lips from her shoulder to her ear. "You were very disobedient."

"Yes," she says, as if she's proud of herself.

"Hmm. What are we going to do about that?" She tastes exquisite.

"Learn to live with it?" she counters, and I grin against the pulse point beneath her ear.

No backing down from my girl.

God, she's hot.

"Ah, Mrs. Grey. You are ever the optimist." I kiss her neck once more, then set to braiding her hair. Once it's done, I use her hair tie to finish up. Tugging her head to the side once more, I whisper in her ear, "I am going to teach you a lesson." Abruptly, I grab her around the waist and sit down on the bed, pulling her over my knee. I smack her beautiful behind. Once. Hard. Then toss her, faceup, onto the bed. Leaning over her, I run my fingertips up her thigh as we drink each other in.

"Do you know how beautiful you are?" I whisper, as she squirms on the bed, panting.

Waiting.

Her eyes dark with longing.

Keeping my gaze on her, I stand and reach for the cuffs. I grasp her left ankle and cuff it with one set of the cuffs. I take the other set and fasten a cuff to her right ankle. "Sit up."

She does.

"Now hug your knees."

With a quizzical look at me, she draws her legs up and wraps her arms around her knees. Reaching down, I lift her chin and brush her lips with a soft, wet kiss before slipping the eye mask over her eyes.

"What's the safe word, Anastasia?"

"Popsicle."

"Good." I snap the left cuff on around her left wrist, and the one attached to her right ankle around her right wrist. She yanks on both and realizes she's unable to straighten her legs.

This is going to be intense.

For you. And for me.

"Now," I whisper. "I'm going to fuck you till you scream."

And I can't wait.

She gasps, and I grab both her heels and tip her feet up so she falls backward onto the bed. I ease her ankles apart, and for a moment I enjoy the sight of her, open and helpless before me. Frankly, I could come over her right now. I'm tempted to. But I kneel down at her altar, and kiss my way up her inner thigh. She moans, pulling on the cuffs.

Careful, Ana. They will bite you.

"You're going to have to absorb all the pleasure, Anastasia. No moving." I shift so I can reach her bikini briefs, and run my lips over her taut belly. The string fastenings on both sides unravel with a simple tug, and her briefs are no more.

I kiss her belly, my tongue dipping into her navel.

"Ah!" Ana groans. Her breasts rise and fall rapidly, as I continue with my trail of wet kisses across her stomach.

"Shh," I murmur. "You're so beautiful, Ana."

She moans, louder this time, and tugs against her metal restraints. "Argh!" she cries as she feels the bite of the cuffs while I continue my conquest of her body, kissing and grazing my teeth against her fragrant skin.

"You drive me crazy," I whisper. "So I'm going to drive you crazy." I kiss her breasts, my tongue, my lips, and my teeth provoking Ana's passionate cries, her heavy breathing, her head thrashing from side to side. I roll each of her nipples between a thumb and forefinger and feel them harden and lengthen under my not-so-tender ministration. I suck hard around each nipple, leaving a telltale little mark each time.

She's breathless now.

Trying to move.

She can't.

She's mine.

And I don't stop.

"Christian," she pleads, and I know I'm driving her crazy.

"Shall I make you come this way?" I blow on her nipple. "You know I can." I take it in my mouth, sucking. Hard.

She cries out, a guttural cry of pleasure.

And I'm fully aroused.

Straining to be inside her.

"Yes," she whimpers.

"Oh, baby, that would be too easy."

"Oh, please."

"Hush." My teeth graze her chin, then I capture her mouth with mine, thrusting my tongue between her lips to meet hers. She tastes of Ana and fresh gin and tonic with a hint of lemon.

Delicious.

But she's greedy. Kissing me back. Wanting more. And more.

Fuck. She tastes so good. She gives as good as she takes. Her head lifting off the sheets.

Oh, baby.

I release her lips and grasp her chin. "Still, baby. I want you still," I whisper.

"I want to see you," she breathes, desperate and needy.

"Oh, no, Ana. You'll feel more this way." I ease my hips forward, knowing we're lined up, and ease my way inside her, just a little.

She can't move.

And I ease back, teasing her.

"Ah! Christian, please!"

"Again?" I ask, and I don't recognize my own voice.

"Christian!"

I push myself into her again, a little farther this time, but pull back and let my fingers tease her right nipple.

"No!" she wails in disappointment. She does not want me to withdraw.

"Do you want me, Anastasia?"

"Yes!" she cries.

"Tell me." My voice is hoarse. I need to hear her say it, and I tease her with my cock once more. In. Out.

"I want you," she whimpers. "Please."

I love it when she begs.

"And have me you will, Anastasia." I slam into her and she screams, pulling against the cuffs.

I know she's helpless.

And I take full advantage. Stilling. Feeling her around me, then circling my hips. She groans.

"Why do you defy me, Ana?"

"Christian, stop."

It's not the safe word. I circle my hips once more, deep, deep inside her. Then pull out and slam into her once more.

Don't come! I will myself. "Tell me. Why?" *I need to know.*

She cries out, and her pleasure is my pleasure.

"Tell me," I plead.

"Christian!"

"Ana, I need to know." I thrust into her once more.

Tell me. Please.

"I don't know!" she wails. "Because I can! Because I love you! Please, Christian."

I groan loudly, and finally let myself love her, cocooning her head beneath my hands as I claim her. Pleasure her. And pleasure myself. She's fighting against the cuffs. Gasping. Keening. Building beneath me.

She's close. I feel it.

She cries out.

"That's it," I grind out between gritted teeth. "Feel it, baby!"

Ana screams as she comes. And comes. And comes. Shattering beneath me. Her head back. Her mouth open. Her face screwed up. I kneel up, taking her with me, pulling her into my lap. Riding out her climax. Holding her tightly, burying my head against her neck as I let go.

FUCK!

My orgasm is relentless.

When I'm finally spent, I rip off her blindfold and kiss my wife.

Her eyelids. Her nose. Her cheeks.

Thank you, Ana.

She's crying. I kiss the tracks of her tears while I cup her face. "I love you, Mrs. Grey," I whisper. "Even though you make me so mad—I feel so alive with you."

She's exhausted—listless in my arms—so I lay her down on the bed and ease out of her. "No," she mumbles, feeling the loss of contact, I think.

Oh, baby.

You're so done.

From the nightstand I grab the key and release her from each of the cuffs, rubbing her wrists and ankles as I do. I lay down beside her as she stretches out her legs, and wrap her in my arms. She sighs, a small, satisfied smile on her lips, and her breathing slows. She's gone to sleep. I kiss her hair and cover us both.

Boy, that was intense for me, too.

Ana. What you do to me.

I WAKE FIFTEEN MINUTES later from my doze. Ana is still in my arms, sleeping soundly. I kiss her forehead, untangle myself from her limbs, and get up to use the bathroom. She's still out for the count when I return from my shower. I dress quickly, unlock the cabin door, and head up on deck to find the captain to discuss staying on board this evening.

She's still asleep when I return. I put away the cuffs and grab my laptop to check through my e-mails, and also check on the brownfield sites in Detroit, just to make sure that I made the correct call with Ros earlier.

On deck and around the boat, the crew ready the *Fair Lady.* I hear the loud clanking of the anchor as it's winched on board and the distant rumble of the engines as they're fired up. We're setting sail.

DUSK HAS BEEN AND gone and it's dark outside when Ana stirs.

"Hi," I murmur, eager to see her. *I've missed you while you were sleeping.*

"Hi." Her voice is hesitant, and she pulls the cover up to her chin. *Has she gone all shy on me?*

"How long have I been asleep?" she asks.

"Just an hour or so."

"We're moving?"

"I figured since we ate out last night, and went to the ballet and the casino, that we'd dine on board tonight. A quiet night à deux."

She grins—relieved, I think, to be spending the evening on board. "Where are we going?"

"Cannes."

"Okay." She stretches out beside me, then gets up, grabs her robe, and slips it on.

Shit.

She has a few love-bites. It's what I planned, but now, seeing the purple blotches on her skin, I'm not so sure it was a good idea.

This could go either way.

She ambles into the en suite bathroom and closes the door.

Hours. Minutes. Seconds. I don't know how long she's in there, but it takes forever. Eventually, she appears, but deliberately—it seems—she avoids eye contact with me as she darts into the closet.

This does not look good.

Maybe she's just tired.

I wait. Again.

She's in there for too long.

I can't bear it. "Anastasia, are you okay?"

No answer.

Damn.

Suddenly, she bursts out of the closet, a blur of arms and hair, and hurls a hairbrush at me. *Shit.* I raise my arm in time to protect my head, and the hairbrush smacks me below my wrist. Ana storms out of the room and slams the cabin door.

Fuck.

She's not impressed.

I don't think I've ever seen her this mad. Not even over the vows, when she threatened to cancel the wedding.

Grey, what have you done?

My good humor evaporates, replaced by an anxiety I've not felt since before we got married. Warily, I get up, dump my laptop on the nightstand, and go in search of my furious wife.

She's leaning on the rail at the bow, staring at the distant shore. It's a beautiful evening and the *Fair Lady*, like the Queen of the Seas that she is, coasts effortlessly over the Mediterranean.

Ana looks desolate. It's chastening.

"You're mad at me," I whisper.

"No shit, Sherlock!" she hisses, but she doesn't turn to look at me.

"How mad?"

"Scale of one to ten, I think I'm at fifty. Apt, huh?"

Wow. "That mad."

"Yes. Pushed-to-violence mad," she seethes. Finally, she looks at me, her expression raw and angry…and I know she sees me. Sees me for who I am. *You are one fucked-up son of a bitch.* Her recrimination from months ago echoes in my head.

Hell. It's been weeks since I've felt as shitty as this.

Flynn's words float back to me: *communicate and compromise.*

Ana takes a deep breath and stands taller, squaring her shoulders. "Christian, you have to stop unilaterally trying to bring me to heel. You made your point on the beach. Very effectively, as I recall."

"Well, you won't take your top off again," I grunt, and even to my own ears I sound like a petulant teen.

She glares at me. "I don't like you leaving marks on me. Well, not this many, anyway. It's a hard limit!" She spits at me like a cornered kitten.

"I don't like you taking your clothes off in public. That's a hard limit for me," I counter.

I warned you, Ana.

"I think we've established that," she continues in the same vein. "Look at me!" She tugs down her top, exposing the love-bites I've left on her. I count six. I didn't know my plan would be quite so effective.

But I don't want to fight.

I raise my hands, palms up in surrender. "Okay, I get it."

Maybe I overreacted.

"Good!" she snaps.

I run my hand through my hair, feeling helpless.

I'm lost. What more can I do? "I'm sorry. Please don't be mad at me." *I don't want to fight. Ana. Please.*

"You are such an adolescent sometimes." Ana shakes her head, but she sounds more resigned than forthright. I take a step forward and tuck a loose tendril behind her ear.

"I know, I have a lot to learn."

"We both do." She sighs and slowly raises her hand and places it over my heart.

Ana.

I place my hand over hers and give her an apologetic smile. "I've just learned that you've got a good arm and a good aim, Mrs. Grey. I would never have figured that, but then I constantly underestimate you. You always surprise me."

Her lips form a half smile and she arches a brow. "Target practice with Ray. I can throw and shoot straight, Mr. Grey, and you'd do well to remember that."

"I will endeavor to do that or ensure that all potential projectile objects are nailed down and that you don't have access to a gun."

She narrows her eyes. "I'm resourceful."

Oh, Ana. I don't doubt it. "That you are," I whisper, and releasing her hand, I fold her into my arms. Her hands move over my back and she returns my embrace. I plant my nose in her hair, inhaling her soothing scent. "Am I forgiven?" I ask, quietly.

"Am I?"

"Yes," I respond.

"Ditto."

We stand at the bow, the French Riviera passing us by, and we just…*are.*

For a moment, it's the best feeling in the world.

"Hungry?" I ask.

"Yes. Famished. All the, um, activity has given me an appetite. But I'm not dressed for dinner."

"You look good to me, Anastasia. Besides, it's our boat for the week. We can dress how we like. Think of it as dress-down Tuesday on the Côte d'Azur. Anyway, I thought we'd eat on deck."

"Yes, I'd like that."

I reach under her chin and raise her lips to mine and kiss her. Slowly. Gently.

Forgive me, Ana.

She smiles and together we walk hand in hand back to where our dinner awaits.

"**WHY DO YOU ALWAYS** braid my hair?" Ana asks as I'm about to tuck into my crème brûlée.

I frown, because the answer's obvious. "I don't want your hair catching in anything." *I've always done it. Hair and toys don't mix.* "Habit, I think, I add. And from nowhere a vision of a young woman singing an eighties pop song as she brushes out her long dark hair comes to mind. She turns and smiles at me, the dust motes circling in the air around her.

Hey, Maggot. Do you want to brush my hair?

And I'm back in a godforsaken slum in Detroit, a lifetime ago. Ana caresses my chin and runs a finger across my lips, bringing me back to the *Fair Lady.*

Why is the crack whore haunting me now?

"It doesn't matter," Ana whispers. "I don't need to know. I was just curious." She smiles and leans forward to kiss the corner of my lips. "I love you," she whispers. "I'll always love you, Christian."

"And I you." I'm thankful that she's here to drag me back from the dark abyss of my early childhood.

"In spite of my disobedience?" She smirks, immediately lightening the mood.

I chuckle, feeling better. "Because of your disobedience, Anastasia."

She bashes the caramelized sugar of her dessert with her spoon and scoops up a mouthful, and all thoughts of the crack whore fade.

ONCE REBECCA HAS CLEARED our plates, I offer Ana more rosé. She looks past me to check we're alone, then leans toward me with a conspiratorial air. "What's with the no-going-to-the-bathroom thing?" she asks.

Always curious. "You really want to know?"

"Do I?"

I smile. "The fuller your bladder, the more intense your orgasm, Ana."

"Oh. I see." A sweet blush colors her cheeks, and I know she's embarrassed.

Don't be, baby.

"Yes. Well…" She takes a swift gulp of wine.

"What do you want to do for the rest of the evening?" I ask, to move us on to a more comfortable topic. She raises her right shoulder in a shrug, a suggestive shrug, I think.

Again, Ana?

And I know I could make up for my transgression in bed. But I want more. "I know what I want to do." I pick up my glass of wine and stand, holding out my hand to her. "Come."

We move to the main salon and I guide her to the dresser, where my iPod is plugged into an impressive speaker. I select a song, something sweet and romantic for my girl. "Dance with me," I ask, and sweep her into my arms.

"If you insist."

"I insist, Mrs. Grey."

Michael Bublé is singing the Lou Rawls classic "You'll Never Find Another Love Like Mine."

We start to move, Ana following my lead. I dip her low and she giggles. I right her, then spin her around beneath my arm. She laughs. "You dance so well." Her voice is a little husky. "It's like I can dance."

I love dancing with you, baby.

Elena flits, unwelcome, into my mind, and while I'm grateful to her for teaching me to dance, I'm not happy that she's in my head.

Don't go there, Grey.

She's history.

Let's just enjoy this.

I dip Ana again, then kiss her when she's upright once more.

"I'd miss your love," she whispers, echoing the lyrics.

"I'd more than miss your love," I respond, and sing the next few lines softly in her ear. The song fades and we stop moving, and just gaze at each other.

I watch as her pupils grow larger and darker.

It's magic. Our special alchemy bubbling between us.

"Come to bed with me," I beg her.

Her coy smile brightens her face, and she places her hand on my heart. Beneath my chest, it starts hammering with my love for her—my wife—a beautiful woman who knows how to forgive me.

Wednesday, August 17, 2011

Mommy is pretty today. She laughs as she sits on her bed. It is sunny and lots of little dots float in the air around her like she's a princess. *Hey, Maggot, brush my hair.* I pull the brush through her long hair. It is hard for me because of tangles. But Mommy likes it. She sings. *What's love got to do, got to do with it.* She smiles her special smile. It is her smile for me. Only me. She shakes her hair so it is silky down her back. I stroke it. It smells of clean. She splits it into three snakes. And then she ties them together to make one bumpy snake. *There, it's out of the way, Maggot.* She picks up her hairbrush. And she brushes my hair. No! Mommy. It hurts. Too many tangles. *Don't fight, Maggot.* No! Mommy. I try to make her stop. There is a loud noise. A crash. He's back. No! *Where the fuck are you, bitch? Got a friend here. A friend with dough.* Mommy stands and takes my hand and pushes me into her closet. I sit on her shoes. I am quiet. Like a mouse. I cover my ears and close my eyes. If I am small he won't see me. The clothes smell of Mommy. I like the smell. I like being here. Away from him. He is shouting. *Where is the little fucking runt?* He has my hair and he pulls me out of the closet. He waves the hairbrush at Mommy. *Don't want this little prick spoiling the party.* He slaps Mommy hard on her face with her hairbrush. *Put your fucking hooker heels on and make it good for my friend, then you get your fix, bitch.* Mommy looks at me and she has tears. Don't cry, Mommy. Another man comes into the room. A big man with dirty coveralls. Blue coveralls. The big man smiles at Mommy. I am pulled into the other room. He pushes me onto the floor and I hurt my knees. He waves the hairbrush at me. *Now, what am I going to do with you, you piece of shit?* He smells bad. He smells of beer and he is smoking a cigarette.

I wake suddenly, fear clawing at my throat.

Where am I?

Gasping, I suck precious air into my lungs and try to steady my racing heart. It takes me a moment to orient myself.

I'm on the *Fair Lady.* With my fair lady. I look frantically to my right, and Ana is fast asleep in the shadows beside me.

Thank heavens.

I'm immediately calmed, just by the sight of her.

I take a deep, cleansing breath.

Why am I having nightmares?

Arguing with Ana?

I hate fighting with her.

Judging by the light that's seeping through the curtains over the portholes, it's early dawn. I should sleep some more. I cuddle up to Ana, and put my arm around her, breathing in her unique calming fragrance…and I drift.

IT'S MUCH LIGHTER IN the cabin when I wake later, with Ana still slumbering beside me. I watch her for a few moments, enjoying this quiet time.

Will she ever really know what she means to me?

I kiss her hair, get up, and slip on a pair of swim trunks. I'm going for a swim around the boat. Maybe I can shake the unease that lingers.

AS I SHAVE, I'M still rattled by my nightmare.

Why? I don't get it.

I've had these dreams before.

Why am I so hung up on this one, now?

The bathroom door opens and Ana stands before me, a ray of light, and I mute my dark thoughts. "Good morning, Mrs. Grey." I welcome her with a cheery smile.

"Good morning yourself." She grins and leans against the wall, raising her chin, imitating me as I shave under my jaw. From the corner of my eye, I watch her as she mimics my actions.

"Enjoying the show?" I ask.

"One of my all-time favorites."

She's forgiven me.

I lean over and kiss her, grateful that she's with me, and leave a small smudge of shaving foam on her face. "Shall I do this to you again?" I whisper, brandishing my razor, recalling the moment when I shaved her in our suite at Brown's Hotel.

Ana purses her lips. "No. I'll wax next time."

"But that was fun."

You beguiled me, Ana.

"For you maybe." She pouts, but there's a spark of amusement and perhaps carnal appreciation in her eyes.

I see you, Ana.

"I seem to recall the aftermath was very satisfying." I continue shaving, but Ana's gone very quiet. "Hey, I'm just teasing. Isn't that what husbands who are hopelessly in love with their wives do?" I tip her chin up and scrutinize her expression. Perhaps she's still mad at me.

She squares her shoulders.

Uh-oh.

"Sit," she orders.

What?

She splays her hands on my naked chest and pushes me gently toward a stool in the bathroom.

Okay, I'll play. I sit down and she takes my razor.

"Ana," I warn. But she ignores me and leans down and kisses me.

"Head back," she says against my lips.

When I hesitate, she cocks her head to one side. "Tit for tat, Mr. Grey." And I know she's provoking me. How can I walk away from a challenge when my wife never does?

"You know what you're doing?" I ask.

She shakes her head.

Well, what's she going to do, Grey?

Slit my throat?

Taking a deep breath, I close my eyes and raise my chin, offering myself to her. She slides her fingers into my hair and grips hard while I scrunch my eyes tighter. She's standing so close to me. I can smell her. Sea. Sunshine. Sex. Sweetness. Ana.

It's heady.

With the utmost tenderness she glides my razor from my neck to my chin, shaving me. I release the breath I was holding.

"Did you think I was going to hurt you?" I hear the tremor in her voice.

"I never know what you're going to do, Ana, but no—not intentionally."

Sliding the razor across my skin again, she says quietly, "I would never intentionally hurt you, Christian." She sounds so sincere. Opening my eyes, I curl my arms around her as she shaves my cheek.

"I know," I whisper.

She hurt me when she left, that one time.

And I deserved it. I hurt her.

You are one fucked-up son of a bitch!

Grey, don't go there.

I angle my cheek, making it easier for her to finish the job, and two strokes of the razor later, she's completed her work. "All done, and not a drop of blood spilled." She beams at me.

I run my hands up her leg and ease her onto my lap until she's sitting astride me. "Can I take you somewhere today?"

"No sunbathing?" Ana's tone is disingenuous, but I ignore it.

"No. No sunbathing today. I thought you might prefer something else."

"Well, since you've covered me in hickeys and effectively put the kibosh on that, sure, why not?"

Hickeys? We're not in high school!

"You never really had an adolescence—emotionally speaking. I think you're experiencing it now."

Hell.

Ignoring Flynn's words and Ana's reference to my bad behavior, I continue, "It's a drive, but it's worth a visit, from what I've read. My dad recommended we visit. It's a hilltop village called

Saint-Paul-de-Vence. There are some galleries there. I thought we could pick out some paintings or sculptures for the new house, if we find anything we like."

She presses her lips together and leans back to study me.

"What?" I ask, alarmed at her expression.

"I know nothing about art, Christian."

I shrug. "We'll buy only what we like. This isn't about investment."

She looks a little less alarmed, but preoccupied nevertheless.

"What?" I ask again. "Look, I know we only got the architect's drawings the other day—but there's no harm in looking, and the town is an ancient, medieval place."

Her expression remains the same.

"What now?" I ask. *Fuck, Ana. Are you still angry about yesterday?*

She shakes her head.

"Tell me," I beg, but she gives nothing away. "You're not still mad about what I did yesterday?" I can't look her in the eye; instead, I bow my head and nuzzle between her breasts.

"No. I'm hungry," she says.

"Why didn't you say?" I ease her off my lap.

ANA AND I FALL under Saint-Paul-de-Vence's spell. We wander the narrow, cobbled streets, breathing in the Gallic wonder of it all, followed from a discreet distance by Taylor and Philippe Ferreux. Ana is tucked under my arm, where she fits perfectly. "How did you know about this place?" she asks.

"Dad e-mailed me when we were in London. He and Mom came here back in the day."

"It's beautiful." Ana waves her hand in homage to our spectacular surroundings.

We stop at a small gallery with some striking abstract art in the window and decide to venture in. I'm taken by some erotic photographs that are on display inside. They're beautifully composed. "Not quite what I had in mind," Ana says, her tone wry.

I grin down at her. "Me neither." My hand finds hers as we study some still-life paintings, all vegetables and fruit. They're good.

"I like those." Ana points to some peppers. "They remind me

of you chopping vegetables in my apartment." She giggles, her eyes alive with mischief and memories—of our reconciliation—maybe?

"I thought I managed that quite competently. I was just a bit slow, and anyway"—I embrace her and nuzzle her ear—"you were distracting me. Where would you put them?"

Ana gasps, distracted by my teasing lips. "What?"

"The paintings—where would you put them?" I graze her earlobe with my teeth.

"Kitchen," she breathes.

"Hmm. Nice idea, Mrs. Grey."

"They're really expensive!"

"So?" I kiss the spot behind her ear. "Get used to it, Ana." I release her and approach the sales assistant to purchase all three of the paintings and give her my credit card and our address in Escala for shipping.

"Merci, monsieur," she simpers, with a flirtatious smile.

Sweetheart, I'm married.

I raise my left hand to stroke my chin, making my ring obvious, then return to Ana, who is looking at the nudes.

"Changed your mind?" I ask.

She laughs. "No. They're good, though. And the photographer's female."

I cast my eye over them again. One catches my attention: a woman kneels up on a chair, her back to the camera. She's naked, except for hooker heels, her long, dark hair loose. A memory I don't want stirs in the back of my mind and I'm reminded of the bleak black-and-white photo on my bulletin board.

The crack whore.

Fuck.

I look away and take Ana's hand. "Let's go. Are you hungry?"

"Sure," she says with an uncertain look as I open the door and step out into the fresh air. I'm grateful to get back outside where I can breathe again.

What the hell is wrong with me?

PROTECTED FROM THE FIERCE Mediterranean sun, we sit beneath bright red parasols on an archaic stone terrace at a hotel restaurant. We're surrounded by geraniums and ancient ivied walls. It really is stunning. The food is off the charts, too. Damn, but the French can cook. I hope Mia's learned some of these skills. I'll have to persuade her to make dinner for us someday.

When I pay the check, I give the waiter a hefty tip.

Ana is sipping coffee, admiring the view. She's been quiet, and I wonder once more what she's thinking about.

Yesterday?

I shift in my seat.

I'm still trying to shake off my nightmare. Fragments keep haunting me and it's unsettling. I'm reminded of Ana's question yesterday evening about braids. Did it stir something from my subconscious?

Communicate and compromise. Flynn's words circle my brain.

Maybe I should talk to Ana. Tell her the truth. Perhaps that's why I'm getting these vivid flashbacks. I take a deep breath. "You asked me why I braid your hair."

Ana looks up, expectant. "Yes."

"The crack whore used to let me play with her hair, I think. I don't know if it's a memory or a dream."

Ana blinks, in that way she does when she's processing information, but her eyes are wide and clear, and all I see in them is her compassion. "I like it when you play with my hair," she says, but her voice wavers, and I think she's just trying to reassure me.

"Do you?"

"Yes!" The vehemence in her tone surprises me. She clasps my hand. "I think you loved your birth mother, Christian."

Time stills, and it's like she's knocked all the air out of my lungs.

I'm in free-fall.

Why does she say shit like this?

She says she doesn't want to hurt me.

And yet…

My eyes stay glued to hers, because in spite of what she's just said, Ana's my life raft, and I'm drowning in a wave of uncertainty that I don't understand or know how to process.

I can't do this.

I don't want to think about the past.

It's been. It's done.

It's too painful.

My gaze drifts to her hand in mine and to the red mark around her wrist. It's a stark reminder of what I did to her yesterday.

I hurt her.

"Say something," she whispers.

I need to get out of here. "Let's go."

In the street, feeling adrift and unsure of myself, I reach for her hand once more. "Where do you want to go?" I ask, but it's more to distract myself from what's hovering at the edge of my memory. Whatever it is, it's dredging up these unwanted and unsettling… feelings.

She smiles. "I'm just glad you're still speaking to me."

Only just! You mentioned "love" and the crack whore in the same sentence.

"You know I don't like talking about all that shit. It's done. Finished."

I'm expecting her to sulk or berate me, but as I watch a kaleidoscope of emotions cross her face, what settles in her gaze is love.

Her love.

For me.

I think.

All the wrongs right themselves, and my world spins on its proper axis once more. I fold my arm around her and she slips her hand into my back pocket, her palm against my ass. It's a possessive gesture, and I live for it.

We walk down one of the cobbled streets, stalked by our security, when a fine jeweler's store catches my eye. We pause outside, and I have a sudden urge to buy Ana a piece. Grasping her free hand, I rub my thumb along the red wheal left by the handcuff yesterday. "It's not sore," Ana says, correctly interpreting my look of concern. I shift so Ana has no choice but to take her other hand out of my pocket. Around *that* wrist, she's wearing my wedding gift to her, which I purchased in the crazy rush to buy our rings from Astoria Fine Jewelry. It's a white gold Omega De Ville with diamonds; I had it inscribed.

Anastasia
You Are My More
My Love, My Life
Christian

And that was never truer than now.

Yet beneath the strap lies a red mark.

That I gave her.

And all those hickeys, too.

Because I was pissed at her.

Damn. Releasing her, I gently grasp her chin and raise her eyes to mine. She stares back at me, as guileless as ever, and with the same look of love.

"They don't hurt," she whispers, and I take her hand again, and plant a soft kiss on her wrist.

I'm sorry, Ana.

"Come." We head into the shop because there's a Chanel bracelet that's caught my eye in the window. Once inside, I waste no time and purchase it. I know if I ask Ana, she'll politely refuse. It's pretty—white gold with small diamonds—and it'll look lovely on her.

"Here." I fasten it around her wrist. It covers the red line. "There, that's better," I mutter.

"Better?" Her brow creases a little.

"You know why."

"I don't need this." She rotates her wrist and the diamonds on the bracelet sparkle in the sunlight, throwing little rainbows around the store.

"*I* do," I whisper.

It's an apology. I just don't know how to do this, Ana.

"No, Christian, you don't. You've given me so much already. A magical honeymoon, London, Paris, the Côte d'Azur, and you. I'm a very lucky girl."

"No, Anastasia, I'm a very lucky man."

"Thank you." She stretches up and puts her arms around my neck and kisses me, properly. In front of everyone.

Oh, baby.

I love you.

"Come. We should head back," I murmur against her lips. She slips her hand into my back pocket again, and together we make our way back to the car.

THE MERCEDES CRUISES BACK to Cannes. Taylor is in the passenger seat up front and Ferreux is driving, but we're hampered by the traffic. I stare out of the window, trying to figure out why I'm so agitated.

It can't have just been my dream.

My argument with Ana, yesterday?

The fact that I've marked her?

I don't understand why this feels so weird. I've marked women before. Not permanently. *Fuck, no. Never!* That's not my scene. Two of my submissives hated it, so that was fine, and I didn't do it. And, of course, I never marked Elena. That was impossible. She was married. And then there was Susannah. She loved that shit. Whenever she was marked, she liked me to photograph her.

Ana grips my hand, distracting me from my thoughts. She's wearing a short skirt that exposes her legs. I look across at her and caress her knee. She has such lovely legs.

Her ankles!

They're probably marked, too.

Shit.

Reaching down, I grasp her ankle and gently ease her foot onto my lap. She swivels in her seat and faces me. "I want the other one, too." I need to see for myself. She looks toward Taylor and Ferreux.

She's shy?

What does she think I'm going to do?

I press the privacy screen button and it slowly rises out of the panel in front of us until we're partitioned off from them. "I want to look at your ankles."

She frowns and places her other foot in my lap. I skim my thumb up her instep and she squirms.

She's ticklish. I don't know why I haven't registered this before.

I undo the strap on her sandal. And there it is. Another mark. Darker than those on her wrists. "Doesn't hurt," she says.

I'm an inconsiderate asshole.

I massage the line in the hope that it will disappear, and look back out of the window at the passing countryside. She wriggles her foot, and her sandal falls into the footwell. But I ignore it.

"Hey. What did you expect?" she asks.

She's gazing at me as if I've beamed down from Mars.

I shrug. "I didn't expect to feel like I do looking at these marks."

"How do you feel?"

Shitty.

"Uncomfortable," I mutter.

And I don't really know why.

Suddenly she unbuckles her seat belt and scoots closer to me and grabs both of my hands. "It's the hickeys I don't like," she hisses. "Everything else…what you did"—her voice drops lower—"with the handcuffs, I enjoyed that. Well, more than enjoyed. It was mind-blowing. You can do that to me again anytime."

Oh.

"Mind-blowing?" Her words are a small boost to my mood and my libido.

"Yes." She grins and curls her toes around my more-than-interested dick.

"You should really be wearing your seat belt, Mrs. Grey."

She teases me with her toes once more.

I glance at the glass. Could we…? But my lascivious thoughts are interrupted by my phone vibrating. *Shit.* I remove it from my shirt pocket.

It's work. I check my watch. It's early in Seattle.

"Barney," I answer, while Ana tries to withdraw her feet from the close proximity of my dick. I tighten my hold on her feet.

"Mr. Grey. There's been a fire in the server room."

What? "In the server room?" *How the hell did that happen?*

"Yes, sir."

The servers? Fuck! "Did it activate the fire-suppression system?"

Ana removes her feet from my lap, and this time I let her.

"Yes, sir. It did."

I hit the button to lower the privacy glass so Taylor can hear me. "Anyone injured?"

"No, sir," Barney responds.

"Damage?"

"Very little, from what I've been told."

"I see."

"Security were quick to call."

"When?" I glance at my watch again.

"Just now. The fire's out, but they want to know if we should call the fire department."

"No, not the fire department or the police. Not yet anyway."

I need to think.

"Welch has just called me on the other line," Barney says.

"Has he?"

"He's probably trying to get ahold of you. I'll text him."

"Good."

"I'm heading to Grey House now."

"Okay. I want a detailed damage report. And a complete rundown of everyone who had access over the last five days, including the cleaning staff."

"Yes, sir."

"Get ahold of Andrea and get her to call me."

"Will do. It was a good move to change from the outdated suppression system," Barney says as he blows out a breath.

"Yeah, sounds like the argon is just as effective, worth its weight in gold."

"Yes, sir."

"I realize it's early."

"I was awake. There'll be no traffic now," Barney continues. "I'll be there in no time. And I'll see what's up."

"E-mail me in two hours."

"I hope you don't mind that I called."

"No, I need to know. Thank you for calling me." I hang up and call Welch, who is heading to Grey House as we speak. During a brief exchange, we agree to increase security at the off-site data center as a precaution, and that we'll talk in an hour. When I end my call with him, I direct Philippe to get us back on board as soon as possible.

"Monsieur." Ferreux speeds up.

I wonder what could have gone wrong in the server room? An electrical fault? Something overheated? Arson?

Ana looks wary. "Anyone hurt?" she asks.

I shake my head. "Very little damage." Though I haven't had a damage report, I want to reassure her. Reaching over, I take her hand and give it a comforting squeeze. "Don't worry about this. My team is on it."

"Where was the fire?"

"Server room."

"Grey House?"

"Yes."

"Why so little damage?"

"The server room is fitted with a state-of-the-art fire-suppression system. Ana, please, don't worry."

"I'm not worried," she whispers, but I'm not convinced.

"We don't know for sure that it was arson." And that's my biggest fear.

I'M IN THE SMALL study aboard *Fair Lady.* Welch and Barney are at GEH and Andrea is making her way into the office early. Now that Welch has inspected the damage, he's advised that we get the fire department in so an expert can establish what started the fire. He doesn't want a stream of people in the server room contaminating any evidence. We run through a list of protocols, and as I feared, he's not ruling out arson. He's compiling lists of everyone who has had access to the server room in advance of the fire department's report.

Andrea calls when she arrives at the office and I pace the floor as I talk her through what's happened. I'm leaning against the desk when there's a knock on the door. It's my wife. "Andrea, hold please."

Ana's expression is one of determination—it's a look I know well, the one she wears when we're going to fight. My shoulders tense in preparation for a showdown. "I'm going shopping. I'll take security with me," she says with a too-bright smile.

Is that it? "Sure, take one of the twins and Taylor, too," I reply. She doesn't leave. "Anything else?"

"Can I get you anything?"

"No, baby, I'm good. The crew will look after me."

"Okay." She hesitates, then strides toward me, places her hands on my chest, and gives me a quick peck on my lips.

"Andrea, I'll call you back."

"Yes, Mr. Grey," Andrea says, and I'm sure she's smiling on the other end of the phone. Hanging up, I place my phone on the desk, pull Ana into my arms, and kiss her. Properly. Her mouth is sweet and wet and warm, and a welcome diversion. She's breathless when I stop. "You're distracting me," I whisper, staring down into dazed eyes. "I need to sort this out, so I can get back to my honeymoon." I run my finger down her cheek and clasp her chin.

"Okay. I'm sorry."

"Please don't apologize, Mrs. Grey. I love your distractions." I kiss the corner of her mouth. "Go spend some money." I step back, letting her go.

"Will do." With a girlish smile, she sashays to the door and is gone, though there's something about her demeanor that makes me pause.

What isn't she telling me?

Dismissing the thought, I call Andrea back.

"Mr. Grey, while I have you on the phone, Ros mentioned that you might go to New York next week. If so, I wanted to remind you that the Telecommunications Alliance Organization fundraiser is on Thursday in Manhattan. They really want you there."

"That trip's not definite. But let them know that I'm considering their invitation, and if I accept it, it will be for two. We might want to think about any other meetings I could do in New York while I'm there."

"Yes, sir."

"I think that's all for now. Can you put me through to Ros?"

"Will do."

I update Ros and ask her to liaise with Barney and Welch.

From somewhere close to the yacht, the sound of a Jet Ski starting up sidetracks me. It stalls. It starts and stalls again. I peer through the windows on the starboard side and Ana is on one of the Jet Skis. Fully clothed.

I thought she was going shopping.

"Ros. I'll call you back!" I hang up and scramble out of the study to the starboard walkway, but she's gone. I dash around to the port side, and Ana's tearing across the water on the Jet Ski with the tender in hot pursuit. She waves at me.

No. Ana! Don't let go. My heart leaps into my mouth.

Hesitantly, I raise my hand and wave back.

This was her plan?

I watch as she races toward the marina with the tender in her wake. I pull out my phone and call Taylor.

"Sir."

"What the hell are you and Anastasia playing at!" I shout.

"Mr. Grey, Mrs. Grey wanted to try the Jet Ski."

"But she could fall. Drown—fuck!" Words fail me.

"She's quite competent on it, sir."

"For fuck's sake, don't let her come back on it!"

I hear Taylor's sigh. But I don't give a fuck. "Yes, sir."

"Thank you!" I press end call.

In the salon, I find the binoculars and watch as Ana pulls up beside the tender. Taylor helps her in, then onto the dock.

I call her number and watch as she fumbles in her purse for her phone.

"Hi," she answers, a little breathlessly.

"Hi."

"I'll come back on the boat. Don't be mad."

Oh. I'm expecting a fight. "Um."

"It was fun, though," she whispers, sounding exhilarated. And I see her once more in my head, flying past the boat, the wind in her hair and a huge smile on her face.

I sigh. "Well, far be it for me to curtail your fun, Mrs. Grey. Just be careful. Please."

"I will. Anything you want from town?"

"Just you, back in one piece."

"I'll do my best to comply, Mr. Grey."

"I'm glad to hear it, Mrs. Grey."

"We aim to please." She giggles, and the sweet sound makes me smile. My phone beeps.

"I have another call. Laters, baby."

"Laters, Christian."

I hang up and Grace is on the line. "Hello, darling, how are you?"

"I'm good, Mom."

"I'm just calling to check that you're all okay."

"Why wouldn't I be okay?" *Shit. Maybe she knows.* "Are you calling about the fire?"

"What fire?" she asks, suddenly terse.

"It's nothing, Mother."

"What. Fire. Christian." Her tone is intimidating.

Sighing, I quickly fill her in on what's happened at Grey House, sparing no details. "Mom, it's no big deal. No damage." The last thing I want to do is worry Grace.

"Will you come home?"

"I don't see any reason to cut my honeymoon short. The fire was contained and hasn't done any damage."

She's quiet for a moment.

"Grace. It's okay."

She sighs. "If you say so, darling. How is your honeymoon going?"

"Well, up until this incident—it's been wonderful. Ana loves London and Paris and the yacht, she's yar."

"Sounds heavenly. Did you go to Saint-Paul-de-Vence?"

"We did. Today. It was magical."

"I fell in love with the place. I won't keep you, I know you'll have a lot to think about and do. The reason I called was to invite you and Ana to lunch on Sunday, when you're home."

"Sure. That sounds great."

"Lovely. See you then. And, Christian, remember, we love you."

"Yes, Mom. Thanks for the call."

WHEN I HANG UP there's an e-mail from Ana.

From: Anastasia Grey
Subject: Thank You
Date: August 17 2011 16:55
To: Christian Grey

For not being too grouchy.
Your loving wife
xxx

I type back.

From: Christian Grey
Subject: Trying to Stay Calm
Date: August 17 2011 16:59
To: Anastasia Grey

You're welcome.
Come back in one piece.
This is not a request.
x

Christian Grey
CEO & Overprotective Husband, Grey Enterprises Holdings, Inc.

A COUPLE OF HOURS later, I'm sitting at the small desk in the study and I get the call I've been dreading. "It's arson," Welch says.

"Fuck." My heart sinks.

Who the hell is doing this to me? What do they want?

"Exactly. A small incendiary device was placed beside one of the server cabinets. Interestingly, it was designed to set off smoke, but that's it. I think it's a warning."

A *warning?*

"Any idea when it was placed?" I ask.

"We don't have that information, yet. We've already doubled security. I'll post a guard 24/7 outside the server room. I know it's the lifeblood of the company."

"Good idea."

"Will you come back early?"

"Do I need to?" I don't want to end our honeymoon.

"No. I don't think so. I think the biggest question for me right now is if this is linked to your EC135."

"Let's assume it is. That's the worst-case scenario."

"Yes. I think that's prudent," Welch responds.

"There's nothing I can achieve there that I can't do here. Besides, I think we're safer on the boat."

"There's that," he agrees, then pauses. "I know all our leads for a potential suspect have led to nothing. But we'll double-check all the footage in and around Grey House. We will find this person."

"Do. Nail the prick."

"The police forensics team are in the server room right now, dusting for prints."

"I bet Barney's thrilled about that."

Welch's laugh is wry. "He's not."

"Goddamn it, this is frustrating," I mutter into the phone.

"I know, Christian. The EC135 was dusted for prints by the FBI a few weeks ago. We're still waiting to see if that yields a suspect. Eurocopter have the helicopter now. They're assessing the damage to see if it can be repaired."

"Okay."

"I'll call if there's an update."

"Thank you." I hang up and stare at the coastline, where the city lights of Cannes are beginning to wake and welcome the dusk.

What the hell am I going to do?

What have I done to deserve this?

Grey, don't go there.

The tender is being craned onto the bridge deck, which means Ana must have returned.

Ana. My girl.

She might get caught in this crossfire. I put my head in my hands in an attempt to drive the image of Ana lying unmoving on the floor from my psyche.

If anything happened to her…

The thought is torture. I need to see that she's back in one piece. Now.

Quelling my morbid thoughts, I go in search of her. Stopping outside the master cabin door, I take a deep breath to calm my anxiety, and step inside. Ana is sitting on the bed with a parcel beside her. "You were gone some time."

Startled, she looks up and eyes me warily. "Everything in control at your office?"

"More or less." I don't tell her more; I don't want to worry her.

"I did a little shopping," she says with a sweet smile.

"What did you buy?"

"This." She places her foot on the bed, and around her ankle there's a silver ankle chain.

"Very nice." I run my fingers over the little bells that hang from the chain. They have a sweet, delicate chime, but the chain doesn't hide the faint red line from the cuff yesterday.

The mark I left on her.

Hell.

"And this." She holds out a wrapped gift box, a little too eagerly—to distract me, I think. Of course, she's bought me something, and my mood switches to curious delight.

"For me?" The package is surprisingly heavy. Sitting down beside her, I give it a quick shake. Grinning, I clasp her chin and kiss her. "Thank you."

"You haven't opened it yet."

"I'll love it, whatever it is. I don't get many presents."

"It's hard to buy you things. You have everything."

"I have you."

"You do." She smiles.

I unwrap the paper to find a digital SLR camera. "A Nikon?"

"I know you have your compact digital camera, but this is for… portraits and the like. It comes with two lenses."

Portraits?

Where is she going with this?

My anxiety returns in full force, prickling my scalp.

"Today in the gallery you liked the Florence D'elle photographs. And I remember what you said in the Louvre. And, of course, there were those other photographs." Her voice drops.

Oh good God. I don't want to talk about them!

"I thought you might, um, like to take pictures of me."

"Pictures? Of you?"

She nods, blinking, her uncertainty obvious, and I examine the box, playing for time. It's a state-of-the-art camera, a thoughtful gift from my thoughtful wife, but it makes me uncomfortable. Really uncomfortable

Why does she think I want to photograph her naked?

That isn't my life anymore.

I look up at her. "Why do you think I want this?" I whisper.

A frisson of alarm crosses her face. "Don't you?" she asks.

No, Ana. You've got this all wrong.

Suddenly, I see it clearly: my old life and my new one careening together like a car crash and inflicting untold damage. Those photographs were fundamentally to protect me—to protect my position and my family. I have to make her understand that I don't need this from her...but I don't want to hurt her feelings.

Try the truth, Grey. Communicate.

"For me, photos like those have usually been an insurance policy, Ana."

And for your pleasure, Grey. Yes. It felt intimate, but deep down I knew I was safe viewing my subject through a lens. I was always at a remove; the camera put a wall between me and my sub, even though it was a thrill to capture them in the most intimate poses.

Fuck. Shame washes over me, and I'm in the confessional spilling my darkest secrets. "I know I've objectified women for so long."

Ana tucks her hair behind her ear, and looks as confounded as I feel. "And you think taking pictures of me is objectifying me?" she whispers.

I close my eyes. *What is happening here?*

Why wouldn't I do this with her?

"I'm so confused," I murmur.

"Why do you say that?" she asks gently.

Opening my eyes, I look down at her wrist, which still bears the marks that I left on her. I'm trying to protect her from my old life. And this is what I do?

How can I keep her safe, when I can't even keep her safe from me?

"Christian, these don't matter." She holds up her hand so the welt is on show. "You gave me a safe word. Shit—yesterday was fun. I enjoyed it. Stop brooding about it. I like rough sex, I've told you that before." She sounds panicked. "Is this about the fire? Do you think it's connected somehow to *Charlie Tango*? Is this why you're worried? Talk to me, Christian, please."

Don't frighten her further, Grey.

She frowns. "Don't overthink this, Christian." She reaches for the box, opens it, and removes the camera. Switching it on, she takes the lens cap off, and raises the Nikon to her face, pointing it at me.

I loathe having my photograph taken. The last time I did it willingly was at the wedding, and before that it was for her, not so long ago, at The Heathman. That was before my life changed irrevocably. Before I knew her. She presses the button and holds it, taking a burst of photographs.

"I'll objectify you, then," she mutters. And once more I know she's laughing at me, and not putting up with my bullshit. She edges closer, still looking at me through the lens. One, two, three, she takes several photos. She pokes her tongue between her teeth as she snaps each one, but I know she's unaware that she's doing it and I'm beguiled. She smiles and captures my answering smile.

Only you, Ana.

Only you can drag me back into the light.

I pose for her, pursing my lips in an exaggerated fashion.

Her grin broadens and she giggles, and it's such a wonderful sound.

"I thought it was *my* present," I grumble.

"Well, it was supposed to be fun, but apparently, it's a symbol of women's oppression." She takes more photographs.

She's laughing at me!

Game on, Ana.

"You want to be oppressed?" A delightful vision of her kneeling in front of me, hands tied while she services my cock, forms in my mind.

"Not oppressed. No," she whispers, continuing to take photographs.

"I could oppress you big-time, Mrs. Grey."

"I know you can, Mr. Grey. And you do, frequently."

Oh. Fuck. She's serious!

She lowers the camera and stares at me. "What's wrong, Christian?"

I just want to keep you safe.

She frowns and lifts the camera to her eye once more. "Tell me," she insists.

Get a grip, Grey.

I damp down my feelings. I can't deal with them right now. "Nothing," I answer, and drop out of her line of sight, remove the camera box from the bed, and grab Ana, dragging her down onto the comforter and sitting astride her.

"Hey!" she protests, and takes more photographs of me smiling down at her until I take the camera from her and frame her beautiful face in the viewfinder. I press the shutter and capture her loveliness for posterity.

"So, you want me to take pictures of you, Mrs. Grey?" She looks so earnest, through the lens. "Well, for a start, I think you should be laughing." Reaching down, I start to tickle her with my free hand. She squeals and struggles beneath me and I take picture after picture.

This is fun.

She laughs and laughs. "No! Stop!"

"Are you kidding?" I've never tickled anyone, and hers is a particularly gratifying reaction. I put the camera down and use both hands.

"Christian!" she squeals, and thrashes around beneath me. "Christian, stop!" she pleads, and I take pity on her. Grabbing both her hands, I hold them down on either side of her head. She's winded, flushed, her eyes dark, her hair a mess. She's stunning. She takes my breath away.

"You. Are. So. Beautiful," I whisper.

I don't deserve her.

Leaning down, I close my eyes and kiss her. Her lips are soft. Her mouth welcoming. I cradle her head in my hands, my fingers weaving into her hair, and I deepen our kiss, wanting more, wanting to lose myself in her. She responds, her body rising, her hands traveling up my arms and grasping my biceps.

Her response is a torch to my arousal.

No, it's more than that.

I want her, yes, but I *need* her more.

My body stands at attention, hungering for her. She's my life raft, while I'm adrift, trying to make sense of what's happening to me. When I'm with her, in her, all is right with the world. "Oh, what you do to me." I groan, yearning for her. I shift quickly so I'm lying on top of her, feeling her body along the length of mine. My hand skates down to her breast, her waist, her hip, and her behind, squeezing as I go. I kiss her again, pushing my knee between her legs, running my hand down her thigh and hitching her leg over my hip. I grind against her, wanting her. Her fingers are in my hair and she tugs and holds me to her mouth, while I take all I want.

I think I'm going to combust, I want her so badly.

Fuck.

Abruptly, I stop. *I need her. Now.*

Standing, I pull her off the bed and undo her shorts. Kneeling down, I drag them and her panties off, then we're back on the bed with her beneath me. My fingers make light work of my fly and free my impatient dick.

With one move, I'm inside her. Hard. Deep.

"Yes!" I hiss as she cries out.

I still and examine her face. Her eyes are closed, her head tipped back and her mouth open. I swivel my hips and drive myself deeper.

She groans and wraps her arms around me.

"I need you," I growl, and graze my teeth along her jaw, and then I'm kissing her again, taking her mouth and all she has to give while she binds herself to me, wrapping her legs and arms around me. I'm unleashed. My need for her greater than I ever imagined. I want to crawl inside her skin so she can keep me in one piece; keep me whole. She meets me stroke for stroke. Encouraging me with her soft cries of need. Her passion, loud and hot in my ear.

I feel her. She's close. So close. Reaching. With me. As I drive her higher. As she drives me higher.

"Come with me," I rasp, and rear up over her. "Open your eyes. I need to see you." She peers up at me, eyes dazed with longing, and she lets go, tipping her head back and screaming her orgasm for all to hear.

It pushes me over the edge and I climax, driving myself into her and calling out her name. I collapse to the side, bringing her with me, and turn us both so that she's sprawled on top of me. I drag precious air into my lungs while still inside her, holding her tightly.

My beacon. My dream catcher. My love. My life.

Someone wants to kill us. Damn them.

She kisses my chest, soft, sweet kisses. "Tell me, Christian, what's wrong?"

I tighten my hold on her and close my eyes.

I don't want to lose you.

"I give you my solemn vow," she whispers, "to be your faithful partner in sickness and in health, to stand by your side in good times and in bad, to share your joy as well as your sorrow."

I still. She's reciting her vows. I open my eyes. Her face is a picture of sincerity and her love-light shines so bright from her beautiful face. "I promise to love you unconditionally, to support you in your goals and dreams, to honor and respect you, to laugh with you and cry with you, to share my hopes and dreams with you, and bring you solace in times of need. And to cherish you for as long as we both shall live." She sighs, gazing at me and willing me to speak.

"Oh, Ana," I murmur, and move, easing out of her, so that we're lying side by side, lost in each other's eyes. I stroke her face with my knuckles and thumb. From memory, I recite my vows, my voice hoarse as I try to contain my emotion. "I solemnly vow that I will safeguard and hold dear and deep in my heart our union and you. I promise to love you faithfully, forsaking all others, through the good times and the bad, in sickness and in health, regardless of where life takes us. I will protect you, trust you, and respect you. I will share your joys and sorrows and comfort you in times of need. I promise to cherish you and uphold your hopes and dreams and keep you safe at my side. All that is mine is now yours. I give you my hand, my heart, and my love from this moment on for as long as we both shall live."

Tears well in her eyes.

"Don't cry," I whisper, brushing away a stray tear with my thumb.

"Why won't you talk to me? Please, Christian."

I close my eyes.

Talking about it makes it real, Ana.

"I vowed I would bring you solace in times of need. Please don't make me break my vows," she pleads.

I have no defenses against her.

I love her.

Before Ana, I didn't feel *anything*. And now, I feel *everything*. Every emotion is so heightened. It's hard to process. Hard to understand.

Her expression hasn't changed. She's begging me.

I sigh, defeated. "It's arson," I whisper, as if this is a huge failing on my part. "And my biggest worry is that they are after me. And if they are after me—" The next thought is unbearable.

"They might get me," Ana finishes the sentence in a whisper and caresses my face as her eyes soften. "Thank you."

"What for?"

"For telling me."

I shake my head. "You can be very persuasive, Mrs. Grey."

"And you can brood and internalize all your feelings and worry yourself to death. You'll probably die of a heart attack before you're forty, and I want you around far longer than that."

"You'll be the death of me. The sight of you on the Jet Ski—I nearly did have a coronary." I flop back on the bed and cover my eyes with the back of my hand to blot out the memory. But it doesn't work. In my mind, she's lying on the cold, hard floor. I shudder.

"Christian, it's a Jet Ski. Even kids ride Jet Skis. Can you imagine what you'll be like when we visit your place in Aspen and I go skiing for the first time?"

I gasp and turn to look at her, alarmed. *Skiing. No!*

"Our place," I remind her.

She's wearing that smile—the one I stare at every day in my office. Is she laughing at me? No. I don't think so. It's her compassion. "I'm a grown-up, Christian, and much tougher than I look. When are you going to learn this?"

I shrug. She doesn't look tough to me—not when I see her out cold on a sticky green rug.

"So, the fire. Do the police know about the arson?"

"Yes," I respond.

"Good."

"Security is going to get tighter," I tell her.

"I understand." Her eyes sweep down over my body, and suddenly her lips quirk up.

"What?"

"You."

"Me?"

"Yes. You. Still dressed."

"Oh." I glance down. I'm still dressed. I grin when I look back at Ana and let her know how hard it is for me to keep my hands off of her, especially when she's giggling.

Her eyes brighten immediately and she moves quickly, straddling me.

Shit. I grab her wrists, somehow knowing what she's going to do.

"No," I whisper, as the darkness makes an unwelcome return to my chest, ready to claw its way out. I take a deep breath. "Please don't," I plead. "I couldn't bear it. I was never tickled as a child." Ana puts her hands down and I continue, "I used to watch Carrick with Elliot and Mia, tickling them, and it looked like such fun, but I, I—"

She puts her finger on my lips. "Hush, I know." She removes her finger and plants a sweet kiss in its place. Scooting down, she rests her cheek to my chest, and I hold her, pressing my nose into her hair. Her scent is soothing, mixed with the pungent fragrance of sex. We lie for several minutes in our calm after the storm, before she interrupts our quiet, comfortable silence. "What is the longest you've gone without seeing Dr. Flynn?"

"Two weeks. Why? Do you have an incorrigible urge to tickle me?"

"No." She laughs. "I think he helps you."

I snort. "He should. I pay him enough." I stroke her hair and she turns her face to me. "Are you concerned for my well-being, Mrs. Grey?"

"Every good wife is concerned for her beloved husband's well-being, Mr. Grey."

"Beloved?" I whisper, wanting to say the word out loud, to hear it ring between us with all its significance.

"Very much beloved." She leans up to kiss me.

It's a relief that she knows the truth and yet she still loves me. My anxiety has evaporated, replaced by hunger. I smile down at her. "Do you want to go ashore to eat?"

"I want to eat wherever you're happiest."

"Good. Aboard is where I can keep you safe. Thank you for my present." I reach for it and, turning it around, hold it at arm's length and snap a picture of the two of us wrapped around each other.

WE TAKE COFFEE POST-DINNER inside the impressive dining room on the *Fair Lady*. "What are you thinking about?" I ask, as Ana looks wistfully out the window.

"Versailles."

"Ostentatious, wasn't it?"

Ana looks at our surroundings.

"This is hardly ostentatious," I observe.

"I know. It's lovely. The best honeymoon a girl could want."

"Really?" I smile. Pleased.

"Of course it is."

"We only have two more days. Is there anything you'd like to see or do?"

"Just be with you," she says.

I rise and come around the table and drop a kiss on her forehead

"Well, can you do without me for about an hour? I need to check my e-mails, find out what's happening at home."

"Sure," she says.

"Thank you for the camera."

As I head into the study, I notice that for some reason, I'm feeling far more settled. Could it be the delicious dinner, the sex, or telling Ana about the arson? It could be a combination of all those. I pull my phone out of my pocket and notice a missed call from my dad.

"Son," he says when he answers his phone.

"Hi, Dad."

"How's the South of France?"

"It's great."

"And Ana?"

"She's great, too." I can't help my smile.

"You sound happy."

"Yes. The only fly in the ointment is the fire."

"Your mother told me about that. But not much damage, I hear."

"No."

"What's the matter, Christian?" He adopts a serious tone, probably in response to my monosyllabic reply.

"It was arson."

"Shit. Police involved?"

"Yes."

"Good. This and your helicopter. It's a lot to deal with."

"Welch is on it. But we don't have a clue who it might be. Have you noticed anything unusual?"

"No, I can't say that I have. But I'll keep a watchful eye."

"Do," I insist.

"Is the jet safe?" he asks.

"The Gulfstream? Yes. I think so."

"Perhaps you should fly back commercial."

Why?

"It's just a thought. I don't want to worry you. I'll let you go."

"Thanks for checking in, Dad."

"Christian. I'm here for you. Always. Enjoy the rest of your evening." He hangs up, and I wonder what he's going to do with the information I've just given him. I don't dwell on it, but call Ros for an update.

I'M STILL ON THE phone when Ana pops her head around the door later. She blows a kiss at me and leaves me to my conversation with Andrea, who is sorting our flights back to Seattle.

Ana is curled up asleep when I return to our cabin. I slip into bed beside her and pull her into my arms without waking her. I kiss her hair and close my eyes.

I have to keep her safe. I have to keep her safe…

SATURDAY, AUGUST 20, 2011

Through the lens, I watch my wife sleep soundly at last. Earlier, Ana was talking, begging someone in her dreams not to go. I wonder who? Me? Where would I go without her? She's been plagued by nightmares since the arson at Grey House was confirmed. She's even taken to sucking her thumb on the odd occasion while she sleeps. I wonder if it might have been better for us to fly home earlier. But I was reluctant to leave the tranquility of *Fair Lady,* and so was Ana. And at least I've been able to comfort her after her night terrors—hold her. Soothe her. Like she holds me, when I have mine.

We have to catch this asshole.

How dare he, or she, frighten my wife.

I've taken my father's advice and we're flying commercial. It's been a while for me, but Ana has never flown international first class, so it will be a new experience for her. We're leaving out of London, and I've grounded the jet in Nice until it's had a thorough inspection. I'm not taking any chances, not with my crew and not with my wife.

Apart from the nightmares, the remaining days of our honeymoon have been blissful. Reading. Eating. Swimming. Sunbathing on board. Making love. These have been magical days. There's just one more activity I want to do, before we go.

I push the shutter and hope that the sound won't wake her. The camera's been a welcome gift, and I've rediscovered my passion for photography. We're in such a splendid, photogenic setting after all; the *Fair Lady* is yar.

Ana stirs and stretches her hand out, to my side of the bed, looking for me. The gesture warms my heart.

I'm not far away, baby.

She opens her eyes, startled, I think, so I put the camera on the floor and quickly lie down beside her. "Hey, don't panic. Everything's fine," I whisper. I hate her wary look. I push her hair off her face. "You've been so jumpy these last couple of days."

"I'm okay, Christian," she lies. Her forced smile is for my sake. "Were you watching me sleep?"

"Yes. You were talking."

"Oh?" Her eyes widen.

"You're worried." I kiss the soft spot above her nose to try to reassure her. "When you frown, a little *v* forms just here. It's soft to kiss. Don't worry, baby, I'll look after you."

"It's not me I'm worried about, it's you," she grumbles. "Who's looking after you?"

"I'm big enough and ugly enough to look after myself. Come. Get up. There's one thing I'd like to do before we head home."

Something fun.

I slap her ass, and I'm rewarded with a gratifying squeal.

I bound off the bed, and she follows.

"Shower later. Put your swimsuit on."

"Okay."

THE CREW HAVE LOWERED the Jet Ski into the water. My life vest is on, and I'm helping Ana into hers. I strap the ignition key and kill cord to her wrist.

"You want me to drive?" she asks, incredulous.

"Yes." I grin. "That's not too tight?"

"It's fine. Is that why you're wearing a life jacket?" She arches a brow, unimpressed.

"Yes."

"Such confidence in my driving capabilities, Mr. Grey."

"As ever, Mrs. Grey."

"Well, don't lecture me," she warns, and I know she's talking from bitter experience.

I hold up my palms in surrender. "Would I dare?"

"Yes, you would, and yes, you do, and we can't pull over and argue on the sidewalk here."

"Fair point well made, Mrs. Grey. Are we going to stand on this platform all day debating your driving skills, or are we going to have some fun?"

"Fair point well made, Mr. Grey." She climbs onto the craft, and I slide on behind her and look up to find we've attracted a small audience on deck: the crew, our French security, and Taylor. I kick us away from the small pontoon and wrap my arms and clamp my thighs around Ana. She inserts the ignition key, presses the start button, and the engine powers into life with a gutsy roar. "Ready?" she shouts.

"As I'll ever be."

Slowly, she opens up the accelerator and the Jet Ski glides away from the ship.

Steady, Ana.

I tighten my hold on her as Ana increases our speed and we shoot across the water. "Whoa!" I shout, but it doesn't stop her. She leans forward, taking me with her, and speeds toward the open sea, then veers toward the shore, where the runway at Nice airport juts out into the Mediterranean.

"Next time we do this we'll have two Jet Skis," I shout.

That would be fun. Racing together.

Ana soars across the waves. We bounce a little, as it's choppier on the water today with the brisk summer breeze. As she nears the shore, a plane flies overheard. The noise is deafening.

Shit.

Ana swerves suddenly. I shout, but I'm too late, and we're both bucked off the craft and into the Mediterranean. The water closes over my head, into my eyes and my mouth, but I kick up and surface immediately, shaking my head and looking for Ana. The Jet Ski bobs, lifeless and harmless, not far from us, and Ana is wiping the water from her eyes. I swim toward her, relieved she's surfaced. "You okay?" I ask when I get close.

"Yes," she croaks. And she's grinning from ear to ear.

Why is she smiling? She just catapulted us into the cold sea.

I pull her into my wet embrace and hold her face between my palms, checking to see that she wasn't hit by the Jet Ski.

"See, that wasn't so bad!" she gushes, and I know she's okay.

"No, I guess it wasn't. Except I'm wet."

"I'm wet, too."

"I like you wet." I leer at her.

"Christian!" She admonishes me for my lewd look, and I can't help myself. I kiss her.

No.

I consume her. We're both winded when I pull away.

"Come. Let's head back. We have to shower. I'll drive." I swim over to the Jet Ski, vault onto it, and pull her up behind me.

"Was that fun, Mrs. Grey?"

"It was. Thank you."

"No, thank *you*. Shall we go home now?"

"Yes. Please."

ANASTASIA IS SIPPING CHAMPAGNE and reading off her iPad as we sit in the Concorde lounge at Heathrow and wait for our connecting flight to Seattle. This is one of the things I loathe about traveling on a scheduled flight: the waiting. But Ana seems happy enough. Occasionally, from the corner of my eye, I notice her surreptitious glances in my direction.

Inside, I'm dancing. I love that she's watching me.

I'm reading the *Financial Times*. It makes for sober reading. The global markets are still skittish in the wake of the recent budget deficit issues and Black Monday. The dollar is sinking. Also there's an article on whether the rich should pay more tax; Warren Buffett seems to think we should, and maybe he's right.

Ana takes a photograph, with the flash on, surprising me. I blink the blur of the bright lights out of my eyes and watch as she switches the flash off.

"How are you, Mrs. Grey?" I ask.

"Sad to be going home." She pouts. "I like having you to myself."

I take her hand and kiss her knuckles in turn. "Me, too," I whisper.

"But?" she asks.

Damn. She heard my unspoken doubt. Her eyes narrow, shrewd and interrogative. She's not going to let this go until I tell her. I sigh. "I want this arsonist caught and out of our lives."

"Oh."

Exactly.

"I'll have Welch's balls on a platter if he lets anything like that happen again." My tone sounds cold and sinister, even to me.

But this has gone on too long. We need to catch the fucker.

Ana gapes at me, then raises the camera and takes a quick shot. "Gotcha."

I smile, relieved that she's lightened the mood. "I think it's time to board our flight. Come."

"SAWYER, CAN WE GO through the front?" I ask, and he pulls the Audi up to the curb outside Escala. Taylor climbs out and opens my door. Ana is fast asleep.

"Thanks, Taylor," I say as I stretch my legs. "It's good to be back."

"It is, sir."

"I'll wake Ana." Opening her door, I lean over her. "Hey, sleepy-head, we're home." I unbuckle her seat belt.

"Hmm," she hums, and I lift her into my arms. "Hey, I can walk," she grumbles sleepily.

Oh, no, baby. "I need to carry you over the threshold."

She puts her arms around my neck. "Up all thirty floors?"

"Mrs. Grey, I am very pleased to announce that you've put on some weight."

"What?"

"So, if you don't mind, we'll use the elevator."

Taylor opens the doors to the Escala lobby and smiles. "Welcome home, Mr. Grey, Mrs. Grey."

"Thanks, Taylor," I answer.

We head into the lobby. "What do you mean I've put on weight?" Ana glares at me.

She's pissed.

"Not much." I grin to reassure her. Tightening my hold on her as I walk to the elevator, I recall how she looked when I picked her up from SIP, after we split up. How thin and sad she was. The memory is sobering.

"What is it?" she asks.

"You've put on some of the weight you lost when you left me." My answer is quiet. *That was me. I was responsible for her sadness.*

I never want to see her like that again.

I press the call button.

"Hey." Ana caresses my face and her fingers entwine in my hair. "If I hadn't gone, would you be standing here, like this, now?"

And just like that, she pours oil on my troubled waters.

"No." I smile. Because it's true. I step into the elevator, holding my wife, and lightly brush my lips over hers. "No, Mrs. Grey, I wouldn't. But I would know I could keep you safe, because you wouldn't defy me."

"I like defying you," she says with her coquettish smile.

I chuckle. "I know. And it's made me so happy."

"Even though I'm fat?" She pouts.

I laugh. "Even though you're fat." My lips capture hers once more, and she tightens her hold on my hair as we lose ourselves in each other.

The elevator pings, and we are back at Escala for the first time as husband and wife. "Very happy," I whisper, my body stirring. I carry her into the foyer and I want to bypass everything and everyone and take her to bed. "Welcome home, Mrs. Grey." I kiss her once more.

"Welcome home, Mr. Grey." Her face is alight with joy.

I carry her into the main living room and set her down on the kitchen island. From the cupboard, I take down two champagne flutes, and from the fridge I retrieve a chilled bottle of Grand Année Bollinger, our favorite rosé. Opening the bottle with a quick twist of the cork, I pour the pale pink sparkling liquid into each glass. I hand one to Ana, who's still sitting on the counter, and stand between her legs. "Here's to us, Mrs. Grey."

"To us, Mr. Grey," she answers with a shy smile.

We clink glasses and each take a sip.

"I know you're tired." I run my nose against hers. "But I'd really like to go to bed, and not to sleep." I kiss the corner of her sweet mouth. "It's our first night back here, and you're really mine."

She moans, closes her eyes, and raises her head, giving me access to her throat.

Ana. You goddess.

My love.

My life.

My wife.

SUNDAY, AUGUST 21, 2011

I'm expecting the smooth roll of the *Fair Lady* as she floats on the Mediterranean, and the sounds of the crew readying her for the day. But when I open my eyes, I'm at home. Outside, the golden dawn heralds a beautiful morning, and beneath my arm Ana tenses. She's staring at the ceiling, trying to stay still.

"What's wrong?" I whisper.

Her eyes meet mine, and for a moment she looks lost. "Nothing." Her face softens as she smiles. "Go back to sleep." My dick responds enthusiastically to her smile, far more roused than me. Blinking, I rub my face and stretch my limbs in an effort to wake my mind and the rest of my body.

"Jet lag?" I ask.

"Is that what this is? I can't sleep."

"I have the universal panacea right here, just for you, baby." Grinning, I nudge her hip with my erection. She giggles, rolling her eyes, and her teeth tease my earlobe as her hand skates down my body to my waiting cock.

WHEN I STIR AN hour or so later, it's early morning. I've slept well, and Ana is still asleep beside me. I let her rest and get up quietly; a quick run in my gym is what I need. While I'm on the treadmill with Four Tet blaring in my ears, I check the markets and watch the news. It's going to be quite the adjustment to return to my routine. Ana and I have been in a blissful bubble for the last few weeks, but now I'm ready to go back to work. I'm excited. My wife and I are going to forge this new life together, and as of yet I have no idea what that will entail. Maybe we could travel; I could take Ana to see the Great Wall of China, the Pyramids—hell, all the Wonders of the World. I could ease up at the office—Ros has done a great job since I've been away—and Ana could stop working. After all, she won't need the money.

But she loves her job, and she's good at it.

Maybe she has great ambitions in publishing.

I shake my head; she would be safer if she stayed at home.

Damn. Don't dwell on the negative, Grey.

ANA IS IN THE shower when I enter the bathroom, and I cannot resist. I step in behind her. "Good morning. Let me scrub your back, Mrs. Grey." She hands me the sponge and body wash with a distracted smile. Lathering up the sponge, I start soaping her neck. "Don't forget we're going to my parents' for lunch. I hope you don't mind. Kate will be there." I kiss her ear.

"Hmm," she murmurs, eyes closed.

"You okay?" I ask. "You're quiet."

"I'm good, Christian. Getting pruny." She wiggles her fingers.

"I'll let you go."

She smiles, exits the shower cubicle, and grabs her robe on the way out. She seems happy enough, but I think my girl is preoccupied. Something's up.

Ana is in the kitchen making breakfast when I enter. She looks lovely wearing a black strappy top and the skirt she wore on our walk around Saint-Paul-de-Vence.

"Coffee?" she asks.

"Please."

"Sourdough toast?"

"Please."

"Preserves?"

"Apricot. Thanks." I kiss her cheek. "I've got some things to do before we leave for lunch."

"Okay, I'll bring breakfast to you."

IN MY STUDY, I find Gia Matteo's latest plans for the house on my desk where Gail must have left them. Setting them aside to review later, I fire up my iMac and get to work. Welch and Barney are combing through all of the past week's footage from the CCTV cameras at

Grey House, but there's no news on the arsonist yet. Welch has been rolling out additional security at each of the GEH sites. I read through the schedule for our personal protection, to find it includes an additional operative. Her name is Belinda Prescott. But today, it's Ryan and Sawyer who will accompany us to my parents' place—Taylor, quite rightly, has gone to visit his daughter after so many weeks away.

Ana pushes the door open using her back, and places coffee and toast on my desk.

"Thank you, wife."

"You're welcome, husband." Her smile is thin. "I'm going to unpack."

"You don't have to, Gail can do it."

"It's okay. I want to be busy."

"Hey." I get up and catch her hand before she leaves, scrutinizing her face. "What's wrong?"

"Nothing." She leans up to kiss my cheek. "I'll be ready to leave midday."

I frown and release her. "Okay."

Something's up.

But I have no idea what it could be.

It's unsettling.

Perhaps Ana needs time to readjust to this time zone. She leaves, and I turn my attention to work, setting aside my disquiet for now. I have an e-mail from Gia Matteo, who wants to see us tomorrow to discuss her latest plans. I let her know that's fine and suggest a meeting for early evening.

There's good news from Eurocopter: they can replace both of *Charlie Tango*'s engines, so she should be back, fully functioning, within a couple of weeks; however, there's still no progress in the FBI investigation into her sabotage. It's irritating.

Why is it taking so long?

I move on and review the latest e-mails from Ros; the sooner I get through these, the sooner I can get back to my wife.

THE DRIVE TO MY parents' home is a joy. I haven't driven my R8 for weeks, and with my wife by my side, I'm enjoying the lush greenery of urban Seattle. After the old-world charm of the South of France, the landscape is pleasingly familiar. It's good to be home. I've missed driving, especially in this car. I check the rearview mirror and, sure enough, Sawyer and Ryan are on our tail.

Ana is quiet beside me, gazing at the scenery that's dappled with summer sun as we speed, top down, along I-5. "Would you let me drive this?" she asks out of the blue.

Is that what she's been thinking about?

"Of course. What's mine is yours. If you dent it, though, I will take you into the Red Room of Pain." I give her a wolfish grin, knowing that I'm using her spurious name for the playroom, not mine.

Her mouth drops open. "You're kidding. You'd punish me for denting your car? You love your car more than you love me?" She sounds incredulous.

"It's close," I tease, reaching over to squeeze her knee. "But she doesn't keep me warm at night."

"I'm sure it could be arranged. You could sleep in her," Ana retorts.

I laugh, loving her banter. "We haven't been home one day and you're kicking me out already?"

"Why are you so pleased?"

I flash her a quick grin, while keeping my eyes on the road. "Because this conversation is so…normal."

Isn't this what marriage is all about? The to and fro between us?

"Normal!" she scoffs. "Not after three weeks of marriage! Surely."

What? My smile withers. *She was serious? She's gonna kick me out?*

"I'm kidding, Christian."

Hell. So was I!

She presses her lips together, looking sullen, then mutters, "Don't worry, I'll stick to the Saab." She turns to stare at the scenery once more.

So much for marital banter. "Hey. What's wrong?" I ask.

"Nothing."

"You're so frustrating sometimes, Ana. Tell me."

She turns her head to me, a smirk twisting her lips. "Back at you, Grey."

I'm the problem? Me?

Shit.

"I'm trying," I respond.

"I know. Me, too." She smiles, and I think she's okay. But I'm not sure. Maybe her heart is still in the Côte d'Azur.

Or perhaps she's upset over the arson?

Maybe the increased security?

Hell, I wish I knew.

"BRO!" IT'S ELLIOT WHO answers the front door at my parents' home. "How's it hanging?" He grabs my hand and pulls me into a bear hug.

"Perpendicular," I mutter. "How are you, Elliot?"

"It's great to see you, hotshot. You're looking good. You got a little sun." Then he turns his attention to Ana. "Sister!" he bellows, and he sweeps my wife off her feet.

"Hello, Elliot." She giggles, and it's a relief to hear her laugh. He sets her down.

"Looking beautiful, Ana. He treating you well?"

"Mostly."

"Come in." Elliot steps aside. "Dad's in charge of the BBQ."

MY PARENTS ARE EXPERT hosts and love entertaining. We're on the terrace in the backyard, sitting around the table. Across the lawn, there's the familiar view of the bay and Seattle's skyline in the distance. It's still stunning. Grace has gone all out, as usual, so there's plenty of food. Carrick holds us captive with family camping stories and his BBQ skills, and we're seated with Elliot, Kate, Mia, and Ethan. It's weird, I've always felt removed from my family, not that they excluded me—it's more that I siloed myself, to protect myself. Sitting here now, watching them laugh and tease one another—and me—and take such a keen interest in my wife and our honeymoon—I kind of regret having been so guarded. To think of all those years I missed locked in an ivory tower of my own making—an accusation that Ana frequently levels at me.

Perhaps she's right.

Our hands are entwined, and I fondle the rings on her finger, reluctant to release her. She seems to have brightened up, the way she's laughing with Kate, whatever was bothering her forgotten, I hope.

Elliot is talking about the new house. "So if you can get the plans finalized with Gia, I have a window September through to mid-November and can get the whole crew on it." Elliot puts his arm around Kate and clasps her shoulder. His thumb lightly brushes her skin. I think he really likes her. This has to be a first.

"Gia is due to come over to discuss the plans tomorrow evening," I reply. "I hope we can finalize everything then." I look at Ana.

"Sure." She smiles, but some of the light in her eyes fades.

What is it?

She's driving me crazy.

"To the happy couple." Dad raises a glass, and a smile, and everyone seconds the sentiment.

"And congratulations to Ethan for getting into the psych program at Seattle," Mia interjects, pride ringing in her voice. She's obviously smitten, and I wonder if she's gotten into his pants yet. It's difficult to tell from the smirk he gives her.

My family is thirsty for information about our honeymoon, so I give them an executive summary of the last three weeks.

Ana remains quiet.

Is she regretting all this?

No, I can't let myself go there.

Grey, get a grip.

Elliot makes some crude joke and stretches his arms, sending his glass flying onto the flagstones, where it smashes rather dramatically. My mother leaps up, as do Mia and Kate, while Elliot sits there like the dope he is.

Seizing the opportunity this distraction presents, I lean over and whisper to Ana, "I am going to take you to the boathouse and finally spank you in there if you don't snap out of this mood."

She gasps and checks that no one is listening. "You wouldn't dare!" she challenges, her voice husky.

I raise a brow.

Bring it, Ana.

"You'd have to catch me first—and I'm wearing flats," she hisses for my ears only.

"I'd have fun trying."

Ana turns a delightful and familiar shade of pink and stifles her smile.

There she is, my girl.

Mom serves us strawberries and whipped cream, which reminds me of London; this and Eton mess were the staple summer desserts there. As we finish up, we're caught short by a sudden shower. "Ah! Everyone inside," Grace cries as she gathers the serving dish.

We all grab plates, cutlery, and glasses and bolt back into the kitchen.

Ana looks happier, her hair a little wet, while she giggles with Mia. It warms my heart to see her with my family—they have fallen in love with her, like I have. Perhaps Mia will tell her what's happening with Ethan. I smile; inquiring minds need to know.

We head into the den to shelter from the rain and I take a seat at the upright piano. It's an old, worn, but much-loved Steinway, with a warm, rich tone. I press the middle C key and the sound rings through the room perfectly in tune. I smile, thinking of Grace. I suspect she keeps it tuned, as she plays on the odd occasion, though I haven't heard her play for years. And I haven't played here for so long—I can't even remember the last time. As a child, music was my refuge. It was somewhere I could escape and lose myself, at first in the tedious repetition of scales and arpeggios, and then in each piece I learned.

Music and literature got me through puberty.

There's sheet music on the rest, and I wonder who it belongs to, maybe Grace, maybe her housekeeper—she plays, I think. It's a song I know, "Wherever You Will Go" by The Calling. My family gathers, continuing their conversations, while I read the music. My fingers flex, instinctively following the song.

I could play this.

And before I know it, I've started to play. The words are on the sheet music and I sing along. A few bars later I'm lost in the melody and the poignant lyrics—it's just me and the piano and the music.

It's a beautiful song. About loss…and love.

"I'll go wherever you go…"

Slowly, the silence in the room intrudes into my consciousness.

The chatting has ceased. I stop playing, and turn around on the stool to find out what has caught everyone's attention. All eyes are on me.

What the hell!

"Go on," Grace prompts, her voice wavering with emotion. "I've never heard you sing, Christian. Ever." She's almost inaudible, but I can hear her because of the oppressive silence in the room. Her face glows with pride and wonder and love.

It's a gut punch.

Mom.

A well of feeling pours from my heart into my chest, filling me up and threatening to drown me.

I can't breathe.

No. I cannot do this.

I shrug and surreptitiously take a deep breath and look at my wife, my anchor. She seems puzzled, possibly by the weird reaction of my family. In an effort to blot them out for a moment, I turn and stare through the French windows.

This is why I distance myself.

This.

To escape these...*feelings.*

There's a sudden and almost spontaneous burst of chatter, and I get up and stand at the window. From the corner of my eye, I see Grace embrace my wife with an unbridled enthusiasm that surprises Ana. My mother whispers in her ear, and my throat burns with the same choking emotion from a moment ago. With a beseeching look, Grace kisses Ana's cheek, then announces in a throaty voice, "I am going to make some tea."

Ana takes pity on me and comes to my rescue. "Hi," she says.

"Hi." I slip my arm around her and tug her to my side, finding comfort in her warmth. She slides her hand in the back pocket of my jeans. Together, we watch the rain through the French window, the sun still in the distance. Somewhere there must be a rainbow.

"Feeling better?" I ask her.

She nods.

"Good."

"You certainly know how to silence a room," she says.

"I do it all the time." I grin down at her.

"At work, yes, but not here."

"True, not here."

"No one's ever heard you sing? Ever?"

"It appears not." My tone is wry.

She stares up at me as if she's trying to solve a puzzle.

It's just me, Ana. "Shall we go?"

"You going to spank me?" she whispers.

What?

Ana is, as ever, unexpected. Her words twist and turn through me, awakening my desire. "I don't want to hurt you, but I'm more than happy to play."

Ana nervously scans the room.

Baby, no one can hear us. I tilt my head and whisper in her ear, "Only if you misbehave, Mrs. Grey."

She squirms in my arms, and her face breaks into an impish grin. "I'll see what I can do."

Does she know how adrift I felt a moment ago?

Does she say this stuff to bring me back?

I don't know, but right now, my heart swells with my love for her.

My answering grin is just as broad. "Let's go."

"IT'S SO GOOD TO see you so happy, darling," Grace says, her gaze unwavering as she presses her palm against my cheek.

"Thanks for lunch." I give her a quick peck.

"You are welcome, always, Christian. This is your home, too."

"Thank you, Mom." I pull her into an impulsive hug. She beams up at me, then turns her attention to Ana, hugging her hard. When I manage to pry Ana from my mother's clutches, we wave our goodbyes to everyone else and head to the car. As we do, it occurs to me that her decrepit Beetle must have been a stick shift too.

Let's do this, Grey.

"Here." I toss the R8 key at Anastasia. She catches it with one hand. "Don't bend it or I will be fucking pissed."

"Are you sure?" Her voice is full of excitement.

"Yes, before I change my mind."

What's mine is yours, baby. Even this...I think.

She lights up like Christmas, and rolling my eyes at her elation, I open the driver's door to let her in. She starts the engine before I'm even in the car.

"Eager, Mrs. Grey?" I ask as I fasten my seat belt.

"Very." She flashes me a wild-eyed smile and I wonder if I've made a huge mistake. She doesn't take the top down—my girl is not wasting any time. Slowly, she reverses so that she can turn the car around in the driveway. I glance behind us, and Sawyer and Ryan are scrambling into the SUV.

Where were they?

Ana reaches the end of the driveway and glances nervously at me. Her early bravado has slipped a little. "You're sure about this?"

"Yes," I lie.

She inches out into the road and I brace myself. As soon as she's on the pavement, she puts the pedal to the metal and we shoot down the street.

Fuck. "Whoa! Ana! Slow down! You'll kill us both!"

She eases off the accelerator. "Sorry," she says, but I know from her tone she's anything but, and I'm reminded of our time, only yesterday, on the Jet Ski.

I smirk at her. "Well, that counts as misbehaving."

Ana slows down a little more.

Good. That's got her attention.

She drives steadily along Lake Washington Boulevard and through the Tenth Street intersection. My phone buzzes. "Shit." I struggle to retrieve it from my jeans. It's Sawyer. "What?" I snap.

"Sorry to disturb you, Mr. Grey. Are you aware of the Black Dodge following you?"

"No." Turning around, I survey the street behind us through the cramped rear window of the R8, but as we're on a bend, I don't see any cars.

"Mrs. Grey is driving?"

"Yes. She is." Ana turns onto Eighty-Fourth Avenue.

"The Dodge set off after you left. The driver was waiting in the car. We ran the plates. They're fake. We don't want to take any chances. Could be nothing. Or it could be something."

"I see." Myriad thoughts dart through my mind. Maybe this is just a coincidence. *No.* After everything that's happened recently, this can't be a coincidence. And whoever is following us could be armed. My scalp prickles with alarm. How could this have happened? Sawyer and Ryan were out there the whole time. Weren't they? They didn't think it odd that someone was sitting in a car? Did it follow us to my parents' place?

"Do you want to try to lose them?" Sawyer asks.

"Yes."

"Will Mrs. Grey be okay?"

"I don't know."

When has she ever let me down?

Ana is concentrating on the road ahead, but her earlier spirit has vanished and her grip on the steering wheel has tightened; she's figured out something's wrong. "We're fine. Keep going," I tell her in the most soothing tone I can muster.

Her eyes widen, and I know I've failed to reassure her.

Shit. I pick up the phone again. Sawyer is talking. "We haven't been able to get a close look at the driver. The 520 is probably the best place to try. Mrs. Grey could try to lose them there, too. The Dodge is no match for the R8."

"Okay, on the 520. As soon as we hit it." I say.

Damn, I wish I was driving.

"We'll be right behind the Dodge. We'll try to come alongside it. Are you okay with this?

"Yes."

"Do you want to put us on speaker, so Mrs. Grey can hear us?"

"I will."

I slot the phone onto the speaker cradle.

"What's wrong, Christian?"

"Just look where you're going, baby," I murmur gently. "I don't want you to panic, but as soon as we're on the 520 proper, I want you to step on the gas. We're being followed."

Ana blinks several times as she absorbs this news, and the color drains from her cheeks

Shit.

She sits up straighter and squints into the rearview mirror, no doubt trying to identify our pursuer.

"Keep your eyes on the road, baby." I speak softly. Calmly. I don't want to spook Ana any more than she's spooked already. We just need to get back to Escala as quickly as possible and lose this asshole.

"How do we know we're being followed?" Her voice is high-pitched and breathless.

"The Dodge behind us has false license plates."

She drives carefully across the Twenty-Eighth Street intersection, around the roundabout and up the 520 on-ramp. Traffic is light, so that's something. Ana's eyes flick to the rearview mirror, then she takes a deep breath and abruptly seems to slow down.

Ana, what are you doing?

She's studying the flow of traffic; suddenly she drops a gear and floors the gas so we shoot forward through a break in the traffic onto the highway. The Dodge has to slow right down to a crawl to wait for a gap to follow us.

Whoa. Ana. Clever girl!

But we're going too fast!

"Steady, baby." I keep my voice even, though inside my stomach is in knots. She drops her speed and starts to weave between the two lanes. Knotting my hands together, I hold them in my lap so I don't distract her. "Good girl." I glance behind us. "I can't see the Dodge."

"We're right behind the unsub, Mr. Grey," Sawyer's voice says over the speaker. "He's trying to catch up with you, sir. We're going to try to come alongside. Put ourselves between your car and the Dodge."

"Good. Mrs. Grey is doing well. At this rate, provided the traffic remains light, and from what I can see it is, we'll be off the bridge in a few minutes."

"Sir."

We speed past the bridge control tower. We're halfway. Ana is traveling fast, but smoothly and confidently. She's got this. "You're doing really well, Ana."

"Where am I headed?"

"Mrs. Grey, head for I-5 and then south. We want to see if the Dodge follows you all the way."

The lights on the bridge are green, thank goodness, and Ana continues at speed. "Shit." There are cars backed up coming off the bridge. Ana slows, and I see her glance in the rearview mirror, looking for the Dodge.

"Ten or so cars back?" she says.

Staring behind us, I spot it. "Yeah, I see it. I wonder who the fuck it is?"

"Me, too. Do we know if it's a man driving?" Ana directs her comment to my phone.

"No, Mrs. Grey. Could be a man or woman. The tint is too dark."

"A woman?" I ask.

Ana shrugs. "Your Mrs. Robinson?"

What? No!

I've not heard from Elena since—well, since the wedding, when she sent that fucking text. I reach for my phone and pull it out of the cradle to mute it.

"She's not my Mrs. Robinson," I grumble. "I haven't spoken to her since my birthday."

That's not right, Grey. I called her when I gifted her the business, but now is not the time to mention that. "Elena wouldn't do this. It's not her style."

"Leila?"

"She's in Connecticut with her parents. I told you."

"Are you sure?"

"No. But if she'd absconded, I'm sure her folks would have let Flynn know. Let's discuss this when we're home. Concentrate on what you're doing."

"But it might just be some random car."

"I'm not taking any risks. Not where you're concerned." I sound brusque, but I don't care. Ana, as ever, is challenging. Unmuting my BlackBerry, I place it back in the speaker cradle.

The traffic starts to ease, and Ana's able to increase her speed along the intersection.

"What if we get stopped by the cops?" she asks.

"That would be a good thing."

"Not for my license."

"Don't worry about that." The arson attempt and *Charlie Tango*'s sabotage are all part of a police investigation. I'm sure any police officer would be more interested in our stalker.

"He's cleared the traffic and picked up speed." Sawyer's disembodied voice is calm and informative. "He's doing ninety."

Ana accelerates and my beautiful car responds like the finely honed machine she is, climbing to ninety-five with ease.

"Keep it up, Ana," I assure her.

Ana coasts onto I-5 and immediately crosses several lanes to get into the fast lane.

Smooth, baby. Smooth.

"He's hit one hundred miles per hour, sir."

Fuck. "Stay with him, Luke," I bark at Sawyer.

A semi lurches into our lane and Ana hits the brakes, so we're thrown forward. "Fucking idiot!" I shout.

Christ. He could have killed us!

"Go around him, baby," I grit between clenched teeth. Ana maneuvers across three lanes, past several cars and the fucking semi, then back into the passing lane, leaving the asshole behind us. "Nice move, Mrs. Grey. Where are the cops when you need them?"

"I don't want a ticket, Christian," she says without heat. "Have you had a speeding ticket driving this?"

"No." But nearly.

"Have you been stopped?"

"Yes."

"Oh."

"Charm. It all comes down to charm."

Yes, Mrs. Grey. Believe it or not, I can be charming.

"Now concentrate. Where's the Dodge, Sawyer?" I ask.

"He's just hit one hundred and ten, sir," Sawyer says.

Ana gasps and she puts her foot down so the Audi picks up speed. There's a Ford Mustang in our way.

Fucking hell.

"Flash the headlights," I yell.

"But that would make me an asshole."

"So be an asshole!" I hiss, trying to keep my anger at the Mustang and my spiraling anxiety in check.

"Um, where are the headlights?" Ana asks.

"The indicator. Pull it toward you."

The prick gets the message and moves over, giving us the finger. "He's the asshole," I mutter. "Get off on Stewart," I tell Ana. "We're taking the Stewart Street exit," I inform Sawyer.

"Head straight to Escala, sir."

Ana glances in the mirror, her brow furrowed. She signals and moves across four lanes of the highway, straight down the off-ramp, slowing down and then turning smoothly onto Stewart Street.

She's amazing.

"We've been damned lucky with the traffic. But that means the Dodge has, too. Don't slow down, Ana. Get us home."

"I can't remember the way," she squeaks.

"Head south on Stewart. Keep going until I tell you when."

She cruises down the street.

Shit, the lights at Yale are on yellow.

"Run them, Ana," I urge.

Ana overreacts and we're thrown back as we speed through the intersection. The light on red.

"He's taking Stewart," Sawyer says.

"Stay with him, Luke."

"Luke?"

"That's his name." Didn't you know?

She glances at me.

"Eyes on the road!" I yell.

"Luke Sawyer?"

"Yes!" *Why are we talking about this now?*

"Ah."

"That's me, ma'am," Sawyer says. "The unsub is heading down Stewart, sir. He's really picking up speed."

"Go, Ana. Less of the fucking chitchat."

"We're stopped at the first light on Stewart," Sawyer informs us.

"Ana—quick—in here." I point to the parking lot on the south side of Boren Avenue. She turns sharply, gripping the steering wheel, and the expensive tires on my magnificent R8 squeal in disapproval, but Ana holds it, and swerves into the crowded lot.

Shit. That must have been a quarter-inch off the tread.

"Drive around. Quick."

Ana takes us to the back of the parking lot. "In there." I point to an empty space. Ana gives me a quick, panicked look. "Just fucking do it," I growl. And she does. Perfectly. As if she'd spent her whole life driving my car.

Well done, Ana.

"We're hidden in the parking lot between Stewart and Boren," I tell Sawyer.

"Okay, sir. Stay where you are; we'll follow the unsub." He sounds a little irritated.

Tough.

I turn to Ana. "You okay?"

"Sure." Her voice is deathly quiet, and I know she's really shaken.

I try for humor to calm us both. "Whoever's driving that Dodge can't hear us, you know."

Ana laughs. Loudly. Too loudly. She's masking her fear.

"We're passing Stewart and Boren now. I see the lot. He's gone straight past you, sir."

Thank Christ. The relief is instant, for Ana, too. I blow out a breath. "Well done, Mrs. Grey. Good driving." Reaching up, I startle her when I stroke my fingertips down her face. She takes a huge gulp of air.

"Does this mean you'll stop complaining about my driving?" she asks.

I laugh, and it's cathartic. "I wouldn't go so far as to say that."

"Thank you for letting me drive your car. Under such exciting circumstances, too." She's trying to stay bright, but she sounds brittle as if she's about to break.

I switch off the ignition, as she's made no attempt to do so. "Maybe I should drive," I offer.

"To be honest, I don't think I can climb out right now, to let you sit here. My legs feel like Jell-O." Her hands are shaking.

"It's the adrenaline, baby. You did amazingly well, as usual. You blow me away, Ana. You never let me down." I stroke her cheek again with the back of my hand because I need to touch her, to reassure her and me that we're safe. Tears well in her eyes, and her choked sob surprises us both as tears start coursing down her face. "No, baby, no. Please don't cry." I can't bear to see her cry. Reaching over, I unbuckle her seat belt, grasp her waist, and pull her over the center console into my lap; her feet remain on the driver's seat. Smoothing her hair off her face, I kiss her eyelids, and her cheeks, then bury my nose in her hair as she curls her arms around my neck and sobs into my throat. Cradling her close, I let her cry it out.

Ana. Ana. Ana. You did so well.

Sawyer's voice startles us. "The unsub has slowed outside Escala. He's casing the joint."

"Follow him," I order.

Ana wipes her nose with the back of her hand, sniffles, and takes a deep breath.

"Use my shirt," I offer, and kiss her temple.

"Sorry," she says.

"What for? Don't be."

She wipes her nose again, and I hold her chin, tipping it up and kissing her tenderly. "Your lips are so soft when you cry, my beautiful, brave girl." I keep my voice low, conscious of our security at the other end of the phone.

"Kiss me again," she whispers, and all I hear is the need in her voice. It lights a fire in my soul. "Kiss me." Her voice is husky and insistent. Retrieving my BlackBerry from its cradle, I hang up and toss it on the seat, next to her feet. I weave my fingers through her hair, holding her in place while my lips find hers and my tongue finds hers. She welcomes it, her tongue caressing mine and kissing me back with an intensity that steals my breath away. She clutches my face, her fingers skimming over stubble as she takes all I have to offer.

I groan. And my body responds. All the adrenaline heading south.

Fuck. I want her.

I move my hand down her body, feeling her, brushing her breast, her waist, and landing on her backside. She moves, sliding on top of my trapped dick. "Ah!" I pull away, panting.

"What?" she says against my lips.

"Ana, we're in a car lot in Seattle."

"So?"

"Well, right now I want to fuck you, and you're shifting around on me; it's uncomfortable."

"Fuck me, then." She kisses the corner of my mouth, as her words take me by surprise. I stare into her dark, dark eyes that are nearly all pupil. All lust. All need.

"Here?" I breathe, shocked.

"Yes. I want you. Now."

I can't believe she's said that. "Mrs. Grey, how very brazen." I scan our environs. We're well hidden. There's no one here. We won't be seen. We can do this. My hunger for her goes into overdrive. I tighten my grip on her hair, holding her where I want her, and kiss her again. Harder. Deeper. Taking. Taking. More and more.

My other hand skims again down her body to her thigh.

She grips my hair.

"I'm so glad you're wearing a skirt." My hand travels up her thigh. She wriggles on top of me.

Ah!

"Keep still," I grunt, tightening my grasp on her hair at the nape.

She's going to unman me.

I cup her through her lace panties; they're damp already.

Oh, baby.

With my thumb, I circle her clitoris, once, twice, and she groans, her body quivering at my touch. "Still," I whisper, and capture her lips with mine while my thumb teases the swollen bud beneath the dewy lace. I move the material aside and sink two fingers inside her.

She groans and tips her hips toward my hand in greeting.

Oh, my greedy girl.

"Please," she whispers.

"Oh. You're so ready," I murmur in appreciation, and slowly slide my fingers in. And out. And in. And out. And in. "Do car chases turn you on?"

"You turn me on."

Her words feed my hunger, and I withdraw my hand and slide my arm beneath her knees and lift her so she's fully on my lap, facing the windshield.

She gasps. But she starts grinding down on me.

I groan. "Place your legs either side of mine," I order, and run my hands down her outer thighs, then back up, yanking her skirt out of the way. "Hands on my knees, baby. Lean forward, lift that glorious ass in the air. Mind your head." She raises her beautiful behind and I unzip my jeans, freeing my heavy cock. Putting one arm around her waist, with my other hand I tug her panties sideways and, lifting my hips, force her down and thrust balls-deep inside her in one swift move.

My breath whistles through my lips. *Yes!*

"Ah," Ana cries out for anyone to hear, and she grinds down on me.

I groan, teeth clenched. She feels out of this world. I grasp her jaw and lean her back against me and angle her head so I can kiss her throat. Grabbing her hip with my other hand to keep her steady, I move into her, and I'm in deep. She pushes up and starts to ride me. Hard. Fast. Frantic.

Ah… I bite down on her earlobe.

She moans and moves and together we set a heady, desperate pace.

Her rising and falling. Me, bucking into her.

I move my fingers to her clitoris and start to tease her through her panties.

Ana makes a garbled cry, and the sound does nothing for my restraint.

Shit. I'm going to come. "Be. Quick," I rasp in her ear. "We need to do this quick, Ana."

Sweat beads on my brow, and I increase the pressure on her clitoris, circling around and around with my fingers.

"Oh," Ana cries.

"Come on, baby. I want to hear you."

We move. And move. And then I feel her. Building. Ready.

Oh, thank God. I slam into her once more and she tips her head back on my shoulder so she's facing the roof of the car.

"Yes!" I grind out between my teeth and she comes. Loudly.

"Oh, Ana." I wrap her in my arms and climax deep inside her.

When I return to reality, my head is bent against hers, and she's limp on top of me. I run my nose along her jaw and kiss her throat, her cheek, and her temple. "Tension relieved, Mrs. Grey?" I tug her earlobe. She whimpers, in a good way, and I smile. That's a great sound. "Certainly helped with mine," I murmur, and shift her forward, withdrawing from her. "Lost your voice?"

"Yes," she breathes.

"Well, aren't you the wanton creature? I had no idea you were such an exhibitionist."

She sits up immediately, watchful and wary. Her fatigue, a memory. "No one's watching, are they?" She scours the parking lot.

"Do you think I'd let anyone watch my wife come?" I stroke my hand down her back and she calms, turning around to give me a sweet playful smile.

"Car sex!" she exclaims, and her eyes flare with a sense of achievement, I think.

I grin. *Yes. It's a first for me, too, Ana.* I tuck a wayward strand of hair behind her ear. "Let's head back. I'll drive." Leaning forward, I open the car door, and Ana clambers off my lap so I can do up my fly.

When I'm back in the driver's seat I call our security detail.

"Mr. Grey, it's Ryan."

"Where's Sawyer?" I snap.

"At Escala."

"And the Dodge?"

"I'm following the Dodge south on I-5."

"How come Sawyer's not with you?"

"He thought it better to wait at Escala once we saw her—"

"Her?" I gasp.

"Yes. The driver is a woman," says Ryan. "I was going to follow her to see if we can ID her."

"Stick with her."

"Will do."

I hang up and look at Ana.

"The driver of the Dodge is female?" She sounds shocked.

"So it would appear." I have no idea who it might be. It can't be

Elena, and surely not Leila. Not after all the work that Flynn has put in with her. "Let's get you home."

The R8 growls to life, and I reverse out of the space and head home.

"Where's the, um, unsub? What does that mean, by the way? Sounds very BDSM."

"It stands for *unknown subject.* Ryan is ex-FBI."

"Ex-FBI?"

"Don't ask." That's a long story about doing the right thing, protecting an innocent, and getting fired for it. I'll tell her over dinner. He's probably why we know the plates on the Dodge were false. He has extensive connections.

"Well, where is this female unsub?" Ana continues.

"On I-5, heading south." Whoever it is drove past our place, scouted it out, and left. Who the hell is it?

Ana reaches over and runs her fingers down my inner thigh.

Whoa.

We're stopped at a red. I scoop her hand into mine to stop its progress to my dick. "No. We've made it this far. You don't want me to have an accident three blocks from home." I kiss her index finger and release her, and concentrate on getting us back in one piece. I need a thorough debrief from Sawyer. I'm pissed that there was someone waiting for us outside my parents' house. Surely they should have seen the Dodge.

What the hell am I paying them for?

Ana is quiet until we approach the garage at Escala. "Female?" she says out of nowhere. She sounds incredulous.

"Apparently so." I sigh and punch in the code to raise the gate to the garage.

Yeah. I wish I knew who. Welch has investigated all my ex-submissives, even those from the private club I used to frequent. They're all in the clear, as I knew they would be. I'll check on Leila via Flynn, but last I heard she was happy back in the bosom of her family.

I ease the R8 into her designated space.

"I really like this car," Ana says, giving me a welcome break from my dark thoughts.

"Me too. And I like how you handled it—and how you managed not to break it."

She smirks. "You can buy me one for my birthday."

Anastasia Ste…Grey! I gape at her, shocked. I don't think she's ever asked me for anything, but she steps out of the car before I can respond. I'm so astonished I don't know what to say. Once out, before she closes the door, she bends down and flashes me a sassy grin. "A white one, I think."

I laugh. White. Apt choice. She is the light to my darkness. "Anastasia Grey, you never cease to amaze me."

She shuts the door and I get out after her. She's waiting by the trunk, looking every bit the just-fucked goddess who wants a two-hundred-thousand-dollar car.

She's never asked me for anything.

Why is that so hot?

Leaning down, I whisper, "You like the car. I like the car. I've fucked you in it. Perhaps I should fuck you on it."

She gasps and her cheeks pink in that delightful way I love. The sound of a car pulling into the garage distracts me. It's a silver 3 Series BMW.

Cockblocker.

"But it looks like we have company. Come." Taking her hand, I guide her to the elevator. Sadly, we have to wait and we're joined by Mr. BMW Cockblocker. He looks my age. Maybe younger.

"Hi," he says, with an appreciative smile aimed at my wife.

I put my arm around Ana.

Back off, bud.

"I've just moved in. Apartment sixteen," he gushes at her.

"Hello," Ana says, her tone nothing but friendly.

We're saved by the elevator. Once inside, I keep Ana close. I glance down at her, willing her not to engage with this stranger.

"You're Christian Grey," he says.

Yep. That's me.

"Noah Logan." He holds out his hand. Reluctantly, I extend mine and he gives me a damp, overenthusiastic handshake. "Which floor?" he asks.

"I have to input a code."

"Oh."

"Penthouse."

"Oh. Of course." He presses the button for his floor and the doors close. "Mrs. Grey, I presume." He simpers like a nervous eighth-grader with an epic crush.

"Yes." She gives him a sweet smile, and they shake hands and the fucker blushes.

Blushes!

"When did you move in?" Ana asks, and I tighten my hold on her.

Don't encourage him.

"Last weekend. I love the place."

She smiles. *Again!*

Mercifully, the elevator stops at his floor. "Great to meet you both," he says, sounding relieved, and steps out. The doors close behind him, and I enter the code for the penthouse into the keypad.

"He seemed nice," Ana says. "I've never met any of the neighbors before."

I grimace. "I prefer it that way."

"That's because you're a hermit. I thought he was pleasant enough."

"A hermit?"

"Hermit. Stuck in your ivory tower," Ana says, deadpan.

I try, really try, to suppress my smile. "*Our* ivory tower," I correct her. "And I think you have another name to add to the list of your admirers, Mrs. Grey."

She rolls her eyes heavenward. "Christian, you think everyone is an admirer."

Oh. Sweet. Joy.

"Did you just roll your eyes at me?"

She looks up at me from beneath her lashes. "I sure did," she whispers.

Oh, Mrs. Grey.

I cock my head to one side. The day has just improved one thousand percent. "What shall we do about that?"

"Something rough."

Fuck. Her words are arousing.

"Rough?" I swallow.

"Please."

"You want more?"

She nods, not taking her eyes off me. It's so fucking hot.

The doors of the elevator open, but neither of us step out. We just stare at each other, our attraction, our yearning, sparking between us like static. Ana's eyes darken, like mine, I'm sure.

"How rough?" I ask.

Ana's teeth sink into her full lower lip, but she says nothing.

Oh. Dear. God.

I close my eyes to savor this sensual moment, then grab her hand and march out of the elevator and through the double doors of the foyer. Sawyer is waiting.

Hell.

"Sawyer, I'd like to be debriefed in an hour," I state, wanting him gone.

"Yes, sir." He heads back into Taylor's office.

Good. I look down at my wife. "Rough?"

She nods, her expression serious.

"Well, Mrs. Grey, you're in luck. I'm taking requests today." My mind races with possibilities. "Do you have anything in mind?"

She raises her left shoulder in a coquettish shrug.

What does that mean? "Kinky fuckery?" I ask, to be clear.

She nods an emphatic yes, but her face flushes.

"Carte blanche?" I ask.

Her eyes flick to mine, and they're brimming with curiosity and sensuality. "Yes." Her husky affirmation feeds the flames of my desire.

"Come." We head upstairs to the playroom. "After you, Mrs. Grey." I unlock the door and step aside, and Ana strolls into my favorite room. I follow her in, switching on the lights. Ana turns, watching me as I lock the door.

Take a breath, Grey.

I love this moment.

Building anticipation.

It's exhilarating.

She stands there, waiting. Wanting. *Mine.*

Last time we were in here, I put her in the harness.

A memory of that flits through my mind. That was fun.

What shall I do with her today?

"What do you want, Anastasia?"

"You."

"You've got me. You've had me since you fell into my office."

"Surprise me, then, Mr. Grey."

She's so bold. "As you wish, Mrs. Grey." Folding my arms, I tap my index finger against my lip.

I know what I'd like to do.

I've wanted to do it for a long, long time.

But first things first.

"I think we'll start by ridding you of your clothes." Stepping forward, I grasp her short denim jacket, ease it off her shoulders, and drop it to the floor; her camisole is next. "Lift your arms." She does as she's told and I peel it off her lovely body. I offer her a soft, sweet kiss, then discard her top so it lands on her jacket. She's wearing a lacy black bra, her nipples visible and pressing through the fabric.

My wife is hot.

"Here," she says and, to my surprise, offers me a hair tie.

My dark confession in Saint-Paul-de-Vence has done nothing to discourage her, or to keep her away from me.

Don't overthink this, Grey.

I take it from her. "Turn around."

She does, with a small, private smile, and I wonder what she's thinking about.

Don't go there, either, Grey.

Quickly, I braid her hair and fasten it. With a tug, I pull her head back. "Good thinking, Mrs. Grey," I murmur, my lips brushing her ear, then I nip her earlobe. "Now turn around and take your skirt off. Let it fall to the floor."

She steps forward, turns on her heel, and with her eyes on mine, she unfastens her skirt and slides the zipper down, slowly. Her skirt flares out like a parasol and drifts to her feet.

She is Aphrodite.

"Step out from your skirt."

She complies and I kneel at her feet and grasp her ankle, unbuckling each of her sandals in turn. Once they're off, I sit back on my heels and gaze up at my wife. In black lacy underwear, she's spectacular. "You're a fine sight, Mrs. Grey." Kneeling up, I grab her hips and yank her forward, burying my nose at the blessed junction of her thighs.

She gasps as I inhale. "And you smell of you and me and sex. It's intoxicating." I kiss the top of her sweet cleft through the lace, then release her and gather her clothes and shoes before standing. With my hands full, I point with my chin. "Go and stand beside the table." I make my way to the chest of drawers. When I glance back at Ana, she's watching me like a hawk.

This will never do.

"Face the wall. That way you won't know what I'm planning. We aim to please, Mrs. Grey, and you wanted a surprise."

Ana obeys, and I drop her shoes beside the door and place her clothes on the chest. I strip off my shirt, remove my own shoes, and glance at her. She's still facing the wall. *Good.* From the butt drawer, I extract what I need, and leave the items on the chest while I find some music on the iPod: Pink Floyd, "The Great Gig in the Sky."

Okay. Let's see if she goes for this.

Moving back to Ana, I place my haul on the table, out of her sight line.

"Rough, you say, Mrs. Grey?" I whisper into her ear.

"Hmm."

"You must tell me to stop if it's too much. If you say stop, I will stop immediately. Do you understand?"

"Yes."

"I need your promise."

"I promise," she whispers, her tone husky with want.

"Good girl." I kiss her shoulder and then hook my finger beneath the bra strap across her back and gently run my finger under it, skimming over her flesh. "Take it off," I order.

I want her naked.

Hastily, she unhooks the back and lets it fall. Coasting my hands down her back to her hips, I hook my thumbs into her panties and slip them down her lovely legs. When I reach her ankles, I ask her to step out of them, and she obliges.

At eye level with her beautiful behind, I kiss one cheek, knowing that we're about to get better acquainted, and I stand. A thrill runs through me; I've been waiting for this moment.

"I'm going to blindfold you so that everything will be more intense," I murmur, and slip an airline eye mask over her eyes. Around us, the music swells and the singer lets loose, as if she's mid-climax.

Apt.

"Bend down and lie flat on the table. Now."

Ana's shoulders rise and fall quickly as her breathing escalates, but she does as she's told and lays down over the table.

"Stretch your arms up and hold on to the edge."

She reaches up and clutches the far edge. The table is wide, so her arms are fully extended.

"If you let go, I will spank you. Do you understand?"

"Yes."

"Do you want me to spank you, Anastasia?"

Her lips part as she takes in a breath. "Yes," she whispers, her voice hoarse.

"Why?" I ask.

She doesn't answer, though I think she's trying to shrug.

"Tell me," I prompt.

"Um."

I smack her hard across her ass, the sound echoing over the music and through the playroom. "Ah!" she cries out. For me, both sounds are deeply, deeply satisfying.

"Hush now." I gently rub her backside. Standing right behind her, I bend over her body, my cock straining against my jeans, and my fly digging into the soft swell of her behind as I plant a kiss between her shoulder blades. Slowly, I leave a trail of wet kisses across her back. When I stand, my saliva glistens in little patches on her skin.

"Open your legs."

She shuffles her feet apart.

"Wider."

She moans and does as she's told.

"Good girl," I whisper, and run my index finger down her spine, down to her coccyx, and over her anus. It shrinks and puckers beneath my touch. "We're going to have some fun with this," I whisper.

She tenses. But she doesn't stop me, so I skim my finger over her perineum and slowly ease it into her vagina.

Sweet. Heaven.

"I see you're very wet, Anastasia. From earlier or from now?"

She groans as I slip my finger in and out and she pushes back against my hand, wanting more. "Oh, Ana, I think it's both." My fingers move back and forth. "I think you love being here. Like this. Mine."

She moans, closing her eyes, and I withdraw my finger and smack her fine ass once more.

"Ah."

"Tell me." My voice is hoarse with my passion.

"Yes, I do," she whispers. I spank her again and she cries out, then I slide two fingers inside her and twist them once around to lubricate them. When I withdraw, I spread her essence up, and over and around her anus.

She tenses a little, once more. "What are you going to do?"

"It's not what you think," I reassure her. "I told you, one step at a time with this, baby." I reach for the lube and squirt a generous amount on my fingers, then massage it around her small, puckered hole. She squirms, her back rising and falling more rapidly with her accelerated breathing. Her lips part. She's excited. I smack her hard, aiming slightly lower, so my fingertips strike her labia that's soaked from her passion.

She moans and wiggles her ass, begging for more.

"Keep still," I order. "And don't let go." I squirt more lube on my fingers.

"Ah."

"This is lube." I spread some more over and around her anus. "I have wanted to do this to you for some time now, Ana." I grab the small, metal butt plug.

She groans and I drag the plug slowly down her spine. "I have a small present for you here," I whisper, and slide it down between her buttocks. "I am going to push this inside you, very slowly."

She inhales, breathless. "Will it hurt?"

"No, baby. It's small. Once it's inside you, I'm going to fuck you real hard."

Her lips part and she quivers. Leaning over her, I kiss her once again between her shoulder blades.

"Ready?"

Because I am.

My cock is almost bursting.

"Yes," she breathes.

With the plug in my left hand, I quickly coat it in lube, then skim my right thumb down between her buttocks, over her anus, and sink it into her vagina, circling inside her. My fingers brush against her clitoris, slowly, methodically taunting her eager bud while I move my thumb. She groans loudly with pleasure. And that's my cue. Very slowly, I push the plug into her ass.

"Ah!" she moans.

I'm met with a little resistance, so I circle my thumb inside her vagina, teasing the sweet spot inside her with the tip of my thumb, and push harder on the plug. Joy of joys, it slips inside her. Easily.

"Oh, baby." I swirl my thumb inside her again and feel the weight of the plug inside her butt. Slowly, I twist the plug, and Ana mewls, a strange sound of pure pleasure.

Whoa.

"Christian," she whimpers, lewd and needy, and I withdraw my thumb.

She's breathless.

"Good girl," I murmur. Leaving the plug in its place, I trace my fingers down her side until I reach her hip. Undoing my fly and freeing my dick, I grasp her hips with both hands, and pull her ass toward me. With my foot, I force her to widen her stance. "Don't let go of the table, Ana."

"No," she pants.

"Something rough? Tell me if I'm too rough. Understand?"

"Yes," she whispers. And in one swift move, I yank her toward me and slam inside her, to the hilt.

"Fuck!" she cries.

And I still, relishing the feel of my girl around me.

She's doing good, her breathing as harsh as mine. I reach between us and gently tug on the plug.

She lets out a breathtaking moan of pleasure.

It almost tips me over the edge.

"Again?" I whisper.

"Yes," she says, and she sounds desperate, begging for more.

"Stay flat," I insist, and ease out of her, then slam into her again.

"Yes," she hisses with loud, sibilant fervor. I pick up the pace, slamming inside her with a wild abandon that's exhilarating.

It's never felt like this.

Taking Ana to a darker side.

I fucking love it.

"Oh, Ana," I pant, and twist the plug around again.

She cries out as I keep rocking into her. Taking her. Consuming her. Owning her.

"Oh, fuck," she cries.

And I know she's close.

"Yes, baby," I whisper.

"Please," she begs.

"That's right."

You goddess, Ana.

I slap her hard and she lets go, screaming out loud and proud as she's gripped by her orgasm. I tug the plug out and toss it in the bowl.

"Fuck!" she screams, and I tighten my hold on her hips and let go, holding her to me and losing myself in my release.

I sag over her, spent but elated. Pulling her into my arms, I sink to the floor, curling her into my embrace as I catch my breath. She's gulping in air, her head resting on my chest.

"Welcome back," I say, removing the blindfold. She blinks, a little dazed, as her eyes adjust to the muted light. She looks okay. I tip her head back and press my lips to hers, anxiously trying to gauge how she's feeling.

Reaching up, she strokes my face.

I smile with relief. "Well, did I fulfill the brief?" I ask.

Her brow creases. "Brief?"

"You wanted rough." My tone is cautious.

Her face brightens. "Yes. I think you did."

Her words wrap around my soul. "I'm very glad to hear it. You look thoroughly well fucked and beautiful at this moment." I caress her cheek.

"I feel it," she hums. Holding her face, I kiss her with all the tenderness that she deserves. Because I love her.

"You never disappoint." *Ever.* "How do you feel?" I breathe.

"Good," she whispers and a telltale flush crosses her face. "Thoroughly well fucked." Her smile is shy and sweet and telling. And totally at odds with her profanity.

"Why, Mrs. Grey, you have a dirty, dirty mouth."

"That's because I'm married to a dirty, dirty boy, Mr. Grey."

I can't argue with that.

And I'm buoyant, grinning back at her. I must resemble the Cheshire Cat. "I'm glad you're married to him." My fingers grasp her braid, and I lift the end to my lips and kiss it. *I love you, Ana. Never leave me.*

She reaches for my left hand and, raising it to her lips, kisses my wedding ring. "Mine," she whispers.

"Yours," I answer, and I tighten my hold on her and drive my nose in her hair. "Shall I run you a bath?"

"Hmm. Only if you join me in it."

"Okay." I help Ana to her feet and stand up.

She points to the jeans I'm still wearing. "Will you wear your, er, other jeans?"

"Other jeans?"

"The ones you used to wear in here."

"Those jeans?" *My Dom jeans. The DJs.*

"You look very hot in them."

"Do I?"

"Yeah. I mean, really hot."

How could I refuse? I want to look hot for my wife.

"Well, for you, Mrs. Grey, maybe I will." I kiss her and grab the small bowl that contains our afternoon's entertainment, and I walk over to the chest of drawers to switch off the music.

"Who cleans these toys?" Ana asks.

Oh. Ah. "Me. Mrs. Jones."

"What?" Ana gasps in shock.

Yep. Gail knows everything, all my dirty little secrets, and she still works for me.

Ana is still gaping at me as if she expects more information. I switch off the iPod. "Well. Um—"

"Your subs used to do it?" Ana says, finally figuring it out.

All I have is an apologetic shrug. "Here." I offer her my shirt and she dons it quickly, and says no more about toy-cleaning. I leave our stuff on the chest and, taking Ana's hand, unlock the playroom door, and we head downstairs to our bathroom. She pauses on the threshold, yawns and stretches, a secret smile etched on her face.

"What is it?" I ask, turning on the faucets.

Ana shakes her head, avoiding eye contact.

Is she feeling shy all of a sudden?

"Tell me," I coax, as I pour bath oil into the running water.

Her cheeks develop a rosy flush. "I just feel better."

"Yes, you've been in a strange mood today, Mrs. Grey." I embrace her. "I know you're worrying about these recent events. I'm sorry you're caught up in them. I don't know if it's a vendetta, an ex-employee, or a business rival. If anything were to happen to you because of me—" The horrific image, of her lying in place of the crack whore, haunts me.

Stop, Grey. Stop.

She hugs me. "What if something happens to you, Christian?" She sounds bleak.

"We'll figure this out. Now let's get you out of this shirt and into this bath."

"Shouldn't you talk to Sawyer?"

"He can wait." My tone is clipped; I have a few choice words for him.

I slip my shirt off Ana.

Shit. The marks I left on her body are still there. Faded. But still present, reminding me that I'm an asshole.

"I wonder if Ryan has caught up with the Dodge?" Ana says, and I know she's ignoring my reaction.

"We'll see, after this bath. Get in." I offer her my hand, and she steps into the foam-filled tub. Gingerly, she sits down.

"Ow." She winces as her ass hits the hot water.

"Easy, baby," I whisper, but she smiles when she settles, submerged in the water. I strip out of my jeans and join her, sinking down behind her and gathering her to my chest.

Slowly I let myself relax.

Be in the moment, Grey.

That was really something.

Ana did so well. I nuzzle her hair and marvel at how easy it is to just *be* in her company. I don't have to talk; she doesn't have to talk. We can just lie and unwind in a bath together.

I close my eyes and reflect on the day.

What a crazy end to our honeymoon.

A car chase, which Ana handled brilliantly, like a pro.

I run the end of her braid through my fingers, absently.

And she let me have fun in the playroom, doing something I've wanted to do forever, and she's never done before.

My girl. My beautiful girl.

A few moments later, I remember that Gia Matteo will be joining us tomorrow evening. I break the comfortable silence between us. "We need to go over the plans for the new house. Later this evening?"

"Sure," Ana responds, and she sounds resigned. "I must get my things ready for work," she adds.

Her braid slips through my fingers. "You know you don't have to go back to work."

Ana's shoulders tense against me. "Christian, we've been through this. Please don't resurrect that argument."

Okay. I gently tug her braid, slanting her face toward me. "Just saying." I brush my lips over hers.

LEAVING ANA TO SOAK a little longer in the bath, I get dressed and wander through to my study for Sawyer's debrief. Mrs. Jones is in the kitchen.

"Evening, Gail."

"Mr. Grey. Welcome home, and congratulations once again."

"Thank you. Your sister okay?"

"All good, sir. Would you like anything?"

"No, thanks. I have some work to do."

"Mrs. Grey?"

I grin. "She's in the bath."

Gail smiles and nods. "I'll ask her when she's out, sir."

At my desk, I check my e-mails. Then buzz Sawyer. A moment later there's a brisk knock at my door.

"Come in."

Sawyer enters and stands before me, looking cool, calm, and professional in his suit and tie. His demeanor makes me so mad. Slowly, I get up from my desk and, placing both hands on it, lean toward him. "Where the fuck were you?" I shout.

He takes a small step back, surprised by my outburst.

"What the hell were you doing that you weren't ready to leave when we were?" I fold my arms, keeping a rein on my temper.

"Mr. Grey." He holds up his hands. "We were patrolling the grounds, like you asked us to do. And we didn't know you were leaving."

Oh.

"Also," he adds, getting into his stride, "I'd noticed the unsub. It arrived while we were out patrolling and I was going to investigate, when you came out of the house."

Ah.

I sigh, somewhat mollified. "I see. Okay." I should have told them we were leaving. And I know if Taylor had been with us, he would have left his colleague in the car.

"And Mrs. Grey set off at one hell of a pace." He raises a disapproving eyebrow.

I want to laugh at his response. I feel his pain, but I remain impassive. "She did," I admit. "Though you should have caught up. You're both trained in defensive driving."

"Yes, sir."

"Don't let it happen again."

"Yes, Mr. Grey." He looks a little contrite. "Sir," he says. "The unsub didn't follow us. He or she arrived shortly before you were leaving. I logged the exact time I noticed the car. It was 14:53 and they did not exit the vehicle. They knew where you were."

I pale. "What does that mean?"

"That someone could be watching your parents' house, sir. Or watching us here. Though I think we would have noticed if we were followed to Bellevue."

"Shit."

"Precisely. I've written a report for you and forwarded it to Taylor and Mr. Welch."

"I'll read it. Where's Ryan?"

"He's still on the road to Portland."

"Still?"

"Yes. Let's hope the unsub runs out of gas," Sawyer says.

"Why do you think the driver's a woman?" I ask.

"From the brief glimpse I got, I thought their hair was tied back."

"That's not definitive."

"No, sir."

"Keep me updated."

"Will do."

"Thank you, Luke. You can go."

He turns without a word and leaves my study while I sit back down at my desk, relieved that I don't have to fire him or Ryan, though I'll be glad when Taylor's back with us tomorrow evening. I contemplate Sawyer's theory; perhaps someone is watching my parents' place. But why? I should call my father, but I don't want to worry him, or my mother.

Shit. What to do?

My iMac has been nagging me about the latest update to its operating system, so I decide to install it, and open my laptop to check my e-mails and Sawyer's report.

I'm reading when my phone buzzes.

"Barney," I answer, surprised that he's contacting me on a Sunday.

"Welcome home, Mr. Grey."

"Thank you. What is it?"

"I've been going through the CCTV footage in the server room and I've uncovered something."

"You have?"

"Yes, sir. I couldn't wait until tomorrow to share it with you. I hope you don't mind. But I figured you'd want to know. I'll e-mail you a link and you can take a look yourself."

"You figured right. E-mail it to me now."

"Doing it."

"Will you stay on the line?"

"Yes, sir. I'm anxious for you to see it."

I smile. Barney is protective of his server room. I bet he's as pissed as I am by the unwelcome breach. His e-mail pops into my inbox; I open it and click on the link and I'm taken to a site I've not seen before. There are four different boxes that look like they might be monochrome views of my server room at Grey House. "Barney, you there?"

"Yes, Mr. Grey."

"What am I looking at?"

"This is the GEH security hub. If you click the play button in the menu on the left-hand side of the screen at the top, the footage from all the cameras within the server room will play." I do as I'm asked, and the footage plays four different views of the room. At the bottom center of each feed there's a date with a timer. It reads 08/10/11 07:03:10:05 and the milliseconds on the clock fly by. Via these four views, I watch a tall, slim man enter the room. He has scruffy dark hair and he's in pale, possibly white, coveralls. He walks to one of the servers, bends to the floor, and places a small black item that's hard to identify between two of the server cabinets. He stands and glances down at his handiwork, then, keeping his face fixed on the door, leaves.

"This is him?"

"I believe so, sir. It's not anyone we can identify. And that's where the incendiary device was found."

"That's over a week ago. How the fuck did he get in there?"

"The pass that correlates to that time of entry to the server room was issued to the cleaning crew."

"What?" How the hell did he get ahold of that?

"Exactly. We'll have to check that out tomorrow." The footage freezes.

"Did you just stop the feeds?" I ask.

"Yes, sir."

"Can you put these in a sequence?"

"Yes, sir."

"Quickly?"

"I can do it now."

"Has Welch seen this?"

"His team notified me of it. They've been combing the footage."

"Good."

A moment or so later my screen changes so I'm only looking at one feed. I press play again, and this time the sequence is longer, cutting between views. Each time one view finishes, I press play for the next.

"I can try and enhance the image," Barney says, his enthusiasm bubbling over in his tone. He wants to nail this son of a bitch, too.

"Do."

The image on my screen changes. It's sharper.

Suddenly, my study door opens. I look up, surprised, about to rebuke the intruder. It's Ana.

"So, you can't enhance it further?" I ask Barney.

"Let me try something." He's silent as Ana walks toward me with a look of quiet determination, and before I can do or say anything she crawls into my lap.

"I think that's as good as it's going to get," Barney says.

Ana puts her arms around my neck and snuggles beneath my chin, and I tighten my hold on her.

Is something wrong?

"Um, yes, Barney. Could you hold one moment?"

"Yes, sir."

I lift one shoulder to trap and hold my phone.

"Ana, what's wrong?"

She shakes her head, refusing to answer me. I grasp her chin and study her face, but her expression is unreadable. She frees her chin from my fingers and cuddles into me. I have no idea what's wrong, and frankly, I'm too engrossed in what Barney has found. I drop a kiss on her head. "Okay, Barney, what were you saying?"

"I can enhance the picture a little more."

I press play. The grainy black-and-white image of the arsonist appears on-screen. I press play once more, the arsonist moves closer to the camera, and I freeze the frame. "Okay, Barney, one more time."

"Let me see what I can do."

A dashed box appears around the head of the arsonist and suddenly zooms in.

Ana sits up and stares at the image. "Is Barney doing this?" she asks.

"Yes." And I know I sound as awed as she looks by Barney's technical prowess. "Can you sharpen the picture at all?" I ask him. The picture blurs, then refocuses moderately sharper on the asshole. He's looking down at the floor. Ana tenses and squints at the screen.

"Christian," she whispers. "That's Jack Hyde."

What!

"You think?" I squint at the image.

"It's the line of his jaw." Ana points at the screen following the monochromatic line of his chin. "And the earrings and the shape of his shoulders. He's the right build, too. He must be wearing a wig, or he's cut and dyed his hair."

I feel the blood drain from my face. *Hyde. Jack fucking Hyde!*

"Barney, are you getting this?" I put the phone down and switch to hands-free, then whisper to Ana, "You seem to have studied your ex-boss in some detail, Mrs. Grey."

Ana grimaces and shudders while anger surges like sulfuric acid through me.

"Yes, sir. I heard Mrs. Grey. I'm running facial-recognition software on all the digitized CCTV footage right now. See where else this asshole—I'm sorry, ma'am—this man has been within the organization."

"Why would he do this?" Ana asks.

I shrug, trying to mask my rage.

Fucking Hyde.

I put a stop to his creepy shit. Fired him. Punched him and broke his nose.

"Revenge, perhaps," I offer, darkly. "I don't know. You can't fathom why some people behave the way they do. I'm just angry that you ever worked so closely with him."

We have to get this information to the police, the FBI, and Welch, though he has some explaining to do. Hyde is obviously not in Florida. Why the hell did Welch think he was? I need to talk to him. And maybe, given all this time, Hyde may have skulked back to his apartment, here in Seattle. Welch needs to find him sooner rather than later, and if he does, I hope I get to punch that fucker's lights out again. One thing's for sure, I need to keep him away from my wife, keep her safe. I curl my arm around her waist.

"We have the contents of his hard drive, too, sir," Barney adds.

I interrupt Barney with the first thought that comes into my head. "Yes, I remember. Do you have an address for Mr. Hyde?" I don't want to alarm Ana with the details of what was on Hyde's old computer.

"Yes, sir, I do," Barney says.

"Alert Welch." Welch needs to make sure Hyde's not back home.

"Sure will. I'm also going to scan the city CCTV and see if I can track his movements."

"Check what vehicle he owns."

"Sir."

"Barney can do all this?" Ana whispers, clearly impressed.

I nod, feeling a little smug that he works for me.

"What was on his hard drive?" she asks.

I shake my head. "Nothing much."

"Tell me."

"No."

"Was it about you, or me?"

She is not going to drop this.

"Me." I sigh.

"What sort of things? About your lifestyle?"

No. I shake my head and place my index finger on her lips.

We are not alone, Ana.

She scowls at me but keeps quiet.

"It's a 2006 Camaro," Barney pipes up, excited. "I'll send the license details to Welch, too."

I'm sure he has them, but it doesn't hurt to be sure. "Good. Let me know where else that fucker has been in my building. And check this image against the one from his SIP personnel file. I want to be sure we have a match."

"Already done, sir, and Mrs. Grey is correct. This is Jack Hyde."

Ana grins, practically preening, she's so pleased with herself.

As she should be.

I run my hand down her back, proud of her. "Well done, Mrs. Grey." To Barney, I add, "Let me know when you've tracked all his movements at HQ. Also check out any other GEH property he may have had access to, and let the security teams know so they can make another sweep of all those buildings."

"Sir."

"Thanks, Barney." I hang up the phone. "Well, Mrs. Grey, it seems that you are not only decorative, but useful, too," I tease.

"Decorative?"

"Very." I press a soft kiss to her lips.

"You're much more decorative than I am, Mr. Grey."

I wind her braid around my wrist and hold her, pouring my gratitude into a deep and tender kiss. She's done so much today. And identified our perpetrator!

She pulls away.

"Hungry?" I ask.

"No."

"I am," I confess.

"What for?" She eyes me warily.

"Well—food, actually."

She giggles. "I'll make you something."

"I love that sound."

"Of me offering you food?"

"Your giggling." I kiss her head, and she eases herself off my lap.

"So, what would you like to eat, Sir?" she asks with faux sweetness.

She's making fun of me. Again.

I narrow my eyes. "Are you being cute, Mrs. Grey?"

"Always, Mr. Grey, Sir."

I see how it is.

"I can still put you over my knee," I whisper. Frankly, not much would give me greater pleasure.

"I know." Ana grins and places her hands on the arms of my office chair. She bends down and kisses me. "That's one of the things I love about you. But stow your twitching palm, you're hungry."

"Oh, Mrs. Grey, what am I going to do with you?"

"You're going to answer my question. What would you like to eat?"

"Something light. Surprise me."

"I'll see what I can do." She turns and struts out of my office, like she owns the place, which, of course, as my wife, she does.

I call Welch to interrogate him about what Barney and Ana have uncovered.

"Hyde?" While usually gruff, his voice is high-pitched with incredulity.

"Yes. In my fucking server room."

"We tracked his cell phone to Orlando. It's been there ever since. We assumed he'd been staying with his mother, as the phone was tracked to her condominium in Orlando. There are no records of him traveling elsewhere."

"Well. He's here." I take a deep breath, trying to keep a lid on my frustration.

He sighs, obviously annoyed. "So it would seem. I'll put the team straight on this. I don't know how he slipped through our fingers. I'll make inquiries and find out how and where we messed up."

"You do that. I want to know."

"It's a damned shame there are no prints from the server room," he says.

"None?

"No."

"Hell. He was probably wearing gloves, though it's difficult to tell from the footage," I speculate. "Perhaps Hyde's prints are on file somewhere."

"Interesting thought. In fact, the FBI recovered a partial print but has no match."

"From *Charlie Tango*?" I ask.

"Yes."

"Why didn't you let me know?"

"They didn't have a match, and it's only a partial print," Welch explains.

"Could Hyde be behind the sabotage of my EC135?"

"In the absence of any other suspects, I think it's a possibility," Welch's gravelly voice echoes over the phone.

"We had him on our list of suspects and he was right there this whole time."

I can't believe it.

"We dismissed him for three reasons," Welch clarifies. "First, we thought he was in Florida. He'd not been in his apartment in Seattle for some time, but we'll check on that now. Second, he's not withdrawn any cash from an ATM in the Seattle area. And third, his misdeeds seemed limited to harassing female colleagues."

"You should let the FBI know about all this," I say.

"I'll brief them," he says, and then changes tack. "Sawyer's informed me about the chase."

"He thinks my parents' house was being watched."

"It's a possibility. We'll need to track this Dodge down to be sure."

"The driver could have been Hyde."

"Yes. In light of what you've uncovered, could be."

"Given that he still poses a threat, I think we should provide security for all my family."

"That's a good idea. There were extensive details about all of them on Hyde's computer. You should consider letting your parents know."

I sigh. I don't want to alarm my family.

"We'll concentrate our efforts on locating Hyde."

"Find him."

"We'll redouble our efforts."

"You'd better," I warn. "Barney will be in touch and you can submit the server room footage as evidence to the police. I'll talk to my dad and get back to you."

"Yes, sir. We'll get on it." He hangs up.

I call my parents' landline, but it diverts to the answering machine. I try my dad's cell, but that goes straight to voice mail, too. They must be at evening Mass. I leave a message asking Dad to call me in the morning.

I gather Gia Matteo's plans and go in search of my wife and food.

Placing the plans on the kitchen island, I stroll over to Ana, who I have to say looks fetching even in sweatpants and her camisole. She's preparing some food; the mashed avocado looks good. I fold my arms around her and kiss her neck. "Barefoot and in the kitchen," I whisper into her fragrant skin.

"Shouldn't that be barefoot and pregnant in the kitchen?"

Pregnant! I tense. Shit. No. Kids. Hell no. "Not yet," I state, as I try to calm my suddenly spiked heart rate.

"No. Not yet!" Ana sounds as panicked as me.

I take a deep breath. "On that we can agree, Mrs. Grey."

She stops mashing the avocado. "You do want kids, though, don't you?"

"Sure, yes. Eventually. But I'm not ready to share you yet." I kiss her neck.

One day. Sure.

"What are you making? Looks good." I nuzzle her ear. She quivers and gives me a wicked grin.

"Subs." She smirks.

God, I love this woman's sense of humor.

I nip her earlobe. "My favorite," I whisper in her ear, and am rewarded with a poke in my side from her elbow. "Mrs. Grey, you wound me." I clutch my damaged side in a performance worthy of an Oscar winner.

"Wimp," Ana teases.

"Wimp?" Playfully, I slap her behind. "Hurry up with my food, wench. And later I'll show you how wimpy I can be." I spank her again and head to the fridge. "Would you like a glass of wine?" I ask.

Ana flashes me a quick smile. "Please."

ANA DOES GOOD SUB. What can I say?

Taking both our plates, I leave them in the sink for Gail. I top off both our wineglasses, then spread out Gia's plans over the breakfast bar. We pore over her drawings; she's worked hard and produced thorough and detailed elevations. Her designs are impressive. But what does my wife think?

Ana looks up at me. "I love her proposal to make the entire downstairs back wall glass, but…"

"But?" I prompt.

She sighs. "I don't want to take all the character out of the house."

"Character?"

"Yes. What Gia is proposing is quite radical, but, well, I fell in love with the house as it is, warts and all."

Oh. I think this house is in need of a serious update.

"I kind of like it the way it is," she says quietly, her expression serious.

In that moment, everything becomes clear to me. "I want this house to be the way you want. Whatever you want. It's yours."

She frowns. "I want you to like it, too. To be happy in it, too."

"I'll be happy wherever you are. It's that simple, Ana." *I mean it. You* are what will make the house a home, and I want you happy. *Always.*

"Well—" Her breath catches in her throat. "I like the glass wall. Maybe we could ask her to incorporate it into the house a little more sympathetically."

"Sure. Whatever you want. What about the plans for upstairs and the basement?"

"I'm cool with those."

"Good."

She bites her lip. "Do you want to put in a playroom?" she blurts, and her question completely takes me by surprise. She flushes.

Ana, Ana, Ana, even after today, you're still shy about what we do?

I hide my smile. "Do you?" I ask.

She raises one narrow shoulder, trying to look nonchalant. "Um, if you want."

I think she does.

"Let's leave our options open for the moment. After all, this will be a family home. Besides, we can improvise."

"I like improvising," she whispers.

Me, too, baby.

"There's something I want to discuss." I don't want separate bathrooms. I like showering with Ana too much.

Fortunately, she agrees.

"Are you going back to work?" Ana asks as I roll up the plans.

"Not if you don't want me to. What would you like to do?"

"We could watch TV."

"Okay." I deposit the plans on the dining table and we both head into the TV room.

On the couch, I pick up the remote and switch on the TV and start flicking through the channels, while Ana curls up beside me and rests her head on my shoulder.

This is nice.

"Any specific drivel you want to see?" I ask her.

"You don't like TV much, do you?" Ana says.

I shake my head. "Waste of time. But I'll watch something with you."

"I thought we could make out."

"Make out?" I stop flicking and stare at her.

"Yes." Ana frowns.

"We could go to bed and make out."

"We do that all the time. When was the last time you made out in front of the TV?" she asks with a shy smile.

Um… Never?

I shrug and shake my head, embarrassed to answer. I didn't do the make-out thing. I would have liked to. I remember Elliot bringing home girl after girl and making out with them

I used to burn with envy.

But I couldn't bear to be touched.

How can you kiss and cuddle someone when you can't tolerate their hands on you?

Fuck. Those were tough years.

I flick through the channels, and an old episode of *The X-Files* pops up.

Ha! Scully, my first adolescent crush.

"Christian?" Ana asks, bringing me back from my fucked-up past.

"I've never done that," I answer, quickly. *Can we move on?*

"Never?"

"No."

"Not even with Mrs. Robinson?"

I laugh. "Baby, I did a lot of things with Mrs. Robinson. Making out was not one of them." Ana looks horrified, and I want to kick myself for allowing Elena into our conversation. And then it occurs to me—maybe Ana has made out with countless boys. I narrow my eyes. "Have you?"

"Of course." She's scandalized that I would think otherwise.

"What! Who with?"

Ana clams up.

What the fuck? Does she have some first great love? I know nothing about her love life. I assumed, stupidly, that she didn't have one, because she was a virgin. "Tell me," I press her.

She gazes down at her hands, knotted in her lap. I place my hand over hers, and she glances up at me.

I'm just curious, Ana. "I want to know. So, I can beat whoever it was to a pulp."

She giggles. "Well, the first time—"

"The first time! There's more than one fucker?"

"Why so surprised, Mr. Grey?"

I run a hand through my hair. The thought of anyone touching Ana is...annoying. "I just am. I mean—given your lack of experience."

"I've certainly made up for that since I met you."

"You have." I grin. "Tell me. I want to know."

"You really want me to tell you?"

I'm interested in everything about you, Ana.

She takes a deep breath. "I was briefly in Texas with Mom and Husband Number Three. I was in tenth grade. His name was Bradley, and he was my lab partner in physics."

"How old were you?"

"Fifteen."

"And what's he doing now?"

"I don't know."

"What base did he get to?"

"Christian!" she chastises me, and we stare at each other.

Fuck this Bradley. What kind of a name is that, anyway?

I grab her knees, then her ankles, and tip her up so she falls back on the couch, and I lay down on top of her.

"Ah," she cries out.

I grab both her hands and raise them above her head. "So, this Bradley. Did he get to first base?" I whisper and run my nose down hers and leave soft kisses at the corner of her mouth.

"Yes," she breathes. I release one of her hands and clasp her chin and kiss her, properly, my tongue caressing hers, and her body rises to meet mine, her tongue twisting with mine.

"Like this?" I whisper.

"No. Nothing like that." Ana is breathless.

Releasing her chin, I skim my fingers down her body, then back to her breast. "Did he do this? Touch you like this?" Through the soft material of her top, my thumb skates repeatedly over her nipple, and it perks up at my touch.

"No." She writhes beneath me.

"Did he get to second base?" I blow the words gently in her ear as my hand travels down to her hip. My lips suck gently on her earlobe before my teeth tug it into my mouth.

"No." The word is a husky whisper.

I mute the TV. *The X-Files* can wait. I gaze down at Ana; she's tousled and dazed and looking up at me with big blue eyes that I could drown in. "What about Joe Schmo number two? Did he make it past second base?"

I move to her side and slip my hand into her sweatpants, keeping her pinned with my gaze.

"No."

"Good." I hold her in the palm of my hand, the gateway to heaven. "No underwear, Mrs. Grey. I approve." I kiss her again, and my thumb strokes her clitoris in a steady rhythm and I ease my index finger inside her.

"We're supposed to be making out," she murmurs with a moan.

I stop. "I thought we were?"

"No. No sex."

"What?" *Why?*

"No sex."

"No sex, huh?" I gently ease my finger out of her and remove my hand from her pants. "Here." I circle her mouth with my finger, then push it between her lips and onto her tongue. Once. Twice. Again.

Taste good, Ana?

I shift so I'm lying on top of her, between her legs, and I rock against her, giving my cock some relief.

She groans.

Oh, wow.

I grind against her. "This what you want?" And I repeat the action, hitting her sweet spot with my erection.

It feels good.

"Yes."

I tease her nipple with my fingers, tugging gently, feeling it lengthen beneath my touch. My teeth graze her jaw. She smells of Ana and jasmine and her arousal. "Do you know how hot you are, Ana?"

Her mouth opens, slack and wanting, as I tantalize her further, pushing at the junction of her thighs. She lets out an inarticulate moan and I seize the moment, tugging at her bottom lip, then invading her mouth with my tongue, tasting her arousal on mine.

It's so fucking hot.

I release her remaining hand and her fingers feel their way over my biceps and over my shoulders and into my hair. She tugs and I groan, staring down at her.

"Do you like me touching you?" she asks.

Why would she ask me that now?

I stop rubbing against her. "Of course I do." I'm breathless. "I love you touching me, Ana. I'm like a starving man at a banquet when it comes to your touch." Kneeling up between her legs, I maneuver her to a sitting position and remove her top in one swift move. I do the same with my shirt, yanking it over my head and throwing our clothes on the floor. While still kneeling, I seat her on my lap and rest my hands on her behind. "Touch me," I whisper.

She takes full advantage, brushing the tips of her fingers over my sternum and over my scars. I inhale sharply as her touch radiates through my body with the promise of fulfilment. My eyes stay on hers as she skims her fingers over my skin to my nipple, then to its twin; each react to her touch, hardening, erect, mirroring another part of my anatomy. She leans forward and presses her lips in a soft, sweet line across my chest. Her hands hold my shoulders, and she squeezes, and I feel her nails pinching my skin.

It's heady.

And to think a few months ago I would have said this was impossible.

Yet, here she is. Touching me. Loving me.

And I welcome it. All of it.

"I want you," I whisper, and her hands move to my head, her fingers in my hair. She yanks my head back and takes my mouth with hers. Claiming my tongue with hers.

Fuck. I groan loudly and push Ana back down on the couch, divesting her of her sweatpants in one hasty move, and freeing my erection at the same time. I move on her. "Home run," I murmur, and fill her in one rapid move.

She lets out a deep, guttural cry and I still, holding her face between my hands. "I love you, Mrs. Grey." And very slowly, I make sweet love to my wife until she cries out and falls apart in my arms, taking me with her and cocooning me with her limbs and keeping me safe.

ANA IS SPRAWLED ON my chest. I think it's the end of *The X-Files*.

"You know, we completely bypassed third base." Her fingers trace a pattern on my chest.

I chuckle. "Next time." I nuzzle her hair, inhaling her magical scent, and kiss her head. The end credits roll for *The X-Files* and, using the remote, I switch the sound back on.

"You liked that show?" Ana asks.

"When I was a kid."

Ana goes quiet.

"You?" I ask.

"Before my time."

"You're so young." I hug her tightly. "I like making out with you, Mrs. Grey."

"Likewise, Mr. Grey." She kisses my chest and the commercials start on the TV.

Why are we watching these?

Because I like being here, with her lying on me.

This is married life.

I could get used to this...

"It's been a heavenly three weeks," she says airily. "Car chases and fires and psycho ex-bosses notwithstanding. Like being in our own private bubble."

"Hmm." I tighten my arms around her. "I'm not sure I'm ready to share you with the rest of the world yet."

"Back to reality tomorrow." She sounds a little sad.

"Security will be tight—"

Ana silences me with her index finger. "I know. I'll be good. I promise." She leans up on her elbows, scrutinizing me. "Why were you shouting at Sawyer?"

"Because we were followed."

"That wasn't Sawyer's fault."

"They should never have let you get so far in front. They know that."

"That wasn't—"

"Enough." Sawyer fucked up and he knows it. "This is not up for discussion, Anastasia. It's a fact, and they won't let it happen again."

"Okay," she says. "Did Ryan catch up with the woman in the Dodge?"

"No. And I'm not convinced it was a woman."

"Oh?"

"Sawyer saw someone with their hair tied back, but it was a brief look. He assumed it was a woman. Now, given that you've identified that fucker, maybe it was him. He wore his hair like that."

That piece of shit is dead if I ever get ahold of him.

I run my hand down Ana's back, my fingers stroking her skin. Grounding me. Calming me. "If anything happened to you." The thought is unbearable.

"I know. I feel the same about you." She shivers.

"Come. You're getting cold." I sit up, taking her with me. "Let's go to bed. We can cover third base there."

Monday, August 22, 2011

To our relief, there are no photographers outside SIP when we pull up in the Q7. I'm hoping that the intense press scrutiny and intrusion into our lives will now ease off. Ana gathers up her briefcase when Ryan stops the car, and I can't resist one more try. "You know you don't have to do this."

"I know," she answers quietly, so Ryan and Sawyer can't hear. "But I want to. You know this." Her sweet kiss does little to mollify me. We both have to go back to reality. Don't we?

"What's wrong?" she asks, and I realize I'm frowning.

I'm not going to see her until this evening. We've spent the last three weeks or so in each other's company, and it's been the best time of my life. Sawyer climbs out of the car to open her door, and I seize my opportunity. "I'll miss having you to myself."

She places her palm on my cheek. "Me, too." Her lips brush mine. "It was a wonderful honeymoon. Thank you."

It was for me as well, Ana.

"Go to work, Mrs. Grey."

"You, too, Mr. Grey."

Sawyer opens her door, she squeezes my hand, and I watch both of them head into the building.

"Take me to Grey House," I instruct Ryan, and stare out of the window. It's a cooler, cloudy day—a precise match for my mood. I'm strangely out of sorts. Perhaps this is what Ana was feeling yesterday, though she never managed to articulate it to me.

If this was what you were experiencing, Ana, I get it. It's a case of the post-honeymoon blues.

AS RYAN AND I walk up to the entrance at Grey House I notice Barry and an additional security guard who I don't recognize on the other side of the glass doors. Barry typically stands by the elevator, and is usually the only security operative in reception.

"Good morning, Mr. Grey. Welcome back," he says as he holds open the door.

"Thank you, Barry. Good morning."

They are checking that all GEH staff are wearing their passes. I'm not wearing mine, but then I'm the exception to the rule. Welch was not lying when he said he was doubling down on all our security measures.

Greeting both of the receptionists with a salute, I head to the elevators. They both wave back, and I notice they're wearing their passes, too. It's reassuring.

Andrea and Sarah look up as the elevator doors open; each have ID lanyards. "Welcome back, Mr. Grey," Andrea says.

"Good morning. How are you? Oh, these are for you and Sarah." I place a bag that contains a large box of chocolates—from Ladurée, near the Jardin des Tuileries in Paris—that Ana insisted I buy for them on the desk. Andrea blushes, speechless.

Yes. I don't blame her. Apart from her wedding present, this is a first.

"Thank you," Sarah blurts, eyeing the bag with keen interest.

"You're welcome. I would have bought some of their world-famous macarons, too, but was advised that the chocolates have a longer shelf life."

"Thank you, Mr. Grey," Andrea says, recovering her composure. "Coffee?"

"Please. Black."

"Coming up."

I head into my office, leaving Sarah's giggles and Andrea's quiet hushing behind me. Rolling my eyes, I shut the door and cut off their chatter.

At my desk, I call Welch for an update on Jack Hyde.

Once that call is over, I e-mail Ana, wondering how she is adapting to life back at SIP.

From: Christian Grey
Subject: Bubble
Date: August 22 2011 09:32
To: Anastasia Grey

Mrs. Grey
Love covering all the bases with you.
Have a great first day back.
Miss our bubble already.
x

Christian Grey
Back in the Real World CEO, Grey Enterprises Holdings, Inc.

My phone buzzes. "Mr. Grey, I have your father on the line," Andrea says.

"Put him through."

"Christian, you called?"

"Dad." I tell him everything that has happened with Jack Hyde since I fired him in mid-June. "His vendetta against me is out of hand. We're submitting the server room footage to the FBI and the police. They can press charges. They just have to locate him first. But given what we found on his hard drive, I think I should extend our security protocols to you, Mom, Mia, and Elliot."

"That seems excessive."

"Dad, he's a bright guy. I wouldn't put anything past him."

Carrick blows out a breath. "Well, if you think it's necessary."

"I do. We were followed from your house yesterday. He knows where you live."

"Fuck!"

Dad!

My father sighs. "Get on it. I'll talk to Mom and Mia."

"I'll tell Elliot."

"Thanks, Christian. I'm sorry it's come to this."

"Me, too."

With my father's reluctant agreement secured, I phone Welch back to implement enhanced security measures for my family.

I just have to tell Elliot. I don't know how he'll take the news.

When I look at my e-mails I notice the one I sent to Ana has bounced. Maybe she hasn't had a chance to change her e-mail address at work.

Let's have some fun with this.

I forward the e-mail I sent her.

From: Christian Grey
Subject: Errant Wives
Date: August 22 2011 09:56
To: Anastasia Steele

Wife
I sent the e-mail below and it bounced.
And it's because you haven't changed your name.
Something you want to tell me?

Christian Grey
CEO, Grey Enterprises Holdings, Inc.

Andrea knocks on the door with another coffee.

"Thanks, Andrea. Shall we go through the schedule?"

She takes the chair opposite my desk and we discuss my appointments for the week and the coming month.

"…You have the Seattle Assistance Union Gala for Hope on Wednesday evening, I have two tickets. Your mother is involved with that charity," she says.

"Okay."

"And the Telecommunications Alliance Organization fundraiser is on Thursday evening in New York," Andrea continues. "I have tickets for two. The Gulfstream will be back. Everything has checked out. Stephan is flying in from Maine tomorrow."

"My plans aren't set yet. I'll talk to Ros to see if a visit to GEH Fiber Optics is still required."

"Okay. Stephan will be on standby should you decide to go. And I'll have your Tribeca apartment serviced, too, unless you'd like me to make a reservation at The Lowell."

My mind whirrs. "If I do go to New York, then I could come back via DC. There are two meetings we could set up for Friday, one with the Securities and Exchange Commission, the other with Senator Blandino."

"Do you want me to arrange those?"

"I'll talk to Vanessa about the Securities and Exchange Commission. But provisionally yes for Blandino."

"Sir."

"Okay. I should see Ros, and can you get Flynn on the line for me? Oh, and find time for Bastille tomorrow. Please."

"Will do." She gets up and leaves, and I turn my attention to my computer. An e-mail from Ana arrived a short while ago.

From: Anastasia Steele
Subject: Don't Burst the Bubble
Date: August 22 2011 09:58
To: Christian Grey

Husband
I am all for a baseball metaphor with you, Mr. Grey.
I want to keep my name here.
I'll explain this evening.
I am going into a meeting now.
Miss our bubble, too…
PS: Thought I had to use my BlackBerry?

Anastasia Steele
Editor, SIP

I stare at her e-mail.

She's not going to take my name.

She's. Not. Going. To. Take. My. Name.

Why?

She doesn't want my name.

Not now, Maggot.

It's a gut punch.

I gape at the screen, shocked and momentarily paralyzed.

Don't fight, Maggot!

Why didn't she tell me? This is how I find out?

Damn it. To hell with this.

I'm going to get her to change her mind.

Like you did about her obeying you, Grey?

My phone buzzes. It's Andrea. "Ros is on the way up."

"Thanks. Send her in when she gets here."

I don't know what to say to Ana, so I push her e-mail from my thoughts and await my meeting with my chief operating officer.

Ros is in sparkling form. She sails through a concise agenda and brings me up to speed on everything within an hour.

"You've done a great job," I tell her.

"Christian, I've loved it. But in all honesty, I missed you."

I smile, because I don't know how I should react. I'm not used to compliments from my staff. "In all honesty, I can't say the same," I reply.

She grins. "That's as it should be. I'm sure you had a wonderful time."

"I did, thank you."

Except my wife doesn't want my name.

She gives me a brief speculative look, but I force a smile. "I'll get on to the Detroit people," she says, "and I'll give Hassan a call about whether you need to visit the New York operation this week."

"Thursday would be good if they need me to go."

"I'll let you know."

After she's gone, I reread Ana's e-mail. It's as discouraging as it was the first time I read it. While I'm contemplating how to respond, Andrea puts Flynn through.

"Christian. Welcome back. How was your honeymoon?" He sounds hale and hearty, and very British. He must have been back to the UK recently.

"Good. Thanks."

He hesitates, and I know he senses something's wrong.

"Can I come and see you?" I ask.

"I'm sorry, but my schedule is full today."

When I don't respond, he sighs. "Janet, my secretary, will kill me, but I can squeeze you in at lunchtime, though you'll have to watch me eating my cheese-and-pickle sandwiches."

"Okay. What time is that?"

"Twelve thirty."

"I'll see you then." I hang up and call Elliot to give him the full story on Hyde and brief him about security.

"What a fucker!" Elliot sneers.

"Yes. That's him in a nutshell. Don't tell Kate about this. I know what a newshound she is."

"Dude—" Elliot protests, but I cut him off.

"Elliot, I don't want to argue. She's tenacious. I met my wife because of Kate's constant badgering, and I don't want her fucking up the police investigation by becoming involved."

Elliot is silent.

"No disrespect meant," I add.

He sighs. "Okay, man. Hope the police catch the bastard."

"Me, too."

"I've got to be on-site, but let me know how your meeting with Gia goes this evening. I can't wait to see the plans and we can start ordering the materials we'll need."

"Will do."

"I HAVE HALF AN hour, Christian," Flynn says when I march into his office.

"She won't take my name."

"What?"

"Anastasia."

"She won't take your name?" He looks momentarily confused. "Anastasia Grey?"

"Yes. She sent me an e-mail this morning, telling me so."

"Sit," he says, and points to the couch, and rather than take his usual chair, he sits down on the couch opposite. There is a plate of sandwiches, their crusts removed, and what looks like cola in a glass in front of him on the coffee table. "Lunch," he says.

"Please, go ahead. Don't mind me."

"So, Christian, let's just back up a bit. I last saw you on your wedding day. It was a joyous occasion. How was the honeymoon?" He takes a large bite out of a sandwich while my mind casts back to a few days ago. I relax, a little, remembering the calm waters of the deep blue Med; the scent of the bougainvillea, how accommodating and efficient the crew of *Fair Lady* were…how much I loved being in Anastasia's company.

"It was sublime."

John smiles. "Good. Any issues?"

"None that I want to discuss." I'm not prepared to tell him about the hickey incident yet.

He gives me a direct, level look. "Because you are encroaching on my lunchtime, I'm going to tell you that's not very helpful."

I sigh. "Nothing serious. We had one fight."

"Was that about your name?"

I flush. "Um. No."

"Okay, when and if you want to discuss that, we can. So, what's happened since then?"

I tell him at length about Hyde, about firing him, about the incendiary device, and the fact that he had information about me, my family, and Ana on his SIP hard drive. I tell him about the car chase.

"Crikey!" Flynn exclaims when I finish.

"He's now the chief suspect in my helicopter's sabotage."

"Holy crap," he mouths, and takes a bite of his sandwich.

"But that's not the reason I'm here. This morning I got an e-mail from Ana saying she doesn't want to take my name. I would have expected a discussion at least. Not just an e-mail."

"I see." His expression is thoughtful. "Finding out your wife's ex-boss is trying to burn down your building, and may be responsible for a near-fatal accident in your helicopter is a big deal, Christian. Plus, a car chase. Have you considered that you may be channeling your stress from all these incidents into your reaction to the e-mail that you received from your wife?"

I frown. "I don't think so."

He strokes his chin. "Knowing how anxious you are about Ana's safety, all of these events had to have had an effect on you. As I've learned over the last few months, she is your primary concern. Always."

"True."

"You do a great deal for her," he says gently.

I do.

"You've given up a great deal for her."

I say nothing. *Where is he going with this?*

"Then you might be interpreting her e-mail as a rejection, especially after all that you've done for her, and that wounds you."

I take a deep breath.

Yes. It does. "I just can't believe she didn't talk to me about it. It's like she's dismissing me and all that I have worked to become. I wasn't born a Grey."

Flynn frowns. "There's a lot to unpack in that sentence, Christian. And, sadly, I don't have the time to do that right now. I hate to break it to you, but Anastasia keeping her name might be more about how she feels about herself, and may have nothing to do with you."

How could this not be about me? It's my name. It's the only one I have…the only one I acknowledge.

There you are, Maggot.

I gaze at him, remaining impassive.

"The best thing to do is to talk to her. Tell her how you feel," Flynn adds. "We spoke about this before. Ana is not an unreasonable person."

She's not. Except about the obey vow.

"This obviously means a great deal to you. Talk to her. I think we have an appointment on Wednesday. We can discuss this in more detail then. And maybe, in the meantime, you'll have worked out some kind of compromise."

"Compromise?"

She either takes my name or she doesn't. Where's the compromise in that?

"Ask her why, Christian," he says gently. "Communicate and compromise."

"Yeah, yeah. 'It's better to concede the battle to win the war.'" I parrot his words from one of our earlier sessions.

"Precisely."

I get up. "Thanks for seeing me at such short notice."

"Well, I hope I've been helpful."

"I think so." *I'm going to talk to Ana right now.*

"I'll see you Wednesday."

"One more thing. Leila Williams—is she in Connecticut?" I ask.

"I think so. She starts college today in Hamden. I had an e-mail from her last night. She's excited to begin her studies." He angles his head to one side in an unspoken "why?"

"It's nothing. See you Wednesday."

"RYAN, TAKE ME TO SIP."

"Yes, sir."

On the short journey to Ana's workplace, I contemplate what I'm going to say to her. We had three weeks to discuss the issue of her name while we were on our honeymoon. Why didn't she bring it up then? I've done nothing but call her Mrs. Grey. She didn't object. Maybe I've made a stupid assumption about her name, but she knows I have…issues. I've told her to manage my expectations.

I want people to know she's *my* wife, even where she works.

My name does that. It represents all that is good in my life.

My parents. *My father.*

It represents everything he's done for me. For Elliot and for Mia, too.

Even though he's an asshole sometimes.

I still want to emulate him.

And every time I stood in front of his desk while he gave me a dressing-down, I knew I'd failed and disappointed him.

He has pushed me to be a better person, a better man.

I admire him.

I love him.

Fuck.

Maybe I should wait until this evening.

No. It can't wait. I will burst a blood vessel.

This is too important to me.

As I stare out of the car window, looking at everyone going about their business, my resentment simmers. Why the hell didn't she tell me?

By the time I stalk into SIP, I'm hanging on to my temper by a silken thread. The first person I meet is Jerry Roach, who's standing in the reception area and talking to a willowy woman with long, out-of-control dark hair.

"Christian Grey," he says in disbelief.

"Jerry. How are you?"

"Um. Good. This is Elizabeth Morgan, our head of HR."

"Hi," I mutter tightly, as we shake hands.

"Mr. Grey. I've heard a great deal about you." Her smile doesn't reach her eyes, and I doubt Ana's confided in her about me—so where she's heard about me, I don't know, but I've got no time to speculate on this now.

"What can we do for you?" Roach asks, pleasantly.

"I need a quick word with Ms. Steele."

"Ana? Of course. I'll take you to her. Follow me." His fawning small talk leaves a lot to be desired, and I listen with half an ear as we head through the double doors behind reception and through to Ana's office. I recall her saying that he went a little crazy when he found out that we were engaged. This does not endear him to me. Idly, I wonder how he would feel if he worked for Ana. That would surely make him crazy.

There's a thought.

That would teach him.

Ana is in Hyde's old office. I nod in greeting to Sawyer, who's standing outside, while Roach raps on the door. Ana calls, "Come in." The office is as small and shabby as I remember—still in need of updating and a lick of paint—though there are flowers on Ana's desk, and the shelves are ordered and tidy. She's eating her lunch with a young woman who I assume is her assistant. Both of them gape at me. I turn to her PA. "Hello, you must be Hannah. I'm Christian Grey."

Hannah leaps to her feet and offers me her hand. "Mr. Grey. H-how nice to m-meet you," she says as we shake hands. "Can I fetch you a coffee?"

"Please." I give her a polite smile and she rushes out of the room. I turn to Roach. "If you'll excuse me, Roach, I'd like a word with *Ms.* Steele."

"Of course, Mr. Grey. Ana." Roach leaves, closing the door behind him. I turn my attention to my wife, who looks guilty—like I've caught her doing something illicit—though she's as lovely as ever.

A little pale, perhaps.

A little hostile, perhaps.

Shit. My anger recedes, leaving anxiety in its wake, as she squares her shoulders.

"Mr. Grey, how nice to see you." Her smile is saccharine, and I know our honeymoon is over, and I have a fight on my hands. My spirit nosedives once more.

"*Ms.* Steele, may I sit down?" I nod toward the worn leather chair facing Ana's desk that's been vacated by Hannah.

"It's your company." Ana offers me the chair with a dismissive wave of her hand.

"Yes, it is." I grin back with an equally saccharine look.

Yes, baby. Mine.

We are circling each other—boxers in a ring—sizing each other up. Dampening down my bitterness, I steel myself for the battle ahead. This issue is important to me. "Your office is very small," I note as I take the seat.

"It suits me." Her tone is clipped and irritated; she's mad at me. "So, what can I do for you, Christian?"

"I'm just looking over my assets."

"Your assets?" she scoffs. "All of them?"

"All of them. Some of them need rebranding."

"Rebranding?" Her eyebrows shoot up. "In what way?"

"I think you know."

She sighs. "Please don't tell me you have interrupted your day, after three weeks away, to come over here and fight with me about my name."

That's exactly what I've done.

I cross my legs and remove a speck of lint from my pants, playing for time.

Steady, Grey. "Not exactly fight. No."

She narrows her eyes. Pissed. "Christian, I'm working."

"Looked like you were gossiping with your assistant to me."

"We were going through our schedules," she hisses, as her cheeks color. "And you haven't answered my question."

There's a knock on the door. "Come in!" Ana yells, surprising us both. Hannah enters, bearing a small tray with coffee, which she places on Ana's desk.

"Thank you, Hannah," Ana mutters, subdued.

"Do you need anything else, Mr. Grey?" Hannah asks.

"No, thank you. That's all." Deliberately, I give her my most excellent smile. It has the desired effect, and she scuttles out. "Now, *Ms.* Steele, where were we?"

"You were rudely interrupting my workday to fight with me about my name." Ana spits the words at me, her fervor taking me by surprise.

She is really mad.

So. Am. I.

She should have told me.

"I like to make the odd impromptu visit. It keeps management on their toes, wives in their place. You know."

"I had no idea you could spare the time," she retorts.

Enough. Cut to the chase, Grey.

Striving to keep my tone respectful, I ask, quietly, "Why don't you want to change your name here?"

"Christian, do we have to discuss this now?"

"I'm here. I don't see why not." *This is important to me, Ana.*

"I have a ton of work to do, having been away for the last three weeks."

"Are you ashamed of me?" I inquire, surprising myself, and inadvertently revealing the darkness that resides in my soul.

I hadn't intended to go here.

I hold my breath.

Don't fight, Maggot.

"No! Christian, of course not." She grimaces, appalled. "This is about me, not you."

"How is this not about me?" I cock my head, willing her to explain. Of course this is about me; it's my name.

Her expression softens. "Christian, when I took this job, I'd only just met you." It's like she's talking to a child. "I didn't know you were going to buy the company—" She closes her eyes, as if this is a particularly painful memory, and puts her head in her hands. "Why is it so important to you?" she asks and looks up, beseeching me.

"I want everyone to know that you're mine."

"I am yours—look." She holds up her hand, which bears her wedding and engagement rings.

"It's not enough," I whisper.

"Not enough that I married you?" Her voice is almost inaudible, and her eyes widen.

"That's not what I mean." *Ana, don't distort what I'm trying to say to you.*

"What do you mean?" she demands.

"I want your world to begin and end with me."

Her eyes are impossibly blue. "It does," she says, and I don't know if I've ever heard two words filled with such quiet passion before; they suck the air out of the room and take my breath away. "I'm just trying to establish a career," she continues, warming to her subject, "and I don't want to trade on your name. I have to do something, Christian."

I swallow down my rising emotion, listening hard, as she speaks.

"I can't stay imprisoned at Escala or the new house with nothing to do. I'll go crazy. I'll suffocate. I've always worked, and I enjoy this. This is my dream job; it's all I've ever wanted. But doing this doesn't mean I love you less. You are the world to me." Her voice is hoarse and her eyes dewy with unshed tears.

We hold each other's gaze, testing the silence between us.

You are my world, Ana.

But I want you bound to me in every way.

I need that.

I need you…maybe too much.

"I suffocate you?" I whisper.

"No. Yes. No." She sounds exasperated; she closes her eyes and rubs her forehead. "Look, we were talking about my name. I want to keep my name here because I want to put some distance between you and me, but only here, that's all. You know everyone thinks I got the job because of you, when the reality is—" She stops and sits back, staring at my expression in shock.

Shit. How does she read me so well?

Fess up, Grey.

"Do you want to know why you got the job, Anastasia?"

"What? What do you mean?"

"The management here gave you Hyde's job to babysit. They didn't want the expense of hiring a senior executive when the company was mid-sale. They had no idea what the new owner would do with it once it passed into his ownership, and, wisely, they didn't want an expensive redundancy. So they gave you Hyde's job to caretake until the new owner—namely, me—took over."

That's the truth.

"What are you saying?" She looks offended and horrified.

Baby. Don't sweat this. "Relax. You've more than risen to the challenge. You've done very well."

You're very good at what you do, Anastasia Steele.

"Oh," she says, and she looks lost.

And it all becomes crystal clear.

This is what she wants.

This is her dream, and I can make it come true.

I vowed I would uphold her dreams during our wedding.

I don't want to stifle her; I want to help her reach her full potential. I want her to fly...but just not too far away from me.

"I don't want to suffocate you, Ana. I don't want to put you in a gilded cage. Well... Well, the rational part of me doesn't."

It's a gamble, but I play my most ambitious hand yet, voicing the idea that I've had on the spur of this moment. "So, one of the reasons I'm here—apart from dealing with my errant wife—is to discuss what I am going to do with this company."

Ana scowls. "So, what are your plans?" Her sarcasm is threaded through each word and she cocks her head to one side, like I do... copying me, laughing at me, I suspect.

God, I love her; she's recovered her backbone.

"I'm changing the name of the company—to Grey Publishing."

Ana blinks.

"And in a year's time, it will be yours."

Her mouth drops open.

"This is my wedding present to you."

She shuts her mouth, opens it again, then shuts it again, looking shell-shocked.

"So, do I need to change the name to Steele Publishing?"

"Christian, you gave me a watch. I can't run a business."

"I ran my own business from the age of twenty-one."

"But you're, *you*. Control freak and whiz-kid extraordinaire. Jeez, Christian, you majored in economics at Harvard before you dropped out. At least you have some idea. I sold paint and cable ties for three years on a part-time basis, for heaven's sake. I've seen so little of the world, and I know next to nothing!"

Well, that's not true.

"You're also the most well-read person I know." I have to pitch this to her. "You love a good book. You couldn't leave your job while we were on our honeymoon. You read how many manuscripts? Four?"

"Five," she whispers.

"And you wrote full reports on all of them. You're a very bright woman, Anastasia. I'm sure you'll manage."

"Are you crazy?"

"Crazy for you." *Always.*

She snorts, trying not to laugh. "You'll be a laughingstock. Buying a company for the little woman, who has only had a full-time job for a few months of her adult life."

I dismiss her concerns with a wave of my hand. "Do you think I give a fuck what people think? Besides, you won't be on your own."

"Christian, I—" She stalls, lost for words, and I cherish the moment—it doesn't happen often. She lays her head in her hands again. When she looks up, she's trying not to laugh.

"Something amusing you, *Ms.* Steele?"

"Yes. You."

Her amusement is contagious, and I find myself smiling. This is what she does. Disarms me.

Every time.

"Laughing at your husband? That will never do." Her teeth sink into her lovely lower lip. "And you're biting your lip," I mutter darkly; it's a stirring sight.

She sits back. "Don't even think about it," she warns.

"Think about what, Anastasia?"

Fucking you in your office? Lust streaks through my bloodstream like lightning.

"I know that look. We're at work," she whispers.

Can't you feel this, Ana? The sorcery between us is potent. Raw.

I lean forward to get closer to her, to catch her scent, to touch her. "We're in a small, reasonably soundproofed office with a lockable door," I whisper.

I want to seduce my wife.

"Gross. Moral. Turpitude." Each word is a bullet forming a shield around her.

"Not with your husband."

"With my boss's boss's boss," she hisses.

"You're my wife."

"Christian, no. I mean it. You can fuck me seven shades of Sunday this evening. But not now. Not here!"

Hell. I take a deep breath as I come to my senses and the temperature in the room drops back to normal. I laugh, releasing my tension. "Seven shades of Sunday?" I arch a brow, intrigued. "I may hold you to that, *Ms.* Steele."

"Oh, stop with the Ms. Steele!" she snaps and hammers her hand on her desk, making us both jump. "For heaven's sake, Christian. If it means so much to you, I'll change my name!"

What?

She's agreeing?

I feel a sudden rush of relief.

My face erupts in a huge grin. I've succeeded in a negotiation with my wife. I think this might be a first.

Thank you, Ana.

"Good." I clap my hands and stand. "Mission accomplished. Now, I have work to do. If you'll excuse me, Mrs. Grey."

She gawks at me. "But—"

"But what, Mrs. Grey?"

She shakes her head and closes her eyes, looking thoroughly exasperated. "Just go."

"I intend to. I'll see you this evening. I'm looking forward to seven shades of Sunday." I ignore her scowl. "Oh, and I have a stack of business-related social engagements coming up, and I'd like you to accompany me."

She frowns.

"I'll have Andrea call Hannah to put the dates in your calendar.

There are some people you need to meet. You should get Hannah to handle your schedule from now on."

"Okay," she mumbles, sounding bewildered.

I lean over the desk, staring straight into her dazed baby blues. "Love doing business with you, Mrs. Grey." She doesn't move, and I plant a soft kiss on her lips. "Laters, baby," I whisper, then turn and leave.

Outside SIP, I sink into the plush leather in the back of the waiting Audi and ask Ryan to take me back to Grey House.

Thank heavens.

My relief is proportionate to the anxiety I felt before I went into the building. It appears my wife can be reasonable. I reach for my phone to send her an e-mail, and find that she's beaten me to it.

From: Anastasia Steele
Subject: NOT AN ASSET!
Date: August 22 2011 14:23
To: Christian Grey

Mr. Grey
Next time you come and see me, make an appointment, so I can at least have some prior warning of your adolescent overbearing megalomania.
Yours

Anastasia Grey <— please note name.
Editor, SIP

Overbearing megalomaniac, eh?
My wife has a way with words.

From: Christian Grey
Subject: Seven Shades of Sunday
Date: August 22 2011 14:34
To: Anastasia Steele

My Dear Mrs. Grey (emphasis on My)
What can I say in my defense? I was in the neighborhood.
And no, you are not an asset, you are my beloved wife.
As ever, you make my day.

Christian Grey
CEO & Overbearing Megalomaniac, Grey Enterprises Holdings, Inc.

In a calmer frame of mind, I head back to my office. I need lunch.

THROUGHOUT THE AFTERNOON, I check my e-mails to see if she's responded. She hasn't, and I presume that's the end of it, I hope.

LATER, I'M SITTING IN the car waiting for Ana outside SIP. Ryan is tapping his index fingers on the steering wheel, and it's driving me crazy.

For fuck's sake.

Taylor will be back this evening, so I'm endeavoring to keep my cool. I keep glancing toward the door to see if Ana is on her way. According to my watch, it's 5:35, precisely. She's five minutes late. We have a meeting with Gia later; I hope Ana hasn't forgotten.

Where is she?

Sawyer appears, holding the office door open for Ana. Ryan gets out and strolls around the car to the rear passenger door.

What's he playing at?

Head down, Ana walks briskly toward us, followed by Sawyer, who heads to the driver's seat while Ana climbs into the car. Ryan takes the passenger seat.

"Hi," she says, avoiding eye contact.

"Hi."

"Disrupt anyone else's work today?" Her tone is frostier than an arctic night.

"Only Flynn's."

Her eyes flick to me in surprise, but she looks ahead. "Next time you go to see him, I'll give you a list of topics I want covered." She's bristling like a feral kitten beside me.

She's still mad.

I clear my throat. "You seem out of sorts, Mrs. Grey."

She doesn't answer. She just stares ahead, ignoring me. I shuffle a little closer and reach for her hand. "Hey," I whisper. But she snatches her hand out of mine. "You're mad at me?"

"Yes," she spits, and folds her arms, turning away from me and staring through the window.

Damn.

Seattle streams past my window, and I stare out, unseeing, feeling miserable and out of my depth. I thought we'd resolved this.

Sawyer stops outside Escala, and Ana grabs her briefcase and is out of the car before any of us are ready.

"Ana!" I call.

"I've got this," Ryan says, and scoots out in pursuit.

Not waiting for Sawyer to open my door, I scramble out after them, in time to watch Ana stomp into the building with Ryan at her heels.

I'm right behind them when he dashes ahead to reach the elevator before her, to press the call button.

"What?" she snaps at him.

He flushes, shocked, I think, by her tone. "Apologies, ma'am," he says. He steps back when I join them.

"So, it's not just me you're mad at?" I observe, wryly.

"Are you laughing at me?" she seethes, her eyes narrowing.

"I wouldn't dare." I hold my hands up in surrender. I am no match for my wife's bad mood.

"You need a haircut." She scowls as she steps into the elevator.

"Do I?" Taking my life in my hands and brushing my hair off my forehead, I follow her in.

"Yes." She stabs the code for our floor into the keypad.

"So, you're talking to me now?"

"Just."

"What exactly are you mad about? I need an indication." *So I'm sure.*

She stares at me, horrified. "Do you really have no idea? Surely, for someone so bright, you must have an inkling? I can't believe you're that obtuse."

Wow.

I take a step back. "You really are mad. I thought we had sorted all this in your office."

"Christian, I just capitulated to your petulant demands. That's all."

I have no answer to that.

The elevator doors open and Ana storms out. "Hi, Taylor," I hear her say.

I follow her into the foyer. "Mrs. Grey," Taylor says, and glances at me with raised eyebrows. She dumps her briefcase in the hallway.

"Good to see you," I quietly address Taylor.

"Sir," he says, and I follow my wife into the living room.

"Hi, Mrs. Jones," Ana says, and stomps straight to the fridge.

I nod at Gail, who's at the stove, preparing dinner.

Ana pulls out a bottle of wine and a glass from the cupboard while I remove my jacket, wondering what to say to her. "Do you want a drink?" she asks in a syrupy tone.

"No thanks." I watch her as I take off my tie and undo my shirt collar. She pours herself a large glass of wine while Mrs. Jones, with a swift, unreadable look at me, exits the kitchen.

So, Ana's frightened off all the staff.

I am the last man standing.

I run my hand through my hair, feeling helpless, while she takes a sip of wine, closing her eyes and enjoying the taste, or so it would seem.

Enough.

"Stop this," I whisper, stepping toward her. Tucking her hair behind her ear, I then gently tug on her earlobe, because I want to touch her. She takes a breath, then shakes me off. "Talk to me," I whisper.

"What's the point? You don't listen to me."

"Yes, I do. You're one of the few people I listen to."

Her eyes don't leave mine as she takes another swig of wine.

"Is this about your name?" I ask.

"Yes and no. It's about how you dealt with the fact that I disagreed with you." She sounds surly.

"Ana, you know I have...issues. It's hard for me to let go where you're concerned. You know that."

"But I'm not a child, and I'm not an asset."

"I know." I sigh.

"Then stop treating me as though I am," she beseeches me with quiet fortitude.

I can't bear not touching her. Brushing my fingers down her cheek, I run the tip of my thumb across her bottom lip. "Don't be mad. You're so precious to me. Like a priceless asset. Like a child."

"I'm neither of those things, Christian. I'm your wife. If you were hurt that I wasn't going to take your name, you should have said."

"Hurt?" I frown. *Hurt? Yes. I am. Was…shit.*

This is confusing. This is what Flynn said. I glance at my watch. "The architect will be here in just under an hour. We should eat."

Ana looks dismayed, the *v* between her brows deeper than usual. "This discussion isn't finished."

"What else is there to discuss?"

"You could sell the company."

"Sell it?" I scoff.

"Yes."

Why would I do that? "You think I'd find a buyer in today's market?"

"How much did it cost you?"

"It was relatively cheap."

"So, if it folds?"

"We'll survive. But I won't let it fold, Anastasia. Not while you're there."

"And if I leave?"

"And do what?"

"I don't know. Something else."

"You've already said this is your dream job. And forgive me if I'm wrong, but I promised before God, Reverend Walsh, and a congregation of our nearest and dearest to 'cherish you, uphold your hopes and dreams, and keep you safe at my side.'"

"Quoting your wedding vows to me is not playing fair."

"I've never promised to play fair where you're concerned. Besides, you've wielded your vows at me like a weapon before."

She scowls.

"Anastasia, if you're still angry with me, take it out on me in bed later." Her mouth pops open, and I know how I'd like to fill it.

Right now.

Here.

Then I remember. "Seven shades of Sunday," I whisper. "Looking forward to it."

She closes, then opens her mouth again.

Oh, baby. What I'd like to do to that mouth.

Stop, Grey.

"Gail!" I call, and a few moments later she comes back into the kitchen.

"Mr. Grey?" she says.

"We'd like to eat now, please."

"Very good, sir."

I watch Ana, who has gone worryingly quiet, as she takes another sip of wine.

"I think I'll join you in a glass," I mutter, and run a hand through my hair. She's right, it's too long, but I don't think she'd approve if I went to Esclava to have it cut.

Ana is monosyllabic as we eat. Well, I'm eating, Ana is pushing her food around her plate, but given how mad she is at me, I decide not to chide her about it.

It's frustrating.

Hell. I can't stay quiet. "You're not going to finish?"

"No."

I wonder if she's doing this on purpose. But before I can ask her, she stands and takes my empty plate and hers from the dining table.

"Gia will be with us shortly," she says.

"I'll take those, Mrs. Grey," Mrs. Jones says.

"Thank you."

"You didn't like it?" Gail asks, concerned.

"It was fine. I'm just not hungry."

Mrs. Jones gives Ana a pitying smile, and I suppress my eye roll. "I'm going to make a couple of calls," I mumble, to escape them both.

The spectacular sunset over the distant Sound does little to improve my temper. I wish for a moment that Ana and I were on *The Grace* or back on the *Fair Lady.* We didn't argue then. Well, apart from after the hickey incident.

I dwell on Flynn's words. *Marriage is a serious business.*

It sure is.

Sometimes too serious, especially if your wife doesn't agree with you.

Communicate and compromise.

This should be my new mantra.

Why is this so hard?

"I don't want you to sabotage your happiness, Christian."

Flynn is still in my head.

Shit, is that what I'm doing?

Sullenly, I pick up the phone and call my dad to let him know that all the arrangements are in place for additional security. It's a short conversation, and when I'm done, I gather up Gia Matteo's designs and head back into the living room.

There's no sign of Ana, or Mrs. Jones, who has cleaned up the kitchen and dining area. I spread the plans out on the dining table, then, using the remote, I scroll through the list of music. I chance upon Fauré's Requiem.

This should soothe my soul.

And maybe Ana's, too.

I press play and wait. The notes from a church organ echo through the living room, and they're joined by the celestial voice of the choir, their voices rising and falling to the lament.

It's stunning.

Calming.

Elevating.

Perfect.

Ana appears on the threshold, where she stops and inclines her head, listening to the music. She looks different; she's shrouded in silver-gray, her hair backlit and shining from the hall lights. She looks like an angel.

"Mrs. Grey."

"What's this?" she asks.

"Fauré's Requiem. You look different."

"Oh. I've not heard it before."

"It's very calming, relaxing. Have you done something to your hair?"

"Brushed it," she says, and there's too much distance between us. Transported by my stunning wife and the music, I make my way over to her. "Dance with me?" I whisper.

"To this? It's a requiem," she squeaks, shocked.

"Yes." *And?*

I tug her into my arms and hold her, my nose in her hair, inhaling her sweet but stirring fragrance. She wraps her arms around me and nuzzles my chest, and together we start to sway. Slowly. Side to side.

Ana. This is what I've missed. You. In my arms.

"I hate fighting with you," I whisper.

"Well, stop being such an arse."

I chuckle and draw her closer. "Arse?"

"Ass."

"I prefer arse."

"You should. It suits you."

I laugh and kiss the top of her head, remembering that she was very taken with the word when she overheard it in Harrods.

London. Happy times.

"A requiem?" There's a trace of censure in her murmur.

I shrug. "It's just a lovely piece of music, Ana." *And I get to hold you.*

Taylor coughs, and grudgingly I release her. "Miss Matteo is here," he announces.

"Show her in." I clasp Ana's hand as Gia enters.

"Christian. Ana." She beams at us, and we each shake her hand.

"Gia," I respond, politely.

"You both look so well after your honeymoon," she purrs.

I pull Ana close. "We had a wonderful time, thank you." I plant a soft kiss on my wife's temple and she slips her hand into my back pocket, and, to my delight, squeezes my butt.

Gia's smile falters a little. "Have you managed to look over the plans?" she asks brightly.

"We have," Ana says with a quick glance at me. I can't help my grin. Ana's gone all territorial and is laying claim to me. I like it.

"Please, the plans are here." I wave in the direction of our dining table. Reluctantly, I pull away from Ana, but hold her hand.

"Would you like something to drink?" Ana asks Gia. "A glass of wine?"

"That would be lovely. Dry white if you have it," she responds.

I switch off the music as Gia joins me by the table.

“Would you like some more wine, Christian?” Ana calls.

“Please, baby.” I watch as she retrieves the wineglasses.

Gia stands beside me. “This is good work, Gia,” I say, as she moves a little too close. “This especially.” I point at the rear elevation of her CAD drawing. “I think Ana has some opinions on the glass wall, but generally we’re both pleased with the ideas you’ve come up with.”

“Oh, I’m glad,” Gia coos, and she pats my arm.

Keep your fucking distance. She’s wearing a cloying, rich perfume that’s almost suffocating.

I step out of her reach and call to Ana. “Thirsty here.”

“Coming right up,” Ana responds.

A beat later, she’s back with glasses of wine for each of us, and she inserts herself between Gia and me—deliberately, I think. Has she noticed how Gia is incapable of keeping her hands to herself?

“Cheers.” I offer up my glass in thanks to Ana and take a sip of wine.

“Ana, you have some issues with the glass wall?” Gia prompts.

“Yes. I love it—don’t get me wrong. But I was hoping that we could incorporate it more organically into the house. After all, I fell in love with the house as it was, and I don’t want to make any radical changes.”

“I see.” Gia’s eyes flick to mine, and I look at Ana.

She continues, “I just want the design to be sympathetic, you know, more in keeping with the original house.” Ana glances at me.

“No major renovations?” I say.

“No.”

“You like it as it is?”

“Mostly, yes. I always knew it just needed some TLC.”

Ana’s eyes are glowing, reflecting mine, I’m sure.

Are we talking about the house, or me?

“Okay.” Gia gives us a quick glance before pitching a revised plan. “I think I get where you’re coming from, Ana. How about if we retain the glass wall, but have it open out onto a larger deck that’s in keeping with the Mediterranean style. We have the stone terrace there already. We can put in pillars in matching stone, widely spaced so you’ll still have the view. Add a glass roof, or tile it as per the rest of the house. It'll also make a sheltered alfresco dining and seating area."

Ana looks impressed.

Gia continues, "Or instead of the deck, we could incorporate a wood color of your choice into the glass doors—that might help to keep the Mediterranean spirit."

"Like the bright blue shutters in the South of France," Ana says, looking at me.

I'm not keen on the idea, but I'm not going to shoot her down in front of Ms. Matteo. Besides, if that's what Ana wants, she can have it. I'll learn to live with it. I ignore Gia, preening beside me.

"Ana, what do you want to do?" I ask.

"I like the deck idea."

"Me, too."

Ana turns her attention to Gia. "I think I'd like to see revised drawings, showing the bigger deck and pillars that are in keeping with the house."

"Sure," Gia says to Ana. "Any other issues?"

"Christian wants to remodel the master suite," Ana says.

Another discreet cough interrupts us.

"Taylor?" He's standing on the threshold.

"I need to confer with you on an urgent matter, Mr. Grey."

I squeeze Ana's shoulders and address Gia. "Mrs. Grey is in charge of this project. She has absolute carte blanche. Whatever she wants, it's hers. I completely trust her instincts. She's very shrewd." Ana reaches up and pats my hand.

"If you'll excuse me." I leave them, and follow Taylor into his office. Prescott is there, seated at the CCTV monitor bank. Over her shoulder, all the feeds from around the apartment and also from the perimeter of Escala and the garage are on display.

"Mr. Grey," Prescott greets me.

"Evening. What gives?"

Taylor grabs a chair from his small conference table and places it beside Prescott. He gestures to me to sit down. I comply and look at them expectantly.

"Prescott has been going through all the tapes from over the weekend from downstairs and outside. She found this." Taylor nods at her, and using her mouse, Prescott clicks start on one of the screens.

A grainy image begins to play. It shows a man in coveralls walking toward the front entrance of the building, and inspecting the camera itself. She freezes it as the man looks directly at the camera.

Fuck. "It's Jack Hyde," I murmur, and he has his hair tied back. "When was this?"

"It's Saturday, August 20, at around nine forty-five in the morning."

His hair is lighter here; he must have been wearing a wig in the server room at Grey House.

"Sir, I've isolated all the footage I can find of him at around this time," Prescott says.

"Interesting. What else do you have?"

She runs through several clips of Hyde: at the front door, at the opening to the garage, at the fire escapes. He's carrying a broom, which he uses occasionally so he looks like a street cleaner.

Cunning bastard.

It's weirdly fascinating to watch him.

"Have you sent this to Welch?"

"Not yet," Taylor says. "I thought you'd better see it first."

"Send it to him. Perhaps he can track where he goes from here."

"Will do. This might be just the clue they need. Though, I learned today they haven't found him yet. He's still not been to his apartment, sir."

"Oh, that's news."

"I spoke with Welch for a full update about an hour ago," Taylor clarifies.

"No doubt he'll fill me in tomorrow. This is good work. Well done, Prescott." I give her a quick smile.

"Thank you, sir."

"We'll have to be extra careful, knowing that he's prowling around the building."

"Indeed," Taylor agrees.

"I'd better head back. Thank you. Both of you."

It looks like Ana and Gia are finishing up when I enter the living room. "All done?" I ask, as I put my arm around Ana.

"Yes, Mr. Grey." Gia smiles brightly, though her smile looks forced. "I'll have the revised plans to you in a couple of days."

Oh. I'm Mr. Grey now.

Interesting.

"Excellent. You're happy?" I ask Ana, and I want to know what she's said to Gia. Ana nods, looking rather pleased with herself.

"I'd better be going," Gia says, again too brightly. She offers her hand to Ana first, then to me.

"Until next time, Gia," Ana says with a charming smile.

"Yes, Mrs. Grey. Mr. Grey."

Taylor appears at the entrance of the great room.

"Taylor will see you out," Ana says, and arm in arm, we watch her join Taylor in the hallway.

When she's out of earshot, I look down at my wife. "She was noticeably cooler."

"Was she? I didn't notice." Ana shrugs, trying and failing miserably to look nonchalant. My wife is an appalling liar. "What did Taylor want?" She's changing the subject.

Releasing her, I turn and start rolling up the plans. "It was about Hyde."

"What about Hyde?" She pales.

Shit. I don't want to add to her nightmares.

"It's nothing to worry about, Ana." Abandoning the plans, I draw her into my arms. "It turns out he hasn't been in his apartment for weeks, that's all." I kiss her hair and go back to rolling up Gia's designs. "So, what did you decide on?"

"Only what you and I discussed. I think she likes you," Ana says quietly.

I think so, too! "Did you say something to her?"

She stares down at her hands. She's knotting her fingers.

"We were Christian and Ana when she arrived, and Mr. and Mrs. Grey when she left," I prompt.

"I may have said something," she admits.

Oh, baby, you're going into battle for me?

I've met Gia's type before. Always in a business context. "She's only reacting to this face."

Ana looks alarmed.

"What? You're not jealous, are you?" I'm shocked that she could even think this. Her cheeks color, and she doesn't answer me, but looks down at her hands again, and I know I have my answer. I remember Elliot alluding to Gia's nature and it reminded me of Elena—a woman who doesn't take no for an answer. A woman who gets what she wants. "Ana, she's a sexual predator. Not my type at all. How can you be jealous of her? Of anyone? Nothing about her interests me." I run a hand through my hair, at a loss. "It's only you, Ana. It will only ever be you."

Abandoning the drawings again, I move quickly toward her and grasp her chin. "How can you think otherwise? Have I ever given you any indication that I could be remotely interested in anyone else?"

"No," she whispers. "I'm being silly. It's just today. You—" She stops.

"What about me?"

"Oh, Christian." Tears well in her eyes. "I'm trying to adapt to this new life, that I had never imagined for myself. Everything is being handed to me on a plate—the job, you, my beautiful husband, who I never…I never knew I'd love this way, this hard, this fast, this… indelibly."

I stare at her, paralyzed, as she takes a deep breath. "But you're like a freight train, and I don't want to get railroaded because the girl you fell in love with will be crushed. And what'll be left? All that would be left is a vacuous social X-ray, flitting from charity function to charity function."

Whoa! Ana!

"And now you want me to be a company CEO, which has never even been on my radar. I'm bouncing between all these ideas, struggling. You want me at home. You want me to run a company. It's so confusing." She fights down a sob. "You've got to let me make my own decisions, take my own risks, and make my own mistakes, and let me learn from them. I need to walk before I can run, Christian, don't you see? I want some independence. That's what my name means to me."

This is about her!

Shit.

"You feel railroaded?" I whisper.

She nods.

I close my eyes. "I just want to give you the world, Ana, everything and anything you want. And save you from it, too. Keep you safe. But I also want everyone to know you're mine. I panicked today when I got your e-mail. Why didn't you tell me about your name?"

She flushes. "I only thought about it while we were on our honeymoon, and, well, I didn't want to burst the bubble, and I forgot about it. I only remembered yesterday evening. And then Jack—you know—it was distracting. I'm sorry, I should have told you or discussed it with you, but I could never seem to find the right time."

I study her, measuring her words. Yes. It would have resulted in an argument on our honeymoon.

"Why did you panic?" she asks.

I want to be worthy of you and your e-mail derailed me.

Stop, Grey. "I just don't want you to slip through my fingers."

"For heaven's sake, I'm not going anywhere. When are you going to get that through your incredibly thick skull? I. Love. You." She waves her hand in the air looking for inspiration—like I do. "More than 'eyesight, space, or liberty.'"

Shakespeare? "A daughter's love?" *I hope not!*

"No." She laughs. "It's the only quote that came to mind."

"Mad King Lear?"

"Dear, dear mad King Lear." She reaches up and strokes my cheek and I lean in to her hand, closing my eyes and reveling in her touch. "Would you change your name to Christian Steele, so everyone would know that you belong to me?"

Opening my eyes, I stare at her. "Belong to you?"

"Mine," she says.

"Yours," I repeat. "Yes, I would. If it meant that much to you." I remember surrendering myself to her here, before we were married, when I thought she was leaving.

"Does it mean that much to you?" she asks.

"Yes."

"Okay," she says.

"I thought you'd already agreed to this."

"Yes, I have, but now that we've discussed it further, I'm happier with my decision."

"Oh."

Flynn was right. This was about her and how she feels.

But I'm glad she's come around. It's a relief—our feud is over. I beam at her and she smiles back, so I swoop down, grab her by her waist, and swing her high.

Thank you, Anastasia.

She giggles, and I set her on her feet. "Mrs. Grey, do you know what this means to me?"

"I do now."

I kiss her, threading my fingers through the softness of her hair, and whisper against her lips, "It means seven shades of Sunday." I run my nose down hers.

"You think?" She leans back, her eyes narrowed, but she's trying to hide her smile.

"Certain promises were made. An offer extended, a deal brokered," I whisper.

And I want you.

After this fight, I need to know we're okay.

"Um..." Ana regards me as if I've lost mind.

Hell, she's backing out. "You reneging on me?" A plan pops, fully formed, into my mind. "I have an idea. A really important matter to attend to."

Ana's expression intensifies; she thinks I'm crazy.

"Yes, Mrs. Grey. A matter of the gravest importance." I'm sure there's a wicked gleam in my eye. This is a means to an end.

She narrows hers, once more. "What?" she asks.

"I need you to cut my hair. Apparently, it's overlong, and my wife doesn't like it."

"I can't cut your hair!" she exclaims, in amused disbelief.

"Yes, you can." I shake my head and my hair falls into my eyes.

How have I not noticed this?

"Well, if Mrs. Jones has a pudding bowl." Ana giggles.

I laugh. "Okay, good point well made. I'll get Franco to do it."

Her laugh turns to a grimace, and after a moment's hesitation she grabs my hand with surprising strength. "Come." She drags me all the way to our bathroom and releases me there.

Looks like she's going to cut my hair.

I stand watching her as she drags the bathroom chair in front of her sink. Her high heels emphasize her legs and the tight pencil skirt sculpts her beautiful behind. This is a show worth watching.

She turns and points to the chair. "Sit."

"Are you going to wash my hair?"

She nods.

Whoa. I can't remember anyone washing my hair. Ever.

"Okay." Without taking my eyes off hers, I slowly unbutton my shirt, and when it's undone I present her with my right wrist. The cuff is held together with one of my cuff links.

Undo this, baby.

With a darkening look, she undoes the right, then the left cuff, her fingertips tantalizing my skin with a soft sweep or two over each pulse. Her blouse is undone, one button too far, and I glimpse the soft swell of her breasts encased in fine lace.

It's a most inspiring sight. She steps closer, and I catch a hint of her lovely fragrance as she pushes my shirt off my shoulders and lets it drop to the floor.

"Ready?" she whispers, and that one word holds so much promise. It's arousing. Deeply arousing.

"For whatever you want, Ana."

Her eyes stray to my lips and she leans in for a kiss.

"No," I breathe, and in a monumental act of self-sacrifice, I grasp her shoulders. "Don't. If you do that, I'll never get my hair cut."

Her mouth forms a perfect o.

"I want this," I whisper, surprising myself.

"Why?"

Because no one's washed my hair… Ever. "Because it'll make me feel cherished."

She gasps at my softly spoken confession, and before I can do so much as blink, she embraces me, holding me close. She kisses my chest with soft, gentle kisses, where only two months ago I couldn't bear to be touched.

"Ana. My Ana." Closing my eyes, I gather her in my arms while my heart overflows.

I think I'm forgiven for railroading her.

I think we're okay.

We stand in our embrace in the middle of our bathroom for an age, her warmth and her love soaking into me.

Eventually, Ana leans back, the love-light shining in her eyes. "You really want me to do this?"

I nod, and her smile matches mine. She steps out of my arms and points to the chair again. "Then sit." I do as she asks while she kicks off her shoes and retrieves my shampoo from the shower. "Would Sir like this?" She holds it up as if she's on a cheesy shopping channel, selling it to me. "Hand-delivered from the South of France. I like the smell of this." She pops the top. "It smells of you."

"Please."

She places the shampoo on the vanity unit, then reaches for a small towel. "Lean forward," she orders, and drapes the towel over my shoulders and turns the taps on behind me.

"Lean back."

She's bossy.

I like it.

I try to lean back, but it doesn't work because I'm too tall. I shuffle the chair forward and then tip it so it rests against the sink.

Success. I tilt my head backward over the sink and watch Ana.

Slowly, using a glass to scoop up the warm water, she anoints my head, leaning over me. "You smell so good, Mrs. Grey." I close my eyes, enjoying her hands on me as she continues to wet my hair.

Abruptly, she pours water over my forehead and it flows into my eyes.

"Sorry!" she squeals.

I laugh and wipe the excess off with the corner of my towel. "Hey, I know I'm an arse, but don't drown me."

She giggles and plants a tender kiss on my forehead. "Don't tempt me," she whispers. Reaching up, I place my hand on her neck and guide her lips to mine. Her breath is sweet; she tastes of Ana, and sauvignon blanc. An enticing combination.

"Mm," I murmur, savoring the taste. Releasing her, I lean back, ready for her to continue. She smiles down at me, and I hear the sound of liquid squirting from the tube as she squeezes it into her hand. Gently, she starts to massage the shampoo into my scalp—from my temples, she works her way over my head—and I close my eyes, relishing her touch.

Sweet Jesus.

Who knew heaven resided in my wife's fingertips?

When Franco's cut my hair, he's always used a spray. I've never had my hair washed.

Why not, Grey? This is so relaxing.

Or perhaps it's just Ana—I'm so acutely aware of her. Her leg grazing mine, her arm skimming my cheek, her touch, her scent…"That feels good," I murmur.

"Yes, it does." Her lips graze my forehead.

"I like it when you scratch my scalp with your fingernails."

"Head up," she says, and I lift my head so she soaps the back using her fingernails on my scalp.

Bliss.

"Back."

I do as I'm told, and she pours water over my head again, rinsing out the suds.

"Once more?" she asks.

"Please." When I open my eyes, she's smiling down at me.

"Coming right up, Mr. Grey." She releases me and fills my sink. "For rinsing," she explains.

Closing my eyes, I surrender myself to her ministrations. She washes my hair again, anointing me with more water, massaging more shampoo into my scalp, and using her fingernails.

I have found nirvana.

This is pure paradise.

Her fingers caress my cheek and I open heavy eyelids to watch her. She kisses me, and her kiss is soft, sweet, chaste.

I sigh, my contentment complete.

She moves over me and her breasts brush my face.

Fuck.

Hello!

Behind me, the water gurgles down the drain, but with my eyes closed, I reach up and grab her hips, then slide my fingers over her magnificent behind.

"No fondling the help," she warns.

"Don't forget I'm deaf." Slowly I start to hitch up her skirt, but she swats my arm. I grin, feeling like I've been caught with my hand in the cookie jar. I stop misbehaving, but I keep my hands on her fine backside while she rinses my hair. I imagine I'm playing the Moonlight Sonata on her ass, my fingers flexing through the notes. She wiggles deliciously against my fingers and I growl in appreciation.

"There, all rinsed," she announces.

"Good." My fingers tighten around her hips and I sit up, dripping water everywhere and pulling Ana sidesaddle onto my lap. I curl my fingers around her nape, and with my other hand I hold her jaw. She gasps and I take full advantage, pressing my lips to hers and kissing her. My tongue seeking more.

Hot. Hungry. Ready.

I don't care that I'm spraying water all over the bathroom and soaking my wife. Ana's fingers tighten in my wet hair as she returns my kiss with a ferocity of her own.

Desire courses through my veins.

Demanding release.

I'm tempted to rip off her blouse, but I tug the top button. "Enough of this primping. I want to fuck you seven shades of Sunday, and we can do it in here or in the bedroom. You decide."

Ana's expression is dazed.

"What's it to be, Anastasia?"

"You're wet," she whispers.

Holding her hips, I tip my head forward and rub my wet hair all over the front of her blouse. She squeals once more and squirms, but I tighten my hold. "Oh, no you don't, baby."

When I look up, her blouse is sticking to her like a second skin, her lacy bra obvious, her nipples pert beneath the lace. She's gorgeous, but she's also outraged, amused, and aroused at once. "Love the view," I whisper, and lean down to run my nose around her wet, waiting nipple. She groans and wriggles on me. "Answer me, Ana. Here or the bedroom?"

"Here," she whispers.

"Good choice, Mrs. Grey," I murmur against the corner of her mouth, and move my hand from her jaw to her leg. Skimming my fingers over her pantyhose toward her thigh, I raise her skirt higher and higher while placing tender kisses along her jaw. "Oh, what shall I do to you?" I murmur.

Oh. My fingers reach the firm flesh of her thighs.

She's wearing stockings!

Deep joy.

"I like these." I run a finger under the stocking top and across the soft skin of her upper thigh. Ana squirms in delight. I groan. "If I'm going to fuck you seven shades of Sunday, I want you to keep still."

"Make me," she demands, and the challenge in her eyes goes straight to my cock.

"Oh, Mrs. Grey. You have only to ask." I slide my hand up to her panties, glad that she's wearing them over her garter belt. "Let's divest you of these." I tug gently, and she shifts on top of my erection.

Fuck. My breath hisses through my teeth. "Keep still," I grumble.

"I'm helping." She pouts in protest, and I suck her bottom lip between my teeth.

"Still," I warn, then release her lip and tug her panties down her legs, crushing them into my hand; I have a plan for them. I raise Ana's skirt so it's bunched up around her hips and take a brief moment to appreciate how beautiful her legs are in stockings with lacy tops. I lift her. "Sit. Astride me."

Keeping her darkening eyes on mine, she obeys, but tilts her chin up wearing her *Bring it* expression.

Oh, Ana.

"Mrs. Grey, are you goading me?"

We could have some fun with this.

My pants feel two sizes too small.

"Yes. What are you going to do about it?"

God, I love a challenge.

"Clasp your hands together behind your back."

She does, and I bind her wrists with her panties and pull them tight. Now she's helpless. "My panties? Mr. Grey, you have no shame," she chides me, breathless.

"Not where you're concerned, Mrs. Grey, but you know that."

I love the provocation in her smoky blue eyes. It's such a turn-on. I push her backward on my lap so I have more room to work. She chews her lip, her eyes on mine, and gently I skim my hands down to her knees, pushing her legs wider apart. Then I widen my legs, to give my dick some more room and to make her more available to me.

Also, it will be more intense for her this way.

My fingers move to the buttons on her wet blouse. "I don't think we need this." Slowly, I undo each button, revealing her breasts, still slick from their earlier soaking. They rise and fall rapidly as she inhales sharply, and I leave her blouse gaping open.

Desire shines in her eyes and they stay glued to mine.

I caress her face and brush my thumb across her bottom lip, then abruptly push it into her mouth. "Suck." She closes her mouth around me and does exactly what she's been told to do.

Hard.

My girl does not back down.

This I know.

She scrapes her teeth gently over my skin and bites the pad.

I moan, then ease my thumb from her mouth and paint her chin, her throat, and her sternum with her saliva. I hook my thumb into her bra cup and tug it down, freeing her breast, then tuck the cup beneath, pushing her breast up so it's poised and ready for me. We stare at each other, her mouth opens and closes, her eyes filled with yearning. I love watching her reaction to everything I do. She bites down on her lip as I free her other breast, so it, too, is helpless and waiting for me. They are too tempting. I hold both of them and slowly graze my thumbs over her nipples in a tight circle, torturing each one so that they stand proud beneath my touch. Ana starts panting and arching her back, thrusting her breasts into my palms. I don't stop, but continue to tease her so that she throws her head back and lets out a long, low moan of pleasure.

"Shh," I whisper, not letting up on the slow, sweet rhythm I've set for my thumbs. Ana's hips shift. "Still, baby, still." Reaching behind her head, I gather her hair in one hand and hold her neck.

I want her still.

Leaning down, I tease her right nipple with my lips, then suck hard as my fingers move to continue taunting its twin, gently tugging and twisting.

"Ah! Christian!" she groans, and rocks her hips forward on my lap.

Oh, no, baby.

I don't let up. My lips tasting and teasing, my fingers tweaking and tugging.

"Christian, please," she mewls.

"Hmm. I want you to come like this," I whisper against my captive peak, and I return to it, but this time I tug tenderly and carefully with my teeth.

"Ah!" Ana calls, and writhes on my lap, but I hold her still and I don't stop.

"Please." She's breathless and begging, and I watch her, her mouth slack, her head back, as she has no choice but to absorb all the pleasure.

I know she's close. "You have such beautiful breasts, Ana. One day I'll fuck them."

She arches her back fully, surrendering to me, her breathing rapid. Her thighs straining against mine.

She's close.

So close.

"Let go," I whisper, and she does, her eyes scrunched closed as she cries out and her body quivers through her orgasm. I tighten my hold on her as she sails down from her high.

Her eyes flicker open, dazed, and beautiful.

"God, I love to watch you come, Ana."

"That was…" She stops, overwhelmed, I think.

"I know." I kiss her, angling her head so I can claim her, and tell her with my tongue that she is everything to me.

She blinks up at me when I pull away.

"Now I'm going to fuck you, hard." I grab her around the waist and move her farther back on my lap once more. With one hand on her thigh, I reach for my pants zipper and free my impatient cock. Ana's eyes darken, her pupils dilating. "You like?" I whisper.

"Hm." She makes a delicious rumbling noise of approval in throat.

I wrap my fingers around my erection and move them up and down as she watches.

"You're biting your lip, Mrs. Grey."

"That's because I'm hungry."

"Hungry?"

Anastasia Grey, my day's just improved a thousandfold.

She makes that noise again, the sexy one deep in her throat, and licks her lips while I continue to pleasure myself.

"I see. You should have eaten your dinner." I'm almost tempted to spank her, but I'm not sure that would be welcome. "But maybe I can oblige." I put my hands around her waist so that she keeps her balance. "Stand," I order.

She does, indecently quickly. She's keen.

"Kneel," I murmur, watching her. Her eyes flick to mine shining with sensuous delight and she does, surprisingly gracefully, considering her hands are tied. I slide forward on the chair, holding my erection. "Kiss me," I order, offering her my cock. She glances from my dick to my face, and I run my tongue over my teeth.

Come on, baby.

She leans forward and plants a soft kiss on the tip. Her eyes on mine.

It's so fucking hot. I could come over her right now.

I lay my hand against her cheek and she runs her tongue around the head of my erection. I gasp, and suddenly she pounces, pulling my dick into her mouth and sucking, really hard.

"Ah!" Ana's mouth is heaven.

I flex my hips forward, diving deeper into her throat, and she takes me, all of me.

Fuck.

She moves her head, up and down, consuming me.

Ah. She's so good at this.

But I don't want to come in her mouth. I hold her head with both hands to slow her down and control her pace.

Easy, baby.

Panting hard, I guide her mouth. Down. Up. On. Me. Her tongue works its magic. "Jesus, Ana," I whisper, and screw my eyes up, and lose myself in her rhythm.

She draws her lips back, so I feel her teeth.

Fuck. I stop and grab her, moving her onto my lap. "Enough!" I growl. I tug her panties off her wrists and she looks so fucking pleased with herself. As she should. She's a goddess, her expression sultry beneath her long lashes. She licks her lips and wraps her fingers around my dick and scoots forward and lowers herself oh-so-fucking-slowly onto me.

Oh, the feel of her.

Groaning, in tribute to her, I tug her blouse off so it falls to the floor. I steady her hips with my hands to stall her. "Still," I order. "Please, let me savor this. Savor you."

She stops moving, and her dark, dark eyes glow with her love and innate sensuality; her lips are parted and moist where she's been biting her bottom lip.

She is my life.

I flex my butt, driving deeper into her, and she moans and closes her eyes. "This is my favorite place," I murmur. "Inside you. Inside my wife."

Ana's fingers fist in my wet hair, her lips find mine, and her tongue finds mine as she starts to move, rising up and down, riding me.

Riding me, fast. Her pace frantic.

I moan, weaving my hands in her hair, and my tongue welcomes hers, as they dance a dance they know so well.

She's greedy.

Like me.

Too fast, baby.

My hands move to her ass, and I guide her once more, to a quick but even tempo.

"Ah!" she cries out.

"Yes. Yes, Ana," I hiss through my teeth, as I try to prolong this exquisite pleasure. "Baby," I murmur as my passion builds, and I take her mouth once more.

Ana. Ana. Will it always be like this?

This. Hot.

This. Elemental.

This. Extreme.

"Oh, Christian, I love you. I will always love you."

Her words are my undoing. I can't hold on, after all the tension between us today. I clasp her to me and let go, crying out as I come hard and fast, triggering her release. She cries out and surrenders herself to me, shuddering around me, until we're both still.

Together, we resurface.

She's crying. "Hey." I tip her chin back. "Why are you crying? Did I hurt you?"

"No," she says in a breathless rush of denial. I push her hair off her face and wipe the tear that's slipped down her cheek with my thumb, and kiss her. I shift, pulling out of her, and she winces as I do.

"What's wrong, Ana? Tell me."

Watery eyes stare into mine. "It's just, it's just sometimes I'm overwhelmed by how much I love you," she whispers.

My heart melts and mends into one glorious whole. "You have the same effect on me." I touch my lips to hers in the softest of kisses.

"Do I?"

Ana. "You know you do."

"Sometimes I know. Not all the time."

"Back at you, Mrs. Grey."

What a pair we make, Anastasia.

Her smile lights a path for my dark soul and she leaves a trail of soft, sweet kisses over my chest and cuddles up to me, her cheek against my heart. I stroke her hair and run my fingers down her back. She's still wearing her bra. It can't be very comfortable; I undo it, tug down each of the straps so it falls to the floor, joining her blouse.

"Hmm. Skin on skin." I fold her into my arms and graze my lips over her shoulder and up to her ear. "You smell like heaven, Mrs. Grey."

"So do you, Mr. Grey." She kisses my chest again and relaxes into me, letting out what I think is a sigh of contentment.

I don't know how long we sit, wrapped around each other, but it's a balm to my soul. We are one. The tension between us gone. I kiss her hair, inhale my wife's scent, and all is right in my world once more.

"IT'S LATE." I'M STROKING her back and I don't want to move.

"Your hair still needs cutting."

I laugh. "That it does, Mrs. Grey. Do you have the energy to finish the job you started?"

"For you, Mr. Grey, anything." She drops another kiss on my chest and stands up.

"Don't go." I capture her hips and turn her around. Quickly, I unzip her skirt so it falls to the floor and I offer Ana my hand so she steps free of it. I take a moment to appreciate my wife wearing nothing but her stockings and garter belt. "You are a mighty fine sight, Mrs. Grey." Sitting back in the chair, I cross my arms and gawk.

She opens her arms and twirls for me.

"God, I'm a lucky son of a bitch," I whisper in awe.

"Yes, you are."

"Put my shirt on and you can cut my hair. Like this, you'll distract me, and we'll never get to bed."

Her wicked smile is sexy. What is she planning? I zip up my pants as she waltzes over to where my shirt lies on the floor, her hips swaying in a sensual rhythm. She bends from her waist, in a pose worthy of *Penthouse* magazine, leaving nothing to my imagination, collects my shirt, smells it, then, with a coy glance at me, shrugs it on.

Down, boy.

"That's quite a floor show, Mrs. Grey."

"Do we have any scissors?" she asks, wearing my shirt and a cheeky smile.

"My study." My voice is hoarse.

"I'll go search." She prances out of the bathroom, leaving me with a semi-hard-on.

Mrs. Mrs. Mrs. Grey.

While Ana is finding scissors, I collect her clothes, fold them, and place them on the vanity. I glance at myself in the mirror, hardly recognizing the man staring back at me.

Giving up a little control in matters sexual with Ana, is extremely satisfying.

I like frantic Ana.

And greedy Ana.

I love that she loves my dick.

Yes. Especially that.

And she's agreed to be Mrs. Grey in name, too.

I'd call that a good result.

We just have to get better at communicating with each other.

Communicate and compromise.

Ana dashes into the bathroom, catching her breath.

"What's wrong?" I ask.

"I just ran into Taylor."

"Oh." I frown. "Dressed like that?"

Ana's eyes widen in alarm at my expression. "That's not Taylor's fault," she says quickly.

"No. But still." I don't want anyone eyeing my nearly naked wife.

"I'm dressed."

"Barely."

"I don't know who was more embarrassed, me or him."

I bet. Poor Taylor. Or lucky Taylor. I'm not sure how I feel about that. I remember the bikini-top incident and push that quickly from my mind.

"Did you know he and Gail are, well, together?" she says, sounding a little shocked.

I laugh. "Yes, of course I knew."

"And you never told me?"

"I thought you knew, too."

"No."

"Ana, they're adults. They live under the same roof. Both unattached. Both attractive."

She blushes. Why, I don't know. I'm glad they have each other.

"Well, if you put it like that," she mutters. "I just thought Gail was older than Taylor."

"She is, but not by much. Some men like older women—"

Shit.

"I know that," Ana snaps, scowling.

Shit. Why did I say that? Will Elena always loom over and between us?

"That reminds me," I change the subject.

"What?" Ana sounds sulky. She takes the chair and turns it so it faces the sinks. "Sit," she orders.

My bossy wife.

I do as I'm told, trying to hide my amusement.

See. I can behave.

"I was thinking we could convert the rooms over the garages for them at the new place," I say. "Make it a home. Then maybe Taylor's daughter could stay with him more often." I watch Ana's reaction in the mirror as she combs my hair.

She frowns. "Why doesn't she stay here?"

"Taylor's never asked me."

"Perhaps you should offer. But we'd have to behave ourselves."

"I hadn't thought of that." *Kids. They ruin all the fun.*

"Perhaps that's why Taylor hasn't asked. Have you met her?"

"Yes. She's a sweet thing. Shy. Very pretty. I pay for her schooling."

Ana stops combing my hair, and our eyes meet in the mirror. "I had no idea."

I shrug it off. "Seemed the least I could do. Also, it means he won't quit."

"I'm sure he likes working for you."

"I don't know."

"I think he's very fond of you, Christian." She runs the comb through my hair again. It feels nice.

"You think?" I ask. It's never crossed my mind.

"Yes. I do."

Well, how about that? I have enormous respect for Taylor. I'd like him to stay working for me—for us, indefinitely. I trust him. "Good. Will you talk to Gia about the rooms over the garage?"

"Yes, of course." Her lips curl in a secret smile, and I wonder what she's thinking about. She glances at me in the mirror. "You sure about this? Your last chance to bail."

"Do your worst, Mrs. Grey. I don't have to look at me, you do."

Her smile illuminates the room. "Christian, I could look at you all day."

I shake my head. "It's just a pretty face, baby."

"And behind it is a very pretty man." She kisses my temple. "My man."

Her man.

I like that.

I sit still and let her work. Her tongue escapes between her teeth while she concentrates. It's cute and arousing, so I close my eyes, and think back to our honeymoon, enjoying the many memories we made. Occasionally, I crack open an eyelid to take a quick peek at her.

"Finished," she announces. I open my eyes and check her handiwork.

It's a haircut. And it looks fine.

"Great job, Mrs. Grey." I pull her to me and nuzzle her belly. "Thank you."

"My pleasure." She gives me a quick kiss.

"It's late. Bed." I smack her behind, because she's waving it in front of me and it's too tempting.

"Ah! I should clean up in here," she exclaims.

There are small clumps of my hair all over the floor. "Okay, I'll get the broom," I mutter, and stand up. "I don't want you embarrassing the staff with your lack of appropriate attire."

"Do you know where the broom is?"

I stare at Ana. "Um, no."

She laughs. "I'll go." And with a quick grin, she sashays out of the bathroom.

How do I not know where the broom is?

I turn to the sink and check my hair again. Ana's done a good job. It looks fine. Smiling, impressed by her handiwork, I reach for my toothbrush.

ANA IS LAUGHING TO herself when I join her in bed.

"What?" I ask.

"Nothing. Just an idea."

"What idea?" I turn on my side and watch her.

"Christian, I don't think I want to run a company."

I shift onto my elbow. "Why do you say that?"

"Because it's not something that has ever appealed to me."

"You're more than capable, Anastasia."

"I like to read books, Christian. Running a company will take me away from that."

"You could be the creative head."

She looks pensive, and I don't know if she hates the idea or is considering it. I persist. "You see, running a successful company is all about embracing the talent of the individuals you have at your disposal. If that's where your talents and your interests lie, then you structure the company to enable that. Don't dismiss it out of hand, Anastasia. You're a very capable woman. I think you could do anything you wanted if you put your mind to it."

She's not convinced. "I'm also worried it will take up too much of my time."

I hadn't considered that.

"Time I could devote to you," she murmurs.

I see your game, Mrs. Grey. "I know what you're doing."

"What?"

"You're trying to distract me from the issue at hand. You always do that. Just don't dismiss the idea, Ana. Think about it. That's all I ask." I plant a swift kiss on her lips and run my thumb down her cheek.

You are so lovely.

You are more than capable.

"Can I ask you something?" Ana says.

"Of course."

"Earlier today you said if I was angry with you, I should take it out on you in bed. What did you mean?"

"What did you think I meant?" I ask.

"That you wanted me to tie you up."

What? "Um…no. That's not what I meant at all." I just want some…resistance in bed.

"Oh." Ana looks disappointed.

"You want to tie me up?" I ask.

I'm not sure I could do that…not yet, anyway.

Ana blushes. "Well."

"Ana, I—" That would mean complete loss of control, and total surrender. I offered that to her once before, and she didn't want it. I'm not sure I could deal with that kind of rejection from her again. Besides, I've only just learned to tolerate—no, revel—in her touch. I don't want to derail that.

"Christian," she whispers, and scrambles up so she's facing me. She places her palm on my cheek. "Christian, stop. It doesn't matter. I thought that's what you meant."

Taking her hand, I place it on my chest, where beneath my skin and bone my heart is hammering with my anxiety. "Ana, I don't know how I'd feel about you touching me if I were restrained."

Her eyes grow wider.

"This is still too new." I'm confessing my darkest fears to her again.

Ana leans toward me, and I don't know what she's going to do, but she kisses the corner of my mouth. "Christian, I got the wrong idea. Please don't worry about it. Please don't think about it." She kisses me again, and I close my eyes and kiss her back, hungrily. I grab the back of her head, holding her in place, and press her into the mattress, banishing my demons as I do.

TUESDAY, AUGUST 23, 2011

Scarlet nails rake across my chest. I can't move. I can't see. I can only feel. *You don't like this, do you?* I can't speak. Silenced by the ball gag. Frantically I shake my head as the darkness slithers inside me, trying to crawl its way out, while her talons wreak their havoc on the outside. *Hush, now. You'll get your reward.* The flogger strikes my chest, the small beads pinching my skin in a stinging rebuke that silences the darkness with pain. Sweat beads on my brow. *Such beautiful skin.* She hits me again. Lower. And I pull against the restraints as the flogger sings its song across my belly. *Fuck.* She's going lower. The pain will be hard to take. I steel myself. Waiting. Ana stands over me. She's caressing my face while wearing my fur glove. Her hand moves down my throat, across my chest, the fur sliding over my skin. Soothing. Quieting the darkness. Ana watches me, her hair mussed, her eyes shining with her love. *Ana.* Her hand moves lower to my belly and sweeps over my stomach with the softest caress. Then her fingers are in my hair.

Opening my eyes, I find I'm wrapped around Ana like swaddling, my head on her chest. My gray eyes meet sparkling summer blue. "Hi," I murmur, delighted to see her.

"Hi." My joy is mirrored in her face.

Her satin nightgown is perfectly designed, revealing that special valley between her breasts. I kiss her there as the rest of my body wakes…fully. My hand skims over her hip. "What a tempting morsel you are," I mutter. "But, tempting though you are"—the radio alarm reads 7:30—"I have to get up." Reluctantly, I disentangle myself from my wife and climb out of bed. She puts her hands behind her head and watches me as I strip, teasing her top lip with her tongue.

"Admiring the view, Mrs. Grey?"

"It's a mighty fine view, Mr. Grey." Her mouth twists into a smug grin, so I throw my pajama pants at her.

She catches them, giggling.

To hell with work.

I hoist the duvet off of her, kneel on the bed, and grab Ana's ankles, drawing her toward me so that her nightgown rides up over her thighs, and up, and up, revealing my favorite place.

She squeals. It's a stimulating sound, and I lean down and start a path of kisses from her knee, to her thigh, to my favorite place.

Good morning, Ana.

Ah! She groans.

MRS. JONES IS BUSYING herself in the kitchen when I stroll in. "Good morning, Mr. Grey. Coffee?"

"Good morning, Gail. Please."

"And what would you like for breakfast?"

I'm famished after this morning's, and yesterday evening's, activities. "Omelet. Please."

"Ham, cheese, and mushrooms?"

"Great."

"Mrs. Grey did an excellent job on your hair, sir." Mrs. Jones smiles, and there's a teasing glint in her eye.

I grin back. "That she did." I perch on one of the barstools at the kitchen counter, where she's laid two place settings. "Ana will be with us shortly."

"Very good, sir." She hands me a coffee, and while my omelet is cooking she lays out granola, yogurt, and blueberries for Ana. I check the markets on my phone.

"Good morning, Mrs. Grey." Gail hands Ana a cup of tea as she greets her.

My wife is wearing a pretty blue shift dress that complements her eyes. She looks ever the cool publishing executive, and not the sex siren that I know, intimately, and often. She sits down beside me. "How are you, Mrs. Grey?" I ask, knowing that she was well pleasured, and loud about it, this morning.

"I think you know, Mr. Grey." She gazes up at me through her lashes, giving me that look that goads my libido.

I smirk. "Eat. You didn't eat yesterday."

"That's because you were being an arse."

Mrs. Jones drops a plate that she's washing beneath a tap into the sink; the sound startles Ana.

"Arse or not—eat."

Don't fuck with me on this, Ana.

Ana rolls her eyes. "Okay! Picking up spoon, eating granola." She sounds exasperated, but proceeds to serve herself yogurt and blueberries and makes a start on her breakfast.

I relax and remember what I wanted to talk to her about. "I may have to go to New York later in the week."

"Oh."

"It'll mean an overnight. I want you to come with me."

"Christian, I won't get the time off."

I peer down at her. *Oh, I think we can work that out.*

She sighs. "I know you own the company, but I've been away for three weeks. Please. How can you expect me to run the business if I'm never there? I'll be fine here. I'm assuming you'll take Taylor with you, but Sawyer and Ryan will be here—" She stops.

As ever, my wife makes a good point.

"What?" she asks.

"Nothing. Just you." *And your negotiation skills.*

She gives me a sideways look, but the amusement in her expression abruptly vanishes.

"How are you getting to New York?"

"The company jet, why?"

"I just wanted to check if you were taking *Charlie Tango.*" Her face loses color as she shudders.

"I wouldn't fly to New York in *Charlie Tango.* She doesn't have that kind of range. Besides, she won't be back from the engineers for another two weeks."

She looks relieved. "Well, I'm glad she's nearly fixed, but—" She stops and looks down at her granola.

"What?" I ask.

She shrugs.

I hate it when she does this. "Ana?" *Tell me.*

"I just…you know. Last time you flew in her…I thought, we th-thought, you'd—" She stutters and then stops.

Oh.

Ana.

"Hey." I brush my fingers down her face. "That was sabotage."

And we suspect your ex-boss.

"I couldn't bear to lose you," she says.

"Five people have been fired because of that, Ana. It won't happen again."

"Five?"

I nod.

She frowns. "That reminds me. There's a gun in your desk."

How the hell does she know that?

The scissors.

Shit.

"It's Leila's."

"It's fully loaded."

"How do you know?" I ask.

"I checked it yesterday."

What! "I don't want you messing with guns. I hope you put the safety back on."

She looks at me as if I've grown an additional head. "Christian, there's no safety on that revolver. Don't you know anything about guns?"

"Um, no."

Taylor clears his throat. He's waiting for us at the entrance. I check my watch; it's later than I thought.

That's because you made love to your wife this morning, Grey.

"We have to go." Standing up, I don my jacket, and Ana follows me out to the hallway, where we both greet Taylor.

"I am just going to brush my teeth," Ana says, and Taylor and I watch her retreat toward the bathroom.

I turn to Taylor. "That reminds me. It's Ana's birthday in September. She wants an R8. A white one."

Taylor raises his eyebrows.

I laugh. "Yeah. Surprised me, too. Can you order one?"

Taylor grins. "With great pleasure, sir. A Spyder like yours?"

"Yes. I think so. Same spec."

Taylor rubs his hands in ill-disguised glee. "I'll get onto it."

"We need it by the latest September 9."

"I'm sure I can source one in time."

Ana returns and we head into the elevator. "You should ask Taylor to teach you how to shoot," she says.

"Should I, now?" My tone is wry.

"Yes."

"Anastasia, I despise guns. My mom has patched up too many victims of gun crime, and my dad is vehemently antigun. I grew up with their ethos. I support at least two gun-control initiatives here in Washington."

"Oh. Does Taylor carry a gun?"

I glance at Taylor and hope that the utter disdain I feel for firearms doesn't show on my face. "Sometimes."

"You don't approve?" Ana asks, as I usher her out of the elevator.

"No. Let's just say that Taylor and I hold very different views with regard to gun control."

In the car, Ana reaches over and grasps my hand. "Please," she says.

"Please what?"

"Learn how to shoot."

I roll my eyes. "No. End of discussion, Anastasia."

She opens her mouth, but closes it again, and folds her arms and gazes out of the window. I suppose being an ex-soldier's daughter will give you a different perspective on guns. Being a doctor's son formed mine.

"Where is Leila?" Ana pipes up.

Why is she thinking about my ex-sub?

"I told you. She's in Connecticut with her folks."

"Did you check? After all, she does have long hair. It could have been her driving the Dodge."

"Yes, I checked. She's enrolled in an art school in Hamden. She started this week."

"You've spoken to her?" Ana pales, her voice quietly ringing with shock.

"No. Flynn has."

"I see," she mutters.

"What?"

"Nothing."

I sigh. This is the second time this morning she's done this. "Ana. What is it?"

Communicate and compromise.

She shrugs, and I have no idea what she's thinking. About Leila? Maybe Ana needs reassuring. "I'm keeping tabs on her," I say, "checking that she stays on her side of the continent. She's better, Ana. Flynn has referred her to a shrink in New Haven, and all the reports are very positive. She's always been interested in art, so..." I stop, trying to find a clue in Ana's face as to what she's thinking. "Don't sweat this, Anastasia." I squeeze her hand, and I'm heartened when she returns the gesture.

"NICE HAIRCUT, MR. GREY." Barry is effusive as he opens the glass door to Grey House.

"Er, thank you, Barry."

Well, that's a first.

"How's your boy?" I ask.

"He's great, sir. Doing well at school." Barry glows with paternal pride.

I can't help my smile. "Good to hear it."

Ros and Sam are in the elevator.

"Haircut?" Ros asks.

"Yes. Thanks."

"Looks good."

"Yes," says Sam.

"Thanks."

What the hell has gotten into my staff?

AFTER MY UPDATE WITH Barney on the tablet prototype, I send an e-mail to Ana. I take a gamble that she's managed to have her e-mail name changed.

From: Christian Grey
Subject: Flattery
Date: August 23 2011 09:54
To: Anastasia Grey

Mrs. Grey
I have received three compliments on my new haircut. Compliments from my staff are new. It must be the ridiculous smile I'm wearing whenever I think about last night. You are indeed a wonderful, talented, beautiful woman.
And all mine.

Christian Grey
CEO, Grey Enterprises Holdings, Inc.

I'm delighted when it doesn't bounce, though I don't get an immediate answer.

I'm between meetings when her response arrives.

From: Anastasia Grey
Subject: Trying to Concentrate Here
Date: August 23 2011 10:48
To: Christian Grey

Mr. Grey
I am trying to work and don't want to be distracted by delicious memories.
Is now the time to confess that I used to cut Ray's hair regularly? I had no idea it would be such useful training.
And yes, I am yours and you, my dear, overbearing husband who refuses to exercise his constitutional right under the Second Amendment to bear arms, are mine. But don't worry because I shall protect you. Always.

Anastasia Grey
Editor, SIP

She used to cut Ray's hair. Well, damn it, that's why she did such a good job. And she's going to protect me.

Of course, she is. I turn to my computer and Google "gun phobia."

From: Christian Grey
Subject: Annie Oakley
Date: August 23 2011 10:53
To: Anastasia Grey

Mrs. Grey
I am delighted to see you have spoken to the IT dept and changed your name. :D
I shall sleep safe in my bed knowing that my gun-toting wife sleeps beside me.

Christian Grey
CEO & Hoplophobe, Grey Enterprises Holdings, Inc.

From: Anastasia Grey
Subject: Long Words
Date: August 23 2011 10:58
To: Christian Grey

Mr. Grey
Once more you dazzle me with your linguistic prowess.
In fact, your prowess in general, and I think you know what I'm referring to.

Anastasia Grey
Editor, SIP

Her reply makes me grin.

From: Christian Grey
Subject: Gasp!
Date: August 23 2011 11:01
To: Anastasia Grey

Mrs. Grey
Are you flirting with me?

Christian Grey
Shocked CEO, Grey Enterprises Holdings, Inc.

From: Anastasia Grey
Subject: Would you rather...
Date: August 23 2011 11:04
To: Christian Grey

I flirted with someone else?

Anastasia Grey
Brave Editor, SIP

From: Christian Grey
Subject: Grrrrr
Date: August 23 2011 11:09
To: Anastasia Grey

NO!

Christian Grey
Possessive CEO, Grey Enterprises Holdings, Inc.

From: Anastasia Grey
Subject: Wow...
Date: August 23 2011 11:14
To: Christian Grey

Are you growling at me? 'Cause that's kinda hot.

Anastasia Grey
Squirming (in a good way) Editor, SIP

I love making her squirm via e-mail.

From: Christian Grey
Subject: Beware
Date: August 23 2011 11:16
To: Anastasia Grey

Flirting and toying with me, Mrs. Grey?
I may pay you a visit this afternoon.

Christian Grey
Priapic CEO, Grey Enterprises Holdings, Inc.

From: Anastasia Grey
Subject: Oh No!
Date: August 23 2011 11:20
To: Christian Grey

I'll behave. I wouldn't want my boss's boss's boss getting on top of me at work. ;)
Now let me get on with my job. My boss's boss's boss may fire my ass.

Anastasia Grey
Editor, SIP

From: Christian Grey
Subject: &*%$&*&*
Date: August 23 2011 11:23
To: Anastasia Grey

Believe me when I say there are a great many things he'd like to do to your ass right now. Firing you is not one of them.

Christian Grey
CEO & Ass man, Grey Enterprises Holdings, Inc.

From: Anastasia Grey
Subject: Go Away!
Date: August 23 2011 11:26
To: Christian Grey

Don't you have an empire to run?
Stop bothering me.
My next appointment is here.
I thought you were a breast man…
Think about my ass, and I'll think about yours…
ILY x

Anastasia Grey
Now Moist Editor, SIP

Moist? There's that word again. I shake my head. I like her wet. Moist doesn't do it for me, at all. But sadly, I must cease, as my meeting with Marco and his team starts in four minutes.

It's a great meeting. Marco has gone aggressively after Geolumara and our bid has been successful. This acquisition will take us into a new area of green energy, via a cheaper and easier-to-manufacture solar panel.

It's also looking likely that either I'll have to go to Taiwan or the shipyard owners will come to us. But first they want a phone conference. Ros is arranging a time.

When we finish up, she asks for a word. We wait for the others to leave.

"Hassan would like you to go to New York," she says. "Morale is low because of how Woods left. He wasn't well liked, and because he kicked up a fuss in the press, the tech team is skittish. We don't want to lose any of them. They're all good people."

"Hassan can't reassure them?"

"He can only do so much, Christian. Your visit would signal real support. You're good at rallying the troops."

"Okay."

"I'll let him know you'll be there Thursday."

"Thanks."

"Oh, and Gwen is pregnant."

"Wow. Congratulations!"

I wonder how all that works, but I don't want to pry.

"Yes. She's at twelve weeks, so we're telling people."

"Three kids! Wow!"

"Yes. We'll probably stop there."

I grin. "Well, congratulations once more."

When I get back to my desk, I call Welch for an update. He's viewed the footage from outside Escala. "Mr. Grey, I'd like to talk to Hyde's former assistants again. See if they'll talk this time."

"Couldn't do any harm."

"My thoughts exactly."

"Let me know how you get on."

"Will do."

I hang up and let Ana know I'm off to New York.

From: Christian Grey
Subject: The Big Apple
Date: August 23 2011 12:59
To: Anastasia Grey

Dearest Wife
My empire requires that I go to NYC on Thursday.
I'll be back on Friday evening.
Are you sure I can't persuade you to come with me?
Your boss's boss's boss needs you.

Christian Grey
CEO, Breast & Ass man, Grey Enterprises Holdings, Inc.

From: Anastasia Grey
Subject: NYC NoNo
Date: August 23 2011 13:02
To: Christian Grey

I think my boss's boss's boss can manage a night without me and my breasts and ass!
As they say, absence makes the…heart grow fonder.
I'll behave. I promise.

Anastasia Grey
Editor, SIP

THURSDAY, AUGUST 25, 2011

It's pre-dawn, and my wife is curled up beneath the covers. Beside her on the floor is the remains of a cable tie. I pick it up, smirking, remembering last night, and slip it into my pants pocket.

Fun times.

Leaning over her, I catch a hint of her scent. Ana and sex; the most seductive perfume in the world. I plant a gentle kiss on her forehead.

"Too early," she grumbles.

Damn. I've woken her, and I know from experience that Ana is not a fan of the early morning. "I'll see you tomorrow night," I whisper.

"Don't go," she says sleepily, and she's so tempting.

"I have to." I stroke her cheek. "Miss me."

"I will." She gives me a sleepy smile and puckers her lips.

I grin. An early morning good-bye kiss from my girl. "Bye," I whisper against her lips, and reluctantly, I leave her to sleep.

FROM THE BACK OF the car I send Ana an e-mail while Ryan drives Taylor and me to Boeing Field.

From: Christian Grey
Subject: Miss You Already
Date: August 25 2011 04:32
To: Anastasia Grey

Mrs. Grey
You were adorable this morning.
Behave while I'm away.
I love you.

Christian Grey
CEO, Grey Enterprises Holdings, Inc.

Captain Stephan and First Officer Beighley are on hand, and we're soon airborne for NYC. I strip down in the small bedroom, hoping to catch an hour or so of sleep. As I lay down, I recall our evening. Ana and I went to the Seattle Assistance Union Gala; she looked elegant in her pale pink dress and second-chance earrings. She looked even more elegant when I undressed her last night.

She should be with me now. I close my eyes and my mind drifts to our honeymoon night, on board this Gulfstream.

Hmm…I hope to dream of my wife.

I WAKE WHEN WE'RE about an hour out of New York and, feeling refreshed, dress quickly. Taylor is in the main cabin, eating what looks like a ham-and-cheese croissant.

"Good morning, sir."

"Hi. Breakfast. Great. Did you get some sleep?"

Taylor nods, looking his usual, immaculate self. "I did, thank you."

I take my seat as the captain joins us.

"Sleep well, sir?" Stephan asks.

"Yes. Thanks. Everything okay?" I ask.

"We're being rerouted to JFK. There's been an incident at Teterboro."

"An incident?"

"As far as I know, it's nothing major, it's just hit our landing time."

"This will give me less time at GEH Fiber Optics," I say to Taylor.

"I've been in touch with the ground crew at Sheltair, and we're rerouting your car from Teterboro," Stephan says.

"Good. Will you get the Gulfstream to Teterboro after we land? It's more convenient to leave from there."

"I'll see what we can do." Stephan smiles and heads back into the cockpit.

FORTY MINUTES LATER WE land at JFK. As we taxi to the terminal, I check my e-mails. There's one from Ana.

From: Anastasia Grey
Subject: Behave Yourself!
Date: August 25 2011 09:03
To: Christian Grey

Let me know when you land—I'll worry until you do.
And I shall behave. I mean, how much trouble can I get into with Kate?

Anastasia Grey
Editor, SIP

Kate? I imagine she could get into a lot of trouble with Kate. The second time I met Miss Kavanagh, Ana was inebriated. That's how we spent our first night together. *Shit!* I press call.

"Ana St—Grey."

It's such a pleasure to hear her voice. "Hi."

"Hi! How was your flight?"

"Long. What are you doing with Kate?"

"We're just going out for a quiet drink."

Out? With Hyde at large? Fuck!

"Sawyer and the new woman—Prescott—are coming to watch over us," she says sweetly.

Then I remember. "I thought Kate was coming to the apartment."

"She is, after a quick drink."

I sigh. "Why didn't you tell me?" I'm not in Seattle. If something happens to them…to her, and I'm not there, I'll never forgive myself.

"Christian, we'll be fine. I have Ryan, Sawyer, and Prescott here. It's a quick drink. I've seen her only a few times since you and I met. Please. She's my best friend."

"Ana, I don't want to keep you from your friends. But I thought she was coming back to the apartment."

She sighs. "Okay. We'll stay in."

"Only while this lunatic is out there. Please."

"I've said okay," she mutters, and I know by the tone of her voice she's exasperated.

I chuckle, relieved that she's reverting to type. "I always know when you're rolling your eyes at me."

"Look, I'm sorry. I didn't mean to worry you. I'll tell Kate."

"Good." I blow out a breath. I can go about the rest of my day and not worry about her.

"Where are you?"

"On the tarmac at JFK."

"Oh, so you just landed?"

"Yes. You asked me to call the moment I landed."

"Well, Mr. Grey, I'm glad one of us is punctilious."

"Mrs. Grey, your gift for hyperbole knows no bounds. What am I going to do with you?"

"I am sure you'll think of something imaginative. You usually do," she whispers.

"Are you flirting with me?"

"Yes." She sounds breathless and even from this far away, and over the phone her voice is arousing.

I grin. "I'd better go. Ana, do as you're told, please. The security team knows what they're doing."

"Yes, Christian, I will." I sense more eye rolling.

"I'll see you tomorrow evening. I'll call you later."

"To check up on me?"

"Yes."

"Oh, Christian!" she chides me.

"Au revoir, Mrs. Grey."

"Au revoir, Christian. I love you."

Hearing her say those three words will never get old. "And I you, Ana."

Neither of us hangs up.

"Hang up, Christian," she murmurs.

"You're a bossy little thing, aren't you?"

"Your bossy little thing."

"Mine," I whisper. "Do as you're told. Hang up."

"Yes, Sir," she purrs, and hangs up.

And the disappointment is real.

Ana.

I type a quick e-mail.

From: Christian Grey
Subject: Twitching Palms
Date: August 25 2011 13:42 EDT
To: Anastasia Grey

Mrs. Grey
You are as entertaining as ever on the phone.
I mean it. Do as you're told.
I need to know you're safe.
I love you.

Christian Grey
CEO, Grey Enterprises Holdings, Inc.

The plane pulls to a stop outside the terminal. Our car is waiting for us on the tarmac. It's time to head to the Flatiron district and rally the troops.

I loathe the tedious drive from JFK to Manhattan. The traffic is always gridlocked, and even when it's moving, it's slow. That's why I prefer to travel from Teterboro. I occupy myself with e-mails until I glance out of the car window. We're driving through Queens on the expressway, heading to the Midtown Tunnel, and there she is—Manhattan. There is something magical about her skyline. I've not been to New York for a few months; well, since before I met Ana. And I know I must bring her here soon, as she's never been before, if only to see this iconic view.

We head straight to the GEH Fiber Optics division, which is based in an old building on East Twenty-Second Street. We pull up outside, and I can feel the bustling energy of the city. It's invigorating. As I step out of the car into the Manhattan throng, I'm hyped for my first meeting of the day.

The engineering team blows me away. Young. Creative. Energetic. I feel at home here. Over a long lunch of sandwiches and beer, I tell them how their technology is going to revolutionize Kavanagh Media's operation and how the work they're doing now is vital in future-proofing Kavanagh's expansion plans. His will be the first major media outlet to use their technology, and when I show them how we intend to deploy their expertise in other fields, they're all buzzing with excitement.

Ros was right—I needed to do this. Hassan, who is now the senior vice president of the company, is smart, young, and driven; he reminds me of myself. He's far superior to Woods, an inspiring and worthy successor with vision and drive. One only has to see the premises that Woods has inflicted on his team to know he had a short-term, narrow perspective. What was he thinking? While the reception area is remarkably upscale and frankly pretentious, the offices are cramped, shabby, and in need of substantial refurbishment. We need to relocate. I've instructed Rachel Morris, their logistics chief, to get on that. She's keen to do so, which is great, but it's no wonder morale is low; the place is grim. I e-mail Ros and ask her to go through the lease to see if we can get out before the end of the term, which has another two years to run.

When I leave it's after 6 p.m., and we're behind schedule. I have just enough time to get to my apartment in Tribeca, change into my tux, then head out again to the Telecommunications Alliance Organization fundraiser near Union Square.

In the car I try to call Ana, but I can't get a signal.

Hell.

The irony is not lost on me. I'll try again later.

The event, as I expected, is convivial enough, and it gives me a chance to network with fellow senior executives and entrepreneurs in my field. But yesterday I attended a charity gala in Seattle with Ana, and it was more enjoyable for that reason alone.

While the gathered guests enjoy canapés and cocktails, I call her once more, but her phone goes to voice mail. I'm about to leave a message when I'm interrupted by the host, Dr. Alan Michaels, who is delighted to see me.

At 9:30 p.m., during the entrée, Taylor sidles up to me.

"Sir. Mrs. Grey is having a drink with Kate Kavanagh at the Zig Zag Café."

"Really?" Ana said she would go back to the apartment. I check my watch. It's 6:30 p.m. in Seattle. "Who's with her?"

"Sawyer and Prescott."

"Okay." *Maybe it's just one drink.* "Let me know when she leaves."

She said she would stay at home.

Why would she do this?

She knows I'm concerned about her welfare.

Hyde is at large. He's obviously crazy and unpredictable.

My mood sours, and I find it difficult to concentrate on the conversation that floats around me. I'm sitting at a table occupied by some of the titans of our industry and their wives—and a husband, in one case. We are here to raise money to provide technology for schools in less privileged and underserved communities across the country. But there are only nine of us at our table and one empty seat; my wife is conspicuous by her absence.

She's also absent from our home.

"Where's your wife this evening?" Callista Michaels asks me. Seated on my left, she's the organizer of the event and Dr. Michaels's wife. She's older, maybe in her late fifties, and dripping in diamonds.

"She's in Seattle."

At a fucking bar.

"Shame she couldn't come tonight," she says.

"She works. And she enjoys her job."

"Oh. How quaint. What does she do?"

I grit my teeth. "She's in publishing."

And I wish she were here.

Or I were back in Seattle.

My mood grows bleaker. My sirloin with béarnaise sauce doesn't taste quite as good as it did. It's weird. I've always attended these events without a date; now I don't know what possessed me to accept the invitation without Ana.

Well, I thought Ana would come with me.

Though, now that I think about it, she was a little bored at the benefit we attended yesterday.

And tonight, she's out drinking. With Kate.

Having fun.

Shit.

Every time I've known them to go out together, Ana has had too much to drink. The first night we slept together in Portland she was so drunk she passed out in my arms. She was totally inebriated when she got home after her bachelorette party. An image of her naked in bed, her arms beckoning me, her sweet, seductive tone, calls to me. "*You can do anything you want to me.*"

Fuck!

It's always when she's out with Kavanagh.

Keep it together, Grey. The security team is with her.

What harm can she come to?

Hyde. He's out there, somewhere. And he wants revenge? I don't know.

He's a maniac.

I look up at Taylor, who is standing on the other side of the room. He shakes his head.

She's still out. She's still drinking. With Kavanagh.

I'm dragged back into the now, and a conversation about conflict minerals and reliable sources of ethically mined materials.

After the delicious and frankly comforting dark chocolate torte, I look up at Taylor again.

He shakes his head.

Hell.

That's time for how many drinks?

I hope she's had something to eat.

"Excuse me, I have to make a call." I leave the table and call Ana from the lobby. She doesn't pick up. I try her again. No answer. I try once more. Still no answer.

Fuck.

I text her.

WHERE THE HELL ARE YOU!

She should be home. Or here.

And I know I'm being petulant, but she won't even pick up my calls.

I storm back into the ballroom, where a charity auction is about to begin. I listen to the first two lots. Both involve golf.

Fuck this.

I write a check for one hundred thousand dollars and hand it to Mrs. Michaels. "I am sorry, Callista, but I have to go. Thank you for hosting a lovely evening. I'll pledge the same again for next year. It's a worthy cause."

"Christian, that's so generous. Thank you." I get up to leave, as does she, and she kisses me on both cheeks, which I'm not expecting.

"Good night," I say to Callista, and I shake her husband's hand.

I eye Taylor at the edge of the room, and I think he's already calling the car.

Even with its high ceilings and great views over the city, the place suddenly feels claustrophobic, and I'm grateful when we get outside into the balmy evening heat of New York.

"Sir, the car will be a couple of minutes."

"Okay. She's still there? At the Zig Zag?"

"Yes, sir."

"Let's go home."

Taylor tilts his head. "Tribeca?"

"No, Seattle."

He stares at me, his face giving nothing away, but I know he thinks I'm crazy.

I sigh. "Yes. I'm sure. I want to go home." I answer his unspoken question.

"I'll call Stephan," he says.

He wanders over to the side of the main entrance and makes the call. I try Ana again, and her phone goes to voice mail. I don't trust myself to leave a message. I realize I could call Sawyer, but I have only a flimsy hold on my temper.

Taylor could call him. But what would that achieve? It's not like Sawyer can physically remove Ana from the bar.

Could he?

Grey! Behave.

Taylor finishes his call and walks back to me, his expression grim.

What the hell?

"Sir, the Gulfstream is at Teterboro. It can be ready to fly in an hour."

"Good. Let's go."

"Do you want to go back to the apartment?" he asks.

"No, I don't need anything there. Do you need to go back there?"

"No, sir."

"We'll go straight to the airport."

In the car I brood. I have a nagging suspicion that I'm behaving badly, but not as badly as my wife. Why can't she do what she says? Or let me know?

Hyde is out for revenge, and I'm scared.

For her.

And for me, if I lose her.

FRIDAY, AUGUST 26, 2011

Once we're on board, I remove my bow tie, fold it, and stuff it into the outside breast pocket of my tux. Taylor hangs my jacket with his in the small closet, and I grab a blanket for each of us, then take a seat in the main cabin.

I gaze out into the New Jersey darkness, tension leaching from my muscles into my bones. While we were in the terminal waiting for the Gulfstream, I managed to restrain myself from calling Ana again. But I can bear it no longer, and as Stephan and Beighley do their final checks, I call Sawyer.

"Mr. Grey," he says, above the background hum of the bar. People are out, enjoying themselves. Like Ana.

"Sawyer, good evening. Is Mrs. Grey still with you?"

"She is, sir."

I'm tempted to ask him to hand his phone to her, but I know I will lose my shit and she's probably having a good time. I'm reassured that she's under Sawyer's watchful eye.

"Do you want to talk to her?" he asks.

"No. Stick close to her. Keep her safe."

Hyde could be anywhere.

"Yes, sir. Prescott and I have her covered," Sawyer replies. I hang up and glance at Taylor, who is sitting diagonally opposite me, watching me impassively.

I look back down at my phone and I'm so mad at my wife, I didn't even tell Sawyer that we were on our way home. Taylor must think I'm crazy.

I am crazy—crazy for my fucking wife, who cannot be trusted to do as she says. Taylor's seen me sitting on the floor of my foyer, staring at the elevator, after she left me. And he had glue for the little glider.

"Sir, she'll be fine," he says gently.

I look up at him again and bite my tongue.

This is none of his goddamn business.

This is between me and my wife.

Deep down I think she's going to be fine.

But I have to be sure.

Why the hell couldn't she do what I needed her to do?

Just once.

Just now.

My temper simmers and I fire off a quick e-mail to her.

From: Christian Grey
Subject: Angry. You've Not Seen Angry
Date: August 26 2011 00:42 EST
To: Anastasia Grey

Anastasia
Sawyer tells me that you are drinking cocktails in a bar when you said you wouldn't.
Do you have any idea how mad I am at the moment?
I'll see you tomorrow.

Christian Grey
CEO, Grey Enterprises Holdings, Inc.

Beighley announces that we will be taking off shortly. I buckle up as Taylor does the same. "You can take the bed, if you'd like to sleep," I offer. "I think it will elude me."

"I'm good, sir."

Okay. I lay back and close my eyes, grateful that Beighley likes a nap and has slept all afternoon. She's going to fly us home.

I SLEEP FITFULLY, MY dreams a tangled mess of dominance and submission—standing over Ana with a cane in my hand. Elena standing with a cane over me.

It's confusing and unsettling.

I try not to sleep.

To stay awake, I pace. Feeling like a caged animal, though that sense is exacerbated because the Gulfstream is not exactly designed for pacing.

Hell. I want to howl at the moon.

I want to be home.

I want to curl up with Ana.

THE PLANE LANDING AT Boeing Field wakes me from my restless sleep. Opening my eyes, which are gritty from lack of sleep and dry from the air-conditioning, I pick up my phone.

Taylor is awake. I wonder if he's slept at all. "What's the time?" I ask as Beighley brings the plane to a stop at the end of the runway.

"It's ten after four."

"That's early. Will we be met?"

"I did e-mail Ryan. Let's hope he got the message." We both switch on our phones at the same time.

Shit. I have several messages. And judging by the irritating notifications coming from his phone, so does Taylor. There's a text and missed call from Ana. I read her text first.

> ANA
> I'M STILL IN ONE PIECE. I HAD A NICE TIME. MISSING YOU—PLEASE DON'T BE MAD.

Too late, Ana.

At least she missed me.

She's left a voice mail, which I listen to next. Her voice is breathy and anxious. "Hi. It's me. Please don't be mad. We've had an incident at the apartment. But it's under control, so don't worry. No one is hurt. Call me."

What the fuck?

And my first thought is Leila has broken in again. Maybe it *was* her driving the Dodge. When I glance at Taylor, his face is ashen. "Hyde was caught in the apartment. Ryan took him down. He's in police custody," he says.

My world grinds to a screeching halt.

"Ana?" I whisper, as all the breath evaporates from my body.

"She's fine."

"Gail?"

"She's fine, too."

"What the hell?"

"Exactly." Taylor looks as shaken as I feel. The plane taxies to a stop, and I call Ana immediately, but her phone goes straight to voice mail.

Shit.

Hyde. In the apartment? How? Why? What?

I'm trying to wrap my head around this, but exhaustion is clouding my thinking. Ana's not answering; she must be asleep. I hope so. I'm relieved she's okay, but I need to see her to make sure. Stephan has opened the aircraft door, and the early morning chill seeps into the main cabin and my bones. Shivering, I get up, and take my jacket from Taylor, who is first off the plane.

"Thanks, Beighley. Stephan," I say, as I don my tux jacket to ward off the cool pre-dawn air.

"You're welcome, sir," she says.

"No. I mean it. Thank you. For the last-minute scramble of it all."

"It's not a problem."

"Get some rest." I shake both their hands and follow Taylor out to where Sawyer is waiting with the Audi.

Sawyer gives us a debrief during the drive back to Escala. While Ana and Kate were carousing at the Zig Zag Café, Hyde, dressed in coveralls, arrived at Escala and buzzed the apartment service entrance. Ryan recognized him. Let him in. And took him down. This all happened just before Ana, Sawyer, and Prescott returned home. The police and paramedics came. Took Hyde away. They questioned everyone.

What the actual fuck!

"Was he armed?" Taylor asks.

"Yes," Sawyer responds.

"Is Ryan okay?" I ask.

"Yes. But there was an altercation. One of the doors needs repair."

"Altercation?" *I don't believe it!*

"They fought."

Fuck. "But Ryan's okay?"

"Yes, sir."

"And Gail. She was there?" Taylor presses.

"In the panic room."

Thank you, Ros Bailey! I glance at Taylor, who rubs his forehead, his eyes screwed shut.

Hell. Both of our women threatened by that evil motherfucker Hyde.

"Who called the police?" Taylor asks.

"I did. Mrs. Grey insisted."

"She did the right thing," I mutter. "What the hell was he hoping to achieve?"

"I don't know, sir," Sawyer replies. "One more thing. The press were outside last night."

Damn. And after they'd lost interest in us. This day just keeps getting better and better, and it's only—I glance at my watch—4:40 a.m.

"Ryan didn't get your e-mail until he turned in," Sawyer says. "It was too late to let everyone know you were on your way back."

"So Ana and Gail don't know," I ask.

"No, sir."

"Okay."

We're quiet for the rest of the short journey. Each of us with our own haunting thoughts. If Ana had been home, she'd have been in the panic room with Gail, and Ryan would have had backup and wouldn't have had to face Hyde alone.

Why can't she do as she's told?

Sawyer parks the Audi in the garage, and both Taylor and I fly out of the car and into the elevator.

"Glad we came home when we did," I say to Taylor.

"Yes, sir." He nods in agreement.

"What a fucking mess."

"Indeed." He remains tight-lipped.

"We should have a full debrief when everyone has had some sleep."

"Agreed."

The elevator doors open and we spill out into the foyer, each of us with one goal: to check on our woman. I head straight for our bedroom, and I know that's exactly what Taylor is doing. I barrel down the hallway and into the room, grateful that the thick carpet absorbs the sound of my footsteps.

Ana is fast asleep on my side of the bed. She's curled up in a small ball, wearing one of my T-shirts.

She's here.

She's fine.

My relief almost brings me to my knees, but I stand and watch her. I can't risk touching her, as I know I'll wake her if I do.

Wake her and bury myself in her.

I wonder how drunk she was last night.

Ana. Ana. Ana.

What a shock to come back here to Hyde.

I steel myself and brush my forefinger over her cheek. She mumbles something in her sleep, and I freeze. I don't want to wake her. When she settles, I slink out and head back to the living room. I need a drink.

As I pass the foyer door I notice that it's hanging off its hinges. There are scuff marks over the walls. But no blood, that I can see.

Thank God. An altercation? It looks like it was a full-on fight.

And Hyde had a gun. He could have murdered Ryan right here in my home.

The thought is sickening.

In the living room I head over to the bar cart and pour myself a Laphroaig. I toss the contents of the glass down in one swallow, appreciating the burn as it sears my throat, the warmth spreading downward and joining the maelstrom in my gut. I take a deep breath and pour another, larger glass and head back into the bedroom.

I should really get some sleep, but I'm too wired.

And too mad.

No. Not mad. I'm raging.

The sanctity of my home invaded by that cocksucking, motherfucking asshole.

Quietly, I drag the bedroom chair from its position by the window to my side of the bed. Sitting down, I watch Ana sleep as I slowly sip my scotch and pinch the bridge of my nose, trying to quiet the ferocious storm inside me.

It doesn't work.

He wanted to harm my wife.

That's the only conclusion I can come to.

Kidnap her? Kill her?

To get back at me.

And Ana…she wasn't here.

Where I asked her to be.

Told her to be.

My anger simmers, curdling into bitter rage.

And I have no outlet.

Only this drink, and the fire it leaves in its wake with each sip.

I re-cross my legs and tap my finger against my lip as I think of all the ways I'd like to end Hyde.

Strangulation. Suffocation. Beat him to death. Shoot him. I have Leila's gun.

And punish Ana for not doing as she's told.

Paddle. Flogger. Cane… Belt.

But I can't. She won't let me.

Fuck.

As dawn breaks, it gradually lights the room.

Ana stirs, and her eyes flutter open. Her lips part as she gasps in surprise when she realizes I'm sitting and watching her. "Hi," she whispers. I finish my drink and place the glass on the bedside table while I contemplate what I'm going to say to her. "Hello," I murmur, and it feels like someone else is talking. Someone robotic. Someone without feeling.

"You're back."

"It would appear so."

She sits up, eyes bright, and blue, and lovely. "How long have you been sitting there watching me sleep?"

"Long enough."

"You're still mad," she whispers.

Oh, I wish I was just *mad.* Robotic me says the word out loud, testing it. But it's not enough. "No, Ana. I am way, way beyond mad."

"Way beyond mad. That doesn't sound good."

No. It's not. We gaze at each other and I wish I could stand up and yell and scream and tell her how I feel. How disappointed and relieved I am.

How frightened I am.

How fucking furious I am.

I don't think I've ever experienced the depth of these conflicting feelings that plague me right now. But robotic me doesn't know what to do; all systems are offline, trying to contain my rage.

She reaches over, grabs her glass, and takes a sip of water. "Ryan caught Jack," she says, placing the glass back down.

"I know."

Her brow creases. "Are you going to be monosyllabic for long?"

Is she trying to be funny? "Yes," I respond, because it's all I can manage.

Her frown deepens. "I'm sorry I stayed out."

"Are you?"

"No."

"Why say it, then?"

"Because I don't want you to be mad at me."

It's too late for that, Ana. I sigh and run a hand through my hair.

"I think Detective Clark wants to talk to you," she says.

"I'm sure he does."

"Christian, please..."

"Please what?"

"Don't be so cold."

Cold? "Anastasia, cold is not what I'm feeling at the moment. I'm burning. Burning with rage. I don't know how to deal with these"—I wave my hand seeking inspiration—"feelings."

Her eyes widen farther, and before I can stop her, she clambers out of bed and onto my lap. It's so unexpected—a welcome, disarming diversion from my rage. Slowly and carefully, so I don't break her, I wrap my arms around her and bury my nose in her hair, inhaling her unique Ana scent.

She's here.

She's okay.

My throat burns with my unshed tears of gratitude.

Thank heavens she's safe.

She embraces me and kisses my neck.

"Oh, Mrs. Grey. What am I going to do with you?" My voice is hoarse, and I kiss the top of her head.

"How much have you had to drink?"

"Why?"

"You don't normally drink hard liquor."

"This is my second glass. I've had a trying night, Anastasia. Give a man a break."

I sense her smile. "If you insist, Mr. Grey." She nuzzles my throat, once more. "You smell heavenly. I slept on your side of the bed because your pillow smells of you."

Oh, Ana.

I kiss her hair. "Did you, now? I wondered why you were on this side. I'm still mad at you."

"I know," she whispers. My hand moves rhythmically down her back; touching her brings me solace and starts to ground me in the now. "And I'm mad at you," she says.

I stop caressing her back. "And what, pray, have I done to deserve your ire?"

"I'll tell you later when you're no longer burning with rage." She kisses my neck and I close my eyes and hold her.

Tight.

I never want to let her go.

I could have lost her. She could have been killed by that asshole. "When I think of what might have happened..." I squeeze the words past the knot of fury that's still lodged in my throat.

"I'm okay."

"Oh, Ana," I choke out, and I want to cry.

"I'm okay. We're all okay. A bit shaken. But Gail is fine. Ryan is fine. And Jack is gone."

"No thanks to you," I mutter.

She leans back and glares at me. "What do you mean?"

"I don't want to argue about it right now, Ana."

I think she's weighing my words, and for whatever reason, she cuddles into me once more. She wouldn't if she knew the truth.

She knows the truth.

She knows me.

The bad seed.

She's seen the monster. "I want to punish you." I whisper, like it's a deep, dark confession, "really beat the shit out of you."

She stills. "I know," she whispers.

That's not what I expect her to say. "Maybe I will."

"I hope not," she says, her voice quiet but unwavering.

I sigh. It's never going to happen. This I know and I reconciled myself to that when she came back after leaving me.

But I want to.

Really fucking want to.

But she left the last time I did.

Now she's my wife and here we are.

I hug her tighter. "Ana, Ana, Ana. You'd try the patience of a saint."

"I could accuse you of many things, Mr. Grey, but being a saint isn't one of them."

And there she is.

My girl.

I chuckle, and though it sounds hollow, even to my ears, it's cathartic. "Fair point well made as ever, Mrs. Grey." I kiss her forehead. "Back to bed. You had a late night, too." I pick her up and deposit her back on the bed.

"Lie down with me?" she says, her eyes imploring me to stay.

"No. I have things to do." I reach for my empty glass. "Go back to sleep. I'll wake you in a couple of hours."

"Are you still mad at me?"

"Yes."

"I'll go back to sleep, then."

"Good." I tuck her in and kiss her forehead. "Sleep."

I stride out of the room before I change my mind.

And I know that I'm running from her, because she has the power to wound me like no other. If Hyde had gotten to her…*shit.* Her absence from this world would hurt me more than anything I've experienced so far.

I wander into the kitchen, deposit the glass by the sink, and head into my study. I need an action plan. I scribble down everything that I need to do, then send Andrea an e-mail to cancel my meetings in Washington, DC. I tell her I've had to return to Seattle, but can still have the meetings via WebEx or phone. I press send, knowing that once the news cycle picks up on Hyde's arrest, it will be self-explanatory.

I pull out Hyde's file to have another look through the information Welch has provided, to see if there are any clues to Hyde's insanity.

I keep coming back to one detail that's been nagging at me since I read it the first time. I wonder if it's a coincidence or material to this mess.

Jackson "Jack" Daniel Hyde.

DOB: Feb 26, 1979, Brightmoor, Detroit, MI

Hell. I'm so tired my brain is fried, but I know I won't sleep. I need some fresh air to clear the fear and anxiety from my system.

Quietly, I sneak into the closet and change into my running gear, but before I go out, I check on Ana. She's fast asleep. With my iPod strapped to my arm, I head down to the lobby in the elevator.

As the doors open, I note the two photographers outside. I slip through the rear doors to the utility area, then through a series of corridors and out into the passage behind the building. I hit the early morning streets of Seattle, The Verve's "Bitter Sweet Symphony" playing loud and proud through my earbuds.

I run and run and run, down Fifth Avenue to Vine. I run past Ana's old apartment, where Kate Kavanagh should be sleeping off her hangover. I run along Western, veering off to go through Pike Place Market. It's grueling. But I don't stop until I'm back outside Escala. And then I do it all over again.

I return a sweaty mess with my Mariners cap pulled low over my face. I make my way unrecognized through the press gathered outside the building and safely into the elevator.

Mrs. Jones is in the kitchen.

"Gail! How are you?" I ask as soon as I see her.

"Good, Mr. Grey. Glad you and Taylor are back."

"Tell me what happened."

As I fill and drink a glass of water, she gives me a quick run-through of last night's events. How Ryan ushered her into the panic room. And afterward, once Hyde was caught, what happened with the police and paramedics. "I never thought we'd have to use that room."

"I'm glad I had it installed."

"Yes, sir. I'm grateful, too. Do you want a coffee?"

"Not yet. I'll have some orange juice for Ana."

She smiles. "Coming right up."

"Is Taylor awake?"

"No, sir."

"Good. Let him rest."

She hands me the juice, and I leave her to go wake Ana.

She's still asleep.

"There's some orange juice for you here." I place it on her bedside table and she stirs, her eyes are on me, her teeth toying with her bottom lip. "I'm going to take a shower," I mutter and leave.

I strip quickly, leaving my clothes on the bathroom floor. My run has done little to improve my temper. I start washing my hair vigorously, and mentally run through a checklist of what I have to do this morning. I sense Ana before I hear her. She closes the shower door, then steps up behind me and places her arms around me. I stiffen at her touch.

Everywhere.

Don't touch me.

Ignoring my reaction, she pulls me closer, so that I feel her warm, naked body against me. She presses her cheek to my back.

We're skin on skin.

And it's unbearable.

I'm too mad at you right now.

I'm too mad at myself.

I shift so we're both under the water and continue rinsing the suds out of my hair. She presses her lips against me in small, soft kisses.

No. "Ana," I caution her.

"Hmm."

Stop.

I burn for her.

But my thoughts are too dark.

I'm too angry.

Her hand skims down over my belly, and I know what she has in mind. But I want none of it.

I want all of it.

All of her.

No!

I place both of mine on hers and shake my head. "Don't," I whisper.

She steps back, immediately, as if I've slapped her, so I turn around and her eyes flit to my erection.

It's just biology, baby.

I clasp her chin. "I'm still fucking mad at you," I whisper, and rest my forehead against hers, closing my eyes.

And I'm fucking mad at myself.

I should have stayed in Seattle.

She reaches up and strokes my cheek, and I desperately want to give in to her tender touch.

"Don't be mad at me, please. I think you're overreacting," she says.

What!

I straighten, so her hand falls to her side, and glare at her. "Overreacting?" I rant. "Some fucking lunatic gets into my apartment to kidnap my wife, and you think I'm overreacting!"

She gazes up at me, but she doesn't back away. "No, um, that's not what I was referring to. I thought this was about me staying out."

Oh. I close my eyes. I left her for one night, and she could have been kidnapped or worse. Murdered by that asshole.

"Christian, I wasn't here," she whispers in the gentlest of tones.

"I know." I open my eyes, feeling hopeless and worthless at once. "And all because you can't follow a simple fucking request. I don't want to discuss this now, in the shower. I am still fucking mad at you, Anastasia. You're making me question my judgment."

I leave her and grab a towel as I stalk out of the bathroom. I want to hang on to my anger. It protects me and keeps her away from me.

It keeps me safe.

Safe from more complex and difficult feelings.

I towel myself dry. I'm still damp as I dress, but I don't give a damn.

I storm out of the closet and along the corridor to the kitchen.

"Coffee?" Gail calls after me, as I head toward my study.

"Please."

At my desk I look once more through Hyde's background check.

There's something here. I can feel it. Gail appears and leaves a black coffee on my desk.

"Thanks."

I take a sip; it's hot and dark. Damn, it tastes good.

I call Welch.

"Good morning, Grey. I hear you're back in Seattle," Welch says.

"I am. Who told you?"

"I just got an update from Taylor."

"So you've heard about Hyde."

"Yes. I've put a call in to my contact at King County PD. Find out what's going on."

"Thanks."

"And I've heard from the FBI."

There's a knock at my door, and Ana stands in the doorway, wearing the purple dress that reveals every womanly curve she possesses. Her hair is in a bun, and there are diamonds in her ears. She looks prim and proper, hiding her inner freak, and it's arousing as hell. I shake my head, dismissing her, noting the downturn of her mouth as she turns away.

"Sorry, Welch—what did you say?"

"The FBI. There's a match. The partial print in the EC135."

"It's Hyde?"

"Yes, sir. The FBI uncovered his convictions as a minor in Detroit."

Detroit again.

"They match," he says, "though those documents are supposed to be sealed, which is why it's taken a few days."

"What does that mean?"

"They may be inadmissible."

"Shit, really? Well, there's also the footage we have of Hyde outside Escala that Prescott found earlier this week. It's obvious he was checking the place out. And, of course, the CCTV from GEH's server room."

"The police have been wanting to question him about the incident at GEH, but they hadn't been able to locate him."

"They have him now."

"Indeed," Welch growls. "And the two investigations are going to compare Hyde's prints for a match."

"About time. Did you get anything out of his former assistants?"

"No. They're reluctant to talk. They all say he was an excellent boss."

"I find that hard to believe."

"Agreed, given the hushed-up harassment claims," Welch mutters. "We've only spoken to four. I'll keep pushing."

"Okay."

"What do you want to do about the heightened security around your family?"

"Let's keep it for now and see where this goes with Hyde. We have no idea if he's working alone or with someone."

"Okay. I'll report back when I've heard from my contact."

"Great. Thanks."

I check my e-mails. There's one from Sam letting me know that he's been inundated with press inquiries about last night. I respond, telling him to send all inquiries to the King County PD press office.

Taylor enters. "Good morning, sir."

"Did you get some sleep?"

He blows out a breath. "A few hours. Enough."

"Good. We have a great deal to cover."

He pulls up a chair and we run through my to-do list.

"…and, finally, get a carpenter to fix the door."

"Will do. Briefing at ten with the entire team. I'll let them know," Taylor says.

"Please."

"Sawyer and Ryan are in their racks. I'm assuming they're still asleep. Prescott is sifting through the CCTV from last night to find out how Hyde got into the building."

"Good."

"Sir," he says, in a way that gets my immediate attention.

"Yes?"

"I'm grateful we came home last night. Maybe you have a sixth sense or something."

I'm taken aback. "Taylor, I was just mad at my wife."

His sudden smile is wry and world weary. "Happens to us all, sir."

I nod, but his words are not reassuring; he's divorced.

Don't go there, Grey.

"Thank God Ana and Gail are safe," I add, as I get up. I'm hungry for my breakfast.

"Yes, sir." He follows me out of the study.

"I've made you an omelet," Gail says to me, and she gives us both a huge smile.

Maybe Taylor and Gail will tie the knot.

Who knows?

Ignoring them, I take a seat at the kitchen counter, and once Taylor has left the room I ask Gail if Ana ate. "She did, Mr. Grey. An omelet, too."

"Good."

As if I've conjured her by mentioning her name, Ana appears in the doorway wearing her jacket.

"You're going?" I ask in disbelief.

"To work? Yes, of course." She moves closer. "Christian, we've hardly been back a week. I have to go to work."

"But—" I rake my hand through my hair, feeling anxious.

What about yesterday? Hyde! The kidnapping!

Out of the corner of my eye, I notice Gail leave the kitchen. "I know we have a great deal to talk about," Ana continues. "Perhaps if you've calmed down, we can do it this evening."

"Calmed down?" I whisper and I'm immediately incandescent again. This woman is pressing every single button I have this morning.

She flushes, embarrassed. "You know what I mean."

"No, Anastasia, I don't know what you mean."

"I don't want to fight. I was coming to ask you if I could take my car."

"No. You can't," I snap.

"Okay," she says, quietly.

And just like that all the wind is out of my sails, and I'm no longer mad, just tired. I was expecting a battle. "Prescott will accompany you." My tone is softer.

"Okay," she says, and she steps toward me again.

Ana. What are you doing? She leans up and kisses me, sweetly, at the corner of my mouth. As her lips press against my skin, I close my eyes, savoring her touch. I don't deserve this.

I don't deserve her.

"Don't hate me," she whispers.

I grab her hand. "I don't hate you." *Ana, I could never hate you.*

"You haven't kissed me," she whispers.

"I know." *But I want to.*

Damn, Grey. Carpe diem.

Standing abruptly, I grasp her face between my hands and raise her mouth to mine. Her lips part in surprise and I pounce, pushing my tongue into her mouth, tasting and testing her.

She tastes of heaven, and better times and minty toothpaste.

Ana. I love you.

You. Just. Drive. Me. Crazy.

I release her before she can properly respond. I know she'll never get to work if I don't back away. I'm breathing harder. "Taylor will take you and Prescott to SIP." I fight to recover my composure and dampen my desire.

Ana blinks at me, her breathing labored, too.

"Taylor!" I call.

"Sir." Taylor is standing in the doorway.

"Tell Prescott Mrs. Grey is going to work. Can you drive them, please?"

"Certainly." Taylor turns on his heel and disappears.

Feeling more myself, I look back at Ana. "If you could try to stay out of trouble today, I would appreciate it," I mutter.

"I'll see what I can do." Her eyes shine with amusement, and it's impossible not to respond.

"I'll see you later, then," I reply.

"Laters," she whispers, and leaves with Taylor and Prescott in tow.

After breakfast I head back into my study and call Andrea. I tell her I'll be working from home, as I wasn't planning to be in the office anyway. She puts me through to Sam and we have a tedious discussion about "owning the message" with regard to Hyde's break-in.

"No, we don't, Sam, not in this instance."

"But—" he protests.

"No buts. This is a police matter. All press inquiries about this incident to them. End of discussion."

He sighs. Sam is such a publicity whore. "Very well, Mr. Grey." He sounds sullen, but I don't care. I hang up and call my dad to tell him about Hyde. We agree to keep up the security for the next week just in case.

"Will you tell Mom?"

"Yes, son. You take care."

"Will do."

I hang up and my phone buzzes with a text from Elliot.

> ELLIOT
> Yo Bro! You ok? Hyde! Fuck!

He's brief and to the point, as ever. He must have seen the news, or Ana's told Kate. I call to fill him in on events, and we agree to meet up over the weekend. He wants to talk about something, but not over the phone.

"Whatever, dude," I say. "And by the way, your girlfriend has been leading my wife astray. She should have been here in the panic room—instead, she was out getting drunk with Katherine."

"Katherine, eh?"

"Kate." I roll my eyes. "Whatever."

"And you're telling me this why?"

"I don't know, dude, just sharing my thoughts."

Elliot sighs. "You'll have to take it up with her."

Oh. Have they split up? What does that mean?

He continues before I can ask any questions. "This guy who follows me around. Do I still need him?"

"Let's see what happens with Hyde over the next few days."

"Okay, hotshot. It's your money."

"Laters, Elliot."

RYAN AND SAWYER GIVE Taylor and me a full debrief. I can't decide if Ryan is a hero or an idiot for letting Hyde into the apartment. His face is pretty battered, and he has a cut over one eye after their "altercation." Judging from his bruised face, he must have had quite the skirmish with our intruder. He says he only let Hyde in because Ana wasn't here. I glance at Taylor, whose mouth is set in a grim line. Ryan put Gail at risk, panic room or not.

The good news is that Prescott, before she left this morning, located the CCTV footage of Hyde arriving in the basement garage. His van is still down there.

I ask Sawyer to let Detective Clark know.

"Yes, sir."

"Is that all?" Taylor asks Ryan and Sawyer.

"Yes, sir," they say in unison.

"Thank you. For everything," I tell them. "I'm grateful you caught the bastard, Ryan."

"I felt an enormous sense of satisfaction knowing I brought the guy down."

"Let's hope the police charge him," I add.

Ryan and Sawyer leave.

"I have a carpenter arriving in about half an hour to repair the broken door," Taylor informs me.

"Good. I'm going to scour what was on Hyde's computer to see if I can find any further clues as to what could be behind all this."

"Sir, we have a potential problem," Taylor says.

"What?"

"Technically, Ryan did grant Hyde access to the apartment."

I pale. "Only under unique circumstances. And Hyde was armed."

"True. But it's something to bear in mind when speaking with the cops."

"Yes. Agreed. Talk to Ryan."

"Will do."

"Taylor, take the night off. Gail, too. In fact, all of you."

"Mr. Grey—"

"You had a very late night and little sleep, as did Sawyer and Prescott, watching my wife last night."

Taylor looks grim. "I'd like to leave Ryan on lookout. He's in no fit state to go out."

"Okay."

"Thank you, sir." Taylor nods and exits while I turn my attention to my computer. Specifically, the files that Barney recovered from Hyde's hard drive.

At 10:45 I stop combing through his creepy, obsessive collection of all things Grey, and log on to WebEx. Vanessa is online, too, and we start our conference with the Securities and Exchange Commission. It's a brief and convivial chat, and GEH is co-opted onto a task force that will examine the issue of conflict minerals in tech.

When we hang up with the SEC, Vanessa informs me that she's located Sebastian Miller, the truck driver who rescued Ros and me when *Charlie Tango* went down. She's introduced him to our logistics team and he'll shortly become an affiliate with the haulage contractor that GEH uses.

"That's great news."

"Mr. Grey, he was stunned to get the call."

"I bet. Thanks for tracking him down."

When that's over I call Senator Blandino.

Our conversation is short and we resolve to have lunch next time she's in Seattle.

Taylor is standing in the doorway when I finish the call.

"Yes?"

"Detective Clark is here, sir."

"Show him in."

Detective Clark has a firm handshake and a curmudgeonly, hangdog appearance. "Mr. Grey, thank you for seeing me."

"Please sit." I direct him to the chair in front of my desk.

"Thank you. I was hoping to get a brief history of your dealings with Jackson Hyde."

"Of course." I explain that I own SIP, and that Ana used to work for him, until he was fired, and all the circumstances around that, including my run-in with him at SIP.

"You assaulted him?" Clark's eyebrows are raised.

"I taught him some manners. He attacked my wife."

"I see."

"If you check his employment history, he has a track record of being fired for assaulting his female colleagues."

"Hmm… You think he's behind the GEH arson attempt?"

"I do. We have the CCTV from Grey House."

"Yes. I've seen it. And thank you for the CCTV from the garage. The forensic team have been examining the van."

"Did they find anything?"

"This." He pulls out a plastic evidence bag. In it is a note. He shows it to me so I can read the note through the bag. It's scrawled in black Sharpie:

Grey, Do you know who I am?
Because I know who you are, Baby Bird.

I look at the words blankly.

What a weird note.

"Do you know what this means?" Clark asks.

I shake my head. "No idea."

He slides it back into the inside breast pocket of his jacket.

"I have some more questions for Mrs. Grey. How is she?"

"She's good. She's remarkably tough."

"Hmm… Is she here?"

"She's at work. You could phone her."

"I see. I prefer a more hands-on approach. I'd like to talk to her again, face-to-face," Clark grunts.

"I'm sure I can make that happen. Given the intense press interest in my wife and me, I would request that you go to her office."

"I can do that." He nods and sits quietly while I send a quick e-mail to Hannah to see when Ana might be free.

"Hyde had a gun. Does he have a license for it?"

"We're checking."

"Have you spoken with the FBI team investigating the sabotage of my helicopter?"

"We've been in touch."

"Good. I suspect he might be behind that, too."

"Hmm… He does seem a little obsessed."

"A little." I tell him about Hyde's computer hard drive, and all the information he had accumulated about my family.

Clark frowns. "Interesting. Can we have access to that?"

"By all means. I'll ask my IT people to send it to you."

My computer pings, announcing a response from Hannah.

"My wife is free at three this afternoon at her office."

"Excellent. Well, I won't keep you, Mr. Grey."

He stands, as do I. "I'm relieved you have him. And hopefully he'll stay behind bars for a long time."

Clark's smile is menacing, and I suspect he's thinking the same. "Great view you have from up here," he says.

"Thank you."

Taylor shows him out and I compose an e-mail.

From: Christian Grey
Subject: Statement
Date: August 26 2011 13:04
To: Anastasia Grey

Anastasia
Detective Clark will be visiting your office today at 3 p.m. to take your statement.
I have insisted that he should come to you, as I don't want you going to the police station.

Christian Grey
CEO, Grey Enterprises Holdings, Inc.

I go back to searching through the contents of Hyde's computer. An e-mail arrives from Ana.

From: Anastasia Grey
Subject: Statement
Date: August 26 2011 13:12
To: Christian Grey

Okay.
A x

Anastasia Grey
Editor, SIP

At least I get a kiss.

I open up Hyde's files once more. He has a great deal about Carrick in one of the files. *Why is he so interested in my dad? I don't get it.*

Notification of an e-mail from Ana pops up on my screen.

From: Anastasia Grey
Subject: Your Flight
Date: August 26 2011 13:24
To: Christian Grey

What time did you decide to come back to Seattle yesterday?

Anastasia Grey
Editor, SIP

The kiss is missing. I respond.

From: Christian Grey
Subject: Your Flight
Date: August 26 2011 13:26
To: Anastasia Grey

Why?

Christian Grey
CEO, Grey Enterprises Holdings, Inc.

From: Anastasia Grey
Subject: Your Flight
Date: August 26 2011 13:29
To: Christian Grey

Call it curiosity.

Anastasia Grey
Editor, SIP

What is she trying to find out? I send a glib answer.

From: Christian Grey
Subject: Your Flight
Date: August 26 2011 13:32
To: Anastasia Grey

Curiosity killed the cat.

Christian Grey
CEO, Grey Enterprises Holdings, Inc.

From: Anastasia Grey
Subject: Huh?
Date: August 26 2011 13:35
To: Christian Grey

What is that oblique reference to? Another threat?
You know where I am going with this, don't you?
Did you decide to return because I went out for a drink with my friend after you asked me not to, or did you return because a madman was in your apartment?

Anastasia Grey
Editor, SIP

Hell. I stare at the screen, uncertain what to say. It wasn't a threat. *Jesus.*

She knows I came back before I knew about Hyde. If she doesn't, she hasn't done the time-zone math.

What can I say?

I'm staring blankly out of the window when Mrs. Jones knocks on my office door.

"Would you like some lunch?"

"Yeah. Sure. Thank you, Gail."

"Very good, Mr. Grey." With a polite smile she leaves me with my thoughts. I'm still trying to think of something to respond to Ana, when I hear the ping of a new message arriving from my iMac.

From: Anastasia Grey
Subject: Here's the Thing…
Date: August 26 2011 13:56
To: Christian Grey

I will take your silence as an admission that you did indeed return to Seattle because I CHANGED MY MIND. I am an adult female and went for a drink with my friend. I did not understand the security ramifications of CHANGING MY MIND because YOU NEVER TELL ME ANYTHING. I found out from Kate that security has, in fact, been stepped up for all the Greys, not just us. I think you generally overreact where my safety is concerned, and I understand why, but you're like the boy crying wolf.

I never have a clue about what is a real concern or merely something that is perceived as a concern by you. I had two of the security detail with me. I thought both Kate and I would be safe. Fact is, we were safer in that bar than at the apartment. Had I been FULLY INFORMED of the situation, I would have taken a different course of action.

I understand your concerns are something to do with material that was on Jack's computer here—or so Kate believes. Do you know how annoying it is to find out my best friend knows more about what's going on with you than I do? And I am your WIFE. So are you going to tell me? Or will you continue to treat me like a child, guaranteeing that I continue to behave like one?

You are not the only one who is fucking pissed. Okay?
Ana

Anastasia Grey
Editor, SIP

Cursing and shouty capitals, too. Two can play at that game.

From: Christian Grey
Subject: Here's the Thing…
Date: August 26 2011 13:59
To: Anastasia Grey

As ever, Mrs. Grey, you are forthright and challenging in e-mail. Perhaps we can discuss this when you get home to **OUR** apartment. You should watch your language. I am still fucking pissed, too.

Christian Grey
CEO, Grey Enterprises Holdings, Inc.

Fuck it. I don't want an e-mail fight with Ana. I storm out of my office and into the living area. My temper eases at the sight of the cold chicken salad that Mrs. Jones has prepared for my lunch.

Maybe I'm so mad because I'm hungry.

"Thanks," I mumble.

"I'm going to the Greek deli that Mrs. Grey likes, to pick up her favorite foods from there for this evening. She'll just have to pop them in the oven or microwave to heat them up."

"Great," I say, distracted. *Why are Ana and I always fighting these days?*

"Mr. Grey—" Mrs. Jones is trying to get my attention.

"Yes."

"Thank you for this evening. But I must say you look tired. Have you thought about taking a quick nap?"

I frown. A nap? I'm not a child. "No."

"It's just an idea."

"I'll take it under advisement," I mutter, and bring my salad into my office.

Welch calls while I'm eating.

"Welch."

"Interesting development in the Hyde case," he rasps in his gruff voice. "Turns out Hyde's van in the garage was kitted out with a mattress and enough ketamine to fell a Texas rodeo."

"Ketamine. Shit." *I was right!*

"Yes, sir. And syringes."

I grimace. I loathe syringes.

Welch continues, "Looks like our boy will be charged with attempted kidnapping, first degree. They'll probably throw in criminal trespass, robbery, and illegal possession of a firearm, too. Also, there was a note."

"Clark showed me the note."

"Mean anything to you?"

"No. And Hyde left it in the van. Maybe he changed his mind about that, because it's nonsensical."

"Maybe. He was delivering lights to one of the new tenants in the building," Welch growls.

"Delivering lights? What do you mean?"

"Yes. He was working for a courier company. The client lives at apartment sixteen."

"Oh, yes. I've met him. Young guy. That's how Hyde got access; he's a wily bastard."

"That he is, sir," Welch agrees. "One more thing. I've heard from King County PD and the FBI. The prints match."

"We have him!"

"It looks like it."

"There must be a Detroit connection, but I'm damned if I know what it is," I mutter.

"I'll keep digging," Welch responds. "That's it for now."

"Thanks for the update."

He hangs up, and I look at the remains of my lunch. My appetite has evaporated. What the hell did that evil motherfucker have planned for my wife? Kidnap. Rape. Murder. And he had syringes. Perhaps he was going to inject her with a filthy, dirty syringe. Bile rises in my throat, but I swallow it down.

Fuck.

I have to get out of here and get some fresh air. Abandoning my lunch, I walk out through the living room and, ignoring Gail's anxious look, take the elevator down to the main lobby. The photographers have gone, so I slip out the front entrance and walk. And walk. And walk.

Life in the Emerald City goes on. People are going about their business; the streets are crowded, but I manage to weave my way through the throng.

My poor wife.

He could have killed her.

If I ever get my hands on that evil, twisted asshole. I will end him.

Once more I imagine all the ways I could do that.

Shit.

Grey, get a grip.

I'm outside Nordstrom. Maybe I should buy something for Ana. Anything. I check that my wallet's in my back pocket and head in. I'm in the scarf section. A silk scarf… Yeah. That works.

I'M CALMER WHEN I get back to the apartment.

"You didn't like your lunch? Would you like something else?" Gail offers.

"No, thanks. I think I'll take your advice. I'm going to lie down. I'm exhausted."

Gail's smile is sympathetic.

Once in our bedroom, I take off my shoes, lie down, and close my eyes.

> Ana is laid out before me, naked. She holds out her arms. *You can do anything you want to me. A punishment fuck.* She's in the harness. In the playroom. *What will you do to me?* I stand behind her, a cane in my hand. *Whatever I want.* She's on the table. Facedown. She cannot move. She's tied. I slap a paddle against my hand. Her buttocks clench in anticipation. She's on her knees, her forehead pressed to the floor. Her hands tied behind her back. *I want your mouth. Your cunt. Your ass. Your body. Your soul.* She kneels before me. *I'm yours. I will always be yours, husband of mine. Mine. Yours.*

I wake. Disoriented.

I'm at home. It's late afternoon, by the look of the light. I check the time; it's 5:30. Ana won't be home yet. I rub my face and walk into the bathroom, a plan hatching in my mind. I'm anticipating one hell of a fight. Ana says she's pissed at me. In the closet I remove my shirt, replace it with a T-shirt, and change into my playroom jeans in readiness for her return. I tuck the new scarf into my pocket.

Maybe we can both get what we want.

In my office, I print out her e-mail and notice that she hasn't sent me any messages since our last exchange. My wife does not back down from a challenge. This evening will be interesting.

Gail is absent. As is Taylor. Idly, I wonder what they are doing.

Ryan is in Taylor's office; he stands when I enter. "Good evening, Mr. Grey."

"You can hang out upstairs. I'd like to give everyone the night off. We'll call you if we need you."

He hesitates before agreeing. "Okay, sir."

And with that I wander back into the living room and over to the piano to await my wife's return.

Behind me, the late-afternoon sun is drifting toward the horizon, and I'm in my corner of the ring, waiting for the match to start. Gloves on. Mouth guard in.

How many rounds will I go with Mrs. Grey?

The soft ping of the elevator rings through the foyer.

She's here.

Showtime, Grey.

The thud of Ana's briefcase hitting the floor in the hall is followed by her footsteps into the living room. She stops when she sees me.

"Good evening, Mrs. Grey." Barefoot, I swagger toward her, like a gunfighter in an old black-and-white movie, my eyes fixed on her. "Good to have you home. I've been waiting for you."

"Have you, now?" she whispers. She's as beautiful as she looked this morning, though her eyes are wide and wary; her guard is up.

Game on, Ana.

"I have," I answer.

"I like your jeans," she murmurs, eyeing me from head to toe.

I wore them for you. I give her a wolfish grin and halt in front of her. She licks her lips, and swallows, but she doesn't look away.

"I understand you have issues, Mrs. Grey." From my back pocket I pull out her shouty-capped e-mail and unfold it in front of her, trying to intimidate her with a look.

I fail.

"Yes, I have issues," she responds, gazing at me, her manner forthright but her voice betraying her, all breathy and sexy.

Leaning down, I run my nose along hers, relishing the contact. Her eyes close and she utters the softest of sighs.

"So do I," I murmur against her fragrant skin.

Her eyes flutter open and I straighten up.

"I think I'm familiar with your issues, Christian." She raises a brow, and humor hovers behind her eyes.

I narrow mine.

Don't make me laugh, Ana.

I remember her saying that to me, not so long ago.

She takes a step back. "Why did you fly back from New York?" she asks, her voice kitten-soft, belying the lioness I know.

"You know why."

"Because I went out with Kate?"

"Because you went back on your word, and you defied me, putting yourself at unnecessary risk."

"Went back on my word? Is that how you see it?"

"Yes."

She looks heavenward, then stops when she notices my scowl, but I'm not sure a spanking would be a good idea right now. "Christian," she says in the same soft voice, "I changed my mind. I'm a woman. We're renowned for it. That's what we do." When I don't respond, she continues, "If I had thought for one minute that you would cancel your business trip…" She stops, seemingly at a loss.

"You changed your mind?"

"Yes."

"And you didn't think to call me?"

How could you be so inconsiderate?

"What's more, you left the security detail short here and put Ryan at risk."

Her cheeks pink. "I should have called, but I didn't want to worry you. If I had, I'm sure you would have forbidden me to go, and I've missed Kate. I wanted to see her. Besides, it kept me out of the way when Jack was here. Ryan shouldn't have let him in."

But he did.

And had you been here…

Fuck. Enough, Grey.

I reach for her, pulling her into my arms. "Oh, Ana," I whisper, and hold her as close as I can. "If something were to happen to you—"

He had a gun.

He had a syringe.

"It didn't," she whispers.

"But it could have. I've died a thousand deaths today, thinking about what might have happened. I was so mad, Ana. Mad at you. Mad at myself. Mad at everyone. I can't remember being this angry…except—"

"Except?" she asks.

"Once in your old apartment. When Leila was there."

Someone else with a fucking gun.

"You were so cold this morning." Her voice breaks into a sob on the last word.

No. Ana. Don't cry. I loosen my grip and tip her head up. "I don't know how to deal with this anger," I whisper.

I used to have a way. But that's lost to me now.

Shit. Don't go there, Grey.

I gaze down into troubled blue eyes that draw the truth from me. "I don't *think* I want to hurt you." That's why I was cold. I was raging. "This morning, I wanted to punish you, badly, and—"

How do I explain that?

I want to rage at the world, and you are my world.

"You were worried you'd hurt me?" she asks.

"I didn't trust myself."

"Christian, I know you'd never hurt me. Not physically, anyway." She clasps my face.

"Do you?"

"Yes. I knew what you said was an empty, idle threat. I know you're not going to beat the shit out of me."

"I wanted to."

"No, you didn't. You just thought you did."

"I don't know if that's true."

"Think about it," she says, embracing me and nuzzling my chest. "About how you felt when I left. You've told me often enough what that did to you. How it altered your view of the world, of me. I know what you've given up for me. Think about how you felt about the cuff marks on our honeymoon."

She has a point. Thinking back, I felt like an asshole, and I don't want her to leave me again. She tightens her arms around me and gently rubs my back, and slowly, oh-so-slowly, my tension eases. She presses her cheek to my chest, and I can resist her no more. Leaning down, I kiss her hair, and she turns her face up, offering her mouth to me. I kiss her, my lips begging her to do as she's told, begging her not to go, begging her to stay. She kisses me back.

"You have such faith in me," I murmur.

"I do."

I stroke her face, staring into her beautiful eyes, seeing her compassion, her love, and her desire.

What did I do to deserve her?

She smiles. "Besides," she whispers, an impish look on her face, "you don't have the paperwork."

I laugh and clutch her to my chest. "You're right. I don't." We hold each other, and a quiet peace settles between us; it's the first time I've felt any tranquility since my trip to New York. Is this the end of hostilities?

"Come to bed," I whisper.

"Christian, we need to talk."

"Later."

"Christian, please. Talk to me."

Damn. I sigh as my spirits sink. Perhaps we're just in the eye of the storm. "About what?" Even to my own ears, I sound petulant.

"You know. You keep me in the dark."

"I want to protect you."

"I'm not a child."

"I am fully aware of that, Mrs. Grey." I skim my hands over her body and fondle her backside, pressing my interested cock against her.

"Christian!" she scolds. "Talk to me."

Ana is as persistent as ever. "What do you want to know?" Releasing her, I pick up her e-mail that's fallen to the floor and take her hand.

"Lots of things," she says, as I lead her to the couch.

"Sit." She obeys, and I take a seat beside her. Putting my head in my hands, I steel myself for her onslaught of questions. Then I turn to face her. "Ask me."

"Why the additional security for your family?"

"Hyde was a threat to them."

"How do you know?"

"From his computer. It held personal details about me and the rest of my family. Especially Carrick."

"Carrick? Why him?"

"I don't know yet." This feels like the Inquisition. I change tack. "Let's go to bed."

"Christian, tell me!"

"Tell you what?"

"You are so exasperating," she says, holding up her hands.

"So are you."

She sighs. "You didn't ramp up the security when you first found out there was information about your family on the computer. So what happened? Why now?"

"I didn't know he was going to attempt to burn down my building, or—" I stop. I don't want to tell her about *Charlie Tango*. She'll worry. I change tack again. "We thought it was an unwelcome obsession, but you know"—I shrug—"when you're in the public eye, people are interested. It was random stuff: news reports on me from when I was at Harvard—my rowing, my career. Reports on Carrick—following his career, following my mom's career—and, to some extent, Elliot and Mia."

She frowns. "You said 'or.'"

"Or what?"

"You said 'attempt to burn down my building, or…' Like you were going to say something else."

She misses nothing.

"Are you hungry?" I try distraction and, on cue, her stomach rumbles. "Did you eat today?" She flushes, and I have my answer. "As I thought. You know how I feel about you not eating. Come." Standing, I hold out my hand, and my mood softens. "Let me feed you."

"Feed me?"

I guide Ana over to the kitchen, and I grab a barstool and drag it around to the other side of the island. "Sit."

"Where's Mrs. Jones?" Ana perches on the stool.

"I've given her and Taylor the night off."

"Why?" She looks incredulous.

They deserve an evening off after last night. "Because I can." Simple.

"So you're going to cook?" Now she sounds incredulous.

"Oh, ye of little faith, Mrs. Grey. Close your eyes."

She looks at me askance, still unsure.

"Close them!"

With a withering look, she complies.

"Hmm. Not good enough." From my back pocket I pull out the scarf I bought earlier, and I'm pleased to see it's a good match for her dress. She raises a brow. "Close. No peeking."

"You're going to blindfold me?" Her voice is soft and high-pitched.

"Yes."

"Christian—" She's about to object, but I gently press a finger to her lips.

"We'll talk later. I want you to eat now. You said you were hungry." I skim my lips over hers, then place the scarf over her eyes, tying it behind her head. "Can you see?"

"No," she grumbles, lifting her head in that way she does when she rolls her eyes. It makes me chuckle. She's so predictable sometimes.

"I can tell when you're rolling your eyes, and you know how that makes me feel."

She huffs and purses her lips. "Can we just get this over and done with?"

"Such impatience, Mrs. Grey. So eager to talk."

"Yes!"

"I must feed you first." I place a soft kiss on her temple. She has no idea how hot she looks perched primly on the stool, blindfolded and with her hair restrained in its bun. I'm almost tempted to grab my camera.

But I must feed her.

From the fridge I extract a bottle of Sancerre and the various serving dishes into which Gail has transferred the Greek deli food; the lamb is in a Pyrex bowl.

Shit. How long do I cook this for?

I pop it in the microwave and set it to heat for five minutes on full power. That should be enough. I place two pitas in the toaster.

"Yes. I am eager to talk," Ana says, and the way she's tilting her head, it's obvious she's listening to what I'm doing. I grab the bottle of wine and a corkscrew as Ana shifts in her chair.

"Be still, Anastasia—I want you to behave," I murmur, close to her ear. "And don't bite your lip." I tug her bottom lip free from her teeth and she smiles.

Finally!

A smile.

I open the bottle, easing out the cork, and fill a glass.

Now for some musical accompaniment. I switch on the surround speakers and select Chris Isaak's "Wicked Game" from the iPod. The pluck of a guitar string resonates through the room.

Yes. This song works.

I turn it down and pick up the glass of wine. "A drink first, I think," I say, almost to myself. "Head back." She lifts her chin. "Farther." Ana obliges and I take a swig of cool, crisp wine and kiss her, pouring the wine into her mouth.

"Mm." She swallows.

"You like the wine?"

"Yes," she breathes.

"More?"

"I always want more, with you."

I grin. *More.* Our word. She grins, too.

"Mrs. Grey, are you flirting with me?"

"Yes."

Good. I love it when she flirts with me.

I take another large sip of wine, then, holding the knot of the scarf, gently tug her head back. I kiss her, drizzling the wine into her mouth. She drinks, greedily. "Hungry?" I ask her against her lips.

"I think we've already established that, Mr. Grey." Her voice is dripping with sarcasm.

Ah, there she is again…my girl.

The microwave pings, announcing that the lamb is ready. Its appetizing aroma has filled the kitchen. I pick up a cloth, open the microwave door, and grab the dish. "Shit! Christ!" It's scalding hot where my finger touches it without the cloth. I drop it and it clatters on the counter.

"You okay?" Ana asks.

"Yes!"

No.

Ow!

I abandon the dish, wanting some TLC. "I just burned myself. Here." I ease my poor finger into her mouth. "Maybe you could suck it better."

Ana grabs my hand and slowly draws my finger out of her mouth.

"There, there," she whispers, and pouts prettily and blows gently on my smarting skin.

Oh.

She might as well be blowing on my dick.

She kisses my knuckle, twice, then slowly reinserts my digit into her mouth, her tongue cradling and sucking me.

She might as well be sucking my dick.

Lust surges like a tidal wave, south.

Ana.

As she fellates my finger her forehead creases.

"What are you thinking?" I whisper, as I draw my finger out of her mouth and attempt to bring my body under control.

"How mercurial you are."

This is not news. "Fifty Shades, baby." I plant a kiss at the corner of her mouth.

"My Fifty Shades." She grabs my T-shirt and tugs me closer.

"Oh, no you don't, Mrs. Grey. No touching. Not yet." I pry her hand from my shirt and kiss each of her fingers. "Sit up." Ana pouts. "I will spank you if you pout."

I stick a fork into the lamb dish, then into the accompanying sauce of yogurt and mint. "Now open wide." She opens her mouth and I slide a forkful between her lips.

"Hmm," she hums in appreciation.

"You like?"

"Yes."

I try some, too, and it's a party of delicious flavors in my mouth. I realize how hungry I am. "More?" I ask Ana. She nods, and I feed her another forkful. While she's chewing, I tear some of the pita bread and dip it into the hummus. "Open." Ana indulges me and eats this latest morsel with enthusiasm.

I join her.

This really is the best hummus in Seattle.

"More?" I ask.

She nods. "More of everything. Please. I'm starving."

Her words are music to my soul. I feed her and myself, alternating between the bread and hummus and the lamb. Ana is lapping it up, thoroughly enjoying the feast, and it's a pleasure to watch her savor the food and to feed her. Occasionally I offer her more wine, using my tried-and-trusted mouth-to-mouth technique.

When the lamb is finished, I turn to the stuffed grape leaves. "Open wide, then bite."

She does. "I love these," she mumbles with a full mouth.

"I agree. They're delicious."

When I finish feeding her, she licks my fingers clean. One by one. "More?" My voice is husky.

She shakes her head.

"Good," I murmur against her ear, "because it's time for my favorite course. You." I pick her up suddenly and she squeaks with surprise.

"Can I take the blindfold off?"

"No. Playroom." Ana stills in my arms while I cradle her to my chest. "You up for the challenge?" I ask.

"Bring it on," she says, as I knew she would. She feels a little lighter in my arms as I carry her upstairs. "I think you've lost weight," I mutter. She smiles, pleased, I think. Outside the playroom, I slide her down my body and onto her feet, keeping my arm around her waist while I unlock the door. I usher her inside, turning on the lights as we enter.

In the middle of the room, I release her, undo the scarf, and slowly draw the hairpins from her bun, freeing her braid. Grasping it as it swings between her shoulder blades, I tug gently so she steps back against me. "I have a plan," I whisper in her ear.

"I thought you might," she answers, as I kiss that spot beneath her ear where her pulse beats.

"Oh, Mrs. Grey, I do." Still holding her braid, I tilt Ana's head, exposing her neck, and skim my lips down her throat. "First we have to get you naked." When I turn her around, her eyes flit down to the unfastened top button on my jeans. Before I can stop her, she inserts her finger into the waistband, teasing the hair at the base of my belly.

Ah!

She glances up at me from behind long lashes. "You should keep these on," she says.

"I fully intend to, Anastasia." I fold her in my arms, one hand at her neck, the other splayed on her backside, and I kiss her, my tongue testing and tasting her. While we kiss, I walk her backward until she's against the playroom cross, where I press my body into hers. Her lips are greedy, her tongue as eager as mine. I pull back. "Let's get rid of this dress." I grasp the hem and slowly divest her of her dress, revealing her body an inch at a time as I peel it off. "Lean forward," I say, and she complies. The dress ends up on the floor as my wife stands before me in her seductive lingerie and her sandals. Threading my fingers through hers, I raise her hands over her head and incline mine in a question.

Restraints, Ana?

Her gaze is intense, missing nothing. I bathe in it, feeling it in my groin. She swallows and then nods.

My sweet girl. She never lets me down.

I clip her wrists in the leather cuffs above her head and take the scarf from my back pocket once more. "Think you've seen enough," I whisper, and blindfold her again. I run my nose down hers and deliver a promise: "I'm going to drive you wild."

Grasping her hips, I run my hands down her body, removing her panties as I go. "Lift your feet, one at a time." She obliges and I remove her panties, then each of her sandals in turn. Sliding my fingers around her ankle, I tug her right leg to the right. "Step," I order. She does, and I cuff her right ankle to the cross. I repeat the process with her left ankle, buckling her up tight. When she's secure I stand and step close to her, bathing in her warmth and her growing excitement. Holding her chin, I plant a soft, chaste kiss on her lips. "Some music and toys, I think. You look beautiful like this, Mrs. Grey. I may take a moment to admire the view." Stepping back, I do exactly that, knowing that the longer I look at her and do nothing, the wetter she'll get…and the harder I'll get.

She is a mighty fine sight.

But right now, I want to teach her about orgasm denial.

I pad over to the drawers and pull out a wand and the iPod. There's a small tin of Tiger Balm beside the wand, and I contemplate spreading a little on her clitoris.

That would heat her up.

No. Not right now. That's too next-level.

I switch on the music system and choose something unsettling, to suit my mood.

Yes. Bach. Aria from Goldberg Variations. Perfect.

I press play, and the crisp, bright, cool notes sing out through my playroom.

Our playroom.

I put the wand in my back pocket, pull off my T-shirt, and return to my wife, who is biting her lip. Taking her chin between my fingers, I startle her, then tug so that she releases her bottom lip. Her smile is shy and sweet, and I know she was unaware of what she was doing.

Oh, Ana. What I have in store for you.

Maybe I'll let you come.

Maybe I won't.

I run the backs of my fingers over the soft skin of her throat to her sternum, then, using my thumb, I tug her bra cup down, freeing her breast. She has such beautiful breasts. While I kiss her throat, I release her other breast from its bra cup and toy with her nipple. My lips and my fingers tug and tease each of them, until they're both erect and begging for more.

Ana squirms against her restraints. "Ah," she groans. But I don't stop; my mouth and fingers continue their slow, sensual torment. I know how easy it is to arouse her to orgasm this way.

She's breathing hard. "Christian," she begs.

"I know." My voice is husky with want. "This is what you make me feel."

She gasps.

And I continue.

Her hips press forward and her legs start to tremble. "Please," she pleads.

Oh, baby. Feel it.

My cock is pressing against soft denim, wanting release. *All in good time, Grey.*

I stop and stand up, looking down at her face. Her mouth is hanging open as she drags air in to her lungs, and she writhes against the leather cuffs. I run my hands down the side of her body, leaving one to linger at her hip while I skirt the fingers of my other hand down her belly. Again, she pushes her hips forward, offering herself to me. "Let's see how you're doing," I murmur. I brush my fingers over her sex, and she soaks my fingers.

My jeans get tighter.

I skate my thumb over the excited little nub at the junction of her thighs and she cries out, pushing herself into my hands.

Oh, Ana. So keen. So wet for me.

And you're so far from coming.

If—and it's a big if—I let you come at all.

Slowly, I insert my middle, then index finger inside her. She groans and continues to strain against my hand, searching for release. "Oh, Anastasia, you're so ready." I circle my fingers inside her, stroking her, tantalizing her, while my thumb continues to rouse her clitoris. Her legs start to tremble again as she strains toward me. It's the only part of her body I'm touching. Her head is thrown back as she absorbs the pleasure. She's close.

With my other hand, I pull out the wand from my back pocket and switch it on.

"What?" she murmurs at the sound.

"Hush." My lips swoop down on hers, and she kisses me greedily. I pull back while my fingers still work away inside her. "This is a wand, baby. It vibrates." I hold it against her sternum and let it float over her so it oscillates against her skin. My thumb and fingers still tease her sex, and I drag the vibrating wand down between her breasts, then across each nipple in turn.

"Ah!" she moans out loud, and her legs stiffen as she throws her head back once more and groans loudly. I stop moving my fingers and lift the wand from her skin.

"No! Christian," she cries, and pushes her hips fruitlessly toward me.

So close. And yet so far.

"Still, baby," I whisper, and kiss her. "Frustrating, isn't it?"

She gasps. "Christian, please."

"Hush." I kiss her and slowly start to move my fingers inside her, grazing the wand across her skin between the two peaks of her breasts. I move so I'm leaning into her, my cock hard and ready against her.

She starts to climb again and I bring her close.

So close.

Then stop once more.

"No," she whimpers, and I plant kisses on her shoulder as I withdraw my fingers from inside her and stop teasing her clitoris with my thumb. Instead, I increase the speed of the wand and let it travel down her stomach, over her belly and over the tiny swollen bud between her thighs.

"Ah!" she cries out, and pulls on her shackles.

And I stop once more, removing the wand from her skin.

"Christian!" she calls.

"Frustrating, yes?" I whisper against her throat. "Just like you. Promising one thing and then…"

"Christian, please!"

I let the wand touch her again.

And stop.

And start.

And stop.

She's panting hard.

"Each time I stop, it feels more intense when I start again. Right?"

"Please," she begs, and I switch the wand off and place it on the small shelf beside the cross and kiss her. Her lips are eager—no, *desperate*—for my touch. I run my nose down hers and whisper, "You are the most frustrating woman I have ever met."

She shakes her head. "Christian, I never promised to obey you. Please, please—" I grab her behind and push my still clothed cock against her; rubbing myself over her. She groans, and I peel off the blindfold and grasp her chin; wild blue eyes meet mine.

"You drive me crazy." My voice is hoarse as I flex my hips against her, once, twice, thrice, and she tips her head back, ready to come—and I stop. She closes her eyes and takes a deep breath.

"Please," she whispers, and looks up at me.

Oh, baby, you can take more. I know you can.

My fingers skim her breast as they travel down her body, and she stiffens beneath my touch, and turns her face away from me. "Red," she whimpers. "Red. Red." As tears spill down her face.

I freeze.

Fuck.

No. No.

"No!" I breathe. "Jesus Christ, no." I unclip her hands, and, holding her, I bend down and unclip her ankles. She puts her head in her hands and starts to weep.

"No, no, no. Ana, please. No." I've gone too far. I pick her up and sit down on the bed, cradling her in my lap while she sobs. Reaching for the satin sheet behind me, I pull it off the bed and wrap it around her, and I hug her close, rocking her gently, backward and forward. "I'm sorry. I'm sorry," I whisper, feeling like an asshole, and shower her hair with kisses. "Ana, forgive me, please."

She says nothing. She continues to weep; each sob a twist of the knife in my dark, dark soul.

What was I thinking?

Ana. I'm sorry.

I'm a fucking asshole.

She buries her face in my neck, and her tears scorch my skin. "Please switch the music off."

"Yes, of course." I move with her on my lap, easing the remote out of my back pocket, and switch off the music. All I hear is her quiet keening interspersed with her shuddering breaths.

It's hell.

"Better?" I ask.

She nods, and gently I wipe away her tears with my thumb. "Not a fan of Bach's Goldberg Variations?" I make a desperate attempt at humor.

"Not that piece." She looks up at me, her eyes dulled by her inner pain, and shame washes over me in a torrent.

"I'm sorry," I whisper.

"W-why did you d-do that?" she stutters between shudders.

I shake my head and close my eyes. "I got lost in the moment."

Her brows knit together.

I sigh. I have to explain. "Ana, orgasm denial is a standard tool in— You never—"

What's the use?

I stop and she shifts; her weight slams against my semi-erect dick and I wince.

"Sorry," she mumbles, as her pale cheeks pink. Even now, she's apologizing to me. This woman puts me to shame. Disgusted with myself, I lie back and take her with me so that we're both lying on the bed, my arms around her.

She squirms and starts to readjust her bra.

"Need a hand?" I ask.

She shakes her head vehemently, and I know she doesn't want me to touch her.

Fuck.

Ana. I'm. Sorry.

I can't bear it. I move so that we're facing each other. I raise my hand and wait a beat to see if she withdraws, but she doesn't, and I stroke the backs of my fingers gently down her tearstained face. Tears well in her eyes again.

"Please don't cry," I mutter, as we gaze at each other.

She looks so damned hurt. It's heartrending.

"I never what?" she asks, and it takes me a split second to realize what she's referring to—my unfinished sentence.

"Do as you're told. You changed your mind; you didn't tell me where you were. Ana, I was in New York, powerless and livid. If I'd been in Seattle, I'd have brought you home."

"So you are punishing me?"

Yes. No. Yes. I close my eyes, unable to face her.

"You have to stop doing this," she says.

I frown.

"For a start, you only end up feeling shittier about yourself."

I snort. "That's true. I don't like to see you like this."

"And I don't like feeling like this. You said on the *Fair Lady* that you hadn't married a submissive."

"I know. I know."

"Well, stop treating me like one. I'm sorry I didn't call you. I won't be so selfish again. I know you worry about me."

We stare at each other while I weigh her words. "Okay. Good." I lean over to kiss her. But I stop before my lips touch hers, asking for permission and begging for forgiveness. She raises her lips to mine and I kiss her with tenderness.

"Your lips are always so soft when you've been crying."

"I never promised to obey you, Christian."

"I know."

"Deal with it, please. For both our sakes. And I will try to be more considerate of your controlling tendencies."

I have no answer to that, except "I'll try."

She sighs. "Please do. Besides, if I *had* been here…" Her eyes grow wide.

"I know," I whisper, feeling like all the blood is draining from my face. I lie back and fling my arm across my eyes, imagining for the thousandth time what could have happened.

He could have killed her.

She curls around me and lays her head on my chest while I hold her. My fingers twirl her braid, then untie it and slowly untangle her hair. It's soothing, feeling her soft hair spill through my fingers.

Ana, I'm so sorry.

We lie for several moments, until Ana interrupts my thoughts. "What did you mean earlier, when you said 'or'?"

"Or?" I ask.

"Something about Jack."

I peer at her. "You don't give up, do you?"

She rests her chin on my sternum. "Give up? Never. Tell me. I don't like being kept in the dark. You seem to have some overblown idea that I need protecting. You don't even know how to shoot—I do." She's on a roll. "Do you think I can't handle whatever it is you won't tell me, Christian? I've had your stalker ex-sub pull a gun on me, your pedophile ex-lover harass me—"

Ana!

"And don't look at me like that. Your mother feels the same way about her."

What? "You talked to my mother about Elena?" I don't believe it.

"Yes, Grace and I talked about her."

I gape at her, and Ana continues, "She's very upset about it. Blames herself."

"I can't believe you spoke to my mother. Shit!" I put my arm over my face again, as yet more shame washes through me.

"I didn't go into any specifics."

"I should hope not. Grace doesn't need all the gory details. Christ, Ana. My dad, too?"

"No!" she says, shocked, I think. "Anyway, you're trying to distract me—again. Jack. What about him?"

I lift my arm to check on her and she's sporting her expectant talk-to-me-now, I'm-taking-none-of-your-bullshit look. Sighing, I put my arm back over my eyes, and I let the words spill out in a rush. "Hyde is implicated in *Charlie Tango*'s sabotage. The investigators found a partial print—just partial, so they couldn't make a match. But then you recognized Hyde in the server room. He has convictions as a minor in Detroit, and the prints matched his. This morning, a cargo van was found in the garage here. Hyde was the driver. Yesterday, he delivered some shit to that new guy who's moved in. The guy we met in the elevator."

"I don't remember his name," Ana mutters.

"Me neither. But that's how Hyde managed to get into the building legitimately. He was working for a delivery company—"

"And? What's so important about the van?"

Damn.

"Christian, tell me," Ana insists.

"The cops found things in the van." I stop. I don't want to give her nightmares. I tighten my hold around her.

"What things?" she presses.

I stay silent. But then I know she'll keep pushing me. "A mattress, enough horse tranquilizer to take down a dozen horses, and a note." I try to hide my horror, and I don't tell her about the syringes.

"Note?"

"Addressed to me."

"What did it say?"

I shake my head. *It was gibberish.*

"Hyde came here last night with the intention of kidnapping you."

She shudders. "Shit."

"Quite."

"I don't understand why," she says. "It doesn't make sense to me."

"I know. The police are digging further, and so is Welch. But we think Detroit is the connection."

"Detroit?" Ana sounds confused.

"Yeah. There's something there."

"I still don't understand."

I raise my arm and gaze at her, realizing that she doesn't know. "Ana, I was born in Detroit."

"I thought you were born here in Seattle."

No. Reaching behind me, I grab one of the pillows and place it under my head. With my other hand, I continue to run my fingers through her hair. "No. Elliot and I were both adopted in Detroit. We moved here shortly after my adoption. Grace wanted to be on the West Coast, away from the urban sprawl, and she got a job at Northwest Hospital. I have very little memory of that time. Mia was adopted here."

"So, Jack is from Detroit?"

"Yes."

"How do you know?"

"I ran a background check when you went to work for him."

She gives me a sideways look. "Do you have a manila file on him, too?" She smirks.

I hide my smile. "I think it's pale blue."

"What does it say in his file?"

I stroke her cheek. "You really want to know?"

"Is it that bad?"

I shrug. "I've known worse." My sad and sorry start in life springs to mind.

Ana cuddles into me, pulling the red satin sheet over the two of us before laying her cheek on my chest. She looks thoughtful.

"What?" I ask. Something's on her mind.

"Nothing," she murmurs.

"No, no. This works both ways, Ana. What is it?"

She glances at me, her eyebrows drawn together. She rests her cheek on my chest once more. "Sometimes I picture you as a child before you came to live with the Greys."

I tense beneath her. I do not want to talk about this. "I wasn't talking about me. I don't want your pity, Anastasia. That part of my life is done. Gone."

"It's not pity. It's sympathy and sorrow, sorrow that anyone could do that to a child." She stops and swallows, then continues, her voice soft and low. "That part of your life is not done, Christian. How can you say that? You live every day with your past. You told me yourself—fifty shades, remember?"

I sigh and run my hand through my hair. *Drop it, Ana.*

"I know it's why you feel the need to control me. Keep me safe."

"And yet you choose to defy me." I'm bewildered. This is what I find most confusing about her. She knows that I have issues, yet she still challenges me.

"Dr. Flynn said I should give you the benefit of the doubt. I think I do, I'm not sure. Perhaps it's my way of bringing you into the here and now—away from your past," she mutters. "I don't know. I just can't seem to get a handle on how far you'll overreact."

"Fucking Flynn," I mumble.

"He said I should continue to behave the way I've always behaved with you."

"Did he, now?" I observe wryly.

I have him to blame.

She takes a deep breath. "Christian, I know you loved your mom, and you couldn't save her. It wasn't your job to do that. But I'm not her."

Fuck. What? Stop. Now.

I lay paralyzed beneath her. "Don't," I whisper.

I don't want to discuss the fucking crack whore.

I'm floating above a deep well of harrowing, painful feelings that I don't want to acknowledge, and I certainly don't want to *feel.*

"No, listen. Please." Ana lifts her head, her bright blue eyes penetrating my shield, and I realize I'm holding my breath. "I'm not her," Ana says. "I'm much stronger than she was. I have you, and you're so much stronger now, and I know you love me. I love you, too."

"Do you still love me?" I whisper.

"Of course I do. Christian, I will always love you. No matter what you do to me."

Ana, you're crazy.

I close my eyes and place my arm over my eyes again, holding her closer to me.

"Don't hide from me," she says, and she pries my arm off my face. "You've spent your life hiding. Please don't, not from me."

Me?

I stare at her, bewildered. "Hiding?"

"Yes."

I roll onto my side, smooth her hair off her face, and tuck it behind her ear. "You asked me earlier today if I hated you. I didn't understand why, and now—"

"You still think I hate you?" she asks.

"No." I shake my head. "Not now. But I need to know, why did you safe-word, Ana?"

She swallows, and I watch the play of emotions that cross her face. "Because...because you were so angry and distant and cold. I didn't know how far you'd go."

I realize that she asked me and asked me and asked me to let her come. And I didn't.

I betrayed her trust.

Thank heaven for safe words.

"Were you going to let me come?" Her gaze is unwavering, in spite of her blush.

Yes. No. I don't know.

"No," I answer. But the truth is, I don't know.

"That's harsh."

I caress her cheek with my knuckle, the one with the burn. "But effective," I whisper.

And you stopped me.

We will always have safe words. If I go too far.

Even when I said we didn't need them.

"I'm glad you did," I mutter.

"Really?" She doesn't believe me.

I try to smile at her. "Yes. I don't want to hurt you. I got carried away." I kiss her. "Lost in the moment." I kiss her again. "Happens a lot with you."

Her face brightens with a grin.

It's catching. "I don't know why you're grinning, Mrs. Grey."

"Me neither."

I embrace her, holding her close, and place my head on her chest. She strokes my naked back with one hand and runs her fingers through my hair with the other. And I crave her touch.

"It means I can trust you, to stop me. I never want to hurt you," I confess. "I need—"

Tell her, Grey.

"You need what?"

"I need control, Ana. Like I need you. It's the only way I can function. I can't let go of it. I can't. I've tried. And yet, with you…" I shake my head in exasperation.

"I need you, too," she says, hugging me tighter. "I'll try, Christian. I'll try to be more considerate."

"I want you to need me."

"I do!" she says emphatically.

"I want to look after you."

"You do. All the time. I missed you so much while you were away."

"You did?"

"Yes, of course. I hate you going away."

I smile. "You could have come with me."

"Christian, please. Let's not rehash that argument. I want to work."

I sigh as she runs her fingers through my hair, chasing away my tension, helping me relax. "I love you, Ana."

"I love you, too, Christian. I will always love you."

We lie entwined in red satin, almost naked, me wearing jeans, Ana in her bra.

What a pair we are…

Her breathing evens out, she's sleeping. I close my eyes.

Mommy is sitting on the couch. She is quiet. She looks at the wall and blinks sometimes. I stand in front of her with my cars, but she doesn't see me. I wave and she sees me, but she waves me away. *No, Maggot, not now.* He comes here.

He hurts Mommy. *Get up, you stupid Bitch.* He hurts me. I hate him. He makes me so mad. I run to my kitchen and hide under the table. *Get up, you stupid Bitch.* He shouts. He is loud. Mommy screams. *No.* I put my hands over my ears. *Mommy.* He comes into the kitchen with his boots and smell. *Where are you, little shit? There you are. Stay here, you little prick. I'm going to fuck your bitch of a mother. I don't want to see your fuck-ugly face for the rest of the evening. Understand?* When I don't reply, he slaps my face. Hard. My cheek stings. *Or you get the burn, you little prick.* No. No. I don't like that. I don't like the burn. It hurts. He smokes his cigarette and waves it in front of me. *Do you want the burn, you little shit? Do you?* He laughs. He has some teeth gone. He laughs. And laughs. *I'm going to cook something for that bitch. Gonna need a spoon. Then it's going into this.* He holds an in-jec-shun up for me to see. *She loves this. She loves this more than she loves you or me, you little shit.* He turns away. He changes. He's Jack Hyde and Ana lies on the floor beside him and he's plunging the syringe into her thigh.

"No!" I bellow to the world.

"Christian, please. Wake up!"

I open my eyes. She is here. Shaking me. "Christian, you're having a nightmare. You're home. You're safe." I look around. We're on the bed in the playroom.

"Ana!" She's here. She's safe. I grab her face and pull her lips to mine, seeking the comfort and solace of her mouth. She is everything wholesome in my life. My love. My light.

Ana.

Desire rockets through my body like lightning; I'm aroused. I roll us over, pressing her into the mattress.

I want her. I need her.

Holding her chin, I place my hand on her head to keep her still while I part her legs with my knee, resting my bursting dick, still clad in denim, against her sex. "Ana," I breathe, and gaze down into her startled blue eyes. Her pupils grow bigger and darker.

She feels it, too.

She wants it, too.

My lips capture her mouth again, tasting her, taking her. And I rock my dick against her. I kiss her face, her eyelids, her cheeks, along her jawline. I want her.

Now.

"I'm here," she whispers, and wraps her arms around my shoulders and grinds against me.

"Oh, Ana. I need you." I'm breathless, yearning for her.

"Me, too," she rasps, clutching at my back.

I rip open my button fly, freeing my dick, and I shift, ready to take her.

Yes? No? Ana? I gaze into her dark, dark eyes and see a reflection of my need and want.

"Yes. Please," she says.

I bury myself in her in one thrust.

"Ah!" she cries, and I groan, cherishing the feel of her.

Ana. I honor her mouth once more, my tongue insistent as I drive into her, chasing away my fear and my nightmare. Losing myself in her love and lust. She is frantic, too. Needy. Greedy. Joining me, thrust for thrust, on and on.

"Ana!" I growl and let go, coming inside her over and over, losing all sense of self and falling under her powerful spell. She makes me whole.

She heals me. She is my light.

She holds me, hard and tight, while I drag air into my lungs.

I ease out of her and tighten my arms around her while the earth rights itself on its axis.

Wow.

That was…

Quick!

I shake my head and lean up on my elbows, staring down into her beautiful face. "Oh, Ana. Sweet Jesus." I kiss her.

"You okay?" She places her palm on my cheek.

I nod as I finally settle back on earth. "You?" I ask.

"Um…" She wriggles beneath me, pressing herself against my

sated cock. I give her a wicked, carnal smile. I know what she's trying to tell me. This is a language I understand.

"Mrs. Grey, you have needs," I whisper. I drop a quick kiss on her lips, and before she can say anything, I get up. Kneeling at the end of the bed, I grab Ana's legs and tug her toward me so that her ass hangs on the edge of the bed. "Sit up," I tell her, and she does as she's told. Her hair tumbles down to her breasts, and with my eyes on hers, I gently push her legs apart. She leans back on her hands, her breasts rising and falling as her breathing quickens. Her lips are parted. I don't think she can quite believe what I'm going to do.

"You are so fucking beautiful, Ana," I murmur, and press soft kisses up her inner thigh. I glance at her through my lashes, like she does to me.

"Watch," I breathe, as my tongue laps at her clitoris.

"Ah!" she cries out. She tastes of Ana and sex and me and I don't let up. After what I did to her earlier, she must be wound up tighter than an old-fashioned watch. I keep her legs apart, holding her in place while my mouth works its magic, lavishing her with unyielding attention.

Her body starts to tremble.

"No…ah!" she says, and it's my cue to slowly slide a finger inside her. She groans and collapses onto the bed while I stoke the fire inside her, taunting her sweet spot over and over, my tongue continuing to bathe her clitoris.

She's so close. Her legs stiffen.

Ana. Let it go.

She cries out my name, her back arching off the bed as she comes and comes and comes. I ease my finger out of her and strip out of my jeans. Leaning up, I nuzzle her belly as she runs her fingers through my hair. "I'm not finished with you yet," I whisper, and kneeling back, I tug her off the bed, onto my lap and my waiting erection.

She gasps as I fill her. "Oh, baby," I breathe, as I wrap my arms around her while cradling her head and raining soft kisses on her face. I flex my hips, and she clutches my upper arms, with a wild-eyed look at me. I grab her ass and lift her, flexing my butt once more and driving into her.

"Ah," she groans, and we kiss while I slowly ease in and out of her. She tightens her thighs around me as we ride each other.

Slowly. Sweetly.

She raises her face to the ceiling, her mouth open wide in a silent cry of joy.

"Ana," I murmur against her throat as I kiss her.

We move.

Together.

In bliss.

"I love you, Ana."

She folds her hands around my neck. "I love you, too, Christian." She opens her eyes and we watch each other.

Building.

Climbing.

Higher.

She's there.

"Come for me, baby," I whisper, and she screws her eyes shut and she hollers out as she submits to her release.

Ah!

I lean my forehead against hers, and whisper her name as her body pulls mine into a sweet, slow orgasm.

When I've come down from my high, I lift her onto the bed and we lie in each other's arms. "Better now?" I ask, as I nuzzle her neck.

"Hmm."

"Shall we go to bed, or do you want to sleep here?"

"Hmm."

I grin. "Mrs. Grey, talk to me."

"Hmm."

"Is that the best you can do?"

"Hmm."

"Come. Let me put you to bed. I don't like sleeping here."

She moves. "Wait," she murmurs.

What now?

"Are you okay?" she asks.

I can't help my smug smile. "I am now."

"Oh, Christian," she admonishes me, and reaches up to stroke my face. "I was talking about your nightmare."

Nightmare?

Shit.

Fleeting visions of the horror I witnessed in my sleep flicker through my mind. I hold her close, and hide from them by burying my face in her neck. "Don't," I mutter.

Ana. Don't remind me.

She gasps. "I'm sorry." She holds me, running her hands through my hair and down my back. "It's okay. It's okay," she whispers.

"Let's go to bed," I say. Getting up, I pick my jeans up off the floor and slip them on. She follows me, keeping the sheet wrapped around herself to preserve her modesty. "Leave those," I say, as she bends to gather her clothes. I scoop her into my arms, cradling her against my chest. "I don't want you to trip over this sheet and break your neck." I carry her downstairs to the bedroom and set her down. She slips on her nightdress while I take off my jeans and drag on my pajama bottoms, and together we climb into bed. "Let's sleep," I mutter. She gives me a sleepy smile and nestles into my arms.

I lie staring at the ceiling, trying to rid my mind of my morbid thoughts. We have Hyde, now. I should be asleep, like Ana is beside me. It never takes her long. I envy her that.

I close my eyes, grateful that she's still here, in one piece, in our bed.

Saturday, August 27, 2011

Ana's on her knees. Bowed. Naked. In front of me. Her forehead pressed to the playroom floor. Her hair a burnished coronet against the wooden boards. Her hand stretched out. Splayed. She's begging. I stand with a crop in hand. I want more. I always want more. But she can't take it. *Red. Red. Red.* No! There's a crash. The door flies open. His frame fills the doorway. He roars and the bloodcurdling sound fills the room. *Fuck. No. No. No.* He's here. He knows. *Ana screams. Red. Red. Red.* He hits me. A right hook to my chin. I fall. And fall. My head spins. I'm faint. No. Stop the screaming. *Red. Red. Red.* Stop. It goes on. And on. Then it stops. I open my eyes and Hyde looms over her body. Syringe in hand. He leers. Ana is still. Pale. Cold. I shake her. She doesn't move. *Ana!* She lies unresponsive in my arms. I shake her once more. *Wake up.* She's gone. Gone! *Gone! No.* Kneeling on a sticky green rug, I clutch her to me and tip my head back and howl. Ana. Ana. *Ana!*

I'm startled awake, dragging air into my lungs.

Ana!

A quick twist of my head confirms that she's peacefully asleep beside me.

Thank Christ.

Clasping my head in my hands, I stare up at the ceiling.

What the hell?

Why am I letting that asshole into my psyche?

He's in custody. We've got him.

I take a long, calming breath as my thoughts wander.

Baby Bird? What the hell does that mean? From the depths of my brain something stirs but vanishes instantly. My mind spins, trying to chase it through the shadows, but without success. I suspect it's from a part of my psyche that stores all the memories I try to forget. I shudder.

Don't go there.

I know I'm not going back to sleep anytime soon. With a sigh, I get up, grab my phone, and pad into the kitchen for a glass of water. Standing by the sink, I run my hand through my hair.

Get it together, Grey.

Tomorrow we could do something special. Take our minds off Hyde.

Sailing? Soaring?

New York? No, it's too far and given that I've just been there—and all the shenanigans that have ensued since I returned—I don't think it's a good idea.

Aspen.

I could take her to Aspen. She's never seen the house. The press won't find us there. What's more, I could ask Elliot and Mia to join us. She said she wanted to see more of Kate.

Yes.

From my study, I send e-mails to Stephan, to Taylor, and to Mr. and Mrs. Bentley, the caretakers of our Aspen property, about a possible trip in the morning. Then I e-mail Mia and Elliot.

From: Christian Grey
Subject: Aspen TODAY!
Date: August 27 2011 02:48
To: Elliot Grey; Mia G. Chef Extraordinaire

Mia, Elliot
As a surprise for Ana, I'm taking the jet to Aspen just for the night, Sat 27.
Come with us. Kate and Ethan are welcome to join us. We'll be back Sunday evening.
Let me know if you're up for it.

Christian Grey
CEO, Grey Enterprises Holdings, Inc.

I press send and a few seconds later my phone buzzes.

ELLIOT
Sounds great, hotshot.

He's awake.

Why the hell is he up at this time? He normally sleeps like the dead.

Can't sleep?

ELLIOT
No. You?

I roll my eyes.

Obviously!

ELLIOT
All the Hyde shit?

Yeah.

My phone vibrates. Elliot is calling me.

What the hell?

"Dude, it's late," I answer.

"I can't believe I'm doing this," he mutters.

"Doing what?"

"Taking advice from someone who married the first girl they dated. But how did you know?"

"How did I know what?"

"That Ana was the one," he says.

What? Why's he asking me this?

How did I know?

"It was instant," I respond.

"What do you mean?"

I conjure an image of Ana falling into my office during *that* interview.

It's a lifetime ago.

"When I met her, she looked at me with her big blues eyes, and I knew. She saw past all the bullshit. She saw *me*. It was terrifying."

"Yeah. I get that."

"Why are you asking me?" *Please don't tell me it's about Kavanagh!*

"It's Kate, man."

Shit.

He continues, "I remember when I first saw her. I mean, she's hot—no arguments there. And then we were dancing in that bar in Portland, and I thought…You don't have to try so hard. You've got me, and what's more, it's only been her since then."

I blow out a breath. This is not Elliot's usual M.O.—he's the most promiscuous person I know. "So, what's the problem?" I ask.

"I dunno. Is she the one? I dunno."

We've never had this kind of conversation before; there have been so many women in Elliot's life. I don't know what to say. "Well, as you know, she kept Ana out late last night, and whenever she's with Ana, Ana comes back drunk," I grumble. And she's a major pain in the ass, but I can't say that to him.

"Kate's a good-time girl. Maybe that's it. I just don't know how she feels."

"Dude, I am not the person to ask for advice. Believe me. You'll have to figure this out for yourself."

"I guess," he says.

"Aspen might be the place."

"Yes. I'll text her."

"She's not with you?"

"No. But I want her to be. I'm just playing it cool."

"Whatever, dude. I'll send details of where to go in the morning."

"It is the morning, bro."

"True. This trip is a surprise for Ana. Tell Kate. I don't want her blowing it."

"Copy."

"Good night, Elliot."

"Dude." He hangs up.

I stand staring at my phone, not quite believing the conversation we've just had. Elliot's never asked me for advice on his love life. Ever. And as I suspected, he's really fallen for Kavanagh. I don't get it. She's the most irritating woman on the planet.

It's late, and I should head back to bed. But I'm drawn to the piano; some music will quiet my mind. I lift the lid, sit down, and focus. The keys are cool and familiar beneath my fingers, and I start to play Chopin. Melancholic music wraps around me like a soothing blanket, smothering my thoughts, the plaintive, somber notes a perfect match for my frame of mind. I play it once, twice, three times, losing myself in the melody and forgetting everything; it's just me and the music. While I'm playing the piece for a fourth time, Ana appears at the edge of my vision dressed in her robe. I don't stop, but I shift to make room for her on the stool. She sits down beside me and lays her head on my shoulder. Kissing her hair, I continue to play.

When I finish, I ask if I woke her.

"Only because you were gone. What's that piece called?"

"It's Chopin. It's one of his preludes in E minor. It's called 'Suffocation.'" I almost smile at the irony: it's what she accuses me of doing to her.

She takes my hand. "You're really shaken by all this, aren't you?"

"A deranged asshole gets into my apartment to kidnap my wife. She won't do as she's told. She drives me crazy. She safe-words on me." I close my eyes. "Yeah, I'm pretty shaken up."

She squeezes my hand. "I'm sorry."

I press my forehead to hers, and I'm in the confessional, whispering my darkest fear. "I dreamed you were dead. Lying on the floor—so cold—and you wouldn't wake up." I swallow down the image that lingers from my nightmare.

"Hey." Ana's voice is soothing. "It was just a bad dream." She holds my head, her hands on my cheeks. "I'm here, and I'm cold without you in bed. Come back to bed, please." She stands, taking my hand, and after a heartbeat, I follow her.

She slips out of her robe, and we both climb into bed. I hold her close. "Sleep," she whispers, and kisses my hair, and I shut my eyes.

IT'S THE WARMTH I become aware of first, the warmth of her body and the scent of her hair. When I open my eyes, I am wrapped around my wife. I lift my head off her chest.

"Good morning, Mr. Grey," she says with a soft smile.

"Good morning, Mrs. Grey. Did you sleep well?" I stretch out beside her, feeling remarkably fresh after such a disturbed night.

"Once my husband stopped making that terrible racket on the piano, yes, I did."

"Terrible racket? I'll be sure to e-mail Miss Kathie and let her know." I grin back at her.

"Miss Kathie?"

"My piano teacher."

She giggles.

"That's a lovely sound. Shall we have a better day today?"

"Okay," she agrees. "What do you want to do?"

"After I have made love to my wife, and she's cooked me breakfast, I'd like to take her to Aspen."

Ana looks dumbfounded. "Aspen?"

"Yes."

"Aspen, Colorado?"

"The very same. Unless they've moved it. After all, you did pay twenty-four thousand dollars for the experience."

She gives me her most superior smile. "That was your money."

"Our money," I correct her.

"It was your money when I made the bid." She rolls her eyes.

"Oh, Mrs. Grey, you and your eye rolling." I run my hand up her thigh.

"Won't it take hours to get to Colorado?" she asks.

"Not by jet," I mutter, as my hand cradles my favorite place.

MY PLAN HAS COME together, with surprising ease. I have a full crew and our guests are on board, waiting for us; I'm excited to see Ana's reaction. As we pull up to the Gulfstream, I squeeze her hand. "I have a surprise for you." I kiss her knuckles.

"Good surprise?"

"I hope so."

She tilts her head, amused but curious, as Sawyer and Taylor simultaneously climb out of the car to open our doors.

With Ana behind me, I greet Stephan at the top of the plane

steps. "Thanks for doing this on such short notice." I grin back at him. "Our guests here?"

"Yes, sir."

Ana looks around to see Kate, Elliot, Mia, and Ethan all seated in the main cabin. She gapes at me.

"Surprise!"

"How? When? Who?" she says in a breathless rush.

"You said you didn't see enough of your friends." I shrug.

So, here we are, with your friends.

"Oh, Christian, thank you." She throws her arms around me, planting her lips firmly on my mine. *Whoa.* I'm stunned by her unexpected ardor, but soon lost in her passion, taking all that she has to give. My hands find her hips, pulling her to me. "Keep this up and I'll drag you into the bedroom," I whisper.

"You wouldn't dare." Her breath is soft and sweet against my lips.

"Oh, Anastasia."

Gauntlet. Thrown.

When will she learn that neither of us will back down from a challenge? Grinning, I stoop quickly, grab her thighs, and carefully hoist her over my shoulder. "Christian, put me down!" She smacks my behind as I wave a welcome to our guests and walk through the cabin.

"If you'll excuse me, I need to have a word with my wife in private." I think Mia, Kate, and Ethan are shocked. Elliot is cheering like the Mariners are about to score a home run. *Ha! Maybe I will.*

"Christian!" Ana shouts. "Put me down!"

"All in good time, baby."

Carrying her into the rear cabin, I close the door and slide her down my body to set her on her feet. She looks less than impressed. "That was quite a show, Mr. Grey." She crosses her arms, and I think she's pretending to be pissed.

"That was fun, Mrs. Grey."

"Are you going to follow through?" There's a dare in her tone, but I'm not sure if she's serious. She glances at the bed and blushes. Perhaps she's remembering our wedding night. Her gaze returns to mine, and a slow smile spreads across her face until we're grinning at each other like idiots. I think that's exactly what she's remembering.

"I think it might be rude to keep our guests waiting," I murmur.

Tempting though you are.

I step toward her and run my nose down hers. "Good surprise?" I ask, because I need to know.

She looks delighted. "Oh, Christian, fantastic surprise." She kisses me once more. "When did you organize this?" Her fingers linger in my hair.

"Last night, when I couldn't sleep. I e-mailed Elliot and Mia, and here they are."

"It's very thoughtful. Thank you. I'm sure we'll have a great time."

"I hope so. I thought it would be easier to avoid the press in Aspen than at home. Come. We'd better take our seats—Stephan will be taking off shortly." I offer her my hand and together we go back into the main cabin.

Elliot cheers when we enter. "That sure was speedy in-flight service!"

Dude! Calm the hell down.

I ignore him and nod greetings at Mia and Ethan, as Stephan announces our imminent takeoff. Taylor has taken a seat at the rear.

"Good morning, Mr. Grey, Mrs. Grey," says Natalia, our flight attendant. Returning her welcoming smile, I sit down opposite Elliot. Ana hugs Kate before sitting down beside me. I ask if she's packed her hiking boots.

"We're not going skiing?"

"That would be a challenge, in August."

She rolls her eyes, and I wonder if she was being sarcastic.

"Do you ski, Ana?" Elliot asks her.

"No."

The thought of Ana on skis as a beginner is troubling. I grasp her hand.

"I'm sure my little brother can teach you." Elliot winks at her. "He's pretty fast on the slopes, too." I ignore him and watch Natalia run through the safety procedures as our plane taxis to the runway.

"You okay?" I overhear Kate ask Ana. "I mean, following the Hyde business?"

Ana nods.

"So why did he go postal?" she asks.

"I fired his ass," I intervene, hoping that will shut her up.

"Oh? Why?" Kate looks intently at both of us.

Damn. More questions.

"He made a pass at me," Ana says tightly.

"When?" Kate's eyes are on stalks. She's shocked.

"Ages ago."

"You never told me he made a pass at you!"

Ana shrugs.

"It can't just be a grudge about that, surely," Kate says. "I mean, his reaction is way too extreme." She turns her attention to me. "Is he mentally unstable? What about all the information he has on you Greys?"

She really doesn't let up. I sigh. "We think there's a connection with Detroit."

"Hyde is from Detroit, too?"

I nod. *How the hell does she know all this stuff?*

Ana grips my hand as the plane accelerates. My fearless girl is not a fan of takeoffs and landings. I brush my thumb across her knuckles.

We're okay, baby.

"What *do* you know about him?" Elliot is serious for once, and I have no choice but to reveal what I know. I shoot Kate a warning look.

"This is off the record," I tell her, and rattle off what I remember from his background check. "We know a little about him. His dad died in a brawl in a bar. His mother drank herself into oblivion. He was in and out of foster homes as a kid. In and out of trouble, too. Mainly boosting cars. Spent time in juvie. His mom got back on track through some outreach program, and Hyde turned himself around. Won a scholarship to Princeton."

"Princeton?" Kate squeaks, surprised.

"Yep. He's a bright boy." I shrug.

"Not that bright. He got caught," Elliot observes wryly.

"But surely he can't have pulled this stunt alone?" Kate asks.

Christ, she's irritating. This is none of her damned business. "We don't know yet," I growl, trying to keep a rein on my temper. Ana looks up at me in alarm. I squeeze her hand to reassure her as we sail into the air. She leans in to me.

"How old is he?" she whispers, so neither Kate or Elliot hear us.

"Thirty-two. Why?"

"Curious, that's all."

"Don't be curious about Hyde. I'm just glad the fucker's locked up."

"Do you think he's working with someone?" She sounds anxious.

"I don't know."

"Maybe someone who has a grudge against you? Like Elena?"

For fuck's sake, Ana. I check that Kate and Elliot aren't listening, but they're deep in their own conversation. "You do like to demonize her, don't you?" I mutter. "She may hold a grudge, but she wouldn't do this kind of thing. Let's not discuss her. I know she's not your favorite topic of conversation."

"Have you confronted her?"

"Ana, I haven't spoken to her since my birthday party." *Well, I haven't spoken to her in person.* "Please, drop it. I don't want to talk about her." I kiss her knuckles.

"Get a room," Elliot interrupts my thoughts. "Oh, right—you already have, but you didn't need it for long."

"Fuck off, Elliot."

"Dude, just telling you how it is." Elliot looks so pleased with himself.

"Like you'd know," I retort.

"You married your first girlfriend." Elliot gestures to Ana.

"Can you blame me?" I kiss Ana's hand again, and give her a smile.

"No." Elliot laughs and shakes his head.

Kate slaps Elliot's thigh. "Stop being an ass."

"Listen to your girlfriend." Maybe Kavanagh can keep him in line. She scowls at Elliot while Stephan announces our altitude and flight time, and tells us we're free to move around the cabin.

Natalia appears from the galley. "May I offer anyone coffee?"

WHEN THE GULFSTREAM PULLS to a stop at Aspen Pitkin airport, Taylor is off the plane first.

"Good landing." I shake Stephan's hand as the rest of our guests prepare to disembark.

"It's all about the density altitude, sir. Beighley here is good at math."

"You nailed it, Beighley. Smooth landing."

"Thank you, sir." Her grin is rightly smug.

"Enjoy your weekend, Mr. Grey, Mrs. Grey. We'll see you tomorrow." Stephan steps aside to let us deplane, and we descend the aircraft steps to where Taylor is waiting with our ride.

"Minivan?" I raise a brow. With an apologetic smile, he slides open the door. "Last minute, I know," I offer. I turn to Ana. "Want to make out in the back of the van?"

She giggles.

"Come on, you two. Get in," Mia nags from behind us. We climb on board, scrambling to the backseat, where we sit down. I put my arm around Ana as she cuddles into me.

"Comfortable?"

"Yes." Ana smiles and I kiss her forehead, delighted that we're here together. I've been on trips like this before, with my parents, to their place in Montana, and with Mia and Elliot when they've included their friends. But I've always gone solo.

This is another first.

As a teenager I didn't have friends, and as an adult I've been too busy and too solitary to enjoy this kind of outing.

And I still don't have many friends.

Once Elliot and Taylor have loaded the luggage, we set off toward town. As I enjoy the scenery, my thoughts drift to our house on Red Mountain. I wonder if Ana will like it.

I hope so. I love it here.

Aspen in late summer is as green as Seattle, more so at this time of year. It's what I love about the place. The grass in the pastures is lush and tall and the mountains are smothered in forests in full leaf. Today, the sun is high in the sky, though there are dark clouds on the horizon toward the west. I hope that's not an omen.

Ethan turns in his seat to face us. "Have you been to Aspen before, Ana?"

"No, first time. You?"

"Kate and I used to come here a lot when we were teens. Dad's a keen skier. Mom less so."

"I'm hoping my husband will teach me how to ski." She peers at me.

"Don't bet on it," I mutter.

"I won't be that bad!"

"You might break your neck." A shiver runs down my spine.

"How long have you had this place?" she asks.

"Nearly two years. It's yours now, too, Mrs. Grey."

"I know," she whispers, and kisses my jaw before settling in to my side once more.

Ethan asks me which are my favorite slopes, and I run through them. I'm not as fearless as Elliot, though. He could ski downhill, backward, with his eyes closed, anywhere.

"I can ski, too," Mia pipes up, glaring at Ethan. He smiles indulgently at her and I wonder how her campaign to capture his heart—*or his dick*—is going. He says she's not his type, but the way she's making eyes at him, he's definitely hers.

"Why did you choose Aspen?" Ana asks me as we cruise down Main Street.

"What?"

"To buy a place."

"Mom and Dad used to bring us here when we were kids. I learned to ski here, and I like the place. I hope you do, too—otherwise, we'll sell the house and choose somewhere else." I tuck a loose strand of her hair behind her ear. "You look lovely today." She blushes prettily and I cannot resist kissing her.

The traffic is fairly light, and Taylor reaches the center of town in good time. He turns north on Mill Street and we cross the Roaring Fork River and head up on Red Mountain. Taylor steers around the bend at the ridge and I inhale sharply.

"What's wrong?" Ana asks.

"I hope you like it," I answer. "We're here." Taylor parks in the driveway and Ana turns to look at the house, while our guests pile out of the van. When she turns back to me, her eyes are luminous with excitement. "Home," I mouth.

"Looks good."

"Come. See." I grab her hand, anxious to show her around.

Mia has dashed ahead, into the arms of Carmella Bentley.

"Who's that?" Ana asks of the slight figure in the doorway who's welcoming our guests.

"Mrs. Bentley. She lives here with her husband. They look after the place."

Mia introduces Ethan and Kate to Mrs. Bentley, while Elliot gives her a hug.

"Welcome back, Mr. Grey." Carmella smiles.

"Carmella, this is my wife, Anastasia."

"Mrs. Grey."

Ana beams at her as they shake hands.

"I hope you've had a pleasant flight. The weather is supposed to be fine all weekend, though I'm not sure." She eyes the darkening gray clouds behind us. "Lunch is ready whenever you want," she says with a warm welcome.

I think she approves of my wife.

"Here." I grab Ana and swing her into my arms.

"What are you doing?" she squeals.

"Carrying you over yet another threshold."

Everyone stands aside as I carry my wife into the wide hallway where I give her a swift kiss and set her onto the hardwood floor.

Behind us, Mia grabs Ethan's hand and drags him toward the stairs.

Where the hell is she going?

Kate whistles loudly. "Nice place."

"Tour?" I ask Ana.

"Sure." She offers me a brief smile.

I take her hand, excited to show her around and guide her through a whistle-stop tour of her vacation home: kitchen, sitting room, dining area, nook, downstairs den complete with bar and billiard table. Ana blushes at the sight of it. "Fancy a game?" I ask with a husky timbre to my voice.

I thoroughly enjoyed the last game we played.

She shakes her head.

"Through there is a home office, and Mr. and Mrs. Bentley's rooms."

She nods, distracted.

Maybe she doesn't like the place.

I find the thought depressing.

Feeling a little deflated, I take her up to the second floor, where there are four guest bedrooms and the master suite. The view from the picture window in the master bedroom is stunning and the reason I bought the house. Ana wanders in and stares out at the scenery. "That's Ajax Mountain, or Aspen Mountain, if you like," I inform her from the doorway.

She nods.

"You're very quiet." My voice is tentative.

"It's lovely, Christian." Her gaze is wide-eyed and wary. Striding over to her, I tug her chin, freeing her lip from her teeth.

"What is it?" I ask, searching her eyes for a clue.

"You're very rich."

Is that all?

I temper my relief. "Yes." I'm reminded of how quiet she was when I first took her to Escala; that's where I've seen her like this before.

"Sometimes it just takes me by surprise how wealthy you are."

"We are," I remind her, yet again.

"We are," she breathes, her eyes widening further.

"Don't stress about this, Ana, please. It's just a house."

"And what did Gia do here, exactly?"

"Gia?"

"Yes. She remodeled this place?" Ana asks.

"She did. She designed the den downstairs. Elliot did the build." I rake my hand through my hair, wondering where she is going with this. "Why are we talking about Gia?"

"Did you know she had a fling with Elliot?"

I pause for a second, wondering what I should tell her. She knows nothing of Elliot's dissolute habits. I sigh. "Elliot's fucked most of Seattle, Ana."

She gasps.

"Mainly women, I understand." I shrug and hide my amusement at her shocked expression.

"No!"

"It's none of my business." I hold up my palms; I don't really want to discuss this.

"I don't think Kate knows," Ana squeaks, appalled.

"I'm not sure he broadcasts that information. Kate seems to be holding her own." He's discreet, so that's a plus. Her eyes are on mine, and I'm trying to work out what she's thinking. "This can't just be about Gia's or Elliot's promiscuity," I whisper.

"I know. I'm sorry. After all that's happened this week, it's just…" She lifts her shoulder as tears well in her eyes.

No. Ana. Don't cry. I fold her into my embrace. "I know," I murmur into her hair. "I'm sorry, too. Let's relax and enjoy ourselves, okay? You can stay here and read, watch godawful TV, shop, go hiking—fishing, even. Whatever you want to do. And forget what I said about Elliot. That was indiscreet of me."

"Goes some way to explain why he's always teasing you," she says, her cheek against my chest.

"He really has no idea about my past. I told you, my family assumed I was gay. Celibate, but gay."

She giggles. "I thought you were celibate. How wrong I was." She draws me closer, and I sense her smile.

"Mrs. Grey, are you smirking at me?"

"Maybe a little. You know what I don't understand is why you have this place."

"What do you mean?" I kiss her hair.

"You have the boat, which I get, you have the place in New York for business—but why here? It's not like you shared it with anyone."

"I was waiting for you."

"That's…that's such a lovely thing to say," she whispers; bright blue eyes meet mine.

"It's true. I didn't know it at the time."

"I'm glad you waited."

"You are worth waiting for, Mrs. Grey." I run my finger beneath her jaw, tip her lips toward mine, and kiss her.

"So are you." She smiles. "Though I feel like I cheated. I didn't have to wait long for you at all."

I grin in disbelief. "Am I that much of a prize?"

"Christian, you are the state lottery, the cure for cancer, and the three wishes from Aladdin's lamp all rolled into one."

What? Even after yesterday?

I still, trying to wrap my head around her compliment.

"When will you realize this?" She semi-scowls at me. "You were a very eligible bachelor. And I don't mean all this." She waves an arm at the view. "I mean in here." She rests her hand on my heart while I flounder for something to say. "Believe me, Christian, please." Holding my face, she brings my lips to hers, and we're soon lost in a healing, searing kiss, her tongue sparring with mine.

I want to christen the bed.

But we can't. Not yet.

I pull away, my eyes burning into hers, knowing how strong she is and how much she could wound me if she chose to…by leaving.

Don't go there, Grey.

"When are you going to get it through your exceptionally thick skull that I love you?"

I swallow. "One day."

Her smile is heartwarming—lighting me up on the inside. "Come." I'm uncomfortable with our conversation. "Let's have some lunch—the others will be wondering where we are. We can discuss what we all want to do."

DURING THE IMPRESSIVE MEAL that Mrs. Bentley has laid out for us, we decide on an afternoon walk. But as we finish up, the room darkens. "Oh no!" Kate says suddenly. "Look." Outside, the threatened rain has arrived.

"There goes our hike," Elliot says, but he sounds relieved.

"We could go into town," Mia says.

"Perfect weather for fishing," I suggest.

"I'll go fish," Ethan says.

"Let's split up." Mia claps her hands. "Girls, shopping—boys, outdoor boring stuff."

"Ana, what do you want to do?" I ask.

"I don't mind," she says. "But I'm more than happy to go shopping." She smiles at Kate and Mia.

She hates shopping.

"I can stay here with you, if you'd like," I offer, thinking again about how we could christen the bed.

"No, you go fish," she says, but she gives me a scorching look, her eyes smoky, making me think she'd prefer to stay home.

With me. I feel ten feet tall.

"Sounds like a plan." Kate rises from the table.

"Taylor will accompany you," I announce. He'll keep Ana safe.

"We don't need babysitting," Kate huffs, her irritation obvious.

Ana puts her hand on her arm. "Kate, Taylor should come."

Listen to my wife. This is not up for discussion. That woman makes my hackles rise; I don't know what my brother sees in her.

Elliot frowns. "I need to pick up a battery for my watch in town."

Today? Can't he do that at home?

"Take the Audi, Elliot. When you come back we can go fishing."

"Yeah." His voice wavers. "Good plan."

What's up with him?

TAYLOR MANEUVERS THE MINIVAN carrying Ana and Co. out of the driveway and sets off toward town. I hand Mrs. Bentley's Audi keys to Elliot. He's told me and Ethan to go ahead without him. "We'll be on the Roaring Fork. Usual place, I think," I say.

As he takes the keys, his expression is odd, like he's about to face a firing squad. "Thanks, bro," he mutters.

I frown. "You okay?"

He swallows. "I'm going to do it."

"What?"

"A ring."

"Ring?"

"I'm going to buy a ring. I think it's time."

Shit. "You're going to ask Kate to marry you?"

He nods.

"Are you sure?"

"Yeah. She's the one."

I think my mouth drops open. *Kavanagh?*

"Hey, hotshot, marital bliss seems to be working for you." He grins, recovering his usual devil-may-care demeanor in an instant. "You're gonna catch flies with that mouth open, dude. Go catch some fish instead." He laughs as I shut my mouth, and dumbfounded, I watch him climb into the A4 wagon.

Hot damn. He's going to marry Kavanagh. That woman will be a thorn in my side forever. Maybe she'll say no. But as I watch him reverse out of the driveway, something tells me she won't. With a brisk wave, he's gone. I shake my head. *Elliot Grey, I hope to God you know what you're doing.*

Ethan is in the mudroom, checking out the line of fishing rods. "Float or fly?" I ask him.

"Let's wade. We'll be wet anyway, with this rain," Ethan replies with a grin.

"The gear's there." I point to one of the cupboards. "I'm going to get changed. You can wear what you like from whatever's in there."

"Cool." Ethan opens the cupboard and pulls out a pair of waders.

WE LOAD OUR BACKPACKS and our fishing gear into my pickup and I reverse out of the garage and head down the mountain; even in the rain, the scenery is inspiring. Our first stop is the local angling store, where I purchase our fishing licenses. From there we drive to one of my favorite spots on the Roaring Fork River.

"You fished around here before?" I ask Ethan as we make our way to the bank.

"Here, no. But around the Yakima. My dad's a big fan."

"He is?" *Now, there's another reason to like Eamon Kavanagh.*

"Yeah. Dad told me you're working with him," Ethan says.

"GEH is updating his fiber-optic network."

"He's pleased."

I grin. "I enjoy working with him. He's got a good head on his shoulders."

Ethan nods. "He says the same about you."

"I'm glad to hear that." From my backpack, I remove a box of flies. Inside is an impressive collection. "Carmella's husband makes these. They're great for trout."

"Cool." He selects one and examines it closely.

"Yeah." I choose one. "The mayflies are hatching around now."

"These should do it. Let's hook some lips. I'll give you some room," he says, and we both move over the rock-strewn bank in opposite directions.

My reel is attached, but I quickly assemble the rest of the rod and run the fly-line through the guides and attach my fly to the tippet. I'm ready. A glance at Ethan, who must be twenty-five feet away, tells me he's ready, too. He makes his first cast. It's smooth and graceful, and the fly lands in what looks like a sweet spot in the water. He knows what he's doing.

The Roaring Fork gurgles westward at my feet, flanked by rocks and silver birches. It's a perfect, peaceful setting. The mere sight of this wilderness is enough to make me exhale. I gaze intently at the water as it rushes past me, and slowly wade into the shallows.

Dad is standing with me in the water.

We're in waders. He scans the river.

Here, son, you've got to learn to read the water like you do a book.

Look for those telltale signs of Mr. Trout.

He could be hiding under rocks in the river.

He could be in the seam.

You see the seam, where the slow water hits the fast water.

And look for the bubbles. He could be feeding there.

He loves to eat mayflies, especially this time of year.

This guy, he holds up a fly. We'll fool him with this.

Take your fly and fasten to the tippet. Here. Like this. Dad knots the fly.

Now you do it. After a few goes, I do. It's a good knot because Dad's shown me how.

Good going, Christian. Remember to cast like you're flicking paint off a brush. It's all in your wrist.

The mayfly lands and I let her drift on top of the water like Dad said. I get a bite. A trout.

Good going, Christian!

Together we reel it in.

My dad was a good teacher. I make a couple of casts upstream to the far bank and let the fly drift toward me, and soon I'm lost in concentration. Everything slips from my mind as I set about conquering the river.

A heron lands upstream.

The drizzle eases.

It's so quiet. In spite of the weather, it's great out here.

I get a bite.

It's a trout.

A big one.

Hell yes.

The trout backflips and snaps the line.

Shit. Lost him. And the fly.

ETHAN HAS BETTER LUCK than me. I suspect he hooks the same fish I lost.

"The one that got away," I complain.

Ethan grins. "This one had my name on it."

I check the time; we should go.

"He's big enough to eat. Can we take him?" Ethan says.

"We shouldn't."

He grimaces. "Just this once?"

I smile. "Let's load up. And head back."

"Elliot never showed," Ethan says, as we climb into the truck.

"His business in town must have taken longer than he thought."

Ethan nods, pensive. "He's a good guy. I think my sister is pretty stuck on him."

"I think he's pretty stuck on her, too. Speaking of sisters, how are things with Mia?" I hope I sound casual.

"Your sister is a real force of nature." He shakes his head, amused by something. "But we're still just friends."

"I think she'd like to be more than friends."

"Yeah. I think so, too." He blows out a breath.

We pull into the driveway and I activate the garage door. We both climb out of the truck to start unloading, as the garage door slowly rises to reveal Ana and Kate standing beside Elliot astride one of my

KTM dirt bikes. They're all staring at us. "Garage band?" I ask, as I saunter toward Ana. She's a little flushed, as if she's been drinking. She grins as her eyes travel down my body; she's amused at my attire.

Fishing gear, baby. Or maybe she recognizes the coveralls she sold me at Clayton's. "Hi," I say, wondering what the hell they're all doing in the garage.

"Hi. Nice coveralls," coos Ana.

"Lots of pockets. Very handy for fishing." I remember how attractive but awkward she was when I was at the hardware store. Her cheeks grow rosier.

Oh, baby, we've come a long way since then.

From the corner of my eye, I see Kate roll her eyes, but I ignore her.

"You're wet," Ana breathes.

"It was raining. What are you guys doing in the garage?"

"Ana came to fetch some wood." Elliot smirks.

Dude!

"I tried to tempt her to take a ride." He pats the bike.

Fuck. No. In this weather? And enough of the smut talk, bro!

"She said no. That you wouldn't like it," Elliot says quickly.

I slide my eyes to Ana. "Did she, now?"

Her cheeks grow rosier still.

"Listen, I'm all for standing around discussing what Ana did next, but shall we go back inside?" Kate snaps. She picks up two logs and marches out of the garage. Elliot sighs and swings his leg off the bike and follows her.

I turn back to Ana. "You can ride a motorcycle?"

"Not very well. Ethan taught me."

Did he, now? My sister and my wife…

"You made the right decision. The ground's very hard at the moment, and the rain's made it treacherous and slippery."

"Where do you want the fishing gear?" Ethan asks.

"Leave it, Ethan—Taylor will take care of it."

"What about the fish?" Ethan continues, his voice vaguely taunting.

"You caught a fish?" Ana asks.

No. "Not me. Kavanagh did." I pout.

Ana starts laughing.

"Mrs. Bentley will deal with that," I call. With a smug grin, Ethan takes it into the house. "Am I amusing you, Mrs. Grey?"

"Very much so. You're wet. Let me run you a bath."

"As long as you join me." I plant a kiss on her lips. "I'll see you up in the bedroom. I've just got to get out of my coveralls."

Ana cocks her head to the side.

"Do you want to watch?" I grin at her.

"Always. But right now, I'll go run your bath, Sir."

I smirk and watch her leave, then head into the mudroom.

"Man, that was great," Ethan says, as he strips out of his waders.

"Yeah. It's a good spot."

"I'm happy to sort the gear." He sounds sincere.

"Okay. I'll help you."

"No, man. Your wife is waiting for you. I'll bring it in." He waves me away as he goes back out to the truck. I don't argue; instead, I strip out of my gear and leave the coveralls on a peg in the mudroom.

On my way to join Ana, I run into Mia at the bottom of the stairs.

"Hey, big brother." She hugs me, taking me by surprise.

"Mia." I think she's a little tipsy.

"Where's Ethan?"

"He's outside. Unloading the truck."

She puts her hands on her hips. "Christian Grey, did you make him unload it on his own?"

"He offered."

"You know, I don't hear from you at all since you got married. It's like I don't exist." She sounds sullen.

"Hey." I kiss her forehead. "You exist. How about I take you for lunch next week?"

She claps her hands in delight.

"What have you been drinking?" I call after her.

"Strawberry daiquiris." She dashes out to find Ethan and I shake my head.

Taking the stairs two at a time, I go in search of my wife.

Ana is hanging a silvery-looking garment in the closet. She must have bought it in town. "Did you have a good time?" I ask, as I enter and close the door.

"Yes," she says, staring at me.

"What is it?"

"I was thinking how much I've missed you."

My heart skips a beat at the warmth in her voice. "You sound like you have it bad, Mrs. Grey."

"I have, Mr. Grey," she whispers.

I stroll over and stand before her, feeling the heat emanating from her body. "What did you buy?" I whisper, basking in her warmth.

"A dress, some shoes, a necklace. I spent a great deal of your money." She peers up at me as if she's guilty of some terrible crime.

Oh, this will never do.

"Good," I stress quietly while my fingers ease a stray lock of her hair behind her ear. "And for the billionth time, *our* money." The scent of jasmine and the sound of the bath filling with water drift from the en suite. With a gentle tug, I release her bottom lip from her teeth. I run my index finger down the front of her T-shirt, between her breasts, over her stomach and belly, to the hem. "You won't be needing this in the bath." I grip her T-shirt with both hands and slowly pull it up. "Lift your arms." Ana cooperates, her luminous eyes on mine, and I tug off her top, dropping it on the floor.

"I thought we were just having a bath." Her voice is breathy with desire.

"I want to make you good and dirty first. I've missed you, too." I lean down and kiss her. Her hands creep into my hair as she welcomes the touch of my lips, and we're soon lost in each other.

ANA'S HEAD IS OFF the side of the bed, tipped back as she cries out her orgasm. Her response triggers mine, and I come fast and hard inside her. Panting, I pull her onto my chest and we lie dazed and replete while I stare up at the ceiling.

"Shit, the water!" Ana cries, and tries to sit up. I keep hold of her.

Don't go.

"Christian, the bath!" She stares down at me in horror.

I laugh. "Relax—it's a wet room." I roll onto her, pressing her into the mattress once more and kiss her, quickly. "I'll switch off the faucet." Feeling far more relaxed than I have for days, I get up, saunter into the bathroom, and turn off the water. Sure enough, the bath is overflowing, which will make for a fun time with my wife. She follows me in and gapes at the floor.

"See?" I point to where the water is circling the drain. She grins, and together we climb in, laughing as the water splashes out around us. She's piled her hair into an impossible topknot perched precariously on her head, tendrils falling around her face.

She looks lovely.

And she's all mine.

We sit at opposite ends of the overflowing tub. "Foot," I command, and she places her left foot in my hand. I start massaging her sole with my thumbs. She closes her eyes and, as earlier, tips her head back and groans. "You like?" I whisper.

"Yes," she breathes. Tugging each of her toes, I watch her lips pucker as she absorbs the pleasure. I kiss each toe in turn and graze my teeth along her little toe.

"Aaah!" she groans once more, and her eyes pop open.

"Like that?"

"Hmm." I start massaging again, and she closes her eyes. "I saw Gia in town," she says airily.

"Really? I think she has a place here."

"She was with Elliot."

My hands still, and Ana opens her eyes.

"What do you mean 'with Elliot'?"

"We were in a boutique opposite a jeweler. I saw him go in alone, and I thought he must be buying the watch battery. He came out with Gia Matteo. She laughed at something he said, then he kissed her cheek and left."

Maybe Gia helped him select a ring?

"Ana, they're just friends. I think Elliot is pretty stuck on Kate." Unfortunately. "In fact, I know he's pretty stuck on her." Though why, I have no idea.

"Kate is gorgeous." Ana bridles, and I wonder once more if she can read my mind.

"Still glad it was you who fell into my office." I kiss her big toe, pick up her right foot, and begin the process over again. Ana lays back once more as I lavish attention on her sole and we stop talking about Elliot and Gia and Kate.

I wonder when he's going to propose?

I LEAVE ANA TO get ready for dinner while I head down to my study to check my e-mails. I sit down at my desk and open my laptop. As I go through my inbox, there are a couple of irritating work issues that I need to deal with, but I shelve them for the moment. It's the e-mail from Leila that stops me in my tracks. My scalp tingles with apprehension. What the hell does she want?

From: Leila Williams
Subject: Thank you
Date: August 27 2011 14:00 EST
To: Christian Grey

Sir, or should I just call you Mr. Grey?
I don't know anymore.
I wanted to say thank you.
For everything.
In person.
Please.
Leila

I scowl at the screen, and at Leila's audacity. I've asked her, via Flynn, not to contact me directly, and yet she's sent me this e-mail. I send it on to Flynn and ask him to remind her of my precondition to paying for her treatment and her tuition fees. Hopefully she won't contact me again.

To add to my annoyance, there's an e-mail from Ros telling me that the Taiwanese would like to talk tomorrow at 2:30 p.m. their time. On a Sunday? What time is that here?

I google it—shit. That's half-past midnight, tonight.

What the hell?

I call Ros.

"Christian, hi. How are you?" She sounds upbeat, which only adds to my annoyance.

"Pissed. Can you change the time of this call?"

"I know. It's ridiculous. But no. One of their execs is only available then."

"On a Sunday?"

"It's something to do with them having to be off-site when they make this call."

I sigh. "Okay."

"I'll be on the call, too," she says, in an attempt to mollify me, I suspect. "And we'll have an interpreter."

"Okay, I'll speak to you then." I hang up, irritated.

To hell with this.

I head into the den, where Elliot and Ethan are playing pool and drinking beer. I join them for a drink. Taylor has booked a table at a local restaurant for the six of us, but they have time for a game.

"So, what's the deal with you and Mia?" Elliot asks Ethan.

Ethan chuckles. "You're as bad as your brother." He eyes me. "Like I said to Christian, we're just friends."

Elliot raises an eyebrow and directs a look at me.

I take a long swig of cool, clean-tasting beer.

"Did you get what you needed from town?" I ask Elliot as we watch Ethan slam in a couple of solids.

"Yeah." He grins.

"Did you get some help?"

Elliot cocks his head to one side. "Why do you ask?"

"Little bird told me."

Elliot scowls and Ethan fouls the white ball, so he goes to take his shot.

My phone buzzes in my back pocket. I have an e-mail from my wife.

From: Anastasia Grey
Subject: Does My Butt Look Big in This?
Date: August 27 2011 18:53 MST
To: Christian Grey

Mr. Grey
I need your sartorial advice.
Yours
Mrs. G x

Now, this I have to see. I type a quick response.

From: Christian Grey
Subject: Peachy
Date: August 27 2011 18:55 MST
To: Anastasia Grey

Mrs. Grey
I seriously doubt it.
But I will come and give your butt a thorough examination just to make sure.
Yours in anticipation
Mr. G x

Christian Grey
CEO, Grey Enterprises Holdings and Butt Inspectorate, Inc.

I abandon my beer, bound up two sets of stairs, and open our bedroom door.

Wow.

Anastasia Grey. Wow.

Paralyzed, I stand on the threshold. Ana's in front of the full-length mirror. She's dressed—in a sense—in a tiny silver dress, and towering stilettos. Her hair is a glossy veil edging her beautiful face. Kohl frames her eyes, and dark red lipstick paints her mouth.

She looks sensational; my body comes alive in response.

She flicks her hair to the side. "Well?" she whispers.

"Ana, you look… Wow."

"You like it?"

"Yes, I guess so." My voice is husky, betraying my desire. I want to mess up her hair and smudge her lipstick. I want her to be my Ana, not this version of her. This powerful, seductive woman is, frankly, a little intimidating.

And hot.

Ball-tighteningly hot.

I enter the room, bewitched by my wife, and close the door behind me, glad that I put my jacket back on. She has endless, shapely legs. A vision of her feet in those shoes, hooked over my shoulders, comes to the forefront of my mind.

Fuck.

Placing my hands on her naked shoulders, I turn her around so we're both facing the mirror.

Christ!

This *dress* hardly has a back.

At least it covers her backside. Just.

Our eyes meet in the glass, smoky blue to darkening gray.

She looks every inch the goddess I know. And tall. Really tall!

I glance down at her naked back, and I cannot resist her. I glide a knuckle down her spine and she slowly arches her back into my touch.

Oh, Ana.

I stop where the dress starts at the small of her back. "This is very revealing," I whisper. My hand skates lower, over her pert behind, which is provocatively accentuated in the tight clinging material, to the hem. My fingers hover over her skin at her thigh. Gently, I caress her, teasing her flesh as my fingers move around her thigh, her eyes following their path. She inhales sharply, her mouth forming a perfectly fuckable o.

"It's not far from here." I run my fingers around the hem, then higher up her thigh. "To here." I touch her panties and stroke her through the thin material. She gasps as I ease my fingers against her, feeling the fabric dampen beneath my touch.

Oh, baby.

"And your point is?" Her voice is hoarse.

"My point is…it's not far from here"—I glide my fingers over her panties to the edge and slip my index finger around the fabric so we're skin on skin—"to here. And then…to here." As we gaze at each other, I slide my finger inside her.

She's warm and wet around me, and she closes her eyes as she groans.

"This is mine." I drip the words into her ear and, closing my eyes, slowly move my finger in and out of her. "I don't want anyone else to see this."

She starts to pant, and I open my eyes to watch as I pleasure her. "So be a good girl and don't bend down, and you should be fine."

"You approve?" she breathes.

"No, but I'm not going to stop you from wearing it. You look stunning, Anastasia."

Enough.

I want to fuck her. But we don't have time. And as much as I want to smudge her makeup, I'm sure she won't appreciate it. Slowly, I withdraw my hand, and move so I'm in front of her. Gently I trace her bottom lip with the slick tip of my index finger. She puckers her scarlet lips to kiss it.

The contact echoes in my groin.

I grin. A wicked grin.

This is what I love about my girl.

She does not back down from a challenge.

I slip my finger in my mouth.

She tastes mighty fine. I lick my lips and Ana flushes.

Yes. There she is. My girl.

Grinning, I take her hand. "Come."

Hand in hand, we head downstairs to join our guests, and I'm not immune to the admiring looks they all give my wife.

"Ana! You look like a million dollars," Mia gushes, giving her a hug.

I release Ana and open the closet door. "Whose coat is this?" I ask, holding up a trench coat.

"Mine," Mia says.

"Were you going to wear it?"

"Not tonight."

"Good. Can I borrow it?"

"It'll be a bit small for you," Mia quips.

Ignoring her, I hold up the coat for Ana. She rolls her eyes, but acquiesces and lets me slip it on her.

Good.

She might be cold later.

And no one will see her ass.

THE FOOD AT MONTAGNA is excellent, as is—to my surprise—the conversation. It must be the company. I've discovered that I love watching my wife interact with people; she's charming, funny, and smart. Well, I knew that before I married her, but today her shyness is in check and she's making it look easy. I wonder if it's the amount of alcohol she's consumed that's making her more gregarious, but right now I don't care. I could watch her all day. She is bewitching and she offers me hope for our future together. We could do this more often: bring friends here, entertain them, enjoy time with them. I never thought that would be my thing, but maybe it is.

I'm warming more and more to Ethan. He's passionate about his academic field and excited to be joining the postgraduate psychology program at Seattle U. "Man, you know a lot about this shit," he says as we await dessert.

I chuckle. "I should. I've seen enough shrinks."

He frowns as if he doesn't quite believe me. "Really?"

You have no idea.

Elliot stands suddenly, his chair scraping across the floor, the noise ringing over the general level of chatter. We all turn to look at him. He's gazing down at Kate, and she's gazing up at him as if he's grown an extra head. Elliot drops to one knee.

Oh, fuck.

Dude.

Here?

He takes her hand, and I think he has the attention of the entire restaurant. "My beautiful Kate, I love you. Your grace, your beauty, and your fiery spirit have no equal, and you have captured my heart. Spend your life with me. Marry me."

There's a collective intake of breath. Ana grabs my hand, and all eyes turn to Kavanagh, who just gapes at Elliot in shock. A tear trickles down her cheek and she splays her hand on her chest, as if she's trying to contain her emotion. Finally, she smiles. "Yes," she whispers.

The patrons in the place erupt with cheers, applause, catcalls. This is so Elliot—in a crowded restaurant, in front of everyone. The guy is fearless. My admiration for him grows exponentially. From his pocket he produces a ring box and opens it, showing her the ring inside. Kate throws her arms around him and they kiss.

I laugh as their audience goes wild. Elliot stands, takes a

well-deserved bow, and sits down beside his fiancée with a ridiculous grin plastered on his face.

Ana is crying and squeezing my hand.

Shit.

I remember when I first asked her to marry me. She cried then, too. We were on the floor of the living room in Escala, and I had confessed my worst. I wonder what Ethan Kavanagh would make of that if he knew.

Don't go there, Grey.

Elliot is sliding the ring onto Kate's finger—which reminds me that I have lost the feeling in mine. I squeeze Ana's hand, and she lets go, letting the blood rush back into my fingertips. Ana has the grace to look embarrassed. "Ow." I mouth the word.

"Sorry. Did you know about this?" she whispers.

I give her my best sphinxlike smile and summon the waiter. "Two bottles of the Cristal, please. The 2002, if you have it." He gives me a wide grin and rushes off.

Ana smirks.

"What?" I ask.

"Because the 2002 is so much better than the 2003," she teases me.

I laugh. She's right. But I don't have to tell her that. "To the discerning palate, Anastasia."

"You have a very discerning palate, Mr. Grey, and singular tastes."

"That I do, Mrs. Grey." I lean closer, catching a trace of her scent. "You taste best." I kiss the pulse point beneath her ear.

Mia is up and hugging Kate and Elliot. Ana follows.

"Kate, I am so happy for you. Congratulations," Ana says while she clutches Kate.

I hold out my hand to Elliot, he grins, and he looks so relieved and happy that I pull him into a hug, surprising us both. "Way to go, Lelliot."

Elliot stills for a nanosecond, no doubt shocked by my sudden display of affection, then he embraces me. "Thanks, Christian," he says, his voice cracking on my name.

I hug Kate, quickly. "I hope you are as happy in your marriage as I am in mine."

"Thank you, Christian. I hope so, too," she says sweetly.

She can be sweet!

Maybe she's not as annoying as I thought she was.

The waiter opens the champagne and pours it into our flutes. Taking mine, I hold it up to the happy couple in a toast. "To Kate and my dear brother, Elliot—congratulations."

"Kate and Elliot," we all murmur.

Ana is smiling.

"What are you thinking about?" I ask.

"The first time I drank this champagne."

I frown, filing through the myriad memories I have of Ana.

"We were at your club," she says.

The elevator. I grin. Ana with no panties. "Oh, yes. I remember." I wink at her.

"Elliot, have you set a date?" Mia pipes up.

Elliot shakes his head, his exasperation obvious. "I've only just asked Kate, so we'll get back to you on that, 'kay?"

"Oh, make it a Christmas wedding. That would be so romantic, and you'd have no trouble remembering your anniversary." Mia claps her hands.

"I'll take that under advisement." Elliot smirks at her.

"After the champagne, can we please go clubbing?" Mia turns and gives me her most pleading look.

"I think we should ask Elliot and Kate what they'd like to do."

Elliot shrugs and Kate blushes. I think she wants to return home to the seclusion of their room.

I WALK TO THE front of the line with our guests and we're ushered into Zax, the nightclub that Mia has set her heart on attending. The music is already thumping through the small lobby. I don't know how long I'm going to last here.

"Mr. Grey, welcome back," the receptionist says. "Max will take your coat." Her words are directed at Ana. A young man dressed in black appears at her side. I think he approves of my wife's appearance—a little too much, for my liking.

"Nice coat," he says, admiring Ana's…physique.

I glare at the little prick. *Back off, bud.*

He hastily hands me a coat-check ticket.

"Let me show you to your table." The hostess bats her eyelashes at me, and Ana tightens her grip on my arm. I glance down at her, but her eyes are on the hostess, and we follow her into the club to a VIP seating area near the dance floor. "There'll be someone along to take your order shortly." The hostess waltzes off while we sit down.

"Champagne?" I ask, as Ethan and Mia both head to the dance floor, holding hands. Ethan gives me a thumbs-up.

"Show me your ring," Ana asks Kate, while I turn my attention to my sister and Ethan on the dance floor. She's making her usual crazy moves, but Ethan seems unconcerned and is following her lead.

The waitress arrives for our drink order.

Ignoring Elliot's protest about paying, I reel off, "Bottle of Cristal, three Peronis, and a bottle of iced mineral water, six glasses."

"Thank you, sir. Coming right up."

Ana is shaking her head.

"What?" I ask her.

"She didn't flutter her eyelashes at you."

I must be losing my touch. I try hard not to grin. "Oh. Was she supposed to?"

"Women usually do."

I smile. "Mrs. Grey, are you jealous?" And tipsy?

"Not in the slightest." Though she pouts. I take her hand and bring it to my lips, kissing each knuckle.

"You have nothing to be jealous of, Mrs. Grey."

"I know."

"Good."

The waitress returns with our drinks and opens the bottle of champagne with little fuss. She pours it, and Ana takes a sip.

"Here." I hand her a glass of water. "Drink this."

Ana frowns and I sigh. "Three glasses of white wine at dinner and two of champagne, after a strawberry daiquiri and two glasses of Frascati at lunchtime. Drink. Now, Ana."

She scowls at me, probably because I'm keeping score. But she does as she's told. I'm hoping she'll avoid a hangover tomorrow. She wipes her hand over her mouth in a less-than-decorous way. I'm assuming it's her version of a protest at my high-handedness. "Good girl. You've vomited on me once already. I don't wish to experience that again in a hurry."

"I don't know what you're complaining about. You got to sleep with me."

This is true. "Yeah, I did."

"Ethan's had enough, for now," Mia exclaims when they return from the dance floor. "Come on, girls. Let's hit the floor. Strike a pose, throw some shapes, work off the calories from the chocolate mousse."

Kate stands up. "Coming?" she asks Elliot.

"Let me watch you," he says.

"I'm going to burn some calories," Ana says, then leans down so I get a glimpse of some fine cleavage, and she whispers, "You can watch me."

"Don't bend over," I warn.

"Okay." She stands upright quickly and grabs my shoulder.

Shit. I reach up to support her as she sways, but I don't think she notices. She's dizzy or drunk or both. "Perhaps you should have some more water," I offer.

Perhaps I should take her home.

"I'm fine. These seats are low and my heels are high." She smiles, and Kate takes her hand as they head onto the dance floor.

I'm not sure how I feel about this.

Kate hugs Ana.

And then they both start to move.

Mia is…well, Mia. I'm used to watching her lost in her own world, dancing around the room. She rarely keeps still.

Kavanagh can dance.

And so can my wife. She sets the dance floor alight, in that scrap of material she calls a dress. Legs, back, ass, hair: she's letting loose in a most provocative way.

She closes her eyes and surrenders herself to the thumping beat.

Fuck. My mouth dries as I watch her move.

In my previous life, I enjoyed watching dancing like this, but it was always in the privacy of my apartment, and always at my command. I run my thumb over my bottom lip and shift in my chair as my body responds to my wife. Maybe I could persuade Ana to do this at home. For my eyes only. The lyrics of the song are apt.

Damn, you's a sexy bitch.

As the music pulses through the club, more and more people crowd onto the dance floor. I glance at Elliot, who grins back at me, and we both laugh. "This is a good game," I mutter.

"Sure is." His grin is wicked, and I know exactly what he's thinking.

Dirty dog.

"You did it," I say over the thumping music.

"What?"

"Proposed. In public."

"Yeah. It was a now-or-never moment."

"Happy?"

He nods, beaming. "Very."

I glance back at Ana just in time to see a haystack of a man looming over her, and Ana smacking him across his face.

What the fuck?

Adrenaline courses through my veins, followed closely by a rage that's baying for blood. Springing up from my seat, I knock over my beer, but I don't give a shit.

Did he put his hands on my wife?

I'm going to fucking kill him.

At lightning speed I weave through the throng as Ana looks around frantically. *I'm here, baby.* Slipping my arm around her waist, I move her to my side. The motherfucker in front of her is half a head taller than me, and too broad, like he's overdone the steroids. He's young. And stupid. "Keep your fucking hands off my wife."

"She can take care of herself," he shouts.

I hit him. Hard. An uppercut to his chin.

And he drops to the floor.

Stay down, asshole.

I'm wound so tight, every sinew and muscle on high alert.

I'm ready. Bring it.

"Christian, no!" Ana moves in front of me and I'm vaguely aware of the panic in her voice. "I already hit him," she shouts, her hands pushing at my chest. But I don't take my eyes off the cocksucker on the floor. He scrambles hastily to his feet, and I feel another hand tighten around my arm. I tense, ready to hit that person, too.

It's Elliot.

The haystack holds up his palms in defeat. "Take it easy, okay? Didn't mean any harm." He moves away, tail between his legs, and I have to quell the urge to follow him and teach him some fucking manners. My heart is pounding to the same beat that's shaking the room. I hear it, the blood thumping against my eardrums.

Or is it the music? I don't know.

Elliot eases his hold on me and finally lets go.

I'm frozen. In place. Battling to stay afloat and not descend into the abyss.

I take a deep breath, and finally look down at Ana. Her arms are around my neck, her eyes wide and fearful.

Shit. "Are you okay?" I ask.

"Yes." She slides her hands from my neck to my chest, her eyes searing my soul. She's scared.

For me?

For her?

For the haystack?

"Do you want to sit down?" I ask.

Ana shakes her head. "No. Dance with me."

She wants to dance? Now?

I remain impassive as I fight to bring my fury under control, my mind replaying the last fifteen seconds in a loop.

"Dance with me," she says again, pleading. "Dance. Christian, please." She takes my hands while I watch the asshole make his way to the exit. Ana starts to move against me. Her warmth, her heat, brushing up against me and seeping into my veins.

It's…distracting.

"You hit him?" I want to check that I didn't imagine that.

"Of course I did." My hands fist, because I want to smack him again. She continues, "I thought it was you, but his hands were hairier. Please dance with me." Her fingers curl around my balled fists and she moves closer so I catch a trace of her scent.

Ana. Grabbing her wrists, I haul her against my body and pin her hands beneath mine. "You wanna dance? Let's dance," I growl in her ear, and roll my hips against her, enjoying the feel of her against my groin. I don't let go, but when she smiles, I release her and she moves her hands up my arms to my shoulders.

We move.

Together.

Forehead against forehead.

Eye to eye.

Body to body

Soul to soul.

I keep her close.

As she relaxes, she throws her head back.

God, she's sexy. I am one lucky man.

I spin her across the floor to watch her hair fly out around her.

Then pull her back to me as the throbbing rhythm infects us both.

I've never done this.

In a club.

We danced at our wedding…but not like this.

It's liberating.

When the song changes, she's breathless, her eyes shining.

And my equilibrium has returned. I must download this song onto my iPod. I think it's called "Touch Me."

Apt. I've not heard it before.

"Can we sit?" she gasps.

"Sure." We head back toward our table.

"You've made me rather hot and sweaty," she whispers.

I wrap my arms around her. "I like you hot and sweaty. Though I prefer to make you hot and sweaty in private." Exhilarated, we sit down. I'm relieved to see that my spilled beer has been cleaned up and replenished. As has our water.

The others are still on the dance floor. Ana takes a sip of her champagne.

"Here." I place a glass of sparkling mineral water in front of her, and I'm relieved to watch her down the entire glass. I grab myself a beer from the ice bucket and take a long swig.

What a night.

"What if there had been press here?" Ana asks.

I shrug. "I have expensive lawyers."

She frowns. "But you're not above the law, Christian. I did have the situation under control."

Really? "No one touches what's mine." I insert the right amount of venom into that statement. Ana takes another sip of champagne and closes her eyes. Suddenly she looks weary. I grasp her hand. "Come, let's go. I want to get you home."

"You going?" asks Kate, as she and Elliot arrive back at the table.

"Yes."

"Good, we'll come with you."

ANA FALLS ASLEEP IN the minivan on the way back, her head on my shoulder. She's fried. I shake her gently when Taylor pulls up outside the house. "Wake up, Ana."

She staggers out into the cool air, where Taylor is waiting patiently.

"Do I need to carry you?" I ask her.

She shakes her head.

"I'll go fetch Miss Grey and Mr. Kavanagh," Taylor says.

Ana clings to me as she tiptoes up the stone steps to the oak front door. Taking pity on her, I bend down, unstrap and remove each of her shoes. "Better?"

She nods and gives me a bleary smile. She's tipsy.

"I had delightful visions of these around my ears," I whisper, looking wistfully down at her fuck-me heels, but she's too tired for that. I open the door and we head upstairs to our bedroom. She stands, swaying, beside our bed, eyes closed, hands loose at her sides. "You're wrecked, aren't you?" I stare down into her sleepy face.

She nods and I start to unbuckle her coat.

"I'll do it," she mumbles, and tries to brush me off.

"Let me."

She sighs and resigns herself to her fate.

"It's the altitude. You're not used to it. And the drinking, of course." I smirk down at her and ease her out of her coat, tossing it aside onto a chair. Taking her hand, I lead her into the bathroom.

She frowns.

"Sit," I order.

She slumps onto the chair and closes her eyes. She might fall asleep if I'm not quick enough. In the vanity I find the Advil, cotton balls, and moisturizer that Mrs. Bentley has supplied, and fill a small glass with water. I turn back to Ana and gently tip her head back. She opens eyes that are smudged with makeup. "Eyes closed," I order.

She obliges, and gently I clean the makeup off until, finally, she's smudge-free. "Ah. There's the woman I married."

"You don't like makeup?"

"I like it well enough, but I prefer what's beneath it." I kiss her forehead. "Here. Take these." I place the tablets on her palm and hand her the water.

She gazes up at me, pouting.

What?

"Take them." *You'll feel worse tomorrow if you don't.*

She rolls her eyes but does as she's told.

"Good. Do you need a private moment?"

She scoffs. "So coy, Mr. Grey. Yes, I need to pee."

I laugh. "You expect me to leave?"

She giggles. "You want to stay?"

I cock my head to one side. It's tempting.

"You are one kinky son of a bitch. Out. I don't want you to watch me pee. That's a step too far." She stands up and waves me out of the bathroom.

I suppress my laughter and leave her to it. In the bedroom, I strip out of my clothes, change into my pajama bottoms, and hang my jacket in the closet. When I turn around, Ana is watching me. Grabbing a T-shirt, I stroll up to her, appreciating her frankly lascivious appraisal of my body. "Enjoying the view?"

"Al-ways," she slurs.

"I think you're slightly drunk, Mrs. Grey."

"I think, for once, I have to agree with you, Mr. Grey."

"Let me help you out of what little there is of this dress. It really should come with a health warning." I turn her around, sweep her hair to the side, and undo the single button at the halter neck.

"You were so mad," she says.

"Yes. I was."

"At me?"

"No. Not at you." I kiss her shoulder. "For once."

"Makes a nice change."

"Yes. It does." I kiss her other shoulder, then tug her dress over her behind. Hooking my thumbs into her panties, I bend down and remove them together. I take her hand. "Step." She does, tightening her fingers around mine as she wobbles. I toss her clothes on top of the coat. "Arms up." I slip the T-shirt over her head and pull her into my arms and kiss her. She tastes of champagne and toothpaste and my favorite flavor, Ana. "As much as I'd love to bury myself in you, Mrs. Grey—you've had too much to drink, you're at nearly eight thousand feet, and you didn't sleep well last night. Come. Get into bed." I pull back the duvet and let her climb in. She snuggles down as I cover her up and kiss her forehead.

"Close your eyes. When I come back to bed, I'll expect you to be asleep."

"Don't go."

"I have some calls to make, Ana."

"It's Saturday. It's late. Please." She looks up at me with her soul-searching eyes.

I run my hand through my hair. "Ana, if I come to bed with you now, you won't get any rest. Sleep." She pouts once more, but without any real passion. She's too tired. I brush my lips against her forehead again. "Good night, baby." I turn and leave her. I have to get Taipei on the line.

SUNDAY, AUGUST 28, 2011

Ana is comatose when I return to bed. Slipping beneath the covers, I lean over and kiss her hair. She mumbles something unintelligible, but remains fast asleep. I close my eyes. My conversation with the owners of the Taiwanese shipyard was a success: a brother and sister in business together—it's a first for me—and they're keen to discuss terms in person. We just have to settle on a date. It's the icing on the cake of a good day. Well, apart from losing it at the club and punching that asshole's lights out. I grin into the darkness. No, that felt pretty good, too. With a self-satisfied smile on my face, I drift.

ANA SQUIRMS AGAINST ME and I wake, fully. As usual, my limbs are entwined with hers. "What's wrong?" I ask.

"Nothing." She's luminous in the early morning sunshine. "Good morning." She runs her fingers through my hair.

"Mrs. Grey, you look lovely this morning." I press my lips to her cheek.

Her eyes search mine. "Thank you for taking care of me last night."

"I like taking care of you. It's what I want to do." *Always.*

"You make me feel cherished." Her smile warms my heart.

"That's because you are." More than you'll ever know. I grasp her hand and she winces. I release her immediately. *Shit!* "The punch?" I ask.

I knew I should have hit that prick again.

"I slapped him. I didn't punch him."

"That fucker! I can't bear that he touched you." My temper flares.

"He didn't hurt me—he was just inappropriate, Christian. I'm okay. My hand's a little red, that's all. Surely you know what that's like?" She smirks, laughing at me as usual, and my brief burst of anger dissolves.

"Why, Mrs. Grey, I am very familiar with that. I could reacquaint myself with that feeling this minute, should you so wish."

"Oh, stow your twitching palm, Mr. Grey." She runs her fingertips over my cheek and then tugs the little hairs of my sideburn. I'm not sure I like the feeling. I take her hand and kiss her palm.

"Why didn't you tell me this hurt last night?"

"Um, I didn't really feel it last night. It's okay now."

Ah, yes. Alcohol deadened the pain. "How are you feeling?"

"Better than I deserve."

"That's quite a right arm you have there, Mrs. Grey."

"You'd do well to remember that, Mr. Grey." And there's a challenge in her tone.

"Oh, really?" I roll onto her and grab her wrists, holding them above her head. "I'd fight you any day. In fact, subduing you in bed is a fantasy of mine." I kiss her throat, wondering what that would be like. The idea is arousing.

"I thought you subdued me all the time."

"Hmm, but I'd like some resistance," I murmur, running my nose along her jaw, wondering if she'd ever agree to that. She stills beneath me and I know I have her attention, and possibly her interest. Releasing her hands, I lean up on my elbows.

"You want me to fight you? Here?" she whispers, trying to contain her surprise.

I nod. *Why not?* I've always wanted to do this but couldn't—because I couldn't bear to have anyone touch me.

"Now?" she asks.

I shrug. Part of me can't believe she's even entertaining the idea, but I'm thrilled that she might. I nod again, as my dick grows rigid against her soft flesh. Ana toys with her bottom lip as she gazes at me, and I know she's considering the notion.

"Is this what you meant about coming to bed angry?"

Yes. Exactly. I nod. "Don't bite your lip."

She narrows her eyes, but there's a flash of amusement, and possibly desire, in their depths as her pupils enlarge. "I think you have me at a disadvantage, Mr. Grey." She wriggles beneath me and flutters her lashes, and I want her all the more.

"Disadvantage?"

"Surely you've already got me where you want me?" Her smile is coy as I press my eager cock against her.

"Good point well made, Mrs. Grey." I kiss her quickly and roll over, taking her with me so she's astride my belly. She grabs my hands, pinning them to the bed on each side of my head. Her eyes sparkle with carnal mischief, and her hair tumbles down over my face. She shakes her head to torture me, the ends of her hair tickling my face.

"So, you want to play rough?" she asks while she teases me, her groin skimming over mine.

I inhale suddenly. "Yes."

She sits up and releases my hands. "Wait." Reaching for the glass of sparkling water I left for her on the nightstand, she takes a long draft, while I skate my fingers in circles up her thighs to her ass. I give it a good squeeze. She leans down and kisses me, pouring cool water into my mouth.

"Very tasty, Mrs. Grey," I murmur, trying to contain my excitement at our new game. Placing the glass back on the nightstand, she grabs my hands from her behind and pins them on either side of my head once more.

"So I'm supposed to be unwilling?" She sounds amused.

"Yes."

"I'm not much of an actress."

I grin. "Try."

Leaning down, she kisses me once more. "Okay, I'll play," she murmurs, and I close my eyes, inwardly rejoicing as she skims her teeth along my jaw. I groan deep in my throat and move, quickly, pinning her beneath me. Ana cries out in surprise and I make a play to grab her hands, but she's too quick. She pushes against my chest as I try to part her legs with my knee, but her thighs are firmly clamped together. I capture her wrist, but she grabs my hair with her other hand and yanks it. Hard.

Fuck. This. Is. Hot.

"Ah!" I twist my head free and stare down at her.

Her eyes are wide and wild, her breathing erratic.

She's turned on, too.

It's a torch to my libido. "Savage," I whisper, my lust laced through each syllable. Ana is unleashed—she tries to wrest her hand from mine as she attempts to buck me off. I grab her free hand with my left, so I have both of her wrists pinned above her head, leaving my right hand to linger over her body. My fingers travel down, my aim to lift the hem of her T-shirt, but I love the feel of her flesh beneath the soft material. Her nipple is hard, ready for me, and I greet it with a tweak.

Ana yelps and tries in vain to buck me off once more.

I lean down to kiss her and she turns her face away from me.

No.

I clasp her chin and hold her in place while my teeth graze her jaw, as she did to me earlier. "Oh, baby, fight me." My voice is husky with need.

She twists and writhes one more, trying to free herself, but I keep my hold on her and it's such a kick—a heady, euphoric feeling of dominance. Teasing her lower lip with my teeth, I try to invade her mouth, but suddenly she softens beneath me, granting my tongue access and kissing me back, her passion taking me by surprise. I release her wrists, and her hands are in my hair while she wraps her legs around me, her heels at my ass, pushing down my pajamas. She tips her pelvis up to me as we kiss. "Ana," I whisper, her name a talisman as she bewitches me. We're no longer fighting. We're surrendering to each other. I cannot get enough of her. She's on me, I'm on her. We're lips and tongues, and mouths and hands.

Fuck. I want her.

"Skin," I mumble, panting. I haul her up and remove her T-shirt in one fast move, throwing it on the floor.

"You," she whispers, and she yanks down my pajamas and grabs my cock, squeezing me hard as she tightens her hand around me.

"Fuck!"

I grab her thighs, lifting them so she falls back on the bed, but she doesn't let go of me. Her fingers move over me, hot and fevered, her thumb teasing me, while my hands caress her body: her hips, her stomach, her breasts.

She slips her thumb in her mouth.

"Taste good?" I ask, as she stares at me, her eyes burning with desire.

"Yes. Here." She shoves her thumb into my mouth as I hover over her. Tasting and biting the pad, I suck her thumb and marvel at her audacity. She groans, her fingers tugging on my hair, bringing my mouth to hers. She folds around me, pushing my pajamas off with her feet. My teeth skim her jaw, nipping gently.

"You're so beautiful." My lips continue their journey down her throat. "Such beautiful skin." Across her chest and onward to her breasts.

Ana writhes beneath me. "Christian," she begs, tightening her hands in my hair.

"Hush." My tongue circles her nipple, honoring it, before my lips close around it and I tug.

"Ah!" she moans, tilting her hips so that we're slick against each other. I grin against her skin. I'm going to make her wait. Gliding my lips to her other breast, I greet its erect and eager nipple with my mouth.

"Impatient, Mrs. Grey?" I suck hard on her, and Ana yanks hard on my hair, eliciting a long groan from me. I narrow my eyes in warning. "I'll restrain you."

"Take me," she beseeches.

"All in good time." My lips and tongue pay homage to her breast and nipple, while Ana continues to squirm beneath me. She moans, loudly, her pelvis thrusting against my ready dick.

Suddenly she twists and bucks, trying to throw me off her again. "What the—" I grab her hands and pin her down into the mattress.

Ana is panting underneath me. "You wanted resistance," she rasps.

I take some of my weight on my elbows and gaze down at her, trying to understand her sudden change of heart…again. Her heels dig into my ass.

She wants me.

Now.

"You don't want to play nice?" My cock is straining.

"I just want you to make love to me, Christian," she says through gritted teeth. "Please." Her heels press into my ass again, with more force this time.

Fuck. What's going on here?

Releasing her hands, I sit back on my haunches, pulling her into my lap. "Okay, Mrs. Grey, we'll do this your way." Lifting her, I lower her onto my waiting erection.

"Ah," she groans, closing her eyes and tipping back her head.

God, she feels so good.

She curls her arms around my neck, her fingers clamped over my head, and she starts to move. Fast. Frantic. My lips find hers, and I surrender to her pace, and her supercharged rhythm, until we both shout out as we come, and collapse back on the bed.

Wow.

That was…different.

We both lie there, catching our breath. She runs her fingertips through my chest hair and I thrum my fingers down her back, enjoying the contact.

"You're quiet," Ana says eventually, and kisses my shoulder. I turn to look at her, trying to understand what just happened. "That was fun," she says, but as her eyes search mine, she looks uncertain.

"You confound me, Ana."

"Confound you?"

I turn so we're face-to-face. "Yes. You. Calling the shots. It's different."

The small *v* forms between her brows as she frowns. "Good different or bad different?" She traces her finger over my lips, and I pucker them to kiss her fingertip as I contemplate her question.

"Good different." *Frantic, though.* I would have liked that to last longer.

"You've never indulged this little fantasy before?"

"No, Anastasia. You can touch me." *And it was fucking hot. I'd like to do it again.*

"Mrs. Robinson could touch you."

My eyes find hers while I wonder why she would bring up Elena at this time. "That was different," I whisper.

Ana's eyes widen, seeing through me, as ever. "Good different or bad different?" she asks.

The searing pain of Elena's touch flares in my imagination.

Her hands on me. Her nails scraping my skin while the darkness flailed and clawed at me from within, trying to throw her off.

It was unbearable.

I swallow, trying to dispel the memory. "Bad, I think." The words are less than a whisper.

"I thought you liked it."

"I did. At the time."

"Not now?"

Ana's eyes are a guileless blue, impossible to escape. Slowly, I shake my head.

"Oh, Christian." She launches herself at me, an unstoppable force of good, kissing my face, my chest, each of my scars. I groan and answer her kiss with my own passion and my love. And we're soon lost, making love at my pace. Slowly, tenderly, so I can show her how much I love her.

ANA IS BRUSHING HER teeth as I finish dressing. "I'll go and check on our guests."

Her eyes meet mine in the bathroom mirror. "I have a question."

I lean against the doorjamb. "Pray, what do you wish to know, Mrs. Grey?"

She turns to face me, dressed only in a towel. "Does Mrs. Bentley know about your…um…your—"

"Predilections?" I offer.

Ana flushes and I laugh, because Ana can still blush at anything to do with sex, and because Mr. and Mrs. Bentley have no idea.

"No. No playroom here. We'll have to bring some toys." I wink at her and turn to go, leaving her mouth open.

Kate and Mrs. Bentley are chatting in the kitchen. They're the only ones up, it seems, on such a beautiful morning. I greet them both.

"Good morning, Mr. Grey," Carmella says.

Kate smiles, and frankly it's unnerving. I'm more used to her snarling at me.

"We could go for a hike and a picnic before heading home," I suggest to Kate.

"Sounds great."

"Waffles okay today?" Mrs. Bentley asks.

"Great. Picnic for later, would that be possible?"

"Of course," she says, with a look that tells me I shouldn't dare doubt her culinary abilities. "Oh, and Martin would like a word with you," she continues. "He's somewhere in the yard."

"I'll go find him."

Martin Bentley is weeding what Mrs. Bentley calls the kitchen garden. We exchange pleasantries and he takes me on a tour of the grounds. He's a thoughtful, introspective man with some ideas on how to improve the yard. Not only does he maintain my property, but also a couple of the other properties in the near vicinity, and he's a volunteer for the fire department.

While we walk, we discuss putting in a hot tub, and maybe a pool. I notice a bamboo cane that's been discarded, and I pick it up as we continue to talk. It's been a while since I held a cane. It's a little heavy, and not very flexible. Absentmindedly, I swipe it through the air.

"It'll be expensive," Martin says, referring to the notional pool, "and, to be honest, how often would you use it?"

"Good point. Perhaps we could go for a tennis court instead."

"Or you could leave it all be and let the meadow flowers bloom." His grin is infectious.

I survey the yard: pool, or tennis court, or meadow flowers? I wonder which Ana would prefer. I swipe the cane through the air once more as Mr. Bentley opens the door into the basement. I don't know what it is that makes me glance up, but I do, to discover Ana is watching me from the kitchen window. She waves, but looks guilty for some reason—why? I don't know. She turns away, and I hand the cane to Martin and head back into the house. I'm hungry for waffles.

THE FLIGHT HOME IS smooth. Ana slumbers beside me while I go through the draft deal terms for the acquisition of Geolumara. I think everyone is tired after the forced-march hike up the Red Mountain Road trail that Elliot led us on. But it was worth it for the view. The late night, the altitude, and the alcohol are catching up with all of us: Elliot and Ana are sleeping, Kate and Ethan are dozing, Mia is reading. She and Ethan appear to have had an argument. I suspect Ethan's "we're just friends" has finally registered in Mia's stubborn mind.

Stephan announces that we're beginning our descent into Seattle. "Hey, sleepyhead." I wake Ana. "We're about to land. Buckle up."

She stirs and fumbles for her belt, but I fasten it for her and kiss her forehead. She snuggles against me and I drop a kiss in her hair.

This trip has been a success, I think. But for me, it's also been disturbing. I'm sensing a growing feeling of…contentment. It's a strange and frightening sentiment. One that could disappear in a heartbeat. I glance down at Ana, trying to dismiss the worrisome feeling. It's too new. And too fragile. Turning my attention back to the paperwork in front of me, I continue to read, making notes in the margins with my queries.

Don't dwell on your happiness, Grey.

It will only lead to pain.

Flynn's recent advice echoes in my mind. *Nurture and treasure it.*

Shit. How?

Hell.

Elliot wakes and teases Ana while First Officer Beighley announces our final approach. I take Ana's hand.

"Christian, Ana. Thank you for a fantastic weekend," Kate says, threading her fingers through Elliot's.

"You're welcome," I answer. And there it is again, that *contentment.*

"HOW WAS YOUR WEEKEND, Mrs. Grey?" I ask once we're en route to Escala.

Ryan is driving, with Taylor in the passenger seat. Even he looks relaxed.

"Good, thank you."

"We can go anytime. Take anyone you wish to take."

"We should take Ray. He'd like the fishing."

"That's a good idea."

"How was it for you?" she asks.

I glance at her.

Fantastic. Scarily so…

"Good," I say, eventually. "Real good."

"You seemed to relax."

"I knew you were safe."

She frowns. “Christian, I’m safe most of the time. I’ve told you before, you’ll keel over at forty if you keep up this level of anxiety. And I want to grow old and gray with you.” Ana reaches out taking my hand. I raise it to my lips and kiss her fingers.

I will always worry about you, baby.

You are my life.

“How’s your hand?” I ask, to change the subject.

“It’s better, thank you.”

“Very good, Mrs. Grey. You ready to face Gia again?”

Ana rolls her eyes. “I might want to keep you out of the way, keep you safe.”

“Protecting me?” Well, how the tables have turned. I want to laugh.

“As ever, Mr. Grey. From all sexual predators,” she teases, keeping her voice low, so Ryan and Taylor don’t overhear her.

I BRUSH MY TEETH, glad that we’ve approved Gia’s plans. Elliot’s team will start on the build Monday. I tick through a mental checklist. I have much to do over the coming week, but chiefly I want to make sure we nail Hyde’s ass to the wall and keep him incarcerated. Welch will need to keep digging to see if the asshole’s been working with anyone.

I hope not.

I hope this is over.

“Everything okay?” Ana asks, when I join her in the bedroom. She’s wearing one of her satin nightdresses and looks every inch a goddess.

I nod as I climb into bed beside her, putting aside my thoughts about next week.

“I’m not looking forward to going back to reality,” she says.

“No?”

She shakes her head and caresses my face. “I had a wonderful weekend. Thank you.”

“You’re my reality, Ana.” I kiss her.

“Do you miss it?”

“Miss what?”

"You know. The caning, and stuff," she whispers.

Why is she asking me this? I rack my brain. The bamboo cane. This morning?

"No, Anastasia, I don't." I stroke her cheek with the back of my knuckles. "Dr. Flynn said something to me when you left, something that's stayed with me. He said I couldn't be that way if you weren't so inclined. It was a revelation." John encouraged me to try our relationship her way.

And look where we are…

"I didn't know any other way, Ana. Now I do. It's been educational."

"Me, educate you?" she scoffs.

I smile. "Do you miss it?"

"I don't want you to hurt me, but I like to play, Christian. You know that. If you wanted to do something…" She lifts her left shoulder in a coy shrug.

"Something?"

"You know, with a flogger or your crop—" She stops as her face colors.

Crops and floggers, eh?

"Well, we'll see. Right now, I'd like some good old-fashioned vanilla." My thumb skims her bottom lip, and I kiss her once more.

THURSDAY, SEPTEMBER 1, 2011

Bastille is kicking my ass. "Marriage is making you soft, Grey," he taunts, flicking his dreads to the side as I struggle to my feet once more. That is the third time he has knocked me on my butt. "Maybe this is what happiness looks like." His face brightens with a benign grin and he comes at me again with a roundhouse kick. But I block him and feint right, then bring him down with my left leg.

"Yeah," I respond, adrenaline flying through my veins. "Maybe it does." I bounce on my feet, fists raised, ready to take him down once more, as he leaps to his feet.

"That's more like it, man."

AS I SIP MY coffee at my desk, I contemplate the last few days and Bastille's words. *Maybe this is what happiness looks like.*

Happiness.

It's a strange and unsettling emotion, one that I've felt often enough since I met Ana. But I've always thought of those as fleeting moments, sometimes euphoric, sometimes just pure joy. It's never been my constant companion. It's crept up on me, and now it's with me, always—but it's an uneasy feeling, a tightness in my chest. And I know it's because it could be snatched from me at any moment, and I'd be left devastated.

"*I don't want you to sabotage your happiness, Christian. I know you feel you don't deserve it.*" Flynn's words echo once more through my thoughts.

Sabotage my happiness?

How and why would I do that?

It's like love. That was a frightening prospect, too, yet I let that in.

Shit. Why can't I just accept this feeling and enjoy it? I could bathe in its fire and rise reborn like a phoenix…or will I perish in its flames, with what's left of my heart destroyed?

Flowery, Grey. I snort. *Get a grip.*

Maybe Bastille has a point. These last few days have been idyllic. Work is going well. I've not had any further arguments with my wife, just fun and frolics.

She's been...*Ana. My Ana.*

I recall the Shipbuilding Association dinner, a few nights back, where—at my request—Ana wore Kegel balls throughout the long meal. How she held it together I'll never know. She didn't when we got home. I shift in my seat, remembering her need.

My phone buzzes, interrupting my erotic reminiscence.

"Yes?"

"I have Welch for you."

"Thanks, Andrea."

"Mr. Grey." His gravelly voice kills any residual lust that's lingering in my body. "Hyde's bail hearing is this afternoon. I'll report back when the judge has given her verdict."

"Let's hope she makes the right decision."

He clears his throat, "He's a flight risk. I think she will."

"Great. Let me know."

As I put the phone down, my BlackBerry buzzes with a text.

LEILA
I wanted to thank you personally for everything you've done for me. I am trying to understand why you won't see me. It's hard. I owe you so much. Leila.

What the hell?

I switch my phone off and return to my coffee. I am not in the mood to deal with Leila Williams. She shouldn't be texting me at all. I had hoped that Flynn had talked to her, but I'll discuss Leila's persistence with him later today when I see him.

MIA IS MORE ANIMATED than usual when we meet for an early lunch at my favorite sushi restaurant. She hurls herself at me, fizzing with excitement, kissing my cheek. "It's so good to see you," she gushes.

"You saw me last weekend." I return her hug, my tone wry.

"But I get you to myself—and I have news! I have a job." She raises her hands and does a celebratory twirl before she takes her seat.

"What! Finally?" Her joy is contagious, and I'm eager to hear the details.

"It's taken forever. But I'm thrilled. I'm working for Crissy Scales."

"The caterer?"

"Yes. Weddings. Events. All those gigs. I want to start my own business one day, but she's going to show me the ropes. I'm super-excited."

"Great. When do you start?"

"Next Friday."

"Tell me everything."

No one can enthuse like my little sister, and I can't remember the last time we spent a long lunch together, just the two of us. Over our sashimi and maki rolls she regales me with her hopes for her new career, and with her latest attempts to win Ethan Kavanagh's heart.

"Mia, I'm not sure I can deal with you having a love life."

"Oh, Christian, of course I have a love life. I had so much fun in Paris."

"What?"

"Yes. There was Victor, Alexandre—"

"There's a list? Christ. Stop."

"Don't be such a prude, Christian," she scolds.

"Moi?" I place my hands on my chest in feigned outrage.

She laughs.

"So, you think you have a chance with Ethan?" I ask.

"Yes." She's definitive, and that's one of the many things I love about her, her determination and resilience.

"Okay. Good luck with that." I signal for the check.

"Can we do this again? I miss you."

"Of course. But right now I have to get back to work for a meeting."

I'M SITTING WITH BARNEY and Fred in the lab, examining the latest prototype of the solar tablet—the lighter, simpler, cheaper version for struggling economies in the developing world. This is the part of my job that I love most. Barney is in full flow. "Took eight hours to charge and it's giving us three days of use."

"Can we get more?"

"I think we're at our limit with the battery technology at the moment." Fred glides his glasses up his nose. "It's the black-and-white E-ink screen that saves us on power. And it's more robust."

"And for the home market?"

"Color touchscreen." Barney hands me the other prototype.

I weigh it in my hands. "It's quite a bit heavier."

"Color screens are."

"Feels expensive." I grin.

"We're only getting four hours from it so far, with eight hours in the sun."

"Makes sense. But it can be charged conventionally?"

"Yes. Here." Barney points out the charging port on the bottom of the device. "It's standard, nonproprietary USB. Saves on landfill."

"That's a good marketing angle." My phone buzzes, and Welch's name pops up on the screen.

"Guys, I've got to get this." I step away from the workbench and answer. "What gives?"

"He didn't make bail. No trial set yet."

"He doesn't deserve bail. Thanks for letting me know." I hang up and send a quick e-mail to Ana.

From: Christian Grey
Subject: Hyde
Date: September 1 2011 15:24
To: Anastasia Grey

Anastasia
For your information, Hyde has been refused bail and remanded in custody. He's charged with attempted kidnapping and arson. As yet no date has been set for the trial.

Christian Grey
CEO, Grey Enterprises Holdings, Inc.

I turn back to Fred and Barney to continue our discussion of the tablet and next steps.

BACK IN MY OFFICE, I notice Ana's reply to my earlier message.

From: Anastasia Grey
Subject: Hyde
Date: September 1 2011 15:53
To: Christian Grey

That's good news.
Does this mean you'll lighten up on security?
I really don't see eye to eye with Prescott.
Ana x

Anastasia Grey
Editor, SIP

From: Christian Grey
Subject: Hyde
Date: September 1 2011 15:59
To: Anastasia Grey

No. Security will remain in place. No arguments.
What's wrong with Prescott? If you don't like her, we'll replace her.

Christian Grey
CEO, Grey Enterprises Holdings, Inc.

There's a knock on the door. I'm expecting Ros for our four o'clock, but it's Andrea who pops her head around the door. "Mr. Grey, Ros is running late. She'll be with you in ten minutes. Can I get you anything?"

"I'm good, Andrea, thanks." She closes the door and I open the revised deal terms for Geolumara. I need to read it through and check that all my suggestions have been incorporated. When I look up, I have a response from Ana.

From: Anastasia Grey
Subject: Keep Your Hair On!
Date: September 1 2011 16:03
To: Christian Grey

I was just asking (rolls eyes). And I'll think about Prescott.

Stow that twitchy palm!
Ana x

Anastasia Grey
Editor, SIP

From: Christian Grey
Subject: Don't Tempt Me
Date: September 1 2011 16:11
To: Anastasia Grey

I can assure you, Mrs. Grey, that my hair is very firmly attached—has this not been demonstrated often enough by your good self?
My palm, however, is twitching.
I might do something about that tonight.
x

Christian Grey
Not Bald Yet CEO, Grey Enterprises Holdings, Inc.

I send a quick e-mail to Ros to bring signature copies for the Geolumara deal with her, and there's another e-mail from my wife.

From: Anastasia Grey
Subject: Squirm
Date: September 1 2011 16:20
To: Christian Grey

Promises, promises...
Now stop pestering me. I am trying to work. I have an impromptu meeting with an author. Will try not to be distracted by thoughts of you during the meeting.
A x

Anastasia Grey
Editor, SIP

There's a knock on the door, and this time it's Ros, twenty minutes late.

"YOU LOOK WELL." FLYNN motions me into his office.

"I am, thank you." I take my usual seat and wait patiently for him to take his. When he's ready, he gives me his expectant look.

"So, what's occurring?" he asks.

I fill him in on the week's events, starting with my rushed flight back from New York. Hiding my amusement, I watch his eyebrows ascend farther up his forehead as my tale unfolds.

"That's it?" he asks, when I finish.

"More or less."

"So, let me get this straight. You canceled two important meetings to fly home to check on Anastasia, because you were angry with her that she hadn't followed your instructions, only to find this Hyde character had broken into your apartment to kidnap your wife."

"In a nutshell. Yes."

"She safe-words on you, and that's never happened before—I don't want to know the details, unless you really feel a need to tell me—but you resolve your differences, and following that, you have a nightmare that she dies."

I nod, trying to dampen my sudden anxiety as I remember fragments of my dream.

"Anything else?"

"I took her to Aspen with some friends. I punched a guy's lights out because he touched her. And this afternoon Hyde was refused bail. And I got a text from Leila."

He closes his eyes, and I don't know if it's because he can't believe what he's just heard, or because he's collecting his thoughts, or because he's pissed at Leila.

"Christian, that's a hell of a lot to take on board. I'm surprised you're not more stressed."

"Yes. You'd think. But my stress has been tempered by something altogether unfamiliar and frankly alarming."

"Oh?"

"Yes. Something you alluded to in our last couple of meetings."

"Go on," Flynn prompts.

"I have a general and creeping sense of happiness. It's quite unsettling."

"Ah. I see."

"You do?"

"It's obvious. To me anyway." His expression, frustratingly, gives nothing away.

"Please. Enlighten me."

"Well, I would hazard a guess that Jack Hyde's kidnap attempt and his subsequent incarceration have justified your feelings about Ana's security, but the threat he posed has now been eliminated. So, you've been able to let down your guard. Ana's safe."

Ah! Makes sense.

"But I would also say this is not a new phenomenon. You've experienced a great deal of happiness over the last few months. Your engagement. The wedding. The honeymoon. We've talked about this before. You have a tendency to focus on the end result and not the journey to get there. You were focused on getting married and anxious that wouldn't happen. Yet it did." He pauses, I imagine for emphasis. "Christian, you are the master of your own happiness. I imagine that in your subconscious you don't think you deserve to be happy. But let me set you right on that. You do. You are *allowed* to be happy. After all, it's an unalienable right written into your constitution."

"I think you'll find it's the *pursuit* of happiness that's enshrined in the Constitution."

"Hmm…semantics. But what I'm reading into this situation is that you hold the key to your happiness. You're in control. You just need to let it in. And not deliberately put obstacles in its way."

I glance down at the mini orchids on his coffee table. "Can I?" The words are out before I realize I've said them out loud.

"Can you what?"

"Let it in."

"That's entirely up to you."

"But what if she leaves?"

He sighs. "There are no certainties in life except death and taxes. Everyone runs the risk of being hurt; you know this. You've had more than your fair share of that as a child. But you're not a child anymore. Give yourself permission to enjoy your life and your wife."

Is it as simple as that?

"Now. Leila," he says, and I know we've moved on.

MONDAY, SEPTEMBER 5, 2011

Taylor pulls away from the curb as I watch Ana and Prescott disappear into SIP. My uneasy sense of bliss lingers. We've had an amazing weekend…more fun and frolics with Mrs. Grey. This is what I've been missing from my life.

"Sir." Taylor distracts me from my happy place.

"Yes?"

"The R8 Spyder for Mrs. Grey will be ready at the end of the week."

"Excellent. Thanks."

His gaze does not leave mine in the rearview mirror.

"What?"

"Gail has a suggestion for you, with regard to Mrs. Grey's birthday."

"Oh?" I wait for him to tell me more, but he continues to drive. "Are you going to tell me?"

His eyes flick back to mine in the rearview mirror, and in them I see a silent plea. He doesn't want to rain on her parade.

"I'll talk to her."

"Thank you, sir."

My phone buzzes.

> ELLIOT
> It begins!

He's attached a photograph of his team taking down one of the rear walls of our house on the coast. It's a dramatic shot: blue skies, a gaping hole in a wall, clouds of brick dust, and five hulking men in yellow hard hats wielding sledgehammers.

> Whoa! Leave some of it standing!

ELLIOT
Don't get your panties in a wad. We're following the plans.

I'd expect no less. Good luck.

IN THE ELEVATOR AT Grey House, I check my e-mails.

From: Anastasia Grey
Subject: Sailing & Soaring & Spanking
Date: September 5 2011 09:18
To: Christian Grey

Husband
You sure know how to show a girl a good time.
I shall of course be expecting this kind of treatment every weekend.
You are spoiling me. I love it.
Your wife
xox

Anastasia Grey
Editor, SIP

At my desk, I respond.

From: Christian Grey
Subject: My Life's Mission...
Date: September 5 2011 09:25
To: Anastasia Grey

Is to spoil you, Mrs. Grey.
And keep you safe because I love you.

Christian Grey
Smitten CEO, Grey Enterprises Holdings, Inc.

Smitten doesn't cover it. I want to do something special for her birthday, and I wonder what Mrs. Jones has in mind. I'll talk to her this evening. In the meantime, I'd like to get Ana something other than the car...a gift that requires a little more creative thought.

As I sip my coffee, an idea slowly forms in my mind.

Something to celebrate all our *firsts*.

When I finish my coffee, her response is in my inbox.

From: Anastasia Grey
Subject: My Life's Mission…
Date: September 5 2011 09:33
To: Christian Grey

Is to let you—because I love you, too.
Now stop being so sappy.
You are making me cry.

Anastasia Grey
Equally Smitten Editor, SIP

I grin. We're both smitten.

TUESDAY, SEPTEMBER 6, 2011

Astoria Fine Jewelry has outdone itself. My lunchtime quest was a success, and I'm delighted with the gift I've bought for Ana. I hope she likes it, too. Glancing at her beautiful face on my office wall, I admire her secret smile as she peers down at me, but as ever, she gives nothing away.

Lord, she is lovely.

I find myself grinning at her portrait like the lovesick fool I am.

A man in love with his wife.

Get a grip, Grey.

My plans for Ana's birthday are falling into place. Mrs. Jones has volunteered to cook a surprise dinner party for Ana, and I'm waiting to hear if all our guests can make it. I've offered to send the jet to collect Carla and Bob, Ray is on, and my siblings have both said yes, but I've yet to hear from my folks. Ana knows nothing of this, and the event will be the first surprise party I've ever organized. I remember, when I bought my apartment pre-construction, how the real estate agent had waxed lyrical about the expansive entertainment space within. I never thought I'd actually get to use it. That wasn't my life. And now, two years later, I'm hosting a party.

For my wife. Who knew.

It should be fun.

Perhaps we could take everyone to see the new house on Sunday after lunch and check out how Elliot and his team are doing. Or perhaps we could go before, just Ana and me. Maybe on Friday. I check my schedule, but I'm interrupted by a text from Taylor, and a nanosecond later, an e-mail from Ana. I open the e-mail first.

From: Anastasia Grey
Subject: Visitors
Date: September 6 2011 15:27
To: Christian Grey

Christian
Leila is here to see me. I will see her with Prescott.
I'll use my newly acquired slapping skills with my now-healed hand, should I need to.
Try, and I mean try, not to worry.
I am a big girl.
Will call once we've spoken.
A x

Anastasia Grey
Editor, SIP

What!

Leila?

Fuck!

I dial Ana's number immediately.

No fucking way is she meeting with Leila.

The phone rings and rings, ignored by Ana, and my blood pressure climbs with each unanswered chime until it reaches a dizzying height. Eventually her voice mail kicks in, asking me to leave a message. I hang up, not trusting myself to speak.

Hell.

I check Taylor's text.

TAYLOR
Mrs. Grey is meeting with Leila Williams. Prescott is attending the meeting. I'm heading to the car.

Prescott must have told him. "Andrea!" My bellow practically shakes the window behind me. I text Taylor back.

You going to SIP?

Andrea doesn't bother to knock and comes barreling into my office.

"Mr. Grey?"

"Get me Ana's assistant on the line. Now."

"Yes, sir."

What the hell is Leila playing at? She knows this is forbidden. And as for Prescott—Leila is on the watch list, she knows this is prohibited.

My office phone buzzes and Andrea puts Hannah through.

"Mr. Grey, good afternoon." Hannah sounds irritatingly cheery.

"I need to speak to my wife. Now." I am not in the mood for pleasantries.

"Oh. Um. I'm afraid she's in a meeting."

I'm going to have a coronary. "I'm fully aware of that. Get her out of the meeting."

"Um. I'm not—"

"Do it, now, or you're fired," I seethe through gritted teeth.

"Yes, sir," she squeaks, and the phone clatters to her desk, the noise an assault on my eardrum.

Shit.

I'm left hanging. Waiting once more for Anastasia Stee—Grey.

My fingers drum a frantic tattoo on my desk.

Perhaps I should just get up and go.

That's absurd.

Did John speak to Leila?

My BlackBerry buzzes.

TAYLOR
I'm in the car. Outside.

Wait for me.

TAYLOR
Copy.

I don't understand what Prescott is playing at. How did she let this happen?

The phone scrapes along the desk and is dropped back onto the hard surface, the noise deafening again.

Fucking hell. Hannah is clumsy!

"Um. M-Mr. Grey?"

"Yes." The word hisses out at her in frustration.

Get on with it!

"Ana says she's sorry, but she's b-busy and she'll c-call you b-back shortly."

Jesus Christ. She's a tongue-tied mess.

"Fine," I snap, and hang up.

Shit. What to do?

Prescott! Of course.

Ana said Prescott would be in the meeting with her. She has a phone, though I don't think I have her number. "Andrea!" I shout once more, and a moment later she's in the doorway, her demeanor tentative. "Get me Prescott on her mobile."

Andrea looks momentarily baffled, and I think I'm going to explode.

"Belinda Prescott, Ana's security," I snap. "Now!"

"Ah, yes." Andrea disappears.

Don't be an asshole, Grey.

Taking a deep breath in an effort to calm myself, I get up and pace behind my desk, knowing it will be a moment before Andrea has Prescott's number. I'm suffocated by my anxiety. Loosening my tie, I undo my top button to ameliorate the situation. But an image of Leila—bedraggled and destitute, holding a gun at Ana—remains at the forefront of my mind.

It's torture.

My anger and apprehension rise several notches on the Richter scale.

When my phone rings, I grab it. "Mrs. Grey's security for you," Andrea says.

"Mr. Grey," Prescott says.

"Prescott, I cannot begin to articulate how disappointed I am in you right now. Let me talk my wife."

"Yes, sir," she answers.

There's a beat of muffled chatter. "Christian," Ana snaps, and from her tone I know she's on her high-fucking-horse, condescending to talk to me.

"What the fuck are you playing at?" I bark down the phone.

"Don't shout at me." Her retort only fuels my temper.

"What do you mean, don't shout at you?" My voice bellows around the room and into the phone. "I gave specific instructions, which you have completely disregarded—again. Hell, Ana, I am fucking furious."

"When you are calmer, we will talk about this."

Oh, no! "Don't you hang up on me!"

"Good-bye, Christian."

"Ana! Ana!" The line is dead, and I think I'm going to erupt like Mount St. Helens. Incandescent with fury, I grab my jacket and my phone, and storm out of my office. "Cancel the rest of my meetings today," I growl at Andrea. "And let Taylor know I'm on my way down."

"Yes, sir."

The elevator takes an eternal sixteen seconds to arrive. I know because I count each and every one in an effort to rein in my temper. After I step in and jab the button for the lobby, I clench my fists so tightly that my fingernails dig into my palms, and I know I have lost the fight. Andrea glances up, consternation writ large on her face, but I remain impassive, ignoring her as the doors close.

I am ready to do battle.

With my wife.

Again.

And with Leila. *What the fuck is she thinking?*

Taylor is standing by the car, holding the door open. I'm grateful that at least he's on the case. We drive in silence to SIP as my anger simmers, ready to boil over at the slightest provocation. From the back of the car I call Flynn's office, but I get his secretary Janet's voice mail. I hang up, frustrated that I can't even vent my anger on Flynn.

Was this Leila's plan all along?

She knew that if she accosted my wife, then I would come running.

I'm playing into her hands, but I don't give a fuck.

After an agonizing journey, Taylor pulls up outside SIP and I'm out of the car as soon as he stops at the curb. I don't bother with reception, but head straight through the double doors toward Ana's office. At her desk, Hannah looks up. I ignore her, too.

"Mr. G-Grey—"

I burst into Ana's office, so forcefully that a few papers fall to the floor, amplifying the room's emptiness.

Shit.

Feeling like a complete idiot, I turn around and glare at Hannah. "Where is she?" I snap, trying not to lose it. She pales and points toward the opposite end of the open-plan floor.

"In the meeting room. I-I'll take you."

"I'll manage, thank you." Scowling at her, my tone glacial and clipped, I blaze back in the direction I've come from, a storm cloud about to burst. I have to remind myself that it's not her fault. Ignoring the curious glances from the staff at their desks, I pass by the double doors to reception. They open, and Taylor stalks through to join me, but beyond him I catch a glimpse of Susannah Shaw sitting on one of the Chesterfields in the waiting area.

What the hell?

Are all my ex-submissives here?

She's reading a magazine, so she doesn't see me.

I haven't got time for this.

I spot Leila through the glass wall of the conference room. Without knocking, I barge in and am met by three surprised pairs of eyes. Ana stares at me in shock, then fury. Leila's eyes widen, but she drops her gaze to the table, as she should. Prescott stares ahead. My first response is relief that Ana is unharmed, but it's swiftly swept aside by my anger.

"You," I address Prescott. "You're fired. Get out now." Prescott nods—resigned, I think—and makes her way around the table to leave.

Ana gapes at me. "Christian—" She pushes her chair back, and I know she's going to stand up and berate me. I hold a finger up in warning.

"Don't." I keep my voice low while I struggle to contain my fury. Prescott, her face expressionless, walks past me out of the room. Shutting the door behind her, I turn to confront Leila.

She looks as I remember when she was with me: healthy and well adjusted. It's a relief to see her looking like her old self, and I'd tell her that, if I wasn't so fucking angry with her right now. Splaying my fingers onto the cool surface of the polished wood, I lean forward, tension tightening every muscle in my body, and snarl, "What the fuck are you doing here?"

"Christian!" Ana exclaims, shocked, I think, but I ignore her and concentrate my attention on Miss Leila Williams.

"Well?" I demand.

Leila's eyes dart to mine, her face slowly draining of color. "I wanted to see you, and you wouldn't let me," she whispers.

"So you came here to harass my wife?"

Leila examines the tabletop again.

Well, I'm here now. You got what you wanted.

I'm mad that I've been played, but more livid that she's here with Ana.

"Leila, if you come anywhere near my wife again, I will cut off all support. Doctors, art school, medical insurance—all of it—gone. Do you understand?"

"Christian!" Ana tries to interject. She looks distraught, but right now I don't give a shit, and I silence her with a look.

"Yes," Leila says, her voice almost inaudible.

"What's Susannah doing in reception?"

"She came with me."

I stand upright and run a hand through my hair.

What am I going to do with her?

"Christian, please," Ana interjects again. "Leila just wants to say thank you. That's all."

Ignoring Ana, I direct a question at Leila. "Did you stay with Susannah while you were sick?"

"Yes."

"Did she know what you were doing while you were staying with her?"

"No. She was away on vacation."

I can't imagine that Susannah would have stood by and let Leila lose her mind. She always struck me as a caring and considerate person.

I sigh. "Why do you need to see me? You know you should send any requests through Flynn. Do you need something?"

Leila traces her finger along the edge of the table and the silence fills the room. Abruptly, she looks up. "I had to know," she declares, looking directly at me.

"Had to know what?"

"That you're okay."

What the fuck? "That I'm okay?" I don't believe her.

"Yes." She's not backing down.

"I'm fine. There, question answered. Now Taylor will run you to Sea-Tac so you can go back to the East Coast. And if you take one step west of the Mississippi, it's all gone. Understand?"

"Yes. I understand," Leila says quietly, her expression finally contrite. It goes a long way to calming me.

"Good," I mutter.

"It might not be convenient for Leila to go back now. She has plans," Ana intervenes again.

"Anastasia." My tone is arctic. "This does not concern you." The stubborn scowl that I know so well forms on her face.

"Leila came to see me, not you," she snaps.

Leila turns to look at Ana. "I had my instructions, Mrs. Grey. I disobeyed them." She glances at me, then back to my wife. "This is the Christian Grey I know," she says, and her tone is almost wistful.

What?

That's not fair.

We role-played a relationship, for fuck's sake. And the last time she was in a room with my wife, she had her at gunpoint! I will go to the ends of the earth to keep Anastasia safe. Leila rises, and I want to leap to my own defense, but if that's how she'd like to rewrite history, then so be it. I don't give a flying fuck.

"I'd like to stay until tomorrow. My flight is at noon," she states.

"I'll have someone collect you at ten to take you to the airport."

"Thank you."

"You're at Susannah's?"

"Yes."

"Okay."

Leila turns to Ana. "Good-bye, Mrs. Grey. Thank you for seeing me."

Ana rises and holds out her hand, and they shake. "Um, good-bye. Good luck," she says.

Leila nods with a faint, sincere smile and turns to me. "Good-bye, Christian."

"Good-bye, Leila. Dr. Flynn, remember."

"Yes, Sir."

I open the door for her to leave, but she pauses in front of me. "I'm glad you're happy. You deserve to be," she says, and then she's out the door. I watch her leave, baffled by our exchange.

What the hell was that all about?

I close the door and, taking a deep breath, turn to face my wife.

"Don't even think about being angry with me," she snarls. "Call Claude Bastille and kick the shit out of him, or go see Flynn." Her cheeks pink with her rising anger.

Wow. Attack as the first form of defense.

But that's not what this is about.

"You promised you wouldn't do this."

"Do what?" she spits at me.

"Defy me."

"No, I didn't. I said I'd be more considerate. I told you she was here. I had Prescott search her, and your other little friend, too. Prescott was with me the entire time. Now you've fired the poor woman, when she was only doing what I asked." Ana is on a roll. "I told you not to worry, yet here you are. I don't remember receiving your papal bull decreeing that I couldn't see Leila. I didn't know that my visitors were subject to a proscribed list." She's mad, really mad, her voice rising and her eyes flashing with righteous indignation.

Impressive, Mrs. Grey.

I marvel at how she always stands up to me and remains as disarming as ever. And she's funny, sucking the venom of the room with her choice of words. "Papal bull?" I ask, because it's the most amusing and disrespectful thing I've heard in a while, and I hope to raise a smile.

Ana remains stony-faced.

Shit. "What?" I ask, exasperated. I had hoped that we could move on, now that she's got everything off her chest.

"You. Why were you so callous toward her?"

What? I wasn't callous, I was mad. She shouldn't be here.

Hell.

Sighing, I lean against the table. "Anastasia, you don't understand. Leila, Susannah—all of them—they were a pleasant, diverting pastime. But that's all. You are the center of my universe. And the last time you two were in a room together, she had you at gunpoint. I don't want her anywhere near you."

"But, Christian, she was ill."

"I know that, and I know she's better now, but I'm not giving her the benefit of the doubt anymore. What she did was unforgivable."

"But you've just played right into her hands. She wanted to see you again, and she knew you'd come running if she came to see me."

I shrug. "I don't want you tainted with my old life."

Ana frowns. "Christian, you are who you are because of your old life, your new life, whatever. What touches you touches me. I accepted that when I agreed to marry you, because I love you."

Where is she going with this?

Her expression is raw, full of compassion.

But this time it's not for me, but for Leila.

Who knew Leila would find an advocate in my wife?

"She didn't hurt me. She loves you, too."

"I don't give a fuck."

And no, she doesn't love me. How could she?

Leila knows only too well what I'm capable of...

Ana stares at me as if she's seeing me for the first time.

Oh, baby. I told you a long time ago. Fifty Shades.

"Why are you championing her cause all of a sudden?" I ask, baffled.

"Look, Christian, I don't think Leila and I will be swapping recipes and knitting patterns anytime soon. But I didn't think you'd be so heartless to her."

"I told you once, I don't have a heart," I mutter, and even to my own ears I sound petulant.

She rolls her eyes. "That's just not true, Christian. You're being ridiculous. You do care about her. You wouldn't be paying for art classes and the rest of that stuff if you didn't."

I remember Leila, broken and filthy as I bathed her in Ana's old apartment and how I felt seeing her like that.

Hell. I've had enough of this shit.

"This discussion is over. Let's go home."

Ana glances at her watch. "It's too early."

"Home!" I insist.

Please. Ana.

"Christian, I'm tired of having the same argument with you." She sounds weary.

What argument?

"You know," she continues, correctly interpreting my frown, "I do something you don't like, and you think of some way to get back at me. Usually involving some of your kinky fuckery, which is either mind-blowing or cruel." She shrugs.

Cruel? Shit.

Yeah, she safe-worded on you, Grey.

Fuck.

"Mind-blowing?" I ask, because I don't want to dwell on *cruel*.

"Usually, yes."

"What was mind-blowing?"

Ana looks exasperated. "You know."

"I can guess." Various erotic memories cloud my imagination. Ana in a spreader bar, shackled to the bed, the cross…in my childhood bedroom…

"Christian, I—" She sounds breathless; distracting her has worked.

"I like to please you." I brush my thumb over her bottom lip.

"You do." Her voice is petal-soft, caressing me. *Everywhere.*

"I know." I whisper in her ear, "It's the one thing I *do* know." When I stand, Ana's eyes are closed. She opens them abruptly and purses her lips, probably in response to my wicked smile.

I want her.

I don't want to argue.

"What was mind-blowing, Anastasia?" I coax her.

"You want the list?"

"There's a list?"

"Well, the handcuffs," she mumbles, and for a moment she looks lost in the memory of our honeymoon tryst.

No. I grab her hand and skim my thumb around her wrist. "I don't want to mark you." My eyes meet hers, imploring her. "Come home."

"I have work to do."

"Home."

Please, Ana. I don't want to fight.

We gaze at each other, our battlefield the space between us as I try desperately to understand what she might be thinking. I know I've angered her, and at the back of my mind I'm concerned that I might be doing exactly what Flynn has warned me against—sabotaging our relationship and killing my own happiness.

I need to know we're okay.

Her pupils widen, growing larger and darkening her eyes. I can't resist her. Raising my hand, I caress her cheek with the back of my fingers. "We could stay here." My voice is hoarse, betraying my desire and my need to reconnect with my wife.

Ana blinks and shakes her head, stepping back. "Christian, I don't want to have sex here. Your mistress has just been in this room."

"She was never my mistress."

Only Elena fits that title.

Don't go there, Grey.

"That's just semantics, Christian." She sounds weary, once more.

"Don't overthink this, Ana. She's history." And I don't know if I'm referring to Leila or Elena, but the same applies to both of them. *They're history.*

Ana sighs, and she regards me as if I'm a complex riddle to solve, her eyes beseeching me, but for what I don't know. Suddenly, her expression changes to one of alarm, and she gasps, and I think she says no.

But she *is* history. "Yes," I implore her, and press my lips to hers, to drive away her doubt.

"Oh, Christian," she whispers, "you scare me sometimes." She grasps my head in her hands and pulls my lips to hers, kissing me.

I'm lost. *Scare her?*

I fold her in my arms and whisper against her lips, "Why?"

"You could turn away from her so easily."

This time I know she's referring to my attitude to Leila. "And you think I might turn away from you, Ana? Why the hell would you think that? What's brought this on?"

"Nothing. Kiss me. Take me home." Her lips find mine once more, but this time there's a desperate edge to her kiss.

What's wrong, Ana?

The thought is fleeting as I surrender to her tongue.

ANA WRITHES BENEATH ME. "Oh, please," she begs.

"All in good time." I have her exactly where I want her, on our bed in Escala, trussed up and available. She groans and pulls on the leather restraints that bind each elbow to each knee. She's completely open to me, and helpless, as I focus my attention and the tip of my tongue on her clitoris. She groans as I tease the potent powerhouse buried in her flesh, feeling it harden under my relentless ministration.

God, I love this.

Her fingers find my hair, tugging it hard.

But I don't stop.

She's trying to straighten her legs. She's close. "Don't come." My words float over her wet flesh. "I will spank you if you come."

She groans and tugs harder.

"Control, Ana. It's all about control." And I double down on my efforts, my tongue continuing to provoke her, bringing her closer and closer. I know this is a losing battle for her, she's so near.

"Ah!" she cries, and her climax spirals through her body. She raises her face to the ceiling and arches her back as she comes.

Yes!

I don't stop until she screams. "Oh, Ana," I chide her, nipping her thigh. "You came." Flipping her onto her front, I smack her hard on her behind, so she cries out.

"Control," I repeat, and grabbing her hips, I drive into her.

She cries out again.

And I still.

Reveling in her.

This is where I want to be.

My happy place.

Leaning forward, I unclip each cuff in turn so she's free, and pull her fully onto my lap, driving deeper inside her.

Ana. I wrap my arm around her and caress her jaw, enjoying the feel of her back against my front.

"Move." I whisper my demand in her ear.

She moans and rises on my lap, then back down.

Too slow.

"Faster," I order.

And she moves. Fast. Faster. Faster still. Taking me with her.

Ah, baby.

This is heaven.

The feel of her.

I ease her head back, kissing her throat as my other hand skims down her body, caressing her skin. From her hip I trail my fingers down to cup her vulva. She whimpers as I brush my fingers against her already-sensitized clitoris. "Yes. Ana. You are mine. Only you."

"Yes," she cries out, and I can't believe she's so close. Her readiness fuels my desire. She tips her head back.

And the first shocks are there. "Come for me," I whisper.

She lets go, and I hold her still while I ride out her orgasm.

"Christian!" she calls, my name tipping me over the edge.

"Oh, Ana, I love you." I groan, and I come, all the tension from earlier spiraling out of my body as I find my release.

WE LIE SPRAWLED TOGETHER, and we're a tangle of limbs and cuffs. I kiss her shoulder and stroke her hair from her face before propping myself up on my elbow. While I knead her backside where I smacked her, I ask, "Does that make the list, Mrs. Grey?"

"Hmm."

"Is that a yes?"

"Hmm." Her lips lift in a glorious smile.

I grin. She's incoherent.

Job done, Grey.

I kiss her shoulder again and she rolls over to face me. "Well?" I ask.

"Yes. It makes the list." Her eyes sparkle with mischief. "But it's a long list."

She makes me feel ten feet tall.

My earlier anger is forgotten.

Thank you, Ana. I kiss her. "Good. Shall we have dinner?"

She nods and her fingers dance over my chest. "I want you to tell me something." Sincere, curious blue eyes meet mine.

"What?"

"Don't get mad."

"What is it, Ana?"

"You *do* care." She says the words with such compassionate sincerity that all the air is sucked from my lungs. "I want you to admit that you care. Because the Christian I know and love would care."

Why does she do this?

From nowhere images of Leila, and Susannah, and the rest of my subs cloud my brain. All that we did. All that they did. For me. All that I did, and do for them.

Leila broken and filthy.

Hell.

That was torture. I wouldn't want her or any of them to experience that. *Ever.*

"Yes. Yes, I care. Happy?"

Ana's eyes soften. "Yes. Very."

I frown. "I can't believe I'm talking to you now, here in our bed, about—"

She places a finger on my lips. "We're not. Let's eat. I'm hungry."

I sigh and shake my head.

This woman confounds me. In every way.

Why is this so important to her?

My sweet, compassionate wife. "You beguile and bewilder me, Mrs. Grey."

"Good." She kisses me, her tongue finding mine, and soon we're lost in each other again.

Friday, September 9, 2011

"Good morning, Mr. Grey." Andrea is bright and chirpy.

A little like me. Married life agrees with her, too, it would seem. "Good morning, Andrea." I give her a quick, sincere smile.

"Coffee?"

"Please. Where's Sarah?"

"On an errand for the meeting this morning. Black?"

"Yes. And let's go through the preparations for today and the weekend."

Sitting down at my desk, I review the documents laid out in front of me. Today we meet the Hwangs from Taiwan to discuss our joint venture with their shipyard. I have their stats, their management structure, details of their suppliers and subcontractors, and a list of their clients. It's impressive, but part of me is still wondering why they would want to partner with a company in the U.S. In fact, this is what has been nagging me throughout our discussions with them. They told us during our recent call that they want to expand throughout the Pacific rim to be less reliant on the domestic and East Asian market. But GEH could be entering a political minefield.

Well, today we get to ask all the difficult questions.

Andrea joins me. She makes a mighty fine cup of coffee. "This is great." I raise my cup to her, and am rewarded with a smile. "Where are you with the travel arrangements for Ana's surprise party?"

"Your family arrives tomorrow. Raymond Steele will be driving in from his fishing trip in Oregon tomorrow. The Gulfstream is due to take off this afternoon for Savannah to collect Mr. and Mrs. Adams. They'll fly into Seattle tomorrow afternoon. I wanted to check that you didn't need hotel reservations for them."

"No, thanks. They'll be staying with us."

"I think that's all with regard to the weekend. I've been liaising with Mrs. Jones."

"Great. Now, the Taiwanese delegation." I check my watch. "They should be here by eleven."

"Everything's in place." Andrea is exuding her usual efficiency. "They're coming from the Fairmont Olympic. In addition to the owners, Mr. and Miss Hwang, and their chief operating officer, Mr. Chen, they're bringing their interpreter; I'm sorry that I don't have his or her name yet. Marco will meet them in reception and escort them to the conference room."

"Odd that they are bringing an interpreter. They all speak fluent English."

Andrea shrugs. "Lunch is booked in your name, at the Four Seasons at one thirty p.m."

"Thanks, Andrea, sounds like everything is in hand."

"Will that be all?"

"For now."

Once she's gone, I turn to my iMac and check my e-mail. The title of Ana's jumps out at me.

From: Anastasia Grey
Subject: The List
Date: September 9 2011 09:33
To: Christian Grey

That's definitely at the top.
:D
A x

Anastasia Grey
Editor, SIP

I laugh out loud and shift in my seat as I remember the spreader bar and how exceptionally accommodating my wife was last night. Then again, she has been every night since Leila intruded on our lives. Thankfully, that drama is over—Leila is home and Flynn has reassured me that she's happily settled back into her life in Connecticut.

Ana is as insatiable as ever.

I am a lucky, lucky man.

From: Christian Grey
Subject: Tell Me Something New
Date: September 9 2011 09:42
To: Anastasia Grey

You've said that for the last three days.
Make your mind up.
Or...we could try something else.
;)

Christian Grey
CEO, Enjoying This Game, Grey Enterprises Holdings, Inc.

Our only source of conflict has been Ana's campaign to rehire Prescott, in spite of the fact that Ana herself said she wasn't certain about her. I've reassured Ana that I'll give Prescott a good reference, but that's it, and for me the matter is closed. I return to the documents in front of me for a reread; I need to be on my game.

That done, I check for any further e-mails from Ana, but there are none. I'm restless for the meeting to start, but with forty-five minutes to go, I need to stretch my legs. Leaping up, I grab my phone and head out of my office.

"Andrea, I'm just going to see Ros. I've got my phone." I wave it in front of her, and notice it needs charging.

Damn. "Can you charge this for me?"

"Yes, Mr. Grey."

With a need to burn off some of my excess energy prior to the meeting, I vault down the stairs to Ros's office.

ROS HAS A REAM of final questions for the Hwangs, and we're discussing tactics when there's a knock on the door. It's Andrea. "Mrs. Grey called you. She wanted to talk to you urgently. I thought you would want to know." She hands me my phone.

"Thank you." Frowning, I step out of Ros's office and dial Ana's number.

"Christian," Ana gasps, breathless and choked.

A frisson runs up my spine. "Christ, Ana. What's wrong?"

"It's Ray—he's been in an accident."

"Shit!"

"I'm on my way to Portland."

"Portland? Please tell me Sawyer is with you."

"Yes, he's driving."

"Where's Ray?"

"At OHSU."

Ros steps out of her office, distracting me. "Christian, they'll be here shortly." My eyes dart to the clock on the wall. It's 10:48.

"Yes, Ros, I know!" The meeting will take at least two hours. *Hell.* I was going to take them to lunch.

Ros and Marco can do it.

"Sorry, baby—I can be there in about three hours. I have business I need to finish here. I'll fly down." Thank God *Charlie Tango* is back in operation. "I have a meeting with some guys over from Taiwan. I can't blow them off. It's a deal we've been hammering out for months. I'll leave as soon as I can."

"Okay," she whispers, her voice small and scared.

A fist tightens around my heart. This is not Ana's usual demeanor. "Oh, baby," I murmur, overwhelmed with the need to drop everything and join her.

She needs me.

But I can't. I have responsibilities here.

Sawyer is with her.

"I'll be okay, Christian. Take your time. Don't rush. I don't want to worry about you, too. Fly safely."

"I will."

"Love you."

"I love you, too, baby. I'll be with you as soon as I can. Keep Luke close."

"Yes, I will."

"I'll see you later."

"Bye." She hangs up.

"Everything okay?" Ros asks.

I shake my head. "No. Ana's dad has had an accident."

"Oh no…"

"He's in OHSU hospital in Portland. She's heading there now. I have to make a quick call." I speed-dial my mother, and by some miracle Grace answers her cell.

"Christian, darling. How lovely to hear from you."

"Mom, Ana's dad has been in an accident."

"Oh no, poor Ray. Is he okay? Where is he?"

"OHSU."

"Is it serious?"

"I don't know. Ana's on her way down there. Unfortunately, I have a meeting here that I need to take before I can join her."

"I see. A friend from Yale works there. I'll make some calls."

"Thanks, Mom. I've got to go."

I call Andrea, hoping that she's back at her desk.

"Mr. Grey."

"Ana's dad has been in an accident. I'll need Stephan to fly with me to Portland in *Charlie Tango* after my meeting. Can you ask Beighley to fly the Gulfstream to Savannah? We'll need to find a second pilot to go with her. And liaise with Taylor—I need him to come with me."

"Yes, sir. I'll get right on it." I hang up. Ros is gathering her papers from her desk. "You'll have to entertain the Hwangs after this meeting. Take them to lunch. I have a table booked at the Four Seasons. I'll have to join Ana."

"Of course. I'll ask Marco to join me."

"We'd better head up."

RYAN DRIVES TAYLOR AND me to the helipad in downtown Seattle. It was Andrea's idea that we leave from here, rather than Boeing Field, to save time. The meeting with the Hwangs has been a huge success. I've acquired a shipyard, and the settlement we've reached appears to be satisfactory to all parties, but I've left Ros and Marco to iron out the details. Ros and I have an invitation to visit the shipyard next week, but right now I need to support my wife and find out about my father-in-law's condition.

As Ryan parks the Audi outside the building, I'm reminded of the last time I used this helipad—to take Ana to José's exhibition in Portland. All part of my campaign to win her back.

I allow myself a brief moment of triumph.

I succeeded.

She's now my wife.

Who would have thought, Grey?

Taylor and I make our way to the elevator, which whisks us up to the rooftop helipad. The doors slide open and there she is: *Charlie Tango.*

My pride and joy restored to her former glory.

I left her burnt out and abandoned in a clearing in a wild and desolate corner of Gifford National Forest. Now she has two new engines, and after a thorough cleanup at Eurocopter, she stands tall and proud, gleaming like new in the early afternoon sun. It's a joy to see her. Stephan climbs out of the cockpit, beaming, as we walk toward him. "She's handling just like she used to, and she's looking good, too," he says by way of a greeting.

"I can't wait to take her up." In spite of my anxiety about Ana, I can barely contain my excitement to be at *Charlie Tango*'s controls again.

"Thought you'd say that." With a grin, he holds the pilot's door open, then takes the seat beside me while Taylor hops into the back. Once I've buckled up, I don my headphones and run through my preflight checks.

"Have I forgotten anything?" I ask Stephan.

"No, sir. Well remembered."

I check the rotor rpm then radio the tower.

"Okay, guys. You ready?"

"Copy," Taylor says over his headset, and Stephan gives me a thumbs-up. Gently, I ease back the collective, and *Charlie Tango* rises like a phoenix into the Seattle sunshine. It's a rush and a relief, knowing I'll be with my wife in just over an hour.

The flight to Oregon is a welcome diversion from my worries about Ana and her dad. *Charlie Tango* is as responsive, smooth, and elegant as she's always been. She lands with her usual grace on the Portland helipad.

"You'll keep her warm?" I ask Stephan.

"With pleasure, sir." He's agreed to stand by for further instructions, as I don't know when, or if, we'll be heading home today.

Outside the building, there's a Suburban waiting for us. The rental agent hands the keys to Taylor, and we set off for the hospital. While he drives, I fish out my phone to contact Ana, but there's a missed call and voice mail from my mother. I call Grace, rather than listen to her message, but she doesn't pick up. *Hell.* I hang up and listen to her voice mail. Her tone is crisp and concise, her doctor's voice. "Christian, I don't have much information on your father-in-law. I know he's in the OR and has been there for some time. He's in serious condition. We'll find out more when they're finished with him. I don't have a time yet. If you're at the hospital, call me."

I scowl at my phone. My mother's message is disturbing; *serious* does not sound good. "Taylor, we may have to stay overnight. Can you pick up some essentials for Ana and me?"

"Toiletries?"

"Yes. And a change of clothes or two. For both of us. Casual attire. Please."

"Yes, sir."

I call Andrea and she picks up on the first ring. "Mr. Grey."

"Andrea, we may need to stay in Portland tonight. Check that The Heathman has a suite."

"Will do. Shall I courier your laptop to you?"

"I have it. Taylor picked it up."

Shit. It's Ana's birthday tomorrow.

"Call Mrs. Jones. I'm not sure we'll be able to make dinner tomorrow. I'll update her later."

"Shall I turn the Gulfstream around?"

"No. Let them land in Savannah. Ana may want her mother here. I'll come back to you when I know more." I hang up.

What to do?

Taylor catches my eye.

"What is it?" I ask.

"Sir, I could drop you at the hospital. Shop for your essentials. Leave the shopping bags at your hotel, then fly back to Seattle with

Stephan and bring the R8 down for Mrs. Grey so it's here tomorrow morning."

"That's an idea. Let's see how her father is before we do anything. But yes, that's a good plan. You could also collect a few items for me, too."

"Yes, sir."

Perhaps we'll have to reschedule Ana's birthday celebrations to later in the month. While I chew on that, I remember that Mia starts her new job today. I send her a quick good-luck text as Taylor pulls up outside the main OHSU building.

I gird my loins. In spite of my mother's chosen profession, I loathe hospitals.

IN THE ELEVATOR, on my way to the OR floor, my phone buzzes with a text from Andrea. She's reserved my usual suite at The Heathman. A nurse at the reception desk on the third floor directs me to the waiting room. Taking a deep breath, I open the door. Inside the stark, utilitarian room I find Ana seated on a plastic chair. Pale, scared, and swamped in a man's leather jacket, she's clutching José Rodriguez's hand. His father sits in a wheelchair beside him.

"Christian," she cries. The relief and hope on her face as she leaps up to greet me extinguish the brief flash of jealousy that flared in my gut. When she's in my arms, I close my eyes and hold her close. She smells of apples and orchards and Ana, and the unmistakable aroma of cheap cologne and sweaty nights out.

José's jacket?

I wrinkle my nose and hope no one notices. José stands, but José Rodriguez senior remains in the wheelchair, looking pretty banged up.

Shit. He must have been in the accident, too.

"Any news?" I direct my question at Ana.

She shakes her head.

"José." I nod a greeting while keeping hold of my wife. Sawyer is seated in the corner. He acknowledges me with a quick nod; I'm grateful that he's been here with Ana.

"Christian, this is my father, José Senior," José says.

"Mr. Rodriguez—we met at the wedding. You were in the accident, too?" Gently, I shake his free hand.

"We all were," José replies. "We were driving to Astoria for a day's fishing." His face hardens, and his fresh-faced boyishness disappears, revealing the menacing man beneath. "But we were hit by a drunk driver on the way. He totaled my dad's car. Miraculously, I was unharmed. My dad got beat up, but Ray—" He stops and swallows to collect himself, then, with a swift, anxious glance at Ana, continues, "He was bad. He was airlifted from Astoria community hospital to here."

I tighten my arm around Ana.

"After they patched my father up, we followed," he finishes, and I raise my brows in surprise. Mr. Rodriguez Senior has a leg and an arm in casts, and one side of his face is bruised. He doesn't look fit to travel.

"Yeah." José shakes his head in exasperation, as if he can read my mind. "My dad insisted."

"Are you both well enough to be here?" I ask.

"We don't want to be anywhere else." Mr. Rodriguez's face contorts; he looks and sounds like he's in pain.

Maybe they should go home.

But I don't press them; they're here for Ray. Taking Ana's hand, I guide her back to one of the seats and sit down beside her. "Have you eaten?"

She shakes her head.

"Are you hungry?"

She shakes her head.

"But you're cold?" I ask, catching another whiff of José's jacket. She nods and wraps the offending garment more snugly around her. The door opens and a man in scrubs enters—dark-haired, tall, and with a weary air of battle fatigue; his expression is grave.

Shit.

Ana stumbles to her feet, and I stand quickly to steady her. All eyes in the room are on the young doctor.

"Ray Steele," Ana says with quiet trepidation.

"You're his next of kin?" the doctor asks.

"I'm his daughter, Ana."

"Miss Steele—"

"Mrs. Grey," I mutter, correcting him.

"My apologies," the doctor stammers. "I'm Dr. Crowe. Your father is stable, but in critical condition."

Ana crumples in my arms as the doctor delivers each blow about Ray's condition. "He suffered severe internal injuries, principally to his diaphragm, but we've managed to repair them, and we were able to save his spleen. Unfortunately, he suffered a cardiac arrest during the operation because of blood loss. We managed to get his heart going again, but this remains a concern."

Jesus!

"However," Dr. Crowe continues, "our gravest concern is that he suffered severe contusions to the head, and the MRI shows that he has swelling in his brain. We've induced a coma to keep him quiet and still while we monitor the brain swelling."

Ana gasps, sagging against me some more.

"It's standard procedure in these cases. For now, we just have to wait and see."

"And what's the prognosis?" I ask, trying to mask the distress in my voice.

"Mr. Grey, it's difficult to say at the moment. It's possible he could make a complete recovery, but that's in God's hands now."

"How long will you keep him in a coma?"

"That depends on how his brain responds. Usually seventy-two to ninety-six hours."

"Can I see him?" Ana's breathless with anxiety.

"Yes, you should be able to see him in about half an hour. He's been taken to the ICU on the sixth floor."

"Thank you, Doctor."

Dr. Crowe nods a good-bye and leaves us.

"Well, he's alive," Ana whispers, trying to sound hopeful, but tears pool in her eyes and spill down her ashen face.

No. Ana, baby. "Sit down," I tell her, easing her back to the seat.

"Papa," José says to his father, "I think we should go. You need to rest. We won't know anything for a while. We can come back this evening, after you've rested. That's okay, isn't it, Ana?" José turns to Ana.

"Of course," she responds.

"Are you staying in Portland?" I ask, and José nods. "Do you need a ride home?"

José frowns. "I was going to order a cab."

"Luke can take you."

Sawyer stands, while José looks confused.

"Luke Sawyer," Ana says.

"Oh. Sure. Yeah, we'd appreciate it. Thanks, Christian."

Ana offers Mr. Rodriguez a careful hug, and a less careful one to José. He whispers in her ear, but I'm close enough to hear. "Stay strong, Ana. He's a fit and healthy man. The odds are in his favor."

"I hope so," she replies, her voice distressingly small. Her words slice through me like a scythe, because there's nothing I can do to help. She shrugs off José's pungent jacket and hands it back to him.

Thank God.

"Keep it, if you're still cold," he offers.

"No, I'm okay. Thanks," she says, and I take her hand. "If there's any change, I'll let you know right away."

José gives her a faint smile and wheels his father toward the door that Sawyer props open. Mr. Rodriguez raises his hand, and José stops. "He'll be in my prayers, Ana." The older man's voice cracks. "It's been so good to reconnect with him after all these years. He's become a good friend."

"I know," Ana says, her voice strained with emotion.

The three of them exit, and we're finally alone. I caress her cheek. "You're pale. Come here." Taking a seat, I gather her onto my lap, folding my arms around her. She burrows into my chest, and I kiss her hair.

We sit.

Together.

Each of us with our own thoughts.

What do I say to comfort her?

I have no idea. I'm helpless and I hate it.

Taking her hand, I offer her what I hope is a reassuring squeeze.

Ray is a strong man. He'll pull through; he's got to.

"How was *Charlie Tango*?" she asks eventually, and I marvel that even in this situation she's thinking of me. I think my spontaneous grin is answer enough.

My EC135 is back. And what a joy she was to fly. "Oh, she was yar."

She smiles. "Yar?"

"It's a line from *The Philadelphia Story.* Grace's favorite film."

"I don't know it."

"I think I have it on Blu-Ray at home. We can watch it and make out." Brushing my lips against her hair, I inhale her fragrance, sweeter now that José's jacket has left with him. "Can I persuade you to eat something?"

"Not now. I want to see Ray first."

I don't push her.

"How were the Taiwanese?" she asks, and I think she's steering the conversation to stop me from brooding about food.

"Amenable."

"Amenable how?"

"They let me buy their shipyard for less than the price I was willing to pay."

"That's good?"

"Yes. That's good."

"But I thought you had a shipyard over here."

"I do. We're going to use that to do the fitting-out. Build the hulls in the Far East. It's cheaper."

"What about the workforce at the shipyard here?"

Good question, Mrs. Grey.

"We'll redeploy. We should be able to keep redundancies to a minimum."

I hope.

I kiss her once more. "Shall we check on Ray?"

RAYMOND STEELE IS IN the last bed in the ICU ward. It's a shock to see him out cold and hooked up to a range of high-tech medical equipment. This man intimidates me more than anyone I know, but right now, he looks vulnerable and sick. *Real sick.* He's in an induced coma and on a ventilator; his leg is in plaster and his chest is wrapped in a surgical dressing. His modesty's protected by a thin blanket.

Jesus. Ana is stunned when she sees him and blinks back tears of shock.

Her anguish is hard to witness.

What do I do? What do I say?

I can't make this better for her.

A nurse is checking his various monitors. Her badge identifies her as KELLIE RN.

"Can I touch him?" Ana asks, and she reaches for Ray's hand without waiting for a response.

"Yes," Kellie says kindly. Standing at the end of the bed, I watch as Ana carefully covers Ray's hand with hers. Abruptly, she sinks into the chair beside the bed, lays her head on his arm, and starts sobbing.

Oh no.

I move quickly to comfort her.

"Oh, Daddy. Please get better," she pleads quietly. "Please."

Feeling utterly fucking powerless, I place my hand on her shoulder and clasp it tightly, trying to offer her some reassurance. "All Mr. Steele's vitals are good," Kellie says quietly.

"Thank you," I mutter, because I don't know what else to say.

"Can he hear me?" Ana asks.

"He's in a deep sleep. But who knows?"

"Can I sit for a while?"

"Sure thing." Kellie gives Ana a warm smile.

Ana is where she needs to be right now, and I should make arrangements for us to stay in Portland. There's no way we're going home tonight. I squeeze her shoulder once more and she raises her eyes to mine. "I need to make a call." I drop a kiss on her head. "I'll be outside. I'll give you some alone time with your dad."

FROM THE SIXTH FLOOR waiting room I call my mother. This time she answers, and I update her on Raymond Steele's condition.

She takes a deep breath. "It sounds critical. I want to come and see him—"

"Mom. You don't—"

"No. Christian. I want to. Ana is family. I have to come down and check on him myself. Carrick and I will drive down."

"I can fly you down."

"What?"

"My helicopter is here, but Taylor is taking it back to Seattle. Stephan can fly you down here."

"That sounds good. Let's do that."

"Okay. I'll let Taylor know, and you can liaise with him."

"I'll do that. Christian, Ray is in good hands."

"Thanks, Mom."

I call Taylor and let him know about my mother.

Then I call Andrea. "Mr. Grey. How's Mr. Steele?"

"He's in serious condition. We'll be here for at least two nights. I'm going to have to do something for Ana's birthday here, if we do anything at all. Maybe a private dinner, if she's up to it. I'd like her family and our friends to attend, too. But we should see how Ray does during the night."

"I can talk to The Heathman and see if they'll accommodate a private dinner."

"Good. Ana needs her mom, so let's bring her and her husband out as planned. Book rooms for them, for my folks and the rest of our guests, and make provisional arrangements to get them here. My mother will be joining us this evening. Please book her into The Heathman tonight."

"Will do."

"Find out José Rodriguez's cell number. I'd like to invite him, too."

"I'll text you."

"Thanks, Andrea." I hang up and call Mrs. Jones to confirm that tomorrow's surprise dinner party at Escala is canceled.

"I hope Mr. Steele makes a swift recovery," Gail says.

"Yes. I do, too. I'm sorry about tomorrow."

"It's no trouble, Mr. Grey. There'll be another time."

"There will. Thanks, Gail." I hang up and return to the ICU. At the nurses' station I give Kellie my cell number and Ana's, with instructions to call us if there's a change in Ray's condition. It's time I took my wife for something to eat.

When I return to Ray's bedside, Ana is talking to him and her tears have ceased. She's composed and her face shines with her love for the man out cold and prostrate beside her.

It's an affecting sight.

And I feel I'm intruding.

But I don't want to go.

Quietly, I take a seat and listen to her soft, sweet voice. She's asking him to come to Aspen, where I'll take him fishing. Her words tug at my heart. Ana is my family now, like my mother said, and by extension, so is Ray. I see us side by side, casting flies in the Roaring Fork River or up on Snowmass Lake. Ray taciturn. Me relaxed and equally taciturn.

The two of us sharing a beer later.

"Mr. Rodriguez and José will be welcome, too. It's such a beautiful house. There's room for all of you. Please be here to do that, Daddy. Please."

Okay. Ray, José Senior, José, and me fishing together.

Yes. I could do that.

She turns and notices me.

"Hi," I murmur.

"Hi."

"So, I'm going fishing with your dad, Mr. Rodriguez, and José?"

She nods.

"Okay." I smile in agreement. "Let's go eat. Let him sleep." Ana frowns, and I know she doesn't want to leave her father. "Ana, he's in a coma. I've given our cell numbers to the nurses here. If there's any change, they'll call us. We'll eat, check in to a hotel, rest up, then come back this evening."

She looks longingly at Ray, then back at me. "Okay," she capitulates.

ANA STANDS IN THE doorway of our suite at The Heathman, surveying the familiar room. She looks shell-shocked.

Or perhaps she's remembering the first time I brought her here, though that's doubtful, as she was blind drunk at the time. I place her briefcase beside one of the sofas. "Home away from home," I murmur.

It was certainly home to me while I was pursuing Miss Steele to be my submissive.

And now here we are.

Husband and wife.

Finally she enters, and stands in the middle of the room, looking lost and forlorn.

Oh, Ana. What can I do? "Do you want a shower? A bath? What do you need, Ana?" I'm desperate to help her in any way I can.

"A bath. I'd like a bath," she mutters.

"Bath. Good. Yes." I stride into the en suite, relieved to have a purpose, and turn on the faucets. The water pours in, and I add some sweet-smelling bath oil, which instantly begins to foam. I slip out of my jacket and take off my tie as my phone buzzes. It's a text from Andrea with José's mobile number. I'll deal with that later.

Ana's in the bedroom, staring at the Nordstrom bags, when I reenter. "I sent Taylor to get some things. Nightwear. You know." She nods but says nothing, her desolation obvious in her blank look. My heart yearns to take her pain away. "Oh, Ana, I've not seen you like this. You're normally so brave and strong."

She returns my gaze, mute and helpless.

Slowly, she crosses her arms, hugging herself as if caught in an icy draft, and I can bear it no more. I fold her into my embrace, offering her the warmth of my body. "Baby, he's alive. His vital signs are good. We just have to be patient." She shudders, and I don't know if she's cold, or if it's the shock of seeing Ray brought so low. "Come." Taking her hand, I lead her into the bathroom, slowly undress her, and help her into the bath. She fastens her hair in a gravity-defying bun, slips beneath the foam, and closes her eyes. I take it as my cue to undress and join her. Climbing in behind her, I settle into the hot water and pull her against my front so we're both lying in the warm, soothing waters, her feet on mine.

As time moves on, Ana relaxes against me.

I let out a sigh of relief and allow myself a moment of respite from the dread that lingers in the pit of my stomach.

I hope to God that Ray will be okay.

Ana will fall apart if he's not.

And I'm powerless to help.

Idly I kiss her hair, grateful that she can take a moment to unwind as she pops the bubbles in the foam.

"You didn't get into the bath with Leila, did you? That time you bathed her?" she asks out of the blue.

"Um, no!"

"I thought so. Good."

Where is this coming from?

Tugging her haphazard topknot of hair, I angle her head so I can see her face. I'm curious. "Why do you ask?"

She shrugs. "Morbid curiosity. I don't know…seeing her this week."

Hopefully you'll never see her again. "I see. Less of the morbid."

"How long are you going to support her?"

"Until she's on her feet. I don't know. Why?"

"Are there others?"

"Others?" I ask.

"Exes who you support."

"There was one, yes. No longer, though."

"Oh?"

"She was studying to be a doctor. She's qualified now and has someone else."

"Another Dominant?"

"Yes."

"Leila says you have two of her paintings," Ana mutters.

"I used to. I didn't really care for them. They had technical merit, but they were too colorful for me. I think Elliot has them. As we know, he has no taste."

Ana giggles, and it's such a wonderful sound that I wrap both arms around her, with a little too much enthusiasm, and the bath water slops over the sides and onto the floor with a satisfying splash.

"That's better." I kiss her temple.

"He's marrying my best friend."

"Then I'd better shut my mouth." I smile down at her and am rewarded with her answering smile. "We should eat."

Ana's face falls, but I'm not going to take no for an answer. I sit her up and clamber out of the bath, grabbing a robe as I do.

"You soak. I'm going to order some room service."

Once I've ordered some food, I rummage through the shopping bags and change into fresh clothes. Taylor has done well. I like the black jeans and a grey cashmere sweater that he's chosen. In the living room, I unpack my laptop and fire it up to check e-mails. While I'm scrolling through them, I have an idea.

From: Christian Grey
Subject: Drunk Driver. Astoria PD.
Date: September 9 2011 17:34
To: Grey, Carrick

Hi, Dad
Mom has probably told you that Raymond Steele was in an accident. His car was hit by a drunk driver this morning in Astoria. Ray is now in the ICU. Can you use your police department contacts to find out any information about the guy who hit him?
Thanks.

Christian Grey
CEO, Grey Enterprises Holdings, Inc.

I saunter back toward the bedroom and lean against the door frame, watching Ana search through the Nordstrom bags.

"Apart from harassing me at Clayton's, have you ever actually gone into a store and just bought stuff?" she asks.

"Harassing you?" I amble over to her, trying to hide my amusement.

She half smiles. "Yes. Harassing me."

"You were flustered, if I recall. And that young boy was all over you. What was his name?"

"Paul."

"One of your many admirers."

She rolls her eyes, and I cannot help my smile. I plant a quick kiss on her lips. "There's my girl." I knew she couldn't be far away. "Get dressed. I don't want you getting cold again."

ANA IS NOT SEDUCED by the food I ordered. She eats two fries and half a crab cake, but that's all. Sighing in disappointment, I watch her leave the table and head back into the bedroom. I know I can't force her to eat, but it worries me when she doesn't. While I debate what to do, I text José to invite him and his father to Ana's surprise birthday dinner if—and it's a big if—it goes ahead tomorrow and if José Senior is up for it, too.

At my laptop I check e-mails. There's one from Carrick.

From: Grey, Carrick
Subject: Drunk Driver. Astoria PD.
Date: September 9 2011 17:42
To: Christian Grey.

Will do. Your mother should be in Portland now.
Dad.

Carrick Grey, Partner
Grey, Krueger, Davis, and Holt LLP

This is good news. My mom should be with Ray by the time we're back at the hospital.

When Ana returns to the living room, she's wearing a light blue hooded sweatshirt, chucks, and jeans. "Ready," she murmurs. Maybe it's because she's sad and anxious, and her face is pale, but she looks younger.

But then, she's still only twenty-one.

"You look so young—and to think you'll be a whole year older tomorrow," I murmur.

Her sad smile tears me in two. "I don't feel much like celebrating. Can we go see Ray now?"

"Sure. I wish you'd eat something. You barely touched your food."

"Christian, please. I'm just not hungry. Maybe after we've seen Ray. I want to wish him good night."

JOSÉ IS LEAVING THE ICU as we arrive. "Ana, Christian, hi."

"Where's your dad?" Ana asks.

"He was too tired to come back. He was in a car accident this morning."

I think that's José's idea of a joke as he forces a grin.

"And his painkillers have kicked in," he continues. "He was out for the count. I had to fight to get in to see Ray, since I'm not next of kin."

"And?" Ana's voice cracks with anxiety.

"He's good, Ana. Same, but all good."

She nods, relieved, I think.

"See you tomorrow, birthday girl."

Hell. Don't blow the surprise!

"Sure. We'll be here," Ana responds.

José glances at me, then pulls her into a brief hug, closing his eyes as he holds her. "Mañana," he whispers.

Dude. Are you still holding a torch for my wife?

He releases her, and we wish him good night, watching him walk down the corridor toward the elevators.

I sigh. "He's still nuts about you."

"No, he's not. And even if he is…" She shrugs. She doesn't care. "Well done," she says.

What?

"For not frothing at the mouth," she clarifies, her eyes sparkling with amusement.

Even now, she's making fun of me. "I've never frothed!" I try to sound offended, but her lips twitch in a slight smile, which was my intention. "Let's see your dad. I have a surprise for you."

"Surprise?"

"Come." I take her hand.

My mother is standing at the end of Ray's bed, her head bowed, as she listens to Dr. Crowe and a woman dressed in scrubs. Grace perks up when she sees us.

"Christian." She kisses my cheek, then hugs my wife. "Ana. How are you holding up?"

"I'm finc. It's my father I'm worried about."

"He's in good hands. Dr. Sluder is an expert in her field. We trained together at Yale."

"Mrs. Grey." Dr. Sluder shakes Ana's hand. She has a soft southern accent, her words sounding like a lullaby. "As the lead physician for your father, I'm pleased to tell you that all is on track. His vital signs are stable and strong. We have every faith that he'll make a complete recovery. The brain swelling has stopped and shows signs of decreasing. This is very encouraging after such a short time."

"That's good news," Ana says, a little color returning to her cheeks.

"It is, Mrs. Grey. We're taking real good care of him. Great to see you again, Grace."

"Likewise, Lorraina."

"Dr. Crowe, let's leave these good people to visit with Mr. Steele." Crowe follows Dr. Sluder out of the ward.

Ana looks down at Ray, who is still sleeping peacefully. Grace takes her hand. "Ana, sweetheart, sit with him. Talk to him. It's all good. I'll visit with Christian in the waiting room."

"HOW'S SHE DOING?" GRACE asks.

"It's hard to tell. She's bearing up, but I know she's extremely anxious. She's normally so strong."

"It must be a shock to her, darling. Thank heavens you're here with her."

"Thank you for coming, Mom. What you said was really reassuring, and I'm sure it made a huge difference to Ana."

Grace smiles at me. "You love her so."

"I do."

"What will you do for her birthday tomorrow?"

"I'm undecided, but I thought we might go ahead and have a low-key celebration here."

"I think that's a good idea. I'll stay in Portland tonight. It's not often I get some time to myself."

"Andrea has booked a room for you and dad at The Heathman."

She smiles. "Christian, you're so capable. You think of everything."

Her words spread like warm summer sunshine through my body.

I STRIP OUT OF my white T-shirt, and Ana grabs it and slips it over her head before climbing into bed.

"You seem brighter." I don my pajamas, pleased that Ana wants to wear my T-shirt.

"Yes. I think talking to Dr. Sluder and your mom made a big difference. Did you ask Grace to come here?"

Sliding into bed, I pull her into my arms, her back to my front; it's the best position to spoon with my girl. "No. She wanted to come and check on your dad herself."

"How did she know?"

"I called her this morning."

Ana sighs.

"Baby, you're exhausted. You should sleep."

"Hmm," she mumbles, then turns her head to look at me, frowning.

What?

She turns over and curls herself around me, her warmth permeating my skin as I stroke her hair. Whatever she was thinking about, it seems to have gone.

"Promise me something," I ask.

"Hmm?"

"Promise me you'll eat something tomorrow. I can just about tolerate you wearing another man's jacket without frothing at the mouth, but, Ana, you must eat. Please."

"Hmm," she grunts in agreement and I kiss her hair. "Thank you for being here," she mumbles, and kisses my chest.

"Where else would I be? I want to be wherever you are, Ana."

Always.

You are my wife. My family now.

And family comes first.

I stare up at the ceiling, remembering the first time we slept together in this room.

So long ago. And yet, not so long ago.

It was a revelation.

Sleeping with someone.

Sleeping with her.

"Being here makes me think of how far we've come. And the night I first slept with you." I whisper, "What a night that was. I watched you for hours. You were just…yar."

I sense Ana's tired smile against my chest.

Oh, baby.

"Sleep," I murmur, and it's not a request.

Saturday, September 10, 2011

> Grandpa Theodore hands me an apple. It's bright red. And tastes sweet; of home and long rich summers when the days went on forever. There's a light breeze on my face. It's cooling in the sunshine. We stand eye to eye in the orchard. His face sun-worn and weather-beaten, the etched lines in his skin telling a thousand stories. He reaches up, and a tremor runs through his hand. He's not as steady as he once was…*Grandpa!* He grasps my shoulder, his eyes hooded but still shining with wisdom and love… For me. I see it now. *Remember how we made the sweet apples when you were a boy?* I grin. They're still sweet. The trees are still giving. He smiles, his skin crinkling around his eyes. *Boy, you were an odd one. Wouldn't talk. Awful shy. Now look at you. Master of your own universe. I'm proud of you, son. You done good.* The warmth of his words matches the warmth of the sun. Behind him, Mom, Dad, Elliot, Mia, and Ana are walking through the long, lush grass to join us with a blanket and a picnic basket. Ana laughs at something Mia says. She tips her head back, her hair free and catching the golden light. My mom joins in. Laughing, too. *It's all about family, boy. Always. Family first.* Ana turns and beams at me. The sunshine of her smile lighting me from within. My light. My love. My family. *Ana.*

I wake, but before I open my eyes, I savor my contentment. All is right in the world, everything is as it should be, and I know I'm enjoying the remnants of a now-forgotten dream.

I open my eyes.

Where am I?

The Heathman.

Shit—Ray.

Grim reality intrudes, but I turn my head and am comforted to see Ana curled up beside me, still slumbering. From the light filtering through the curtains I know it's early. I lie still for a moment, making a mental list of all that I need to do today.

It's her birthday.

And Ray is lying injured in the hospital.

It will be a delicate balancing act, to celebrate and commiserate all at once with her.

I slip out of bed carefully.

Don't wake the wife!

When I'm showered and dressed, I move quietly into the living room and let Ana sleep. I have to make a decision on whether to proceed with Ana's birthday dinner, so my first task of the day is to call the ICU. I speak to one of Ray's nurses, who reports that he's spent a comfortable night and that his vitals are good. She then hands me over to the attending physician, who explains that all is as it should be and we should remain optimistic. At this encouraging news, and Dr. Sluder's report yesterday, I decide to go ahead with the dinner.

In the meantime, I need her gifts—both of which are in Taylor's hands. I check my watch—7:35 a.m.—and text Taylor, who's staying somewhere in the hotel.

Good morning.
Do you have Ana's present?

TAYLOR
Yes, sir.
Shall I bring the box up?

Please. She's still asleep!

A few moments later there's a gentle tap on the door, and Taylor is his usual smart-suited self on the other side. "Hello," I whisper, mindful of sleeping beauty. I prop the door open with my foot and join Taylor in the corridor.

"Good morning," he says, whispering, too. "Here." He places a beautifully wrapped package, all pale pink paper and satin ribbons, in my palm.

"Nice wrapping. Your handiwork?" I raise a brow, and Taylor flushes.

"For Mrs. Grey," he mutters, and I know this is reason enough. "Here's the card that came with the box."

"Thanks. I'm taking a gamble and going ahead with the small dinner party for Ana. We'll need to coordinate the arrival of our guests today."

"Andrea has been keeping me up-to-date, and Sawyer is here. Between the two of us I think we've got this," he says.

"And we'll have the new car, so Ana and I won't need ferrying around."

"I took the liberty of bringing both keys." He holds up the R8 key. "The spare is with the valet."

"Smart thinking." I slip the key into my pocket. "I think we'll be at least an hour. I'll text you when we're ready to leave so you can bring the Audi around to the front."

"I may not get a signal in the garage. I'll liaise with the concierge and he can call me at the valet station."

"Okay. I'll give him a sign when we're in the foyer. How was she?"

"The R8?"

I nod, and his broad grin tells me all I need to know.

"Great." I grin back. "I'll see you later."

He turns on his heel and I smile at his departing figure. Have I ever had a whispered conversation in a hotel corridor before? With Taylor? Ex-Marine? I shake my head at the ridiculousness of the two of us, and step back inside the suite.

When I check on Ana, she's still out for the count. I'm not surprised; she must be shattered from yesterday. I have time to e-mail Andrea.

From: Christian Grey
Subject: Ana's Birthday Dinner
Date: September 10 2011 07:45
To: Andrea Parker

Good morning, Andrea.
I want to go ahead with the surprise dinner for Ana.

Please confirm with the hotel and organize a cake (chocolate!).
Keep me informed about the travel arrangements for everyone.
Sawyer and Taylor are here so will be able to do airport pickups.
Coordinate with them.
Thanks.

Christian Grey
CEO, Grey Enterprises Holdings, Inc.

What else do I need to do?

Sitting down at the desk with Ana's gift in my hand, I stare at the blank card. Fortunately, I know exactly what I want to say.

For all our firsts on your first birthday
as my beloved wife.
I love you.
C x

I slide the card into its envelope and turn to my laptop. Ana will want something a little dressier for dinner, and bearing in mind what she said yesterday, I'd rather pick a dress for her myself than send Taylor. I check out the Nordstrom website and discover that the local store has a "buy and pick up" service. And it's two blocks from The Heathman.

Perfect.

I start browsing.

Twenty minutes later I've purchased everything Ana will need; I hope she likes my choices. I text Taylor to let him know, and he texts me back that he'll send Luke to Nordstrom when we're out visiting Ray.

Time to wake Ana.

She stirs as I sit down on the edge of the bed, and opens her eyes, blinking in the morning light. For a moment she looks relaxed and well rested, but abruptly her expression changes. "Shit! Daddy!" she exclaims in alarm.

"Hey." I stroke her cheek, so that she looks directly up at me. "I called the ICU this morning. Ray had a good night. It's all good." She thanks me as she sits up, looking relieved. Leaning in, I kiss her forehead and, closing my eyes, inhale her scent.

Sleep and Ana.

Delectable.

"Good morning, Ana." I kiss her temple.

"Hi."

"Hi. I want to wish you happy birthday. Is that okay?"

Her smile is uncertain, but she caresses my cheek, her eyes bright with sincerity. "Yes, of course. Thank you. For everything."

"Everything?"

"Everything," she says with conviction.

Why is she thanking me? It's bewildering. But I'm anxious to give her my gift, so I ignore the feeling. "Here."

Ana's eyes dart to mine, shining with excitement as she takes the package and opens the card. Her expression softens as she reads it. "I love you, too."

I grin. "Open it."

Returning my smile, she unravels the ribbon and gently removes the wrapping paper, revealing the Cartier leather box. Her eyes widen when she opens it to find a white-gold bracelet with charms that represent our firsts we've experienced together: a helicopter, a catamaran, a glider, a London black cab, the Eiffel Tower, a bed. Her forehead creases as she examines the sugar cone, and she glances up at me with a bemused expression.

"Vanilla?" I offer with a sheepish shrug.

She laughs. "Christian, this is beautiful. Thank you. It's yar." Her fingers fondle the small heart on the bracelet. It's a locket: I thought it appropriate, as I've never given anyone my heart before. Ana's been the one to unlock it, walk right in, and make herself at home there.

Sappy, Grey. "You can put a picture or whatever in that."

"A picture of you." She peers at me through her lashes. "Always in my heart."

She makes me feel ten feet tall.

Her fingertips brush over the C and A letter charms that signify the two of us, then over the white-gold key. She looks up again, a question burning in her bright blue eyes.

"To my heart and soul," I whisper. She lets out a strangled cry and launches herself at me, taking me by surprise as she throws her arms around my neck. I cradle her in my lap.

"It's such a thoughtful present. I love it. Thank you." Her voice breaks on the last word.

Oh, baby. I tighten my arms around her.

"I don't know what I'd do without you," she says through her tears.

I swallow, trying to digest her words and ignore the pang deep in my chest. "Please don't cry." My voice is husky with emotion. I love that she needs me.

She sniffs. "I'm sorry. I'm just so happy and sad and anxious at the same time. It's bittersweet."

"Hey." I tip her head back and press my lips to hers. "I understand."

"I know," she says with a sad smile.

"I wish we were in happier circumstances, and at home. But we're here." I give her an apologetic hug. Neither of us could have foreseen this situation. "Come, up you go. After breakfast, we'll check on Ray."

"Okay." Her smile is a little cheerier when I leave her so she can dress.

In the living room I order granola, yogurt, and berries for Ana, an omelet for me.

IT'S GRATIFYING TO SEE that Ana's appetite has returned. She wolfs down her breakfast, a woman on a mission, but I don't comment. It's her birthday and I want her happy.

Actually, I want her happy pretty much all the time.

"Thank you for ordering my favorite breakfast."

"It's your birthday. And you have to stop thanking me."

"I just want you to know that I appreciate it."

"Anastasia, it's what I do."

I want to take care of you. I've told you more than once.

She smiles. "Yes, it is."

Once she's finished her breakfast, I ask as nonchalantly as possible if we should go. I'm excited to give her the car.

"I'll just brush my teeth."

I smirk. "Okay."

The little *v* forms between her brows as she frowns—I think she suspects something's afoot—but she says nothing and heads to the bathroom. I text Taylor to let him know that we're leaving imminently.

As we walk to the elevators, I notice that Ana is wearing her new charm bracelet. Grasping her hand, I kiss her knuckles. My thumb grazes the helicopter charm. "You like?"

"More than like. I love it. Very much. Like you."

I kiss her fingers once more while we wait for the elevator.

The elevator.

Where it all started. Where I lost control.

Ceded control, Grey.

Yes. She's had you on a tight leash since you met her.

Ana's eyes flit to mine as we enter.

Is she thinking what I'm thinking? "Don't," I whisper, as I push the button for the lobby and the doors slide shut.

"Don't what?" She peeks at me through her lashes, coy and provocative at once.

"Look at me like that."

"Fuck the paperwork," she says, with a wide grin.

I laugh and tug her into my arms and tilt her face to mine. "Someday, I'll rent this elevator for a whole afternoon."

"Just the afternoon?" She raises an eyebrow, and it's a challenge.

"Mrs. Grey, you're greedy."

"When it comes to you, I am."

"I'm very glad to hear it." I plant a tender kiss on her lips, but as I pull away, Ana's fingers curl around the nape of my neck, pulling my mouth to hers. Her tongue is insistent, demanding access, and she pushes me against the wall, pressing her body against mine. I kiss her back as desire flares like a comet inside me.

What I thought would be a courtly, respectful expression of affection becomes darker, needier, hotter.

More.

So much more.

Her tongue is relentless, mating with mine.

Fuck.

I want her. Here. In this elevator.

Again.

We kiss. Tongues. Lips. Hands. All playing a role.

My fingers tightening in her hair while her hands caress my face. "Ana," I breathe, fighting my desire.

"I love you, Christian Grey." She's breathy and restless, her eyes full of promise. "Don't forget that." The elevator stops, the doors open, and she puts some space between us.

Hell.

My blood is running fast and thick through my body.

"Let's go see your father before I decide to rent this today." I kiss her quickly and, taking her hand, head out into the lobby. I'm grateful that I'm wearing my jacket.

The concierge sees us, and I give him a nod. Ana notices our exchange, but I give my girl my patented I-so-own-you-and-I've-got-a-surprise-for-you smile, and she frowns. "Where's Taylor?" she asks.

"We'll see him shortly."

"Sawyer?"

"Running errands."

We head outside and stop on the wide sidewalk. It's a beautiful late-summer day; the trees on Broadway are in full leaf, but there's a hint of the coming fall in the air. There's no sign of Taylor. Ana looks up and down the street, following my lead. "What is it?" she asks. I lift my shoulders, trying for nonchalance, not wanting to give the game away.

Then I hear it: the growl of the R8's throaty engine. Taylor steers the white, pristine vehicle that is Ana's brand-new Audi to a stop in front of us.

Ana takes a step back, and in stunned disbelief looks from the car to me.

Okay, last time I tried to give her a car, it didn't go so well.

This could go either way.

You said it, Ana. *You can buy me one for my birthday. A white one.*

"Happy birthday," I murmur, and from my pocket I produce the key.

Her mouth drops open. "You are completely over the top." Each word is a quiet staccato, then she turns to admire the marvel of engineering parked at the curb. Her consternation is short-lived; her face lights up and she jumps up and down on the spot. She turns and barrels into my waiting arms, and I swing her around, delighted at her reaction.

"You have more money than sense!" she cries. "I love it! Thank you."

I dip her low, surprising her, so she gasps and grips my biceps. "Anything for you, Mrs. Grey." I kiss her. "Come. Let's go see your dad."

"Yes!" she exclaims. "And I get to drive?"

Smiling down at her, and against my better judgment, I acquiesce. "Of course. It's yours." I pull her to her feet, and she dances to the driver's door, which Taylor is holding open for her.

"Happy birthday, Mrs. Grey." He beams.

"Thank you, Taylor." She hugs him while I roll my eyes and climb into the passenger seat. Ana clambers in beside me and slides her hands around the steering wheel, grinning with glee, as Taylor closes her door.

"Drive safe, Mrs. Grey," he says, his affection obvious despite the gruff tone. For some unfathomable reason it makes me smile.

"Will do," Ana replies, buzzing with excitement. She puts the key in the ignition, and I tense beside her.

I hate being driven.

Except by Taylor.

But she knows this.

"Take it easy," I caution. "Nobody chasing us now." She turns the key, and the R8 roars to life. Ana quickly adjusts the side and rearview mirrors, puts the car in drive, and pulls out into the street at a harrowing speed.

"Whoa!" I cry out, clutching my seat.

"What?"

"I don't want you in the ICU beside your father. Slow down," I yell, wondering if the R8 was a good idea. She slows immediately.

"Better?" She gives me a dazzling smile.

"Much," I mutter, grateful that we're both still alive. "Take it easy, Ana."

SEVEN MINUTES LATER WE'RE in the hospital parking lot, and I've aged at least ten years with each minute of the journey. My pulse must be at 180 bpm; being driven by my wife is not for the faint of heart. "Ana, you have to slow down. Don't make me regret buying you this." I glare at her as she turns off the ignition. "Your dad is upstairs because he was involved in a car accident."

"You're right," she whispers, reaching over and clasping my hand. "I'll behave."

I want to say more, but I don't. It's her birthday and her dad's in the ICU.

And you bought her the car, Grey.

"Okay. Good. Let's go."

WHILE ANA IS VISITING with Ray, I hole up in the waiting room and make some calls. First, Andrea.

"Mr. Grey. Good morning."

"Good morning. What news?"

"Everyone is lined up to come to Portland. I'm liaising with Stephan later this morning. I'm still waiting to hear from The Heathman, and if they can't source a cake, I've found a bakery in Portland that can do it today."

"Good work."

"Mr. and Mrs. Adams will take off at ten thirty this morning Pacific time. They should be in Portland by four thirty."

"Do they know why we've moved the surprise party to Portland?"

"I haven't elaborated."

Good. I don't want Carla to spend the flight worrying about Ray.

Andrea continues, "Mrs. Adams said she's deliberately not contacting Mrs. Grey, to add to the surprise."

"Okay. Let me know when they've left Savannah."

"Will do."

"Thanks for organizing all this."

"It's a pleasure, sir. I hope Mr. Steele continues to improve."

"We'll talk later." I hang up and open the e-mail that has caught my attention.

From: Grey, Carrick
Subject: Drunk Driver. Astoria PD.
Date: September 10 2011 09:37
To: Christian Grey

Your mother says that Raymond Steele is in good hands.
I'll be joining her later for Ana's birthday celebrations.
With regard to the driver, I have some information which I'd rather talk you through, either in person or over the phone.
See you this evening, son.
Dad.

Carrick Grey, Partner
Grey, Krueger, Davis, and Holt LLP

I call Carrick but get his voice mail. I leave a message, then sit down and peruse the notes Ros has sent me regarding our meeting yesterday with the Hwangs.

Half an hour later my dad calls.

"Christian."

"Dad. Hello. You have news?" I stare out at the Portland skyline.

"I spoke with one of my contacts at the Astoria PD. The perpetrator's name is Jeffrey Lance. He's well known to the police, not only in Astoria but also in southeast Portland, where he's from. He lives in a trailer park there."

"He was a long way from home."

"His blood alcohol level was 0.28 percent."

"What does that mean?"

I turn around; unbeknownst to me, Ana has crept into the waiting room and is watching me warily.

"It means he was three and a half times over the legal limit," Dad says, pulling me back into the conversation.

"*How* far above the limit?" I don't believe it. *Fucking drunks. I loathe them.* From deep in that part of my brain that holds my most painful memories, the smell of stale Camel cigarette smoke, bourbon, and body odor seeps into my consciousness.

"There you are, you little prick."

Fuck. The crack whore's pimp.

"Three and half times," Dad mutters, disgusted.

"I see."

"And it isn't his first offense. His driver's license was suspended. He has no insurance. The police are assessing all the charges and his lawyer is trying to get a plea bargain, but—"

"All charges, everything," I interrupt. My blood's boiling. *What an asshole.* "Ana's father is in the ICU. I want you to throw the fucking book at him, Dad."

"Son—I can't get involved, because of the family connection. But one of the women I work with specializes in this kind of law. With your permission, she can act on behalf of your father-in-law, and she'll press for the heaviest penalties."

I blow out a breath, trying to calm down. "Good," I mutter.

"I have to go, son. There's another call on the line. See you later."

"Keep me informed."

"Will do."

"The other driver?" Ana asks, when I've hung up.

"Some drunken asshole from southeast Portland."

Her eyes widen, probably at my tone, but Jeffrey Lance deserves it. Taking a deep breath to calm myself, I amble over to her. "Finished with Ray? Do you want to go?"

"Um, no." She looks anxious.

"What's wrong?"

"Nothing. Ray's being taken to radiology for a CT scan to check the swelling in his brain. I'd like to wait for the results."

"Okay. We'll wait." Sitting down, I hold out my arms and she climbs into my lap. I stroke her back and inhale the scent of her hair. It's soothing. "This is not how I envisaged spending today," I murmur against her temple.

"Me neither, but I'm feeling more positive now. Your mom was very reassuring. It was kind of her to come last night."

"My mom is an amazing woman." I continue caressing her back and rest my chin on her head.

"She is. You're very lucky to have her."

I couldn't agree more, Ana.

"I should call my mom. Tell her about Ray," she says.

Uh-oh. At this moment her mom should be en route to Portland.

"I'm surprised she hasn't called me." She frowns, and I feel a little guilty about my subterfuge.

"Maybe she did," I offer.

Ana fishes her phone out of her pocket but finds no missed calls. She looks through her texts, and from what I can see she's received birthday wishes from her friends, but as I suspected, nothing from her mother. She shakes her head.

"Call her now," I say, knowing she won't get a reply. Ana does, but she soon hangs up.

"She's not there. I'll call later when I know the results of the brain scan."

Drawing her closer, I kiss her hair. I long to tell her, but that would blow the surprise. My own phone buzzes. Without letting go of Ana, I tug it out of my pocket.

"Andrea."

"Mr. Grey. Just to let you know that Mr. and Mrs. Adams took off from Savannah fifteen minutes ago."

"Good."

"Taylor is primed to pick them up from the airport."

"ETA is what time?" I don't want Ana and me to run into them at the hotel.

"At present, four thirty-five."

"And the other, um"—I glance down at Ana, not wanting to give the game away—"packages?"

"They're all set. Your father is driving down. Your brother, sister, Kate, and Ethan Kavanagh will be flying down with Stephan. They can't leave until five thirty because of your sister's new job, but they should be with you by six thirty."

"Does The Heathman have all the details?"

"Rooms have been booked for all of them. Dinner is booked for twelve people at seven thirty. They are offering the full menu and a cake—chocolate, as requested."

"Good."

"Ros wanted to know if you got her notes on the shipyard deal. If you're happy with them, she can send the Heads of Agreement for signing."

"Yes. It can hold until Monday morning, but e-mail it just in case—I'll print, sign, and scan it back to you."

"Samir and Helena have an HR issue they want to discuss, and Marco needs two minutes."

"They can wait. Go home, Andrea."

I think I hear her smile on the end of the phone. "Is there anything else you need? I'm on my cell if you do."

"No, we're good, thank you." I hang up.

"Everything okay?" Ana asks.

"Yes."

"Is this your Taiwan thing?"

"Yes."

"Am I too heavy?"

As if! "No, baby."

She asks me if I'm worried about the Taiwan deal and I assure her I'm not.

"I thought it was important."

"It is. The shipyard here depends on it. There are lots of jobs at stake. We just have to sell it to the unions. That's Sam and Ros's job. But the way the economy's heading, none of us have a lot of choice."

Ana yawns.

"Am I boring you, Mrs. Grey?" Amused, I kiss her hair once more.

"No! Never. I'm just very comfortable on your lap," she murmurs. "I like hearing about your business."

"You do?"

"Of course. I like hearing any bit of information you deign to share with me." She smirks, and I know she's teasing me.

"Always hungry for more information, Mrs. Grey."

"Tell me." She rests her head against my chest again.

"Tell you what?"

"Why you do it."

"Do what?"

"Work the way you do."

I snort, amused, because it's obvious, isn't it? "A guy's got to earn a living."

"Christian, you earn more than a living," she says, her eyes as guileless as ever, demanding the truth.

"I don't want to be poor. I've done that. I'm not going back there again."

The hunger.

The insecurity.

The vulnerability.

...The fear.

Grey, lighten up. It's her birthday.

"Besides, it's a game. It's about winning. A game I've always found very easy."

"Unlike life," she mutters, almost to herself.

"Yes, I suppose." I've never thought of it that way. I smile at her. *Perceptive, Mrs. Grey.* "Though it's easier with you."

She hugs me. "It can't all be a game. You're very philanthropic."

I shrug. "About some things, maybe." Ana, don't lionize me. I can afford to be generous.

"I love philanthropic Christian," she whispers.

"Just him?"

"Oh, I love megalomaniac Christian, too, and control-freak Christian, sexpertise Christian, kinky Christian, romantic Christian, shy Christian—the list is endless."

"That's a whole lot of Christians."

"I'd say at least fifty."

I laugh. "Fifty Shades," I whisper into her hair.

"My Fifty Shades."

I sit back, tip her head up, and kiss her. "Well, Mrs. Shades, let's see how your dad is doing."

"Okay."

Dr. Sluder has good news. The swelling in Ray's brain has subsided, so she's decided to wake him from his coma tomorrow morning.

"I'm pleased with his progress. He's come a long way in a short period of time. His recovery is proceeding well. It's all good, Mrs. Grey."

"Thank you, Doctor," Ana gushes, her eyes shining with gratitude.

I take Ana's hand. "Let's go get some lunch."

"**CAN WE GO FOR** a drive?" she asks as she starts the ignition.

"Sure. It's your birthday—we can do anything you want." For a moment I'm transported to a parking lot in Seattle, where an insatiable Ana took matters into her own hands.

She stares at me, her eyes darkening. "Anything?" Her voice is husky.

"Anything," I offer.

"Well." Her tone is seductive. "I want to drive."

"Then drive, baby." We grin at each other like the fools we are, and I resist the urge to pounce on her.

Behave, Grey.

Ana steers us out of the lot, and at a sedate speed that keeps my blood pressure normal she takes us to I-5. Once there, she puts her foot down, throwing us back into our seats. *Damn!* She was lulling me into a false sense of security. "Ana! Steady, baby," I warn, and she slows down. We cruise over the bridge; luckily, the traffic is light. I stare down at the Willamette River and remember all the times I went running along its banks when I stayed in Portland during my pursuit of Miss Anastasia Steele.

And now here we are and she's Mrs. Anastasia Grey.

"Have you planned lunch?" she asks.

"No. You're hungry?" I hear the hope in my voice.

"Yes."

"Where do you want to go? It's your day, Ana."

"I know just the place."

She diverts off I-5, back across the river, and into downtown Portland. Eventually she pulls up outside the restaurant where we ate after José Rodriguez's photography exhibition. *The day I won her back.*

"For one minute I thought you were going to take me to that dreadful bar you drunk-dialed me from," I tease her.

"Why would I do that?"

"To check the azaleas are still alive." I give her a sideways look, and she blushes.

Oh, yes, baby. You vomited at my feet.

"Don't remind me! Besides, you still took me to your hotel room." Smirking, she lifts her chin in that stubborn, triumphant way that she has.

"Best decision I ever made."

"Yes. It was." She leans over and kisses me.

"Do you think that supercilious fucker is still waiting tables?" I ask.

"Supercilious? I thought he was fine."

"He was trying to impress you."

"Well, he succeeded."

Ana, you're too easily impressed.

"Shall we go see?" she says, amused.

"Lead on, Mrs. Grey."

I PINCH THE BRIDGE of my nose. For the last couple of hours I've been working in the confines of the ICU waiting room. Ana has been at Ray's bedside since we returned from lunch; last time I checked, she was reading to him. She's a kind and considerate daughter—he must have been a wonderful father to inspire such devotion.

I've read through the Shipyard Heads of Agreement, and I have a list of questions, which I've e-mailed to Ros. I'm not signing anything until we've spoken, but all that can wait until Monday at the earliest.

My phone buzzes. It's Taylor, calling to say he's delivered Ana's mother and her husband to The Heathman. I check the time, noting it's just after 5 p.m. Carla needs to know about Ray—I can't put that off any longer. Reluctantly, I call the hotel and ask to be put through to the Adamses' room.

I'm not looking forward to this.

"Hello," Carla answers.

I take a deep breath. "Carla, it's Christian."

"Christian," she gushes. "We had such a wonderful flight over here. Thank you so much."

"I'm glad you had a pleasant journey. I have some bad news, though."

"Oh no! Is Ana okay?"

"Ana's fine. It's Ray. He was involved in a car accident and he's in the ICU here in Portland. That's why we're in Portland and not Seattle. His condition is improving. Though he's in an induced coma at the moment, but he'll be coming out of it tomorrow."

"Oh no," she breathes. "How's Ana?"

"She's holding up. And because all the news from the ICU is good, I thought we'd go ahead and celebrate her birthday."

"Yes. Yes, of course."

"I thought you should know before this evening. But I'd still like to keep your arrival a surprise."

"Yes. Yes," she says. "I've deliberately not called or texted Ana to keep the surprise."

"I appreciate that, and I'm sorry to be the bearer of this news. It must be upsetting."

"No. Christian. Thank you for telling me. I'm very fond of Ray."

"I'll see you later this evening."

"Yes. You will. Bye for now." She hangs up.

That was not as bad as I anticipated.

It's time to go back to the hotel. I pack up my laptop, then stand and stretch. These are not the most comfortable seats.

Ana is still reading off her phone to Ray. I watch from the end of the bed as she caresses his hand and glances at him occasionally, her lovelight burning bright.

She notices me as Nurse Kellie approaches.

"It's time to go, Ana," I say gently.

She tightens her hold on Ray's hand, making it clear she doesn't want to leave him.

"I want to feed you. Come. It's late," I insist.

"I'm about to give Mr. Steele a sponge bath," Nurse Kellie says.

"Okay," Ana acquiesces. "We'll be back tomorrow morning." Leaning over, she kisses Ray's cheek.

SHE'S QUIET AND THOUGHTFUL as we walk across the parking lot.

"Do you want me to drive?" I ask.

Her face whips to mine. "No. I'm good," she says, and opens the driver's door.

There's my girl.

I grin and climb in beside her.

IN THE ELEVATOR SHE'S quiet again. Her mind is with Ray, I'm sure of it. Wrapping her in my arms, I offer her the only comfort I can.

Me. And the warmth of my body.

I hold her close as we travel up to our floor.

"I thought we'd dine downstairs. In a private room." I open the door to our suite and usher her in.

"Really? Finish what you started a few months ago?" Ana raises a brow.

"If you're very lucky, Mrs. Grey."

She laughs. "Christian, I don't have anything dressy to wear."

Oh, ye of little faith, Ana.

In the bedroom, I open the closet door. There, hanging where Sawyer said it would be, is a dress bag.

"Taylor?" Ana's surprised.

"Christian," I state, feeling a little aggrieved that she would doubt me.

She laughs, in that indulgent way she has sometimes, unzips the bag, and takes out the dress. She draws a sharp breath as she holds it up. "It's lovely," she says. "Thank you. I hope it fits."

"It will." *I hope*. "And here." From the depths of the closet I retrieve the box. "Shoes to match."

High-heeled fuck-me pumps. My favorite.

"You think of everything. Thank you." She kisses me, a sweet, chaste peck, and I flash her a quick grin, pleased.

"I do." I hand her a second, smaller Nordstrom bag that weighs nothing and seems to be all tissue. Ana ferrets around inside and discovers the black lace lingerie to complement the dress. Tilting her chin up, I plant a soft kiss on her lips. "I look forward to taking this off you later."

"So do I," she whispers, and her words inspire my cock.

Not now, Grey.

"Shall I run you a bath?" I ask.

"Please."

WHILE ANA IS SOAKING in the tub, I check with the hotel that all of Andrea's arrangements are in place. It seems she's thought of everything, right down to the decorations.

Give the woman a raise, Grey.

I have to wait for Ana, so I open my laptop, pull up Geolumara's P&L, and spend several minutes running through it.

Hmm…their sales could be better—but their cash deposits are healthy, given it's a fairly new company. However, with their considerable expenses their profit margins aren't as high as I would expect. We can get them there. I make a few notes of what we could do, until the sound of a hair dryer coming to life next door pulls me from the spreadsheet.

I've lost track of time.

Ambling into the bedroom I find a squeaky clean Ana sitting on the edge of the bed wrapped in a towel, drying her hair. "Here, let me," I offer, and point to the chair by the dressing table.

"Dry my hair?" Her disbelief is obvious.

Ana, this is not my first rodeo.

But I'm not sure she'd like to hear that I used to do this for my submissives as a reward for good behavior.

"Come," I coax her. She seats herself in the chair, throwing me a quizzical look in the mirror. But as I brush her hair she surrenders herself to my ministrations. It's an absorbing task, and I soon find myself lost in it…detangling strands of her hair, then drying them. It takes me back, much further back than I want to go.

To a small, shabby room in a slum in Detroit.

I halt those thoughts immediately.

"You're no stranger to this." Ana interrupts my reverie, and I smile at her in the mirror, but say nothing.

You don't want to know, Ana.

When I'm finished, her hair is soft and lush, capturing the light from a lamp on the dressing table.

Beautiful.

"Thank you," she says, shaking her head and letting her hair tumble down her back. I drop a kiss on her naked shoulder and tell her that I'll have a quick shower. She smiles, though I see her sadness and it makes me wonder if I've made the right decision to host this party.

Hell.

These thoughts weigh heavily on me as I step under the cascade of hot water.

So much so that I offer a silent prayer to God.

Make Ray better.

Please, Lord.

WHEN I COME OUT of the bathroom, Ana's waiting for me. She looks stunning. The dress fits perfectly, accentuating her beautiful body, and the bracelet sparkles on her wrist. She does a quick twirl, then stops so I can zip her up. "You look gorgeous, as you should on your birthday," I whisper.

She turns and places her hands on my naked chest. "So do you." She peeks up at me, through long lashes, in that way that heats my blood.

Ana.

"I'd better get dressed, before I change my mind about dinner and unzip that dress."

"You chose well, Mr. Grey."

"You wear it well, Mrs. Grey."

MIA HAS TEXTED TO let me know everyone has gathered in the room. Squeezing Ana's hand as we step out of the elevator onto the mezzanine level, I hope she likes surprises. I steer us toward the private dining rooms, my stunning wife seemingly oblivious to the admiring glances she's attracting. At the end of the corridor, I pause for the briefest moment before I open the door, then in we go—to a rousing chorus of "Surprise!"

Mom, Dad, Kate, Elliot, both Josés, Mia, Ethan, Bob, and Carla all raise their glasses, cheering, as we stand together before our family and friends. Ana turns and gawks at me. I grin, squeezing her hand, delighted that this has all come together, and Carla steps forward, sweeping Ana into her arms.

"Darling, you look beautiful. Happy birthday."

"Mom!" Ana sobs. It's a bittersweet sound and I step away to give them some privacy, and to greet the rest of our guests.

I'm actually pleased to see everyone—even José. He and his father are looking well rested, and less battered than yesterday. Elliot and Ethan rave about *Charlie Tango*, Mia and Kate about The Heathman.

"And I got to fly in your helicopter! Thank you so much!" Mia throws her arms around me. I ask her how her job's going. "So far so good." She grins. "Oh, my turn for Ana!" She darts off to pester my wife.

"Thanks for all this, Christian," Kate says. "I'm sure Ana appreciates it."

"I hope so."

When I return to her, Elliot has Ana in a tight embrace. Taking her hand, I ease her to my side. "Enough fondling my wife. Go fondle your fiancée," I say without rancor. Elliot winks at Kate.

A waiter presents Ana and me with flutes of rosé champagne—our usual, Grande Année, of course. I clear my throat; the general hum in the room dies down as everyone gives me their attention. "This would be a perfect day if Ray were here with us, but he's not far away. He's doing well, and I know he'd like you to enjoy yourself, Ana. To all of you—thank you for coming to share my beautiful wife's birthday, the first of many to come. Happy birthday, my love." I raise my glass to my girl, amid a chorus of "happy birthdays," and tears shine in her eyes.

Oh, baby.

I kiss her temple, longing to take her hurt away. "Good surprise?" I ask, suddenly nervous.

"Very good surprise. Thank you, you darling man." She raises her lips to mine, and I give her a quick, chaste peck, suitable for family viewing.

Ana is not her usual self during dinner—she's subdued, but I understand; she's worried about her father. She follows the conversations, laughs in the right places, and I *think* she's buoyed by the merriment of our family and friends. But deep down my girl is aching: she's pale, she's chewing her lip, and occasionally, she's distracted—probably lost in her dark thoughts.

I see her pain and I'm powerless to help.

It's frustrating.

She picks at her food, but I don't nag her. I'm just grateful she ate a hearty lunch.

Elliot and José are in top form. I had no idea the photographer had such a sharp sense of humor. Kate, too, has noticed Ana's state; she's solicitous, and during a hushed conversation I watch them laughing. Ana shows off her new bracelet and Kate makes the right appreciative noises. My feelings toward Kavanagh thaw a little more.

Make my wife laugh. She needs the distraction right now.

Finally, a magnificent chocolate cake with twenty-two candles ablaze is delivered by two waitstaff. Elliot starts a spirited rendition of "Happy Birthday," and we all join in. Ana's smile is wistful.

"Make a wish," I whisper to her, and she screws her eyes shut like a child might, then blows out every candle in one breath. She looks up at me, anxiously, and I know she's thinking of Ray. "He'll be fine, Ana. Just give him time."

BIDDING GOOD NIGHT TO all our guests, we wander up to our hotel room. I think the night has been a success. Ana seems more content, and I'm surprised, given the circumstances, how much I enjoyed everyone's company. I close the door to our suite and lean against it as Ana turns to face me. "Alone at last," I mutter.

She must be exhausted.

She steps toward me and runs her fingers over my lapels. "Thank you for a wonderful birthday. You really are the most thoughtful, considerate, generous husband."

"My pleasure."

"Yes, your pleasure. Let's do something about that," she whispers, and raises her lips to mine.

Sunday, September 11, 2011

Ana is curled up on the sofa in our suite, reading a manuscript that she's had printed out at the hotel. She's calm and focused, that little *v* forming between her brows as she scribbles her blue-penciled hieroglyphics in the margins. Occasionally she chews her plump lower lip, and I don't know if it's a judgment on what she's reading or if she's immersed in the narrative, but it has the usual effect on my body.

I want to bite that lip.

Smiling to myself, I remember my surprise wake-up call this morning. Ana is becoming more and more proactive when it comes to sex, but as the beneficiary of her passion, I'm not complaining. I think seeing her nearest and dearest at this difficult time has been therapeutic.

Having said that, it's been an emotional morning. After a convivial breakfast with our family and friends, we said good-bye to everyone, except Carla and Bob. My parents have driven back to Seattle; Stephan has flown Elliot, Mia, Kate, and Ethan back home in *Charlie Tango*. Ryan, who's still in Seattle, will pick them up at Boeing Field.

After everyone left, Carla, Ana, and I visited Ray. Well, Carla and Ana did; I gave them some privacy and worked in the waiting room until it was time to take Carla and Bob to the airport. We delivered them into the safe hands of First Officer Beighley and her copilot, who were standing by with the Gulfstream. Ana said a tearful farewell to her mother, and now we're back in our suite, cooling our heels after a light lunch. I think Ana is reading to distract herself from thinking about Ray.

I'd just like to go home.

But I guess that depends on Ray's recovery.

I hope he wakes shortly, and we can make plans to move him to

Seattle and return to Escala. I don't mention this to Ana, though—I don't want to add to her worries.

I've had my fill of reading, so to pass the time, I've started assembling a collage of photographs of my wife to use as a screensaver on my laptop and phone. I have so many photographs of her from our honeymoon—and in all of them, Ana is stunning. I'm delighted to have captured her in so many different moods: laughing, pensive, pouting, amused, relaxed, happy, and in some, she's scowling at me. Those are the photos that make me grin.

I'm reminded of the shock at seeing her image, large and lovely, at José Rodriguez's exhibition, and our conversation afterward.

I want you that relaxed with me.

I glance over at her again. Here she is. Relaxed. Absorbed in her work.

Mission accomplished, Grey.

We'll hang the other photographs in our new house, and maybe I'll put one of them in the study at Escala.

She looks up. "What?"

I tap my index finger against my lips and shake my head. "Nothing. How's the book?"

"It's a political thriller. Set in a dystopian surreal future."

"Sounds riveting."

"It is. It's a take on Dante's *Inferno* by a new writer who's based in Seattle. Boyce Fox." Ana's eyes shine, animated with the thrill of a good book.

"I can't wait to read it."

She smiles and returns to her manuscript.

Smiling, I return to my collage.

A LITTLE LATER SHE gets up and wanders over to me, her expression hopeful. "Can we go back?"

"Of course." I close my laptop, pleased with my photomontage of Mrs. Anastasia Grey.

"Will you drive?" she asks.

"Sure." Taylor is visiting his daughter, and I've given Sawyer the day off.

"I want to grab a copy of *The Oregonian* on the way, so I can read Dad the sports page."

"Good idea. I'm sure they'll have one at reception. Let's go." I grab my jacket and my laptop, and we head out.

RAY LIES PEACEFULLY ASLEEP in his hospital bed, and it takes a few seconds for Ana and me to realize that he's no longer on a ventilator. The repetitive, measured blast of air that had been his constant companion is no more; he's breathing on his own. Ana's face glows in relief. With infinite tenderness she strokes his stubbled chin and wipes his spittle with a tissue.

I look away.

I'm intruding. This wordless expression of love from a daughter to her father is too intimate for me to witness. I know Ray would be mortified if he knew I was standing here watching him at his most vulnerable. I stalk off to find one of his doctors for an update. Nurse Kellie and her colleague Liz are at the nurses' station. "Dr. Sluder is in surgery." Kellie picks up the phone. "She's due out any minute. Do you want me to page her?"

"No. That's fine. Thanks." I leave both nurses and head back to the all-too-familiar waiting room. Again, I'm here alone; slumping into one of the chairs I open my laptop and pull up the latest iteration of my Ana collage. I've decided I want to add a few photographs from our wedding.

I'm completely absorbed in the task when Ana bursts into the room, dragging me from the screen. Her eyes are red-rimmed from fresh tears, but she's brimming with elation. "He's awake," she exclaims.

Thank God. At last.

Setting aside my laptop, I stand up to embrace her. "How is he?"

She snuggles against my chest, her eyes closed, as she wraps her arms around me. "Talking, thirsty, bewildered. He doesn't remember the accident at all."

"That's understandable. Now that he's awake, I want to get him moved to Seattle. Then we can go home, and my mom can keep an eye on him."

"I'm not sure he's well enough to be moved."

"I'll talk to Dr. Sluder. Get her opinion."

"You miss home?" Ana looks up at me.

"Yes." *Very much.*

"Okay." She smiles, and together we return to the ward, where we find Ray is sitting up in bed. He looks a little shell-shocked, and frankly embarrassed that I'm there.

"Ray. It's good to see you back with us."

"Thanks, Christian," he grumbles. "Awful lot of trouble for you kids to be here."

"Dad, it's no trouble. We don't want to be anywhere else." Ana tries to reassure him.

Dr. Sluder joins us, bristling with efficiency. "Mr. Steele. Welcome back," she says.

"YOU HAVEN'T STOPPED SMILING." I tuck a strand of Ana's hair behind her ear as she pulls up outside The Heathman in the R8.

"I'm very relieved. And happy." She flashes me a smile.

"Good." We climb out and Ana hands her keys to the valet. It's getting darker and cooler and Ana shivers, so I drape my arm around her shoulders, and we wander into the hotel. From the foyer, I eye the Marble Bar. "Shall we celebrate?"

"Celebrate?" Ana frowns.

"Your dad."

She chuckles. "Oh, him."

"I've missed that sound." I kiss her hair.

"Can we just eat in our room? You know, have a quiet night in?"

"Sure. Come." Taking her hand, we walk to the elevators.

ANA DEVOURS HER DINNER. "That was delicious." She pushes her plate away. "They sure know how to make a fine tarte tatin here."

That they do, Ana. "That's the most I've seen you eat the entire time we've been here."

"I was hungry." She sits back, replete, and it's most gratifying to witness. She's fresh and clean from our bath earlier and wearing nothing but my T-shirt and her panties. She's all eyes and smiles and ponytail and legs…especially legs.

Lifting my glass of wine, I take a sip. "What would you like to do now?" I keep my tone gentle, and hopefully a little seductive. My iPod is playing some serene tunes in the background. I know what I want to do, but she's had an emotional day.

"What do *you* want to do?"

Is this a trick question?

I raise a brow, amused. "What I always want to do."

"And that is?"

"Mrs. Grey, don't be coy."

She purses her lips with her secret smile and, reaching across the table, grasps my hand and turns it over. With great care, she skates her index finger over my palm, which tingles in response. It's an odd feeling that takes my breath away.

"I'd like you to touch me with this." Her voice is low and provocative as her fingertip continues brushing over my index finger.

Her touch echoes. *Everywhere.*

Fuck.

I shift in my chair. "Just that?"

"Maybe this." She traces a line along my middle finger and back to my palm. "And this." She weaves a path up to my wedding ring. "Definitely this." She stops, her finger pressed against my platinum ring. "This is very sexy."

"Is it, now?"

"It sure is. It says 'this man is mine.'"

Hell. I'm hard.

Yes. Ana. Yours.

Using her fingernail, she outlines the small callus that's formed where my palm rubs against my ring, her eyes on mine. Her pupils dilate—the dark overcoming the bright blue.

She beguiles me.

Leaning forward, I capture her chin in my hand. "Mrs. Grey, are you seducing me?"

"I hope so."

"Anastasia, I'm a given." *Always.* "Come here." I pull her into my lap and hold her. "I like having unfettered access to you." To prove it, I run my hand up her naked thigh to her behind, then clasping the nape of her neck with my other hand, I angle her head and kiss her. Thoroughly. Exploring her mouth and savoring the feel of her tongue against mine, as her fingers find my hair.

She tastes of apple pie and Ana.

With a hint of fine Chablis.

It's a stimulating combination in every sense. We're both breathing hard when I pull away. "Let's go to bed," I whisper against her lips.

"Bed?" she scoffs.

Oh!

I lean back and tug her hair so I'm looking directly into her eyes. "Where would you prefer, Mrs. Grey?"

She shrugs, nonchalant. Challenging. "Surprise me."

"You're feisty this evening." I run my nose down hers while a list of possibilities forms in my mind.

"Maybe I need to be restrained."

"Maybe you do. You're getting mighty bossy in your old age."

"What are you going to do about it?" She squares her shoulders, in that way she does, ready for battle.

Oh, Ana. "I know what I'd like to do about it. Depends if you're up to it."

"Oh, Mr. Grey, you've been very gentle with me these last couple of days. I'm not made of glass, you know."

"You don't like gentle?"

"With you, of course. But you know…variety is the spice of life." She flutters her eyelashes.

"You're after something less gentle?"

"Something life-affirming."

Wow. "Life-affirming?" Astonished, I gaze at her, as all manner of sexual scenarios pop most welcome into my mind. She nods, gazing into my eyes and teasing her lower lip with her teeth.

On purpose.

She's goading me.

She wants life-affirming, I can oblige. "Don't bite your lip." I tighten my grip on her and rise, holding her close. She gasps in surprise and grabs my arms while I carry her across the room and settle her on the farthest sofa.

I have a plan. I want to see how far her newfound sexual confidence extends.

And I want to watch.

"Wait here. Don't move." She turns her head, her eyes tracking me as I head to the bedroom. I scan the room and remember one of the presents she opened this morning at breakfast—some fancy toiletries from Kate. In the smart presentation box, I discover a small bottle of scented moisturizing oil, dark amber and sandalwood.

Perfect. I slip it into the rear pocket of my jeans. From the bathroom I retrieve both belts from our hotel bathrobes and grab one of the largest bath towels.

Back in the living room, I'm pleased to find Ana has stayed on the couch.

Obedience! At last!

She can't see me as I approach her from behind, or hear me, as I'm barefoot. She gasps when I lean over and grab the hem of her T-shirt. "I think we'll dispense with this." I drag it over her head and toss it on the floor, admiring how her nipples peak in response to the brush of the material and the cooler temperature in the room. I grab her ponytail, tipping her head back and claiming her mouth with a brief kiss.

"Stand up," I murmur against her skin. She obliges, naked except for her panties. I lay the towel over the sofa, not wishing to get oil, or anything else, on the fabric.

"Take your panties off." I look directly at Ana. She swallows, but with her eyes fixed on mine she obeys, without hesitating.

I like this version of Ana.

"Sit."

She does as she's told, and I grasp her ponytail once more, twirling her soft hair between my fingers. I tug it, pulling back her head, and stand over her. "You'll tell me to stop if this gets too much, yes?"

She nods.

Damn it, Ana. "Say it."

"Yes," she answers, her voice a little shrill and breathy, betraying her excitement.

I smirk and pitch my voice low. "Good. So, Mrs. Grey—by

popular demand, I'm going to restrain you." I've chosen this, the only sofa that has finials, for a reason. "Bring your knees up. And sit right back." Once more she complies, without hesitation. Taking her left leg, I wrap a belt from one of the robes around her lower thigh and tie a slip knot above her knee.

"Bathrobes?" Ana asks.

"I'm improvising." I tie the other end to the finial at the back left-hand corner of the sofa and tug, parting her thighs. "Don't move." I do the same with her right leg, tying the other belt to the back-right finial.

Ana is splayed out, her legs spread wide, revealing all she has to offer, her hands by her sides.

"Okay?" I ask, drinking in the view from above.

She nods and looks up at me, soft, sweet, vulnerable. *Mine.*

Bending down, I kiss her. "You have no idea how hot you look right now." I rub my nose against hers, fighting my anticipation of what's to come. "Change of music, I think." I wander over to my iPod.

I scroll through artists. Select a track. Press repeat and play.

"*Sweet About Me.*" Perfect.

As Gabriella Cilmi's sugared, sultry voice fills the room, I turn and lock eyes with my trussed-up, naked wife and saunter back to her. Her gaze doesn't leave mine, as I sink down onto my knees in front of her, to worship at her altar.

Her mouth parts as she inhales.

Oh, Ana. Let's see how far your confidence has grown.

I know what she's feeling. "Exposed? Vulnerable?" I ask.

She licks her lips and nods.

"Good," I whisper.

Baby, you've got this. "Hold out your hands." From my back pocket I withdraw the small bottle of oil. Ana holds up her cupped palms and I pour a little oil into her hands. The scent is heavy but not unpleasant. "Rub your hands."

She wriggles on the couch.

Oh, this will never do. "Keep still," I warn.

Ana stops squirming.

"Now, Anastasia, I want you to touch yourself."

She blinks—surprised, I think.

"Start at your throat and work down."

Her teeth dig into that bottom lip.

"Don't be shy, Ana. Come. Do it."

Come on, Ana.

She places her hands on either side of her neck, then glides them down to the tops of her breasts, leaving a slick shine over her skin in their wake.

"Lower," I whisper.

After a beat, her hands embrace her breasts.

"Tease yourself."

Tentatively, her darkening eyes on mine, she takes each of her nipples between thumb and forefinger and gently tugs on both.

"Harder," I urge her, feeling like the serpent in the garden. "Like I would," I add, gripping my own thighs to keep myself from touching her. She groans in response and squeezes and tugs harder. I watch each pucker and lengthen under her touch.

Damn, she's hot.

"Yes. Like that. Again."

She closes her eyes and moans, and rolls and twists them between her fingers and thumbs.

"Open your eyes." My voice is hoarse.

She blinks them open.

"Again," I order. "I want to see you. See you enjoy your touch."

She continues, her eyes clouded with dark longing—her breathing increasing as desire consumes her—while my yearning matches hers.

This must be making her so wet…

My pants are getting tighter by the second. *Enough.* "Hands. Lower."

She squirms.

"Keep still, Ana. Absorb the pleasure. Lower."

"You do it," she whispers.

"Oh, I will. Soon. You. Lower. Now." She has no idea how fucking hot she looks right now. She glides her hands beneath her breasts, over her stomach, toward her belly, as she writhes, pulling on the robe restraints.

No. No. I shake my head. "Still." Placing my hands on each of her knees, I hold her in place. “Come on, Ana—lower.” Her hands slide down to her belly.

“Lower,” I mouth.

“Christian, please,” she begs. I skim my hands from her knees, along her thighs, toward the exposed junction at the top of her legs.

My end goal.

Her goal.

“Come on, Ana. Touch yourself.”

Her left hand grazes her vulva, then she starts to rub her fingers in a slow circle over her clitoris. “Ah!” she breathes, her mouth forming a badly drawn *o*.

“Again.” The word is a whisper and a command.

She groans, gasping for air, and closes her eyes, tipping her head back against the sofa as her hand moves.

“Again.”

She groans again, and I don’t want her to come without me. Grabbing her hands, I hold them firmly, and bend down between her thighs, running my nose and tongue over her clitoris. Back and forth. Again. Taking her higher.

She’s so wet. Dripping with her lust.

“Ah!” she cries and tries to move her hands. I tighten my fingers around her wrists while I continue my sensual onslaught.

“I’ll restrain these, too. Keep still,” I breathe, against her most intimate place.

Ana groans, and I release her, then slowly ease two fingers inside her.

So wet.

So ready.

So greedy.

The heel of my hand pushes up against her clitoris.

“I’m going to make you come quickly, Ana. Ready?”

“Yes,” she breathes, nodding frantically.

I move my hand. Hard. Fast. Stimulating her both inside and out. She mewls above me. Her head twisting to and fro, her toes curling, and her fingers clawing at the towel beneath her. I know she wants to straighten her legs to lessen the intense feeling. But she can’t; she’s close.

So close.

But I don't stop.

And I feel it.

The beginning.

Of the end.

Her orgasm. Coming.

"Surrender," I whisper, and she cries out. Loud and proud, and I press the heel of my hand against her clitoris, and ride out her orgasm, which goes on and on.

Wow. Ana.

With my other hand I untie the robe belts, one at a time.

As she descends back to earth, I murmur, "My turn." Withdrawing my fingers from inside her, I ease back and I flip her over so she's facedown on the sofa, her knees on the floor. I yank open my jeans, spread her legs with my knee, and slap her hard across her beautiful backside.

"Ah!" she cries, and I drive into her, as deep as I can. She cries out again.

"Oh, Ana," I breathe, and gripping her hips, I start to move. Hard. Fast.

Again. Taking my pleasure. She wanted it rough.

We. Aim. To. Please.

I drive into her. Losing myself. In her. *So in her.*

Her cries taking me higher.

Fuck.

She's building again.

I feel it.

"Come on, Ana!" I shout, and she comes once more, taking me over the edge with her.

I EASE HER OFF the sofa and we lie down on the floor, where she sprawls on top of me, facing the ceiling. We're quiet, catching our collective breath.

"Life-affirming enough for you?" I ask eventually, as I kiss her hair.

"Oh, yes." Her hands settle on my thighs, and she tugs at the material of my jeans. "I think we should go again. No clothes for you this time."

Again! "Christ, Ana. Give a man a chance."

She giggles, and I can't help laughing with her. "I'm glad Ray's conscious. Seems all your appetites are back."

She turns over, still on top of me, and scowls. "Are you forgetting about last night and this morning?" she pouts and rests her chin on her hands, on my chest.

"Nothing forgettable about either of those." I grin and grab her bountiful behind with both hands. "You have a fantastic ass, Mrs. Grey."

"So do you." She arches a brow. "Though yours is still under cover."

"And what are you going to do about that, Mrs. Grey?"

"Why, I'm going to undress you, Mr. Grey. All of you."

Her enthusiasm is infectious.

"And I think there's a lot that's sweet about you," she whispers, repeating the song lyric, her eyes radiating her warmth and love.

Shit.

"You are," she stresses, and kisses the corner of my mouth. Closing my eyes, I tighten my arms around her.

Why are you talking about this?

"Christian, you are. You made this weekend so special—in spite of what happened to Ray. Thank you."

Large, luminous eyes meet mine.

"Because I love you," I murmur.

"I know," she says. "I love you, too." She runs her fingertips down my cheek. "And you're precious to me, too. You do know that, don't you?"

Precious. *Me?*

Suddenly, I'm helpless and panicked. And completely disarmed.

What do I say?

Not now, Maggot.

Fuck. I close my eyes. I don't want that in my head.

"Believe me," she whispers, and I open them once more, gray eyes to blue.

"It's not easy." My words are almost inaudible.

I don't want to talk about this.

It's too raw. Right now. For some reason I don't understand.

She holds such power over me. That's why.

"Try. Try hard, because it's true." She caresses my face, and I know she means what she says. If only I could hear it without panicking inside.

"You'll get cold. Come." I move her to one side and stand, pulling her to her feet, too.

Leaving the detritus of our lovemaking, Ana slips her arm around me. I switch off the iPod and we stroll back into the bedroom, while I wonder about my reaction.

Why is it still so hard to hear her declarations of love sometimes?

I shake my head.

"Shall we watch TV?" Ana asks, and I know she's trying to recapture our former levity.

"I was hoping for round two."

She eyes me speculatively. "Well, in that case, I think I'll be in charge."

Oh!

She pushes me suddenly with such force that I fall onto the bed. Before I know it, she's straddled me and is pinning my arms down on either side of my head.

"Well, Mrs. Grey, now that you've got me, what are you going to do with me?"

Leaning down, her breath tickling my ear, she whispers, "I am going to fuck you with my mouth."

Oh boy.

I close my eyes as she runs her teeth along my jaw, and I surrender to her. I surrender to the love of my life.

Monday, September 12, 2011

Ana is still asleep when I step out of the en suite. Frankly, I'm not surprised; she was persistent last night.

Sex-mad and insatiable indeed.

I'm not complaining.

That delectable memory fresh in my mind, I gather my clothes together and step into the living room to get dressed. The remnants from last night's tryst are still all over the sofa. I untie the bathrobe belts and grab the towel, wondering what housekeeping would have made of this scenario if they'd come in early to clean. Folding the items, I place them on the console beside the bedroom door.

I order breakfast—it will take half an hour and I'm hungry. To distract myself, I sit down at the desk and open my laptop. Today, I want to arrange moving Ray to Northwest Hospital, where my mother can watch over him. I fire up my e-mails, and to my surprise there's one from Detective Clark. He has questions for Ana about that asshole Hyde.

What the hell?

I send a brief reply to let him know we're in Portland and he'll have to wait until we return to Seattle. I call my mom and leave a message about moving Ray, then breeze through my other e-mails. There's one from Ros: the Hwangs are inviting us to visit later this week.

That will depend on Ray.

I guess.

I e-mail Ros to say that it's likely that I'll be able to go, but I can't confirm yet, as we're not sure what's happening with my father-in-law.

I don't want to leave Ana to deal with this on her own.

As I press send, I receive a reply from Clark.

He's coming to Portland.

Shit.

What can be that important?

"Good morning." Ana's sweet tone interrupts my thoughts. When I turn around she's standing in the bedroom doorway, wearing nothing but a sheet and a shy smile. Her hair is a tousled mess that falls to her breasts, her bright eyes intent on me.

She looks like a Greek goddess.

"Mrs. Grey. You're up early." I hold out my arms, and in spite of the sheet, she bolts across the room, offering me a welcome flash of legs, and lands in my lap.

"As are you," she says.

I cradle her against me and kiss her hair. "I was just working."

"What?" she asks, leaning back to scrutinize me. She knows something is off.

I blow out a breath. "I got an e-mail from Detective Clark. He wants to talk to you about that fucker Hyde."

"Really?"

"Yes. I told him you're in Portland for the time being, so he'll have to wait. But he says he'd like to interview you here."

"He's coming here?"

"Apparently so."

She frowns. "What's so important that it can't wait?"

"Exactly."

"When's he coming?"

"Today. I'll e-mail him back."

"I have nothing to hide. I wonder what he wants to know?"

"We'll find out when he gets here. I'm intrigued, too." I move in my chair. "Breakfast will be here shortly. Let's eat, then we can go see your dad."

"You can stay here if you want. I can see you're busy."

"No, I want to come with you."

"Okay." She grins, pleased, I think, that I want to accompany her. She kisses me, then waltzes back toward the bedroom and, with a suggestive glance at me, lets the sheet drop as she crosses the doorway.

Damn. Goddess indeed.

That's my cue. E-mails and breakfast can wait.

I follow her into the bedroom to make good on her invitation.

RAY IS AWAKE, BUT it would appear that he's not in the best of tempers. After saying good morning, I leave Ana to deal with him and head to the waiting room—my new office, or so it seems. I've already received tentative approval from Dr. Sluder to move Ray to Seattle, and I'm waiting for my mother to confirm that there's a bed for him at Northwest before I organize the helicopter transfer. Dr. Sluder thinks we can relocate him as early as tomorrow, but she'll confirm that later today, once she's run more tests.

I call Andrea.

"Good morning, Mr. Grey."

"Andrea, hello. I'm hoping we can move Raymond Steele tomorrow. Can you find an air ambulance service, please? Portland OHSU to Northwest Hospital. My mother should know a reliable company. I'll ask Ray's doctor if there's any specific medical equipment that should be on board. Either she or I will send that through."

"I'll call Dr. Grey."

"Do. I'm waiting to hear from her if there's a room available."

"Okay, I'll take care of it."

"Taiwan. Ros and I may fly out on Thursday evening. We'll need the jet."

"You're at WSU on Thursday morning."

"I know. But get Stephan and the crew prepped. It's still tentative."

"Yes, sir. Actually, Ros wants a word."

"Okay. Thanks. Put me through."

Ros and I have a quick catch-up and decide that signatures on the Heads of Agreement for the Taiwan shipyard can wait until tomorrow, when I'm hopefully back in Seattle. As soon as I hang up, my phone buzzes. It's Clark.

"Mr. Grey. Thank you for seeing me today. Is four o'clock a good time?"

"Sure. We're at The Heathman."

"I'll see you then."

Ana wanders into the waiting room. She looks serious.

Is there a problem?

"Okay," I respond to Clark, and hang up. "Clark will be here at four this afternoon."

She frowns. "Okay. Ray wants coffee and doughnuts."

I laugh, not expecting that response. "I think I would, too, if I'd been in an accident. Ask Taylor to go."

"No, I'll go."

"Take Taylor with you."

Ana rolls her eyes. "Okay." She sounds like an exasperated teen.

I smirk and cock my head to one side. "There's no one here."

Her eyes widen a fraction as she catches my drift; her interest is clearly piqued. She sets her shoulders as if she's going to challenge me and raises that stubborn Steele chin.

A young couple enters the room behind her and the man has his arms around his weeping companion. The woman is visibly distraught. *Shit, something is seriously wrong.*

Ana's eyes widen with compassion, then she turns to me and lifts a shoulder in regret.

Oh. Maybe she was game for a spanking. The thought is appealing. *Very appealing.*

Picking up my laptop, I take her hand, and we head out of the room. "They need the privacy more than we do," I mutter. "We'll have our fun later."

Taylor is outside, waiting in the car. "Let's all go get coffee and doughnuts," I say. We could use a treat.

Ana returns my smile. "Voodoo Doughnut in Portland. Best doughnuts in the world," she says, and climbs into the back of the SUV.

DETECTIVE CLARK IS PUNCTUAL. Taylor shows him into our suite and he wanders in, looking as rumpled and curmudgeonly as ever. "Mr. Grey, Mrs. Grey, thank you for seeing me."

"Detective Clark." I shake his hand and direct him to sit down, then step over to join Ana on the sofa that I tied her to last night.

"It's Mrs. Grey I wish to see," Clark says, his tone a little abrasive, and I know he's addressing Taylor and me.

Oh. Now I definitely want to hear what he has to say.

I nod to Taylor, who acknowledges my cue and leaves, closing the door behind him.

"Anything you wish to say to my wife you can say in front of me." If this is about Hyde, I'm not leaving my wife's side.

"Are you sure you'd like your husband to be present?" Clark asks Ana.

She looks puzzled. "Of course. I have nothing to hide. You are just interviewing me?"

"Yes, ma'am."

"I'd like my husband to stay."

There. Told you so. I glare at him, pleased that Ana has taken my side. I sit down beside her, trying to mask my simmering irritation.

"All right," murmurs Clark. He coughs to clear his throat, and I wonder if he's nervous. "Mrs. Grey, Mr. Hyde maintains that you sexually harassed him and made several lewd advances toward him."

What the fuck!

Ana looks both shocked and amused at once. She places her hand on my thigh, but it doesn't stop me. "That's preposterous," I exclaim. Her fingernails dig into my leg—I suspect in an attempt to shut me up.

"That's not true." Ana looks him squarely in the eye, the embodiment of serenity as she addresses Clark. "In fact, it was the other way around. He propositioned me in a very aggressive manner, and he was fired."

Clark's mouth flattens, as if he'd been expecting this response. "Hyde alleges that you fabricated a tale about sexual harassment in order to get him fired. He says that you did this because he refused your advances and because you wanted his job."

Ana's face twists in disgust. "That's not true."

This is fucking absurd.

"Detective, please don't tell me you have driven all this way to harass my wife with these ridiculous accusations."

Clark graces me with a resigned look. "I need to hear this from Mrs. Grey, sir." Ana grasps my thigh again, and I know she wants me to shut up.

"You don't have to listen to this shit, Ana."

"I think I should let Detective Clark know what happened." She pins me with bright blue eyes, imploring me to shut the fuck up.

Okay, baby. Have it your way.

Waving at her to continue, I endeavor to stay quiet and keep my temper in check. She folds her hands in her lap and continues, "What Hyde says is simply not true." Her voice rings calm and clear through the room. "Mr. Hyde accosted me in the office kitchen one evening. He told me that it was thanks to him that I'd been hired, and that he expected sexual favors in return. He tried to blackmail me, using e-mails that I'd sent to Christian, who wasn't my husband then. I didn't know Hyde had been monitoring my e-mails. He's delusional. He even accused me of being a spy sent by Christian, presumably to help him take over the company. He didn't know that Christian had already bought SIP." She shakes her head and knits her hands together. "In the end, I–I took him down."

"Took him down?" Clark interjects, puzzled.

"My father is ex-army. Hyde, um, touched me, and I know how to defend myself." Her eyes flick to mine, and I can't hide my pride and awe for my girl.

Don't mess with my girl.

She's a warrior.

"I see." Clark huffs out a breath and sits back on the sofa.

"Have you spoken to any of Hyde's former personal assistants?" I ask. I'm curious to know if the cops have made more progress than Welch.

"Yes, we have. But the truth is, we can't get any of his assistants to talk to us. They all say he was an exemplary boss, even though none of them lasted more than three months."

Damn. "We've had that problem, too. My security chief, he's interviewed Hyde's past five PAs."

This news piques Clark's interest. He frowns, his eyes boring into me. "And why's that?"

"Because my wife worked for him, and I run security checks on anyone my wife works with."

Clark's face reddens. "I see." His bushy brows draw together. "I think there's more to this than meets the eye, Mr. Grey. We are conducting a more thorough search of his apartment tomorrow, so maybe something will present itself then. Though by all accounts he hasn't lived there for some time."

"You've searched already?"

"Yes. We're doing it again. A fingertip search this time."

"You've still not charged him with the attempted murder of Ros Bailey and myself?"

Maybe that's the FBI's prerogative?

"We're hoping to find more evidence in regard to the sabotage of your aircraft, Mr. Grey. We need more than a partial print, and while he's in custody, we can build a case."

"Is this all you came down here for?"

Clark stiffens. "Yes, Mr. Grey, it is, unless you've had any further thoughts about the note?"

Again, Ana's eyes scrutinize mine, but this time she's frowning.

"No. I told you. It means nothing to me." *My wife does not need to know about that!* "And I don't see why we couldn't have done this over the phone."

"I think I told you, I prefer a hands-on approach. And," he adds, slightly sheepishly, "I'm visiting my great-aunt, who lives in Portland. Two birds—one stone."

"Well, if we're all done, I have work to attend to." I stand, hoping that Clark will take the hint.

He does. "Thank you for your time, Mrs. Grey."

Ana nods.

"Mr. Grey."

I open the door and he shuffles out.

Thank fuck.

Ana leans back into the sofa.

"Can you believe that asshole?" I run my hands through my hair.

"Clark?" Ana says.

"No. That fucker, Hyde."

"No, I can't." She looks bemused.

"What's his fucking game?"

"I don't know. Do you think Clark believed me?"

"Of course he did. He knows Hyde is a fucked-up asshole—"

"You're very sweary," Ana chastises me.

"Sweary? Is that even a word?"

"It is now."

And just like that, her humor smothers my anger, and it's gone.

Marveling at the spell she casts, I sit down beside her and pull her into my arms. "Don't think about that fucker. Let's go see your dad and try to talk about the move tomorrow."

"He was adamant that he wanted to stay in Portland and not be a bother," Ana says.

"I'll talk to him."

She fingers the buttons on my shirt. "I want to travel with him."

That should be possible. "Okay. I'll come, too. Sawyer and Taylor can take the cars. I'll let Sawyer drive your R8 tonight."

She offers me a sweet smile of thanks, and I feel ten feet tall.

RAY HAS CAPITULATED; HE'S in far better spirits than he was this morning. The doughnuts must have worked their magic, and I think he's secretly pleased that he'll get to ride in a helicopter tomorrow. He doesn't remember anything of his flight here from Astoria. I make a mental note to take him up in *Charlie Tango* at some point.

While Ana sits with him, I head to the waiting room to finalize Ray's move.

Andrea has everything organized. She is, without doubt, the best PA I've ever had.

"Thanks, Andrea."

"You're welcome, Mr. Grey. Anything else?"

"No, it's all good. Go home."

"Will do, sir."

I fire off a quick e-mail to Samir to review Andrea's salary and recommend a generous raise.

Before I head back to the ward, I reflect on Clark's visit and what he did and didn't say. He's obviously liaising with the FBI with regard to *Charlie Tango*'s sabotage, but mentioned that he's searching Hyde's apartment again. Why? Does he have another lead? Or is it something else that he's not telling us? And where *was* Hyde while he was planning his kidnap attempt? It's obvious he was still in Seattle; I have the CCTV footage to prove it. This is worth exploring.

I e-mail Welch and Barney and ask them if they tracked the movements of the white van that Hyde used before he arrived at Escala.

Perhaps they'll come up with something.

TUESDAY, SEPTEMBER 13, 2011

I hang up from my phone conversation with my mother and catch Ana's monochrome eye. She's gazing down at me from my office wall with her disarming smile, her eyes bright and brimming with intelligence. It's been only three hours since I saw her, but I miss her already. I wonder what she's doing right now? She's probably at work and if all has gone to plan, Ray should be settled in his room at Northwest Hospital where my mother will keep an eye on him. I hope he's comfortable, or as comfortable as he can be. He seemed to enjoy the flight from OHSU to Boeing Field, but he's not a man who likes to be the center of attention—quite the opposite, in fact. A little like his daughter.

And here I am, missing her.

Last time I saw her, she was heading to the hospital in an ambulance with her father.

I glance at my watch.

She'll definitely be at work.

I type a quick e-mail.

From: Christian Grey
Subject: Missing You
Date: September 13 2011 13:58
To: Anastasia Grey

Mrs. Grey
I've been back in the office for only three hours, and I'm missing you already.
Hope Ray has settled into his new room okay. Mom is going to see him this afternoon and check up on him.
I'll collect you around six this evening, and we can go see him before heading home.
Sound good?

Your loving husband

Christian Grey
CEO, Grey Enterprises Holdings, Inc.

I press send, then open the report on my desk and start to read. But almost immediately the ping of a new e-mail distracts me. Ana?

No. It's from Barney.

From: Barney Sullivan
Subject: Jack Hyde
Date: September 13 2011 14:09
To: Christian Grey

CCTV around Seattle tracks the white van from South Irving Street. Before that I can find no trace, so Hyde must have been based in that area.

As Welch has told you, the unsub car was rented with a false license by an unknown female, though nothing that ties it to the South Irving Street area.

Details of known GEH and SIP employees who live in the area are in the attached file, which I have forwarded to Welch, too.

There was nothing on Hyde's SIP computer about his former PAs.

As a reminder, here is a list of what was retrieved from Hyde's SIP computer.

Greys' Home Addresses:
Five properties in Seattle
Two properties in Detroit

Detailed Résumés for:
Carrick Grey
Elliot Grey
Christian Grey
Dr. Grace Trevelyan
Anastasia Steele
Mia Grey

Newspaper and online articles relating to:
Dr. Grace Trevelyan
Carrick Grey
Christian Grey
Elliot Grey

Photographs:
Carrick Grey
Dr. Grace Trevelyan
Christian Grey
Elliot Grey
Mia Grey

I'll continue my investigation, see what else I can find.

B Sullivan
Head of IT, GEH

I gaze at the contents of his e-mail and wonder when Hyde started scouring the internet for information on my family. Was it before Ana started working with him? Or was it after he'd met me? I'm about to pen a response to Barney when Ana's reply to my earlier e-mail pops into my inbox.

From: Anastasia Grey
Subject: Missing You
Date: September 13 2011 14:10
To: Christian Grey

Sure.
x

Anastasia Grey
Editor, SIP

Oh. Feeling a tad deflated, I glance at the enigmatic, smiling goddess on the wall. I thought we might indulge in some e-mail banter.

She's normally so good at that.

This is not like her.

From: Christian Grey
Subject: Missing You
Date: September 13 2011 14:14
To: Anastasia Grey

Are you okay?

Christian Grey
CEO, Grey Enterprises Holdings, Inc.

While I wait for her reply, I sift through the address file that Barney has attached to his e-mail. A couple of GEH employee names, and one from SIP, jump out at me: the highest-profile name is Elizabeth Morgan, the HR director at SIP. Her name stirs something in the back of my brain, but whatever it is, it remains elusive. I'll ask Welch to follow up on her when we next speak, but it's hard to conceive that any of these people could be involved with Hyde.

I dismiss that train of thought and wonder what's up with Ana. I'm tempted to pick up the phone and call her, but as I reach for it, another e-mail arrives from her.

From: Anastasia Grey
Subject: Missing You
Date: September 13 2011 14:17
To: Christian Grey

Fine. Just busy.
See you at six.
x

Anastasia Grey
Editor, SIP

Of course she's busy. She's missed a few days of work, and my girl is nothing but conscientious.

Grey, keep it together.

I go back to Barney's e-mail and read through his list one more time. It doesn't yield any further insights, but maybe he can answer a question for me.

From: Christian Grey
Subject: Jack Hyde
Date: September 13 2011 14:23
To: Barney Sullivan

Barney
Thanks for the e-mail. Can you track when Hyde began these internet searches?

Christian Grey
CEO, Grey Enterprises Holdings, Inc.

I check the time; I have a catch-up with Ros.

TAYLOR AND I WAIT for Ana outside SIP. I glance anxiously toward the entrance, hoping that she'll be out at any moment. An e-mail alert appears on my phone.

From: Barney Sullivan
Subject: Jack Hyde
Date: September 13 2011 17:35
To: Christian Grey

Internet searches on the topics in Hyde's e-mail happened between 19:32 Monday, June 13, 2011, and 17:14 Wednesday, June 15, 2011.

B Sullivan
Head of IT, GEH

Hmm… Interesting. I remember I'd met him the Friday before, at the bar when I'd arranged to meet Ana. He was a loudmouthed asshole then. I wonder if he was looking for anything specific on my family, and if he found it. I glance out of the window, and finally Ana appears. She dashes toward the car, dodging the rain, Sawyer at her heels. I smile as I watch her, but my heart sinks when she glances into the car.

Her face is a stark alabaster in the gray rain.

Shit!

Sawyer opens her door, and she slides in beside me.

"Hi." The inflection in my voice is tentative. *What is it, Ana?*

"Hi." Her eyes flick to my face, briefly—too briefly, and all I see is her turmoil flashing back at me.

"What's wrong?"

She shakes her head as Taylor pulls into traffic. "Nothing."

I don't think that's true. "Is work all right?"

"Yes. Fine. Thanks." Her tone is clipped.

Tell me! "Ana, what's wrong?" My words are harsher than I intend, as they're loaded with my anxiety.

"I've just missed you, that's all. And I've been worried about Ray."

Oh, of course. Thank God. I brighten immediately. "Ray's good." I try to reassure her. "I spoke to Mom this afternoon, and she's impressed with his progress." I reach for her hand. It's freezing. "Boy, your hand is cold. Have you eaten today?"

She flushes.

"Ana." *Why does she do this?*

"I'll eat this evening. I haven't really had time."

I rub her hand in an attempt to warm it. "Do you want me to add 'feed my wife' to the security detail's list of duties?" I catch Taylor's eye in the rearview mirror.

"I'm sorry. I'll eat. It's just been a weird day. You know, moving Dad and all."

I guess. She turns away and stares out the window, leaving me to flounder.

Something's not right.

It *has* been a weird day.

Take her at her word, Grey.

I give her my news to test the water. "I may have to go to Taiwan."

"Oh. When?" This gets her attention.

"Later this week. Maybe next week."

"Okay."

"I want you to come with me."

Her lips thin. "Christian, please. I have my job. Let's not rehash this argument again."

I blow out a breath, unable to conceal my disappointment. "Thought I'd ask."

"How long will you go for?" Ana's voice is soft, but distracted.

This is not my girl. She's too quiet and hesitant.

"Not more than a couple of days. I wish you'd tell me what's bothering you."

"Well, now that my beloved husband is going away..." Her voice fades as I raise her hand to my lips and kiss her knuckles.

"I won't be away for long."

"Good." She gives me a thin smile, but I know she's preoccupied.

I gaze out the window and go through several scenarios that might be bothering Ana. Only one rings true: her father has just been in a major accident and his recovery will take some time.

Yes.

That's it.

Grey, get a grip.

RAYMOND STEELE IS HAPPY to see us. "Can't thank you enough for organizing all this." He waves at the airy room, his dark eyes full of quiet sincerity.

"Ray, you're most welcome." Uncomfortable with his gratitude, I change the subject. "I see you have a stack of sports magazines."

"From Annie. I've been reading about the Mariners, and the season they've been having." Ray launches into a diatribe about how disappointed he is with the M's this year. I have to say, I'm with him; it's not been a stellar season. Our conversation moves on to fishing. He's sorry to miss out on his angling trip in Astoria, and I mention my recent fishing expedition in Aspen.

"Roaring Fork—I know it," he says.

"You should come and stay. Maybe for a weekend, once you're up and about."

"I'd appreciate that, Christian."

Throughout our discussion Ana is quiet.

Too quiet. She's tuning out and going elsewhere.

It's frustrating. *Ana. What's wrong?*

Ray yawns. Ana glances at me, and I know it's time to go. "Daddy, we'll leave you to sleep."

"Thanks, Ana honey. I like that you drop by. Saw your mom today, too, Christian. She was very reassuring. And she's a Mariners fan!"

"She's not crazy about fishing, though."

"Don't know many women who are, eh?" Ray's smile is weary. He needs to rest.

"I'll see you tomorrow, okay?" Ana kisses his forehead, and there's a trace of sadness in her voice.

Hell. Why is she sad? "Come." I hold out my hand. Is she tired? Maybe what she needs is an early night.

ANA WAS QUIET IN the car and quiet when we got home, and now she's just chasing her food around her plate with her fork, taciturn and distracted. My anxiety has climbed to DEFCON 1.

"Damn it! Ana, will you tell me what's wrong?" I push my empty plate away. "Please. You're driving me crazy."

She turns apprehensive eyes to mine.

"I'm pregnant."

What? I stare at her as a frisson of disbelief skitters down my spine, and for some unknown reason, I'm suddenly at the door of the skydiving plane, hanging over the world without a parachute, about to leap out.

Into the air.

Into nothing.

"What?" I don't recognize my voice.

"I'm pregnant."

That's what I thought you said.

But I thought we took care of this.

"How?"

She tilts her head to one side and raises a brow.

Fuck. Anger like I've never felt before erupts inside me. "Your shot?" I snarl. "Did you forget your shot?"

She just stares at me, eyes glassy, as if she's looking right through me, and says nothing.

I don't want kids.

Not yet.

Not now. Panic knots in my chest and tightens around my throat, feeding my fury. "Christ, Ana!" I bang my fist on the table and stand. "You have one thing, one thing to remember. Shit! I don't fucking believe it. How could you be so stupid?"

She closes her eyes, then stares down at her fingers. "I'm sorry," she whispers.

"Sorry? Fuck!" A *child. What do I do with a child?*

"I know the timing's not very good."

"Not very good!" My bellow echoes around the room. "We've known each other five fucking minutes! I wanted to show you the fucking world and now… Fuck! Diapers and vomit and shit—!" I close my eyes.

You won't love me anymore.

"Did you forget? Tell me. Or did you do this on purpose?"

"No." Her word is a quiet rush of denial.

"I thought we'd agreed on this!" And I don't give a fuck who can hear me.

She cringes, folding in on herself. "I know. We had. I'm sorry."

"This is why! This is why I like control—so shit like this doesn't come along and fuck everything up!"

"Christian, please don't shout at me."

Fuck.

I'll be displaced.

She starts to cry.

Don't you dare, Ana. "Don't start with waterworks now! Fuck." I run a hand through my hair, trying to comprehend this colossal fuckup. "You think I'm ready to be a father?" My voice cracks on the last word.

She turns tear-filled eyes to me. "I know neither one of us is ready for this," she mumbles, "but I think you'll make a wonderful father. We'll figure it out."

"How the fuck do you know!" My voice clamors around the room. "Tell me how!"

She opens her mouth, and closes it again as tears stream down her face.

And there it is—her regret.

Regret that's writ large in every feature of her face. Regret that she's saddled with me.

I can't bear it.

My fury is drowning me.

"Oh, fuck this!" I rage at the world and back away, holding up my hands in defeat.

I cannot do this—

I'm out of here.

Grabbing my jacket, I storm out of the room, slamming the foyer door. Frantically, I stab the call button, and even though the elevator is on our floor the doors take far too fucking long to open.

A child?

A fucking child?

I step into the elevator, but in my head I'm underneath a kitchen table, in a shambolic, grimy, neglected hovel, waiting for him to find me.

There you are, you little shit.

Hell and damnation.

Fuck, no.

On the ground floor, I slam through the main doors out of Escala and onto the sidewalk. I drag in a lungful of fresh fall air, but it does little to assuage the anger and fear that surge in equal measure through my veins. I need to get away. Instinctively, I turn right and start walking, barely noticing that it's stopped raining.

I walk.

And walk.

In a daze.

Concentrating on the simple act of placing one foot in front of the other.

Blotting out all other thoughts.

Except one.

How could she do this to me?

How?

How can I love a child?

I've only just learned to love her.

When I look up, I'm at Flynn's office. There's no way he's going to be here. The door doesn't shift—it's locked. I call him but get his voice mail. I don't leave a message. I can't trust myself.

Jamming my hands into the pockets of my jacket and ignoring the commuters on the streets, I trudge on.

Aimless.

When I look up, Elena is locking up the salon, shrouded in her usual black attire. We gaze at each other; she's on one side of the glass, I'm on the other. She unlocks and opens the door.

"Hello, Christian. You look like shit."

I stare at her, not knowing what to say.

"Are you coming in?"

I shake my head and step back.

Grey, what are you doing?

Somewhere deep in my subconscious an alarm is sounding.

I ignore it.

Elena sighs and taps a scarlet nail against scarlet lips, her silver ring catching the evening light. "Shall we go for a drink?"

"Yes."

"The Mile High?"

"No. Somewhere less crowded."

"I see." She tries and fails to hide her surprise. "Okay."

"There's a bar around the corner."

"I know the one. It's a quiet place. Let me grab my purse."

Standing on the sidewalk while I wait for her, I feel numb.

I've just walked out on my pregnant wife.

But right now I'm too mad at her to care.

Grey, what are you doing?

I shake the disquieting voice from my head, and Elena steps out of her salon, locks the door, and with a slight nod of her head indicates right. I jam my hands farther into my pockets and together we walk the rest of the block, around the corner, and into the bar.

It's had a considerable makeover since I was last here—it's no longer a dive, but an upscale watering hole, all paneled wood and plush velvet seating. Elena was right—it is quiet except for Billie Holiday's soft, melancholic voice over the sound system.

Apt.

We slide into a booth, and Elena signals for the waitress.

"Good evening, my name's Sunny. What can I get you folks?"

"I'd like a glass of your Willamette pinot noir," Elena says.

"A bottle," I order, without looking at the waitress. Elena's eyebrows rise a fraction, but she maintains her familiar air of cool detachment. Maybe that's why I'm here; that's what I'm looking for—cool detachment personified.

"Coming right up." The young woman leaves us.

"So, all is not well in the world of Christian Grey," Elena observes. "I knew I'd see you again." Her eyes are fixed on mine and I don't know what to say. "Like that, is it?" Elena fills the silence between us. "Did you get my text?"

"On my wedding day?"

"Yes."

"I did. I deleted it."

"Christian, I can feel your enmity from here. It's coming off you in waves. But you wouldn't be here if I was the enemy."

I blow out a breath and sit back in the booth.

"Why are you here?" she asks, not unreasonably.

Fuck. "I don't know." Could I sound any more sullen?

"She's left you?"

"Don't." I give her a glacial stare.

I don't want to talk about Ana.

Elena purses her lips as the waitress returns. We both sit back and watch as she uncorks our wine and pours a sample into my glass. "I'm sure it's fine." I wave in Elena's direction and the waitress fills each of our glasses in turn.

"Enjoy," she says brightly, leaving us with the bottle.

Elena reaches for her glass and raises it. "To old friends." She smirks and takes a sip.

I snort, feeling some of my tension leave my shoulders. "Old friends." I raise my glass and gulp down a few mouthfuls of wine, not tasting it. Elena frowns and presses her lips together but says nothing, her eyes not leaving mine.

I sigh. She wants me to fill the silence. I'm going to have to say something. "How's the business?"

"Good. It was generous of you to gift it to me. Thank you for that."

"It was the least I could do."

She glances down at her glass as the silence between us expands.

Eventually, she breaks it. "As you're here, I think I should apologize for how I behaved at your parents' house."

Well, this is a surprise. It's not like Mrs. Lincoln to apologize for anything. Her mantra has always been "never apologize, never explain."

"I said several things that I regret," she adds quietly.

"We both did, Elena. It's in the past."

I offer her more wine, but she declines—her glass is still half full, while mine is empty. I pour myself another.

She sighs. "My social circle is considerably diminished. I miss your mother. It hurts that she won't see me."

"It's probably not a good idea for you to get in contact with her."

"I know. I understand. I never meant for her to overhear us. Grace was always most fearsome when it came to protecting her brood." She looks wistful for a moment. "We shared some good times, though. Your mother knows how to party."

"I don't wish to know that."

Elena laughs. "You've always placed her on such a pedestal."

"I'm not here to talk about my mother."

"What are you here to talk about, Christian?" She cocks her head to the side and runs a scarlet nail around the rim of her glass, icy blue eyes on mine.

I shake my head and take another long draft of the pinot.

"Has she left you?"

"No!" I snap. If anything, it was *me* who walked out.

What kind of man walks out on his pregnant wife?

Hell. Maybe my father was right.

His words come back to haunt me. *It's about you. You living up to your responsibilities. You being a trustworthy and decent human being. You being husband material.*

Maybe I'm not husband material.

I shake off the thought as Elena gazes at me, and I know she's trying to work out what's wrong. "You miss it? The lifestyle? Is that it? The little woman not giving you what you want?"

Fuck you, Elena.

I don't have to listen to her bullshit.

I start to slide out of the booth.

"Christian. Don't go. I'm sorry." She reaches for my hand, then changes her mind, so her outstretched hand becomes a fist on the table. "Please. Don't go," she pleads.

Two apologies from Mrs. Lincoln in such a short time.

I settle back in my seat. Warier.

"I'm sorry," she says once more, for emphasis. Then tries a different tack. "How is Anastasia?"

"She's good," I answer, eventually, and hope that I haven't given anything away.

Elena narrows her eyes; she doesn't believe me.

I exhale and confess. "She wants children."

"Ah," Elena says, as if she's solved the riddle of the Sphinx. "This shouldn't be a surprise to you. Though I will say she's a little young to be producing your spawn."

"Spawn?" I scoff, because she's said the last word with such malicious invective. Elena's never wanted children. I suspect she doesn't have a maternal bone in her body.

"Baby Grey," she muses. "That *will* put an end to your predilections." She looks amused. "Or maybe they've come to an end already."

I scowl at her. "Elena. Shut up. I'm not here to discuss my sex life with you." I drain my glass and pour more wine for us both, finishing the bottle. The pinot noir is beginning to work its magic. I'm already feeling hazy around the edges. It's not a sensation I normally enjoy, but right now, I welcome the oblivion that beckons from the bottom of my glass. I signal the waitress for another bottle.

"Has she done something specific to upset you? I haven't seen you drink like this in years." Elena sounds most disapproving. But I don't give a fuck.

"How's Isaac?" I ask, to move the focus to her lover and away from my wife. My marriage is none of her business.

She half smiles and folds her arms. "Okay. I get it. You really don't want to talk." She pauses, and I know she's waiting for me to spill my guts. But my secrets are mine. Not hers.

"Isaac is fine," she continues, finally. "Thank you for asking. In fact, we're really good at the moment." She launches into a tale of their latest sexual escapade, but to what end, I don't know. I half listen and half let the wine carry me away.

"So, is it the business? Is that your issue?" she asks when I don't react.

"No, it's going great. I bought a shipyard."

She nods, impressed, I think, and I refill both our glasses from the latest bottle, and give her a rundown of what I've been doing at work: the solar-powered tablet, the fiber-optic business takeover, Geolumara, and of course the shipyard.

"You've been busy."

"Always."

"So, you're talkative about your business, but not your wife."

"And?" *Is this a problem?*

"I knew you'd come back," she whispers.

What?

"Why are you drinking so much?"

"Because I'm thirsty." *And I want to forget how I behaved two hours ago.*

She regards me through half-closed eyes. "Thirsty?" she breathes. "How thirsty?" She leans in and reaches over, taking my hand. I tense as her fingers slide under my palm, and beneath the cuffs of my jacket and shirt. Her fingernails digging into my flesh over my pulse. "Maybe I could make you feel better? I'm sure you miss it." Her breath is stale, not sweet like Ana's. Her hand tightens around my wrist, and from nowhere the darkness circles my chest and starts spiraling into my throat. It's a feeling I haven't experienced for a while, and now it's back, amplified, echoing through my body and screaming for release.

"What are you doing?" I squeeze the words out.

It's tightening its hold on me.

Don't touch me.

This was how it was.

Always.

Me fighting my fear as she laid her hands on me.

"Don't touch me." I withdraw my hand from hers.

She pales and frowns, her eyes on mine. "Isn't this what you want?"

"No!"

"That's not why you're here?"

"No, Elena. No. I haven't thought about you like that for years." I shake my head, wondering how she could have so badly misread my intentions, but my thoughts aren't as clear as they should be. "I love my wife," I whisper.

Ana.

Elena studies me, her formerly pale cheeks reddening with wine or embarrassment or both. She frowns and looks down at the table. "I'm sorry," she mutters.

Apology number three.

My cup runneth over.

"I don't know…what came over me." She laughs—but her laughter is loud, forced. "I have to go." She gathers her purse. "Christian, I wish you and your wife well." She stops and looks me squarely in the eye. "I miss you, though. More than you know."

"Good-bye, Elena."

"The way you say that has a finality about it."

I don't answer her.

She nods. "It would be difficult. I get it. I'm glad you came to see me. I think we've cleared the air."

Have we? Cleared the air about what? Us? There is no us.

"Good-bye, Mrs. Lincoln." I know it's the last time I'll ever say these words to her.

She nods. "Good luck, Christian Grey." She slides out of the booth. "It was good to see you. I hope whatever it is that's bothering you sorts itself out. I'm sure it will. If it's about being a dad, you'll do great." She tosses her sleek hair over her shoulder and exits the bar without a backward glance, leaving me with a half-empty bottle of pinot noir and an uneasy feeling of guilt.

I want to go home.

To Ana.

Shit.

I put my head in my hands. Ana will be mad as hell when I get home.

Grabbing the bottle and my glass, I head toward the bar to settle my tab. There's a stool free, so I sit down and replenish my glass.

Waste not, want not.

I nurse my drink. Slowly.

Hell. I hate it when Ana's mad at me. If I go home now, I may say something else I'll regret. Besides, I've had too much to drink, and I don't think Ana's ever seen me drunk. Of course, I've seen *her* drunk—that first night I slept with her at The Heathman, and the night of her bachelorette party…

Her words float through my slow, intoxicated brain.

Are you going to punish me?

Punish you?

For getting so drunk. A punishment fuck. You can do anything you want to me.

Stop. Grey.

I wonder when she got pregnant.

On our honeymoon? In our bed? In the Red Room?

Fuck…

Junior.

We'll need a fucking minivan.

Will he have Ana's blue eyes? My temper? *Shit.* My glass is empty. I refill it, finishing the bottle.

There will be hell to pay if Ana ever finds out I've had a drink with Elena. She loathes Elena.

Christian—if that were your son, how would you feel?

Oh, Ana, Ana, Ana.

I don't want to think about that.

Not now. It's too raw and too painful.

I need oblivion.

I want to forget who I am, and how I've behaved.

The way I used to…before…everything.

Before Mrs. Robinson.

The barman looks my way.

"Bourbon, please."

WEDNESDAY, SEPTEMBER 14, 2011

"We're here." The driver turns and flashes me a wide big-toothed grin.

"Wha?" I'm in a car… A cab. My face is pressed against cool glass. My head is spinning. *Shit.* Closing one eye, I squint up at the building we're parked outside. The brass lantern beckons bright in the darkness.

"Escala?" the driver says.

"Oh. Yeah." From my inside pocket I fumble for my wallet and paw through the notes. I hand one to the cabdriver and hope it's enough.

"Wow! Thanks!"

I open the car door and fall onto the sidewalk.

"Fuck."

"You okay?" he calls.

"Yeah." I lay there for a second, staring up at the night sky, waiting for the world to stop spinning. It's clear and there are a few stars shining down, winking at me. It's peaceful.

I'm lying on the sidewalk.

Get up, Grey.

A man looms over me, blotting out the light from the lantern, and for a moment a chill grips my heart. "Here." He offers me his hand.

Oh, he's here to help… Cab guy? Maybe. He hauls me to my feet.

"One too many, eh?"

"Yeah. More than one. I think." I make a half-assed attempt to brush myself down, and the driver climbs back into his car. Turning around, I start to sway and use forward momentum to stagger into the building and over to the elevator. I'll be okay if I can just get to bed. The elevator doors open and I stumble inside. I punch in the code… the elevator doesn't move.

I try again.

Nothing.

Hell.

One more time.

I close one eye and jab at the buttons. That does the trick! The doors slide shut and the elevator hums, indicating some movement on its part… Wait, no—everything is moving. I lean against the wall and close my eyes to stop the spinning. The ping sounds. I'm here! I open my eyes and stumble out into the foyer.

Fuck. I bump into something.

Who the hell moved the foyer table?

"Shit!" Placing my hands on the table, I steady myself, but it fucking moves again, the scraping sound grating on what's left of my nerves.

"Shit!" I make it to the double doors.

"Christian, are you okay?"

I look up, and there she is, dressed like a goddess on the silver screen.

Ana. My own Aphrodite. My wife. My heart fills with love and light. She's so beautiful. "Mrs. Grey." The doorjamb holds me up. "Oh, you look mighty fine, Anastashia."

Suddenly she's closer and I have to squint to bring her into focus.

"Where have you been?" She sounds worried.

Oh, no. I mustn't tell her. She'll be mad as hell. I bring my fingers to my lips. "Shh!"

"I think you'd better come to bed."

Bed. With Ana. There is nowhere I would rather be. "With you." I give her my best smile, but she's frowning.

"Let me help you to bed. Lean on me." She wraps her arm around my middle, and I lean against her, catching the scent of her hair.

Nectar. "You are very beautiful, Ana."

"Christian, walk! I am going to put you to bed."

She's so bossy! But I want her happy. "Okay." We move. Together. Down the corridor. One slow step at a time. And then we're in our bedroom. "Bed." It is a most welcome sight.

"Yes, bed," Ana says. Her face is a blur. But it's still lovely. I hold her to me.

"Join me."

"Christian, I think you need some sleep."

Oh, no. "And so it begins. I've heard about this."

"Heard about what?"

"Babies mean no sex."

"I'm sure that's not true. Otherwise we'd all come from one-child families."

Mrs. Grey has an answer for everything, with her smart mouth. "You're funny."

"You're drunk."

"Yes." *Very.*

To forget.

There you are, you little shit.

"Come on, Christian," Ana says. Gentle, compassionate Ana. "Let's get you into bed."

Suddenly I am on the bed.

It's so comfortable.

I should just stay here.

She stands over me, dressed in silk or satin, as tempting as Eve herself. I hold my arms out to her. "Join me."

"Let's get you undressed first."

Hmm… Naked. With Ana. "Now you're talking."

"Sit up. Let me take your jacket off."

"The room is spinning."

"Christian. Sit up!"

I smile up at her. "Mrs. Grey, you are a bossy little thing."

"Yes. Do as you're told and sit up." She places her hands on her hips. She's trying to look stern…I think. But she just looks lovely.

My wife.

My beloved wife.

Slowly, I wrestle with the bed, to sit up.

I win.

She grabs my tie.

And I think she's trying to undress me. She's close. So close. I drink in her unique scent. "You smell good."

"You smell of hard liquor."

"Yes. Bour. Bon." Oh shit—the room is a carousel again. To keep myself anchored to the bed, I rest my hands on Ana, and the spinning slows. Her nightgown is warm and soft, augmenting her body heat. "I like the feel of this fabric on you, Anastay-shia. You should always be in satin or silk."

Of course. It's not just her now. I jerk her closer. I want to talk to Junior. We need to set some ground rules. "And we have an invader in here. You're going to keep me awake, aren't you?"

Ana's hands are in my hair. I raise my face up to her. My Madonna. Mother of my child. And in that moment, I tell her my darkest fear. "You'll choose him over me."

"Christian, you don't know what you're talking about. Don't be ridiculous—I am not choosing anyone over anyone. And he might be a she."

"A she. Oh God."

A girl?

A baby girl?

No. The room won't stop spinning and I fall back on the bed…

Baby Mia, with her shock of dark hair and watchful dark eyes. Ana holds her. There's a light breeze on my face. It's cooling in the sunshine. We're in the orchard. Ana's face radiates with love as she smiles down at Mia, then aims sad eyes to me. She walks away, not turning back to look, as I stand watching her. She doesn't look back. She continues and disappears into the garage at The Heathman. She doesn't look back. Every sinew, every bone, every atom of my marrow is aching. *No.* I want to call out. But I can't speak. I have no words. I'm curled on the floor. Bound. Gagged. Aching. Everywhere. The clip of red heeled stilettos echoes off the flagstones. *So, you got drunk. Again.* Elena's wearing a strap-on and wielding a long, thin cane. No. No. This will be hard to take. *I'm sorry. I didn't say you could speak.* Her tone is clipped. Formal. I brace myself. Digging deep. She trails the cane down my spine, and suddenly it disappears from my skin, offering me a brief respite before she strikes me across my back. I take a deep breath as I embrace its fiery bite across my skin. She pokes the tip of the cane at my skull. Pain radiates through my head. The door crashes open and his bulk fills the frame. Elena screams. And screams. And screams. The sound splitting my head in two. He's here. And he hits me, a good left hook to my jaw, and my skull explodes with pain. *Shit.*

My eyes crack open, and light slices through my brain like a scalpel. I shut them immediately. *Fuck.* My head—my throbbing, aching head.

What the hell?

I'm lying on top of the bed, cold and stiff.

Dressed?

Why? I open my eyes again, slowly this time, allowing the daylight to creep in. I'm home.

What happened? I struggle to remember, but something, a misdeed maybe, is chafing on my conscience.

Grey. What did you do?

Slowly, my mind draws back the curtains on last night, revealing some of my transgressions.

Drinking.

A keg full.

I sit up, too quickly—my head swims and bile rises in my throat. I force it down while I rub my temples, racking what's left of my brain to recall what happened. Vague images of the previous evening flash fuzzy and malformed through my mind. Red wine and bourbon?

What was I thinking?

The baby. Fuck.

I lift my head to check on Ana, but she's not here, and it's obvious she didn't sleep in this bed last night.

Where is she?

I take stock of myself. No injuries, but I'm still in yesterday's clothes, and I stink.

Hell. Did I drive Ana away?

What time is it? I glance at the clock and it's 7:05 a.m. Shakily, I get to my feet, which are bare. I don't remember removing my socks.

I rub my forehead.

Where is my wife? Unease yawns in my gut, accompanied by a burning sense of guilt.

Damn, what did I do?

My phone is on the nightstand; I pick it up and stagger to the bathroom. Ana's not there. Nor is she in the spare room.

Mrs. Jones is in the kitchen. She gives me a cursory glance, then returns to her work. Ana is nowhere to be seen. "Good morning, Gail. Ana?"

"I haven't seen her, sir." Her tone is arctic. Mrs. Jones is pissed.

At me?

Why?

Ignoring her, I check the library. Nothing.

My unease blooms.

Studiously avoiding Gail's frosty gaze, I head back through the living room to check my study and the TV room. Ana is not in there either.

Fuck.

In spite of feeling like shit, I hurry back through the living room, bolt upstairs, and check both of the guest rooms. *No Ana.*

She's gone. She's fucking gone. I dash downstairs, ignoring the stabbing at my temples, and burst into Taylor's office. He looks up, surprised, I think.

"Ana?"

His face is impassive. "I haven't seen her, sir."

"For fuck's sake, we have how many security personnel here? Where the fuck is my wife?" I explode, and my head pounds. I close my eyes as Taylor's face pales.

Shit. Get a grip, Grey.

"Did she go out?" I ask, in as measured a tone as I can manage.

"There's nothing in the log, sir."

"I can't find her." I'm at a loss.

He casts his eyes over the CCTV monitors. "All the vehicles are accounted for. And no one can get in."

I blanch as I grasp his meaning. Has she been kidnapped?

Taylor notices my expression. "No one can get in, sir," he repeats for emphasis.

"Leila Williams and Jack Hyde got in!" I snap.

"Miss Williams had a key, and Ryan let Hyde in," Taylor counters. "I'll check the apartment, Mr. Grey."

I nod and follow him out into the hallway.

She wouldn't leave. Would she? I rack my addled, aching brain and recall a vision of Ana—from last night, I think—dressed in the softest satin, fragrant and beautiful, smiling down at me. Taylor heads off to our bedroom, no doubt to look there, and I don't stop him. I might have missed something.

My phone!

I could call her.

Wait. There's a text from her, in very shouty capitals.

> ANA
> WOULD YOU LIKE MRS. LINCOLN
> TO JOIN US WHEN WE EVENTUALLY
> DISCUSS THIS TEXT SHE SENT
> YOU? IT WILL SAVE YOU RUNNING
> TO HER AFTERWARD.
> YOUR WIFE
>
> FORWARDED: ELENA
> It was good to see you. I understand now.
> Don't fret. You'll make a wonderful father.

Oh, shit.

Ana's been reading my texts.

When?

How dare she?

Anger flares inside me. I press call, and Ana's phone rings, and rings. And fucking rings. Eventually it diverts to voice mail. "Where the hell are you?" I snarl into my BlackBerry, furious that she's been reading my texts, furious that she knows about Elena, furious *with* Elena—but most of all, I'm furious at myself and at the clawing fear that threatens to choke me. She's missing.

Ana, where the fuck are you? Perhaps she's left me.

Where would she go? *Kate.* Of course. I call Kavanagh.

"Hello." Kate answers after several rings, her voice thick with sleep.

"It's Christian."

"Christian? What is it? Is Ana okay?" Kate is fully awake and instantly adopts her familiar badgering tone, which I do not need right now.

"She's not with you?" I ask.

"No. Should she be?"

"No. Don't worry. Go back to sleep."

"Chris—" I hang up.

My head is pounding and my wife is missing. This is hell. I'm in hell. I try Ana's phone and again it diverts to voice mail. I storm into the kitchen where Gail is making coffee. "Can you get me some Advil, please?" I'm as gracious as a man with a missing wife can be. She stifles a smile.

Is she smiling because I'm suffering?

I scowl at her as she wordlessly places a container of Advil on the counter and turns to fill a glass of water, leaving me to struggle with the childproof lid. Eventually, I manage to pry two tablets from the plastic tub as stony-faced Mrs. Jones places water in front of me.

Glaring at her, I tip both pills into my mouth, but she turns back to the stove. I take a sip.

Hell. The water is lukewarm; it tastes awful.

I glower at her; she's done this on purpose. Slamming the glass down on the counter, I turn and stomp back upstairs to look for Ana, hoping that the capsules will settle the storm in my head.

Taylor is emerging from what was the submissives' room. He looks grim. I try the playroom door. It's locked, but in my frustration, I rattle it anyway just to make sure, and bellow Ana's name down the corridor. Immediately I regret raising my voice, as pain lances through my head.

"Any luck?" I ask Taylor.

"No, sir. I've checked the gym, and roused Sawyer and Ryan. They're searching the staff quarters."

"Good. We need a plan."

"We'll meet downstairs."

Back in the kitchen, we're joined by Sawyer and Ryan; Ryan looks like he's had less sleep than me.

"Mrs. Grey is missing," I growl at them. "Sawyer, check the CCTV footage and see if you can track her movements. Ryan, Taylor, let's search the apartment again."

All of them suddenly look shocked—their eyes wide, their mouths dropping open.

What?

A movement from the corner of my eye catches my attention.

It's Ana.

Thank Christ. She's here. For a moment my relief is overwhelming, but as Ana stands and surveys us, I see she's cool and distant, her eyes wide, but with telltale dark circles beneath. She's wrapped in a duvet—small, pale, and utterly beautiful.

And mad as hell.

As I drink her in, a sense of foreboding creeps up my spine, raising all the hair on the back of my head. She squares her narrow shoulders, raises her chin in that stubborn way she does, and completely ignoring me, addresses Luke. "Sawyer, I'll be ready to leave in about twenty minutes." She tightens the duvet around her, keeping her chin high.

Oh, Ana. I'm just so glad she's still here. *She hasn't left me.*

"Would you like some breakfast, Mrs. Grey?" Gail asks, in such a sweet, solicitous tone that I turn to look at her in surprise. Her eyes slide to me, as frigid as ever.

Ana shakes her head. "I'm not hungry, thank you." Her voice is soft and clear, but her expression's implacable. Is she not eating in order to punish me? Is that what this is? But now is not the time for that argument.

"Where were you?" I ask, bemused. Behind me there's a sudden burst of activity as my staff make themselves scarce. I ignore them, as does Ana. She turns and heads toward our bedroom.

"Ana! Answer me!"

Don't fucking ignore me!

I follow in her stately wake down the hallway, into our suite, until she turns into our bathroom, shuts the door, and locks it.

Shit!

"Ana!" I thump on the door, then try the handle. "Ana, open the damned door."

Why is she doing this? Because I walked out last night? Because I saw Elena?

"Go away!" she shouts over the sound of gushing water from the shower.

"I'm not going anywhere!"

"Suit yourself."

"Ana, please." I rattle the door once more in an effort to express my anger, but I feel nothing except impotent rage. How dare she lock the door? It takes all my self-control not to break it down, but given her attitude, and my headache, that probably wouldn't be a wise choice.

Why is she so mad?

She's mad?

After the ten-fingered, ten-toed bombshell she dropped on me?

Or is it because I got drunk?

Deep down I know the problem.

Elena. Why couldn't Mrs. Lincoln keep her thoughts to herself?

I knew it was a mistake to see her.

I knew it in the bar.

This is a fuckup, Grey.

Well, as my mother always likes to say, it takes two to tango. Wives get mad at their husbands all the time. Don't they? This is normal, surely. I scowl at the locked door.

What can I do?

Find your happy place. Flynn's words invade my thoughts as I lean against the wall.

Well, my happy place is not fucking standing here.

My happy place is in the shower.

But I don't have a choice.

My head is thumping. At least the sound of the rushing water from the shower is less painful than my shouting. Otherwise, it's all quiet. I contemplate going to have a shower myself, in the spare room. But she might duck out on me. Sighing, I run my hand through my hair, reconciled to waiting for Mrs. Grey.

Again.

Like I always do.

My mind drifts to the previous evening. To Elena. What did we talk about? As I try to remember, my sense of unease returns. What did we discuss? My business. Yes. Her business. Isaac. The fact that Ana wants kids. I didn't actually tell Elena that Ana was pregnant. Did I?

No. *Thank Christ.*

Spawn. I snort. That's the term Elena used.

And she apologized. Now, that is a first.

What else did we talk about? There's something hovering at the edge of my consciousness. Damn. *Why did I get so drunk?* I loathe being out of control. I loathe drunks.

A darker memory surfaces—not from last night, one that I try to bury. That man. The crack whore's fucking pimp, drunk on cheap liquor and whatever he could jack into his system and the crack whore's system.

Fuck.

This is not my happy place. A cold sweat breaks out over my skin as I recall the stench emanating from his unwashed body, and from the Camel cigarette jammed between his teeth. I take a deep, long breath to quell my rising panic.

It's in the past, Grey.

Stay calm.

The door clicks and I open my eyes to see Mrs. Anastasia Grey, wrapped in two towels, emerge from the bathroom. She strides right past me as if I'm invisible and disappears into the closet. I follow her and stand on the threshold, watching as she ever-so-casually selects her outfit for the day.

"Are you ignoring me?" The disbelief is evident in my voice.

"Perceptive, aren't you?" she mutters, as if I'm some kind of afterthought.

I watch her. Helpless. *What do I do?*

Her clothes are in her hands as she waltzes toward me and halts, finally looking me in the eye, a "get out of my way, asshole" expression on her face. I really am in deep shit. I've never seen her this mad, except maybe that time she threw a hairbrush at me on the *Fair Lady.* I step out of her way, when really all I want to do is grab her, press her against the wall, and kiss her—kiss her senseless. Then bury myself inside her. But I follow her like a fucking lapdog into the bedroom and stand in the doorway as she saunters over to her chest of drawers. How can she be so nonchalant?

Look at me! I will her.

She loosens the towel that's cloaked around her body and drops it to the floor. My dick stirs in response, making me angrier. Christ, she's beautiful; her flawless skin, the soft flare of her hips, the swell of her behind, and her long, long legs that I want wrapped around me. Her body shows no sign of the invader yet. Christ, I have no idea how pregnant she is.

Shit. I put Junior out of my mind.

How long will it take me to get her into bed?

Grey, no—keep it together.

She's still ignoring me. "Why are you doing this?" I try to hide the desperation in my voice.

"Why do you think?" She fishes some lingerie out of a drawer.

"Ana—" My breath catches in my throat as she bends and tugs on her panties, wiggling her fine, fine ass. She's doing this on purpose. And in spite of my aching head, and my filthy mood, I want to fuck her. *Now.* Just to make sure we're okay. My growing erection concurs.

"Go ask your Mrs. Robinson. I'm sure she'll have an explanation for you." She rifles through her drawer, dismissing me, as if I'm some fucking lackey.

As I thought, it's Elena.

What did you expect, Grey?

"Ana, I've told you before, she's not my—"

"I don't want to hear it, Christian." Ana holds up her hand. "The time for talking was yesterday, but instead you decided to rant, and get drunk with the woman who abused you for years. Give her a call. I'm sure she'll be more than willing to listen to you now."

What?

Ana chooses a bra—the black lacy one—and slides it on and fastens it. I stride farther into the room and place my hands on my hips, glaring at her. She's crossed a line.

"Why were you snooping on me?" I can't believe she went through my texts.

"That's not the point, Christian," she hisses. "Fact is, the going gets tough, and you run to her."

"It wasn't like that—"

"I'm not interested!" She stalks over to the bed while I gaze at her. Lost. She's so cold. *Who is this woman?*

Sitting down, she stretches out a long, shapely leg, points her toes, and slowly eases one thigh-high up over her skin. My mouth goes from parched to desert as I watch her hands glide up her leg.

"Where were you?" It's the only coherent sentence I can form. Ignoring me, she pulls on the other thigh-high with the same slow, sensual ease. Then she stands, turns away from me, and bends over to towel-dry her hair, her back in a perfect curve. It takes every remaining shred of my self-control not to grab her and toss her onto the bed. She stands up straight again, flicking her thick, wet mane of chestnut hair, so it cascades down her back below her bra line.

"Answer me," I murmur. But she merely stalks back to the chest of drawers, picks up her hair dryer, and switches it on, wielding it like a weapon. The noise grates on my frayed nerves, unraveling them further.

What do I do when my wife ignores me?

I'm at a loss.

She rakes her fingers through her hair as she dries it and I fist my hands to stop myself from reaching out to her. I'm desperate to touch her and end this nonsense. But the memory of her hissing at me with such venom after the belting in the playroom comes to mind.

You are one fucked-up son of a bitch.

I pale. I don't want a repeat of that.

Ever.

I watch her, wordless and mesmerized. It was only a few days ago that she let me dry her hair. She finishes with a flourish, her hair a riotous crown of chestnut streaked with red and gold that tumbles down over her shoulders. She *is* doing this on purpose. The thought revives my anger.

"Where were you?" I whisper.

"What do you care?"

"Ana, stop this. Now."

She shrugs, like she doesn't care, and my blood boils. I move quickly toward her, unsure what I'm going to do, but she whirls to face me like an avenging angel. "Don't touch me," she snarls through clenched teeth, and I'm catapulted back to that moment in my playroom when she left.

It's sobering.

"Where were you?" I clench my fists to stop my hands from shaking.

"I wasn't out getting drunk with my ex." Her eyes blaze with righteous indignation. "Did you sleep with her?"

It's like she's punched me in the face.

I gasp. "What? No!" *How could she think that? Sleep with Elena?* "You think I'd cheat on you?" Christ, she thinks so little of me. A knot twists in my gut, and a memory, lost in a mist of red wine and bourbon, stirs.

"You did," Ana continues. "By taking our very private life and spilling your spineless guts to that woman."

"Spineless. That's what you think?" Jesus, I thought I'd fucked up, but this is so much worse than I'd feared.

"Christian, I saw the text. That's what I know."

"That text was not meant for you!"

"Well, fact is I saw it when your BlackBerry fell out of your jacket, while I was undressing you because you were too drunk to undress yourself. Do you have any idea how much you've hurt me by going to see that woman?" She doesn't pause for breath. "Do you remember last night when you came home? Remember what you said?"

Hell. No. *What did I say last night?* I was just mad at you, Ana. Shocked by your revelation. I want to say it, but I can't find the words.

"Well, you were right. I do choose this defenseless baby over you."

My world grinds to an abrupt halt.

What does that mean?

"That's what any loving parent does. That's what your mother should have done for you. And I'm sorry that she didn't—because we wouldn't be having this conversation right now if she had. But you're an adult now. You need to grow up and smell the fucking coffee, and stop behaving like a petulant adolescent." She's on a roll.

I frown, and gape at her in all her glory. She's naked except for sensational underwear, her hair a mahogany cloud spilling down to her breasts, dark eyes wide and desolate. The anger and hurt roll off her in waves, and in spite of all that, she's stunning, and I am utterly lost. "You may not be happy about this baby," she exclaims. "I'm not ecstatic, given the timing and your less-than-lukewarm reception to this new life, this flesh of your flesh. But you can either do this with me, or I'll do it on my own. The decision is yours. While you wallow in your pit of self-pity and self-loathing I'm going to work. And when I return, I'll be moving my belongings to the room upstairs."

She's moving out. She's leaving.

She *is* choosing the baby over me.

Panic overwhelms me. It's like a knife in my guts.

"Now, if you'll excuse me, I'd like to finish getting dressed."

My scalp prickles as I edge toward the abyss. *She's leaving.* I step back. "Is that what you want?" My voice is a shocked whisper.

Her wounded eyes are impossibly wide as she scrutinizes me. "I don't know what I want anymore," she says quietly, and turning back to the mirror she smooths some face cream over her cheeks.

"You don't want me?" There's no oxygen in the room.

"I'm still here, aren't I?" she says, as she opens and applies her mascara.

How can she be so cold?

"You've thought about leaving." The abyss opens and yawns in front of me.

"When one's husband prefers the company of his ex-mistress, it's usually not a good sign." Her disdain drips from every word and pushes me closer to the abyss. Pursing her lips, she dabs on some lip gloss oh-so-fucking casually while I'm poised on the edge of this awful precipice.

She reaches for her boots, strides to the bed, and sits down. I watch her, completely at a loss. She pulls them on and stands to face me, her hands on her hips, her expression aloof.

Fuck.

In her boots and lingerie, her hair wild, she's a woman to tame.

A Dom's wet dream.

My wet dream.

My only dream.

I want her. I want her to tell me that she loves me. The way I love her.

Seduce her, Grey.

It's my only weapon.

"I know what you're doing here," I murmur, pitching my voice lower.

"Do you?" Her voice cracks. Is that a chink in her armor? Hope flares briefly in my gut.

She feels.

I can do this. I step forward, but she steps back and holds up her hands, palms toward me. "Don't even think about it, Grey." Her words are bullets aimed at my heart.

"You're my wife," I murmur.

"I'm the pregnant woman you abandoned yesterday, and if you touch me I will scream the place down."

What the fuck? No!

"You'd scream?"

"Bloody murder."

This is too much! Or—does she want to play? Maybe that's it—that's what she wants. "No one would hear you," I murmur.

"Are you trying to frighten me?"

What? No. Never. I back away. "That wasn't my intention."

I'm in free-fall.

Tell her. Just come clean, Grey.

And tell her what—that Elena reached for me, her intention clear? *I don't think so.*

"I had a drink with someone I used to be close to. We cleared the air. I'm not going to see her again." *Believe me, please. Ana.*

"You sought her out?"

"Not at first. I tried to see Flynn. But…I found myself at the salon."

Ana's eyes narrow, fury smoldering in their depths. "And you expect me to believe you're not going to see her again?" She raises her voice. "What about the next time I step across some imaginary line? This is the same argument we have over and over again. Like we're on some Ixion's wheel. If I fuck up again, are you going to run back to her?"

It's not like that! "I am not going to see her again. She finally understands how I feel."

Elena saw me recoil. She knows I don't want her.

"What does that mean?"

If I tell her Elena made a pass at me, Ana will go into meltdown.

Shit. Why the fuck did you go to see her, Grey?

I gaze at my furious, beautiful wife. What can I say?

"Why can you talk to her and not to me?" Ana whispers.

No. It's not like that. You don't understand. She was my only *friend.*

"I was mad at you. Like I am now." The words come in a desperate rush.

"You don't say," Ana shouts. "Well, *I* am mad at you right now. Mad at you for being so cold and callous yesterday, when I needed you. Mad at you for saying I got knocked up deliberately when I didn't. Mad at you for betraying me."

I didn't!

"I should have kept better track of my shots," she continues, quieter. "But I didn't do it on purpose. This pregnancy is a shock to me, too. It could be that the shot failed."

You're shocked! I'm shocked, too.

We're not ready for a baby.

I'm not ready for a baby.

"You really fucked up yesterday," she whispers. "I've had a lot to deal with over the last few weeks."

I fucked up? What about you? Cornered again, I lash out. "You really fucked up three weeks ago. Or whenever you forgot your shot."

"Well, God forbid I should be perfect like you."

Touché, Anastasia. "This is quite a performance, Mrs. Grey."

"Well, I'm glad that even knocked up I'm entertaining."

Fuck this! "I need a shower," I grit between my teeth.

"And I've provided enough of a floor show."

"It's a mighty fine floor show," I whisper, stepping forward. One more try. She steps back. *No dice.*

"Don't."

"I hate that you won't let me touch you."

"Ironic, huh?"

I gasp as her words slice through me. Who knew she could be such a…bitch? My sweet Ana, hurt and aching, unleashing her claws. Is this what I've driven her to?

This is getting us nowhere.

"We haven't resolved much, have we?" My voice is bleak and flat. I don't know what else to say; I have failed to turn her around.

"I'd say not. Except that I'm moving out of this bedroom."

So…she's not leaving me. I grasp on to this hope as I hang over the abyss.

One more pitch, Grey. This is your marriage.

"She doesn't mean anything to me," I whisper. *Not like you do.*

"Except when you need her."

"I don't need her. I need you."

"You didn't yesterday. That woman is a hard limit for me, Christian."

"She's out of my life."

"I wish I could believe you."

"For fuck's sake, Ana."

"Please let me get dressed."

Sighing, I run my hand through my hair. What can I do? She won't let me touch her. She's too mad. I have to regroup and come up with a different strategy. And right now, I need to put some distance between us, before I do something I'll regret. "I'll see you this evening." I storm out and into the bathroom, shutting the door behind me. Like her, I lock it, for the first time ever, protecting myself. Ana has the power to wound me like no other. Standing against the door, I tip my head back and close my eyes.

I have really fucked up. The last time I really fucked up she left me.

"You don't want me?"

"I'm still here, aren't I?"

I clutch on to that hope. Right now I need a shower to wash last night's stink off me.

The water is blistering, the way I like it. I tilt my face into the stream, welcoming its stinging heat as it douses me.

Christ, I'm confused. Nothing is simple where Ana is concerned;

I should know that by now. She's mad because I shouted at her and left, and she's mad because I saw Elena.

That woman is a hard limit for me, Christian.

Elena has been a thorn in Ana's side from the beginning. And now, because of that careless fucking text, she's a thorn in mine. Last night should have put an end to it. All of it. But she had to send that text.

Elena's words haunt me. *Maybe I could make you feel better? I'm sure you miss it.*

I shudder at the memory.

Shit, what a mess.

WHEN I EMERGE FROM the bathroom, Ana's gone. I'm not sure if I'm relieved or disappointed.

Disappointed.

With a heavy heart, I dress, choosing my favorite tie as a talisman for the day. It's brought me luck before.

In the kitchen, Mrs. Jones is still emitting glacial disapproval. It's irritating and chastening at the same time. However, she's prepared a substantial fried breakfast for me.

"Thank you," I mutter. Her only reply is a tight smile. I suspect she heard Ana and me fighting last night.

Grey, you were shouting.

Everyone heard you.

Shit.

I STARE OUT OF the car window as Taylor drives through the morning rush-hour traffic. Ana didn't even say good-bye; she just fucking left, with Sawyer. "Taylor, tell Sawyer I want him to stick to Mrs. Grey like glue. I need to know if she's eating."

"Yes, sir." His words are clipped. Even Taylor is frosty this morning.

I wonder if Ana will follow through with her threat to move upstairs.

I hope not.

She fucks up her contraception, saddling us with a child before we're ready, before we've done anything—and *I'm* in the fucking doghouse? I don't even know how pregnant she is. I resolve to call Dr. Greene when I get to the office. Maybe she can shed some light on how my wife came to miss her shot.

My phone buzzes, and immediately my heart starts pounding. *Ana?* No, it's Ros.

"Grey," I snap.

"You're bright and breezy this morning, Christian."

"What is it, Ros?" I snap again.

She pauses for a nanosecond, then she's all business. "Hansell from the shipyard wants a meeting. And Senator Blandino, too."

Damn. The unions and the politicians. *Could this day get any better?*

"They have wind of the Taiwan deal already?"

"So it would seem, and they want to talk."

"Okay, this afternoon. Set it up. I want you and Samir there, too."

"Will do, Christian."

"That's all?"

"Yes."

"Good." I hang up.

What am I going to do about my wife? Truth is, I'm still smarting from angry Anastasia. Who knew she had such gumption? I don't think anyone's bawled me out like that since…forever. Apart from my mother *and* father—at my own birthday party, no less. And that was because of fucking Elena, as well. I snort at the irony. Yeah, fucking Elena.

I shake my head in disgust. Why did I seek her out? Why?

The Advil has kicked in, and Mrs. Jones's fried breakfast has helped. I feel almost human, but miserable…utterly miserable.

What is Ana doing now? I picture her in her tiny office, wearing her purple dress. Perhaps she's sent me an e-mail. I scramble for my phone, but there's nothing.

Is she thinking about me like I'm thinking about her? I hope so. I want to be in her thoughts, always.

Taylor pulls up outside GEH, and I brace myself for a long day.

"GOOD MORNING, MR. GREY." Andrea smiles as I step out of the elevator, but her smile fades when she sees my expression.

"Get me Dr. Greene on the line and tell Sarah to bring me some coffee."

"Yes, sir."

"After I've finished with Greene, I need to talk to Flynn. Then you can bring in my schedule for the day. Has Ros spoken to you about Hansell and Blandino?"

"Yes."

"Good."

"Dr. Flynn left for a conference in New York early this morning."

Fuck! "I forgot. See if he can find a moment for me on the phone."

"Will do. The flat screen you requested for Mr. Steele will be installed this afternoon."

"And the additional PT?"

"That will start tomorrow."

"Okay. Put Dr. Greene through when you have her." I don't wait for an answer, but stalk into my office and sit down, under the watchful gaze of my wife. I let out a long, slow breath, wondering if her photographer friend ever witnessed her the way she was this morning. From Aphrodite to Athena, goddess of war—a scolding, angry, alluring Athena.

My phone buzzes. "I have Dr. Greene for you."

"Thanks, Andrea. Dr. Greene?"

"Mr. Grey, what can I do for you?"

"I thought the shot was a reliable form of contraceptive," I hiss. There's a prolonged silence on the other end of the line. "Dr. Greene?"

"Mr. Grey, no form of contraception is one hundred percent effective. That would be abstinence, or sterilization for yourself or your wife." Her tone is icy. "I can send you some literature if you'd like to read up on it."

I sigh. "No. That won't be necessary."

"What can I do for you, Mr. Grey?"

"I would like to know how pregnant my wife is."

"Can't Mrs. Grey tell you that herself?"

What is this? Just answer the question!

"I'm asking you, Dr. Greene. That's what I pay you for."

"My patient is Mrs. Grey. I suggest you talk to your wife, and she can give you the details. Is there anything else you need?"

My temper reaches boiling point.

Take a deep breath, Grey.

"Please," I ask through gritted teeth.

"Mr. Grey. Talk to your wife. Good day." She hangs up, and I glare at the phone, expecting it to shrivel to ashes under my gaze; some bedside manner she has.

There's a knock at my door and Sarah appears with my coffee. "Thanks," I mutter, trying to rein in my fury at the goddamned, officious, unhelpful so-called doctor. "Ask Andrea to come in—I want to go through my schedule."

Sarah dashes out and I stare at monochrome Ana on my wall.

Even your doctor is pissed at me.

MISERY IS MY CONSTANT companion, all the way through my meetings, my lunch, and my kickboxing session with Bastille.

"You look like a wet weekend, Grey."

"I feel it."

"Let's see if we can turn that frown upside down."

Really?

I knock him on his ass twice; he deserves to go down for that comment alone.

BY 4:30 I'VE HEARD nothing from my wife, not even an angry hectoring e-mail liberally sprinkled with shouty capitals. Sawyer has reported in to let me know that she had a bagel for lunch. That's something. I have fifteen minutes before showtime with Brad Hansell, the head of the shipbuilders' union, and Senator Blandino. This is going to be a tough meeting. I'm briefed but I can't focus; instead, I'm sitting here staring at my computer, willing an e-mail to arrive from my wife. I can't believe I've heard nothing from Ana all day. Nothing.

I don't like this. I don't like being the object of her anger. I put my head in my hands. Maybe...maybe I should apologize. What did Flynn say? *It's better to concede the battle to win the war.*

And deep down, I know I've fucked up. But I'd hoped that she would have forgiven me by now.

I type out an e-mail.

From: Christian Grey
Subject: I'm Sorry
Date: September 14 2011 16:45
To: Anastasia Grey

I'm Sorry. I'm Sorry. I'm Sorry. I'm Sorry. I'm Sorry. I'm Sorry.
I'm Sorry. I'm Sorry. I'm Sorry. I'm Sorry. I'm Sorry. I'm Sorry.
I'm Sorry. I'm Sorry. I'm Sorry. I'm Sorry. I'm Sorry. I'm Sorry.
I'm Sorry. I'm Sorry. I'm Sorry. I'm Sorry. I'm Sorry. I'm Sorry.
I'm Sorry. I'm Sorry. I'm Sorry. I'm Sorry. I'm Sorry. I'm Sorry.
I fucked up. Please forgive me.

Christian Grey
CEO & Penitent Husband, Grey Enterprises Holdings Inc.

I don't want to go home to face her anger again. I want her smiles, her laughter, and her love. I gaze up at her smiling face in the photo. I want her to look at me like she does in this portrait. I return to the e-mail, wondering whether to hit send. This meeting could go on for a while. I call Mrs. Jones.

"Mr. Grey."

"I may not be home for dinner. Please make sure Mrs. Grey eats."

"Yes, sir."

"Cook her something nice."

"I will."

"Thank you, Gail." I hang up and delete the e-mail—it's not going to be enough. I could try jewelry. Flowers? My phone buzzes.

"Yes, Andrea."

"Mr. Hansell and Senator Blandino are here with their teams."

"Call Ros and Samir to join us."

"Yes, sir."

This will be a fight about layoffs. I grit my teeth. Sometimes I hate my job.

BLANDINO IS APPEALING FOR calm. "These are our economic realities in 2011," she says to Hansell, who sits red-faced on the other side of my boardroom table.

I just want to go home. But we're not finished here.

My phone buzzes, and my heart rate spikes. It's my wife. "Excuse me." I rise from the table, feeling seven pairs of eyes on me as I exit the room.

She's called. I'm almost giddy with relief—my heart feels like it will escape my chest. "Ana!"

"Hi." It's so good to hear her voice.

"Hi."

I can't think what else to say, but I want to beg her to stop being mad at me.

Please don't be mad. I'm sorry.

"Are you coming home?" she asks.

"Later."

"Are you in the office?"

I frown. "Yes. Where did you expect me to be?"

"I'll let you go."

What? But— There's so much I want to say, but neither of us speaks. The silence is a chasm between us and I have a boardroom of people locked in crisis talks waiting for me.

"Good night, Ana." *I love you.*

"Good night, Christian." I hang up before she can, thinking about all those times we've stayed on the line and neither of us hangs up. I couldn't bear to hear her end the call first. I stare despondently at my phone. At least she asked if I was coming home. Perhaps she misses me. Or she's checking up on me. Either way. She cares. Maybe. A small ember of hope glows deep in my heart. I need to wrap this meeting up and get home to my wife.

IT'S LATE WHEN WE agree on a potential compromise. With hindsight, I see that confrontation with the union was inevitable, but it's been good for all sides to air their grievances. Samir and Ros will now take the negotiations from here and hammer out a deal. Compared to the battle I'm facing at home, this wasn't so bad. Ros was an impressive negotiator, and I've persuaded her to go to Taiwan tomorrow evening without me.

"Okay, Christian. I'll go. But they'll really want you there."

"I'll find time. Later this month."

Her lips tighten, but she says nothing.

I can't tell her that I don't want to leave Ana when she's not even talking to me. Deep down, I know it's because I'm petrified my wife might not be there when I return.

THE APARTMENT IS DARK when I get home; Ana must be in bed. I head into our bedroom, and my heart sinks when I find she's not there. Stifling my panic, I head upstairs. In the dim light from the hallway, I make out her form curled up beneath the duvet in her old bedroom.

Old bedroom?

It's hardly that; she's slept in it, what, twice?

She looks so small. I flick the dimmer switch on to see her better, but keep the lights low, and carry the armchair over so I can sit down and gaze at her. Her skin is pale, translucent, almost. She's been crying; her eyelids and lips are swollen. My heart freefalls through my body with despair.

Oh, baby—I'm sorry.

I know how soft her lips are to kiss when she's been crying...when I make her cry. I want to climb in beside her, to pull her into my arms and hold her, but she's asleep, and she needs her sleep, especially now.

I settle into the chair and match my breathing to Ana's. The rhythm soothes me, that and my proximity to her. For the first time since I woke up this morning I feel a little calmer. The last time I sat and watched her sleep was when Hyde broke into our apartment; she'd been out with Kate. I was mad as hell then.

Why do I spend so much time mad at my wife?

I love her.

Even though she never does as she's told.

That's why.

God grant me the serenity to accept the things I cannot change;
The courage to change the things I can;
And the wisdom to know the difference.

I grimace as Dr Flynn's oft-quoted serenity prayer pops into my head: a prayer for alcoholics and fucked-up businessmen. I check my watch, though I know it's far too late to call him in New York. I'll try him tomorrow. I can discuss my impending fatherhood with him.

I shake my head.

Me, a dad?

What could I possibly offer a child? I undo my tie and the top button of my shirt as I lean back. I suppose there's the material wealth. At least he won't go hungry. No—not on my fucking watch. Not my child. She says she'll do this on her own. How could she? She's too…and I want to say *fragile*, because sometimes she looks fragile, but she's not. She's the strongest woman I know, stronger even than Grace.

Gazing at her as she lies here, sleeping the sleep of the innocent, I realize what an asshole I was yesterday. She's never backed down from a challenge, ever. She was hurt by what I said and what I did. I see that now. She knew I'd overreact when she told me about the baby.

She knows me better than anyone.

Did she find out before we were in Portland? I don't think so; she would have told me. She must have found out yesterday. And when she told me, everything turned to shit. My fear took over.

How am I going to make it up to her?

"I'm sorry, Ana. Forgive me," I whisper. "You scared the living shit out of me yesterday." Leaning forward, I kiss her forehead.

She stirs and frowns. "Christian," she murmurs, her voice wistful and full of longing. The hope kindled by her earlier call ignites into a fire.

"I'm here," I whisper.

But she turns over, sighs, and falls back into a deep slumber. I'm so tempted to strip down and join her, but I don't think I'd be welcome. "I love you, Anastasia Grey. I'll see you in the morning."

Damn. No, I won't.

I have to fly to Portland and see the finance committee at WSU in Vancouver. That means leaving early.

I place my favorite tie beside her on the pillow so she'll know I've been here. As I do, I recall the first time I tied her hands. The thought travels straight to my cock.

I wore it to tease her at her graduation.

I wore it at our wedding.

I'm a sentimental fool. "Tomorrow, baby," I whisper. "Sleep well."

I forgo the piano, even though I want to play. I don't want to wake her. But as I head alone into our bedroom, I'm more hopeful. She whispered my name.

Yes. There's hope for us yet.

Don't give up on me, Ana.

THURSDAY, SEPTEMBER 15, 2011

It's 5:30 in the morning and I'm in the gym, pounding away on the treadmill. Sleep eluded me last night, and when I did drift off, I was haunted by my dreams:

Ana disappearing into the garage at The Heathman without looking back at me.

Ana an enraged siren, holding a thin cane, eyes blazing, wearing nothing but expensive lingerie and leather boots, her angry words like barbs.

Ana lying unmoving on a sticky green rug.

I shake off that last image and run harder, pushing my body to its limits. I don't want to feel anything except the pain of my bursting lungs and aching legs. With Bloomberg's rolling business news on the TV and "Pump It" in my ears, I blot out the world... I blot out thoughts of my wife, sleeping soundly two rooms away from me.

Dream of me, Ana. Miss me.

In the shower while I hose off my workout sweat, I contemplate waking her just to say good-bye. I fly to Portland in *Charlie Tango* this morning, and I'd like a sweet smile to take with me.

Let her sleep, Grey.

And given how pissed she is at me, there's no guarantee of a sweet smile.

Mrs. Jones is still giving me the cold shoulder, but I grill her anyway. "Did Ana eat last night?"

"She did." Mrs. Jones's attention is on the omelet she's preparing for me. I think that's all the information I'm going to get this morning. I sip my coffee and sulk, feeling fifty shades of miserable.

In the car on the way to Boeing Field I write an e-mail to Ana.

Keep it factual, Grey.

From: Christian Grey
Subject: Portland
Date: September 15 2011 06:45
To: Anastasia Grey

Ana,
I am flying down to Portland today.
I have some business to conclude with WSU.
I thought you would want to know.

Christian Grey
CEO, Grey Enterprises Holdings, Inc.

But I know my real intention in sending an e-mail isn't to inform her...but to get a response.

I live in hope.

Stephan is on hand to fly us down to Portland. After my sleepless night, I'm dog-tired. If I fall asleep, I'll be more comfortable in the rear, so for the first time ever, I offer Taylor the front passenger seat, remove my jacket, and take a back seat in *Charlie Tango.* I leaf through the notes I have for the meeting, and once I've done that, I lean back and close my eyes.

> Ana is running through the meadow at the new house. She's laughing as I chase her. I'm laughing, too. I catch her and pull her down into the long grass. She giggles and I kiss her. Her lips are soft, because she's been crying. No. Don't cry. Baby, don't cry. Please don't cry. She closes her eyes. She sleeps. She won't wake. Ana! *Ana!* She's lying on a thread worn rug. Pale. Unmoving. Ana. Wake up. *Ana!*

Gasping, I wake, and I'm momentarily disoriented. Wait—I'm in *Charlie Tango,* and we've just landed in Portland. The rotors are still spinning, and Stephan is talking to the tower. I rub my face to rouse myself and unbuckle my harness.

Taylor opens his door and steps out onto the helipad while I don my jacket, careful not to snag the cable of my headphones.

"Thanks, Stephan," I say over the cans.

"No problem, Mr. Grey."

“We should be back around one this afternoon.”

“We’ll be ready and waiting.” He frowns, his concern evident in the creases across his brow, while Taylor, head down, opens my door

Shit. I hope that concern is not directed at me. I remove my headphones and clamber out to join Taylor. It’s a crisp morning, brighter than Seattle, but with a brisk breeze that carries the scent of fall. There’s no sign of Joe, the old-timer who’s normally here to oversee arrivals and departures. Maybe it’s too early in the day, or he’s not slated to work this morning…or it’s an omen or some shit.

For fuck’s sake, Grey. Pull yourself together.

Our driver is waiting outside the helipad building. Taylor opens the door of the Escalade and I slide in, then he takes the passenger seat up front.

With my bad dream about Ana still in mind, I call Sawyer.

“Mr. Grey.”

“Luke. Stay close to Mrs. Grey today.”

“Will do, sir.”

“Is she having breakfast?” I keep my voice low as I’m a little embarrassed to be asking. But I want to know she’s okay.

“I believe so, sir. We’re leaving in about fifteen minutes for the office.”

“Good. Thanks.” I hang up and stare morosely out the window at the Willamette River. Its metallic gray waters look chilly as we cross over the Steel Bridge. I shudder. This is hell. I need to talk to Ana. We can’t go on like this.

I have one option that might work.

Apologize, Grey.

Yeah. It’s my only option.

Because I behaved like an asshole.

Ana’s words come back to me: *You need to grow up and smell the fucking coffee, and stop behaving like a petulant adolescent.*

Fuck. She’s not wrong.

Now is not the time. I have to help the WSU Environmental Science Department nail additional funding from the USDA. It’s vital to progress the work that Professor Gravett and her team are undertaking in soil technology. Her work is reaping huge benefits in our test sites in Ghana. This is a game changer. Soil could be a key initiative not only in feeding the planet and alleviating food insecurity and poverty, but also through carbon sequestration reversing climate change. From my briefcase I pull out my notes and scan them once more.

THE MEETING HAS BEEN a resounding success—we've secured an additional million dollars from the USDA. It appears that feeding the world is quite high on the federal government's agenda, too. With the gratitude of Professors Choudury and Gravett ringing in my ears, Taylor and I head back to Portland. I check my phone, but there's no word from my wife—not even a snarky response to my e-mail. It's depressing. I'm anxious to get home and find some way to smooth her ruffled feathers…if I can.

Maybe a meal out?

A movie?

Soaring?

Sailing?

Sex?

What can I do?

I miss her.

The Escalade parks outside the helipad building, as Taylor makes a call.

"Sawyer, I read your text," he murmurs, and he has my full attention.

Text? Is Ana okay?

He frowns as he listens. "Copy." Taylor's eyes meet mine. "I see. Hold on," he says to Luke, then addresses me. "Mrs. Grey is feeling unwell. Sawyer is taking her back to the apartment."

"Is it serious?"

"No reason to think so."

"Okay. We'll fly straight to Escala."

"Yes, sir. Sawyer, we're leaving shortly. We'll divert directly to Escala, land there."

"Keep her safe!" I shout, loud enough for Sawyer to hear me.

"You heard Mr. Grey. Text me if the situation changes." Taylor hangs up.

With a renewed sense of urgency, Taylor and I enter the building, and I'm pleased that the elevator is waiting for us.

I hope Ana's okay…and the baby.

Maybe I should call my mom, ask her to go over and check on Ana. Or Dr. Greene—though I'm not sure she'd take my call. It will take us an hour to get home, and I can't wait that long; I try my mother, but there's no phone signal—we're in the elevator. I can't call Ana, either.

Surely if it were serious she'd have called me?

Damn. I have no idea, given she's not talking to me.

The elevator doors open, *Charlie Tango* is where we left her, and Stephan is waiting at the controls.

To hell with this. I'm going to fly her. I can direct my attention to the flight, rather than dwell on what's happening at Escala.

I hope Ana goes to bed. *Our bed.*

Stephan steps down from the cockpit to greet us.

"Stephan, hi. I'd like to fly her home. We need a new course, for Escala."

"Yes, sir." He opens the pilot's door for me, and I think he's surprised by the change in my attitude. I climb aboard, buckle up, and begin the final preflight checks.

"All checks done?" I ask Stephan as he takes the seat beside me.

"Just the transponder."

"Oh, yes. I see. I need to get home to my wife. Taylor, you strapped in?"

"Yes, sir." His disembodied voice is loud and clear in my cans. I radio the tower, and they're ready for us.

"Right, gentlemen, let's get home." Pulling back the collective, I float *Charlie Tango* smoothly into the sky and head for Seattle.

As we cut through the air at speed, I know I've made the right decision to pilot. I have to focus on keeping us airborne, but deep down, my anxiety continues to gnaw at my insides. I hope Ana's okay.

We touch down right on schedule at 2:30.

"Good flying, Mr. Grey," Stephan says.

"Enjoy taking her back to Boeing Field."

"Will do." He grins.

I unbuckle my harness, switch on my phone, and follow Taylor out onto Escala's rooftop. Taylor frowns down at his phone. I halt as he listens to a message.

"It's from Sawyer. Mrs. Grey is at the bank." Taylor raises his voice to be heard over the wind that whips around us on the roof.

What? I thought she was ill. What the fuck is she doing at the bank?

"Sawyer followed her there. She tried to give him the slip."

Anxiety spirals into my chest, tightening around my heart. My rebooted phone beeps and vibrates with a flood of alerts. There's a text from Andrea, sent four minutes ago, and a couple of missed calls from my bank, and one from Welch.

What the fuck?

> ANDREA
> Troy Whelan at your bank needs
> to speak with you urgently.

I have Whelan on speed dial. He picks up immediately.

"Whelan, it's Christian Grey. What's going on?" I shout over the rush of the wind.

"Mr. Grey, good afternoon. Um, your wife is here requesting to withdraw five million dollars."

What?

My blood turns to ice.

"Five million?" I can't quite believe what he's said.

What does she need five million for?

Fuck. She's leaving me.

My world crashes and burns, a cavern of despair opening at my feet.

"Yes, sir. As you know, under current banking legislation I can't cash five million."

"Yes, of course." I'm in shock, teetering on the brink of the abyss. "Let me talk to Mrs. Grey." I sound robotic.

"Certainly, sir. If you'll hold for a minute."

This is agony. I head to shelter out of the wind, beside the elevator doors, and stand quietly waiting to hear from my wife…dreading to hear from my wife.

She's going. She's leaving me.

What am I going to do without her? The phone clicks and my panic overwhelms me.

"Hi." Ana's voice is breathy and high-pitched.

"You're leaving me?" The words are out before I can stop them.

"No!" she rasps, and it sounds like an agonized appeal.

Oh, thank fuck. But my relief is short-lived.

"Yes," she whispers, as if she's just made her decision.

What!

"Ana, I—" I don't know what to say. I want to beg her to stay.

"Christian, please. Don't."

"You're going?" *You're really going.*

"Yes."

No! No! NO! I free-fall, tumbling down into the abyss. Falling. Falling. Falling. Reaching out, I splay my hand on the wall to support myself. The pain is visceral.

Don't leave me.

Shit, was this always going to happen? Did she ever love me?

Was it my fucking money?

"But why the cash? Was it always the money?" Tell me it wasn't the money. Please. The pain is indescribable.

"No!" She sounds emphatic.

Do I believe her?

Is it because I saw Elena? For God's sake! And in this moment, I don't think I could loathe Elena more. I breathe deep, trying to get a handle on my thoughts.

"Is five million enough?" *How will I live without Ana?*

"Yes."

"And the baby?" *She'll take our baby away?* The knife twists in my soul.

"I'll take care of the baby."

"This is what you want?"

"Yes." Her voice is barely audible. But I hear her. The pain is crippling. She wants me off the phone—I can tell. She wants it done. She wants away from *me.*

"Take it all," I whisper.

"Christian," she sobs. "It's for you. For your family. Please. Don't."

I can't stand this.

"Take it all, Anastasia," I snarl and tilt my head back and silently howl at the gray sky above me.

"Christian—" Her desperation is laced through every syllable of my name. I can't bear to hear her.

"I'll always love you," I murmur, because it's true. They're the last words of a condemned man. I hang up and take a deep, steadying breath, feeling hollow…nothing more than a husk.

I told her that once.

In a shower.

And then I told her I loved her.

"Mr. Grey?" Taylor's trying to attract my attention. Ignoring him, I call Whelan again.

"Troy Whelan."

"It's Christian Grey. Give my wife the money. Whatever she wants."

"Mr. Grey, I can't—"

"I know you hold the reserve for the Pacific Northwest. Just transfer it from the main holding account. Or liquidate some of my assets. I don't care. Give her the money."

"Mr. Grey, this is highly irregular."

"Just fucking do it, Whelan. Find a way, or I'll close all the accounts and move GEH's business elsewhere. Understand?"

He's silent on the other end of the phone.

"We'll sort the fucking paperwork out later," I add, in a more conciliatory tone.

"Yes, Mr. Grey."

"Just give her whatever she wants."

"Yes, Mr. Grey." I hang up.

I want to cry. I want to break down here on the roof and weep. But I can't. I close my eyes and wish that I were here on my own.

"Mr. Grey." Taylor's voice cuts through my pain.

I turn to face him, and he blanches. "What?" I snarl.

"Hyde has been granted bail. He's free."

I glare at him. *What fresh hell is this?*

Hyde is free? *How?* I thought we'd dealt with that.

Taylor and I eyeball each other, wondering, *What the hell?*

"You're leaving me?"

"No!"

"It's for you. For your family. Please. Don't."

"Ana!" I whisper. "She's trying to withdraw five million dollars."

Taylor's eyes widen. "Shit!" he says.

We reach the same conclusion at the same instant. Whatever the hell she's doing, deep down I know it has something to do with that fucker Hyde. I punch the elevator button, as my utter despair congeals into fear. Fear for my wife. "Where's Sawyer?"

"He's at the bank. He tracked her car." We leap into the elevator and I jab the button for the garage as *Charlie Tango*'s rotors start again. It's deafening.

"You have the car keys?" I shout to Taylor as the doors close.

"Yes, sir."

"Let's get to the bank. Do we know where Hyde is?"

"No. I'll text Welch."

"He left a message. Shit—it must have been the news about Hyde."

The elevator takes forever to descend to the garage. What is Ana playing at? Why can't she tell me if she's in trouble? Fear wraps around my heart and my gut, strangling me from the inside. What could be worse than Ana leaving me? The distressing picture from my earlier dream slips into my head, drawing on older—much older—disturbing memories: a woman lifeless on the floor. I screw my eyes shut.

No. Please. No.

"We'll find her," Taylor says with grim determination.

"We have to."

"I'll track her cell," he states.

At last the doors open and Taylor tosses me his Q7 keys. He wants me to drive?

Get a grip, Grey. You have to get your wife out of this mess.

Perhaps that fucker is blackmailing her.

We climb into the car and I switch on the ignition. The tires scream as I reverse out of the space and speed up to the garage entrance, only to wait agonizing seconds for the barrier to rise. "Come on. Come on. Come on. Come on!"

Barely clearing the barrier, we roar out onto the street in the direction of the bank.

Taylor puts his phone on the dash, waiting for a signal, cursing impatiently under his breath.

"She's still at the bank," he says eventually.

"Good."

The traffic is heavier than I expected. It's frustrating.

Come on, come on, come *on*!

Why does Ana do this? Keep this shit to herself? Doesn't she trust me?

I think about my behavior over the last couple of days.

Okay, it hasn't been exemplary, by any means, but she takes all this crap on her shoulders. Why can't she ask for help?

"Ana Grey," I shout into the phone's Bluetooth system. After a few moments her phone starts to ring, and ring, and ring…then it goes to voice mail. My heart sinks.

"Hi, you've reached Ana. I can't take your call right now, but please leave a message after the beep, and I'll call you right back."

Christ!

"Ana! What the fuck is going on?" I yell. It feels good to yell. "I'm coming to get you. Call me. Talk to me." I hang up.

"She's still at the bank," Taylor says.

"Sawyer's still there?"

"Yes, sir."

"Call Sawyer!" I shout into the hands-free, and moments later his cell is ringing.

"Mr. Grey?"

"Where's Ana?"

"She's just turned around and gone back into one of the offices."

"Go get her."

"Sir, I'm armed. I can't go through the detectors. I'm standing by the entrance watching Anast—Mrs. Grey, and looking very suspicious. If I go back to the car to stow my gun, I may lose her."

Fucking firearms.

"How the hell did she give you the slip?"

"She's a very resourceful woman, Mr. Grey." He sounds like he's speaking through gritted teeth, and I recognize his frustration. It makes me feel slightly more sympathetic to him; she drives me crazy, too.

"I want a thorough briefing when we have her back. Jack Hyde has been granted bail, and both Taylor and I have a hunch that Ana's actions have something to do with him."

"Shit!" Luke says.

"Exactly. We're about five minutes away. Don't let her go again, Sawyer."

"Sir."

I hang up.

Taylor and I sit in silence as I weave through traffic.

What are you up to, Anastasia Grey?

What am I going to do to you when I get you back?

Various scenarios cross my mind. I shift in my seat.

For fuck's sake, Grey. Now is not the time.

Taylor startles me. "She's on the move."

"What?" My heart jump-starts as adrenaline courses through my body.

"She's heading south, on Second."

"Call Sawyer!" I shout. Moments later, his cell rings again.

"Mr. Grey," he answers immediately.

"She's on the move!"

"What? She hasn't come out through the main entrance." He sounds confused.

"She's heading south on Second," Taylor interjects.

"I'm on it. I'll call from the car." Sawyer is obviously running. "She's not in her car. It's still here."

"Hell!" I shout.

"Still heading south on Second," Taylor says. "Wait. She's turned left onto Yesler."

We pass my bank. There's no point stopping. "That's three blocks?" I ask him.

"Yes, sir."

For the billionth time I thank God Taylor's with me. He knows this city like the back of his hand—which is odd, given he's from some rural town in the middle of nowhere in Texas.

Three minutes later, we're heading east on Yesler.

"She's still on Yesler," Taylor growls, eyes glued to his phone. "She's turned south. Onto Twenty-Third. That's eight blocks from here."

"I'm right behind you," Sawyer pipes up through the hands-free.

"Stay close. I'm going to try and dodge through this traffic." I glance at Taylor. "I wish you were driving."

"You're doing fine, sir."

Where the fuck is she going? And who with?

We're silent for several minutes. I focus on the road, while Taylor occasionally calls out directions. We head south, then east again, now through mainly residential streets.

"She's turned south down Thirtieth."

We follow for a few blocks, then turn east.

"It's stopped. South Day Street. Two more blocks."

Dread sits heavy and caustic in my stomach as I race through the back streets.

Three minutes later, I swing onto South Day Street.

"Slow down," Taylor orders, surprising me, but I do as he says. "She's here somewhere." He leans forward, and we scan each side of the road. There is a row of derelict buildings on my side.

"Fuck!" There's a potholed parking lot where a woman is standing with her hands in the air beside a black Dodge. *The Dodge!* I wrench the wheel and swing into the parking lot, and there she is—

On the ground. Unmoving. Eyes closed.

Ana. My Ana… No! Everything moves in slow motion as all the air is sucked from my lungs. My worst fear realized. Here. Now.

Taylor is out of the car before I've screeched to a halt. I follow him, leaving the engine running.

"Ana!" I shout. *Please, God. Please, God. Please, God.*

She is lifeless on the concrete. In front of her, that fucker Hyde is rolling on the ground, screaming in agony as he clutches his upper leg. Blood seeps through his fingers. The woman steps back, keeping her hands in the air as Taylor draws his gun.

But it's Ana who has my whole attention. She's lying unmoving on the cold, hard ground.

No!

This is what I've dreaded since I met her. This moment. I kneel beside her, terrified to touch her. Taylor picks up the gun lying beside her and orders the woman to lie facedown on the ground. "Don't shoot me, don't shoot me," she gibbers.

Shit! That's Elizabeth Morgan, from SIP.

How the hell is she involved in this clusterfuck?

Sawyer is suddenly with us. He draws his gun on Elizabeth and stands guard over her.

Hyde screams in agony. "Help me! Help me! The bitch shot me!" We ignore him.

Taylor bends and checks the pulse point beneath Ana's jaw.

"She's alive. Strong pulse," he says. *Thank God.* Then he barks at Sawyer, "Call 911 now. Ambulance and police."

Sawyer reaches for his phone, while Taylor quickly and gently runs his hands over Ana, checking for injuries.

"I don't think she's bleeding."

"Can I touch her?"

"She may have broken something. Best leave it to the paramedics."

Oh no. My wife. My girl. My beautiful girl.

I stroke her hair and gently tuck a strand behind her ear. She looks like she's asleep, though she has a red mark on her face. *Did he fucking hit you? Did he do this to you?*

Now my attention turns to Hyde, who's still fucking screaming. A fresh shot of adrenaline-fueled rage streaks through my bloodstream.

The fucker. He put his hands on my wife, and she shot him.

My God, Ana shot him.

I stand and move so I tower over him as he writhes on the ground.

And before I know what I'm doing, I lean on the Dodge, draw

back my leg, and kick him with all my might in his stomach, hard. Twice. Three times, with all my weight behind each kick.

He screams.

"You do this to my wife, you fucker?" I bellow my rage and kick him again. He drags his hands up to protect his stomach, and I stamp with all my weight on the seeping wound on his thigh. He screams again—a different, louder, feral cry of agony. Leaning down, I grab the lapels of his jacket and bounce his head off the ground. Once. Twice. His eyes are wide and wild with fear as he grips my hands, smearing his blood on me.

"I'm going to fucking kill you, you twisted, sick motherfucker!"

From the far end of the tunnel, I hear voices. "Mr. Grey! Mr. Grey! Christian! Christian, stop!" It's Taylor. He and Sawyer are pulling me away—pulling me off the vermin that is Hyde. Taylor grabs me by both shoulders and shakes me.

"Christian! Stop! Now!" He shakes me once more.

I blink at him and shrug him off.

Don't touch me!

Taylor puts himself between Hyde and me, watching me like I'm unhinged, lethal and ready to strike. I take a breath while the murderous red mist clears.

"I'm okay," I whisper.

"Look after your wife, sir." Taylor's tone is emphatic.

I nod. And glance once more at the fucker on the ground. He's rocking gently, sniveling like the weasel-turd he is and clutching his thigh. He's pissed himself, disgusting fuck. "Let him bleed to death," I mutter to Taylor, and turn away.

I kneel beside Ana and lean down to hear her breathing, but I hear nothing. Panic swamps me once more. "Is she still breathing?" I glance up at Taylor.

"Look at her chest, rising and falling." Taylor leans down again and checks her pulse. "Still strong."

Oh, Ana. What were you thinking? What about the baby?

Tears prick my eyes. I loathe this feeling of helplessness. I want to fold her into my arms and sob into her hair—but I can't touch her. This is agony. Where is the fucking ambulance?

"The girl. The girl." Elizabeth suddenly pipes up.

What girl? We all turn to look at her, prone on the ground.

"Inside," she says. "There. That building." She points with her chin.

Is this a trick?

I hear Taylor's quiet command. "Sawyer, check inside."

In the distance, sirens wail. Thank God!

"Taylor!" When I turn, Sawyer is standing in the doorway. "They have Miss Grey in here."

"Stay here, Christian!" Taylor raises a finger in warning.

Mia? My baby sister? Fear blooms in my gut. What has that fucker done to my sister? I watch, paralyzed, as Taylor disappears into the building, Sawyer regarding him from the doorway.

"It's for you. For your family. Please. Don't…"

And what Ana said all becomes clear. I stare down at her, and I know in this moment that she could have been murdered by the sick fuck. Bile rises in my throat, and time suspends, until Taylor emerges from the building. "She's okay, I think. She's drugged. Asleep. No obvious signs of injury or assault. She's fully clothed. I don't want to move her. We'll let the paramedics do that."

"Mia?" I ask, not quite believing the awfulness of this situation.

He nods. His mouth set in a grim line.

The sirens are louder.

What the fuck was Hyde planning to do to my sister? He's still whimpering like a wounded dog, quieter now, and I suspect he's lost a lot of blood. I don't give a shit. I want to kill him, slowly, painfully—but two ambulances, two police patrol vehicles, and a fire truck pull up in blaze of flashing lights and a cacophony of sirens, shattering the peace of the neighborhood, and saving Hyde's skin.

I'M IN A WAKING nightmare, sitting between Mia and Ana in the ambulance as we speed through Seattle. My head is in my hands, my heart is in my mouth, as I pray for both of them. I'm not a religious man, but right now I'd do anything, even plead with God, to know that my wife, our baby, and my sister are okay.

"Vital signs are good, Mr. Grey, for both your wife and your sister," the paramedic says, his dark eyes full of compassion.

"My wife's pregnant."

The paramedic looks down at Ana. "Sir, there are no obvious signs of bleeding."

I pale, knowing that he's trying to reassure me, but it's not working. "Why is she still unconscious?" My voice is a whisper.

"The doctors should be able to determine that when we arrive."

Mia stirs, mumbling incoherently. She's coming around. It's obvious she's been drugged. But at least she's calm. I grasp her hand and squeeze. "It's okay, Mia. We're here."

She mumbles something, but still hasn't opened her eyes, but she squeezes my hand in return and relaxes back into what I hope is sleep.

My sister, my wife, my unborn child. I should have killed Hyde when I had the chance. Impotent rage curdles in my stomach once more and I screw up my eyes, trying to dispel it. I want to weep. I want to howl to release this pain, but I can't.

Hell. I'm wrung out. The last words I exchanged with Ana…

"You're leaving me?"

"No!"

"It's for you. For your family. Please. Don't."

I told her I would always love her. At least I did that.

Please wake up, Ana.

Nagging me, deep down, is concern for the baby. Was Ana really ill, or did she make that up? This…stress, fuck. It can't be good for him.

Junior. Is he okay?

Finally, we reach the ER, and I'm immediately sidelined as the paramedics swing into action.

Mom and Dad are there, waiting. They rush to the gurney carrying my sleeping or unconscious sister. Grace takes one look at Mia and tears spring to her eyes. She takes her hand. "I love you, baby," she wails, as the paramedics whisk Mia toward the double doors where Dad can't follow. He stands aside and watches as Mom follows them through into the ER triage.

A nurse and doctor take Ana's gurney.

"Careful with my wife. She's pregnant." My voice is hoarse and hushed with worry.

"We'll take good care of her," the attending says. I release Ana's hand, and they wheel her through after Mia.

Carrick joins me, ashen-faced, looking every inch his age.

We stare at each other. "Dad," I whisper, my voice cracking.

"Oh, son." Carrick opens his arms and for the first time in my life I step into them, and he holds me. I swallow my welling emotion and grip his jacket, beyond grateful for his quiet strength, his reassuring presence, his familiar scent, but most of all his love. "It's going to be okay, son. They're both going to be okay."

"They're going to be okay," I repeat like a mantra, while my throat burns with my suppressed anguish. "They're going to be okay."

But he doesn't know that for sure.

I just pray it's true.

I pull back, suddenly conscious that we're two grown men hugging at the entrance of the ER. Carrick smiles and squeezes my shoulder. "Let's go to the waiting room. You can tell me what's happened, and we can get you cleaned up."

"Sure." I nod and look down at my hands. Shit! They're still stained with that cocksucker's blood.

ANA IS PALE, EXCEPT for the bruise on her cheek where the motherfucker must have hit her. Her eyes are closed as if she's merely asleep, but she's still unconscious. She looks heartbreakingly young and small. Numerous tubes wind into and out of her body. My heart clenches and twists in fear, but Dr. Bartley is calm as she looks down at my broken wife.

"Her ribs are bruised, Mr. Grey, and she has a hairline fracture to her skull, but her vital signs are stable and strong."

"Why is she still unconscious?"

"Mrs. Grey has had a major contusion to her head. But her brain activity is normal, and she has no cerebral swelling. She'll wake when she's ready. Just give her some time."

"And the baby?" I whisper.

"The baby's fine, Mr. Grey."

"Oh, thank God." Relief crashes through me like a cyclone.

Thank God.

"Mr. Grey. Do you have any further questions?"

"Can she hear me?"

Dr. Bartley's smile is benign. "Who knows? If she can, I'm sure she'd love to hear your voice."

I'm not so sure. She'll be mad. I thought she was leaving me.

"My colleague Dr. Singh will look in on your wife later."

"Thank you," I mutter, and she leaves.

Pulling up a chair I sit down beside Ana. Tenderly I take her hand, glad to find it's warm. I squeeze it gently, hoping to rouse her. "Wake up, baby, please," I whisper. "Be mad at me, but be awake, please." Leaning forward, I brush my lips against her knuckles. "I'm sorry. Sorry for everything. Please wake up."

Please. I love you.

I cup her hand in both of mine and press my forehead to my fingers and pray.

Please, God. Please. Bring my wife back to me.

ANA SLEEPS, HER ROOM shrouded in darkness, save for the pool of light from her bedside lamp and the faint illumination from beneath the door. Using my jacket as a blanket, I doze in my chair, fighting sleep. I want to be awake when she comes back to me.

The door opens, rousing me, and Grace enters. "Hello, darling," she whispers, her face pale—devoid of makeup. She looks as tired and drained as I feel.

"Mom." I'm too weary to stand.

"I'm just checking in, as I'm leaving to get some sleep. Carrick is here to watch over Mia."

"How is she?"

"She's okay. Angry. Still suffering from the effects of the drugs. Trying to sleep. Ana?"

"No change."

Grace picks up Ana's medical chart from the end of her bed and scans the notes. Her eyes widen and she gasps. "She's pregnant!"

I nod, too shattered and anxious to do anything else.

"Oh, Christian, that's wonderful news. Congratulations." She steps forward and grasps my shoulder.

"Thanks, Mom. It's early days." *I think.*

"I understand. Couples usually announce at twelve weeks. Darling, you're exhausted. Go home and sleep."

I shake my head. "I'll sleep when Ana wakes."

She presses her lips together but doesn't comment, and bending down she kisses my head. "She'll wake, Christian. Just give her a little time. Try and get some sleep."

"Bye, Mom."

She ruffles my hair. "I'll see you in the morning." She exits as quietly as she arrived, leaving me more bereft than ever.

Just to torture myself, and also to stay awake, I replay my misdemeanors of the last couple of days.

I've been an asshole.

About the baby.

Seeing Elena.

Not apologizing.

And to cap it all, I believed Ana…believed her when she said she was leaving me.

My eyes droop, and my head drops forward, jolting me awake.

Fuck.

I gaze at my wife, willing her to open her eyes.

Ana. Please. Come back to me. "And then I can apologize. Properly. Please, baby." Taking her hand, I bring it to my lips once more and kiss each knuckle. "I miss you."

Leaning back, I close my eyes, just for a second.

FRIDAY, SEPTEMBER 16, 2011

I wake a moment later. *Shit.* How long have I slept? I check my watch—nearly three hours. Glancing over at my wife, I see she's still slumbering peacefully.

Except she's not asleep. She's unconscious.

"Come back to me, baby," I whisper.

"Christian."

"Dad! You startled me."

"Sorry." Carrick emerges from the shadows.

"How long have you been standing there?"

"Not long. I didn't want to wake you. The nurse was just here checking Ana's vitals. It's all good." He stares down at my wife. "Grace tells me she's carrying my grandchild." His eyes shine in reverence as he gazes at Ana.

"Yes. She is."

"Congratulations, son."

I give him a bleak smile. "She put the child and herself at risk." I shiver, and don't know if it's because the night air is cooler or because Ana could so easily be dead.

Carrick presses his lips together, his expression grave, then turns his attention to me. "You're exhausted. You should go home and rest."

"I'm not leaving her."

"Christian, you should sleep."

"No, Dad. I want to be here when she wakes up."

"I'll sit with her. It's the least I can do after she saved my daughter."

"How's Mia?"

"She's asleep. She was groggy, scared, and angry. It'll be a few hours before the Rohypnol is completely out of her system."

"Christ." *Hyde is a sick, twisted, cocksucking son of a bitch.*

"I know. I'm feeling seven kinds of foolish for relenting on her security. You warned me, but Mia is so stubborn. If it wasn't for Ana here…"

"We all thought Hyde was out of the picture. And my crazy, stupid wife—why didn't she tell me?" My unshed tears scald my throat.

"Christian, calm down," he says, gently moving toward me. "Ana's a remarkable young woman. She was incredibly brave."

"Brave and headstrong and stubborn and stupid." My voice breaks on the last word as I fight to contain my emotion.

But what would have happened to Mia, if not for Ana?

This is so confusing. I place my head in my hands, conflicted.

"Hey." Dad rests his hand on my shoulder. I welcome his comforting touch. "Don't be so hard on her, or yourself, son.. I'd better get back to your mom. It's after three in the morning, Christian. You really should try to sleep."

"I thought Mom went home."

Carrick blows out a breath in frustration. "She couldn't leave Mia. She's stubborn, like you. Congratulations again on the baby. That's some good news, in all this mess."

I feel the blood drain from my head—I'll never be as good a father as Carrick.

"Hey," he says gently. "You've got this."

And because I'm weary and despondent, I'm annoyed that he's diagnosed my anxiety so precisely.

Perceptive, Dad.

"You'll make a great father, Christian. Stop worrying. You have several months to get used to the idea." He pats my shoulder again. "I'll be back later this morning."

"Good night, Dad." I watch him quietly close the door.

A great father, eh?

I put my head in my hands.

Right now, I just want my wife back. I don't want to think about the baby.

I stand and stretch. It's late. I'm stiff and sore and heartsick with worry.

Why won't she wake up? Bending, I kiss her cheek. Her skin is soft and reassuringly warm against my lips.

"Wake up, baby," I whisper. "I need you."

"GOOD MORNING, MR. GREY."

What? Again I'm startled from my doze as the nurse opens the curtains, letting the golden fall light invade the room. It's the older nurse—I can't remember her name. "I'm going to check your wife's IV fluids."

"Sure," I mumble. "Do I need to leave?"

"It's up to you."

"I'll stretch my legs." Feeling like shit, I get up, and with a last glance at my wife, I stagger out into the corridor. Maybe I can find some coffee.

TAYLOR ARRIVES AROUND 8:30 with my phone charger and some breakfast (courtesy of Mrs. Jones). I wonder if it's a peace offering from her. One peek into the brown paper bag confirms that it is: two ham-and-cheese croissants. They smell divine. And I have a thermos of proper coffee. "Please thank Gail for me."

"Will do. How is Mrs. Grey?" He looks toward Ana, his concern obvious in the tight line of his jaw.

"All signs are good. We're just waiting for her to wake up. I can't believe we spent last weekend at OHSU, and this weekend we're at Northwest."

Taylor nods sympathetically.

"You may as well stay and update me here. I don't want to leave her side." I offer him the seat beside me. While I eat my breakfast, he recounts all that happened after the ambulances left the crime scene.

"...and the police have recovered Mrs. Grey's cell phone."

"Oh."

"She placed it in one of the duffel bags with the cash."

"Really?" I glance at my sleeping wife. That's genius. "We were following the money?"

"Indeed," Taylor responds, and it's obvious he's impressed with Ana's ingenuity. "The police have the cash."

It's the first time I've thought about the five million dollars.

"Will we get it back?"

"Eventually, sir."

I roll my eyes. It's the least of my problems. "I'll get Welch onto the police and let him liaise with them for the return of the money."

"Hyde is here, being patched up. He's under police guard," Taylor says.

"I wish she'd finished him off."

Taylor holds his counsel, and I remember him wrestling me off Hyde while I was beating that fucker to a pulp. I can't decide if Taylor's actions were a good thing or not.

Hell. If he hadn't, I'd be in a police cell now.

"Detective Clark would like a word with you at some point." Taylor wisely changes the subject as I take a bite of the second croissant.

"Now is not the time."

"Ryan has collected Mrs. Grey's car. Apart from a parking ticket, it's all good." His smile is wry. "Sawyer's mad he let her get away."

"I'm sure."

"There are photographers camped outside the hospital."

Hell.

My phone buzzes. It's Ray. *Shit.*

"Ray. Good morning."

"I need to see Annie."

Ray has heard about Ana's heroics, courtesy of the media, and now insists on seeing her. As he's the only man in the world who intimidates me, I cannot say no.

I dispatch Taylor, and thirty minutes later Ray's sitting at the end of her bed in his wheelchair.

"Annie," he whispers as I wheel him in closer to her bed. "What was she thinking?" he says, his voice hoarse. He's shaved and is wearing loose shorts and a shirt, so in spite of the broken leg and bruising, he looks more like himself.

"I don't know, Ray. We'll have to wait for her to wake up before we can ask her."

"If you don't take her across your knee, I sure as hell will. What the hell was she thinking?" He's more adamant this time.

"Trust me, Ray, I just might do that." *If she'll let me.* I clutch her hand while Ray shakes his head.

"She shot him, you know."

His mouth drops open. "The kidnapper?"

"Yes."

"Well, I'll be damned."

"Thanks for teaching her how to use a gun. Maybe you can teach me to shoot one day."

"Christian, I'd be honored." We both gaze at my headstrong, reckless, brave wife. Each of us nursing our own fearful thoughts while Ana remains unconscious.

"Let me know when she wakes up."

"Will do, Ray."

"I'll call Carla," he mutters.

"I'd appreciate it. Thanks."

He kisses Ana's hand, his eyes glistening with tears, and I have to look away.

When he leaves, I call the office, then Welch, who is in Detroit, following a lead on Hyde. He can't believe Hyde found someone to post bail. Finding out who and why they did is next on his agenda. He's going to call his contact at the Seattle Police Department to ascertain what they know.

I pace back and forth in front of the window to shake off my fatigue as I talk on the phone and watch my wife. She sleeps through my calls, she sleeps through the frequent arrival of flowers from our family and friends—so by mid-afternoon her room resembles a florist's, and she sleeps through their calls inquiring about her well-being.

Everyone loves Ana.

What's not to love? I brush her soft, translucent cheek with my knuckles, fighting the urge to cry. "Baby, wake up. Please. Wake up and be mad at me again. Anything. Hate me…whatever. Just wake up. Please."

I sit beside her and wait.

Kate barges into the room without knocking.

"Kate. Hi."

She nods a greeting and strides straight to Ana's bed and takes her hand. "How is she?"

I'm too tired for this. "Unconscious."

"Ana! Ana! Wake up," Kate barks.

For fuck's sake. The tenacious Ms. Kavanagh is here. "I've tried, Kate. I've been assured that she'll wake in her own time."

Kate presses her lips together. "She doesn't have the sense that she was born with."

I can't argue with that.

She turns to me. "How are you holding up?"

Her inquiry into my well-being is a surprise. "I'm fine. Anxious. Tired."

She nods. "You look it. You two make up?"

I sigh. "Not exactly. When she wakes…" I trail off.

Weirdly, Kate seems to accept this, and doesn't give me a hard time. "So, what happened? How did she end up here?" She folds her arms, and because it looks like I won't get rid of her any other way, I give her the executive summary of Hyde's kidnapping of my sister and Ana's heroic but utterly foolhardy rescue.

"Shit!" Kate says when I finish. "What the hell was she thinking? She's supposed to be the smart one."

"Yeah."

"You know, Christian—she loves you very much."

"I know. She wouldn't be here like this if she didn't." I clench my jaw in self-loathing for doubting her.

"Tell her I was here."

"I will."

"Hope you get some sleep." She gives Ana a last glance and squeeze of her hand, and then she's gone.

Thank God.

A KNOCK ON THE door wakes me, and Detective Clark appears. He's the last person I want to see. I don't want to share my wife with anyone, not when she's like this.

"Sorry to disturb you. I was hoping there might be a chance to talk to Mrs. Grey."

"Detective, as you can see, my wife is in no state to answer any of your questions." I stand to greet him, feeling like shit. I just want this man to go.

Fortunately, his visit is brief but informative. He tells me that

Elizabeth Morgan is cooperating fully with the police. It seems Hyde had compromising videos of her, so he was able to coerce her into helping him. It was Morgan who lured Mia out at the gym.

"Hyde's a twisted son of a bitch," mutters Clark. "He has a serious grudge against your father, and you."

"Do you know why?"

"Not yet. I'll be back when Mrs. Grey wakes. She's safe here. We have Hyde handcuffed to the bed, under police guard 24/7. He's not going anywhere."

"That's reassuring. Will we get our money back?"

Clark frowns.

"The ransom."

He smiles, briefly. "Eventually, Mr. Grey."

"That's reassuring."

"I'll leave you to rest," he says.

"Thank you."

I grimace at Detective Clark's back as he closes the door.

Hyde is here, somewhere in this hospital, because my wife put a bullet in him.

Anger surges through me again.

I could find him and finish the job.

He's under guard, Grey. I hope to God he's incarcerated for a very long time.

Dr. Bartley returns. "How are you doing, Mr. Grey?"

"I'm fine. It's my wife I'm concerned about."

"Well, I'm here to take a look at her."

I stand back and let her do her checks.

"Why hasn't she woken?" I ask.

"It's a good question. I would have expected her to by now. What she's been through was traumatic, though, so maybe she needs a little more down time to process it all. Was she under any other stress?" Dr. Bartley gives me a direct look and I flush, guiltily.

"Well, um…the pregnancy?" I keep my answer vague.

"I have an idea that may bring her around, but it might take a while to see if it works. Besides, I'm not happy catheterizing pregnant women for a long period of time. It runs the risk of UTI."

"Okay, sure. Do I need to leave?"

"It's up to you."

"I'll go fetch some coffee."

Out in the corridor, my phone buzzes. It's John Flynn.

"Christian. I heard about Ana. How is she?"

I sigh and give him the bullet-point summary. "She's expected to wake at any time. It's just—"

"I know. This must be hard on you. I'm sure she's in capable hands. I got a missed call from you the other day. I was at my son's parent-teacher conference."

Ah. The night of my transgressions. It would have been great if he'd answered the phone.

"We'll talk next week?" Flynn asks.

"Yes."

"If you need me, I'm here."

"Thanks, John."

"HELLO, DARLING." GRACE ARRIVES during the evening carrying a small cooler bag.

"Mom."

She hugs me briefly, then scrutinizes my face, her eyes full of concern. "When did you last eat?"

I gaze at her blankly while I try to remember. "Breakfast?"

"Oh, Christian, it's after eight. You must be famished." She strokes my cheek. "I've brought macaroni and cheese. I made it for you."

I'm so tired that the burning in my throat moves to my eyes. "Thanks," I whisper, and in spite of the fact that my wife has still not surfaced, I'm hungry.

No. I'm fucking starving.

"I'll go heat this up. The nurses' kitchen has a microwave. I'll be a couple of minutes."

My mother makes the best mac and cheese in America—better even than Gail's. When she returns, the room fills with its mouthwatering aroma and we sit side by side, and she chats aimlessly while we watch my beautiful wife, who stubbornly refuses to wake.

"We took Mia home late this morning. Carrick's with her."

“How is she?” I ask.

“Christian! Don’t talk with your mouth full.”

“Sorry,” I mumble, with my mouth full—and she laughs. For the first time in forever, my lips lift in a reluctant smile.

“That’s better.” Grace’s eyes glow with maternal love, and I have to confess I feel more hopeful with her here. I finish the last forkful and place my plate on the floor, too tired to move any farther.

“That was delicious. Thanks, Mom.”

“My pleasure, darling. She’s very brave, your wife.”

“Stupid,” I mutter.

“Christian!”

“She is.”

Grace’s eyes narrow and she regards me speculatively. “What is it?”

“What do you mean?”

“Something’s up. I mean, something other than Ana lying here unconscious and you being exhausted.”

How does she know?

Grace says nothing, her penetrating gaze doing all the talking. Silence fills the room, broken only by the hum of the machine monitoring Ana’s blood pressure.

Fuck.

Interfering woman.

It’s no good—I crack under her scrutiny, like I always do. “We had a fight.”

“A fight?”

“Yes. Before all this happened. We weren’t talking.”

“What do you mean, you weren’t talking? What did you do?”

“Mom—” *Why does she automatically assume it was my fault?*

“Christian! What did you do?”

I swallow, and my throat burns with unshed tears, exhaustion, and anxiety. “I was so angry.”

“Hey.” Grace takes my hand. “Angry with Ana? Why, what did she do?”

“She didn’t do anything.”

“I don’t understand.”

“The baby. It was a shock. I stormed out.”

Mom grasps my hand, and suddenly I'm overcome with an urge to confess all. "I saw Elena," I whisper, and shame washes over me like a riptide. My mother's eyes widen, and she releases my hand.

"What do you mean, 'saw'?" she hisses, emphasizing the last word with such scorn that it rocks me. *Did you sleep with her?* I recall Ana's question from…when, yesterday? The day before?

First Ana, now my mother!

"Nothing like that! Fuck, Mom!"

"Don't curse at me, Christian. What was I supposed to think?"

"We just talked. And I got drunk."

"Drunk? Shit!"

"Mom! Don't *you* curse! It sounds wrong."

She presses her lips together. "You are the only one of my children that makes me use such vulgar language. You told me you would cut all ties." Her glare is loaded with censure.

"I know. But seeing her finally put it all in perspective for me. You know, with the child. For the first time I felt…uncomfortable. More than uncomfortable. What we did. It was wrong."

"What *she* did, darling. You were a child!" She purses her lips again and then sighs. "Christian, children will do that to you. They make you look at the world in a different light."

"She finally got the message. I think. And so did I. I'm done with her. I hurt Ana." Shame douses me once more.

"We always hurt the ones we love, darling. You'll have to tell her you're sorry. And mean it, and give her time."

"She said she was leaving me."

"Did you believe her?"

"At first, yes."

"Darling, you always believe the worst of everyone, including yourself. You always have. Ana loves you very much, and it's obvious you love her."

"She was mad at me."

"I'm sure she was. I'm pretty mad at you right now. I think you can only be truly mad at someone you really love."

"I thought about it, and she's shown me over and over how much she loves me, to the point of putting her own life in danger."

"Yes, she has, darling."

"Oh, Mom, why won't she wake up?" Suddenly, it's all too much. The lump in my throat swells, choking me, and I'm overwhelmed—the fight, Ana leaving, nearly dying, Hyde, Mia—*fuck*...and though I've tried to hold back my tears, I can't. "I nearly lost her." The words are strangled and barely audible as I voice my worst fear, and the dam breaks.

"Oh, Christian," Mom gasps. She wraps her arms around me as I break down, and for the first time in my life, I weep in my mother's arms: for my wife, my broken wife, and for myself, and the asshole I've been.

Hell. Hell. Hell.

Grace rocks me to and fro, kissing my hair and crooning soft words as she lets me cry. "It's going to be okay, Christian. It's going to be okay."

She holds me. Tight. And I don't want her to let go.

Mom.

The first woman to save me.

I SIT UP AND wipe my face, and find she's crying, too.

"For fuck's sake, Mom, stop crying."

Her tears turn to smiles. She hands me a tissue from her purse and takes one for herself. Reaching up, she caresses my face. "It's taken twenty-four years for you to let me hold you like this," she says sadly.

"I know, Mom."

"Better late than never." She pats my face, and I give her a watery smile.

"I'm glad we talked."

"Me, too, darling. I'm always here." She looks at me with nothing but love, and she grins with a hint of glee. "I can't believe I'm going to be a grandmother!"

IT'S DARKER. LATER. I don't know what time, and I'm too exhausted to look. Ana lies in her own private world.

"Oh, baby, please come back to me. I'm sorry. Sorry for everything.

Just wake up. I miss you. I love you." I kiss her knuckles and rest my head on my arms, on her bed.

IT'S A SOFT TOUCH, fingers running through my hair, and in this dream, I revel in her touch. *Shit.* I wake instantly and sit up. Ana is gazing at me with big, beautiful blue eyes. Joy bursts in my heart. I have never been so pleased to see those eyes as I am now.

"Hi," she croaks, her voice hoarse.

"Oh, Ana." *Oh, thank God, thank God, thank God.* I grasp her hand and hold her palm to my face so she's caressing me.

"I need to use the bathroom," she whispers.

"Okay."

Ana tries to sit up.

"Ana, stay still. I'll call a nurse." Standing, I reach for the buzzer at her bedside.

"Please," she whispers. "I need to get up."

"Will you do as you're told for once?" I snap.

"I really need to pee," she rasps.

The nurse arrives, and she's pleased to see Ana's finally conscious. "Mrs. Grey, welcome back. I'll let Dr. Bartley know you're awake." She makes her way to Ana's bedside. "My name is Nora. Do you know where you are?" Her blue eyes twinkle kindly.

"Yes. Hospital. I need to pee."

"I'll fetch a bedpan," Nurse Nora offers

Ana screws up her face in revulsion. "Please. I want to get up."

"Mrs. Grey—" Nora is not convinced.

"Please."

"Ana," I warn as she struggles to sit up.

"Mr. Grey, I am sure Mrs. Grey would like some privacy." Nora raises an eyebrow, and from her tone I know she's dismissing me.

In your dreams, sweetheart. "I'm not going anywhere."

"Christian, please—" Ana grasps my hand, and I give hers a squeeze, beyond grateful that she's back. "Please," she says once more.

Shit.

"Fine!" I run my hand over my scalp, frustrated that she wants to be rid of me already. "You have two minutes," I snap at Nurse

Nora. I lean down and kiss my wife's forehead and storm out of the room.

I pace the corridor.

Ana doesn't want me anywhere near her.

Perhaps she's can't stand the sight of me.

I wouldn't blame her.

Fuck. I can't bear this.

I storm back into the room as Nora is helping Ana out of bed.

"Let me take her," I say.

"Mr. Grey, I can manage," Nurse Nora scolds, giving me an icy look.

"Damn it, she's my wife. I'll take her." I move her IV stand out my way.

"Mr. Grey!" Nora chastises me, but I ignore her and carefully place my arms around and under my wife and lift her.

Ana wraps her arms around my neck, and I carry her into the adjacent bathroom. Nurse Nora follows, pushing the IV stand.

"Mrs. Grey, you're too light." I set Ana on her feet, keeping one hand on her so she doesn't fall. She seems a little unsteady. I flip on the light and Ana staggers.

Hell! "Sit, before you fall." I don't let go of her. Gingerly, she does as she's told, and once she's seated, I release her.

"Go." She waves me out.

"No. Just pee, Ana."

"I can't, not with you here." She peers up, beseeching me with wide, dark eyes.

"You might fall."

"Mr. Grey!" Nora is not happy, but we both ignore her.

"Please," Ana says.

Fuck. Get a grip, Grey.

"I'll stand outside, door open." I step outside with Nora while she glares at me.

"Turn around, please," Ana says, and I want to smile. We've done all manner of things to each other but this is a hard limit for her? I roll my eyes, but do as she asks.

Nora mutters something under her breath and I think I catch

the word *interfering* but I'm too relieved that Ana's woken up to let it bother me.

After a minute or two, Ana pipes up that she's done. I scoop her into my arms once more, and I'm thrilled when she curls her arms around me. I bury my nose in her hair, but I'm alarmed to find that she doesn't smell of Ana—she smells of chemicals and hospitals and fucking trauma. But I don't care. She's back. "Oh, I've missed you, Mrs. Grey," I whisper, and I lay her back on her bed, Nurse Nora trailing behind me with the IV, a scowling chaperone.

"If you've quite finished, Mr. Grey, I'd like to check over Mrs. Grey now." Nurse Nora is hatchet-faced when mad.

I stand back and hold up my hands in surrender. "She's all yours."

Nora huffs, unimpressed, but she smiles at Ana. "How do you feel?"

"Sore and thirsty. Very thirsty."

"I'll fetch you some water once I've checked your vitals and Dr. Bartley has examined you." She reaches for a blood pressure cuff and wraps it around Ana's upper arm while I watch. Ana's eyes stay on me. She frowns.

What is it?

Does she want me to leave?

Grey, you must look a sight.

I sit down on the edge of the bed, out of Nora's reach. "How are you feeling?" I ask Ana.

"Confused. Achy. Hungry."

"Hungry?"

She nods.

"What do you want to eat?"

"Anything. Soup."

"Mr. Grey, you'll need the doctor's approval before Mrs. Grey can eat."

Nora and I are not on the same wavelength. I pull my phone from my pocket and call Taylor.

"Mr. Grey."

"Ana wants chicken soup."

"I'm delighted to hear that, sir." I know he's smiling. "Gail's gone to her sister's, but I'll call the Olympic Hotel—they'll still have room service at this time."

"Good."

"I'll be right there."

"Thank you." I hang up.

Nora looks grimmer than ever. But I don't care.

"Taylor?" Ana asks.

I nod.

"Your blood pressure is normal, Mrs. Grey. I'll fetch the doctor." Nora removes the cuff and, without so much as another word, stalks out of the room, radiating disapproval at me.

"I think you made Nurse Nora mad."

"I have that effect on women." I smirk at Ana, and she laughs, but stops abruptly, her face stricken, as she clutches her side. "Yes, you do," she says, gently.

"Oh, Ana, I love to hear you laugh." *But not if it pains you.*

Nora returns with a pitcher of water and Ana and I fall silent, gazing at each other as she pours a glass. "Small sips now," Nora warns.

"Yes, ma'am." Ana takes a sip and closes her eyes for a moment. When she opens them, she looks directly at me. "Mia?"

"She's safe. Thanks to you."

"They did have her?"

"Yes."

"How did they get her?"

"Elizabeth Morgan."

"No!"

I nod. "She picked her up at Mia's gym."

Ana frowns, as if she can't quite comprehend the magnitude of Morgan's and Hyde's treachery.

"I'll fill you in on the details later. Mia is fine, all things considered. She was drugged. She's groggy now and shaken up, but by some miracle she wasn't harmed." My anger flares once more; Ana put herself and Junior in jeopardy. "What you did"—I drag my fingers through my hair, choosing my words carefully, and trying to hang on to my temper—"was incredibly brave and incredibly stupid. You could have been killed."

"I didn't know what else to do," she whispers, and glances down at her fingers.

"You could have told me!"

"He said he'd kill her if I told anyone. I couldn't take that risk."

I close my eyes as I imagine the most awful outcome. *No Mia. No Ana.* "I have died a thousand deaths since Thursday." My voice is hoarse.

"What day is it?"

"It's almost Saturday." I check my watch. "You've been unconscious for more than twenty-four hours."

"And Jack, and Elizabeth?"

"In police custody. Although Hyde is here under guard. They had to remove the bullet you left in him." Once more I wish she'd ended him. "I don't know where in this hospital he is, fortunately, or I'd probably kill him myself."

Ana's eyes grow wide, and she shudders, her fear evident as her shoulders tense and tears prick her eyes.

"Hey." I move forward, taking the glass from her hand, placing it on the nightstand, and gently folding her into my arms. "You're safe now."

"Christian, I'm so sorry." She starts to cry.

No. Ana. You're safe. "Hush." I stroke her hair and let her weep.

"What I said. I was never going to leave you."

"Hush, baby, I know."

"You do?" She pulls away and studies me through her tears.

"I worked it out. Eventually. Honestly, Ana, what were you thinking?"

She places her head on my shoulder. "You took me by surprise. When we spoke at the bank. Thinking I was leaving you. I thought you knew me better. I've said to you over and over I would never leave."

Slowly, I blow out a breath. "But after the appalling way I've behaved—" I tighten my arms around her. "I thought for a short time that I'd lost you."

"No, Christian. Never. I didn't want you to interfere and put Mia's life in danger."

Interfere!

"How did you work it out?" she asks.

I tuck her hair behind her ear. "I'd just touched down in Seattle when the bank called. Last I'd heard, you were ill and going home."

"So, you were in Portland when Sawyer called you from the car?"

"We were just about to take off. I was worried about you."

"You were?"

"Of course I was." I skim her lower lip with my thumb. "I spend my life worrying about you. You know that."

This earns me a half smile. That's something. "Jack called me at the office," she says, her eyes wide once more. "He gave me two hours to get the money." She shrugs. "I had to leave, and it just seemed the best excuse."

Fucking Hyde. "And you gave Sawyer the slip. He's mad at you, as well," I mutter.

"As well?"

"As well as me."

She raises her hand, her fingertips once more caressing my face. Closing my eyes, I lean in to her touch, savoring the feel of her fingers skating over my stubble. "Don't be mad at me. Please," she whispers.

"I am so mad at you. What you did was monumentally stupid. Bordering on insane."

"I told you, I didn't know what else to do."

"You don't seem to have any regard for your personal safety. And it's not just you now."

But before she or I can say anything further, the door opens and Dr. Bartley strides in. "Good evening, Mrs. Grey. I'm Dr. Bartley."

I give her a nod and step away so she has room to examine my wife. While she's doing that, I call Dad to let him know that Ana is awake.

"Oh, that's great news, son." He pauses, and I know he's listening to Grace. "Your mother says to apologize."

"I'll do that, Dad."

"Why? What's happened?" Carrick sounds confused.

"It's a long story."

"Okay. Give Ana our love. We'll come see her tomorrow."

I call Carla to give her the good news.

"Thank you, Christian!" she sobs through her tears.

Next, Kavanagh. "Thank God," Kate says. "And I hope you two have made up."

"Yeah," I mutter, though it's none of her fucking business. "I've got to call Ray."

"Okay," Kate says. "And tell Ana no more chasing kidnappers."

"Will do."

Ray is so relieved, he's silent for several seconds while he gathers himself. Eventually he says, "I appreciate the call, Christian. Tell Annie I love her."

"Will do, Ray."

When I finish my call to my father-in-law, Dr. Bartley is prodding my wife's ribs. Ana winces. "These are bruised, not cracked or broken. You were very lucky, Mrs. Grey."

Ana glances at me. "Foolhardy," I mouth.

I'm still fucking angry with you, Ana.

"I'll prescribe some painkillers. You'll need them for this, and for the headache you must have. But all's looking as it should, Mrs. Grey. I suggest you get some sleep. Depending on how you feel in the morning, we may let you go home. My colleague Dr. Singh will be attending you then."

"Thank you."

A loud knock, and Taylor enters carrying a hefty box from the Fairmont Olympic.

"Food?" Dr. Bartley says, surprised.

"Mrs. Grey is hungry," I inform her. "This is chicken soup."

"Soup will be fine, just the broth. Nothing heavy." She looks pointedly at both of us, then exits the room with Nurse Nora.

There's a wheeled tray in the corner. I maneuver it over to Ana, and Taylor places the box on it. "Welcome back, Mrs. Grey," he says with a fond smile.

"Hello, Taylor. Thank you."

"You're most welcome, ma'am—" He stops, and I glance up at him as I unpack the box. I think he wants to say more. Perhaps to scold Ana? I wouldn't blame him, but he just smiles at her.

In addition to the thermos with soup, there's a small basket of bread rolls, a linen napkin, a china bowl, and a silver spoon.

"This is great, Taylor," Ana says.

"Will that be all?" Taylor asks.

"Yes, thanks," I say. He can go back to bed.

"Taylor, thank you."

"Anything else I can get you, Mrs. Grey?"

She looks at me and arches a brow. "Just some clean clothes for Christian."

Taylor glances at me and smiles. "Yes, ma'am."

What? I check my shirt. I've not spilled anything down it.

But I haven't washed or shaved for days.

I must look like shit.

"How long have you been wearing that shirt?" Ana asks.

"Since Thursday morning." I give her an apologetic shrug and Taylor leaves us. "Taylor's real pissed at you, too," I add, and unscrew the lid of the thermos to pour the soup into the bowl.

Ana dives in with an eagerness I've never seen before. At the first mouthful she closes her eyes as if in ecstasy.

"Good?" I perch on the bed once more.

She nods enthusiastically and takes another spoonful, then pauses to wipe her mouth on a linen napkin. "Tell me what happened—after you realized what was going on."

"Oh, Ana, it's good to see you eat."

"I'm hungry. Tell me."

I frown, trying to remember the order in which everything happened. "Well, after the bank called, and I thought my world had completely fallen apart—"

Ana stops and gazes at me, looking lost.

"Don't stop eating, or I'll stop talking." I sound far sterner than I intend. She flattens her lips, but continues to eat. "Anyway, shortly after you and I had finished our conversation, Taylor informed me that Hyde had been granted bail. How, I don't know; I thought we'd managed to thwart any attempts at bail. But that gave me a moment to think about what you'd said, and I knew something was seriously wrong."

"It was never about the money," she snaps, suddenly raising her voice. "How could you even think that? It's never been about your fucking money!"

Whoa! "Mind your language," I exclaim. "Calm down and eat."

She glares at me, eyes blazing with anger.

"Ana."

"That hurt me more than anything, Christian," she whispers. "Almost as much as you seeing that woman."

Shit. I close my eyes, as my remorse returns full-blown. "I know." I sigh. "And I'm sorry. More than you know. Please, eat. While your soup is still hot." My tone is contrite and gentle. I owe her that.

She picks up her spoon, and I blow out a breath of relief.

"Go on," Ana encourages me, between bites of soft bread roll.

"We didn't know Mia was missing. I thought maybe he was blackmailing you or something. I called you back, but you didn't answer." I scowl, remembering how impotent I felt. "I left you a message and then called Sawyer. Taylor started tracking your cell. I knew you were at the bank, so we headed straight there."

"I don't know how Sawyer found me. Was he tracking my cell, too?"

"The Saab is fitted with a tracking device. All our cars are. By the time we got near the bank, you were already on the move, and we followed. Why are you smiling?"

"On some level I knew you'd be stalking me."

"And that is amusing because?"

"Jack had instructed me to get rid of my cell. So I borrowed Whelan's cell, and that's the one I threw away. I put mine into one of the duffel bags so you could track your money."

I sigh. "Our money, Ana. Eat."

Once again, I'm amazed by her cool head and quick thinking, but I merely watch as she wipes the last piece of bread around the bowl and pops it into her mouth. "Finished."

"Good girl."

There's a knock on the door and Nurse Nora enters once more, carrying a small paper cup. "Pain relief," Nora announces, while I pack the detritus from Ana's meal back into the box from the Olympic.

"Is this okay to take? You know, with the baby?"

"Yes, Mrs. Grey." She hands Ana the pills and a fresh glass of water. "It's Tylenol—it's fine; it won't affect the baby."

Ana swallows the tablet, yawns, and blinks sleepily.

"You ought to rest, Mrs. Grey." Nurse Nora looks pointedly at me.

I nod. *Yes. She should.*

"You're going?" Ana exclaims with a look of alarm.

I snort. "If you think for one moment I'm going to let you out of my sight, Mrs. Grey, you are very much mistaken."

Nora gives me a withering look as she adjusts Ana's pillows so Ana can lie down. "Good night, Mrs. Grey," she says, and with one last censorious glance at me she leaves.

"I don't think Nurse Nora approves of me." I look down at my wife. Awake. Present. Fed. And my relief is overwhelming, but I'm utterly drained and bone-weary. I don't think I've ever felt so tired in my life.

"You need rest, too, Christian. Go home. You look exhausted."

"I'm not leaving you. I'll doze in this armchair." I can ease up on my vigil for a little while.

She scowls, then smiles as if she's had a mischievous idea and shifts over. "Sleep with me."

What! No way! "No. I can't."

"Why not?"

"I don't want to hurt you."

"You won't hurt me. Please, Christian."

"You have an IV."

"Christian. Please."

It's so tempting. I shouldn't…but I can hold her, and my urge to hold her supersedes my common sense.

"Please." She lifts the blankets, inviting me into her bed.

"Fuck it." I slip out of my shoes and socks and climb into my wife's bed, facing her. Gently, I put an arm around her, and she lays her head on my chest.

Oh. The. Feel. Of. Her.

Ana.

I kiss her hair. "I don't think Nurse Nora will be very happy with this arrangement."

Ana giggles and stops abruptly. "Don't make me laugh. It hurts."

"Oh, but I love that sound." *And I love you, Ana. With all my heart.* "I'm sorry, baby. So, so sorry." I kiss her once more and inhale her scent. I catch a trace of my Ana. She's there, beneath the chemicals.

My wife. My beautiful wife.

She rests her hand on my heart, and I place my hand on hers and close my eyes.

"Why did you go see that woman?"

"Oh, Ana," I groan. "You want to discuss that now? Can't we drop this? I regret it, okay?"

"I need to know."

"I'll tell you tomorrow," I mutter, too tired to be pissed about her question. "Oh, and Detective Clark wants to talk to you. Just routine. Now go to sleep." I kiss her hair again.

"Do we know why Jack was doing all this?"

"Hmm…" I murmur as sleep beckons, hard and fast. And after hours and hours of worry, regret, and exhaustion, I submit, and fall into a deep, dreamless slumber.

SATURDAY, SEPTEMBER 17, 2011

> Ana is out cold. I can't wake her. *Wake up, Ana. Wake up.* Elena struts over to sit down beside me. She's naked but for long, tight leather gloves that stop just above her elbows. And her black stilettos with red soles. She takes my hand. *No.* Her fingers clasp my thigh. *No. Don't touch me. No more. Only Ana.* Her eyes blaze in anger, but the fire in them dies. Defeated, she stands. Clothed now in black. *Good-bye, Christian.* She flips her hair to the side and stalks to the door without looking back. I turn. Ana is awake, smiling at me. *Join me. Sleep with me. Stay with me.* My heart soars. Her words bring me joy. She caresses my cheek. *Stay with me. Please.* She begs. How can I resist? She loves me. She does. And I love her.

When I wake, it takes me a moment to remember that I'm in Ana's hospital bed. She slumbers at my side, facing me, her head on the pillow. Eyes closed, lips parted, her cheek pale except for the faint purple blemish from Hyde's cruel blow. The sight of it twists my gut in anger.

Don't dwell, Grey.

She's here. She's safe.

I blink the sleep from my eyes, feeling rested but grimy. I'm in dire need of a shower, a shave, and clean clothes. My watch says 6:20 a.m. I have time. Now that Ana's back in the world of the living, I don't mind leaving her for a little while. With any luck, she'll continue to sleep until I return. Carefully, so as not to wake her, I slide out of bed and slip on my shoes. I brush my lips to her forehead in the semblance of a kiss, then grab my phone, charger, and jacket and tiptoe out of the room as if I'm fleeing a crime scene.

I'm doing the walk of shame.

The thought amuses me.

We're married, for fuck's sake.

Fortunately, Nora and her colleagues are not at the nurses' station, so my escape is unnoticed.

It's my lucky day—there's a cab waiting at the entrance of the hospital, and no photographers. And because it's early, I make good time to Escala. By the time the elevator doors open to the penthouse, my mood is buoyant.

Taylor is in the foyer, on his way out. He steps back, mouth open, surprised to see me, but he recovers quickly. "Mr. Grey. Welcome back."

"Good morning, Taylor."

"I would have picked you up—I was bringing you a change of clothes as per Mrs. Grey's instructions, and *The Seattle Times*." He brandishes a leather duffel.

"It's fine. I need a shower. We'll head back when I'm done."

"Yes, sir. I'll ask Sawyer to join us."

"We'll pick up some breakfast for her on the way."

He nods.

THE STEAMING WATER CASCADES over me.

Washing away my sins.

Damn. After all that I've done, I wish it were that simple. And to cap it off, Ana wants to know everything about my discussion with Elena. What the hell am I going to tell her?

The truth, Grey.

She's not going to like it. But I owe her that, especially considering my recent awful behavior. My effervescent humor fizzles and dies. While I shave, I contemplate the asshole who stares back at me in the mirror.

You owe her more than that.

After all that Ana's done for you.

She saved your sister.

She saved YOU.

I close my eyes.

It's true. This woman has disarmed me at every turn. She's broken through all my barriers, cracked me wide open, and shined her light inside. She doesn't take any of my shit. She's driven out my darkness like the warrior she is—and offered me hope because she loves me. I know it.

And she's carrying my child.

Fuck. A *child.*

The gray-eyed asshole stares back at me, bewildered.

She's done all of this for the simple reason that she loves me, and because she's a decent human.

And how do I treat her?

Badly doesn't cover it, Grey.

Her words haunt me. *I do choose this defenseless baby over you. That's what any loving parent does. That's what your mother should have done for you. And I'm sorry that she didn't—because we wouldn't be having this conversation right now if she had. But you're an adult now. You need to grow up and smell the fucking coffee, and stop behaving like a petulant adolescent.*

And I thought she was leaving me.

I wipe my face.

Make this right, Grey.

ON THE WAY TO the hospital, we stop and Taylor hurries into the café that he phoned for takeout. He returns with what looks like a breakfast feast for Ana; I hope she's hungry. Sawyer pulls up at the entrance to the hospital, but when I climb out of the car, I'm ambushed by a couple of photographers, who start snapping away.

"How's your wife, Mr. Grey?"

"Mr. Grey, will you be pressing charges?"

I ignore the assholes and dart inside the lobby. Taylor follows, carrying Ana's breakfast.

We head to the nurses' kitchen on Ana's ward, where we lay out her breakfast on a tray. Damn, why didn't I bring a small vase, and I could steal a flower from one of the many bouquets she's received. It would go some way toward an apology.

"Sir," says Taylor, as I lift the loaded tray, "before she left, Gail made Mrs. Grey's favorite chicken stew, if I need to bring that in later for lunch, sir."

"Good to know. I'm hoping I can take her home this morning."

Taylor nods his affirmation and pushes open the door to Ana's room to let me in, and I'm hoping for a warm welcome.

She's gone.

Shit.

"Ana!" I shout as my heart catapults into overdrive.

"I'm in the bathroom!"

Oh, thank God.

Taylor bursts through the door, as alarmed as I was. "We're good," I reassure him, and he steps out again, presumably to sit in the corridor. I place the food on Ana's rolling tray and wait, again, for Mrs. Grey…patiently, this time. A moment later she appears and rewards me with a broad grin—I'm relieved to see her up and about.

"Good morning, Mrs. Grey. I have your breakfast."

She climbs into bed, while I pull the tray on wheels over toward her and lift the cover. One wide-eyed, grateful glance from Ana is all the confirmation I need as she gulps down the orange juice and starts on the oatmeal. I sit on the edge of her bed, taking vicarious pleasure in her enjoyment as she eats. Not only is she ravenous, but there's some color in her cheeks. She's on the mend. "What?" she asks, with her mouth full.

"I like to watch you eat. How are you feeling?"

"Better."

"I've never seen you eat like this."

She looks up, her expression serious. "It's because I'm pregnant, Christian."

I snort. "If I knew getting you knocked up was going to make you eat, I might have done it earlier." My smartass remark is an effort to distract her from a serious conversation that I'm not ready to have.

I don't know how I feel about this yet.

"Christian Grey!" She drops the spoon in her oatmeal.

"Don't stop eating."

"Christian, we need to talk about this."

"What's there to say? We're going to be parents." I shrug, hoping she'll change the subject.

Ana's not impressed. She pushes the tray aside, crawls down the bed, and takes my hands in hers. I sit staring at her, paralyzed. "You're scared. I get it," she says gently, pinning me with deep blue eyes. "I am, too. That's normal."

I'm aware that I'm holding my breath.

How can I love a child?

I've only just learned to love you.

"What kind of father could I possibly be?" I whisper, forcing the words through my tightening throat.

"Oh, Christian." My name's almost a sob, and it twists my heart. "One that tries his best. That's all any of us can do."

"Ana—I don't know if I can."

"Of course you can. You're loving, you're fun, you're strong, you'll set boundaries. Our child will want for nothing." Her eyes widen, imploring me.

Ana. It's just so soon…

Is there room in my heart for someone else?

Is there room in your heart for both of us?

She continues, "Yes, it would have been ideal to have waited. To have longer, just the two of us. But we'll be three of us, and we'll all grow up together. We'll be a family. Our own family. And your child will love you unconditionally, like I do." Tears pool in her eyes and slowly trickle down her cheeks.

"Oh, Ana." I gasp while keeping my own tears lodged in my throat. "I thought I'd lost you. Then I thought I'd lost you again. Seeing you lying on the ground, pale and cold and unconscious—it was all my worst fears realized. And now here you are—brave and strong, giving me hope. Loving me…after all that I've done."

"Yes, I do love you, Christian, desperately. I always will."

Reaching up, I take her head in my hands and gently wipe away her tears with my thumbs. "I love you, too." I draw her lips to mine and kiss her, beyond grateful that she's still here and whole. Grateful that she's mine. "I'll try to be a good father."

"You'll try, and you'll succeed. And let's face it: you don't have much choice in the matter, because Blip and I are not going anywhere."

"Blip?"

"Blip."

Blip. "I had the name Junior in my head."

"Junior it is, then."

"But I like Blip." I kiss her again, tentatively teasing her lips—and it's a match to dry kindling. My reaction immediate. Innate.

No. I pull away. "Much as I'd like to kiss you all day, your breakfast is getting cold." Ana's eyes shine the color of a summer sky. She's amused, I think. "Eat," I insist.

She shuffles back into bed and I push the tray in front of her. A barrier between us. She starts on the pancakes with enthusiasm. "You know," she says between mouthfuls, "Blip might be a girl."

Christ. I run my hand through my hair. "Two women, eh?"

"Do you have a preference?"

"Preference?"

"Boy or girl."

"Healthy will do." *Jesus. A girl? Who looks like Ana?* "Eat," I snap.

"I'm eating, I'm eating. Jeez, keep your hair on, Grey."

I move off the bed and take a seat in the armchair beside her, cheered that we've finally broached the subject of…Blip.

Blip.

Yeah. I like the name.

I reach for the newspaper.

Shit! Ana is on the front page. "You made the papers again, Mrs. Grey." Inside, I'm seething. Why can't they leave us alone? *Fucking press.*

"Again?"

"The hacks are just rehashing yesterday's story, but it seems factually accurate. You want to read it?"

She shakes her head. "Read it to me. I'm eating."

Anything to keep you eating, wife.

I read the article out loud as Ana tucks into her breakfast. She doesn't comment on what's been written, but asks me to read more. "I like listening to you."

Her words warm my soul.

She finishes her breakfast, sits back, and listens as I continue, but we're interrupted by a knock on the door. My spirits sink when Detective Clark shambles in. "Mr. Grey, Mrs. Grey. Am I interrupting?"

"Yes," I snap. He's the last person I want to see.

Clark ignores me, which sets my teeth on edge, the arrogant asshole. "Glad to see you're awake, Mrs. Grey," he says. "I need to ask you a few questions about Thursday afternoon. Just routine. Is now a convenient time?"

"Sure," Ana mumbles, but she looks wary.

"My wife should be resting."

"I'll be brief, Mr. Grey. And it means I'll be out of your hair sooner rather than later." He has a point. Giving Ana an apologetic look, reluctantly I stand and offer him my chair, then perch on the other side of her bed and take Ana's hand. I listen quietly as Clark lets my wife tell her side of Hyde's kidnapping and extortion horror story; the words are at odds with her soft, sweet voice. Occasionally, I tighten my grip on her hand as I rein in my anger, and I'm relieved when it's over. Ana's done well to remember so many details.

"That's great, Mrs. Grey." Clark seems pleased.

"I wish you'd aimed higher," I mutter.

"Might have done womankind a service if Mrs. Grey had," he agrees.

Ana's puzzled look skims from Clark to me. She doesn't know what we're talking about, but I'm not going to explain that right now.

"Thank you, Mrs. Grey. That's all for now." Clark shifts in his seat, ready to leave.

"You won't let him out again, will you?" Ana flinches, visibly at the thought.

"I don't think he'll make bail this time, ma'am."

"Do we know who posted his bail?" I ask.

"No, sir. It was confidential."

I'll chase Welch for an update to see if he's found Hyde's benefactor. Clark rises to leave just as Dr. Singh and two interns enter the room, and I follow the detective out, taking Ana's tray with me.

"Good day, Mr. Grey," Clark says, saluting me, then walks on up the corridor.

Taylor rises from his chair outside Ana's room and follows me into the nurses' kitchen, where I deposit the tray. "Sir, I'll take care of that."

"Thanks." I leave him to wash up and return to Ana's room, where I hang back while Dr. Singh completes her examination.

"You're good. I think you can go home," she says, with a pleasant smile to Ana.

Thank God.

"Mrs. Grey, you'll have to watch for worsening headaches and blurry vision. If that occurs, you must return to the hospital immediately."

Ana nods, beaming, clearly as grateful as I am that she's being discharged.

"Dr. Singh, can I have a word?"

"Of course."

We step into the corridor, and I'm relieved that Taylor is still away from his station on the chair outside. "My wife… Um—"

"Yes, Mr. Grey?"

"Her injuries… Will they stop us…"

Dr. Singh frowns.

"Sexual act—"

She interrupts me, finally understanding my gist. "Yes, Mr. Grey, that's fine." She smiles and adds in a quieter tone, "Provided your wife is…you know. Willing."

I give her a broad smile.

"What was all that about?" Ana asks as I close the door.

"Sex!" I give her a wicked grin.

Ana colors. "And?"

"You're good to go."

Ana can't hide her amusement. "I have a headache." Her teasing smirk makes me doubt if she's being entirely truthful.

"I know. You'll be off-limits for a while. I was just checking."

She frowns, and if I'm interpreting her look correctly, I'd say she's disappointed. Nurse Nora bustles into the room, and after a haughty glance at me, she removes Ana's IV.

Ana thanks her and Nora exits. I smile as she leaves. I don't begrudge her at all; she's taken good care of my wife. I resolve to make a substantial donation to the hospital staff appreciation fund.

"Shall I take you home?" I turn to Ana.

"I'd like to see Ray first."

Grey, of course, she wants to see her dad! "Sure."

"Does he know about the baby?"

"I thought you'd want to be the one to tell him. I haven't told your mom, either."

"Thank you."

"My mom knows. She saw your chart. I told my dad, but no one else. Mom said couples normally wait for twelve weeks or so to be sure." I shrug. This is her decision.

"I'm not sure I'm ready to tell Ray."

That's probably a good idea. "I should warn you, he's mad as hell. Said I should spank you."

Ana's mouth drops open. It's such a gratifying response, I laugh. "I told him I'd be only too willing to oblige."

"You didn't!" Ana gapes at me, but her eyes shine with amusement.

Will this ever get old?

Shocking my wife?

I'm glad I still can.

I wink at her. "Here, Taylor brought you some clean clothes. I'll help you dress."

RAY IS QUIETLY OVERJOYED to see his daughter. It shows in his eyes, unmasked for a moment when he sets them on Ana—fear, relief, love, and anger are all reflected in their dark depths. I beat a hasty retreat, knowing he's going to reprimand Ana as she deserves to be reprimanded. Taylor is waiting outside by her door. "Sir, there are still photographers outside the main entrance."

"Find a back way out, and have Sawyer meet us there with the car."

"Will do." He strides off, and I reach for my phone to call Welch.

"Mr. Grey," he answers.

"Welch. Any news?"

"Yes. I'm waiting to board my plane. Let me find a quiet corner." There's rustling, and I hear a muffled airline departure announcement—but not to Seattle. "Right," he grunts. "I have uncovered some information about Hyde. I'll bring that to you. I'd rather you see it in person than have me go through it over the phone."

"Can't you tell me now?"

"I'd rather not. It's a little public here, and this is not a secure line."

What the hell could it be?

"Also, the police discovered several USB sticks in Hyde's apartment during their fingertip search. Sex tapes. All of them. With his old assistants. With Morgan. It's some pretty heavy stuff."

Fuck. My scalp crawls.

"My guess is he used the footage to buy their silence, and also to blackmail Morgan." Welch's gruff voice drives the point home.

I knew about Morgan—but his former assistants?

Thank God I stopped Ana from going to New York with him.

"They'll probably charge him with that, too," Welch continues. "But they're still building their case."

"I see. Any word on who posted bail yet?'

"Nothing certain. But I'll get into that when I'm back."

"What time can I expect you?"

"I'll be there around five p.m."

"See you then." I hang up and wonder what he's found that connects me to Hyde.

ANA IS SUBDUED AS we head down to the rear entrance of the hospital. I think she's been chastened by the reunion with her father, and even though I'm with her dad all the way on this, a very small part of me feels sorry for her. I would not like to be on the receiving end of Raymond Steele's ire.

Once in the car, Ana calls her mother. "Hi, Mom..." Her voice is husky with controlled emotion; Carla, on the other hand, I can hear through the phone as she sobs and wails.

"Mom!"

Ana doesn't stand a chance. Her eyes fill, and I reach over to take her hand and give her a supportive squeeze, brushing my thumb over her knuckles. But I tune their conversation out as my thoughts turn to Welch and what he might have discovered. I'm irritated that he didn't give me a clue over the phone.

Do I even want to know?

I stare out of the window and wonder.

"What's wrong?" Ana asks, and I realize she's finished her call with her mom.

"Welch wants to see me."

"Welch? Why?"

"He's found something out about that fucker Hyde." My lips form a snarl around his name. I loathe the man with every fiber of my being. *Loathe* is not strong enough. *Hate* is not strong enough. I detest him and everything he's done. Ana is still looking at me expectantly. "He didn't want to tell me on the phone."

"Oh."

"He's coming here this afternoon from Detroit."

"You think he's found a connection?"

I nod.

"What do you think it is?"

"I have no idea." It's frustrating, but I shelve the thought, as right now, I need to concentrate on my wife.

"GLAD TO BE HOME?" I ask Ana, as we step into the elevator at Escala.

"Yes." Ana's reply is pin-drop quiet, and I watch as the blood slowly drains from her face. She raises glazed eyes to me and starts to tremble.

Hell. It's finally hitting her.

She's traumatized.

"Hey—" I gather her into my arms. "You're home. You're safe." I kiss her hair, thankful that she smells more like Ana, without the synthetic tang of drugs and disinfectant.

"Oh, Christian." A sob bubbles up through her lips, and she starts to weep.

"Hush, now." I cradle her head against my chest, wanting to chase away the hurt and fear. She must have been holding all this emotion inside.

For my benefit?

I hope not.

I hate to see her cry—but I understand the need right now.

Let it all out, baby. I'm here.

When the elevator doors slide open, I lift her into my arms, and she clings to me, sobbing still, each sound a lesion in my heart. I carry her through the foyer, down the corridor, and into our en suite, where I deposit her on the white chair as if she's made of glass. "Bath?"

Ana shakes her head, then winces.

Shit. Her head aches.

"Shower?"

She nods, tears still streaming down her face. The sight claws at my soul, and I suck in a breath to contain my warring emotions—rage at Hyde, and fury at myself for letting this happen. I switch on the shower, and when I turn back, Ana's rocking slowly, keening into her hands. "Hey." I kneel at her feet and cover each of her hands in mine, easing them away from her tearstained cheeks. I cradle her face, and she blinks away her tears as we gaze into each other's eyes. "You're safe. You both are," I murmur.

Her grief wells in her eyes once more and renders me helpless. "Stop, now. I can't bear it when you cry." My voice is hoarse; my words are honest yet woefully inadequate against the tide of her anguish. I wipe her cheeks once more with my thumbs, but it's a losing battle. Her tears still flow.

"I'm sorry, Christian. Just sorry for everything. For making you worry, for risking everything—for the things I said."

"Hush, baby, please." I kiss her forehead. "I'm sorry. It takes two to tango, Ana." I try a crooked smile to cheer her. "Well, that's what my mom always says. I said things and did things I'm not proud of."

My words come back to haunt me.

This is why I like control.

So shit like this doesn't come along and fuck everything up!

Shame burns like a pyre in my chest. *Grey, this is not helping.*

"Let's get you undressed."

Ana wipes her nose with the back of her hand, and the raw gesture endears her to me even more. I kiss her forehead, because I need her to know that I love her, no matter what she does. Taking her hand, I support her as she staggers to her feet, and quickly undress her, taking particular care as I tug her T-shirt over her head. I guide her to the shower and open the door, where we pause as I strip out of my clothing. When I'm naked, I take her hand again and we both step in.

Beneath the waterfall of steaming water, I hold her hard and tight against me.

I never want to let her go.

She continues to cry, her tears washed away by the cascade flowing over us. I rock her gently from side to side, the rhythm soothing me and, I hope, Ana.

I'm rocking my child, too…inside her.

Whoa. That's a strange thought.

I kiss her hair, so grateful that she's back home with me, when I'd feared…

Shit. Don't go there, Grey.

All of a sudden, I hear a loud sniff, and Ana steps out of my arms. She seems to have stopped crying.

"Better?"

She nods, her eyes clear.

"Good. Let me look at you."

Her brow furrows, and I hope she won't stop me as I need to see for myself what that asshole prick has done to my wife. Taking her hand, I turn it over. My gaze travels from the graze on her wrist to the abrasion at her elbow, to the large fist-sized bruise on her shoulder. The sight of these marks infuriates me, igniting the embers of my earlier anger at Hyde. I bend to kiss each scrape and bruise, planting the barest of kisses at each site. Grabbing the washcloth and shower gel from the rack, I soap the cloth, inhaling the sweet fragrance of jasmine. "Turn around."

Ana does as she's told and, knowing she's fragile and wounded, I wash her arms, neck, shoulders, and back, as tenderly as I'm able. Absorbed in the task, I keep my touch light. She doesn't complain, and the tension in her shoulders eases little by little as I wash them. I turn her so I have a clearer view of the bruise on her hip; my fingers skate over the livid purple mark. She winces.

Motherfucker.

"It doesn't hurt," Ana says quietly, and I raise my head to meet her brilliant gaze.

I don't believe her.

"I want to kill him. I nearly did." The rage I felt, when Hyde was on the ground, burns deep inside my soul.

I should have kicked him to a pulp.

To shield Ana from my murderous thoughts, I concentrate on the washcloth and soap it again with shower gel. I bathe her body once more—her sides and her behind, and I kneel at her feet and wash her legs. I pause at the bruise on her knee, lean in and brush my lips against it before moving on to soap her feet. Her fingers tangle in my hair, distracting me from my task. When I look up, her expression is raw and tender, and it twists my heart. Standing, I trace the bruise at her ribs with my fingertips, the sight stoking my fury once more, but I dampen it down. It's not helping either of us.

"Oh, baby." I push the words past the anguish in my throat.

"I'm okay." Her fingers weave into my hair again, and she pulls my head down and kisses me. Soft. Sweet. I hold myself back. She's hurt. But her tongue teases me, and the fire flares once more, blazing through my body in a different way.

"No," I whisper against her lips, and pull back. "Let's get you clean."

Ana regards me through her lashes, that way she does, and her eyes flick down to my growing erection, then back to my eyes. She pouts, so prettily, and the mood between us lightens immediately. Grinning, like the clown I am, I kiss her quickly. "Clean. Not dirty."

"I like dirty."

"Me, too, Mrs. Grey. But not now, not here." I grab the shampoo and squirt some into my hands. Using only my fingertips, I gently wash her hair, remembering how gentle she was when she last washed mine, and how cherished I felt then.

After I've rinsed out the suds, I switch off the shower and exit, taking her with me. I cloak her in a warm towel, wrap one around my own waist, and hand her a towel for her hair. "Here." She can judge how vigorous to be—she's the one with a hairline fracture in her skull. My lighter mood takes a nose dive.

That asshole.

"I still don't understand why Elizabeth was involved with Jack." Ana intrudes on my dark thoughts.

"I do," I offer.

She peers at me, and I'm expecting a question, but she seems to lose her train of thought as her eyes study me…all of me.

Mrs. Grey! I smirk. "Enjoying the view?"

"How do you know?"

"That you're enjoying the view?"

"No." She sounds exasperated. "About Elizabeth."

I sigh. "Detective Clark hinted at it."

Ana's brows knit together and her gaze goads me, demanding more information.

"Hyde had videos. Videos of all of them. On several USB flash drives. Videos of him fucking her, and fucking all his PAs."

Her mouth drops open.

"Exactly. Blackmail material. He likes it rough."

So do I. Fuck.

Christ.

Self-disgust sweeps over me like an avenging angel.

"Don't," Ana interrupts, the word like the crack of a whip.

"Don't what?"

"You aren't anything like him."

How did she guess?

"You're not." Ana's tone is insistent.

Oh, but, Ana, I am. "We're cut from the same cloth."

"No you're not!" Ana's fervent denial silences me. "His dad died in a brawl in a bar. His mother drank herself into oblivion. He was in and out of foster homes as a kid, in and out of trouble, too—mainly boosting cars. Spent time in juvie." My God, she's remembered everything I told her on the plane to Aspen and she doesn't stop—she's on a roll. "You both have troubled pasts, and you were both born in Detroit. That's it, Christian." She fists her hands and places them on her hips.

She's trying to intimidate me, dressed only in a towel.

It's not going to work.

Because I know who I am.

But I don't want to rile her. Now is not the time for an argument. It's not good for her or the baby. "Ana, your faith in me is touching, especially in light of the last few days. We'll know more when Welch is here."

"Christian—"

Bending, I plant a swift kiss on her lips to end the discussion. "Enough." Her expression is sullen. "And don't pout," I add. "Come. Let me dry your hair."

She presses her lips together, but to my relief, she drops the subject. I lead her into the bedroom, then head into the closet, where I dress quickly, dragging on jeans and a T-shirt. I grab a pair of her sweatpants and one of my T-shirts for her.

While she slips on the clothes, I plug in the hair dryer, sit down on the bed, and gesture to her to join me. Ana perches between my legs and I start to brush through her wet hair.

I love combing out her hair.

It's so soothing.

Soon, the only sound in our bedroom is the high-pitched whine of the hair dryer. Ana's shoulders slump as she relaxes against me, and she's quiet for a while.

"So, did Clark tell you anything else while I was unconscious?" Her words drag me from my absorbing task.

"Not that I recall."

"I heard a few of your conversations."

"Did you?" I stop brushing.

"Yes. My dad, your dad, Detective Clark, your mom."

"And Kate?"

"Kate was there?"

"Briefly, yes. She's mad at you, too."

She jerks around. "Stop with the 'Everyone is mad at Ana' crap, okay?" Her tone is as high-pitched as the hair dryer.

"Just telling you the truth." I shrug.

I'm still a little mad at you myself, Ana.

"Yes, it was reckless, but you know—your sister was in danger."

"Yes. She was," I murmur, as a bleak morbid fantasy of what could have happened plays out once more in my head.

Disarmed with a simple truth. Ana, you humble me at every turn.

I switch off the hair dryer and grasp her chin, gazing into clear but vibrant eyes, eyes I could drown in.

No. I'm not mad.

I'm in awe of my brave, brave woman.

She had the courage to save Mia.

"Thank you." The words are inadequate. "But no more recklessness. Because next time, I will spank the living shit out of you."

She sucks in a breath. "You wouldn't!"

Oh, baby. My palm is twitching right now. "I would." I can't hold back my smug smile. "I have your stepfather's permission."

Ana's pupils dilate, and her lips part.

And it's there between us, that electricity that crackles invisibly—I feel it everywhere, and I know she does, too.

Ana. No.

Suddenly, she launches herself at me.

Fuck! Ana!

I catch her and twist so that we fall together on the bed, Ana in my arms.

But her face crumples in pain, and she gasps.

"Behave!" I growl, my tone harsher than I intend.

"Sorry." She caresses my cheek and I take her hand and kiss her palm.

"Honestly, Ana, you really have no regard for your own safety." I lift the hem of her T-shirt and rest my fingertips on her belly.

A thrill of the unknown sharpens all my senses.

There is life. Here. Inside her.

What did she say? *Flesh of my flesh.*

Our child.

"It's not just you anymore," I whisper, and skate my fingers across her taut, warm skin. Ana tenses beneath me, dragging air into her lungs. I know that sound. My eyes move to hers, and I lose myself in their fathomless blue depths.

It's Ana's desire. I feel it, too.

Our special alchemy.

But it's impossible. She's hurt. Reluctantly, I lift my fingertips from her skin, tug down her T-shirt, then tuck a stray lock of hair behind her ear, because I still need to touch her. But I can't give her what we both want. "No," I breathe.

Ana's face falls, her expression forlorn.

"Don't look at me like that. I've seen the bruises. And the answer's no." I kiss her forehead and she squirms beside me.

"Christian," she moans, needling me.

"No. Get into bed." I sit up to remove myself from temptation.

"Bed?" She looks crestfallen.

"You need rest."

"I need you." The whine has gone, leaving only a husky come-on in her voice.

Closing my eyes, I shake my head at her audacity and my desire.

She's hurt. I open my eyes and glare at her. "Just do as you're told, Ana."

"Okay," she mutters, with an exaggerated pout that immediately lifts my spirits and makes me want to laugh.

"I'll bring you some lunch."

"You're going to cook?" She blinks, incredulous.

"I'm going to heat something up. Mrs. Jones has been busy."

"Christian, I'll do it. I'm fine. Jeez, I want sex—I can certainly cook." She struggles to sit up but winces.

Damn it! Ana!

"Bed!" I point at the pillow, all carnal thoughts banished.

"Join me." She makes one last-ditch attempt.

I don't know what's gotten into her.

Not you recently, Grey.

"Ana, get into bed. Now." I scowl.

She answers with a scowl of her own, stands, and drops her sweatpants to the floor in a dramatic gesture. In spite of her glower, she looks lovely. I hide my smile, and part of me is beyond pleased that she still wants me, after all that's transpired over the last few days.

She loves me.

I draw back the duvet. "You heard Dr. Singh. She said rest."

Still pouting, Ana complies, sliding into bed and folding her arms, conveying her frustration. I want to laugh, but I don't think my mirth would be well received.

"Stay," I order, and with the memory of her beautiful, sour face, I hurry into the kitchen to find the fabled chicken stew Taylor mentioned this morning.

IT'S GOOD TO SEE Ana wolfing down Mrs. Jones's cooking. I sit cross-legged in the middle of the bed, watching her as I devour my lunch. It's delicious, and nourishing, too—perfect for Ana.

"That was very well heated." She smacks her lips, looking replete and a little drowsy. I beam at her, feeling pleased. I managed not to burn myself this time—so, yeah, it was!

"You look tired." I place my bowl on her tray and, standing, take both from her.

"I am," she admits.

"Good. Sleep." I kiss her quickly. "I have some work I need to do. I'll do it in here, if that's okay with you."

She nods and closes her eyes, and seconds later she's out.

ROS HAS SENT ME a preliminary report of her visit to Taiwan. She reassures me that while it was the right decision for her to go, I'll still need to travel there myself, and soon. It's strange reading her quick summary. It's been days since I thought about my business, my company, the shipyard, or even the world at large—I've lost track of time. My attention has been solely concentrated on my wife. I glance over at her. She's still fast asleep.

I read through my other e-mails, and there's a detailed earnings projection on Geolumara, and a remarkably upbeat e-mail from Hassan at GEH Fiber-Optics—morale there is up since my visit and business is going well. My trip to see them was worth it.

Taylor's gentle tap at the door disturbs my reading. "Welch is here, sir."

I can barely hear him, he's speaking so softly. I nod and, with another quick check on my sleeping beauty, follow him out to the living room.

Welch is standing and admiring the view from the window. He's grasping a large manilla envelope.

Showtime, Grey.

"Welch."

He turns. "Mr. Grey."

"Shall we head into my study?"

I LISTEN TO ANA'S breathing as I watch her, timing each of my breaths to hers. In. Out. In. Out. Focusing on her means that I don't have to focus on the photographs Welch has left with me.

Why didn't Carrick and Grace tell me?

I lived with Jackson Hyde!

How did I not know this?

My thoughts have been racing, searching through all the nooks and crannies of my troubled mind, trying to shine a light in the shadows, but I've found nothing. My foster care experience is hidden in the murky depths of the past.

I cannot remember any of it. A chunk of my life. Gone. No. Not gone. *Erased.*

In its place is a dark, gaping hole of nothing but uncertainty.

It's deeply unsettling. Surely I should remember…*something*?

Ana stirs. Her eyes flicker open and find mine.

Thank God.

"What's wrong?" She blanches, and she sits up, her face strained by her concern.

"Welch has just left."

"And?"

"I lived with the fucker." The words are barely audible.

"Lived? With Jack?"

Swallowing down my agitation, I nod.

"You're related?" Ana's shock is palpable.

"No. Good God, no."

Frowning, she moves over and tugs back the duvet; it's an invitation to join her. I don't hesitate. I need her—to anchor me to the now and to help me make sense of this alarming news and this huge gap in my memory.

Right now, I'm untethered.

From everything.

Kicking off my shoes and clutching the photographs, I slip in beside her and drape an arm over her upper thighs as I lay my head in her lap. Slowly she trails her fingers through my hair; the gesture is comforting, and it calms my troubled soul. "I don't understand," she says.

Closing my eyes, I picture Welch and recall the throaty rasp of his voice as he briefed me. I repeat his words for Ana, editorializing a little. "After I was found with the crack whore, before I went to live with Carrick and Grace, I was in the care of the state of Michigan. I lived in a foster home." I pause and take a gulp of air. "But I can't remember anything about that time."

Ana's hand stops and rests on my head. "For how long?"

"Two months or so. I have no recollection."

"Have you spoken to your mom and dad about it?"

"No."

"Perhaps you should. Maybe they could fill in the blanks."

I tighten my hold on Ana, my life raft. "Here." I pass her the photographs. I've been poring over them in the hope that they might stir a dormant memory that's buried deep. The first depicts a scrubby little house with a cheery, yellow front door. The second shows an ordinary working-class couple, and their three scrawny, unremarkable children—plus Jackson Hyde as an eight-year-old, and…me. I'm four years old, a small scrap of humanity, with wild, haunted eyes and threadbare clothes, clutching a filthy blanket. It's obvious that the four-year-old is severely malnourished—no wonder I'm always nagging Ana to eat.

"This is you," Ana gasps, and stifles a sob.

"That's me." My voice is bleak; right now, I've no words of comfort left for her.

I've got nothing. I'm numb.

I stare out at the dusk. The sky is streaked in pale pink and orange that heralds the coming darkness. A darkness that claims me as one of its own.

A husk of a man once more. Hollowed and empty.

I'm missing time. Missing a part of myself that I didn't even know existed.

And I don't understand why.

I'm scared to know why.

What happened to me back then? How could I have forgotten it all?

I cling to the residual anger that simmers beneath the surface. It's aimed at Carrick and Grace.

Why the fuck didn't they tell me?

I close my eyes. I don't want the darkness. I've lived in it too long. I want the light that Ana brings.

"Welch brought these photos?" she asks.

"Yes. I don't remember any of this."

"Remember being with foster parents? Why should you? Christian, it was a long time ago. Is this what's worrying you?"

"I remember other things, from before and after. When I met my mom and dad. But this… It's like there's a huge chasm."

"Is Jack in this picture?"

"Yes, he's the older kid."

Ana's silent for a moment, and I hug her harder.

"When Jack called to tell me he had Mia," she murmurs, "he said if things had been different, it could have been him."

Revulsion shudders through me. "That fucker!"

"You think he did all this because the Greys adopted you instead of him?"

"Who knows? I don't give a fuck about him."

"Perhaps he knew we were seeing each other when I went for that job interview. Perhaps he planned to seduce me all along." Ana's dread echoes in her voice.

"I don't think so. The searches he did on my family didn't start until a week or so after you began your job at SIP. Barney knows the exact dates. And, Ana, he fucked all his assistants and taped them."

Ana's quiet, and I wonder what she's thinking.

About Hyde? About me?

I could have ended up like Hyde if I hadn't been adopted.

Is she comparing me to him?

Fuck. I *am* like Hyde. A *monster.* Is that what she sees?

That we're the same?

What a repulsive thought.

"Christian, I think you should talk to your mom and dad." She squirms, and I release her legs, but she shuffles down into the bed so we're facing each other.

"Let me call them," she offers in a tender whisper. I shake my head. "Please," she pleads. Her expression is as compassionate and sincere as ever. Her eyes brimming with love.

Perhaps she's not comparing me to Hyde.

Should I call my parents? Maybe they can offer the missing pieces on these fragments of my past. They're bound to remember, surely.

"I'll call them," I murmur.

"Good. We can go see them together, or you can go. Whichever you prefer."

"No. They can come here."

"Why?"

"I don't want you going anywhere."

"Christian, I'm up for a car journey."

"No." I give her a lopsided smile. "Anyway, it's Saturday night; they're probably at some function."

"Call them. This news has obviously upset you. They might be able to shed some light." Ana's words are stirring. As I gaze into her eyes, there's no judgment there, only her love shining through the cracks into my darkness.

"Okay." I'll play it her way. I pick up the bedside phone and call my parents' home. Ana snuggles up to me while I wait for an answer.

"Christian." Carrick's voice has never been more welcome.

They're home! "Dad!" I can't hide my surprise.

"Great to hear from you, son. How's Ana?"

"Ana's good. We're home. Welch has just left. He found out the connection."

"Connection? With what? With who? Hyde?"

"The foster home in Detroit."

Carrick is silent on the other end of the phone.

"I don't remember any of that." My voice wavers as my shame and simmering anger surface, a poisonous cocktail. Ana hugs me tighter.

"Christian. Why should you? It was long ago. But your mother and I can fill in the gaps, I'm sure."

"Yeah?" I hate the hope in my voice.

"We'll come over. Now, if you like?"

"You will?" I can scarcely believe it.

"Of course. I'll bring some paperwork from that time with me. We'll be there soon. It will be good to see Ana, too."

Paperwork?

"Great." I hang up and regard Ana's curious expression. "They're on their way." I still can't hide my surprise.

I ask my parents for help…and they come running.

"Good. I should get dressed," Ana says.

I tighten my hold on her. "Don't go."

"Okay." She bathes me in a loving smile, and she snuggles once more into my side.

ANA AND I STAND arm in arm in the doorway of the living room to welcome my parents. My mother lights up when she sees Ana, her joy and gratitude obvious to each of us. Reluctantly, I release my wife into my mother's embrace. "Ana, Ana, darling Ana," she says, and I have to strain to hear her. "Saving two of my children. How can I ever thank you?"

Yep. Mom's right. She's saved me, too.

Dad hugs Ana, his eyes shining with paternal affection. He kisses her forehead. From behind them Mia, whom I wasn't expecting, appears and pulls Ana into a fierce hug.

"Thank you for saving me from those assholes!"

Ana winces.

"Mia! Careful! She's in pain." My shout startles everyone.

Of course. They brought Mia because Mom doesn't want to let her out of her sight. She was drugged and kidnapped only a few days ago. My irritation at my baby sister evaporates.

"Oh! Sorry," she says goofily.

"I'm good," Ana says, giving Mia a tight smile.

Mia barrels over to me and curls her arm around me. "Don't be so grumpy!" she scolds me quietly.

I scowl at her and she pouts playfully at me.

Damn. I hug her tightly to my side.

Thank God she's okay.

My mother joins us, and I hand her the photographs from Welch. Grace examines the picture of the family. She sucks in a breath and covers her mouth. Dad joins us and winds his arm around her shoulders as he also scrutinizes the family picture.

"Oh, darling." Grace reaches up and places her palm against my cheek, her eyes stricken with shock and dismay.

Why? Did she not want me to know about this?

Taylor interrupts us. "Mr. Grey, Miss Kavanagh, her brother, and your brother are coming up, sir."

What the hell? "Thank you, Taylor."

"I called Elliot and told him we were coming over," Mia pipes up. "It's a welcome-home party."

Mom and Dad share an exasperated look. Ana's glance is sympathetic. "We'd better get some food together. Mia, will you give me a hand?"

"Oh, I'd love to." She grabs Ana's hand and they head over into the kitchen area.

Mom and Dad follow me into my study, and I offer them each a seat in front of my desk. I lean back against it, suddenly aware that this is how my father would perch in his study as I stood in front of him while he lectured me about my latest misdemeanor. The tables have been well and truly turned, and the irony is not lost on me. I need answers and they're here—so presumably they're willing to shed some light on this dark chapter in my life. I mask my anger and gaze at both of them expectantly.

Grace is the first to speak, her voice clear and authoritative, her doctor's voice. "This photograph, these are the Colliers. They were your foster parents. You had to go to them once your biological mother died, because under state law we had to wait to see if you had any relatives who would claim you."

Oh.

Her voice drops. "We had to wait for you. It was agonizing. Two whole months." She closes her eyes, as if reliving the pain. It's sobering. My anger melts away as my breath catches in my throat. I cough to hide my emotion.

"In the picture." I gesture to the photograph Grace is holding. "The boy with red hair. That's Jack Hyde."

Carrick leans in and they examine the photograph together. "I don't remember him," my father muses.

Mom shakes her head, a forlorn look on her face. "No, me, neither. We only had eyes for you, Christian."

"Were… Were they kind?" I ask haltingly, my voice a shadow. "The Colliers?"

Grace's eyes fill with tears. "Oh, darling. They were wonderful. Mrs. Collier doted on you."

Silently, I blow out a breath of relief. "I wondered. I couldn't remember."

Grace's eyes widen with understanding. She reaches out and grips my hand, hazel eyes beseeching mine. "Christian, you were a traumatized child. You wouldn't or couldn't speak. You were skin and bone. I can't even imagine the horrors you endured in your early life. But that ended with the Colliers." She squeezes my hand, willing me to believe her. "They were good people."

"I wish I could remember them," I whisper.

She stands and takes my hand. "There's no reason why you should. It felt like forever for us, because we wanted you so badly, but it was only two months. We'd already been approved to adopt, thank goodness. Otherwise, the process could have been longer."

"Here," Carrick says. "It must be harrowing not knowing, but I have a few things from that time for you. Maybe they might help you remember." From inside his jacket he produces a large envelope. I sit down at my desk, steel myself, and open it. Inside I find a résumé for Mr. and Mrs. Collier and details about their family, a daughter and two sons. Several letters, and two drawings…my drawings?

I gaze down at them, and my scalp tingles with a sense of wonder.

Both pictures are in crayon. They're a scrawled child's view of a house with a yellow door. There are stick figures: two adults, five siblings.

The sun shines over them all. Huge. Bright.

The second picture is similar, but all the children are holding what look like sugar cones with ice cream.

It appears happy enough.

"We had reports on you every week from them. And we visited. Every weekend."

"Why didn't you tell me?"

Grace and Carrick exchange a look.

"It never came up, son." Carrick's jaw tightens, his voice quiet with remorse, I think, as he shrugs. "We wanted you to forget, about all…" He trails off.

I nod. *I get it.*

Forget about my life with the crack whore.

Forget about her pimp.

Forget about my life before them.

I don't blame them. I'd like to forget.

Why would anyone want to remember that?

"I hope this helps with some of your questions," he says.

"It does. I'm glad I called you. It was Ana's idea."

Carrick smiles. "She's one brave woman, Christian." He glances once more at Grace. She nods, and it looks like she's giving him permission. He hands me another envelope.

With a puzzled look at both of them, I open it. Inside is a birth certificate.

STATE OF MICHIGAN

CERTIFICATE OF LIVE BIRTH

121-83-757899	June 29, 1983
STATE FILE NUMBER	DATE FILED

Kristian Pusztai
CHILD'S NAME (FIRST, MIDDLE, LAST, SUFFIX)

June 18, 1983	Male	Detroit, Wayne County
DATE OF BIRTH	GENDER	CHILD'S BIRTHPLACE
Életke Pusztai	19	Budapest, Hungary
MOTHER'S NAME BEFORE FIRST MARRIED	MOTHER'S AGE	MOTHER'S BIRTHPLACE
Unknown	Unknown	Unknown
FATHER'S NAME	FATHER'S AGE	FATHER'S BIRTHPLACE

I hereby certify that the above is a true and correct representation of the birth facts on file with the Division for Vital Records, Michigan Department of Community Health.

Kristian! A tremor runs up my spine. *My name!*

And the crack whore! *She has a name.*

From nowhere I hear her pimp asshole shouting. "Ella!"

Ella…short for Életke.

His usual epithet was *bitch*.

I shake off the thought.

"Why are you giving this to me now?" My voice is hoarse as I gaze at my parents.

"I found it with the letters and the drawings. In Mrs. Collier's letters she calls you Christian with a *K*. So, if you wondered…" My mother's voice trails off.

"Why did you change the spelling?"

"Because you are a gift. To us. From God."

I stare at her. Stupefied. A *gift? Me?* All the shit I gave the two people standing in front of me, and this is what they think?

"We felt we owed Him. You've always been a gift, Christian," Carrick murmurs.

Tears pinch the back of my eyes and I take a deep breath.

A *gift*.

"Children are a gift. Always." Grace's maternal adoration is plain in her glistening eyes, and I know what she's left unsaid—that I'll find this out for myself, in a few months. Leaning over, she smooths my hair off my forehead. I return her smile and, standing, pull her into my arms.

"Thanks, Mom."

"You're welcome, son."

Carrick hugs us both.

I close my eyes, and fighting back my tears, I accept it.

Unconditional love.

From my parents.

As it should be.

Enough. I pull away. "I'll read the letters later." My voice is gruff with emotion.

"Okay."

"We should get back to the others," I mutter.

"Have you remembered anything?" Carrick asks.

I shake my head.

"Maybe you will, maybe you won't, but don't sweat it, son. You have us. You have your family. And like your mother says, the Colliers were good people." Gently, he squeezes my arm, his warmth and affection radiating through my body.

We head back into the main living room, but I'm moving in slow motion, disconnected from my reality, my head ready to explode with all these revelations. I scan the room for Ana; she's standing with Elliot and Kate at the kitchen counter, eating some canapés.

From somewhere deep in my brain, the part that stores my earliest memories, comes a fragment—a vision of a family gathered around a wooden table. Laughing. Teasing. Eating…macaroni and cheese.

The Colliers.

I'm distracted from my reminiscence by the sight of Ana with a flute of pink champagne in her hand.

Junior!

I move to take the alcohol from her, but Kate steps into my path. "Kate." I acknowledge her.

"Christian," she responds, in her usual abrupt way.

"Your meds, Mrs. Grey?" My tone is a warning as I stare at the glass in Ana's hand, trying not to give anything away. But Ana narrows her eyes and raises her chin in defiance. Grace collects a full flute from Elliot, walks up to Ana, and whispers something in her ear. They exchange a furtive smile, and they clink glasses.

Mom! I grimace at both of them. But they ignore me.

"Hotshot!" Elliot claps me on the back and hands me a glass.

"Bro." I keep my eyes on Ana as Elliot and I take a seat on the couch.

"Jesus, you must have been worried sick."

"Yeah."

"Glad that asshole is finally caught. His ass is on its way to jail."

"Yeah."

Elliot frowns. "You missed a great game."

"Game?"

He wants to talk baseball? Is he trying to distract me? He's pissed the Mariners lost to the Rangers today, but I find it difficult to concentrate on what he's saying—my attention is locked on Ana. Carrick joins Ana, and Grace kisses him on the cheek, then moves to sit with Mia and Ethan—who are looking mighty cozy on the couch—leaving Ana to talk to Dad.

My father and my wife enjoy a lively whispered conversation.

What are they talking about? Me?

"You're not listening to a word I'm saying, asshole." Elliot pulls me back into our conversation.

"Sure. The Rangers."

He punches my arm. "You get a pass," he says. "You've had a tough few days. You know, you two should come see your house."

"Yeah. I'd like that. Ana and I were planning to and then all hell broke loose."

"Ana and Mia. Fuck." Elliot's expression is grim. "Glad your wife took that asshole down."

I nod.

"Hi, Christian." Ethan joins us and I'm grateful for the interruption.

"Watch the game?" Elliot asks, and they fall into a debate about Beltré hitting a homer against the Mariners. I tune them out as Ana comes toward us.

"It's great to see everyone," she says to Carrick, as she sits next to me.

"One sip," I scold her under my breath. And you've had that. I take the glass from her hand.

"Yes, Sir." She flutters her eyelashes, her eyes darkening and suddenly full of promise. My body stirs in response, and I ignore it.

Jesus. We're in company.

I wind my arm around her shoulders and shoot her a quick look.

Behave, Ana.

ANA IS CURLED UP in bed, watching me as I strip. "My parents think you walk on water." I toss my T-shirt onto the chair.

"Good thing you know differently."

"Oh, I don't know."

"Did they fill in the gaps for you?"

"Some. I lived with the Colliers for two months while Mom and Dad waited for the paperwork. They were already approved for adoption because of Elliot, but the wait's required by law, to see if I had any living relatives who wanted to claim me."

"How do you feel about that?"

"About having no living relatives?" *Relieved!* "Fuck that. If they were anything like the crack whore." I shake my head.

Thank God for Mom and Dad.

They were—*are*—a gift to me.

I don my pajama pants and climb into bed, cuddling up to my wife, beyond grateful that she's here with me. She inclines her head, her expression warm, but I know she's expecting me to say more. "It's coming back to me," I muse.

Mac and cheese...yeah.

"I remember the food. Mrs. Collier could cook. And at least we know now why that fucker is so hung up on my family." A hazy memory surfaces.

Wait—didn't she use to sit by my bed?

She's tucking me into a small cot bed and holding a book. "Fuck!"

"What?"

"It makes sense now!"

"What?"

"Baby Bird. Mrs. Collier used to call me Baby Bird."

Ana's looks puzzled. "That makes sense?"

"The note. The ransom note that fucker left. It went something like 'Do you know who I am? Because I know who you are, Baby Bird.'"

Ana still looks confused.

"It's from a kid's book. The Colliers had it. It was called *Are You My Mother*? Shit." I imagine the cover in my mind's eye: the little bird and the sad, old dog. "I loved that book. Mrs. Collier used to read it to me. Christ. He knew. That fucker knew."

Though I have no memory of him...thank God.

"Will you tell the police?"

"Yes. I will. Christ knows what Clark will do with that information."

I exhale. They're here, in my brain, the missing memories. It's a relief. And once more I'm grateful that my parents came to see me this evening. They've dislodged whatever was holding these recollections back.

Ana smiles, relieved for me, I think. But enough of my fucked-up history. I owe Ana an explanation. But where to start? She might be too tired; she's worked hard to entertain my family. "Thank you for this evening."

"For what?"

"Catering for my family at a moment's notice."

"Don't thank me, thank Mia. And Mrs. Jones. She keeps the pantry well stocked."

Ana! Take a compliment. She's such an exasperating woman sometimes, but I let it go. "How are you feeling, Mrs. Grey?"

"Good. How are you feeling?"

"I'm fine."

Ana's eyes light up, and her fingers dance over my belly.

I laugh and grab her hand. "Oh, no. Don't get any ideas."

Her lips purse in disappointment, and she stares up at me through her lashes again. "Ana, Ana, Ana, what am I going to do with you?" I kiss her hair.

"I have some ideas." She wriggles beside me and stops suddenly, her face scrunched in pain.

Ana! You're hurt.

She smiles quickly, to reassure me.

"Baby, you've been through enough. Besides, I have a bedtime story for you."

She looks up, expectant.

"You wanted to know..." I close my eyes and swallow, as my mind drifts back to my adolescence.

I'm fifteen again.

"Picture this: an adolescent boy looking to earn some extra money so he can continue his secret drinking habit." I open my eyes, but I can still see myself as I was back then: a tall but scrawny teen, in cut-off shorts, with a shock of copper hair and a belligerent fuck-off attitude.

That was me.

Hell.

I shift onto my side so Ana and I are lying facing each other. Her eyes are wide, and full of questions. I take a deep breath. "So, I was in the backyard at the Lincolns', clearing some rubble and trash from the extension Mr. Lincoln had just added to their place."

Closing my eyes again, I'm there once more. The scent of summer flowers hangs thick in the air. Insects buzz and I swat them away. The heat from the midday sun is beating down on me, so much so that I strip off my T-shirt. And there's Elena. Wearing the lowest-cut dress I've ever seen—it barely sheathes her body.

When I chance a look at Ana, she's still staring at me, hanging on my every word. "It was a hot summer day. I was working hard." I chuckle, remembering this was probably one of the few days I ever did any manual labor. "It was backbreaking work, shifting that rubble. I was on my own, and Ele—Mrs. Lincoln appeared out of nowhere and brought me some lemonade. We exchanged small talk, and I made some smartass remark—and she slapped me. She slapped me so hard." My hand moves automatically to my cheek as I remember the unfamiliar sting. No one had ever slapped me like that.

My eyes are here, boy. Mrs. Lincoln points two fingers at her face.

She caught me staring at her tits.

Well. You couldn't miss them.

Fuck.

I was hard. Instantly. To bursting.

Mrs. Lincoln's gaze drifts to my pants.

Fuck. My boner! It's humiliating.

Like that, do you? she drawls, scarlet lips lifting in a sexy smile.

I think I'm gonna come in my pants.

"But then she kissed me. And when she finished, she slapped me again."

Her mouth is hot. Wet. Strong. Everything I ever wet-dreamed about.

"I'd never been kissed before or hit like that."

Ana gasps.

Fuck. "Do you want to hear this?"

Ana stares, round-eyed, and her words rush out in a breathless whisper. "Only if you want to tell me."

"I'm trying to give you some context."

She nods, but she looks like she's seen a fucking ghost, and I hesitate. Should I continue? I look deeply into her startled eyes, and all

I see are more questions. She's hungry for information; she's always hungry for more.

I roll onto my back and stare at the ceiling and continue my sorry tale. "Well, naturally, I was confused and angry…and horny as hell. I mean, a hot older woman comes on to you like that."

It was the first time I'd ever been kissed.

Ever. It was heaven. And hell, too.

"She went back into the house, leaving me in the backyard. She acted as if nothing had happened. I was at a total loss." *I wanted to rub one out right there. But, of course, I couldn't.* "So I went back to work, loading the rubble into the dumpster. When I left that evening, she asked me to come back the next day. She didn't mention what had happened. The next day I went back. I couldn't wait to see her again." I'm whispering, as if I were in the confessional. "She didn't touch me when she kissed me." *Only my face, where she grabbed me. It was a revelation.*

I turn to face Ana. "You have to understand—my life was hell on earth. I was a walking hard-on, fifteen years old, tall for my age, hormones raging. The girls at school—"

They were interested.

And so was I…but I couldn't bear to be touched.

I fought everyone off.

And pushed everyone away with my rage.

"I was angry, so fucking angry at everyone, at myself, my folks. I had no friends. My therapist at the time was a total asshole. My folks, they kept me on a tight leash; they didn't understand." I gaze at the ceiling, thinking how solicitous Carrick and Grace had been this evening.

"I just couldn't bear anyone touching me. I couldn't. Couldn't bear anyone near me. I used to fight. Fuck, did I fight. I got into some godawful brawls. I was expelled from a couple of schools. But it was a way to let off steam. To tolerate some kind of physical contact." I clench my fists, remembering one particular brawl.

Wilde. That asshole. Picking on smaller kids.

"Well, you get the idea. And when she kissed me, she only grabbed my face. She didn't touch me."

It was such a relief.

To finally experience that kind of contact.

And it was so fucking exciting.

My life changed in that moment.

Everything changed.

"Well, the next day I went back to the house, not knowing what to expect. And I'll spare you the gory details, but there was more of the same."

I could whip a savage like you into shape. Elena's drawl echoes in my mind.

Savage? *She knows!*

She sees me.

The bad seed.

"And that's how our relationship started." Shaking off the memory, I turn to face Ana once more. "And you know something, Ana? My world came into focus. Sharp and clear. Everything. It was exactly what I needed. She was a breath of fresh air. Making the decisions, taking all that shit away from me, letting me breathe. And even when it was over, my world stayed in focus, because of her. And it stayed that way…until I met you." Suddenly a flood of emotion wells inside me, almost engulfing me.

Ana.

My love.

Reaching up, I smooth a stray tendril of her hair behind her ear, because I want—no, *need*—to touch her. "You turned my world on its head." Suddenly, I see her pale, sad face, leaving me as the elevator doors close. "My world was ordered, calm, and controlled, then you came into my life with your smart mouth, your innocence, your beauty, and your quiet temerity and everything before you was just dull, empty, mediocre. It was nothing."

Ana sucks in a breath.

"I fell in love," I whisper, and strum my knuckles across her cheek.

"So did I," she responds, and I feel her breath on my face.

"I know."

"You do?"

"Yes."

You're still here with me, listening to this sorry, disturbing story. You saved me.

Her face breaks into a shy smile. "Finally," she murmurs.

"And it's put everything into perspective for me. When I was younger, Elena was the center of my world. There was nothing I wouldn't do for her. And she did a lot for me. She stopped my drinking. Made me work hard at school. You know, she gave me a coping mechanism I hadn't had before, allowed me to experience things that I never thought I could."

"Touch," Ana asks.

"After a fashion."

Ana's brows pucker together, and her eyes are full of new questions. I have no choice but to tell her. "If you grow up with a wholly negative self-image, thinking you're some kind of reject, an unlovable savage, you think you deserve to be beaten." I pause, gauging her reaction. "Ana, it's much easier to wear your pain on the outside."

It's much harder on the inside.

I don't dwell on that thought. "She channeled my anger. Mostly inward—I realize that now. Dr. Flynn's been on and on about this, for some time. It was only recently that I saw our relationship for what it was. You know, on my birthday."

Ana grimaces.

"For her that side of our relationship was about sex and control, and a lonely woman finding some kind of comfort with her boy toy."

"But you like control," she says.

"Yes. I do. I always will, Ana. It's who I am. I surrendered it for a brief while. Let someone make all my decisions for me. I couldn't do it myself—I wasn't in a fit state. But through my submission to her, I found myself, and found the strength to take charge of my life. Take control and make my own decisions."

"Become a Dom?"

"Yes."

"Your decision?"

"Yes."

"Dropping out of Harvard?"

"My decision, and it was the best decision I ever made. Until I met you."

"Me?"

"Yes. The best decision I ever made was marrying you." I smile at her.

"Not starting your company?" she whispers.

I shake my head.

"Not learning to fly?"

No, baby. "You." I stroke her cheek once more, marveling at its softness. "She knew."

"She knew what?"

"That I was head over heels in love with you. She encouraged me to go down to Georgia to see you, and I'm glad she did. She thought you'd freak out and leave. Which you did."

Ana blinks, and the color drains from her cheeks.

"She thought I needed all the trappings of the lifestyle I enjoyed."

"The Dom?"

Yes. "It enabled me to keep everyone at arm's length, gave me control, and kept me detached, or so I thought. I'm sure you've worked out why."

"Your birth mom?"

"I didn't want to be hurt again. And then you left me." I see the elevator doors closing on Ana once more, and I remember sitting on my foyer floor for what seemed like hours. "And I was a mess." I take a deep breath. "I've avoided intimacy for so long—I don't know how to do this."

"You're doing fine." She sculpts my lips with her finger, and I press a kiss to her fingertip as we gaze at each other. And as ever, I'm drowning in her blue eyes. "Do you miss it?" she asks.

"Miss it?"

"That lifestyle."

"Yes, I do."

From her look, I'm not sure she believes me. "But only insofar as I miss the control it brings. And, frankly, your stupid stunt"—I halt—"that saved my sister."

You mad. Bad. Beautiful woman. "That's how I know."

"Know?" She frowns.

"Really know that you love me."

"You do?"

"Yes. Because you risked so much. For me. For my family."

Her frown deepens, and I can't resist. Reaching over, I skim over her brow with my fingertip. "You have a *v* here when you frown. It's very soft to kiss." Her expression lightens. "I can behave so badly, and yet you're still here," I murmur.

"Why are you surprised I'm still here? I told you I wasn't going to leave you."

"Because of the way I behaved when you told me you were pregnant." Of its own accord, my finger traces her brow and down her cheek. "You were right. I am an adolescent."

She purses her lips. Contrite. "Christian, I said some awful things."

I place my finger over her mouth.

"Hush. I deserved to hear them. Besides, this is my bedtime story." I roll onto my back again. "When you told me you were pregnant—" I stop, fighting my shame and trying to find the words. "I'd thought it would be just you and me for a while. I'd considered children, but only in the abstract. I had this vague idea we'd have a child sometime in the future. You're still so young, and I know you're quietly ambitious. Well, you pulled the rug out from under me. Christ, was that unexpected. Never in a million years, when I asked you what was wrong, did I expect you to be pregnant." I sigh, disgusted at myself. "I was so mad. Mad at you. Mad at myself. Mad at everyone. And it took me back, that feeling of nothing being in my control. I had to get out. I went to see Flynn, but he was at some school parents' evening."

I glance at her as I arch a brow, hoping that she sees the funny side of that. And of course, she does.

"Ironic," she says and we both smirk.

"So I walked and walked and walked, and I just found myself at the salon. Elena was leaving. She was surprised to see me. And, truth be told, I was surprised to find myself there. She could tell I was mad and asked me if I wanted a drink. We went to a quiet bar I know and had a bottle of wine. She apologized for the way she behaved the last time she saw us. She's hurt that my mom will have nothing to do with her anymore—it's narrowed her social circle—but she understands. We talked about the business, which is doing fine, in spite of the recession… I mentioned that you wanted kids."

"I thought you let her know I was pregnant."

"No, I didn't."

"Why didn't you tell me that?"

I shrug. "I never got the chance." *You were too angry.*

"Yes, you did."

"I couldn't find you the next morning, Ana. And when I did, you were so mad at me."

"I was."

"Anyway, at some point in the evening—about halfway through the second bottle—she leaned over to touch me. And I froze." I throw my arm over my eyes. I'm mortified.

Spit it out, Grey.

"She saw that I recoiled from her. It shocked both of us."

Ana tugs at my arm, so I turn and gaze at her.

I'm sorry, baby.

"What?" Ana asks.

I swallow, trying to fight the awkwardness. "She made a pass at me."

Ana's face transforms. She's appalled. And mad. Again.

Fuck.

"It was a moment, suspended in time," I continue hastily. "She saw my expression, and she realized how far she'd crossed the line. I said no, I haven't thought of her like that for years, and besides"—I swallow again, my voice soft—"I love you. I told her I love my wife."

Ana stares at me. Silent.

Oh, my love, what are you thinking? I stumble on. "She backed right off. Apologized again, made it seem like a joke. I mean, she said she's happy with Isaac and with the business and she doesn't bear either of us any ill will. She said she missed my friendship, but she could see that my life was with you now. And how awkward that was, given what happened the last time we were all in the same room. I couldn't have agreed with her more. We said our good-byes—our final good-byes. I said I wouldn't see her again, and she went on her way."

"Did you kiss?"

"No!" *Good God no.* "I couldn't bear to be that close to her. I was miserable. I wanted to come home to you. But I knew I'd behaved badly. I stayed and finished the bottle, then started on the bourbon. While I was drinking, I remembered your saying to me some time ago, *'If that was my son...'* And I got to thinking about Junior, and about how Elena and I started. And it made me feel...uncomfortable. I'd never thought of it like that before."

"That's it?" Ana breathes.

"Pretty much."

"Oh."

"Oh?"

"It's over?"

"Yes. It's been over since I laid eyes on you. I finally realized it that night, and so did she."

"I'm sorry," she says.

"What for?"

"Being so angry the next day."

"Baby, I understand angry."

Angry is my middle name.

I sigh. "You see, Ana, I want you to myself. I don't want to share you. What we have, I've never had before. I want to be the center of your universe, for a while at least."

"You are," she objects. "That's not going to change."

"Ana," I whisper gently, with a resigned smile. "That's just not true. How can it be?"

Tears well in her eyes.

"Shit—don't cry, Ana. Please, don't cry." I lay my hand on her cheek.

"I'm sorry." Her lip trembles, and I brush my thumb over it as my heart swells.

"No, Ana, no. Don't be sorry. You'll have someone else to love as well. And you're right. That's how it should be."

"Blip will love you, too. You'll be the center of Blip's—Junior's world. Children love their parents unconditionally, Christian."

I feel the blood drain from my face.

"That's how they come into the world," Ana continues, her passion clear. "Programmed to love. All babies, even you. Think about that children's book you liked when you were small. You still wanted your mom. You loved her."

Ella.

Hey, Maggot. Let's find your cars.

I'm on the edge of a dark maelstrom.

Teetering over it.

I fist my hand beneath my chin as I gaze at my beautiful wife, floundering for something to say as I fight the current to swim away from the pain. "No," I whisper.

Ana's tears spill down her cheeks. "Yes. You did. Of course you did. It wasn't an option. That's why you're so hurt."

All the air has left the room and my body.

I'm being sucked down.

"That's why you're able to love me," she says. "Forgive her. She had her own world of pain to deal with. She was a shitty mother, and you loved her."

I'm lost in the vortex. It's choking me.

Hey, Maggot. Shall we bake a cake?

Mommy smiles and ruffles my hair.

Here you go. Mommy gives me a brush.

She smiles down at me. Mommy is pretty.

She has long hair. She's singing. Happy.

There you go, Grey.

There *were* happy times..."I used to brush her hair. She was pretty."

"One look at you and no one would doubt that."

"She was a shitty mother."

Ana nods, her tearful eyes brimming with compassion.

I close my eyes and confess. "I'm scared I'll be a shitty father."

Ana's fingers skim over my face, reassuring me. "Christian, do you think for one minute I'd let you be a shitty father?"

I open my eyes and stare at her.

And there it is...the Anastasia Steele glint.

So aptly named.

My warrior, fighting for me, with me, against me...for our child.

She takes my breath away.

I grin. In awe. "No, I don't think you would." I stroke her face. "God, you're strong, Mrs. Grey. I love you so much." I kiss her forehead. "I didn't know I could."

"Oh, Christian," she whispers.

"Now, that's the end of your bedtime story."

"That's some story."

"How's your head?"

"My head?"

"Does it hurt?"

"No."

"Good. I think you should sleep now."

Ana is not convinced.

"Sleep," I exclaim. "You need it."

"I have one question," Ana says.

"Oh? What?"

"Why have you suddenly become all…forthcoming, for want of a better word? You're telling me all this, when getting information out of you is normally a pretty harrowing and trying experience."

"It is?"

"You know it is."

"Why am I being forthcoming? I can't say. Seeing you practically dead on the cold concrete, maybe." I flinch, remembering Ana on the ground outside that derelict warehouse where Hyde was holding my sister. It's traumatic so I turn my thoughts in a happier direction, to Junior. "The fact I'm going to be a father. I don't know. You said you wanted to know, and I don't want Elena to come between us. She can't. She's the past, and I've said that to you so many times."

"If she hadn't made a pass at you, would you still be friends?" Ana asks.

"That's more than one question."

"Sorry. You don't have to tell me." She blushes, and it's good to see some color in her cheeks. "You've already volunteered more than I ever thought you would."

"No, I don't think so, but she's felt like unfinished business since my birthday. She stepped over the line, and I'm done. Please, believe me. I'm not going to see her again. You said she's a hard limit for you. That's a term I understand."

Ana smiles. "Good night, Christian. Thank you for the enlightening bedtime story." She leans over and touches her lips to mine, her tongue teasing me. My body ignites, and I pull away.

"Don't. I am desperate to make love to you," I whisper through my desire.

"Then do."

"No, you need to rest, and it's late. Go to sleep." I switch off the bedside light and we're surrounded by the darkness.

"I love you unconditionally, Christian," Ana whispers, as she snuggles up to me.

"I know," I whisper, bathing in her light.

You…and my parents.

Unconditionally.

Sunday, September 18, 2011

It's almost midnight. Apart from some exercise, I've enjoyed a quiet day with my wife; our only excursion has been to see Ray, who is definitely on the mend. Other than that, I've insisted that Ana stay in bed and rest. She's acquiesced but has been reading a couple of manuscripts, and no amount of cajoling on my part could persuade her otherwise.

Mrs. Jones has returned from her sister's, and this evening she prepared a hearty three-course meal for the two of us. She seems as anxious for Ana's well-being as I am.

Ana fell asleep just after ten.

I've caught up on work, and now I'm poring over the notes that Mrs. Collier wrote to my mother and father while I was in her care. She has a neat and tidy hand, and her words spark small reminiscences that cast light into the dark corners of my memory.

Kristian won't let me wash him, but he does know how to wash himself. It has taken two baths to get him clean and I've had to teach him how to wash his hair. He will not tolerate us touching him at all.

Kristian had a better day today. He still refuses to talk. We don't know if he can or if he's unable. He has a temper, though. The other kids are quite scared of him.

Kristian still doesn't let any of us touch him. He has a meltdown if we do.

Kristian is hungry. He has a huge appetite for such a skinny little kid. His favorites are pasta and ice cream.

Our daughter, Phoebe, has taken a shine to Kristian. She dotes on him, and he's tolerating her attention. She sits and draws with him. I don't think he's had a great deal of experience drawing.

Where Phoebe goes, Kristian will follow.

Today Kristian had a meltdown. He does not like to be parted from his blanket. But it's filthy. I let him sit and watch it in the washing machine. This seemed to be the only thing that calmed him down.

The memories flare and flicker to the surface in fits and starts, but it's the feeling of being overwhelmed that resonates most with me. I was in a strange place, with a strange family—it must have been horribly bewildering. No wonder I chose to forget that time. But, having read through the notes, I know I didn't come to any harm there and I do remember Phoebe. She would sing to me. Silly songs. She was kind and especially sweet to me.

I'm grateful that my parents kept these letters. They remind me just how far removed I am from that frightened little boy. I am not him anymore. He no longer exists.

I contemplate sharing these with Ana, then remember her reaction to the photographs. Her sorrow as she gazed at that starved, neglected child. And they'd remind of her that asshole Hyde...and how much he and I have in common.

To hell with that.

She's had enough to contend with over the last few days.

I tuck the letters, drawings, and the photographs into a manilla folder marked KRISTIAN and file them safely away in my filing cabinet for another day. Maybe when she's fully recovered. Besides, I need to talk this through with Flynn, and I should do that before I share them with Ana. She's my wife, not my therapist.

I lock the filing cabinet and check the time.

It's late, and Ana is dozing when I slip into bed and pull her into my arms. She mumbles something unintelligible while I breathe in her soothing scent and close my eyes.

My dream catcher.

MONDAY, SEPTEMBER 19, 2011

Ana is curled up beside me, still out for the count. It's 7:16 a.m. I'm normally up earlier, but the last few days have taken a toll on me, too. It could also be the workout I did yesterday. Not only did I go for a run, but I did two circuits of the gym and an hour's hard rowing. I smile at the ceiling while I contemplate going for another run this morning. I have all this excess energy.

Perhaps I should let Ana have her wicked way with me.

The thought is appealing.

Fuck.

Too appealing.

Taking a deep breath, I bring my wayward body to heel, grab my phone, and ease myself out of bed. Maybe I'll come back when she's awake. Right now, I'm hungry.

"Good morning, Mr. Grey." Gail is in the kitchen; if she's surprised that I'm still in my pajamas, she doesn't give anything away. She moves straight to the Gaggia to make my coffee.

"Good morning, Mrs. Jones."

"How's Mrs. Grey this morning?"

"Still asleep."

She nods with a satisfied smile. "What can I get you?"

"An omelet. Please."

"Bacon, mushroom, and cheese?"

"Sounds great." She slides over a cup of freshly brewed coffee.

I start leafing through *The Seattle Times*, glad that my wife isn't on the front page, and wonder what Ana and I will do today, when I spot the real estate section.

Of course!

"Gail." I get her attention once more. "Depending on how Ana's feeling, I thought we might go out to the new house later. Could you rustle up a picnic for us?"

"It would be a pleasure, sir. I'll ask Taylor to take it down to the R8 when it's ready."

"Thank you."

I call Andrea to inform her I'm not coming into the office and ask her to reschedule any of today's meetings. She's unfazed. "Yes, Mr. Grey. How is Mrs. Grey?" she asks tentatively.

"Much improved. Thank you."

"That's good to hear."

"I'll be on my cell today, if you need me."

MY OMELET IS EVERYTHING that I hoped it would be. I am happily eating when I look up. Ana has appeared in the doorway. She looks well rested; the bruise on her cheek has faded but she's fully dressed, as if she's going out somewhere. She's wearing a skirt that borders on indecent—she's all legs and high fuck-me heels. I lose my train of thought.

"Good morning, Mrs. Grey. Going somewhere?" I'm hoarse.

"Work." She throws me a smile that illuminates the room.

I scoff at her audacity. "I don't think so. Dr. Singh said a week off."

"Christian, I'm not spending the day lounging in bed on my own." She flashes me a quick, heated look, which I feel in all the right places. "So, I may as well go to work. Good morning, Gail."

"Mrs. Grey." Mrs. Jones flattens her lips, attempting to hide her amusement. "Would you like some breakfast?"

"Please."

"Granola?"

"I'd prefer scrambled eggs with whole-wheat toast."

"Very good, Mrs. Grey," Gail replies, with a broad grin.

"Ana, you are not going to work." I'm amused that she thinks she should.

"But—"

"No. It's simple. Don't argue." *I'm your boss's boss, and the answer is no.*

She narrows her eyes, but her glare becomes a frown as she scrutinizes my attire. "Are you going to work?"

I shake my head and glance down at my pajama pants. "No."

"It is Monday, right?"

I grin. "Last time I looked."

"Are you playing hooky?" From her tone, I think she's intrigued and slightly incredulous.

"I'm not leaving you here on your own to get into trouble. And Dr. Singh said it would be a week before you could go back to work. Remember?"

She sits down on the barstool beside me, her skirt riding up higher, exposing her upper thighs, and I lose my train of thought… again. "You look good," I murmur, and she crosses her legs. "Very good. Especially here." I cannot resist running my finger across the exposed skin between her stocking tops and the hem of her skirt. "This skirt is very short," I murmur.

I can't keep my eyes off your legs, Mrs. Grey.

I'm not sure I approve.

"Is it? I hadn't noticed." Ana waves a nonchalant hand.

Yanking my gaze away from her legs, I look her in the eye. Her cheeks color; she's such a hopeless liar. "Really, Mrs. Grey?" I raise a brow. "I'm not sure this look is suitable for the workplace."

"Well, since I'm not going to work, that's a moot point," she says stiffly.

"Moot?"

"Moot," she mouths, and I hide my smile.

There's *that* word again. I take another bite of my omelet. "I have a better idea."

"You do?"

My eyes meet hers, and suddenly it's there, that look I know so well—her desire responding to mine. The air between us sparks with our own special electricity.

She inhales and I whisper, reeling her in, "We can go see how Elliot's getting on with the house."

A momentary flash of disappointment crosses her face, but then she smiles at my teasing. "I'd love to."

"Good."

"Don't you have to work?"

"No. Ros is back from Taiwan. That all went well. Today, everything's fine."

There are certain advantages to being your own boss.

"I thought you were going to Taiwan."

"Ana, you were in the hospital." *There was no way I was leaving you.*

"Oh."

"Yeah—oh. So today I'm spending some quality time with my wife." I take a sip of Mrs. Jones's great coffee.

"Quality time?" Ana's yearning threads through each syllable.

Oh, baby.

Gail places Ana's scrambled eggs in front of her. "Quality time," I murmur.

Ana's eyes dart from my lips to her breakfast. And her breakfast wins.

Damn. Thwarted by scrambled eggs.

"It's good to see you eat," I murmur, and pushing my plate aside, I step off my barstool and kiss Ana's hair. "I'm going to shower."

"Um…can I come and scrub your back?" she asks through a mouthful of breakfast.

"No. Eat."

I stride off to the bathroom, feeling her eyes on me. As I exit, I strip off my shirt, and I don't know if it's to tempt her to join me in the shower or not. Keeping my hands off her is getting harder and harder in more ways than one.

Grey, grow up.

ANA HAS INSISTED THAT we go visit Ray first, but we don't stay long. Mr. Rodriguez is with him, watching a British soccer match from yesterday—Manchester United vs. Chelsea. Manchester United is two goals up, which seems to please Mr. Rodriguez enormously, judging by his cheer.

I sigh. Try as I might, I don't care for soccer.

Ana takes pity on me and lets Ray know that we're off.

Thank heavens.

I SIT BACK AND relax as we cruise in my R8 to the new house. I'm excited to see the destruction that Elliot has wrought, and hopefully the beginnings of what our home will be.

Ana has changed her sky-high heels for more sensible flats; she's tapping her feet to a Crosby, Stills & Nash song that blares over the Audi's sound system, looking happy to be out and about. Two days of enforced bed rest has been good for her. She has color in her cheeks, and a soft, sweet smile for me when I glance at her, and she seems to have set aside her recent, horrific encounter with the evil Hyde.

I push him out of my mind.

Don't go there, Grey.

I want to preserve my good mood.

Since I unburdened my soul a couple of nights ago, I've felt happier. I had no idea that spilling my guts to my wife would have such a beneficial effect. I don't know if it's because I've finally laid the ghost of Elena Lincoln to rest, or if it's because my parents have provided me with some of the missing pieces from the incomplete puzzle that was my former life, but my heart is lighter somehow—freer, even—but tethered, and as steadfast as ever, to the beautiful woman beside me.

Ana knows me.

She refracts my darkness and turns it to brilliant light.

I shake my head at my fanciful thoughts.

Flowery, Grey.

She's still here, in spite of all that I've done.

The warmth of her love spreads through my veins.

Reaching over, I squeeze her leg, then trail my fingers over her exposed flesh above her thigh-high, relishing the feel of her skin. "I'm glad you didn't change."

Ana covers my hand with her own. "Are you going to continue to tease me?"

I didn't know that's what I was doing.

But, hey, I'll play. "Maybe."

"Why?"

"Because I can." I beam at her.

"Two can play that game," she whispers.

I move my fingers up her inner thigh. "Bring it on, Mrs. Grey."

She takes my hand and places it on my knee. "Well, you can keep your hands to yourself," she says primly.

"As you wish, Mrs. Grey."

I cannot hide my smile. I love playful Ana.

Ha. I love Ana. Period.

STOPPING AT THE GATES to our house, I press the entry code into the keypad. The metal gates swing slowly open, creaking a protest at being disturbed. They need replacing, and we'll get around to it eventually. Speeding along the driveway, I wish I'd taken the top down on the car. The tall grass in the meadow is golden beneath the September sun, and the trees lining the drive are all decked in the colors of the coming fall. The Sound in the distance is a brilliant blue. It's idyllic.

And it's ours.

As the lane meanders around a wide curve, the house appears, surrounded by a number of Elliot's construction trucks. It's hidden behind scaffolding, and several of Elliot's crew are at work on the roof. I park outside the portico, switch off the engine, and turn to Ana. "Let's go find Elliot." I'm buzzing to see what he's accomplished so far.

"Is he here?"

"I hope so. I'm paying him enough."

She laughs and we both exit the car.

"Yo, bro!" I hear Elliot shout, but I can't see him.

"Up here!" I scan the roofline, grateful that I'm wearing aviators against the glare of the sun, and there he is, waving at us. His grin rivals the Cheshire Cat's. "About time we saw you here. Stay where you are. I'll be right down."

I reach out to Ana, and she takes my hand, and while we wait, we study the exterior of what will be our home. It's bigger than I remember.

Plenty of room for our child.

My wayward thought surprises me.

Finally, Elliot appears at the front door caked in grime but still wearing his broad grin. He's clearly over the moon that we're here. "Hey, bro." He pumps my hand like he's trying to drag water from the deepest well. "And how are you, little lady?" He grabs Ana and swings her around.

"Better, thanks," she says, laughing, a little embarrassed, I think.

Dude! Quit manhandling my wife! Her ribs are bruised!

He sets her down and I scowl at him.

Asshole.

But he ignores me—no one is raining on his parade today. "Let's head over to the site office. You'll need one of these." He slaps the hard hat perched on his head.

ELLIOT GIVES US A thorough tour of the house, or what's left of it—it's almost a shell. Meticulously he explains the work in progress, and how long each stage is going to take. When he's in his element like this, he's so engaging. Both Ana and I listen, rapt.

The back wall at the rear has disappeared. This is where Gia Matteo's glass wall will be, and the view is spectacular. There are a few sails out on the Sound, and I'm tempted to go down to *The Grace* after our visit here. But that's not such a good idea, given Ana's recent injuries. She's still recovering and needs to take it easy.

"Hopefully we'll be finished by Christmas," Elliot declares.

"Next year," I interject. *There is no way we'll be in by Christmas.*

"We'll see. With a fair wind it's doable."

In the kitchen, he concludes our tour. "I'll leave you two to roam. Be careful. This is a building site."

"Sure. Thanks, Elliot."

My brother gives us a cheery wave and heads up the covered staircase to join his construction crew, back on the roof. I take Ana's hand. "Happy?"

Ana gives me a dazzling smile. "Very. I love it. You?"

"Ditto."

"Good. I was thinking of the pepper pictures in here." Ana points to one of the walls.

I nod in agreement. "I want to put up José's portraits of you in this house. You need to decide where they should go."

Her cheeks stain that delicious shade of pink. "Somewhere I won't see them often."

"Don't be like that." I brush my thumb across her bottom lip. "They're my favorite pictures. I love the one in my office."

"I have no idea why." She pouts and kisses the pad of my thumb.

"Worse things to do than look at your beautiful smiling face all day. Hungry?"

"Hungry for what?" She peers at me with the come-hither look that I know so well.

Oh, baby. I can only take so much of this.

"Food, Mrs. Grey." I kiss her quickly.

She pouts and sighs. "Yes. These days I'm always hungry."

"The three of us can have a picnic."

"Three of us? Is someone joining us?"

I drop my head to one side.

Forgotten someone, Ana? "In about seven or eight months," I murmur.

She grins goofily at me... *Yeah. Him.*

"I thought you might like to eat alfresco," I suggest, casually.

"In the meadow?"

I nod.

"Sure." Ana lights up. And I feel ten feet tall for thinking of bringing a picnic. We have so much space and privacy here.

"This will be a great place to raise a family." I gaze down at my wife.

Junior will be happy here.

The meadow as his backyard.

I reach out and spread my hand over her belly. Ana's breath hitches and she places her hand on mine.

"It's hard to believe," I whisper.

"I know. Oh—here, I have evidence. A picture."

"You do? Baby's first smile?"

From her wallet she produces a black-and-white image on shiny paper and hands it to me. "See?" she says.

The grainy photograph is mostly gray. But in the middle, there's a small, dark void, and within that, there's a tiny anomaly, anchored to the gray, but visible against the darkness. "Oh, blip," I breathe in wonder. "Yeah, I see."

Our blip. Wow. Our tiny human. Baby Grey.

And I'm surprised by a momentary pang of regret, that I missed this moment with Ana.

"Your child," she whispers.

"Our child," I correct her.

"First of many."

"Many?" *What?*

"At least two." Ana sounds hopeful.

"Two?" *Shit!* "Can we just take this one child at a time?"

She smiles up at me fondly. "Sure."

I take her hand, and together we walk back through the house and out the front door.

It's such a beautiful afternoon. The scents of the Sound, the meadow grass, and flowers hang in the air. My beautiful wife is by my side. It's heaven. And soon there will be three of us. "When are you going to tell your folks?" I ask.

"Soon. I thought about telling Ray this morning, but Mr. Rodriguez was there." Ana shrugs.

I nod. *I get it, Ana.*

Lifting the hood of the R8, I gather up the wicker picnic basket and the tartan blanket that Ana bought from Harrods in London. "Come." Hand in hand, we stroll into the meadow. When we're far enough from the house, I release her, and together we spread the blanket on the ground. I settle down beside her, shrug off my jacket, and slip off my shoes and socks. I take a moment to just breathe, taking in a lungful of fresh air. We're shielded by the long grass, away from the world, truly in our own bubble. As Ana opens the picnic basket to inspect all the goodies that Mrs. Jones has provided, my phone vibrates.

Shit.

It's Ros.

"…THANK YOU FOR ANSWERING my question, and glad to hear that Ana is on the mend," Ros says over the phone.

"You're welcome." It's the second time she's called and the third call I've had since we started our picnic.

"You shouldn't be so indispensable."

I laugh. "You flatter me."

Ana is lying beside me, half listening to my side of the conversation. Her brow puckers at my last remark.

"You should take a couple of days off," I tell Ros. "After all, you spent most of the weekend traveling back from Taiwan."

"That's a great idea. I may take Thursday and Friday, if that's okay with you."

"Sure, Ros, go for it."

"Will do. Thanks, Christian. Good-bye."

I toss my phone down, and resting my hands on my raised knees, I regard my wife. She's lying beside me on our blanket, gazing up with a dreamy expression. Reaching over, I pluck another strawberry from what's left of Mrs. Jones's excellent picnic and trace it along Ana's mouth. She parts her lips, and the tip of her tongue toys with the strawberry, then sucks it into her warm, wet mouth.

I feel it in my groin. "Tasty?" I whisper.

"Very."

"Had enough?"

"Of strawberries, yes." Her tone is low.

Ana, no one can see us here.

Grey, behave.

I grin. *Enough.* I change the subject. "Mrs. Jones packs a mighty fine picnic."

"That she does."

God, I miss my wife—all of her. I lie down, gently resting my head on her belly, and close my eyes, trying not to think of all the things I'd like to do to her right now. Her fingers caress my hair.

Oh, this is bliss.

My BlackBerry starts buzzing again.

Shit. It's Welch. What does he want?

I answer, a little grumpy at the interruption. "Welch."

"Mr. Grey. I have an update. It was Eric Lincoln of Lincoln Timber who paid Hyde's bail."

Fuck.

That motherfucking asshole.

I sit up. My senses switch to high alert as my anger takes hold.

"I'd like to place him under watch, unless you have any objection."

"24/7," I snarl in agreement.

How dare Lincoln get involved with Hyde?

This is a declaration of war.

"Will do. I don't know what else he might have planned, or how the two of them are connected. But I'll find out."

"Thanks." He hangs up, and I can barely contain my fury. Gripping my phone, I realize *now* is the moment for payback. My plans were laid long ago, and as the saying goes, revenge is a dish best served cold. I give Ana a cool smile and call Ros.

"Christian. I thought you were enjoying your day off?"

I kneel up—*I'm not calling for chitchat.*

"Ros, how much stock do we own in Lincoln Timber?"

"Let me just check." She's all business. "We hold sixty-six percent between all the shell companies."

Excellent.

"So, consolidate the shares into GEH, then fire the board."

"All of them? Has something happened?"

"Except the CEO."

"Christian, that doesn't make sense."

"I don't give a fuck."

She gasps. "There'll be no company left. What can the CEO do? If you want to liquidate this company, this isn't the way."

"I hear you, just do it," I growl, keeping a lid on my anger.

She sighs, sounding resigned. "They're your shares." She's not going to argue further.

"Thank you," I reply, feeling a little calmer.

"I'll get Marco on it."

"Keep me informed."

When I hang up, Ana is wide-eyed. "What's happened?" she whispers.

"Linc."

"Linc? Elena's ex?"

"The same. He's the one who posted Hyde's bail."

Ana's mouth drops open in shock. "Well—he'll look like an idiot," she says, dismayed. "I mean, Hyde committed another crime while out on bail."

As ever, Ana has a smart response. "Fair point well made, Mrs. Grey."

"What did you just do?" She kneels up to face me.

"I fucked him over."

She shivers. "Um, that seems a little impulsive."

"I'm an in-the-moment kind of guy."

"I'm aware of that."

"I've had this plan in my back pocket for a while," I explain.

A hostile takeover.

"Oh?" Ana tilts her head, her gaze demanding answers. I debate whether to tell her.

Hell, she knows everything about Elena anyway. I take a deep breath and shoot her a warning look. *This is rough, Ana.* "Several years back, when I was twenty-one, Linc beat his wife to a pulp. He broke her jaw, her left arm, and four of her ribs because she was fucking me. And now I learn he posted bail for a man who tried to kill me, kidnap my sister, and fracture my wife's skull. I've had enough. I think it's payback time." My mind drifts to that awful moment when he beat me, too—I thought he'd dislocated my jaw. My hand moves to my chin as I recall the disturbing incident. I lost consciousness for a few minutes and it was enough time for him to do his worst to Elena.

And I did nothing. I was too shocked...too dazed.

Damn. *Grey, stop. Now.*

Ana's face is pale. "Fair point well made, Mr. Grey," she says.

"Ana, this is what I do. I'm not usually motivated by revenge, but I cannot let him get away with this. What he did to Elena—well, she should have pressed charges, but she didn't. That was her prerogative." My jaw tenses. "But he's seriously crossed the line with Hyde. Linc's made this personal by going after my family. I'm going to crush him, break up his company right under his nose, and sell the pieces to the highest bidder. I'm going to bankrupt him."

Ana gasps.

"Besides," I add, trying to lighten the tone, "we'll make good money out of the deal."

She blinks several times, and I wonder if she's seeing me in a whole new light. *Not a good one.*

Shit. "I didn't mean to frighten you."

"You didn't," she whispers.

I arch a brow. Does she mean that? Or is she trying to make me feel better?

"You just took me by surprise," Ana concedes.

I cup her face in my hands and brush my lips against hers.

I'm not sorry, Ana. "I will do anything to keep you safe. Keep my family safe. Keep this little one safe." I place my hand on her belly, and Ana's breath hitches.

Her eyes meet mine, and in their blue depths, her desire is smoldering, calling to me.

Fuck.

I want her.

She's so enticing. I slip my fingers a little lower, brushing her sex through her clothes with the tips of my fingers, teasing her.

Ana pounces, grabbing my head, entwining her fingers in my hair and tugging my lips to hers. I gasp in surprise, and her tongue is instantly in my mouth.

Desire, hot and heavy, travels at light speed all the way to the end of my cock.

Damn, I'm hard.

I groan and return her kiss, my tongue tangling with hers.

It's been so long.

The taste of her, the feel of her. She's everything. "Ana," I breathe in longing against her lips. I'm bewitched, my hands moving undirected over her beautiful behind to the hem of her skirt and the soft flesh of the thighs.

Thank all that is holy for this short skirt!

Her hands start to unbutton my shirt, as ever all fingers and thumbs.

And for a moment her fumbling fingers distract me.

"Whoa, Ana—stop." With enormous restraint, I pull back and grab her hands.

"No," she cries, distraught, and her teeth clamp over my lower lip. "No." She's insistent, darkening blue eyes staring at me with longing. She releases me. "I want you."

Ana! You're hurt!

My body agrees with Ana.

"Please, I need you." It's a heartfelt plea.

Oh, fuck.

I'm done. I concede, overcome by her ardor and my need. I groan, and my mouth finds hers, kissing her and tasting her once more. Cradling her head, I run my hand down her body to her waist, and gently ease her onto her back and stretch out beside her.

We kiss.

And kiss.

Lips and tongues locked.

Reacquainting ourselves with each other.

When I come up for air, I stare down into eyes dazed with passion. "You are so beautiful, Mrs. Grey."

Her fingers strum my face. "So are you, Mr. Grey. Inside and out."

Oh, I'm not sure that's true.

Her fingers trace the line of my brow. "Don't frown," she whispers. "You are to me, even when you're angry."

She says the sweetest things. I moan and kiss her once more and revel in her response, her body rising to meet mine. "I've missed you." My words are inadequate and no match for the feelings behind them.

She is the world to me.

I skim my teeth over her jaw.

"I've missed you, too. Oh, Christian."

Her passion spurs me on. I run my lips along her throat, leaving soft, wet kisses in their wake, and I unbutton her shirt and tug it open to kiss the soft swell of her breasts.

Sweet Jesus, they're bigger!

Already.

Mm. "Your body's changing," I murmur in appreciation, and rub my thumb over her bra, coaxing her nipple awake until it's begging for my lips. "I like…"

Did I say that out loud?

I don't know. I don't care. I'm just so enamored of my wife. I nuzzle her breast with my nose and my tongue through the white gossamer of her bra. As her nipple strains for release, I use my teeth to drag down the cup, freeing her breast. Her nipple puckers in the gentle breeze, and I draw it slowly into my mouth and suck hard.

"Ah!" Ana groans, then flinches beneath me.

Fuck! Her ribs!

I stop, immediately. "Ana!" *Damn.* "This is what I'm talking about. Your lack of self-preservation. I don't want to hurt you."

Desperate, blazing eyes meet mine. "No! Don't stop," she whimpers. "Please."

Shit. My whole body is screaming don't stop.

But—

Hell!

"Here." Carefully, I lift her and shift so she's sitting astride me, and my hands travel smoothly up her legs to the tops of her thigh-highs.

She is one helluva sight. Her hair falling toward me, eyes soft and full of desire, her breast free. "There. That's better, and I can enjoy the view." I hook my finger into the other bra cup, drag it down so that I have both of her breasts to enjoy. As I take them in my hands, Ana groans and throws her head back, pushing them farther into my palms.

Oh, baby.

I tug and tease each of her nipples, and they lengthen further beneath my touch until she cries out. I want her mouth; I sit up so we're nose to nose and kiss her, my tongue and my fingers teasing and tantalizing her.

Ana's fingers are at my shirt again, scrambling to undo the remaining buttons, and she's kissing me back with such fervor that I'm sure either one or both of us will combust. There's a desperation in her kiss. "Hey—" Gently, I grasp her head and ease back. "There's no rush. Take it slow. I want to savor you."

"Christian, it's been so long." She's breathless.

I know. But you're hurt. Let's not be hasty.

"Slow." And that's not a request. I press my lips to the right corner of her mouth "Slow." The left corner. "Slow, baby." I suck her bottom lip into my mouth. "Let's take this slow." Cradling her head, I continue to kiss her, my tongue subduing hers, hers enticing mine. She glides her fingers across my face, my chin, my throat, and starts on my shirt buttons once more. She tugs my shirt apart, her fingers caressing my chest, then pushing me down so that I'm prostrate beneath her.

She gazes down at me and squirms over my groin.

I push up my hips to enjoy the friction against my eager dick.

Ana watches me, her lips parted as she traces my mouth with the tips of her fingers. She moves on, her fingers skimming over my jaw, down my neck, and to the base of my throat. Leaning down, her tender kisses trail where her fingers have been, grazing my jaw and my throat. I surrender to the sensation, closing my eyes and reclining my head with a moan. Her tongue continues its journey, down my sternum, across my chest, where she stops to kiss a couple of my scars.

Ana.

I want to bury myself deep inside her. Grasping her hips, I meet her dark eyes with a dark look of my own. "You want this? Here?" My voice is husky with need.

"Yes," she murmurs, and dips her head once more, her lips and tongue teasing my nipple. She tugs it gently.

"Oh, Ana," I breathe in awe as pleasure spikes through my body. I circle her waist, lift her clear, and quickly unbutton my jeans, open my fly, and push down my underwear so my cock springs free. I sit her down once more and she grinds against me.

Ah. I need to be inside her. Running my hands up her thighs, I pause at the top of her thigh-highs. I circle my thumbs against her warm flesh and move my hands further up, so I brush the damp seeping through her lace panties.

Ana gasps.

"I hope you're not attached to your underwear," I whisper, and my fingers slide inside her panties, touching her.

Damn. She's soaking.

Ready for me.

I force my thumbs through the fabric and the material rips apart.

Yes!

I move my hands to her upper thighs and let my thumbs brush against her clitoris as I tighten my ass, searching for some friction against my cock. She slides over me. "I can feel how wet you are."

You fucking goddess, Ana.

Sitting up, so we're eye to eye once more, I wrap my arm around her waist and rub my nose to hers. "We're going to take this slow, Mrs. Grey. I want to feel all of you." And before she can argue with me, I lift her again, and gently lower her onto me and fill her, languidly. I close my eyes and relish each delicious inch of her.

She's bliss.

"Ah!" Ana moans, and grasps my arms. She tries to lift up, eager to begin, but I hold her in place and open my eyes again.

"All of me," I murmur, and tilt my pelvis up, claiming all of her.

Ana lets out a strangled moan and throws her head back.

"Let me hear you," I whisper. And she tries to rise again. "No—don't move, just feel." Her eyes spring open, and her mouth is agape in a fixed gasp of pleasure. She gazes at me, barely breathing, it seems. I drive into her once more, but hold her still. She groans while I bend my head to kiss her throat. "This is my favorite place. Buried in you," I whisper to the pulse under her ear.

"Please, move," she begs.

But I want to tease her.

Take it slow.

So she doesn't hurt herself.

"Slow, Mrs. Grey." I flex my ass one more, pushing into her, and she caresses my face and kisses me. Her tongue consuming me.

"Love me. Please, Christian."

My resolve crumbles, and I skim her jaw with my teeth. "Go."

I'm all yours, Ana.

She pushes me to the ground, and she starts to move, up and down. Fast, a little frantic. Taking all I have to give.

Oh God.

I grab her hands and complement her wild pace. Pushing up, again and again. Relishing the feel of her, enjoying the view, my wife, the blue sky behind her in the outdoors. "Oh, Ana." I groan, surrendering completely to her rhythm. I close my eyes and move my hands up her thighs once more, to that precious point between them. There, I press both thumbs against her clitoris, and she cries out, exploding around me, in a gasping, rolling climax that tips me over the edge.

"Ana!" I cry as I succumb to my own heady orgasm.

WHEN I OPEN MY eyes, she's sprawled over me.

I cloak her in my arms, and we lie together. Still joined.

I've missed this.

Her hand is over my heart as it slows to its normal rhythm.

It's weird. Not long ago I couldn't have tolerated her hands on me. Now, I crave her touch.

She kisses my chest.

And I kiss her hair. "Better?" I ask.

She raises her head, her grin reflecting mine.

"Much. You?"

I'm just grateful that she's here and whole and still with me, after everything that's happened. "I've missed you, Mrs. Grey."

"Me, too."

"No more heroics, eh?"

"No," she breathes.

"You should always talk to me," I insist in a soft voice.

"Back at you, Grey."

"Fair point well made. I'll try." I kiss her again, smirking. She's not taking any of my shit, as usual.

"I think we're going to be happy here," Ana says.

"Yep. You, me, and Blip. How do you feel, incidentally?"

"Fine. Relaxed. Happy."

"Good."

"You?"

"Yeah, all those things." *Deliriously happy, Ana.*

She peers at me.

"What?" I ask.

"You know, you're very bossy when we have sex."

Oh. "Are you complaining?"

"No," she says emphatically. "I'm just wondering. You said you missed it."

And I wonder what she means for a moment.

Control? I need that. The playroom? *What we do in there?* A vision of her shackled to the four-poster, the Tallis ringing through the room, comes to mind. Or maybe the cross and a riding crop…the brown leather one. My memories go on and on, seducing me.

"Sometimes," I whisper.

Yeah. Sometimes I miss it.

She smiles. "Well, we'll have to see what we can do about that." She drops a kiss on my lips.

Oh. That sounds interesting.

"I like to play, too," she says, and peeks shyly up at me.

Well. Well. Well. This perfect day just got a whole lot better.

"You know, I'd really like to test your limits," I whisper.

"My limits for what?"

"Pleasure."

"Oh, I think I'd like that."

"Well, maybe when we get home." I hug her gently, marveling at how much she means to me.

How much I love her.

Who knew I could fall so desperately and completely in love?

Wednesday, September 21, 2011

Flynn is at a loss for words.

This might be a first.

I've given him an executive summary of all that has transpired since our last session. "So that's why you came looking for me," he mutters.

"Yes."

He shakes his head in disbelief. "Well, first things first. How's Ana?"

"She's good. On the mend. Desperate to get back to work."

"No PTSD?"

"I don't think so. But it might be too early to tell."

"I can recommend someone, if she needs a therapist." He stops and taps his lip with his index finger. "Shall we take this in stages? Let's start with the pregnancy, and your reaction."

"Not my proudest moment." I stare past him at a space on the wall, embarrassed to look him in the eye.

"No," he agrees, far too readily. "How are you feeling about it now?"

Sighing, I lean forward and rest my elbows on my knees. "Resigned. Excited. Scared. In about equal measure. I would have preferred if we'd waited. But now that Junior is on his way…well." I shrug.

Flynn's expression is sympathetic, I think. "You don't truly learn what unconditional love is until you have a child."

"That's what Ana says. But I've only just learned to love her…" I trail off, unwilling to voice the rest of my thought.

"How can you love someone else, too?" Flynn finishes the sentence for me.

My smile is bleak.

"Christian, knowing your extraordinary need to protect and provide for those who are close to you, those you love, there's no doubt in my mind that you have an innate capacity to love your own child."

"I hope you're right."

John allows himself a small smile. "We'll see. You'll find out in a few months. How are you feeling about Mrs. Lincoln?"

"As if that chapter's closed."

Flynn nods.

"I think it helps that I told Ana everything. How it all began and how it all ended. It feels complete."

"Sounds like it. Any regrets?"

I blow out a breath. "Telling Ana? No. None. Severing my relationship with Elena... Yes. No..."

John purses his lips and I add quickly, "I know you don't agree. I know what Elena and I did was wrong...what she did was wrong. Her behavior was predatory—I understand that now, but I don't wholly regret it. How can I? I've always believed she was what I needed at the time. She taught me so much."

He sighs. "She took advantage of a vulnerable adolescent, Christian. You can't dodge that truth."

I stare at him.

He's not wrong.

But I'm not prepared to admit that...yet.

"Give me time," I state quietly.

He nods. "No doubt we'll keep coming back to this, so let's give you some time and we can dig into that again when you're ready." He blows out a breath. "I'd like to ask you about the conversation with your parents with regard to your foster placement. How that felt?"

"Strange, for several reasons."

"Please, elaborate."

"First of all, I was stunned they were so quick to respond to my call for help."

"Have they not done that before?"

"Well, yes, they have. My mom was really helpful with Ray, when he was in an accident."

"But that's different. She's a doctor."

"Yeah. I'm not sure I've ever asked them about something so personal before. I think I gave up trying a long time ago. As you know, in my teens, I had a difficult relationship with both of them. And they were so disappointed and disapproving after I dropped out of Harvard."

Flynn nods. "But as a parent you always think you know what's best for your child. It's a lesson worth remembering. Dropping out obviously did you no harm."

"But the other evening when they came over, they were more than helpful. They brought all that stuff with them." I point to the manilla folder that Flynn has already leafed through. He reaches for the photograph of the Collier family and their two foster children.

"And that's Hyde?" He indicates the truculent red-haired boy.

I nod.

"And you. The smallest kid."

"Yes."

"It must have been very unsettling for you, not to remember this time."

"It was."

"Do you remember more now?"

"Yes. I think it was my mother's reassurance, that I came to no harm in the foster family's care, that was the most comforting. It enabled me to let the memories in. Before then, my imagination went wild. I was scared to remember. You know…when you don't know."

"Yes. I understand. You believe her?"

"Yes. The recollections I do have are all good."

"And what of Kristian Pusztai?"

I sigh. "He's no more."

Flynn's brow creases. "Are you sure?"

I scoff. "No. But I think it's time I grew up and left him behind. My wife told me in no uncertain terms that I need to grow up and smell the fucking coffee."

Flynn snorts. "Did she, now? Have you told her? About this?" He holds up my birth certificate.

"No."

"Why?"

I shrug. "She knows me as Christian Grey."

John considers my response. "That child is part of you."

"I know. But I want to keep him to myself for a little while longer. Get used to him."

"Will you tell her?"

"One day. Sure."

"You've only known about him for a few days. I think you're entitled to keep him to yourself for as long as you want, Christian. Learn to love him. Forgive him. It's in your power to do so."

I gasp as the full weight of Flynn's words blindside me.

Forgive him.

"What did he do that requires forgiveness?" I whisper.

John smiles at me, kindly. "He survived."

I'm frozen. Staring at him.

"And his poor mother didn't. You might want to direct some of your forgiveness at her, too."

I gaze at him for what feels like minutes, then I glance at the clock. "Okay." I blow out a breath, relieved we're done. "As ever, you've given me a great deal to think about."

"Good. That's my job. We still have so much to discuss, but I'm sorry, we're out of time."

"We're getting there, surely?" I ask.

Flynn's grin is amicable. "Slowly. Now we're at this point, your attachment issues alone could fill a year."

I laugh. "I know."

"But you're beginning to open up to your wife. Making yourself vulnerable. These are giant steps."

I nod, feeling like I got an A in therapy. "I think so."

"I'll see you next time. And congratulations, Christian."

I frown. *What?*

"The baby." Flynn grins.

"Oh, yes. Junior. Thank you."

IT'S DUSK, A GOLDEN pink light filling the room. My hands in the pockets of my pants, I stare out at the Seattle skyline toward the Sound and smile—from my ivory tower, as Ana would say. And I would correct her and tell her it's *our* ivory tower.

She was animated and talkative at dinner, happy to be working. After our meal she returned to her lair—well, the library—to sort through query letters that she had messengered over from SIP. Perhaps she should go into the office tomorrow. I think she's well enough.

My mind shifts to my conversation with Flynn.

Forgive him.

Forgive her.

Perhaps it's time. I've spent so long loathing the crack whore, I'm not sure I can move on from those feelings, but Ana was passionate in her defense… *Forgive her. She had her own world of pain to deal with. She was a shitty mother, and you loved her.*

My shrink and my wife are of one accord. Perhaps I should listen to them.

Idly I walk to the piano, sit down, and start to play Debussy's "Arabesque No. 1." A piece I haven't played in forever. As the upbeat, evocative melody echoes through the room, I disappear into the music.

My phone buzzes, interrupting the second Arabesque.

I have an e-mail from my wife.

From: Anastasia Grey
Subject: My Husband's Pleasure
Date: September 21 2011 20:45
To: Christian Grey

Sir
I await your instructions.
Yours always
Mrs. G x

I stare at it in anticipation as desire wakes my body.

Ana wants to play.

Best not to keep a lady waiting.

I type a response.

From: Christian Grey
Subject: My Husband's Pleasure <— love this title, baby
Date: September 21 2011 20:48
To: Anastasia Grey

Mrs. G
I'm intrigued. I'll come find you.
Be ready.

Christian Grey
Anticipative CEO, Grey Enterprises Holdings, Inc.

She can't be in the playroom—I'd have noticed her moving to the upper floor. I open the bedroom door, and here she is, kneeling at the entrance—eyes downcast, wearing a pale blue camisole and panties, and nothing else. On the bed she's laid out my Dom jeans.

My heart lurches into overdrive as I gaze at her, drinking in every detail: her parted lips, her long lashes, her hair curling in luscious waves below her breasts. Her breathing's accelerated; she's excited. My beautiful girl is offering herself to me, wholly. Again.

Last time we were in the playroom, she safe-worded on me.

And yet she trusts me enough to go again.

What did I do to deserve her?

She's still healing, Grey.

Fuck.

But she's dropped enough hints these last few days.

We'll have to see what we can do about that.

And suddenly a barrage of visions of Ana in the playroom fill my mind.

That first time.

Her nervousness.

My excitement.

Damn. She wants this…so do I. I reach for my jeans and, turning, head into the closet to change. As I strip, I think of what we could do. We'll take it easy…*easy sweet.*

But I'm going to drive her wild.

A frisson of pure excitement runs down my spine to my dick.

Bring it on, Mrs. Grey.

I return to the bedroom and she's still kneeling at the door. "So, you want to play?"

"Yes."

Oh, Ana. You can do better than that.

When I don't respond, she looks up at me and registers my annoyed frown.

"Yes what?" I whisper.

"Yes, Sir," she says quickly.

"Good girl." I stroke her hair. "I think we'd better get you upstairs now." Offering my hand, I help her to her feet, and together we walk to the stairs and up to the playroom.

Outside the door, I bend down and kiss her, then grasp her hair and tip her head back so I can drown in the depths of her eyes. "You know, you're topping from the bottom," I murmur against her lips. But then, she's been doing that since I met her.

She owns me, body and soul.

"What?" she breathes.

"Don't worry. I'll live with it."

Until death do us part, Anastasia Grey.

Because I love you.

More than life itself.

And I know you love me.

I run my nose down her jaw, filling my senses with her sweet scent. I nibble her ear. "Once inside, kneel, like I've shown you."

"Yes, Sir."

Ana peers at me through her lashes, and I don't miss her I-so-own-you smile.

It makes me smile, too.

Because it's true.

She is my everything.

And I'm hers…always.

Now, let's have some fun…

Epilogue

Monday, July 30, 2012

I lie perfectly still, drinking in the sight of my gorgeous wife lying beside me. Early morning light streams through the gap in the curtains, gilding Ana's hair and revealing the adoring glow in her face. She doesn't know I'm awake yet, as she's busy breastfeeding our son—smiling down, murmuring quiet words of love to him, and stroking his soft, plump cheek.

It's a stirring scene.

Ana has a fathomless well of love to give. To him. To me.

She shows me how it should be, and that it's okay to feel this thrill, this passion for someone so small. This flesh of my flesh.

Ted.

My boy.

I'm besotted, with both of them.

She peeks up to check on me, and I'm caught mid-ogle. Her face erupts into an enormous smile. "Good morning, Mr. Grey. Enjoying the view?" She cocks an eyebrow, amused.

"Very much, Mrs. Grey." Leaning up on my elbow, I press a tender kiss to her waiting lips, and another on the coppery down atop Ted's head. Closing my eyes, I breathe in his scent; after Ana's, it's the sweetest fragrance in the world.

"He smells so good."

"That's because I changed his diaper ten minutes ago."

I grimace, then smile.

Rather you than me!

Ana grins but rolls her eyes, knowing full well what I'm thinking. Teddy ignores us, his eyes closed, his hand splayed over the swell of Ana's breast. He's too busy enjoying breakfast.

Lucky boy.

He's a very lucky boy. He sleeps with us.

That was a battle I was never going to win. And while it has somewhat curtailed our bedroom activity at night, it's reassuring to know he's so close when we sleep. It's ironic to think that until I met Ana, I'd never slept with anyone, and now there are two people in my bed.

"Did he wake last night?"

"Not since I fed him at midnight." She strokes his cheek once more and croons. "You slept all night, little man." He pats her breast in response, staring up at her with eyes the same shade as hers, and with a look I know only too well.

Complete adoration.

Yep, Teddy and I suffer from the same fixation.

He closes his eyes and his suckling slows and stops.

She strokes his cheek, then delicately slides her finger into his mouth so he releases her nipple. "That's breakfast done," she whispers. "I'll put him in his crib."

"I'll do it." Today is a special day. Sitting up, I gently scoop him into my arms, enjoying his warmth and weight against my chest. I kiss his head once more and, holding him close, carry him next door to his room, *where he should be sleeping.* Miraculously, he stays asleep as I lay him down in his crib and cover him with his cotton blanket. Gazing down at him, I'm lost in an overwhelming swell of emotion. It hits me now and then—an immense tidal wave of love that washes over and through me. This tiny human has invaded my heart, ensnared it, and trashed all my defenses. Flynn was right: I love him unconditionally.

I shiver, because this feeling still frightens me, and scan his room. It's painted like an apple orchard, and one day, I hope to teach him how to grow sweet red apples from a bitter green apple tree with the help of his namesake, Grandpa Theodore. Switching on the baby monitor, I grab the receiver and take it back to our bedroom.

Ana is fast asleep.

Damn. I never wished her a happy anniversary.

For a moment I contemplate waking her, but deep down I know that wouldn't be fair. Ana is tired most of the time; sleep is prized over everything. Hopefully, now that Ted's nearly three months old, she'll get more rest.

I miss her.

Feeling a pang of regret that I know is completely selfish, I stride into the closet to change into my running gear.

I scroll through the songs on my phone and find one that Ana must have uploaded. It brings a smile to my lips.

With Rihanna's "We Found Love" blaring through my earbuds, I set off for a run down Fourth Avenue. It's early, and the streets are relatively empty, except for the occasional dog walker, and refrigerated trucks delivering to the local restaurants, and early-shift personnel heading to work. My mind empties as I concentrate on finding my rhythm and setting a long run pace. I'm heading northwest, the sun is shining, the trees are in full leaf, and I feel I could run forever. All is right in my world.

An idea occurs to me.

I decide on a nostalgia tour and set my sights on Ana's old apartment, where Kate and Ethan live.

For old times' sake.

Their living arrangements will change shortly; Kate and Elliot are getting married this coming weekend. As soon as Kate found out Ana was pregnant, and her due date, she changed all their plans so that Ana could still be her matron of honor. That woman is as determined as ever—I hope Elliot knows what he's doing.

His bachelor party was epic, far more gregarious than mine. But that's Elliot. And what happens in Cabo San Lucas stays there. And even though as best man it was my responsibility to organize the whole shebang, I spent those few days missing my wife and son. But then, I'm not the party animal—Elliot is—and he had fun. That was the point.

As I round the corner onto Vine Street, I'm reminded of my desperate runs during the dark days when Ana left me.

Damn. I was crazy then.

Crazy in love, Grey.

And I didn't even know it.

Approaching my stalker's hide, I contemplate pausing there, but dismiss the idea. Those dark days are far behind me. And I don't want to be away from Ana for too long.

I turn left at the corner onto Western Avenue, my mind drifting to all that's happened since Ana and I tied the knot—on this day, last year. Of course, the biggest change was the dramatic arrival of Theodore Raymond Grey on May 2, who now rules our hearts and our domain.

God, I love my boy.

Even though I now have to compete with him for my wife's attention.

I do choose this defenseless baby over you. That's what any loving parent does.

Damn right, *Ana.*

Her words still sting, but they resonate with me now. It's hard, surrendering her to someone else. I wouldn't do it for anyone but him.

And to see her care for him!

She loves him so much. She'll do anything for him.

I know that my birth mother, to some degree, must have done the same for me. I wouldn't have survived to age four otherwise. It makes me feel a little more kindly toward Ella…just.

In a way, I envy Ted; he has such an advocate in his mother. She'll fight for him. Always. That's why he's in our bed.

While I'm breastfeeding him, he's here with us. Deal with it, Christian.

My girl does not back down.

And, of course, he has *me.*

I'll do everything in my power to keep him safe.

That fucker Hyde is locked up. The trial was a painful but necessary evil—he was convicted of aggravated kidnapping, arson, extortion, and sabotage and sentenced to thirty years. Not long enough, in my opinion, but at least he's out of our lives and where he deserves to be—behind bars.

Lincoln is bankrupt and currently on remand for felony fraud charges. I hope he, too, rots in jail. Revenge is indeed a most satisfying dish.

Enough, Grey.

I direct my thoughts back to my family as I run through Pike Place Market. I love this time of the morning here: the florists setting up their colorful displays, the fishmongers icing their fresh catch, and the grocers arranging their fruits and vegetables—it's such a vibrant, bustling part of the city, and so much easier to navigate this early, without the tourists in the way.

Next weekend's wedding will be held at Eamon Kavanagh's Medina residence. I still have to write my speech, and much to Kate's irritation, I've refused to give her editorial approval.

She's such a control freak.

I don't know how Elliot puts up with her.

Ana and Mia are both part of the bridal party—Ana as matron of honor and Mia as bridesmaid. I hope it's not going to be too awkward with Ethan.

I shake my head. *He's just not that into you, Mia.*

I continue on and pick up my pace on Stewart Street, running toward Escala.

Running home.

Well, to one of our homes.

We divide our time between our two residences—Escala during the week and the Big House, as Ana calls it, on the weekends. So far, it's working well.

As I reach the main entrance, I check my time. Not bad.

In the elevator I catch my breath and, as I'm alone, stretch out.

Mrs. Jones is busy in the kitchen as I walk past on my way to my bedroom. I check in on Ted and find that he's still fast asleep, his chest rising and falling.

Damn, but I love it when he sleeps.

Hope, his nanny, should be up and with him shortly.

Ana is still out for the count, too.

I strip down in the closet, dumping my sweaty clothes in the laundry basket, then head into the shower.

The hot water douses me, washing off all the sweat from my run. I'm lost in my thoughts as I soap my hair when I hear the sound of the shower door open. Ana snakes her arms around me and kisses my back, pressing her body against mine.

My day just got a whole lot better.

I make to move, but Ana tightens her arms and splays her hands on my chest. "No," she says, between kisses on my back. "I want to hold you here. Properly."

We stand quietly, together, until I can bear it no more. Turning around, I pull her into my arms, enjoying the softness and warmth of her body against mine. She raises her lips to me, her eyes darkening.

"Good morning, Mrs. Grey. Happy anniversary."

"Happy anniversary, Christian." Her voice is husky, laced with desire.

I touch my lips to hers and my body comes alive. As does Ana. She moans as she kisses me back, opening her mouth and granting me access to her tongue, which greets mine with heightened fervor. We kiss, tongues tangling and tussling together, pouring what must be a week's worth of frustration into each other as she runs her hands up my back, over my shoulders, and into my hair, pushing me against the cold tiles.

Breathless, she nips my jaw to my ear. "I've missed you," she murmurs above the rush of the shower.

Fuck.

Her words pour gasoline on the fire. My erection is harder and fuller, pressing against her. Wanting her. My fingers are in her wet hair, angling her lips to mine, while I take more from her mouth.

I'd expected maybe some gentle lovemaking, the way we have recently.

But not this.

Ana is lit and greedy. Her teeth scrape along my stubbled jawline. Her fingers tug at my hair as my hands move to her behind, pressing her to me. She squirms against me, finding some friction, her intent clear.

"Ana? Here?" I gasp.

"Yes. I'm not made of glass, Christian." She's emphatic as she kisses the line of my clavicle, her hands now roaming down my back to my ass. She squeezes hard, and then her hand is on me.

"Fuck," I whisper through clenched teeth.

"I've missed this." She wraps her fingers around my cock and starts to move her hand up and down, her mouth on mine once more.

I pull back to gaze at her; her eyes are dazed with passion. Her hand tightens around me, and I watch and clench my ass with each move, thrusting into her hand.

She licks her lips.

Oh, no. To hell with this.

I want inside her.

She said she's not made of glass.

I lift her. "Wrap your legs around me, baby." She complies, with a surprising agility.

That must be her sessions with Bastille.

And her lust.

I turn, resting her back against the tiles.

"You're so beautiful," I whisper, and slowly ease into her.

She tips her head up against the wall and cries out.

The sound travels to the end of my dick.

And I start to move.

Hard. Fast.

Her heels press into my butt. Spurring me on. Her arms wrap around my neck, cradling me as I drive myself into her. Over and over. Her breathing accelerates, becoming louder and harsher in my ear as she climbs.

"Yes. Yes," she whispers, and I don't know if it's a plea or a promise.

Ana.

My love.

Suddenly she cries out as her orgasm consumes her, and I let go, following her over the edge, coming inside my wife and calling her name.

When I'm sane again, I'm leaning against her, holding both of us up. Ana unhitches her legs and slides them down my body so that we're both standing together in the shower.

I press my forehead to hers.

And together we catch our breath.

Holding each other beneath the stream of hot water.

Ana tilts her head up, cups the back of my neck, and brushes her lips against mine. Gentle. Sweet. "I needed that," she says.

I laugh. "Me, too, baby!" My lips are on hers once more, but this time in thanks.

"Can we enjoy part two in bed?" Her eyes are still smoldering.

"But…work?"

Ana shakes her head. "I've taken the day off. I want to spend it in bed with you. We'll never have this first again, and I want to celebrate our anniversary, doing what we do best."

I beam down at her, feeling all the love in the world. "Mrs. Grey. Your wish is my command." Lifting her into my arms, I carry her back to bed and lay her down, both of us soaking wet.

ANA IS DOZING, FACEDOWN and naked on our bed. I kiss her shoulder and get up. In our closet, I drag on some sweatpants and a T-shirt and go in search of food. I check in on Teddy and find Hope with him, changing his diaper.

"Good morning, Mr. Grey." She has a sweet drawl, betraying her southern roots.

"Good morning, Hope."

Hope minds Teddy when Ana's at work and lives upstairs with the rest of the staff.

She's in her early forties. Never married. Never had kids. I'm sure there's a story there that Ana will unearth one day. Ana has a knack for getting people to talk.

She did it with me.

Hope has been with us for three months, and so far, it's working well. Ana had insisted on someone older—a career nanny, because Ana's so young. *I want someone I can learn from. My mom lives too far away, and your mom is so busy.*

Hope does not approve of Ted sleeping in our bed.

As much as I love him, I'm with Hope on this, but Ana will not be swayed.

Hope kisses Teddy's belly and he chortles with glee.

It's a beautiful sound.

"I'll leave you to it," I tell Hope.

Mrs. Jones is at the stove. "Good morning, Gail."

"Ah! Mr. Grey. Good morning. Happy anniversary."

"Thank you. I'd like to take Ana breakfast in bed."

"Lovely idea. What would the two of you like?"

"Pancakes, bacon. Blueberries. Coffee."

"Coming right up. It'll be about twenty minutes."

"Great." I amble into my study to fetch the first of my anniversary presents for Ana. The second one, an eternity ring—a symbol of my eternal love—I'll give to her over dinner this evening. I open my desk drawer to check that the red box with her ring is still there, but my eyes stray to the photograph of Ella Pusztai adorned by a silver frame that's now tucked away in my drawer. Ana liberated the snap from my childhood bedroom and had it enlarged and placed in the frame as a gift for my last birthday, but no matter how often I open the drawer, the sight of my birth mother catches me unawares.

"You still wanted your mom. You loved her."

My wife is nothing if not persistent. She also found Ella's final resting place and we'll go one day…I think. Maybe I'll find out more about her then, and maybe after that, she'll earn a place on my shelf.

You might want to direct some of your forgiveness at her.

I'm working on it, John. I'm working on it.

Enough, Grey.

I close the drawer and retrieve the first present I'm going to give Ana this morning. I hope she likes it. Placing the gift on my desk, I check the time. It's 8:30. Andrea should be at her desk. My wife has decided to stay home, and so will I. Picking up the phone, I press call.

"Good morning, Mr. Grey."

"Good morning, Andrea. Cancel all my meetings today. I'm taking the day off."

There's a slight pause and a small gasp before she replies, "Yes, sir."

"And don't call me. At all."

"Er…sure. I mean, yes."

I laugh. "Thank you. Tell Ros, too. Whatever it is can wait until tomorrow."

She laughs. "Will do, Mr. Grey. Enjoy your day." That's two of us in a good mood.

ANA IS DOZING WHEN I bring in her tray—the sheet loosely wrapped around her body, so I'm treated to the spectacular view that is my wife. Her hair is tousled from our earlier lovemaking and spreads across the pillows in a lush sprawl. She has one arm raised over her head, one breast and one shapely leg partly exposed. The morning light caresses her body, as if she's been captured by a Grand Master himself. A Titian, or a Velázquez maybe.

Aphrodite.

My goddess.

She's lost weight since Ted's birth, and I know she wants to lose more, but to me, she's as lovely as ever.

The rattle of our coffee cups rouses her, and she rewards me with a breathtaking smile. "Breakfast in bed? You really are spoiling me."

I place the tray on the bed and take my place beside her.

"A feast!" She claps her hand. "I'm famished!" She tucks into her pancakes and bacon.

"You'll have to thank Mrs. Jones for this. I can't take any credit."

"I will," she mumbles, mouth full.

We eat in a companionable silence, enjoying the nearness of each other.

It's a curious feeling.

This utter contentment.

I've only ever felt it with Ana.

And I allow myself a moment to reflect on my extraordinary good fortune.

I have a loving, smart, gorgeous wife.

A beautiful son, who is at present being entertained by Hope.

My business is in good hands. All the companies we've bought over the past few years are highly profitable. The solar tablet is a huge success, and we're creating new technology around it, specifically for the developing world.

Sitting here, with my wife, eating pancakes, is about as good as it gets.

Once I finish, I put my plate down. "I have something for you, which I can take credit for." From beside the bed, I hold up the gift-wrapped package.

"Oh!" Ana grabs a napkin and wipes her hands while I place her empty plate on the tray and push it out of the way.

"Here."

She gives me a quizzical look as I hand her the broad, heavy, oblong package.

"It's our paper anniversary. That's your only clue."

She grins and starts carefully unwrapping the paper, trying not to tear it. Inside is a large leather binder. Ana bites her lip as she unlatches the strap holding it shut and lifts the cover. She gasps, her hand flying to her mouth. Beneath the cover is a black-and-white still of Ana and Ted: she's smiling down at him, and he's gazing up at her in adoration. The light is perfect, illuminating both of them in a warm, loving glow. I took it a couple of weeks ago, specifically for this series of ledger-sized prints, and it reminds me of the Virgin in the small shrine in St. James's cathedral in Seattle. "This is lovely," Ana breathes, her voice ringing with awe.

I'm proud of these stills. My intention is to hang them in place of some of the Madonnas in the foyer. In the next one, she's holding Ted and looking at me, her eyes alight with amusement, and something a little darker…something for me. I love this picture.

There are four prints with Ana and Teddy—and then the last one.

She gasps again. It's me and Ted, in a selfie. He's in my arms, all dimples and baby fat, curled against my naked chest, fast asleep while I gaze into the camera. "Oh, Christian, this is fabulous. I love it." Ana turns to me, tears in her eyes. "My two favorite men, in one exquisite capture."

"They both love you, very much."

"And I love you!" She closes the book and sets it aside carefully and pounces on me, rattling the cups and plates. "You *are* the three wishes from Aladdin's lamp, the state lottery, and the cure for cancer rolled into one!"

I laugh and brush my fingers down her cheek. "No, Ana. You are."

ACKNOWLEDGMENTS

Thanks to:

Dominique Raccah and all the dedicated team at Sourcebooks, for welcoming me into my new home with such warmth and enthusiasm, and for doing such a fabulous job on this book.

My editor, Anne Messitte, for once more steering me with such grace through the mayhem that is Christian Grey.

Kathleen Blandino, for the beta read and for wrangling my website. Ruth Clampett, for the beta read and for your gracious, constant encouragement. Debra Anastasia, for the writing sprints and words of encouragement—we got there in the end! Crissy Maier, for advice on police procedure. And Amy Brosey for all her hard work on the manuscript.

Becca, Bee, Belinda, Britt, Jada, Jill, Kellie, Kelly, Leis, Liz, Nora, Rachel, QT, and Taylor—ladies, you are all amazing and such a safe place. Thank you also for the Americanisms. You constantly remind me that we belong to four great nations divided by a common language. Who knew that a buttonhole is called a boutonnière?

Vanessa, Emma, Zoya, Crissy—for being such wonderful friends and social media advocates.

To all the wonderfully supportive book bloggers out there, of which there are too many to mention! I see you and thank you for all that you do for me and the author community.

Philippa and all the social media allies who amplify and support. Thank you so much.

The Bunker 3.0 ladies, you rock.

And to all my book-world friends for being a constant source of inspiration and support. You know who you are; I only hope that we can get to see each other sometime soon.

Julie McQueen, for all the off-site help and all that you do for me and mine.

Val Hoskins. My agent. My friend. You are a wonderful woman to have in my corner. Thank you for everything.

Niall Leonard, thank you for the initial edit, cups of tea, fud, steadfast support, and most of all your love.

And to my two beautiful boys—my love for you overwhelms me sometimes. You are my joy. Thank you for being such wonderful, supportive young men. (And, Minor, thank you for all the help on the poker game!)

And to my readers, thank you for waiting.
This book took much longer than I intended,
but I hope you enjoyed it.
It was for you.
Thank you for all that you've done for me.

ABOUT E L JAMES

E L James is an incurable romantic and a self-confessed fangirl. After twenty-five years of working in television, she decided to pursue a childhood dream and write stories that readers could take to their hearts. The result was the controversial and sensuous romance *Fifty Shades of Grey* and its two sequels, *Fifty Shades Darker* and *Fifty Shades Freed*. In 2015, she published the #1 bestseller *Grey*, the story of *Fifty Shades of Grey* from the perspective of Christian Grey, and in 2017, the chart-topping *Darker*, the second part of the Fifty Shades story from Christian's point of view. She followed with the #1 *New York Times* bestseller *The Mister* in 2019. Her books have been published in fifty languages and have sold more than 165 million copies worldwide.

E L James has been recognized as one of *Time* magazine's Most Influential People in the World and *Publishers Weekly*'s Person of the Year. *Fifty Shades of Grey* stayed on the *New York Times* bestseller list for 133 consecutive weeks. *Fifty Shades Freed* won the Goodreads Choice Award (2012), and *Fifty Shades of Grey* was selected as one of the 100 Great Reads, as voted by readers, in PBS's The Great American Read (2018). *Darker* was longlisted for the 2019 International DUBLIN Literary Award.

She was a producer on each of the three Fifty Shades movies, which made more than a billion dollars at the box office. The third installment, *Fifty Shades Freed*, won the People's Choice Award for Drama in 2018. E L James is blessed with two wonderful sons and lives with her husband, the novelist and screenwriter Niall Leonard, and their West Highland terriers in the leafy suburbs of West London.

"Passion APLENTY."
—*People* magazine

Fall in love with ***The Mister***, the thrilling romance from #1 *New York Times* bestselling author **E L James**, author of the phenomenal bestselling Fifty Shades trilogy.

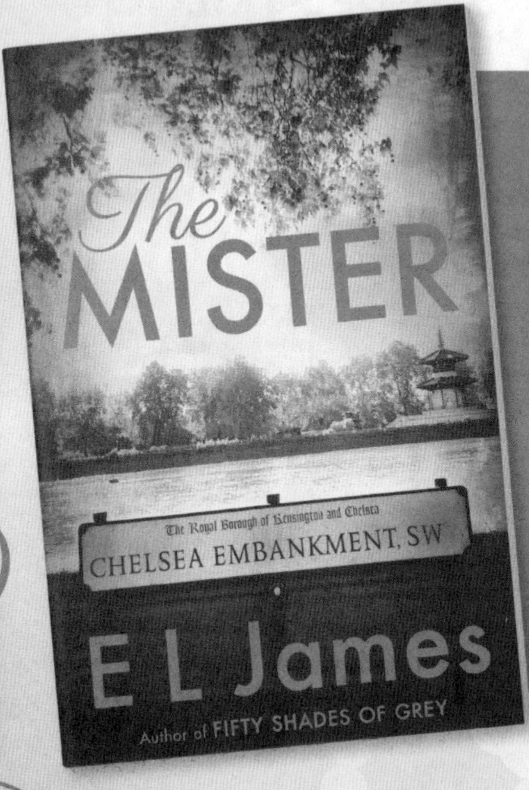

From the heart of London through wild, rural Cornwall to the bleak, forbidding beauty of the Balkans, **THE MISTER** is a roller-coaster ride of danger and desire that leaves the reader breathless to the very last page.

Available wherever books are sold.

Bloom *books*

READ MORE FROM

E L JAMES

Provocative Romance

THE FIFTY SHADES TRILOGY

Erotic, amusing, and deeply moving, the Fifty Shades trilogy is a tale that will *obsess you, possess you, and stay with you forever.*

Available wherever books are sold.

Bloom books

See the world of *FIFTY SHADES OF GREY* anew through the eyes of CHRISTIAN GREY

A fresh perspective on the love story that has enthralled millions of readers around the world.

Collect the other books in the
Fifty Shades of Grey as Told by Christian trilogy

Available wherever books are sold.

Bloom books

See yourself

in Bloom

every story is a celebration.

Visit **bloombooks.com**
for more information about

E L JAMES

and more of your favorite authors!

bloombooks
@read_bloom
@read_bloom
read_bloom

Bloom books

BOOKS BY E L JAMES

Fifty Shades of Grey

Fifty Shades Darker

Fifty Shades Freed

Grey

Darker

Freed

The Mister

Darker

DARKER

E L James

Bloom books

Copyright © 2011, 2017 by Fifty Shades Ltd
Cover design by Sqicedragon and Megan Wilson
Cover images © Petar Djordjevic/Penguin Random House, icepreaw /Shutterstock

Sourcebooks and the colophon are registered trademarks of
Sourcebooks. Bloom Books is a trademark of Sourcebooks.

All rights reserved. No part of this book may be reproduced in any form or by any electronic or mechanical means including information storage and retrieval systems—except in the case of brief quotations embodied in critical articles or reviews—without permission in writing from its publisher, Sourcebooks.

The characters and events portrayed in this book are fictitious or are used fictitiously. Any similarity to real persons, living or dead, is purely coincidental and not intended by the author.

All brand names and product names used in this book are trademarks, registered trademarks, or trade names of their respective holders. Sourcebooks is not associated with any product or vendor in this book.

Portions of this book, including significant portions of the dialogue and email exchanges, have previously appeared in the author's prior works.

Published by Bloom Books, an imprint of Sourcebooks
P.O. Box 4410, Naperville, Illinois 60567-4410
(630) 961-3900
sourcebooks.com

Originally published in 2011 in the United States by Vintage Books, a division of Random House LLC, and in Canada by Penguin Random House of Canada Limited.

Library of Congress Cataloging-in-Publication Data is on file with the publisher.

Printed and bound in the United States of America.
LSC 10 9

For my readers.
Thank you for all that you've done for me.
This book is for you.

Thursday, June 9, 2011

I sit. Waiting. My heart is thumping. It's 5:36 and I stare through the privacy glass of my Audi at the front door of her building. I know I'm early, but I've been looking forward to this moment all day.

I'm going to see her.

I shift in my seat in the rear of the car. The atmosphere feels stifling, and though I'm trying to remain calm, the anticipation and anxiety are knotting my stomach and pressing down on my chest. Taylor sits in the driver's seat, staring straight ahead, wordless, looking his usual composed self, while I can barely breathe. It's irritating.

Damn it. Where is she?

She's inside—inside Seattle Independent Publishing. Set back beyond a wide, open sidewalk, the building is shabby and in need of renovation; the company's name is etched haphazardly in the glass, and the frosted effect on the window is peeling. The business behind those closed doors could be an insurance company or an accounting firm—they're not displaying their wares. Well, that's something I can rectify when I take control. SIP is mine. Almost. I've signed the revised heads of agreement.

Taylor clears his throat and his eyes dart to mine in the rearview mirror. "I'll wait outside, sir," he says, surprising me, and he climbs out of the car before I can stop him.

Maybe he's more affected by my tension than I thought. Am I that obvious? Maybe *he's* tense. But why? Maybe it's because he's had to deal with my ever-changing moods this past week, and I know I've not been easy.

But today has been different. Hopeful. It's the first productive day I've had since she left me, or so it feels. My optimism has driven me through my meetings with enthusiasm. Ten hours until I see her. Nine. Eight. Seven… My patience has been tested by the clock as it ticks closer to my reunion with Miss Anastasia Steele.

And now that I'm sitting here, alone and waiting, the determination and confidence I've enjoyed all day are evaporating.

Perhaps she's changed her mind.

Will it be a reunion? Or am I just the free ride to Portland?

I check my watch again.

5:38.

Shit. Why does time move so slowly?

I contemplate sending her an email to let her know I'm outside, but as I fumble for my phone, I realize I don't want to take my eyes off the front door. Leaning back, I run through her recent emails in my mind. I know them by heart, all of them friendly and concise but without a hint that she's been missing me.

Maybe I *am* the free ride.

I dismiss the thought and stare at the doorway, willing her to appear.

Anastasia Steele, I'm waiting.

The door opens and my heart soars into overdrive but then quickly stutters with disappointment. It's not her.

Damn.

She has always kept me waiting. A humorless smile tugs at my lips: waiting at Clayton's, at The Heathman after the photo shoot, and again when I sent her the Thomas Hardy books.

Tess…

I wonder if she still has them. She wanted to give them back to me; she wanted to give them to a charity.

I don't want anything that will remind me of you.

The image of Ana leaving surfaces in my mind's eye: her sad, ashen face stricken with hurt and confusion. The memory is unwelcome. Painful.

I made her that miserable. I took everything too far, too quickly. And it fills me with a despair that has become all too familiar since she left. Closing my eyes, I try to center myself, but I'm confronted by my deepest, darkest fear: she's met someone else. She's sharing her little white bed and her beautiful body with some fucking stranger.

Damn it, Grey. Stay positive.

Don't go there. All is not lost. You'll be seeing her shortly. Your plans are in place. You are going to win her back. Opening my eyes, I stare at the front door through the window, my mood now as dark as the Audi's tinted glass. More people leave the building, but still no Ana.

Where is she?

Taylor is pacing outside and glancing toward the front door. Christ, he looks as nervous as I feel. *What the hell is it to him?*

My watch says 5:43. She'll be out in a moment. I take a deep breath and tug at my cuffs, then try to straighten my tie, only to find I'm not wearing one. *Hell.* Raking my hand through my hair, I try to dismiss my doubts, but they continue to plague me. *Am I just a free ride to her? Will she have missed me? Will she want me back? Is there someone else?* I have no idea. This is worse than waiting for her in the Marble Bar, and the irony is not lost on me. I thought that was the biggest deal I'd ever negotiate with her and that didn't turn out the way I expected. Nothing turns out as I expect with Miss Anastasia Steele. Panic knots my stomach once more. Today, I have to negotiate a bigger deal.

I want her back.

She said she loved me…

My heart rate spikes in response to the adrenaline that floods my body.

No. No. Don't think about that. She can't feel that way about me.

Calm down, Grey. Focus.

I glance once more at the entrance to Seattle Independent Publishing and she's there, walking toward me.

Fuck.

Ana.

Shock sucks the breath from my body like a kick to the solar plexus. Beneath a black jacket she's wearing one of my favorite dresses, the purple one, and black high-heeled boots. Her hair, burnished by the early-evening sun, sways in the breeze as she moves. But it's not her clothing or her hair that holds my attention. Her face is pale, almost translucent. There are dark circles beneath her eyes, and she's thinner.

Thinner.

Guilt lances through me.

Christ.

She's suffered, too.

My concern at her appearance turns to anger.

No. Fury.

She hasn't been eating. She's lost, what, five or six pounds in the last few days? She glances at some random guy behind her and he gives her a broad smile. He's a good-looking son of a bitch, full of himself. *Asshole.* Their carefree exchange only fuels my rage. He watches her with blatant male appreciation as she walks toward the car, and my wrath increases with each of her steps.

Taylor opens the door and offers her his hand to help her climb inside. And suddenly she is sitting beside me.

"When did you last eat?" I snap, struggling to keep my composure.

Her blue eyes peer up at me, stripping me bare and leaving me as raw as they did the first time I met her. "Hello, Christian. Yes, it's nice to see you, too," she says.

What. The. Fuck.

"I don't want your smart mouth now. Answer me."

She stares at her hands in her lap so I've no idea what she's thinking, then trots out some lame excuse about eating a yogurt and a banana.

That's not eating!

I try, really try, to keep a rein on my temper.

"When did you last have a real meal?" I press her, but she ignores me, looking out the window. Taylor pulls away from the curb, and Ana waves to the prick who followed her out of the building. "Who's that?"

"My boss."

So that's Jack Hyde. I recall the employee details I flipped through this morning: from Detroit, scholarship to Princeton, worked his way up at a publishing firm in New York but has moved on every few years, working his way across the country. He never retains an assistant—they don't last more than three months. He's on my watch list, and I'll have my security adviser Welch find out more.

Focus on the matter at hand, Grey.

"Well? Your last meal?"

"Christian, that really is none of your concern," she whispers.

Shit, I'm the free ride.

"Whatever you do concerns me. Tell me." Don't write me off, Anastasia. *Please.*

I'm the free ride.

She sighs in frustration and rolls her eyes to piss me off. And I see it—a soft smile pulling at the corner of her mouth. She's trying not to laugh. She's trying not to laugh *at me.* After all the heartache I've suffered, it's so refreshing that it cracks through my anger. It's so Ana. I find myself mirroring her, and I try to mask my smile.

"Well?" My tone is much gentler.

"Pasta alla Vongole, last Friday," she answers, her voice subdued.

Jesus H. Christ, she's not eaten since our last meal together! I want to pull her across my knee, right now, here in the back of the SUV—but I know I can't ever touch her like that again.

What do I do with her?

She looks down, examining her hands, her face paler and sadder than it was before. And I drink her in, trying to fathom what to do. An unwelcome emotion blooms in my chest, threatening to overwhelm me but I push it aside. As I study her it becomes achingly clear that my biggest fear is unfounded. I know she didn't get drunk and meet someone. Looking at how she is now, I know she's been on her own, tucked up in her bed, weeping her heart out. The thought is at once comforting and distressing. I'm responsible for her misery.

Me.

I'm the monster. I did this to her. How can I ever win her back?

"I see." The words feel inadequate. My task suddenly feels too daunting. She will never want me back.

Get a grip, Grey.

I damp down my fear and make a plea. "You look like you've lost at least five pounds, possibly more since then. Please eat, Anastasia." I'm helpless. What else can I say?

She sits still, lost in her own thoughts, staring straight ahead, and I have time to study her profile. She's as elfin and sweet and as beautiful as I remember. I want to reach out and stroke her cheek. Feel how soft her skin is… check that she's real. I turn my body toward her, itching to touch her.

"How are you?" I ask, because I want to hear her voice.

"If I told you I was fine, I'd be lying."

Damn. I'm right. She's been suffering—and it's all my fault. But her words give me a modicum of hope. Perhaps she's missed me. Maybe? Encouraged, I cling to that thought. "Me, too. I miss you." I reach for her hand because I can't live another minute without touching her. Her hand feels small and ice-cold engulfed in the warmth of mine.

"Christian. I—" She stops, her voice cracking, but she doesn't pull her hand from mine.

"Ana, please. We need to talk."

"Christian. I… Please. I've cried so much," she whispers, and her words, and the sight of her fighting back tears, pierce what's left of my heart.

"Oh, baby, no." I tug her hand and before she can protest I lift her into my lap, circling her with my arms.

Oh, the feel of her.

"I've missed you so much, Anastasia." She's too light, too fragile, and I want to shout in frustration, but instead I bury my nose in her hair, overwhelmed by her intoxicating scent. It's reminiscent of happier times: An orchard in the fall. Laughter at home. Bright eyes, full of humor and mischief…and desire. My sweet, sweet Ana.

Mine.

At first, she's stiff with resistance, but after a beat she relaxes against me, her head resting on my shoulder. Emboldened, I take a risk and, closing my eyes, I kiss her hair. She doesn't struggle out of my hold, and it's a relief. I've yearned for this woman. But I must be careful. I don't want her to bolt again. I hold her, enjoying the feel of her in my arms and this simple moment of tranquility.

But it's a brief interlude—Taylor reaches the Seattle downtown helipad in record time.

"Come." With reluctance, I lift her off my lap. "We're here."

Perplexed eyes search mine.

"Helipad—on the top of this building." How did she think we were getting to Portland? It would take at least three hours to drive. Taylor opens her door and I climb out on my side.

"I should give you back your handkerchief," she says to Taylor with a coy smile.

"Keep it, Miss Steele, with my best wishes."

What the hell is going on between them?

"Nine?" I interrupt, not just to remind him what time he'll pick us up in Portland, but to stop him from talking to Ana.

"Yes, sir," he says quietly.

Damn right. She's my girl. Handkerchiefs are my business, not his.

Flashes of her vomiting on the ground, me holding back her hair, run through my head. I gave her my handkerchief then. I never got it back. And later that night I watched her sleep beside me. Perhaps she still has it. Perhaps she still uses it.

Stop. Now. Grey.

Taking her hand—the chill has gone, but her hand is still cool—I lead her into the building. As we reach the elevator, I recall our encounter at The Heathman. That first kiss.

Yeah. That first kiss.

The thought wakes my body.

But the doors open, distracting me, and reluctantly I release her to usher her inside.

The elevator is small, and we're no longer touching. But I sense her.

All of her.

Here. Now.

Shit. I swallow.

Is it because she's so near? Darkening eyes look up at mine.

Oh, Ana.

Her proximity is arousing. She inhales sharply and looks at the floor.

"I feel it, too." I reach for her hand again and caress her knuckles with my thumb. She looks up at me, her fathomless eyes clouding with desire.

Fuck. I want her.

She bites her lip.

"Please don't bite your lip, Anastasia." My voice is low, full of longing. Will I always want her like this? I want to kiss her, press her into the elevator wall like I did during our first kiss. I want to fuck her here and make her mine again. She blinks, her lips gently parted, and I suppress a groan. How does she do this? Derail me with a look? I am used to control—and I'm practically drooling over her because her teeth are pressing into her lip. "You know what it does to me." And right now, baby, I want to take you in this elevator, but I don't think you'll let me.

The doors slide open and the rush of cold air brings me back to the now. We're on the roof, and although the day has been warm, the wind has picked up. Anastasia shivers beside me. I wrap my arm around her and she huddles into my side. She feels too slight, but her petite frame fits perfectly under my arm.

See? We fit together so well, Ana.

We head out onto the helipad toward *Charlie Tango*. The rotors are slowly spinning—she's ready for liftoff. Stephan, my pilot, runs toward us. We shake hands, and I keep Anastasia tucked under my arm.

"Ready to go, sir. She's all yours!" he roars above the sound of the helicopter engines.

"All checks done?"

"Yes, sir."

"You'll collect her around eight thirty?"

"Yes, sir."

"Taylor's waiting for you out front."

"Thank you, Mr. Grey. Safe flight to Portland. Ma'am." He

salutes Anastasia and heads to the waiting elevator. We duck down under the rotors and I open the door, taking her hand to help her climb aboard.

As I strap her into the seat, her breath hitches. The sound travels straight to my groin. I cinch the straps extra-tight, trying to ignore my body's reaction to her.

"This should keep you in your place." The thought runs through my head, and I realize I've said it out loud. "I must say, I like this harness on you. Don't touch anything."

She flushes. Finally, some color stains her face—and I can't resist. I run the back of my index finger down her cheek, tracing the line of her blush.

Lord, I want this woman.

She scowls, and I know it's because she can't move. I hand her some headphones, take my seat, and buckle up.

I run through my preflight checks. All instruments are in the green with no advisory lights. I roll the throttles to "fly," set the transponder code, and confirm that the anticollision light is on. It all looks good. I don my headphones, switch on the radios, and check the rotor rpm.

When I turn to Ana, she's watching me intently. "Ready, baby?"

"Yes." She's wide-eyed and excited. I can't help my wolfish grin as I radio the tower to make sure they're awake and listening.

Once I have permission to take off, I check the oil temperature and the rest of the gauges. They're all in normal operating range, so I increase the collective, and *Charlie Tango*, elegant bird that she is, rises smoothly into the sky.

Oh, I love this.

Feeling a little more confident as we gain altitude, I glance at Miss Steele beside me.

Time to dazzle her.

Showtime, Grey.

"We've chased the dawn, Anastasia. Now the dusk." I smile, and I'm rewarded with a shy smile that illuminates her face. Hope stirs in my chest. I have her here when I thought all was lost and she seems happier now than when she walked out of her office. I might just be the free ride, but I'm going to try to enjoy every damn minute of this flight with her.

Dr. Flynn would be proud.

I'm in the moment. And I'm optimistic.

I can do this. I can win her back.

Baby steps, Grey. Don't get ahead of yourself.

"As well as the evening sun, there's more to see this time," I say, interrupting the silence. "Escala's over there. Boeing there—and you can just see the Space Needle."

Curious as ever, she cranes her slim neck to look. "I've never been," she says.

"I'll take you. We can eat there."

"Christian, we broke up." I hear the dismay in her voice.

That is not what I want to hear, but I try not to overreact. "I know. I can still take you there. And feed you." I give her a pointed look and she blushes a lovely pale rose.

"It's very beautiful up here. Thank you." She changes the subject.

"Impressive, isn't it?" I play along—and she's right, I never get tired of the view from up here.

"Impressive that you can do this."

Her compliment surprises me. "Flattery from you, Miss Steele? But I'm a man of many talents."

"I'm fully aware of that, Mr. Grey," she responds tartly, and I suppress a smirk imagining what she's referring to. This is what I've missed: her impertinence, disarming me at every turn.

Keep her talking, Grey. "How's the new job?"

"Good, thank you. Interesting."

"What's your boss like?"

"Oh. He's okay." She sounds less than enthusiastic about Jack Hyde. Has he tried anything with her?

"What's wrong?" I want to know—has that prick done anything inappropriate? I will fire his ass if he has.

"Aside from the obvious, nothing."

"The obvious?"

"Oh, Christian, you really are very obtuse sometimes," she says with playful disdain.

"Obtuse? Me? I'm not sure I appreciate your tone, Miss Steele."

"Well, don't, then," she quips, pleased with herself. I like that she mocks and teases me. She has the ability to make me feel two feet tall or ten feet tall with just a look or a smile—it's refreshing, and unlike anything I've known before.

"I've missed your smart mouth, Anastasia." An image of her on her knees in front of me pops into my mind and I shift in my seat. *Shit. Concentrate, Grey.* She looks away, concealing her smile, and stares down at the suburbs passing beneath us while I check the heading. All is well; we're on track for Portland.

She's quiet, and I steal the occasional glance at her. Her face is lit with curiosity and wonder as she gazes out at the landscape below and the opal sky. Her cheeks are soft and glowing in the evening light. And in spite of her pallor and the dark circles beneath her eyes—evidence of the suffering I've caused her—she's stunning. How could I have let her walk out of my life?

What was I thinking?

While we race above the clouds in our bubble, high in the sky, my optimism grows and the turmoil of the last week recedes. Slowly, I begin to relax, enjoying a serenity I've not felt since she left. I could get used to this. I'd forgotten how content I feel in her company. And it's refreshing to see my world through her eyes.

But as we near our destination my confidence falters. I hope to God that my plan works. I need to take her somewhere private. To dinner maybe. *Damn it.* I should have booked a table somewhere. She needs feeding. If I get her to dinner, I'll just need to find the right words. These last few days have shown me that I need someone—I need her. I want her, but will she have me? Can I convince her to give me a second chance?

Time will tell, Grey—just take it easy. Don't frighten her off again.

WE LAND ON PORTLAND'S downtown helipad fifteen minutes later. As I bring *Charlie Tango*'s engines to idle and switch off the transponder, fuel, and radios, the uncertainty I've felt since I resolved to win her back resurfaces. I need to tell her how I feel, and that's going to be hard—because I don't understand my feelings toward her. I know that I've missed her, that I've been miserable without her, and that I'm willing to try a relationship her way. But will it be enough for her? Will it be enough for me?

Talk to her, Grey.

Once I've unbuckled my harness I lean across to undo hers and catch a trace of her sweet fragrance. As ever, she smells good. Her eyes meet mine in a furtive glance—revealing an inappropriate thought? What exactly is she thinking? As usual I'd love to know but have no idea.

"Good trip, Miss Steele?"

"Yes, thank you, Mr. Grey."

"Well, let's go see the boy's photos." I open the door, jump down, and hold my hand out for her.

Joe, the manager of the helipad, is waiting to greet us. He's an antique: a veteran of the Korean War, but still as spry and acute as a man in his fifties. Nothing escapes his notice. His eyes light up as he gives me a craggy smile.

"Joe, keep her safe for Stephan. He'll be along around eight or nine."

"Will do, Mr. Grey. Ma'am. Your car's waiting downstairs, sir. Oh, and the elevator's out of order. You'll need to use the stairs."

"Thank you, Joe."

As we head for the emergency stairwell, I eye Anastasia's high-heeled boots and remember her less-than-dignified fall into my office.

"Good thing for you this is only three floors—in those heels." I hide my smile.

"Don't you like the boots?" she asks, looking down at her feet. A pleasing vision of them hooked over my shoulders springs to mind.

"I like them very much, Anastasia." I hope my expression doesn't betray my lascivious thoughts. "Come. We'll take it slow. I don't want you falling and breaking your neck." I'm thankful that the elevator is out of order—it gives me a plausible excuse to hold her. Putting my arm around her waist, I pull her to my side and we descend the stairs.

In the car on the way to the gallery my anxiety doubles; we're attending the opening of an exhibition by her so-called friend. The man who, last time I saw him, was trying to push his tongue into her mouth. Perhaps over the last few days they've talked. Perhaps this is a long-anticipated rendezvous between them.

Hell, I hadn't considered that before. I sure hope it's not.

"José is just a friend," Ana explains.

What? She knows what I'm thinking? Am I that obvious? Since when?

Since she stripped me of all my armor and I discovered that I needed her.

She stares at me and my stomach tightens. "Those beautiful eyes look too large in your face, Anastasia. Please tell me you'll eat."

"Yes, Christian, I'll eat." She sounds less than sincere.

"I mean it."

"Do you, now?" Her voice is laced with sarcasm, and I almost have to sit on my hands.

Fuck this.

It's time to declare myself.

"I don't want to fight with you, Anastasia. I want you back, and I want you healthy." I'm honored with her shocked, all-eyes look.

"But nothing's changed." Her expression shifts to a frown.

Oh, Ana, it has—there's been a seismic shift in me.

We pull up at the gallery and I have no time to explain before the show. "Let's talk on the way back. We're here."

Before she can say she's not interested, I exit the car, walk around to her side, and open the door. She looks mad as she climbs out.

"Why do you do that?" she exclaims, exasperated.

"Do what?" *Shit—what's this?*

"Say something like that and then just stop."

That's it—that's why you're mad?

"Anastasia, we're here. Where you want to be. Let's do this and then talk. I don't particularly want a scene in the street."

She presses her lips together in a petulant pout, then gives me a begrudging "Okay."

Taking her hand, I move swiftly into the gallery, and she scrambles behind me.

The space is brightly lit and airy. It's one of those converted warehouses that are fashionable at the moment—all wood floors and brick walls. Portland's cognoscenti sip cheap wine and chat in hushed tones while they admire the exhibition.

A young woman greets us. "Good evening and welcome to José Rodriguez's show." She stares at me.

It's only skin deep, sweetheart. Look elsewhere.

She's flustered but seems to recover when she spies Anastasia. "Oh, it's you, Ana. We'll want your take on all this, too." She hands her a brochure and points us toward the makeshift bar. Ana's brow furrows, and that little *v* that I love forms above her nose. I want to kiss it, like I've done before.

"You know her?" I ask. She shakes her head and her frown deepens. I shrug. *Well, this is Portland.* "What would you like to drink?"

"I'll have a glass of white wine, thank you."

As I head for the bar I hear an exuberant shout. "Ana!"

Turning, I see that *that boy* has his arms wrapped around my girl.

Hell.

I can't hear what they're saying, but Ana closes her eyes, and for one horrible moment I think she's going to burst into tears. But she remains composed as he holds her at arm's length, appraising her.

Yeah, she's that thin because of me.

I fight back my guilt—though it seems she's trying to reassure him. For his part, he looks really fucking interested in her. Too interested. Anger flares in my chest. She says he's just a friend, but it's obvious he doesn't feel that way. He wants more.

Back off, buddy, she's mine.

"The work here is impressive, don't you think?" A balding young man in a loud shirt sidetracks me.

"I've not looked around yet," I answer and turn to the barman. "Is this all you have?"

"Yep. Red or white?" he says, sounding disinterested.

"Two glasses of white wine," I grunt.

"I think you'll be impressed. Rodriguez has a unique eye," the irritating prick with the irritating shirt tells me. Tuning him out, I glance at Ana. She's staring at me, her eyes large and luminous. My blood thickens and it's impossible to look away. She's a beacon in the crowd and I'm lost in her gaze. She looks sensational. Her hair frames her face and falls in a lush cascade to curl at her breasts. Her dress, looser than I remember, still hugs her curves. She might have worn it deliberately. She knows it's my favorite. Doesn't she? Hot dress, hot boots…

Fuck—control yourself, Grey.

Rodriguez asks Ana a question and she's forced to break eye contact with me. I sense she's reluctant to do so, which is pleasing. But damn it, that boy's all perfect teeth, broad shoulders, and sharp suit. He's a good-looking son of a bitch, for a dope smoker, I'll give him that. She nods at something he says and gives him a warm, carefree smile.

I'd like her to smile like that at me. He leans down and kisses her cheek. *Fucker.*

I glare at the bartender.

Hurry up, man. He's taking an eternity to pour the wine, incompetent fool.

Finally, he's finished. I grab the glasses, cold-shoulder the young man beside me who's talking about another photographer or some such crap, and head back to Ana.

At least Rodriguez has left her alone. She's lost in thought, contemplating one of his photographs. It's a landscape, a lake, and not without merit, I suppose. She glances up at me with a guarded expression as I hand her a glass. I take a quick sip from mine. Christ, it's disgusting, a warm over-oaked chardonnay.

"Does it come up to scratch?" She sounds amused, but I have no idea what she's referring to—the exhibition, the building? "The wine," she clarifies.

"No. Rarely does at these kinds of events." I change the subject. "The boy's quite talented, isn't he?"

"Why else do you think I asked him to take your portrait?" Her pride in his work is obvious. It irks me. She admires him and takes an interest in his success because she cares about him. She cares about him too much. An ugly emotion with a bitter sting rises in my chest. It's jealousy, a new feeling, one that I've only ever felt around her—and I don't like it.

"Christian Grey?" A guy dressed like a vagrant thrusts a camera in my face, interrupting my dark thoughts. "Can I have a picture, sir?"

Damned paparazzi. I want to tell him to fuck off but decide to be polite. I don't want Sam, my publicity guy, dealing with a press complaint.

"Sure." I reach out and pull Ana to my side. I want everyone to know she's mine—if she'll have me.

Don't get ahead of yourself, Grey.

The photographer takes a few snaps. "Mr. Grey, thank you." At least he sounds appreciative. "Miss… ?" he asks, wanting to know her name.

"Ana Steele," she answers shyly.

"Thank you, Miss Steele." He slithers off and Anastasia steps out of my grasp. I'm disappointed to let her go and fist my hands to resist the urge to touch her again.

She peers at me. "I looked for pictures of you with dates on the internet. There aren't any. That's why Kate thought you were gay."

"That explains your inappropriate question." I can't help smiling as I remember her awkwardness at our first meeting: her lack of interview skills, her questions. *Are you gay, Mr. Grey?* And my annoyance.

That seems so long ago. I shake my head and continue. "No—I don't do dates, Anastasia, only with you. But you know that."

And I'd like many, many more.

"So you never took your"—she lowers her voice and glances over her shoulder to check that no one's listening—"subs out?" She blanches at the word, embarrassed.

"Sometimes. Not on dates. Shopping, you know." Those occasional trips were just a distraction, maybe a reward for good submissive behavior. The one woman I've wanted to share more with… is Ana. "Just you, Anastasia," I whisper, and I want to plead my case, ask her about my proposition, see how she feels, and if she'll take me back.

However, the gallery is too public a setting. Her cheeks turn that delicious pink that I love, and she stares down at her hands. I hope it's because she likes what I'm saying, but I can't be sure. I need to get her out of here and on her own. Then we can talk seriously and eat. The sooner we've seen the boy's work, the sooner we can leave.

"Your friend here seems more of a landscape man, not portraits. Let's look around." I hold out my hand, and to my delight, she takes it.

We stroll through the gallery, stopping briefly at each photograph. Though I resent the boy and the feelings he inspires in Ana, I have to admit he's quite good. We turn the corner—and stop.

There she is. Seven full-blown portraits of Anastasia Steele. She looks jaw-droppingly beautiful, natural, and relaxed—laughing, scowling, pouting, pensive, amused, and in one of them, wistful and sad. As I scrutinize the detail in each photograph, I know, without a shadow of a doubt, that *he* wants to be much more than her friend. "Seems I'm not the only one," I mutter. The photographs are his homage to her—his love letters—and they're all over the gallery walls for any random asshole to ogle.

Ana is staring at them in stunned silence, as surprised as I am to see them. Well, there's no way anyone else is having these. I want the pictures. I hope they're for sale.

"Excuse me." I abandon Ana for a moment and head to the reception desk.

"May I help you?" asks the woman who greeted us when we arrived.

Ignoring her fluttering eyelashes and provocative, overly red smile, I inquire, "The seven portraits you have hanging at the back, are they for sale?"

A look of disappointment flits across her face but resolves into a broad smile. "The Anastasia collection? Stunning work."

Stunning model.

"Of course they're for sale. Let me check the prices," she gushes.

"I want them all." And I reach for my wallet.

"All of them?" She sounds surprised.

"Yes." *Irritating woman.*

"The collection is fourteen thousand dollars."

"I'd like them delivered as soon as possible."

"But they're due to hang for the duration of the exhibition," she says.

Unacceptable.

I give her my full-kilowatt smile, and she adds, flustered, "But I'm sure we can arrange something." She fumbles with my credit card as she swipes it.

When I return to Ana, I find a blond dude chatting with her, trying his luck. "These photographs are terrific," he says. I place a territorial hand on her elbow and give him my best fuck-off-now glare. "You're a lucky guy," he adds, taking a step back.

"That I am," I answer, dismissing him as I usher Ana over to the wall.

"Did you just buy one of these?" Ana nods toward the portraits.

"One of these?" I scoff. *One? Are you serious?*

"You bought more than one?"

"I bought them all, Anastasia." And I know I sound condescending, but the thought of someone else owning and enjoying these photographs is out of the question. Her lips part in astonishment, and I try not to let it distract me. "I don't want some stranger ogling you in the privacy of their home."

"You'd rather it was you?" she counters.

Her response, though unexpected, is entertaining; she's admonishing me. "Frankly, yes," I respond in kind.

"Pervert," she mouths and bites her lip, I suspect to suppress a laugh.

Lord, she's challenging and funny and right. "Can't argue with that assessment, Anastasia."

"I'd discuss it further with you, but I've signed an NDA." With a haughty look, she turns to study the pictures once more.

And she's doing it again: laughing at me and trivializing my lifestyle. Christ, I'd like to put her in her place—preferably under me or on her knees. I lean in closer and whisper in her ear, "What I'd like to do to your smart mouth."

"You're very rude." She's scandalized, her expression prim, while the tips of her ears turn a fetching pink.

Oh, baby, that's old news.

I glance back at the pictures. "You look very relaxed in these photographs, Anastasia. I don't see you like that very often."

She examines her fingers once more, hesitating as if she's contemplating what to say. I don't know what she's thinking, so, reaching forward, I tilt her head up. She gasps as my fingers make contact with her chin.

Again, that sound; I feel it in my groin.

"I want you that relaxed with me." I sound hopeful.

Damn it. Too hopeful.

"You have to stop intimidating me if you want that," she retorts, surprising me with her depth of feeling.

"You have to learn to communicate and tell me how you feel!" I snap back.

Shit, are we doing this here, now? I want to do this in private. She clears her throat and draws herself up to full height.

"Christian, you wanted me as a submissive," she says, keeping her voice down. "That's where the problem lies. It's in the definition of a submissive—you emailed it to me once." She pauses, glaring at me. "I think the synonyms were, and I quote, 'compliant, pliant, amenable, passive, tractable, resigned, patient, docile, tame, subdued.' I wasn't supposed to look at you. Not talk to you, unless you gave me permission to do so. What do you expect?"

We need to discuss this in private! Why is she doing this here?

"It's very confusing being with you," she continues, in full flow. "You don't want me to defy you, but then you like my 'smart mouth.' You want obedience except when you don't so that you can punish me. I just don't know which way is up when I'm with you."

Okay, I can see how that could be confusing—however, I do not want to discuss it here. We need to leave.

"Good point well made, as usual, Miss Steele." My tone is arctic. "Come, let's go eat."

"We've only been here for half an hour."

"You've seen the photos. You've spoken to the boy."

"His name is José," she asserts, louder this time.

"You've spoken to *José*—the man who, if I am not mistaken, was trying to push his tongue into your mouth the last time I met him, while you were drunk and ill." I grit my teeth.

"He's never hit me," she retaliates with fury in her eyes.

What the hell? She *does* want to do this now.

I can't believe it. *She fucking asked me how bad it could get!* Anger erupts like Mount St. Helens deep in my chest. "That's a low blow, Anastasia." I'm seething. Her face reddens, and I don't know if it's from embarrassment or anger. I run my hands through my hair to prevent myself from grabbing her and dragging her outside so we can continue this discussion in private. I take a deep breath.

"I'm taking you for something to eat. You're fading away in front of me. Find the boy, say goodbye." My tone is clipped as I struggle to control my temper, but she doesn't move.

"Please, can we stay longer?"

"No. Go. Now. Say goodbye." I manage not to shout. I recognize that stubborn, mulish set to her mouth. She's mad as hell, and in spite of all I've been through over the last few days, I don't give a shit. We are leaving if I have to pick her up and carry her. She gives me a withering look and turns with a sharp spin, her hair flying so that it hits my shoulder. She stalks off to find him.

As she moves away I struggle to recover my equilibrium. What is it about her that presses all my buttons? I want to scold her, spank her, and fuck her. Here. Now. And in that order.

I scan the room. The boy—no, Rodriguez—is standing with a flock of female admirers. He notices Ana, and forgetting his fans, he greets her like she's the center of his whole goddamn universe. He listens intently to everything she has to say, then sweeps her into his arms, spinning her around.

Get your fat paws off my girl.

She glances at me, then weaves her hands into his hair and presses her cheek to his and whispers something in his ear. They continue talking. Close. His arms around her. And he's basking in her fucking light.

Before I'm even aware that I'm doing it, I'm striding over, ready to rip him limb from limb. Fortunately for him, he releases her as I approach.

"Don't be a stranger, Ana. Oh, Mr. Grey, good evening," the boy mumbles, sheepish and a little intimidated.

"Mr. Rodriguez, very impressive. I'm sorry *we* can't stay longer, but *we* need to head back to Seattle. Anastasia?" I take her hand.

"Bye, José. Congratulations again." She leans away from me, gives Rodriguez a tender kiss on his reddening cheek, and I'm going to have a coronary. It takes all my self-control not to haul her over my shoulder. Instead I drag her by the hand to the front door and out onto the street. She's stumbling behind me, trying to keep up, but I don't care.

Right now. I just want to—

There's an alley. I hurry us into it, and before I know what I'm doing I've pressed her against the wall. I grab her face between my hands, pinning her body with mine as rage and desire mix in a heady, explosive cocktail. I capture her lips with mine and our teeth clash, but then my tongue is in her mouth. She tastes of cheap wine and delicious, sweet, sweet Ana.

Oh, this mouth.

I have missed this mouth.

She ignites around me. Her fingers are in my hair, pulling hard. She moans into my mouth, giving me more access, and she's kissing me back, her passion unleashed, her tongue entwined with mine. Tasting. Taking. Giving.

Her hunger is unexpected. Desire bursts through my body, like a forest fire licking through dry tinder. I'm so aroused—I want her now, here, in this alley. And what I'd intended as a punishing I-own-you kiss becomes something else.

She wants this, too.

She's missed this, too.

And it's more than arousing.

I groan in response, undone.

With one hand, I hold her at the nape of her neck as we kiss. My free hand travels down her body, and I reacquaint myself with her curves: her breast, her waist, her ass, her thigh. She moans as my fingers find the hem of her dress and start tugging it higher. My goal is to pull it up, fuck her here. Make her mine, again.

The feel of her.

It's intoxicating, and I want her like I've never wanted her before.

In the distance and through the fog of my lust, I hear a police siren wail.

No! No! Grey!

Not like this. Get a grip.

I pull back, gazing down at her, and I'm panting and mad as hell.

"You. Are. Mine!" I growl and push myself away from her as my reason returns. "For the love of God, Ana." I bend over, hands on my knees, trying to catch my breath and calm my raging body. I'm painfully hard for her right now.

Has anyone ever affected me like this? Ever?

Christ! I nearly fucked her in a back alley.

This is jealousy. This is what it feels like: my insides gutted and raw, my self-control absent. I don't like it. I don't like it one bit.

"I'm sorry," she says, hoarse.

"You should be. I know what you're doing. Do you want the photographer, Anastasia? He obviously has feelings for you."

"No." Her voice is soft and breathless. "He's just a friend." At least she sounds contrite, and it goes some way toward pacifying me.

"I have spent all my adult life trying to avoid any extreme emotion. Yet you… you bring out feelings in me that are completely alien. It's very…" Words fail me. I cannot find the vocabulary to describe how I feel. I'm out of control and at a loss. "Unsettling" is the best I can manage. "I like control, Ana, and around you, that just"—I stand and look down at her—"evaporates."

Her eyes are wide with carnal promise, and her hair is mussed and sexy, falling to her breasts. I rub the back of my neck, thankful that I've recovered some semblance of self-control.

See how I am around you, Ana? See?

I run my hand through my hair, taking deep, thought-clearing breaths. I grab her hand. "Come, we need to talk." *Before I fuck you.* "And you need to eat."

There's a restaurant close to the alley. It's not what I would have chosen for a reunion, if that's what this is, but it will suffice. I don't have long, as Taylor will be arriving soon.

I open the door for her. "This place will have to do. We don't have much time." The restaurant looks like it caters to the gallery crowd, and maybe students. It's ironic that the walls are painted the same color as my playroom, but I don't dwell on the thought.

An obsequious waiter leads us to a secluded table; he's all smiles for Anastasia. I glance at the chalkboard menu on the wall and decide to order before the waiter retreats, letting him know we're tight for time. "So we'll each have sirloin steak cooked medium, béarnaise sauce if you have it, fries, and green vegetables, whatever the chef has—and bring me the wine list."

"Certainly, sir," he says and rushes off.

Ana purses her lips, annoyed.

What now?

"And if I don't like steak?"

"Don't start, Anastasia."

"I am not a child, Christian."

"Well, stop acting like one."

"I'm a child because I don't like steak?" She doesn't hide her petulance.

No!

"For deliberately making me jealous. It's a childish thing to do. Have you no regard for your friend's feelings, leading him on like that?"

Her cheeks pink and she examines her hands.

Yes. You should be embarrassed. You're confusing him. Even I can see that.

Is that what she's doing to me? Leading me on?

In the time we've been apart, maybe she's finally recognized that she has power. Power over me.

The waiter returns with the wine list, giving me a chance to regain my cool. The selection is average: only one drinkable wine on the menu. I glance at Anastasia, who looks like she's sulking. I know that look. Perhaps she wanted to select her own meal. And I can't resist toying with her, aware that she has little knowledge of wine. "Would you like to choose the wine?" I ask and I know I sound sarcastic.

"You choose." She presses her lips together.

Yeah. Don't play games with me, baby.

"Two glasses of the Barossa Valley Shiraz, please," I say to the waiter, who's hovering.

"Er, we only sell that wine by the bottle, sir."

"A bottle, then." *You stupid prick.*

"Sir." He retreats.

"You're very grumpy," she says, no doubt feeling sorry for the waiter.

"I wonder why that is?" I keep my expression neutral, but even to my own ears *I'm* now sounding childish.

"Well, it's good to set the right tone for an intimate and honest discussion about the future, wouldn't you say?" She gives me a saccharine smile.

Oh, tit for tat, Miss Steele. She's called me out again and I have to admire her nerve. I realize our bickering will get us nowhere.

And I'm being an ass.

Don't blow this deal, Grey.

"I'm sorry," I say, because she's right.

"Apology accepted. And I'm pleased to inform you I haven't decided to become a vegetarian since we last ate."

"Since that *was* the last time you ate, I think that's a moot point."

"There's that word again, 'moot.'"

"Moot," I mouth. *That word, indeed.* I remember I last used it while discussing our arrangement on Saturday morning. The day my world fell apart.

Fuck. Don't think about that.

Man up, Grey. Tell her what you want.

"Ana, the last time we spoke, you left me. I'm a little nervous. I've told you I want you back, and you've said… nothing."

She bites her lip as the color drains from her face.

Oh no.

"I've missed you… really missed you, Christian," she says, quietly. "The past few days have been… difficult."

Difficult is an understatement.

She swallows and takes a steadying breath. This doesn't sound good. Perhaps my behavior over the last hour has finally driven her away. I tense. Where's she going with this?

"Nothing's changed. I can't be what you want me to be." Her expression is bleak.

No. No. No.

"You are what I want you to be." You are everything I want you to be.

"No, Christian, I'm not."

Oh, baby, please believe me. "You're upset because of what happened last time. I behaved stupidly, and you—so did you. Why didn't you safe-word, Anastasia?"

She looks surprised, as if this isn't something she's considered.

"Answer me," I urge.

This has haunted me. *Why didn't you safe-word, Ana?*

She wilts in her seat. Sad. Defeated.

"I don't know," she whispers.

What?

WHAT?

I'm rendered speechless. I've been in hell because she didn't safe-word. But before I recover, words tumble from her mouth. Soft, quiet, as if she's in a confessional, as if she's ashamed.

"I was overwhelmed. I was trying to be what you wanted me to be, trying to deal with the pain, and it went out of my mind." Her look is raw, her shrug small and apologetic. "You know… I forgot."

What the hell?

"You forgot!" I'm dismayed. We've been through all this shit because she *forgot?*

I can't believe it. I clutch the table for something to anchor me to the now as I let this alarming information register.

Did I remind her of her safe words? *Christ.* I can't remember.

The email she sent me the first time I spanked her comes to mind.

She didn't stop me then.

I'm an idiot.

I should have reminded her.

Wait. She knows she has safe words. I remember telling her more than once.

"We don't have a signed contract, Anastasia. But we've discussed limits. And I want to reiterate we have safe words, okay?"

She blinks a couple times but remains mute.

"What are they?" I demand.

She hesitates.

"What are the safe words, Anastasia?"

"Yellow."

"And?"

"Red."

"Remember those."

She raises an eyebrow in obvious scorn and is about to say something.

"Don't start with your smart mouth in here, Miss Steele. Or I will fuck it with you on your knees. Do you understand?"

"How can I trust you? Ever?" If she can't be honest with me, what hope do we have? She can't tell me what she thinks I want to hear. What kind of relationship is that? My spirits sink. This is the problem in dealing with someone who isn't in the lifestyle. She doesn't get it.

I should never have chased her.

The waiter arrives with the wine as we stare with incredulity at each other.

Maybe I should have done a better job of explaining it to her.

Damn it, Grey. Eliminate the negative.

Yes. It's irrelevant now. I'm going to try a relationship her way, if she'll let me.

The irritating prick takes too much time opening the bottle. Jesus. Is he trying to entertain us? Or is it just Ana he wants to impress? He finally pops the cork and pours a taste for me. I take a quick sip. It needs to breathe, but it's passable.

"That's fine." *Now go. Please.* He fills our glasses and leaves.

Ana and I haven't taken our eyes off each other. Each trying to discern what the other is thinking. She's the first to look away, and she takes a sip of wine, closing her eyes as if seeking inspiration. When she opens them, I see her despair. "I'm sorry," she whispers.

"Sorry for what?" *Hell.* Is she done with me? Is there no hope?

"Not using the safe word," she says.

Oh, thank God. I thought it was over.

"We might have avoided all this suffering," I mutter in response, and also in an attempt to hide my relief.

"You look fine." There's a tremor in her voice.

"Appearances can be deceptive. I'm not fine. I feel like the sun has set and not risen for five days, Ana. I'm in perpetual night here."

Her gasp is just audible.

How did she think I'd feel? She left me when I'd almost begged her to stay. "You said you'd never leave, yet the going gets tough and you're out the door."

"When did I say I'd never leave?"

"In your sleep." Before we went soaring. "It was the most comforting thing I'd heard in so long, Anastasia. It made me relax."

She inhales sharply. Her open and honest compassion is written all over her lovely face as she reaches for her wine. This is my chance.

Ask her, Grey.

Ask her the one question I haven't allowed myself to think about because I know I'll dread her answer, whatever it is. But I'm curious. I need to know.

"You said you loved me," I whisper, almost choking on the words. She can't feel that way about me still. Can she? "Is that now in the past tense?"

"No, Christian, it's not," she says, as if in the confessional again.

I'm unprepared for the relief that rushes through me. But it's relief mixed with fear. It's a confounding combination because I know she shouldn't love a monster.

"Good," I mumble, confused. I want to stop thinking about that right now, and with impeccable timing, the waiter returns with our meal.

"Eat," I demand. The woman needs feeding.

She examines the contents of her plate with distaste.

"So help me God, Anastasia, if you don't eat, I will take you across my knee here in this restaurant. And it will have nothing to do with my sexual gratification. Eat!"

"Okay. I'll eat. Stow your twitching palm, please." She's trying for humor—but I'm not laughing. She's wasting away. She picks up her cutlery with stubborn reluctance but she takes one bite, closes her eyes, and licks her lips in satisfaction. The sight of her tongue is enough to provoke a response from my body—already in a heightened state from our kiss in the alley.

Hell, not again! I stop my response in its tracks. There'll be time for that later, *if* she says yes. She takes another bite and another and I know she'll continue eating. I'm grateful for the diversion that our food has provided. Slicing into my steak, I take a bite. It's not bad.

We continue to eat, watching each other but saying nothing.

She hasn't told me to fuck off. This is good. And as I study her I realize how much I'm enjoying just being in her company. Okay, so I'm tied up in all kinds of conflicting emotions… but she's here. She's with me and she's eating. I'm hopeful we can make my proposition work. Her reaction to the kiss in the alley was… visceral. She still wants me. I know I could have fucked her there and she wouldn't have stopped me.

She interrupts my reverie. "Do you know who's singing?" Over the restaurant sound system, a young woman with a soft lyrical voice can be heard. I don't know who she is, but we both agree she's good.

Listening to this singer reminds me that I have the iPad for Ana. I hope she lets me give it to her, and that she likes it. In addition to the music I uploaded yesterday, I spent some time this morning adding more features—photographs of the glider on my desk and of the two of us at her graduation ceremony and a few apps, too. It's my apology, and I'm optimistic that the simple message I've had engraved on the back conveys my sentiment. I hope she doesn't think it's too cheesy. I just need to give it to her first, but I don't know if we'll get to that point. I suppress my sigh because she's always been difficult about accepting gifts from me.

"What?" she asks. She knows I'm up to something, and not for the first time I wonder if she can read my mind.

I shake my head. "Eat up."

Bright, blue eyes regard me. "I can't manage any more. Have I eaten enough for Sir?"

Is she deliberately trying to goad me? I scrutinize her face, but she seems genuine, and she's eaten more than half of what was on her plate. If she hasn't eaten anything over the last few days she's probably had enough to eat this evening.

"I'm really full," she reiterates.

As if on cue, my phone vibrates in my jacket pocket, signaling a message. It will be from Taylor. He's probably close to the gallery by now.

I glance at my watch. "We have to go shortly. Taylor's here, and you have to be up for work in the morning." I hadn't considered that before. She's working now—she needs sleep. I may have to revise my plans and my body's expectations. The thought of deferring my desire displeases me.

Ana reminds me that I need to be up for work, too.

"I function on a lot less sleep than you do, Anastasia. At least you've eaten something."

"Aren't we going back via *Charlie Tango*?"

"No, I thought I might have a drink—Taylor will pick us up. Besides, this way I have you in the car all to myself—for a few hours, at least. What can we do but talk?" And I can put my proposition to her.

I shift uncomfortably in my chair. Stage three of the campaign has not gone as smoothly as I anticipated.

She's made me jealous.

I've lost control.

Yes. As usual, she's derailed me. But I can turn this around and close the deal in the car.

Don't give up, Grey.

Summoning the waiter, I ask for the check, then call Taylor. He answers on the second ring.

"Mr. Grey."

"We're at Le Picotin, Southwest Third Avenue," I inform him and hang up.

"You're very brusque with Taylor… In fact, with most people."

"I just get to the point quickly, Anastasia."

"You haven't gotten to the point this evening. Nothing's changed, Christian."

Touché, Miss Steele.

Tell her. Tell her now, Grey.

"I have a proposition for you."

"This started with a proposition."

"A different proposition," I clarify.

She's a little skeptical, I think, but maybe she's curious, too. The waiter returns and I give him my card, but I keep my attention on Ana. Well, at least she's intrigued.

Good.

My heart rate accelerates. I hope she goes for this… or I really will be lost. The waiter hands me the credit card slip to sign. I enter an obscene tip and sign my name with a flourish. The waiter seems excessively grateful. And it's still irritating.

My phone buzzes and I scan the text. Taylor's arrived. The waiter gives me my card back and disappears.

"Come. Taylor's outside."

We both stand and I take her hand. "I don't want to lose you, Anastasia," I murmur and raise her hand and brush my lips against her knuckles. Her breathing accelerates.

Oh, that sound.

I glance at her face. Her lips are parted, cheeks pink and eyes wide. The sight fills me with hope and desire. I stifle my impulses and lead her through the restaurant and outside, where Taylor is waiting at the curb in the Q7. It occurs to me that Ana might be reluctant to talk if he's in front.

I have an idea. Opening the rear door, I usher her in and

walk around to the driver's side. Taylor gets out to open the door for me.

"Good evening, Taylor. Do you have your iPod and headphones?"

"Yes, sir, never leave home without them."

"Great. Use them on the way home."

"Of course, sir."

"What will you listen to?"

"Puccini, sir."

"*Tosca*?"

"*La Bohème*."

"Good choice." I smile. As ever, he surprises me. I'd always assumed his musical tastes leaned toward country and rock. Taking a deep breath, I climb into the car. I'm about to negotiate the deal of my life.

I want her back.

Taylor presses play on the car's sound system and the stirring notes from Rachmaninov swell quietly in the background. He regards me for a second in the mirror and pulls out into the light evening traffic.

Anastasia is watching me when I turn to face her. "As I was saying, Anastasia, I have a proposition for you."

She looks anxiously at Taylor, as I knew she would.

"Taylor can't hear you."

"What?" She looks perplexed.

"Taylor," I call. Taylor doesn't respond. I call him again, then lean over and tap his shoulder. He removes an earbud.

"Yes, sir?"

"Thank you, Taylor. It's okay—resume your listening."

"Sir."

"Happy now? He's listening to his iPod. Puccini. Forget he's here. I do."

"Did you deliberately ask him to do that?"

"Yes."

She blinks in surprise. "Okay… your proposition," she says, hesitant and apprehensive.

I'm nervous, too, baby. Here goes. *Don't blow this, Grey.*

How to begin?

I take a deep breath. "Let me ask you something first. Do you want a regular vanilla relationship, with no kinky fuckery at all?"

"Kinky fuckery?" she squeaks in disbelief.

"Kinky fuckery."

"I can't believe you said that." She looks anxiously at Taylor again.

"Well, I did. Answer me."

"I like your kinky fuckery," she whispers.

Oh, baby, so do I.

I'm relieved. Step one… okay. *Keep cool, Grey.*

"That's what I thought. So what don't you like?"

She's silent for a moment, and I know she's scrutinizing me in the light and shadows of the intermittent streetlamps. "The threat of cruel and unusual punishment," she says.

"What does that mean?"

"Well, you have all those"—she stops, glancing at Taylor once more, and her voice lowers—"things in your playroom, the canes and whips, and they frighten the living daylights out of me. I don't want you to use them on me."

This I have worked out for myself.

"Okay, so no whips or canes. Or belts, for that matter," I add, unable to keep the irony out of my voice.

"Are you attempting to redefine the hard limits?" she asks.

"Not as such. I'm just trying to understand you—get a clearer picture of what you do and don't like."

"Fundamentally, Christian, it's your joy in inflicting pain that's difficult for me to handle. And the idea that you'll do it because I have crossed some arbitrary line."

Hell. She knows me. She has seen the monster. I'm not going there or I will blow this deal. I ignore her first comment and concentrate on her second point. "But it's not arbitrary—the rules are written down."

"I don't want a set of rules."

"None at all?"

Fuck—she might touch me. How can I protect myself from that? And suppose she does something stupid that puts herself at risk?

"No rules," she states, shaking her head for emphasis.

Okay, million-dollar question.

"But you don't mind if I spank you?"

"Spank me with what?"

"This." I hold up my hand.

She shifts in her seat, and a silent, sweet joy unfurls deep in my gut. *Oh, baby, I love it when you squirm.*

"No, not really. Especially with those silver balls…"

My cock stirs at the thought. *Damn.* I cross my legs. "Yes, that was fun."

"More than fun," she adds.

"So you can deal with some pain." I can't keep the hope out of my voice.

"Yes, I suppose." She shrugs.

Okay. So we may be able to structure a relationship around this.

Deep breath, Grey. Give her the terms.

"Anastasia, I want to start again. Do the vanilla thing and then maybe, once you trust me more—and I trust you to be honest and to communicate with me—we could move on and do some of the things that I like to do."

That's it.

Fuck. My heart rate escalates; blood thrums through my body, pounding past my eardrums as I wait for her reaction. My well-being hangs in the balance. And she says… nothing! She stares at me as we pass under a streetlight and I see her clearly. She's assessing me. Her eyes still impossibly large in her beautiful, thinner, sadder face.

Oh, Ana.

"But what about punishments?" she says finally.

I close my eyes. It's not a no. "No punishments. None."

"And the rules?"

"No rules."

"None at all? But you have needs…" Her voice trails off.

"I need you more, Anastasia. These last few days have been

hell. All my instincts tell me to let you go, tell me I don't deserve you. Those photos the boy took—I can see how he sees you. You look untroubled and beautiful, not that you're not beautiful now, but here you sit. I see your pain. It's so hard knowing that I'm the one who has made you feel this way."

It's killing me, Ana.

"But I'm a selfish man. I've wanted you since you fell into my office. You are exquisite, honest, warm, strong, witty, beguilingly innocent; the list is endless. I am in awe of you. I want you, and the thought of anyone else having you is like a knife twisting in my dark soul."

Fuck. Flowery, Grey! Real flowery.

I'm like a man possessed. I'm going to scare her off.

"Christian, why do you think you have a dark soul?" she cries out, totally surprising me. "I would never say that. Sad maybe, but you're a good man. I can see that—you're generous, you're kind, and you've never lied to me. And I haven't tried very hard. Last Saturday was such a shock to my system. It was my wake-up call. I realized that you'd been easy on me and that I couldn't be the person you wanted me to be. Then, after I left, it dawned on me that the physical pain you inflicted was not as bad as the pain of losing you. I do want to please you, but it's hard."

"You please me all the time." When will she understand this? "How often do I have to tell you that?"

"I never know what you're thinking."

She doesn't? Baby, you read me like one of your books, except I'm not the hero. I'll never be the hero.

"Sometimes you're so closed off, like an island state," she continues. "You intimidate me. That's why I keep quiet. I don't know which way your mood is going to go. It swings from north to south and back again in a nanosecond. It's confusing and you won't let me touch you and I want so much to show you how much I love you."

Anxiety bursts in my chest and my heart starts hammering. She said it again, the three potent words I cannot bear. And touching. No. No. *No.* She can't touch me. But before I can respond, before the darkness takes hold, she unfastens her seat belt and crawls across the seat and into my lap, ambushing me. She places her hands on either side of my head, staring into my eyes, and I stop breathing.

"I love you, Christian Grey," she says. "And you're prepared to do all this for me. I'm the one who is undeserving. And I'm just sorry that I can't do all those things for you. Maybe with time—I don't know—but yes, I accept your proposition. Where do I sign?" She curls her arms around my neck and hugs me, her warm cheek against mine.

I can't believe what I'm hearing.

Anxiety turns to joy. It expands in my chest, lighting me up from head to toe, spreading warmth in its wake. She's going to try. I get her back. I don't deserve her, but I get her back. I wrap my arms around her and hold her tightly, burying my nose in her fragrant hair, as relief and a kaleidoscope of colorful emotions fill the void that I've carried inside me since she left.

"Oh, Ana," I whisper, and I hold her, too dazed and too… replete to say anything else. She snuggles into my arms, her head on my shoulder, and we listen to the Rachmaninov. I go over her words.

She loves me.

I test the phrase in my head and what's left of my heart and swallow the knot of fear that forms in my throat as those words ring through me.

I can do this.

I can live with this.

I must. I need to protect her and her vulnerable heart.

I take a deep breath.

I can do this.

Except the touching. I can't do that. I have to make her understand—manage her expectations. Gently I stroke her back. "Touching is a hard limit for me, Anastasia."

"I know. I wish I understood why." Her breath tickles my neck.

Shall I tell her? Why would she want to know this shit? My shit? Maybe I can hint at it, give her a clue.

"I had a horrific childhood. One of the crack whore's pimps…"

"There you are, you little shit."

No. No. No. Not the burn.

"Mommy! Mommy!"

"She can't hear you, you fucking maggot." He grabs my hair and pulls me out from under the kitchen table.

"Ow. Ow. Ow."

He's smoking. The smell. Cigarettes. It's a dirty smell. Like old and nasty. He's dirty. Like trash. Like drains. He drinks brown licker. From a bottle.

"And even if she could, she doesn't give a fuck," he shouts. He always shouts.

His hand hits me across my face. And again. And again. No. No.

I fight him. But he laughs. And takes a puff. The end of the cigarette shines bright red and orange.

"The burn," he says.

No. No.

The pain. The pain. The pain. The smell.

Burn. Burn. Burn.

Pain. No. No. No.

I howl.

Howl.

"Mommy! Mommy!"

He laughs and laughs. He has two teeth gone.

I shudder as my memories and nightmares float together like smoke from his discarded cigarette, fogging my brain, dragging me back to a time of fear and impotence.

I tell Ana I remember it all and she tightens her hold on me. Her cheek on my neck. Her soft, warm skin against mine, bringing me back to the now.

"Was she abusive? Your mother?" Ana's voice is hoarse.

"Not that I remember. She was neglectful. She didn't protect me from her pimp."

She was a sad excuse and he was a sick fuck.

"I think it was me who looked after her. When she finally killed herself, it took four days for someone to raise the alarm and find us. I remember that." I close my eyes and see vague, muted images of my mother slumped on the floor, me covering her with my blanket and curling up beside her.

Anastasia gasps. "That's pretty fucked up."

"Fifty shades."

She kisses my neck, a soft, tender press of her lips onto my skin. And I know it's not pity she's offering. It's comfort, maybe even understanding. My sweet, compassionate Ana.

I tighten my hold on her and kiss her hair as she nestles in my arms.

Baby, it was a long time ago.

My exhaustion catches up with me. Several sleepless nights plagued with nightmares have taken their toll. I'm tired. I want to stop thinking. She's my dream catcher. I never had nightmares when she was sleeping at my side. Leaning back, I close my eyes, saying nothing, because I have nothing more to say. I listen to the music, and when it's finished, to her soft, even breathing. She's asleep. She's weary. Like me. I realize I can't spend the night with her. She'll get no sleep if I do. I hold her, enjoying her weight on me, honored that she can sleep on me. I can't help my self-satisfied grin. I've done it. I've won her back. Now all I have to do is keep her, which will be challenging enough.

My first vanilla relationship—who would have thought? Closing my eyes, I imagine the look on Elena's face when I tell her. She'll have plenty to say. She always has…

I can tell by the way you're standing that you have something to tell me.

I dare a quick peek at Elena as her scarlet lips curl into a smile and she crosses her arms, flogger in hand.

Yes, Ma'am.

You may speak.

I have a place at Harvard.

Her eyes flash.

Ma'am, I add quickly and stare down at my toes.

I see. She walks around me as I stand naked in her basement. The chill spring air caresses my skin, but it's the anticipation of what's to come that makes each of my hair follicles stand on end. That, and the smell of her expensive perfume. My body begins to respond.

She laughs. *Control!* she snaps, and the flogger bites across my thighs. And I try, really try, to bring my body to heel. *Though perhaps you should be rewarded for good behavior,* she purrs. And she hits me again, across my chest this time, but soft, more playful. *It's quite the achievement to get into Harvard, my dear, dear pet.* The flogger flies again, stinging my ass, and my legs quiver in response.

Hold still, she warns. And I stand straight, waiting for the next blow. *So you'll leave me,* she whispers, and the flogger strikes my back.

My eyes spring open and I glance at her in alarm.

No. Never.

Eyes down, she commands.

And I stare at my feet as panic overwhelms me.

You'll leave me and find some young college girl.

No. No.

She grabs my face, her nails biting into my skin.

You will. Her ice-blue eyes burn into mine, scarlet lips twisted in a snarl.

Never, Ma'am.

She laughs and pushes me away and raises her hand.

But the blow never comes.

When I open my eyes, Ana stands before me. She caresses my cheek and smiles. *I love you,* she says.

I wake, momentarily disoriented, my heart thudding like a klaxon, and I don't know if it's fear or excitement. I'm in the back of the Q7 and Ana is curled up asleep in my lap.

Ana.

She's mine once more. And for a moment I feel giddy. A stupid grin splits my face and I shake my head. Have I ever felt like this?

I'm excited for the future. I'm excited to see where our relationship will go. What new things we'll try. There are so many possibilities.

I kiss her hair and rest my chin on her head. When I glance out of the window I notice that we've reached Seattle.

Taylor's eyes meet mine in the rearview mirror. "Are we heading to Escala, sir?"

"No, Miss Steele's."

The corners of his eyes crinkle. "We'll be there in five minutes," he says.

Whoa. We're nearly home.

"Thank you, Taylor." I've slept longer than I thought possible in the back of a car. I wonder what time it is, but I don't want to move my arm to check my watch as I'm holding her. I gaze down at my sleeping beauty. Her lips are gently parted, her dark lashes fanned out, shadowing her face. And I remember watching her sleep at The Heathman, that first time. She looked so peaceful then; she looks peaceful now. I'm reluctant to disturb her.

"Wake up, baby." I kiss her hair. Her eyelashes flutter and she opens her eyes. "Hey," I murmur in greeting.

"Sorry," she mumbles as she sits up.

"I could watch you sleep forever, Ana." No need to apologize.

"Did I say anything?" She looks worried.

"No," I reassure her. "We're nearly at your place."

"We're not going to yours?" She sounds surprised.

"No."

She sits up straight and glares at me. "Why not?"

"Because you have work tomorrow."

"Oh." Her pout says all I need to know about her disappointment. I want to laugh out loud.

"Why, did you have something in mind?" I tease her.

She squirms in my lap.

Ow.

I still her with my hands.

"Well, maybe," she says, looking anywhere but at me and sounding a little shy. I can't help my laugh. She's courageous in so many ways, yet still so coy in others. And as I watch her, I realize

I've got to get her to open up about sex. If we're going to be honest with each other, she has to tell me how she feels. Tell me what she needs. I want her to be confident enough to express her desires. All of them.

"Anastasia, I am not going to touch you again, not until you beg me to."

"What!" She sounds a little upset.

"So that you'll start communicating with me. Next time we make love, you're going to have to tell me exactly what you want in fine detail."

That will give you something to think about, Miss Steele.

I lift her off my lap when Taylor pulls up at the curb beside her apartment. I climb out of the car, walk to her door, and open it for her. She looks sleepy and adorable as she struggles out of the car.

"I have something for you."

This is it. Will she accept my gift? This is the final stage of my campaign to win her back. Opening the trunk, I grab the gift box that contains her Mac, her phone, and an iPad. She looks from the box to me with suspicion. "Open it when you get inside."

"You're not coming in?"

"No, Anastasia." As much as I'd like to. We both need to sleep.

"So when will I see you?"

"Tomorrow?"

"My boss wants me to go for a drink with him tomorrow."

What the hell does that fucker want? I must chase Welch for his report on Hyde. There's something off about him that isn't reflected in his employee records. I don't trust him one bit. "Does he, now?" I try to sound nonchalant.

"To celebrate my first week," she says quickly.

"Where?"

"I don't know."

"I could pick you up from there."

"Okay. I'll email or text you."

"Good."

We walk to the lobby door together and I watch, amused, as

she rummages around in her purse for her keys. She unlocks the door and turns to say goodbye—and I can't resist her any longer. Leaning down, I cup her chin in my fingers. I want to kiss her hard, but I hold back and trace soft kisses from her temple to her mouth. She moans and the sweet sound travels straight to my cock.

"Until tomorrow," I say, failing to keep the desire out of my voice.

"Good night, Christian," she whispers, and her longing echoes my own.

Oh, baby. Tomorrow. Not now.

"In you go," I order, and it's one of the hardest things I've ever done: letting her leave knowing that she's mine for the taking. My body ignores my noble gesture and stiffens in anticipation. I shake my head, amazed as ever by my lust for Ana.

"Laters, baby," I call after her, and turning toward the street I head to the car, determined not to look back. Once I'm inside the car, I allow myself to look. She's still there, standing on the doorstep, watching me.

Good.

Go to bed, Ana, I will her. As if she hears me, she closes the door, and Taylor starts the car to head home to Escala.

I lean back in my seat.

What a difference a day makes.

I grin. She's mine once more.

I imagine her in her apartment, opening the box. Will she be pissed? Or will she be delighted?

She'll be pissed.

She never took kindly to gifts.

Shit. Was it a step too far?

Taylor heads into the garage at Escala and we pull into the vacant parking space next to Ana's A3. "Taylor, will you deliver Miss Steele's Audi to her place tomorrow?" I hope she will accept the car, too.

"Yes, Mr. Grey."

I leave him in the garage, doing whatever he does, and head for the elevator. Once inside, I check my phone to see if she has anything to say about the gifts. Just as the elevator doors open and I step into my apartment, there's an email.

From: Anastasia Steele
Subject: iPad
Date: June 9 2011 23:56
To: Christian Grey

You've made me cry again.
I love the iPad.
I love the songs.
I love the British Library app.
I love you.
Thank you.
Good night.

Ana xx

I grin at the screen. *Happy tears, great!*
She loves it.
She loves me.

FRIDAY, JUNE 10, 2011

She loves me.

It's taken a three-hour car ride for me not to flinch at this thought. But then again, she doesn't really know me. She doesn't know what I'm capable of, or why I do what I do. No one can love a monster, no matter how compassionate they are.

I put the thought out of my mind because I don't want to dwell on the negative.

Flynn would be proud.

Quickly, I type a response to her email.

From: Christian Grey
Subject: iPad
Date: June 10 2011 00:03
To: Anastasia Steele

I'm glad you like it. I bought one for myself.

Now, if I were there, I would kiss away your tears.

But I'm not—so go to sleep.

Christian Grey
CEO, Grey Enterprises Holdings, Inc.

I want her well rested for tomorrow. I stretch, feeling a contentment that's entirely unfamiliar, and wander into my bedroom.

Looking forward to collapsing into bed, I put my phone on the nightstand and notice there's another email from her.

From: Anastasia Steele
Subject: Mr. Grumpy
Date: June 10 2011 00:07
To: Christian Grey

You sound your usual bossy and possibly tense, possibly grumpy self, Mr. Grey.

I know something that could ease that. But then, you're not here—you wouldn't let me stay, and you expect me to beg...

Dream on, Sir.

Ana xx

P.S. I also note that you included the Stalker's Anthem, "Every Breath You Take." I do enjoy your sense of humor, but does Dr. Flynn know?

And there it is. The Anastasia Steele wit. I have missed it. I sit down on the edge of the bed and compose my reply.

From: Christian Grey
Subject: Zen-Like Calm
Date: June 10 2011 00:10
To: Anastasia Steele

My Dearest Miss Steele

Spanking occurs in vanilla relationships, too, you know.

Usually consensually and in a sexual context… but I am more than happy to make an exception.

You'll be relieved to know that Dr. Flynn also enjoys my sense of humor.

Now, please go to sleep, as you won't get much tomorrow.

Incidentally—you will beg, trust me. And I look forward to it.

Christian Grey
Tense CEO, Grey Enterprises Holdings, Inc.

I watch my phone, waiting for her reply. I know she won't let this go. And, sure enough, her response appears.

From: Anastasia Steele
Subject: Good Night, Sweet Dreams
Date: June 10 2011 00:12
To: Christian Grey

Well, since you ask so nicely, and I like your delicious threat, I shall curl up with the iPad that you have so kindly given me and fall asleep browsing in the British Library, listening to the music that says it for you.

A xxx

She likes my threat? Lord, she's confusing. Then I remember her squirming in the car while we talked of spanking.

Oh, baby, it's not a threat. It's a promise.

I get up and wander into my closet to take off my jacket while I think of something to say.

She wants a softer approach; surely I can think of something. And then it comes to me.

From: Christian Grey
Subject: One more request
Date: June 10 2011 00:15
To: Anastasia Steele

Dream of me.

x

Christian Grey
CEO, Grey Enterprises Holdings, Inc.

Yes. Dream of me. I want to be the only one in her head. Not that photographer. Not her boss. Just me. I change quickly into PJ bottoms and brush my teeth.

As I slip into bed, I check my phone once more, but there's nothing from Miss Steele. She must be asleep. When I close my eyes it occurs to me that I've not thought about Leila all evening. Anastasia has been so diverting, beautiful, funny…

THE RADIO ALARM WAKES me for the first time since she left me. I've slept a soundless and dreamless sleep and I awake refreshed. My first thought is of Ana. How is she this morning? Has she changed her mind?

No. Stay positive.

Okay.

I wonder what her morning routine is?

Better.

And I get to see her this evening. I bound out of bed and into my sweats. My run will take me on my usual route to check on her building. But this time, I won't linger. I'm a stalker no more.

MY FEET POUND THE pavement. The sun is peeping through the buildings as I make my way to Ana's street. It's still quiet, but I have the Foo Fighters turned up loud and proud as I run. I wonder if I should be listening to something that's more in sync with my mood. Maybe "Feeling Good." Nina Simone's version.

Too sappy, Grey. Keep running.

I dash past Ana's building, and I don't have to stop. I'll see her later today. All of her. Feeling particularly pleased with myself, I wonder if perhaps we'll end up here tonight.

Whatever we do, it will be up to Ana. We're doing this her way.

I run up Wall Street, back home to begin my day.

"GOOD MORNING, GAIL." Even to my own ears I sound unusually hearty. Gail stops in her tracks in front of the stove and stares at me as if I've grown three heads. "I'll have scrambled eggs and toast this morning," I add and wink at her as I head toward my study. Her chin drops, but she says nothing.

Ah, speechless Mrs. Jones. This is novel.

In my study, I check emails on my computer and there's nothing that can't wait until I get into the office. My thoughts stray to Ana and I wonder if she's had breakfast.

From: Christian Grey
Subject: So Help Me...
Date: June 10 2011 08:05
To: Anastasia Steele

I do hope you've had breakfast.

I missed you last night.

Christian Grey
CEO, Grey Enterprises Holdings, Inc.

In the car, on the way to the office, I get a response.

From: Anastasia Steele
Subject: Old books...
Date: June 10 2011 08:33
To: Christian Grey

I am eating a banana as I type. I have not had breakfast for several days, so it is a step forward. I love the British Library app—I started rereading *Robinson Crusoe*... and, of course, I love you.

Now leave me alone—I am trying to work.

Anastasia Steele
Assistant to Jack Hyde, Editor, SIP

Robinson Crusoe? A man alone, stranded on a deserted island. Is she trying to tell me something?

And she loves me.

Loves. Me. And I'm surprised that those words are getting easier to hear... but not *that* easy.

So I shift my focus to what irritates me most about her email.

From: Christian Grey
Subject: Is that all you've eaten?
Date: June 10 2011 08:36
To: Anastasia Steele

You can do better than that. You're going to need your energy for begging.

Christian Grey
CEO, Grey Enterprises Holdings, Inc.

Taylor pulls up at the curb in front of Grey House.

"Sir, I'll take the Audi to Miss Steele's this morning."

"Great. Until later, Taylor. Thank you."

"Good day, sir."

In the elevator at Grey House, I read her response.

From: Anastasia Steele
Subject: Pest
Date: June 10 2011 08:39
To: Christian Grey

Mr. Grey—I am trying to work for a living—and it's you who will be begging.

Anastasia Steele
Assistant to Jack Hyde, Editor, SIP

Ha! I don't think so.

"Good morning, Andrea." I give her a friendly nod as I stride past her desk.

"Um," she stalls, but recovers quickly, because she's ever the adept PA. "Good morning, Mr. Grey. Coffee?"

"Please. Black." I close my office door and when seated at my desk respond to Ana.

From: Christian Grey
Subject: Bring It On!
Date: June 10 2011 08:42
To: Anastasia Steele

Why, Miss Steele, I love a challenge…

Christian Grey
CEO, Grey Enterprises Holdings, Inc.

I love that she's so feisty over email. Life is never boring with Ana. I lean back in my chair with my hands behind my head, trying to understand my effervescent mood. When have I ever felt this cheerful? It's frightening. She has the power to give me hope, and the power to make me despair. I know which I prefer. There's a blank space on my office wall; perhaps one of her portraits should fill the void. Before I can brood on this further, there's a knock on the door.

Andrea enters, carrying my coffee. "Mr. Grey, may I have a word?"

"Of course."

She perches on the chair opposite me, looking nervous. "Do you remember I'm not here this afternoon and I'm not in on Monday?"

I stare at her, completely blank. *What the hell?* I don't remember this. I hate it when she's not here.

"I thought I should remind you," she adds.

"Do you have someone covering for you?"

"Yes. HR is sending someone from another department. Her name is Montana Brooks."

"Okay."

"It's only a day and a half, sir."

I laugh. "Do I look that worried?"

Andrea gives me a rare smile. "Yes, Mr. Grey, you do."

"Well, whatever you're up to, I hope it's fun."

She stands. "Thank you, sir."

"Do I have anything scheduled for this weekend?"

"You have golf tomorrow with Mr. Bastille."

"Cancel it." I'd rather have fun with Ana.

"Will do. You also have the masquerade ball at your parents' place for Coping Together," Andrea reminds me.

"Oh. Damn."

"It's been in the schedule for months."

"Yes. I know. Leave that."

I wonder if Ana will come as my date?

"Okay, sir."

"Did you find someone to replace Senator Blandino's daughter?"

"Yes, sir. Her name is Sarah Hunter. She starts on Tuesday when I'm back."

"Good."

"You have a nine o'clock with Miss Bailey."

"Thanks, Andrea. Get me Welch on the line."

"Yes, Mr. Grey."

ROS IS CONCLUDING HER report on the Darfur airdrop. "Everything has gone as scheduled and early reports from the NGOs on the ground are that it's come at the right time and to the right place," Ros says. "Frankly, it's been a huge success. We're going to help so many people."

"Great. Perhaps we should do it every year where it's needed."

"It's expensive, Christian."

"I know. But it's the right thing to do. And it's only money."

She gives me a slightly exasperated look.

"Are we done?" I ask.

"For now, yes."

"Good."

She continues to regard me with curiosity.

What?

"I'm glad you're back with us," she says.

"What do you mean?"

"You know what I mean." She gets up and gathers her papers. "You've been absent, Christian." Her eyes narrow.

"I was here."

"No, you weren't. But I'm glad you're back and focused, and you seem happier." She gives me a broad smile and heads for the door.

Is it that obvious?

"I saw the photo in the paper this morning."

"Photo?"

"Yes. You and a young woman at a photo exhibition."

"Oh, yes." I can't hide my smile.

Ros nods. "I'll see you later this afternoon for the meeting with Marco."

"Sure."

She leaves, and I'm left wondering how the rest of my staff will react to me today.

BARNEY, MY TECH WIZARD and senior engineer, has produced three prototypes of the solar tablet. It's a product I hope we'll sell at a premium globally and also underwrite philanthropically in the developing world. Democratizing technology is one of my passions—making it cheap, functional, and available in the poorest nations to help bring these countries out of poverty.

Later that morning we're gathered in the lab discussing the prototypes that are scattered over the workbench. Fred, the VP of our telecom division, is making a pitch to incorporate the solar cells into the rear casing of each device.

"Why can't we incorporate them into the entire casing of the tablet, even into the screen?" I ask.

Seven heads turn my way in unison.

"Not the screen, but a cover…maybe?" says Fred.

"Expense?" Barney pipes up at the same time.

"This is blue sky, people. Don't concern yourselves with the economics," I answer. "We'll sell it as a premium brand here and practically give it away in the third world. That's the point."

The room erupts in creativity and two hours later we have three ideas about how to cover the device in solar cells.

"Of course we'll make it WiMAX-enabled for the home market," Fred states.

"And incorporate the capability for satellite internet access for Africa and India," Barney adds. "Provided we can get access." He looks quizzically toward me.

"That's a little down the line. I'm hoping we can piggyback on the EU GPS system Galileo." I know this will take a while to negotiate, but we have time. "Marco's team is looking into it."

"Tomorrow's technology today," Barney states proudly.

"Excellent." I nod in approval. I turn to my VP of procurement. "Vanessa, where are we with the conflict mineral issue? How are you dealing with it?"

LATER, WE'RE SITTING AROUND the table in my boardroom and Marco is running through the modified business plan for SIP and their contract stipulations following the signing of our revised heads of agreement yesterday.

"They want to embargo the acquisition news for a month," he says. "Something about not freaking out their authors."

"Really? Will their authors care?" I ask.

"This is a creative industry," Ros says gently.

"Whatever." And I want to roll my eyes.

"You and I have a call scheduled with Jeremy Roach, the owner, at four thirty today."

"Good. We can hash out remaining details then." My mind drifts to Anastasia. How is her day going? Has she rolled her eyes at anyone today? What are her work colleagues like? Her boss? I've asked Welch to investigate Jack Hyde; just reading Hyde's employee file, I know there's something odd about his career trajectory. He started in New York, and now he's here. Something doesn't add up. I need to know more about him, especially if Ana is working for him.

I'm also waiting for an update on Leila. Welch has nothing new to report on her whereabouts. It's like she's disappeared completely. I can only hope that wherever she is, she's in a better place.

"Their email monitoring is almost as stringent as ours," Ros says, interrupting my reverie.

"So?" I ask. "Any company worth its equity has a rigorous email policy."

"It surprises me for such a small operation. All emails are checked by the HR function."

I shrug. "I don't have an issue with that." Though I should warn Ana. "Let's go through their liabilities."

Once we've dealt with SIP, we move to the next item on the agenda. "We're going to make a tentative inquiry about the shipyard in Taiwan," Marco says.

"I don't see what we've got to lose," Ros agrees.

"My shirt and the goodwill of our workforce?"

"Christian, we don't have to do it," Ros says with a sigh.

"It makes financial sense. You know it. I know it. Let's see how far we can run with this."

My phone flashes, announcing an email from Ana.

At last!

I've been so busy I haven't managed to contact her since this morning, but she's been hovering at the edge of my consciousness all day, like a guardian angel. My guardian angel. Ever present but not intrusive.

Mine.

Grey, get a grip.

As Ros lists next steps for the Taiwan project, I read Ana's email.

From: Anastasia Steele
Subject: Bored...
Date: June 10 2011 16:05
To: Christian Grey

Twiddling my thumbs.
How are you?

What are you doing?

Anastasia Steele
Assistant to Jack Hyde, Editor, SIP

Twiddling her thumbs? The thought makes me smile as I recall her fumbling with the tape recorder when she came to interview me.

Are you gay, Mr. Grey?

Ah, sweet, innocent Ana.

No. Not gay.

I love that she's thinking about me and has taken time out of her day to make contact. It's… distracting. An unfamiliar warmth seeps into my bones. It makes me uneasy. Really uneasy. Ignoring it, I quickly type a response.

From: Christian Grey
Subject: Your thumbs
Date: June 10 2011 16:15
To: Anastasia Steele

You should have come to work for me.

You wouldn't be twiddling your thumbs.

I am sure I could put them to better use.

In fact, I can think of a number of options…

Fuck. Not now, Grey.

My eyes meet Ros's, and I sense her disapproval.

"Urgent response required," I tell her. She shares a look with Marco.

I am doing the usual humdrum mergers and acquisitions.

It's all very dry.

Your emails at SIP are monitored.

Christian Grey
Distracted CEO, Grey Enterprises Holdings, Inc.

I can't wait to see her this evening, and she's yet to email where we'll meet. It's frustrating. But we've agreed to try our relationship her way, so I put my phone down and turn my attention back to my meeting.

Patience, Grey. Patience.

We've moved on to discuss the mayor of Seattle's visit to Grey House next week, an appointment I set up when I met him earlier this month.

"Is Sam on this?" Ros asks.

"Like a rash," I respond. Sam never misses a PR opportunity.

"Okay. If you're ready I'll get Jeremy Roach on the line from SIP to go through those final details."

"Let's do it."

BACK IN MY OUTER office, Andrea's replacement is applying yet more lipstick to her scarlet mouth. I don't like it. And the color reminds me of Elena. One of the things I love about Ana is that she doesn't cake herself in lipstick, or any other makeup for that matter. Hiding my disgust, and ignoring the new girl, I head into my office. I can't even remember her name.

Fred's revised proposal for Kavanagh Media is open on my desktop, but I'm preoccupied and finding it hard to concentrate. Time is moving on and I've not heard from Anastasia; as ever, I'm waiting for Miss Steele. I check my email once more.

Nothing.

I check my phone for texts.

Nothing.

What's keeping her? I hope it's not her boss.

There's a knock on my door.

What now?

"Come in."

Andrea's replacement pokes her head around the door and, *ping*, there's an email, but it's not from Ana.

"What?" I bark, trying to remember the woman's name.

She's unfazed. "I'm just about to leave, Mr. Grey. Mr. Taylor left this for you." She holds up an envelope.

"Just leave it on the console there."

"Do you need me for anything else?"

"No. Go. Thanks." I give her a thin smile.

"Have a good weekend then, sir," she offers, simpering.

Oh, I fully intend to.

I dismiss her, but she doesn't leave. She pauses for a moment, and I realize she's expecting something from me.

What?

"I'll see you Monday," she says with an annoying, nervous giggle.

"Yes. Monday. Shut the door behind you."

Looking a little crestfallen, she does as she's told.

What was that about?

I pick up the envelope from the console. It's the key to Ana's Audi, and written in Taylor's tidy hand are the words: *Parked in allocated parking space at rear of apartment building.*

Back at my desk, I turn my attention to my emails, and finally there's one from Ana. I grin like the Cheshire Cat.

From: Anastasia Steele
Subject: You'll Fit Right In
Date: June 10 2011 17:36
To: Christian Grey

We are going to a bar called Fifty's.
The rich seam of humor that I could mine from this is endless.
I look forward to seeing you there, Mr. Grey.

A. x

Is this a reference to fifty shades?
Weird. Is she making fun of me?
Okay. Let's have some fun with this.

From: Christian Grey
Subject: Hazards
Date: June 10 2011 17:38
To: Anastasia Steele

Mining is a very, very dangerous occupation.

Christian Grey
CEO, Grey Enterprises Holdings, Inc.

Let's see what she makes of that.

From: Anastasia Steele
Subject: Hazards?
Date: June 10 2011 17:40
To: Christian Grey

And your point is?

So obtuse, Anastasia? That's not like you. But I don't want to fight.

From: Christian Grey
Subject: Merely...
Date: June 10 2011 17:42
To: Anastasia Steele

Making an observation, Miss Steele.

I'll see you shortly.

Sooners rather than laters, baby.

Christian Grey
CEO, Grey Enterprises Holdings, Inc.

Now that she's been in contact, I relax and concentrate on the Kavanagh proposal. It's good. I send it back to Fred and tell him to send it on to Kavanagh. Idly I speculate whether Kavanagh Media might be ripe for a takeover. It's a thought. I wonder what Ros and Marco would say. I shelve the idea for now and head down to the lobby, texting Taylor to let him know where I'm meeting Ana.

50'S IS A SPORTS bar. It's vaguely familiar, and I realize I've been here before with Elliot. But then Elliot is a jock, a real guy's guy, who's the life and soul of any party. This is his type of place, a shrine to team sports. I was too hotheaded to play on a team at any of my schools. I preferred more solitary pursuits like sculling and full-contact sports like kickboxing, where I could kick the shit out of someone… or have the shit kicked out of me.

Inside, it's crowded with young office workers starting their weekends with a quick drink or five, and it takes me only two seconds to spot her by the bar.

Ana.

And he's there. *Hyde.* Crowding her.

Asshole.

Her shoulders are tense. She's obviously uncomfortable.

Fuck him.

With great effort I keep my walk casual, trying to maintain my cool. When I'm by her side, I drape my arm over her shoulder and pull her toward me, freeing her from his unwanted advances.

I kiss her, just behind her ear. "Hello, baby," I whisper into her hair. She melts against me as the asshole stands taller, appraising me. I want to rip the "fuck you" expression off his rugged, smug face, but I deliberately ignore him to focus on my girl.

Hey, baby. Is this guy bothering you?

She beams at me. Eyes shining, lips moist, her hair cascading over her shoulders. She's wearing the blue blouse that Taylor bought her, and it complements her eyes and skin. Leaning in, I kiss her. Her cheeks color, but she turns to the asshole who's taken the hint and stepped back a little.

"Jack, this is Christian. Christian, Jack," she says, waving between us.

"I'm the boyfriend," I state, so there's no confusion, and hold out my hand to Hyde.

See. I can play nice.

"I'm the boss," he responds as we shake. His grip is tight, so I tighten mine.

Keep your hands off my girl.

"Ana did mention an ex-boyfriend," he says with a patronizing drawl.

"Well, no longer ex." I give him a slight fuck-off smile. "Come on, baby, time to go."

"Please, stay and join us for a drink," Hyde says, emphasizing the word "us."

"We have plans. Another time, perhaps."

Like. Never.

I don't trust him, and I want Ana far away from him. "Come," I say when I take her hand.

"See you Monday," she says as she tightens her fingers around mine. She's addressing Hyde and an attractive woman, who must be one of her colleagues. At least Ana wasn't on her own with him. The woman gives Ana a warm smile while Hyde scowls at us both. I sense his eyes boring into my back as we leave. But I don't give a fuck.

Outside, Taylor is waiting in the Q7. I open the rear door for Ana.

"Why did that feel like a pissing contest?" she asks as she gets in.

Perceptive as ever, Miss Steele.

"Because it was," I confirm and close her door.

When I'm in the car, I reach for her hand because I want to touch her and raise it to my lips. "Hi," I whisper. She looks so good. The dark circles beneath her eyes have disappeared. She's slept. She's eaten. Her healthy glow has returned. From her bright smile, I'd say she's brimming with happiness, and it washes over me.

"Hi," she says, all breathy and suggestive. Damn, I want to jump her now—though I'm sure Taylor wouldn't appreciate it if I did. I glance at him and his eyes dart to mine in the rearview mirror. He's waiting for instruction.

Well, we're doing this Ana's way.

"What would you like to do this evening?" I ask.

"I thought you said we had plans."

"Oh, I know what I'd like to do, Anastasia. I'm asking you what you want to do."

Her smile widens into a salacious grin that speaks directly to my cock.

Hot damn.

"I see. So… begging it is, then. Do you want to beg at my place or yours?" I tease.

Her face shines with humor. "I think you're being very presumptuous, Mr. Grey. But by way of a change, we could go to my apartment." She bites down on her plump lower lip and peers at me through her dark lashes.

Fuck.

"Taylor, Miss Steele's please." *And hurry!*

"Sir," Taylor acknowledges, and he pulls out into traffic.

"So how has your day been?" I ask and brush my thumb across her knuckles.

Her breath hitches. "Good. Yours?"

"Good, thank you." Yes. Really good. I've done more work today than I've done all week. I kiss her hand, because I have her to thank for that. "You look lovely."

"As do you."

Oh, baby, it's just a pretty face.

Speaking of pretty faces… "Your boss, Jack Hyde. Is he good at his job?"

She frowns and the *v* I like to kiss forms above her nose. "Why? This isn't about your pissing contest?"

"That man wants into your panties, Anastasia," I warn her, trying to sound as neutral as possible. She looks shocked. Jesus, she's so innocent. It was obvious to me and anyone who was paying attention at the bar.

"Well, he can want all he likes," she says, her tone prim. "Why are we even having this conversation? You know I have no interest in him whatsoever. He's just my boss."

"That's the point. He wants what's mine. I need to know if he's good at his job." Because if not, I'll fire his sorry ass.

She shrugs but looks down at her lap.

What? Has he tried something already?

She tells me she thinks he's good at what he does, but she sounds like she's trying to convince herself.

"Well, he'd better leave you alone, or he'll find himself on his ass on the sidewalk."

"Oh, Christian, what are you talking about? He hasn't done anything wrong."

Why is she frowning? Does he make her uncomfortable? Talk to me, Ana. Please. "He makes one move, you tell me. It's called gross moral turpitude—or sexual harassment."

"It was just a drink after work."

"I mean it. One move and he's out."

"You don't have that kind of power," she scoffs, amused. But her smile fades and she regards me with skepticism. "Do you, Christian?"

I do, actually. I smile at her.

"You're buying the company?" she whispers, and she looks appalled.

"Not exactly." This is not the reaction I was expecting, nor is the conversation going the way I thought it would.

"You've bought it. SIP. Already." Her face pales.

Christ! She's pissed.

"Possibly," I answer cautiously.

"You have or you haven't?" she demands.

Showtime, Grey. Tell her.

"Have."

"Why?" Her voice is shrill.

"Because I can, Anastasia. I need you safe."

"But you said you wouldn't interfere in my career!"

"And I won't."

She snatches her hand back. "Christian!"

Shit. "Are you mad at me?"

"Yes. Of course I'm mad at you," she yells. "I mean, what kind of responsible business executive makes decisions based on who he is currently fucking?" She glances nervously at Taylor, then glares at me, her expression full of recrimination.

And I want to admonish her for her foul mouth and for overreacting. I start to tell her so, then decide that it might not be a good idea. Her lips are set in the mulish Steele pout that I know so well… I have missed that, too.

She folds her arms in disgust.

Fuck.

She's really mad.

I glare back at her, wanting nothing more than to drag her across my knee—but, sadly, that's not an option.

Hell, I was only doing what I thought was best.

Taylor parks outside her apartment, and before he's stopped, it seems, she's out of the car.

Shit! "I think you'd better wait here," I say to Taylor, and I scramble after her. My evening may be about to take a radically different course than the one I'd planned. I may have blown it already.

When I reach her at the lobby door, she's rummaging around in her purse for keys while I stand behind her, helpless.

What to do?

"Anastasia," I entreat her as I try to remain calm.

She lets out an exaggerated sigh and turns to face me, her mouth pressed in a hard line.

Following up what she said in the car, I try for humor. "First, I haven't fucked you for a while—a long while, it feels—and second, I wanted to get into publishing. Of the four companies in Seattle, SIP is the most profitable." I keep talking about the company but what I really want to say is… *Please don't fight with me.*

"So you're my boss now?" she snaps.

"Technically, I'm your boss's boss's boss."

"And technically, it's gross moral turpitude—the fact that I am fucking my boss's boss's boss."

"At the moment, you're arguing with him." My voice is beginning to rise.

"That's because he's such an ass."

Ass. Ass!

She's calling me names! The only people who do that are Mia and Elliot.

"An ass?" Yes. Maybe I am. And suddenly I want to laugh. Anastasia called me an ass—Elliot would approve.

"Yes." She's trying to stay mad at me, but her mouth is lifting at the corners.

"An ass?" I repeat, and I cannot help my smile.

"Don't make me laugh when I'm mad at you!" she shouts, trying and failing to stay serious. I give her my best one-thousand-watt smile and she unleashes an uninhibited, spontaneous laugh that makes me feel ten feet tall.

Success!

"Just because I have a stupid damn grin on my face doesn't mean I am not mad as hell at you," she claims between giggles.

Leaning forward, I nuzzle her hair and inhale deeply. Her scent and her proximity stir my libido. I want her. "As ever, Miss Steele, you are unexpected." I gaze down, treasuring her flushed face and shining eyes. She's beautiful. "So are you going to invite me in, or am I to be sent packing for exercising my democratic right as an American citizen, entrepreneur, and consumer to purchase whatever I damn well please?"

"Have you spoken to Dr. Flynn about this?"

I laugh. Not yet. It will be a mindfuck when I do.

"Are you going to let me in or not, Anastasia?"

For a moment she looks undecided, making my heartbeat spike. But she bites her lip, then smiles and opens the door for me. I wave Taylor off and follow Ana upstairs, enjoying the fantastic view of her ass. The gentle sway of her hips as she climbs each step is beyond seductive—more so, I think, because she has no idea she's so alluring. Her innate sensuality stems from her innocence: her willingness to experiment, and her ability to trust.

Damn. I hope I still have her trust. After all, I drove her away. I will have to work hard to rebuild it. I don't want to lose her again.

Her apartment is neat and tidy, as I would expect, but it has an unused, uninhabited vibe about it. It reminds me of the gallery: it's all old brick and wood. The concrete kitchen island is a stark and novel design statement. I like it.

"Nice place," I remark with approval.

"Kate's parents bought it for her."

Eamon Kavanagh has indulged his daughter. It's a stylish place—he's chosen well. I hope Katherine appreciates it. I turn and stare at Ana as she stands by the island. I wonder how she feels living with such a well-off friend. I'm sure she pays her way… but it must be tough to play second fiddle to Katherine Kavanagh. Maybe she likes it, or maybe she finds it a struggle. She certainly doesn't squander her money on clothes. But I've remedied that; I have a closetful for her at Escala. I wonder what she'll think about that? She'll likely give me a hard time.

Don't think about that now, Grey.

Ana's studying me, her eyes dark. She licks her bottom lip, and my body lights up like a firework.

"Er… would you like a drink?" she asks.

"No thank you, Anastasia." I want you.

She clasps her hands together, seemingly at a loss and looking a little apprehensive. Do I still make her nervous? This woman can bring me to my knees, and she's the one who's nervous?

"What would you like to do, Anastasia?" I ask and move closer to her, my eyes not leaving hers. "I know what I want to do."

And we can do it here, or in your bedroom, or your bathroom. I don't care—I just want you. Now.

Her lips part as her breath hitches and her breathing quickens.

Oh, that sound is beguiling.

You want me, too, baby.

I know it.

I feel it.

She backs up against the kitchen island with nowhere else to go.

"I'm still mad at you," she asserts, but her voice is tremulous and soft. She doesn't sound mad at all. Wanton, maybe. But not mad.

"I know." I give her a wolfish grin.

Her eyes widen.

Oh, baby.

"Would you like something to eat?" she whispers.

I nod slowly. "Yes. You."

Standing over her, staring into eyes that are dark with desire, I feel the heat from her body. It's searing me. I want to be wrapped in it. Bathed in it. I want to make her scream and moan and call out my name. I want to reclaim her and wipe the memory of our breakup from her mind.

I want to make her mine. Again.

But first things first.

"Have you eaten today?" I need to know.

"I had a sandwich at lunch."

That will do. "You need to eat," I chide her.

"I'm really not hungry right now…for food."

"What are you hungry for, Miss Steele?" I lower my face so our lips are almost touching.

"I think you know, Mr. Grey."

She's not wrong. I stifle my groan and it takes all my self-control not to grab her and toss her onto the concrete counter. But I was serious when I said she'd have to beg. She has to tell me what she wants. She has to vocalize her feelings, her needs, and her desires. I want to learn what makes her happy. I lean down as if to kiss her, fooling her, and whisper in her ear instead.

"Do you want me to kiss you, Anastasia?"

She inhales sharply. "Yes."

"Where?"

"Everywhere."

"You're going to have to be a bit more specific than that. I told you I'm not going to touch you until you beg me and tell me what to do."

"Please," she pleads.

Oh no, baby. I'm not going to make this easy on you. "Please what?"

"Touch me."

"Where, baby?"

She reaches for me.

No.

The darkness erupts inside me and grips my throat with its claws. Instinctively, I step back, my heart pounding as fear courses through my body.

Don't touch me. Don't touch me.

Fuck.

"No. No," I mutter.

This is why I have rules.

"What?" She's confused.

"No." I shake my head. She knows this. I told her yesterday. I have to make her understand she can't touch me.

"Not at all?" She steps toward me and I don't know what she intends. The darkness stabs at my insides, so I take another step back and hold up my hands to ward her off.

With a smile, I beseech her, "Look. Ana…" But I can't find the right words.

Please. Don't touch me. I can't handle it.

Damn, it's frustrating.

"Sometimes you don't mind," she protests. "Perhaps I should find a marker pen, and we could map out the no-go areas."

Well, that's an approach I've not considered before. "That's not a bad idea. Where's your bedroom?" I need to move her on from this subject.

She nods to the left.

"Have you been taking your pill?"

Her face falls. "No."

What!

After all the trouble we went through to get her on the fucking pill! I can't believe she just stopped taking it.

"I see."

This is a disaster. What the hell am I going to do with her? Damn it. I need condoms. "Come, let's have something to eat," I say, thinking we can go out and I can replenish my supply.

"I thought we were going to bed. I want to go to bed with you." She sounds sullen.

"I know, baby."

But with us it's two steps forward and one step back.

This evening is not going as planned. Maybe it was too much to hope. How can she be with a fucked-up asshole who can't bear to be touched? And how can I be with someone who forgets to take their damned pill? I hate condoms.

Christ. Maybe we are incompatible.

Enough of the negative thinking, Grey. Enough!

She looks crestfallen, and part of me is suddenly absurdly pleased that she does. At least she wants me. I bound forward and grab her wrists, pinning her hands behind her and pulling her into my arms. Her slender body against the length of mine feels good. But she's slim. Too slim. "You need to eat and so do I." And you've completely thrown me by trying to touch me. I need to recover my composure, baby. "Besides… anticipation is the key to seduction, and right now I'm really into delayed gratification." Especially with no contraception.

She looks a little skeptical.

Yes, I know. I just made that up.

"I'm seduced and I want my gratification now. I'll beg. Please," she whimpers.

She is Eve herself: temptation incarnate. I tighten my hold and there's definitely less of her. It's disconcerting, more so because I know I'm to blame. "Eat. You're too slender." I kiss her forehead and release her, wondering where we can dine.

"I'm still mad that you bought SIP, and now I'm mad at you because you're making me wait." She purses her lips.

"You are one angry little madam, aren't you?" I state, knowing she won't understand the compliment. "You'll feel better after a good meal."

"I know what I'll feel better after."

"Anastasia Steele, I'm shocked." I feign outrage and hold my palm against my heart.

"Stop teasing me. You don't fight fair." All of a sudden her stance changes. "I could cook something," she says, "except we'll have to go shopping."

"Shopping?"

"For groceries."

"You have no food here?" For heaven's sake—no wonder she hasn't eaten! "Let's go shopping, then." I stride to the door of her apartment and open it wide, gesturing for her to exit. This could work in my favor. I just need to find a pharmacy or a convenience store.

"Okay, okay," she says and scurries out the door.

As we walk down the street hand in hand, I wonder at how, in her presence, I can run through an entire spectrum of emotion: from angry, to carnal, to fearful, to playful. Before Ana, I was calm and stable, but boy, was my life monotonous. That changed the moment she fell into my office. Being with her is like being inside a storm, my feelings colliding and crashing together, then surging and ebbing away. I hardly know which way is up. Ana's never dull. I just hope what's left of my heart can cope.

We walk two blocks to Ernie's Supermarket. It's small and packed with too many people; mostly singles, I think, judging from the contents of their shopping baskets. And here I am, single no more.

I like that idea.

I follow in Ana's wake, holding a wire basket and enjoying the view of her ass, all tight and taut in her jeans. I especially like it when she leans over the vegetable counter and picks up some onions. The fabric stretches across her behind and her blouse rides up, revealing a sliver of pale, flawless skin.

Oh, what I'd like to do to that ass.

Ana is looking at me, perplexed and asking me questions about when I was last in a supermarket? I have no idea. She wants to cook stir-fry because it's quick. Quick, huh? I smirk and follow her through the store, enjoying how adept she is at choosing her ingredients: a squeeze of a tomato here, the sniff of a pepper there. As we walk to the checkout she asks me about my staff and how long they've been with me. *Why does she want to know?* "Taylor, four years, I think. Mrs. Jones, about the same."

I ask her a question of my own. "Why didn't you have any food in the apartment?"

Her expression clouds. "You know why."

"It was you who left me," I remind her. If you'd stayed we might have worked things out and avoided all the misery.

"I know," she says, sounding contrite.

I stand in line beside her. There's a woman in front of us, trying to wrangle two small children, one of whom is whining incessantly.

Jesus. How do people do this?

We could have gone out to eat. There are enough restaurants around here. "Do you have anything to drink?" I ask, because after this real-life experience, I'm going to need alcohol.

"Beer, I think."

"I'll get some wine."

I put as much distance as I can between me and the screaming boy, but after a brief look around the store I realize there's no alcohol or condoms for sale here.

Damn it.

"There's a good liquor store next door," Anastasia says when I return to the line which doesn't seem to have moved and is still dominated by the wailing child.

"I'll see what they have."

Relieved to be out of the hellhole that is Ernie's, I notice a small convenience store beside Liquor Locker. Inside, I find the only two remaining packs of condoms.

Thank heavens. Two packs of two.

Four fucks if I'm lucky.

I can't help my grin. That should be enough even for the insatiable Miss Steele.

I grab them both and pay the old guy behind the counter and leave. I'm lucky in the liquor store, too. It has an excellent selection of wine and I find an above-average pinot grigio in the fridge.

Anastasia is staggering out of the grocery store when I return.

"Here, let me carry that." I take both grocery bags and we walk back to her apartment.

She tells me a little about what she's been doing during the week. She's obviously enjoying her new job. She doesn't mention my takeover of SIP, and I'm grateful. And for my part I don't mention her asshole of a boss.

"You look very domestic," she says with ill-concealed amusement when we're back in her kitchen.

She's laughing at me. Again. "No one has ever accused me of that before." I place the bags on the kitchen island and she sets to work unloading them. I grab the wine. The grocery store was enough reality for today. Now, where would she keep a corkscrew?

"This place is still so new. I think the opener is in that drawer there." She points using her chin. I smile at her multitasking and locate the corkscrew. I'm pleased that she hasn't been drowning her sorrows during my absence. I've seen what happens when she gets drunk.

When I turn to look at her, she's blushing.

"What are you thinking about?" I ask as I shrug out of my jacket and toss it on the couch. I make my way back to the waiting bottle of wine.

"How little I know you."

"You know me better than anyone." She can certainly read me like no one else. It's unsettling. I open the bottle, mimicking the cheesy flourish of the waiter in Portland.

"I don't think that's true," she responds as she continues to unpack the bags.

"It is, Anastasia. I'm a very, very private person." It comes with the territory, doing what I do. *What I did.*

I pour two glasses and hand one to her.

"Cheers." I raise my glass.

"Cheers." She takes a sip and then starts busying herself in the kitchen. She's in her element. I remember her telling me how she used to cook for her dad.

"Can I help you with that?" I ask.

She gives me a sideways I've-got-this look. "No, it's fine. Sit."

"I'd like to help."

She can't hide her surprise. "You can chop the vegetables." It sounds like she's making a huge concession. Perhaps she's right to be wary. I know nothing about cooking. My mother, Mrs. Jones, and my submissives—some with more success than others—have all fulfilled that role.

"I don't cook," I tell her while examining the razor-sharp knife she hands me.

"I imagine you don't need to." She places a chopping board and some red peppers in front me.

What the hell am I supposed to do with these? They are such a weird shape.

"You've never chopped a vegetable?" Anastasia asks in disbelief.

"No."

She looks smug all of a sudden.

"Are you smirking at me?"

"It appears this is something that I can do and you can't. Let's face it, Christian, I think this is a first. Here—I'll show you."

She brushes past me, her arm touching mine, and my body springs to life.

Christ.

I step out of her way.

"Like this." She demonstrates, slicing into the red pepper and removing all the seeds and shit from the inside with one smooth twirl of her knife.

"Looks simple enough."

"You shouldn't have any trouble with it." Her tone is teasing but ironic. Does she think I'm not capable of chopping a vegetable? With careful precision, I start to slice.

Damn, these seeds get everywhere. It's more difficult than I thought. Ana made it look easy. She pushes past me, her thigh brushing against my leg as she collects the ingredients. It's deliberate, I'm sure, but I try to ignore the effect she's having on my libido, and I continue to slice with care. This blade is evil. She moves past me again, this time skimming her hip against me, then again, another touch, and all below my waist. My cock approves, big-time. "I know what you're doing, Anastasia."

"I think it's called cooking," she says with disingenuous sincerity.

Oh. Playful Anastasia. Is she finally realizing the power she has over me?

Grabbing another knife, she joins me at the chopping board, peeling and slicing garlic, shallots, and French beans. She takes every opportunity to bump into me. She's not subtle.

"You're quite good at this," I concede as I start on my second pepper.

"Chopping?" She bats her eyelashes. "Years of practice," she states and brushes up against me with her behind.

That's it. Enough.

She takes the vegetables and places them beside the gently smoking wok.

"If you do that again, Anastasia, I'm going to take you on the kitchen floor."

"You'll have to beg me first," she counters.

"Is that a challenge?"

"Maybe."

Oh, Miss Steele. Bring it on.

I put down the knife and meander over to where she's standing, keeping her pinned with my gaze. Her lips part as I lean past her, an inch away, but I don't touch her. With a twist, I switch off the gas for the wok. "I think we'll eat later." *Because right now I'm going to fuck your brains out.* "Put the chicken in the fridge."

Swallowing hard, she picks up the bowl of diced chicken, rather clumsily places a plate over the top, and puts the whole thing in the fridge. I step up behind her silently so that when she turns I'm right in front of her.

"So, you're going to beg?" she whispers.

"No, Anastasia." I shake my head. "No begging." I look down at her, lust and need thickening my blood.

Fuck, I want to be buried in her.

I watch as her pupils dilate and her cheeks flush with desire. She wants me. I want her. She bites her lip and I can bear it no more. Grabbing her hips, I pull her against my growing erection. Her hands are in my hair and she's pulling me down to her mouth. I push her against the fridge and kiss her hard.

She tastes so good, so sweet.

She moans into my mouth and it's like a wake-up call that makes me harder still. I move my hand into her hair, pulling her head back so I can angle my tongue deeper into her mouth. Her tongue wrestles with mine.

Fuck—it's erotic, raw, intense. I pull back.

"What do you want, Anastasia?"

"You."

"Where?"

"Bed."

Needing no further prompting, I scoop her into my arms and carry her into her bedroom. I want her naked and yearning beneath me. Putting her gently on the floor, I switch on her bedside light and draw her curtains. As I glance through the window to the street below, I realize this is indeed the room I stared at during my silent vigils, from my stalker's hideout.

She was here, alone, curled up in her bed.

When I turn, she's watching me. Wide-eyed. Waiting. Wanting.

"Now what?" I ask.

She flushes.

And I stay absolutely still.

"Make love to me," she says after a beat.

"How? You have got to tell me, baby."

She licks her lips, a nervous gesture, and lust surges through me.

Shit—focus, Grey.

"Undress me," she says.

Yes! Hooking my index finger into the top of her blouse, careful not to touch her soft skin, I tug gently, forcing her to step toward me. "Good girl."

Her breasts rise and fall as her breathing accelerates and her dark eyes are full of carnal promise. Deftly I start to unbutton her blouse. She puts her hands on my arms—to steady herself, I think—and glances at me.

Yeah, that's fine, baby. Don't touch my chest.

I undo the last button, slip the blouse off her shoulders, and let it fall to the floor. Making a conscious effort not to touch her beautiful breasts, I reach down to the waistband of her jeans. I undo the top button and pull down the zipper.

I resist the urge to throw her onto the bed. This is going to be a waiting game. She needs to talk to me. "Tell me what you want, Anastasia."

"Kiss me from here to here." She trails her finger from the base of her ear down her throat.

My pleasure, Miss Steele.

Smoothing her hair out of the way, I gather her soft tresses in my hand and pull her head gently to the side, exposing her slender neck. Leaning in, I nuzzle her ear and she squirms as I trail soft kisses following the path of her finger and back again. She makes a soft noise in the back of her throat.

It's arousing.

Boy, I want to lose myself in her. Rediscover her.

"My jeans… and panties," she rasps, breathy and flustered, and I grin against her throat. She's getting the idea.

Talk to me, Ana.

I kiss her throat one final time and kneel down in front of her, taking her by surprise. I push my thumbs into the waistband of her jeans and her panties and slowly pull them down. Sitting back on my knees, I admire her long legs and delectable ass as she steps out of her shoes and pants. Her eyes meet mine, and I await my command.

"What now, Anastasia?"

"Kiss me," she answers, her voice barely audible.

"Where?"

"You know where."

I stifle my smile. She really can't say the word.

"Where?" I coax.

She blushes once more, but with a determined yet mortified expression, she points to the top of her thighs.

"Oh, with pleasure," I chuckle, enjoying her embarrassment. Slowly I let my fingers travel up her legs until my hands are at her hips, then I tug her forward, onto my mouth.

Fuck. I smell her arousal.

I'm already uncomfortable in my jeans, but suddenly they're several sizes too small. I push my tongue through her pubic hair, wondering if I'll ever persuade her to get rid of this, but I find my goal and begin tasting her.

Lord, she's sweet. So fucking sweet.

She groans and fists her fingers in my hair and I don't stop. Swirling my tongue, around and around, teasing and testing her.

"Christian, please," she begs.

I stop.

"Please what, Anastasia?"

"Make love to me."

"I am," I answer, and blow gently on her clitoris.

"No. I want you inside me."

"Are you sure?"

"Please."

No. I'm having too much fun. I continue the slow, lascivious torture of my exquisite, precious girl.

"Christian—please!" she moans.

I release her and stand, my mouth wet from her arousal, and stare down at her through hooded eyes.

"Well?" I ask.

"Well what?" she pants.

"I'm still dressed."

She seems at a loss, not understanding, and I hold my arms out in surrender.

Take me—I'm yours.

She reaches for my shirt.

Shit. No. I step back.

I forget myself.

"Oh no," I protest. I mean my jeans, baby. She blinks as she realizes what I'm asking and suddenly drops to her knees.

Whoa! Ana. What are you doing?

Rather awkwardly—her usual fingers and thumbs—she undoes my waistband and fly and tugs my jeans down.

Ah! My cock has some room.

I step out of my pants and remove my socks while she stays kneeling in her submissive position on the floor. What is she trying to do to me? Once I've dropped my pants, she reaches up and grabs my erection and squeezes me tightly like I've shown her.

Fuck.

She pushes her hand back. Ah! Almost too far. Almost painfully. I groan and tense and close my eyes; the sight of her on her knees and the feel of her hand around me is nearly too much. Suddenly, her warm, wet mouth is around me. She sucks hard.

"Ah. Ana. Whoa, gently." As I cup her head she pushes me deeper into her mouth, sheathing her teeth with her lips, pressing down on me. "Fuck," I whisper in veneration, and I flex my hips so I'm deeper in her mouth. That feels so good. She does it over and over, and it's beyond arousing. She swirls her tongue around the end, repeatedly, teasing me. She's all tit for tat today. I groan, reveling in the feel of her adept mouth and tongue.

Christ. She's too good at this. She takes me deep into her mouth once more.

"Ana, that's enough. No more," I insist through clenched teeth.

She's unraveling my control. I do not want to come now; I want to be inside her when I explode, but she ignores me and does it again and again.

Fucking tease.

"Ana, you've made your point. I do not want to come in your mouth," I grunt. And still she disobeys me.

Enough, woman.

Grasping her shoulders, I drag her to her feet, lift her quickly, and toss her onto her bed. I reach for my jeans and fish out a condom from the back pocket and dispense with my shirt, dragging it over my head and leaving it beside my jeans. She's lying sprawled and wanton on the bed.

"Take your bra off." She sits up and hurriedly does as she's told, for once.

"Lie down. I want to look at you."

She lies back on her sheets, eyes on me. Her hair is tousled and free, a luscious chestnut halo spilled across the pillow. Her body is flushed a delicate pink with arousal. Her nipples are hard, calling to me; her long legs are parted.

She's stunning.

I rip the foil packet open and roll on the rubber. She watches my every move, still panting. Waiting for me.

"You're a fine sight, Anastasia Steele."

And you're mine. Again.

Crawling up the bed, I kiss her ankles, the insides of her knees, her thighs, her hip, her soft belly; my tongue swirls around her navel and she rewards me with a loud moan. I lick the underside of one breast, then the other. And take her nipple in my mouth, teasing it, elongating it as it hardens between my lips. I tug hard, and she writhes brazenly beneath me, calling out.

Patience, baby.

Releasing that nipple, I lavish my attention on its twin.

"Christian, please."

"Please what?" I murmur between her breasts, enjoying her need.

"I want you inside me."

"Do you, now?"

"Please." She's all breathy and desperate, just how I like her.

I push her legs apart with my knees. Oh, I want you, too, baby. I hover over her, poised and ready. I want to savor this moment, this moment when I reclaim her beautiful body, reclaim my beautiful girl. Her dark, smoky eyes meet mine and slowly, slowly, I sink into her.

Fuck. She feels so good. So tight. So right.

She tilts her pelvis up to meet me, throws her head back, her chin in the air, and her mouth is open in soundless adulation. She grasps my upper arms and groans without restraint. What a wonderful sound it is. I place my hands around her head to hold her in place, ease out of her, then slide into her again. Her fingers find my hair, tugging and twisting, and I move slowly, feeling her tight, wet warmth around me as I relish every single fucking inch of her.

Her eyes are dark, her mouth slack, as she pants beneath me. She looks gorgeous.

"Faster, Christian, faster. Please," she pleads.

Your wish is my command, baby.

My mouth finds hers, claiming that, too, and I start to move, really move, pushing and pushing. She's so damned beautiful. I have missed this. Missed everything about her. She feels like home. She *is* home. She's everything. And I lose myself, burying myself in her over and over again.

She starts building around me, reaching her peak.

Oh, baby, yes. Her legs tense. She's close. So am I.

"Come on, baby. Give it to me," I whisper through my gritted teeth.

She cries out as she detonates around me, clenching and drawing me deep inside her, and I come, pouring my life and soul into her.

"Ana! Oh, fuck—Ana!"

I collapse on her, pressing her into the mattress, and bury my face in her neck, inhaling her delicious, intoxicating Ana perfume.

She's mine once more.

Mine.

No one will take her away from me, and I'll do everything in my power to keep her.

Once I've caught my breath I lean up and take her hands in mine as her eyes flutter open. They are the bluest of blue, clear and sated. She gives me a shy smile and I trail the tip of my nose down the length of hers, trying to find the words to express my gratitude. In lieu of any suitable words, I offer her a swift kiss as I reluctantly ease out of her. "I've missed this."

"Me, too," she says.

I grip her chin and kiss her once more.

Thank you, thank you, thank you for giving me a second chance.

"Don't leave me again," I whisper. *Ever.* And I'm in the confessional, disclosing a dark secret: *my need for her.*

"Okay," she answers with a tender smile that flips my heart into overdrive. With one simple word she stitches my torn soul together. I'm elated.

My fate is in your hands, Ana. It's been in your hands since I met you.

"Thank you for the iPad," she adds, interrupting my fanciful thoughts. It's the first gift I've given her that she's accepted with grace.

"You're most welcome, Anastasia."

"What's your favorite song on there?"

"Now, that would be telling," I tease her. I think it might be the Coldplay, because it's the most apt.

My stomach growls. I'm starving, and it's not a condition I tolerate well. "Come cook me some food, wench. I'm famished." I sit up and pull her onto my lap.

"Wench?" she repeats, giggling.

"Wench. Food. Now. Please," I order, like the caveman I am, while nuzzling her hair.

"Since you ask so nicely, sire, I'll get right on it."

She wriggles in my lap as she gets up.

Ow!

When she climbs off the bed she shifts her pillow. Beneath it is a rather sad, much deflated helicopter balloon. I pick it up and look at her, wondering where it's from.

"That's my balloon," she stresses.

Oh yes, Andrea sent a balloon with flowers when Ana and

Katherine moved into this apartment. What is it doing here? "In your bed?"

"Yes. It's been keeping me company."

"Lucky *Charlie Tango*."

She returns my smile as she wraps a robe around her beautiful body.

"My balloon," she warns before she sashays out of the bedroom.

Proprietary, Miss Steele!

Once she's left I remove the condom, knot it, and toss it in the trash basket at Ana's bedside. I fall back onto the pillows, examining the balloon. She kept it and slept with it. Every time I stood outside her apartment pining for her, she was curled up in this bed and pining for me, holding this.

She loves me.

I'm suddenly awash with mixed, bewildered emotions and panic rising in my throat.

How can this be?

Because she doesn't know you, Grey.

Shit.

Don't dwell on the negative. Flynn's words fog my brain. *Focus on the positive.*

Well, she's mine once more. I just have to keep her. Hopefully we'll have the whole weekend together to get to know each other again.

Hell. I have the Coping Together Ball tomorrow.

I could skip it—but then my mother would never forgive me.

I wonder if Ana will accompany me?

She'll need a mask if she agrees.

On the floor, I find my phone and text Taylor. I know he's seeing his daughter in the morning, but I hope he can source a mask.

I'm going to need a mask for
Anastasia for tomorrow's event.
Do you think you can source something?

TAYLOR
Yes, sir.
I know just the place.

Excellent.

TAYLOR
What color?

Silver or dark blue.

And as I text I have an idea, which may or may not work.

Could you get me a lipstick, too?

TAYLOR
Any particular color?

No. I'll leave that to you.

ANA CAN COOK. The stir-fry is delicious. I'm calmer now that I've had something to eat and I can't remember being this casual or relaxed with her. We're both sitting on the floor, listening to music from my iPod, as we eat and sip chilled pinot grigio. What's more, it's gratifying to see her devour her food. She's as hungry as I am.

"This is good." I'm appreciating every forkful.

She glows in response to my compliment and tucks a stray strand of unruly hair behind her ear. "I usually do all the cooking. Kate isn't a great cook." She's cross-legged beside me, her legs on display. Her rather worn robe is a fetching shade of cream. When she leans forward it hangs open and I glimpse the soft swell of her breast.

Grey, behave.

"Did your mother teach you?" I ask.

"Not really." She laughs. "By the time I was interested in

learning how to, my mom was living with Husband Number Three in Mansfield, Texas. And Ray, well, he would've lived on toast and takeout if it weren't for me."

"Why didn't you stay in Texas with your mom?"

"Her husband, Steve, and I—" She stops, and her face clouds with what I assume is an unpleasant memory. I regret asking her and want to change the subject, but she continues. "We didn't get along. And I missed Ray. Her marriage to Steve didn't last long. She came to her senses, I think. She never talks about him," she adds quietly.

"So you stayed in Washington with your stepfather."

"I lived very briefly in Texas. Then went back to Ray."

"Sounds like you looked after him."

"I suppose," she says.

"You're used to taking care of people."

It should be the other way around.

She turns to study my face. "What is it?" she asks, concerned.

"I want to take care of you." In every way. It's a simple statement, but it says everything for me.

She's taken aback. "I've noticed," she says wryly. "You just go about it in a strange way."

"It's the only way I know how." I'm feeling my way in this relationship. It's new to me. I don't know the rules. And right now, all I want is to take care of Ana and give her the world.

"I'm still mad at you for buying SIP."

"I know, but you being mad, baby, wouldn't stop me."

"What am I going to say to my work colleagues, to Jack?" She sounds exasperated. But an image of Hyde at the bar, leaning over her, leering, crowding her, springs to mind.

"That fucker better watch himself," I grumble.

"Christian. He's my boss."

Not if I have anything to do with it.

She's scowling at me and I don't want her mad. We're having such a chill time. *What do you do to chill out?* she asked me during the interview. Well, Ana, this is what I do: eat chicken stir-fry with you while we're sitting on the floor. She's still fretting, dwelling on her work situation, no doubt, and what she should tell them about GEH acquiring SIP.

I offer a simple solution. "Don't tell them."

"Don't tell them what?"

"That I own it. The heads of agreement was signed yesterday. The news is embargoed for four weeks while the management at SIP makes some changes."

"Oh." She looks alarmed. "Will I be out of a job?"

"I sincerely doubt it." Not if you want to stay.

Her eyes narrow. "If I leave and find another job, will you buy that company, too?"

"You're not thinking of leaving, are you?" Jesus, I'm about to spend a small fortune on acquiring this firm and she's talking about leaving!

"Possibly. I'm not sure you've given me a great deal of choice."

"Yes, I will buy that company, too."

This could get expensive.

"Don't you think you're being a tad overprotective?" There's a hint of sarcasm in her voice.

Maybe…

She's right.

"Yes. I am fully aware of how this looks," I concede.

"Paging Dr. Flynn," she says, rolling her eyes. And I want to reprimand her for that, but she stands and holds her hand out for my empty bowl. "Would you like dessert?" she says with an insincere smile.

"Now you're talking!" I grin, ignoring her attitude.

You can be dessert, baby.

"Not me," she says quickly, as if she can read my mind. "We have ice cream. Vanilla," she adds and smiles as if she's privy to some inside joke.

Oh, Ana. This just gets better and better.

"Really? I think we could do something with that." This is going to be fun. I rise to my feet in anticipation of what's to come and who's to come.

Her.

Me.

Both of us.

"Can I stay?" I ask.

"What do you mean?"

"The night."

"I assumed that you would."

"Good. Where's the ice cream?"

"In the oven." Her smirk is back.

Oh, Anastasia Steele, my palm is twitching.

"Sarcasm is the lowest form of wit, Miss Steele. I could still take you across my knee."

She arches a brow. "Do you have those silver ball things?"

I want to laugh. This is good news. It means she's amenable to the occasional spanking. But that's for another time. I pat down my shirt and jeans pockets as if in search for some kegel balls. "Funnily enough, I don't carry a spare set around with me. Not much call for them in the office."

She gasps with faux outrage. "I'm very glad to hear it, Mr. Grey, and I thought you said that sarcasm was the lowest form of wit."

"Well, Anastasia, my new motto is 'If you can't beat 'em, join 'em.'"

Her mouth drops open. And she's dumbfounded.

Yes!

Why is it so much fun to spar with her?

I head toward the fridge, grinning like the fool that I am, open the freezer door, and pull out a pint of vanilla ice cream. "This will do just fine." I hold up the container. "Ben. And. Jerry's. And. Ana." From the cutlery drawer, I grab a spoon.

When I look up, Ana has a greedy look and I don't know if it's for me or the ice cream. I hope it's for a combination of both.

It's playtime, baby.

"I hope you're warm. I'm going to cool you down with this. Come." I hold out my hand, and I'm thrilled when she takes it. She wants to play, too.

The light from her bedside lamp is insipid and her room's a little dark. She might have preferred this ambiance at one time, but judging by her behavior earlier this evening, she seems less shy and more comfortable with her nudity. I place the ice cream on her bedside table and drag the duvet and pillows off the bed and onto the floor. "You have a change of sheets, don't you?"

She nods, watching me from the threshold of her room. *Charlie Tango* lies crumpled on the bed. "Don't mess with my balloon," she warns when I pick it up. I let it go and watch as it floats to the duvet on the floor.

"Wouldn't dream of it, baby, but I do want to mess with you and these sheets." We're going to get sticky and so is her bedding.

Now to the important question: Will she or won't she? "I want to tie you up," I whisper. In the silence that stretches between us I hear her soft gasp.

Oh, that sound.

"Okay," she says.

"Just your hands. To the bed. I need you still."

"Okay," she repeats.

I stalk toward her, our eyes locked. "We'll use this." I grab the sash from her robe, tug gently, and her robe opens, revealing a naked Ana; a further tug and the sash is free. With a gentle push at the shoulders, her robe falls to the floor. She doesn't take her eyes off mine and she doesn't make any attempt to cover herself.

Well done, Ana.

My knuckles graze her cheek; her face is smooth like satin beneath my touch. I give her a quick peck on the lips. "Lie on the bed, faceup."

Showtime, baby.

I sense Ana's anticipation as she does what she's told, lying down on the bed for me. Standing over her, I take a moment to admire her.

My girl.

My stunning girl. Long legs, narrow waist, perfect tits. Her flawless skin is radiant in the dusky light and her eyes glint darkly with carnal longing as she waits.

I'm a lucky guy.

My body stiffens in agreement.

"I could look at you all day, Anastasia."

The mattress dips as I crawl onto it and straddle her. "Arms above your head," I demand. She complies immediately, and using the sash, I fasten her wrists together, then to the metal spindles of her headboard.

There.

What a mighty fine sight she is…

I give her a quick and grateful peck on the lips and climb off the bed. Once I'm standing, I pull off my shirt and jeans and place a condom on the bedside table.

Now. What to do?

At the end of the bed once more, I grab her ankles and pull her down the mattress so that her arms are fully extended. The less she can move, the more intense the sensations will be.

"That's better," I mutter to myself.

Grabbing the ice cream and spoon, I straddle her again. She bites her lip as I lift the lid and try to scoop out a spoonful. "Hmm, it's still quite hard." I contemplate smearing some of this on me and inserting myself into her mouth. But as I taste how cold it is, I fear it might have a negative, shriveling effect on my body.

That would be inconvenient.

"Delicious." I lick my lips for effect as it melts in my mouth. "Amazing how good plain old vanilla can taste." I watch her and she grins at me, her expression luminous. "Want some?"

She nods—a little uncertain, I think.

I take another spoonful and offer her the contents so that she opens her mouth. I change my mind and pop it into my mouth. *It's like taking candy from a baby.* "This is too good to share," I declare, teasing her.

"Hey," she starts.

"Why, Miss Steele, do you like your vanilla?"

"Yes," she exclaims and surprises me by trying to buck me off, but my weight is no match for her.

I laugh. "Getting feisty, are we? I wouldn't do that if I were you."

She stills. "Ice cream," she whines, pouting in frustration.

"Well, as you've pleased me so much today, Miss Steele." I scoop some more onto the spoon and present it to her. She regards me with amused uncertainty, but she parts her lips and I acquiesce, tipping the vanilla into her mouth. My erection hardens as I imagine her lips around me.

All in good time, Grey.

Gently, I ease the spoon from her mouth and scoop up more ice cream. She takes the second spoonful greedily. It's a little runnier, as it's beginning to melt from the warmth of my hand around the tub. Slowly, I feed her another spoonful.

"Hmm, well, this is one way to ensure you eat. Force-feed you. I could get used to this."

She clamps her mouth shut when I offer her more and there's a defiant gleam in her eye as she shakes her head. She's had enough. I tip the spoon and oh-so-slowly the melted ice cream drips onto her throat and as I move the spoon the drips fall on her sternum. Her mouth opens.

Oh yes, baby.

Bending down, I lick her clean with my tongue.

"Mmm. Tastes even better off you, Miss Steele."

She tries to flex her arms, pulling against her robe tie, but it holds, keeping her in place. The next spoonful I dribble artfully over her breasts and nipples, watching with fascination as each nipple hardens under the cold assault. With the back of the spoon I spread the vanilla over each pebbled peak and she squirms beneath me.

"Cold?" I ask, and not waiting for an answer, I gorge myself, licking and lapping wherever there are rivulets of ice cream, sucking at her breasts, elongating her nipples further. She closes her eyes and groans.

"Want some?" I take a large mouthful, swallowing some, then kissing her, thrusting my tongue and ice cream into her waiting mouth.

Ben. And. Jerry's. And. Ana.

Exquisite.

I sit up and scoot back so I'm straddling her thighs and dribble melted ice cream off the spoon from the bottom of her sternum and down the center of her abdomen. I leave a large dollop of vanilla in her navel. Her eyes spring open in heated surprise.

"Now, you've done this before," I warn. "You're going to have to stay still, or there will be ice cream all over the bed." I pop a large spoonful of vanilla into my mouth and return to her breasts, sucking each of her nipples in turn with my cool lips and tongue. I crawl down her body, following the melted ice cream, lapping it up. She writhes beneath me, her hips pulsing in a familiar rhythm.

Oh, baby, if you kept still you'd feel so much more.

I devour what's left of the ice cream in her navel using my tongue.

She's sticky. But not everywhere.

Yet.

I kneel between her thighs and trail another spoonful of ice cream down her belly and into her pubic hair, to my ultimate goal. I dribble the remaining vanilla onto her swollen clitoris. She cries out and tenses her legs.

"Hush now." Leaning down, I slowly lick and suck her clean.

"Oh. Please. Christian."

"I know, baby, I know," I whisper against her sensitive skin but continue my lascivious invasion. Her legs tense again. She's close.

Abandoning the tub of vanilla so that it falls to the floor, I ease one finger inside her, then another, enjoying how wet, warm, and welcoming her body feels, and concentrate on her sweet, sweet spot, caressing her, feeling her, knowing she's nearly there. Her climax is imminent.

"Just here," I murmur as my fingers slowly pump in and out of her.

She lets out a strangled cry as her body convulses around my fingers.

Yes.

I withdraw my hand and reach over for the foil packet. And even though I hate these things, it takes only a second to put on. I hover over her while she's still in the throes of her orgasm and thrust into her. "Oh yes!" I moan.

She's heaven.

My heaven.

But she's sticky. All over. My skin is sticking to hers and it's disconcerting. I withdraw and flip her onto her elbows and knees. "This way," I mutter and reach forward to undo the sash, freeing her hands. When she's free I pull her up so she's sitting astride me: her back to my front. I palm her breasts and tug on her nipples as she groans and tilts her head back so that it's resting on my shoulder. I nuzzle her neck and begin flexing my hips, driving deeper inside her. She smells of apples and vanilla and Ana.

My favorite fragrance.

"Do you know how much you mean to me?" I whisper into her ear as her head is thrown back in ecstasy.

"No," she breathes.

I gently wrap my fingers around her jaw and throat, stilling her. "Yes you do. I'm not going to let you go."

Never.

I love you.

"You are mine, Anastasia."

"Yes, yours."

"I take care of what's mine," I whisper, and my teeth graze her earlobe.

She cries out.

"That's right, baby, I want to hear you."

I want to take care of you.

I curl my arm around her waist, holding her against me while I grasp her hip with my other hand. And I continue to thrust inside her. She rises and falls with me, crying out, moaning, groaning. Sweat beads on my back, on my forehead, and on my chest, so we're slipping and sliding against each other as she rides me. She fists her hands and stops moving, her legs braced around me, her eyes closed as she lets out a silent cry.

"Come on, baby," I growl through clenched teeth, and she comes, screaming a garbled version of my name. I let go, coming inside her and losing all sense of self.

We sink onto the bed and I wrap her in my arms as we lie in

a sticky, sugary, panting mess together. I take a deep breath as her hair brushes against my lips.

Will it always be this way?

Mind-blowing.

I close my eyes and enjoy this lucid, quiet moment of peace.

After a while she stirs. "What I feel for you frightens me," she says, a little hoarse.

"Me, too, baby." More than you know.

"What if you leave me?"

What? Why would I leave her? I've been lost without her. "I'm not going anywhere. I don't think I could ever have my fill of you, Anastasia."

She turns in my arms and studies me, her eyes dark and intense, and I have no idea what she's thinking. She leans up and kisses me, a soft, tender kiss.

What the hell is she thinking?

I tuck a wisp of hair behind her ear. I have to make her believe I'm here for the long haul, for as long as she'll have me. "I've never felt the way I felt when you left, Anastasia. I would move heaven and earth to avoid feeling like that again."

The nightmares. The guilt. The despair sucking me into the abyss, drowning me.

Shit. Pull yourself together, Grey.

No. I never want to feel like that again.

She kisses me once more, a gentle, beseeching kiss, comforting me.

Don't think about it, Grey. Think about something else.

I remember my parents' summer ball. "Will you come with me to my father's summer party tomorrow? It's an annual charity thing. I said I'd go." I hold my breath.

This is a date.

A real date.

"Of course I'll come." Ana's face lights up but then falls.

"What?"

"Nothing."

"Tell me," I insist.

"I have nothing to wear."

Yes. You do. "Don't be mad, but I still have all those clothes for you at home. I'm sure there are a couple of dresses in there."

"Do you, now?" She purses her lips.

"I couldn't get rid of them."

"Why?"

You know why, Ana. I caress her hair, willing her to understand. I wanted you back and I kept them for you.

She shakes her head, resigned. "You are, as ever, challenging, Mr. Grey."

I laugh because it's true and also because it's something I might say to her.

Her expression lightens. "I'm gooey. I need a shower."

"We both do."

"Sadly, there's no room for two. You go and I'll change this bedding."

HER BATHROOM IS THE size of my shower, and this has to be the smallest shower cubicle I've ever been in; I'm practically face to face with the showerhead. However, I discover the source of her fragrant hair. Green apple shampoo. As the water trickles over me, I open the lid and, closing my eyes, take a long sniff.

Ana.

I may have to add this to Mrs. Jones's shopping list. When I open my eyes, Ana is staring at me, hands on hips. To my disappointment, she's wearing her robe.

"This shower is small," I complain.

"I told you. Were you smelling my shampoo?"

"Maybe." I grin.

She laughs and hands me a towel that is designed with the spines of classic books. Ana is ever the bibliophile. I wrap it around my waist and give her a swift kiss. "Don't be long. That's not a request."

Lying in her bed, waiting for her return, I look around her room. It doesn't feel lived in. Three walls are stark exposed brick, the fourth smooth concrete, but there's nothing on them. Ana's not had time to make this place home. She's been too miserable to unpack. And that's my fault.

I close my eyes.

I want her happy.

Happy Ana.

I smile.

SATURDAY, JUNE 11, 2011

Ana is beside me. Radiant. Lovely. Mine. She's dressed in a white satin robe. We're in *Charlie Tango*, chasing the dawn. Chasing the dusk. Chasing the dawn. The dusk. High above the clouds we fly. Night a dark shroud arching over us. Ana's hair is burnished, titian, bright from the setting sun. We have the world at our feet and I want to give her the world. She's entranced. I do a wingover and we're in my glider. See the world, Ana. I want to show you the world. She laughs. Giggling. Happy. Her braids pointing to the ground when she's upside down. Again, she calls. And I oblige. We roll and roll and roll. But this time she starts screaming. She's staring at me in horror. Her face contorted. Horrified. Disgusted. At me.

Me?

No.

No.

She screams.

I WAKE AND MY heart is pounding. Ana is tossing and turning beside me, making an eerie, unworldly sound that rouses every hair follicle on my body. In the glow of the ambient streetlight I see she's still asleep. I sit up and shake her gently.

"Jesus, Ana."

She wakes suddenly. Gasping. Eyes wild. Terrified.

"Baby, are you okay? You were having a bad dream."

"Oh," she whispers as she focuses on me, her lashes fluttering like the wings of a hummingbird. I reach over her and switch on her lamp. She squints in the half-light. "The girl," she says, her eyes searching mine.

"What is it? What girl?" I resist the urge to gather her in my arms and kiss away her nightmares.

She blinks once more, and her voice is clearer, less fearful. "There was a girl outside SIP when I left this evening. She looked like me, but not really."

My scalp tingles.

Leila.

"When was this?" I ask, sitting upright.

"When I left work this evening." She's shaken. "Do you know who she is?"

"Yes." What the hell is Leila doing confronting Ana?

"Who?" Ana asks.

I should call Welch. During our update this morning, he had nothing to report on Leila's whereabouts. His team is still trying to find her.

"Who?" Ana persists.

Damn. I know she won't stop until she has some answers. Why the hell didn't she tell me earlier?

"It's Leila."

Her frown deepens. "The girl who put 'Toxic' on your iPod?"

"Yes. Did she say anything?"

"She said, 'What do you have that I don't?' and when I asked who she was, she said, 'I'm nobody.'"

Christ, Leila, what are you playing at? I have to call Welch.

I stumble out of bed and slip on my jeans.

In the living room, I retrieve my phone from my jacket pocket. Welch answers in two rings and any hesitation I had about calling him at five in the morning disappears. He must have been awake.

"Mr. Grey," he says, his voice hoarse as usual.

"I'm sorry to call you so early." I begin pacing what space I have in the kitchen.

"Sleep's not really my thing, Mr. Grey."

"I figured. It's Leila. She accosted my girlfriend, Anastasia Steele."

"Was it at her office? Or at her apartment? When did it happen?"

"Yes. Outside SIP. Yesterday. Early evening." I turn, and Ana, dressed only in my shirt, is standing by the kitchen counter, watching me. I study her as I continue my conversation, her expression a mixture of curious and haunted. She looks beautiful.

"What time, exactly?" Welch asks.

I repeat the question to Ana.

"About ten to six?" she says.

"Did you get that?" I ask Welch.

"No."

"Ten to six," I repeat.

"So she's tracked Miss Steele to her work."

"Find out how."

"There are press photographs of the two of you together."

"Yes."

Ana tilts her head to one side and tosses her hair over her shoulder as she listens to my side of the conversation.

"Do you think we should be concerned for Miss Steele's safety?" Welch inquires.

"I wouldn't have said so, but then I wouldn't have thought she could do this."

"I think you should consider additional security for her, sir."

"I don't know how that will go down." I look at Ana as she folds her arms, accentuating the outline of her breasts as they strain against the white cotton of my shirt.

"I'd like to increase your security, too, sir. Will you talk to Anastasia? Tell her of the danger she might be in?"

"Yes, I'll talk to her."

Ana bites her lip. I wish she'd stop. It's distracting.

Welch continues, "I'll brief Mr. Taylor and Mrs. Jones at a more reasonable hour."

"Yes."

"In the meantime, I'm going to need more personnel on the ground."

"I know." I sigh.

"We'll start with the stores in the vicinity of SIP. See if anyone saw anything. This could be the lead we've been waiting for."

"Follow it up and let me know. Just find her, Welch. She's in trouble. Find her." I hang up and look at Ana. Her tangled hair tumbles over her shoulders; her long legs are pale in the dim light from the hallway. I imagine them wrapped around me.

"Do you want some tea?" she asks.

"Actually, I'd like to go back to bed." And forget all this crap about Leila.

"Well, I need some tea. Would you like to join me for a cup?" She moves to the stove, picks up the kettle, and begins to fill it with water.

I don't want fucking tea. I want to bury myself in you and forget about Leila.

Ana gives me a pointed look and I realize she's waiting for an answer about tea.

"Yes. Please." Even to my own ears I sound surly.

What does Leila want with Ana?

And why the hell hasn't Welch found her?

"What is it?" Ana asks a few minutes later. She's holding a familiar-looking teacup.

Ana. Please. I don't want you to worry about this.

"You're not going to tell me?" she persists.

"No."

"Why?"

"Because it shouldn't concern you. I don't want you tangled up in this."

"It shouldn't concern me, but it does. She found me and accosted me outside my office. How does she know about me? How does she know where I work? I think I have a right to know what's going on."

She has an answer for everything.

"Please?" she presses.

Oh, Ana. Ana. Ana. Why do you do this?

Her bright, blue eyes beseech me.

Fuck. I can't say no to that look.

"Okay." You win. "I have no idea how she found you. Maybe the photograph of us in Portland. I don't know." With some reluctance I continue, "While I was with you in Georgia, Leila turned up at my apartment unannounced and made a scene in front of Gail."

"Gail?"

"Mrs. Jones."

"What do you mean 'made a scene'?"

I shake my head.

"Tell me." She puts her hands on her hips. "You're keeping something back."

"Ana, I—" Why is she so mad? I don't want her mixed up in this. She doesn't understand that Leila's shame is my shame. Leila chose to attempt suicide in *my* apartment and I wasn't there to help her; she cried out to me for a reason.

"Please?" Ana prompts again.

She won't give up. I sigh with exasperation and tell her in the sparsest terms what happened to Leila.

"Oh no!"

"Gail got her to the hospital. But Leila discharged herself before I could get there. The shrink who saw her called it a typical cry for help. He didn't believe her to be truly at risk—one step from suicidal ideation, he called it. But I'm not convinced. I've been trying to track her down since then to get her some help."

"Did she say anything to Mrs. Jones?"

"Not much."

"You can't find her? What about her family?"

"They don't know where she is. Neither does her husband."

"Husband?" she exclaims.

"Yes." *That lying asshole.* "She's been married for about two years."

"So she was with you while she was married?"

"No! Good God, no. She was with me nearly three years ago. Then she left and married this guy shortly afterward." *I told you, baby, I don't share.* I've only tangled with one married woman and that didn't end well.

"So why is she trying to get your attention now?"

"I don't know. All we've managed to find out is that she ran out on her husband about four months ago."

Ana picks up a teaspoon and waves it as she talks. "Let me get this straight. She hasn't been your submissive for three years?"

"About two and a half years."

"And she wanted more."

"Yes."

"But you didn't?"

"You know this."

"So she left you."

"Yes."

"So why is she coming to you now?"

"I don't know." She wanted more, but I couldn't give her that. Maybe she's seen me with you?

"But you suspect—"

"I suspect it has something to do with you." But I could be wrong. *Now can we go back to bed?*

Ana studies me, surveying my chest. But I ignore her scrutiny and ask the question that's been nagging me since she told me she'd seen Leila. "Why didn't you tell me yesterday?"

Ana has the grace to look guilty. "I forgot about her. You know, drinks after work, at the end of my first week. You turning up at the bar and your testosterone rush with Jack." She gives me a shy smile. "And then when we were here. It slipped my mind. You have a habit of making me forget things."

I'd like to forget this now. Let's go back to bed.

"Testosterone rush?" I repeat, amused.

"Yes. The pissing contest."

"I'll show you a testosterone rush." My voice is low.

"Wouldn't you rather have a cup of tea?" She offers me a cup.

"No, Anastasia, I wouldn't." *I want you. Now.* "Forget about her. Come." I hold out my hand.

She sets the teacup back on the counter and puts her hand in mine.

Back in her bedroom, I slide my shirt over her head. "I like you wearing my clothes," I whisper.

"I like wearing them. They smell of you."

I grasp her head between my hands and kiss her.

I want to make her forget about Leila.

I want to forget about Leila.

I pick her up and walk her to the concrete wall.

"Wrap your legs around me, baby," I order.

WHEN I OPEN MY eyes the room is bathed with light and Ana is awake beside me, tucked in the crook of my arm. "Hi," she says, grinning as if she's up to some mischief.

"Hi," I respond cautiously. Something is off. "What are you doing?"

"Looking at you." She skims her hand down my belly. And my body comes to life.

Whoa!

I grab her hand.

Surely she's sore after yesterday.

She licks her lips and her guilty grin is replaced with a knowledgeable, carnal smile.

Maybe not.

Waking up beside Anastasia Steele has definite advantages. Rolling on top of her, I grab her hands and pin her to the bed as she wriggles beneath me. "I think you're up to no good, Miss Steele."

"I like being up to no good near you."

She may as well be addressing my groin directly.

"You do?" I give her a quick peck on the lips.

She nods.

Oh, you beautiful girl. "Sex or breakfast?"

She tilts her hips to meet me and it takes all my self-control not to take what she's offering straightaway.

No. Make her wait.

"Good choice." I kiss her throat, her clavicle, her sternum, her breast.

"Ah," she breathes.

WE LIE IN THE afterglow.

I don't remember moments like this before Ana. I didn't lie in bed just… being. I nuzzle her hair. All that's changed.

She opens her eyes.

"Hi."

"Hi."

"Are you sore?" I ask.

Her cheeks pink. "No. Tired."

I stroke her cheek. "You didn't get much sleep last night."

"Neither did you." Her smile is one hundred percent coy Miss Steele, but her eyes cloud. "I haven't been sleeping well recently."

Remorse—swift and ugly—flares in my gut. "I'm sorry," I reply.

"Don't apologize. It was my—"

I place my finger on her mouth. "Hush."

She purses her lips to kiss my finger.

"If it's any consolation," I confess, "I haven't slept well this past week, either."

"Oh, Christian," she says and, taking my hand, kisses each knuckle in turn. It's an affectionate, humble gesture. My throat constricts as my heart expands. I'm on the edge of something unknown, a plain where the horizon disappears and the territory is new and unexplored.

It's terrifying.

It's confusing.

It's exciting.

What are you doing to me, Ana?

Where are you leading me?

I take a deep breath and focus on the woman beside me. She gives me a sexy smile and I can see us spending the entire day in bed, but I realize I'm hungry. "Breakfast?" I ask.

"Are you offering to make breakfast or demanding to be fed, Mr. Grey?" she teases.

"Neither. I'll buy you breakfast. I'm no good in the kitchen, as I demonstrated last night."

"You have other qualities," she says with a playful smirk.

"Why, Miss Steele, whatever do you mean?"

She narrows her eyes. "I think you know." She's teasing me. She sits up slowly, swinging her legs out of bed. "You can shower in Kate's bathroom. It's bigger than mine."

Of course it is.

"I'll use yours. I like being in your space."

"I like you being in my space, too." She winks, gets up, and struts out of the bedroom.

Brazen Ana.

WHEN I RETURN FROM the cramped shower, I find Ana dressed in jeans and a tight T-shirt that leaves little to my imagination. She's messing with her hair.

As I yank on my jeans I feel the Audi key in my pocket. I wonder how she'll react when I give it back to her. She seemed to take the iPad well.

"How often do you work out?" she asks, and I realize she's watching me in the mirror.

"Every weekday."

"What do you do?"

"Run, weights, kickboxing." Sprinting to and from your apartment for the past week.

"Kickboxing?" she queries.

"Yes, I have a personal trainer, an ex–Olympic contender who teaches me. His name is Claude. He's very good." I tell Ana that she'd like him as a trainer.

"Why would I need a personal trainer? I have you to keep me fit."

I walk over to where she stands, still fiddling with her hair, and I embrace her. Our eyes meet in the mirror. "But I want you fit, baby, for what I have in mind. I'll need you to keep up." *That's if we ever get back into the playroom.*

She arches a brow.

"You know you want to." I mouth the words at her reflection.

She toys with her lip but then breaks our eye contact.

"What?" I ask, concerned.

"Nothing," she says and shakes her head. "Okay, I'll meet Claude."

"You will?"

That was easy!

"Yes, jeez. If it makes you that happy," she says and laughs.

I squeeze her and give her a peck on her cheek. "You have no idea." I kiss her behind her ear. "So what would you like to do today?"

"I'd like to get my hair cut, and, um, I need to deposit a check and buy a car."

"Ah."

Here goes. From my jeans pocket I fish out the Audi key. "It's here," I inform her.

She looks blank, but then her cheeks pink and I realize she's upset.

"What do you mean 'it's here'?"

"Taylor brought it back yesterday."

She steps out of my embrace, scowling at me.

Shit. She's pissed. Why?

From the back pocket of her jeans she brandishes an envelope. "Here, this is yours."

I recognize it as the envelope that I put the check in for her ancient Beetle. I lift both hands and step away. "Oh no. That's your money."

"No it isn't. I'd like to buy the car from you."

What. The. Hell.

She wants to give *me* money! "No, Anastasia. Your money, your car."

"No, Christian. My money, your car. I'll buy it from you."

Oh. No. You. Don't.

"I gave you that car for your graduation present." And you said you'd accept it.

"If you'd given me a pen, that would be a suitable graduation present. You gave me an Audi."

"Do you really want to argue about this?"

"No."

"Good. Here are the keys." I place her keys on the dresser.

"That's not what I meant!"

"End of discussion, Anastasia. Don't push me."

The look she's giving me now says it all. If I were dry tinder I would burst into flame, and not in a good way. She's mad. Really mad. Suddenly she narrows her eyes and gives me a wicked smile. Taking the envelope, she holds it aloft and, in a rather theatrical manner, rips it in half and in half again. She drops the contents in her trash basket and gives me a victorious fuck-you look.

Oh. Game on, Ana.

"You are, as ever, challenging, Miss Steele." I echo the words she used yesterday and turn on my heel and head into the kitchen.

Now I'm pissed. Fucking pissed.

How dare she?

I find my phone and call Andrea.

"Good morning, Mr. Grey." She sounds a little breathless when she answers.

"Hi, Andrea."

In the background, on her side of the call, I hear a woman shouting, "Doesn't he realize you're getting married today, Andrea?"

Andrea's voice comes through, "Excuse me, Mr. Grey."

Married!

There's the sound of muffled fumbling. "Mom, be quiet. It's my boss." The muffling ceases. "What can I do for you, Mr. Grey?" she says.

"You're getting married?"

"Yes, sir."

"Today?"

"Yes. What is it you want me to do?"

"I wanted you to deposit twenty-four thousand dollars into Anastasia Steele's bank account."

"Twenty-four thousand?"

"Yes, twenty-four thousand dollars. Directly."

"I'll take care of it. It will be in her account on Monday."

"Monday?"

"Yes, sir."

"Excellent."

"Anything else, sir?"

"No, that's all, Andrea."

I hang up, aggravated that I've disturbed her on her wedding day and more aggravated that she didn't tell me she was getting married.

Why wouldn't she tell me? Is she pregnant?

Will I have to find a new PA?

I turn to Miss Steele, who is fuming on the threshold.

"Deposited in your bank account Monday. Don't play games with me."

"Twenty-four thousand dollars!" she shouts. "And how do you know my account number?"

"I know everything about you, Anastasia," I reply, trying to keep my cool.

"There's no way my car was worth twenty-four thousand dollars," she counters.

"I would agree with you, but it's about knowing your market, whether you're buying or selling. Some lunatic out there wanted that deathtrap and was willing to pay that amount of money. Apparently, it's a classic. Ask Taylor if you don't believe me."

We glower at each other.

Impossible woman.

Impossible. Impossible.

Her lips part. She's breathless, her pupils dilated. Drinking me in. Consuming me.

Ana.

Her tongue licks her lower lip.

And it's there in the air between us.

Our attraction, a living force. Building. Building.

Fuck.

I grab her and push her against the door, my lips seeking and finding hers. I claim her mouth, kissing her greedily, my fingers closing around the nape of her neck, holding her. Her fingers are in my hair. Pulling. Directing me while she kisses me back, her tongue in my mouth. Taking. Everything. I cup her behind and pull her against my erection and grind my body into hers. I want her. Again.

"Why, why do you defy me?" I say out loud as I kiss her neckline. She tilts her head back to give me full access to her throat.

"Because I can," she whispers.

Ah. She stole my line.

I'm panting when I lean my forehead against hers.

"Lord, I want to take you now, but I'm out of condoms. I can never get enough of you. You're a maddening, maddening woman."

"And you make me mad," she breathes. "In every way."

I take a deep breath and look down into dark, hungry eyes that promise me the world, and I shake my head.

Steady, Grey.

"Come. Let's go out for breakfast. And I know a place you can get your hair cut."

"Okay." She smiles.

And we fight no more.

WE WALK HAND IN hand up Vine Street and turn right on First Avenue. I wonder how normal it is to go from seething at each other to this casual calm I feel as we walk through the streets. Maybe most couples are like this. I look down at Ana beside me. "This feels so normal," I tell her. "I love it."

"Christian, I think Dr. Flynn would agree that you are anything but normal. Exceptional, maybe." She squeezes my hand.

Exceptional!

"It's a beautiful day," she adds.

"It is."

She briefly closes her eyes and turns her face to the morning sun.

"Come, I know a great place for brunch."

One of my favorite cafés is only a couple of blocks from Ana's on First. When we get there I open the door for Ana and pause to inhale the smell of fresh bread.

"What a charming place," she says when we sit down at a table. "I love the art on the walls."

"They support a different artist every month. I found Trouton here."

"Raising the ordinary to extraordinary," Ana says.

"You remembered."

"There's very little I could forget about you, Mr. Grey."

And I you, Miss Steele. You are extraordinary.

I chuckle and hand her a menu.

"I'LL GET THIS." Ana grabs the check before I do. "You have to be quick around here, Grey."

"You're right, I do," I grumble. Someone who owes more than fifty thousand dollars in student-loan debt should not be paying for my breakfast.

"Don't look so cross. I'm twenty-four thousand dollars richer than I was this morning. I can afford"—she inspects the bill—"twenty-two dollars and sixty-seven cents for breakfast."

Short of wrestling the check from her, there's little I can do. "Thank you," I mutter.

"Where to now?" she asks.

"You really want your hair cut?"

"Yes, look at it."

Dark tendrils have escaped from her ponytail, framing her beautiful face. "You look lovely to me. You always do."

"There's your father's function this evening."

I remind her that it's black tie and at my parents' home. "They have a tent. You know, the works."

"What's the charity?"

"It's a drug-rehab program for parents with young kids called Coping Together." I hold my breath, hoping she doesn't start asking about the Grey connection to this cause. It's personal and I don't need her pity. I've told her all I want to tell her about that time in my life.

"Sounds like a good cause," she says with compassion and thankfully leaves it there.

"Come, let's go." I stand and hold out my hand, ending the conversation.

"Where are we going?" she asks as we continue our walk down First Avenue.

"Surprise."

I can't tell her it's Elena's place. I know she'll freak. From our conversation in Savannah, I know the mere mention of her name is a hot button for Ana. It's Saturday and Elena doesn't work on weekends, and when she does work it's at the salon in the Bravern Center.

"Here we are." I open the door at Esclava and usher Ana in. I haven't been here for a couple of months; the last time was with Susannah.

"Good morning, Mr. Grey," Greta greets us.

"Hello, Greta."

"Is this the usual, sir?" she asks politely.

Fuck. "No." I give Ana a nervous look. "Miss Steele will tell you what she wants."

Ana's eyes are on me, burning with insight. "Why here?" she demands.

"I own this place, and three more like it."

"You own it?"

"Yes. It's a sideline. Anyway, whatever you want, you can have it here, on the house." I run through all the spa treatments available. "All that stuff that women like—everything. It's done here."

"Waxing?"

For a split second I think about recommending the chocolate wax for her pubic hair, but given our détente, I keep my suggestion to myself. "Yes, waxing, too… everywhere."

Ana blushes.

How will I ever convince her that penetrative sex would be more pleasurable for her without the hair?

One step at a time, Grey.

"I'd like a haircut, please," she says to Greta.

"Certainly, Miss Steele."

Greta concentrates on her computer and punches a few keys. "Franco is free in five minutes."

"Franco's fine," I confirm, but notice Ana's demeanor has suddenly changed. I'm about to ask what's wrong when I glance up and see Elena walking out of the back office.

Hell. What's she doing here?

Elena has a quick word with one of her employees, then she

spies me and lights up like Christmas, her expression one of wicked delight.

Shit.

"Excuse me," I say to Ana and hurry to meet Elena before she makes her way to us.

"Well, this is an unexpected pleasure," Elena purrs in greeting as she kisses me on both cheeks.

"Good morning, Ma'am. I wasn't expecting to see you here."

"My aesthetician called in sick. So, you *have* been avoiding me."

"I've been busy."

"I can see. Is that someone new?"

"That is Anastasia Steele."

Elena beams at Ana, who is watching us intently. She knows we're talking about her, and she responds with a lukewarm smile.

Damn.

"Your little southern belle?" Elena asks.

"She's not southern."

"I thought you went to Georgia to see her."

"Her mom lives there."

"I see. She certainly looks like your type."

"Yeah." *Let's not go there.*

"Are you going to introduce me?"

Ana is talking to Greta—grilling her, I think. *What's she asking?*

"I don't think that's a good idea."

Elena looks disappointed. "Why not?"

"She's named you Mrs. Robinson."

"Oh really? That's funny. Though I'm surprised someone that young knows the reference." Elena's tone is wry. "I'm also astonished you told her about us. What happened to confidentiality?" She taps a scarlet fingernail against her lips.

"She's not going to talk."

"I hope so. Look, don't worry. I'll back off." She holds her hands up in surrender.

"Thank you."

"But is this a good idea, Christian? She's hurt you once already." Elena's face is etched with concern.

"I don't know. I missed her. She missed me. I've decided I'm going to try it her way. She's willing."

"Her way? Are you sure you can? Are you sure you want to?"

Ana is still staring at us. She's alarmed.

"Time will tell," I answer.

"Well, I'm here if you need me. Good luck." She gives me a soft but calculated smile. "Don't be a stranger."

"Thanks. Are you going to my parents' soirée this evening?"

"I don't think so."

"That's probably a good idea."

She looks momentarily surprised but says, "Let's catch up later this week when we can talk more freely."

"Sure."

She squeezes my arm and I head back to Ana, who is still waiting by the reception desk. Her face is pinched and her arms are folded across her body as she radiates her displeasure.

This is not good.

"Are you okay?" I ask, knowing full well she isn't.

"Not really. You didn't want to introduce me?" she replies in a tone that's both sarcastic and indignant.

Christ. She knows it's Elena. How? "But I thought—"

Ana interrupts me. "For a bright man, sometimes—" She stops midsentence, too angry to continue. "I'd like to go, please." She taps her foot against the marble floor.

"Why?"

"You know why," she snaps and rolls her eyes as if I'm the biggest idiot she's ever met.

You are *the biggest idiot she's ever met, Grey.*

You know how she feels about Elena.

Everything was going so well.

Make this right, Grey.

"I'm sorry, Ana. I didn't know she'd be here. She's never here. She's opened a new branch at the Bravern Center, and that's where she's normally based. Someone was sick today."

Ana turns abruptly and storms to the door.

"We won't need Franco, Greta," I inform the receptionist,

annoyed that she may have heard our exchange. Hastily, I go after Ana.

She wraps her arms around herself defensively and marches up the street with her head down. I'm forced to take longer strides to catch up with her.

Ana. Stop. You're overreacting.

She simply doesn't understand the nature of Elena's and my relationship.

As I walk beside her, I'm floundering. What do I do? What do I say? Perhaps Elena is right.

Can I do this?

I've never tolerated this kind of behavior from any submissive; what's more, none of them have been this petulant.

But I hate it when she's angry with me.

"You used to take your subs there?" she asks, but I don't know if it's a rhetorical question. I chance a reply.

"Some of them, yes."

"Leila?"

"Yes."

"The place looks very new."

"It's been refurbished recently."

"I see. So Mrs. Robinson met all your subs."

"Yes."

"Did they know about her?"

Not in the way you're thinking. They never knew about our D/s relationship. They just thought we were friends. "No. None of them did. Only you."

"But I'm not your sub."

"No, you most definitely are not." Because I certainly wouldn't indulge this behavior from anyone else.

She stops suddenly and whirls around to face me, her expression bleak. "Can you see how fucked up this is?" she says.

"Yes. I'm sorry." I didn't know she was going to be there.

"I want to get my hair cut, preferably somewhere where you haven't fucked either the staff or the clientele." Her voice is hoarse and she's on the verge of tears.

Ana.

"Now, if you'll excuse me." She turns to go.

"You're not running. Are you?" Panic starts to well inside me. This is it. She's out before we've even had a second chance.

Grey, you've blown it.

"No," she shouts, exasperated. "I just want a damn haircut. Somewhere I can close my eyes, have someone wash my hair, and I can forget about all this baggage that accompanies you."

She's not leaving me. I take a deep breath. "I can have Franco come to the apartment, or your place," I offer.

"She's very attractive."

Christ. Not this. "Yes, she is." So what? Give it up, Ana.

"Is she still married?"

"No. She got divorced about five years ago."

"Why aren't you with her?"

Ana! Let it go. "Because that's over between us. I've told you this." How many times do I need to tell her? My phone vibrates in my jacket pocket. I hold my finger up to stop her tirade and answer my phone. The caller ID says it's Welch. I wonder what he has to report.

"Mr. Grey."

"Welch."

"Three things. We've tracked Mrs. Leila Reed to Spokane, where she'd been living with a man named Geoffrey Barry. He was killed in an auto accident on I-90."

"Killed in a car crash? When?"

"Four weeks ago. Her husband, Russell Reed, knew about Barry but still won't disclose where Mrs. Reed has gone."

"That's twice that bastard's not been forthcoming. He must know. Does he have no feelings for her whatsoever?" I'm staggered that her ex could be so heartless.

"He has feelings for her, but they're certainly not matrimonial."

"This is beginning to make sense."

"Did the psychiatrist give you anything to go on?" Welch asks.

"No."

"Could she be suffering a kind of psychosis?"

I agree with Welch that this might be her condition, but it still doesn't explain where she is, which is what I really want to know. I look around. *Where are you, Leila?* "She's here. She's watching us," I mutter.

"Mr. Grey, we're close. We'll find her." Welch tries to reassure me and asks if I'm at Escala.

"No." I wish Ana and I weren't so exposed here on the street.

"I'm considering how many people you need for your close protection team."

"Two or four, 24/7."

"Okay, Mr. Grey. Have you told Anastasia?"

"I haven't broached that yet."

Ana's watching me, listening. Her expression is intense but inscrutable.

"You should. There's something else. Mrs. Reed has obtained a concealed-weapons license."

"What?" Fear grips my heart.

"The details came up in our search this morning."

"I see. When?"

"It's dated yesterday."

"That recently? But how?"

"She forged the papers."

"No background checks?"

"All the forms are faked. She's using a different name."

"I see. Email the name, address, and photos if you have them."

"Will do. And I'll organize the additional security."

"24/7, from this afternoon. Establish liaison with Taylor." I hang up. This is serious.

"Well?" Ana asks.

"That was Welch."

"Who's Welch?"

"My security adviser."

"Okay. So, what's happened?"

"Leila left her husband about three months ago and ran off with a guy who was killed in a car accident four weeks ago."

"Oh."

"The asshole shrink should have found that out. Grief, that's what this is."

Damn. That hospital could have done a better job.

"Come." I hold out my hand and Ana takes it without thinking. Then, just as abruptly, she snatches her hand away.

"Wait a minute. We were in the middle of a discussion about 'us.' About her, your Mrs. Robinson."

"She's not my Mrs. Robinson. We can talk about it at my place."

"I don't want to go to your place. I want to get my hair cut!" she yells.

I take my phone and call the salon. Greta answers immediately.

"Greta, Christian Grey. I want Franco at my place in an hour. Ask Mrs. Lincoln."

"Yes, Mr. Grey." She puts me on hold for a nanosecond. "That's fine. He can be there at one."

"Good." I hang up. "He's coming at one."

"Christian!" Ana glares at me.

"Anastasia, Leila is obviously suffering a psychotic break. I don't know if it's you or me she's after, or what lengths she's prepared to go to. We'll go to your place, pick up your things, and you can stay with me until we've tracked her down."

"Why would I want to do that?"

"So I can keep you safe."

"But—"

Give me strength.

"You are coming back to my apartment if I have to drag you there by your hair."

"I think you're overreacting."

"I don't. We can continue our discussion back at my place. Come."

She glowers at me. Intractable. "No," she says.

"You can walk or I can carry you. I don't mind either way, Anastasia."

"You wouldn't dare."

"Oh, baby, we both know that if you throw down the gauntlet, I'll be only too happy to pick it up."

She narrows her eyes.

Ana. You give me no choice.

I scoop her up and throw her over my shoulder, ignoring the startled look of a couple walking past us.

"Put me down!" she rages and starts to struggle. I tighten my hold on her and slap her behind.

"Christian!" she screeches. She's mad. But I don't give a fuck. An alarmed man—a father, I presume—pulls his young children out of our path.

"I'll walk! I'll walk," she shrieks, and I put her down immediately. She whirls around so fast her hair hits my shoulder. She stomps off in the direction of her apartment and I follow, but I keep watch. Everywhere.

Where are you, Leila?

Behind a parked car? A tree?

What do you want?

Ana comes to a sudden stop. "What's happened?" she demands.

"What do you mean?" *What now?*

"With Leila."

"I've told you."

"No, you haven't. There's something else. You didn't insist that I go to your place yesterday. So what's happened?"

Perceptive, Miss Steele.

"Christian! Tell me!"

"She managed to obtain a concealed-weapons permit yesterday."

Her whole demeanor changes. Anger turns to fear. "That means she can just buy a gun," she whispers, horrified.

"Ana." I pull her into my arms. "I don't think she'll do anything stupid, but I just don't want to take that risk with you."

"Not me. What about you?" she says, her voice filled with anguish. She wraps her arms around me and hugs me hard. She's scared for me.

Me!

And a moment ago I thought she was leaving.

This is unreal.

"Let's get back." I kiss her hair. As we move on, I extend my arm around her shoulders and pull her to my side to protect her. She slips her hand into the belt loop of my jeans, holding me close, her fingers curled around my hip.

This... proximity is new. I could get used to it.

We walk back to her apartment and I keep an eye out for Leila.

I CONTEMPLATE THE RANGE of emotions I've experienced since waking as I watch Ana pack a small suitcase. In the alley the other day I tried to articulate how I felt. The best I could do was "unsettled." And that still describes my psyche right now. Ana is not the mild woman I remember—she's far more audacious and volatile.

Has she changed so much since she left me? *Or have I?*

It doesn't help that there's a whole new level of disquiet because of Leila. For the first time in a long time, I'm fearful. What if something were to happen to Ana because of my association with Leila? That whole situation is out of my control. And I don't like it.

Ana, for her part, is solemn and unusually quiet. She folds the balloon into her backpack.

"*Charlie Tango*'s coming, too?" I tease.

She nods and gives me a tepid smile. She's either scared or still mad about Elena. Or she's pissed for being hoisted over my shoulder in the street. Or maybe it's the twenty-four thousand dollars.

Damn, there's a great deal to choose from. I wish I knew what she was thinking.

"Ethan is back Tuesday," she says.

"Ethan?"

"Kate's brother. He's staying here until he finds a place in Seattle."

Ah, the other Kavanagh progeny. The beach bum. I met him at her graduation. He had his hands all over Ana. "Well, it's good that you'll be staying with me. Give him more room."

"I don't know that he's got keys. I'll need to be back then. That's everything," she says.

Taking her case, I have a quick look around before we lock up. I note with displeasure that the apartment has no intruder alarm.

THE AUDI IS PARKED out back where Taylor said it would be. I open the passenger door for Ana, but she stays rooted to the ground, staring at me.

"Are you getting in?" I ask, confused.

"I thought I was driving."

"No. I'll drive."

"Something wrong with my driving?" she asks, and there's that tone again. "Don't tell me you know what I scored on my driving test. I wouldn't be surprised, with your stalking tendencies."

"Get in the car, Anastasia." My patience is running thin.

Enough. You're making me crazy. I want you home where you'll be safe.

"Okay," she huffs and climbs in. She doesn't live far from me, so our ride shouldn't take long. Normally I would enjoy driving the small Audi. It's nimble in Seattle's traffic. But I'm distracted by every pedestrian. One of them could be Leila.

"Were all your submissives brunettes?" Ana asks out of nowhere.

"Yes." But I don't really want to discuss this. Our fledgling relationship is moving into dangerous territory.

"I just wondered." She's fidgeting with a tassel on her backpack; fidgeting means she's apprehensive.

Put her at ease, Grey.

"I told you. I prefer brunettes."

"Mrs. Robinson isn't a brunette."

"That's probably why. She put me off blondes forever."

"You're kidding." Ana's disbelief is obvious.

"Yes. I'm kidding." Do we really have to talk about this? My anxiety multiplies. If she keeps digging, I'll confess my darkest secret.

No. I can never tell her. She'll leave me.

Without a backward glance.

And I recall watching her walk up the street and into the garage at The Heathman after our first coffee.

She never looked back.

Not once.

If I hadn't contacted her about the photographer's show… I wouldn't be with her now.

Ana's strong. If she says goodbye, she means it.

"Tell me about her," Ana says, interrupting my thoughts.

What now? Is she talking about Elena? Again? "What do you want to know?" More information about Mrs. Lincoln will only worsen her mood.

"Tell me about your business arrangement."

Well, that's easy enough. "I'm a silent partner. I'm not particularly interested in the beauty business, but she's built it into a successful venture. I just invested and helped get her started."

"Why?"

"I owed it to her."

"Oh?"

"When I dropped out of Harvard, she loaned me a hundred grand to start my business."

"You dropped out?"

"It wasn't my thing. I did two years. Unfortunately, my parents were not so understanding."

"You're what?" Grace scowls at me, her expression apoplectic.

"I want to leave. I'm going to start my own company."

"Doing what?"

"Investments."

"Christian, what do you know about investments? You need to finish college."

"Mom, I have a plan. I think I can do this."

"Look, son, this is a huge step that could affect your entire future."

"I know, Dad, but I can't do it anymore. I don't want to live in Cambridge for another two years."

"Transfer. Come back to Seattle."

"Mom, it's not the place."

"You just haven't found your niche."

"My niche is out in the real world. Not in academia. It's stifling."

"Have you met someone?" Grace asks.

"No," I lie smoothly. I knew Elena before I went off to Harvard.

Grace narrows her eyes and the tips of my ears burn.

"We cannot condone this reckless move, son." Carrick is summoning his full-on pompous-prick dad mode, and I worry he's going to give me his signature "study hard, work hard, and family first" lecture.

Grace emphasizes her point. "Christian, you're gambling with the rest of your life."

"Mom. Dad. It's done. I'm sorry to disappoint you again. My decision is already made. I'm just informing you."

"But what about the wasted tuition?" My mother is wringing her hands.

Shit.

"I'll pay you back."

"How? And how in heaven's name are you going to start a business? You need capital."

"Don't worry about that, Mom. It's in hand. And I will pay you back."

"Christian, darling, it's not about the money..."

The only lesson I learned at college was how to read a balance sheet, and I found the peace that single sculls brought me.

"You don't seem to have done too badly dropping out. What was your major?" Ana says, bringing me back to our conversation.

"Politics and economics."

"So, she's rich?" Ana is fixated on Elena's loan to me.

"She was a bored trophy wife, Anastasia. Her husband was wealthy—big in timber." This always makes me smile. I give Ana a sideways smirk. Lincoln Timber. What an unpleasant asshole he turned out to be. "He wouldn't let her work. You know, he was controlling. Some men are like that."

"Really? A controlling man?" Ana sounds scornful. "Surely a mythical creature." Sarcasm drips off every word. She's in a sassy mood, but her response makes me grin.

"She lent you her husband's money?"

She sure did.

"That's terrible."

"He got his own back."

The asshole.

My thoughts take a dark turn. He nearly killed his wife because she was fucking me. I shudder to think what he'd have done to her if I hadn't come around. Fury surges through my body and I clutch the steering wheel as we wait for the Escala garage barrier to open. Blood drains from my knuckles. Elena was in the hospital for three months and she refused to press charges.

Control yourself, Grey.

I relax my hold on the steering wheel.

"How?" asks Ana, as curious as ever, wanting to know about Linc's revenge.

I'm not telling her that story. I shake my head and park in one of my allotted spaces and turn off the ignition. "Come—Franco will be here shortly."

In the elevator, I glance down at her. The little *v* is there between her brows. She's pensive, maybe processing what I told her—or is it something else?

"Still mad at me?" I ask.

"Very."

"Okay." At least I know.

Taylor has returned from visiting Sophie, his daughter. He greets us when we arrive in the foyer.

"Good afternoon, sir," he says quietly to me.

"Has Welch been in touch?"

"Yes, sir."

"And?"

"Everything's arranged."

"Excellent. How's your daughter?"

"She's fine, thank you, sir."

"Good. We have a hairdresser arriving at one—Franco De Luca."

"Miss Steele," Taylor greets Ana.

"Hi, Taylor. You have a daughter?"

"Yes, ma'am."

"How old is she?"

"She's seven."

Ana looks confused.

"She lives with her mother," Taylor explains.

"Oh, I see," she says, and he gives her a rare smile.

I turn and head into my living room. I'm not sure I appreciate Taylor charming Miss Steele or vice versa. I hear Ana behind me.

"Are you hungry?" I ask and look back at her.

She shakes her head and her eyes scan the room. She hasn't been here since the awful day she left me. I want to tell her I'm glad she's back, but she's mad at me right now.

"I have to make a few calls. Make yourself at home."

"Okay," she says.

IN MY STUDY, on my desk, I find a large cloth bag. Inside is a stunning silver mask with navy plumes for Ana. Beside it there's a small Chanel bag containing a red lipstick. Taylor has done well. However, I don't think Ana will be too impressed with my lipstick idea—at least not at the moment. I place the mask on a shelf and pocket the lipstick, then sit down at my computer.

It was an enlightening and diverting morning with Anastasia. She's been as challenging as ever since we woke, whether it was about the check for her death trap of a Beetle, my relationship with Elena, or who pays for breakfast.

Ana's fiercely independent and still doesn't seem interested in my money. She doesn't take, she gives, but then she's always been that way. It's refreshing. All my submissives used to love their gifts. *Grey, who are you kidding?* They said they did, but perhaps that was because of the role they were playing.

I put my head in my hands. This is difficult. I'm on an uncharted course with Ana.

Her anger toward Elena is unfortunate. Elena is a friend.

Is Ana jealous?

I can't help my past, and after all that Elena has done for me, it's going to be awkward dealing with Ana's hostility.

Is this what my life will be like from now on, mired in this uncertainty? It will make an interesting topic to discuss with Flynn the next time I see him. Perhaps he can coach me through this.

Shaking my head, I wake up the iMac and check my emails. Welch has sent through a copy of Leila's forged concealed-weapons license. She's using the name Jeanne Barry and an address in Belltown. The photograph is her likeness, though she looks older, thinner, and sadder than she did when I knew her. It's depressing. The woman needs help.

I print out a couple of spreadsheets from SIP—P&Ls for the last three years that I will examine later. Then I review the résumés of the additional close protection team that Taylor has approved; two of them are ex-feds and two are ex–Navy Seals. But I have yet to broach the subject of additional security with Ana.

One step at a time, Grey.

WHEN I'VE FINISHED RESPONDING to a few work emails, I go in search of Ana.

She's not in the living room or my bedroom but while there I collect a couple of condoms from my bedside and continue my search. I want to go upstairs to check whether she's in the sub's room, but I hear the elevator doors and Taylor greeting someone. My watch reads 12:55. Franco must have arrived.

The doors of the foyer open, and before Taylor opens his mouth I say, "I'll fetch Miss Steele."

"Very good, sir."

"Let me know as soon as the security detail gets here."

"Will do, Mr. Grey."

"And thanks for the mask and lipstick."

"You're welcome, sir." Taylor closes the door.

Upstairs, I can't see her, but I hear her.

Ana's talking to herself in the closet.

What the hell is she doing in there?

Taking a deep breath, I open the door and she's sitting cross-legged on the floor. "There you are. I thought you'd run off."

She holds up a finger and I realize she's on the phone and not talking to herself at all. Leaning against the doorjamb, I watch as she tucks her hair behind her ear and starts winding a strand around her index finger.

"Sorry, Mom, I have to go. I'll call again soon..." She's jittery. Do I make her feel that way? Perhaps she's hiding in here to get away from me. She needs some space? The thought is disheartening.

"Love you, too, Mom." She hangs up and turns to me, her expression expectant.

"Why are you hiding in here?" I ask.

"I'm not hiding. I'm despairing."

"Despairing?" Anxiety pricks my skin. She *is* thinking of running.

"Of all this, Christian." She gestures toward the dresses hanging in the closet.

The clothes? She doesn't like them?

"Can I come in?" I ask.

"It's your closet."

My closet. Your clothes, Ana.

Slowly I sink to the floor opposite her, trying to gauge her mood. "They're just clothes. If you don't like them, I'll send them back." I sound resigned rather than conciliatory.

"You're a lot to take on, you know?"

She's not wrong. Scratching my unshaved chin, I consider what to say.

Be real. Be truthful. Flynn's words ring in my head.

"I know. I'm trying," I reply.

"You're very trying," she quips.

"As are you, Miss Steele."

"Why are you doing this?" She gestures between us.

Her and me.

She and I.

Ana and Christian.

"You know why." *I need you.*

"No, I don't," she insists.

I scrape my hands through my hair, looking for inspiration.

What does she want me to say? What does she want to hear? "You are one frustrating female."

"You could have a nice brunette submissive. One who'd say 'How high?' every time you said 'Jump,' provided of course she had permission to speak. So why me, Christian? I just don't get it."

What should I tell her? Because I've woken up since I met her? Because my whole world has changed. It's rotating on a different axis. "You make me look at the world differently, Anastasia. You don't want me for my money. You give me…" I search for the word. "Hope."

"Hope for what?"

Everything.

"More," I answer. It's what Ana wanted. And now I want it, too.

Give her your whole pitch, Grey.

I tell her she's right. "I'm used to women doing exactly what I say, when I say, doing exactly what I want. It gets old. There's something about you, Anastasia, which calls to me on some deep level I don't understand. It's a siren's call. I can't resist you, and I don't want to lose you."

Whoa. Flowery, Grey.

I take her hand. "Don't run, please. Have a little faith in me and a little patience. Please."

And it's there in her sweet smile. Her compassion. Her love. I could bask in that look all day. Every day. She places her hands on my knees, surprising me, and leans up to plant a kiss on my lips. "Okay. Faith and patience, I can live with that," she says.

"Good. Because Franco's here."

She flips her hair over her shoulder. "About time!" Her girlish laugh is infectious, and together we stand.

Hand in hand, we make our way downstairs and I think we might be over whatever was making her mad.

FRANCO MAKES AN EMBARRASSING fuss over my girl. I leave them in my bathroom. I'm not sure Ana would appreciate me micromanaging a haircut.

Heading back to my study, I feel tension in my shoulders. I feel it everywhere. This morning has been out of my control, and though she says she's going to try faith and patience, I'll have to see if she's as good as her word.

But Ana has never given me a reason to doubt her.

Except when she left.

And she hurt me…

I dismiss the dark thought and quickly check my emails. There's one from Flynn.

From: Dr. John Flynn
Subject: Tonight
Date: June 11 2011 13:00
To: Christian Grey

Christian
Are you attending your parents' benefit this evening?

JF

I respond immediately.

From: Christian Grey
Subject: Tonight
Date: June 11 2011 13:15
To: Dr. John Flynn

Good afternoon, John.
I am indeed, and I'll be accompanied by Miss Anastasia Steele.

Christian Grey
CEO, Grey Enterprises Holdings, Inc.

I wonder what he'll make of that. I think it's the first time I've really followed his advice—and I am trying my relationship with Ana her way.

So far, so confusing.

I shake my head and retrieve the spreadsheets I printed out and a couple of bound reports I have to read about the shipping business in Taiwan.

I'M LOST IN THE figures for SIP. They are hemorrhaging money. Their overhead is too high, their write-offs are astronomical, their production costs are rising, and their staff—

A movement out of the corner of my eye distracts me.

Ana.

She stands at the entrance of the living room, twisting one foot inward and looking awkward and shy. She's staring anxiously at me, and I know she's seeking my approval.

She's stunning, her hair a glossy mane.

"See! I tell you he like it." Franco has followed her into the living room.

"You look lovely, Ana," I say, and my compliment induces a fetching flush on her cheeks.

"My work 'ere is done," Franco says, clapping his hands.

It's time to see him out.

"Thank you, Franco," I say and attempt to direct him out of my living room. He grabs Ana and kisses her on both cheeks in a rather dramatic display of affection. "Never let anyone else be cutting your hair, *bellissima* Ana!"

I glare at him until he lets her go. "This way," I say to get him out.

"Mr. Grey, she is a jewel."

I know.

"Here." I hand him three hundred dollars. "Thank you for coming at such short notice."

"It was a pleasure. A real pleasure." He pumps my hand, and not a moment too soon Taylor appears to escort him to the foyer.

Thank God.

Ana is standing where I left her.

"I'm glad you kept it long." I take a strand of her hair and caress it between my fingers. "So soft," I whisper. She watches me—anxious, I think. "Are you still mad at me?" I ask.

She nods.

Oh, Ana.

"What precisely are you mad at me about?"

She rolls her eyes at me… and I recall a moment in her bedroom in Vancouver when she made exactly the same mistake. But that was a lifetime ago in our short relationship, and I'm sure she wouldn't let me spank her right now. Though I want to. Yes. I want to very much.

"You want the list?" she says.

"There's a list?" I'm amused.

"A long one."

"Can we discuss it in bed?" Thoughts of spanking Ana have gone to my groin.

"No."

"Over lunch, then. I'm hungry, and not just for food."

"I am not going to let you dazzle me with your sexpertise."

Sexpertise!

Anastasia, you flatter me.

And I like it.

"What is bothering you specifically, Miss Steele? Spit it out." I've lost track.

"What's bothering me?" she scoffs. "Well, there's your gross invasion of my privacy, the fact that you took me someplace where your ex-mistress works and you used to take all your lovers to have their bits waxed, you manhandled me in the street like I was six years old." She's on a roll with a litany of all my misbehavior. I feel like I'm in first grade again. "And to cap it all, you let your Mrs. Robinson touch you!"

She didn't touch me! *Christ.* "That's quite a list. But just to clarify once more, she's not my Mrs. Robinson."

"She can touch you," she stresses, and her voice wavers, full of hurt.

"She knows where."

"What does that mean?"

"You and I don't have any rules. I have never had a relationship without rules, and I never know where you're going to touch me. It makes me nervous." She's unpredictable and she has to understand that her touch disarms me. "Your touch completely... It just means more. So much more."

You can't touch me, Ana. Please just accept this.

She steps forward, raising her hand.

No. The darkness squeezes my ribs. I step back. "Hard limit," I whisper.

She masks her disappointment. "How would you feel if you couldn't touch me?"

"Devastated and deprived."

Her shoulders fall and she shakes her head but gives me a resigned smile. "You'll have to tell me exactly why this is a hard limit one day, please."

"One day," I answer. And I push the vision of a burning cigarette out of my head.

"So, the rest of your list. Invading your privacy. Because I know your bank account number?"

"Yes, that's outrageous."

"I do background checks on all my submissives. I'll show you." I head into my study and she follows. Wondering if this is a good idea, I pull Ana's file from the cabinet and hand it to her. She glances at her neatly typed name and gives me a withering look.

"You can keep it," I tell her.

"Well, gee, thanks," she sneers and starts flipping through and scanning the contents.

"So, you knew I worked at Clayton's?"

"Yes."

"It wasn't a coincidence. You didn't just drop by?"

Fess up, Grey.

"No."

"This is fucked up. You know that?"

"I don't see it that way. What I do, I have to be careful."

"But this is private."

"I don't misuse the information. Anyone can get ahold of it if they have half a mind to, Anastasia. To have control, I need information. It's how I've always operated."

"You do misuse the information. You deposited twenty-four thousand dollars that I didn't want into my account."

"I told you. That's what Taylor managed to get for your car. Unbelievable, I know, but there you go."

"But the Audi—"

"Anastasia, do you have any idea how much money I make?"

"Why should I? I don't need to know the bottom line of your bank account, Christian."

"I know. That's one of the things I love about you. Anastasia, I earn roughly one hundred thousand dollars an hour."

Her lips form the letter *o*.

And for once she remains silent.

"Twenty-four thousand dollars is nothing. The car, the Tess books, the clothes, they're nothing."

"If you were me, how would you feel about all this… largesse coming your way?" she asks.

This is irrelevant. We're talking about her, not me.

"I don't know." I shrug because it's such a ludicrous question.

She sighs as if she's had to explain a complex equation to a simpleton. "It doesn't feel great. I mean, you're very generous, but it makes me uncomfortable. I have told you this often enough."

"I want to give you the world, Anastasia."

"I just want you, Christian. Not all the add-ons."

"They're part of the deal. Part of what I am." Who I am.

She shakes her head, seeming subdued. "Shall we eat?" she asks, changing the subject.

"Sure."

"I'll cook."

"Good. Otherwise, there's food in the fridge."

"Mrs. Jones is off on the weekends?"

I nod.

"So, you eat cold cuts most weekends?"

"No."

"Oh?"

I take a deep breath, wondering how the piece of information I'm going to give Ana will go down. "My submissives cook, Anastasia." Some well, some not so well.

"Oh, of course." She fakes a smile. "What would Sir like to eat?"

"Whatever Madam can find," I reply, knowing she won't get the reference.

She nods and exits my study, leaving her file. Placing it back in the filing cabinet, I catch sight of Susannah's file. She was a hopeless cook, even worse than me. But she tried… and we had some fun with that.

"You've burned this?"

"Yes. Sorry, Sir."

"Well, what are we going to do with you?"

"Whatever pleases you, Master."

"Did you burn this deliberately?"

Her flush and the twitch of her lips as she masks her smile are answer enough.

Those were pleasurable and simpler times. My previous relationships were dictated by a set of rules that were followed, and if they weren't, there were consequences. I had peace. And I knew what was expected of me. They were intimate relationships, but none of my previous submissives thrilled me as Ana does, even though she's so difficult.

Maybe it's because she's so difficult.

I remember our contract negotiation. She was difficult then.

Yes. Look how that turned out, Grey.

She's had me on my toes since I met her. Is this why I like her so much? How long will I feel this way? Probably as long as she stays. Because deep down I know she'll leave me eventually.

They all do.

Music starts blaring from the living room. "Crazy in Love" by Beyoncé. Is Ana sending me a message?

I stand in the corridor that leads to my study and the TV room and watch her cook. She's whisking some eggs, but she stops suddenly, and from what I can see, she's grinning like a fool.

I creep up behind her and slip my arms around her, startling her. "Interesting choice of music," I croon in her ear and plant a kiss behind it. "Your hair smells good."

She shimmies out of my arms. "I'm still mad at you," she says.

"How long are you going to keep this up?" I ask and rake my hand through my hair in frustration.

"At least until I've eaten." Her tone is haughty but playful.

Good.

Picking up the remote, I switch off the music.

"Did you put that on your iPod?" Ana asks.

I shake my head. I don't want to say it was Leila, because she might get mad again.

"Don't you think she was trying to tell you something back then?" she says, guessing correctly that it was Leila.

"Well, with hindsight, probably," I reply. *Why didn't I see this coming?*

Ana asks why it's still on my iPod, and I offer to remove it.

"What would you like to hear?"

"Surprise me," she says, and it's a challenge.

Very well, Miss Steele. Your wish is my command. I scroll through the iPod, dismissing several tunes. I consider "Please Forgive Me" by David Gray, but that's too obvious and frankly too apologetic.

I know. What did she call it earlier? Sexpertise? Yes.

Use it. *Seduce her, Grey.*

I've had enough of her crankiness. I find the song I want, hit play. *Perfect.* The orchestra swells and music fills the room with a cool, sultry intro, and then Nina Simone sings. *"I put a spell on you."*

Ana whirls around, armed with a whisk, and I catch and hold her gaze as I move toward her.

"You're mine," Nina sings.

You're mine.

"Christian, please," Ana whispers when I reach her.

"Please what?"

"Don't do this."

"Do what?"

"This." She's breathless.

"Are you sure?" I take the whisk out of her hand before she decides to use it as a weapon.

Ana. Ana. Ana.

I'm close enough to smell her. I shut my eyes and take a deep breath. When I open them, the telltale flush of desire stains her cheeks.

And it's there between us.

That familiar pull.

Our intense attraction.

"I want you, Anastasia," I whisper. "I love and I hate, and I love arguing with you. It's very new. I need to know that we're okay. It's the only way I know how."

She closes her eyes. "My feelings for you haven't changed," she says, her voice low and reassuring.

Prove it.

Her eyelashes flutter and her eyes flit to the exposed skin above my shirt and she bites her lip. I suppress my groan as the heat radiating from her body warms us both.

"I'm not going to touch you until you say yes." My voice is thick with my hunger. "But right now, after a really shitty morning, I want to bury myself in you and just forget everything but us."

Her eyes meet mine. "I'm going to touch your face," she says, surprising me.

Okay. I ignore the frisson that runs down my spine. Her hand caresses my cheek and I close my eyes, enjoying the feel of her fingertips teasing my stubble.

Oh, baby.

No need for fear, Grey.

Instinctively, I press my face into her touch, experiencing it, luxuriating in it. I lean down, my lips close to hers, and she raises her face to mine.

"Yes or no, Anastasia?"

"Yes." The word is no more than an audible sigh.

And I lower my mouth to hers, my lips brushing hers, coaxing her. Tasting her. Teasing her until she opens up for me. I embrace her, one hand on her behind pushing her against my arousal and my other hand running up her back, into her soft hair, where I tug gently. She moans as her tongue meets mine.

"Mr. Grey." We're interrupted.

Christ.

I release Ana.

"Taylor," I acknowledge through gritted teeth as he stands on the threshold of the living room, looking suitably embarrassed but resolute.

What. The. Fuck.

We have an understanding that he makes himself scarce when I'm not alone in the apartment. Whatever he has to say must be important.

"My study," I indicate, and Taylor walks briskly across the room. "Rain check," I whisper to Ana and follow Taylor out.

"I'm sorry to interrupt you, sir," he says when we're in my office.

"You'd better have a good reason."

"Well, your mother called."

"Please don't tell me that's the reason."

"No, sir. But you should call her back sooner rather than later. It's about this evening."

"Okay. What else?"

"The security team is here, and knowing how you feel about guns, I thought I should inform you that they're armed."

"What?"

"Mr. Welch and I both think it's a precautionary measure."

"I loathe guns. Let's hope they don't have to use them." I sound pissed, and I am—I was making out with Anastasia Steele.

When have I ever been interrupted while making out?

Never.

The thought suddenly amuses me.

I'm living the adolescence I never had.

Taylor relaxes, and I know it's because my mood has changed.

"Did you know Andrea was getting married today?" I ask him, because this has been bugging me since this morning.

"Yes," he answers with a puzzled expression.

"She didn't tell me."

"Probably just an oversight, sir."

Now I know he's patronizing me. I raise an eyebrow.

"The wedding is at The Edgewater," he says quickly.

"Is she staying there?"

"I believe so."

"Can you discreetly inquire if the happy couple has a room there and get them upgraded to the best suite available? And pay for it."

Taylor smiles. "Certainly, sir."

"Who's the lucky guy?"

"That I don't know, Mr. Grey."

I wonder why Andrea has been so mysterious about her wedding. I brush aside the thought as the aroma of something delicious filters into the room and my stomach growls in anticipation.

"I'd better get back to Anastasia."

"Yes, sir."

"Was that all?"

"Yes."

"Great." We both exit my study. "I'll brief them in ten," I say to Taylor when we're back in the living room. Ana is bending over the stove, retrieving a couple of plates.

"We'll be ready," Taylor says and departs, leaving me alone with Anastasia.

"Lunch?" she offers.

"Please." I sit down at one of the barstools where she's laid our places for lunch.

"Problem?" she inquires, as curious as ever. I have yet to tell her about the additional security.

"No."

She doesn't push me for any answers as she busies herself plating our lunch of Spanish omelet with salad. I'm impressed she's so capable and at ease in my kitchen. She sits beside me as I take a bite and the food melts in my mouth.

Hmm. Delicious.

"This is good. Would you like a glass of wine?"

"No thank you," she replies and gingerly starts eating her lunch.

At least she's eating.

I forgo the wine, as I know I'll be drinking this evening. Which reminds me that I have to call my mother. I wonder what she wants. She doesn't know I split up with Ana—and now we're back together. I should let her know that Ana is coming to the ball this evening.

Using the remote, I switch on some relaxing music.

"What's this?" Ana asks.

"Canteloube, *Songs of the Auvergne*. This is called 'Bailero.'"

"It's lovely. What language is it?"

"It's in old French—Occitan, in fact."

"You speak French; do you understand it?"

"Some words, yes. My mother had a mantra: 'musical instrument, foreign language, martial art.' Elliot speaks Spanish; Mia and I speak French. Elliot plays guitar, I play piano, and Mia the cello."

"Wow. And the martial arts?"

"Elliot does judo. Mia put her foot down at age twelve and refused." Ana knows I kickbox.

"I wish my mother had been that organized."

"Dr. Grace is formidable when it comes to the accomplishments of her children."

"She must be very proud of you. I would be," Ana says warmly.

Oh, baby, you couldn't be more wrong. Nothing is that simple. I've been a big disappointment to my folks: school expulsions, dropping out of college, no relationships that they knew of… If Grace only knew the truth about my lifestyle.

If *you* only knew the truth, Ana.

Don't go there, Grey.

"Have you decided what you'll wear this evening? Or do I need to come pick something for you?"

"Um, not yet. Did you choose all those clothes?"

"No, Anastasia, I didn't. I gave a list and your size to a personal shopper at Neiman Marcus. They should fit. Just so you know, I have ordered additional security for this evening and the next few days. With Leila unpredictable and unaccounted for somewhere on the streets of Seattle, I think it's a wise precaution. I don't want you going out unaccompanied. Okay?"

She looks a little stunned but agrees, surprising me by acquiescing without argument.

"Good. I'm going to brief them. I shouldn't be long."

"They're here?"

"Yes."

She looks puzzled. But she hasn't objected to the additional security, so while I have the upper hand, I pick up my empty plate and place it in the sink and leave Ana to finish her meal in peace.

The security team is gathered in Taylor's office, seated at his round table. After our introductions I sit down and run through the evening's event.

BRIEFING FINISHED, I RETURN to my study to call my mother.

"Darling, how are you?" she enthuses into the phone.

"I'm well, Grace."

"Are you coming this evening?"

"Of course. And Anastasia is coming, too."

"She is?" She sounds surprised, but she recovers quickly. "That's wonderful, sweetheart. I'll make room at our table." She sounds too exuberant. I can only imagine her delight.

"I'll see you this evening, Mother."

"I look forward to it, Christian. Goodbye."

There's an email from Flynn.

From: Dr. John Flynn
Subject: Tonight
Date: June 11 2011 14:25
To: Christian Grey

I look forward to meeting Anastasia.

JF

I bet you do, John.

It seems everyone is thrilled I have a date tonight.

Everyone, including me.

ANA IS LYING ACROSS the bed in the submissive's room, staring at her Mac. She's engrossed in reading something on the web.

"What are you doing?" I ask.

She startles, and for some reason looks guilty. I lie down beside her and see she's on a website with a page titled "Multiple Personality Disorder: The Symptoms."

I understand I have many issues, but fortunately schizophrenia is not one of them. I can't hide my amusement at her amateur psychological sleuthing. "On this site for a reason?"

"Research. Into a difficult personality."

"A difficult personality?"

"My own pet project."

"I'm a pet project now? A sideline. Science experiment, maybe. When I thought I was everything. Miss Steele, you wound me."

"How do you know it's you?"

"Wild guess," I tease.

"It's true you are the only fucked-up, mercurial control freak that I know intimately."

"I thought I was the only person you know intimately."

"Yes. That, too," she replies, and an embarrassed flush turns her cheeks a fetching pink.

"Have you reached any conclusions yet?"

She turns to scrutinize me, her expression warm. "I think you're in need of intense therapy."

I tuck her hair behind her ear, pleased that she's kept it long and I can still do this. "I think I'm in need of you," I counter. "Here." I give her the lipstick.

"You want me to wear this?"

I laugh. "No, Anastasia, not unless you want to. Not sure it's your color."

Scarlet red is Elena's color. Though I don't tell Ana that. She'll combust. And not in a good way.

I sit up on the bed, cross my legs, and pull my shirt over my head. This is either a brilliant brain wave—or a stupid one. We'll see. "I like your road-map idea."

She looks puzzled.

"The no-go areas," I prompt.

"Oh. I was kidding," she says.

"I'm not."

"You want me to draw on you, with lipstick?" She's bewildered.

"It washes off. Eventually."

She considers my proposition and a smile tugs at her lips. "What about something more permanent, like a Sharpie?"

"I could get a tattoo."

"No to the tattoo!" She laughs, but her eyes are wide in horror.

"Lipstick, then," I retort. Her laugh is infectious and I beam at her.

She shuts the Mac and I hold out my hands. "Come. Sit on me."

She peels her shoes off and crawls over to me. I lay back, keeping my knees upright. "Lean against my legs."

She sits astride me, excited at this new challenge.

"You seem…enthusiastic for this," I note with irony.

"I'm always eager for information, Mr. Grey, and it means you'll relax, because I'll know where the boundaries lie."

I shake my head. I hope this is a good idea. "Open the lipstick," I instruct.

For once, she does as she's told.

"Give me your hand."

She holds up her free hand.

"The one with the lipstick!"

"Are you rolling your eyes at me?" she chides.

"Yep."

"That's very rude, Mr. Grey. I know some people who get positively violent at eye rolling."

"Do you, now?" My tone is wry.

She places her hand with the lipstick in mine and I sit up suddenly, surprising her, so we're nose to nose.

"Ready?" I whisper, trying to curb my anxiety, but panic starts to spread.

"Yes," she responds, the word as soft as a summer breeze.

Knowing I'm about to overstep my bounds, the darkness is circling like a vulture, waiting to consume me. Taking her hand, I move it to the top of my shoulder and fear squeezes my ribs, expelling the air from my lungs.

"Press down." I struggle to get the words out. She does, and I guide her hand around my arm socket and down the side of my chest. The darkness slides into my throat, threatening to choke me. Ana's amusement is gone, replaced by her solemn and determined concentration. I fix my eyes on hers and read every nuanced thought and emotion in the depths of her irises, each a life buoy, keeping me from drowning, holding the darkness at bay.

She is my salvation.

I stop at the bottom of my rib cage and move her hand across my abdomen, the lipstick spilling its red trail as she paints my body. I'm panting, trying desperately to hide my fear. Each muscle is tense and standing proud as the red slices my flesh. I lean back, supporting myself on flexed, straining arms as I fight my demons and surrender myself to her gentle illustration. She's halfway done when I let go and give her total control. "And up the other side," I whisper.

With the same single-minded focus, Ana draws up my right side. Eyes impossibly large. Anguished. But holding my attention. When she reaches the top of my shoulder, she stops. "There, done," she breathes, her voice husky with repressed emotion. She lifts her hand away from my body, giving me a brief respite.

"No you're not." I draw a line with my finger around the base of my neck above my clavicle. Ana takes a deep breath and traces the lipstick along the same line. When she finishes, blue eyes meet gray.

"Now my back," I instruct and shift so she clambers off me. I turn around, my back to her, and cross my legs. "Follow the line from my chest, all the way around to the other side." My voice is hoarse and alien to me, like I've left my body entirely to watch a beautiful young woman tame a monster.

No. No.

Be in the moment, Grey.

Live this.

Feel this.

Conquer this.

I am at Ana's mercy.

The woman I love.

The tip of the lipstick crosses my back as I hunch over and screw my eyes shut, tolerating the pain. It disappears.

"Around your neck, too?" Her voice is plaintive. Full of reassurance. *My life buoy.* I nod and the pain is back, piercing my skin beneath my hairline.

Then, just as suddenly, it's gone again.

"Finished," she says, and I want to shout my relief from the helipad on Escala. I turn to face her and she's watching me. And I know I'll shatter like a shard of glass if I see any pity on her face… but there's none. She's waiting. Patient. Kind. Controlled. Compassionate.

My Ana.

"Those are my boundaries," I whisper.

"I can live with those. Right now I want to launch myself at you," she says, her eyes shining.

At last!

My relief is a wicked smile, and I hold out my hands in invitation. "Well, Miss Steele, I'm all yours."

She squeals with glee and throws herself into my arms.

Whoa!

She knocks me off balance, but I recover and twist so she lands on the bed beneath me, grasping my biceps. "Now, about that rain check." I kiss her, hard. Her fingers curl in my hair and tug as I consume her. She moans, her tongue entwined with mine, and there's a reckless, wild abandon in our kissing. She's driving the darkness out and I'm drinking in her light. Adrenaline is fueling my passion and she's matching me kiss for kiss. I want her naked. I sit her up and drag her T-shirt over her head and toss it to the floor.

"I want to feel you." My words are feverish against her lips as I undo her bra and throw it aside. I lay her back down on the bed and kiss her breast, my lips toying with one nipple while my fingers tease the other. She cries out when I suck and tug hard.

"Yes, baby, let me hear you," I breathe against her skin.

She squirms beneath me as I continue my sensual worship of her breasts. Her nipples respond to my touch, growing longer and harder as Ana writhes to a rhythm set by her passion.

She is a goddess.

My goddess.

I undo the button on her jeans as she twists her hands in my hair. I make short work of her zipper and slip my hand inside her panties. My fingers slide with ease to their goal.

Fuck.

She thrusts her pelvis up to meet the heel of my hand and I press against her clitoris as she mewls beneath me. She's slick and ready. "Oh, baby," I whisper and lean up and hover over her, watching her wild expression. "You're so wet."

"I want you," she whimpers.

I kiss her again as my hand moves against and inside her. I'm greedy. I want all of her. I need all of her.

She's mine.

Mine.

I sit up and grab the hem of her jeans, and in one swift tug they're off. I hook my fingers in her panties and they follow. I stand and out of my pocket take a foil packet and toss it at her. I'm relieved to remove my jeans and underwear.

Ana rips open the packet and eyes me hungrily when I lie down beside her. Slowly she rolls the condom over me and I grab her hands and roll onto my back.

"You. On top," I insist, and I sit her astride me. "I want to see you."

Slowly I ease her down onto me.

Fuck. She. Feels. So. Good.

I close my eyes and flex my hips as she takes me, and I exhale with a long, loud groan. "You feel so good." I tighten my fingers around hers. I don't want to let her go.

And she rises and falls, her body embracing mine. Her breasts bouncing as she does. I let go of her hands, knowing she'll respect the road map, and I grab her hips. She places her hands on my arms as I rise up and thrust into her.

She cries out.

"That's right, baby, feel me," I whisper.

She tips her head back and becomes the perfect counterpoint.

Up. Down. Up. Down. Up. Down.

I lose myself in our shared rhythm, reveling in every precious inch of her. She's panting and moaning. And I watch her take me, over and over. Eyes closed. Head back in ecstasy. She's magnificent. She opens her eyes.

"My Ana." My lips form the words.

"Yes. Always," she cries.

And her words call to my soul and tip me over the edge. I close my eyes and surrender to her once more.

She cries out as she finds her own release, pulling me to mine as she collapses on top of me.

"Oh, baby," I grunt, and I'm spent.

Her head lolls on my chest, but I don't care. She's subdued the darkness. I caress her hair and with tired fingers I stroke her back as we both catch our breath.

"You are so beautiful," I murmur, and it's only when Ana lifts her head that I realize I've said the words out loud. She eyes me with skepticism.

When will she learn to take a compliment?

I sit up quickly, catching Ana off-guard. But I hold her in place and we're face-to-face again.

"You. Are. Beautiful." I emphasize each word.

"And you're amazingly sweet sometimes." She leans forward and gives me a chaste kiss.

I lift her up and she winces as I ease out of her. I kiss her gently. "You have no idea how attractive you are, do you?"

She looks nonplussed.

"All those boys pursuing you, that isn't enough of a clue?"

"Boys? What boys?"

"You want the list? The photographer, he's crazy about you; that boy in the hardware store; your roommate's older brother. Your boss." That untrustworthy fucker.

"Oh, Christian, that's just not true."

"Trust me. They want you. They want what's mine." I tighten my hold on her and she rests her forearms on my shoulders, her hands in my hair. And she studies me with amused tolerance.

"Mine," I assert.

"Yes. Yours." She gives me an indulgent smile. "The line is still intact," she continues. And draws her finger over the lipstick mark on my shoulder.

I stiffen, alarmed.

"I want to go exploring," she whispers.

"The apartment?"

"No." She shakes her head. "I was thinking of the treasure map we've drawn on you."

What?

She rubs her nose against mine, distracting me.

"And what would that entail exactly, Miss Steele?"

She raises her hand and tickles my stubble with her fingertips. "I just want to touch you everywhere I'm allowed."

Her index finger brushes my lips and I capture it between my teeth.

"Ow," she yelps when I bite down, and I grin as I growl.

So she wants to touch me. I've given her my boundaries.

Try it her way, Grey.

"Okay," I acquiesce, but I hear the uncertainty in my voice. "Wait." I lift her and remove the condom and drop it beside the bed. "I hate those things. I've a good mind to call Dr. Greene around to give you a shot."

"You think the top ob-gyn in Seattle is going to come running?"

"I can be very persuasive." I smooth her hair behind her ear. She has the most beautiful small, impish ears. "Franco's done a great job on your hair. I like these layers."

"Stop changing the subject," she warns.

I lift her so she's astride me once more. Watching her carefully, I recline onto the pillows while she rests her back against my upright knees. "Touch away," I murmur.

Her eyes never leave mine and she places her hand on my belly, beneath the lipstick line. I tense as her finger explores the valleys between my abdominal muscles. I flinch and she lifts her finger.

"I don't have to," she says.

"No, it's fine. Just takes some readjustment on my part. No one's touched me for a long time."

"Mrs. Robinson?"

Shit. Why did I allude to her?

Warily, I nod. "I don't want to talk about her. It will sour your good mood."

"I can handle it."

"No you can't, Ana. You see red whenever I mention her. My past is my past. It's a fact. I can't change it. I'm lucky that you don't have one, because it would drive me crazy if you did."

"Drive you crazy? More than you are already?"

"Crazy for you," I declare.

She grins, a large, genuine grin. "Shall I call Dr. Flynn?"

"I don't think that will be necessary."

She wriggles on top of me and I drop my legs. With her eyes on mine, she places her fingers on my belly.

I tense.

"I like touching you," she says, and her hand slips down to my navel, teasing the hair there. Her fingers quest lower.

Whoa.

My cock twitches in approval.

"Again?" she says with a carnal smile.

Oh, Anastasia, you insatiable woman.

"Oh yes, Miss Steele, again."

I sit up and clasp her head in my hands and kiss her, long and hard. "You're not too sore?" I whisper against her lips.

"No."

"I love your stamina, Ana."

SHE DOZES BESIDE ME. Replete, I hope. After all of today's arguments and recriminations, I'm now feeling more at peace.

Perhaps I can do this vanilla thing.

I look down at Ana. Her lips are parted and her lashes leave little shadows across her pale cheek. She looks serene and beautiful, and I could watch her sleep forever.

Yet she can be really fucking difficult.

Who knew?

And the irony is—I think I like it.

She makes me question myself.

She makes me question everything.

She makes me feel alive.

BACK IN THE LIVING room, I gather my papers from the sofa and head into my study. I've left Anastasia asleep. She must be exhausted after last night, and we have a long night ahead at the ball.

At my desk I fire up my computer. One of Andrea's many virtues is that she keeps my contacts up-to-date and synced across all my devices. I look up Dr. Greene and, sure enough, I have her email address. I'm so over condoms—I'd like her to see Ana as soon as possible. I send her an email, but I don't imagine I'll hear from her until Monday—after all, it's the weekend.

I send a couple of emails to Ros and make some notes on the reports I read earlier. Opening a drawer to put away my pen, I spy the red box with the earrings I bought Ana for the gala that we never attended.

She left me.

Taking out the box, I examine the earrings once more. They are perfect for her. Elegant. Simple. Stunning. I wonder if she'd accept them today. After the fight about the Audi and the twenty-four thousand dollars, it seems unlikely. But I'd like to give them to her. I put the box in my pocket and check my watch. It's time to wake Ana as I'm sure she'll need a while to get ready for tonight.

SHE'S CURLED UP IN the middle of the bed, looking small and lonely. She's in the sub's room. I wonder why she's up here. She's not my submissive. She should be asleep in my bed, downstairs.

"Hey, sleepyhead." I kiss her temple.

"Mmm," she grumbles, and her eyelids flicker open.

"Time to get up," I whisper, and kiss her quickly on the lips.

"Mr. Grey." Her fingers caress my stubble. "I've missed you."

"You've been asleep." How can she have missed me?

"I missed you in my dreams."

Her simple, sleepy statement floors me. She is so unpredictable and bewitching. I grin as an unexpected warmth spreads through my body. It's becoming familiar but I don't want to put a name to the feeling. It's too new. Too scary.

"Up," I order, and I leave her to get ready before I'm tempted to join her.

AFTER A QUICK SHOWER, I shave. Usually I try to avoid eye contact with the asshole in the mirror, but today he looks happier, though somewhat ridiculous with a smeared red lipstick line around his neck.

My thoughts turn to the night ahead. I usually loathe these events and find them intensely dull, but this time I'll have a date. Another first with Ana. I hope having her on my arm will ward off the flocks of Mia's friends who try desperately to get themselves noticed. They have never learned that I'm just not interested.

I wonder how Ana will find it—perhaps she'll think it's dull, too. I hope not. Maybe I should liven up the evening.

As I finish shaving, an idea comes to mind.

A few minutes later, wearing my dress pants and shirt, I head upstairs, pausing outside my playroom.

Is this a good idea?

Ana can always say no.

I unlock the door and step inside.

I've not been in my playroom since she left me. It's quiet, and ambient light glows on the red walls, giving the place an illusion of warmth. But today this room is not my sanctuary. It hasn't been since she left me alone and in darkness. It holds the memory of her tearstained face, her anger, and her bitter words. I close my eyes.

You need to sort your shit out, Grey.

I'm trying, Ana. I'm trying.

You are one fucked-up son of a bitch.

Fuck.

If she only knew. She'd leave. Again.

I discard the unpalatable thought and from the chest fetch what I need.

Will she go for this?

I like your kinky fuckery. Her hushed words from the night of our reconciliation give me some consolation. With Ana's confession in mind, I turn to leave. For the first time ever, I don't want to linger in here.

As I lock the door I wonder when or if Ana and I will revisit this room. I know I'm not ready. How Ana will feel about the—what does she call it?—Red Room of pain, we'll have to see. The thought that I may never use it again depresses me. Brooding on this, I walk to her room. Perhaps I should get rid of the canes and belts. Maybe that would help.

I open the submissive's room door and stop.

A startled Ana whirls around to face me. She's dressed in a black corset, tiny lace panties, and thigh-highs.

All thought is erased from my mind.

My mouth dries as I stare.

She's a walking wet dream.

She's Aphrodite.

Thank you, Caroline Acton.

"Can I help you, Mr. Grey? I assume there is some purpose to your visit other than to gawk mindlessly at me." There's a haughty edge to her voice.

"I am rather enjoying my mindless gawk, thank you, Miss Steele." I step into the room. "Remind me to send a personal note of thanks to Caroline Acton."

Ana gestures with her hands. She's wondering what I'm talking about.

"The personal shopper at Neiman's," I clarify.

"Oh."

"I'm quite distracted."

"I can see that. What do you want, Christian?" she says, sounding impatient, but I think she's teasing me. I pull the kegel balls out of my pocket for her to see, and her expression changes from playful to alarmed.

She thinks I want to spank her.

I do…

But.

"It's not what you think," I reassure her.

"Enlighten me."

"I thought you could wear these, tonight."

She blinks several times. "To this event?"

I nod.

"Will you spank me later?"

"No."

Her face falls and I can't help but laugh. "You want me to?"

I watch her swallow, indecision plain on her face.

"Well, rest assured I am not going to touch you like that, not even if you beg me." I pause and let that information sink in before I continue. "Do you want to play this game?" I hold them up. "You can always take them out if it's too much."

Her eyes darken and a small, wicked smile teases her lips. "Okay," she says.

And once again I'm reminded that Anastasia Steele is not a woman to back away from a challenge.

I spy the Louboutins on the floor. "Good girl. Come here, and I'll put them in once you've put your shoes on."

Ana in fine lingerie and Louboutins—all my dreams are coming true.

I hold out my hand to help her into her shoes. She steps into them and turns from elfin and gamine to tall and willowy.

She's gorgeous.

Man, what they do for her legs.

I lead her to the bedside and fetch the bedroom chair and place it in front of her.

"When I nod, you bend down and hold on to the chair. Understand?"

"Yes."

"Good. Now open your mouth."

She does, and I slide my index finger between her lips.

"Suck," I order. She clasps my hand, and with a lustful glance at me, she does exactly as I ask.

Christ.

Her look is scorching. Wanton. Unwavering. And her tongue teases and pulls at my finger.

I might as well have my cock in her mouth.

I'm hard.

Instantly.

Oh, baby.

I've known very few women who have had this instant effect on me, but none as instant as Ana… and given her naivete, it surprises me. But she's had this hold on me since I met her.

Get to the matter in hand, Grey.

To lubricate the balls, I slip them into my mouth while she continues to pleasure my finger. When I try to withdraw it, her teeth clamp down and she gives me a winsome smile.

No you don't, I warn, shaking my head, and she loosens her grip, releasing me.

I nod, indicating she should bend over the chair, and she obliges.

Kneeling behind her, I move her panties to one side and slide my fellated finger inside her and circle slowly, feeling the tight, wet walls of her vagina. She moans and I want to tell her to be quiet and to stay still, but that's not the relationship we have anymore.

We're doing things her way.

I withdraw my finger, then gently ease each ball inside her, carefully pushing them as deep as they can go. As I slip her panties back in place, I kiss her delectable derrière. I sit back on my heels and run my hands up her legs and kiss each thigh where her stockings stop.

"You have fine, fine legs, Miss Steele." I stand and grasp her hips, pulling her against my arousal. "Maybe I'll have you this way when we get home, Anastasia. You can stand now."

She does, her breath quickening once she's upright, and she shimmies in front of me, her ass brushing my erection. I kiss her shoulder and extend my arm around her, palm up, holding out the Cartier box.

"I bought these for you to wear to last Saturday's gala. But you left me, so I never had the opportunity to give them to you." I take a deep breath. "This is my second chance."

Will she accept them?

It seems symbolic somehow. If she's serious about us, she'll accept them. I hold my breath. She reaches for the box and opens it and stares at the earrings for the longest time.

Please take them, Ana.

"They're lovely," she whispers. "Thank you."

She *can* play nice. I grin as I relax, knowing I won't have to fight to get her to keep them. I kiss her shoulder and spot the silver satin dress on the bed. I ask her if that's what she's chosen to wear.

"Yes. Is that okay?"

"Of course. I'll let you get ready."

I'VE LOST COUNT OF the number of these events I've attended, but for the first time I'm excited. I get to show Ana off to my family and all of their well-heeled friends.

I finish tying my bow tie with ease and grab my jacket. Slipping it on, I take one last look in the mirror. The asshole looks happy, but he needs to straighten his tie.

"Keep still," Elena snaps.

"Yes, Ma'am." I stand before her, getting ready for prom. I've told my parents I'm not going and that I'm seeing a friend. It will be our own personal prom. Just Elena and I. She moves, and I hear the rustle of expensive silk and inhale the provocative scent of her perfume.

"Open your eyes."

I do as I'm instructed. She's poised behind me and we're facing a mirror. I look at her, not at the idiot boy standing in front of her.

She takes the ends of my bow tie. "And this is how you do this." Slowly, she moves her fingers. Her nails are bright scarlet. I watch. Fascinated.

She pulls the ends and I'm wearing a most respectable bow tie.

"Now, let's see if you can do it. And if you do, I'll reward you." She smiles her secret I-so-own-you smile and I know it will be good.

I'M REHASHING THE NIGHT'S arrangements with the security team when I hear her footfalls behind me. All four men are suddenly distracted. Taylor smiles. When I turn around, Ana is standing at the bottom of the stairs.

A vision. Wow.

She's stunning in her silver gown and reminiscent of a silent-movie siren.

I saunter over to her, feeling a disproportionate sense of pride, and kiss her hair. "Anastasia. You look breathtaking." I'm delighted that she's wearing the earrings.

She flushes.

"A glass of champagne before we go?" I offer.

"Please."

I nod to Taylor, who leads his three colleagues out to the foyer, and with my arm around my date we head into the living room. From the fridge, I take a bottle of Cristal Rosé and open it.

"Security team?" Ana asks as I pour the bubbling liquid into champagne flutes.

"Close protection. They're under Taylor's control. He's trained in that, too." I hand her a glass.

"He's very versatile."

"Yes, he is. You look lovely, Anastasia. Cheers." I raise my glass to meet hers. She takes a sip and closes her eyes, savoring the wine.

"How are you feeling?" I ask, noting the pink flush on her cheeks, the same blush of the champagne, and I wonder how long she'll tolerate the balls.

"Fine, thank you." She gives me a coy smile.

Tonight will be entertaining.

"Here, you're going to need this." I give her the velvet bag that contains her mask. "Open it."

Ana does and pulls out the delicate silver masquerade mask and runs her fingers through the plumes.

"It's a masked ball."

"I see." She examines the mask in wonder.

"This will show off your beautiful eyes, Anastasia."

"Are you wearing one?"

"Of course. They're very liberating, in a way."

She grins.

I have one more surprise for her. "Come. I want to show you something." I hold out my hand and lead her back out to the corridor and into my library. I can't believe I haven't shown her this room.

"You have a library!" she exclaims.

"Yes, the balls room, as Elliot calls it. The apartment is quite spacious. I realized today, when you mentioned exploring, that I've never given you a tour. We don't have time now, but I thought I'd show you this room and maybe challenge you to a game of billiards in the not-too-distant future."

Her eyes are bright with wonder as she takes in the collection of books and the billiard table. "Bring it on," she says with a self-satisfied grin.

"What?" She's hiding something. Can she play?

"Nothing," she says quickly, and I know that's probably the answer. She really is a hopeless liar.

"Well, maybe Dr. Flynn can uncover your secrets. You'll meet him this evening."

"The expensive charlatan?"

"The very same. He's dying to meet you. Shall we go?"

She nods, and excitement shines in her eyes.

WE TRAVEL IN COMPANIONABLE silence in the back of the car. I skim my thumb across her knuckles, sensing her growing anticipation. She crosses and uncrosses her legs, and I know the balls are taking their toll.

"Where did you get the lipstick?" she asks out of the blue.

I point to Taylor and mouth his name.

She laughs. Then stops abruptly.

And I know it's the kegel balls.

"Relax," I whisper. "If it's too much…" I kiss each of her knuckles and suck the tip of her little finger, rolling my tongue around it, as she did with my finger earlier. Ana closes her eyes, tips her head back, and inhales. Her smoldering eyes meet mine when she opens them again. She rewards me with a wicked grin and I respond in kind.

"So what can we expect at this event?" she asks.

"Oh, the usual stuff."

"Not usual for me."

Of course. When would she have been to an event like this? I kiss her knuckles once more as I explain. "Lots of people flashing their cash. Auction, raffle, dinner, dancing—my mother knows how to throw a party."

The Audi joins the line of cars arriving at my parents' house. Ana strains to have a look. I glance out the back window to see Reynolds from the security detail following us in my other Audi Q7.

"Masks on." I retrieve mine from the black silk bag beside me.

When we pull up into the driveway, we are both in disguise. Ana looks spectacular. She's dazzling, and I want to show her off to the world. Taylor comes to a stop and one of the valets opens my door.

"Ready?" I ask Ana.

"As I'll ever be."

"You look beautiful, Anastasia." I kiss her hand and climb out of the car.

I put my arm around my date, and we walk alongside the house on a green carpet my mother has rented for the occasion. I glance once over my shoulder and observe our four security personnel walking behind us, looking everywhere. It's reassuring.

"Mr. Grey!" a photographer calls out to me, and I pull Ana close and we pose.

"Two photographers?" Ana observes, curious.

"One is from *The Seattle Times*; the other is for a souvenir. We'll be able to buy a copy later."

We pass a line of servers holding flutes of champagne and I hand a glass to Ana.

My parents have gone all-out, like they do every year. Pavilion, pergolas, lanterns, checkered dance floor, ice swans, and a string quartet. I watch Ana as she takes in the surroundings with awe. It's gratifying to see my parents' generosity through her eyes. It's not often that I get the opportunity to stand back and appreciate how lucky I am to be part of their world.

"How many people are coming?" she asks, sizing up the elaborate tent next to the shoreline.

"I think about three hundred. You'll have to ask my mother."

"Christian!" I hear the shrill, not-so-dulcet tones of my sister, then she's throwing her arms around my neck in a melodramatic display of affection. She's a vision in pink.

"Mia." I return her enthusiastic hug. She spies Ana, and I'm forgotten.

"Ana! Oh, darling, you look gorgeous! You must come meet my friends. None of them can believe that Christian finally has a girlfriend." She hugs Ana and takes her hand. Ana gives me a quick apprehensive look before Mia drags her to a group of women who coo over her. All except one.

Shit. I recognize Lily, Mia's friend since kindergarten. Spoiled, wealthy, gorgeous, but spiteful, she embodies all the worst attributes of privilege and entitlement. And there was a time when she thought she was entitled to me. I shudder.

I watch Ana as she's gracious with Mia's friends, but she steps back suddenly looking uncomfortable. I think Lily is being an asshole. This will never do. I walk over and put my arm around Ana's waist. "Ladies, if I could claim my date back, please?"

"Lovely to meet you," Ana says to the throng as I pull her away. "Thank you," she mouths.

"I saw that Lily was with Mia. She is one nasty piece of work."

"She likes you," Ana observes.

"Well, the feeling is not mutual. Come, let me introduce you to some people."

Ana is impressive—the perfect date. Gracious, elegant, and sweet, she listens attentively to anecdotes, she asks intelligent questions, and I love the way she defers to me.

Yes. I especially love that. It's novel and unexpected.

But then she's always unexpected.

What's more, she's oblivious to the many, many admiring glances she receives from both men and women, and she stays close to my side. I attribute her rosy glow to the champagne and maybe the kegel balls, and if the latter are bothering her, she hides it well.

The master of ceremonies announces that dinner is served, and we follow the green carpet across the lawn to the pavilion. Ana is looking toward the boathouse.

"Boathouse?" I ask.

"Maybe we can go there later."

"Only if I can carry you over my shoulder."

She laughs, then stops abruptly.

I grin. "How are you feeling?"

"Good," she says with a superior air, and my grin broadens.

Game on, Miss Steele.

Behind us, Taylor and his men follow at a discreet distance and, once in the tent pavilion, position themselves so they have a good view of the crowd.

My mother and Mia are already at our table with a friend of Mia's.

Grace welcomes Ana warmly. "Ana, how delightful to see you again! And looking so beautiful, too."

"Mother." I greet Grace and kiss her on both cheeks.

"Oh, Christian, so formal!" she chides.

My maternal grandparents join us, and after the obligatory hugs I introduce them both to Ana.

"Oh, he's finally found someone, how wonderful, and so pretty! Well, I do hope you make an honest man of him," my grandmother enthuses.

Inappropriate, Grandma.

Fuck. I stare at my mother. *Help. Mom. Stop her.*

"Mother, don't embarrass Ana," Grace admonishes her mom.

"Ignore the silly old coot, m'dear. She thinks because she's so old, she has a God-given right to say whatever nonsense pops into that woolly head of hers." My grandfather gives me a wink.

Theodore Trevelyan is my hero. We have a special bond. This man has patiently taught me how to plant, cultivate, and graft apple trees, and in doing so has won my eternal affection. Quiet. Strong. Kind. Patient with me. Always.

"Here, kiddo," Grandpa Trev-yan says. "You don't talk much, do you?"

I shake my head. No. I don't talk at all.

"That's no problem. Folks around here talk too much anyway. Do you want to help me in the orchard?"

I nod. I like Grandpa Trev-yan. He has kind eyes and a loud laugh. He holds out his hand, but I tuck my hands under my arms.

"As you like, Christian. Let's go make some green apple trees make red apples."

I like red apples.

The orchard is big. There are trees. And trees. And trees. But they are small trees. Not big. And they have no leaves. And no apples. Because of winter. I have big boots on and a hat. I like my hat. I'm warm.

Grandpa Trev-yan looks at a tree.

"See this tree, Christian? It makes bitter green apples. But we can fool the tree to make sweet red apples for us. These twigs are from the red apple tree. And here are my pruning shears."

Prew-nig sheers. They are sharp.

"Do you want to cut this one?"

I say yes with my head.

"We're going to graft this twig you've cut. It's called a scion."

Si-yon. Si-yon. I say the word in my head. He takes a knife and makes one end of the twig sharp. And he cuts a branch on the tree and sticks the si-yon in the cut.

"Now we tape it up."

He takes green tape and ties the twig to the branch.

"And we put melted beeswax on the wound. Here. You take this brush. Steady now. That's right."

We make many grafts.

"You know, Christian, apples are second only to oranges as the most valuable fruit grown in the U.S. of A. Here in Washington, though, there's not really enough sun for oranges."

I'm sleepy.

"Tired? You want to head back to the house?"

I say yes with my head.

"We've done a lot of grafting. This tree will yield a huge crop of sweet red apples come autumn. You can help me pick them."

He smiles and holds out a big hand and I take it. It's big and rough but warm and gentle.

"Let's go have some hot chocolate."

Grandpa gives me a crinkled smile and I turn my attention to Mia's date, who seems to be checking out mine. His name is Sean and I think he's from Mia's old high school. I shake his hand, squeezing hard.

Keep your eyes on your own date, Sean. And by the way, you're with my sister. Treat her well or I will end you. I think I manage to convey all that information in my pointed look and the tight grip I have on his hand.

He nods and swallows. "Mr. Grey."

I pull out Ana's chair and we sit.

My dad is standing on the stage. He taps the mic and rattles off a welcome and an introduction to the great and the good gathered before him. "Welcome, ladies and gentlemen, to our annual charity ball. I hope that you enjoy what we have laid out for you tonight and that you'll dig deep into your pockets to support the fantastic work that our team does with Coping Together. As you know, it's a cause that is very close to my wife's heart, and mine."

The plumes on Ana's mask quiver as she turns to look at me, and I wonder if she's thinking about my past. Should I answer her unspoken question?

Yes. This charity exists because of me.

My parents formed it because of my miserable start in life. And now they help hundreds of addicted parents and their kids by offering them refuge and rehabilitation.

But she says nothing and I remain impassive, as I'm not sure how I should feel about her curiosity.

"I'll hand you over now to our master of ceremonies. Please be seated, and enjoy," Dad says, and he hands the microphone to the MC, then wanders over to our table, making a beeline for Ana. He greets her with a kiss on each cheek. She blushes. "Good to see you again, Ana," he says.

"Ladies and gentlemen: please nominate a table head," the MC calls out.

"Ooh. Me, me!" cries Mia, bouncing like a child in her seat.

"In the center of the table you will find an envelope," the MC continues. "Would everyone find, beg, borrow, or steal a bill of the highest denomination you can manage, write your name on it, and place it inside the envelope? Table heads, please guard these envelopes carefully. We will need them later."

"Here." I give a hundred-dollar bill to Ana.

"I'll pay you back," she whispers.

Sweetheart.

I don't want that argument again. Saying nothing because a scene would be unseemly, I hand her my Mont Blanc so she can sign her name on the note.

Grace signals a couple of servers standing at the front of the pavilion and they pull back the canvas, revealing a picture-postcard view of Seattle and Meydenbauer Bay at dusk. It's a great view, especially at this time of the evening, and I'm glad the weather has remained fine for my parents.

Ana gazes at the cityscape and its reflection in the water with delight.

And I examine it anew. It's stunning. The darkening sky ablaze with the setting sun mirrored in the water, the lights of Seattle twinkling in the distance. Yeah. Stunning.

Seeing all this through Ana's eyes is humbling. For years I've taken it for granted. I glance at my parents. My father clasps his wife's hand as she laughs at something her friend says. The way he looks at her… the way she looks at him.

They love each other.

Still.

I shake my head. Is it weird that I'm having a strange and new appreciation for my upbringing?

I was lucky. Very lucky.

Our servers arrive, ten of them in total, and as one they present the table with our first course. Ana peeks at me from behind her mask.

"Hungry?"

"Very," she replies with serious intent.

Damn. All other thoughts evaporate as my body responds to her bold statement and I know she's not referring to the food. My grandfather diverts her and I shift in my seat, trying to bring my body to heel.

The food is good.

But then it always is at my parents' place.

I have never been hungry here.

I'm startled by the direction of my thoughts and I'm glad when Lance, my mother's friend from college, engages me in a conversation about what GEH is developing.

I'm acutely aware of Ana's eyes on me as Lance and I debate the economics of technology in the developing world.

"You can't just give this technology away!" Lance scoffs.

"Why not? Ultimately, whose benefit is it for? As human beings, we all have to share finite space and resources on this planet. The smarter we are, the more efficiently we'll use them."

"Democratizing tech is not what I'd expect from someone like you." Lance laughs.

Dude. You don't know me very well.

Lance is engaging enough, but I'm distracted by the beautiful Miss Steele. She moves beside me as she listens to our conversation, and I know the kegel balls are having the desired effect.

Perhaps we should go to the boathouse.

My conversation with Lance is interrupted a few times by various business associates offering a handshake and the odd anecdote. I don't know if they're checking out Ana or trying to ingratiate themselves with me.

By the time dessert is served, I'm ready to leave.

"If you'll excuse me," Ana says suddenly, breathless. And I know she's had enough.

"Do you need the powder room?" I ask.

She nods, and in her eyes I see a desperate plea.

"I'll show you," I offer.

She stands and I start to get up, but Mia stands, too. "No, Christian! You're not taking Ana—I will."

And before I can say anything, she grabs Ana's hand.

Ana gives me an apologetic shrug and follows Mia out of the pavilion. Taylor signals that he's on it and trails behind them both; I'm sure Ana is unaware of her shadow.

Fuck. I wanted to go with her.

My grandmother leans in to talk to me. "She's delightful."

"I know."

"You look happy, dear."

Do I? I thought I was sulking at a missed opportunity.

"I don't think I've ever seen you so relaxed." She pats my hand; it's an affectionate gesture, and for once I don't withdraw from her touch.

Happy?

Me?

I test the word to see if it fits, and an unexpected warmth flares in my gut.

Yes. She makes me happy.

It's a new feeling. I've never described myself in those terms.

I smile at my grandmother and squeeze her hand. "I think you're right, Grandmother."

Her eyes twinkle and she squeezes mine back. "You should bring her to the farm."

"I should. I think she'd like that."

Mia and Ana return to the pavilion, giggling. It's a pleasure to watch them together and to witness my whole family embrace my girl. Even my grandmother has concluded that Ana makes me happy.

She's not wrong.

As Ana takes her seat, she gives me a swift carnal look.

Ah. I mask my smile. I want to ask if she's still wearing the kegel balls, but I presume she's removed them. She's done well to wear them this long. Taking Ana's hand in mine, I give her a list of auction prizes.

I think Ana will enjoy this part of the evening—Seattle's elite flashing their cash.

"You own property in Aspen?" she asks, and everyone at the table turns to look at her.

I nod and put my finger to my lips.

"Do you have property elsewhere?" she whispers.

I nod. But I don't want to disturb everyone at the table with conversation. This is the part of the evening when we raise a sizable sum for the charity.

As everyone applauds a sale price of $12,000 for a signed Mariners baseball bat, I lean over and say, "I'll tell you later."

She licks her lips and my earlier frustration returns.

"I wanted to come with you."

She shoots me a quick aggrieved look, which I think means that she's of the same mind, but she settles down to listen to the bidding.

I watch her get caught up in the excitement of the auction, turning her head to see who's bidding on what and applauding at the conclusion of each lot.

"And up next is a weekend stay in Aspen, Colorado. What are my starting bids, ladies and gentlemen, for this generous prize courtesy of Mr. Christian Grey?" There's a smattering of applause and the master of ceremonies continues. "Do I hear five thousand dollars?"

The bidding begins.

I contemplate taking Ana to Aspen. I don't even know if she skis. The thought of her on skis is unsettling. She's not a coordinated dancer, so she might be a disaster on the slopes. I wouldn't want her to get hurt.

"Twenty thousand dollars, we are bid. Going once, going twice," the MC calls. Ana puts her hand up and calls.

"Twenty-four thousand dollars!"

And it's like she's kicked me in the solar plexus.

What. The. Fuck.

"Twenty-four thousand dollars, to the lovely lady in silver, going once, going twice. Sold!" the master of ceremonies declares to rapturous applause. Everyone at our table gapes at her while my anger spirals out of control. That money was for her. Taking a deep breath, I lean forward and kiss her cheek. "I don't know whether to worship at your feet or spank the living shit out of you," I hiss in her ear.

"I'll take option two, please," she says quickly. Breathlessly.

What?

For a moment I'm confused, and then I realize the kegel balls have done their work. She's needy, really needy, and my anger is forgotten. "Suffering, are you?" I whisper. "We'll have to see what we can do about that." I run my fingers along her jaw.

Make her wait, Grey.

That should be punishment enough.

Or perhaps we could prolong the agony. A wicked thought comes to mind.

She wriggles beside me as my family congratulates her on her win. I drape my arm over her chair and begin to stroke her naked back with my thumb. With my other hand I take hers and kiss her palm, then rest her hand on my thigh. Slowly, I ease her hand up my thigh until her fingers are resting on my erection.

I hear her gasp, and from beneath her mask her shocked eyes meet mine.

I will never tire of shocking sweet Ana.

As the auction continues, my family returns their attention to the next prize. Ana, emboldened, no doubt, by her need, surprises me and starts to caress me through my pants.

Hell.

I keep my hand over hers so no one will be the wiser as she fondles me and I continue to stroke her neck.

My pants are becoming uncomfortable.

She's turned the tables on you, Grey. Again.

"Sold, for one hundred and ten thousand dollars!" the MC declares, bringing me back into the room. The prize is a week in my parents' place in Montana, and it's a colossal amount of money.

The whole room erupts with cheers and applause, and Ana takes her hands off me and joins in the clapping.

Damn.

Reluctantly, I applaud, too, and now that the auction is over, I plan to give Ana a tour of the house.

"Ready?" I mouth to her.

"Yes," she says, her eyes shining through her mask.

"Ana!" Mia says. "It's time!"

Ana looks confused. "Time for what?"

"The First Dance Auction. Come on!" Mia stands and holds out her hand.

Fucking hell. My annoying little sister.

I glower at Mia. Cockblocker extraordinaire.

Ana looks at me and starts to giggle.

It's infectious.

I stand, grateful for my jacket. "The first dance will be with me, okay? And it won't be on the dance floor," I murmur against the pulse beneath her ear.

"I look forward to it." She kisses me in full view of everyone.

I grin and then notice that the entire table is staring at us.

Yes, people. I have a girlfriend. Get used to it.

They, as one, look away, embarrassed to be caught gawking.

"Come on, Ana." Mia is persistent and leads Ana toward the small stage, where several women are assembled.

"Gentlemen, the highlight of the evening!" the MC booms over the PA system and the excited hum of the crowd. "The moment you've all been waiting for! These twelve lovely ladies have all agreed to auction their first dance to the highest bidder!"

Ana is uncomfortable. She looks down at the ground, then at her knotted fingers. She looks anywhere but at the group of young men approaching the stage.

"Now, gentlemen, pray gather around and take a good look at what could be yours for the first dance. Twelve comely and compliant wenches."

When did Mia get Ana involved in this fucking charade?

It's a meat market.

I know it's for a good cause, but still.

The MC announces the first young woman, giving her a hyperbolic introduction. Her name is Jada, and her first dance is quickly sold for $5,000. Mia and Ana are talking. Ana looks engaged in what Mia is saying.

Shit.

What is Mia telling her?

Mariah is up next. She seems embarrassed by the MC's introduction, and I don't blame her; it's inappropriate. Mia and Ana continue to talk—and I know it's about me.

For fuck's sake, Mia, shut up.

Mariah's first dance is sold for $4,000.

Ana glances at me, then back at Mia, who appears to be in full flow.

Jill is up next, and her first dance is sold for $4,000.

Ana stares at me, and I see her eyes glitter inside her mask, but I have no idea what she's thinking.

Shit. What did Mia say?

"And now, allow me to introduce the beautiful Ana."

Mia ushers Ana to the center of the stage and I make my way to the front of the crowd. Ana does not like to be the center of attention.

Damn Mia for making her do this.

But Anastasia is beautiful.

The MC makes another overblown and ridiculous introduction. "Beautiful Ana plays six musical instruments, speaks fluent Mandarin, and is keen on yoga… well, gentlemen—"

Enough. "Ten thousand dollars," I shout.

"Fifteen." There's a call from some random guy.

What the hell?

I turn to look at who is bidding on my girl, and it's Flynn, the expensive charlatan, as Ana calls him. I'd recognize his gait anywhere. He gives me a polite nod.

"Well, gentlemen! We have high rollers in the house this evening," the MC announces to the assembled patrons.

What is Flynn's game? How far does he want to take this?

The chatter in the pavilion dies as the crowd watches us and waits to hear my reaction.

"Twenty," I offer, my voice low.

"Twenty-five," counters Flynn.

Ana looks anxiously from me to Flynn. She's mortified. And, frankly, so am I. I've had enough of whatever game Flynn is playing.

"One hundred thousand dollars," I call so the entire audience can hear me.

"What the fuck?" one of the women behind Ana calls out, and I hear gasps from people in the crowd around me.

Come on, John.

I give Flynn a level stare and he laughs and graciously holds up both his hands. He's done.

"One hundred thousand dollars for the lovely Ana! Going once. Going twice." The MC invites Flynn to bid again, but he shakes his head and bows.

"Sold!" the MC cries out triumphantly, and the applause and cheering are deafening. I step forward and hold out my hand to Ana.

I've won my girl.

She beams at me with relief when she places her hand in mine. I help her down from the stage and kiss the back of her hand, then tuck it under my arm. We make our way to the exit of the pavilion, ignoring the catcalls and the shouts of congratulations.

"Who was that?" she asks.

"Someone you can meet later. Right now, I want to show you something. We have about twenty minutes until the First Dance Auction finishes. Then we have to be back on the dance floor so that I can enjoy that dance I've paid for."

"A very expensive dance," she observes dryly.

"I'm sure it'll be worth every single cent."

At last. I have her. Mia is still on the stage and unable to stop me now. I guide Ana across the lawn toward the dance floor, aware that two of the close protection guys are tailing us. The sounds of revelry fade behind us as I take her through the french doors that lead into the sitting room. I leave the doors open so the guys can follow us. From there we head into the hall and up two flights of stairs to my childhood bedroom.

It will be another first.

Inside, I lock the door. Security can wait outside. "This was my room."

Ana stands in the center, drinking it all in: my posters, my bulletin board. Everything. Her eyes scan it all, then settle on me.

"I've never brought a girl in here."

"Never?"

I shake my head. There's an adolescent thrill running through me. A girl. In my room. What would my mom say?

Ana's lips part in invitation. Her eyes are dark beneath her mask and they don't leave mine. I saunter over to her.

"We don't have long, Anastasia, and the way I'm feeling right this moment, we won't need long. Turn around. Let me get you out of that dress."

She spins around immediately.

"Keep the mask on," I whisper in her ear.

She groans and I haven't even touched her. I know she'll be craving relief after wearing the kegel balls for so long. I unzip her dress and help her out of it. I step back, drape it over a chair, and remove my jacket.

She's wearing the corset.

And thigh-highs.

And heels.

And the mask.

She's driven me to distraction during dinner.

"You know, Anastasia." I move toward her, undoing my bow tie and then the shirt buttons at the collar. "I was so mad when you bought my auction lot. All manner of ideas ran through my head. I had to remind myself that punishment is off the menu. But then you volunteered." Standing close, I stare down at her. "Why did you do that?"

I need to know.

"Volunteer?" Her voice is husky, revealing her desire. "I don't know. Frustration. Too much alcohol. Worthy cause."

She shrugs, and her eyes move to my mouth.

"I vowed to myself I would not spank you again, even if you begged me."

"Please."

"But then I realized you're probably very uncomfortable at the moment, and it's not something you're used to."

"Yes," she answers, breathy and sexy and pleased, I think, that I know how she feels.

"So there might be a certain latitude. If I do this, you must promise me one thing."

"Anything."

"You will safe-word if you need to, and I will just make love to you, okay?"

She agrees readily.

I lead her to the bed, throw the comforter aside, and sit down as she stands before me in her mask and corset.

She looks sensational.

I grab a pillow and place it beside me. Taking her hand, I tug so that she falls across my lap, her chest on the pillow. I sweep her hair off her face and the mask.

There.

She looks glorious.

Now, to spice this up. "Put your hands behind your back."

She scrambles to do my bidding and squirms on top of me.

Eager. I like that.

I tie her wrists with my tie. She's helpless. In my power.

It's exhilarating.

"You really want this, Anastasia?"

"Yes," she stresses, clarifying her need.

But I still don't get it. I thought all this was off the table.

"Why?" I ask as I caress her behind.

"Do I need a reason?"

"No, baby, you don't. I'm just trying to understand you."

Be in the moment, Grey.

She wants this. And so do you.

I stroke her ass once more, preparing myself. Preparing her.

Leaning over, I hold her down with my left hand and I smack her once with the other, just at the junction of her fine, fine ass and her thighs.

She moans an incoherent word.

It's not a safe word.

I smack her again.

"Two. We'll go with twelve." I start counting.

I smooth her behind and spank her twice, once on each cheek. And I pull off her lacy panties, trailing them down her thighs, her knees, her calves, and over her Louboutins, where I discard them on the floor.

It's arousing.

In every way.

Noting she's no longer wearing the kegel balls, I spank her again, numbering each blow. She groans and writhes across my knees, her eyes shut beneath her mask. Her ass is a lovely shade of pink.

"Twelve," I whisper when I'm done.

I caress her glowing ass and sink two fingers into her.

She's wet.

So fucking wet.

So ready.

She moans as I rotate my fingers inside her and she comes, loudly, frantically, around them.

Wow. That's quick. She's such a sensual creature.

"That's right, baby," I murmur, and I untie her wrists. She's panting, trying to catch her breath. "I've not finished with you yet, Anastasia."

I'm now uncomfortable. I want her.

Badly.

Lowering her so her knees touch the floor, I kneel behind her. I undo my zipper and yank down my pants and underwear, freeing my eager erection. From my pants pocket, I extract a condom and pull my fingers out of my girl.

She whimpers.

I wrap my cock in latex. "Open your legs." She complies and I ease into her. "This is going to be quick, baby," I whisper. I hold her hips and slowly pull out of her, then I slam into her.

She cries out. With joy. With abandon. With ecstasy.

This is what she wants, and I'm only too happy to oblige. I thrust and thrust, and then she's meeting me. Thrusting back.

Shit.

This is going to be even quicker than I thought. "Ana, no," I warn. I want to prolong her pleasure. But she's a greedy girl and she takes all she can. A voracious counterpoint to me.

"Ana, shit." It's a strangled cry as I come and it sets her off. She screams as her orgasm rips through her, pulling on me as I sink onto her.

Man, that was good.

I'm spent.

After all the teasing and the anticipation during that meal... this was inevitable. I kiss her shoulder and pull out of her and remove the condom, tossing it into the wastebasket by the bed. That will give my mother's housekeeper something to think about.

Ana's still in her mask, panting, smiling. She looks satiated. I kneel over her, resting my forehead on her back as we both find our equilibrium.

"Mmm," I murmur in satisfaction and plant a kiss on her flawless back. "I believe you owe me a dance, Miss Steele."

She hums a contented response from somewhere deep in her throat. I sit back and pull her onto my lap.

"We don't have long. Come on." I kiss her hair. She moves off my lap and sits on the bed, beginning to dress as I do up my shirt and redo my bow tie.

Ana gets up and walks over to where I've placed her dress. Wearing only her mask, corset and shoes, she embodies sensuality. I knew she was a goddess, but this… She's beyond all my expectations.

I love her.

I turn away, feeling suddenly vulnerable, and straighten the comforter on my bed.

The uneasy feeling ebbs like a receding tide as I finish and see Ana examining the photographs on my bulletin board. There are many—from all over the world. My parents were fond of a foreign vacation.

"Who's this?" Ana asks, pointing to an old black-and-white photograph of the crack whore.

"No one of consequence." I slip on my jacket and straighten my mask. I'd forgotten about that picture. Carrick gave it to me when I was sixteen. I'd tried several times to throw it away, but I could never quite bring myself to dispose of it.

"Son, I have something for you."

"What?" I'm in Carrick's study, expecting a dressing-down. But for what I don't know. I hope he hasn't found out about Mrs. Lincoln.

"You seem calmer, more collected, more yourself these days."

I nod, hoping my expression gives nothing away.

"I was going through some old files and I found this." He hands me a black-and-white photograph of a sad young woman. It's like a gut punch.

The crack whore.

He studies my reaction. "We were given this at the time of the adoption."

"Oh," I manage to say through my closing throat.

"I thought you might want to see it. Do you recognize her?"

"Yes." I squeeze the word out.

He nods, and I know he has something else to say.

What more does he have?

"I don't have any information on your biological father. By all accounts he wasn't part of your mother's life in any way."

He's trying to tell me something… It wasn't her fucking pimp?

Please tell me it wasn't him.

"If you want to know anything else… I'm here."

"That man?" I whisper.

"No. Nothing to do with you," my dad says, to reassure me.

I close my eyes.

Thank fuck. Thank fuck. Thank fuck.

"Is that all, Dad? Can I go?"

"Of course." Dad looks troubled, but he nods.

Clutching the photo, I leave his office. And I run. Run. Run. Run…

The crack whore was a sad and pathetic creature. She looks every bit the victim in this old black-and-white. I think it's a police mug shot but with the numbers cut off. I wonder if things would have ended up differently for her if my parents' charity had existed then. I shake my head. I don't want to talk about her with Ana. "Shall I zip you up?" I ask, to change the subject.

"Please," Ana says and turns her back to me so I can zip up her dress. "Then why is she on your bulletin board?"

Anastasia Steele, you have an answer and a question for everything.

"An oversight on my part. How's my tie?"

She examines my tie and her eyes soften. She reaches up and straightens it, pulling on both ends. "Now it's perfect," she says.

"Like you." I fold her in my arms and kiss her. "Feeling better?"

"Much, thank you, Mr. Grey."

"The pleasure was all mine, Miss Steele."

I'm feeling grateful. Content.

I hold out my hand and she takes it with a shy but satisfied grin. I unlock the door and we head downstairs and back out to the gardens. I don't know at which point our security joins us, but they follow us onto the terrace through the sitting room's french doors. A few smokers are gathered there, puffing away, and they watch us with interest, but I ignore them and lead Ana toward the dance floor.

The MC announces, "And now, ladies and gentlemen, it's time for the first dance. Mr. and Dr. Grey, are you ready?" Carrick nods, my mother in his arms. "Ladies and gentlemen of the First Dance Auction, are you ready?" I circle Ana's waist and peer down at her, and she grins.

"Then we shall begin," the MC declares with gusto. "Take it away, Sam!" The band leader bounds across the stage, turns to the band and snaps his fingers, and the band begins a cheesy version of "I've Got You Under My Skin."

I pull Ana close as we start to dance and she falls easily into step with me. She's captivating as I twirl her around the dance floor, and we grin at each other like the lovesick fools we are…

Have I ever felt like this?

Buoyant?

Happy?

Master of the fucking universe.

"I love this song," I tell her. "Seems very fitting."

"You're under my skin, too. Or you were in your bedroom."

Ana! I'm shocked.

"Miss Steele, I had no idea you could be so crude."

"Mr. Grey, neither did I. I think it's all my recent experiences," she says with a mischievous smile. "They've been an education."

"For both of us." I take her for a spin around the dance floor once more. The song finishes, and reluctantly I release her to applaud.

"May I cut in?" Flynn asks, appearing from nowhere. He has some explaining to do after the charade at the auction, but I step aside.

"Be my guest. Anastasia, this is John Flynn. John, Anastasia."

Ana shoots me a nervous look and I retreat to the sidelines to watch. Flynn opens his arms and Ana takes his hand as the band strikes up "They Can't Take That Away from Me."

Ana is animated in John's arms. I wonder what they are talking about.

Me?

Shit.

My anxiety returns in full force.

I have to face the reality that once Ana knows all my secrets, she'll leave and that trying things her way is just prolonging the inevitable.

But John wouldn't be so indiscreet, surely.

"Hello, darling," Grace says, interrupting my dark thoughts.

"Mother."

"Are you enjoying yourself?" She's also watching Ana and John.

"Very much."

Grace has taken off her mask. "What a generous donation from your young friend," she says, but there's a slight edge to her voice.

"Yes," I respond dryly.

"I thought she was a student."

"Mom, it's a long story."

"I figured as much."

Something is off. "What is it, Grace? Spit it out."

She tentatively reaches out to touch my arm. "You look happy, darling."

"I am."

"I think she's good for you."

"I think so, too."

"I hope she doesn't hurt you."

"Why would you say that?"

"She's young."

"Mother, what are you—"

A female guest wearing the most garish gown I've ever seen approaches Grace.

"Christian, this is my friend Pamela, from book club."

We exchange pleasantries, but I want to grill my mother. What the hell is she trying to imply about Ana? The music is coming to an end, and I know I need to rescue Anastasia from my psychiatrist.

"This conversation isn't over," I warn Grace and head over to where Ana and John have stopped dancing.

What is my mother trying to tell me?

"It's been a pleasure to meet you, Anastasia," Flynn says to Ana.

"John." I nod in greeting.

"Christian." Flynn acknowledges me and excuses himself—to find his wife, no doubt. I'm confounded by the exchange I've just had with my mother. I sweep Ana into my arms for the next dance.

"He's much younger than I expected," Ana says. "And terribly indiscreet."

Fuck. "Indiscreet?"

"Oh yes, he told me everything," she discloses.

Shit. Did he really do this? I test Ana to see how much damage he's done. "Well, in that case, I'll get your bag. I'm sure you want nothing more to do with me."

Ana stops dancing. "He didn't tell me anything!" she exclaims, and I think she wants to shake me.

Oh, thank God.

I place my hand on the small of her back as the band launches into "The Very Thought of You." "Then let's enjoy this dance."

And I'm an idiot. Of course Flynn wouldn't break any professional confidences. And as Ana matches me step for step, my spirit soars and my anxiety dissipates. I had no idea I could enjoy dancing so much.

It amazes me how poised Ana is tonight on the dance floor, and for a moment I'm back in the apartment after our first night together, watching her doing a little jig with her headphones on. She was so uncoordinated then—such a contrast to the Ana who's here with me now, following my lead perfectly and enjoying herself.

The band segues into "You Don't Know Me."

It's slower. It's melancholy. It's bittersweet.

It's a warning.

Ana. *You don't know me.*

And as I hold her and we sway together, I silently beg her forgiveness for a sin she knows nothing about. For something she must never know about.

She doesn't know me.

Baby, I'm sorry. I inhale her scent and it offers me some solace. Closing my eyes, I commit it to my memory so I'll always be able to recall it once she's gone.

Ana.

The song finishes and she gives me a winsome smile.

"I need to go to the restroom," she says. "I won't be long."

"Okay." I watch her leave with Taylor following and note the other three security officers standing at the edges of the dance floor. One of them peels off to trail after Taylor.

I spot Flynn talking with his wife.

"John."

"Hello again, Christian. You've met my wife, Rhian."

"Of course. Rhian," I say as we shake hands.

"Your parents know how to throw a party," she says.

"That they do," I respond.

"If you'll excuse me, I'm going to run to the powder room. John. Behave," she warns, and I have to laugh.

"She knows me well," Flynn remarks dryly.

"So what the fuck was all that about?" I ask. "Are you having some fun at my expense?"

"Definitely at your expense. I love to see you parted with your money."

"You're lucky that she's worth every single penny."

"I had to do something to make you see that you're not afraid of commitment." Flynn shrugs.

"That was the reason you bid against me, to test me? It's not my lack of commitment that scares me." I give him a bleak look.

"She seems well equipped to deal with you," he says.

I'm not so sure.

"Christian, just tell her. She knows you have issues. It's not because of anything I've said." He holds his hands up. "And this isn't really the time or the place to have this discussion."

"You're right."

"Where is she?" Flynn glances around.

"Powder room."

"She's a lovely young woman."

I nod in agreement.

"Have some faith," he says.

"Mr. Grey." We're interrupted by Reynolds from the security team.

"What is it?" I ask him.

"Could I have a private word?"

"You can speak freely," I answer. This is my shrink, for fuck's sake.

"Taylor wanted you to know that Elena Lincoln is talking to Miss Steele."

Shit.

"Go," says Flynn, and from the look he gives me, I know he'd like to be a fly on the wall for that conversation.

"Laters," I mutter and follow Reynolds to the pavilion.

Taylor is standing by the tented doorway. Beyond him, inside the large tent, Ana and Elena are in a tense discussion. Ana suddenly whirls around and storms toward me.

"There you are," I say, trying to gauge her mood when she reaches us. She completely ignores me and brushes past both Taylor and me.

This is not good.

I give Taylor a quick look, but he remains impassive.

"Ana," I call and hurry to catch up with her. "What's wrong?"

"Why don't you ask your ex?" she seethes. She's furious.

I check to make sure no one is in listening distance. "I'm asking you," I persist.

She glares at me.

What the hell have I *done?*

She squares her shoulders. "She's threatening to come after me if I hurt you again—probably with a whip," she snarls.

And I don't know if she's being intentionally funny, but the image of Elena threatening Ana with a riding crop is ridiculous. "Surely the irony of that isn't lost on you," I tease Ana in an attempt to lighten her mood.

"This isn't funny, Christian!" she snaps.

"No, you're right. I'll talk to her."

"You will do no such thing." She crosses her arms.

What the hell am I supposed to do?

"Look," she says, "I know you're tied up with her financially, forgive the pun, but—" She stops and huffs because she seems at a sudden loss for words. "I need the restroom," she growls. Ana is pissed. Again.

I sigh. *What can I do?* "Please don't be mad," I urge. "I didn't know she was here. She said she wasn't coming." I reach up and Ana lets me run my thumb across her bottom lip. "Don't let Elena ruin our evening, please, Anastasia. She's really old news." I tip her chin up and plant a gentle kiss on her lips.

She relents with a sigh and I think our fight is over. I take her elbow. "I'll accompany you to the powder room so you don't get interrupted again."

I fish out my phone as I wait for her outside the portable luxury restrooms my mother has rented for the event. There's an email from Dr. Greene saying she can see Ana tomorrow.

Good. I'll deal with that later.

I punch Elena's number into my phone and walk several steps away to a quiet corner of the backyard. She answers on the first ring.

"Christian."

"Elena, what the hell are you doing?"

"That girl is unpleasant and rude."

"Well, maybe you should leave her alone."

"I thought I should introduce myself," Elena says.

"What for? I thought you said you weren't coming. Why did you change your mind? I thought we'd agreed."

"Your mother called and begged me to come, and I was curious about Anastasia. I need to know she's not going to hurt you again."

"Well, leave her alone. This is the first regular relationship I've ever had, and I don't want you jeopardizing it through some misplaced concern for me. Leave. Her. Alone."

"Chris—"

"I mean it, Elena."

"Have you turned your back on who you are?" she asks.

"No, of course not." I look up, and Ana is watching me. "I have to go. Good night." I hang up on Elena, probably for the first time in my life.

Ana raises a brow. "How's the old news?"

"Cranky." I decide a change of subject is for the best. "Do you want to dance some more? Or would you like to go?" I check my watch. "The fireworks start in five minutes."

"I love fireworks," she says, and I know she's being conciliatory.

"We'll stay and watch them, then." I fold her in my arms and pull her close. "Don't let her come between us, please."

"She cares about you," Ana says.

"Yes, and I her, as a friend."

"I think it's more than a friendship to her."

"Anastasia, Elena and I—" I stop. What can I tell Ana to reassure her? "It's complicated. We have a shared history. But it is just that, history. As I've said to you time and time again, she's a good friend. That's all. Please, forget about her." I kiss her hair and she says no more.

I take her hand, and we wander back to the dance floor.

"Anastasia," my father says in his smooth tone. He's standing behind us. "I wondered if you'd do me the honor of the next dance." Carrick holds his hand out to her.

I give him a smile and watch him lead my date onto the dance floor as the band starts "Come Fly with Me."

They're soon enjoying a spirited conversation and I wonder again if it's about me.

"Hello, darling." My mother sidles up to me, holding a glass of champagne.

"Mother, what were you trying to say?" I ask without any preamble.

"Christian, I—" She stops and looks anxiously at me, and I know she's prevaricating. She never likes to give bad news.

My anxiety level rises. "Grace. Tell me."

"I spoke with Elena. She told me that you and Ana had split up and that you were heartbroken."

What?

"Why didn't you tell me?" she continues. "I know you run a business together, but I was upset hearing it from her."

"Elena is exaggerating. I wasn't heartbroken. We had a falling-out. That's all. I didn't tell you because it was temporary. It's fine now."

"I hate to think of you being hurt, darling. I hope she's with you for the right reasons."

"Who? Ana? What are you implying, Mother?"

"You're a wealthy man, Christian."

"You think she's a gold-digger?" And it's like she's struck me.

Fuck.

"No, that's not what I said—"

"Mom. She's not like that at all." I'm trying not to lose my temper.

"I hope so, darling. I'm just watching out for you. Be careful. Most young people experience heartbreak during their adolescence." She gives me a knowing look.

Oh, please. My heart was broken way, way before I hit puberty.

"Darling, you know we only want you happy, and I have to say, on the evidence of this evening, I've never seen you happier."

"Yeah. Mother, I appreciate the concern, but it's all good." I almost cross my fingers behind my back. "Now I'm going to rescue my gold-digging girlfriend from the clutches of my father." My voice is arctic.

"Christian—" My mother tries to call me back, but frankly she can fuck off. How dare she think that of Ana. And why the hell is Elena gossiping about me and Ana to Grace?

"That's enough dancing with old men," I announce to Ana and my dad.

Carrick laughs. "Less of the 'old,' son. I've been known to have my moments." He winks at Ana and swaggers away to join his distressed-looking wife.

"I think my dad likes you," I mutter, feeling murderous.

"What's not to like?" Ana says with a coy smile.

"Good point well made, Miss Steele." I pull her into an embrace as the band starts to play "It Had to Be You." "Dance with me." My voice is low and husky.

"With pleasure, Mr. Grey," she replies. We dance and my thoughts of gold-diggers, overanxious parents, and interfering ex-Dommes are forgotten.

Sunday, June 12, 2011

At midnight, the MC declares that we can remove our masks. We stand on the banks of the bay and watch the astonishing fireworks display, Ana in front of me, cloaked in my arms. Her face is lit by a kaleidoscope of colors as the fireworks explode in the sky above us. She marvels at each dazzling burst, a huge grin on her face. The display is perfectly timed to the music, Handel's "Zadok the Priest."

It's stirring.

My parents have gone overboard for their guests, and it makes me feel a little less annoyed with them. The final volley of rockets bursts into golden stars that light up the bay. The crowd spontaneously applauds as sparks rain down from the sky, illuminating the black water.

It's spectacular.

"Ladies and gentlemen," the MC calls out as the cheers and whistles fade. "Just one note to add at the end of this wonderful evening: your generosity has raised a total of $1,853,000!"

The news is met with rousing cheers from the crowd. It's an impressive total. I imagine my mother has been busy all evening extracting money from her wealthy friends and guests. My contribution of $600,000 has helped. The applause is deafening, and on the pontoon where the fireworks technicians have been busy, the words *Thank You from Coping Together* light up in silver sparklers and shimmer over the dark mirror of the bay.

"Oh, Christian, that was wonderful," Ana exclaims, and I kiss her. I suggest to her that it's time to go. I can't wait to get home and curl up with her. It's been a long day. I'm hoping that I don't need to persuade her to stay the night. For a start, Leila is still at large.

Also, in spite of everything, I've enjoyed today, and I want more. I want her to stay through Sunday, and maybe next week, too.

Tomorrow Ana can see Dr. Greene and, depending on the weather, we could either go soaring or go sailing. I could show her *The Grace*.

Spending more time with Ana is appealing.

Very appealing.

Taylor approaches, shaking his head, and I know he wants us to stay put until the crowd disperses. He's been vigilant all evening and must be exhausted. I follow his direction and ask Ana to wait with me.

"So, Aspen?" I ask to divert her.

"Oh, I haven't paid for my bid," she says.

"You can send a check. I have the address."

"You were really mad."

"Yes, I was."

"I blame you and your toys."

"You were quite overcome, Miss Steele. A most satisfactory outcome, if I recall. Incidentally, where are they?"

"The silver balls? In my bag."

"I'd like them back. They are far too potent a device to be left in your innocent hands."

"Worried I might be quite overcome again, maybe with somebody else?" she says with a wicked gleam in her eye.

Ana, don't tease me about these things.

"I hope that's not going to happen. But no, Ana, I want all your pleasure."

Always.

"Don't you trust me?" she asks.

"Implicitly. Now, can I have them back?"

"I'll think about it."

Miss Steele is playing hardball.

In the distance, the DJ has started his set.

"Do you want to dance?" I ask.

"I'm really tired, Christian. I'd like to go, if that's okay."

I motion to Taylor. He nods and talks into his sleeve microphone to the other security personnel, and we make our way across the lawn. Mia gallops toward us with her shoes in hand. "You're not going, are you? The real music's just beginning. Come on, Ana." She grabs Ana's free hand.

"Mia, Anastasia's tired. We're going home. Besides, we have a big day tomorrow."

Ana looks at me in surprise.

Mia pouts because she's not getting her way, but she doesn't push it. "You must come by sometime next week. Maybe we can hit the mall?"

"Sure, Mia," Ana replies, and I hear the fatigue in her voice. I must get her home.

Mia kisses Ana goodbye, then grabs me and hugs me, hard. Her face shines as she stares up at me. "I like seeing you this happy," she says, and she kisses me on the cheek. "Bye. You guys have fun." She runs off to her waiting friends, who start making their way to the dance floor.

My parents are nearby, and I'm now feeling guilty about the outburst with my mother. "We'll say good night to my parents before we leave. Come." We stroll toward them.

Grace's face lights up when she sees us. Reaching up, she touches my face, and I try not to scowl at her. She smiles. "Thank you for coming and bringing Anastasia. It was wonderful watching the two of you together."

"Thanks for a great evening, Mom," I manage. I don't want to bring up our earlier conversation in front of Ana.

"Good night, son. Ana," says Carrick.

"Please do come again, Anastasia. It's been lovely having you here," Grace enthuses. She seems sincere, and the sting of her gold-digger comment begins to fade. Perhaps she is just looking out for me. But they don't know Ana at all. She's the least acquisitive woman I've ever met.

We walk around to the front of the house. Ana runs her hands up and down her arms. "Are you warm enough?" I ask.

"Yes, thank you."

"I really enjoyed this evening, Anastasia. Thank you."

"Me, too… Some parts more than others." And clearly she's thinking about our tryst in my childhood bedroom.

"Don't bite your lip," I warn.

"What did you mean about a big day tomorrow?" she asks.

I tell her that Dr. Greene will make a house call and that I have a surprise for her.

"Dr. Greene?"

"Yes."

"Why?"

"Because I hate condoms."

"It's my body," she grumbles.

"It's mine, too," I whisper.

Ana. Please. I. Hate. Them.

Her eyes shine in the soft glow of paper lanterns that are strung up over the front yard, and I wonder if she's going to continue this argument. She raises her hand, and I still. She tugs the corner of my bow tie, and it unravels. With gentle fingers, she undoes the top button of my shirt. Fascinated, I watch her and stay rooted to the ground.

"You look hot like this," she says quietly, surprising me.

I think she's moved on from Dr. Greene. "I need to get you home. Come."

The Q7 pulls up, and the valet gets out and gives the keys to Taylor. One of our security guys, Sawyer, hands me an envelope. It's addressed to Ana.

"Where did this come from?" I ask him.

"One of the servers gave it to me, sir."

Is it from an admirer? The handwriting seems familiar. Taylor ushers Ana into the car and I slide in beside her, handing her the note. "It's addressed to you. One of the staff gave it to Sawyer. No doubt from yet another ensnared heart."

Taylor follows the line of cars out of my parents' driveway. Ana rips the envelope open and casts her eyes over the note inside.

"You told her?" she exclaims.

"Told who what?"

"That I call her Mrs. Robinson."

"It's from Elena? This is ridiculous." I told Elena to leave Ana alone. Why is she ignoring me? And what has she said to Ana? What the hell is her problem? "I'll deal with her tomorrow. Or Monday." I want to read the note, but Ana doesn't give me the opportunity. She stuffs it in her purse but fishes out the kegel balls.

"Until next time," she says, handing them back to me.

Next time?

Now, that is good news. I squeeze her hand and she returns the gesture as she stares out the window into the darkness.

Midway across the 520 bridge, she's asleep. I take a moment to relax. So much has happened today. I'm tired, so I put my head back and close my eyes.

Yeah. It's been quite a day.

Ana and the check. Her bad temper. Her willfulness. The lipstick. The sex.

Yes. The sex.

And of course I will have to deal with my mother's anxiety and her offensive concern that Ana is an opportunist who's after my fortune.

And then there's Elena, interfering, behaving badly. What the hell am I going to do about her?

I look at my image reflected in the car window. The sallow, ghoulish figure stares back at me and disappears only when we exit I-5 onto a well-lit Stewart Street. We are close to home.

Ana is still asleep when we pull up outside. Sawyer jumps out of the car and opens my door.

"Do I need to carry you in?" I ask Ana, squeezing her hand. She wakes and sleepily shakes her head. With Sawyer in front of us, keeping vigil, we walk into the building together as Taylor takes the car into the garage.

Ana leans on me in the elevator and closes her eyes.

"It's been a long day, eh, Anastasia?"

She nods.

"Tired?"

She nods.

"You're not very talkative," I observe.

She nods once more, making me smile.

"Come. I'll put you to bed." My fingers curl around hers, and we follow Sawyer out of the elevator and into the foyer. Sawyer halts in front of us and holds up his hand. I tighten my grip on Ana's fingers.

What the hell?

"Will do, T," Sawyer says and turns to face us. "Mr. Grey, the tires on Ms. Steele's Audi have been slashed and paint thrown all over it."

Ana gasps.

What?

My immediate thought is that some mindless vandal has broken into the garage… then I remember Leila.

What the hell has she done?

Sawyer continues. "Taylor is concerned that the perp may have entered the apartment and may still be there. He wants to make sure."

How can anyone be in the apartment?

"I see. What's Taylor's plan?"

"He's coming up in the service elevator with Ryan and Reynolds. They'll do a sweep, then give us the all-clear. I'm to wait with you, sir."

"Thank you, Sawyer." I tighten my hold on Ana. "This day just gets better and better." There's no way Leila could be in the apartment. Is there?

And I recall those moments when I thought I saw something move at the periphery of my vision… and when I woke because I thought someone had ruffled my hair, only to find Ana fast asleep beside me. A shiver of doubt runs down my spine.

Shit.

If Leila's here, I need to know. I don't think she'll hurt me. I kiss Ana's hair. "Listen, I can't stand here and wait. Sawyer, take care of Miss Steele. Don't let her in until you have the all-clear. I'm sure Taylor is overreacting. She can't get into the apartment."

"No, Christian." Ana tries to stop me, her fingers clasping my lapels. "You have to stay with me."

"Do as you're told, Anastasia. Wait here." I sound sterner than I mean to, and she releases me. "Sawyer?" He's standing in my way, uncertain. I raise a brow, and after a moment's hesitation he opens the double doors into the apartment and lets me go through. He closes them behind me.

In the hallway outside the living room it's dark and quiet. I stand and listen, straining my ears for anything unusual. All I hear is the sigh of the wind as it wraps itself around the building and the hum of the electrical appliances from the kitchen. Far below in the street there's a police siren, but apart from that, Escala is still and quiet, as it should be.

If Leila were here, where would she go?

My first thought is the playroom, and I'm about to dash upstairs when there's a rumble and a ping from the service elevator, and Taylor and the two other security guys spill out into the corridor wielding guns, as if they're in some macho action movie.

"Are those strictly necessary?" I ask Taylor, who's leading the charge.

"We're taking the necessary precautions, sir."

"I don't think she's here."

"We'll do a quick sweep."

"Okay," I reply, resigned. "I'll check upstairs."

"I'll come with you, Mr. Grey." I suspect that Taylor is being unduly concerned for my safety.

He issues swift instructions to the other two and they scatter to search the apartment. I switch on all the lights so that the living room and corridor are well lit and bright, and I head upstairs with Taylor.

He's thorough. He checks under the four-poster bed, the table, and even the couch in the playroom. He does the same in the sub's room and in each of the spare rooms. No sign of any intruder. He proceeds into his and Mrs. Jones's quarters, and I head downstairs. My bathroom and walk-in closet are clear, as is my bedroom. Standing in the middle of the room, I feel like a fool, but I squat down and check under the bed.

Nothing.

Not even dust. Mrs. Jones is doing a stellar job.

The balcony door is locked, but I open it. Outside, the breeze is cool and the city is laid out, dark and somber, at my feet. There's the hum of distant traffic and the faint moan of the wind, but that's it. Inside again, I lock the door.

Taylor comes back downstairs. "She's not here," he says.

"You think it's Leila?"

"Yes, sir." His mouth forms a hard, flat line. "Do you mind if I search your room?"

Though I've already done this, I'm too tired to argue. "Sure."

"I want to check all the closets and cupboards, sir," he says.

"Fine." I shake my head at the preposterous situation we're in, and I open the foyer doors to find Ana. Sawyer brandishes his gun but lowers it when he sees it's me.

"All clear," I tell him. He holsters his pistol and stands aside. "Taylor is overreacting," I say to Ana. She looks exhausted, and she doesn't move—she just stares at me pale-faced, and I realize she's scared. "It's all right, baby." I fold her in my arms and kiss her hair. "Come on, you're tired. Bed."

"I was so worried," she says.

"I know. We're all jumpy."

Sawyer has disappeared, presumably into the apartment.

"Honestly, your exes are proving to be very challenging, Mr. Grey," she asserts.

"Yes. They are." They really are. I lead her into the living room. "Taylor and his crew are checking all the closets and cupboards. I don't think she's here."

"Why would she be here?" Ana sounds bewildered, and I reassure her that Taylor is thorough and that we've searched everywhere, including the playroom.

To calm her, I offer her a drink, but she declines. She's tired. "Come. Let me put you to bed. You look exhausted."

In my bedroom, she empties the contents of her evening bag on top of the chest of drawers. "Here." She passes Elena's note to me. "I don't know if you want to read this. I want to ignore it."

I scan the note.

Anastasia,
I may have misjudged you. And you have definitely misjudged me. Call me if you need to fill in any of the blanks—we could have lunch. Christian doesn't want me talking to you, but I would be more than happy to help. Don't get me wrong, I approve, believe me—but so help me, if you hurt him.. He's been hurt enough.
Call me: (206) 279-6261.

Mrs. Robinson

It provokes my temper.

Is this one of Elena's games?

"I'm not sure what blanks she can fill in." I put the note in my pants pocket. "I need to talk to Taylor. Let me unzip your dress."

"Are you going to call the police about the car?" she asks as she turns around.

I move her hair out of the way and pull down the zipper. "No. I don't want the police involved. Leila needs help, not police intervention, and I don't want them here. We just have to double our efforts to find her." I kiss her shoulder. "Go to bed."

IN THE KITCHEN, I pour myself a glass of water.

What the hell is going on? My world seems to be imploding. Just when I'm beginning to get back on track with Ana, my past is coming back to haunt me: Leila and Elena. I wonder for a moment if they might be colluding with each other, but then I realize that I'm being paranoid. What an absurd notion. Elena is not that crazy.

I rub my face.

Why would Leila be targeting me?

Is it jealousy?

She wanted more. I didn't.

But I would have been happy to continue our relationship as it was... She was the one who ended it.

"Master. May I speak freely?" Leila says. She's sitting at my right at the dinner table, wearing a fetching lacy La Perla one-piece.

"Of course."

"I have developed feelings for you. I had hoped you would collar me and that I would stay by your side forevermore."

Collar? Forevermore? I think to myself. What's this once-upon-a-time bullshit?

"But I think that is beyond my dreams," she continues.

"Leila. You know that's not for me. We've discussed this."

"But you're lonely. I can see it."

"Lonely? Me? I don't feel that way. I have my work. My family. I have you."

"But I want more, Master."

"I can't give you more. You know this."

"I see." She raises her face to look at me, her amber eyes scrutinizing me. She's broken the fourth wall—she has never looked at me without permission. But I don't scold her.

"I can't. It's not within me." I've always been honest with her. This is nothing she doesn't know.

"It is within you, Sir. But maybe I'm not the person to make you realize it." She sounds sad. She looks back down at her clean plate. "I'd like to terminate our relationship."

She's caught me by surprise. "Are you sure? Leila, this is a big step. I'd like to continue our arrangement."

"I can't do this anymore, Master." Her voice cracks on the last word, and I don't know what to say. "I can't," she whispers, clearing her throat.

"Leila—" I stop, bewildered by the emotion I hear in her voice. She's been an impeccable sub. I thought we were compatible. "I'll be sorry to see you go," I say, because it's true. "I've really enjoyed our time together. I hope you have, too."

"I'll be sorry, too, Sir. I've more than enjoyed everything. I had hoped…" Her voice trails off and she gives me a sad smile.

"I wish I felt differently." But I don't. I have no need of a permanent relationship.

"You've never given me any indication that you would." Her voice is quiet.

"I'm sorry. You're right. Let's end this as you wish. It's for the best, especially if you've developed feelings for me."

Taylor and the security team arrive back in the kitchen. "There's no sign of Leila in the apartment, sir," Taylor says.

"I didn't think there would be, but I appreciate you checking. Thanks."

"We're going to monitor the cameras in turn. Ryan first. Sawyer and Reynolds are going to sleep."

"Good. As you should."

"Yes, Mr. Grey. Gentlemen." Taylor dismisses the three men.

"Good night."

Once they've left, Taylor turns to me. "The car's a mess, sir."

"Write-off?"

"I think so. She's done a real number on it."

"That's if it's Leila."

"I'll speak to the building security in the morning and check their CCTV. Do you want to involve the police?"

"Not yet."

"Okay." Taylor nods.

"I'll need to get Ana another car. Can you talk to Audi tomorrow?"

"Yes, sir. I'll have the wreck collected in the morning."

"Thanks."

"Is there anything else, Mr. Grey?"

"No. Thanks. Get some rest."

"Good night, sir."

"Good night."

Taylor leaves and I head into my study. I'm wired. I can't possibly sleep. I contemplate calling Welch just to keep him up-to-date, but it is too late. Slipping off my jacket, I hang it on my chair, then sit down at my computer and write him an email.

As I press send my phone buzzes. Elena Lincoln's name flashes up on the screen.

What now?

I answer. "What do you think you're doing?"

"Christian!" She's surprised.

"I don't know why you're calling at this hour. I have nothing to say to you."

She sighs. "I just wanted to tell you—" She stops and changes tack. "I was hoping to leave a message."

"Well, you can tell me now. You don't have to leave a message." I'm finding it impossible to keep my composure.

"You're angry. I can tell. If it's about the note, listen—"

"No, you listen. I asked you, and now I am telling you. Leave her alone. She has nothing to do with you. Do you understand?"

"Christian, I only have your best interests at heart."

"I know you do. But I mean it, Elena. Leave her the fuck alone. Do I need to put it in triplicate for you? Are you hearing me?"

"Yes. Yes. I'm sorry." I've never heard her so contrite. It goes some way to cooling my anger.

"Good. Good night." I slam my phone down on the desk. Interfering woman. I put my head in my hands.

I'm so fucking tired.

There's a knock on my door.

"What?" I shout. I look up. It's Ana. She's dressed in my T-shirt, and she's all legs and big fearful eyes. She's bearding the lion in his den.

Oh, Ana.

"You should be in satin or silk, Anastasia. But even in my T-shirt you look beautiful."

"I missed you. Come to bed." Her voice is sexy and cajoling.

How can I sleep with all this shit going on? I stand and walk around my desk to gaze down at her. What if Leila wants to hurt her? What if she succeeds? How could I live with that?

"Do you know what you mean to me? If something happened to you, because of me..." I'm overwhelmed by a familiar, uncomfortable feeling that expands in my chest, becoming a lump in my throat that I have to swallow.

"Nothing's going to happen to me," she says in a soothing tone.

She strokes my cheek, her fingers scratching my stubble. "Your beard grows quickly." There's wonder in her voice. I love her tender touch on my cheek. It's soothing and sensual. It tames the darkness. She caresses my bottom lip with her thumb, her eyes following her fingers. Her pupils are large and the small *v* has appeared between her brows as she concentrates. She traces a line from my bottom lip, down my chin, down my throat, to the base of my neck, where my shirt is open.

What is she doing?

She runs her finger along what I can only assume is the lipstick line. I close my eyes, waiting for the darkness to constrict my chest. Her finger touches my shirt.

"I'm not going to touch you. I just want to undo your shirt," she says.

Opening my eyes, I keep my panic in check and focus on her face. I don't stop her. The material of my shirt lifts and she unfastens a second button. Keeping the fabric off my skin, her fingers move to the next button down and she undoes that one, then the next. I don't move. I daren't. My breathing is shallow as I suppress my fear; my whole body is tense and waiting.

Don't touch me.

Please, Ana.

She opens the next button down and smiles up at me. "Back on home territory," she says, and her fingers trail along the line she made much, much earlier in the day and I tense my diaphragm as her fingers skim across my skin.

She undoes the final button and opens my shirt fully and I let out the breath I'm holding. Next she grabs my hand and, grasping my shirt cuff, removes my left cuff link, followed by the right. "Can I take your shirt off?" she asks.

I nod, totally disarmed, and she lifts my shirt up off my shoulders and pulls it from my body. She's done. She looks pleased with herself, and I'm standing half naked in front of her.

Slowly I relax.

That wasn't so bad.

"What about my pants, Miss Steele?" I manage a lascivious smirk.

"In the bedroom. I want you in your bed."

"Do you, now? Miss Steele, you are insatiable."

"I can't think why," she says, taking my hand. I let her lead me across the living room, through the corridor, and into my bedroom. It's cold. My nipples pucker against the chill in the room.

"You opened the balcony door?" I ask.

"No," Ana replies, looking at the open door with a bewildered expression. Then she turns to me, her face ashen. She's alarmed.

"What?" I ask as every hair on my body stands on end—not from cold but from fear.

"When I woke," she whispers, "there was someone in here. I thought it was my imagination."

"What?" I scan the room quickly, then dash to the balcony and look outside. No one there—but I distinctly remember locking this door during the search. And I know Ana's never been on the balcony. I lock it again. "Are you sure?" I ask her. "Who?"

"A woman, I think. It was dark. I'd only just woken up."

Fuck!

"Get dressed. Now!" I order. Why the hell didn't she tell me when she came into my office? I have to get her out of here.

"My clothes are upstairs," she whimpers.

From my chest of drawers I pull out some sweatpants. "Put these on." I toss them at her, pull out a T-shirt, and dress quickly. I pick up the phone at my bedside.

"Mr. Grey?" Taylor answers.

"She's still fucking here," I bark.

"Shit," says Taylor, and he hangs up.

Moments later he barrels into the bedroom with Ryan.

"Ana says she saw someone in the room. A woman. She came to see me in my study and neglected to tell me this." I give her a pointed look. "Then when we got back here the balcony door was open. I remember closing and locking it myself during the search. It's Leila. I know it is."

"How long ago?" Taylor asks Ana.

"About ten minutes," she answers.

"She knows the apartment like the back of her hand. I'm taking

Anastasia away now. She's hiding here somewhere. Find her. When is Gail back?"

"Tomorrow evening, sir."

"She's not to return until this place is secure. Understand?"

"Yes, sir. Will you be going to Bellevue?"

"I'm not taking this problem to my parents. Book me somewhere."

"Yes. I'll call you."

"Aren't we all overreacting slightly?" Ana asks.

"She may have a gun," I growl.

"Christian, she was standing at the end of the bed. She could have shot me then if that's what she wanted to do."

I take a deep breath, because now isn't the time to lose it. "I'm not prepared to take the risk. Taylor, Anastasia needs shoes."

Taylor leaves, but Ryan stays to watch over Ana.

I hurry into my closet, strip out of my pants, and pull on some jeans and my jacket. From my dress-pants pocket I grab the condoms I'd slipped in there earlier and stuff them into my jeans pocket. I pack some clothes and as an afterthought grab my denim jacket.

Ana is where I left her, looking lost and anxious. My sweatpants are far too big on her, but there's no time for her to change. I place the denim jacket over her shoulders and grab her hand.

"Come."

I lead her into the living room to wait for Taylor.

"I can't believe she could hide somewhere in here," Ana says.

"It's a big place. You haven't seen it all yet."

"Why don't you just call her? Tell her you want to talk to her?"

"Anastasia, she's unstable, and she may be armed," I stress, irritated.

"So we just run?"

"For now, yes."

"Supposing she tries to shoot Taylor?"

Jesus. I hope she doesn't.

"Taylor knows and understands guns. He'll be quicker with a gun than she is." I hope.

"Ray was in the army. He taught me to shoot."

"You, with a gun?" I scoff. I'm shocked. I loathe guns.

"Yes." She sounds offended. "I can shoot, Mr. Grey, so you'd better beware. It's not just crazy ex-subs you need to worry about."

"I'll bear that in mind, Miss Steele."

Taylor comes down the stairs and we join him in the foyer. He gives Ana a carry-on suitcase and her Chucks. She hugs him, taking him and me by surprise.

"Be careful," she says.

"Yes, Miss Steele," Taylor replies, embarrassed yet pleased by her concern and her spontaneous affection.

I give him a look and he adjusts his tie. "Let me know where I'm going."

Taylor takes out his wallet and passes me his credit card. "You might want to use this when you get there."

Whoa. He's really taking this seriously. "Good thinking."

Ryan joins us. "Sawyer and Reynolds found nothing," he tells Taylor.

"Accompany Mr. Grey and Miss Steele to the garage," Taylor says.

The three of us enter the elevator, where Ana has a chance to pull on her Chucks. She looks a little comical in my jacket and sweatpants. But as cute as she looks, I can't find the funny in our situation; the fact is I've placed her in harm's way.

Ana blanches when she sees her car in the garage. It's a mess—the windshield is shattered and the bodywork is covered in dents and cheap white paint. My blood boils at the sight, but for Ana's sake I control my rage. I usher her quickly into the R8. She's staring straight ahead when I climb into the car beside her, and I know it's because she can't bear to look at her car.

"A replacement will arrive on Monday," I assure her, hoping that might make her feel better. I start the engine and put on my seat belt.

"How could she have known it was my car?"

I sigh. This is not going to go down well. "She had an Audi A3. I buy one for all my submissives. It's one of the safest cars in its class."

"So, not so much a graduation present, then," she says quietly.

"Anastasia, despite what I hoped, you have never been my submissive, so technically it is a graduation present." I back out of the parking space and head to the garage exit where we pause, waiting for the barrier to lift.

"Are you still hoping?" she asks.

What?

The in-car phone rings. "Grey," I answer.

"Fairmont Olympic. In my name," Taylor informs me.

"Thank you, Taylor. And Taylor, be careful."

"Yes, sir," he says and hangs up.

It's eerily quiet in downtown Seattle. That's one of the advantages of driving at nearly three in the morning. I take a detour on I-5 just in case Leila is following us. Every few minutes I check the rearview mirror, anxiety gnawing at my gut.

Everything is out of control. Leila might be dangerous. Yet she had the opportunity to harm Ana and didn't. She was a gentle soul when I knew her, artistic, bright, mischievous. And when she ended our relationship as a means of self-preservation, I admired her for that. She was never destructive, not even to herself, until she turned up at Escala and cut herself in front of Mrs. Jones and tonight when she vandalized Ana's car.

She's not herself.

And I don't trust her not to hurt Ana.

How could I live with myself if that happened?

Ana is swimming in my clothes, looking small and miserable, staring out the car window. She asked me a question and I was interrupted. She wanted to know if I'm still hoping for a submissive.

How can she ask that?

Reassure her, Grey.

"No. It's not what I hope for, not anymore. I thought that was obvious."

She turns to look at me, huddling down in my jacket so that she looks even smaller. "I worry that, you know, that I'm not enough."

Why is she bringing this up now? "You're more than enough. For the love of God, Anastasia, what do I have to do?"

She fiddles with a button on my denim jacket. "Why did you think I'd leave when I told you Dr. Flynn had told me all there was to know about you?"

Is this what she's brooding about?

Keep it vague, Grey.

"You cannot begin to understand the depths of my depravity, Anastasia. And it's not something I want to share with you."

"And you really think I'd leave if I knew? Do you think so little of me?"

"I know you'll leave," I answer, and the thought is untenable.

"Christian, I think that's very unlikely. I can't imagine being without you."

"You left me once. I don't want to go there again."

She pales and begins fiddling with the drawstring on my sweatpants.

Yeah. You hurt me.

And I hurt you…

"Elena said she saw you last Saturday," she whispers.

No. That's bullshit. "She didn't." Why the hell would Elena lie?

"You didn't go to see her when I left?"

"No. I just told you I didn't, and I don't like to be doubted." And I realize I'm taking my anger out on her. In a gentler tone I add, "I didn't go anywhere last weekend. I sat and made the glider you gave me. Took me forever."

Ana looks down at her fingers. She's still fiddling with the drawstring.

"Contrary to what Elena thinks," I continue, "I don't rush to her with all my problems, Anastasia. I don't rush to anybody. You may have noticed, I'm not much of a talker."

"Carrick told me you didn't talk for two years."

"Did he, now?" Why can't my family keep quiet?

"I kind of pumped him for information," she confesses.

"So what else did Daddy say?"

"He said your mom was the doctor who examined you when you were brought into the hospital. After you were discovered in your apartment. He said learning the piano helped. And Mia."

A vision of Mia as a baby, a shock of black hair and a gurgling smile, comes to mind. She was someone I could take care of, someone I *could* protect. "She was about six months old when she arrived. I was thrilled, Elliot less so. He'd already had to contend with my arrival. She was perfect. Less so now, of course."

Ana giggles. And it's so unexpected.

I immediately feel more at ease. "You find that amusing, Miss Steele?"

"She seemed determined to keep us apart."

"Yes, she's quite accomplished." And annoying. She is… Mia. My baby sister. I squeeze Ana's knee. "But we got there in the end." I offer her a brief smile, then check the rearview mirror. "I don't think we've been followed."

I take the next off-ramp and head back into downtown Seattle.

"Can I ask you something about Elena?" Ana asks when we're stopped at a red light.

"If you must." But I really wish she wouldn't.

"You told me ages ago that she loved you in a way you found acceptable. What did that mean?"

"Isn't it obvious?"

"Not to me."

"I was out of control. I couldn't bear to be touched. I can't bear it now. For a fourteen-, fifteen-year-old adolescent boy with hormones raging, it was a difficult time. She showed me a way to let off steam."

"Mia said you were a brawler."

"Christ, what is it with my loquacious family?" We're stopped at the next red. I glare at her. "Actually, it's you. You inveigle information out of people."

"Mia volunteered that information. In fact, she was very forthcoming. She was worried you'd start a brawl in the tent if you didn't win me at the auction," she says.

"Oh, baby, there was no danger of that. There was no way I would let anyone else dance with you."

"You let Dr. Flynn."

"He's always the exception to the rule."

I turn into the driveway of the Fairmont Olympic Hotel. A valet scrambles out to meet us and I pull up toward him.

"Come," I say to Ana and get out of the car to retrieve our luggage. I toss the keys to the enthusiastic young man. "Name of Taylor," I inform him.

The lobby is quiet, save for some random woman and her dog. At this time? Odd.

The receptionist checks us in. "Do you need a hand with your bags, Mr. Taylor?" she asks.

"No, Mrs. Taylor and I can manage."

"You're in the Cascade Suite, Mr. Taylor, eleventh floor. Our bellboy will help with your bags."

"We're fine. Where are the elevators?"

She directs us, and as we wait, I ask Ana how she's holding up. She looks worn out.

"It's been an interesting evening," she says with her usual gift for understatement.

Taylor has booked us into the largest suite in the hotel. I'm surprised to discover it has two bedrooms. I wonder if Taylor is expecting us to sleep apart, as I do with my submissives. Maybe I should tell him this doesn't apply to Ana.

"Well, Mrs. Taylor, I don't know about you, but I'd really like a drink," I say as Ana follows me into the master bedroom, where I set our overnight bags on the ottoman.

Back in the main living room there's a fire burning in the hearth. Ana warms her hands while I fix a drink at the bar. She looks gamine, adorable, and her dark hair shines coppery and bright in the firelight.

"Armagnac?"

"Please," she says.

By the fire, I hand her a brandy glass. "It's been quite a day, huh?" I gauge her reaction. I'm amazed, given all the drama of the evening, that she hasn't broken down and wept by now.

"I'm okay," she says. "How about you?"

I'm wired.

Anxious.

Angry.

I know of one thing that will give me relief.

You, Miss Steele.

My panacea.

"Well, right now I'd like to drink this and then, if you're not too tired, take you to bed and lose myself in you." I'm really chancing my luck. She must be exhausted.

"I think that can be arranged, Mr. Taylor," she says and rewards me with a shy smile.

Oh, Ana. You're my heroine.

I slip out of my shoes and socks. "Mrs. Taylor, stop biting your lip," I murmur.

She takes a sip of her Armagnac and closes her eyes. She hums her appreciation for her drink. The sound soft and mellow and oh so sexy.

I feel it in my groin.

She really is something else.

"You never cease to amaze me, Anastasia. After a day like today, or yesterday, rather, you're not whining or running off into the hills screaming. I am in awe of you. You're very strong."

"You're a very good reason to stay," she whispers.

That strange feeling swells in my chest. Scarier than the darkness. Bigger. More potent. It has the power to wound.

"I told you, Christian, I'm not going anywhere, no matter what you've done. You know how I feel about you."

Oh, baby, you'd run if you knew the truth.

"Where are you going to hang José's portraits of me?" she asks, throwing me for a loop.

"That depends," I respond, bemused that she can change tack so quickly.

"On what?"

"Circumstances." It'll depend on whether she stays. I don't think I could bear to look at them when she's no longer mine.

If. If she's no longer mine.

"His show's not over yet, so I don't have to decide straightaway." I still don't know when the gallery will deliver them, in spite of my request.

She narrows her eyes, studying me, as if I'm hiding something.

Yeah. My fear. That's what I'm hiding.

"You can look as sternly as you like, Mrs. Taylor. I'm saying nothing," I tease.

"I may torture the truth from you."

"Really, Anastasia, I don't think you should make promises you can't fulfill."

She narrows her eyes once more, but this time, she's amused. She places her glass on the mantelpiece, then takes mine and sets it beside hers. "We'll just have to see about that," she says with cool determination in her voice. Grasping my hand, she guides me into the bedroom.

Ana is taking the lead.

This hasn't happened since that time in my study when she jumped me.

Go with it, Grey.

At the foot of the bed, she stops.

"Now that you have me in here, Anastasia, what are you going to do with me?"

She looks up at me, eyes shining, full of love, and I swallow, awed at the sight of her. "I'm going to start by undressing you. I want to finish what I started earlier."

All the breath leaves my body.

She grasps the lapels of my jacket and gently eases it off my shoulders. She turns and places it on the ottoman and I catch a trace of her fragrance.

Ana.

"Now your T-shirt," she says.

I feel bolder. I know she won't touch me. Her road-map idea was a good one, and I still have the smudged remains of the lipstick on my chest and back. I raise my arms and take a step back as she tugs my T-shirt over my head.

Her lips part as she surveys my torso, and I itch to touch her, but I'm loving her slow, sweet seduction.

We're doing it her way.

"Now what?" I murmur.

"I want to kiss you here." She runs a fingernail across my belly from hipbone to hipbone.

Fuck.

I tense everywhere as all the blood in my body heads south. "I'm not stopping you," I whisper.

Grabbing my hand, she instructs me to lie down.

With my pants on?

Okay.

I remove the covers on the bed and sit down, my eyes on Ana, waiting to see what she'll do next. She shrugs out of my denim jacket and lets it fall to the floor; my sweatpants follow, and it takes all my self-control not to grab her and toss her onto the bed.

Squaring her shoulders, her gaze fixed on mine, she grips the hem of my T-shirt and tugs it over her head, wiggling to get it free.

Naked before me, she's beautiful. "You are Aphrodite, Anastasia."

She cradles my face in her hands and stoops to kiss me, and I can resist her no more. When her lips touch mine, I reach for her hips and pull her onto the bed so she's beneath me. As we kiss, I push her legs apart so I'm resting at the junction of her thighs: my favorite place. She kisses me back with a ferocity that fires my blood, her mouth voracious, her tongue wrestling with mine. She tastes of Armagnac and Ana. My hands are on her. With one, I cup her head and I trail the other up her body, kneading and squeezing as I go. Palming her breast, I tweak her nipple and marvel as it hardens between my fingers.

I need this. I crave this contact.

She groans and tilts her pelvis, compressing my hardening denim-clad cock.

Fuck.

I suck in my breath. And stop kissing her.

What are you doing?

She's panting, gazing up at me with a scorching, imploring expression.

She wants more.

I flex my hips, pushing my erection against her while watching her reaction. She closes her eyes and moans with carnal appreciation and tugs at my hair. I do it again, and this time she slides against me.

Whoa.

The feeling's exquisite.

Her teeth scrape my chin and she claims my lips and my tongue in a passionate wet kiss as she and I grind against each other, moving in perfect opposition, creating a sweet, sweet friction that is delicious torture. The heat builds and burns between us, concentrated at our point of connection. Her fingers grasp my arms as her breathing accelerates. Panting, she moves her hand to my lower back and into the waistband of my jeans, where she cups my ass and urges me on.

I'm going to come.

No.

"You're going to unman me, Ana." I kneel up and tug down my pants, freeing my erection, and grab a condom from my pocket. I hand it to Ana, who lies, breathless, on the bed.

"You want me, baby, and I sure as hell want you. You know what to do."

With greedy fingers she rips open the foil packet and unfurls the condom over my straining dick.

She's so keen. I grin at her when she lies back down.

Insatiable Ana.

I run my nose along hers and slowly, slowly sink into her, claiming her.

She's mine.

She grasps my arms and tilts her chin up, her mouth open in a wide *o* of pleasure. Gently, I slide into her again, my arms and hands on either side of her face.

"You make me forget everything. You are the best therapy." I ease out of her again and ease back inside her.

"Please, Christian, faster." She pushes her pelvis up to meet me.

"Oh no, baby. I need this slow."

Please. Let's do this slowly.

I kiss her and tug her bottom lip. She twines her fingers in my hair and holds me and lets me continue at my slow, tender pace. On and on and on. She begins to build, her legs stiffening, and she throws her head back as she comes, taking me with her.

"Oh, Ana," I call, and her name is a prayer on my lips. That unfamiliar feeling is back, swelling in my chest, fighting to get out. And I know what it is. I've known forever. I want to tell her I love her.

But I can't.

The words burn to ashes in my throat.

I swallow and rest my head on her belly, my arms coiled around her. Her fingers tangle in my hair. "I will never get enough of you. Don't leave me." I kiss her belly.

"I'm not going anywhere, Christian, and I seem to remember that I wanted to kiss your belly," she says. And she sounds a little grumpy.

"Nothing stopping you now, baby."

"I don't think I can move. I'm so tired."

I stretch out beside her and pull the comforter over us. She looks radiant but exhausted.

Let her sleep, Grey.

"Sleep now, sweet Ana." I kiss her hair and hold her.

I never want to let her go.

I WAKE TO BRILLIANT sunshine filtering through the sheers that shroud the windows and Ana soundly asleep beside me. In spite of our late night I feel refreshed; I sleep well when I'm with her.

I climb out of bed, grab my jeans and my T-shirt, and drag them on. If I stay in bed, I know I'll wake her. She's too tempting to leave alone, and I know she needs sleep.

In the main room, I sit down at the escritoire and take my laptop out of the bag. My first job is to email Dr. Greene. I ask her if she can come to the hotel to attend to Ana. She responds that the only time she can do is ten fifteen.

Great.

I confirm the time and then call Mac, who's the first mate on my yacht.

"Mr. Grey."

"Mac. I'd like to take *The Grace* out this afternoon."

"You'll have fine weather."

"Yes. I'd like to head to Bainbridge Island."

"I'll get her ready, sir."

"Great. We'll see you around lunchtime."

"We?"

"Yes, I'm bringing my girlfriend, Anastasia Steele."

There's a slight hesitation in Mac's voice before he says, "Look forward to it."

"Me, too."

I hang up, excited that I can show *The Grace* to Ana. I think she'll love sailing. She loved the soaring and the flight in *Charlie Tango.*

I call Taylor for an update, but his phone goes to voice mail. I hope he's getting some well-deserved sleep or having Ana's wrecked Audi removed from the garage as he promised. It reminds me that I need to replace her car. I wonder if Taylor has spoken to the Audi dealership. It's a Sunday, so maybe not.

My phone buzzes. It's a text from my mother.

GRACE
Darling, it was so lovely to see you and Anastasia last night.
As ever, thank you, and Ana, for your generosity.
Mom X

I'm still smarting over her gold-digger comments. It's obvious she doesn't know Ana well. But then, she's only met Ana three times. It was Elliot who was always bringing girls around, not me. Grace couldn't keep up.

"Elliot, darling, we get attached to them and then they're history. It's heartbreaking."

"Don't get attached." He shrugs, chewing with his mouth open. "I don't," he mutters so only I can hear him.

"One day someone will break your heart, Elliot," Grace says as she hands Mia a plate of mac and cheese.

"Whatever, Mom. At least I bring girls home." He eyes me with disdain.

"Lots of my friends want to marry Christian. Ask them," Mia pipes up in my defense.

Ugh. What an unpleasant thought—her poisonous little eighth-grade friends.

"Don't you have exams to study for, douchebag?" I give Elliot the finger.

"Study. Not me, dickless. I'm out tonight," he brags.

"Boys! Enough! This is your first night home from college. You haven't seen each other in ages. Stop arguing. Eat up."

I take a bite of mac and cheese. Tonight I get to see Mrs. Lincoln…

It's 9:40 so I order breakfast for Ana and me, knowing it will take at least twenty minutes. I turn back to my emails and decide to ignore my mother's text for now.

Room service arrives just after ten. I ask the young man to keep everything in the cart's warming drawers and, after he's set the table, I dismiss him.

Time to wake Ana.

She's still fast asleep. Her hair is a mess of mahogany on the pillow, her skin luminous in the light, and her face soft and sweet in repose. I lie down beside her and watch her, drinking in every detail. She blinks and opens her eyes.

"Hi."

"Hi." She tugs the comforter up to her chin as her cheeks turn rosy. "How long have you been watching me?"

"I could watch you sleep for hours, Anastasia. But I've only been here about five minutes." I kiss her temple. "Dr. Greene will be here shortly."

"Oh."

"Did you sleep well?" I ask. "Certainly seemed like it to me, with all that snoring."

"I do not snore!"

I put her out of her misery, grinning. "No. You don't."

"Did you shower?" she asks.

"No. Waiting for you."

"Oh. Okay."

"What time is it?"

"Ten fifteen. I didn't have the heart to wake you earlier."

"You told me you didn't have a heart at all."

That at least is true. But I ignore her comment.

"Breakfast is here. Pancakes and bacon for you. Come, get up, I'm getting lonely out here." I swat her behind, clamber off the bed, and leave her to get up.

In the dining room I remove the dishes from the cart and lay out the plates. I sit down and within moments my toast and scrambled eggs are history. I pour myself some coffee, wondering whether to hurry Ana along but decide against it and open *The Seattle Times*.

She shuffles into the dining room wearing an oversize robe and sits down beside me.

"Eat up. You're going to need your strength today," I say.

"And why is that? You going to lock me in the bedroom?" she teases.

"Appealing as that idea is, I thought we'd go out today. Get some fresh air." I'm excited about *The Grace*.

"Is it safe?" she quips.

"Where we're going it is," I mutter, unamused by her comment. "And it's not a joking matter," I add.

I want to keep you safe, baby.

Her mouth sets in that stubborn way she has and she stares down at her breakfast.

Eat, Ana.

As if she can read my mind, she grabs her fork and starts picking at her breakfast, allowing me to relax a little.

A few minutes later there's a knock on the door. I glance at my watch. "That'll be the good doctor," I say and stroll to the door to answer it.

"Good morning, Dr. Greene, come in. Thank you for coming at such short notice."

"Again, Mr. Grey, thank you for making it worth my while. Where's the patient?" Dr. Greene is all business.

"She's having her breakfast and will be ready in a minute. Do you want to wait in the bedroom?"

"That'll be fine."

I show her into the master, and soon after Ana wanders in and gives me a disapproving look. I choose to ignore it and close the door, leaving her with Dr. Greene. She can be as annoyed as she likes, but she stopped taking her pills. And she knows I hate condoms.

My phone buzzes.

At last.

"Good morning, Taylor."

"Good morning, Mr. Grey. You called?"

"What news?"

"Sawyer has been through the CCTV footage from the garage and I can confirm it was Leila who vandalized the car."

"Shit."

"Quite, sir. I've updated Welch on the situation, and the Audi has been removed."

"Good. Have you checked the apartment CCTV?"

"We're doing that now, but we haven't found anything yet."

"We need to know how she got in."

"Yes, sir. She's not here now. We've done a thorough check, but I understand that until we're certain that she can't get in again you should stay away. I'm having all the locks changed. Even on the fire escape."

"The fire escape. I always forget about that."

"It's easily done, sir."

"I'm taking Ana to *The Grace*. We'll stay on board if we need to."

"I'd like to do a security check of *The Grace* before you get there," Taylor says.

"Okay. I can't imagine we'll be there before one."

“We can collect your luggage from the hotel after that.”

“Great.”

“And I’ve emailed Audi about a replacement vehicle.”

“Okay. Let me know how that goes.”

“Will do, sir.”

“Oh, and Taylor, in the future, we only need a one-bedroom suite.”

Taylor hesitates. “Very good, sir,” he says. “Will that be all for now?”

“No, one more thing. When Gail returns, can you ask her to move all of Miss Steele’s clothes and belongings into my room?”

“Certainly, sir.”

“Thanks.”

I hang up and sit back down at the dining table to finish the newspaper. I note with displeasure that Ana has hardly touched her breakfast.

Plus ça change, Grey. Plus ça change.

HALF AN HOUR LATER Ana and Dr. Greene emerge from the bedroom. Ana looks subdued. We exchange goodbyes with the doctor and I close the suite door behind her.

“Everything okay?” I ask Ana as she stands, looking sullen, in the hallway. She nods but won’t look at me. “Anastasia, what is it? What did Dr. Greene say?”

She shakes her head. “You’re good to go in seven days.”

“Seven days?”

“Yes.”

“Ana, what’s wrong?”

“It’s nothing to worry about. Please, Christian, just leave it.”

Normally I have no idea what she’s thinking, but something is troubling her, and because it’s troubling her, it’s troubling me. Maybe Dr. Greene warned her away from me. I tilt her chin back so we’re eye to eye. “Tell me,” I persist.

“There’s nothing to tell. I’d like to get dressed.” She jerks her chin out of my hand.

Fuck. What's wrong?

I run my hands through my hair in an effort to remain calm.

Perhaps it's the Leila scare?

Or maybe the doctor gave her some bad news?

She gives nothing away.

"Let's shower," I suggest eventually. She agrees but is hardly enthusiastic. "Come." I take her hand and move into the bathroom with a reluctant Ana trailing behind me. I turn on the shower and strip out of my clothes while she stands in the middle of the bathroom sulking.

Ana, what the hell is wrong?

"I don't know what's upset you, or if you're just bad-tempered through lack of sleep," I say quietly as I unfasten her robe. "But I want you to tell me. My imagination is running away with me, and I don't like it."

She rolls her eyes, but before I can rebuke her she says, "Dr. Greene scolded me about missing the pill. She said I could be pregnant."

"What?"

Pregnant!

And I'm free-falling. Fuck.

"But I'm not," she says. "She did a test. It was a shock, that's all. I can't believe I was that stupid."

Oh, thank God.

"You're sure you're not?"

"Yes."

I exhale. "Good. Yes, I can see how news like that would be very upsetting."

"I was more worried about your reaction."

"My reaction? Well, naturally, I'm relieved. It would be the height of carelessness and bad manners to knock you up."

"Then maybe we should abstain," she snaps.

What the hell?

"You are in a bad temper this morning."

"It was just a shock, that's all," she says, sullen again.

I haul her into my embrace. She's tense and stiff with

indignation. I kiss her hair and hold her. "Ana, I'm not used to this," I whisper. "My natural inclination is to beat it out of you, but I seriously doubt you want that."

She could cry it out if I did. In my experience, women feel better after a good cry.

"No, I don't," she responds. "This helps." And she puts her arms around me and hugs me tighter, her warm cheek against my chest. I rest my chin on top of her head. We stand like this for an age and slowly she relaxes in my arms.

"Come, let's shower." I strip her out of her robe and she follows me into the hot water. It's welcome. I've felt grimy all morning. I shampoo my hair and hand the bottle to Ana. She looks happier now, and I'm glad the showerhead is big enough for both of us. She surrenders herself to the water, tipping up her lovely face, and begins to wash her hair.

I take the body wash, lather up my hands, then begin washing Ana. Her earlier bad mood has rattled me. I feel responsible. She's tired and she had a trying evening. As she rinses her hair, I massage and wash her shoulders, arms, underarms, back, and her beautiful breasts. Turning her around, I continue with her stomach and belly, between her legs, and her ass. She makes a noise of approval deep in her throat.

My smile is broad.

That's better.

I turn her to face me. "Here." I give her the body wash. "I want you to wash off the remains of the lipstick."

Her eyes flicker open and her expression is serious and earnest.

"Don't stray far from the line, please," I add.

"Okay."

She squeezes soap onto her palm and rubs her hands together to make a frothy lather. Placing her hands on my shoulders, she begins to wash away the line with a gentle circular motion. I close my eyes and take a deep breath.

Can I do this?

My breathing shallows, and panic wells in my throat. She continues down my side, her nimble fingers tenderly administering to me. But it's unbearable. Like tiny razor blades on my skin. Every muscle in my body is tense. I stand like a hollow bronze, counting the seconds until she's finished.

It's taking an eternity.

My teeth are clenched.

Suddenly her hands are no longer on my body and that alarms me more. I open my eyes and she's soaping her hands again. She glances up at me and I see my pain reflected in her eyes and on her sweet, anxious face. And I know it's not pity but compassion. My agony is her agony.

Oh Ana.

"Ready?" she asks, her voice hoarse.

"Yes," I whisper, determined not to let the fear win, and I close my eyes.

She touches my side and I freeze, as fear fills my gut, my chest, and my throat, leaving nothing but the darkness. It's a gaping, aching void that consumes me, all of me.

Ana sniffles and I open my eyes.

She's crying, her tears lost in the cascade of hot water, her nose pink. Her compassion is spilling down her face—her compassion and her anger as she washes away my sins.

No. Don't cry, Ana.

I'm just a fucked-up man.

Her lip trembles.

"No. Please, don't cry." I fold her into my arms and hold her. "Please don't cry for me."

She starts sobbing. Really sobbing. And I cradle her head in my hands and lean down to kiss her. "Don't cry, Ana, please," I whisper against her mouth. "It was long ago. I am aching for you to touch me, but I just can't bear it. It's too much. Please, please don't cry."

"I…want to touch you, too…" she stutters between sobs. "More than you'll ever know. To see you like this. So hurt and afraid, Christian. It wounds me deeply. I love you so much."

I run my thumb across her bottom lip. "I know. I know."

And she squints at me with a look of dismay, because she knows my words have no conviction.

"You're very easy to love. Don't you see that?" she says as the water falls around us.

"No, baby, I don't."

"You are. And I do," she stresses. "And so does your family. So do Elena and Leila. They have a strange way of showing it, but they do. You are worthy."

"Stop."

I can't bear it. I put my finger over her lips and shake my head. "I can't hear this. I'm nothing, Anastasia." I'm a lost boy, standing before you. Unloved. Abandoned by the one person who was supposed to protect me, because I'm a monster.

That's me, Ana.

That's all I am.

"I'm a husk of a man. I don't have a heart."

"Yes, you do," she cries passionately. "And I want it, all of it. You're a good man, Christian, a really good man. Don't ever doubt that. Look at what you've done. What you've achieved." She continues to sob. "Look what you've done for me. What you've turned your back on, for me. I know. I know how you feel about me." Her blue, blue eyes, filled with love, filled with compassion, leave me as raw and exposed as they did the first time I met her.

She sees me. She thinks she knows me.

"You love me," she says.

Every ounce of oxygen evaporates from my lungs.

Time suspends and all I can hear is my own blood thrumming in my ears and the splash of the water as it washes the darkness away.

Answer her, Grey. Tell her the truth.

"Yes," I whisper, "I do."

It's a deep, dark confession wrenched from my soul. And yet as I say the words out loud it all becomes clear. Of course I love her. Of course she knows. I've loved her since I met her. Since I watched her sleep. Since she gave herself to me and only me. I'm addicted. I can't get enough. That's why I tolerate her attitude.

I'm in love. This is what it feels like.

Her reaction is instant. Her smile is dazzling, lighting up her beautiful face. She's breathtaking. She clasps my head, bringing my mouth to hers, and kisses me, pouring all her love and sweetness into me.

It's humbling.

It's overwhelming.

It's hot.

And my body responds. The only way it knows how.

Groaning against her lips, I encircle her with my arms. "Oh, Ana, I want you, but not here."

"Yes," she says feverishly against my mouth.

I switch off the water and lead her out of the shower. I wrap her in her bathrobe and secure a towel around my waist. Taking a smaller one, I begin to dry her hair.

This is what I love. Taking care of her.

And what's more, for a change, she's letting me.

She stands patiently while I squeeze the water from her hair and rub her head. When I look up she's watching me in the mirror above the sink. Our eyes meet and I'm lost in her loving look.

"Can I reciprocate?" she asks.

What does she have in mind?

I nod and Ana reaches for another towel. Standing on tiptoe, she wraps it around my head and starts to rub. I lower my head, giving her easier access.

Mmm. This feels good.

She uses her nails, rubbing hard.

Oh man.

I grin like a fool, feeling…cherished. When I raise my head to look at her she's peeking at me through the towel, and she grins, too. "It's a long time since anyone did this to me. A very long time," I tell her. "In fact, I don't think anyone's ever dried my hair."

"Surely Grace did? Dried your hair when you were young?"

I shake my head. "No. She respected my boundaries from day one, even though it was painful for her. I was very self-sufficient as a child."

Ana stills for a moment and I wonder what she's thinking. "Well, I'm honored," she says.

"That you are, Miss Steele. Or maybe it is I who am honored."

"That goes without saying, Mr. Grey."

She tosses the damp towel onto the vanity unit in front of us and reaches for a new one. As she stands behind me our eyes meet once more in the large mirror.

"Can I try something?" she asks.

We're doing this your way, baby.

I nod, giving her permission, and she runs the towel down my left arm, removing all the drops of water that cling to my skin. She looks up, watching me intently, and then leans forward and kisses my bicep.

My breathing stalls.

She dries my other arm and leaves a trail of feather-light kisses over my right bicep. Dodging behind me so I can no longer see what she's doing, she wipes my back, respecting the lipstick lines.

"Whole back," I offer, feeling brave, "with the towel." I take a deep breath and shut my eyes.

Ana does as she's told and briskly dries my back. When she finishes she gives me a swift kiss on my shoulder.

I exhale. That wasn't so bad.

She puts her arms around me and dries my belly.

"Hold this," she says and hands me a face towel. "Remember in Georgia? You made me touch myself using your hands," she explains. She wraps her arms around me and stares at me in the mirror. With the towel draped over her head, she looks like a biblical character.

The Virgin.

She's soft enough and sweet enough, but a virgin no more.

Grasping my hand that holds the face towel, she guides it across my chest, drying a spot. As soon as the towel touches me, I freeze. My mind empties and I will my body to endure this touch. I stand tense before her, unmoving. We're doing this her way. I start to pant with a strange mixture of fear, love, and fascination, and my eyes follow her fingers as she gently guides my hand and wipes my chest dry.

"I think you're dry now," she says and drops her hand.

In the mirror's reflection we fix our eyes on each other.

I want her. I need her. I tell her.

"I need you, too," she says, her eyes darkening.

"Let me love you."

"Yes," she replies, and I scoop her up in my arms, my lips on hers, and carry her into the bedroom. I lay her down on the bed, and with infinite care and tenderness I show her how much I honor her, cherish her, and treasure her.

And love her.

I AM A NEW being. A new Christian Grey. I am in love with Anastasia Steele, and what's more, she loves me. Of course, the girl needs to have her head examined, but right now I'm grateful, spent, and happy.

I lie beside her, imagining a world of possibility. Ana's skin is soft and warm. I cannot stop touching her while we gaze at each other in the calm after the storm.

"So, you can be gentle." Her eyes are alight with amusement.

Only with you.

"Hmm. So it would seem, Miss Steele."

She grins, showing perfect white teeth. "You weren't particularly the first time we, um, did this."

"No?" I take a strand of her hair and wind it around my index finger. "When I robbed you of your virtue."

"I don't think you robbed me. I think my virtue was offered up pretty freely and willingly. I wanted you, too, and if I remember correctly, I rather enjoyed myself." Her smile is shy but warm.

"So did I, if I recall, Miss Steele. We aim to please. And it means you're mine, completely."

"Yes, I am. I wanted to ask you something."

"Go ahead."

"Your biological father, do you know who he was?"

Her question is completely unexpected. I shake my head. She's surprised me again. I never know what's going on in that smart brain of hers. “I have no idea. Wasn’t the savage who was her pimp, which is good.”

“How do you know?”

“Something my dad—something Carrick said to me.”

Her look is expectant, urging me on.

“So hungry for information, Anastasia.” I sigh and shake my head. I don’t like thinking about this time in my life. It’s difficult to separate the memories from the nightmares. But she’s persistent. “The pimp discovered the crack whore’s body and phoned it in to the authorities. Took him four days to make the discovery, though. He shut the door when he left. Left me with her. Her body.”

Mommy is asleep on the floor.
She has been asleep for a long time.
She doesn’t wake up.
I call her. I shake her.
She doesn’t wake up.

I shudder and continue. “Police interviewed him later. He denied flat-out I had anything to do with him, and Carrick said he looked nothing like me.”

Thank God.

“Do you remember what he looked like?”

“Anastasia, this isn’t a part of my life I revisit very often. Yes, I remember what he looked like. I’ll never forget him.” Bile rises in my throat. “Can we talk about something else?”

“I’m sorry. I didn’t mean to upset you.”

“It’s old news, Ana. Not something I want to think about.”

She looks guilty and, knowing she’s gone too far with these questions, changes the subject. “So, what’s this surprise, then?”

Ah. She remembered. Now, this I can deal with. “Can you face going out for some fresh air? I want to show you something.”

“Of course.”

Great! I swat her behind. “Get dressed. Jeans will be good. I hope Taylor’s packed some for you.”

I leap out of bed, excited to take Ana sailing, and she watches me pull on my underwear.

"Up," I nag, and she grins.

"Just admiring the view," she says.

"Dry your hair," I tell her.

"Domineering as ever," she observes, and I bend down to kiss her.

"That's never going to change, baby. I don't want you sick."

She rolls her eyes.

"My palms still twitch, you know, Miss Steele."

"I am glad to hear it, Mr. Grey. I was beginning to think you were losing your edge."

Oh. Mixed signals from Miss Steele.

Don't tempt me, Ana. "I could easily demonstrate that is not the case, should you so wish." I grab a sweater from my bag, fetch my phone, and pack the rest of my belongings.

Once I'm done, I find Ana dressed and drying her hair.

"Pack your things. If it's safe, we'll go home tonight; if not, we can stay again."

ANA AND I STEP into the elevator. An elderly couple moves aside for us. Ana looks up at me and smirks. I squeeze her hand and grin, remembering that kiss.

Oh, fuck the paperwork.

"I'll never let you forget that," she says so only I can hear. "Our first kiss."

I'm tempted to do a repeat performance and scandalize the elderly couple, but I settle for a discreet peck on her cheek that makes her giggle.

We check out at reception and walk hand in hand through the foyer to the valet.

"Where are we going, exactly?" Ana asks as we wait for my car.

I tap the side of my nose and wink, trying to hide my excitement. Her face lights up with a huge smile, matching mine. Leaning down, I kiss her. "Do you have any idea how happy you make me feel?"

“Yes. I know exactly. Because you do the same for me.”

The valet appears with my R8.

“Great car, sir,” he says as he gives me my keys. I tip him and he opens Ana’s door.

As I turn onto Fourth Avenue, the sun is shining, my girl is beside me, and there’s good music playing on my car stereo.

I overtake an Audi A3 and suddenly remember Ana’s wrecked car. I realize I’ve not thought about Leila and her crazy behavior for the last few hours. Ana’s a good distraction.

She’s more than a distraction, Grey.

Perhaps I should buy her something else.

Yes. Something different. Not an Audi.

A Volvo.

No. My dad has one.

A BMW.

No. My mom has one.

“I need to make a detour. It shouldn’t take long,” I inform her.

“Sure.”

We pull into the Saab dealership. Ana looks perplexed. “We need to get you a new car,” I say.

“Not an Audi?”

No. I’m not getting you the car I’ve bought all my subs. “I thought you might like something else.”

“A Saab?” She’s amused.

“Yeah. A 9-3. Come.”

“What is it with you and foreign cars?”

“The Germans and the Swedes make the safest cars in the world, Anastasia.”

“I thought you’d already ordered me another Audi A3?”

“I can cancel that. Come.” I climb out of the car, walk to her side, and open the door. “I owe you a graduation present.”

“Christian, you really don’t have to do this.”

I make it clear to her that I do and we stroll into the car showroom where a salesman greets us with a well-rehearsed smile. “My name’s Troy Turniansky. Are you after a Saab, sir? Pre-owned?” He rubs his hands, sensing a sale.

"New," I inform him.

"Did you have a model in mind, sir?"

"9-3 2.0T Sport Sedan."

Ana shoots a questioning look at me.

Yeah. I've been meaning to test drive one of these.

"An excellent choice, sir."

"What color, Anastasia?" I ask.

"Er, black?" she says with a shrug. "You really don't need to do this."

"Black's not easily seen at night."

"You have a black car."

This is not about me. I give her a pointed look.

"Canary yellow, then," she says and flips her hair over her shoulder—irritated, I think.

I scowl at her.

"What color do you want me to have?" She crosses her arms.

"Silver or white."

"Silver, then," she says but reiterates that she'd be fine with the Audi.

Now, sensing the loss of a sale, Turniansky pipes up. "Perhaps you'd like the convertible, ma'am?"

Ana lights up and Turniansky claps his hands.

"Convertible?" I ask, raising a brow. And her cheeks redden with embarrassment. Miss Steele would like a convertible, and I'm beyond pleased that I've found something she wants. "What are the safety stats on the convertible?" I ask the salesman, and he's prepared, reeling off a brochure's worth of stats and other information. I glance at Ana, and she's all smiles and teeth.

Turniansky hurries to his desk to consult his computer on the availability of a brand-new convertible 9-3.

"Whatever you're high on, I'd like some, Miss Steele." I pull her close.

"I'm high on you, Mr. Grey."

"Really? Well, you certainly look intoxicated." I kiss her. "And thank you for accepting the car. That was easier than last time."

"Well, it's not an Audi A3."

"That's not the car for you."

"I liked it."

"Sir, the 9-3? I've located one at our Beverly Hills dealership. We can have it here for you in a couple of days." Turniansky is bursting at the seams with his achievement.

"Top of the range?" I ask.

"Yes, sir."

"Excellent." I hand him my credit card.

"If you'll come this way, Mr…" Turniansky glances at the name on the card. "Grey."

I follow him to his desk. "Can you get it here tomorrow?"

"I can try, Mr. Grey." He nods and we begin to fill out the paperwork.

"THANK YOU," ANA SAYS as we set off.

"You're most welcome, Anastasia."

The soulful, sad voice of Eva Cassidy fills the R8 when I turn on the engine.

"Who's this?" Ana asks, and I tell her.

"She has a lovely voice."

"She does. She did."

"Oh."

"She died young." Too young.

"Oh." Ana gives me a wistful look.

I remember that she didn't finish her breakfast earlier and I ask her if she's hungry.

I'm keeping track, Ana.

"Yes."

"Lunch first, then."

I speed along Elliott Avenue, heading to Elliott Bay Marina. Flynn was right. I like trying things her way. I look at Ana, who's lost in the music, staring out at the passing scenery. I feel content and excited for what I have planned this afternoon.

The car lot is crowded at the marina, but I find a space. "We'll eat here. I'll open your door," I say as Ana makes a move to get out of the car. Together we walk toward the waterfront, arms around each other.

"So many boats," she says.

And one of them is mine.

We stand on the promenade and watch the sailboats out in the Sound. Ana tugs her jacket around herself.

"Cold?" I tuck her under my arm, closer to my side.

"No, just admiring the view."

"I could stare at it all day. Come, this way."

We head into SP's, the waterfront restaurant and bar, for lunch. Inside, I search for Dante, Claude Bastille's brother.

"Mr. Grey!" He sees me before I see him. "What can I get you this afternoon?"

"Dante, good afternoon." I usher Ana onto one of the stools at the bar. "This lovely lady is Anastasia Steele."

"Welcome to SP's Place." Dante grins at Ana, his dark eyes intrigued. "What would you like to drink, Anastasia?"

"Please, call me Ana," she says, then, eyeing me, adds, "and I'll have whatever Christian's drinking."

Ana is deferring to me, like she did at the ball. I like it.

"I'm going to have a beer. This is the only bar in Seattle where you can get Adnams Explorer."

"A beer?"

"Yes. Two Explorers, please, Dante."

Dante nods and sets up the drinks on the bar and I tell Ana that the seafood chowder that's served here is delicious. Dante writes down our food order and gives me a wink.

Yes, I'm here with a woman I'm not related to. It's a first, I know.

I turn my attention to Ana.

"How did you get started in business?" she asks and takes a sip of her beer.

I give her the executive summary: With Elena's money and some shrewd but risky investments I was able to build a capital fund. The first company I acquired was about to go under; it had been developing power units for cell phones using graphene technology, but the R&D had exhausted the company's capital. The patents they held were worth exploiting, and I kept their key talent, Fred and Barney, who are now my two chief engineers.

I tell Ana about our work on solar and wind-up technology for the home market and the developing world and our innovative research to develop battery storage. All critical initiatives, given the depletion of fossil fuels.

"You still with me?" I ask when our chowder arrives. I love that she's interested in what I do. Even my parents struggle not to glaze over when I tell them about my work.

"I'm fascinated," she says. "Everything about you fascinates me, Christian."

Her words are encouraging, so I continue my story of how I bought and sold more companies, keeping those that shared my ethos, breaking up and selling the others.

"Mergers and acquisitions," she muses.

"The very same. I moved into shipping two years ago, and from there into improving food production. Our test sites in Africa are pioneering new agricultural techniques for higher crop yields."

"Feed the world," Ana teases me.

"Yeah, something like that."

"You're very philanthropic."

"I can afford to be."

"This is delicious," Ana says as she takes another spoonful of chowder.

"One of my favorites," I respond.

"You told me you like sailing." Ana motions to the boats outside.

"Yes. I've been coming here since I was a kid. Elliot and I learned to sail at the sail school here. Do you sail?"

"No."

"So what does a young woman from Montesano do to keep herself amused?" I take a sip of my beer.

"Read."

"It always comes back to books with you, doesn't it?"

"Yes."

"What happened between Ray and your mom?"

"I think they drifted apart. My mom is such a romantic, and Ray, well, he's more practical. She'd been in Washington all her life. She wanted adventure."

"Did she find any?"

"She found Steve." Her expression darkens, as if the mention of his name leaves a nasty taste in her mouth. "But she never talks about him."

"Oh."

"Yes. I don't think that was a happy time for her. I wondered if she regretted leaving Ray after that."

"And you stayed with him."

"Yes. He needed me more than my mom did."

We talk freely and easily. Ana is a good listener and much more forthcoming about herself this time. Perhaps it's because she now knows that I love her.

I love Ana.

There. That's not so painful, is it, Grey?

She's explaining how much she disliked living in Texas and Vegas because of the heat. She prefers the cooler climate in Washington.

I hope she stays in Washington.

Yes. With me.

Like moving in?

Grey, you're getting way ahead of yourself here.

Take her sailing.

I glance at my watch and drain my beer. "Shall we go?"

We settle up for lunch and head out into the mild summer sunshine. "I wanted to show you something."

Holding hands, we amble past the smaller boats anchored in the marina. I spot *The Grace*'s mast towering above the smaller boats as we near her mooring. My anticipation escalates. I haven't been sailing for a while, and now I get to take my girl.

Leaving the main promenade, we step onto the dock, then down onto a narrower pontoon. At *The Grace*, I stop. "I thought we'd go sailing this afternoon. This is my boat."

My catamaran. My pride and joy.

Ana's impressed.

"Built by my company. She's been designed from the ground up by the very best naval architects in the world and constructed here in Seattle at my yard. She has hybrid electric drives, asymmetric dagger boards, a square-topped mainsail—"

"Okay!" Ana says, holding up her hands. "You've lost me, Christian."

Don't get carried away, Grey.

"She's a great boat." I can't conceal my admiration.

"She looks mighty fine, Mr. Grey."

"That she does, Miss Steele."

"What's her name?"

I take her hand and show her *The Grace* written in an elaborate scroll on the side. "You named her after your mom?" Ana sounds surprised.

"Yes. Why do you find that strange?"

She shrugs, at a loss for words.

"I adore my mom, Anastasia. Why wouldn't I name a boat after her?"

"No, it's not that. It's just—"

"Anastasia, Grace Trevelyan-Grey saved my life. I owe her everything."

Her smile is uncertain, and I wonder what's going through her head and what I might have done to make her think I don't love my mother.

Okay, so I once told Ana I didn't have a heart—but there's always been room for my family in what's left of it. Even Elliot.

I didn't know there was space for anyone else.

But there's an Ana-shaped space.

And she's filled it to overflowing.

I swallow as I try to contain the depth of feeling I have for her. She's bringing my heart back to life, bringing me back to life.

"Do you want to come aboard?" I ask before I say something sappy.

"Yes, please."

Taking my hand, she follows me as I stride up the gangplank

onto the aft deck. Mac appears, startling Ana when he opens the sliding doors to the main saloon.

"Mr. Grey! Welcome back." We shake hands.

"Anastasia, this is Liam McConnell. Liam, my girlfriend, Anastasia Steele."

"How do you do?" she says to Liam.

"Call me Mac. Welcome aboard, Miss Steele."

"Ana, please."

"How's she shaping up, Mac?" I ask.

"She's ready to rock and roll, sir," he says with a huge grin.

"Let's get underway, then."

"You going to take her out?" he asks.

"Yep," I reply. I wouldn't miss this for the world. "Quick tour, Anastasia?"

We go through the sliding doors. Ana scans the inside, and I know she's impressed. The interior has been created by a Swedish designer based in Seattle, all clean lines and light oak that give the saloon a bright and airy feel. I've adopted the same look throughout *The Grace*. "This is the main saloon. Galley beside." I wave in its direction. "Bathrooms on either side." I point them out, then lead her through the small door to my cabin. Ana gasps at the sight of the bed. "This is the master cabin. You're the first girl in here, apart from family." I hold her and kiss her. "They don't count. Might have to christen this bed," I whisper against her lips. "But not right now. Come, Mac will be casting off." I lead Ana back into the main saloon. "Office in there, and at the front here, two more cabins."

"So how many can sleep on board?"

"It's a six-berth cat. I've only ever had the family on board, though. I like to sail alone. But not when you're here. I need to keep an eye on you." From the chest by the sliding door I extract a bright-red life jacket.

"Here." I slip it over her head and tighten the straps.

"You love strapping me in, don't you?"

"In any form." I wink at her.

"You are a pervert."

"I know."

"My pervert," she teases.

"Yes, yours."

Once I've fastened the buckles I grab the side of the life jacket and kiss her quickly. "Always," I say and release her before she can respond. "Come." We go outside and up the steps to the top deck and the cockpit.

Below, at the dock, Mac is casting off the bowline. He leaps back on board.

"Is this where you learned all your rope tricks?" Ana is pretending to be naive.

"Clove hitches have come in handy. Miss Steele, you sound curious. I like you curious. I'd be more than happy to demonstrate what I can do with a rope."

Ana goes quiet, and I think I've upset her.

Damn.

"Gotcha." She giggles, pleased with herself.

Well, that's not fair. I narrow my eyes. "I may have to deal with you later, but right now I've got to drive my boat." I sit down at the captain's chair and fire up the twin fifty-five-horsepower engines. I switch off the blower and Mac scoots along the top deck, grabbing the guardrail, then bounces down to the aft deck to release the stern lines. He waves at me and I radio the Coast Guard to get the all-clear.

I take *The Grace* out of idle, move the shifter forward, and ease the throttle. And my beautiful boat glides out of her berth.

Ana is waving to the small crowd that has gathered on the dock to witness our departure. I tug her back between my legs.

"See this." I point to the VHF. "That's our radio. Our GPS, our AIS, the radar."

"What's the AIS?"

"That identifies us to shipping. This is our depth gauge. Grab the wheel."

"Aye, aye, Captain." She salutes me.

I pilot us slowly out of the marina, Ana's hands beneath mine on the wheel. We turn into open water and sweep across the Sound in a large arc until we're heading northwest toward the Olympic Peninsula and Bainbridge Island. The wind is moderate at fifteen knots, but I know once we get the sheets up *The Grace* will fly. I love this. Challenging myself against the elements in a boat I've helped design, using the skills I've spent a lifetime perfecting. It's thrilling.

"Sail time," I say to Ana, and I cannot contain my excitement. "Here, you take her. Keep her on this course."

Ana looks freaked out.

"Baby, it's really easy. Hold the wheel and keep your eye on the horizon over the bow. You'll do great; you always do. When the sails go up, you'll feel the drag. Just hold her steady. I'll signal like this"—I make a slashing motion with my hand across my throat—"and you can cut the engines. This button here." I point to the engines' kill button. "Understand?"

"Yes." But she looks uncertain. I know she's got this. She always does. I give her a quick kiss and bound onto the top deck to prep and hoist the main sail. Mac and I crank in unison, making light work of it. When the wind catches the sheet we lurch forward and I glance at Ana, but she's holding us steady. Mac and I work on the headsail and it flies up the mast, welcoming the wind and harnessing its power.

"Hold her steady, baby, and cut the engines!" I shout over the roar of the wind and the waves, and I motion to her. Ana presses the button and the roar of the engines ceases as we whip across the sea, flying northwest.

I join Ana at the wheel. The wind is lashing her hair around her face; she's exhilarated, her cheeks flushed with joy. "What do you think?" I yell above the call of the sea and the wind.

"Christian! This is fantastic."

"You wait until the spinney's up." With my chin I point to Mac, who is raising the spinnaker.

"Interesting color," Ana shouts.

I give her a knowing wink. Yep, the color of my playroom.

The wind pumps up the spinney and *The Grace* charges ahead, unleashing her power and giving us a thrilling ride. Ana looks from the spinnaker to me. "Asymmetrical sail. For speed," I call out. I've pushed *The Grace* to twenty knots, but the wind has to be in our favor for that kind of speed.

"It's amazing!" she shouts. "How fast are we going?"

"She's doing fifteen knots."

"I have no idea what that means."

"It's about seventeen miles an hour."

"Is that all? It feels much faster."

Ana is radiant. Her joy is infectious. I squeeze her hands on the wheel. "You look lovely, Anastasia. It's good to see some color in your cheeks, and not from blushing. You look like you do in José's photos."

She turns in my arms and kisses me. "You know how to show a girl a good time, Mr. Grey."

"We aim to please, Miss Steele." She turns back to face the bow and I smooth the hair away from her neck and kiss her. "I like seeing you happy," I murmur in her ear, and we race across Puget Sound.

WE ANCHOR IN THE cove near Hedley Spit on Bainbridge Island. Together, Mac and I lower the dinghy so he can go ashore and visit a friend in Point Monroe. "I'll see you in about an hour, Mr. Grey." He descends into the small boat, gives Ana a wave, and fires up the outboard motor.

I vault up to the aft deck where Ana is standing and grab her hand. I don't need to watch Mac speed toward the lagoon; I have more pressing business to attend to.

"What are we going to do now?" Ana asks as I take her into the saloon.

"I have plans for you, Miss Steele." And with indecent haste, I drag her into my cabin. She's smiling as I make quick work of her life jacket and toss it to the floor. Once it's off, she stares at me, remaining mute, but her teeth tease her bottom lip, and I don't know if it's deliberate or an unconscious lure.

I want to make love to her.

On my boat.

It will be another first.

Caressing her face with the tips of my fingers, I slowly move them down to her chin, her neck, and her sternum to the first closed button on her blouse. Her eyes never waver from mine. "I want to see you." With my thumb and forefinger, I undo the button. She stands absolutely still, her breathing accelerated.

I know she's mine to do with as I please. My girl.

I stand back to give her some room. "Strip for me," I whisper. Her lips part and her eyes blaze with desire. Slowly she brings her fingers up to her next fastened button and at a snail's pace undoes it, then moves at the same infuriating pace to the next one.

Fuck.

She's taunting me. Minx.

When the final button is undone she pulls her shirt apart and shrugs out of it, letting it fall to the floor.

She's wearing a white lacy bra, her nipples taut against the lace, and she's a fine, fine sight. Her fingers run down past her navel and toy with the top button of her jeans.

Sweetheart, you need to take your shoes off.

"Stop. Sit." I point to the edge of the bed and she complies.

I fall to my knees and undo the laces of first one and then the other sneaker, pulling them off, followed by her socks.

I pick up her foot and kiss the soft pad of her big toe, then graze it with my teeth.

"Ah," she breathes, and the sound is music to my dick.

Let her do this her way, Grey.

Standing, I hold out my hand and pull her up from the bed. "Continue." I give her the floor and step back to enjoy the show.

With a wanton look at me, she undoes the button and tugs down her zipper at the same slow pace. She hooks her thumbs into her waistband and slowly shimmies out of her jeans, sliding them down her legs.

She's wearing a thong.

A thong.

Wow.

She unfastens her bra and slides the straps down her arms before dropping it on the floor.

I want to touch her.

And I clench my fists to stop myself.

She slips off her thong and lets it fall to her ankles, where she steps out of it and stands before me.

She is all woman.

And I want her.

All of her.

Her body, her heart, and her soul.

You have her heart, Grey. She loves you.

I grab the hem of my sweater and pull it over my head, then my T-shirt. I slip out of my shoes and socks. Her eyes never leave mine.

Her look is scorching.

I move to undo my jeans. She puts her hand over mine. "Let me," she whispers.

I'm impatient to get out of my jeans, but I give her a big smile. "Be my guest."

She steps forward and slips her hand over the waistband of my jeans and tugs so I'm forced to take a step closer to her. She undoes the top button, but she doesn't undo the zipper. Instead, her intrepid fingers meander from the zipper to trace the straining outline of my cock. Instinctively, I flex my hips, pushing my erection into her hand.

"You're getting so bold, Ana, so brave." I cradle her face with my hands and kiss her, easing my tongue into her mouth while she places her hands on my hips and circles her thumbs against my skin, just above the waistband of my jeans.

"So are you," she breathes against my lips.

"Getting there," I answer.

She tugs down my fly, pushes her hand inside my pants, and takes hold of my cock. I growl in appreciation and my lips find hers as I fold her in my arms, feeling her soft skin against mine.

The darkness is gone.

She knows where to touch me.

And how to touch me.

Her hand tightens around me, squeezing hard, and her hand moves up and down, pleasuring me. I tolerate a few moves, then whisper, “Oh, I want you so much, baby.” I step back and remove my pants and underwear and stand before her naked, ready.

Her eyes scan my body, but as she does that *v* appears between her brows.

“What’s wrong, Ana?” I ask and gently stroke her cheek. Is she reacting to my scars?

“Nothing. Love me, now,” she says.

Embracing her, I kiss her with fervor, my fingers tangling in her hair. I’ll never get enough of her mouth. Her lips. Her tongue. I walk her backward and gently lower both of us onto the bed. Lying by her side, I run my nose along her jawline, inhaling deeply.

Orchards. Apples. Summer and a mellow fall.

She’s all of those things.

“Do you have any idea how exquisite your scent is, Ana? It’s irresistible.” With my lips, I trace a line down her throat, across her breasts, kissing her as I go, breathing in her essence as I travel down her body.

“You are so beautiful.” I suck gently on a nipple.

She moans and her body bows off the bed.

The sound makes me harder. “Let me hear you, baby.” I cup her breast, then move to her waist, enjoying the feel of her smooth skin under my fingers. I move past her hip, her ass, down to her knee while I kiss and suckle her breasts. Holding her knee, I hitch up her leg and curl it over my hips.

She gasps, and I revel in her reaction.

Rolling over, I take her with me so she’s on top of me. I hand her a condom from the side table.

Her delight is clear and she scoots down so she’s sitting on my thighs. She grabs my erection and leans down and kisses the tip. Her hair falls, forming a curtain around my cock as she takes me into her mouth.

Fuck. It’s erotic.

She consumes me, sucking hard, skimming her teeth over me.

I groan and flex my hips so I’m deeper in her mouth.

She lets me go, tears open the foil packet, and unrolls the condom on my rigid dick. I hold out my hands to help her balance, and she takes them both, and slowly, oh-so-slowly, sinks down on me.

Oh God.

It's so good.

I close my eyes and tip my head back as she takes me. And I give myself over to her.

She moans and I place my hands on her hips and move her up and then down as I push up, consuming her. "Oh, baby," I whisper, and I want more. So much more.

I sit up so we're nose to nose and I'm cradling her ass with my thighs, and I'm buried deep inside her. She gasps and grabs my arms as I hold her head and stare into her beautiful eyes, eyes that shine with her love and desire.

"Oh, Ana. What you make me feel," I say and kiss her with unbridled passion.

"Oh, I love you," she says, and I close my eyes.

Ana loves me.

I roll her over, her legs locked around my waist, and look down at her in wonder.

I love you, too. More than you'll ever know.

Slowly, tenderly, gently, I start to move, relishing every treasured inch of her.

This is me, Ana.

All of me.

And I love you.

I place my arm around her head, cocooning her in my embrace while she touches my arms, my hair, and my ass with her fingers. I kiss her mouth, her chin, her jaw. I push her higher and higher until she's on the brink. Her body starts to tremble. She's panting; she's ready.

"That's right, baby. Give it up for me. Please. Ana."

"Christian!" she cries out as she comes around me, and I let go.

THE AFTERNOON SUN FILTERS through the portholes, casting watery reflections over the cabin ceiling. It's so peaceful out here on the water. Maybe we could sail around the world, just Ana and me.

She dozes beside me.

My beautiful, passionate girl.

Ana.

I remember thinking those three letters had the power to wound, but now I know they also have the power to heal.

She doesn't know the real you.

I frown at the ceiling. This thought keeps plaguing me. Why?

It's because I want to be honest with her. Flynn thinks I should trust her and tell her, but I don't have the nerve.

She'll leave.

No. I banish the thought and enjoy lying with her for a few more minutes. "Mac will be back soon." I'm sorry to have broken the peaceful silence between us.

"Hmm," she mumbles, but her eyes open and she smiles.

"As much as I'd like to lie here with you all afternoon, he'll need a hand with the dinghy." I kiss her lips. "Ana, you look so beautiful right now, all mussed up and sexy. Makes me want you more."

She strokes my face.

She sees me.

No. Ana, you don't know me.

Reluctantly, I clamber out of bed, and she turns and lies on her stomach.

"You ain't so bad yourself, Captain," she says with appreciation as I dress.

I sit down beside her to put on my shoes.

"Captain, eh?" I muse. "Well, I am master of this vessel."

"You are master of my heart, Mr. Grey."

I wanted to be your master in a different way, but this is good. I think I can do this. I kiss her. "I'll be on deck. There's a shower in the bathroom if you want one. Do you need anything? A drink?"

She's amused, and I know it's at my expense.

"What?" I ask.

"You."

"What about me?"

"Who are you and what have you done with Christian?"

"He's not very far away, baby," I answer, and anxiety knots like ivy around my heart. "You'll see him soon enough, especially if you don't get up." I smack her ass so that she laughs and yelps at once.

"You had me worried." She feigns concern.

"Did I, now? You do give off some mixed signals, Anastasia. How's a man supposed to keep up?" I give her a swift kiss. "Laters, baby." I leave her to get dressed.

Mac arrives five minutes later, and together we get the dinghy fastened onto its rig at the stern.

"How was your friend?" I ask.

"In good spirits."

"You could have stayed longer," I say.

"And miss the trip back?"

"Yes."

"Nah, I can't stay away from this lady too long," Mac says, and he pats the hull of *The Grace*.

I grin. "I get it."

My phone buzzes.

"Taylor," I answer, and Ana opens the sliding doors to the saloon. She's holding her life jacket.

"Good afternoon, Mr. Grey. The apartment is clear," Taylor says.

I pull Ana close and kiss her hair. "That's great news."

"We've been through every room."

"Good."

"We've also been through all the CCTV footage of the last three days."

"Yes."

"It's been illuminating."

"Really?"

"Miss Williams was coming through the stairwell."

"The fire-escape stairwell?"

"Yes. She had a key and climbed all those floors to get there."

"I see." Wow, that's some climb.

"The locks have been changed and it's safe for you to return. We have your luggage. Will you be coming back this evening?"

"Yes."

"When can we expect you?"

"Tonight."

"Very good, sir."

I hang up and Mac fires up the engines.

"Time to head back." I give Ana a swift kiss and strap her into her life jacket.

ANA IS A KEEN and willing deckhand. Between us, we hoist and stow the mainsail, the headsheet, and the spinney while Mac steers. I teach her how to tie three knots. This she's not so good at, and I find it hard to keep a straight face.

"I may tie you up one day," she promises.

"You'll have to catch me first, Miss Steele." It's a long time since anyone tied me up, and I'm not sure I'd like it anymore. I shudder, thinking how defenseless I'd be against her touch. "Shall I give you a more thorough tour of *The Grace*?"

"Please, she's so beautiful."

ANA STANDS IN MY arms at the wheel, just before we make the turn into the marina. She looks so happy.

And that makes me happy.

She's been fascinated by *The Grace* and all that I've shown her. Even the engine room.

It's been fun. I take a deep breath, the salt water in the air cleansing my soul. And I'm reminded of a quote from one of my favorite books—a memoir, *Wind, Sand and Stars*. "'There is a poetry of sailing as old as the world,'" I murmur in her ear.

"That sounds like a quote."

"It is. Antoine de Saint-Exupéry."

"Oh, I adore *The Little Prince*."

"Me, too."

I pilot us into the marina, then slowly turn *The Grace* and reverse into the berth. The crowd that gathered to watch has dispersed by the time Mac jumps onto the dock and ties the stern lines to two dock cleats.

"Back again," I say to Ana, and as usual, I'm a little reluctant to leave *The Grace.*

"Thank you. That was a perfect afternoon."

"I thought so, too. Perhaps we can enroll you in sailing school so we can go out for a few days, just the two of us."

Or we could sail around the world, Ana, just you and me.

"I'd love that. We can christen the bedroom again and again."

I kiss her under her ear. "Hmm, I look forward to it, Anastasia." She squirms with pleasure. "Come, the apartment is clean. We can go back."

"What about our things at the hotel?"

"Taylor has collected them already. Earlier today, after he did a sweep of *The Grace* with his team."

"Does that poor man ever sleep?"

"He sleeps. He's just doing his job, Anastasia, which he's very good at. Jason is a real find."

"Jason?"

"Jason Taylor."

Ana's smile is tender.

"You're fond of Taylor," I observe.

"I suppose I am. I think Taylor looks after you very well. That's why I like him. He seems kind, reliable, and loyal. He has an avuncular appeal to me."

"Avuncular?"

"Yes."

"Okay, avuncular."

Ana laughs. "Oh, Christian, grow up, for heaven's sake."

What?

She's scolding me.

Why?

Because I'm possessive? Maybe that's childish.

Maybe. "I'm trying," I respond.

"That you are. Very," she says, looking toward the ceiling.

"What memories you evoke when you roll your eyes at me, Anastasia."

"Well, if you behave yourself, maybe we can relive some of those memories."

"Behave myself? Really, Miss Steele—what makes you think I want to relive them?"

"Probably the way your eyes lit up like Christmas when I said that."

"You know me so well already," I say.

"I'd like to know you better."

"And I you, Anastasia. Come, let's go." Mac has lowered the gangplank, allowing me to lead Ana onto the dock. "Thanks, Mac." I shake his hand.

"Always a pleasure, Mr. Grey, and goodbye. Ana, great to meet you."

"Good day, Mac, and thank you," Ana replies, and she looks a little shy.

Together Ana and I walk up to the promenade, leaving Mac on *The Grace*.

"Where's Mac from?" Ana asks.

"Ireland. Northern Ireland."

"Is he your friend?"

"Mac? He works for me. Helped build *The Grace*."

"Do you have many friends?"

What would I need friends for?

"Not really. Doing what I do, I don't cultivate friendships. There's only—" *Shit.* I stop myself. I don't want to mention Elena. "Hungry?" I ask, feeling food might be a safer topic.

Ana nods.

"We'll eat where I left the car. Come."

ANA AND I ARE seated at a table in Bee's, an Italian bistro next to SP's. She reads the menu while I take a sip of a fine chilled Frascati. I like watching her read.

"What?" Ana asks when she looks up.

"You look lovely, Anastasia. The outdoors agrees with you."

"I feel rather windburned, to tell the truth. But I had a lovely afternoon. A perfect afternoon. Thank you."

"My pleasure."

"Can I ask you something?"

"Anything, Anastasia. You know that."

"You don't seem to have many friends. Why is that?"

"I told you, I don't really have time. I have business associates, though that's very different from friendships, I suppose. I have my family, and that's it." I shrug. "Apart from Elena."

Thankfully, she ignores my Elena comment. "No male friends your own age that you can go out with and let off steam?"

No. Just Elliot.

"You know how I like to let off steam, Anastasia." My voice is low. "And I've been working, building up the business. That's all I do, except sail and fly occasionally." *And fuck, of course.*

"Not even in college?"

"Not really."

"Just Elena, then?"

I nod. *Where is she going with this?*

"Must be lonely."

Leila's words come back to me: *"But you're lonely. I can see it."* I frown. The only time I felt lonely was when Ana left me.

It was crippling.

I never want to feel like that again.

"What would you like to eat?" I ask, hoping to move the subject on.

"I'm going for the risotto."

"Good choice." I beckon the waiter over.

We place our order. Risotto for Ana, penne for me.

The waiter scurries off and I notice Ana staring down at her lap, knotting her fingers. Something is on her mind. "Anastasia, what's wrong? Tell me."

She looks at me, continuing to fidget, and I know there's something bothering her. "Tell me," I demand. I hate it when she's anxious.

She sits up, straightening her back. She means business.

Shit. Now what?

"I'm just worried that this isn't enough for you. You know, to let off steam."

What? Not this again. "Have I given you any indication that this isn't enough?" I ask.

"No."

"Then why do you think that?"

"I know what you're like. What you, um, need." Her voice is hesitant, and she rounds her shoulders and crosses her arms like she's folding in on herself.

I close my eyes and rub my forehead. I don't know what to say. I thought we were having a good time. "What do I have to do?" I whisper.

I'm trying, Ana. I'm really trying.

"No, you misunderstand," she says, suddenly animated. "You have been amazing, and I know it's just been a few days, but I hope I'm not forcing you to be someone you're not."

Her response is reassuring, but I think she's missing the point. "I'm still me, Anastasia, in all my fifty shades of fucked up… ness," I say, searching for the word. "Yes, I have to fight the urge to be controlling, but that's my nature, how I've dealt with my life. Yes, I expect you to behave a certain way, and when you don't it's both challenging and refreshing. We still do what I like to do. You let me spank you after your outrageous bid yesterday."

The thought of last night's arousing encounter preoccupies me for a moment.

Grey!

Keeping my voice low, I try to unravel how I feel. "I enjoy punishing you. I don't think the urge will ever go, but I'm trying, and it's not as hard as I thought it would be."

"I didn't mind that," Ana says quietly, and she's referring to our assignation in my childhood bedroom.

"I know. Neither did I."

I take a deep breath and tell her the truth. "But let me tell you, Anastasia, this is all new to me, and these last few days have been the best in my life. I don't want to change anything."

Her face brightens. "They've been the best in my life, too, without exception."

I'm sure my relief is reflected in my smile.

She persists. "So, you don't want to take me into your playroom?"

Fuck. I swallow. "No, I don't."

"Why not?" she asks.

Now I'm really in the confessional. "The last time we were in there you left me. I will shy away from anything that could make you leave me again. I was devastated when you left. I explained that. I never want to feel like that again. I've told you how I feel about you."

"But it hardly seems fair. It can't be very relaxing for you to be constantly concerned about how I feel. You've made all these changes for me, and I—I think I should reciprocate in some way. I don't know, maybe try some role-playing games." She's blushing.

"Ana, you do reciprocate, more than you know. Please, please don't feel like this. Baby, it's only been one weekend. Give us some time. I thought a great deal about us when you left. We need time. You need to trust me, and I you. Maybe in time we can indulge, but I like how you are now. I like seeing you this happy, this relaxed and carefree, knowing that I had something to do with it. I have never—" I stop.

Don't give up on me, Ana.

I hear Dr. Flynn's voice, nagging me. "We have to walk before we can run," I say out loud.

"What's so funny?" she asks.

"Flynn. He says that all the time. I never thought I'd be quoting him."

"A Flynnism."

I laugh. "Exactly."

The waiter arrives with the appetizers and our heavy conversation ceases, turning to the much lighter subject of travel. We discuss all the countries Ana would love to visit and the places I've been. Talking to Ana reminds me how lucky I am. My parents took us all over the world: to Europe, to Asia, and to South America. My father in particular considered travel a vital part of our education.

Of course, they could afford it. Ana's never left the U.S. and has always longed to visit Europe. I'd like to take her to all these places; I wonder how she'd feel about sailing the world with me.

Don't get ahead of yourself, Grey.

TRAFFIC IS LIGHT DURING our drive back to Escala. Ana admires the passing sights, her foot tapping in time to the music that fills the car.

I can't help thinking about our earlier intense conversation about our relationship. The truth is, I don't know if I can maintain a vanilla relationship, but I'm willing to try. I don't want to push her into something she doesn't want to do.

But she's willing, Grey.

She said so.

She wants the Red Room, as she calls it.

I shake my head. I think, for once, I'm going to take Dr. Flynn's advice.

Walk before we run, Ana.

I glance out the window and catch sight of a young woman with long brown hair and she reminds me of Leila. It's not her, but as we near Escala I begin to scan the streets, searching for her.

Where the fuck is she?

By the time I pull into the garage at Escala, my hands are gripping the steering wheel and tension has tightened every muscle in my body. I'm wondering if it was a good idea to come back to the apartment with Leila still at large.

Sawyer is in the garage, prowling around my parking spaces like a caged lion. This is overkill surely, but I'm relieved to see the Audi A3 is gone. He opens Ana's car door as I switch off the engine.

"Hello, Sawyer," she says.

"Miss Steele. Mr. Grey," he says in greeting.

"No sign?" I ask him.

"No, sir," he responds, and even though I knew that would be the answer, it's vexing. I grasp Ana's hand and we step into the elevator.

"You are not allowed out of here alone. You understand?" I caution Ana.

"Okay," she says as the doors close, and her lips twitch in amusement.

"What's so funny?" I'm floored that she agreed so readily.

"You are."

"Me?" My tension starts to dissolve. She's laughing at me? "Miss Steele? Why am I funny?" I purse my lips, trying to stop my smile.

"Don't pout," she says.

I'm pouting?

"Why?"

"Because it has the same effect on me as I have on you when I do this." She lets her teeth toy with her bottom lip.

"Really?" I do it once more and lean down to give her a swift kiss. When my lips touch hers, it sparks my desire. I hear her sharp intake of breath, then her fingers are twisting in my hair. Holding my lips to hers, I grab her and push her against the elevator wall, my hands cradling her face. Her tongue is in my mouth and mine in hers as she takes what she wants and I give her all that I have.

It's explosive.

I want to fuck her. Now.

I pour all my anxiety into her, and she takes everything.

Ana…

The elevator doors open with the familiar ping and I pull my face away from her, but I'm still pinning her to the wall with my hips and my hardening erection.

"Whoa," I whisper, dragging air into my lungs.

"Whoa," she answers, panting.

"What you do to me, Ana." I trace my thumb across her lower lip. Ana's eyes flit to the foyer and I sense rather than see Taylor.

She kisses the corner of my mouth. "What you do to me, Christian," she says.

I step back and take her hand. I haven't jumped her in an elevator since that day at The Heathman.

Get a grip, Grey.

"Come," I say.

As we exit the elevator, Taylor is standing to one side.

"Good evening, Taylor."

"Mr. Grey, Miss Steele."

"I was Mrs. Taylor yesterday," Ana says, all smiles for Mr. Taylor.

"That has a nice ring to it, Miss Steele," Taylor responds.

"I thought so, too."

What the hell is going on?

I scowl at Ana and Taylor. "If you two have quite finished, I'd like a debriefing." Ana and Taylor exchange a look. "I'll be with you shortly. I just want a word with Miss Steele," I say to Taylor.

He nods.

And I take Ana into my bedroom and close the door. "Don't flirt with the staff, Anastasia."

"I wasn't flirting. I was being friendly. There is a difference."

"Don't be friendly with the staff or flirt with them. I don't like it."

She sighs. "I'm sorry." She tosses her hair over her shoulder and looks down at her fingernails.

I cup her chin and lift her head so I can see into her eyes. "You know how jealous I am."

"You have no reason to be jealous, Christian. You own me body and soul." She looks at me as if I've lost my mind, and suddenly I feel foolish.

She's right.

I'm completely overreacting.

I give her a chaste kiss. "I won't be long. Make yourself at home." I go to find Taylor in his office. He stands when I enter.

"Mr. Grey, about—"

I hold up my hand. "Don't. It's I who should apologize."

Taylor looks surprised.

"What's occurring?" I ask.

"Gail will return later tonight."

"Good."

"I've informed the facilities management at Escala that Miss Williams had a key. I felt they should know."

"How did they respond?"

"Well, I stopped them from calling the police."

"Good."

"The locks have all been changed and a contractor is coming to look at the emergency stairwell door. Miss Williams shouldn't have been able to get in from the outside even with a key."

"And you found nothing in your sweep?"

"Nothing, sir. I couldn't tell you where she was hiding. But she's not here now."

"Have you spoken to Welch?"

"I've briefed him."

"Thank you. Ana's going to stay here tonight. I think it's safer."

"Agreed, sir."

"Cancel the Audi. I've decided on a Saab for Ana. It should be here soon. I have asked them to expedite delivery."

"Will do, sir."

When I return to my bedroom, Ana is standing on the threshold of my closet. She looks a little stunned. I poke my head around the closet door. Her clothes are here.

"Oh, they managed the move." I thought Gail was going to handle Ana's clothes. I shrug it off.

"What's wrong?" she asks.

I give her a quick rundown of what Taylor has just told me about the apartment and Leila. "I wish I knew where she was. She's evading all our attempts to find her, when she needs help."

Ana puts her arms around me, holding me, calming me. And I embrace her and kiss the top of her head.

"What will you do when you find her?" she asks.

"Dr. Flynn has a place."

"What about her husband?"

"He's washed his hands of her." *Asshole.* "Her family is in Connecticut. I think she's very much on her own out there."

"That's sad."

Ana's compassion knows no bounds. I tighten my hold on her. "Are you okay with all your stuff being here? I want you to share my room."

"Yes."

"I want you sleeping with me. I don't have nightmares when you're with me."

"You have nightmares?"

"Yes."

She squeezes me tighter, and we stand in my closet wrapped around each other. A few moments later, she says, "I was just getting my clothes ready for work tomorrow."

"Work?" I release her.

"Yes, work," she says, confused.

"But Leila, she's out there." Doesn't Ana understand the risk? "I don't want you to go to work."

"That's ridiculous, Christian. I have to go to work."

"No, you don't."

"I have a new job, which I enjoy. Of course I have to go to work."

"No, you don't." *I can look after you.*

"Do you think I am going to stay here twiddling my thumbs while you're off being master of the universe?"

"Frankly, yes," I respond.

Ana closes her eyes and rubs her forehead as if she's calling on all her inner strength. "Christian, I need to go to work," she says.

"No, you don't."

"Yes. I. Do." Her tone is forthright and determined.

"It's not safe." *Suppose something happens to you?*

"Christian, I need to work for a living, and I'll be fine."

"No, you don't need to work for a living, and how do you know you'll be fine?"

Fuck. This is why I like having submissives. This would not be an argument if she'd signed the fucking contract.

"For heaven's sake, Christian, Leila was standing at the end of your bed, and she didn't harm me, and yes, I do need to work. I don't want to be beholden to you. I have my student loans to pay." She places her hands on her hips.

"I don't want you going to work."

"It's not up to you, Christian. This is not your decision to make."

Fuck.

She's made up her mind.

And of course she's right.

I run my hand through my hair, trying to hold on to my temper, and eventually I have an idea. "Sawyer will come with you."

"Christian, that's not necessary. You're being irrational."

"Irrational?" I snap. "Either he comes with you or I will be really irrational and keep you here."

"How, exactly?"

"Oh, I'd find a way, Anastasia. Don't push me." I'm about to explode.

"Okay!" she shouts, holding up both her hands. "Okay, Sawyer can come with me if it makes you feel better."

I want to kiss her or spank her or fuck her. I step forward and she immediately takes a step back, watching me.

Grey! You're frightening the poor girl.

I take a deep cleansing breath and offer Ana a tour of my apartment. If she's going to stay, she should really get to know this place.

She gives me an uncertain look, as if I've caught her off guard. But she agrees and takes my outstretched hand. I give her hand a squeeze.

"I didn't mean to frighten you," I offer as an apology.

"You didn't. I was just getting ready to run," she says.

"Run?"

You've pushed her too far again, Grey.

"I'm joking!" she cries.

That's not funny, Ana.

I sigh and lead her through the apartment. I show her the spare room next to mine, then take her upstairs to the additional spare rooms, the gym, and the staff quarters.

"Are you sure you don't want to go in here?" she asks coyly as we walk past the playroom door.

"I don't have the key." I'm still smarting from our argument. I hate arguing with her. But as usual, she's calling me out on my shit.

But what if something happens to her?

It will be my fault.

All I can do is hope Sawyer will protect her.

Downstairs, I show her the TV room.

"So you *do* have an Xbox." She laughs. I love her laugh. It immediately makes me feel better.

"Yes, but I'm crap at it. Elliot always beats me. That was funny, when you thought I meant this room was my playroom."

"I'm glad you find me amusing, Mr. Grey," she says.

"That you are, Miss Steele, when you're not being exasperating, of course."

"I'm usually exasperating when you're being unreasonable."

"Me? Unreasonable?"

"Yes, Mr. Grey. 'Unreasonable' could be your middle name."

"I don't have a middle name."

"Unreasonable would suit, then."

"I think that's a matter of opinion, Miss Steele."

"I would be interested in Dr. Flynn's professional opinion."

Lord, I love sparring with her.

"I thought Trevelyan was your middle name," she asks.

"No. Surname. Trevelyan-Grey."

"But you don't use it."

"It's too long. Come."

Next I take her to Taylor's office. He stands when we enter.

"Hi, Taylor. I'm just giving Anastasia a tour."

He nods at both of us.

Ana looks around, surprised, I think, by the size of the room and the bank of CCTV monitors. We move on.

"And, of course, you've been in here." I open the door to the library, where Ana spies the billiards table.

"Shall we play?" she challenges.

Miss Steele is up for a game.

"Okay. Have you played before?"

"A few times," she says, avoiding eye contact.

She's lying.

"You're a hopeless liar, Anastasia. Either you've never played before or—"

"Frightened of a little competition?" she interrupts me.

"Frightened of a little girl like you?" I scoff.

"A wager, Mr. Grey."

"You're that confident, Miss Steele?" This is a new side to Ana I've not seen before.

Game on, Ana.

"What would you like to wager?"

"If I win, you'll take me back into the playroom."

Shit. She's serious.

"And if I win?" I ask.

"Then it's your choice." She shrugs, trying to act nonchalant, but her eyes shine with mischief.

"Okay, deal." How hard could this be? "Do you want to play pool, English snooker, or carom billiards?"

"Pool, please. I don't know the others."

I retrieve the pool balls from a cupboard under the bookshelves and rack them on the green baize. I choose a cue for Ana that should be right for her height. "Would you like to break?" I ask as I hand her the chalk.

She is so going down.

Hmm. Maybe that could be my prize.

An image of her on her knees in front of me, hands bound, servicing my cock, comes to mind. *Yeah. That would work.*

"Okay," she says, her voice breathy and soft as she chalks her cue. She purses her lips, and while watching me through her lashes, she slowly, deliberately blows off the excess.

I feel it in my dick.

Damn.

She lines up the cue ball, then hits it with such force and mastery that it scatters the rack. The corner ball, the yellow-striped number nine, dives into the top right pocket.

Oh, Anastasia Steele, you are so full of surprises.

"I choose stripes," she says and has the gall to give me a coy smile.

"Be my guest." This is going to be fun.

She prowls around the table, seeking her next victim. I like this new Ana. Predatory. Competitive. Confident. Sexy as hell. She leans over the table, stretching out her arm so that her blouse rides up, showing a little skin between the hem and the top of her jeans. She hits the cue ball and the maroon stripe bites the dust. Circling the table again, she gives me a cursory glance before leaning over, stretching across the table again, ass in the air, as she pockets the purple.

Hmm. I may need to revise my plans.

She's good.

She makes short work of the blue but misses the green.

"You know, Anastasia, I could stand here and watch you leaning and stretching across this billiard table all day," I tell her.

She flushes.

Yes!

That's the Ana I know.

I slip off my sweater and examine what's left on the table.

Showtime, Grey.

I proceed to pocket as many solids as I can; I have some catching up to do. I sink three and line up to pocket the orange. I hit the cue ball and the orange hurtles into the bottom left pocket, followed by the white.

Shit.

"A very elementary mistake, Mr. Grey."

"Ah, Miss Steele, I am but a foolish mortal. Your turn, I believe." I wave my hand in the direction of the table.

"You're not trying to lose, are you?" She cocks her head to one side.

"Oh no. For what I have in mind as the prize, I want to win, Anastasia. But then, I always want to win."

Blow job on her knees or…

I could stop her from going to work. Hmm… A wager that could cost her her job. I don't think that would be a popular choice.

She narrows her eyes, and I would pay good money to know what she's thinking. At the top of the table she bends down to take a closer look at the lie of the balls. Her blouse gapes and I catch sight of her breasts.

She stands and there's a little smile on her lips. She moves next to me and bends over, shifting her ass first left, then right. She walks back to the top of the table and leans over again, showing me all she has to offer. As she bends over, she peeks up at me.

"I know what you're doing," I whisper.

And my cock approves, Ana.

Big-time.

I adjust my stance to accommodate my growing erection.

She straightens up and tilts her head to one side while running her hand up and down the cue, slowly. "Oh. I am just deciding where to take my next shot."

Fuck. She's a temptress.

She leans over, taps the orange stripe with the cue ball so it aligns with the pocket, then takes the rest from under the table and lines up the shot. As she takes aim at the white, I can see the swell of her breasts down her blouse. I inhale, sharply.

She misses.

Good.

I stroll around to stand behind her while she's still bent over the table and place my hand on her behind. "Are you waving this around to taunt me, Miss Steele?" I smack her hard.

Because she deserves it.

She gasps. "Yes," she whispers.

Oh, Ana. "Be careful what you wish for, baby."

I aim the cue ball at the red, and it sinks into the left top pocket. Then I try for the top right with the yellow. I hit the cue ball gently. It kisses the yellow, but the ball stops just short of its destination.

Shit. Miss.

Ana grins at me. "Red Room, here we come," she crows.

I like your kinky fuckery.

She really does.

It's confusing. I signal to her to continue, knowing that I don't want to take her to the playroom. The last time we were there, she left me.

She pockets the green stripe. She gives me a triumphant smile and sinks the orange.

"Name your pocket," I mutter.

"Top left-hand," she says as she wiggles her ass in front of me. She takes the shot and the black skirts wide of its target.

Oh, joy.

Quickly I dispatch the remaining two solids, and now I'm left with the black. I chalk my cue, gazing at Ana. "If I win, I am going to spank you, then fuck you over this billiard table."

Her lips part.

Yes. She's excited by the idea. That's what she's been asking me for all day. She thinks I've lost my edge?

Well, we'll see.

"Top right," I announce and bend to take the shot. My cue taps the white and it sails up the table and pecks the black, which rolls toward the top-right pocket. It balances on the edge for a moment, and I stop breathing until it drops with a satisfying clunk into its goal.

Yes!

Anastasia Steele, you are mine.

I swagger over to where she stands with her mouth open, looking a little crestfallen. "You're not going to be a sore loser, are you?" I ask.

"Depends how hard you spank me," she murmurs.

Taking the cue from her, I place it on the table, hook my finger into the top of her blouse, and tug so she steps toward me.

"Well, let's count your misdemeanors, Miss Steele." Holding up my fingers, I number her misdeeds. "One, making me jealous of my own staff." Her eyes widen. "Two, arguing with me about working. And three, waving your delectable derrière at me for the last twenty minutes."

Leaning down, I rub my nose against hers. "I want you to take your jeans and this very fetching shirt off. Now." I kiss her gently on her lips, stroll over to the library door, and lock it.

When I turn, she's frozen to the spot. "Clothes, Anastasia. You appear to still be wearing them. Take them off, or I will do it for you."

"You do it," she breathes, and her voice is as soft as a summer breeze.

"Oh, Miss Steele. It's a dirty job, but I think I can rise to the challenge."

"You normally rise to most challenges, Mr. Grey." She bites her lip.

Innuendo from Ana.

"Why, Miss Steele, whatever do you mean?" On the library desk I spy a Perspex ruler.

Perfect.

All day long she's been making not-so-veiled remarks about missing this side of me. Let's see how she fares with this. I hold it up so she can see it and flex it between my hands, then slip it into my back pocket and stroll over to her.

Shoes off, I think.

I drop to my knees and undo both her Chucks, removing them and her socks. I undo the top button of her jeans and pull down her zipper. I look up at her as I slowly tug them off. Her eyes don't leave mine. She steps out of her pants, and she's wearing her white thong.

That thong.

I'm a fan.

So is my cock…

I grab the back of her thighs and run my nose up the front of her panties. "I want to be quite rough with you, Ana. You'll have to tell me to stop if it's too much," I whisper and through the lace plant a kiss on her clitoris.

She moans.

"Safe word?" she says.

"No, no safe word, just tell me to stop and I'll stop. Understand?" I kiss her again and swirl my nose around the potent little bud at the apex of her thighs. I stand before I get carried away. "Answer me."

"Yes, yes, I understand."

"You've been dropping hints and giving me mixed signals, Anastasia. You said you were worried I'd lost my edge. I'm not sure what you meant by that, and I don't know how serious you were, but we are going to find out. I don't want to go back into the playroom yet, so we can try this now, but if you don't like it, you must promise to tell me."

"I'll tell you. No safe word," she says—to reassure me, I think.

"We're lovers, Anastasia. Lovers don't need safe words." I frown. "Do they?" This is something I know nothing about.

"I guess not," she responds. "I promise."

I need to know she will communicate with me if I go too far. Her expression is earnest and full of desire. I unbutton her shirt and let it fall open, and the sight of her breasts is arousing. Very arousing. She looks amazing. From behind her I pick up the cue.

"You play well, Miss Steele. I must say I'm surprised. Why don't you sink the black?"

She purses her lips, then with a defiant look, she reaches for the cue ball and, bending over the table, lines up the shot. As she does I go to stand behind her and place my hand on her right thigh. She tenses as I run my fingers to her ass and back down her thigh, lightly teasing her.

"I am going to miss if you keep doing that," she complains, her voice husky.

"I don't care if you hit or miss, baby. I just wanted to see you like this, partially dressed, stretched out on my billiard table. Do you have any idea how hot you look at this moment?"

She blushes and toys with the white as she tries to line it up. I caress her ass. Her beautiful ass, visible because she's wearing a thong.

"Top left," she says and hits the cue ball with the tip of the cue. I smack her hard and she yelps. The white kisses the black, but the black bounces off the cushion, missing the pocket.

I caress her ass again. "Oh, I think you need to try that again. You should concentrate, Anastasia."

She wiggles her behind beneath my hand, like she's begging for more.

She's enjoying this far too much, so I stroll to the end of the table to reset the black ball, and picking up the white, I run it along the table back to her.

She catches the ball and starts lining it up once more.

"Uh-uh," I warn. "Just wait."

Not so fast, Miss Steele.

I wander back and stand behind her again, but this time I stroke my hand over her left thigh and her ass.

I love her ass.

"Take aim," I whisper.

She moans and puts her head on the table.

Don't give up yet, Ana.

She takes a deep breath and, raising her head, moves to her right and I follow her. She bends, stretches over the table again, and hits the cue ball. As the ball flies up the baize, I smack her again. Hard. The black misses.

"Oh no," she says and groans.

"Once more, baby. And if you miss this time, I'm really going to let you have it." I set up the black again and wander back until I'm standing behind her and caressing her beautiful behind again. "You can do it," I breathe.

She pushes her backside into my hand and I give her a playful smack.

"Eager, Miss Steele?" I ask.

She moans in reply.

"Well, let's get rid of these." I slide the thong down her legs, removing it and dropping it on her discarded jeans. While kneeling behind her, I kiss each cheek of her ass. "Take the shot, baby."

She's agitated, all fingers and thumbs, and she fumbles for the cue ball, lines it up, hits it, but in her impatience misses the shot. She scrunches up her eyes, waiting for me to spank her, but instead I lean over her, pressing her onto the baize. I take the cue from her hand and push it to the side.

Now for some real fun.

"You missed," I whisper in her ear. "Put your hands flat on the table."

My erection is fighting with my fly.

"Good. I'm going to spank you now, and next time, maybe you won't." I move beside her so I have a better aim. She groans and closes her eyes, and her breathing is getting louder. I caress her behind with one hand. With the other I hold her down and twist my fingers in her hair.

"Open your legs," I tell her and reach for the ruler in my pocket. She hesitates, so I smack her with the ruler. It makes a really satisfying noise as it cracks across her ass, and she gasps but says nothing, so I hit her again. "Legs," I order. She complies and I strike her again. She scrunches up her eyes as she takes the pain, but she doesn't ask me to stop.

Oh, baby.

I spank her again, and again, and she moans. Her skin is turning pink beneath the ruler and my jeans are becoming impossibly tight as they restrict my arousal. I smack her again and again. And I'm lost. Lost in her. Owned by her. She's doing this for me. And I love it. I love her.

"Stop," she says.

And I drop the ruler without thinking and release her.

"Enough?" I ask.

"Yes."

"I want to fuck you now," I whisper, my voice hoarse.

"Yes," she pleads.

She wants this, too.

Her ass is pink and she's dragging air into her lungs.

I tug my fly open, allowing my cock some room, and then insert two fingers inside her, moving them in circles, reveling in her readiness.

I make quick work of putting on a condom, then steady myself behind her and slowly ease myself into her. *Oh yes.* This is without a doubt my favorite place in the world.

I ease out of her, holding her hips, then slam into her hard so that she cries out.

"Again?" I ask.

"Yes," she breathes. "I'm fine. Lose yourself. Take me with you."

Oh, Ana, with pleasure.

I slam into her once more and set up a slow but grueling rhythm, taking her again and again and again. She moans and cries out as I claim her. Every inch. Mine.

She starts to quicken—she's nearly there—and I increase the pace, listening to her cries until she orgasms around me, crying out and taking me with her, so I call out her name and empty my soul inside her.

I collapse on top of her as I catch my breath. I'm filled with gratitude and humility. I love her. I want her. Always.

I pull her into my arms and we sink to the floor, where I cradle her against my chest. I never want to let her go. "Thank you, baby," I whisper and cover her face in soft kisses. She opens her eyes and gives me a drowsy, sated smile. I tighten my hold on her and stroke her cheek. "Your cheek is pink from the baize."

Matches your ass, baby.

Her smile widens under my tender ministration. "How was that?" I ask.

"Teeth-clenchingly good," she says. "I like it rough, Christian, and I like it gentle, too. I like that it's with you."

I close my eyes and marvel at the beautiful young woman in my arms. "You never fail, Ana. You're beautiful, bright, challenging, fun, sexy, and I thank Divine Providence every day that it was you who came to interview me and not Katherine Kavanagh." I kiss her hair and she yawns, making me smile. "I'm wearing you out. Come. Bath, then bed." I stand and pull her to her feet. "Do you want me to carry you?"

She shakes her head.

"I'm sorry, but you'd better get dressed—we don't know who we'll meet in the hallway."

IN THE BATHROOM, I turn on the faucet and pour a copious amount of bath oil into the streaming water.

I help Ana out of her clothes and hold her hand as she steps in. I quickly follow her and we sit at opposite ends while the bath fills with hot water and fragrant foam.

I grab some body wash and with it begin to massage Ana's left foot, my thumbs rubbing her instep.

"Oh, that feels so good." She closes her eyes and tips back her head.

"Good." I'm enjoying her pleasure. Her hair is tied in a ponytail that sits precariously in a loose bun on top of her head. A few tendrils escape, and her skin looks dewy and a little sun-kissed from our afternoon on *The Grace.*

She's stunning.

It's been a bewildering couple of days; Leila's aberrant behavior, Elena's interference, and Ana, steadfast and strong through it all. It's been humbling. She humbles me. Most of all I've enjoyed sharing her happiness. I like to see her happy. Her joy is my joy.

"Can I ask you something?" she murmurs, cocking one eye open.

"Of course. Anything, Ana, you know that."

She sits up and squares her shoulders.

Oh no.

"Tomorrow, when I go to work, can Sawyer just deliver me to the front door of the office, then pick me up at the end of the day? Please, Christian. Please," she says quickly.

I stop my massage. "I thought we agreed."

"Please."

Why does she feel so passionately about this?

"What about lunchtime?" I ask, anxious once more about her safety.

"I'll make myself something to take from here so I don't have to go out. Please."

"I find it very difficult to say no to you," I admit, kissing her instep. I want her safe, and until Leila's apprehended, I'm not sure she will be.

Ana's giving me the big blue eyes.

"You won't go out?" I ask.

"No."

"Okay."

She smiles, grateful, I think. "Thank you," she says, spilling water over the side of the bath as she moves to her knees. She places her hands on my upper arms and kisses me.

"You're most welcome, Miss Steele. How's your behind?"

"Sore. But not too bad. The water is soothing."

"I'm glad you told me to stop," I say.

"So is my behind."

I grin. "Let's go to bed."

I BRUSH MY TEETH and wander back into my bedroom, where Ana is in bed.

"Didn't Ms. Acton provide any nightwear?" I ask. I'm sure she has some silk and satin nightgowns.

"I have no idea. I like wearing your T-shirts," she replies, and her eyelids droop.

Boy, she's exhausted. I lean forward and kiss her forehead.

I still have some work to do, but I want to stay with Ana. I've been in her company all day, and it's been lovely.

I never want this day to end.

"I need to work. But I don't want to leave you alone. Can I use your laptop to log in to the office? Will I disturb you if I work from here?"

"S'not my laptop," she mumbles and closes her eyes.

"Yes it is," I whisper, and I sit down beside her and open her MacBook Pro. I click on Safari, log in to my email, and begin to work through them.

Once that's done, I email Taylor and let him know that I'd like Sawyer to accompany Ana tomorrow. The only outstanding detail is deciding where Sawyer will be while Ana is at work.

This we will figure out in the morning.

I check my schedule. I have a meeting at 8:30 with Ros and Vanessa in procurement to discuss the conflict mineral issue.

I'm tired.

Ana is fast asleep as I lay down beside her. I watch her chest rise and fall with each breath. Over such a short time she has become so dear to me.

"Ana, I love you," I whisper. "Thank you for today. Please stay." And I close my eyes.

Monday, June 13, 2011

Seattle's morning news wakes me with a report about the Angels' upcoming game with the Mariners. When I turn my head, Ana is awake and watching me. "Good morning," she says with a bright smile. She caresses my stubbly cheek with her fingers and kisses me.

"Good morning, baby." I'm surprised I've slept so long. "I usually wake before the alarm goes off."

"It's set so early," Ana whines.

"That it is, Miss Steele. I have to get up." I kiss her and bound out of bed.

In my closet, I pull on my sweats and grab my iPod. I check on Ana before I leave; she's gone back to sleep.

Good. She's had an action-packed weekend. As have I.

Yes. What a weekend.

I resist the urge to kiss her goodbye, and let her sleep. Glancing through the windows, I see the sky is overcast, but I don't think it's raining. I'll chance a run rather than my gym.

"Mr. Grey?" Ryan accosts me in the foyer.

"Good morning, Ryan."

"Sir. You're going out?" He probably thinks he needs to join me.

"I'll be fine, Ryan. Thank you."

"Mr. Taylor—"

"I'll be fine." I step into the elevator and leave Ryan in the foyer looking uncertain, probably second-guessing his decision. Leila was never one for an early morning… just like Ana. I think I'll be safe.

It's drizzling outside. But I don't care. With "Bittersweet Symphony" blasting in my ears I set off, sprinting down Fourth Avenue.

My mind clouds with chaotic images of all that has happened over the last few days: Ana at the ball, Ana on my boat, Ana at the hotel.

Ana. Ana. Ana.

My life has been completely overturned to the point that I'm not sure I recognize myself.

Elena's words come back to me: *"Have you turned your back on who you are?"*

Have I?

"I can't change—" The words from the song echo through my head.

The truth is, I like being in her company. I like having her in my home. I'd like her to stay. Permanently. She's brought humor, restful sleep, vitality, and love into my monochrome existence. I didn't know I was lonely until I met her.

But she won't want to move in, will she? While Leila is still at large it makes sense for her to stay, but once she's found, Ana will go. I can't make her stay, though part of me would like to. But in the interim, if she ever finds out the truth about me, she'll leave and never want to see me again.

No one can love a monster.

And when she leaves…

Hell.

I run harder and faster, trying to clear my confusion until I'm conscious only of my bursting lungs and my Nikes hitting the ground.

MRS. JONES IS IN the kitchen when I get back from my run. "Good morning, Gail."

"Mr. Grey, good morning."

"Did Taylor tell you about Leila?"

"Yes, sir. I hope you find her. She needs help." Gail's face is full of concern.

"She does."

"I understand Miss Steele is still here." She gives me that weird little smile she has whenever we talk about Ana.

"I think she'll be staying as long as Leila is a threat. She'll need a packed lunch today."

"Okay. What would you like for breakfast?"

"Scrambled eggs, toast."

"Very good, sir."

ONCE I'M SHOWERED AND dressed, I decide to wake Ana. She's still fast asleep. I kiss her temple. "Come on, sleepyhead, get up."

Her eyes open and close again, and she takes a deep breath.

"What?" I ask.

"I wish you'd come back to bed."

Don't tempt me, baby.

"You are insatiable, Miss Steele. As much as that idea appeals, I have an eight-thirty meeting, so I have to go shortly."

Startled, Ana looks at the clock, pushes me aside to leap out of bed, and dashes into the bathroom. Shaking my head, amused at her sudden burst of energy, I pop a few condoms into my pants pocket, then saunter into the kitchen for some breakfast.

You never know, Grey. I've learned that it's good to be prepared around Anastasia Steele.

Mrs. Jones is making coffee.

"Your scrambled eggs will be ready in a moment, Mr. Grey."

"Great. Ana will join me shortly."

"Shall I make her scrambled eggs?"

"I think she likes pancakes and bacon."

Gail places a coffee and my breakfast at one of the places she's set at the kitchen counter.

Ana appears about ten minutes later, wearing some of the clothes I bought her.

A silk blouse and a gray skirt. She looks different.

Sophisticated.

Elegant.

She's beautiful. Not a gauche student but a confident young working woman.

I approve and wrap my arm around her. "You look lovely,"

I say, kissing her behind her ear. My only misgiving about her appearance is that she has to spend time, looking like this, with her boss.

Don't dwell, Grey. This is her choice. She wants to work.

I release her when Gail places her breakfast on the bar. "Good morning, Miss Steele," she says.

"Oh, thank you. Good morning," Ana replies.

"Mr. Grey says you'd like to take lunch with you to work. What would you like to eat?"

Ana shoots me a look.

Yeah, baby. I was serious. No going out.

"A sandwich. Salad. I really don't mind." She gives Gail an appreciative smile.

"I'll rustle up a packed lunch for you, ma'am."

"Please, Mrs. Jones, call me Ana."

"Ana," Gail says.

"I have to go, baby. Taylor will come back and drop you at work with Sawyer."

"Only to the door," she reiterates.

"Yes. Only to the door." That's what we agreed. "Be careful, though," I add in a hushed tone. Standing, I grasp her chin and give her a swift kiss. "Laters, baby."

"Have a good day at the office, dear," she calls after me, and though it's a corny thing to say, it delights me.

This feels so *normal.*

In the elevator Taylor greets me with an update. "Sir, there's a coffee shop opposite SIP. I think Sawyer can station himself there during the day."

"If he needs backup? You know, bathroom breaks."

"I'll send Reynolds or Ryan."

"Okay."

I'D FORGOTTEN THAT ANDREA is out for her wedding but she won't be having much of a honeymoon if she's back at work tomorrow. The woman who's replaced her and whose name I still can't remember is browsing the *Vogue* Facebook page when I arrive. "No social media during office hours," I say with a grunt.

Rookie mistake. But she should know this. She's already an employee here.

She's startled. "I'm so sorry, Mr. Grey. I didn't hear you arrive. Can I get you some coffee?"

"Yes. You may. A macchiato."

I shut my office door and, at my desk, switch on my computer. There's an email from the Saab dealership: Ana's car will arrive today. I forward the email to Taylor so he can organize delivery, thinking it will be a nice surprise for Ana this evening. Next, I email Ana.

From: Christian Grey
Subject: Boss
Date: June 13 2011 08:24
To: Anastasia Steele

Good morning, Miss Steele
I just wanted to say thank you for a wonderful weekend in spite of all the drama.

I hope you never leave, ever.

And just to remind you that the news of SIP is embargoed for four weeks.

Delete this email as soon as you've read it.

Yours

Christian Grey
CEO, Grey Enterprises Holdings, Inc.
& your boss's boss's boss

I check Andrea's notes. The replacement's name is Montana Brooks. She knocks and brings in my coffee.

"Ros Bailey is running a little late, but Vanessa Conway is here."

"Let her wait for Ros."

"Yes, Mr. Grey."

"I need some ideas for wedding presents."

Ms. Brooks looks taken aback. "Well, it depends how well you know the person and how much you'd like to spend and—"

I don't need a lecture. I hold up my hand. "Write them down. It's for my PA."

"Does she have a bridal registry?"

"A what?"

"A bridal registry at a store?"

"I don't know. Find out."

"Yes, Mr. Grey."

"That will be all."

She leaves. *Thank God Andrea's back tomorrow.*

Welch's report on Jack Hyde is in my inbox. While I wait for Ros, I take the opportunity to look it over.

MY MEETING WITH ROS and Vanessa is brief. Vanessa and her team are conducting a thorough audit of all our supply chains, and they are proposing we source our cassiterite and wolframite from Bolivia and our tantalum from Australia to avoid the conflict mineral problem. It will be more expensive but will keep us on the right side of the U.S. Securities and Exchange Commission. And it's what we, as a company, should be doing.

When they leave, I check my email. There's one from Ana.

From: Anastasia Steele
Subject: Bossy
Date: June 13 2011 09:03
To: Christian Grey

Dear Mr. Grey

Are you asking me to move in with you? And, of course, I remembered that the evidence of your epic stalking capabilities is embargoed for another four weeks. Do I make a check out to Coping Together and send to your dad? Please don't delete this email. Please respond to it.

ILY xxx

Anastasia Steele
Assistant to Jack Hyde, Editor, SIP

Am I asking her to move in with me?

Shit.

Grey, this is a bold, sudden move.

I could look after her. Full-time.

She'd be mine. Really mine.

And deep down I know there is only one answer.

A resounding yes.

I ignore all her other questions and respond.

From: Christian Grey
Subject: Me, Bossy?
Date: June 13 2011 09:07
To: Anastasia Steele

Yes. Please.

Christian Grey
CEO, Grey Enterprises Holdings, Inc.

While I wait for her response I read through the rest of the report on Jack Hyde. On the surface, his background check seems fine. He's successful and earns a decent salary. He's from humble beginnings and seems bright and ambitious, but there's something unusual about his career path. Who in publishing starts in New York, then works at various publishers across the U.S., ending up in Seattle?

It makes no sense.

He doesn't seem to have had any long-term relationships, and he never keeps an assistant for more than three months.

That means Ana's time with him is limited.

From: Anastasia Steele
Subject: Flynnisms
Date: June 13 2011 09:20
To: Christian Grey

Christian
What happened to walking before we run?
Can we talk about this tonight, please?
I've been asked to go to a conference in New York on Thursday.
It means an overnight stay on Wednesday.
Just thought you should know.

A x

Anastasia Steele
Assistant to Jack Hyde, Editor, SIP

She doesn't want to move in with me. This is not the news I wanted.

What did you expect, Grey?

At least she wants to discuss it this evening, so there's hope. But then she also wants to fuck off to New York.

Well, that sucks.

I wonder if this is a conference on her own.

Or with Hyde?

From: Christian Grey
Subject: WHAT?
Date: June 13 2011 09:21
To: Anastasia Steele

Yes. Let's talk this evening.

Are you going on your own?

Christian Grey
CEO, Grey Enterprises Holdings, Inc.

Jack Hyde must be a prick to work for if he doesn't keep an assistant for more than three months. I know I'm an asshole, but Andrea's worked for me for nearly a year and a half.

I didn't know she was getting married.

Yes. That's pissed me off, but before her there was Helena. She was with me for two years, and now she works in HR, recruiting our engineers.

While I wait for Ana's answer, I read the final page of the report.

And there it is. Three hushed-up harassment claims at his previous publishers and two official warnings at SIP.

Three?

He's a fucking creep. *I knew it.* Why wasn't this in his employee file?

He was all over Ana at the bar. Invading her space. Like the photographer.

From: Anastasia Steele
Subject: No Bold Shouty Capitals on a Monday Morning!

Date: June 13 2011 09:30
To: Christian Grey

Can we talk about this tonight?

A x

Anastasia Steele
Assistant to Jack Hyde, Editor, SIP

Evasive, Miss Steele.
It's a trip with him.
I know it.
She looked sensational this morning.
He's planned it, I bet.

From: Christian Grey
Subject: You Haven't Seen Shouty Yet.
Date: June 13 2011 09:35
To: Anastasia Steele

Tell me.

If it's with the sleazeball you work with, then the answer is no, over my dead body.

Christian Grey
CEO, Grey Enterprises Holdings, Inc.

I hit send and then buzz Ros.

"Christian," she answers immediately.

"There's a lot of unnecessary expenditure at SIP. They're hemorrhaging money and we need to put a stop to it. I want a moratorium on all nonessential peripheral spending. Travel. Hotels. Hospitality. All the T&E. Especially for junior staff. You know the drill."

"Really? I don't think we'll save much money."

"Just call Roach. Make it happen. Immediately."

"What's brought this on?"

"Just do it, Ros."

She sighs. "If you insist. Do you want me to add it to the contract?"

"Yes."

"Okay."

"Thanks." I hang up.

There. Now, that should put a stop to Ana and New York. Besides, I'd like to take her there myself. She told me yesterday she's never been there.

There's a ping and Ana has responded.

From: Anastasia Steele

Subject: No YOU haven't seen shouty yet.

Date: June 13 2011 09:46

To: Christian Grey

Yes. It is with Jack.

I want to go. It's an exciting opportunity for me.

And I have never been to New York.

Don't get your knickers in a twist.

Anastasia Steele

Assistant to Jack Hyde, Editor, SIP

I'm about to reply when I hear a knock. "What?" I bark.

Montana pokes her head around the door and lingers, which is especially irritating—either come in or don't. "Mr. Grey, the registry for Andrea…"

For a moment I have no idea what she's talking about.

"It's at Crate & Barrel," she continues, simpering.

"Okay." What the hell am I supposed to do with that information?

"I've made a list of the items still available and their prices."

"Email it to me," I say through gritted teeth. "And get me another coffee."

"Yes, Mr. Grey." She smiles as if we're discussing the fucking weather and shuts the door.

Now I can respond to Miss Steele.

From: Christian Grey
Subject: No YOU haven't seen shouty yet.
Date: June 13 2011 09:50
To: Anastasia Steele

Anastasia
It's not my fucking knickers I am worried about.

The answer is NO.

Christian Grey
CEO, Grey Enterprises Holdings, Inc.

Montana places another macchiato on my desk. "You have a meeting at ten with Barney and Fred in the lab," she says.

"Thanks, I'll take my coffee with me." I know I sound surly. But right now a certain blue-eyed woman is getting under my skin. Montana leaves and I take a sip of coffee.

Fuck. Shit.

It's scalding hot.

I drop the cup, the coffee, everything.

Hell.

Fortunately, it misses me and my keyboard, but it's all over the damn floor.

"Ms. Brooks!" I yell. Jesus, I wish Andrea was here.

Montana pops her head around the door. Neither in. Nor out. And still wearing too much freshly applied lipstick.

"I've just dropped my coffee all over the floor because it was scalding hot. Get it cleaned up, please."

"Oh, Mr. Grey. I'm so sorry."

She scurries in to survey the mess and I leave her to deal with it. For a moment I wonder whether she might have done this on purpose.

Grey, you're paranoid.

I grab my phone and decide to take the stairs.

Barney and Fred are sitting at the lab table.

"Good morning, gentlemen."

"Mr. Grey," Fred says. "Barney's cracked it."

"Oh?"

"Yes. The cover."

"We put this through the 3D printer, and voilà."

He hands me a compact, hinged plastic cover that's attached to the tablet. "This is great," I say. "This must have taken you all weekend." I stare at Barney.

He shrugs. "Nothing better to do."

"You need to get out more, Barney. But this is good work. Is that all you wanted to show me?"

"We could easily adapt it and put this on a mobile phone cover, too."

"I'd like to see that."

"I'll get on it."

"Great. Anything else?"

"That's it for now, Mr. Grey."

"Might be worth showing the 3D printer to the mayor when he visits."

"We've got quite the show planned for him," says Fred.

"Without giving anything away," adds Barney.

"Sounds great. Thanks for the show-and-tell. I'll head back upstairs."

Waiting for the elevator, I check my email. There's a reply from Ana.

From: Anastasia Steele
Subject: Fifty Shades
Date: June 13 2011 09:55
To: Christian Grey

Christian
You need to get a grip.
I am NOT going to sleep with Jack—not for all the tea in China.
I LOVE you. That's what happens when people love each other.
They TRUST each other.
I don't think you are going to SLEEP WITH, SPANK, FUCK, or WHIP anyone else.
I have FAITH and TRUST in you.
Please extend the same COURTESY to me.

Ana

Anastasia Steele
Assistant to Jack Hyde, Editor, SIP

What the hell! I told her the emails at SIP were monitored.

We stop at several floors and I try, really try, to contain my anger. There's that irritating, expectant hush within the elevator as my staff enter and exit, because I'm in there.

"Good morning, Mr. Grey."

"Good morning, Mr. Grey."

I nod my hellos.

But I'm not in the mood.

Beneath my polite smile, my blood is simmering.

As soon as I'm back in my office I check her work number and call her.

"Jack Hyde's office, Ana Steele speaking," she answers.

"Will you please delete the last email you sent me and try to be a little more circumspect in the language you use in your work email? I told you, the system is monitored. I will endeavor to do some damage limitation from here," I snarl and hang up.

I call Barney.

"Mr. Grey."

"Can you delete Miss Anastasia Steele's email to me at nine fifty-five from the SIP server and all mine to her?"

There's silence at the other end of the phone.

"Barney?"

"Um. Sure, Mr. Grey, I was just working out how I can do it. I have an idea."

"Great. Let me know when it's done."

"Yes, sir."

My phone lights up. *Anastasia.*

"What?" I answer, and I think she can tell I'm more than grumpy.

"I am going to New York whether you like it or not."

"Don't count on it."

Silence.

"Ana?"

She's hung up on me.

Fuck. Again.

Who does that?

Well, I might have just done it to her, but that's not the point.

And I remember she did it when she drunk-dialed me.

I put my head in my hands.

Ana. Ana. Ana.

My office phone buzzes.

"Grey."

"Mr. Grey, Barney. It was much easier than I thought. Those emails are no longer on the SIP server."

"Thanks, Barney."

"No worries, Mr. Grey."

At least something is going right.

There's a knock on the door.

What now?

Montana opens the door; she's holding a can of carpet cleaner and some tissue.

"Later," I snap. I've had enough of her. She quickly reverses out of the office. I take a deep breath. Today is turning into a shit day and it's not even lunchtime. There's another email from Ana.

From: Anastasia Steele
Subject: What have you done?
Date: June 13 2011 10:43
To: Christian Grey

Please tell me you won't interfere with my work.
I really want to go to this conference.
I shouldn't have to ask you.
I have deleted the offending email.

Anastasia Steele
Assistant to Jack Hyde, Editor, SIP

I respond immediately.

From: Christian Grey
Subject: What have you done?
Date: June 13 2011 10:46
To: Anastasia Steele

I am just protecting what is mine.

The email that you so rashly sent is wiped from the SIP server now, as are my emails to you.

Incidentally, I trust you implicitly. It's him I don't trust.

Christian Grey
CEO, Grey Enterprises Holdings, Inc.

Her response is almost as immediate.

From: Anastasia Steele
Subject: Grown Up
Date: June 13 2011 10:48
To: Christian Grey

Christian
I don't need protecting from my own boss.
He may make a pass at me, but I would say no.
You cannot interfere. It's wrong and controlling on so many levels.

Anastasia Steele
Assistant to Jack Hyde, Editor, SIP

"Controlling" is my middle name, Ana. I think I've told you this already, along with "unreasonable" and "weird."

From: Christian Grey
Subject: The Answer is NO
Date: June 13 2011 10:50
To: Anastasia Steele

Ana
I have seen how "effective" you are at fighting off unwanted attention. I remember that's how I had the pleasure of spending my first night with you. At least the photographer has feelings for you. The sleazeball, on the other hand, does not. He is a serial philanderer, and he will try to seduce you. Ask him what happened to his previous PA and the one before that.

I don't want to fight about this.

If you want to go to New York, I'll take you. We can go this weekend. I have an apartment there.

Christian Grey
CEO, Grey Enterprises Holdings, Inc.

She doesn't reply immediately, and I distract myself with phone calls.

Welch has nothing new on Leila. We discuss whether to involve the police at this stage; I'm still reluctant to do it.

"She's close, Mr. Grey," Welch says.

"She's clever. She's managed to evade us so far."

"We're watching your place, SIP, Grey House. She won't slip past us again."

"I hope she doesn't. And thanks for the report on Hyde."

"You're welcome. I can dig deeper if you wish."

"It's fine for now. But I may get back to you."

"Okay, sir."

"Bye." I hang up.

My phone buzzes before I've let go of the receiver. "I have your mother on the line," Montana chirps in a singsong voice.

Shit. That's all I need. I'm still a little pissed at my mom and her comment about Ana being after my money.

"Put her through," I mutter.

"Christian, darling," Grace says.

"Hello, Mother."

"Darling, I just wanted to apologize for what I said on Saturday. You know I think the world of Ana, it's just… all of this is so sudden."

"It's fine." But it's not fine.

She's quiet for a moment and I think she's doubting the sincerity of my response.

However, I'm already arguing with one woman in my life; I don't want to argue with another. "Grace?"

"Sorry, darling. It's your birthday on Saturday and we wanted to organize a party."

An email from Ana appears on my computer screen.

"Mom, I can't talk now. I have to go."

"Okay, call me." She sounds melancholy, but I don't have time for her right now.

"Yes. Sure."

"Bye, Christian."

"Bye." I hang up.

From: Anastasia Steele
Subject: FW Lunch date or Irritating Baggage
Date: June 13 2011 11:15
To: Christian Grey

Christian
While you have been busy interfering in my career and saving your ass from my careless missives, I received the following email from Mrs. Lincoln. I really don't want to meet with her—even if I did, I am not allowed to leave this building. How she got ahold of my email address, I don't know. What would you suggest I do? Her email is below:

Dear Anastasia, I would really like to have lunch with you. I think we got off on the wrong foot, and I'd like to make that right. Are you free sometime this week?
Elena Lincoln

Anastasia Steele
Assistant to Jack Hyde, Editor, SIP

Oh, this day just gets better and better. What the hell is Elena doing now? And Ana is calling me out on my shit as usual.

I didn't know arguing could be so tiresome. And discouraging.

And worrying. She's mad at me.

From: Christian Grey
Subject: Irritating Baggage
Date: June 13 2011 11:23
To: Anastasia Steele

Don't be mad at me. I have your best interests at heart.

If anything happened to you, I would never forgive myself.

I'll deal with Mrs. Lincoln.

Christian Grey
CEO, Grey Enterprises Holdings, Inc.

Irritating baggage? I smile for the first time since I left Ana this morning. She has a way with words.

I call Elena.

"Christian," she answers on the fifth ring.

"Do I have to get a banner and attach it to a plane and fly it over your office?"

She laughs. "My email?"

"Yes, Ana sent it to me. Please. Leave her alone. She doesn't want to see you. And I understand and respect that. You're making my life really difficult."

"You understand her?"

"Yes."

"I think she needs to know how hard you are on yourself."

"No. She doesn't need to know anything."

"You sound exhausted."

"I'm just tired of you going behind my back and chasing my girlfriend."

"Girlfriend?"

"Yes. Girlfriend. Get used to it."

She sighs long and hard.

"Elena. Please."

"Okay, Christian, it's your funeral."

What the fuck?

"I have to go," I answer.

"Goodbye," she says, and she sounds annoyed.

"Bye." I hang up.

The women in my life are vexing. I turn in my chair and stare out of the window. The rain is relentless. The sky is dark and drab, reflecting my mood. Life has become complicated. It used to be easier when everything and everyone stayed where I placed them, in their designated compartments. Now, with Ana, everything's changed. This is all new, and so far everyone, including my mother, seems to be pissed at me or pissing me off.

When I turn to face my computer there's another email from Ana.

From: Anastasia Steele
Subject: Laters
Date: June 13 2011 11:32
To: Christian Grey

Can we please discuss this tonight?
I am trying to work, and your continued interference is very distracting.

Anastasia Steele
Assistant to Jack Hyde, Editor, SIP

Okay. I'll leave you alone.

What I really want to do is go over to her office and take her somewhere splendid for lunch. But I don't think she'd appreciate that.

With a heavy sigh, I open the email that lists Andrea's bridal registry. Pots, pans, dishes—nothing appeals to me. And again I wonder why she didn't tell me about her nuptials.

Feeling morose, I call Flynn's office and make an appointment to see him later this afternoon. It's overdue. Then I summon Montana and ask her to go buy me a wedding card and some lunch. Surely she can't screw that up.

AS I'M EATING MY lunch, Taylor calls.

"Taylor."

"Mr. Grey, everything's okay."

My heart goes into overdrive as adrenaline powers through my body.

Ana.

"What is it? Is Ana okay?"

"She's fine, sir."

"Do you have news on Leila?"

"No, sir."

"Then what is it?"

"I'm just letting you know that Ana went to the deli on Union Square. She's back in the office. She's fine."

"Thank you for letting me know. Anything else?

"The Saab will be here this afternoon."

"Great." I put the phone down and try, really try, not to be mad as hell. I fail. She told me she'd stay put.

Leila could put a bullet through her.

Doesn't she understand that?

I call her.

"Jack Hyde's office—"

"You assured me you wouldn't go out."

"Jack sent me out for some lunch. I couldn't say no. Are you having me watched?" She sounds incredulous.

I ignore her question. "This is why I didn't want you going back to work."

"Christian, please. You're being so suffocating."

"Suffocating?"

"Yes. You have to stop this. I'll talk to you this evening. Unfortunately, I have to work late because I can't go to New York."

"Anastasia, I don't want to suffocate you."

"Well, you are. I have work to do. I'll talk to you later." She sounds as miserable as I feel and she hangs up.

I'm suffocating her?

Maybe I am…

I just want to protect her. I saw what Leila did to her car.

Don't push her too far, Grey.

She'll leave.

FLYNN HAS A REAL log fire burning in his office. It's June. It spits and crackles as we talk.

"You bought the company where she works?" Flynn asks with raised eyebrows.

"Yes."

"I think Ana has a point. I'm not surprised she feels suffocated."

I shift in my chair. This is not what I want to hear. "I wanted to get into publishing."

Flynn remains impassive, giving nothing away, waiting for me to speak.

"It's over the top, isn't it?" I concede.

"Yes."

"She wasn't impressed."

"Did you set out to impress her?"

"No. That wasn't my intention. Anyway, SIP is mine now."

"I understand that you're trying to protect her, and I know why you're trying to do that. But this is an out-of-the-ordinary reaction. You have a bank account that allows you to do this, but you will drive her away if you continue on this path."

"That's what I'm worried about."

"Christian, you have a great deal to contend with at the moment. Leila Williams—and yes, I will help you when you find her—Anastasia's animosity toward Elena… I think you can understand why Ana feels that way." He gives me a pointed look.

I shrug, unwilling to agree with him.

"But there's something much bigger you're not telling me, and I've been waiting for you to tell me since you arrived here. I saw it on Saturday."

I stare at him, wondering what he's talking about. He sits patiently. Waiting.

He saw it on Saturday?

The bidding?

The dancing?

Shit.

"I'm in love with Ana."

"Thank you. I know."

"Oh."

"I could have told you that when you came to see me after she left you. I'm glad you worked it out for yourself."

"I didn't know I was capable of feeling like this."

"Of course you're capable." He sounds exasperated. "That's why I was so interested in your reaction when she told you that she loved you."

"It's getting easier to hear."

He smiles. "Good. I'm glad."

"I've always been able to separate the different aspects of my life. My work. My family. My sex life. I understood what each of these meant to me. But since I met Ana, it's not as simple anymore. It's entirely unfamiliar and I feel out of my depth and out of control."

"Welcome to falling in love." Flynn smiles. "And don't be too hard on yourself. You have an ex on the loose with a gun who has already tried to get your attention by attempting suicide in front of your housekeeper. And she's vandalized Ana's car. You've put measures in place to keep Ana and you safe. You've done all you can. You can't be everywhere, and you can't keep Ana locked up."

"I want to."

"I know you do. But you can't. Simple."

I shake my head, but deep down I know John's right.

"Christian, I've long held the belief that you never really had an adolescence—emotionally speaking. I think you're experiencing it now. I can see how agitated you are," he continues, "and since you won't let me prescribe you any anti-anxiety medication, I'd like you to try the relaxation techniques we discussed."

Oh, not that shit. I roll my eyes, but I know I'm behaving like a sulky teenager. He just said as much.

"Christian, it's your blood pressure. Not mine."

"Okay." I hold my hands up in surrender. "I'll try my *happy* place." I sound sarcastic, but it will appease John, who's looking at the clock.

Where is my happy place?

My childhood in the orchard.

Sailing or soaring. Always.

It used to be with Elena.

But now my happy place is with Ana.

In Ana.

Flynn stifles a smile. "Time's up," he says.

FROM THE BACK OF the Audi, I call Ana.

"Hi," she says, her voice quiet and breathy.

"Hi. When will you be finished?"

"By seven thirty, I think."

"I'll meet you outside."

"Okay."

Thank God. I thought she might say she wanted to go back to her own apartment.

"I'm still mad at you, but that's all," she whispers. "We have a lot to talk about."

"I know. See you at seven thirty."

"I have to go. See you later." She hangs up.

"Let's sit here and wait for her," I say to Taylor and glance at the front door of SIP.

"Okay, sir."

And I sit and listen to the rain as it drums an uneven tattoo on the roof of the car, drowning out my thoughts. Drowning out my happy placc.

AN HOUR LATER, the door to SIP opens and there she is. Taylor climbs out of the car and opens the door as Ana hurries toward us, head down to avoid the rain.

I have no idea what she's going to do or say as she shuffles in beside me, but she's shaking her head and scattering droplets of water over me and the backseat.

I want to hold her.

"Hi," she says, and her anxious eyes meet mine.

"Hi," I respond, and reaching over, I grasp her hand and squeeze it.

"Are you still mad?" I ask.

"I don't know," she says.

I bring her hand to my lips and kiss each knuckle in turn. "It's been a shitty day."

"Yes, it has." Her shoulders slump and she seems to relax into the car seat as she lets out a deep breath.

"It's better now that you're here." I run my thumb across her knuckles, craving the contact. As Taylor drives us home, the day's woes seem to dissipate and at last I start to relax.

She's here. She's safe.

She's with me.

Taylor stops outside Escala and I'm not sure why. But Ana is already opening the door, so I jump out after her and we run into the building and out of the rain. I grasp her hand as we wait for the elevator, surveying the street through the plate glass. Just in case.

"I take it you haven't found Leila yet," Ana says.

"No. Welch is still looking for her."

We step into the elevator and the doors close. Ana looks up at me, elfin-faced and wide-eyed—I can't look away. Our gaze holds my longing and her need. She licks her lips. A come-on.

And suddenly our attraction is in the air between us, like static, surrounding us.

"Do you feel it?" I whisper.

"Yes."

"Oh, Ana." I cannot bear the distance between us. I reach for her so she's in my arms and angle her head. My lips seek and find hers. She groans into my mouth, her fingers in my hair as I push her against the elevator wall. "I hate arguing with you." I want every inch of her. Right here. Right now. To know that we're okay.

Ana's response is immediate. Her hunger and passion are unleashed in our kiss, her tongue demanding and urgent. Her body rises and presses against mine, seeking relief as I lift up her skirt, my fingertips skimming her thigh and feeling lace and warm, warm flesh. "Sweet Jesus, you're wearing stockings." My voice is hoarse as I slide my thumb across her stocking line. "I want to see this." And I pull her skirt up so I can see the tops of her thighs.

I step back to enjoy the view and press the elevator's emergency stop button. I'm panting. I'm wanting, and she stands there like the fucking goddess she is, staring me down, her eyes dark, carnal, her breasts rising and falling as she drags air into her lungs.

"Take your hair down."

Ana yanks at her hair tie and her hair spills down over her shoulders and curls at her breasts. "Undo the top two buttons of your shirt," I whisper, growing harder and harder.

Her lips parted, she reaches up and slowly, too slowly, undoes the first one. Pausing for a beat, she lowers her fingers to the second button and undoes it. Unhurried. Tantalizing me further and finally revealing the soft swell of her breasts.

"Do you have any idea how alluring you look right now?" I hear the need in my voice.

She sinks her teeth into her bottom lip and shakes her head.

I think I'm going to explode. I close my eyes and try to bring my body to heel. Stepping forward, I place my hands on the wall on either side of her face. She tilts her face up, and her eyes meet mine.

I lean closer. "I think you do, Miss Steele. I think you like to drive me wild."

"Do I drive you wild?"

"In all things, Anastasia. You are a siren, a goddess." I reach down and grasp her leg above her knee and hitch it up around my waist. Slowly I lean down, pressing my body into hers. My erection sitting at the sacred junction of her thighs. I kiss her throat, my tongue tasting and savoring her. She wraps her arms around my neck and she arches her back, pressing into me.

"I'm going to take you now." I groan and lift her higher. Grabbing a condom from my pocket, I undo my fly. "Hold tight, baby."

She tightens her arms around my neck and I show her the condom. She bites down on the corner and I tug, and together we rip open the foil packet.

"Good girl."

I step back a little and manage to slide on the damn condom. "God, I can't wait for the next six days."

No more condoms.

I run my thumb over her underwear.

Lace. Good.

"I do hope you're not overly fond of these panties." And the only reply is her heavy breathing in my ear. I push my thumbs through the seam at the back and they tear apart, allowing me access to my happy place.

With my eyes on hers, I take her, slowly.

Fuck, she feels good.

She arches her back and closes her eyes and groans.

I pull back and sink slowly into her once more.

This is what I want.

This is what I needed.

After such a shitty day.

She didn't run.

She's here.

For me.

With me.

"You're mine, Anastasia." The words wash against her throat.

"Yes. Yours. When will you accept that?"

Her words are a sigh. And it's what I want to hear. What I need to hear. I take her, fast, furious. I need her. With each little cry, each pant, each tug of my hair, I know she needs me, too. I lose myself in her and I feel her spiral out of control. "Oh, baby," I moan, and she comes around me, crying out, and I follow, whispering her name.

I kiss her, holding her, as my composure returns. We are forehead to forehead and her eyes are closed. "Oh, Ana, I need you so much." I close my eyes and kiss her forehead, thankful that I've found her.

"And I you, Christian," she whispers.

I release her and straighten her skirt and I do up the top two buttons of her shirt. I punch the override code into the elevator keypad and it jolts to life. "Taylor will be wondering where we are." I give her a wicked grin and she tries in vain to smooth out her hair. After a few futile attempts she gives up and opts for a ponytail.

"You'll do," I reassure her and zip up my fly and slip the condom and her ruined panties into my pocket for disposal later.

Taylor is waiting when the doors open.

"Problem with the elevator," I say as we step out, but I avoid eye contact with him. Ana scampers off to the bedroom, no doubt to freshen up, and I make my way into the kitchen, where Mrs. Jones is preparing dinner.

"The Saab is here, Mr. Grey," Taylor says, having followed me into the kitchen.

"Great. I'll let Ana know."

"Sir." He smiles. He and Gail exchange a look before he turns to leave.

"Good evening, Gail," I say, ignoring their look as I slip off my jacket. I hang it on the barstool and sit down at the counter.

"Good evening, Mr. Grey. Dinner will be ready shortly."

"Smells good."

Damn, I'm hungry.

"Coq au vin, for two." She gives me a fond sideways glance as she takes two plates out of the warming drawer. "I'm just checking that Miss Steele will be with us tomorrow."

"Yes."

"I'll fix lunch for her again."

"Great."

Ana returns to join me at the kitchen counter and Mrs. Jones serves us our dinner.

"Enjoy, Mr. Grey, Ana," she says and exits the kitchen.

I fetch a bottle of Chablis from the fridge and pour each of us a glass. Ana tucks into her food. She's hungry.

"I like to see you eat."

"I know." She pops a piece of chicken into her mouth. I grin and take a sip of wine. "Tell me something good about your day," she says when she's finished chewing.

"We had a breakthrough today with the design of our solar-powered tablet. It has so many different applications. We'll be able to make solar-powered phones, too."

"You're excited about that?"

"Very. And they'll be cheap to produce and distribute in developing countries."

"Careful, your philanthropy is showing," she teases, but her expression is warm. "So is it just in New York and Aspen that you have property?"

"Yes."

"Where in New York?"

"Tribeca."

"Tell me about it."

"It's an apartment. I rarely use it. In fact, my family uses it more than I do. I'll take you, whenever you want to go."

Ana stands, collects my plate, and puts it in the sink. I think she's about to wash up. "Leave that. Gail will do it." She looks happier than when she got into the car.

"Well, now that you are more docile, Miss Steele, shall we talk about today?"

"I think you're the one who's more docile. I think I'm doing a good job in taming you."

"Taming me?" I snort, amused that she thinks I need taming.

She nods. She's serious.

Taming me.

Well, I'm certainly more docile since our assignation in the elevator. And she was more than happy to contribute to that encounter. Is that what she means?

"Yes. Maybe you are, Anastasia."

"You were right about Jack," she says and leans across the kitchen counter, regarding me seriously.

My blood runs cold. "Has he tried anything?"

She shakes her head. "No, and he won't, Christian. I told him today that I'm your girlfriend, and he backed right off."

"You're sure? I could fire the fucker."

He's history. I want him out.

Ana sighs. "You really have to let me fight my own battles. You can't constantly second-guess me and try to protect me. It's stifling, Christian. I'll never flourish with your incessant interference. I need some freedom. I wouldn't dream of meddling in your affairs."

"I only want you safe, Anastasia. If anything happened to you, I—"

"I know," she says, "and I understand why you feel so driven to protect me. And part of me loves it. I know that if I need you, you'll be there, as I am for you. But if we are to have any hope of a future together, you have to trust me and trust my judgment. Yes, I'll get it wrong sometimes—I'll make mistakes, but I have to learn." It's a passionate plea, and I know she's right.

It's just… It's just…

Flynn's words come to mind. *You will drive her away if you continue on this path.*

She comes toward me with quiet determination and, taking my hands, places them around her waist. Gently, she puts her hands on my arms. "You can't interfere in my job. It's wrong. I don't need you charging in like a white knight to save the day. I know you want to control everything, and I understand why, but you can't. It's an impossible goal. You have to learn to let go." She strokes my face. "And if you can do that—give me that—I'll move in with you."

"You'd do that?"

"Yes," she says.

"But you don't know me," I blurt, suddenly panicked. I have to tell her.

"I know you well enough, Christian. Nothing you tell me about yourself will frighten me away."

I doubt that. She doesn't know why I do what I do.

She doesn't know the monster.

She touches my cheek again, trying to reassure me. "But if you could just ease up on me."

"I'm trying, Anastasia. I couldn't just stand by and let you go to New York with that sleazeball. He has an alarming reputation. None of his assistants have lasted more than three months, and they're never retained by the company. I don't want that for you, baby. I don't want anything to happen to you. You being hurt, the thought fills me with dread. I can't promise not to interfere, not if I think you'll come to harm." I take a deep breath. "I love you, Anastasia. I will do everything in my power to protect you. I cannot imagine my life without you."

Quite the speech, Grey.

"I love you, too, Christian." She folds her arms around my neck and kisses me, her tongue teasing my lips.

Taylor coughs in the background, and I stand with Ana by my side.

"Yes?" I ask Taylor, a little more sharply than intended.

"Mrs. Lincoln is on her way up, sir."

"What?"

Taylor gives me an apologetic shrug.

I shake my head.

"Well, this should be interesting," I mutter and give Ana a contrite smile. Ana looks from me to Taylor and I don't think she quite believes him. He gives her a nod and leaves.

"Did you talk to her today?" she asks me.

"Yes."

"What did you say?"

"I said that you didn't want to see her and that I understood your reasons why. I also told her that I didn't appreciate her going behind my back."

"What did she say?"

"She brushed it off in a way that only Elena can."

"Why do you think she's here?"

"I have no idea."

Taylor returns to the living room. "Mrs. Lincoln," he says, and Elena stands staring at the two of us. I pull Ana closer to my side.

"Elena?" I say, wondering why the hell she's here.

She looks from me to Ana. "I'm sorry. I didn't realize you had company, Christian. It's Monday," she says.

"Girlfriend," I clarify.

Submissives only on the weekend, Mrs. Lincoln. You know this.

"Of course. Hello, Anastasia. I didn't know you'd be here. I know you don't want to talk to me. I accept that."

"Do you?" Ana's tone is deadly.

Hell.

Elena walks toward us. "Yes, I get the message. I'm not here to see you. Like I said, Christian rarely has company during the week." She pauses and addresses Ana directly. "I have a problem, and I need to talk to Christian about it."

"Oh? Do you want a drink?" I ask.

"Yes, please," she says.

I fetch a glass. When I turn they are both sitting in awkward silence at the kitchen island.

Shit.

This day. This day. This day. It just gets better and better.

I pour wine into both of their glasses and take a seat between them.

"What's up?" I ask Elena.

Elena's eyes dart to Ana.

"Anastasia's with me now." I reach across and give Ana's hand a reassuring squeeze in the hope she keeps quiet. The sooner Elena says her piece, the sooner she'll be gone.

Elena looks nervous, unlike her usual self. She twists her ring, a sure sign that something is agitating her. "I'm being blackmailed."

"How?" I ask, appalled. She pulls a note out of her purse. I don't want to touch it. "Put it down, lay it out." I point with my chin at the marble top and tighten my hold on Ana's hand.

"You don't want to touch it?" Elena asks.

"No. Fingerprints."

"Christian, you know I can't go to the police with this." She puts the note on the counter. It's written in capital letters.

MRS LINCOLN
FIVE THOUSAND
OR I TELL ALL.

"They're only asking for five thousand dollars?" That doesn't seem right. "Any idea who it might be? Someone in the community?"

"No," she responds.

"Linc?"

"What, after all this time? I don't think so."

"Does Isaac know?"

"I haven't told him."

"I think he needs to know."

Ana tugs at her hand. She wants out.

"What?" I ask Ana.

"I'm tired. I think I'll go to bed," she says.

I search her face to see what she's really thinking, and as usual I have no idea.

"Okay," I answer. "I won't be long." I release her hand and she gets up.

"Good night, Anastasia," Elena says.

Ana responds, her voice frigid, and she stalks out of the room.

I turn my attention back to Elena. "I don't think there's a great deal I can do, Elena. If it's a question of money…" I stop. She knows I'd give her the money. "I could ask Welch to investigate?"

"No, Christian, I just wanted to share. You look very happy," she adds, changing the subject.

"I am." Ana just agreed to move in.

"You deserve to be."

"I wish that were true."

"Christian." Elena's tone is chastising. "Does she know how negative you are about yourself? About all your issues?"

"She knows me better than anyone."

"Ouch! That hurts."

"It's the truth, Elena. I don't have to play games with her. And I mean it, leave her alone."

"What is her problem?"

"You. What we were. What we did. She doesn't understand."

"Make her understand."

"It's in the past, Elena, and why would I want to taint her with our fucked-up relationship? She's good and sweet and innocent, and by some miracle she loves me."

"It's no miracle, Christian. Have a little faith in yourself. You really are quite a catch. I've told you often enough. And she seems lovely, too. Strong. Someone to stand up to you."

"She's stronger than both of us."

Elena's eyes cool. She looks thoughtful. "Don't you miss it?"

"What?"

"Your playroom."

"That really is none of your fucking business."

"I'm sorry." Her sarcasm is irritating. She's anything but sorry.

"I think you'd better go. And please, call before you come again."

"Christian, I am sorry," she says again, sincerely this time. "Since when are you so sensitive?"

"Elena, we have a business relationship that has profited us both immensely. Let's keep it that way. What was between us is part of the past. Anastasia is my future, and I won't jeopardize it in any way, so cut the fucking crap."

"I see." Elena gives me a hard stare, as if she's trying to get under my skin. It makes me uncomfortable.

"Look, I'm sorry for your trouble. Perhaps you should ride it out and call their bluff."

"I don't want to lose you, Christian."

"I'm not yours to lose, Elena."

"That's not what I meant."

"What did you mean?" I snap.

"Look, I don't want to argue with you. Your friendship means a lot to me. I'll back off from Anastasia. But I'm here if you need me. I always will be."

"Anastasia thinks that you saw me last Saturday. You called, that's all. Why did you tell her otherwise?"

"I wanted her to know how upset you were when she left. I don't want her to hurt you."

"She knows. I've told her. Stop interfering. Honestly, you're like a mother hen."

Elena laughs, but it's hollow, and I really want her to go. "I know. I'm sorry. You know I care about you. I never thought you'd end up falling in love, Christian. It's very gratifying to see. But I couldn't bear it if she hurt you."

"I'll take my chances," I state wryly. "Now, are you sure you don't want Welch to sniff around?"

"I suppose it wouldn't do any harm."

"Okay. I'll call him in the morning."

"Thank you, Christian. And I am sorry. I didn't mean to intrude. I'll go. Next time I'll call."

"Good."

I stand and she takes the hint and gets up, too. We walk into the foyer and she gives me a peck on the cheek. "I'm just watching out for you," she says.

"I know. Oh, and another thing: Can you not gossip to my mother about my relationship with Ana?"

"Okay," she says, but her mouth is pinched. She's irritated now.

The elevator doors open and she steps inside.

"Good night."

"Good night, Christian."

The doors close and Ana's words from her email earlier today come to mind.

Irritating baggage.

I chuckle in spite of myself. *Yes, Ana. You are so right.*

Ana is sitting on my bed. Her look is inscrutable. "She's gone," I say, anxious about Ana's reaction. I don't know what she's thinking.

"Will you tell me all about her? I am trying to understand why you think she helped you." She glances down at her fingernails, then up at me, her eyes clear with conviction. "I loathe her, Christian. I think she did you untold damage. You have no friends. Did she keep them away from you?"

Oh Christ. I've really had enough of this. I do not need this now. "Why the fuck do you want to know about her? We had a very long-standing affair, she beat the shit out of me often, and I fucked her in all sorts of ways you can't even imagine. End of story."

She's taken aback. Eyes flashing, she tosses her hair over her shoulder. "Why are you so angry?"

"Because all of that shit is over!" And I'm shouting.

Ana looks away, her mouth a hard line.

Damn it.

Why am I so volatile around her… ?

Calm down, Grey.

I sit down beside her. "What do you want to know?"

"You don't have to tell me. I don't mean to intrude."

"Anastasia, it's not that. I don't like talking about this shit. I've lived in a bubble for years with nothing affecting me and not having to justify myself to anyone. She's always been there as a confidante. And now my past and my future are colliding in a way I never thought possible. I never thought I had a future with anyone, Anastasia. You give me hope and have me thinking about all sorts of possibilities."

You've said you'd move in with me.

"I was listening," she whispers, and I think she's embarrassed.

"What? To our conversation?" *Christ. What did I say?*

"Yes."

"Well?"

"She cares for you."

"Yes, she does. And I for her in my own way, but it doesn't come close to how I feel about you. If that's what this is about."

"I'm not jealous," she says quickly and tosses her hair over her shoulder again.

I'm not sure I believe her.

"You don't love her?"

I sigh. "A long time ago, I thought I loved her."

"When we were in Georgia you said you didn't love her."

"That's right."

She's perplexed.

Oh, baby, do I have to spell it out for you?

"I loved you then, Anastasia. You're the only person I'd fly three thousand miles to see. The feelings I have for you are very different from any I ever had for Elena." Ana asks me when I knew this. "Ironically, it was Elena who pointed it out to me. She encouraged me to go to Georgia."

Ana's expression changes. She looks wary. "So you desired her? When you were younger."

"Yes. She taught me a great deal. She taught me to believe in myself."

"But she also beat the shit out of you."

"Yes, she did."

"And you liked that?"

"At the time I did."

"So much that you wanted to do it to others?"

"Yes."

"Did she help you with that?"

"Yes."

"Did she sub for you?"

"Yes."

Ana's shocked. *Don't ask me if you don't want to know.*

"Do you expect me to like her?"

"No. Though it would make my life a hell of a lot easier. I do understand your reticence."

"Reticence! Jeez, Christian—if that were your son, how would you feel?"

What a ridiculous question.

Me. With a son?

Never.

"I didn't have to stay with her. It was my choice, too, Anastasia."

"Who's Linc?"

"Her ex-husband."

"Lincoln Timber?"

"The very same."

"And Isaac?"

"Her current submissive. He's in his midtwenties, Anastasia. You know, a consenting adult."

"Your age," she says.

Enough. Enough.

"Look, Anastasia, as I said to her, she's part of my past. You are my future. Don't let her come between us, please. And quite frankly, I'm really bored of this subject. I'm going to do some work." I stand and look down at her. "Let it go. Please."

She sticks her chin out in that obstinate way she does. I choose to ignore it.

"Oh, I almost forgot," I add. "Your car arrived a day early. It's in the garage. Taylor has the key."

Her eyes light up. "Can I drive it tomorrow?"

"No."

"Why not?"

"You know why not."

Leila. Do I have to spell it out?

"And that reminds me," I continue. "If you're going to leave your office, let me know. Sawyer was there, watching you. It seems I can't trust you to look after yourself at all."

"Seems I can't trust you, either," she says. "You could have told me Sawyer was watching me."

"Do you want to fight about that, too?" I ask.

"I wasn't aware we were fighting. I thought we were communicating," she replies, glaring at me.

I close my eyes, struggling to keep my temper. This is getting us nowhere. "I have to work." I walk out, leaving her sitting on the bed, before I say something I'll regret.

All these questions.

If she doesn't like the answers, why does she ask me?

Elena is pissed, too.

I sit down at my desk and already there's an email from her.

From: Elena Lincoln
Subject: Tonight
Date: June 13 2011 21:16
To: Christian Grey

Christian
I'm sorry. I don't know what possessed me to come over.
I feel that I'm losing you as a friend. That's all.
I value your friendship and advice so much.
I wouldn't be where I am without you.
Just know that.

Ex

ELENA LINCOLN
ESCLAVA
For The Beauty That Is You™

I think she's also telling me that I wouldn't be where I am without her. And that's true.

She grabs a handful of my hair, tugging my head back.

"What do you want to tell me?" she purrs, icy blue eyes boring into mine.

I'm broken. My knees are sore. My back is covered in welts. My thighs ache. I can't take any more. And she's looking directly into my eyes. Waiting.

"I want to leave Harvard, Ma'am," I say. And it's a dark confession. Harvard had always been a goal. For me. For my folks. Just to show them I could do it. Just to prove to them I wasn't the fuckup they thought I was.

"Leave? School?"

"Yes, Ma'am."

She lets go of my hair and swings the flogger from side to side.

"What will you do?"

"I want to start my own business."

She runs a scarlet fingernail down my cheek, to my mouth. "I knew something was bothering you. I always have to beat it out of you, don't I?"

"Yes, Ma'am."

"Get dressed. Let's talk about this."

I shake my head. Now is not the time to think about Elena. I turn to other emails.

WHEN I LOOK UP, it's ten thirty.

Ana.

I've been lost in the final SIP contract. I wonder if I should make it a condition of sale to get rid of Hyde, but that might be actionable.

I get up, stretch, and head into the bedroom.

Ana's not there.

She wasn't in the living room. I run upstairs to the submissive's room, but it's empty. *Shit.*

Where could she be? Library?

I hurtle back down the stairs.

I find her curled up asleep in one of the wing-backed library chairs. She's dressed in pale-pink satin, her hair spilling down over her chest. On her lap is an open book.

Daphne du Maurier's *Rebecca.*

I smile. My grandfather Theodore's family comes from Cornwall, hence my Daphne du Maurier collection.

I lift Ana into my arms. "Hey. You fell asleep. I couldn't find you." As I kiss her hair she puts her arms around my neck and says something I don't understand. I carry her through to my bedroom and tuck her into bed.

"Sleep, baby." I softly kiss her forehead and head for the shower.

I want to wash this day off my body.

Tuesday, June 14, 2011

Suddenly I'm awake; my heart is pounding and a deep unease tightens my gut. I'm lying naked beside Ana, and she's fast asleep. Lord, I envy her ability to sleep. My bedside light is still on, the clock reads 1:45, and I cannot shake my disquiet.

Leila?

I dart into my closet and drag on pants and a T-shirt. Back in the bedroom I check under the bed. The balcony door is locked. I hurry down the corridor to Taylor's office. The door is open, so I knock and look in. Ryan stands, surprised to see me. "Good evening, sir."

"Hi, Ryan. Everything okay?"

"Yes, sir. All's quiet."

"Nothing on the—" I point to the CCTV monitors.

"Nothing, sir. The place is secure. Reynolds just did a walk-through."

"Good. Thanks."

"You're welcome, Mr. Grey."

I shut his door and go into the kitchen for a glass of water. Looking out across the living room toward the windows and the darkness beyond, I take a sip.

Where are you, Leila?

I see her in my mind's eye, head bowed. Willing. Waiting. Wanting. Kneeling in my playroom, asleep in her room, kneeling by my side as I work in my study. And now for all I know she's wandering the streets of Seattle, cold and lonely and acting crazy.

Maybe I'm uneasy because Ana's agreed to move in.

I can protect her. But she doesn't want that.

I shake my head. Anastasia is challenging.

She's very challenging.

Welcome to falling in love. Flynn's words haunt me. So this is what it's like. Confusing, exhilarating, exhausting.

I walk over to my grand piano and lower the top board to cover the strings as quietly as I can. I don't want to wake her. I sit down and stare at the keys. I haven't played for a few days. I place my fingers on the keys and start to play. As Chopin's B-flat Nocturne quietly fills the room, I'm alone with the melancholy music and it soothes my soul.

A movement in my peripheral vision distracts me. Ana is standing in the shadows. Her eyes glint from the light in the hallway, and I continue to play. She walks toward me, dressed in the pale-pink satin robe. She's stunning: a diva who's stepped off the silver screen.

When she reaches me, I take my hands off the keys. I want to touch her.

"Why did you stop? That was lovely," she says.

"Do you have any idea how desirable you look at this moment?"

"Come to bed," she says.

I offer her my hand, and when she takes it I pull her into my lap and embrace her, kissing her exposed neck and tracing my lips to the pulse point at her throat. She trembles in my arms.

"Why do we fight?" I ask as my teeth tease her earlobe.

"Because we're getting to know each other, and you're stubborn and cantankerous and moody and difficult." She tilts her head to give me better access to her neck. I smile against her skin as I run my nose down her throat.

Challenging.

"I'm all those things, Miss Steele. It's a wonder you put up with me." I graze her earlobe with my teeth.

"Mmm..." She lets me know it feels good.

"Is it always like this?" I whisper against her skin. Will I ever get enough of her?

"I have no idea," she says, her voice little more than a sigh.

"Me neither." I untie the sash on her robe and it falls open, revealing the gown beneath. It clings to her body, showing every curve, every dip, every hollow. My hand skims from her face to her breast and her nipples harden, crowning against the satin when I circle them with my fingers. I move my hand to her waist, then to her hip.

"You feel so fine under this material, and I can see everything—even this." I tug gently on her pubic hair, visible as a slight mound beneath the fabric.

She gasps and I cradle her neck and coil my hand in her hair, drawing her head back. I kiss her, coaxing open her mouth and testing her tongue with mine.

She moans once more and her fingers curl around my face, stroking my stubble as her body rises beneath my touch.

Gently I lift up her nightgown, enjoying the feel of rich, soft satin as it inches up her beautiful body, revealing her long lovely legs. My hands find her ass. She's naked. I cup her in my hand, then move and run my thumbnail down the length of her inner thigh.

I want her. Here. On my piano.

Abruptly I stand, surprising Ana, and I lift her onto the piano so she's sitting on the front of the top board, her feet on the keys. Two discordant chords ring through the room as she gazes at me. Standing between her legs, I take her hands. "Lie back." I ease her down onto the piano. The satin spills like fluid over the edge of the gleaming black wood and onto the keys.

Once she's on her back I let go, strip off my T-shirt, and push her legs apart. Ana's feet play a staccato melody on the low and high keys. I kiss the inside of her right knee and trail kisses and soft nips up her leg to her thigh. Her nightgown inches up, revealing more and more of my beautiful girl. She groans. She knows what I have in mind. Her feet flex, and the dissonant sounds from the keys resonate through the room, an uneven accompaniment to her accelerated breathing.

I reach my goal: her clitoris. And I kiss her once, relishing the jolt that shoots through her body. Then I blow on her pubic hair to make a small space for my tongue. I push her knees wider and hold her in place. She's mine. Exposed. At my mercy. And I love it.

Slowly, I start circling my tongue around her sensitive sweet spot. She cries out and I continue over and over and over, while she's writhing beneath me, tilting her pelvis up for more.

I don't stop.

I consume her.

Until my face is soaked.

From me.

From her.

Her legs start to tremble.

"Oh, Christian, please."

"Oh no, baby, not yet." Pausing, I take a deep breath. She's laid out before me in satin, her hair spilling over the polished ebony; she's gorgeous, lit only from the reading light.

"No," she whimpers. She doesn't want me to stop.

"This is my revenge, Ana. Argue with me and I am going to take it out on your body somehow." I kiss her belly, feeling her muscles tighten beneath my lips.

Oh, baby, you are so ready.

My hands travel up her thighs, stroking, kneading, teasing.

With my tongue I circuit her navel while my thumbs reach the junction of her thighs.

"Ah!" She lets out a gargled cry as I push one thumb inside her while the other teases her clitoris, around and around and around.

She arches off the piano.

"Christian!" she cries.

Enough, Grey.

I lift her feet off the keys and push them so she slides effortlessly over the top board. I undo my fly, grab a condom, and let my pants fall to the floor. I climb up and kneel between her legs as I put on the condom. She watches me, her expression intense and filled with longing. I crawl up her body until we are face-to-face. My love and desire are reflected in her dark, dark eyes.

"I want you so badly," I whisper and slowly claim her.

And ease back.

And ease in.

She clutches my biceps and tips her head, her mouth open wide.

She's so close.

I build up speed and her legs flex beneath me and she lets out a strangled cry as she comes and I let go. Losing myself in the woman I love.

I STROKE HER HAIR as she rests her head on my chest.

"Do you drink tea or coffee in the evening?" Ana asks.

"What a strange question."

"I thought I could bring you tea in your study, and then I realized I didn't know what you would like."

"Oh, I see. Water or wine in the evening, Ana. Though maybe I should try tea." I move my hand from her hair to her back, stroking, touching, caressing her.

"We really know very little about each other," she whispers.

"I know." She doesn't know me. And when she does…

She leans up, frowning. "What is it?"

I wish I could tell you. But if I do, you'll leave.

I cup her beautiful, sweet face. "I love you, Ana Steele."

"I love you, too, Christian Grey. Nothing you tell me will drive me away."

We'll see, Ana. We'll see.

I move her to my side, sit up and vault off the piano, then lift her down.

"Bed," I whisper.

Grandpa Trev-yan and I are picking apples.

See these red apples on this green apple tree?

I nod.

We put these here. You and me. Remember?

We fooled this old apple tree.

It thought it would make bitter green apples.

But it makes these sweet red apples.

Remember.

I nod.

He holds the apple to his nose and sniffs.

Smell it.

It smells of good. It smells of full.

He rubs the apple against his shirt and gives it to me.

Taste it. I take a bite.

It is crunchy and yummy and apple pie.

I smile. My tummy is happy.

These apples are called fu-gee.

Here, you want to try the green one?

I don't know.

Grandpa takes a bite and his shoulders shake.

He makes a yuck face. *That's nasty.*

He offers it to me. He smiles. I smile and take a bite.

A shiver goes from my head to my toes.

NASTY.

I make a yuck face, too. He laughs. I laugh.

We pick the red apples and put them in the bucket.

We fooled the tree.

It's not nasty. It's sweet.

Not nasty. Sweet.

The smell is evocative. My grandfather's orchard. I open my eyes and I'm wrapped around Ana like swaddling. Her fingers are in my hair and she's smiling shyly at me.

"Good morning, beautiful," I murmur.

"Good morning, beautiful, yourself."

My body has another greeting in mind. I give her a swift kiss before disentangling my legs from hers. Balanced on one elbow, I look down at her. "Sleep okay?"

"Yes, despite the interruption to my sleep last night."

"Hmm. You can interrupt me like that anytime." I kiss her again.

"How about you? Did you sleep well?"

"I always sleep well with you, Anastasia."

"No more nightmares?"

"No."

Only dreams. Pleasant dreams.

"What are your nightmares about?"

Her question catches me off guard, and suddenly I'm thinking of my four-year-old self—helpless, lost, lonely, hurting, and filled with rage. "They're flashbacks of my early childhood, or so Dr. Flynn says. Some vivid, some less so."

I was a neglected, abused child.

My mother didn't love me.

She didn't protect me.

She killed herself and abandoned me.

The crack whore dead on the floor.

The burn.

Not the burn.

No. Don't go there, Grey.

"Do you wake up crying and screaming?" Ana's question brings me back, and I'm running my finger along her collarbone, keeping contact with her. My dream catcher.

"No, Anastasia. I've never cried. As far as I can remember."

Even that evil fucking bastard couldn't make me cry.

"Do you have any happy memories of your childhood?"

"I recall the crack whore baking. I remember the smell. A birthday cake, I think. For me."

Mommy is in the kitchen.

It smells of nice.

Nice and warm and chocolate.

She sings.

Mommy's happy song.

She smiles. "This is for you, Maggot."

For me!

"And then there's Mia's arrival with my mom and dad. My mom was worried about my reaction, but I adored baby Mia immediately. My first word was 'Mia.' I remember my first piano lesson. Miss Kathie, my tutor, was awesome. She kept horses, too."

"You said your mom saved you. How?"

Grace? Isn't it obvious?

"She adopted me. I thought she was an angel when I first met her. She was dressed in white and so gentle and calm as she examined me. I'll never forget that. If she'd said no, or if Carrick had said no…"

Fuck. I'd be dead by now.

I glance at my alarm clock: 6:15. "This is all a little deep for so early in the morning."

"I have made a vow to get to know you better," Ana says, looking both earnest and mischievous at once.

"Did you, now, Miss Steele? I thought you wanted to know if I preferred coffee or tea. Anyway, I can think of one way you can get to know me." I nudge her with my erection.

"I think I know you quite well enough that way."

I grin. "I don't think I'll ever get to know you well enough that way. There are definite advantages to waking up beside you." I nuzzle her ear.

"Don't you have to get up?"

"Not this morning. Only one place I want to be up right now, Miss Steele."

"Christian!"

I roll on top of her and grab her hands so they are above her head and kiss her throat. "Oh, Miss Steele." Holding both her hands in one of mine, I skim my other hand down her body and at a leisurely pace hitch up her satin nightgown until my arousal is cradled against her sex. "Oh, what I'd like to do to you," I whisper.

She smiles and tilts her pelvis up to meet me.

Naughty girl.

First, we need a condom.

I reach over to my bedside table.

ANA JOINS ME AT the breakfast bar. She's wearing a light-blue dress and high-heeled pumps. Again, she looks stunning. I watch her devour her breakfast. I'm relaxed. Happy, even. She's said she'll move in with me and I started my day with a bang. I smirk and wonder if Ana would find that funny. She turns to me. "When am I going to meet your trainer, Claude, and put him through his paces?"

"Depends if you want to go to New York this weekend or not—unless you'd like to see him early one morning this week. I'll ask Andrea to check on his schedule and get back to you."

"Andrea?"

"My PA."

She's back today. What a relief.

"One of your many blonds?"

"She's not mine. She works for me. You're mine."

"I work for you."

Oh yes! "So you do."

"Maybe Claude can teach me to kickbox," Ana says, but she's grinning like a fool, too.

Clearly she wants to improve her odds against me. Now, this could be interesting. "Bring it on, Miss Steele."

Ana takes a bite of her pancake and glances behind her. "You put the lid of the piano back up."

"I closed it last night so as not to disturb you. Guess it didn't work, but I'm glad it didn't."

Ana blushes.

Yes. There's a lot to be said for piano sex. And sex first thing in the morning. It's great for my mood.

Mrs. Jones interrupts our moment. She leans over and places a paper bag with Ana's lunch in front of her. "For later, Ana. Tuna, okay?"

"Oh yes. Thank you, Mrs. Jones." Ana gives her a broad smile, which Gail reciprocates, and then Gail leaves the room to give us some privacy. This is new to Gail, too. It's unusual for me to have anyone here during the week. The only other time has been with Ana.

"Can I ask you something?" Ana interrupts my thoughts.

"Of course."

"And you won't be angry?"

"Is it about Elena?"

"No."

"Then I won't be angry."

"But I now have a supplementary question."

"Oh?"

"Which is about her."

My sense of humor evaporates. "What?"

"Why do you get so mad when I ask you about her?"

"Honestly?" I ask.

"I thought you were always honest with me."

"I endeavor to be."

"That sounds like a very evasive answer."

"I am always honest with you, Ana. I don't want to play games. Well, not those sorts of games," I add.

"What sort of games do you want to play?" Ana blinks, pretending to be clueless.

"Miss Steele, you are so easily distracted."

She laughs, and the sight and sound of her doing so restore my good humor. "Mr. Grey, you are distracting on so many levels."

"My favorite sound in the whole world is your giggle, Anastasia. Now, what was your original question?"

"Oh yes. You only saw your subs on the weekends?"

"Yes, that's correct." *Where is she going with this?*

"So no sex during the week." She glances at the living room entrance; she's checking that no one can hear.

I laugh. "Oh, that's where we're going with this. Why do you think I work out every weekday?"

Today is different. Sex on a workday. Before breakfast. The last time that happened was on a desk in my study with you, Anastasia.

"You look very pleased with yourself, Miss Steele."

"I am, Mr. Grey."

"You should be. Now eat your breakfast."

WE RIDE DOWN IN the elevator with Taylor and Sawyer, and our collective good mood continues in the car. Taylor and Sawyer are up front when we set off for SIP.

Yes, I could definitely get used to this.

Ana is buoyant. She steals glances at me, or is it me who's stealing glances at her?

"Didn't you say your roommate's brother was arriving today?" I ask her.

"Oh, Ethan," she exclaims. "I forgot. Oh, Christian, thank you for reminding me. I'll have to go back to the apartment."

"What time?"

"I'm not sure what time he's arriving."

"I don't want you going anywhere on your own."

She gives me a pained look. "I know," she says. "Will Sawyer be spying, um, patrolling today?"

"Yes." I stress the word.

Leila's still out there.

"If I were driving the Saab it would be easier," she mutters, sounding sullen.

"Sawyer will have a car, and he can drive you to your apartment, depending on what time." I glance at Taylor in the rearview mirror. He nods.

Ana sighs. "Okay. I think Ethan will probably contact me during the day. I'll let you know what the plans are then."

This arrangement leaves a great deal to chance.

But I don't want an argument.

I'm having too good a day.

"Okay. Nowhere on your own. Do you understand?" I wag a finger at her.

"Yes, dear," she says, each word dripping with sarcasm.

Oh, what I'd give to spank her right now.

"And maybe you should just use your BlackBerry—I'll email you on it. That should prevent my IT guy having a thoroughly interesting morning, okay?"

"Yes, Christian." She rolls her eyes.

"Why, Miss Steele, I do believe you're making my palm twitch."

"Ah, Mr. Grey, your perpetually twitching palm. What are we going to do with that?"

I laugh. She's funny.

My phone vibrates.

Shit. It's Elena.

"What is it?"

"Christian. Hi. It's me. I'm sorry to disturb you. I wanted to make sure you didn't call your guy. That note was from Isaac."

"You're kidding."

"Yes. This is so embarrassing. It was for a scene."

"For a scene."

"Yes. And he didn't mean five thousand in cash."

I laugh. "When did he tell you this?"

"This morning. I called him first thing. I told him I'd been to see you. Oh, Christian, I'm sorry."

"No, don't worry. You don't have to apologize. I'm glad there's a logical explanation. It did seem a ridiculously low amount of money."

"I'm mortified."

"I have no doubt you've something evil and creative planned for your revenge. Poor Isaac."

"Actually, he's furious with me. So I may have to make it up to him."

"Good."

"Anyway. Thank you for listening yesterday. Talk soon."

"Goodbye." I hang up and turn to Ana, who's watching me.

"Who was that?" she asks.

"You really want to know?"

She shakes her head and stares out the window, the corners of her mouth turning down. "Hey." I take her hand and kiss each knuckle, then take her little finger, slip it into my mouth, and suck it. Hard. Then bite down gently.

She wriggles beside me and gives a nervous look to Taylor and Sawyer in the front seat. I have her attention.

"Don't sweat it, Anastasia. She's in the past." I plant a kiss in the center of her palm and release her hand. She opens the door and I watch her stride into SIP.

"Mr. Grey, I'd like to do a sweep of Miss Steele's apartment if she's returning there today," Taylor says, and I agree it's a good idea.

ANDREA GIVES ME A broad smile when I step out of the elevator at Grey House. A mousy-looking young woman stands beside her.

"Good morning, Mr. Grey. This is Sarah Hunter. She'll be interning with us."

Sarah looks me squarely in the eye and holds out her hand. "Good morning, Mr. Grey. Pleased to meet you."

"Hello, Sarah. Welcome." We exchange firm handshakes.

Her grip is surprising.

Not so mousy, then.

I extract my hand.

"Could I see you in my office, Andrea?"

"Of course. Would you like Sarah to make you a coffee?"

"Yes. Black. Please."

Sarah sashays off toward the kitchen with an enthusiasm that I hope I won't find irritating, and I hold the door to my office open for Andrea. Once she's inside, I close the door.

"Andrea—"

"Mr. Grey—"

We both stop talking.

"Go," I say.

"Mr. Grey, I just wanted to say thank you for the suite. It was gorgeous. You really didn't—"

"Why didn't you tell me you were getting married?" I sit down at my desk.

Andrea blushes. This I do not see often, and she seems at a loss for what to say.

"Andrea?"

"Well. Um. There's a non-fraternization clause in my contract."

"You married someone who works here!"

How the hell did she keep that to herself?

"Yes, sir."

"Who's the lucky guy?"

"Damon Parker. He works in engineering."

"The Australian."

"He needs a green card. He's on an H1 visa at the moment."

"I see." A marriage of convenience. For some strange reason,

I'm disappointed for and in her. She sees the censure on my face and hurries on.

"That's not the reason I married him. I love him," she says in a most uncharacteristic blurt, and she blushes. The stain on her cheeks restores my faith in her.

"Well, congratulations. Here you go." I hand her the "happily ever after" card I signed yesterday and hope she doesn't open it in front of me. "How's married life so far?" I ask, to prevent her from doing just that.

"I recommend it, sir." She's glowing. I recognize that look. It's how I feel myself. And now I'm at a loss as to what to say.

Andrea shifts back into work mode. "Shall we go through your schedule?" she asks.

"Please."

MARRIAGE. I CONTEMPLATE THE institution when Andrea leaves. It obviously agrees with her. It's what most women want. Isn't it? I wonder what Ana would do if I asked her to marry me. I shake my head, feeling ambushed by the thought.

Don't be ridiculous, Grey.

In my mind I replay this morning. I could wake up every day beside Anastasia Steele and I could close my eyes beside her every night.

You're smitten, Grey.

You've got it bad.

Enjoy this while it lasts.

I email her.

From: Christian Grey
Subject: Sunrise
Date: June 14 2011 09:23
To: Anastasia Steele

I love waking up with you in the morning.

Christian Grey
Completely & Utterly Smitten CEO,
Grey Enterprises Holdings, Inc.

I grin when I press send.

I hope she'll read this on her BlackBerry.

Sarah brings me my coffee and I open the latest draft of the SIP agreement and start to read.

My phone buzzes. It's a text from Elena.

ELENA
Thank you for being so understanding.

I ignore it and go back to my document. When I look up, there's a response from Ana. I take a swig of coffee.

From: Anastasia Steele
Subject: Sundown
Date: June 14 2011 09:35
To: Christian Grey

Dear Completely & Utterly Smitten
I love waking up with you, too. But I love being in bed with you and in elevators and on pianos and billiard tables and boats and desks and showers and bathtubs and strange wooden crosses with shackles and four-poster beds with red satin sheets and boathouses and childhood bedrooms.

Yours

Sex Mad and Insatiable xx

Shit. Laughing and choking at the same time, I spit coffee onto my keyboard at "Sex Mad and Insatiable." I can't believe she's written that in an email. Fortunately, I have tissues left over from yesterday's coffee fiasco.

From: Christian Grey
Subject: Wet Hardware
Date: June 14 2011 09:37
To: Anastasia Steele

Dear Sex Mad and Insatiable
I've just spat coffee all over my keyboard.

I don't think that's ever happened to me before.

I do admire a woman who concentrates on geography.

Am I to infer you just want me for my body?

Christian Grey
Completely & Utterly Shocked CEO, Grey Enterprises Holdings, Inc.

I continue my read of the SIP agreement but don't get very far before there's a new email from her.

From: Anastasia Steele
Subject: Giggling—and wet too
Date: June 14 2011 09:42
To: Christian Grey

Dear Completely & Utterly Shocked
Always.
I have work to do.

Stop bothering me.

SM&I xx

From: Christian Grey
Subject: Do I have to?
Date: June 14 2011 09:50
To: Anastasia Steele

Dear SM&I
As ever, your wish is my command.

Love that you are giggling and wet.

Laters, baby.

x

Christian Grey
Completely & Utterly Smitten, Shocked, and Spellbound
CEO, Grey Enterprises Holdings, Inc.

LATER, I'M IN MY monthly meeting with Ros and Marco—my M&A guy—and his team. We're going through a list of companies that Marco's people have identified as potential targets for takeovers.

He is discussing the last on the list. "They are floundering, but they have four patents pending, which might be useful in the fiber-optic division."

"Has Fred reviewed them?" I ask.

"He's excited," Marco replies with an avaricious grin.

"Let's do it."

My phone buzzes and Ana's name flashes on my screen.

"Excuse me," I say as I pick up the phone. "Anastasia."

"Christian, Jack has asked me to get his lunch."

"Lazy bastard."

"So I'm going to get it. It might be handy if you gave me Sawyer's number so I don't have to bother you."

"It's no bother, baby."

"Are you on your own?"

I look around the table. "No. There are six people staring at me right now wondering who the hell I'm talking to." Everyone looks away.

"Really?" she squeaks.

"Yes. Really." I pause. "My girlfriend," I tell the room.

Ros shakes her head.

"They probably all thought you were gay, you know."

I laugh as Ros and Marco exchange a look. "Yeah, probably."

"Er—I'd better go."

"I'll let Sawyer know." I laugh at the reactions around the table. "Have you heard from your friend?"

"Not yet. You'll be the first to know, Mr. Grey."

"Good. Laters, baby."

"Bye, Christian."

I get up. "I just need to make a quick call."

Outside the boardroom, I call Sawyer.

"Mr. Grey."

"Ana's leaving to get some lunch. Please stick close."

"Yes, sir."

Back in the room, the meeting is wrapping up. Ros approaches me.

"Your private merger?" she says with a curious look.

"The very same."

"No wonder you're so upbeat. I approve," she says.

I grin, feeling smug.

BASTILLE IS ON FIRE. He's knocked me down three fucking times. "So Dante told me you brought a beautiful girl into the bar. This why you're soft today, Grey?"

"Maybe." I grin. "And she needs a trainer."

"Your PA spoke to me this morning. I can't wait to meet her."

"She wants to learn to kickbox."

"Keep your ass in line?"

"Yeah. Something like that." I lunge for him, but he feints left, his dreads flying, and he knocks me down with a swift roundhouse kick.

Shit. I'm on the floor again.

Bastille's pumped up. "She'll have no trouble punishing your sorry ass if you fight like this, Grey," he crows.

Enough is enough. He's going down.

I RETURN TO MY office showered after my bout with Bastille, and Andrea is waiting for me.

"Mr. Grey. Thank you. You really are too generous."

I dismiss her gratitude with a wave as I head into my office. "You're welcome, Andrea. If you use it for a proper honeymoon, make sure I'm away, too." She gives me a rare smile and I close my office door.

I notice a new email from Ana when I sit down at my desk.

From: Anastasia Steele
Subject: Visitors from Sunny Climes.
Date: June 14 2011 14:55
To: Christian Grey

Dearest Completely & Utterly SS&S
Ethan is back, and he's coming here to collect keys to the apartment.

I'd really like to make sure he's settled in okay.

Why don't you pick me up after work? We can go to the apartment, then we can ALL go out for a meal maybe?

My treat?

Your

Ana x
Still SM&I

Anastasia Steele
Assistant to Jack Hyde, Editor, SIP

She's still using her work computer.
Damn it. Ana.

From: Christian Grey
Subject: Dinner Out
Date: June 14 2011 15:05
To: Anastasia Steele

I approve of your plan. Except the part about you paying!

My treat.

I'll pick you up at 6:00.

x

P.S. Why aren't you using your BlackBerry!!!

Christian Grey
Completely and Utterly Annoyed CEO,
Grey Enterprises Holdings, Inc.

From: Anastasia Steele
Subject: Bossiness
Date: June 14 2011 15:11
To: Christian Grey

Oh, don't be so crusty and cross.
It's all in code.
I'll see you at 6:00.

Ana x

Anastasia Steele
Assistant to Jack Hyde, Editor, SIP

From: Christian Grey
Subject: Maddening Woman
Date: June 14 2011 15:18
To: Anastasia Steele

Crusty and cross!

I'll give you crusty and cross.

And look forward to it.

Christian Grey
Completely and Utterly More Annoyed,
but Smiling for Some Unknown Reason CEO,
Grey Enterprises Holdings, Inc.

From: Anastasia Steele
Subject: Promises. Promises.
Date: June 14 2011 15:23
To: Christian Grey

Bring it on, Mr. Grey.
I look forward to it too. ;D

Ana x

Anastasia Steele
Assistant to Jack Hyde, Editor, SIP

Andrea buzzes me. "I have Professor Choudury on the phone from WSU." The professor is the head of the Environmental Sciences Department. It's rare that he calls. "Put him through."

"Mr. Grey. I wanted to give you some good news."

"Please, go ahead."

"Professor Gravett and her team have made a breakthrough with regard to the microbes that are responsible for nitrogen fixation. I wanted to give you a heads-up because she'll be presenting her findings to you on Friday."

"That sounds impressive."

"As you know, our research has been directed at making soils more productive. And this is a game-changer."

"I'm pleased to hear it."

"It's thanks to you, Mr. Grey, and the funding from GEH."

"I look forward to hearing more about it on Friday."

"Good day, sir."

AT 5:55 P.M. I'M outside SIP's offices, in the back of the Audi, looking forward to seeing Ana.

I call her.

"Crusty and Cross here."

"Well, this is Sex Mad and Insatiable. I take it you're outside?" she answers.

"I am indeed, Miss Steele. Looking forward to seeing you."

"Ditto, Mr. Grey. I'll be right out."

I sit and wait, reading a report on the fiber-optic patents Marco was talking about earlier today.

Ana appears a few minutes later. Her hair, shining in the late-afternoon sun, bounces in thick waves over her shoulders as she walks toward me. My spirits lift, and I'm completely under her spell.

She's everything to me.

I climb out of the car to open the door for her. "Miss Steele, you look as captivating as you did this morning." Embracing her, I plant a kiss on her lips.

"Mr. Grey, so do you."

"Let's go get your friend."

I open her door, and as she climbs in, I acknowledge Sawyer, who's standing outside the SIP office, unseen by Ana. He nods and heads to the SIP parking lot.

TAYLOR STOPS OUTSIDE ANA'S apartment and I reach for the door handle of the Q7, but I'm stopped by the buzz of my phone.

"Grey," I answer as Ana reaches for the door.

"Christian."

"Ros, what is it?"

"Something's come up."

"I'll go get Ethan. I'll be two minutes," Ana mouths to me as she exits the car.

"Hold on a moment, Ros." I watch Ana as she presses the entry phone and speaks to Ethan. The door buzzes and in she goes.

"What is it, Ros?"

"It's Woods."

"Woods?"

"Lucas Woods."

"Oh yes. The idiot who ran his fiber-optic company into the ground and then blamed everyone else."

"The same. He's doing some rather negative press."

"And?"

"Sam is concerned about the PR fallout. Woods has gone public about the takeover. How we came in and didn't let him continue to run the company the way he wanted."

I snort my derision. "There's a good reason for that. He'd be bankrupt by now if he'd continued the way he was going."

"True."

"Tell Sam that I know Woods sounds convincing to those who don't know his story, but those who know him realize that he reached a level beyond his ability and made some really bad decisions. He's got no one to blame but himself."

"So you're not worried."

"About him? No. He's a pretentious asshole. The community knows."

"We could go after him for defamation, and he's breached his NDA."

"Why would we do that? He's the kind that feeds off publicity. He's been given enough rope to hang himself. Though he should grow some balls and let it go."

"I thought you'd say that. Sam is agitated."

"Sam just needs some perspective. He always overreacts to bad press."

As I glance out the window, there's a young man with a duffel bag walking with purpose toward the apartment door.

Ros is continuing to talk, but I ignore her. The man looks familiar. He's sporting the beach-bum look: long blond hair, tanned. Recognition and apprehension hit me at once.

It's Ethan Kavanagh.

Shit. *Who let Ana into the apartment?*

"Ros, I have to go," I bark into the phone as fear grips my chest.

Ana.

I fly out of the car. "Taylor, follow me," I shout, and we rush toward Ethan Kavanagh, who's about to put the key in the lock. He turns in alarm to see us barreling toward him.

"Kavanagh. I'm Christian Grey. Ana's upstairs with someone who could be armed. Wait here." There's a spark of recognition in his expression, but wordlessly—confused I think—he relinquishes hold of the key. I'm through the door and running up the stairs, taking two steps at a time.

I burst into the apartment and there they are.

A face-off.

Ana and Leila.

And Leila's holding a gun.

No. No. No. A fucking gun.

And Ana is here. Alone. Vulnerable. Panic and fury burst inside me.

I want to lunge at Leila. Take the gun. Bring her down. But I freeze and check Ana. Her eyes are wide with fright and something I can't name. Compassion, maybe? But to my relief, she's unharmed.

The sight of Leila is a shock. Not only does she have her fingers wrapped around a gun, but she's lost so much weight. She's filthy. Her clothes are in tatters and her clouded brown eyes are expressionless. A lump forms in my throat and I don't know if it's fear or empathy.

But my biggest concern is that she's still holding a gun with Ana in the room.

Does she mean to harm her?

Does she mean to harm me?

Leila's eyes are on me. Her stare intensifies, no longer lifeless. She's drinking in every detail, as if she can't believe I'm real. It's unnerving. But I stand my ground and return her look.

Her eyelashes flutter as she collects herself. But her grip tightens around the gun.

Shit.

I wait. Ready to pounce. My heart thumping, the metallic taste of fear in my mouth.

What are you going to do, Leila?

What are you going to do with that gun?

She stills and lowers her head a fraction, but her eyes stay on me, gazing at me through her dark lashes.

I sense a movement behind me.

Taylor.

I hold up my hand, warning him to be still.

He's agitated. Furious. I can feel it. But he doesn't move.

My eyes never leave Leila.

She looks like a wraith; there are dark circles beneath her eyes, her skin is translucent like parchment, and her lips are chapped and flaking.

Christ, Leila, what have you done to yourself?

Time passes. Seconds. Minutes. And we stare at each other.

Slowly, the light in her eyes changes; the brightness increases, from dull brown to hazel. And I see a flash of the Leila I knew. There's a spark of connection. A kindred spirit who enjoyed everything we shared. Our old bond, it's there. I sense it between us.

She's giving this to me.

Her breathing quickens and she licks her chapped lips, yet her tongue leaves no moisture.

But it's enough.

Enough to tell me what she needs. What she wants.

She wants me.

Me at what I do best.

Her lips part, her chest rises and falls, and a trace of color appears in her cheeks.

Her eyes brighten, her pupils enlarging.

Yes. This is what she wants.

To cede control.

She wants a way out.

She's had enough.

She's weary. She's mine.

"Kneel," I whisper, for her ears only.

She drops to her knees like the natural submissive she is. Immediate. Unquestioning. Her head bowed. The gun falls from her hand and skids across the wooden floor with a clatter that breaks the silence around us.

Behind me I hear Taylor breathe a sigh of relief.

And it's echoed in mine.

Oh, thank God.

Slowly I move toward her and pick up the gun, slipping it into my jacket pocket.

Now that she's no longer an immediate threat, I need to get Ana out of the apartment and away from her. Deep down I know I will never forgive Leila for this. I know she's unwell—broken, even. But to threaten Ana?

Unforgivable.

I stand over Leila, putting myself between her and Ana. Still not taking my eyes off Leila as she kneels with quiet grace on the floor.

"Anastasia, go with Taylor," I say.

"Ethan?" she whispers, and there's a tremor in her voice.

"Downstairs," I inform her.

Taylor is waiting for Ana, who doesn't move.

Please, Ana. Go.

"Anastasia," I prompt.

Go.

She remains rooted to the floor.

I step beside Leila—and still Ana won't move. "For the love of God, Anastasia, will you do as you're told for once in your life and go!" Our eyes lock and I implore her to leave. I can't do this with her here. I don't know how stable Leila is; she needs help, and she might hurt Ana.

I try to convey this to Ana with my beseeching look.

But she's ashen. She's in shock.

Shit. She's had a fright, Grey. She can't move.

"Taylor. Take Miss Steele downstairs. Now."

Taylor nods and makes a move to Ana.

"Why?" Ana whispers.

"Go. Back to the apartment. I need to be alone with Leila."

Please. I need you out of harm's way.

She looks from me to Leila.

Ana. Go. Please. I need to take care of this problem.

"Miss Steele. Ana." Taylor holds his hand out to Anastasia.

"Taylor," I urge. Without hesitation, he scoops Ana into his arms and leaves the apartment.

Thank fuck.

I let out a deep breath and caress Leila's filthy, matted hair as the door to the apartment closes.

We are on our own.

I step back. "Get up."

Awkwardly, Leila rises to her feet, but her eyes remain on the floor.

"Look at me," I whisper.

Slowly, she lifts her head, and her pain is visible on her face. Tears spring to her eyes and start to trickle down her cheeks.

"Oh, Leila," I whisper, and I embrace her.

Fuck.

The smell.

She stinks of poverty and neglect and homelessness.

And I'm back in a small, badly lit apartment above a cheap liquor store in Detroit.

She smells of him.

His boots.

His unwashed body.

His squalor.

Saliva pools in my mouth and I gag. Once. It's hard to bear.

Hell.

But she doesn't notice. I hold her as she weeps and weeps and weeps, snot-sobbing all over my jacket.

I hold her.

Trying not to retch.

Trying to banish the stench.

A stench so achingly familiar. And so unwelcome.

"Hush," I whisper. "Hush."

When she's gasping for air and her body is racked with dry sobs, I release her. "You need a bath."

Taking her hand, I lead her to Kate's bedroom and the en suite. It's roomy like Ana said. There's a shower, a bath, and a selection of expensive toiletries on display. I shut the door and I'm tempted to lock it; I don't want her to run. But she stands, meek and quiet, as she shudders with each dry sob. "It's okay," I murmur. "I'm here."

I turn on the faucet and hot water buckets into the spacious bath. I squirt some bath oil into the cascade, and soon the stifling fragrance of lilies is overcoming Leila's stench.

She begins to shiver.

"Do you want a bath?" I ask.

She looks down at the foaming suds and then at me. She nods.

"Can I take off your coat?"

She nods once more. And using only the tips of my fingers, I peel it from her body. It's beyond salvation. It'll need burning.

Beneath, her clothes hang off her. She's wearing a grubby pink blouse and a pair of grungy slacks of an indeterminate color. They're also beyond rescue. Around her wrist is a tattered, soiled bandage.

"These clothes, they need to come off. Okay?"

She nods.

"Arms up."

Dutifully she complies, and I pull off her blouse and try not to register my shock at her appearance. She's emaciated, all jutting bones and pointed angles, a sharp contrast to the Leila of old. It's sickening.

This is my fault; I should have found her earlier.

I tug down her slacks.

"Step out." I hold her hand.

She does, and I add her slacks to the pile of rags.

She's shaking.

"Hey. It's okay. We're going to get you some help. Okay?"

She nods but remains impassive.

I take her hand and undo the bandage. I think it should have been changed; the smell is putrid. I retch but don't vomit. The scar on her wrist is livid but miraculously looks clean. I discard the bandage and dressing.

"You'll need to take those off." I'm referring to her grubby underwear. She looks at me. "No. You do it," I say and turn around to give her a modicum of privacy. I hear her move, a scraping of her flats on the bathroom floor, and when she stops I turn around and she's naked.

Gone are her lush curves.

She must not have eaten for weeks.

It's galling.

"Here." I give her my hand, which she takes, and with the other I test the temperature of the water. It's hot but not too hot.

"Get in."

She steps into the bath and slowly sinks into the foaming, fragrant water. I strip off my jacket, roll up the sleeves of my shirt and sit down on the floor beside the bath. She turns her small, sad face toward me but remains mute.

I reach across for the body wash and a nylon scrubber that Kavanagh must use. Well, she won't miss it—I spy another on the shelf.

"Hand," I say. Leila gives me her hand, and methodically and gently I start to wash her.

She's grimy. She hasn't washed for weeks, it seems. There's grime. Everywhere.

How does someone get this dirty?

"Lift your chin up."

I scrub under her neck and down her other arm, leaving her skin clean and a little pinker. I wash her torso and her back.

"Lie down."

She lies down in the bath and I wash her feet and her legs in turn.

"Do you want me to wash your hair?"

She nods. And I reach for the shampoo.

I've bathed her before. Several times. Usually as a reward for her behavior in the playroom. It was always a pleasure.

This, not so much.

I make brisk work of her hair and use the handheld shower to rinse out the suds.

By the time I'm finished, she looks a little better.

I sit back on my heels.

"Long time since you did this," she says. Her voice low and bleak, devoid of all emotion.

"I know." I reach over and pull the plug to empty the murky water. Standing, I reach for a large towel. "Up you go."

Leila stands, and I offer her my hand so that she can step out of the bath. I fold the towel around her and reach for a smaller one and towel-dry her hair.

She smells better, although in spite of the scented bath oil, the foul odor of her clothes still pervades the bathroom.

"Come." I take her out and leave her on the sofa in the sitting area. "Stay there."

Back in the bathroom, I grab my jacket and from the pocket extract my phone. I call Flynn's cell number. He answers immediately.

"Christian."

"I have Leila Williams."

"With you?"

"Yes. She's in a bad way."

"You're in Seattle?"

"Yes. In Ana's apartment." I give him Ana's address.

"I'll be right there."

I hang up, collect Leila's clothes, and head back to the living room.

Leila is sitting where I left her, staring at the wall.

I go through the kitchen drawers and find a trash bag. Checking the pockets of Leila's coat and the slacks, I find nothing but used tissues. I dump her clothes in the trash bag, knot it, and leave it by the front door.

"I'll find you some clean clothes."

"Her clothes?" Leila says.

"Clean clothes."

In Ana's room, I find some sweatpants and a plain T-shirt. I hope Ana doesn't mind, but I think Leila's need is greater.

She's still on the sofa when I return.

"Here. Put these on." I place the clothes beside her and move to the sink at the kitchen counter. I fill a glass with water and, once she's dressed, offer it to her.

She shakes her head.

"Leila, drink this."

She takes the glass and has a sip.

"And another. Just sips," I say.

She takes another sip.

"He's gone," she says, and her face contorts with pain and grief.

"I know. I'm sorry."

"He was like you."

"Was he?"

"Yes."

"I see."

Well, that explains why she sought me out.

"Why didn't you call me?" I sit down beside her.

She shakes her head and tears well in her eyes once more, but she doesn't answer my question.

"I've called a friend. He can help you. He's a doctor."

She's exhausted and remains impassive, but her tears trickle down her face, and I feel at a loss.

"I've been looking for you," I tell her.

She says nothing but starts shaking, violently.

Shit.

There's a throw on the armchair. I drape it over her shoulders. "Cold?"

She nods. "So cold." She snuggles into the blanket and I head back into Ana's room to find her hair dryer.

I plug it into the socket beside the sofa and sit down. I take a cushion and place it on the floor between my feet.

"Sit. Here."

Leila gets up slowly, pulls the blanket around her, and sinks onto the cushion between my legs, facing away from me.

The high-pitched whir of the hair dryer disrupts the silence between us as I gently dry her hair.

She sits quietly. Not touching me.

She knows she can't. She knows she's not allowed.

How many times have I dried her hair? Ten? Twelve times?

I can't remember the exact number so I concentrate on my task.

Once her hair is dry, I stop. And it's quiet in Ana's apartment again. Leila leans her head against my thigh, and I don't stop her.

"Do your folks know you're here?" I ask.

She shakes her head.

"Have you been in touch with them?"

"No," she whispers.

She was always close to her parents.

"They'll be worried about you."

She shrugs. "They're not speaking."

"To you? Why not?"

She doesn't answer.

"I'm sorry it didn't work out with your husband."

She says nothing, but there's a knock on the door.

"That'll be the doctor." I stand and go to open the door. Flynn enters, followed by a woman in scrubs.

"John, thanks for coming." I'm relieved to see him.

"Laura Flanagan, Christian Grey. Laura is our head nurse."

When I turn, Leila is now sitting on the sofa, still wrapped in the throw.

"This is Leila Williams," I say.

Flynn crouches down beside Leila. She gazes at him, her expression blank.

"Hello, Leila," he says. "I'm here to help you."

The nurse hovers in the background.

"Those are her clothes." I point to the trash bag by the front door. "They need burning."

The nurse nods and picks up the trash bag.

"Would you like to come with me to a place where we can help you?" Flynn asks Leila.

She says nothing, but her subdued brown eyes seek mine.

"I think you should go with the doctor. I'll come with you."

Flynn frowns but keeps his counsel.

Leila looks from me to him and nods.

Good.

"I'll take her," I tell Flynn and reach down and lift her into my arms. She weighs nothing. She closes her eyes and rests her head against my shoulder as I carry her down the stairs. Taylor is waiting for us.

"Mr. Grey, Ana's gone home—" he says.

"Let's talk about it later. I've left my jacket upstairs."

"I'll bring it."

"Can you lock up? The keys are in my jacket."

"Yes, sir."

Outside in the street I put Leila into Flynn's car and climb in beside her. I fasten her seat belt as Flynn and his colleague sit up front. Flynn starts the car and pulls out into the rush-hour traffic.

As I stare out the window, I hope Ana is back at Escala. Mrs. Jones will feed her, and when I get home she'll be there waiting for me. The thought is comforting.

FLYNN'S OFFICE AT THE private psychiatric clinic on the outskirts of Fremont is spartan compared to his office downtown: two sofas, one armchair. No fireplace. That's it.

I pace the length of the small room, waiting for him. I'm itching to get back to Ana. She must have been terrified. My phone has died, so I haven't been able to call her or Mrs. Jones to check on Ana's well-being. My watch says it's nearly eight. I glance out the window. Taylor is parked and waiting in the SUV. I just want to go home.

Back to Ana.

The door opens and Flynn enters. "I thought you'd have left by now," he says.

"I need to know she's okay."

"She's a sick young woman, but she's calm and cooperative. She wants help, and that's always a good sign. Please sit. I need a few details from you."

I sit down on the chair and he takes a seat on one of the couches.

"What happened today?"

I explain all that took place in Ana's apartment prior to his arrival.

"You gave her a bath?" he says, surprised.

"She was filthy. The stench was…" I stop and shudder.

"Okay. We can talk about that another time."

"Is she going to be okay?"

"I think so, though you can't medicate against grief. It's a natural process. But I'll dig a little deeper and find out what we're dealing with here."

"Anything she needs," I state.

"That's very generous of you, considering she's not really your problem."

"She came to me."

"She did," he acknowledges.

"I feel responsible."

"You shouldn't. I'll update you when I know more."

"Great. And thanks again."

"I'm just doing my job, Christian."

TAYLOR IS BROODING ON the way home. I know he's mad that Leila slipped through the cracks once more, in spite of the measures we have in place; Ana's apartment was swept by security this morning. I say nothing. I'm tired and anxious to get back to Escala. Ana's purse and cell phone are still in the car, and Taylor has informed me that she went home with Ethan. The thought is displeasing. So I picture her snuggled in the armchair in the library, asleep, a book in her lap. Alone.

I'm impatient. I want to get home to my girl.

AS WE PULL INTO the garage, Taylor reminds me, "We should review our security requirements now that Miss Williams has been found."

"Yes. I don't think we'll be needing the guys."

"I'll talk to Welch."

“Thanks.” He parks and I’m out of the car in an instant, headed right to the elevator. I don’t wait for him.

As soon as I step into my apartment, I sense Ana’s not home. My place has a ringing emptiness about it.

Where the hell is she?

Ryan is monitoring the CCTV. He looks up when I enter Taylor’s office.

“Mr. Grey?”

“Did Miss Steele come home?”

“No, sir.”

“Fuck.” I thought she might have been and gone. I turn and head for my study. She doesn’t have her purse or her phone? Why hasn’t she come home? Part of me wants to send the entire team combing the city looking for her. But where do I start?

I could call Kavanagh. Taylor says she left with him.

Shit. Ethan and Ana.

The idea does not sit well with me.

I don’t have his number. I contemplate calling Elliot to have him ask Kate for her brother’s number, but it’s after midnight in Barbados. With a frustrated sigh, I stare out at the city skyline. The sun is sinking into the sea off the Olympic Peninsula, reflecting the last of the light into my apartment. It’s ironic that all this week I’ve been looking at this view and wondering where Leila might be. Now I’m wondering about Ana. It’s getting dark. Where is she?

She’s left you, Grey.

No. I’m not willing to believe that.

Mrs. Jones knocks on the door.

“Mr. Grey?”

“Gail.”

“You found her.”

I frown. Ana?

“Miss Williams,” she clarifies.

“In a sense. She’s in the hospital, where she needs to be.”

“Good. Would you like something to eat?”

“No. Thanks. I’ll wait for Ana.”

She studies me for a moment. "I've made some mac and cheese. I'll leave it in the fridge."

Mac and cheese. My favorite.

"Okay. Thanks."

"I'm going to retire to my room now."

"Good night, Gail."

She gives me a sympathetic smile and leaves.

I check the time: 9:15.

Damn it. Ana. Come home.

Where is she?

Gone.

No.

I dismiss the thought and sit down at my desk and activate my computer. I have a few emails, but try as I might, I cannot concentrate. My concern for Ana is growing. Where is she?

She'll be back soon.

She will.

She has to come back.

I call Welch and leave a message that Leila has been found and is now getting the help she needs. I end the call and get up, unable to stay seated. It's been one hell of an evening.

Perhaps I should read.

In my bedroom, I pick up the book I've been reading and take it back into the living room. And wait. And wait.

Ten minutes later, I throw the book onto the sofa beside me.

I'm restless and the uncertainty of Ana's whereabouts is becoming unbearable.

I head into Taylor's office. He's there with Ryan.

"Mr. Grey."

"Can you send one of the guys to Ana's place? I want to check if she's returned to her apartment."

"Of course."

"Thanks."

I head back to the sofa and pick up my book again. I keep glancing at the elevator. But it remains quiet.

Empty.

Like me.

Empty except for my growing unease.

She's gone.

She's left you.

Leila frightened her off.

No. I can't believe that. It's not her style.

It's me. She's had enough.

Having said she'd move in, she's now reneged.

Fuck.

I get up and begin pacing. My phone buzzes. It's Taylor. Not Ana. I quash my disappointment and take the call. "Taylor."

"The apartment's empty, sir. No one here."

There's a ping. The elevator. I turn and Ana walks a little unsteadily into the living room.

"She's here," I snap at Taylor and hang up. Relief. Anger. Hurt. All combine in a rush of emotions that threaten to overwhelm me. "Where the fuck have you been?" I bark at her.

She blinks and steps back. She's flushed.

"Have you been drinking?" I ask.

"A bit."

"I told you to come back here. It's now a quarter after ten. I've been worried about you."

"I went for a drink or three with Ethan while you attended to your ex." She spits out the last word like venom.

Hell. She's mad.

She continues. "I didn't know how long you were going to be with her." She lifts up her chin with a look of righteous indignation.

What?

"Why do you say it like that?" I ask, confused by her response. Did she think I *wanted* to be with Leila?

Ana looks down and stares at the floor, avoiding eye contact.

She hasn't come completely into the room.

What's going on?

My anger subsides as anxiety ripples through my chest.

"Ana, what's wrong?"

"Where's Leila?" She looks around the room, her expression chilly.

"In a psychiatric hospital in Fremont." Where the hell does she *expect* Leila to be? "Ana, what is it?" I take a couple cautious steps toward her, but she stands her ground, distant and aloof, and doesn't reach for me.

"What's wrong?" I press her.

She shakes her head. "I'm no good for you," she says.

My scalp tingles, pricked by fear. "What? Why do you think that? How can you possibly think that?"

"I can't be everything you need."

"You are everything I need."

"Just seeing you with her—"

Christ. "Why do you do this to me? This is not about you, Ana. It's about her. Right now, she's a very sick girl."

"But I felt it. What you had together."

"What? No." I reach for her and she steps back, away from me, her cool eyes on mine, assessing me, and I don't think she likes what she sees… "You're running?" My anxiety rises, tightening my throat.

She looks away and her brow furrows, but she says nothing.

"You can't," I whisper.

"Christian, I—" She stops and I think she's struggling to say her goodbyes.

She's going. I knew it would happen. But so soon?

"No. No!" I'm on the edge of the abyss once more.

I can't breathe.

This is it, what I'd predicted from the beginning.

"I…" Ana mutters.

How do I stop her? I look around the room, for help. What can I do?

"You can't go. Ana, I love you!" It's my last-minute pitch to save this deal, to save us.

"I love you, too, Christian. It's just—"

The vortex is sucking me under.

She's had enough.

I've driven her away.

Again.

I feel dizzy. I put my hands on my head, trying to contain the pain that slices through me. My despair is carving a hole in my chest that gets bigger and bigger and bigger. It's going to take me down. "No. No."

Find your happy place.

My happy place.

When was it easier?

Easier to wear my pain on the outside.

Elena is standing over me. In her hands, she holds a thin cane. The welts on my back burn. Each throbbing with pain as my blood thrums through my body.

I'm on my knees. At her feet.

"More, Mistress."

Quiet the monster.

More. Mistress.

More.

Find your happy place, Grey.

Make your peace.

Peace. Yes.

No.

A tidal wave rises inside my body, crashing and breaking within me, but as it recedes it sucks the fear away.

You can do this.

I drop to my knees.

I take a deep breath and place my hands on my thighs.

Yes. Peace.

I'm in a landscape of calm.

I give myself to you. All of me. I'm yours to do with as you wish.

What will she do?

I look straight ahead, and I'm aware she's watching me. In the far distance, I hear her voice.

"Christian, what are you doing?"

I inhale slowly, filling my lungs. Fall is in the air. *Ana.*

"Christian! What are you doing?" The voice is closer, louder, more high-pitched.

"Christian, look at me!"

I look up. And wait.

She's beautiful. Pale. Worried.

"Christian, please, don't do this. I don't want this."

You must tell me what you want. I wait.

"Why are you doing this? Talk to me," she pleads.

"What would you like me to say?"

She gasps. It's a soft sound and it stirs memories of happier times with her. I shut those down. There is only now. Her cheeks are wet. Tears. She wrings her hands.

And suddenly she's on her knees, facing me.

Her eyes are on mine. The outer rings of her irises are indigo. They lighten toward the middle to the color of a cloudless summer sky. But her pupils are expanding, a deep black darkening each center.

"Christian, you don't have to do this. I'm not going to run. I've told you and told you and told you, I won't run. All that's happened. It's overwhelming. I just need some time to think. Some time to myself. Why do you always assume the worst?"

Because the worst happens.

Always.

"I was going to suggest going back to my apartment this evening. You never give me any time, time to just think things through."

She wants to be on her own.

Away from me.

"Just time to think," she continues. "We barely know each other, and all this baggage that comes with you. I need… I need time to think it through. And now that Leila is… well, whatever she is… she's off the streets and not a threat. I thought. I thought…"

What did you think, Ana?

"Seeing you with Leila…" She closes her eyes as if in pain. "It was such a shock. I had a glimpse into how your life has been… and…" She rips her gaze from mine and looks down at her knees. "This is about me not being good enough for you. It was an insight into your life, and I am so scared you'll get bored with me and then you'll go, and I'll end up like Leila, a shadow. Because I love you, Christian, and if you leave me, it will be like a world without light. I'll be in darkness. I don't want to run. I'm just so frightened you'll leave me."

She's scared of the darkness, too.

She's not going to run.

She loves me.

"I don't understand why you find me attractive," Ana whispers. "You're… Well, you're you and I'm—" She looks at me, troubled. "I just don't see it. You're beautiful and sexy and successful and good and kind and caring—all those things—and I'm not. And I can't do the things you like to do. I can't give you what you need. How could you be happy with me? How can I possibly hold you? I have never understood what you see in me. And seeing you with her, it brought all that home."

She raises her hand and wipes her nose, which is blotchy and pink from crying.

"Are you going to kneel here all night? Because I'll do it, too!"

She's mad at me.

She's always mad at me.

"Christian, please. Please. Talk to me."

Her lips would be soft. They are always soft after she's been crying. Her hair frames her face and my heart expands.

Could I love her any more?

She has all the qualities she says she doesn't. But it's her compassion I love most.

Her compassion for me.

Ana.

"Please," she says.

"I was so scared," I whisper. *I'm scared now.* "When I saw Ethan arrive outside, I knew someone had let you into your apartment. Both Taylor and I leapt out of the car. We knew, and to see her there like that with you—and armed. I think I died a thousand deaths, Ana. Someone threatening you. All my worst fears realized. I was so angry, with her, with you, with Taylor, with myself." I'm haunted by the vision of Leila and her gun. "I didn't know how volatile she would be. I didn't know what to do. I didn't know how she'd react." I stop, remembering Leila's surrender. "And then she gave me a clue; she looked so contrite. And I just knew what I had to do."

"Go on," Ana prompts.

"Seeing her in that state, knowing that I might have something to do with her mental breakdown—"

A memory from years ago surfaces, unwelcome—Leila smirking as she deliberately turned her back on me, knowing the consequences. "She was always so mischievous and lively. She might have harmed you. And it would have been my fault."

If anything happened to Ana…

"But she didn't," Ana says. "And you weren't responsible for her being in that state, Christian."

"I just wanted you gone. I wanted you away from the danger, and… You. Just. Wouldn't. Go." My exasperation returns and I glare at Ana. "Anastasia Steele, you are the most stubborn woman I know." I close my eyes and shake my head. What am I going to do with her?

If she stays.

She's still kneeling in front of me when I open my eyes.

"You weren't going to run?" I ask.

"No!" Now she sounds exasperated.

She's not leaving me. I take a deep breath. "I thought—" I stop. "This is me, Ana. All of me, and I'm all yours. What do I have to do to make you realize that? To make you see that I want you any way I can get you. That I love you."

"I love you, too, Christian, and to see you like this is—" She pauses as she chokes back tears. "I thought I'd broken you."

"Broken? Me? Oh no, Ana. Just the opposite."

You make me whole.

Reaching out, I take her hand in mine. "You're my lifeline," I whisper.

I need you.

I kiss each of her knuckles before pressing my palm against the palm of her hand.

How can I make her see what she means to me?

Let her touch me.

Touch me, Ana.

Yes. And before I overthink it, I take her hand and place it on my chest, over my heart.

I'm yours, Ana.

The darkness expands inside my rib cage and my breathing quickens. But I control my fear. I need her more. I drop my hand, leaving hers in place, and concentrate on her lovely face. Her compassion is there, reflected in her eyes.

I see it.

She flexes her fingers so I briefly feel her nails through my shirt. Then she removes her hand.

"No." My response is instinctive, and I press her hand to my chest. "Don't."

She looks bewildered, but then she shuffles closer so our knees are touching. She reaches up.

Shit. She's going to undress me.

And I'm filled with dread. I can't breathe. With one hand she awkwardly undoes the first button. She flexes the fingers trapped beneath my hand and I let her go. Using both hands, she makes light work of my buttons, and when she pulls open my shirt I gasp, and my breathing returns and starts to accelerate.

Her hand hovers over my chest. She wants to touch me. Skin to skin. Flesh to flesh. Reaching deep within myself and relying on years of control, I steel myself for her touch.

Ana hesitates.

"Yes." I whisper my encouragement and tilt my head to one side.

Her fingertips are featherlight on my sternum, stirring my chest hair. My fear rises in my throat, leaving a knot I can't swallow. Ana removes her hand, but I grab it, pressing it against my skin. "No, I need to." My voice is low and strained.

I must do this.

I'm doing it for her.

She flattens her palm on me, then traces a line with her

fingertips to my heart. Her fingers are gentle and warm, but they're searing my skin. Marking me. I'm hers. I want to give her my love and my trust.

I'm yours, Ana.

Whatever you want.

I'm aware I'm panting, dragging air into my lungs.

Ana shifts, her eyes darkening. She runs her fingers over me again and then places her hands on my knees and leans forward.

Fuck. I close my eyes. This will be hard to bear. I tilt my head up. Waiting. And I feel her lips, with acute tenderness, plant a kiss over my heart.

I groan.

It's excruciating. It's hell. But it's Ana, here, loving me.

"Again," I whisper.

She leans in and kisses me above my heart. I know what she's doing. I know where she's kissing me. She does it again, and then again. Her lips landing soft and gentle on each of my scars. I know where they are. I know where they've been since the day they were burned into my body. And here she is, doing what no one's ever done. Kissing me. Accepting me. Accepting this dark, dark side of me.

She's slaying my demons.

My brave girl.

My beautiful brave girl.

My face is wet. My vision is blurred. But I feel my way to her and pull her into my arms, my hands in her hair. I turn her face up to mine and claim her lips. Feeling her. Consuming her. Needing her. "Oh, Ana," I whisper in veneration as I worship her mouth. I pull her down onto the floor and she cups my face and I don't know if the wet is from her tears or mine.

"Christian, please don't cry. I meant it when I said I'd never leave you. I did. If I gave you any other impression, I'm so sorry. Please, please forgive me. I love you. I will always love you."

I look down at her, trying to accept what she's just said.

She says she loves me, that she will always love me.

But she doesn't know me.

She doesn't know the monster.

The monster is not worthy of her love.

"What is it?" she says. "What is this secret that makes you think I'll run for the hills? That makes you so determined to believe I'll go? Tell me, Christian, please?"

She has a right to know. As long as we are together, this will always be an obstacle between us. She deserves the truth. Against my better judgment, I have to tell her.

I sit up and cross my legs and she sits up, too, staring at me. Her eyes are round and fearful, reflecting my feelings exactly.

"Ana." I pause and take a deep breath.

Tell her, Grey.

Get it out. Then you'll know.

"I'm a sadist, Ana. I like to whip little brown-haired girls like you because you all look like the crack whore—my birth mother. I'm sure you can guess why." The words tumble out of my mouth in a rush like they've been ready and waiting for days.

She remains impassive. Still. Quiet.

Please, Ana.

Finally, she speaks, and her voice is a frail whisper. "You said you weren't a sadist."

"No, I said I was a Dominant. If I lied to you, it was a lie of omission. I'm sorry." I can't look at her. I'm ashamed. I stare down at my fingers. Like she does. But she remains mute, so I'm forced to look at her. "When you asked me that question, I had envisioned a very different relationship between us," I add.

It's the truth.

Ana's eyes widen, and suddenly she covers her face with her hands. She can't bear to look at me.

"So it's true," she whispers, and when she removes her hands, her face is alabaster. "I can't give you what you need."

What? "No, no, no. Ana. No. You can. You do give me what I need. Please believe me."

"I don't know what to believe, Christian. This is so fucked up." Her voice is choked with emotion.

"Ana, believe me. After I punished you and you left me, my

worldview changed. I wasn't joking when I said I would avoid ever feeling like that again. When you said you loved me, it was a revelation. No one's ever said it to me before, and it was as if I'd laid something to rest—or maybe you'd laid it to rest, I don't know. Dr. Flynn and I are still in deep discussion about it."

"What does that all mean?"

"It means I don't need it. Not now."

"How do you know? How can you be so sure?"

"I just know. The thought of hurting you in any real way, it's abhorrent to me."

"I don't understand. What about rulers and spanking and all that kinky fuckery?"

"I'm talking about the heavy shit, Anastasia. You should see what I can do with a cane or a cat."

"I'd rather not."

"I know. If you wanted to do that, then fine, but you don't and I get it. I can't do all that shit with you if you don't want to. I told you once before, you have all the power. And now, since you came back, I don't feel that compulsion at all."

"When we met, that's what you wanted, though?"

"Yes, undoubtedly."

"How can your compulsion just go, Christian? Like I'm some kind of panacea, and you're—for want of a better word—cured? I don't get it."

"I wouldn't say 'cured.' You don't believe me?"

"I just find it…unbelievable. Which is different."

"If you'd never left me, then I probably wouldn't feel this way. Your walking out on me was the best thing you ever did for us. It made me realize how much I want you, just you, and I mean it when I say I'll take you any way I can have you."

She stares at me. Impassive? Confused? I don't know.

"You're still here. I thought you would be out the door by now."

"Why? Because I might think you're a sicko for whipping and fucking women who look like your mother? Whatever would give you that impression?" she snaps.

Fuck.

Ana has her claws out, and she's sinking them into me.

But I deserve it. "Well, I wouldn't have put it quite like that, but yes."

She's angry maybe? Hurt, possibly? She knows my secret. My dark, dark secret. And now I await her verdict.

Love me.

Or leave me.

She closes her eyes. "Christian, I'm exhausted. Can we discuss this tomorrow? I want to go to bed."

"You're not going?" I can't believe it.

"Do you want me to go?"

"No! I thought you would leave once you knew."

Her expression is softer, but she still looks confounded.

Please don't go, Ana.

Life will be unbearable if you go.

"Don't leave me," I whisper.

"Oh, for crying out loud—no!" she shouts, startling me. "I am not going to go!"

"Really?" Unbelievable. She astonishes me, even now.

"What can I do to make you understand I will not run? What can I say?" She's exasperated.

And to my surprise an idea springs to mind. An idea so wild and out of my comfort zone that I wonder where it came from. I swallow. "There is one thing you can do."

"What?" she snaps.

"Marry me."

Her mouth drops open, and she gapes at me.

Marriage, Grey? Have you taken leave of your senses?

Why would she want to marry you?

She's stunned but then her lips part and she giggles. She bites her lip—I think it's to try to stop herself. But she fails. She flops down on the floor and her giggling turns to peals of laughter that echo through my living room.

This is not the reaction I was expecting.

Her laughter becomes hysterical. She drapes her hand across her face and I think she might be sobbing.

I don't know what to do.

Gently I lift her arm off her face and wipe her tears with the backs of my knuckles. I try for something light. "You find my proposal amusing, Miss Steele?"

She sniffles and, reaching up, caresses my cheek.

Again, not what I expected.

"Mr. Grey," she whispers. "Christian. Your sense of timing is without doubt..." She stops, her eyes searching mine as if I'm a crazy fool. And maybe I am, but I need to know her answer.

"You're cutting me to the quick here, Ana. Will you marry me?"

Slowly she sits up and places her hands on my knees. "Christian, I've met your psycho ex with a gun, been thrown out of my apartment, had you go thermonuclear Fifty on me—"

Fifty?

I open my mouth to plead my case, but she holds up her hand to stop me, so I remain mute.

"You've just revealed some quite frankly shocking information about yourself, and now you've asked me to marry you."

"Yes, I think that's a fair and accurate summary of the situation."

"Whatever happened to delayed gratification?" she asks, confounding me once more.

"I got over it, and I'm now a firm advocate of instant gratification. Carpe diem, Ana."

"Look, Christian, I've known you for about three minutes, and there's so much more I need to know. I've had too much to drink, I'm hungry, I'm tired, and I want to go to bed. I need to consider your proposal just as I considered that contract you gave me. And"—she pauses and purses her lips—"that wasn't the most romantic proposal."

Hope stirs in my chest. "Fair point well made, as ever, Miss Steele. So, that's not a no?"

She sighs. "No, Mr. Grey, it's not a no, but it's not a yes, either. You're only doing this because you're scared and you don't trust me."

"No, I'm doing this because I've finally met someone I want to spend the rest of my life with. I never thought that would happen to me."

And that's the truth, Ana.

I love you.

"Can I think about it, please? And think about everything else that's happened today? What you've just told me? You asked for patience and faith. Well, back at you, Grey. I need those now."

Faith and patience.

I lean forward and smooth a wayward lock behind her ear. I would wait an eternity for her answer, if it meant she wouldn't leave me.

"I can live with that." Leaning forward again, I give her a swift kiss.

She doesn't recoil.

And I feel a brief sense of relief. "Not very romantic, eh?"

She shakes her head, her expression solemn.

"Hearts and flowers?" I ask.

She nods and I give her a smile.

"You're hungry?"

"Yes."

"You didn't eat."

"No, I didn't eat," she says without rancor and sits back on her heels. "Being thrown out of my apartment after witnessing my boyfriend interacting intimately with his ex-submissive considerably suppressed my appetite." She places her hands on her hips.

I get to my feet, still amazed that she's here. I hold out my hand. "Let me fix you something to eat."

"Can't I just go to bed?" She puts her hand in mine and I help her to her feet.

"No, you need to eat. Come."

I lead her a few feet to a barstool, and once she's seated I explore the fridge.

"Christian, I'm really not hungry."

I ignore her as I look through the contents of the fridge. "Cheese?" I offer.

"Not at this hour."

"Pretzels?"

"In the fridge? No," she says.

"You don't like pretzels?"

"Not at eleven thirty. Christian, I'm going to bed. You can rummage around in your refrigerator for the rest of the night if you want. I'm tired, and I've had far too interesting a day. A day I'd like to forget." She slides off the stool just as I find the dish Mrs. Jones prepared earlier this evening.

"Macaroni and cheese?" I hold it up.

Ana gives me a sideways look. "You like macaroni and cheese?" she asks.

Like? I love mac and cheese. "You want some?" I try to tempt her.

Her smile says all she needs to say.

I pop the bowl into the microwave and press heat.

"So, you know how to use the microwave, then?" Ana teases. She's back on the barstool.

"If it's in a packet, I can usually do something with it. It's real food I have a problem with."

I set up two place mats, plates, and cutlery.

"It's very late," Ana says.

"Don't go to work tomorrow."

"I have to go to work tomorrow. My boss is leaving for New York."

"Do you want to go there this weekend?"

"I checked the weather forecast, and it looks like rain," she says.

"Oh, so what do you want to do?"

The microwave pings. Our supper is ready.

"I just want to get through one day at a time right now. All this excitement is…tiring."

Using a cloth, I remove the steaming bowl from the microwave and place it on the kitchen counter. It smells delicious, and I'm pleased that my appetite has returned. Ana dishes a spoonful onto each plate as I take my seat.

It's staggering that she's still with me, in spite of all I've told her. She's so… strong. She never disappoints. Even when facing Leila, she kept her cool.

She takes a bite of her food, as do I. It's exactly how I like it.

"Sorry about Leila," I mutter.

"Why are you sorry?"

"It must have been a terrible shock for you, finding her in your apartment. Taylor swept through it earlier himself. He's very upset."

"I don't blame Taylor."

"Neither do I. He's been out looking for you."

"Really? Why?"

"I didn't know where you were. You left your purse, your phone. I couldn't even track you. Where did you go?"

"Ethan and I just went to a bar across the street. So I could watch what was happening."

"I see."

"So, what did you do with Leila in the apartment?"

"You really want to know?" I ask.

"Yes," she replies but in a tone that makes me think she's not sure. I hesitate, but she glances at me once more and I have to be honest. "We talked, and I gave her a bath. And I dressed her in some of your clothes. I hope you don't mind. But she was filthy."

Ana remains mute and turns away from me. My appetite vanishes.

Shit. I shouldn't have told her.

"It was all I could do, Ana," I try to explain.

"You still have feelings for her?"

"No!" I close my eyes as a vision of Leila, sad and waiflike, comes to mind. "To see her like that—so different, so broken. I care about her, one human being to another." I let go of the image and turn to Ana.

"Ana, look at me."

She stares at her untouched food.

"Ana."

"What?" she whispers.

"Don't. It doesn't mean anything. It was like caring for a child, a broken, shattered child."

She closes her eyes, and for a horrid moment I think she's going to burst into tears.

"Ana?"

She stands, takes her plate to the sink, and scrapes the contents so they fall into the garbage disposal.

"Ana, please."

"Just stop, Christian! Just stop with the 'Ana, please'!" she shouts with exasperation and starts to cry. "I've had enough of all this shit today. I'm going to bed. I'm tired and emotional. Now let me be." She storms out of the kitchen toward the bedroom, leaving me with cooling, congealing macaroni and cheese.

Shit.

WEDNESDAY, JUNE 15, 2011

I put my head in my hands and rub my face. I can't believe I asked Ana to marry me. And she didn't say no. But she didn't say yes, either. She may never say yes.

In the morning, she'll wake and come to her senses.

The day started so well. But it's been a train wreck since this evening, since Leila.

Well, at least *she's* safe and getting the help she needs.

But at what cost? *Ana?*

She now knows everything.

She knows I'm a monster.

But she's still here.

Focus on the positive, Grey.

My appetite has gone the same way as Ana's, and I'm exhausted. It's been an emotional evening. I get up from the kitchen counter. I've experienced more in the last half hour than I would have thought possible.

This is what she does to you, Grey. She makes you feel.

You know you're alive when you're with her.

I can't lose her. I've only just found her.

Confused and overwhelmed, I deposit my plate in the sink and head to my bedroom.

It will be *our* bedroom if she says yes.

Outside the bathroom, I hear a stifled noise. She's weeping. I open the door and she's on the floor, curled up in the fetal position, wearing one of my T-shirts and sobbing. The sight of her in such despair is like a swift kick to my gut that leaves me breathless. It's intolerable.

I crawl onto the floor. "Hey," I murmur as I pull her into my lap. "Please don't cry, Ana, please." She snakes her arms around me and clings to me, but her crying shows no sign of abating.

Oh, baby.

Gently I stroke her back, thinking about how much more her tears affect me than Leila's did.

Because I love her.

She's brave and strong. And this is how I reward her, by making her cry.

"I'm sorry, baby," I whisper, holding her, and I start to rock to and fro as she weeps. I kiss her hair. Eventually, her crying subsides and she shudders, racked with dry sobs. I stand with her in my arms, carry her to the bedroom, and lay her down on the bed. She yawns and closes her eyes while I strip out of my pants and shirt. Leaving my underwear on, I slip into a T-shirt and switch off the lights. In bed, I hold her close. Within seconds, her breathing deepens and I know she's asleep. She's exhausted, too. I dare not move for fear of waking her. She needs sleep.

In the dark I try to make some sense of all that has occurred this evening. So much has happened. Too much, too much…

Leila stands before me. She's a waif and her stench makes me take a step back.

The stench. No.

The stench.

He smells. He smells of nasty. And dirt. It makes sick come into my mouth.

He's mad. I hide under the table. *There you are, you little prick.*

He has cigarettes.

No. I call my mommy. But she doesn't hear me. She lies on the floor.

Smoke comes out of his mouth.

He laughs.

And he holds my hair.

The burn. I scream.

I don't like the burn.

Mommy is on the floor. I sleep beside her. She is cold. I cover her with my blankie.

He's back. He's mad.

Crazy. Stupid. Bitch.

Get out of my way, you stupid fucking runt. He hits me and I fall.

He goes. He locks the door. And it's Mommy and me.

And then she's gone. Where is Mommy? Where is Mommy?

He holds the cigarette in front of me.

No.

He takes a puff.

No.

He presses it against my skin.

No.

The pain. The smell.

No.

"Christian!"

My eyes flick open. There's light. *Where am I?* My bedroom. Ana's out of bed, holding my shoulders, shaking me.

"You left, you left, you must have left," I mumble incoherently.

She sits down beside me. "I'm here," she says and lays her palm on my cheek.

"You were gone."

I only have nightmares when you're not here.

"I just went for a drink. I was thirsty."

Closing my eyes, I rub my face, trying to separate fact from fiction. She hasn't left. She's looking down at me: kind, kind Ana. My girl. "You're here. Oh, thank God." I pull her down beside me on the bed.

"I just went to get a drink," she says as I wrap my arms around her. She strokes my hair and my cheek. "Christian, please. I'm here. I'm not going anywhere."

"Oh, Ana." My mouth claims hers. She tastes of orange juice… sweetness and home.

My body responds as I kiss her, her ear, her throat. I tug her bottom lip with my teeth as I caress her body. My hand pushing up the T-shirt she's wearing. She trembles as I cup her breast and she moans into my mouth as my fingers find her nipple. "I want you," I whisper.

I need you.

"I'm here for you. Only you, Christian."

Her words light a fire inside me. I kiss her again.

Please never leave me.

She grabs my T-shirt and I move so she can pull it off. I pull her upright while kneeling between her legs and drag off her T-shirt. She looks up at me, her eyes dark and full of hunger and longing. Holding her face, I kiss her, and we sink onto the mattress. Her fingers tangle in my hair as she kisses me back, matching my fervor. Her tongue in my mouth, eager to please.

Oh, Ana.

Suddenly, she pulls back and pushes against my arms. "Christian. Stop. I can't do this."

"What? What's wrong?" I murmur against her throat.

"No, please. I can't do this, not now. I need some time, please..."

"Oh, Ana, don't overthink this," I whisper as my anxiety returns. I'm fully awake. She's rejecting me.

No.

I'm desperate.

I tug her earlobe with my teeth and her body bows under my touch and she gasps. "I'm just the same, Ana. I love you and I need you. Touch me. Please." I stop and rub my nose against hers and stare down at her, holding my weight on my arms as I wait for her response.

Our relationship rests on this moment.

If she can't do this...

If she can't touch me.

If I can't have her.

I wait.

Please, Ana.

Tentatively, she reaches up and places her hands on my chest.

Heat and pain spiral across my chest as the darkness unleashes its claws. I gasp and close my eyes.

I can do this.

I can do this for her.

My girl.

Ana.

She runs her hands up to my shoulder, her fingertips scalding my skin. I groan. I want this so much and I dread it so much.

To dread your lover's touch.

What kind of fuckup am I?

She pulls me down to her and moves her hands to my back, holding me. Her palms on my flesh. Branding me. My strangled cry is half groan, half sob. I bury my face in her neck, hiding, seeking solace from the pain but kissing her, loving her, as her fingers cross the two scars on my back.

It's almost unbearable.

I kiss her feverishly, losing myself in her tongue and her mouth as I fight my demons, using only my lips and my hands. They skim over her body while her hands move over mine.

The darkness is swirling, trying to dislodge her, but Ana's fingers are on me. Caressing me. Feeling me. Gentle. Loving. And I steel myself against my fear and the pain.

I trail my lips down to her breasts and close them around one nipple, tugging until it's hard and standing at attention. She groans as her body rises to meet mine and she scrapes her fingernails across the muscles on my back. It's too much. Fear erupts in my chest, hammering my heart. "Oh, fuck, Ana," I cry out and stare down at her. She's panting, eyes bright and brimming with sensuality.

This is turning her on.

Fuck.

Don't overthink this, Grey.

Man up. Go with it.

Taking a deep breath to slow my pounding heart, I skate my hand down her body, over her belly, to her labia. I cup her and my fingers are wet with her anticipation. Easing them inside her, I circle them and she pushes her pelvis up to meet my hand.

"Ana." Her name is an invocation. I release her and sit up, and her hands fall away so she's no longer touching me. I feel relieved and bereft at once. I remove my boxers, freeing my cock, and lean over to the bedside table for a condom. I hand it to her. "You want to do this? You can still say no. You can always say no."

"Don't give me a chance to think, Christian." She's breathless. "I want you, too." She rips open the foil with her teeth and slowly, with trembling fingers, slides it onto me.

Her fingers on my erection are torture. "Steady. You are going to unman me, Ana."

She gives me a quick, possessive smile, and when she's done I stretch over her. But I need to know she wants this, too. I roll us both over, quickly.

"You, take me," I whisper, staring up at her.

She licks her lips and sinks down on me, taking me inch by inch.

"Ah." I tilt my head back and close my eyes.

I'm yours, Ana.

She grabs my hands and starts to move, up and down.

Oh, baby.

Leaning forward, she kisses my chin and runs her teeth over my jaw.

I'm going to come.

Shit.

I still her with my hands on her hips.

Slow, baby. Please, let's take this slow.

Her eyes are full of passion and excitement.

And I steel myself once more. "Ana, touch me, please."

Her eyes widen with sheer delight and she spreads her hands on my chest. It's blistering. I cry out and thrust deep inside her.

"Ah," she whimpers, and her fingernails trail through my chest hair. Tantalizing me. Teasing me. But the darkness is pushing at each point of contact, determined to rupture my skin. It's so painful, so intense, tears spring to my eyes, and Ana's face blurs in a watery vision.

I twist so she's underneath me. "Enough. No more, please."

She reaches up and clasps my face in her hands, wiping my tears, then pulling me down so her lips are on mine. I drive into her. Trying to find my equilibrium, but I'm lost. Lost to this woman. Her breath is at my ear. Short. Panting. She's reaching. She's close. But she's holding back.

"Let go, Ana," I whisper.

"No."

"Yes," I plead, and I shift and roll my hips, filling her.

She moans, loud and clear, her legs tensing.

"Come on, baby, I need this. Give it to me."

We need this.

She lets go, convulsing around me and crying out while she wraps her arms and legs around my body and I find my release.

HER FINGERS ARE IN my hair while my head rests on her chest. She's here. She didn't leave. But I can't shake the feeling that I nearly lost her again. "Don't ever leave me," I whisper. Above me, I feel her move her head, her chin lifting in that mulish way she has. "I know you're rolling your eyes at me," I add, pleased that she's doing so.

"You know me well." There's humor in her tone.

Thank God.

"I'd like to know you better."

"Back at you, Grey," she says and asks me what torments me when I sleep.

"The usual."

She insists I tell her more.

Oh, Ana, do you really want to know?

She remains silent. Waiting.

I sigh.

"I must be about three, and the crack whore's pimp is mad as hell again. He smokes and smokes, one cigarette after another, and he can't find an ashtray."

Does she really want this shit in her head? The burn. The smell. The screaming.

She tenses beneath me.

"It hurt," I mutter. "It's the pain I remember. That's what gives me nightmares. That, and the fact that she did nothing to stop him."

Ana's hold on me tightens.

I lift my head, meeting her eyes. "You're not like her. Don't ever think that. Please."

She blinks a couple of times and I lay my head on her chest again.

The crack whore was weak. *No, Maggot. Not now.*

She killed herself. Abandoning me.

"Sometimes in the dreams she's just lying on the floor. And I think she's asleep. But she doesn't move. She never moves. And I'm hungry. Really hungry. There's a loud noise and he's back, and he hits me so hard, cursing the crack whore. His first reaction was always to use his fists or his belt."

"Is that why you don't like to be touched?"

I close my eyes and hold her tighter. "That's complicated." I nuzzle the space between her breasts, surrounding myself with her essence.

"Tell me," she asks.

"She didn't love me." She can't have loved me. She didn't protect me. And she left me. Alone. "I didn't love me. The only touch I knew was… harsh. It stemmed from there."

I never had a mother's loving touch, Ana.

Never.

Grace respected my boundaries.

I still don't know why.

"Flynn explains it better than I can."

"Can I see Flynn?" she asks.

"Fifty Shades rubbing off on you?" I try to lighten the mood.

"And then some." Ana squirms. "I like how it's rubbing off right now."

I love her levity, and if she can joke about this, there's hope. "Yes, Miss Steele, I like that, too." I kiss her and stare into the warm depths of her eyes. "You're so precious to me, Ana. I was serious about marrying you. We can get to know each other then. I can look after you. You can look after me. We can have kids if you want. I will lay my world at your feet, Anastasia. I want you, body and soul, forever. Please think about it."

"I will think about it, Christian. I will. I'd really like to talk to Dr. Flynn, though, if you don't mind."

"Anything for you, baby. Anything. When would you like to see him?"

"Sooner rather than later."

"Okay. I'll make the arrangements in the morning." I glance at the clock: 3:44. "It's late. We should sleep." I switch off the light and pull her to me so we're spooning. I only spoon with Ana. I nuzzle her neck. "I love you, Ana Steele, and I want you by my side, always. Now go to sleep."

I'M WOKEN BY A commotion. Ana is leaping over me and onto the floor and heading for the bathroom.

She's leaving?

No.

I check the time.

Shit. It's late. I think this is the latest I've ever slept. She's going to work. Shaking my head, I call Taylor through the internal phone system.

"Good morning, Mr. Grey."

"Taylor, good morning. Could you take Miss Steele to work today?"

"With pleasure, sir."

"She's rather late."

"I'll wait for her outside the front door."

"Great."

"Come back for me."

"Will do, sir."

I sit up, and Ana hurries out of the bathroom, drying herself and gathering her clothes at the same time. It's quite the floor show, especially when she dons a pair of black lace panties and a matching lace bra.

Yes. I could watch this all day.

"You look good. You can call in sick, you know," I offer.

"No, Christian, I can't. I am not a megalomaniac CEO with a beautiful smile who can come and go as he pleases."

Beautiful smile? Megalomaniac? I grin. "I like to come as I please."

"Christian!" she sputters and throws the towel at me.

I laugh. She's still here and I don't think she hates me. "Beautiful smile, huh?"

"Yes. You know the effect you have on me." She wraps her watch strap around her wrist and stops to fasten it.

"Do I?"

"Yes, you do. The same effect you have on all women. Gets really tiresome, watching them all swoon."

"Does it?" I can't hide my amusement.

"Don't play the innocent, Mr. Grey. It really doesn't suit you." She yanks her hair up into a ponytail and puts on a pair of high-heeled shoes.

Baby's in black. She looks sensational.

She bends down to kiss me goodbye and I can't resist. I pull her down onto the bed.

Thank you for still being here, Ana.

"What can I do to tempt you to stay?" I whisper.

"You can't," she grumbles and makes a feeble effort to fight me off. "Let me go."

I pout and she grins. Outlining my lips with her finger, she smiles, leans up, and kisses me.

I close my eyes and enjoy the feel of her lips on mine before I release her. She needs to go. "Taylor will take you. Quicker than finding somewhere to park. He's waiting outside the building."

"Okay. Thank you," she says. "Enjoy your lazy morning, Mr. Grey. I wish I could stay, but the man who owns the company I work for would not approve of his staff ditching just for hot sex." She picks up her purse.

"Personally, Miss Steele, I have no doubt that he would approve. In fact, he might insist on it."

"Why are you staying in bed? It's not like you."

Crossing my hands behind my head, I lean back and give her a broad smile. "Because I can, Miss Steele."

She shakes her head in mock disgust. "Laters, baby." She blows me a kiss and hurries out the door. I hear her footsteps clatter down the hallway and then all is quiet.

Ana's left for the day.

And I miss her already.

I grab my phone with the intention of writing an email to her. But what should I say? I told her so much last night—I don't want to frighten her off with any more… revelations.

Keep it simple, Grey.

From: Christian Grey
Subject: Missing you
Date: June 15 2011 09:05
To: Anastasia Steele

Please use your BlackBerry.

x

Christian Grey
CEO, Grey Enterprises Holdings, Inc.

I look around my bedroom and ponder how empty it feels without her. I type an email to her personal account. I need to make sure she's using her phone, because I don't want anyone at SIP reading our emails.

From: Christian Grey
Subject: Missing you
Date: June 15 2011 09:06
To: Anastasia Steele

My bed is too big without you.

Looks like I'll have to go to work after all.

Even megalomaniac CEOs need something to do.

x

Christian Grey
Twiddling His Thumbs CEO, Grey Enterprises Holdings, Inc.

I hope that will elicit a smile. I press send, then call Flynn's office. I leave a message. If Ana wants to see Flynn, she should see Flynn. With that done, I climb out of bed and head into the bathroom. After all, I do have a meeting with the mayor today.

I'M RAVENOUS AFTER YESTERDAY evening's events. I never ate dinner. Mrs. Jones has prepared a full breakfast for me—eggs, bacon, ham, hash browns, waffles, and toast. Gail has gone to town; she's in her element. While I'm eating, I get a response from Ana. Her work email!

From: Anastasia Steele
Subject: All Right for Some
Date: June 15 2011 09:27
To: Christian Grey

My boss is mad.
I blame you for keeping me up late with your... shenanigans.
You should be ashamed of yourself.

Anastasia Steele
Assistant to Jack Hyde, Editor, SIP

Oh, Ana, I'm more ashamed of myself than you will ever know.

From: Christian Grey
Subject: Shenaniwhatigans?
Date: June 15 2011 09:32
To: Anastasia Steele

You don't have to work, Anastasia.

You have no idea how appalled I am at my shenanigans.

But I like keeping you up late ;)

Please use your BlackBerry.

Oh, and marry me, please.

Christian Grey
CEO, Grey Enterprises Holdings, Inc.

Mrs. Jones is hovering about in the background while I eat my breakfast.

"More coffee, Mr. Grey?"

"Please."

Ana's response comes through on my phone.

From: Anastasia Steele
Subject: Living to make
Date: June 15 2011 09:35
To: Christian Grey

I know your natural inclination is toward nagging, but just stop.

I need to talk to your shrink.
Only then will I give you my answer.
I am not opposed to living in sin.

Anastasia Steele
Assistant to Jack Hyde, Editor, SIP

For fuck's sake, Ana!

From: Christian Grey
Subject: BLACKBERRY
Date: June 15 2011 09:40
To: Anastasia Steele

Anastasia, if you are going to start discussing Dr. Flynn, then USE YOUR BLACKBERRY.

This is not a request.

Christian Grey
Now Pissed CEO, Grey Enterprises Holdings, Inc.

My phone rings, and it's Flynn's PA. He can see me tomorrow evening at 7:00. I ask her to have Flynn call me; I'll need to ask him about bringing Ana to the session.

"I'll see if I can schedule a call later."

"Thanks, Janet."

I also want to know how Leila is this morning.

I send another email to Ana's account. This time my tone is a little softer.

From: Christian Grey
Subject: Discretion
Date: June 15 2011 09:50
To: Anastasia Steele

Is the better part of valor.

Please use discretion… your work emails are monitored.

HOW MANY TIMES DO I HAVE TO TELL YOU THIS?

Yes. Shouty capitals as you say. USE YOUR BLACKBERRY.

Dr. Flynn can see us tomorrow evening.

x

Christian Grey
Still Pissed CEO, Grey Enterprises Holdings, Inc.

I hope that will please her.

"Two for dinner?" Gail asks.

"Yes, Mrs. Jones. Thanks."

I take a last swig of coffee and set my cup down. I like bantering with Ana over breakfast. If she marries me, she could be here every morning.

Marriage. A wife.

Grey, what were you thinking?

What changes will I need to make if she agrees to marry me? I get up and stroll to the bathroom. I stop by the stairway to the upper floor. On impulse, I head up the stairs to the playroom. Unlocking the door, I step inside.

My recent memory of this room is not a good one.

Well, you are one fucked-up son of a bitch.

Ana's words haunt me. A vision of her tearstained, anguished face comes to mind. I close my eyes. Suddenly I'm empty and aching, feeling a remorse so deep it cuts through sinew and bone. I never want to see her that unhappy again. Last night she was sobbing; she cried her heart out, but this time she let me comfort her. That's a huge difference from last time.

Isn't it?

I gaze around the room. What will become of it, I wonder?

I've had some amazing times in here…

Ana on the cross. Ana shackled to the bed. Ana on her knees.

I like your kinky fuckery.

I sigh and my phone buzzes. It's a text from Taylor. He's outside waiting for me. With a last lingering look at what was once my safe place, I shut the door.

MY MORNING IS UNEVENTFUL, but there's a certain excitement running through GEH. It's not often that I host delegations to the company, but the mayor's visit is causing a buzz throughout the building. I get through a few early meetings and all seems in place.

At 11:30, when I'm back in my office, Andrea puts Flynn through to me.

"John, thanks for calling me."

"I assumed you wanted to talk about Leila Williams, but I noticed that you're in my schedule and I'm seeing you tomorrow evening."

"I asked Ana to marry me."

John says nothing.

"You're surprised?" I ask.

"Frankly, no."

That's not what I expect him to say. But I let it go.

He continues. "Christian, you're impulsive. And you're in love. What did she say?"

"She wants to talk to you."

"She's not my patient, Christian."

"But I am, and I'm asking you."

He's silent for a moment. "Okay," he says eventually.

"Please, tell her whatever she wants to know."

"If that's what you wish."

"I do. How's Leila?"

"She had a comfortable night and was forthcoming this morning. I think I can help her."

"Good."

"Christian." He pauses. "Marriage is a serious commitment."

"I know."

"Are you sure that's what you want?"

It's my turn to pause. Spend the rest of my life with Ana… "Yes."

"It's not all rainbows and unicorns," John says. "It's hard work."

Rainbows? Unicorns? What the hell!

"I've never shied away from hard work, John."

John laughs. "That's true. I'll see you both tomorrow."

"Thanks."

MY PHONE BUZZES, AND it's another text from Elena.

> ELENA
>
> Can we do dinner?

Not at the moment, Elena. I just can't deal with her at this time. I press delete. It's after midday and I realize I've heard nothing more from Ana. I type a quick email.

From: Christian Grey
Subject: Crickets
Date: June 15 2011 12:15
To: Anastasia Steele

I haven't heard from you.

Please tell me you are okay.

You know how I worry.

I will send Taylor to check!

x

Christian Grey
Overanxious CEO, Grey Enterprises Holdings, Inc.

My next meeting is lunch with the mayor and his delegation. They want a tour of the building, and my PR guy is beside himself. Sam's all about raising the profile of the company, though sometimes I think it's about elevating his own profile.

Andrea knocks and opens the door. "Sam's here, Mr. Grey," she says.

"Show him in. Oh, can you update the contacts on my phone?"

"Sure." I hand her my phone and she stands aside to let Sam enter. He gives me a supercilious smile and starts a run-through of the various photo opportunities he's planned for the tour. Sam is a pretentious man and a recent hire I'm beginning to regret.

There's a knock on the door and Andrea pokes her head around. "I have Anastasia Steele on your phone. But I can't bring it to you—it's downloading your contacts, and I'm not brave enough to stop it mid-sync."

I leap up, ignoring Sam, and follow her to her desk. She hands me the phone, which is on such a short cable I have to bend over her computer.

"Are you okay?" I ask.

"Yes, I'm fine," Ana replies.

Thank goodness.

"Christian, why wouldn't I be okay?"

"You're normally so quick at responding to my emails. After what I told you yesterday, I was worried." I keep my voice low. I don't want Andrea or the new girl to hear me.

"Mr. Grey." Andrea is holding her phone to her neck and trying to get my attention. "The mayor and his delegation are in reception downstairs. Shall I ask them to come up?

"No, Andrea. Tell them to wait."

She looks stricken. "I think it's too late; they're on their way."

"No. I said wait."

Shit.

"Christian, you're obviously busy. I only called to let you know I'm okay, and I mean that, just very busy today. Jack has been cracking the whip. Er... I mean—" She stops.

What an interesting choice of words.

"Cracking the whip, eh? Well, there was a time when I would have called him a lucky man. Don't let him get on top of you, baby."

"Christian!" she scolds.

And I grin. I like shocking her. "Just watch him, that's all. Look, I'm glad you're okay. What time should I pick you up?"

"I'll email you."

"From your BlackBerry," I emphasize.

"Yes, Sir."

"Laters, baby."

"Bye."

I glance up and see the elevator is climbing to the executive floor. The mayor is on his way.

"Hang up," she says, and I hear the smile in her voice.

"I wish you'd never gone to work this morning."

"Me, too. But I am busy. Hang up."

"You hang up." I grin.

"We've been here before," she says in that teasing tone she has.

"You're biting your lip."

She inhales quickly.

"You see, you think I don't know you, Anastasia. But I know you better than you think."

"Christian, I'll talk to you later. Right now, I really wish I hadn't left this morning, too."

"I'll wait for your email, Miss Steele."

"Good day, Mr. Grey."

She hangs up as the elevator doors open.

BY 3:45 I'M BACK in my office. The mayor's visit has been a success and a PR windfall for GEH. Andrea buzzes me.

"Yes?"

"I have Mia Grey on the line for you."

"Put her through."

"Christian?"

"Hi."

"We're having a party for your birthday on Saturday and I want to invite Anastasia."

"Whatever happened to 'Hello? How are you?'"

Mia makes a dismissive noise. "Spare me one of your lectures, big brother."

"I'm busy on Saturday."

"Cancel it. It's happening."

"Mia!"

"No ifs or buts. What's Ana's number?"

I sigh and stay silent.

"Christian!" she shouts down the phone.

Jesus. "I'll text it to you."

"No bailing. You'll disappoint Mom and Dad and me and Elliot!"

I sigh. "Whatever, Mia."

"Great! See you then. Bye." She hangs up and I stare at the phone with frustrated amusement. My sister is a pain in the ass. I hate birthdays. Well, my birthday. Reluctantly, I text Mia Ana's number, knowing I'm unleashing the force that is my little sister on an unsuspecting victim.

I go back to reading a report.

When I finish, I check my email and there's one from Ana.

From: Anastasia Steele
Subject: Antediluvian
Date: June 15 2011 16:11
To: Christian Grey

Dear Mr. Grey

When, exactly, were you going to tell me?
What shall I get my old man for his birthday?
Perhaps some new batteries for his hearing aid?

A x

Anastasia Steele
Assistant to Jack Hyde, Editor, SIP

Mia is as good as her word. She hasn't wasted any time. I have some fun with my response.

From: Christian Grey
Subject: Prehistoric
Date: June 15 2011 16:20
To: Anastasia Steele

Don't mock the elderly.

Glad you are alive and kicking.

And that Mia has been in touch.

Batteries are always useful.

I don't like celebrating my birthday.

x

Christian Grey
Deaf as a Post CEO, Grey Enterprises Holdings, Inc.

From: Anastasia Steele
Subject: Hmmm.
Date: June 15 2011 16:24
To: Christian Grey

Dear Mr. Grey
I can imagine you pouting as you wrote that last sentence.
That does things to me.

A xox

Anastasia Steele
Assistant to Jack Hyde, Editor, SIP

Her reply makes me laugh out loud, but what do I have to do to make her use her phone?

From: Christian Grey
Subject: Rolling Eyes
Date: June 15 2011 16:29
To: Anastasia Steele

Miss Steele
WILL YOU USE YOUR BLACKBERRY!!!

x

Christian Grey
Twitchy Palmed CEO, Grey Enterprises Holdings, Inc.

I await her answer. It does not disappoint.

From: Anastasia Steele
Subject: Inspiration
Date: June 15 2011 16:33
To: Christian Grey

Dear Mr. Grey
Ah… your twitchy palms can't stay still for long, can they?
I wonder what Dr. Flynn would say about that?
But now I know what to give you for your birthday—and I hope it makes me sore…
;)

A x

Finally, she's using her phone. And she wants to be sore. My mind goes into overdrive imagining the possibilities this presents.

I shift in my seat as I type my response.

From: Christian Grey
Subject: Angina
Date: June 15 2011 16:38
To: Anastasia Steele

Miss Steele
I don't think my heart could stand the strain of another email like that, or my pants for that matter.

Behave.

x

Christian Grey
CEO, Grey Enterprises Holdings, Inc.

From: Anastasia Steele
Subject: Trying
Date: June 15 2011 16:42
To: Christian Grey

Christian
I am trying to work for my very trying boss.
Please stop bothering me and being trying yourself.
Your last email nearly made me combust.
x

P.S. Can you pick me up at 6:30?

From: Christian Grey
Subject: I'll Be There
Date: June 15 2011 16:47
To: Anastasia Steele

Nothing would give me greater pleasure.

Actually, I can think of any number of things that would give me greater pleasure, and they all involve you.

x

Christian Grey
CEO, Grey Enterprises Holdings, Inc.

•

TAYLOR AND I PULL up outside her office at 6:27. I should only have a few minutes to wait.

I wonder if she's had any thoughts about my proposal. Of course, she needs to talk to Flynn first. Perhaps he'll tell her not to be a fool. The thought depresses me. I wonder if our days are numbered. But she knows the worst and she's still here. I think there's room for hope. I check my watch—6:38—and stare at the door of her office building.

Where is she?

Suddenly she's in the street, the door swinging behind her. But she doesn't head toward the car.

What gives?

She stops, looks around, and slowly sinks to the ground.

Fuck.

I open the car door and notice out the corner of my eye that Taylor is doing the same.

We both rush to Ana, who is sitting on the sidewalk, looking faint. I sink down beside her. "Ana! Ana! What's wrong?" I pull her into my lap to check what's wrong, holding her head between my hands. She closes her eyes and sags against me as if in relief. "Ana." I grasp her arms and shake her. "What's wrong? Are you sick?"

"Jack," she whispers.

"Fuck." Adrenaline sweeps through my body, leaving a murderous fury in its wake. I glance up at Taylor. He nods and disappears into the building. "What did that sleazeball do to you?"

Ana giggles. "It's what I did to him." And she doesn't stop laughing. She's hysterical. I'm going to kill him.

"Ana!" I give her a shake. "Did he touch you?"

"Only once," she whispers, and her giggling stops.

Rage fuels my muscles as I stand holding her in my arms. "Where is that fucker?" From inside the building we can hear muffled shouts. I set Ana on her feet. "Can you stand?"

She nods. "Don't go in. Don't, Christian."

"Get in the car."

"Christian, no." She clasps my arm.

"Get in the goddamned car, Ana."

I'm going to kill him.

"No! Please!" she begs. "Stay. Don't leave me on my own."

I drag my hand through my hair, trying and failing to hang on to my temper while the muffled shouting inside SIP intensifies. Abruptly it stops.

I pull out my phone.

"Christian, he has my emails," Ana says in a whisper.

"What?"

"My emails to you. He wanted to know where your emails to me were. He was trying to blackmail me."

I think I'm going to have a coronary.

That motherfucking asshole.

"Fuck!" I growl as I call Barney.

"Hello—"

"Barney. Grey. I need you to access the SIP main server and wipe all of Anastasia Steele's emails to me. Then access the personal data files of Jack Hyde and check they aren't stored there. If they are, wipe them."

"Hyde? H-Y-D-E."

"Yes."

"All of them?"

"All of them. Now. Let me know when it's done."

"Will do."

I hang up and dial Roach's number.

"Jerry Roach."

"Roach. Grey."

"Good evening—"

"Hyde. I want him out. Now."

"But—" Roach blusters.

"This minute. Call security. Get him to clear his desk immediately or I will liquidate this company first thing in the morning."

"Is there a reason—" Roach tries again.

"You already have all the justification you need to give him his pink slip."

"You've read his confidential file?"

I ignore his question. "Do you understand?"

"Mr. Grey, I completely understand. Our HR director is always defending him. I'll see to it. Good evening."

I hang up, feeling somewhat mollified, and turn to Ana. "BlackBerry!"

"Please don't be mad at me."

"I am so mad at you right now," I snap. "Get in the car."

"Christian, please—"

"Get in the fucking car, Anastasia, or so help me I'll put you in there myself."

"Don't do anything stupid, please," she says.

"Stupid!" I see red. "I told you to use your fucking BlackBerry. Don't talk to me about stupid. Get in the motherfucking car, Anastasia—now!"

"Okay." She holds up her hands. "But please, be careful."

Stop shouting at her, Grey.

I point to the car.

"Please be careful," she whispers again. "I don't want anything to happen to you. It would kill me."

And there it is. She cares. Her affection for me is plain in her words and in her kind, concerned expression.

Calm down, Grey. I take a deep breath.

"I'll be careful," I say, and I watch her walk to the Audi and climb in. Once she's in the car, I turn on my heel and stride into the building.

I have no idea where to go, but I follow Hyde's voice.

His irritating, whiny voice.

Taylor is standing outside an executive office, beside what must be Ana's desk. Inside, Hyde is on the phone and a security guard stands over him with his arms crossed.

"I don't give a fuck, Jerry." Hyde is protesting into the phone. "The woman is a pricktease."

I've heard enough.

I storm into his office.

"What the—" Hyde says, shocked to see me. He has a cut over his left eye and a purplish bruise is forming on his cheek. I suspect Taylor has been administering his own brand of discipline.

I reach down to the phone cradle and press the hook, ending his call.

"Well, look what the fucking cat dragged in," Hyde says and sneers. "The boy fucking wonder."

"Pack your things. Get out. And she may not press charges."

"Fuck you, Grey. I'll be pressing charges against that little bitch, for kicking me in the balls in a completely unprovoked attack—and I'll be sending your goon here down for assault, too. Hi, handsome," he calls to Taylor and blows him a kiss.

Taylor remains stoic.

"I won't tell you again," I state, glaring at the cocksucker.

"Like I said, fuck you. You can't come in here throwing your fucking weight around."

"I own this company. You are surplus to requirements. Get out while you can still walk." My tone is low.

The color drains from Hyde's face.

Yeah. Mine. Fuck you, Hyde.

"I knew it. I knew something shady was going on. That little bitch your spy?"

"If you mention Anastasia once more, if you even think about her, if you even think about thinking about her, I will end you."

His eyes narrow. "You like it when she kicks you in the balls?"

I hit him square on the nose and he topples backward and smacks his head on the shelves behind him before he slumps onto the floor.

"You mentioned her. Get up. Clear your desk. And get out. You're fired."

Blood is pouring from his nose.

Taylor steps into the office with a box of tissues and places them on the desk for Hyde.

"You saw him," Hyde whines to the security guard.

"I saw you fall," the security guard says. The name on his badge is M. Mathur. *Good job.*

Hyde struggles onto his feet and grabs a handful of tissues to stem his nosebleed. "I'm pressing charges. She attacked me." Hyde continues to snivel, but he begins to put his belongings in the box.

"Three hushed-up harassment cases in New York and Chicago and the two warnings you've had here. I don't think you'd get very far."

He regards me with dark eyes and unadulterated, feral hatred.

"Pack your things. You're done," I spit.

Turning, I head out of his office to wait with Taylor while Hyde packs up his stuff. I need to distance myself.

I want to kill him.

He takes forever, but he does it in silence. He's mad. Real mad. I can almost smell his blood boiling. He gives me the occasional poisonous glance, but I remain impassive. The sight of his messed-up face gives me some satisfaction.

Eventually he's done and he picks up the box. Mathur follows him out of the building.

"Are we finished here, Mr. Grey?" Taylor asks.

"For now."

"I found him groveling on the floor, sir."

"Really?"

"Miss Steele appears to know how to defend herself."

"She's always full of surprises. Let's go."

We follow Hyde out of the building and both of us head to the Audi. Because Ana is already in the front seat, Taylor gives me the key and I slide into the driver's seat. Taylor gets into the back.

Ana is quiet as I pull out into traffic.

I don't know what to say to her.

The car phone rings.

"Grey," I answer.

"Mr. Grey, Barney here."

"Barney, I'm on speakerphone, and there are others in the car."

"Sir, it's all done. But I need to talk to you about what else I found on Mr. Hyde's computer."

"I'll call you when I reach my destination. And thanks, Barney."

"No problem, Mr. Grey." He hangs up and I stop at a red light.

"Are you talking to me?" Ana asks.

I glance at her. "No," I mutter. I'm still too mad. I told her he was trouble. And I told her to use her phone for email. I was right about everything. I feel vindicated.

Grey, grow up. You're behaving like a child.

Flynn's words circle my brain. *I've long held the belief that you never really had an adolescence—emotionally speaking. I think you're experiencing it now.*

I glance across at her in the hope I can say something amusing, but she's staring out the window. I'll wait until we get home.

OUTSIDE ESCALA, I OPEN Ana's car door while Taylor climbs into the driver's seat.

"Come," I say, and she takes my hand.

While we wait for the elevator, Ana whispers, "Christian, why are you so mad at me?"

"You know why."

As we enter the elevator, I punch the code into the keypad. "God, if something had happened to you, he'd be dead by now. As it is, I'm going to ruin his career so he can't take advantage of young women anymore, miserable excuse for a man that he is." If anything had happened to her… *Leila yesterday. Hyde today. Hell.*

Slowly she sinks her teeth into her lower lip while staring at me.

"Jesus, Ana!" I pull her to me and twist so she's pinned in the corner of the elevator. Tugging her hair, upturning her face, I capture her lips with mine and pour my fear and desperation into my kiss. Her hands grasp my biceps as she returns my kiss, her tongue seeking mine. I pull back and we're both breathless. "If anything had happened to you. If he'd harmed you—" I shudder. "BlackBerry. From now on. Understand?" She nods, her expression earnest, and I straighten up and release her. "He said you kicked him in the balls."

"Yes."

"Good."

"Ray is ex-Army. He taught me well."

"I'm very glad he did. I'll need to remember that." As we exit the elevator, I take her hand and we walk through the foyer and into the living room. Mrs. Jones is in the kitchen cooking. It smells good.

"I need to call Barney. I won't be long."

Sitting down at my desk, I pick up the phone.

"Mr. Grey."

"Barney, what did you find on Hyde's computer?"

"Well, sir, it was a little unsettling. There are articles and photographs of you, your mom and dad, and your brother and sister, all stored in one folder called 'Greys.'"

"That's odd."

"That's what I thought."

"Could you send me what he has?"

"Yes, sir."

"And keep this between us for now."

"Will do, Mr. Grey."

"Thanks, Barney. And go home."

"Yes, sir."

Barney's email arrives almost immediately, and I open the "Greys" folder. Sure enough, there are online articles about my parents and their charitable work; articles on me, my company, *Charlie Tango* and the Gulfstream; and photographs of Elliot, my parents, and me taken, I assume, from Mia's Facebook page. And last, two photos of Ana and me—at her graduation and at the photographer's exhibition.

What the hell would Hyde want with all that shit? It makes no sense. I know he has a thing for Ana; that's consistent with his modus operandi. But my family? Me? It's like he's obsessed with us. Or maybe it's all about Ana? This is weird. And frankly disturbing. I resolve to call Welch in the morning to discuss. He can investigate further and get me some answers.

I close the email, and sitting in my inbox are a couple of final acquisition agreements from Marco. I need to read them tonight—but first some dinner.

"Evening, Gail," I call out to her when I'm back in the living room.

"Good evening, Mr. Grey. Dinner in ten, sir?"

Ana is sitting at the kitchen counter with a glass of wine. After dealing with that asshole, I think she's earned it. I'll join her.

I retrieve the open bottle of Sancerre and pour one for myself. "Sounds good," I respond to Gail and raise my glass to Ana. "To ex-military men who train their daughters well."

"Cheers," she says, but she looks a little crestfallen.

"What's wrong?"

"I don't know if I still have a job."

"Do you still want one?"

"Of course."

"Then you still have one."

She rolls her eyes, and I smile and take another sip of my wine.

"So, did you talk to Barney?" she asks as I take a seat beside her.

"I did."

"And?"

"And what?"

"What did Jack have on his computer?"

"Nothing important."

Mrs. Jones places our food in front of us. Chicken pot pie. One of my favorites.

"Thanks, Gail."

"Enjoy, Mr. Grey. Ana," she says pleasantly and departs.

"You're not going to tell me, are you?" Ana persists.

"Tell you what?"

She sighs and purses her lips, then takes a bite of her meal.

The contents of Jack's computer are not something I want Ana to worry about.

"José called," she says, changing the subject.

"Oh?"

"He wants to deliver your photos on Friday."

"A personal delivery." Why is the artist doing this and not the gallery? "How accommodating of him."

"He wants to go out. For a drink. With me."

"I see."

"And Kate and Elliot should be back."

I put my fork down on my plate. "What exactly are you asking?"

"I'm not asking anything. I'm informing you of my plans for Friday. Look, I want to see José, and he wants to stay over. Either he stays here or he can stay at my place, but if he does, I should be there, too."

"He made a pass at you."

"Christian, that was weeks ago. He was drunk, I was drunk, you saved the day—it won't happen again. He's no Jack, for heaven's sake."

"Ethan's there. He can keep him company."

"He wants to see me, not Ethan," Ana says.

I scowl at her.

"He's just a friend," she continues.

She's already endured Hyde. What if Rodriguez gets drunk and tries his luck again with Ana? "I don't like it."

Ana takes a deep breath; she's trying to keep her cool. "He's my friend, Christian. I haven't seen him since his show. And that was too brief. I know you don't have any friends, apart from that god-awful woman, but I don't moan about you seeing her."

What has Elena got to do with this? And I'm reminded that I haven't responded to her texts.

"I want to see him," she continues. "I've been a poor friend to him."

"Is that what you think?" I ask.

"Think about what?"

"Elena. You'd rather I didn't see her?"

"Exactly. I'd rather you didn't see her."

"Why didn't you say?"

"Because it's not my place to say. You think she's your only friend." She's exasperated. "Just as it's not your place to say if I can or can't see José. Don't you see that?"

She has a point. If he stays here, then he can't make a pass at her. Can he?

"He can stay here, I suppose. I can keep an eye on him."

"Thank you! You know, if I am going to live here, too…" Her voice trails off.

Yes. She'll need to invite her friends here. Jesus. I hadn't thought about that.

"It's not like you haven't got the space." She waves a hand in the general direction of my apartment.

"Are you smirking at me, Miss Steele?"

"Most definitely, Mr. Grey." She gets up and clears both of our plates.

"Gail will do that," I say as she sashays over to the dishwasher. But I'm too late.

"I've done it now."

"I have to work for a while."

"Cool. I'll find something to do."

"Come here."

She steps between my legs and puts her arms around my neck.

I hold her close against me. "Are you okay?" I whisper into her hair.

"Okay?"

"After what happened with that fucker? After what happened yesterday?" I lean back and study her expression.

"Yes," she replies, solemn and emphatic.

To try to reassure me?

I tighten my arms around her. What a weird couple of days this has been. Too much too fast, maybe. And my old life impinging on my new one. She still hasn't responded to my marriage proposal. Perhaps I shouldn't push her for an answer right now.

She holds me close, and for the first time since this morning, I feel calm and centered. "Let's not fight." I kiss her hair. "You smell heavenly as usual, Ana."

"So do you." She kisses my neck.

Reluctantly, I release her and stand. I have to read those agreements. "I should only be a couple of hours."

MY EYES ARE TIRED. I rub my face, pinch the bridge of my nose, and glance out the window. It's getting dark, but I've finished going through both documents. I've made notes and forwarded them to Marco.

Now it's time to find Ana.

Maybe she'd like to watch TV or something. I loathe TV, but I'd sit with her and watch a film.

I expect to find her in the library, but she's not there.

Maybe she took a bath?

No. She's not in the bedroom or the en suite.

I decide to check the sub's room but on my way there I notice the playroom door is open. Looking inside, I see Ana is sitting on the bed, gazing with distaste at all the canes. With a grimace she looks away.

I should get rid of them.

I lean against the doorframe in silence and watch her. She slips from the bed onto the couch, her hands running over the soft leather. She spies the chest of drawers, rises, makes her way toward it, and opens the top drawer.

Well, this is unexpected.

From the chest, she pulls out a large butt plug and, fascinated, examines it, then tests the weight in her hand. It's a little big for a newcomer to anal pleasure, but I'm mesmerized by her captivated expression. Her hair is a little damp and she's wearing sweatpants and a T-shirt.

No bra.

Nice.

Glancing up, she spots me by the door. "Hi," she says, all breathy and nervous.

"What are you doing?"

She blushes. "Um, I was bored and curious."

"That's a very dangerous combination." I wander into the room to join her. Leaning over, I glance at the open drawer to see what else is inside. "So, what exactly are you curious about, Miss Steele? Perhaps I could enlighten you."

"The door was open," she says hastily. "I—" She stops, looking guilty.

Put her out of her misery, Grey.

"I was in here earlier today, wondering what to do with it all. I must have forgotten to lock it."

"Oh?"

"But now here you are, curious as ever."

"You're not mad?"

"Why would I be mad?"

"I feel like I'm trespassing. And you're always mad at me."

Am I? "Yes, you're trespassing, but I'm not mad. I hope that one day you'll live with me here, and all this"—I wave my hand around the room—"will be yours, too. That's why I was in here today. Trying to decide what to do." I watch her expression, thinking about what she's just said. I'm mostly angry at myself, not her. "Am I angry with you all the time? I wasn't this morning."

She smiles. "You were playful. I like playful Christian."

"Do you, now?" I ask, raising an eyebrow and returning her smile. I love her compliments.

"What's this?" She holds up the toy she's been examining.

"Always hungry for information, Miss Steele. That's a butt plug."

"Oh." She looks surprised.

"Bought for you."

"For me?"

I nod.

"You buy new, er… toys… for each submissive?"

"Some things. Yes."

"Butt plugs?"

Definitely. "Yes."

She eyes it warily and places it back in the drawer.

"And this?" She waves some anal beads at me.

"Anal beads."

She runs them through her fingers—intrigued, I think.

"They have quite an effect if you pull them out mid-orgasm," I add.

"This is for me?" she asks, referring to the beads. She keeps her voice low, as if she doesn't want to be overheard.

"For you."

"This is the butt drawer?"

I stifle my chuckle. "If you like."

She turns a lovely shade of pink and closes it.

"Don't you like the butt drawer?" I tease.

"It's not top of my Christmas-card list."

There's her smart mouth. She opens the second drawer. Oh, this will be fun. "Next drawer down holds a selection of vibrators."

She shuts it quickly. "And the next?"

"That's more interesting."

Slowly she opens the next one down. She picks out a toy and shows it to me.

"Genital clamp." Hastily, she puts it back in the drawer and chooses something else. I remember they were a hard limit for her. "Some of these are for pain, but most are for pleasure," I reassure her.

"What's this?"

"Nipple clamps—that's for both."

"Both? Nipples?"

"Well, there are two clamps, baby. Yes, both nipples, but that's not what I meant. These are for both pleasure and pain." I take them from her. "Hold out your little finger."

She complies, and I clamp the clip to the tip of her finger. Her breath catches. "The sensation is very intense, but it's when taking them off that they are at their most painful and pleasurable." She removes the clip. "I like the look of these." Her voice is now husky, making me smile.

"Do you, now, Miss Steele? I think I can tell."

She nods and places the clips back in the drawer. I lean forward and remove another set for her consideration.

"These are adjustable." I hold them up to demonstrate.

"Adjustable?"

"You can wear them very tight, or not. Depending on your mood."

Her eyes move from the clamp to my face and she licks her lower lip. She pulls out another toy. "This?" She's intrigued.

"That's a Wartenberg pinwheel." I pop the adjustable clamps back in the drawer.

"For?"

I take it from her. "Give me your hand. Palm up." She does, and I run the spiky wheel over the center of her hand.

"Ah!" She gasps.

"Imagine that over your breasts."

She snatches her hand away, but the quick rise and fall of her chest reveals her excitement.

This is turning her on.

"There's a fine line between pleasure and pain, Anastasia." I place the pinwheel back in the drawer.

She's looking at the other contents. "Clothespins?"

"You can do a great deal with a clothespin."

But I don't think it would be your thing, Ana.

She leans against the drawer, closing it.

"Is that all?" This is turning me on, too—I should take her downstairs.

"No." She shakes her head, and opening the fourth drawer, she retrieves one of my favorite devices. "Ball gag. To keep you quiet," I inform her.

"Soft limit."

"I remember. But you can still breathe. Your teeth clamp over the ball." Taking it from her, I demonstrate with my hands how a ball gag fits into a mouth.

"Have you worn one of these?" she asks, curious as ever.

"Yes."

"To mask your screams?"

"No, that's not what they're about."

She cocks her head to one side, perplexed.

"It's about control, Anastasia. How helpless would you be if you were tied up and couldn't speak? How trusting would you have to be, knowing I had that much power over you? That I had to read your body and your reaction rather than hear your words? It makes you more dependent, puts me in ultimate control."

"You sound like you miss it." Her voice is barely audible.

"It's what I know."

"You have power over me. You know you do."

"Do I? You make me feel… helpless."

"No," she counters, shocked, I think. "Why?"

"Because you're the only person I know who could really hurt me."

You hurt me when you left.

I tuck her hair behind her ear.

"Oh, Christian. That works both ways. If you didn't want me—" A tremor runs through her and she gazes down at her fingers. "The last thing I want to do is hurt you. I love you."

She strokes my face with both her hands and I savor her

touch. It's both arousing and comforting. I drop the ball gag back into the drawer and fold her in my arms. "Have we finished show-and-tell?"

"Why? What did you want to do?" Her tone is suggestive.

I kiss her gently and she presses her body against mine, making her intention clear. She wants me. "Ana, you were nearly attacked today."

"So?" she breathes.

"What do you mean, 'so'?" I feel a rush of annoyance.

"Christian, I'm fine."

Are you, Ana?

I pull her closer, squeezing her. "When I think of what might have happened—" I bury my face in her hair and breathe.

"When will you learn that I'm stronger than I look?"

"I know you're strong." *You put up with me.* I kiss her and release her.

She pouts and to my surprise reaches down and fishes out another toy from the drawer. *I thought we were done?* "That's a spreader bar with ankle and wrist restraints," I tell her.

"How does it work?" She looks up at me through her lashes.

Oh, baby. I know that look.

"You want me to show you?" I close my eyes, briefly imagining her shackled and at my mercy. It's arousing.

Very arousing.

"Yes, I want a demonstration. I like being tied up."

"Oh, Ana," I whisper. *I want to. But I can't in here.*

"What?"

"Not here."

"What do you mean?"

"I want you in my bed, not in here. Come." I take the bar and her hand and lead her out of the room.

"Why not in there?"

I stop on the stairs. "Ana, you may be ready to go back in there, but I'm not. Last time we were in there, you left me. I keep telling you—when will you understand? My whole attitude has changed as a result. My whole outlook on life has radically shifted. I've told you this. What I haven't told you is—" I pause, searching for the right words. "I'm like a recovering alcoholic, okay? That's the only comparison I can draw. The compulsion has gone, but I don't want to put temptation in my way. I don't want to hurt you."

And I can't trust you to tell me when or if I do.

She frowns.

"I can't bear to hurt you because I love you," I add. Her eyes soften, and before I can stop her she launches herself at me, so I have to drop the spreader bar to prevent us both from toppling down the stairs. She pins me to the wall, and because she's standing on the step above me, we are lip to lip. She cups my face with both her hands and kisses me, pushing her tongue in my mouth. Her fingers are in my hair as she molds her body to mine. Her kiss is passionate, forgiving, and unrestrained.

I groan and gently push her away. "Do you want me to fuck you on the stairs?" I growl. "Because right now, I will."

"Yes," she says.

I look at her dazed expression. She wants this, and I'm tempted, as I've never fucked on the stairs, but it will be uncomfortable.

"No. I want you in my bed." Scooping her up over my shoulder, I'm gratified by her squeal of delight. I smack her hard on her backside and she squeals again and laughs. Stooping, I pick up the spreader bar and carry it and Ana through the apartment to the bedroom, where I set her on her feet and drop the spreader bar on the bed.

"I don't think you'll hurt me," she says.

"I don't think I'll hurt you, either." I take her head in my hands and kiss her, hard, exploring her mouth with my tongue. "I want you so much. Are you sure about this, after today?'

"Yes. I want you, too. I want to undress you."

Shit. She wants to touch you, Grey.

Let her.

"Okay." I managed this yesterday.

She reaches for my shirt button and my breathing halts as I endeavor to bring my fear under control.

"I won't touch you if you don't want me to."

"No. Do. It's fine. I'm good."

I steel myself, preparing for the confusion and fear that comes with the darkness. As she undoes one button and her fingers slide down to the next, I watch the concentration on her face, her beautiful face. "I want to kiss you there," she says.

"Kiss me?" My chest?

"Yes."

I inhale sharply as she undoes the next button. She looks up at me, then slowly, slowly, slowly leans forward.

She's going to kiss me.

I hold my breath and watch her, terrified and fascinated at once, as she plants a gentle, sweet kiss on my chest.

The darkness remains quiet.

She undoes the final button and pulls my shirt apart. "It's getting easier, isn't it?"

I nod. It is. Much easier. She pushes my shirt off my shoulders so it drops to the floor. "What have you done to me, Ana? Whatever it is, don't stop." I pull her into my embrace and move my hands into her hair, gripping it and tugging her head back so I can kiss and nip her throat.

She groans, and her fingers are in my waistband, undoing my button and my fly.

"Oh, baby," I whisper and kiss her behind her ear where her pulse beats a fast, steady rhythm of need. Her fingers brush my erection, and abruptly she drops to her knees.

"Whoa!"

Before I can draw a breath, she tugs at my pants and wraps her lips around my eager cock.

Fuck.

She closes her mouth around me and sucks, hard.

I cannot take my eyes off her mouth.

Around me.

Drawing me in.

Out.

She sheaths her teeth and squeezes.

"Fuck." I close my eyes, cradling her head and flexing my hips so I move deeper and deeper into her mouth.

She taunts me with her tongue.

And moves her mouth up and down.

Again and again.

I tighten my grip on her head.

"Ana," I warn and try to step back.

She clamps down on my cock and grabs my hips.

She's not going to let me go.

"Please." And I don't know if I want her to stop or carry on. "I'm gonna come, Ana."

She's merciless. Her mouth and tongue skilled. She's not going to stop.

Oh fuck.

I climax into her mouth, holding her head to steady myself.

When I open my eyes, she's gazing up at me in triumph. She smiles and licks her lips.

"Oh, so this is the game we're playing, Miss Steele?" I reach down and pull her to her feet and my lips find hers. With my tongue in her mouth, I taste her sweetness and my saltiness.

It's heady.

I groan. "I can taste myself. You taste better." I find the hem of her T-shirt and lift it over her head, then I pick her up and toss her on the bed. Grabbing the hem of her sweatpants, I yank them off in one move so she's naked. I take my clothes off, keeping my eyes on hers. They darken, getting larger and larger until I'm naked, too. I stand over her. She's a nymph sprawled out on the bed, her hair a chestnut halo, her eyes warm and welcoming.

My cock recovers, growing and growing as I appreciate every inch of my girl.

Yeah. She's gorgeous.

"You are one beautiful woman, Anastasia."

"You are one beautiful man, Christian, and you taste mighty fine." Her smile is sexy and coquettish.

I give her a wicked grin.

I am going to take my revenge on Miss Steele.

Grabbing her left ankle, I strap the cuff around it, keeping my eyes on hers the whole time. "We'll have to see how you taste. If I recall, you're a rare, exquisite delicacy, Miss Steele."

I grasp her right ankle and cuff that, too. While holding the bar, I stand back to admire my handiwork, happy that she's secure and that the straps aren't too tight. "The good thing about this spreader is it expands," I inform her. I push down on the clip and tug outward, and the bar extends, forcing her legs farther apart.

Ana gasps.

"Oh, we're going to have some fun with this, Ana." Reaching down, I grab the bar and twist it quickly so that Ana flips onto her front. "See what I can do to you?" I twist again and flip her onto her back.

Her breasts rise and fall as she pants.

"These other cuffs are for your wrists. I'll think about that. Depends if you behave or not."

"When do I not behave?" Her voice is husky with desire.

"I can think of a few infractions." I run my fingers up the soles of her feet and she writhes. "Your BlackBerry, for one."

"What are you going to do?"

"Oh, I never disclose my plans."

She has no idea how hot she looks right now. Slowly I crawl up the bed until I'm between her legs.

"Hmm. You are so exposed, Miss Steele," I whisper, our eyes locked together as I run my fingers up her legs, making small circles. "It's all about anticipation, Ana. What will I do to you?"

She tries to wriggle beneath me, but she's trapped.

My fingers travel higher, to her inner thighs. "Remember, if you don't like something, just tell me to stop." I lean down and kiss her belly, my nose ringing her navel.

"Oh, please, Christian."

"Oh, Miss Steele. I've discovered you can be merciless in your amorous assaults upon me. I think I should return the favor." I kiss her belly and my lips move south. My fingers north.

Slowly, I ease my fingers inside her. She jerks her pelvis up to embrace them.

I moan. "You never cease to amaze me, Ana. You're so wet." Her pubic hair tickles my lips, but I persist and my tongue finds her clitoris pert and eager for attention.

"Ah!" she cries and braces against her restraints.

Oh, baby, you're mine.

I swirl my tongue around and around and move my fingers in and out, rotating slowly. She arches off the bed, and from the corner of my eye I see her clutching the sheets.

Absorb the pleasure, Ana.

"Oh, Christian," she cries out.

"I know, baby." I gently blow on her.

"Ah! Please!" she pleads.

"Say my name."

"Christian," she exclaims.

"Again."

"Christian, Christian, Christian Grey," she shouts.

She's close.

"You are mine," I whisper and suck and flick her with my tongue.

She cries out as she comes around my fingers, and while she's in the throes of her orgasm, I crawl back and flip her over onto her stomach and pull her into my lap.

"We're going to try this. If you don't like it, or it's too uncomfortable, tell me and we'll stop."

She's breathless and dazed.

"Lean down, baby. Head and chest on the bed."

She complies immediately and I tug her hands backward and cuff each to the bar next to her ankles.

Oh, man. Her ass is in the air; she's breathing heavily. Waiting. For me.

"Ana, you look so beautiful."

I grab a condom and quickly rip open the packet and roll it on.

I run my fingers down her spine and pause over her ass. "When you're ready, I want this, too." I brush my thumb over her anus, and she tenses and gasps. "Not today, sweet Ana," I reassure her, "but one day. I want you every way. I want to possess every inch of you. You're mine."

Moving on, I ease my finger inside her. She's still wet, and I kneel up behind her and bury myself in her.

"Aagh! Gently," she cries.

I still. *Shit.* I hold her hips. "You okay?"

"Gently," she says. "Let me get used to this."

Gently. I can do gently.

I ease back and then slowly forward, filling her. She groans and I ease back and ease forward. Again.

And again.

And again.

Take it slow.

"Yes, good, I've got it now," she murmurs.

I groan and move a little faster. She starts mewling with each thrust. And I go faster still. She scrunches up her eyes and opens her mouth, breathing in a gulp of air with each thrust.

Fuck. This is exquisite.

I close my eyes and tighten my fingers on her hips and lose myself in her.

Over and over.

Until I feel her pulling me inside.

She cries out and comes, taking me with her so I climax inside her, calling out her name. "Ana, baby."

I collapse beside her feeling utterly spent and lie for a moment, relishing my release. I cannot leave Ana trussed up so I move to unbuckle her from the spreader bar. She curls up beside me while I rub the life back into her ankles and wrists. When she wiggles her fingers and toes, I lie back down, pulling her against me. She mumbles something unintelligible and I realize she's asleep.

I kiss her forehead, tug the duvet over her, and I sit up and watch her. Taking a strand of her hair, I rub it between my fingers.

So soft.

I curl the tendril around my index finger.

See, I'm tied to you, Ana.

I kiss the end of her hair and sit back and look out at the darkening sky. I know on the ground it will be dark, but up here, the last vestiges of the day are staining the sky pink and orange and opal. We're still in the light.

That's what she's done.

Brought light into my life.

Light and love.

But she still hasn't given me an answer.

Say yes, Ana.

Be my wife.

Please.

She stirs and opens her eyes. "I could watch you sleep forever, Ana." I kiss her forehead once more.

She gives me a drowsy smile and closes her eyes.

"I never want to let you go."

"I never want to go," she rambles. "Never let me go."

"I need you," I whisper, and her lips lift in a tender smile as her breathing evens out.

She's asleep.

THURSDAY, JUNE 16, 2011

Grandpa is laughing. Mia has fallen down on her butt. She's a baby.

Mia. Mommy and Daddy sit on a blanket. We are in the orchard.

My favorite place.

Elliot is running between the trees.

I lift up Mia and she walks again. Shaky steps.

But I am behind her. Watching her. Walking with her.

I keep her safe.

We have a picnic.

I like picnics.

Mommy makes apple pie.

Mia walks to the blanket. And everyone cheers.

Thank you, Christian.

You take such good care of her, Mommy says.

Mia is a baby. She needs someone to watch over her, I tell Mommy.

Grandpa looks at me.

He's talking now?

Yes.

Well, that's just great. Grandpa looks at Mommy.

He has tears in his eyes. But he's happy. Happy tears.

Elliot runs past us. He has a football.

Let's play.

Mind the apples.

I look up and behind a tree Jack Hyde is watching us.

I wake. Instantly. My heart racing. Not from fear, but because I was startled by something in my dream.

What was it?

I can't remember. It's light outside, and Ana is fast asleep beside me. I check the time. It's nearly 6:30. I woke up before the alarm. That hasn't happened for a while—not with my dream catcher beside me. The radio comes to life, but I switch it off and snuggle up to Ana, nuzzling her neck.

She stirs.

"Morning, baby," I whisper, grazing her earlobe. I run my hand up to her breast and gently caress her, feeling her nipple harden beneath my palm. She stretches beside me and I trace her skin to her hip and hold her close. My erection sits in the cleft of her behind.

"You're pleased to see me," she says and wiggles, squeezing my dick.

"I'm very pleased to see you." My fingers skate over her belly to her sex and I caress her, there and everywhere, as I remind her that there are advantages to waking up together. She's warm, willing, and ready when I reach over to the bedside table, grab a condom, and lie on top of her, taking my weight on my elbows. I ease her legs apart, then kneel up and rip open the foil packet. "I can't wait until Saturday."

She looks up at me eagerly. "Your party?"

"No. I can stop using these fuckers." I roll the condom on.

"Aptly named." She giggles.

"Are you giggling, Miss Steele?"

"No," she says, trying and completely failing to keep a straight face.

"Now is not the time for giggling." I stare her down, daring her to giggle again.

"I thought you liked it when I giggle."

"Not now. There's a time and a place for giggling. This is neither. I need to stop you, and I think I know how."

Slowly, I ease into her.

"Ah," she says in my ear.

And we make sweet, unhurried love.

No more giggling.

DRESSED AND ARMED WITH a coffee and a large trash bag from Mrs. Jones, I head up to my playroom. I have one duty to perform while Ana has her shower.

I open the door, step inside, and set down my coffee. It took months to design and source everything for this room. And now I don't know when or if I'll use it again.

Don't dwell, Grey.

I face the reason I'm here—in the corner, my canes. I have several, from all over the world. I run my fingers over my favorite, fashioned from rosewood and the finest leather. I bought it in London. The others are made from bamboo, plastic, carbon fiber, wood, and suede. Carefully, I load them all into the trash bag.

I'm sorry to see them go.

There, I've admitted it to myself.

Ana is never going to enjoy these; it's just not her thing.

What is your thing, Anastasia?

Books.

It will never be canes.

I lock up the room and head to my study. Once there, I pack the canes in a closet to be dealt with at a later date, but for now, she won't have to see them again.

At my desk, I finish my coffee, aware that Ana will be ready for breakfast shortly. But before I join her in the kitchen, I call Welch.

"Mr. Grey?"

"Good morning. I wanted to talk to you about Jack Hyde."

ANA IS BEAUTIFUL AND elegant in gray when she enters the kitchen for breakfast. She should wear skirts more often; she has great legs. My heart swells. With love. With pride. And humility. It's a new and exciting feeling that I hope I never take for granted.

"What would you like for breakfast, Ana?" Gail asks her.

"I'll just have some granola. Thank you, Mrs. Jones." She sits beside me at the counter, her cheeks pink.

I wonder what she's thinking about. This morning? Last night? The spreader bar?

"You look lovely," I offer.

"So do you." Her smile is demure. Ana hides her inner freak well.

"We should buy you some more skirts. In fact, I'd love to take you shopping."

She doesn't seem overly impressed with this idea. "I wonder what will happen at work today," she says, and I know she's referring to SIP to change the subject.

"They'll have to replace the sleazeball," I mutter, but when, I don't know. I've placed a moratorium on any hiring until we've conducted a staff audit.

"I hope they take on a woman as my new boss."

"Why?"

"Well, you're less likely to object to me going away with her," she says.

Oh, baby, you'd appeal to women, too.

Mrs. Jones places my omelet in front of me, distracting me from my brief and extremely enjoyable fantasy of Ana with another woman.

"What's so funny?" Ana asks.

"You are. Eat your granola, all of it, if that's all you're having."

She purses her lips but picks up a spoon and devours her breakfast.

"Can I take the Saab today?" she asks when she finishes the last spoonful.

"Taylor and I can drop you at work."

"Christian, is the Saab just for decoration in the garage?"

"No." Of course not.

"Then let me drive it to work. Leila's no longer a threat."

Why is everything a battle?

It's her car, Grey.

"If you want," I concede.

"Of course I do."

"I'll come with you."

"What? I'll be fine on my own."

I try a different tack. "I'd like to come with you."

"Well, if you put it like that," Ana acquiesces with an accepting nod.

ANA IS BEAMING. SHE'S so delighted with the car. I'm not sure she's concentrating on what I'm saying. I show her the ignition on the center console.

"Strange place," she says, but she's practically bouncing in her seat and touching everything.

"You're quite excited about this, aren't you?"

"Just smell that new-car smell. This is even better than the Submissive Special. Um, the A3," she says quickly.

"Submissive Special?" I try not to laugh. "You have such a way with words, Miss Steele." I sit back. "Well, let's go." I wave her in the direction of the exit.

Ana claps her hands, starts the car, and pops the gearshift into drive. If I had known how thrilled she would be about driving this car, I might have relented and let her drive it sooner.

I love seeing her this happy.

The Saab glides up to the barrier and Taylor follows us out onto Virginia Street in the Q7.

This is the first time Ana has ever driven us anywhere, the first time she's driven me. As a driver, she's confident and seems adept; however, I'm not an easy passenger. This I know. I don't like being driven at all, except by Taylor. I prefer to be in the driver's seat.

"Can we have the radio on?" she asks as we pull up at a stop sign.

"I want you to concentrate."

She snaps back, "Christian, please, I can drive with music on."

Choosing to ignore her attitude, I switch on the radio. "You can play your iPod and MP3 discs as well as CDs on this," I inform her.

The sound of the Police fills the car: a golden oldie, "King of Pain." I turn it down—it's too loud.

"Your anthem," Ana says with an impish grin.

She's making fun of me. Again.

"I have this album, somewhere," she says.

And I remember she mentioned "Every Breath You Take" in an email; the Stalker's Anthem, she called it. She's funny—at my expense. I shake my head because she was right. After she left me, I did loiter outside her apartment during my morning run.

She's gnawing at her bottom lip. Is she worried about my reaction? About Flynn? What he might say? "Hey, Miss Smart Mouth. Come back." She stops abruptly at the red light. "You're very distracted. Concentrate, Ana. Accidents happen when you don't concentrate."

"I'm just thinking about work."

"Baby, you'll be fine. Trust me."

"Please don't interfere—I want to do this on my own. Please. It's important to me," she says.

Me? Interfere? Only to protect you, Ana.

"Let's not argue, Christian. We've had such a wonderful morning. And last night was"—her cheeks pink—"heaven."

Last night. I close my eyes and see her ass in the air. I move in my seat as my body reacts. "Yes. Heaven." And I realize I've said it out loud. "I meant what I said."

"What?"

"I don't want to let you go."

"I don't want to go," she says.

"Good." I relax a little. *She's still here, Grey.*

ANA DRIVES INTO THE SIP parking lot and parks the Saab.

Ordeal over.

She's not that bad a driver.

"I'll walk you to work. Taylor will take me from there," I offer as we climb out of the car. "Don't forget we're seeing Flynn at seven this evening." I hold out my hand for her.

She presses the remote, locking the car, and gives the Saab a fond look before taking my hand. "I won't forget. I'll compile a list of questions for him."

"Questions? About me? I can answer any questions you have about me."

Her smile is indulgent. "Yes, but I want the unbiased, expensive charlatan's opinion."

I fold her into my arms, my hands cupping hers and holding them behind her back. "Is this a good idea?" I stare into her startled eyes.

They soften and she offers to forgo seeing Flynn. She shakes one of her hands loose from my grip and tenderly strokes my face. "What are you worried about?"

"That you'll go."

"Christian, how many times do I have to tell you—I'm not going anywhere. You've already told me the worst. I'm not leaving you."

"Then why haven't you answered me?"

"Answered you?"

"You know what I'm talking about, Ana."

She sighs and her expression clouds. "I want to know that I'm enough for you. That's all."

"And you won't take my word for it?" I release her.

When will she realize she's all I'll ever want?

"Christian, this has all been so quick," she says. "And by your own admission, you're fifty shades of fucked up. I can't give you what you need. It's just not for me. But that makes me feel inadequate, especially seeing you with Leila. Who's to say that one day you won't meet someone who likes doing what you do? And who's to say you won't, you know, fall for her? Someone much better suited to your needs." She looks away.

"I knew several women who like doing what I like to do. None of them appealed to me the way you do. I've never had an emotional connection with any of them. It's only ever been you, Ana."

"Because you never gave them a chance. You've spent too long locked up in your fortress. Look, let's discuss this later. I have to go to work. Maybe Dr. Flynn can offer us his insight."

She's right. We shouldn't be discussing this in a parking lot. "Come." I hold out my hand, and together we walk to her office.

TAYLOR PICKS ME UP in the Audi, and on our way to Grey House, I contemplate my conversation with Ana.

Am I locked in a fortress?

Maybe.

I stare out the window. Commuters hurry to work, wrapped up in minutiae of their daily lives. Here, in the back of my car, I'm removed from it all. I've always been that way. Removed: isolated as a child or isolating myself as I grew up, walled off in a fortress.

I've been scared of feeling.

Feeling anything except my anger.

My constant companion.

Is that what she means? If it is, it's Ana who's given me the key to escape. And all that's holding her back is Flynn's opinion.

Maybe once she's heard what he has to say, she'll say yes.

A guy can hope.

I allow myself a brief moment to see what real optimism feels like...

It's terrifying.

It could end badly. Again.

My phone buzzes. It's Ana. "Anastasia. You okay?"

"They've just given me Jack's job—well, temporarily," she says with no preamble at all.

"You're kidding."

"Did you have anything to do with this?" Her tone is accusatory.

"No. No, not at all. I mean, with all due respect, Anastasia, you've only been there for a week or so—and I don't mean that unkindly."

"I know," she says, and she sounds demoralized. "Apparently, Jack really rated me."

"Did he, now?" I'm so glad that asshole is out of her life. "Well, baby, if they think you can do it, I'm sure you can. Congratulations. Perhaps we should celebrate after we've seen Flynn."

"Hmm. Are you sure you had nothing to do with this?"

Does she really think I'd lie to her? Maybe because of my confession last night?

Or maybe they've given her the job because I won't let them recruit outside the company.

Hell.

"Do you doubt me? It angers me that you do."

"I'm sorry," she says quickly.

"If you need anything, let me know. I'll be here. And Anastasia?"

"What?"

"Use your BlackBerry."

"Yes, Christian."

I ignore her sarcastic tone, and saying my head, I take a deep breath. "I mean it. If you need me, I'm here."

"Okay," she says. "I'd better go. I have to move offices."

"If you need me. I mean it."

"I know. Thank you, Christian. I love you."

Those three little words.

They used to terrify me and now I can't wait to hear her say them.

"I love you, too, baby."

"I'll talk to you later."

"Laters, baby."

Taylor pulls up outside Grey House.

"José Rodriquez will be delivering some portraits to Escala tomorrow," I inform him.

"I'll let Gail know."

"He's staying the night."

Taylor checks me in the rearview mirror, surprised, I think.

"Tell Gail that, too," I add.

"Yes, sir."

AS THE ELEVATOR SHOOTS up to my floor, I allow myself a brief fantasy about married life. It's weird, this *hope*. Something I'm not used to. I imagine taking Ana to Europe, to Asia; I could show her the world. We could go anywhere and everywhere. I could take her to England; she'd love that.

And we'd return home to Escala.

Escala? Maybe my apartment has too many memories of other women. Perhaps I should buy a house that would be ours alone, where we can create our own memories.

But keep Escala. It's handy for downtown.

The elevator doors open.

"Good morning, Mr. Grey," the new girl says.

"Good morning—" I can't remember her name.

"Coffee?"

"Please. Black. Where's Andrea?"

"She's around." New Girl smiles and scurries off to make my coffee.

AT MY DESK, I start perusing houses on the web. Andrea knocks and enters a few minutes later with my coffee. "Good morning, Mr. Grey."

"Andrea, good morning. I'd like you to send some flowers to Anastasia Steele."

"What would you like to send?"

"She's had a promotion. Maybe some roses. Pink and white."

"Okay."

"And can you get me Welch on the line?"

"Yes, sir. Do you remember that you're seeing Mr. Bastille today at Escala, not here?"

"Oh, yes. Thanks. Who has the gym booked here?"

"The yoga club, sir."

I make a face.

She stifles her smile. "Ros would like a word, too."

"Thanks."

AFTER MY CALLS, I go back to looking at houses online. I remember when I bought my apartment at Escala, a broker did it all for me—and it was bought off-plan. It seemed like a great investment, so I didn't look further.

Now I'm getting sucked into real-estate websites, looking at property after property. It's addictive.

I've coveted the big houses on the shores of the Sound for all the years I've sailed. I think I'd like a home that looks out across the water. I grew up in a house like that; my parents live on the shores of Lake Washington.

A family house.

Family.

Kids.

I shake my head. Not for a long time. Ana's young. She's only twenty-one. We have years before we have to think about kids.

What kind of father would I be?

Grey, don't dwell.

I'd like to find a plot of land and build a house. Make it ecologically sustainable. Elliot could build it for me. A couple of the listings meet my criteria; one of the homes looks out across the Sound. The house is old, built in 1924, and has only come on the market in the last few days. The photographs are spectacular. Especially at twilight. For me, it will be all about the view. We can knock this house down and start again.

I check what time the sun will set this evening: 9:09 p.m.

Maybe I could get an appointment to see the house at dusk one night this week.

Andrea knocks and enters.

"Mr. Grey, I have a choice of flowers here." She places some printouts on my desk.

"This one." It's a huge basket of white and blush roses. Ana will love it. "And can you get me in to see this house? I'll email you the link. I'd love to do an evening around sunset as soon as possible."

"Sure. What would you like to say on the card?"

"Put the florist through to me when you've ordered the flowers, and I'll tell her directly."

"Very good, Mr. Grey." Andrea exits.

Three minutes later she puts through the florist, who cheerily asks me to dictate a message for the card. "Congratulations,

Miss Steele. And all on your own! No help from your overfriendly, neighborhood, megalomaniac CEO. Love, Christian."

"Got that. Thank you, sir."

"Thank you."

I go back to looking at houses online, and I know that I'm distracting myself from the anxiety I feel about Ana's appointment with Flynn later today. *Displacing*. That's what Flynn would call it. But my happiness hangs in the balance.

And houses are distracting.

What will Flynn say?

After half an hour of looking at houses and not doing any work, I give in and call Flynn.

"You've caught me between patients. Is it urgent?" he says.

"I was calling to find out about Leila."

"She had another comfortable night. I hope to see her later this afternoon. And I'm seeing you, too, yes?"

"Yes. With Ana."

There's a moment of silence between us, and I know this is one of John's tricks. He doesn't speak, hoping I will fill in the ensuing silence.

"Christian, what is it?"

"This evening. Ana."

"Yes."

"What will you say?"

"To Ana? I don't know what she's going to ask me. But whatever she asks, I'll give her the truth."

"That's what I'm worried about."

He sighs. "I have a different perception of you than you have of yourself, Christian."

"I'm not sure whether to be reassured or not."

"I'll see you this evening," he responds.

LATER THAT AFTERNOON I'M back from my meeting with Fred and Barney and I'm about to click on another real-estate agent's website when I notice an email from Ana. I haven't heard from her all day. She must be busy.

From: Anastasia Steele
Subject: Megalomaniac…
Date: June 16 2011 15:43
To: Christian Grey

…is my favorite type of maniac. Thank you for the beautiful flowers. They've arrived in a huge wicker basket that makes me think of picnics and blankets.

x

She's using her phone. Finally!

From: Christian Grey
Subject: Fresh Air
Date: June 16 2011 15:55
To: Anastasia Steele

Maniac, eh? Dr. Flynn may have something to say about that.

You want to go on a picnic?

We could have fun in the great outdoors, Anastasia…

How is your day going, baby?

Christian Grey
CEO, Grey Enterprises Holdings, Inc.

From: Anastasia Steele
Subject: Hectic
Date: June 16 2011 16:00
To: Christian Grey

The day has flown by. I have hardly had a moment to myself to think about anything other than work. I think I can do this! I'll tell you more when I'm home.
Outdoors sounds… interesting.
Love you.

A x

P.S. Don't worry about Dr. Flynn.

How does she know I'm fretting about him?

From: Christian Grey
Subject: I'll try…
Date: June 16 2011 16:09
To: Anastasia Steele

…not to worry.

Laters, baby. x

Christian Grey
CEO, Grey Enterprises Holdings, Inc.

IN THE GYM AT Escala, Bastille is on a roll, but I get a couple of kicks in and knock him on his ass.

"Something is eating you, Grey. Same girl?" he sneers as he springs off the floor.

"None of your goddamn business, Bastille."

We circle each other, looking for an opportunity to take each other down.

"Ah! I love that you have a woman in your life giving you a hard time. When do I get to meet her?"

"I'm not sure that's going to happen."

"Keep your left up, Grey. You're vulnerable."

He comes at me with a front kick, but I feint and skip left, avoiding him.

"Good move, Grey."

AFTER MY SHOWER, I get a text from Andrea.

ANDREA PARKER
Real estate agent can see
you this evening.
8:30 p.m.
Is that okay?
Her name is Olga Kelly.

Great!
Thanks.
Please text me the address.

I wonder what Ana will make of the house. Andrea sends me the address and the access code to the front gates. I memorize the code and find the house on Google Maps. While I'm working out a route from Flynn's place to the house, my phone rings. It's Ros. I stare out of the balcony window as she gives me some good news.

"Fred has come back to me. Kavanagh is a go," she says.

"Ros, that's great."

"He has a few technical issues that he wants his people to discuss with our people. He'd like a meeting tomorrow morning. Breakfast. I've told Andrea."

"Tell Barney and we'll go from there," I respond, and I turn away from the view of Seattle and the Sound to find Ana watching me.

"Will do. I'll see you tomorrow."

"Goodbye." I hang up and stride over to meet my girl, who looks sweet and shy as she stands on the threshold of the living room. "Good evening, Miss Steele." I kiss her and hold her close. "Congratulations on your promotion."

"You've showered."

"I've just had a workout with Claude."

"Oh."

"Managed to knock him on his ass twice." It's a memory to be savored.

"That doesn't happen often?"

"No. Very satisfying when it does. Hungry?"

She shakes her head and seems worried.

"What?" I ask.

"I'm nervous. About Dr. Flynn."

"Me, too. How was your day?" I release her.

"Great. Busy. I couldn't believe it when Elizabeth, our HR person, asked me to fill in. I had to go to the senior editors' lunch meeting and I managed to get two of the manuscripts I was championing considered."

She doesn't stop. She's excited. Her eyes are shining; she's passionate about what she's been doing. It's a pleasure to behold.

"Oh—there's one more thing I should tell you. I was supposed to have lunch with Mia."

"You never mentioned that."

"I know, I forgot. I couldn't make it because of the meeting, and Ethan took her out to lunch instead."

The beach bum, with my sister. I'm not sure how I feel about that. "I see. Stop biting your lip."

"I'm going to freshen up," she says quickly before I can ask her any more about Kavanagh and my baby sister.

I've never really thought about my sister dating. There was that guy at the ball, but she didn't seem particularly interested in him.

“I USUALLY RUN HERE from home,” I mention as I park the Saab. “This is a great car.”

“I think so, too. Christian… I—”

My gut tightens. “What is it, Ana?”

“Here.” From her purse she hands me a small dark box wrapped in a ribbon. “This is for you for your birthday. I wanted to give it to you now—but only if you promise not to open it until Saturday, okay?”

I swallow to contain my relief. “Okay.”

She takes a deep, nervous breath. Why is she anxious about this? I shake it. It sounds small and plastic. What the hell has she given me?

I look up at her.

Whatever it is, I’m sure I’m going to love it. I give her a broad smile.

My birthday is on Saturday. She will be here that day—or so this gift implies. Doesn’t it?

“You can’t open it until Saturday,” she says, waving a finger at me.

“I get it. Why are you giving this to me now?” I place it in my inside pocket.

“Because I can, Mr. Grey.”

“Why, Miss Steele, you stole my line.”

“I did. Let’s get this over with, shall we?”

FLYNN STANDS AS WE enter his office. “Christian.”

“John.” We shake hands. “You remember Anastasia?”

“How could I forget? Anastasia, welcome.”

“Ana, please,” she says as they shake hands.

He directs us toward his sofas.

I wait for Ana to sit down, admiring the fit of the navy dress she’s changed into, and I take the other sofa but sit close to her. Flynn takes his usual chair. I place my hand on Ana’s and give it a squeeze.

“Christian has requested that you accompany him to one of our sessions,” Flynn says. “Just so you know, we treat these sessions with absolute confidentiality—”

He stops when Ana interrupts. "Oh—um, I've signed an NDA," she says quickly.

Shit.

I release her hand.

"A nondisclosure agreement?" Flynn gives me a puzzled look.

I shrug but say nothing.

"You start all your relationships with women with an NDA?" he asks me.

"The contractual ones I do."

Flynn stifles a smile. "You've had other types of relationships with women?"

Shit.

"No," I respond, amused by his reaction. He knows this.

"As I thought." Flynn turns his attention back to Ana. "Well, I guess we don't have to worry about confidentiality, but may I suggest the two of you discuss this at some point? As I understand, you're no longer entering into that kind of contractual relationship."

"Different kind of contract hopefully," I say with a look at Ana.

She blushes.

"Ana. You'll have to forgive me, but I probably know a lot more about you than you think. Christian has been very forthcoming."

She glances at me.

"An NDA? That must have shocked you," Flynn continues.

"Oh, I think the shock of that has paled into insignificance, given Christian's most recent revelations," she says, and her voice is low and husky.

I shift in my seat.

"I'm sure. So, Christian, what would you like to discuss?"

I shrug. "Anastasia wanted to see you. Perhaps you should ask her."

But Ana is staring at a box of tissues on the coffee table in front of her.

"Would you be more comfortable if Christian left us for a while?" Flynn asks her.

What?

Ana's eyes dart to me. "Yes," she says.

Fuck.

But?

Shit.

I stand up. "I'll be in the waiting room."

"Thank you, Christian," Flynn says.

I give Ana a long look, trying to tell her I'm ready for this commitment that I want to make to her. Then I stalk out of the room, closing the door behind me.

Flynn's receptionist Janet looks up, but I ignore her and wander into the waiting room, where I flop into one of the leather armchairs.

What will they discuss?

You, Grey. You.

Closing my eyes, I lean back and try to relax.

Blood thrums through my ears, a thump, thump, thump that's impossible to ignore.

Find your happy place, Grey.

I'm in the orchard with Elliot. We're kids. We're running through the trees. Laughing. Picking apples. Eating apples. Grandpa is watching us. Laughing too.

We're in a kayak with Mom. Dad and Mia are ahead of us. We're racing Dad.

Elliot and I are paddling with all our twelve-year-old fury. Mom is laughing. Mia splashes us with her paddle.

"Fuck! Elliot!" We're on a Hobie Cat. He has the tiller and we're flying the hull, tearing downwind across Lake Washington. Elliot whoops with joy as we trapeze over the side of the hull. We're wet. Exhilarated. And fighting the wind.

I'm making love to Ana. Breathing in her scent. Kissing her throat, her breast.

My body responds.

Fuck. No. I open my eyes and stare at the utilitarian brass chandelier on the white ceiling and shift in my seat.

What are they talking about?

I get up and start pacing. But I sit down again and leaf through one of the *National Geographic* magazines, the only publication that Flynn offers in his waiting room.

I can't concentrate on any of the articles.

Nice photographs, though.

I can't bear this. I pace once more. Then sit down and check the address of the house we're going to visit. And if Ana doesn't like what she hears from Flynn and doesn't want to see me again? I'll just have to get Andrea to cancel.

I get up, and before I know what I'm doing I'm outside, walking away from the conversation. The conversation about me.

I WALK THREE TIMES around the block and return to Flynn's office. Janet says nothing as I stride past her, knock on the door, and enter.

Flynn gives me a benevolent smile. "Welcome back, Christian," he says.

"I think time is up, John."

"Nearly, Christian. Join us."

I sit down beside Ana and place my hand on her knee. She gives nothing away, and that's frustrating, but she doesn't pull her knee out of my reach.

"Did you have any other questions, Ana?"

She shakes her head.

"Christian?"

"Not today, John."

"It may be beneficial if you both come again. I'm sure Ana will have more questions."

If that's what she wants. If that's what it takes. I clasp her hand and her eyes meet mine.

"Okay?" I ask gently.

She nods and gives me a reassuring smile. I hope the squeeze I give her hand lets her know how relieved I am. I turn to Flynn.

"How is she?" I ask him, and he knows I'm referring to Leila.

"She'll get there," he says.

"Good. Keep me updated as to her progress."

"I will."

I turn to Ana. "Should we go celebrate your promotion?"

Her shy nod is a relief.

WITH MY HAND ON the small of her back, I escort Ana out of the office. I'm anxious to hear what was discussed. I need to know if he put her off.

"How was that?" I ask, aiming for nonchalance as we walk out onto the street.

"It was good."

And? I'm dying here, Ana.

She looks at me and I have no idea what she's thinking. It's unnerving, and annoying. I scowl.

"Mr. Grey. Please don't look at me that way. Under doctor's orders I am going to give you the benefit of the doubt."

"What does that mean?"

"You'll see."

Will she marry me or not? Her winsome smile doesn't give me any clues.

Hell. She's not going to tell me. She's leaving me hanging. "Get in the car," I snap and open her door.

Her phone rings and she gives me a wary look before answering. "Hi," she says enthusiastically.

Who is it?

José, she mouths at me, answering my unspoken question. "Sorry I haven't called you. Is it about tomorrow?" she says to him but without looking away from me. "Well, I'm actually staying with Christian right now, and if you want to, he says you can stay at his place."

Oh yes. He's delivering the stunning photographs of Ana, his love letters to her.

Embrace her friends, Grey.

She frowns and turns away, crossing the sidewalk to lean against the building.

Is she okay? I watch her carefully. Waiting.

"Yes. Serious," she answers, her expression stern.

What's serious?

"Yes," she responds, and then she scoffs, indignant, "Of course I am… You could pick me up from work… I'll text you the address… Six?" She grins. "Cool. I'll see you then." She hangs up and walks back toward the car.

"How's your friend?" I ask.

"He's well. He'll pick me up from work, and I think we'll go for a drink. Would you like to join us?"

"You don't think he'll try anything?"

"No!"

"Okay." I hold my hands up. "You hang out with your friend, and I'll see you later in the evening. See? I can be reasonable."

She purses her lips—amused, I think. "Can I drive?"

"I'd rather you didn't."

"Why, exactly?"

"Because I don't like to be driven."

"You managed this morning, and you seem to tolerate Taylor driving you."

"I trust Taylor's driving implicitly."

"And not mine?" she exclaims and puts her hands on her hips. "Honestly, your control-freakishness knows no bounds. I've been driving since I was fifteen."

I shrug. I want to drive.

"Is this my car?"

"Of course it's your car."

"Then give me the keys, please. I've driven it twice, and only to and from work. Now you're having all the fun." She folds her arms, standing firm, stubborn as ever.

"But you don't know where we're going."

"I'm sure you can enlighten me, Mr. Grey. You've done a great job of it so far."

And just like that she defuses the moment. She's the most disarming person I've ever met. She won't answer me. She's left me hanging, and I want to live the rest of my life with her.

"Great job, eh?" I ask through my smile.

She flushes. "Mostly, yes." And her eyes are alight with amusement.

"Well, in that case." I hand her the keys and open the driver's door for her.

I take a deep breath as she pulls into traffic. "Where are we going?" she asks, and I have to remind myself that she hasn't lived in Seattle long enough to know her way around.

"Continue along this street."

"You're not going to be more specific?" she asks.

I give her a slight smile.

Tit for tat, baby.

She narrows her eyes.

"At the light, turn right," I say.

She stops rather too suddenly, throwing us both forward, then indicates and moves on.

"Steady, Ana!"

Her mouth sets in a grim line.

"Left here."

Ana puts her foot down and we speed up the street.

"Hell! Gently, Ana." I grab the dashboard. "Slow down!" She's doing thirty-eight through the neighborhood!

"I am slowing down!" she shouts as she brakes.

I sigh and get to the heart of what I want to talk about, trying and failing to sound casual. "What did Flynn say?"

"I told you. He says I should give you the benefit of the doubt." Ana signals to pull over.

"What are you doing?"

"Letting you drive."

"Why?"

"So I can look at you."

I laugh. "No, no. You wanted to drive, so you drive. And I'll look at you."

She turns to say something to me.

"Keep your eyes on the road!" I shout.

She screeches to a halt just before a traffic light, releases her seat belt, and storms out of the car, slamming the door.

What the hell?

She stands on the sidewalk with arms crossed in what's both a defensive and combative pose, glaring at me.

I scramble out after her. "What are you doing?" I ask, completely thrown.

"No. What are *you* doing?"

"You can't park here." I point to the abandoned Saab.

"I know that."

"So why have you?"

"Because I've had it with you barking orders. Either you drive or you shut up about my driving!"

"Anastasia, get back in the car before we get a ticket."

"No."

I run my hands through my hair. What's gotten into her?

I look down at her. I'm at a loss. Her expression changes, softening. Damn it, is she laughing at me? "What?" I ask.

"You."

"Oh, Anastasia! You are the most frustrating female on the planet." I throw my hands in the air. "Fine. I'll drive."

She grabs my jacket and tugs me against her body. "No. You are the most frustrating man on the planet, Mr. Grey."

She looks up at me with guileless blue eyes that pull me under and I'm drowning and I'm lost. Lost in a different way. I put my arms around her, holding her close. "Maybe we're meant for each other, then." She smells amazing. I should bottle this.

Soothing. Sexy. Ana.

She hugs me hard and rests her cheek against my chest.

"Oh, Ana, Ana, Ana." I kiss her hair and hold her.

It's weird, embracing in the street.

Another first. No. A second. I held her on the street near Esclava.

She moves and I release her, and without saying a word, I open the passenger door and she gets in the car.

At the wheel, I start the car and pull into traffic. There's a Van Morrison song playing over the sound system and I hum along as we head toward the on-ramp for I-5. "You know, if we had gotten a ticket, the title of this car is in your name," I tell her.

"Well, good thing I've been promoted. I can afford the fine."

And I hide my amusement as we head north on I-5.

"Where are we going?" she asks.

"It's a surprise. What else did Flynn say?"

"He talked about FFFSTB or something."

"SFBT. Thc latest therapy option."

"You've tried others?"

"Baby, I've been subjected to them all. Cognitivism, Freud, functionalism, Gestalt, behaviorism. You name it, over the years I've done it."

"Do you think this latest approach will help?"

"What did Flynn say?"

"He said not to dwell on your past. Focus on the future—on where you want to be."

I nod, but I don't understand why she hasn't accepted my proposal.

That's where I want to be.

Married.

Perhaps he said something to discourage her. "What else?" I ask, trying to get an inkling of what he might have said to dissuade her.

"He talked about your fear of being touched, although he called it something else. And about your nightmares and your self-abhorrence." I meet her gaze.

"Eyes on the road, Mr. Grey," she scolds.

"You were talking forever, Anastasia. What else did he say?"

"He doesn't think you're a sadist."

"Really?" Flynn and I have differing views on this. He cannot step into my shoes. He doesn't really understand.

Ana continues. "He says that that term's not recognized in psychiatry. Not since the nineties."

"Flynn and I have differing opinions on this."

"He said you always think the worst of yourself. I know that's true. He also mentioned sexual sadism—but he said that was a lifestyle choice, not a psychiatric condition. Maybe that's what you're thinking about."

Ana, you have no idea.

You will never know the depths of my depravity.

"So, one talk with the good doctor and you're an expert."

She sighs. "Look, if you don't want to hear what he said, don't ask me," she says.

Fair point, Miss Steele.

Grey. Stop hounding the girl.

She turns her attention to the passing cars.

Damn.

"I want to know what you discussed," I say in a tone that I hope sounds conciliatory. I leave I-5 and head west on Northwest Eighty-Fifth Street.

"He called me your lover."

"Did he, now? Well, he's nothing if not fastidious about his terms. I think that's an accurate description, don't you?"

"Did you think of your subs as lovers?"

Lovers? Leila? Susannah? Madison? Each of my submissives comes to mind.

"No. They were sexual partners. You're my only lover. And I want you to be more."

"I know. I just need some time, Christian. To get my head around these past few days."

I look over at her.

Why didn't she say that earlier?

I can live with that.

Of course I can give her some time.

I'd wait until time stands still, for her.

I RELAX AND ENJOY the drive. We're in the suburbs of Seattle but heading west toward the Sound. I think I've timed this appointment just right and we'll catch the sunset over Puget Sound.

"Where are we going?" she asks.

"Surprise."

She gives me a curious smile and turns to take in our surroundings through the window.

Ten minutes later I spy the corroded white metal gates from the photograph I've seen online. I pull in at the bottom of an impressive driveway and punch the security code into the keypad. With a creaky groan, the heavy gates swing open.

I glance at Ana.

Will she like this place?

"What is it?" she asks.

"An idea." I steer the Saab through the gates.

The driveway is longer than I thought. To one side there's an overgrown meadow. It's big enough to install a tennis court or basketball court—or both.

"Hey bro, let's shoot some hoops."

"Elliot, I'm reading."

"Reading is not going to get you laid."

"Fuck off."

"Hoops. Come on, man," he whines.

Reluctantly, I abandon my tattered copy of Oliver Twist *and follow him out to the yard.*

ANA LOOKS STUNNED AS we arrive at the grand entrance portico and I park beside a BMW sedan. The house is sprawling and actually quite imposing from the outside.

I cut the engine, and Ana's baffled.

"Will you keep an open mind?" I ask.

She arches a brow. "Christian, I've needed an open mind since the day I met you."

And I can't disagree. She's right. As ever.

The real estate agent is waiting inside the large vestibule. "Mr. Grey." She greets me warmly and we shake hands.

"Miss Kelly."

"Olga Kelly," she announces to Ana.

"Ana Steele," she responds.

The real estate agent steps aside. The house smells a little musty from what must be months of disuse. But I'm not here to look at the interior. "Come," I direct Ana and take her hand. Having studied the floor plans at length I know where I want to go and how to get there. I lead her from the vestibule through an archway into an inner hallway, past a grand staircase, and into what was once the main living room.

There are several open french doors on the far side, which is great because the place needs airing. Tightening my hold on Ana's hand, I take her through the nearest door, onto the terrace outside.

The view is every bit as arresting and dramatic as the photographs suggested: the Sound in all its glory at dusk. Already there are lights twinkling from the distant shores of Bainbridge Island, where we sailed last weekend, and beyond that, the Olympic Peninsula.

There is so much sky and the sunset is astounding.

Ana and I stand hand in hand and stare, enjoying the spectacular view. Her face is radiant. She loves it.

She turns to look at me. "You brought me here to admire the view?"

I nod.

"It's staggering, Christian. Thank you," she says and stares once more at the opal sky.

"How would you like to look at it for the rest of your life?" My heart starts hammering.

This is one hell of a pitch, Grey.

Her face whips to mine. She's startled.

"I've always wanted to live on the coast," I explain. "I sail up and down the Sound, coveting these houses. This place hasn't been on the market long. I want to buy it, demolish it, and build a new house—for us."

Her eyes grow impossibly large.

"It's just an idea," I whisper.

She looks over her shoulder into the old living room. "Why do you want to demolish it?" she asks.

"I'd like to make a more sustainable home, using the latest ecological techniques. Elliot could build it."

"Can we look around the house?"

"Sure." I shrug. Why does she want to look around?

I follow Ana and the real estate agent as she gives us the tour. Olga is in her element as she takes us through the numerous rooms, describing the features of each. Why Ana wants to see the whole house is a mystery to me.

As we file up the sweeping staircase, she turns to me. "Couldn't you make the existing house more ecological and self-sustaining?"

This house?

"I'd have to ask Elliot. He's the expert in all this."

Ana likes *this* house.

Keeping the house wasn't what I had in mind.

The real estate agent takes us into the master suite. It has full-height windows opening onto a balcony that looks out at the spectacular view. We both pause for a moment and stare at the darkening sky and the last traces of the sun that can still be seen. It's a glorious vista.

We wander through the rest of the bedrooms; there are many, and the last overlooks the front of the house. The real estate agent suggests the meadow might be a suitable place for a paddock and stables.

"The paddock would be where the meadow is now?" Ana asks, looking dubious.

"Yes," the real estate agent replies.

Back downstairs, we make our way through to the terrace once more and I rethink my plans. The house wasn't what I imagined living in, but it looks well built and solid enough and with a comprehensive update, it could serve our needs. I glance at Ana.

Who am I kidding?

Wherever Ana is, that's my home.

If this is what she wants…

Outside on the terrace, I hold her. "Lot to take in?" I ask.

She nods.

"I wanted to check that you liked it before I bought it."

"The view?"

I nod.

"I love the view, and I like the house that's here."

"You do?"

"Christian, you had me at the meadow," she says with a shy smile.

This means she's not leaving.

Surely.

I cup her face, my fingers in her hair, and pour all my gratitude into one kiss.

"THANKS FOR LETTING US look around," I say to Miss Kelly. "I'll be in touch."

"Thank you, Mr. Grey. Ana," she says, eagerly shaking hands with each of us.

Ana likes it!

My relief is palpable as we climb into the Saab. Olga has switched on the external lights and the driveway is edged with winking lamps. The house is growing on me. It has a sprawling, grand quality to it. I'm sure Elliot can work his magic on the place and make it more ecologically sustainable.

"So, you're going to buy it?" Ana asks when we're on our way back to Seattle.

"Yes."

"You'll put Escala on the market?"

"Why would I do that?"

"To pay for—" She stops.

"Trust me, I can afford it."

"Do you like being rich?"

I want to scoff. "Yes. Show me someone who doesn't."

She chews her finger.

"Anastasia, you're going to have to learn to be rich, too, if you say yes."

"Wealth isn't something I've ever aspired to, Christian."

"I know. I love that about you. But then again, you've never been hungry."

In my peripheral vision, I see her turn and look at me, but I can't make out her expression in the darkness.

"Where are we going?" she asks, and I know she's changing the subject.

"To celebrate."

"Celebrate what, the house?"

"Have you forgotten already? Your acting-editor role."

"Oh yes. Where?"

"Up high at my club." They'll still be serving food at this hour, and I'm hungry.

"Your club?"

"Yes. One of them."

"How many do you belong to?"

"Three."

Please don't ask me about them.

"Private gentleman's clubs? No women allowed?" she teases, and I know she's laughing at me.

"Women allowed. At all of them." Especially one. A Dominant's haven. Though I haven't been for a while.

She gives me an inquisitive look.

"What?" I ask.

"Nothing," she says.

I LEAVE THE CAR with the valet and we travel up to the Mile High Club at the top of Columbia Tower. Our table isn't ready immediately, so we sit at the bar.

"Cristal, ma'am?" I hand Ana a glass of chilled champagne.

"Why, thank you, Sir." She stresses the last word and bats her eyelashes at me. She moves her legs, drawing my attention to them. Her dress is hiked up, exposing a little more of her thigh.

"Are you flirting with me, Miss Steele?"

"Yes, Mr. Grey, I am. What are you going to do about it?"

Oh, Ana. I love when you throw down the gauntlet.

"I'm sure I can think of something," I murmur. Carmine, the maître d', gives me a wave. "Come, our table's ready."

I step back and hold out my hand while she gracefully slips off the barstool, and I follow. Her ass looks great in this dress.

Ah. A wicked idea pops into my mind.

Before she sits down at our table, I touch her elbow. "Go take your panties off," I whisper in her ear. "Go." *Now.*

She inhales quickly, and I remember the last time she went pantyless and how she turned the tables on me then; maybe she will again. She gives me a haughty look but, without saying a word, hands me her glass of champagne and saunters to the ladies' restroom.

While I wait at the table I scan the menu. It reminds me of our dinner in the private room at The Heathman. I summon the waiter and hope Ana won't give me a hard time because I'm ordering her meal.

"Can I help you, Mr. Grey?"

"Please. A dozen Kumamotos, to start. And then two orders of the sea bass with hollandaise sauce and sautéed potatoes. And a side of asparagus."

"Very good, sir. Would you like anything from the wine list?"

"Not right now. We'll stick to the champagne."

The waiter scuttles off and Ana appears, a secret smile playing on her lips.

Oh, Ana. She wants to play… but I'm not going to touch her. Yet.

I want to drive her crazy.

Standing, I motion to the seat. "Sit beside me." She slides in and I join her, mindful not to sit too close. "I've ordered for you. I hope you don't mind." Careful not to touch her fingers with mine, I give her back her glass of champagne.

She fidgets beside me but takes a sip of the Cristal.

The waiter returns with the oysters on ice. "I think you liked oysters last time you tried them."

"Only time I've tried them." Her breathing stalls. She's… eager.

"Oh, Miss Steele, when will you learn?" I tease, taking an oyster from the dish. I lift my hand from my thigh and she leans back in anticipation of my touch, but I reach for some lemon.

"Learn what?" she whispers as I squeeze lemon juice over the shellfish.

"Eat." I hold the shell up to her mouth. She parts her lips and I rest the shell on her bottom lip. "Tip your head back slowly."

With a smoldering look, she does as she's told and I tip the oyster into her mouth. She closes her eyes in appreciation, and I help myself to one.

"Another?" I ask.

She nods, and this time I add a little mignonette sauce and still don't touch her. She swallows and licks her lips.

"Good?"

She nods.

I eat another, then feed her one more.

"Hmm..." she says, and the sound resonates the length of my cock.

"Still like oysters?" I ask as she swallows the final one.

She nods again.

"Good."

I place my hands on my thighs, flexing my fingers, and I'm gratified when she shifts beside me. But as much as I want to, I refrain from touching her. The waiter tops off our champagne and clears our plates. Ana squeezes her thighs together and rubs her hands over them. And I think I hear a frustrated sigh.

Oh, baby. Craving my touch?

The waiter returns with our entrées.

Ana eyes me with suspicious recognition as the food is placed on the table. "A favorite of yours, Mr. Grey?"

"Most definitely, Miss Steele. Though I believe it was cod at The Heathman."

"I seem to remember we were in a private dining room then, discussing contracts."

"Happy days. This time I hope to get to fuck you." I reach for my knife and she fidgets beside me. I take a bite of sea bass.

"Don't count on it," she mutters, and I know without looking that she's pouting.

Oh, playing hard to get, Miss Steele?

"Speaking of contracts," she continues. "The NDA."

"Tear it up."

"What? Really?"

"Yes."

"You're sure I'm not going to run to *The Seattle Times* with an exposé?"

I laugh, knowing how shy she is. "No. I trust you. I'm going to give you the benefit of the doubt."

"Ditto," she says.

"I'm very glad you're wearing a dress."

"Why haven't you touched me, then?"

"Missing my touch?" I tease.

"Yes!" she exclaims.

"Eat."

"You're not going to touch me, are you?"

"No." I hide my amusement.

She looks outraged.

"Just imagine how you'll feel when we're home," I add. "I can't wait to get you home."

"It will be your fault if I combust here on the seventy-sixth floor." She sounds pissed.

"Oh, Anastasia. We'd find a way to put the fire out."

She narrows her eyes and takes a bite of her supper. The sea bass is delicious, and I'm hungry. She wriggles in her seat and her dress rides up a little, exposing more of her skin. She takes another bite, then puts down her knife and runs her hand up the inside of her thigh, her fingertips drumming as she does.

She's toying with me. "I know what you're doing."

"I know you know, Mr. Grey. That's the point." She takes an asparagus stalk between her fingers and, with a sideways glance at me, dips the spear into the hollandaise sauce and swirls it around and around.

"You're not turning the tables on me, Miss Steele." I take the asparagus from her. "Open your mouth."

She opens her mouth and runs her tongue across her bottom lip.

Tempting, Miss Steele. Very tempting.

"Wider," I command, and she bites her bottom lip but complies, easing the stalk into her mouth and sucking.

Fuck.

It might as well be my cock.

She moans quietly and takes a bite and reaches for me.

I stop her with my other hand. "Oh no you don't, Miss Steele." I brush my lips across her knuckles. "Don't touch," I scold and place her hand on her knee.

"You don't play fair."

"I know." I raise my champagne glass. "Congratulations on your promotion, Miss Steele." We clink glasses.

"Yes, kind of unexpected," she says, looking a little discouraged. Does she doubt herself? I hope not.

"Eat." I change the subject. "I am not taking you home until you've finished your meal, and then we can really celebrate."

"I'm not hungry. Not for food."

Ana. Ana. So easily distracted.

"Eat, or I'll put you across my knee, right here, and we'll entertain the other diners."

She shifts in her seat, making me think a spanking might be welcome, but her pursed lips tell a different story. Picking up an asparagus stalk, I dip the head into the hollandaise. "Eat this," I tempt her.

She does, keeping her eyes on me.

"You really don't eat enough. You've lost weight since I've known you."

"I just want to go home and make love."

I grin. "So do I, and we will. Eat up."

She sighs as if in defeat and starts tucking into her food.

I follow her example. "Have you heard from your friend?" I ask.

"Which one?"

"The guy staying in your apartment."

"Oh, Ethan. Not since he took Mia out for lunch."

"I'm doing some work with his and Kate's father."

"Oh?"

"Yes. Kavanagh seems like a solid guy."

"He's always been good to me," she answers, and my earlier thoughts about a hostile takeover of Kavanagh's business recede.

She finishes her supper and places her knife and fork on her plate.

"Good girl."

"What now?" she asks, her expression needy.

"Now? We leave. I believe you have certain expectations, Miss Steele. Which I intend to fulfill to the best of my ability."

"The best of your a-a-bility?" she stutters.

I grin and stand up.

"Don't we have to pay?"

"I'm a member here. They'll bill me. Come, Anastasia, after you." I step aside, and Ana gets up from the table, pausing beside me to smooth her dress down over her thighs.

"I can't wait to get you home." I follow her out of the restaurant and stop to talk to the maître d'. "Thanks, Carmine. Superb as always."

"You're welcome. Mr. Grey."

"And can you call down to have the car brought to the front?"

"No problem. Good night."

As we get into the elevator I take Ana's elbow and steer her toward the far corner. I stand behind her and watch as other couples get in.

Hell.

Linc, Elena's ex, joins us, wearing a shit-brown suit.

What an asshole. I loathe him.

"Grey," he acknowledges me.

I nod, and I'm relieved when he turns around. The fact that he's here, only inches away, makes what I'm about to do even more exciting.

The doors close and I kneel quickly, pretending to do up my shoelace. I place my hand around Ana's ankle, and as I stand, I skim my hand up her calf, past her knee, and her thigh to her ass. Her naked ass.

She tenses and I slide my left arm around her waist and pull her to me while my fingers skate down her ass, to her sex. The elevator stops at another floor and we shuffle back as one to let more people on board. But I'm not interested in them. Carefully

I brush her clitoris, once, twice, thrice, and then move my fingers back to her heat. "Always so ready, Miss Steele," I whisper as I inch my middle finger inside her. I hear her faint gasp. "Keep still and quiet," I warn so only she can hear me. Slowly I move my finger in and out, on and on, as my excitement grows. She grabs the arm I have around her waist and squeezes. Holding on. Her breathing accelerates, and I know she's trying to keep quiet as I silently torment her with my fingers.

The sway of the elevator as it stops to pick up more passengers adds to the rhythm. She sags against me, then pushes her ass against my hand, wanting more. Faster.

Oh, my greedy, greedy girl.

"Hush," I breathe and nuzzle her hair. I ease a second finger inside her and continue to pump them in and out. She tips her head back against my chest, exposing her throat. I want to kiss her, but that would draw too much attention to what we're doing. Her grip on me tightens.

Damn. I'm bursting. My jeans are too fucking tight. I want her, but now really is not the place.

Her fingers dig into me.

"Don't come. I want that later," I whisper and splay my hand on her belly and press down, knowing this will emphasize everything she's feeling. Her head is lolling against my chest and she's biting down on her bottom lip.

The elevator stops.

There's a loud ping and the doors open on the first floor.

Slowly I withdraw my hand as the passengers exit, and I kiss the back of her head.

Well done, Ana.

She did not give us away.

I hold her for a moment longer.

Linc turns and nods as he leaves with a woman who I assume is his present wife. When I'm sure Ana is able to stand, I release her. She gazes up at me, her eyes dark and smoky with lust.

"Ready?" I ask, then slip both of my fingers briefly into my mouth. "Mighty fine, Miss Steele." I give her a wicked grin.

"I can't believe you just did that," she whispers, breathless and arousing.

"You'd be surprised what I can do, Miss Steele." Reaching out, I neaten her hair, pushing it behind her ear. "I want to get you home, but maybe we'll only make it as far as the car." I give her a quick smile, check that my jacket is covering the front of my jeans, then take her hand and lead her out of the elevator. "Come," I bid her.

"Yes, I want to."

"Miss Steele!"

"I've never had sex in a car," she says as her heels echo on the marble floor.

I stop and tip her head up so we are eye to eye.

"I'm very pleased to hear that. I have to say I'd be very surprised, not to say mad, if you had."

"That's not what I meant," she huffs.

"What did you mean?"

"Christian, it was just an expression."

"The famous expression 'I've never had sex in a car.' Yes, it just trips off the tongue." I'm teasing her; she's so easy to provoke.

"Christian, I wasn't thinking. For heaven's sake, you've just… um, done that to me in an elevator full of people. My wits are scattered."

"What did I do to you?"

She purses her lips. "You turned me on, big-time. Now take me home and fuck me."

I laugh, taken aback. I had no idea she could be quite so crude. "You're a born romantic, Miss Steele." I take her hand and we head to the valet, who has the Saab parked and ready. I give him a large tip and open the passenger door for Ana.

"So you want sex in a car?" I ask as I switch on the ignition.

"Quite frankly, I would have been happy with the lobby floor."

"Trust me, Ana, so would I. But I don't enjoy being arrested at this time of night, and I didn't want to fuck you in a restroom. Well, not today."

"You mean there was a possibility?"

"Oh yes."

"Let's go back."

I turn to look at her earnest expression. She's so unexpected sometimes. I start to laugh, and soon we are both laughing. It's cathartic after the build-up of sexual tension. I place a hand on her knee, caressing her and she stops laughing and looks at me with large, dark eyes.

I could fall into them and never come back. She's so beautiful.

"Patience, Anastasia," I whisper and we move off, heading up Fifth Avenue.

She's silent but restless as we drive back, though she gives me the occasional come-hither look through her dark lashes.

I know that look.

Yes. Ana. I want you, too.

In every way… Please say yes.

The Saab glides into a parking space in Escala's garage. I switch off the engine, thinking about her wish for sex in a car. I have to admit it's not something I've done, either. She's biting her lip, her expression… wanton.

Groin-tighteningly wanton.

Gently, I release her lip with my fingers. I love that she wants me as much as I want her. "We will fuck in the car at a time and place of my choosing," I whisper. "Right now, I want to take you on every available surface of my apartment."

"Yes," she says, even though it's not a question.

I lean toward her and she closes her eyes and puckers her lips, offering me a kiss. Her cheeks are slightly flushed.

I take a quick look around the car.

We could.

No.

She opens her eyes, waiting impatiently.

"If I kiss you now, we won't make it into the apartment. Come." Resisting the urge to jump her, I climb out of the car, and together we wait for the elevator.

I hold her hand, stroking her knuckles with my thumb. Setting up a rhythm I hope to repeat with my dick in a few minutes.

"So, what happened to instant gratification?" she asks.

"It's not appropriate in every situation, Anastasia."

"Since when?"

"Since this evening."

"Why are you torturing me so?"

"Tit for tat, Miss Steele."

"How am I torturing you?"

"I think you know."

And I watch as realization dawns on her face.

Yes, baby.

I love you. And I want you to be my wife.

But you won't tell me your answer.

"I'm into delayed gratification, too," she whispers and gives me a shy smile.

She *is* torturing me!

I tug her hand and pull her into my arms, and my fingers wrap around her nape as I angle her head to look into her eyes. "What can I do to make you say yes?" I beg her.

"Give me some time, please," she says.

I groan and my lips are on hers, my tongue seeking hers. The elevator doors open and we shuffle in, maintaining our embrace. And she's lit from within. Her hands are on me. Everywhere. In my hair. Around my face. On my ass. And she's kissing me back with such passion.

I burn for her.

Pushing her against the wall, reveling in the fervor of her kiss, I pin her with my hips and my erection. I have one hand in her hair and one on her chin.

"You own me," I whisper against her mouth. "My fate is in your hands, Ana."

She pushes my jacket off my shoulders and the elevator stops and opens onto the foyer. I notice the usual flowers are missing from the foyer table.

Fucking A.

Foyer table, surface number one!

I press Ana against the wall and she finishes the job, pushing my jacket off me onto the floor. My hand runs up her thigh, taking the hem of her dress with it while we kiss. I boost her skirt higher.

"First surface here," I murmur, and lift her suddenly. "Wrap your legs around me."

She does as she's told and I lay her on the hall table. From my jeans pocket I fish out a condom and hand it to Ana and undo my fly.

Her fingers impatiently open the packet.

Her enthusiasm is arousing.

"Do you know how much you turn me on?"

"What? No. I…" She's breathless.

"Well, you do. All the time." I grab the packet from her hands and roll on the condom while staring at her. Her hair is cascading over the edge of the table and she's staring up at me, her eyes brimming with want.

I move between her legs and lift her ass off the table, spreading her legs farther apart. "Keep your eyes open. I want to see you." I take both her hands and slowly sink into her.

It takes all my willpower to keep my eyes open on hers. She's exquisite.

Every fucking inch of her.

She closes her eyes and I thrust hard into her. "Open," I urge, and I tighten my hold on her hands.

She cries out but opens her eyes. They are wild and blue and beautiful. Slowly I pull out of her, then sink into her again. She watches me.

Her eyes on me.

God, I love her.

I move faster. Loving her. The only way I really know how.

Her mouth opens, slack, wide, beautiful. And her legs tense around me.

This is going to be quick.

And she comes around me, taking me with her.

She calls out through her climax.

"Yes, Ana!" I cry. And come and come and come.

I collapse on her, release her hands, and rest my head on her chest. I close my eyes. She cradles my head, running her fingers through my hair as I catch my breath.

I look up at her. "I'm not finished with you yet," I whisper, and I kiss her and disengage myself.

Hastily, I do up my fly and lift her off the table.

We stand in the foyer holding each other. We're under the careful watch of the women in my Madonna and Child paintings that line the walls.

I think they approve of my girl.

"Bed," I whisper.

"Please," she says. And I take her to bed and make love to her once more.

SHE COMES, RIDING ME hard, and I hold her upright as I watch her spiral out of control.

Fuck, it's erotic.

She's naked, her breasts bouncing, and I let go, climaxing inside her, my head back, my fingers digging into her hips. She flops down on my chest, panting hard.

As I recover my breath, I run my fingers down her back, dewy with her sweat.

"Satisfied, Miss Steele?"

She mumbles her agreement. Then she looks up at me; her expression is a little dazed, but she angles her head.

Shit. She's going to kiss my chest.

I take a deep breath and she plants a soft, warm kiss on my chest.

It's okay. The darkness is quiet. Or gone. I don't know.

I relax and roll us onto our sides.

"Is sex like this for everyone? I'm surprised anyone ever goes out," she says with a sated smile.

She makes me feel ten feet tall. "I can't speak for everyone, but it's pretty damned special with you, Anastasia." My lips touch hers.

"That's because you're pretty damned special, Mr. Grey." She caresses my face.

"It's late. Go to sleep." I kiss her and pull her to me so we're spooning, her back to my front, and I tug up the comforter.

"You don't like compliments." Her voice is drifting. She's tired.

No. *I'm not used to them.*

"Go to sleep, Anastasia."

"I loved the house," she mutters.

That means she might say yes. I grin into her hair and nuzzle her. "I love you. Go to sleep."

And I close my eyes as her scent fills my nostrils.

A *house.* A *wife. What more do I need? Please say yes, Ana.*

Friday, June 17, 2011

Ana's cry drags me from my sleep. Opening my eyes, I wake. She's beside me and I think she's asleep. "Flying too close," she whimpers. The early morning light bleeds pink and bright between the blinds, illuminating her hair. "Icarus," she says.

Leaning up on my elbow, I check to see if she's asleep. I haven't heard her talk in her sleep for a while. She turns over so she's facing me. "Benefit of the doubt," she says. And her face relaxes.

Benefit of the doubt?

Is this about me?

She said it yesterday. She said she was going to give me the benefit of the doubt.

It's more than I deserve.

Much more than you deserve, Grey.

I plant a chaste kiss on her forehead, switch off the alarm before it wakes her, and get out of bed. I have an early morning meeting to discuss Kavanagh's fiber-optic requirements.

In the shower, I think about my schedule for the day. I have Kavanagh. Then I fly down to WSU via Portland with Ros. Drinks in the evening with Ana and her photographer friend.

And I'll put an offer on that house today. Ana says she loved it.

I grin as I rinse the shampoo from my hair.

Just give her time, Grey.

IN MY CLOSET, I slip on my pants and notice my jacket from yesterday slung over the chair. I fish through the pockets and grab Ana's present. It still produces a tantalizing rattle.

I slip it into my inside pocket, pleased that it will rest close to my heart.

You're getting sentimental in your old age, Grey.

SHE'S STILL CURLED UP asleep when I check on her. "Gotta go, baby." I sit down beside her and kiss her neck.

She opens her eyes and turns over to face me. In her drowsy state, she smiles up at me, then her expression changes. "What time is it?"

"Don't panic. I have a breakfast meeting."

"You smell good," she whispers. She stretches out beneath me and encircles my neck with her hands. Her fingers trail in my hair. "Don't go."

"Miss Steele, are you trying to keep a man from an honest day's work?"

She gives me a sleepy nod, her eyes a little dazed. Desire blooms in my body; she looks so damn sexy. Her smile is captivating and it takes all my self-control not to strip off my clothes and slip back into bed. "As tempting as you are, I have to go." I kiss her and stand. "Laters, baby." I leave before I change my mind.

Taylor looks troubled when I join him in the garage.

"Mr. Grey. I have a problem."

"What is it?"

"My ex-wife called. My daughter may have appendicitis."

"Is she in the hospital?"

"They're admitting her now."

"You should go."

"Thank you. I'll drop you at work first."

"Thanks. I appreciate it."

TAYLOR IS DEEP IN thought when we pull up outside Grey House.

"Let me know how she is."

"I may not be back until tomorrow morning."

"It's fine. Go. I hope Sophie's okay."

"Thank you, sir."

I watch him zoom off. He's seldom preoccupied…but this is family. Yes. Family comes first. Always.

Andrea is waiting for me when I step out of the elevator.

"Good morning, Mr. Grey. Taylor called. I'll arrange a driver for you here and in Portland."

"Good. Everyone here?

"Yes. In your boardroom."

"Great. Thanks, Andrea."

THE MEETING GOES WELL. Kavanagh looks refreshed, no doubt from his recent vacation in Barbados, where he met my brother for the first time. He says he likes him. Considering Elliot's fucking his daughter, that's a good thing.

When they left, Kavanagh and his people seemed satisfied with our conversation. Now all that remains is to haggle over the price of the contract. Ros will have to take the lead on that with cost projections from Fred's division.

Andrea has laid out the usual breakfast spread. I grab a croissant and head back to my office with Ros. "What time do you want to leave?" Ros asks me.

"Our driver will pick us up at ten."

"I'll see you in the foyer downstairs," Ros confirms. "I'm excited. I've never been in a helicopter."

Her grin is infectious.

"I found a house yesterday and I want to buy it. Will you handle the details?"

"As your lawyer, sure, of course I will."

"Thanks. I owe you."

"You will." She laughs. "See you downstairs."

I stand alone inside my office, feeling elated. I'm buying a house. The Kavanagh contract will be a great boost to the company. And I had a wonderful evening with my girl. At my desk, I send her an email.

From: Christian Grey
Subject: Surfaces
Date: June 17 2011 08:59
To: Anastasia Steele

I calculate that there are at least 30 surfaces to go. I am looking forward to each and every one of them. Then there's the floors, the walls—and let's not forget the balcony.

After that there's my office…

Miss you. x

Christian Grey
Priapic CEO, Grey Enterprises Holdings, Inc.

I take a look around my office. Yes, there's a lot of potential here: the sofa, the desk. Andrea knocks on the door and enters with my coffee. I marshal my wayward thoughts, and my body.

She places the coffee on my desk. "More coffee."

"Thank you. Can you get the real estate agent for the house I saw yesterday on the line?"

"Sure thing, sir."

My discussion with Olga Kelly is brief. We agree on a price to take back to the seller, and I give her Ros's details so we can move quickly with inspections if the offer is accepted.

I check my email. And I'm pleased to see a response from Ana to my earlier missive.

From: Anastasia Steele
Subject: Romance?
Date: June 17 2011 09:03
To: Christian Grey

Mr. Grey
You have a one-track mind.
I missed you at breakfast.
But Mrs. Jones was very accommodating.

A x

Accommodating?

From: Christian Grey
Subject: Intrigued
Date: June 17 2011 09:07
To: Anastasia Steele

What was Mrs. Jones accommodating about?

What are you up to, Miss Steele?

Christian Grey
Curious CEO, Grey Enterprises Holdings, Inc.

From: Anastasia Steele
Subject: Tapping Nose
Date: June 17 2011 09:10
To: Christian Grey

Wait and see—it's a surprise.
I need to work... Let me be.
Love you.

A x

From: Christian Grey
Subject: Frustrated
Date: June 17 2011 09:12
To: Anastasia Steele

I hate it when you keep things from me.

Christian Grey
CEO, Grey Enterprises Holdings, Inc.

From: Anastasia Steele
Subject: Indulging you
Date: June 17 2011 09:14
To: Christian Grey

It's for your birthday.

Another surprise.

Don't be so petulant.

A x

Another surprise? When I pat down my jacket pocket, I'm reassured by the presence of the box Ana's given me.

She's spoiling me.

ROS AND I ARE in the car on the way to Boeing Field. My phone flashes. It's a text from Elliot.

ELLIOT
Hey, asshole. Bar. This evening.
Kate's getting in touch with Ana.
You'd better be there.

Where are you?

ELLIOT
Layover Atlanta.
Missed me?

No.

ELLIOT
Yeah you have. Well I'm back and
you're getting your beer on tonight Bro.

It's been a while since I went drinking with my brother and at least I won't be alone with Ana and her photographer friend.

If you insist.
Safe travels.

ELLIOT
Laters dude.

Our flight to Portland is uneventful, though it's a revelation how giddy Ros can be. She's like a kid in a candy store during the flight. Fidgeting. Pointing. Nonstop commentary on everything she sees. It's a side of Ros I never knew existed. Where's the cool, collected lawyer I know? I'm reminded how quietly appreciative Ana was when I first took her up in *Charlie Tango.*

When we land, I pick up a voice mail from the real estate agent. The seller has accepted my offer. They must want a quick sale.

"What?" asks Ros.

"I've just bought that house."

"Congratulations."

AFTER A LENGTHY MEETING with the president and vice president of economic development at WSU in Vancouver, Ros and I are in conversation with Professor Gravett and her postgraduate team. The professor is in full flow. "We've been able to isolate the DNA of the microbe that's responsible for nitrogen fixation."

"What does that mean, exactly?" I ask.

"In layman's terms, Mr. Grey, nitrogen fixation is essential for soil diversity, and as you know, diverse soils recover from shocks like drought far more quickly. We can now study how to activate the DNA in the microbes that live in the soil in the sub-Saharan region. In a nutshell, we'll be able to get the soil to hold its nutrients for far longer, making it more productive per hectare."

"Our results will be published in the *Soil Science Society of America Journal* in a couple of months," Professor Choudury says. "We're sure to double our funding once the article comes out. And we'll need to get your input on potential funding sources that align with your philanthropic objectives."

"Of course," I say. "As you know, I think your work here should be shared broadly to benefit as many people as possible."

"We've kept that goal front and center in all that we're doing."

"Good to hear."

The president of the university nods in agreement. "We're very excited about this discovery."

"It is quite the achievement. Congratulations, Professor Gravett, and to your team."

She glows in response to the compliment. "Thanks to you."

Embarrassed, I glance at Ros, and it's as if she can read my mind. "We should be going," she says to the group, and we push our chairs back.

The president shakes my hand. "Thank you for your

continued support, Mr. Grey. As you've seen, your contribution to the Environmental Sciences Department makes a huge difference to us."

"Keep up the good work," I say.

I'm anxious to get back to Seattle. The photographer will be delivering those photographs to Escala and then seeing Ana. I'm fighting my jealous impulses and, so far, successfully keeping them under control. But I will be happier when we set back down at Boeing Field and I join them both at the bar. In the meantime, I have a surprise for Ros.

OUR TAKEOFF IS SMOOTH; I pull back the collective and *Charlie Tango* ascends like a graceful bird into the air above the Portland heliport. Ros smiles with girlish delight. I shake my head; I had no idea she could be this excitable, but then again, I always feel a rush on takeoff.

Once I've finished talking to the tower, Ros's disembodied voice asks over my headset, "How is your private merger going?"

"Good, thanks."

"Hence the house?"

"Yeah. Something like that."

She nods and we fly in silence over Vancouver and WSU, homebound toward my goal.

"Did you know Andrea was getting married?" I ask her. This has bothered me since I found out.

"No. When?"

"Last weekend."

"She kept that quiet." Ros sounds surprised.

"She said she didn't tell me because of our non-fraternization policy. I didn't know we had one."

"It's a standard clause within our employment contracts."

"Seems a little harsh."

"She's married someone in-house?"

"Damon Parker."

"Engineering?"

"Yes. Can we help him with a green card? I believe he's on an H-1B visa at the moment."

"I'll look into it. Though I'm not sure there are any shortcuts."

"I'd appreciate it, and I have a surprise for you." I veer a few degrees northeast and we fly for about ten minutes. "There!" I point toward the barnacle on the horizon that will become Mount St. Helens as we get closer.

Ros actually squeals with delight. "You changed the flight plan?"

"Just for you."

As we fly closer, the mountain looms over the landscape. It looks like a child's drawing of a volcano, tipped with snow, craggy at the top, and nestled within the lush green Gifford Pinchot National Forest.

"Wow! It's so much bigger than I thought," Ros says as we get nearer.

It's an impressive sight.

I bank slowly and we circle the crater, which is no longer complete. The north face has gone, a casualty of the 1980 eruption. It looks eerily deserted and otherworldly from up here; the scars of the last eruption are still obvious, running down the mountain, displacing the forest and defacing the landscape beneath it.

"This is amazing. Gwen and I have been meaning to bring the kids to see this place. I wonder if it will erupt again?" Ros speculates as she snaps photos with her phone.

"I have no idea, but let's head home now that you've seen it."

"Good idea, and thank you." Ros gives me a grateful smile, her eyes shining.

I veer west following the South Fork Toutle River. We should be back at Boeing Field in forty-five minutes, which will give me plenty of time to join Ana, the photographer, and Elliot for drinks.

Out the corner of my eye I see the master caution light flicker.

What the fuck?

The fire light in the engine T-handle flashes, and *Charlie Tango* dips.

Shit. We have a fire in engine one. I take a deep breath but smell nothing. Quickly, I execute an S-turn to see if I can see smoke. A trail of gray fog lingers in our flight path.

"What's wrong? What is it?" Ros asks.

"I don't want you to panic. We have a fire in one of the engines."

"What!" She clutches her purse and her seat.

I shut engine one down and blow the first fire bottle while deciding whether to land or carry on with one engine. *Charlie Tango* is equipped to fly with a single engine…

I want to get home.

I give the landscape a quick sweep, looking for a safe place to land, should we need to. We're a little low, but I can see a lake in the distance—Silver Lake, I think. It's clear of trees at the southeast end.

I'm about to radio a distress signal when the second engine fire light flashes.

Motherfucking hell!

My anxiety balloons and I clench my fingers around the collective.

Fuck. Focus, Grey.

Smoke filters into the cabin and I open my windows and quickly check all the instrument stats. The dash is lighting up like fucking Christmas. And it may be that the electronics are failing. I have no choice. We're going to have to land. And I have a split second to decide whether to kill the engine or keep it going to get us down.

I hope to Christ I can do this. Sweat beads on my brow and I dash it away with my hand. "Hang on, Ros. This is going to get rough."

Ros makes a wailing sound, but I ignore her.

We're low. Too low.

But maybe we have time. That's all I need. Some time. Before she blows.

I lower the collective and reduce the throttle to idle and we autorotate, diving down, and I'm trying to maintain speed to keep the rotors spinning. We hurtle toward the ground.

Ana. Ana? Will I see her again?

Fuck. Fuck. Fuck.

We're close to the lake. There's a clearing. My muscles burn as I fight to hold the collective in place.

Fuck.

I see Ana in a kaleidoscope of images like the photographer's portraits: laughing, pouting, pensive, stunning, beautiful. *Mine.*

I can't lose her.

Now! Do it, Grey.

I flare—pitching *Charlie Tango*'s nose up and dipping the tail to reduce the forward speed. The tail clips some treetops. By some miracle, *Charlie Tango* stays in line as I increase the throttle. We crash-land, tail first, on the edge of the clearing, the EC135 skidding and bumping across the terrain before she comes to a complete stop in the middle of the clearing, the rotors whipping branches off some nearby fir trees. I activate the second fire bottle, shut down the engine and the fuel valves, and apply the rotor brake. I switch off all electronics, lean across to punch the buckle on Ros's harness so it releases, lean farther, and open her door. "Get out! Stay low!" I roar and push her so she scuttles out of her seat and falls out to the ground. I grab the fire extinguisher beside me, scramble out my side, and run to the back of the cabin to spray CO_2 over the smoking engines. The fires are quickly subdued and I take a step back.

Ros, bedraggled and deeply shaken, stumbles over to me as I stand and stare with horror at *Charlie Tango*, my pride and joy. In an uncharacteristic show of emotion, Ros throws her arms around me and I freeze. It's only then I notice she's sobbing.

"Hey. Hey. Hush. We're down. We're safe. I'm sorry. I'm sorry." I hold her for a moment to calm her down.

"You did it," she chokes out. "You did it. Fuck. Christian. You got us down."

"I know." And I can't quite believe we're both in one piece. I step away from her and hand her a handkerchief from my pocket.

"What the hell happened?" she says as she wipes away her tears.

"I don't know." I'm stumped. What the fuck happened? Both engines? But I've no time for this now. She could blow. "Let's move away. I've done an emergency shutdown on all the systems, but there's enough fuel on board to give Mount St. Helens a run for her money should it go up."

"But my stuff—"

"Leave it."

We're in a small clearing, the tops of some of the fir trees now missing. The smell of fresh pine, jet fuel, and acrid smoke is in the air. We shelter under the trees at what I assume is a safe distance from *Charlie Tango*, and I scratch my head.

Both engines?

It's rare for both to go. Bringing *Charlie Tango* down intact and using the fire extinguisher means her engines are preserved and we can find out what went wrong.

But a postmortem and crash analysis is for another time, and for the FAA. Right now, Ros and I have to decide what to do.

I wipe my forehead with my jacket sleeve, and I realize I'm sweating like a fucking pig.

"At least I have my purse and my phone," Ros mutters. "Shit. I don't have a signal." She holds her phone skyward, searching for service. "Do you? Will someone come rescue us?"

"I didn't have time for a distress call."

"That's a no, then." Her face falls.

I grab my phone from my inside pocket, and I'm cheered when I hear the rattle of Ana's gift, but I don't have time to think about that now. I just know I have to get back to her.

"When I don't report in, they'll know we're missing. The FAA has our flight plan." My phone has no signal either but I check the GPS on the off chance it's working and set to our current position. "Do you want to stay or go?"

Ros looks nervously around at our rugged surroundings. "I'm a city girl, Christian. There are all kinds of wild animals out here. Let's go."

"We're on the south side of the lake. We're a couple of hours from the road. Maybe we can get help there."

Ros starts in heels but is barefoot by the time we hit the road and it makes our progress slow. Fortunately, the ground is soft, but not so the road.

"There's a visitors' center along here," I inform her. "We could get help there."

"They're probably closed. It's after five," Ros says, her voice wavering. We're both sweating and in need of water. She's had enough, and I'm beginning to wish we'd stayed near *Charlie Tango*. But who knows how long it would have taken for the authorities to find us?

My watch says 5:25 p.m.

"Do you want to stay here and wait?" I ask Ros.

"No way." She hands me her shoes. "Can you?" She makes a snapping-twig motion with her fists.

"You want me to break the heels off? They're Manolos."

"Please, just do it."

"Okay." Feeling that my manhood is on trial, I use all my strength to snap off the first heel. It gives after a moment or two, as does the second. "Here. I'll get you a new pair when we're home."

"I'll hold you to that."

She puts her shoes back on, and we set off down the road.

"How much money do you have?" I ask.

"On me? About two hundred dollars."

"I have about four hundred. Let's see if we can hitch a ride."

WE MAKE FREQUENT STOPS to rest Ros's feet. I offer to carry her at one point, but she refuses. She's quiet but resilient. I'm grateful she's held it together and not succumbed to panic, but I don't know how long that will last.

We're taking a rest break when we hear the thumping rumble of a semi. I stick my thumb out with the hope the vehicle will stop. Sure enough, we hear a grinding of gears and the gleaming rig comes to a standstill a few feet away, the engine rumbling on, growling, waiting for us.

"Looks like we got a ride." I flash a grin at Ros, trying to keep her buoyant. Her smile is thin, but it's a smile. I help her to her feet and almost carry her to the passenger door. A bearded young guy in a Seahawks cap opens the passenger door from the inside. "You folks okay?" he asks.

"We've had better days. Where you heading?"

"I'm taking this empty box back to Seattle."

"That's where we're going. Will you give us a ride?"

"Sure thing. Climb aboard."

Ros frowns and whispers, "I would never do this if I were on my own."

I help Ros scramble up and follow her into the cab. It's clean and smells of new car and pine forest, though I suspect that's from the air freshener hanging from a hook on the dash.

"What are you folks doing down here?" the guy asks as Ros settles on the comfortable-looking couch at the back of the cabin. It looks brand-new.

I glance at Ros, who gives me a small shake of her head.

"We're lost. You know." I keep my answer vague.

"Okay," he says, and I know he doesn't believe us, but he puts the beast into gear and we rumble off in the direction of Seattle.

"Name's Seb," he says.

"Ros."

"Christian."

He leans over and shakes our hands in turn. "You guys thirsty?"

"Yes," we say at once.

"Back of the cabin there's a small fridge. Should find some San Pellegrino in there."

San Pellegrino?

Ros retrieves two bottles and we drink gratefully. I never knew sparkling water could taste so good.

I notice a microphone hanging from above.

"CB radio?" I ask.

"Yep. But it's not working. It's new. Damn thing." He gives it a frustrated knock with his knuckles. "Whole rig is new. This is her maiden voyage."

That's why he's driving so slowly.

I check the time. It's 7:35. My phone is dead. As is Ros's. *Damn.*

"Do you have a mobile?" I ask Seb.

"No way. I want my ex-wife to leave me alone. When I'm out in the cab it's just me and the road."

I nod.

Fuck. Ana might be worried. But I'll worry her more if I tell her what's happened before she sees me. And she's probably at the bar. With José Rodriguez. I hope Elliot and Katherine will keep an eye on him.

Feeling glum and a little helpless, I stare out at the scenery. We'll shortly be on I-5 and on our way home.

"You guys hungry? I have some kale and quinoa wraps in the fridge left over from my lunch."

"That's mighty hospitable. Thank you, Seb."

"You folks mind a little music while we drive?" he asks when we've finished his lunch.

Oh hell.

"Sure," says Ros, but I hear her uncertainty.

Seb has Sirius on his radio and he turns it to a jazz station. The mellow notes of Charlie Parker's saxophone playing "All the Things You Are" fill the cab.

"All the Things You Are."

Ana. Is she missing me?

I'm on the road with a kale-and-quinoa-eating trucker who listens to cool jazz. This is not how I expected my day to go. I give Ros a brief look. She's sunk onto the couch and is fast asleep. I breathe a sigh of relief and close my eyes.

If I hadn't been able to land…

Jesus. Ros's family would have been devastated.

Both engines?

What is the likelihood?

And *Charlie Tango* had just had all her routine checks.

Something doesn't add up.

The rumble of the truck goes on and on and on. Billie Holiday is singing. Her voice is soothing, like a lullaby. "You're My Thrill."

Charlie Tango is hurtling to the ground.

I'm pulling back on the collective.

No. No. No.

There's a woman screaming.

Screaming.

Ana. Screaming.

No.

There's smoke. Choking smoke.

And we're hurtling down.

I can't stop this.

Ana is screaming.

No. No. No.

And *Charlie Tango* hits the ground.

Nothing.

Black.

Silence.

Nothing.

I wake suddenly, gasping. It's dark, except for the occasional light on the freeway. I'm in the cab.

"Hey." It's Seb.

"Sorry, I must have fallen asleep."

"No problem. You two must be bushed. Your friend is still asleep." Ros is out on the couch behind us.

"Where are we?"

"Allentown."

"What? Great." I peer out and we're still on I-5, but the lights of Seattle are in the distance. Cars whiz past us. This has to be the slowest piece of transport I have ever traveled in. "Where are you heading in Seattle?"

"The docks. Pier 46."

"Right. Could you drop us in town? We can pick up a cab."

"No problem."

"So have you always done this?"

"No. I've done a little of everything. But this truck? This one is mine and I'm working for myself."

"Ah. An entrepreneur."

"Exactly."

"I do a little of that myself."

"One day I'd like to own a fleet of these." He slaps his hands on the wheel.

"I hope you do."

SEB DROPS US AT Union Station.

"Thank you, thank you, thank you," Ros says as we climb out of his truck.

I hand him four hundred dollars.

"I can't take your money, Christian," Seb says, holding up his hand and refusing the cash.

"In that case, here's my card." I pull a card from my wallet and hand it to him. "Call me. And we can talk about the fleet you want to own."

"Sure thing," Seb says, without looking at my card. "Nice meeting you folks."

"Thanks. You're a lifesaver." And with that, I shut the door and we wave as he drives away.

"Can you believe that guy?" Ros asks.

"Thank God he turned up. Let's get a cab."

IT TAKES US TWENTY minutes to get to Ros's place, which, fortunately, is near Escala.

"Next time we go to Portland, can we take the train?"

"Sure thing."

"You did good, Christian."

"So did you."

"I'll call Andrea and let her know we're safe."

"Andrea?"

"She can call your family. I'm sure they're worried. I'll see you tomorrow at your birthday party."

My family? They don't worry about me. "See you then."

She leans across and kisses my cheek. "Good night."

I'm touched. It's the first time she's ever done that.

I watch her walk through the courtyard of her apartment building.

"Ros!" I hear Gwen's screech as she comes barreling out the double doors of the entryway, scooping Ros up in her embrace.

I wave and order the cab to take me around the corner.

THERE ARE PHOTOGRAPHERS OUTSIDE my apartment building. Something must be going on. I pay the driver, get out of the cab, and keep my head down as I walk through the front door.

"There he is!"

"Christian Grey!"

"He's here!"

The flashes dazzle me, but I manage to get inside relatively unscathed. Surely they're not here for me? Maybe they are, or is it someone else who's in the building tonight that's worthy of this kind of attention? Fortunately, the elevator is free. Once inside, I take off my shoes and socks. My feet are sore, and it's a relief to be barefoot. I look at my shoes. I probably won't wear them again.

Poor Ros. She's going to have some blisters tomorrow.

I don't imagine Ana will be home. She's probably still at the bar. I'll go find her once I've swapped the battery on my phone, changed my shirt, and maybe had a shower.

I take off my jacket as the doors to the elevator open and I step into the foyer.

The television is blaring from the TV room.

Odd.

I wander into the living room.

My family is all gathered here.

"Christian!" Grace shrieks, and she races toward me like a tropical storm, so I'm forced to drop my jacket and shoes in time to catch her. She wraps her arms around my neck and kisses me vigorously on my cheek, hugging me. Hard.

What the hell?

"Mom?"

"I thought I'd never see you again," Grace rasps.

"Mom, I'm here," I reassure her, bemused. Can't she see I'm fine?

"I died a thousand deaths today." Her voice cracks on the last word and she begins to sob. I hold her tighter in my arms. I've never seen her like this. My mom. Holding me. It feels good. "Oh, Christian," she sobs, and she hugs me like she'll never let me go as she weeps into my neck. Closing my eyes, I rock her gently.

"He's alive! Shit, you're here!" My dad comes out of Taylor's office, followed by Taylor. Carrick barrels toward Mom and me and embraces us both.

"Dad?"

Then Mia joins us. Hugging us all.

Jesus!

A family huddle.

When did this ever happen?

Never!

Carrick pulls away first, and he's wiping his eyes.

He's crying?

Mia and Grace step back. "Sorry," Grace says.

"Hey, Mom, it's okay," I say, uncomfortable with all this unwarranted attention.

"Where were you? What happened?" she cries and puts her head in her hands, still weeping.

"Mom." I pull her into my arms and kiss her head and hold her once more. "I'm here. I'm good. It's just taken me a hell of a long time to get back from Portland. What's with the welcoming committee?"

I look up, and there she is. Wide-eyed and beautiful. Tears streaming down her face. My Ana.

"Mom, I'm good," I tell Grace. "What's wrong?"

She holds my face and addresses me as if I'm still a child. "Christian, you've been missing. Your flight plan—you never made it to Seattle. Why didn't you contact us?"

"I didn't think it would take this long."

"Why didn't you call?"

"No power in my cell."

"You didn't stop? Call collect?"

"Mom, it's a long story."

"Oh, Christian! Don't you ever do that to me again! Do you understand?"

"Yes, Mom." I wipe her tears with my thumbs and give her another hug. It feels good to hold the woman who saved me.

She steps back and Mia hugs me. Hard. And then she slaps me hard on my chest.

Ow.

"You had us so worried!" she shouts through her tears. I comfort her and calm her with the fact that I'm here now.

Elliot, looking nauseatingly tanned and healthy from his holiday, hugs me.

Christ. Et tu, brute? He slaps me hard on my back.

"Great to see you," he says, loud and gruff. His voice full of emotion.

A lump forms in my throat.

This is my family.

They care. They fucking care.

They were all worried about me.

Family first.

I step back and look at Ana. Katherine stands behind her, stroking her hair. I can't hear what she says. "I'm going to say hi to my girl now," I tell my parents before I lose it. My mother gives me a teary smile, and she and Carrick step aside.

I walk toward Ana and she uncurls herself from her seat on the sofa. She's a little unsteady when she stands. I think she's making sure I'm real. She's still crying, but suddenly she bolts toward me and into my arms.

"Christian!" she sobs.

"Hush," I whisper, and holding her close, I'm relieved to feel her small, delicate frame pressed against me. I'm grateful for everything she is to me.

Ana. My love.

I bury my face in her hair and inhale her sweet, sweet scent. She raises her beautiful, tearstained face to me and I plant a quick kiss on her soft lips. "Hi," I whisper.

"Hi," she says, hoarse and husky.

"Miss me?"

"A bit." She sniffles.

"I can tell." I wipe her tears away with my fingers.

"I thought… I thought…" She sobs.

"I can see. Hush. I'm here. I'm here." I hold her close and kiss her again. Her lips are always so tender when she's been crying.

"Are you okay?" she asks, and her hands are on me. Everywhere, it seems. But I don't mind; I welcome her touch. The darkness is long gone.

"I'm okay. I'm not going anywhere."

"Oh, thank God." She wraps her arms around my waist and holds me.

Damn. I need a shower. But she doesn't seem to care.

"Are you hungry? Do you need something to drink?" she asks.

"Yes."

She tries to step back, but I'm not ready to release her. I hold her and extend a hand to the photographer, who's hovering.

"Mr. Grey," says José.

"Christian, please."

"Christian, welcome back. Glad you're okay, and, um…thanks for letting me stay."

"No problem." Just keep your hands off my girl.

Gail interrupts us. She looks a mess. She's been crying, too.

Shit. Mrs. Jones? It rocks me to my soul.

"Can I get you something, Mr. Grey?" She's dabbing her eyes with a tissue.

"A beer, please, Gail. Budvar, and a bite to eat."

"I'll get it," Ana says.

"No. Don't go." I tighten my arm around her.

The Kavanagh kids are next: Ethan and Katherine. I shake his hand and give Katherine a peck on the cheek. She looks well. Barbados and Elliot obviously agree with her.

Mrs. Jones returns and hands me a beer. I refuse the glass and take a long draft of Budvar.

It tastes so good.

All these people are here for me. I feel like the long-lost prodigal son.

Perhaps I am…

"Surprised you don't want something stronger," says Elliot. "So, what the fuck happened to you? First I knew was when Dad called me to say the chopper was missing."

"Elliot!" Grace admonishes him.

"Helicopter!" For fuck's sake, Elliot. I hate the word *chopper*. He knows that. He grins, and I find myself grinning back at him.

"Let's sit and I'll tell you." I sit down with Ana beside me and the clan joins us. I take a long draft of my beer and spot Taylor in the background. I give him a nod and he nods back.

Thank God he's not crying. I don't think I could cope with that.

"Your daughter?" I ask him.

"She's fine now. False alarm, sir."

"Good."

"Glad you're back, sir. Will that be all?"

"We have a helicopter to pick up."

"Now? Or will the morning do?"

"Morning, I think, Taylor."

"Very good, Mr. Grey. Anything else, sir?"

I shake my head and raise my bottle to him. I can brief him in the morning. He gives me a warm smile and leaves us.

"Christian, what happened?" Carrick asks.

As we sit on the sofa I begin to regale them with the executive summary of my crash landing.

"A fire? Both engines?" Carrick is shocked.

"Yep."

"Shit! But I thought—" Dad continues.

"I know," I interrupt him. "It was sheer luck I was flying so low."

Ana shudders beside me and I put my arm around her. "Cold?" I ask her, and she squeezes my hand and shakes her head.

"How did you put out the fire?" asks Katherine.

"Extinguisher. We have to carry them, by law," I answer, but she's so brusque. I don't tell her that I used the fire bottles.

“Why didn’t you call or use the radio?” Mom asks.

I explain that I had to switch everything off because of the fire. With the electronics out, I couldn’t radio and we had no cell coverage. Ana tenses beside me. I lift her onto my lap.

“So how did you get back to Seattle?” Mom says, and I tell them about Seb.

“Took forever. He didn’t have a cell, weird but true.” I look around at the concerned faces of my family and stop at Mom’s. “I didn’t realize.”

“That we’d worry? Oh, Christian! We’ve been going out of our minds!” She’s pissed, and for the first time I feel a tad guilty. Flynn’s lecture on strong familial ties for adoptees comes to mind.

“You’ve made the news, bro,” says Elliot.

“Yeah. I figured that much when I arrived to this reception, and the handful of photographers outside. I’m sorry, Mom—I should have asked the driver to stop so I could phone. But I was anxious to be back.”

Grace shakes her head. “I’m just glad you’re back in one piece, darling.”

Ana sags against me. She must be tired.

“Both engines?” Carrick mutters again with disbelief.

“Go figure.” I shrug and run my hand down Ana’s back. She’s sniffling again.

“Hey,” I murmur and tilt her chin up. “Stop with the crying.”

She wipes her nose with her hand. “Stop with the disappearing,” she says.

“Electrical failure. That’s odd, isn’t it?” Carrick won’t leave it alone.

“Yes, crossed my mind, too, Dad. But right now I’d just like to go to bed and think about all that shit tomorrow.”

“So, the media knows that Christian Grey has been found safe and well,” Katherine comments, looking up from her phone.

Well, they snapped me coming home. “Yes. Andrea and my PR people will deal with the media. Ros called her after we dropped her home.”

Sam will be in his fucking element with all that attention.

"Yes, Andrea called me to let me know you were still alive," Carrick says with a grin.

"I must give that woman a raise," I mutter. "Sure is late."

"I think that's a hint, ladies and gentlemen, that my dear bro needs his beauty sleep." Elliot gives me a teasing wink.

Fuck off, bro.

"Cary, my son is safe," Mom announces. "You can take me home now."

"Yes. I think we could use the sleep," Carrick replies, smiling down at her.

"Stay," I offer. There's enough room.

"No, sweetheart, I want to get home. Now that I know you're safe."

I ease Ana onto the couch and stand as everyone starts making a move. Mom hugs me once more and I embrace her.

"I was so worried, darling," she whispers.

"I'm okay, Mom."

"Yes. I think you are," she says and gives Ana a quick look and a smile.

After some lengthy goodbyes, we usher my family, Katherine, and Ethan into the elevator. The doors close and it's just me and Ana in the foyer.

Shit. And José. He's hovering in the hallway.

"Look, I'll turn in. Leave you guys," he says.

"Do you know where to go?" I ask.

He nods. "Yeah, the housekeeper—"

"Mrs. Jones," Ana says.

"Yeah, Mrs. Jones, she showed me earlier. Quite a place you have here, Christian."

"Thank you," I respond, placing my arm around Ana and kissing her hair. "I'm going to eat whatever Mrs. Jones has put out for me. Good night, José." I turn and leave him with my girl.

He'd be a fool to try anything now.

And I'm hungry.

Mrs. Jones hands me a ham-and-cheese sandwich with lettuce and mayo.

"Thank you," I tell her. "Go to bed."

"Yes, sir," she says with a sweet smile. "I'm glad you're back with us." She leaves, and I wander into the living area and watch Rodriguez and Ana.

I finish my sandwich as he hugs her. He closes his eyes.

He adores her.

Can't she tell?

She waves him off, then turns and sees me watching her. She walks toward me, then stops and stares.

I drink her in. She's crumpled and tearstained, and she's never looked more beautiful to me. She's a welcome, welcome sight.

She's home.

My home.

My throat burns.

"He's still got it bad, you know," I murmur to distract myself from my intense emotion.

"And how would you know that, Mr. Grey?"

"I recognize the symptoms, Miss Steele. I believe I have the same affliction."

I love you.

Her eyes grow larger. Serious. "I thought I was never going to see you again," she whispers.

Oh, baby. The knot in my throat tightens. "It wasn't as bad as it sounds," I try to reassure her. She collects my jacket and shoes from where they lie on the floor and walks toward me.

"I'll take that," I say, retrieving my jacket.

And we stand there, regarding each other.

She's really here.

She was waiting for me.

For you, Grey. When I thought no one would ever wait for me.

I pull her into my arms.

"Christian," she chokes, and she starts crying again.

"Hush." I kiss her hair. "You know, in the few seconds of sheer terror before I landed, all my thoughts were of you. You're my talisman, Ana."

"I thought I'd lost you," she says.

And we stand. In silence. Holding each other. I remember dancing with her in this very room.

Witchcraft.

That was a moment to remember. *Like now.* And I never want to let her go.

She drops my shoes, and it startles me when they bump on the floor.

"Come shower with me." I'm filthy from my marathon trek.

"Okay." She looks up at me but doesn't release me.

I tip her chin back. "You know, even tearstained, you are beautiful, Ana Steele." I kiss her tenderly. "And your lips are so soft." I kiss her again, taking everything she has to offer. She runs her fingers through my hair. "I need to put my jacket down," I whisper.

"Drop it," she orders against my lips.

"I can't."

Leaning back, she cocks her head, bemused.

I let her go. "This is why." And from the inside pocket I pull out her present to me.

SATURDAY, JUNE 18, 2011

Ana glances at her watch and takes one step back as I drape my jacket over the couch and place the box on top.

What's going on?

"Open it," she whispers.

"I was hoping you'd say that. This has been driving me crazy."

Her smile is broad and she bites her lip, and if I'm not mistaken she's a little nervous.

Why?

I give her a reassuring smile, unwrap the box, and open it.

Nestled inside is a key chain that shows a pixelated picture of Seattle that flashes on and off. I take it out of the box, wondering what the significance might be, but I'm lost. I have no idea.

I look to Ana for a clue.

"Turn it over," she says.

I do. And the word *YES* flashes on and off.

Yes.

Yes.

YES.

One simple word. One profound meaning.

A life-changer.

Right here. Now.

My heartbeat spikes and I gawk at her, hoping this means what I think it means.

"Happy birthday," she whispers.

"You'll marry me?"

I don't believe it.

She nods.

I still don't believe it. "Say it." I need to hear it from her lips.

"Yes, I'll marry you."

Joy bursts in my heart—in my head, in my body, in my soul. It's exhilarating. It's overwhelming. Brimming with elation, I lunge forward and gather her in my arms and swing her around, laughing as I do. She clutches my biceps, her eyes shining, as she laughs, too.

I stop, set her on her feet, grab her face, and kiss her. My lips tease hers and she opens for me, like a flower: my sweet Anastasia.

"Oh, Ana," I whisper in adoration, my lips brushing the corner of her mouth.

"I thought I'd lost you," she says, and she looks a little dazed.

"Baby, it will take more than a malfunctioning 135 to keep me away from you."

"135?"

"*Charlie Tango*. She's a Eurocopter EC135, the safest in its class."

But not today.

"Wait a minute." I hold up the key chain. "You gave this to me before we saw Flynn."

Her smile is a little smug as she nods.

What?

Anastasia Steele!

"I wanted you to know that whatever Flynn said, it wouldn't make a difference to me."

"So all yesterday evening, when I was begging you for an answer, I had it already?" I'm feeling breathless—giddy, even—and a little pissed off.

What the hell?

I don't know whether to be angry or celebratory. She confounds me, even now.

Well, Grey, what are you going to do about it?

"All that worry," I murmur darkly. She gives me an impish grin and shrugs once more. "Oh, don't try to get cute with me, Miss Steele. Right now, I want—"

I had the answer all the time.

I want her.

Here.

Now.

No. Wait.

"I can't believe you left me hanging."

She watches my expression as I construct a plan. Something worthy of such audacity. "I believe some retribution is in order, Miss Steele." My voice is low. Ominous.

Ana takes a cautious step back. Is she going to run?

"Is that the game? Because I will catch you." Her smile is playful and infectious. "And you're biting your lip," I add.

She takes another step back and turns to run, but I pounce and grab her. She squeals and I hoist her over my shoulder and head for my—no, *our*—bathroom.

"Christian!" She swats my behind.

I swat hers back. Hard.

"Ow!" she yelps.

"Shower time," I declare as I carry her down the corridor.

"Put me down!" She squirms on my shoulder but my arm is locked over her thighs. What's really making me smile are her gasps and giggles. She's enjoying this.

As am I.

My grin is as broad and as wide as the Puget Sound when I open the bathroom door. "Fond of these shoes?" I ask. They look expensive.

"I prefer them to be touching the floor." Her words are strangled, and I think she's feigning outrage and trying not to laugh at the same time.

"Your wish is my command, Miss Steele." I pull off both her shoes and they clatter onto the tiles. I empty my pockets onto the vanity: phone, keys, wallet, but most precious of all is my new key chain. I don't want to get it wet. With my pockets empty, I march into the shower, carrying Ana over my shoulder.

"Christian!" she cries.

Ignoring her, I turn on the water and it cascades over us both, but mostly over Ana's backside. It's cold. She shrieks and laughs at once, writhing on my shoulder.

"No! Put me down!" she says between giggles. She swats me once more, and I take pity.

Releasing her, I let her wet, clothed body slide down the length of mine.

She's flushed. Her eyes bright and beautiful. She's captivating.

Oh, baby.

You said yes.

I cup her face and kiss her, my lips tender on hers. I worship her mouth, cherishing her. She closes her eyes and accepts my kiss, kissing me back with a sweet hunger under the streaming shower.

The water is warmer now and her hands move to my soaking shirt. She tugs its hem from my pants. And I groan in her mouth, but I can't stop kissing her.

I can't stop loving her.

I won't stop loving her.

Ever.

Slowly, she begins to unbutton my shirt, and I reach for the zipper at the back of her dress. I slide it down, feeling her warm flesh beneath my fingertips.

Oh. The feel of her. I want more. I kiss her hard, my tongue exploring her mouth.

She moans and suddenly yanks my shirt open, the buttons flying off and landing in the shower.

Whoa.

Ana!

She tugs my shirt over my shoulders and pushes me against the tiles. But she can't remove it. "Cuff links." I hold up my wrists.

Her fingers make quick work of each, and she lets them fall to the floor, followed by my shirt. Her feverish fingers reach for my waistband.

Oh no.

Not yet.

Grasping her shoulders, I spin her around, giving me easier access to her zipper. I complete its journey to its bottom and pull her dress down, just below her breasts. Her arms are still in the sleeves, restricting her movement.

I like that.

Smoothing her wet hair away from her neck, I lean forward, and with my tongue, I taste the water running off her skin, from her neck to her hairline.

She tastes so good.

I run my lips along the length of her shoulder, kissing and sucking, as my arousal strains against my zipper. She braces her hands on the tiles and groans while I kiss my favorite spot beneath her ear. I unhook her bra and push it down, then cup her breasts in my hands. I moan my appreciation. She has great tits.

Responsive, too.

"So beautiful," I whisper in her ear.

She rolls her head to one side, exposing her neck and throat, then pushes her breasts into the palms of my hands. She reaches around, still trapped by her dress, and she finds my erection.

Sucking in a breath, I push my impatient cock into her hands. The feel of her fingers through the soaking fabric is erotic.

Gently, I tug on her nipples, first between my thumb and forefinger, then pinch them between my fingers. She whimpers, loud and clear, as they harden and lengthen under my touch.

"Yes," I whisper.

Let me hear you, baby.

I turn her around and capture her lips with mine, peeling off her dress and her underwear until she's naked before me, her clothes a sodden mess at our feet.

She grabs the body wash and squirts some into her hand. Gazing up at me, asking for permission, she waits.

Okay. We're doing this.

I take a deep breath and nod.

With aching tenderness, she places her hand on my chest. I freeze and she slowly rubs in the soap, skimming small circles on my skin. The darkness is quiet.

But I'm tense.

Everywhere.

Damn it.

Relax, Grey.

She means you no harm.

After a beat, I clasp her hips and watch her face. Her concentration. Her compassion. It's all there. My breathing accelerates. But it's cool. I can cope.

"Is this okay?" she asks.

"Yes." I squeeze the word out.

Her hands flow across my body to wash my underarms, my ribs, down over my belly, and down farther, to the waistband of my pants.

I exhale. "My turn." Moving us out of the shower stream, I reach for the shampoo. I squirt some onto her head and begin massaging the soap into her hair. She closes her eyes and makes an appreciative noise deep in her throat.

I chuckle, and it's cathartic. "You like?"

"Hmm…"

"Me, too." I kiss her forehead and continue kneading her scalp. "Turn around." She obeys immediately, and I continue to wash her hair. When I'm done, her head is covered in suds. I ease her under the shower once more. "Lean your head back."

Ana complies, and I rinse out all the soap.

There is nothing I love more than taking care of my girl.

In every way.

She turns around and grabs the waistband of my pants. "I want to wash all of you," she says.

I hold up my hands in surrender.

I'm yours, Ana. Take me.

She undresses me, freeing my erection—and my pants and boxers join the rest of our clothes on the shower floor.

"Looks like you're pleased to see me," she says.

"I'm always pleased to see you, Miss Steele."

We beam at each other while she grabs and soaps a sponge. She surprises me a little when she starts at my chest, and she works her way down to my ready cock.

Oh yes.

She drops the sponge and her hands are on me.

Fuck.

I close my eyes as she tightens her fingers around me. I flex my hips and groan. This is exactly how to spend the early hours of a Saturday morning after a near-death experience.

Wait.

I open my eyes and pin her with my gaze. "It's Saturday." I grasp her waist and pull her against my body and kiss her.

No more condoms.

My hand, wet and slick with soap, travels down her body, over her breasts, her belly, down to her sex. I tease her with my fingers while I consume her mouth and her tongue, keeping her head in place with my other hand.

I slip my fingers inside her and she moans in my mouth.

"Yes," I hiss. She's ready. I lift her, my hands on her backside. "Wrap your legs around me, baby." She does as she's told, wrapping around me like warm, wet silk. I brace her against the wall.

We're skin on skin.

"Eyes open. I want to see you."

She peers up at me, her pupils large and full of need. Slowly I sink into her, keeping my eyes on hers. I pause. Holding her on me. Holding her up. Feeling her.

"You are mine, Anastasia."

"Always."

Her answer makes me feel ten feet tall.

"And now we can let everyone know, because you said yes."

Leaning down, I kiss her and ease out of her, taking my time. Savoring her. She closes her eyes and tilts back her head as we move together.

Us.

Together.

As one.

I speed up. Needing more. Needing her. Enjoying her. Loving her. Her small cries spur me on, telling me she's climbing higher and higher. With me. Taking me.

She cries out when she comes, her head back against the wall, and I follow her, finding my release and burying my face in her neck.

Carefully, I lower us onto the floor as the water stream rains down on us. I hold her face in my hands and I can see she's crying.

Baby.

I kiss away each tear.

She shifts so her back is against me, and neither of us says anything. Our silence is golden. Quiet. After all the anxiety of this afternoon and evening—my crash landing, my marathon trek, the endless road trip—I've found some peace. I rest my chin on her head, my legs wrapped around her while I hold her in my arms. I love this woman—this beautiful, brave young woman who will soon be my wife.

Mrs. Grey.

I grin and nuzzle her wet hair, surrendering us both to the cascading water.

"My fingers are pruny," she remarks, staring down at her hands.

I take her fingers in mine and kiss each one. "We should really get out of this shower."

"I'm comfortable here," she says.

Me, too, baby. Me, too.

She sags back against me and stares, at my toes I think, and then she chuckles.

"Something amusing you, Miss Steele?"

"It's been a busy week."

"That it has."

"I thank God you're back in one piece, Mr. Grey." She's suddenly serious.

I might not have been here.

Shit.

If…

I swallow as my throat constricts, and an image comes to mind of the ground speeding toward me and Ros in the cockpit of *Charlie Tango*. I shudder. "I was scared," I whisper.

"Earlier?"

I nod.

"So you made light of it to reassure your family?"

"Yes. I was too low to land well. But somehow I did."

She turns and stares at me, fear on her face. "How close a call was it?"

"Close. For a few awful seconds, I thought I'd never see you again." This feels like a dark, dark confession.

She moves and puts her arms around me. "I can't imagine my life without you, Christian. I love you so much it frightens me."

Whoa.

But I feel the same. "Me, too. My life would be empty without you. I love you so much." I tighten my arms around her and kiss her hair. "I won't ever let you go."

"I don't want to go, ever." She kisses my throat and I bend down and kiss her.

I'm getting pins and needles in my feet. "Come, let's get you dry and into bed. I'm tired and you look beat."

She lifts an eyebrow.

"You have something to say, Miss Steele?"

She shakes her head and stands, waiting for me.

We clear our clothes and I grab my cuff links. Ana dumps our soaking clothes into her sink. "I'll deal with these tomorrow," she says.

"Good idea." I wrap her in a towel and place one around my waist. As we brush our teeth at my sink, she gives me a frothy grin, and we both try not to laugh and choke on the toothpaste when I reciprocate.

I'm fourteen again.

In a good way.

I FINISH DRYING HER hair and she climbs into bed. She looks the way I feel—exhausted. I take another look at the key chain and at my favorite word ever written in the English language.

A word full of hope and possibilities.

She said yes.

I grin and join her in bed. "This is so neat. The best birthday present I've ever had. Better than my signed Giuseppe DeNatale poster."

"I would have told you earlier, but since it was going to be your birthday..." Ana lifts her shoulder. "What do you give the man who has everything? I thought I'd give you...me."

I place the key chain on my bedside table and snuggle up to Ana, pulling her into my arms. "It's perfect. Like you."

"I am far from perfect, Christian."

"Are you smirking at me, Miss Steele?"

"Maybe." She chuckles.

I can tell, Ana. Your body language gives you away.

"Can I ask you something?" she adds.

"Of course."

"You didn't call on your trip back from Portland. Was that really because of José? You were worried about me being here alone with him?"

Maybe...

I feel like an idiot. I thought she was at the bar having a good time. I had no idea—

"Do you know how ridiculous that is?" she says as she turns to face me, her eyes full of reproach. "How much stress you put your family and me through? We all love you very much."

"I had no idea you'd all be so worried."

"When are you going to get it through your thick skull that you are loved?"

"Thick skull?"

"Yes. Thick skull."

"I don't think the bone density of my head is significantly higher than anywhere else in my body."

"I'm serious! Stop trying to make me laugh. I'm still a little mad at you, though that's partially eclipsed by the fact that you're home safe and sound when I thought—" She stops and swallows and in a quieter tone continues, "Well, you know what I thought."

I caress her face. "I'm sorry. Okay?"

"Your poor mom, too. It was very moving, seeing you with her," she says quietly.

"I've never seen her that way."

Grace sobbing.

Mom.

Mom sobbing.

"Yes, that was really something. She's normally so self-possessed. It was quite a shock."

"See? Everyone loves you. Perhaps now you'll start believing it." She kisses me. "Happy birthday, Christian. I'm glad you're here to share your day with me. And you haven't seen what I've got for you tomorrow…um, today."

"There's more?" I'm astonished. What more could I possibly want?

"Oh yes, Mr. Grey, but you'll have to wait until then."

She cuddles up to me and closes her eyes, and in moments she's asleep. I'm amazed at how she can fall asleep so quickly.

"My precious girl. I'm sorry. I'm sorry to make you worry," I whisper and kiss her forehead. Feeling more content than I've ever felt in my life, I close my eyes.

Ana, burnished hair and broad smiles, is with me in *Charlie Tango.*

Let's chase the dawn.

She laughs. Carefree. Young. My girl.

The light around us is golden.

She's golden.

I'm golden.

I cough. There's smoke. Smoke everywhere.

I can't see Ana. She's gone in the smoke.

And we're diving down. Down.

Hurtling fast. In *Charlie Tango.*

The ground is coming up to meet me.

I close my eyes, waiting for the impact.

It never comes.

We're in the orchard.

The trees are laden with apples.

Ana smiles, her hair free and wafting in the breeze.

She holds out two apples. A red apple. A green apple.

You choose.

Choose.

Red. Green.

I smile. And take the red apple.

The sweeter apple.

Ana takes my hand and we walk.

Hand in hand.

Past the alcoholics and addicts outside the liquor store in Detroit.

They wave and hold up their brown paper bags in salute.

Past Esclava. Elena smiles and waves.

Past Leila. Leila smiles and waves.

Ana takes my apple. She bites into it.

Mmm…tasty. She licks her lips.

Delicious. I love it.

I made it. With Grandpa.

Wow. You're so capable.

She smiles and whirls around, her hair flying.

I love you, she cries. *I love you, Christian Grey.*

I wake, startled by my dream. But I'm left with a sense of contentment when normally I'm terrified of my dreams.

The Anastasia Steele effect.

I grin and look around. She's not in bed. Before I get up, I check my charged phone. I have too many messages, mostly from Sam, but I don't want to deal with him just yet. I switch off my phone and pick up my key chain to examine it once more.

She said yes.

That wasn't the most romantic proposal.

She's right. She deserves better. If she wants the hearts-and-flowers shit, then I need to step up. I have an idea and Google a florist near my parents' home. They're not yet open so I leave a voice mail.

Shit. I'm going to need a ring. Today.

I'll deal with that later.

In the meantime, I go looking for Ana. She's not in the

bathroom. I wander toward the living room and hear her voice. She's talking to her friend. I pause. And listen.

"You really like him, don't you?" José says.

"I love him, José."

That's my girl.

"What's not to love?" José says and I think he's referring to my apartment.

"Gee, thanks!" Ana exclaims, sounding hurt.

What an asshole.

"Hey, Ana, just kidding." José tries to placate her. "Seriously, I'm kidding. You've never been that kind of girl."

No. She's not. You dick.

"Omelet good for you?" she asks him.

"Sure."

"And me," I state, striding into the kitchen, surprising them both. "José." I greet him with a nod.

"Christian." José returns my nod.

Yeah. I heard you, you fucker, disrespecting my girl.

She's giving me an odd look. She knows what I'm doing. "I was going to bring you breakfast in bed," she says.

I saunter over to her, in front of the photographer, then tilt up her chin and kiss her, long, hard, and noisily. "Good morning, Anastasia," I whisper.

"Good morning, Christian. Happy birthday." She gives me a shy smile.

"I'm looking forward to my other present," I state, and she blushes and looks nervously in Rodriguez's direction.

Oh. What does she have planned?

Rodriguez looks like he's swallowed a lemon.

Good.

"So what are your plans today, José?" I ask, keeping it polite.

"I'm heading up to see my dad and Ray, Ana's dad."

"They know each other?" I frown at this new bit of information.

"Yeah, they were in the army together. They lost contact until Ana and I were in college. It's kinda cute. They're best buds now. We're going on a fishing trip."

"Fishing?" He really doesn't look the type.

"Yeah, some great catches in these coastal waters. The steelheads can grow way big."

"True. My brother Elliot and I landed a thirty-four-pound steelhead once."

"Thirty-four pounds?" José says, and he seems genuinely impressed. "Not bad. Ana's father, though, he holds the record. A forty-three-pounder."

"You're kidding! He never said." But Ray wouldn't brag. That's not his thing, just like his daughter.

"Happy birthday, by the way."

"Thanks. So, where do you like to fish?"

"All around the Pacific Northwest. Dad's favorite is the Skagit."

I'm surprised yet again. "Really? That's my dad's favorite, too."

"He prefers the Canadian side. Ray on the other hand prefers the American."

"Lead to some arguments?"

"Sure, after a beer or two." José grins and I settle in beside him at the kitchen counter. Maybe this guy's not such a dick.

"So your dad likes the Skagit. What about you?" I ask.

"I prefer coastal waters."

"You do?"

"Sea fishing is harder. More exciting. More of a challenge. I love the sea."

"I remember the seascapes in your exhibition. They were good. By the way, thanks for dropping those portraits off."

"No problem." He's embarrassed by the compliment. "Where do *you* like to fish?"

We discuss at length the merits of fishing in rivers, in lakes, and at sea. He's passionate about it, too.

Ana makes breakfast and watches us—happy, I think, that we're getting along.

She pops a steaming omelet and a coffee on the counter for each of us and sits down beside me to eat her granola. Our conversation segues from fishing to baseball, and I hope we're not boring her. We talk about the upcoming Mariners game—he's a fan—and I realize José and I have much in common.

Including loving the same woman.

The woman who has agreed to be my wife.

I'm dying to tell him, but I behave.

Once I finish my breakfast, I change quickly into jeans and a T-shirt. When I come back into the kitchen, José is clearing his plate.

"Ana, that was delicious."

"Thank you." She colors in response to José's praise.

"I have to go. I have to drive out to Bandera and meet the old man."

"Bandera?" I ask.

"Yes, we're fishing for trout in the Mount Baker National Forest. One of the lakes near there."

"Which one?"

"Lower Tuscohatchie."

"I don't think I know that one. Good luck."

"Thanks."

"Say hi to Ray for me," Ana adds.

"Will do."

Arm in arm, Ana and I accompany José into the foyer.

"Thanks for letting me crash here." He shakes my hand.

"Anytime," I respond. And I'm surprised that I actually mean it. He seems harmless enough, like a puppy. He hugs Ana, and to my surprise, I don't want to rip his arms off.

"Stay safe, Ana."

"Sure. Great to see you. Next time we'll have a real evening out," she says as he enters the elevator.

"I'll hold you to that." He waves from inside and the doors close.

"See, he's not so bad," Ana says.

Maybe.

"He still wants into your panties, Ana. But can't say I blame him."

"Christian, that's not true!"

"You have no idea, do you? He wants you. Big-time."

"Christian, he's just a friend, a good friend."

I hold up my hands in surrender. "I don't want to fight."

"Me neither."

"You didn't tell him we were getting married."

"No. I figured I ought to tell Mom and Ray first."

"Yes, you're right. And I… Um, I should ask your father."

She laughs. "Oh, Christian, this isn't the eighteenth century."

"It's traditional."

And I never thought I'd have to ask any father for his daughter's hand in marriage. Give me this moment. Please.

"Let's talk about that later," she says. "I want to give you your other present."

Another present?

Nothing can top the key chain.

Her smile is mischievous and her teeth sink into her lower lip.

"You're biting your lip again." I tug gently at her chin.

She gives me her coy look but she squares her shoulders, takes my hand, and drags me back into the bedroom.

From under the bed, she produces two wrapped gift boxes.

"Two?"

"I bought this before the, um…incident yesterday. I'm not sure about it now." She gives me one of the parcels, but she looks anxious about it.

"Sure you want me to open it?"

She nods.

I tear off the wrapping.

"*Charlie Tango,*" Ana whispers.

Inside the box are the parts for a little wooden helicopter. But the bit that blows me away is the rotor. "Solar-powered. Wow." What a thoughtful gift. And from deep in my past, a memory surfaces. My first Christmas. My first proper Christmas with Mom and Dad.

My helicopter can fly.
My helicopter is blue.
It flies around the Christmas tree.

It flies over the piano and lands in the middle of the white.
It flies over Mommy and flies over Daddy.
And flies over Lelliot as he plays with his LEGOs.

With Ana watching, I sit down and start to assemble it. It snaps together easily, and I hold the little blue copter in my hand.

I love it.

I beam at Ana and go over to the balcony window, where I watch the rotors start to spin under the warm rays of the sun. "Look at that. What we can already do with this technology." I hold the helicopter at eye level, watching how easily solar energy is converted to mechanical energy. The rotors spin and spin, faster and faster.

Wow. All this in a child's toy.

There is so much more that we could do with this simple technology. The challenge is how to store this energy. Graphene is the way to go...but can we build efficient enough batteries? Batteries that charge quickly and hold their charge—

"You like it?" Ana interrupts my thoughts.

"Ana, I love it. Thank you." I grab her and kiss her and we watch the rotors spin. "I'll add it to the glider in my office." I move my hand out of the light and the rotors slow and come to a complete stop.

We move in the light.

We slow in the shadows.

We stop in the dark.

Hmm. Philosophical, Grey.

This is what Ana has done for me. She's dragged me into the light and I quite like it.

I place *Charlie Tango Mark II* on the chest of drawers. "It'll keep me company while we salvage *Charlie Tango.*"

"Is it salvageable?"

"I don't know. I hope so. I'll miss her otherwise."

Ana eyes me speculatively.

"What's in the other box?" I ask.

"I'm not sure if this present is for you or me."

"Really?"

She hands me the second box. It's heavier and has a substantial rattle. Ana flicks her hair over her shoulder and shifts from foot to foot.

"Why are you so nervous?"

She seems excited and a little embarrassed, too.

"You have me intrigued, Miss Steele. I have to say I'm enjoying your reaction. What have you been up to?" I remove the lid of the box and on top of some tissue is a small card.

On your birthday
Do rude things to me.
Please.
Your Ana x

My eyes dart to hers.

What does this mean?

"Do rude things to you?" I ask.

She nods and swallows. She's nervous, and deep down I know where this is going. She's talking about the playroom.

Are you ready for this, Grey?

I rip open the tissue that conceals the box's contents and retrieve an eye mask. Okay, she wants to be blindfolded. Next are some nipple clamps. *Oh, not these.* They're vicious. Not beginner level. Beneath the clamps is a butt plug, but this one is way too big. She's enclosed my iPod, too, which pleases me. She must like my music choices. And here's my silver gray Brioni tie, so she wants to be tied up.

Last, as I suspected, there's the key to my playroom.

She's giving me the big blue eyes. "You want to play?" I ask, my voice soft and husky.

"Yes."

"For my birthday?"

"Yes." Her agreement is barely audible.

Is she doing this because she thinks I want to? Is what we do not enough for her? Am I ready for this?

"You're sure?" I prompt.

"Not the whips and stuff."

"I understand that."

"Then yes. I'm sure."

She confounds me. Every day. I stare down at the contents of the box. Sometimes she's just bewildering. "Sex-mad and insatiable," I mutter. "Well, I think we can do something with this lot."

If this is what she wants—and her words come back to me in a swirl. She's asked me and asked me and asked me.

I like your kinky fuckery.

If I win, Christian, you'll take me back into the playroom.

Red Room, here we come.

I want a demonstration. I like being tied up.

I place the items back in the box.

We could have some fun.

And that spark of anticipation flares and ignites in my gut. I haven't felt it since we did our last scene in the playroom. I regard her through narrowed eyes and hold out my hand. "Now," I state. I'll see how willing she really is.

She puts her hand in mine.

Okay, then, we're doing this.

"Come." I have a million things to do since yesterday's crash landing, but I don't give a fuck. It's my birthday and I'm going to have some fun with my fiancée.

Outside the playroom, I pause. "You're sure about this?"

"Yes," she says.

"Anything you don't want to do?"

She's thoughtful for a moment. "I don't want you to take photos of me."

Why the hell would she say that? Why would I want to take pictures of her?

Grey. Of course you would, if she'd let you.

"Okay," I agree, concerned about what has motivated this question. Does she know? That's impossible.

I unlock the door, feeling apprehensive and excited at once—like the first time I brought her in here. I usher her in and close the door.

For the first time since she left me, the room is welcoming.

I can do this.

Placing the gift box on the chest of drawers, I remove the iPod, place it in its dock, and set the Bose sound system so the track plays over the speakers. Eurythmics. Yes. This song came out the year before I was born. It has a seductive beat. I love it. Yeah, I think Ana will like it. Setting it to repeat, I hear the track begin. It's a little loud so I lower the volume a tad.

When I turn to her, she's in the middle of the room, watching me, a hungry, wanton expression on her face. Her teeth are toying with her lower lip, and her hips are swinging in time to the beat of the music.

Oh, Ana, you sensual creature.

I amble over to her and tug her chin, releasing her lip. "What do you want to do, Anastasia?" I whisper and plant a chaste kiss at the corner of her mouth, keeping my fingers on her chin.

"It's your birthday. Whatever you want," she breathes and her darkening eyes flick up to mine, full of promise.

Fuck.

She might as well be addressing my cock.

I skim my thumb across her bottom lip. "Are we in here because you think I want to be in here?"

"No. I want to be in here, too."

She is a siren.

My siren.

In that case, let's begin with the basics. "Oh, there are so many possibilities, Miss Steele. But let's start with getting you naked." I jerk the sash of her robe, undoing it, and it falls open revealing her silk nightdress.

I step back and sit down on the arm of my chesterfield sofa. "Take your clothes off. Slowly."

Miss Steele loves a challenge.

She slips the robe off and lets it fall like a cloud onto the floor while her eyes stay on me. I'm hard. Instantly, as desire sweeps through my body. I run my finger over my lips to keep my hands off her.

She lifts both straps of her nightgown off her shoulders, watching me watching her, and then drops them so her gown floats down her body to join the robe on the floor. She is naked before me in all her glory.

It makes a difference, her eyes on me.

It's more exciting because I can't hide anymore.

I have an idea and stroll over to the chest of drawers to retrieve my tie from her gift box. Running it through my fingers, I walk back to where she's patiently waiting. "I think you're underdressed, Miss Steele." I place it around her neck and quickly tie it in a half Windsor, but I leave the wider end long. My fingers brush her neck and she gasps, and I let the long end fall so that it skims the top of her pubic hair. "You look mighty fine now, Miss Steele." I give her a swift kiss. "What shall we do with you now?" I murmur. Taking the tie in my hand, I tug it sharply and she's forced into my arms. Her naked body against mine is like an incendiary device. My fingers are in her hair. My mouth is on hers and with my tongue I claim her.

Hard. Insistent. I'm taking no prisoners.

She tastes of sweet Anastasia Steele. My favorite flavor.

With my other hand, I cup her behind, feeling her fine ass.

When I release her, we're both panting. Her breasts are rising and falling with each breath.

Oh, baby. What you do to me.

What I want to do to you.

"Turn around," I prompt. She does so immediately, and I pull the tie from her hair and braid it. No loose hair in the playroom.

I gently pull her braid, and her head tilts up. "You have beautiful hair, Anastasia." I kiss her throat and she writhes. "You just have to say stop. You know that, don't you?" I whisper against her skin.

She nods, her eyes closed.

But damn, she looks happy.

I turn her around and take hold of the end of the tie.

"Come." I lead her over to the chest where her gift box sits, displaying its contents. "Anastasia, these objects." I hold up the butt plug. "This is a size too big. As an anal virgin, you don't want to start with this. We want to start with this." I show her my pinkie.

Her eyes grow impossibly large.

And I have to confess, one of my favorite pastimes is shocking Ana.

"Just finger. Singular," I add. "These clamps are vicious." I poke the nipple clamps. "We'll use these." From one of the drawers I take out a kinder pair. "They're adjustable."

She examines them. Fascinated. I love how she's so curious.

"Clear?" I ask.

"Yes. Are you going to tell me what you intend to do?"

"No. I'm making this up as I go along. This isn't a scene, Ana."

"How should I behave?"

It's a strange question. "However you want to." And I wonder out loud if she was expecting my alter ego.

"Well, yes. I like him," she says.

"Do you, now?" I run my thumb across her lower lip, tempted to kiss it again. "I'm your lover, Anastasia, not your Dom. I love to hear your laugh and your girlish giggle. I like you relaxed and happy, like you are in José's photos. That's the girl that fell into my office. That's the girl I fell in love with.

"But, having said all that, I also like to do rude things to you, Miss Steele, and my alter ego knows a trick or two. So do as you're told and turn around."

She obeys, her face glowing with excitement.

I love you, Ana.

Simple.

I take what I need from the drawers, then arrange all the toys on the top. "Come." I tug the tie and lead her to the table. "I want you to kneel up on this." I lift her onto the table, and she folds her legs beneath her and kneels in front of me.

We are nose to nose. She stares at me with shining eyes.

I run my hands down her thighs and at the knees gently part her legs so I can see my goal.

"Arms behind your back. I'm going to cuff you."

I show her the leather elbow cuffs and lean around her to put them on. She turns and runs her parted lips along my jaw, her tongue teasing my stubble. I close my eyes and for a moment revel in the contact, suppressing a groan.

Pulling back, I admonish her. "Stop. Or this will be over far quicker than either of us wants."

"You're irresistible."

"Am I, now?"

She nods, looking impertinent.

"Well, don't distract me or I'll gag you."

"I like distracting you."

"Or spank you," I warn. She grins. "Behave," I scold her and stand back and beat the cuffs across my palm.

It could so easily be your ass, Ana.

She looks modestly down at her knees. "That's better." I try again and this time succeed in putting them on. I ignore her running her nose over my shoulder, but I thank God for our shower in the early hours of the morning.

With the cuffs on, her back arches a little. Her breasts are now prominent and begging to be touched. "Feel okay?" I ask as I admire her.

She nods.

"Good." From my back pocket I take the mask. "I think you've seen enough now." I slide it over her head and over her eyes.

Her breathing accelerates.

And I step back and drink her in.

She looks smoking hot.

Back at the drawers, I gather the items I need and slip off my T-shirt. I keep my jeans on, even though they are a little uncomfortable, because I don't want her distracted by my impatient dick.

In front of her once more, I open the small glass bottle that contains my favorite massage oil and wave it under her nose. Infused with cedarwood, argan, and sage, it's body-safe, and its fragrance reminds me of a crisp fall day after the rain.

"I don't want to ruin my favorite tie," I mutter, as I undo it and pull it gently off Ana's body. She squirms as the material floats up her body, teasing her.

I fold my tie and place it beside her. Her anticipation is almost palpable. Her body is humming with impatience. It's arousing.

I pour a little oil on my hands and rub them together to warm up the oil. She's listening to what I'm doing. I love heightening her senses. Tenderly, I caress her cheek with my knuckles and run them down her jaw.

She startles when I touch her, but she leans into my hand. I start massaging the oil into her skin—her throat, her clavicle, and along her shoulders. I knead the muscles beneath and let my hands glide in small circles across her chest, avoiding her breasts. She bows backward, pressing them toward me.

Oh no, Ana. Not yet.

I move my fingers down her sides, rubbing in the oil in slow, measured strokes in time to the music. She groans and I don't know if it's from pleasure or frustration. Maybe a little of both.

"You are so beautiful, Ana," I whisper, my lips close to her ear. I run them along her jaw as my hands work their magic. I move them beneath her breasts, over her belly, down to my goal. I kiss her quickly and inhale her scent, now mixed with the oil, down her neck and throat.

"And soon you'll be my wife, to have and to hold."

She inhales sharply.

"To love and to cherish." My hands continue. "With my body, I will worship you."

She throws her head back and moans as my fingers run through her pubic hair to her clitoris. I slowly palm her, teasing her and spreading oil over her where she's wet already.

It's intoxicating.

I lean over to pick up a bullet vibrator. "Mrs. Grey."

She moans.

"Yes," I whisper, continuing my ministrations with my hand. "Open your mouth." She's already panting, but she opens her mouth farther and I slip the small vibrator inside. It's attached to a chain and can be worn as jewelry if so required. "Suck. I'm going to put this inside you."

She stills.

"Suck," I repeat and remove my hands from her body.

She flexes her knees and makes a frustrated grunt. Smiling, I pour more oil onto my palms and finally cup her breasts. "Don't stop," I warn as I gently roll her stiffening nipples between my thumbs and forefingers. They harden and lengthen some more under my touch. "You have such beautiful breasts, Ana."

She moans, and I gather one of the nipple clamps in one hand. Trailing my lips from her throat toward her breast, I stop and carefully attach a clamp.

Her garbled groan is my reward as I bring her trapped nipple to full attention with my lips. She writhes under my touch, shifting from side to side, and I clamp the remaining nipple. Ana's groan is just as loud this time.

"Feel it," I insist, and I lean back to take in the beautiful sight. "Give me this." I remove the vibrator from her mouth and my hand skims down her back toward her backside and between her buttocks. She tenses and rises up on her knees. "Hush, easy," I reassure her and kiss her neck as my fingers continue to stroke between the fine, fine cheeks of her ass.

I glide my other hand down the front of her body and start palming her clitoris once more, then ease my fingers into her. "I'm going to put this inside you," I murmur. "Not here." And my fingers circle her anus, spreading the oil. "But here." And I move the fingers of my other hand slowly in and out of her vagina.

"Ah!" she responds.

"Hush now." I stand and slide the vibrator inside her. Capturing her face with my hands, I kiss her, then click the small remote.

When the vibrator starts, she gasps and jolts up on her knees. "Ah!"

"Easy," I whisper against her lips, stifling her gasp. I tug gently on each of the clamps in turn.

She cries out. "Christian, please!"

"Hush, baby. Hang in there."

You can do this, Ana.

She's panting now and dealing with all the stimulation. I'm sure it's intense. "Good girl," I soothe her.

"Christian," she says, and she sounds a little frantic.

"Hush. Feel it, Ana. Don't be afraid." I place my hands on her waist, holding her. *I'm right here, baby. I've got this. You've got this.*

I dip my little finger into the open pot of lube and slowly move my hands down her back to her ass, watching her reaction, checking that she's okay. I massage her skin and knead her ass, her stunning ass, and I slip one hand between her buttocks.

"So beautiful." Gently, I push my finger inside her ass so that I feel the vibrator buzzing through her body. She tenses and I move my finger slowly, easing in and out while my teeth graze her chin. "So beautiful, Ana."

She gasps, then groans and kneels up a little higher, and I know she's close. Her lips start to move, but whatever she's saying, it's soundless. Suddenly she screams as her orgasm strikes. With my free hand I release first one, then the other nipple clamp, and she cries out.

I hold her close as her body pulses through her climax, still easing my finger in and out of her.

"No," she shouts, and I know she's had enough.

I remove my finger and the vibrator, clean both with a wipe, while keeping her in my arms. She sags against me, but her body is still convulsing. Deftly I unstrap the cuffs on one arm and she falls forward against me. Her head rolls on my shoulder as her intense climax begins to subside.

Her legs must be aching. She groans as I lift her and carry her to the bed, where I lay her faceup on the satin sheets. Using the remote, I switch off the music, then remove my jeans, freeing my raging erection. I start to rub the backs of her legs, her knees, her calves, and then her shoulders, and I remove the cuffs. Lying down beside her, I peel off her mask and find her eyes are scrunched closed. With tenderness I untie her braid, freeing her hair. Leaning forward, I kiss her on the lips. "So beautiful," I say.

She opens one dazed eye.

"Hi." I smile down at her.

She grunts in response.

"Rude enough for you?"

She nods and gives me a sleepy grin.

Ana, you never fail.

"I think you're trying to kill me."

"Death by orgasm. There are worse ways to go."

Like plunging to your death in *Charlie Tango.*

She reaches up and caresses my face and my dispiriting thought disappears. "You can kill me like this anytime," she says. Taking her hand, I kiss her knuckles. I'm so proud of her. She never lets me down in here. She cups my face between her hands and kisses me.

I stop, pulling back. "This is what I want to do," I whisper. From beneath the pillow, I pull out the remote and change the song. I press the button, knowing it will play on repeat, and ease Ana onto her back. "The First Time Ever I Saw Your Face," Roberta Flack's classic, fills the room. "I want to make love to you," I murmur. My lips seek and find hers, and her fingers entwine in my hair.

"Please," Ana breathes, and her sensitized body rises to meet mine, opening up for me as I gently ease into her, and we make slow, sweet love.

I watch her fall apart in my arms and her climax takes me with her. I let go, pouring myself into her, throwing my head back and calling out her name in wonder.

I love you, Ana Steele.

I hold her to me. I never want to let her go.

My joy is complete. Have I ever been this happy?

As I come back to planet earth, I smooth her hair from her face and look down at the woman I love.

She's crying.

"Hey." I clasp her head in my hands. Did I hurt her? "Why are you crying?"

"Because I love you so much," she says, and I close my eyes, letting her words wash over me.

"And I you, Ana. You make me…whole." I kiss her once more as the music stops and gather the sheet to wrap it around us both. She looks glorious; her hair is a mess and her eyes are luminous in spite of her tears. She's so full of life.

"What do you want to do today?" she asks.

"My day is made, thank you." I kiss her.

"Mine, too."

I love Ana's inner freak; she's never far away. And I think of the plans I have for her later. I hope they will make her day, too. "Well, I should call my head of PR. But frankly, I'd like to remain in this bubble with you."

"About the crash?"

"I'm playing hooky."

"It is your birthday, Mr. Grey. You're allowed. And I like having you to myself." She leans up and grazes her teeth against my jaw. She looks happy and free, if a little tired. "I love your music choices. Where do you find them?"

"I'm glad you like them. Sometimes, when I can't sleep I'll either play the piano or trawl iTunes."

"I don't like to think about you unable to sleep and on your own. It sounds lonely," Ana says, her compassion showing.

"To be honest, I never felt lonely until you left. I didn't realize how miserable I was."

She cups my face. "I'm sorry."

"Don't apologize, Ana. What I did was wrong."

She puts her finger over my lips. "Hush," she says. "I love you just the way you are."

"That's a song."

She laughs and changes the subject, asking me about work.

"WE'VE COME A LONG way," Ana says, caressing my face.

"We have."

She looks wistful all of a sudden.

"What are you thinking about?" I ask.

"The photo shoot that José did. Kate. How in command she was. And how hot you looked."

"Hot?" *Me?*

"Yeah. Hot. And Kate was all 'Sit here. Do this. Do that.'" Her impersonation of Kavanagh is spot on.

I laugh. "To think it could have been her who came to interview me. Thank the Lord for the common cold." I kiss the tip of her nose.

"I believe she had the flu, Christian," she scolds and unconsciously trails her fingers through my chest hair. It's weird, but I think she's driven the darkness away. I don't even flinch. "All the canes have gone," she says as she glances around the playroom. I tuck a stray strand of hair behind her ear.

"I didn't think you'd ever get past that hard limit."

"No, I don't think I will." She turns and stares at the whips, paddles, and floggers on the wall.

"You want me to get rid of them, too?" I ask.

"Not the crop…the brown one. Or that suede flogger." She gives me a coy smile.

"Okay, the crop and the flogger. Why, Miss Steele, you're full of surprises."

"As are you, Mr. Grey. It's one of the things I love about you." She kisses the corner of my mouth.

Suddenly I need to hear this from her, because I still can't quite believe it. "What else do you love about me?"

Her eyes soften with her affection. "This," she says and traces her finger across my lips, tickling them. "I love this, and what comes out of it, and what you do to me with it. And what's in here." She strokes the side of my head. "You're so smart and witty and knowledgeable, competent in so many things. But most of all, I love what's in here." She presses her palm against my chest. "You are the most compassionate man I've ever met. What you do. How you work. It's awe-inspiring."

"Awe-inspiring?" I repeat her last word, not quite believing it but loving it anyway. A slow smile tugs at my mouth, but before I can say anything she launches herself at me.

ANA DOZES FOR A few minutes in my arms. I lie staring up at the ceiling, enjoying her weight on me. Could I be any more content? I don't think so.

She wakes when I kiss her forehead.

"Hungry?" I ask.

"Hmm, famished."

"Me, too."

She puts her arm on my chest and studies me. "It's your birthday, Mr. Grey. I'll cook you something. What would you like?"

"Surprise me." I run my hand down her back. "I should check my BlackBerry for all the messages I missed yesterday." I sigh when I sit up. I could spend all day with her in here. "Let's shower," I say.

She grins and together, wrapped in one red sheet, we head down to the bathroom.

Once Ana is dressed she takes all the wet clothes from last night out of her sink and heads out the door. Wearing a tiny blue dress, she's all legs.

Too much leg.

Well at least it's just us.

And Taylor.

I stop shaving for a moment. "Leave them for Mrs. Jones," I call after her.

She glances over her shoulder and smiles.

FEELING BUOYANT, I SIT down at my desk. Ana is working in the kitchen, and I have a ton of messages to get through. Most are from Sam, annoyed that I've not called him. But there are others… moving voice mails from my mother, from Mia, my dad, and Elliot, all begging me to call. It's painful to hear their concern.

And Elena.

Shit.

Ana's hesitant voice is next.

Hi… Um… It's me. Ana. Are you okay? Call me. Her concern is obvious. My heart constricts as it becomes blindingly clear that I've put her and my family through hell.

Grey, you're an idiot.

You should have called.

I save all the messages bar Elena's and return to the most

important voice mail, from the florist in Bellevue. I call them back to outline my requirements, and I'm relieved that they can help me, given such short notice.

Then I call my favorite jewelry store. Okay, the only jewelry store I know. I purchased Ana's earrings there, and it looks like they'll be able to help me with the ring.

If I were a superstitious man I would say these are good omens for what's to come.

Next, I call Sam.

"Mr. Grey, where have you been?" He's pissed. Tough.

"Busy."

"The press has been all over the helicopter story. There are several TV news and print outlets that want an interview—"

"Sam, draw up a statement. Tell them Ros and I are fine. And send it through to me for approval. I'm not interested in doing any interviews. Print, TV, or otherwise."

"But, Christian, this is a great opp—"

"The answer's no. Get me the statement."

He's silent for a moment, publicity whore that he is. "Yes, Mr. Grey," he says, tight-lipped. I hear, and ignore, his reluctance, but I'm beginning to think I need a new PR person. His credentials were seriously overstated when we checked his references.

"Thanks, Sam." I hang up.

I buzz Taylor on the internal phone system.

"Good afternoon, Mr. Grey."

"What news?"

"I'll come down, sir."

Taylor tells me that *Charlie Tango* has been found and that a recovery crew is on its way with an FAA official and someone from Airbus, *Charlie Tango*'s manufacturer.

"I hope they'll be able to provide some answers."

"I'm sure they will, sir," says Taylor. "I've emailed you a list of people you should call."

"Thanks. There's one more thing. I'm going to need you to pop down to this store." I explain what I've discussed with the jeweler.

Taylor gives me a broad grin. "With pleasure, sir. Will that be all?"

"For now, yes. And thanks."

"You're most welcome, and happy birthday." He gives me a nod and leaves.

I pick up the phone and start making my way through Taylor's list of calls.

While I'm on the phone giving a report to the FAA, an email from Ana pops up.

From: Anastasia Steele
Subject: Lunch
Date: June 18 2011 13:12
To: Christian Grey

Dear Mr. Grey
I am emailing to inform you that your lunch is nearly ready.
And that I had some mind-blowing, kinky fuckery earlier today.
Birthday kinky fuckery is to be recommended.
And another thing—I love you.

A x
(Your fiancée)

I'm sure Mrs. Wilson on the other end of the phone at the FAA can hear my smile. With one finger, I type a response.

From: Christian Grey
Subject: Kinky Fuckery
Date: June 18 2011 13:15
To: Anastasia Steele

What aspect was most mind-blowing?

I'm taking notes.

Christian Grey
Famished and Wasting Away After the Morning's Exertions CEO, Grey Enterprises Holdings, Inc.

P.S. I love your signature.

P.P.S. What happened to the art of conversation?

I conclude the phone call with Mrs. Wilson and leave my study to find Ana.

She's concentrating hard. I tiptoe up to the kitchen counter as she types into her phone. She presses send, looks up, and jumps when she sees me smirking at her. I bound around the kitchen island, pull her into my arms, and kiss her, taking her by surprise once more. "That is all, Miss Steele," I say when I release her, and I stroll back into my study feeling ridiculously pleased with myself.

Her email is waiting.

From: Anastasia Steele
Subject: Famished?
Date: June 18 2011 13:18
To: Christian Grey

Dear Mr. Grey
May I draw your attention to the first line of my previous email informing you that your lunch is indeed almost ready… so none of this famished and wasting away nonsense. With regard to the mind-blowing aspects of the kinky fuckery… frankly, all of it. I'd be interested in reading your notes. And I like my bracketed signature, too.

A x
(Your fiancée)

P.S. Since when have you been so loquacious? And you're on the phone!

I call my mom to tell her about the flowers.

"Darling, how are you? Recovered? It's all over the news."

"I know, Mom. I'm fine. I have something to tell you."

"What?"

"I've asked Ana to marry me. She's said yes."

My mother is stunned into silence.

"Mom?"

"Christian, I'm sorry. That's wonderful news," she says, but she sounds a little hesitant.

"I know this is sudden."

"Are you sure, darling? Don't get me wrong, I adore Ana. But this is so soon and she's the first girl—"

"Mom. She's not the first girl. She's the first one you've met."

"Oh."

"Exactly."

"Well, I am delighted for you. Congratulations."

"There's one more thing."

"What is it, love?"

"I'm having some flowers delivered, for the boathouse."

"Why?"

"Well, my first proposal was pretty crap."

"Oh, I see."

"And, Mom, don't tell anyone else. I want it to be a surprise. I plan to make an announcement this evening."

"As you wish, darling. Mia is in charge of deliveries for the party. Let me find her."

I wait for what feels like an eternity.

Come on, Mia.

"Hey, big brother. Thank God you are still with us. What gives?"

"Mom tells me you are coordinating deliveries for my party. How big is this bash, anyway?"

"After your near-death experience, we're celebrating."

Oh hell.

"Well, I have a delivery coming for the boathouse."

"Yes? What?"

"From the Bellevue Florist."

"Why? What for?"

Christ, she can be annoying. I look up and Ana is standing in her short, short dress staring at me. "Just let them in and leave them alone. Do you understand, Mia?"

Ana cocks her head to one side, listening.

"Okay. Don't get your panties in a wad. I'll send them to the boathouse."

"Good."

Ana mimes eating.

Food. Great.

"I'll see you later," I say to Mia and hang up. "One more call?" I ask Ana.

"Sure."

"That dress is very short."

"You like it?" Ana pirouettes in the doorway and her skirt flares up, providing a tantalizing glimpse of her lacy underwear.

"You look fantastic in it, Ana. I just don't want anyone else to see you like that."

"Oh!" She looks upset. "We're at home, Christian. No one but the staff."

I don't want to upset her. I nod as graciously as I can manage and she turns and heads back to the kitchen.

Grey, get a grip.

The next call I have to make is to Ana's father. I have no idea what he's going to say when I ask him for his daughter's hand in marriage. From Ana's file, I get Ray's mobile number. José said he was fishing. I just hope he's somewhere with a signal.

No. He isn't. The call goes to voice mail. "Ray Steele. Leave a message."

Short and to the point.

"Hi, Mr. Steele, it's Christian Grey here. I'd like to talk to you about your daughter. Please call me." I give him my number and hang up.

What did you expect, Grey?

He's in the wilds of the Mount Baker Park.

While I have Ana's file on my desk, I decide to deposit some money into her bank account. She'll have to get used to having money.

"Twenty-four thousand dollars!"

"Twenty-four thousand dollars, to the lovely lady in silver, going once, going twice. Sold!"

I chuckle, remembering her audacity at the auction. I wonder what she'll make of this. I'm sure it will be an interesting discussion. On my computer, I transfer fifty thousand dollars to her account. It should show up within the hour.

My stomach growls. I'm hungry. But my phone starts ringing. It's Ray.

"Mr. Steele. Thank you for calling back—"

"Is Annie okay?"

"She's fine. More than fine. She's great."

"Thank the Lord. What can I do for you, Christian?"

"I know you're fishing."

"I'm trying. Not catching much today."

"I'm sorry to hear that." This is more nerve-racking than I anticipated. My palms are sweating and Mr. Steele says nothing, cranking my anxiety up a notch.

Supposing he says no? This is not something I've considered.

"Mr. Steele?"

"I'm still here, Christian, waiting for you to get to the point."

"Yes. Of course. Um. I called because, um, I'd like your permission to marry your daughter." The words tumble out like I've never negotiated or clinched a deal in my life. What's more, they're met with a resounding silence.

"Mr. Steele?"

"Put my daughter on the line," he says, giving nothing away.

Shit.

"Just a minute." I dart out of my study to where Ana is waiting and hold out the phone to her. "I have Ray for you."

Her eyes widen with shock. She takes the phone and covers the mouthpiece. "You told him!" she squeaks.

I nod.

She takes a deep breath and removes her hand from the mouthpiece. "Hi, Dad."

She listens.

She seems calm.

"What did you say?" she asks and listens again, her eyes on me. "Yes. It is sudden. Hang on." She gives me another unreadable look and heads to the other end of the room and out onto the balcony, where she continues her conversation.

She starts pacing up and down, but she stays close to the window.

And I'm helpless. All I can do is watch her.

Her body language gives nothing away. Suddenly, she stops and beams. Her smile could light Seattle. He's either said yes…or no.

Hell.

Damn it, Grey. Stop with the negative.

She says something else. And she looks like she's going to cry.

Shit. That's not good.

She stomps back in and shoves the phone at me, looking several shades of pissed off.

Nervously, I put the phone to my ear. "Mr. Steele?" Feeling Ana's gaze on my back, I wander into my study just in case it's bad news.

"Christian, I think you ought to call me Ray. Sounds like my little girl is crazy about you and I'm not one to get in her way."

Crazy about you. My heart flips and soars.

"Well, thank you, sir."

"You hurt her in any way and I'll kill you."

"I'd expect nothing less."

"Crazy kids," he mutters. "Now you take good care of her. Annie is my light."

"She's mine, too…Ray."

"And good luck with telling her mother." He laughs. "Now let me get back to my fishing."

"I hope you top the forty-three-pounder."

"You know about that?"

"José told me."

"He's a talkative guy. Good day, Christian."

"It is now." I grin.

"I HAVE YOUR STEPFATHER'S rather begrudging blessing," I announce to Ana in the kitchen. She laughs and shakes her head.

"I think Ray is freaked out," she says. "I've got to tell my mom. But I'd like to do that on a full stomach." She waves in the direction of the counter where our food is waiting. Salmon, potatoes, salad, and an interesting dip. She's also selected some wine. A Chablis.

"Well, this looks great." I open the wine and pour us each a small glass. "Damn, you're a good cook, woman." I raise my glass to Ana in appreciation. Her lighthearted expression fades and I'm reminded of the expression on her face outside the playroom this morning. "Ana? Why did you ask me not to take your photo?"

Her consternation deepens, worrying me.

"Ana, what is it?" My tone is sharper than I intended and she jumps.

"I found your photos," she says as if she's committed some terrible sin.

What photos? But as I say the words, I realize exactly what she's talking about. And I feel like I'm back in my father's study, waiting for a pompous dressing-down for some infraction I've committed.

"You've been in the safe?" *How the hell did she do that?*

"Safe? No. I didn't know you had a safe."

"I don't understand."

"In your closet. The box. I was looking for your tie, and the box was under your jeans. The ones you normally wear in the playroom… Except today."

Fuck.

No one should see those photographs. Especially Ana. How did they get there?

Leila.

"It's not what you think. I'd forgotten all about them. That box had been moved. Those photographs belong in my safe."

"Who moved them?" Ana asks.

"There's only one person who could have done that."

"Oh. Who? And what do you mean it's not what I think?"

Confess, Grey.

You've already alluded to the depths of your depravity.

This is it, baby. Fifty shades.

"This is going to sound cold, but—they're an insurance policy."

"Insurance policy?"

"Against exposure."

I watch her face as she realizes what I mean. "Oh." She closes her eyes as if she's trying to erase what I've told her. "Yes. You're right," she says quietly. "That does sound cold." She stands and starts to clear the dishes; it's to avoid me.

"Ana."

"Do they know? The girls? The subs?"

"Of course they know."

Before she can escape to the sink, I fold her into my arms. "Those photos are supposed to be in the safe. They're not for recreational use."

They were once upon a time, Grey.

"Maybe they were when they were taken originally. But they don't mean anything."

"Who put them in your closet?"

"It could only have been Leila."

"She knows your safe combination?"

I guess. "It wouldn't surprise me. It's a very long combination, and I use it so rarely. It's the one number I have written down and haven't changed. I wonder what else she knows and if she's taken anything else out of there." I'll check it. "Look, I'll destroy the photos. Now, if you like."

"They're your photos, Christian. Do with them as you wish." And I know she's offended and hurt.

Christ.

Ana. This was all before you.

I take her head in my hands. "Don't be like that. I don't want that life. I want our life, together." I know she struggles with not being enough for me. Maybe she thinks I want to do those things to her and photograph her.

Grey, be honest, of course you would.

But I'd never do it without her permission. I had all my submissives' consent to having their photographs taken.

Ana's wounded expression reveals her vulnerability. I thought we'd moved on. I want her as she is. She's more than enough. "Ana, I thought we exorcised all those ghosts this morning. I feel that way. Don't you?"

Her eyes soften. "Yes. Yes, I feel like that, too."

"Good." I kiss her and hold her, feeling her body relax against mine. "I'll shred them. And then I have to go to work. I'm sorry, baby, but I have a mountain of business to get through this afternoon."

"It's cool. I have to call my mother," she says and makes a face. "Then I want to do some shopping and bake you a cake."

"A cake?"

She nods.

"A chocolate cake?"

"You want a chocolate cake?"

I grin.

"I'll see what I can do, Mr. Grey."

I kiss her once more. I don't deserve her. I hope, one day, I'll prove that I do.

ANA WAS RIGHT, the photographs are in my closet. I will have to ask Dr. Flynn to find out if Leila moved them. When I walk back into the living room, Ana's not there. I suspect she's calling her mother.

There's a certain irony in sitting at my desk and shredding

these photographs: relics of my old life. The first photograph is of Susannah, bound and gagged, on her knees on the wooden floor. It's not a bad photograph, and briefly I wonder what José would make of this subject matter. The thought amuses me, but I put the first few photographs through the shredder. I turn the rest of the pile over so I can't see the images and within twelve minutes they're all gone.

You still have the negatives.

Grey. Stop.

I'm relieved to find that nothing else is missing from the safe. I turn to my computer and make a start on my emails. My first task is to rewrite Sam's pretentious statement about my crash landing. I edit it—it lacks clarity and detail—and I send it back to him.

Then I scroll through my text messages.

ELENA
Christian. Please call me.
I need to hear it from your lips
that you're okay.

Elena's text must have come through while I was having lunch. The rest are from late last night and yesterday.

ROS
My feet are sore.
But all good.
Hope you are good, too.

SAM PUBLICITY VP
I really need to talk to you.

SAM PUBLICITY VP
Mr. Grey. Call me. Urgently.

SAM PUBLICITY VP
Mr. Grey. Glad you are okay.
Please call me ASAP.

ELENA

Thank God you're okay.
I just saw the news.
Please call me.

ELLIOT

Pick up the phone. Bro.
We're worried here.

GRACE

Where are you?
Call me. I'm worried.
So is your father.

MIA

CHRISTIAN. WTF.
CALL US. :(

ANA

We're at the Bunker Club.
Please join us.

ANA

You've been mighty
quiet Mr. Grey.
Miss you.

ELENA

Are you ignoring me?

Fuck. Just leave me alone, Elena.

TAYLOR

Sir, false alarm with my daughter.
On my way back to Seattle.
Should be there 3 p.m.

I delete them all. I know I'm going to have to deal with Elena at some point, but I don't feel like it now. I open a spreadsheet from Fred with the cost projections for the Kavanagh contract.

The smell of baking drifts into my study. The aroma is mouth-watering and evokes one of the few happy memories I have of my early childhood. It's a bittersweet feeling. The crack whore. Baking.

A movement distracts me from my thoughts and the spreadsheet I'm reading. It's Ana, standing in my study doorway. "I'm just heading to the store to pick up some ingredients," she says.

"Okay." Not dressed like that, surely?

"What?"

"You going to put some jeans on or something?"

"Christian, they're just legs," she says dismissively, and I grit my teeth. "What if we were at the beach?" she says.

"We're not at the beach."

"Would you object if we were at the beach?"

We'd be on a private beach. "No," I respond.

She gives me a wicked smile. "Well, just imagine we are. Laters." She turns and bolts.

What? She's running?

And before I know it, I'm out of my seat and going after her. I see a flash of turquoise exit through the main entrance at speed and I pursue her into the foyer, but she's in the elevator and the doors are closing when I catch up with her. She gives me a wave from inside and then she's gone. Her haste is such an overreaction, I want to laugh.

What did she think I'd do?

Shaking my head, I walk back to the kitchen. The last time we played tag, she left me. The thought is sobering. I stand at the fridge and pour myself some water and I spy my cake cooling on a wire rack. I bend to sniff it and my mouth waters. I close my eyes and a memory of the crack whore resurfaces.

Mommy is home. Mommy is here.

She's wearing her biggest shoes and a short, short skirt. It's red. And shiny.

Mommy has purple marks on her legs. Near her butt.

She smells good. Like candy.

"Come in, big guy, make yourself comfortable."

She's with a man. A big man with a big beard. I don't know him.

"Not now, Maggot. Mommy has company. Go play in your room with your cars. I'll bake you a cake when I'm done."

She closes her bedroom door.

I hear a ping of the elevator and I turn around expecting Ana to walk back in, but it's Taylor with two men, one holding a briefcase, the other as broad as he is tall, carrying himself like hired muscle.

"Mr. Grey." Taylor introduces the younger man carrying the briefcase. "This is Louis Astoria, from Astoria Fine Jewelry."

"Ah. Thank you for coming."

"My pleasure, Mr. Grey." He's animated. His ebony eyes are warm and friendly. "I have some fine pieces to show you."

"Excellent. Let's look at these in my study. If you'd like to follow me."

I know immediately which platinum ring I want. It's not the biggest; it's not the smallest. It's the finest and most elegant ring, with a four-carat diamond of the highest quality, grade D, and internally flawless clarity. It's beautiful, oval in shape, in a simple setting. The others are too fussy or too gaudy—not right for my girl.

"You've made a fine choice, Mr. Grey," he says as he pockets my check. "I'm sure your fiancée will love it. And we can get it resized if necessary."

"Thank you again for coming. Taylor will see you out."

"Thank you, Mr. Grey." He hands me the ring box and leaves my study with Taylor. I take one more look at the ring.

I really hope she likes it. I place it in my desk drawer and sit down. I wonder if I should call Ana, just to say hi, but dismiss the idea. Instead I listen to her message once more. *Hi… Um… It's me. Ana. Are you okay? Call me.*

Just hearing her voice is enough. I return to my work.

WHILE I'M ON THE phone with the Airbus engineer, I stare out the window at the sky. It's the same blue as Ana's eyes. "And the Eurocopter specialist is due in Monday afternoon?"

"He's flying from Marseilles-Provence near our headquarters in Marignane, to Paris, then to Seattle. It's the earliest we can get him there. We're fortunate that our base in the Pacific Northwest is at Boeing Field."

"Good. Just keep me informed."

"We'll have our people all over the aircraft as soon as she arrives here."

"Tell them I'll need their initial findings either Monday evening or Tuesday morning."

"Will do, Mr. Grey."

I hang up and turn back to my desk.

Ana is standing in the doorway, watching me, looking pensive and a little worried.

"Hi," she says, entering my study and walking around my desk until she's standing in front of me. I want to ask her why she ran, but she preempts me. "I'm back. Are you mad at me?"

I sigh and lift her onto my lap. "Yes," I whisper.

You ran from me, and the last time you did that, you left me.

"I'm sorry. I don't know what came over me." She curls into me, resting her hand and her head against my chest. Her weight is a comfort.

"Me, neither. Wear what you like." I place my hand on her knee to reassure her, but as soon as I touch her, I want more. My desire is like an electric current through my body. It jolts me awake and makes me feel alive. I run my hand up her thigh. "Besides, this dress has its advantages."

She looks up, her eyes smoky, and I kiss her.

Our lips touch, and my tongue teases hers and my libido lights up like a solar flare. I feel it in her, too. She grabs my head between her hands as her tongue wrestles with mine.

I groan as my body responds, growing hard. Wanting her. Needing her. I nip her ear, her throat, her lower lip. She moans into my mouth and yanks my hair.

Ana.

I unzip my pants, free my erection, and move her so she's sitting astride me. Stretching her lacy underwear to the side and out of the way, I sink into her. Her hands grip the back of my chair, the creak of the leather giving her away. She stares down at me and begins to move. Up and down. Fast. Her rhythm is quick and frenetic.

There's a desperation in her movements, as if she wants to make amends.

Slow, baby, slow.

I put my hands on her hips and slow her down.

Easy, Ana. I want to savor you.

I capture her mouth and she moves at a gentler pace. But her passion is in her kiss and in her touch as she tugs my head back.

Oh, baby.

She moves faster.

And faster still.

This is what she wants. She's building. I feel it. Climbing higher and higher as she moves, faster and faster.

Ah.

She falls apart in my arms and she takes me with her.

"I LIKE YOUR VERSION of sorry," I whisper.

"And I like yours." She nuzzles my chest. "Have you finished?"

"Christ, Ana, you want more?"

"No! Your work."

"I'll be done in about half an hour." I kiss her hair. "I heard your message on my voice mail."

"From yesterday."

"You sounded worried."

She hugs me. "I was. It's not like you not to respond."

I kiss her once more and we sit in quiet, peaceful togetherness. I hope she always sits in my lap like this. She fits perfectly.

Finally, she shifts. "Your cake should be ready in half an hour," she says as she stands.

"Looking forward to it. It smelled delicious, evocative even, while it was baking."

She leans down and plants a tender kiss at the edge of my mouth.

I watch her sashay out of my study as I zip my jeans and I feel…lighter. I turn and look at the view from the window. It's late afternoon and the sun is shining, although it's beginning to dip toward the Sound. There are shadows on the streets below. Down there it's already dusk, but up here the light is still golden. Maybe that's why I live here. To be in the light. I've been striving for it since I was a small boy. And it's taken an extraordinary young woman to make me realize that. Ana is my guiding light.

I'm her lost boy, now found.

ANA IS STANDING WITH a frosted chocolate cake that's adorned with a solitary flickering candle.

She sings "Happy Birthday" to me in her sweet musical voice, and I realize I've never heard her sing.

It's magical.

I blow out the candle, closing my eyes to make my wish.

I wish that Ana will always love me. And never leave me.

"I've made my wish," I inform her.

"The frosting is still soft. I hope you like it."

"I can't wait to taste it, Anastasia."

She cuts us each a slice and hands me a plate and a fork.

Here goes.

It's heavenly. The frosting is sweet, the cake moist, and the filling… Mmm. "This is why I want to marry you."

She giggles—relieved, I think—and watches me devour the rest of my slice of cake.

ANA IS QUIET IN the car on the way to my parents' place in Bellevue. She stares out the window but gives me an occasional glance. She looks sensational in emerald green.

There's little traffic tonight, and the R8 roars along the 520 bridge. About halfway across, Ana turns to me. "There was an additional fifty thousand dollars in my bank account this afternoon."

"And?"

"You don't—"

"Ana, you're going to be my wife. Please. Let's not fight about this."

She takes a deep breath and is silent for a while as we cruise just above the pink and dusky waters of Lake Washington. "Okay," she says. "Thank you."

"You're most welcome."

I breathe a sigh of relief.

See, that wasn't so hard, was it, Ana?

On Monday, I'll take care of your student loans.

"READY TO FACE MY family?" I switch off the R8 ignition. We're parked in my parents' driveway.

"Yes. Are you going to tell them?"

"Of course. I'm looking forward to seeing their reactions." I'm excited. I step out of the car and open her door. It's a little cool this evening and she pulls her wrap around her shoulders. I take her hand and we head to the front door. The driveway is choked with cars, including Elliot's truck. It's a bigger party than I'd anticipated.

Carrick opens the front door before I can knock.

"Christian, hello. Happy birthday, son." He takes my hand and engulfs me in a surprise hug.

This never happens. "Um…thanks, Dad."

"Ana, how lovely to see you again." He gives Ana a quick affectionate embrace and we follow him into the house. There's a loud clatter of heels, and I expect to see Mia running down the hallway, but it's Katherine Kavanagh. She looks mad.

"You two! I want to talk to you," she gripes.

Ana gives me a blank look and I shrug. I have no idea what Kavanagh's beef is but we follow her into the empty dining room.

She shuts the door and turns on Ana. "What the fuck is this?"

she hisses and waves a piece of paper at her. Ana takes it from her and reads it. Almost immediately she blanches and her startled eyes meet mine.

What the hell?

Ana steps between Katherine and me.

"What is it?" I ask, feeling anxious.

Ana ignores me and addresses Kavanagh. "Kate! This has nothing to do with you."

Katherine is surprised by her reaction.

What the fuck are they talking about?

"Ana, what is it?"

"Christian, would you just go, please?"

"No. Show me." I hold out my hand and reluctantly she passes the piece of paper to me.

It's her email response to the contract.

Shit.

"What's he done to you?" Katherine asks, ignoring me.

"That's none of your business, Kate." Ana sounds exasperated.

"Where did you get this?" I ask.

Kavanagh blushes. "That's irrelevant." But I stare at her and she continues. "It was in the pocket of a jacket, which I assume is yours, that I found on the back of Ana's bedroom door." She scowls at me, ready for battle.

"Have you told anyone?" I ask.

"No! Of course not," she snaps and has the gall to look offended.

Good. I walk over to the fireplace and taking a lighter from the small porcelain bowl on the mantelpiece I set fire to the corner of the printout and let it float, burning, into the grate. Both women are silent, watching me.

Once it's reduced to ashes, I turn my attention back to them.

"Not even Elliot?" Ana asks.

"No one," Katherine says, and she sounds emphatic. She looks a little puzzled and maybe hurt. "I just want to know you're okay, Ana," she says, concerned.

Unseen by them both, I roll my eyes.

"I'm fine, Kate. More than fine. Please, Christian and I are good, really good—this is old news. Please ignore it," Ana pleads with her.

"Ignore it?" she says. "How can I ignore that? What's he done to you?"

"He hasn't done anything to me, Kate. Honestly, I'm good."

"Really?" she asks.

For fuck's sake.

I wrap my arm around Ana and stare at Katherine, trying and probably failing to keep the animosity out of my expression. "Ana has consented to be my wife, Katherine."

"Wife!" she exclaims, her eyes widening in disbelief.

"We're getting married. We're going to announce our engagement this evening," I inform her.

"Oh!" Katherine stares at Ana, stunned. "I leave you alone for sixteen days, and this happens? It's very sudden. So yesterday, when I said—" She stops. "Where does that email fit into all this?"

"It doesn't, Kate. Forget it—please. I love him and he loves me. Don't do this. Don't ruin his party and our night," Ana begs.

Katherine's eyes fill with tears.

Shit. She's going to cry.

"No. Of course I won't. You're okay?"

"I've never been happier," Ana whispers, and my heart quickens.

Katherine grabs her hand, even though I still have my arm wrapped around Ana.

"You really are okay?" she asks, her voice full of hope.

"Yes." Ana sounds happier and she shrugs out of my hold to hug her.

"Oh, Ana, I was so worried when I read this. I didn't know what to think. Will you explain it to me?" she asks.

"One day, not now."

"Good. I won't tell anyone. I love you so much, Ana, like my own sister. I just thought—" She shakes her head. "I didn't know what to think. I'm sorry. If you're happy, then I'm happy." Katherine looks at me. "I'm sorry. I don't mean to intrude."

I give her a nod. Maybe she does care about Ana, but how Elliot puts up with her I'll never know.

"I really am sorry. You're right, it's none of my business," she whispers to Ana. There's a knock that startles us all, and my mom pokes her head around the door.

"Everything okay, darling?" Mom asks, looking directly at me.

"Everything's fine, Mrs. Grey," Katherine offers.

"Fine, Mom," I respond.

She expresses her relief as she enters the room. "Then you won't mind if I give my son a birthday hug." She gives us all a broad smile and walks into my waiting arms. I hold her close. "Happy birthday, darling," she says. "I'm so glad you're still with us."

"Mom, I'm fine." I look into her warm hazel eyes and they're shining with maternal love.

"I'm so happy for you," she says, and she holds her palm against my cheek.

Mom. I love you.

She steps out of my embrace. "Well, kids, if you've all finished your tête-à-tête, there's a throng of people here to check that you really are in one piece, Christian, and to wish you a happy birthday."

"I'll be right there."

Mom looks from Katherine to Ana, satisfied, I think, that nothing is amiss. She winks at Ana as she holds open the door for all of us. Ana takes my hand.

"Christian, I really do apologize," Katherine says.

I acknowledge her with the briefest of nods and we walk into the hallway.

"Does your mother know about us?" asks Ana.

"Yes."

Ana raises her eyebrows. "Oh. Well, that was an interesting start to the evening."

"As ever, Miss Steele, you have a gift for understatement." I kiss her knuckles and we step into the living room.

A deafening, spontaneous round of applause erupts as we enter.

Shit. So many people! Why so many people? My family. Kavanagh's brother, Flynn and his wife. Mac! Bastille. Mia's friend Lily and her mother. Ros and Gwen. Elena.

Elena catches my attention with a little salute while she

applauds. I'm distracted by my mom's housekeeper. She's carrying a tray of champagne. I squeeze Ana's hand and let it go as the applause dies down.

"Thank you, everyone. Looks like I'll need one of these." I take two flutes and hand a glass to Ana.

I raise my glass in tribute to the room. Everyone moves forward, overzealous and eager to greet me because of yesterday's accident.

Elena is first to reach us, and I take Ana's free hand. "Christian, I was so worried." Elena kisses me on both cheeks before I have a chance to react. Ana tries to free her hand but I tighten my hold on her.

"I'm good, Elena," I respond.

"Why didn't you call me?" She sounds aggravated, her eyes searching mine.

"I've been busy."

"Didn't you get my messages?"

I let go of Ana's hand and put my arm around her shoulder, pulling her to me.

Elena gives Ana a smile. "Ana," she purrs. "You look lovely, dear."

"Elena. Thank you." Ana's tone is saccharine and insincere.

Could this be any more awkward?

I catch Mom's eye and she frowns, looking at the three of us.

"Elena, I need to make an announcement," I tell her.

"Of course," she says with a brittle smile.

I ignore her. "Everyone," I call out, and I wait for the hum in the room to die down. When I have everyone's attention, I take a deep breath. "Thank you for coming today. I have to say I was expecting a quiet family dinner, so this is a pleasant surprise." I shoot Mia a pointed look and she waves at me. "Ros and I"—I give Ros and Gwen a nod—"we had a close call yesterday." Ros raises her glass to me. "So, I'm especially glad to be here today to share with all of you my very good news. This beautiful woman"—I look down at my girl beside me—"Miss Anastasia Rose Steele, has consented to be my wife, and I'd like you all to be the first to know."

My announcement is met with a few gasps, a cheer, and

another spontaneous round of applause. I turn to Ana, who looks flushed and beautiful, tip her chin up and give her a swift, chaste kiss. "You'll soon be mine."

"I am already."

"Legally," I mouth at her with a wicked grin.

She chuckles.

Mom and Dad are the first to congratulate us.

"Darling boy. I've never seen you this happy." Mom kisses my cheek and wipes a tear and then gushes over Ana.

"Son, I'm so proud," Carrick says.

"Thanks, Dad."

"She's a lovely girl."

"I know."

"Where is the ring?" exclaims Mia as she hugs Ana.

Ana gives me a startled look.

"We're going to choose one together." I glare at my little sister. She's such a pain in the ass sometimes.

"Oh, don't look at me like that, Grey!" Mia scoffs, and she folds her arms around me. "I'm so thrilled for you, Christian," she says. "When will you get married? Have you set a date?"

"No idea and no we haven't. Ana and I need to discuss all that."

"I hope you have a big wedding here!" Her persistence is overwhelming.

"We'll probably fly to Vegas tomorrow."

She looks pissed, but thankfully I'm saved by Elliot, who gives me a bear hug.

"Way to go, bro." He slaps me on the back, hard.

Elliot turns to Ana and Bastille claps me on my back, too. Harder.

"Well, Grey, I did not see this coming. Congratulations, man." He pumps my hand.

"Thank you, Claude."

"So, when will I start training your fiancée? The thought of her kicking you onto your backside fills me with hope and joy."

I laugh. "I've given her your schedule. I'm sure she'll be in touch."

Lily's mother, Ashley, congratulates me, but she's a little frosty. I hope she and Lily steer clear of my fiancée.

I rescue Ana from Mia as Dr. Flynn and his wife approach. "Christian," says Flynn, holding out his hand, and we shake.

"John. Rhian." I give his wife a kiss.

"Glad you're still with us, Christian," Flynn says. "My life would be most dull—and penurious—without you."

"John!" Rhian scolds him, and I introduce her to Anastasia.

"Delighted to meet the woman who has finally captured Christian's heart," Rhian says warmly to Ana.

"Thank you," she replies.

"That was one googly you bowled there, Christian." Flynn shakes his head in amused disbelief.

What?

"John, you and your cricket metaphors." Rhian scolds him again, wishes me a happy birthday and congratulates us, and soon she and Ana are deep in an animated conversation.

"That was quite the announcement, given your audience," John says, and I know he's referring to Elena.

"Yes. I'm sure she wasn't expecting that," I answer.

"We can talk about it later."

"How's Leila?"

"She's good, Christian, responding well to treatment. Another couple of weeks and we can consider an outpatient program."

"That's a relief."

"She's interested in our art therapy classes."

"Really? She used to paint."

"So she said. I think these classes could really help."

"Great. Is she eating?"

"Yes. Her appetite's fine."

"Good. Ask her something for me."

"Of course?"

"I need to know if she moved some photography I had in my safe."

"Ah. Yes. She told me about that."

"She did?"

"You know how mischievous she can be. Her intention was to rattle Ana."

"Well, it worked."

"We can discuss that later, too."

We're joined by Ros and Gwen, whom I introduce to Ana.

"I'm so glad to finally meet you, Ana," says Ros.

"Thank you. Have you recovered from your ordeal?"

Ros nods and Gwen puts her arm around her. "It was quite something," Ros continues. "How Christian managed to land safely was a miracle. He's an excellent pilot."

"It was luck, and I wanted to get home to my girl," I respond.

"Of course you did. And having met her, who can blame you?" says Gwen.

Grace announces that dinner is served in the kitchen.

Taking Ana's hand, I give it a quick squeeze to see how she's holding up. Her smile reassures me that she's okay, and we follow the guests through to the kitchen. Mia ambushes Ana in the hallway, holding two cocktail glasses, and I know she's up to no good.

Ana gives me a brief panicked look but I let her go, watching as they enter the dining room. Mia closes the door behind them.

In the kitchen, Mac approaches me to offer his congratulations.

"Please, Mac, call me Christian. You're at my engagement party."

"Heard about the crash." He listens intently as I give him the grisly details.

My mother has set out a feast with a Moroccan theme. I load a plate while Mac and I shoot the breeze about *The Grace*.

As I help myself to a second portion of lamb tagine, I wonder what the hell Ana and Mia are doing. I decide to go rescue Ana but outside the dining room, I hear her shouting. "Don't you dare tell me what I'm getting myself into!"

Shit. What gives?

"When will you learn? It's none of your goddamned business!" Ana rages.

I try to open the door, but someone is in the way. The person moves and the door swings open. Ana is bristling with anger, her complexion reddening. She's shaking with fury. Elena stands before her, drenched in what must have been Ana's drink.

I shut the door and stand between them. "What the fuck are you doing, Elena?" I snarl.

I told you to leave her alone.

She wipes her face with the back of her hand. "She's not right for you, Christian."

"What?" I yell and I'm so loud that I'm sure I've startled Ana because Elena jumps, too. But I don't give a fuck.

I've warned her. And warned her.

"How the fuck do you know what's right for me?"

"You have needs, Christian," she says, her voice softer, and I know she's trying to placate me.

"I've told you before, this is none of your fucking business." I'm surprised by my own vehemence. "What is this?" I scowl at her. "Do you think it's you? You? You think you're right for me?"

Elena's expression hardens, her eyes like flint. She stands taller and steps toward me. "I was the best thing that ever happened to you," she hisses with unrestrained arrogance. "Look at you now. One of the richest, most successful entrepreneurs in the United States. Controlled, driven, you need nothing. You are master of your universe."

She's going there.

Fuck.

I step back. Disgusted.

"You loved it, Christian, don't try to kid yourself. You were on the road to self-destruction, and I saved you from that, saved you from a life behind bars. Believe me, baby, that's where you would have ended up. I taught you everything you know, everything you need."

I cannot remember a time when I've felt such rage. "You taught me how to fuck, Elena. But it's empty, like you. No wonder Linc left."

She gasps. Shocked.

"You never once held me. You never once said you loved me."

Her ice-blue eyes narrow. "Love is for fools, Christian."

"Get out of my house," Grace commands in a cold fury.

The three of us jump and turn to see my mother, an avenging

angel, standing on the threshold of the room. She fixates on Elena, and if looks could kill, Elena would be a small mound of ash on the floor.

I look from Grace to Elena, her color now drained from her face. And as Grace stalks toward her, Elena seems powerless to move or say anything while under my mother's withering glare. Grace slaps her hard across her face, astonishing us all. The sound resonates off the walls. "Take your filthy paws off my son, you whore, and get out of my house—now!" Grace seethes through gritted teeth.

Fuck. Mom!

Elena clutches her cheek in shock. She blinks rapidly, staring at Grace, then turns and abruptly leaves the room, not bothering to close the door behind her.

Mom turns to me, and I cannot look away.

I see hurt and anguish written all over her face.

She says nothing as we stare at each other, and an oppressive and unbearable silence fills the room.

Finally she speaks. "Ana, before I hand him over to you, would you mind giving me a minute or two alone with my son?" It's not a request.

"Of course," Ana whispers. I watch Ana leave and close the door.

Mom glowers at me, saying nothing, looking at me as though she's seeing me for the first time.

Seeing the monster she reared but did not create.

Shit.

I'm in big trouble. My scalp prickles in acknowledgment and I feel the blood drain from my face.

"How long, Christian?" she says, her voice low. And I know that tone—it's the calm before the storm.

How much did she hear?

"A year or so," I mumble. I don't want her to know. I don't want to tell her. I don't want to hurt her and I know it will. I've known that since I was fifteen.

"How old were you?"

I swallow and my heart rate accelerates like a Formula One

engine. I have to be careful here. I don't want to cause trouble for Elena. I study Mom's face, trying to judge how she'll react. Should I lie to her? Could I lie to her? And part of me knows I lied to her every time I saw Elena and told her I was studying with a friend.

Mom's eyes are piercing. "Tell me. How old were you when this all started?" she says through clenched teeth. It's the voice I've only heard on rare occasions, and I know I'm doomed. She will not stop until she has an answer.

"Sixteen," I whisper.

She narrows her eyes and cocks her head to one side.

"Try again." Her voice is chillingly quiet.

Hell. How does she know?

"Christian," she warns, prompting me.

"Fifteen."

She closes her eyes like I've stabbed her, her hand flying to her mouth as she stifles a sob. When she opens them, they're filled with pain and unshed tears.

"Mom..." I try to think of something to say to take that pain away. I step toward her and she holds up her hand to stop me.

"Christian. I am so mad at you right now. I suggest you don't come any closer."

"How did you know? That I lied," I ask.

"For heaven's sake, Christian—I'm your mother," she snaps and dashes a tear from her cheek.

I feel myself blushing, feeling stupid and slightly piqued at the same time. Only my mom can make me feel this way. My mom. And Ana.

I thought I was a better liar.

"Yes, you should look shamefaced. How long did this go on for? How long did you lie to us, Christian?"

I shrug. I don't want her to know.

"Tell me!" she insists.

"A few years."

"Years! Years!" she shouts, making me cringe. She so rarely shouts. "I can't believe it. That *fucking* woman."

I gasp. I have never heard Grace swear. Ever. It shocks me.

She turns and paces to the window. I stay standing. Paralyzed. Speechless.

Mom just cursed.

"And to think, all the times she's been here…" Grace groans and puts her head in her hands.

I cannot stand by any longer. I step toward her and wrap my arms around her. This is so new to me, holding my mom. I pull her to my chest, and she starts to weep quietly.

"I've already thought you dead this week, and now this," she sobs.

"Mom, it's not what you think."

"Don't even try it, Christian. I heard you. I heard what you said. That she taught you to fuck."

She's said it again!

I flinch. This isn't her. She doesn't swear. It's mortifying to think I have something to do with this. The thought of hurting Grace is excruciating. I'd never want to hurt her. She saved me. And all at once I'm overwhelmed by my shame and my remorse.

"I knew something happened when you were fifteen. She was the reason, wasn't she? The reason you suddenly calmed down, seemed to focus? Oh, Christian. What did she do to you?"

Mom! Why is she overreacting? Do I tell her that Elena brought me under control? I don't have to tell her how. "Yes," I murmur.

She groans again. "Oh, Christian. I've gotten drunk with that woman, spilled my soul to her so many nights. And to think…"

"My relationship with her has nothing to do with your friendship."

"Don't give me that bullshit, Christian! She abused my trust. She abused my son!" Her voice cracks, and once more she buries her face in her hands.

"Mom, it didn't feel like that."

She stands back and swats me around the head, making me duck.

"Words fail me, Christian. Fail me. Where did I go wrong?"

"Mom, this is not your fault."

"How? How did it start?" She holds her hand up and continues hurriedly. "I don't want to know that. What will your father say?"

Fuck.

Carrick will go batshit.

Suddenly I'm fifteen again, dreading another of his interminable lectures on personal responsibility and acceptable behavior. Christ, that's the last thing I want.

"Yes, he'll be mad as hell," Mom interjects, correctly interpreting my expression. "We knew something had happened. You changed overnight—and to think it was because you got laid by my best friend."

Right now, I want the floor to swallow me up.

"Mom, it's been, it's done, it's gone. She did me no harm."

"Christian, I heard what you said. I heard her cold response. And to think..." She puts her head in her hands once more. Suddenly her eyes fly up to meet mine and widen in horror.

Fuck. What now?

"No!" she breathes.

"What?"

"Oh no. Tell me it's not true, because if it is, I'll find your father's old pistol and I'll shoot the bitch."

Mom!

"What?"

"I know that Elena's tastes run to the exotic, Christian."

For the second time this evening, I feel slightly dizzy. *Shit.* She must not know this.

"It was just sex, Mom," I mutter quickly—let's shut that down right now. No way am I exposing my mother to that part of my life.

She narrows her eyes at me. "I don't want the sordid details, Christian. Because that's what this is—nasty, sordid, squalid. What kind of woman does that to a fifteen-year-old boy? It's disgusting. To think of all the confidences I've shared with her. Well, you can be sure she'll never set foot in this house again." She presses her lips together in determination. "And you should cease all contact with her."

"Mom, um...Elena and I run a very successful business together."

"No, Christian. You cut your ties with her."

I stare at her, speechless. How can she tell me what to do? I'm twenty-eight years old, for fuck's sake.

"Mom—"

"No, Christian—I'm serious. If you don't, I will go to the police."

I pale. "You wouldn't."

"I will. I couldn't stop it then, but I can now."

"You're just really mad, Mom, and I don't blame you—but you're overreacting."

"Don't tell me I'm overreacting," she yells. "You are *not* going to have any kind of relationship with someone who can abuse a troubled, immature child! She should come with a health warning." She's glowering at me.

"Okay." I hold my hands up defensively and she seems to compose herself.

"Does Ana know?"

"Yes, she does."

"Good. You shouldn't start your married life with secrets." She frowns as if she's speaking from personal experience. Vaguely, I wonder what that's about, but she recovers herself. "I'd be interested to hear what she thinks of Elena."

"She's kind of in your camp."

"Sensible girl. You've fallen on your feet with her, at least. A lovely young woman who's the right age. Someone you can find happiness with."

My expression softens.

Yes. She makes me happier than I ever thought possible.

"You are to end it with Elena. Cut all ties. You understand?"

"Yes, Mom. I could do that as a wedding present to Anastasia."

"What? Are you crazy? You'd better think of something else! That's hardly romantic, Christian," she scolds.

"I thought she'd like that."

"Honestly, men! You have no idea sometimes."

"What do you think I should give her?"

"Oh, Christian." She sighs, then offers me a small wan smile. "You really haven't taken in a word, have you? Do you know why I'm upset?"

"Yes, of course."

"Tell me, then."

I gaze at her and sigh. "I don't know, Mom. Because you didn't know? Because she's your friend?"

She reaches up and gently strokes my hair, like she used to when I was small. The only place she would touch me, because it was the only place I let her.

"For all those reasons and because she abused you, darling. And you are so deserving of love. You're so easy to love. You always have been."

There's a burning sensation at the back of my eyes.

"Mom," I whisper.

She puts her arms around me, calmer now, and I hug her in return.

"You'd better go find your bride-to-be. I'm going to have to tell your father when the party's over. No doubt he'll want to talk to you, too."

"Mom. Please. Do you have to tell him?"

"Yes, Christian, I do. And I hope he gives you hell."

Fuck.

"I'm still mad at you. But madder at her." Her face loses all trace of humor. I'd never realized how scary Grace could be.

"I know," I murmur.

"Go on, off you go. Find your girl." She releases me, steps back, and rubs her fingers under her eyes to wipe away her smudged makeup. She looks beautiful. This wonderful woman, who truly loves me, like I love her.

I take a deep breath. "I didn't mean to hurt you, Mom."

"I know. Go."

I lean down and gently kiss her forehead, surprising her.

I walk out of the room to find Ana.

Shit. That was heavy.

ANA'S NOT IN THE kitchen.

"Hey, bro, want a beer?" Elliot asks.

"In a minute. I'm looking for Ana."

"She come to her senses and run off?"

"Fuck off, Lelliot."

She's not in the sitting room.

She wouldn't leave, would she?

My room? I vault up the first flight of stairs, then up the second. She's standing on the landing. I reach the top step and stop when we are eye to eye.

"Hi."

"Hi," she answers.

"I was worried—"

"I know," she interrupts me. "I'm sorry. I couldn't face the festivities. I just had to get away, you know. To think." She caresses my face and I lean my cheek into her touch.

"And you thought you'd do that in my room?"

"Yes."

Stepping up beside her, I reach out to her and we hold each other. She smells amazing…soothing, even. "I'm sorry you had to endure all that."

"It's not your fault, Christian. Why was she here?"

"She's a family friend."

"Not anymore. How's your mom?"

"Mom is pretty fucking mad at me right now. I'm really glad you're here and that we're in the middle of a party. Otherwise I might be breathing my last."

"That bad, huh?"

Complete overreaction.

"Can you blame her?" Ana asks.

I consider this for a moment. Her best friend fucking her son.

"No."

"Can we sit?"

"Sure. Here?"

Ana nods and we both sit at the top of the stairs.

"So, how do you feel?" she asks.

I let out a deep breath.

"I feel liberated." I shrug. It's true. It's like a weight has been lifted. No more worrying about what Elena thinks.

"Really?"

"Our business relationship is over. Done."

"Will you liquidate the salon business?"

"I'm not that vindictive, Anastasia. No. I'll gift them to her. I'll talk to my lawyer Monday. I owe her that much."

She gives me a quizzical look. "No more Mrs. Robinson?"

"Gone."

Ana grins. "I'm sorry you lost a friend."

"Are you?"

"No," she says sardonically.

"Come." I stand and offer her my hand. "Let's join the party in our honor. I might even get drunk."

"Do you get drunk?"

"Not since I was a wild teenager." We walk down the stairs. "Have you eaten?"

Ana looks guilty. "No."

"Well, you should. From the look and smell of Elena, that was one of my father's lethal cocktails you threw on her."

"Christian, I—"

I hold up my hand. "No arguing, Anastasia. If you're going to drink and toss alcohol on my exes, you need to eat. It's rule number one. I believe we've already had that discussion after our first night together."

An image of her lying comatose on my bed at The Heathman comes to mind. We stop in the hallway and I caress her face, my fingers skimming her jaw. "I lay awake for hours and watched you sleep," I whisper. "I might have loved you even then." Leaning down I kiss her, and she melts against me.

"Eat." I motion toward the kitchen.

"Okay," she says.

I CLOSE THE DOOR, having bid farewell to Dr. Flynn and his wife.

Finally. I can be alone with Ana. It's just the family left. Grace has had too much to drink and is in the den, murdering "I Will Survive" on the karaoke machine with Mia and Katherine.

"Do you blame her?" Ana asks.

I narrow my eyes. "Are you smirking at me, Miss Steele?"

“I am.”

“It’s been quite a day.”

“Christian, recently, every day with you has been quite a day.”

“Fair point well made, Miss Steele. Come. I want to show you something.” I lead her through the hall into the kitchen.

Carrick, Elliot, and Ethan Kavanagh are arguing about the Mariners.

“Off for a stroll?” Elliot taunts us as we head to the french doors, but I give him the finger and otherwise ignore him.

Outside, it’s a mild night. I usher Ana up the stone steps to the lawn, where she takes off her shoes and pauses for a moment to admire the view. The half-moon is high above the bay, illuminating a bright silvery path across the water. Seattle is lit up and twinkling as a backdrop.

We walk, hand in hand, toward the boathouse. It’s lit inside and out and the beckoning light is our guide.

“Christian, I’d like to go to church tomorrow,” Ana says.

“Oh?”

When was the last time I was in church? I recall her background information; I don’t remember her being religious.

“I prayed you’d come back alive and you did. It’s the least I could do.”

“Okay.” Maybe I’ll go with her.

“Where are you going to put the photos José took of me?”

“I thought we might put them in the new house.”

“You bought it?”

I stop. “Yes. I thought you liked it.”

“I do. When did you buy it?”

“Yesterday morning. Now we need to decide what to do with it.”

“Don’t knock it down. Please. It’s such a lovely house. It just needs some tender loving care.”

“Okay. I’ll talk to Elliot. He knows a good architect; she did some work on my place in Aspen. He can do the remodeling.”

Ana smiles, then chuckles with amusement.

“What?” I ask.

“I remember the last time you took me to the boathouse.”

Oh yes. I was in the moment. "Oh, that was fun. In fact—" I stop and scoop her up over my shoulder and she squeals.

"You were really angry, if I remember correctly," Ana observes while she bounces on my shoulder.

"Anastasia, I'm always really angry."

"No you're not."

I swat her behind and slide her down my body when I get to the door of the boathouse. I take her head in my hands. "No, not anymore." My lips and tongue find hers and I pour all the anxiety I'm feeling into a passionate kiss. She's breathless and panting when I release her.

Okay. I hope she likes what I have planned. I hope it's what she wants. She deserves the world. She looks a little intrigued and caresses my face, running her fingers along my cheek to my jaw and chin. Her index finger pauses over my lips.

Showtime, Grey.

"I've something to show you in here." I open the door. "Come." I take her hand and lead her to the top of the stairs. Opening the door, I glance inside, and it all looks good. I step aside to let Ana go first, and I follow her into the room.

She gasps at the sight that greets her.

The florists have gone to town. There are wild meadow flowers everywhere, in pinks and whites and blues, all lit by tiny fairy lights and soft pink lanterns.

Yes. This will do.

Ana is stunned. She whips around and gapes at me.

"You wanted hearts and flowers."

She stares at me in disbelief.

"You have my heart." And I wave at the room.

"And here are the flowers," she murmurs. "Christian, it's lovely." Her voice is hoarse and I know she's close to tears.

Plucking up my courage, I lead her farther into the room. In the center of the arbor, I sink onto one knee. Ana catches her breath, and her hands fly to her mouth. From my inside jacket pocket, I pull out the ring and hold it up for her.

"Anastasia Steele. I love you. I want to love, cherish, and protect you for the rest of my life. Be mine. Always. Share my life with me. Marry me."

She is the love of my life.

It will only ever be Ana.

Her tears start to fall in earnest but her smile eclipses the moon, the stars, the sun, and all the flowers in this boathouse.

"Yes," she says.

Taking her hand, I slip the ring on her finger; it fits perfectly.

She looks down at it in wonder. "Oh, Christian," she sobs, her legs buckling, and she falls into my arms. She kisses me, offering me everything, her lips, her tongue, her compassion, her love. Her body is pressed to mine. Giving, like she always does.

Sweet, sweet Ana.

I kiss her back. Taking what she has to offer and giving in return. She's taught me how.

This woman who has dragged me into the light. This woman who loves me in spite of my past, in spite of my wrongdoings. This woman who's agreed to be mine for the rest of her life.

My girl. My Ana. My love.

EXCERPT FROM *Freed*

SUNDAY, JUNE 19, 2011

We lie in postcoital bliss beneath pink paper lanterns, meadow flowers, and fairy lights that twinkle in the rafters. As my breathing slows, I hold Anastasia close. She's sprawled all over me, her cheek against my chest, her hand resting on my racing heart. The darkness is absent, driven out by my dream catcher…my fiancée. My love. My light.

Could I be happier than I am right now?

I commit the scene to memory: the boathouse, the soothing rhythm of the lapping waters, the flora, the lights. Closing my eyes, I memorize the feel of the woman in my arms, her weight on top of me, the slow rise and fall of her back as she breathes, her legs entwined with mine. The scent of her hair fills my nostrils soothing all my corners and jagged edges. This is my happy place. Dr. Flynn would be proud. This beautiful woman has consented to be mine. In every way. Again.

"Can we marry tomorrow?" I whisper near her ear.

"Hmm." The sound in her throat reverberates with a soft strum across my skin.

"Is that a yes?"

"Hmm."

"A no?"

"Hmm."

I grin. She's spent. "Miss Steele, are you incoherent?" I sense her answering smile and my joy erupts in a laugh, as I tighten my arms around her and kiss her hair. "Vegas, tomorrow, it is then." She raises her head, eyes half closed in the soft light from the lanterns—she looks sleepy yet sated.

"I don't think my parents would be very happy with that." She lowers her head and I skim my fingertips across her naked back, enjoying the warmth of her sleek skin.

"What do you want, Anastasia? Vegas? A big wedding with all the trimmings? Tell me."

"Not big. Just friends and family."

"Okay. Where?"

She shrugs, and I'm guessing she hasn't thought about it.

"Could we do it here?" I ask.

"Your folks' place? Would they mind?"

I laugh. Grace would leap at the chance. "My mother would be in seventh heaven."

"Okay, here. I'm sure my mom and dad would prefer that."

So would I.

For once we're in agreement. No arguing.

Is this a first?

Gently, I stroke her hair, that's a little mussed from our spent passion. "So, we've established where, now the when."

"Surely you should ask your mother?"

"Hmm. She can have a month, that's it. I want you too much to wait any longer."

"Christian, you have me. You've had me for a while. But okay, a month it is." She plants a tender kiss on my chest and I'm grateful that the darkness remains quiet. Her presence is keeping it at bay.

"We'd better head back. I don't want Mia interrupting us like she did that time."

Ana laughs. "Ah, yes. That was close. My first punishment fuck." She grazes my jaw with her fingertips and I roll over, taking her with me, and pressing her into the deep-pile rug on the floor.

"Don't remind me. Not one of my finest moments."

Her lips lift in a coy smile, her eyes sparkling with humor. "As punishment fucks go, it was okay. And I won back my panties."

"You did. Fair and square." Chuckling at the recollection, I kiss her quickly and rise. "Come, put your panties on and let's get back to what's left of the party."

I ZIP UP HER emerald dress and drape my jacket over her shoulders. "Ready?" She laces her fingers with mine and we walk to the top of the stairs of the boathouse. Pausing, she looks back at our floral haven as if *she's* memorizing the setting. "What about all the lights and these flowers?"

"It's okay. The florist is returning tomorrow to dismantle this bower. They've done a great job. And the flowers will go to a local seniors' home."

She squeezes my hand. "You're a good man, Christian Grey."

I hope I'm good enough for you.

MY FAMILY IS IN the den, abusing the karaoke machine. Kate and Mia are up dancing, and singing "We Are Family," with my parents as their audience. I think they're all a little tipsy. Elliot is slumped on the couch, sipping his beer and mouthing the lyrics.

Kate spots Ana and beckons her toward the mic. "OMG!" squeals Mia, drowning out the song. "Look at that rock!" She grabs Ana's hand and whistles. "Christian Grey, you delivered."

Ana gives her a shy smile while Kate and my mother gather round to inspect her ring, making the appropriate admiring noises. Inside I feel ten feet tall.

Yeah. She likes it. They like it.

You did good, Grey.

"Christian, could I talk to you?" Carrick asks as he stands up, his expression grim.

Now?

His stare is unwavering as he directs me out of the room.

"Um. Sure." I glance at Grace, but she's studiously avoiding my gaze.

Has she told him about Elena?

Fuck. I hope not.

I follow him to his study, and he ushers me in, closing the door behind him.

"Your mother told me," he says with no preamble whatsoever.

I glance at the clock—it's 12:28. It's too late in the day for this talk…in every sense. "Dad, I'm tired—"

"No. You are not avoiding this conversation." His voice is stern and his eyes narrow to pinpricks as he peers at me over his glasses. He's mad. Really mad.

"Dad—"

"Quiet, son. You need to listen." He sits on the edge of his desk, removes his glasses, and begins to clean them with the lint cloth he pulls from his pocket. I stand before him, as I often have, feeling like I did when I was fourteen years old and I'd just been expelled from school—again. Resigned, I take a deep breath and, sighing as loudly as I can, place my hands on my hips and wait for the onslaught.

"To say I'm disappointed is an understatement. What Elena did was criminal—"

"Dad—"

"No, Christian. You don't get to speak right now." He glares at me. "She deserves to be locked up."

Dad!

He pauses and slides his glasses back into place. "But I think it's your deception that disappoints me the most. Every time you left this house with some lie that you were studying with your friends—friends we never got to meet—you were fucking that woman."

Christ!

"How am I to believe anything you've ever said to us?" he continues.

Oh, for fuck's sake. This is a complete overreaction. "Can I speak now?"

"No. You can't. Of course, I blame myself. I thought I'd given you some semblance of a moral compass. And now I'm wondering if I've taught you anything at all."

"Are you asking a rhetorical question?"

He ignores me. "She was a married woman and you had no respect for that, and you're shortly to become a married man—"

"This has nothing to do with Anastasia!"

"Don't you dare shout at me," he says, with such quiet venom that I'm silenced immediately. I don't think I've ever seen or heard him this angry. It's sobering. "It has everything to do with her. You are about to make a huge commitment to a young woman." His tone softens. "It's a surprise to all of us. And I'm happy for you. But we are talking about the sanctity of marriage. And if you have no respect for that, then you have no business being married."

"Dad—"

"And if you're that cavalier about the sacred vows that you will soon be affirming, you seriously need to consider a prenuptial agreement."

What? I raise my hands to stop him. He's gone too far. I'm an adult, for heaven's sake. "Don't bring Ana into this. She's not some grubby gold-digger."

"This is not about her." He stands and steps toward me. "It's about you. You living up to your responsibilities. You being a trustworthy and decent human being. You being husband material!"

"For fuck's sake, Dad, I was fifteen years old!" I shout, and we're nose to nose, glowering at each other.

Why is he reacting so badly to this? I know I've always been a huge disappointment to him, but he's never spelled it out so plainly.

He shuts his eyes and pinches the bridge of his nose, and I realize that in my moments of stress I do the same. This habit comes from him, but in my case the apple has fallen far, far from the tree.

"You're right. You were a vulnerable child. But what you fail to see is that what she did was wrong, and clearly you still can't see it because you've continued to associate with her, not only as a family friend, but in business. Both of you have been lying to us for all these years. And that's what hurts the most." His voice drops. "She was your mother's friend. We thought she was a good friend. She's the opposite. You *will* cut all financial ties with her."

Fuck off, Carrick.

I want to tell him that Elena was a force for good, and that I wouldn't have continued my association with her if I thought anything else. But I know this will fall on deaf ears. He didn't want to listen when I was fourteen and struggling in school, and it appears he doesn't want to listen now.

"Have you quite finished?" The words hiss with bitterness through my gritted teeth.

"Think about what I've said."

I turn to go. I've heard enough.

"Think about the prenup. It will save you a great deal of grief in the future."

Ignoring him, I stalk out of his office and slam the door.

Fuck him!

Grace is standing in the hallway.

"Why did you tell him?" I spit at her, but Carrick has followed me out of the study so she doesn't answer. Her frosty glare is directed at him.

I'm going to fetch Ana. We're going home.

My mood savage, I follow the sound of caterwauling into the den and find Elliot and Ana at the mic strangling "Ain't No Mountain High Enough." If I wasn't so angry I'd laugh. Elliot's tuneless rumbling can't really be classed as singing, and he's drowning out Ana's sweet voice. Fortunately, the song is nearly over so I'm spared the worst of it.

"I think Marvin Gaye and Tammi Terrell are spinning in their graves," I observe dryly when they finish.

"I thought that was a pretty good rendition." Elliot bows theatrically to Mia and Kate, who are laughing and applauding with exaggerated gusto. They're definitely all inebriated. Ana giggles, looking flushed and lovely.

"We're going home," I tell her.

Her face falls. "I told your mother we'd stay."

"You did? Just now?"

"Yes. She brought down a change of clothes for us. I was looking forward to sleeping in your bedroom."

"Darling, I was really hoping you'd stay." It's a plea from my mother, who stands in the doorway, Carrick behind her. "Kate and Elliot are, too. I like having all my chicks under one roof." She reaches out and clasps my hand. "And we thought we'd lost you this week."

Muttering an expletive beneath my breath, I keep my temper

in check. My siblings seem to be completely oblivious to the drama that is unfolding in front of them. I expect this cluelessness from Elliot but not from Mia.

"Stay, son. Please." My father's eyes bore into me, but he appears genial enough. It's not like he's just told me that I'm a complete and utter disappointment.

Again.

I ignore him and respond to my mother. "Okay." But it's only because Ana's giving me such an imploring look, and I know that if I leave in my present mood it will be a blight on what has been a wonderful day.

Ana wraps her arms around me. "Thank you," she whispers. I smile down at her and the dark cloud that hangs over me begins to dissipate.

"Come on, Dad." Mia thrusts the mic into his hand and drags him in front of the screen. "Last song!" she says.

"Bed." It's not a request to Ana. I've had enough of my family for one night. She nods in agreement and I knit her fingers with mine. "Good night, all. Thanks for the party, Mother."

Grace hugs me. "You know we love you. We only want the best for you. I am so happy with your news. And so happy that you're here."

"Yeah, Mom. Thanks." I give her a swift peck on the cheek. "We're tired. We're going to bed. Good night."

"Good night, Ana. Thank you," she says and gives her a swift hug. I tug Ana's hand to leave as Mia puts on "Wild Thing" for Carrick to sing.

That I do not want to see.

SWITCHING ON THE LIGHT, I close my bedroom door and pull Ana into my arms, seeking her warmth and trying to put Carrick's blistering rebuke out of my mind.

"Hey, are you okay?" she murmurs. "You're brooding."

"I'm just mad at my dad. But that's nothing new. He still treats me like I'm an adolescent."

Ana hugs me tighter. "Your father loves you."

"Well, tonight he's very disappointed in me. Again. But I don't want to discuss that right now." I kiss the top of her head and she tilts her face up, focusing on me, compassion and understanding shining in her eyes, and I know neither of us wants to raise the specter of Elena...*Mrs. Robinson.*

I'm reminded of earlier this evening, when Grace, in all her avenging glory, threw Elena out of the house. I wonder what my mother would have said, back in the day, if she'd caught me with a girl in my room. Suddenly I'm energized by the same teenage thrill I had when Ana and I snuck up here last weekend during the masquerade ball.

"I've got a girl in my room." I grin.

"What are you going to do with her?" Ana's answering smile is seductive.

"Hmm. All the things I wanted to do with girls when I was an adolescent." But couldn't. Because I couldn't bear to be touched. "Unless you're too tired." I trace the soft curve of her cheek with my knuckle.

"Christian. I'm exhausted. But thrilled, too."

Oh, baby. I kiss her quickly and take pity on her. "Maybe we should just sleep. It's been a long day. Come. I'll put you to bed. Turn around."

She complies and I reach for the zipper on her dress.

WHILE MY FIANCÉE SLUMBERS beside me, I text Taylor and ask him to bring us a change of clothes from Escala in the morning. Scooting down beside Ana, I focus on her profile, marveling that she's asleep already...and that she's agreed to be mine.

Will I ever be good enough for her?

Am I husband material?

My father seems to doubt it.

I sigh and lie on my back, staring up at the ceiling.

I'm going to prove him wrong.

He's always been strict with me. More so than with Elliot or Mia.

Fucker. He knows I'm a bad seed. As I replay his earlier tirade in my head, I drift until sleep claims me.

Arms up, Christian. Daddy has a serious face. He is teaching diving into the pool. *That's right. Now curl your toes around the edge of the pool. Good. Arch your back. That's right. Now push off.* I fall. And fall. And fall. Splash. Into the cool, clear water. Into the blue. Into the calm. Into the quiet. But my water wings push me back to the air. And I look for Daddy. *Look, Daddy, look.* But Elliot jumps on him. And they fall on the ground. Daddy tickles Elliot. Elliot laughs. And laughs. And laughs. And Daddy kisses his tummy. Daddy doesn't do that to me. I don't like it. I'm in the water. I want to be up there. With them. With Daddy. And I'm standing in the trees. Watching Daddy and Mia. She shrieks with joy as he tickles her. And he laughs. And she wriggles free and jumps on him. He swings her around and catches her. And I stand in the trees alone. Watching. Wanting. The air smells good. Of apples.

"GOOD MORNING, MR. GREY," Ana whispers as I open my eyes. The morning sun glimmers through the windows and I'm curled around her like a vine. The knot of homesickness and heartache—evoked by a dream, surely—unravels at the sight of her. I'm smitten and aroused, my body rising to greet her.

"Good morning, Miss Steele." She looks impossibly beautiful in spite of the fact that she's wearing Mia's *I ♥ Paris* T-shirt. She cups my face, her eyes sparkling and her hair wild and glossy in the morning light. She runs a thumb along my chin, tickling the stubble.

"I was watching you sleep."

"Were you now?"

"And looking at my beautiful engagement ring." She stretches out her hand and wiggles her fingers. The diamond captures the light and throws tiny rainbows across my old movie and kickboxing posters on the walls.

"Ooh!" she coos. "It's a sign."

A good sign, Grey. Hopefully.

"I'm never going to take it off."

"Good!" I move so that I'm covering her. "Watching me for how long?" I run my nose down hers and press my lips to hers.

"Oh, no." She pushes at my shoulders and my stab of disappointment is real, but she rolls me onto my back and straddles my hips. Sitting up, she sweeps her T-shirt off in one swift move, and throws it to the floor. "I was thinking about giving you a wake-up call."

"Oh?" My cock and I rejoice.

Before I can steel myself against her touch, she leans down and places a soft kiss on my chest, her hair tumbling around us both, creating a chestnut haven. Bright, blue eyes peek at me.

"Starting here." She kisses me again.

I inhale sharply.

"Then moving down to here." She runs her tongue in a wayward line down my sternum.

Yes.

The darkness stays quiet, subdued by the goddess on top of me or by my bursting libido. I don't know which.

"You taste mighty fine, Mr. Grey," she breathes against my skin.

"I'm glad to hear it." The words are hoarse in my throat.

She licks and nips me along the base of my rib cage as her breasts graze over my lower belly.

Ah!

Once, twice, three times.

"Ana!" I clutch her knees as my breathing accelerates, and squeeze. But she squirms on top of my groin, so I let go, and she rises up, leaving me waiting and wanting. I think she's going to take me. She's ready.

I'm ready.

Fuck, I'm so ready.

But she moves down my body, kissing my stomach and my belly, her tongue slipping into my navel, then grazing through my happy trail. She nips me once more and I feel the bite right through my cock.

"Ah!"

"There you are," she whispers and she stares greedily at my eager dick and then peeps up at me with a coquettish grin. Slowly, her eyes on mine, she takes me in her mouth.

Sweet Jesus.

Her head bobs up and down, her teeth sheathed behind her lips, as she pulls me farther into her mouth each time. My fingers find her hair and sweep it out of the way so I can enjoy an uninterrupted view of my future wife with her lips around my cock. I tighten my buttocks, pushing up my hips, seeking more depth, and she takes it, clamping her mouth around me.

Harder.

Harder still.

Ah. Ana. You fucking goddess.

She picks up the rhythm. And, closing my eyes, I fist my hand in her hair.

She is so good at this.

"Yes," I hiss through my teeth and I lose myself in the rise and fall of her exquisite mouth. I'm going to come.

All of a sudden, she stops.

Damn. No! I open my eyes and watch her move above me, then sink oh-so-slowly onto my bursting dick. I groan, relishing every precious inch. Her hair tumbles to her naked breasts and, reaching up, I caress each one, running my thumbs across her hardening nipples, over and over and over.

She lets out a lengthy moan, thrusting her tits into my hands.

Oh, baby.

Then she pitches forward, kissing me, her tongue invading my mouth, and I taste and savor my saltiness in her sweet mouth.

Ana.

I move my hands to her hips and ease her up off me and then pull her down, thrusting up at the same time.

She cries out, grabbing on to my wrists.

And I do it again.

And again.

"Christian," she calls to the ceiling in a quiet plea as she matches my tempo and we move together. In time. As one. Until she falls apart on top of me, taking me with her and triggering my own release.

I NUZZLE HER HAIR and thrum my fingers down her back.

She takes my breath away.

This is still new. Ana in charge. Ana initiating. I like it.

"Now that's my idea of Sunday worship," I whisper.

"Christian!" She whips her head to mine, eyes round with disapproval.

I laugh out loud.

Will this ever get old? Shocking Miss Steele?

I hug her hard and roll us both over so she's beneath me.

"Good morning, Miss Steele. It's always a treat to wake up to you."

She strokes my cheek. "And you, Mr. Grey." Her tone is soft. "Do we have to get up? I like being here in your room."

"No." I glance at my watch on the nightstand. It's 9:15. "My parents will be at Mass." I shift to her side.

"I didn't know they were churchgoers."

I grimace. "Yes. They are. Catholic."

"Are you?"

"No, Anastasia."

God and I went our separate ways a long time ago.

"Are you?" I ask, recalling that Welch could find no religious affiliations during her background check.

She shakes her head. "No. Neither of my parents practice a faith. But I would like to go to church today. I need to thank… someone for bringing you back alive from the helicopter accident."

I sigh, visualizing a bolt of lightning burning me to a cinder if I step onto the hallowed grounds of a church, but for her, I'll go.

"Okay. I'll see what we can do." I kiss her quickly. "Come, shower with me."

THERE'S A SMALL LEATHER duffel outside my bedroom door—Taylor has delivered clean clothes. I scoop up the bag and shut the door. Ana is wrapped in a towel, beads of water glistening on her shoulders. Her attention is focused on my bulletin board, paused at the photograph of the crack whore. She turns her head toward me, a question on her beautiful face…a question I don't want to answer. "You still have it," she says.

Yeah. I still have the photo. What of it?

As her question hangs in the air between us, her eyes grow luminous in the morning sunshine, drinking me in, begging me to say something. But I can't. This is not somewhere I want to go. For a moment, I'm reminded of the gut punch I felt when Carrick handed me the photograph so many years ago.

Hell. Don't go there, Grey.

"Taylor brought a change of clothes for us," I whisper as I sling the duffel onto the bed. There's an impossibly long silence before she responds.

"Okay," she says, and she walks toward the bed and unzips the bag.

I'VE EATEN MY FILL. My parents have returned from Mass and my mother has cooked her traditional brunch: a delicious, coronary-inducing plate of bacon, sausage, hash browns, eggs, and English muffins. Grace is a little quiet, and I suspect that she might have a hangover.

Throughout the morning I have avoided my father.

I haven't forgiven him for last night.

Ana, Elliot, and Kate are in a heated debate—about bacon, of all things—and arguing over who should have the last sausage. I half listen with amusement while I read an article about the failure rate of local banks in the Sunday edition of *The Seattle Times*.

Mia shrieks and reclaims her place at the table, holding her laptop. "Look at this. There's a gossipy item on the *Seattle Nooz* website about you being engaged, Christian."

"Already?" Mom says, surprised.

Don't these assholes have anything better to do?

Mia reads the column out loud. "'Word has reached us here at the *Nooz* that Seattle's most eligible bachelor, *the* Christian Grey, has finally been snapped up, and wedding bells are in the air.'"

I glance at Ana, who pales as she stares, doe-eyed, from Mia to me.

"'But who is the lucky, lucky lady?'" Mia continues. "'The *Nooz* is on the hunt. Bet she's reading one helluva prenup.'" Mia starts giggling.

I glare at her. *Shut the fuck up, Mia.*

She stops and presses her lips together. Ignoring her, and all the anxious looks exchanged at the table, I turn my attention to Ana, who blanches even more.

"No," I mouth, trying to reassure her.

"Christian," Dad says.

"I'm not discussing this again," I snarl at him. He opens his mouth to say something. "No prenup!" I snap with such vehemence that he closes his mouth.

Shut up, Carrick!

Picking up the paper, I find myself rereading the same sentence in the banking article over and over while I fume.

"Christian," Ana murmurs. "I'll sign anything you and Mr. Grey want."

I look up and she's beseeching me, a sheen of unshed tears reflecting in her eyes.

Ana. Stop.

"No!" I exclaim, imploring her to drop this subject.

"It's to protect you."

"Christian, Ana—I think you should discuss this in private," Grace chastises us and scowls at Carrick and Mia.

"Ana, this is not about you," Dad mumbles. "And please call me Carrick."

Don't try and make it up to her now. I seethe, inwardly, and suddenly there's a burst of activity. Kate and Mia get up to clear the table and Elliot quickly stabs the last remaining sausage with his fork.

"I definitely prefer sausage," he roars with forced levity.

Ana is staring at her hands. She looks crestfallen.

Jesus. Dad. Look what you've done.

ACKNOWLEDGMENTS

Thanks to:

Everyone at Vintage, for your dedication and professionalism. I am constantly inspired by your expertise, good humor, and love for the written word.

Anne Messitte, for your faith in me. I will forever be indebted to you.

Tony Chirico, Russell Perreault, and Paul Bogaards for your invaluable support.

The wonderful production, editorial, and design team who brought this project together: Megan Wilson, Lydia Buechler, Kathy Hourigan, Andy Hughes, Chris Zucker, and Amy Brosey.

Niall Leonard, for your love, support, and guidance, and for being less grumpy.

Valerie Hoskins, my agent—thank you for everything every day.

Kathleen Blandino, for the pre-read, and for all things Web.

Brian Brunetti, once again, for your invaluable insight into helicopter accidents.

Laura Edmonston for sharing your knowledge of the Pacific Northwest.

Professor Chris Collins, for enlightening me about soil science.

Ruth, Debra, Helena, and Liv for the encouragement and word challenges, and for making me get this done.

Dawn and Daisy, for your friendship and advice.

Andrea, BG, Becca, Bee, Britt, Catherine, Jada, Jill, Kellie, Kelly, Leis, Liz, Nora, Raizie, QT, Taylor, Susi—how many years is it now? And we're still going strong. Thank you for the Americanisms.

And all my author and book world friends—you know who you are—you inspire me every day.

And lastly, thank you to my children. I love you unconditionally. I will always be so proud of the wonderful young men you have become. You bring me such joy.

Stay golden. Both of you.

E L James

DARKER

E L James is an incurable romantic and a self-confessed fangirl. After twenty-five years of working in television, she decided to pursue a childhood dream and write stories that readers could take to their hearts. The result was the controversial and sensuous romance *Fifty Shades of Grey* and its two sequels, *Fifty Shades Darker* and *Fifty Shades Freed*. In 2015, she published the #1 bestseller *Grey*, the story of *Fifty Shades of Grey* from the perspective of Christian Grey, and in 2017, the chart-topping *Darker*, the second part of the Fifty Shades story from Christian's point of view. She followed with the #1 *New York Times* bestseller *The Mister* in 2019. In 2021, she released the #1 *New York Times, USA Today, Wall Street Journal*, and international bestseller *Freed*, the third novel in the "As Told by Christian" trilogy. Her books have been published in fifty languages and have sold more than 165 million copies worldwide.

E L James has been recognized as one of *Time* magazine's Most Influential People in the World and *Publishers Weekly*'s Person of the Year. *Fifty Shades of Grey* stayed on the *New York Times* bestseller list for 133 consecutive weeks. *Fifty Shades Freed* won the Goodreads Choice Award (2012), and *Fifty Shades of Grey* was selected as one of the 100 Great Reads, as voted by readers, in PBS's The Great American Read (2018). Darker was longlisted for the 2019 International DUBLIN Literary Award.

She was a producer on each of the three Fifty Shades movies, which made more than a billion dollars at the box office. The third installment, *Fifty Shades Freed*, won the People's Choice Award for Drama in 2018. E L James is blessed with two wonderful sons and lives with her husband, the novelist and screenwriter Niall Leonard, and their West Highland terriers in the leafy suburbs of West London.

"Passion APLENTY."

—*People* magazine

Fall in love with ***The Mister***, the thrilling romance from #1 *New York Times* bestselling author **E L James**, author of the phenomenal bestselling Fifty Shades trilogy.

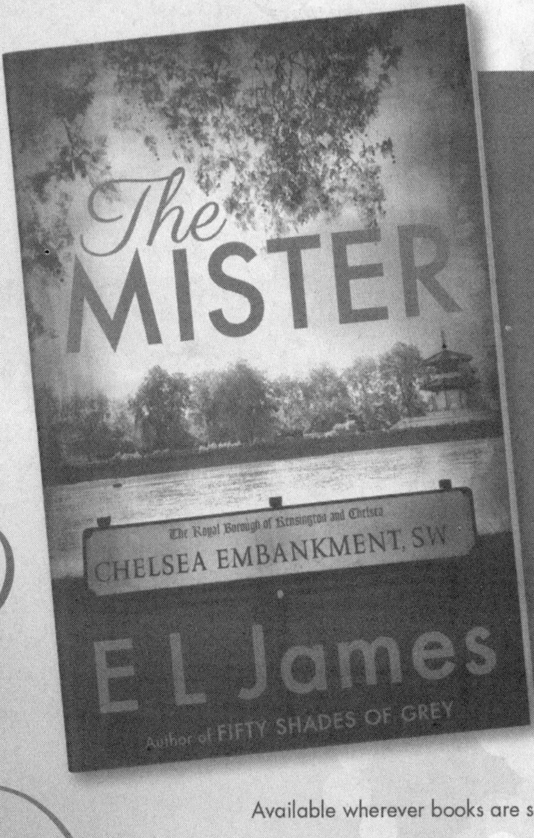

From the heart of London through wild, rural Cornwall to the bleak, forbidding beauty of the Balkans, ***THE MISTER*** is a roller-coaster ride of danger and desire that leaves the reader breathless to the very last page.

Available wherever books are sold.

Bloom *books*

READ MORE FROM

E L JAMES

Provocative Romance

THE FIFTY SHADES TRILOGY

Erotic, amusing, and deeply moving, the Fifty Shades trilogy is a tale that will *obsess you, possess you, and stay with you forever.*

Available wherever books are sold.

Bloom books

See the world of *FIFTY SHADES OF GREY* anew through the eyes of CHRISTIAN GREY

A fresh perspective on the love story that has enthralled millions of readers around the world.

Collect the other books in the
Fifty Shades of Grey as Told by Christian trilogy

Available wherever books are sold.

Bloom books

See yourself in Bloom

every story is a celebration.

Visit **bloombooks.com**
for more information about

E L JAMES

and more of your favorite authors!

bloombooks @read_bloom @read_bloom read_bloom

Bloom books

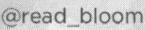

BOOKS BY E L JAMES

Fifty Shades of Grey

Fifty Shades Darker

Fifty Shades Freed

Grey

Darker

Freed

The Mister

GREY

GREY

E L James

Bloom books

Copyright © 2011, 2015 by Fifty Shades Ltd
Cover design by Sqicedragon and Megan Wilson
Cover images © Petar Djordjevic/Penguin Random House, Shutterstock
Book design by Claudia Martinez

Sourcebooks and the colophon are registered trademarks of Sourcebooks. Bloom Books is a trademark of Sourcebooks.

All rights reserved. No part of this book may be reproduced in any form or by any electronic or mechanical means including information storage and retrieval systems—except in the case of brief quotations embodied in critical articles or reviews—without permission in writing from its publisher, Sourcebooks.

The characters and events portrayed in this book are fictitious or are used fictitiously. Any similarity to real persons, living or dead, is purely coincidental and not intended by the author.

All brand names and product names used in this book are trademarks, registered trademarks, or trade names of their respective holders. Sourcebooks is not associated with any product or vendor in this book.

Portions of this book, including significant portions of the dialogue and email exchanges, have previously appeared in the author's prior works.

Published by Bloom Books, an imprint of Sourcebooks
P.O. Box 4410, Naperville, Illinois 60567-4410
(630) 961-3900
sourcebooks.com

Originally published in 2015 in the United States by Vintage Books, a division of Random House LLC, and in Canada by Penguin Random House of Canada Limited.

Library of Congress Cataloging-in-Publication Data is on file with the publisher.

Printed and bound in the United States of America.
LSC 30 29

This book is dedicated to those readers who asked…
and asked…and asked…and asked for this.

Thank you for all that you've done for me.

You rock my world every day.

MONDAY, MAY 9, 2011

I have three cars. They go fast across the floor. So fast. One is red. One is green. One is yellow. I like the green one. It's the best. Mommy likes them, too. I like when Mommy plays with the cars and me. The red is her best. Today she sits on the couch staring at the wall. The green car flies into the rug. The red car follows. Then the yellow. Crash! But Mommy doesn't see. I do it again. Crash! But Mommy doesn't see. I aim the green car at her feet. But the green car goes under the couch. I can't reach it. My hand is too big for the gap. Mommy doesn't see. I want my green car. But Mommy stays on the couch staring at the wall. *Mommy. My car.* She doesn't hear me. *Mommy.* I pull her hand and she lies back and closes her eyes. *Not now, Maggot. Not now,* she says. My green car stays under the couch. It's always under the couch. I can see it. But I can't reach it. My green car is fuzzy. Covered in gray fur and dirt. I want it back. But I can't reach it. I can never reach it. My green car is lost. Lost. And I can never play with it again.

I open my eyes and my dream fades in the early morning light. *What the hell was that about?* I grasp at the fragments as they recede but fail to catch any of them.

Dismissing it, like I do most mornings, I climb out of bed and find some newly laundered sweats in my walk-in closet. Outside, a leaden sky promises rain, and I'm not in the mood to be rained on during my run today. I head upstairs to my gym, switch on the TV for the morning business news, and step onto the treadmill.

My thoughts stray to the day. I've nothing but meetings, though

I'm seeing my personal trainer later for a workout at my office—Bastille is always a welcome challenge.

Maybe I should call Elena?

Yeah. Maybe. We can do dinner later this week.

I stop the treadmill, breathless, and head down to the shower to start another monotonous day.

"TOMORROW," I MUTTER, DISMISSING Claude Bastille as he stands at the threshold of my office.

"Golf this week, Grey." Bastille grins with easy arrogance, knowing his victory on the golf course is assured.

I scowl at him as he turns and leaves. His parting words rub salt into my wounds because, despite my heroic attempts during our workout today, my personal trainer has kicked my ass. Bastille is the only one who can beat me, and now he wants another pound of flesh on the golf course. I detest golf, but so much business is done on the fairways, I have to endure his lessons there, too...and though I hate to admit it, playing against Bastille does improve my game.

As I stare out the window at the Seattle skyline, the familiar ennui seeps unwelcome into my consciousness. My mood is as flat and gray as the weather. My days are blending together with no distinction, and I need some kind of diversion. I've worked all weekend, and now, in the continued confines of my office, I'm restless. I shouldn't feel this way, not after several bouts with Bastille. But I do.

I frown. The sobering truth is that the only thing to capture my interest recently has been my decision to send two freighters of cargo to Sudan. This reminds me—Ros is supposed to come back to me with numbers and logistics. *What the hell is keeping her?* I check my schedule and reach for the phone.

Damn. I have to endure an interview with the persistent Miss Kavanagh for the WSU student newspaper. *Why the hell did I agree to this?* I loathe interviews—inane questions from ill-informed, envious people intent on probing my private life. *And she's a student.* The phone buzzes.

"Yes," I snap at Andrea, as if she's to blame. At least I can keep this interview short.

"Miss Anastasia Steele is here to see you, Mr. Grey."

"Steele? I was expecting Katherine Kavanagh."

"It's Miss Anastasia Steele who's here, sir."

I hate the unexpected. "Show her in."

Well, well…Miss Kavanagh is unavailable. I know her father, Eamon, the owner of Kavanagh Media. We've done business together, and he seems like a shrewd operator and a rational human being. This interview is a favor to him—one that I mean to cash in on later when it suits me. And I have to admit I was vaguely curious about his daughter, interested to see if the apple has fallen far from the tree.

A commotion at the door brings me to my feet as a whirl of long chestnut hair, pale limbs, and brown boots dives headfirst into my office. Repressing my natural annoyance at such clumsiness, I hurry over to the girl who has landed on her hands and knees on the floor. Clasping slim shoulders, I help her to her feet.

Clear, embarrassed eyes meet mine and halt me in my tracks. They are the most extraordinary color, powder blue, and guileless, and for one awful moment, I think she can see right through me and I'm left…exposed. The thought is unnerving, so I dismiss it immediately.

She has a small, sweet face that is blushing now, an innocent pale rose. I wonder briefly if all her skin is like that—flawless—and what it would look like pink and warmed from the bite of a cane.

Damn.

I stop my wayward thoughts, alarmed at their direction. *What the hell are you thinking, Grey?* This girl is much too young. She gapes at me, and I resist rolling my eyes. *Yeah, yeah, baby, it's just a face, and it's only skin deep.* I need to dispel that admiring look from those eyes but let's have some fun in the process!

"Miss Kavanagh. I'm Christian Grey. Are you all right? Would you like to sit?"

There's that blush again. In command once more, I study her.

She's quite attractive—slight, pale, with a mane of dark hair barely contained by a hair tie.

A brunette.

Yeah, she's attractive. I extend my hand as she stutters the beginning of a mortified apology and places her hand in mine. Her skin is cool and soft, but her handshake surprisingly firm.

"Miss Kavanagh is indisposed, so she sent me. I hope you don't mind, Mr. Grey." Her voice is quiet with a hesitant musicality, and she blinks erratically, long lashes fluttering.

Unable to keep the amusement from my voice as I recall her less-than-elegant entrance into my office, I ask who she is.

"Anastasia Steele. I'm studying English literature with Kate…um…Katherine…um…Miss Kavanagh, at WSU Vancouver."

A bashful, bookish type, eh? She looks it: poorly dressed, her slight frame hidden beneath a shapeless sweater, an A-line brown skirt, and utilitarian boots. *Does she have any sense of style at all?* She looks nervously around my office—everywhere but at me, I note with amused irony.

How can this young woman be a journalist? She doesn't have an assertive bone in her body. She's flustered, meek…submissive. Bemused at my inappropriate thoughts, I shake my head and wonder if first impressions are reliable. Muttering some platitude, I ask her to sit, then notice her discerning gaze appraising my office paintings. Before I can stop myself, I find I'm explaining them. "A local artist. Trouton."

"They're lovely. Raising the ordinary to extraordinary," she says dreamily, lost in the exquisite, fine artistry of Trouton's work. Her profile is delicate—an upturned nose, soft, full lips—and in her words she has captured my sentiments exactly. *Raising the ordinary to extraordinary*. It's a keen observation. Miss Steele is bright.

I agree and watch, fascinated, as that flush creeps over her skin once more. As I sit down opposite her, I try to bridle my thoughts.

She fishes some crumpled sheets of paper and a digital recorder out of her large bag. She's all thumbs, dropping the damned thing twice on my Bauhaus coffee table. It's obvious she's never done this before, but for some reason I can't fathom, I find it amusing. Under normal circumstances her maladroitness would irritate the hell out of me, but now I hide my smile beneath my index finger and resist the urge to set it up for her myself.

As she fumbles and grows more and more flustered, it occurs to me that I could refine her motor skills with the aid of a riding crop. Adeptly used, it can bring even the most skittish to heel. The errant thought makes me shift in my chair. She peeks up at me and bites down on her full bottom lip.

Fuck! How did I not notice how inviting that mouth is?

"S-sorry, I'm not used to this."

I can tell, baby, but right now I don't give a damn because I can't take my eyes off your mouth.

"Take all the time you need, Miss Steele." I need another moment to marshal my wayward thoughts.

Grey…stop this, now.

"Do you mind if I record your answers?" she asks, her face candid and expectant.

I want to laugh. "After you've taken so much trouble to set up the recorder, you ask me now?"

She blinks, her eyes large and lost for a moment, and I'm overcome by an unfamiliar twinge of guilt.

Stop being such a shit, Grey. "No, I don't mind." I don't want to be responsible for that look.

"Did Kate, I mean, Miss Kavanagh, explain what the interview was for?"

"Yes, to appear in the graduation issue of the student newspaper, as I shall be giving the commencement address at this year's graduation ceremony." Why the hell I've agreed to do *that*, I don't know. Sam in PR tells me that WSU's Environmental Sciences Department needs the publicity in order to attract additional funding to match the grant I've given them, and Sam will go to any lengths for media exposure.

Miss Steele blinks once more, as if this is news to her—and she looks disapproving. Hasn't she done any background work for this interview? She should know this. The thought cools my blood. It's…displeasing, not what I expect from someone who's imposing on my time.

"Good. I have some questions, Mr. Grey." She tucks a lock of hair behind her ear, distracting me from my annoyance.

"I thought you might," I say dryly. Let's make her squirm. Obligingly, she does, then pulls herself upright and squares her small shoulders. She means business. Leaning forward, she presses the start button on the recorder and frowns as she glances down at her crumpled notes.

"You're very young to have amassed such an empire. To what do you owe your success?"

Surely she can do better than this. What a dull question. Not one iota of originality. It's disappointing. I trot out my usual response about having exceptional people working for me. People I trust, insofar as I trust anyone, and pay well—blah, blah, blah… But Miss Steele, the simple fact is, I'm brilliant at what I do. For me it's like falling off a log. Buying ailing, mismanaged companies and fixing them, keeping some or, if they're really broken, stripping their assets and selling them off to the highest bidder. It's simply a question of knowing the difference between the two, and invariably it comes down to the people in charge. To succeed in business you need good people, and I can judge a person, better than most.

"Maybe you're just lucky," she says quietly.

Lucky? A frisson of annoyance runs through me. *Lucky?* How dare she? She looks unassuming and quiet, but this question? No one has ever suggested that I was lucky. Hard work, bringing people with me, keeping a close watch on them, and second-guessing them if I need to, and if they aren't up to the task, ditching them. *That's what I do, and I do it well. It's nothing to do with luck! Well, to hell with that.* Flaunting my erudition, I quote the words of Harvey Firestone, my favorite industrialist. "The growth and development of people is the highest calling of leadership."

"You sound like a control freak," she says, and she's perfectly serious.

What the hell? Maybe she *can* see through me.

"Control" is my middle name, sweetheart.

I glare at her, hoping to intimidate her. "Oh, I exercise control in all things, Miss Steele." And I'd like to exercise it over you, right here, right now.

That attractive blush steals across her face, and she bites that lip again. I ramble on, trying to distract myself from her mouth.

"Besides, immense power is acquired by assuring yourself, in your secret reveries, that you were born to control things."

"Do you feel that you have immense power?" she asks in a soft, soothing voice, but she arches a delicate brow with a look that conveys her censure. Is she deliberately trying to goad me? Is it her questions, her attitude, or the fact that I find her attractive that's pissing me off? My annoyance grows.

"I employ over forty thousand people. That gives me a certain sense of responsibility—power, if you will. If I were to decide I was no longer interested in the telecommunications business and sell, twenty thousand people would struggle to make their mortgage payments after a month or so."

Her mouth pops open at my response. That's more like it. *Suck it up, baby.* I feel my equilibrium returning.

"Don't you have a board to answer to?"

"I own my company. I don't have to answer to a board." She should know this.

"And do you have any interests outside your work?" she continues hastily, correctly gauging my reaction. She knows I'm pissed, and for some inexplicable reason this pleases me.

"I have varied interests, Miss Steele. Very varied." Images of her in assorted positions in my playroom flash through my mind: shackled on the cross, spread-eagled on the four-poster, splayed over the whipping bench. And behold—there's that blush again. It's like a defense mechanism.

"But if you work so hard, what do you do to chill out?"

"Chill out?" Those words out of her smart mouth sound odd but amusing. Besides, when do I get time to chill out? She has no idea what I do. But she looks at me again with those ingenuous big eyes, and to my surprise I find myself considering her question.

What do *I do to chill out?* Sailing, flying, fucking…testing the limits of attractive brunettes like her and bringing them to heel…The thought makes me shift in my seat, but I answer her smoothly, omitting a few favorite hobbies.

"You invest in manufacturing. Why, specifically?"

"I like to build things. I like to know how things work: what makes things tick, how to construct and deconstruct. And I have a love of ships. What can I say?" They transport food around the planet.

"That sounds like your heart talking, rather than logic and facts."

Heart? Me? Oh no, baby.

My heart was savaged beyond recognition a long time ago. "Possibly. Though there are people who'd say I don't have a heart."

"Why would they say that?"

"Because they know me well." I give her a wry smile. In fact, no one knows me that well, except maybe Elena. I wonder what she would make of little Miss Steele here. The girl is a mass of contradictions: shy, awkward, obviously bright, and arousing as hell.

Yes, okay, I admit it. I find her alluring.

She recites the next question by rote. "Would your friends say you're easy to get to know?"

"I'm a very private person. I go a long way to protect my privacy. I don't often give interviews." Doing what I do, living the life I've chosen, I need my privacy.

"Why did you agree to do this one?"

"Because I'm a benefactor of the university, and for all intents and purposes, I couldn't get Miss Kavanagh off my back. She badgered and badgered my PR people, and I admire that kind of tenacity." But I'm glad it's you who turned up and not her.

"You also invest in farming technologies. Why are you interested in this area?"

"We can't eat money, Miss Steele, and there are too many people on this planet who don't have enough food." I stare at her, poker-faced.

"That sounds very philanthropic. Is that something you feel

passionately about? Feeding the world's poor?" She regards me with a puzzled look, as if I'm a conundrum, but there's no way I want her seeing into my dark soul. This is not an area open to discussion. *Move it along, Grey.*

"It's shrewd business," I mutter, feigning boredom, and I imagine fucking that mouth to distract myself from all thoughts of hunger. Yes, her mouth needs training, and I imagine her on her knees before me. Now, that thought is appealing.

She recites her next question, dragging me away from my fantasy. "Do you have a philosophy? If so, what is it?"

"I don't have a philosophy as such. Maybe a guiding principle—Carnegie's: 'A man who acquires the ability to take full possession of his own mind may take possession of anything else to which he is justly entitled.' I'm very singular, driven. I like control—of myself and those around me."

"So you want to possess things?"

Yes, baby. You, for one. I frown, startled by the thought.

"I want to deserve to possess them, but yes, bottom line, I do."

"You sound like the ultimate consumer." Her voice is tinged with disapproval, pissing me off again.

"I am."

She sounds like a rich kid who's had all she ever wanted, but as I take a closer look at her clothes—she's dressed in clothes from some cheap store like Old Navy or H&M—I know that isn't it. She hasn't grown up in an affluent household.

I could really take care of you.

Where the hell did that thought come from?

Although, now that I consider it, I do need a new sub. It's been, what, two months since Susannah? And here I am, salivating over this woman. I try an agreeable smile. Nothing wrong with consumption—after all, it drives what's left of the American economy.

"You were adopted. How much do you think that's shaped the way you are?"

What does this have to do with the price of oil? What a ridiculous question. If I'd stayed with the crack whore, I'd probably be dead. I blow her off with a non-answer, trying to keep my voice level, but she pushes me, demanding to know how old I was when I was adopted.

Shut her down, Grey!

My tone goes cold. "That's a matter of public record, Miss Steele."

She should know this, too. Now she looks contrite as she tucks an escaped strand of hair behind her ear. *Good.*

"You've had to sacrifice family life for your work."

"That's not a question," I snap.

She startles, clearly embarrassed, but she has the grace to apologize and she rephrases the question: "Have you had to sacrifice family life for your work?"

What do I want with a family? "I have a family. I have a brother, a sister, and two loving parents. I'm not interested in extending my family beyond that."

"Are you gay, Mr. Grey?"

What the hell!

I cannot believe she's said that out loud! Ironically, the question even my own family will not ask. How dare she! I have a sudden urge to drag her out of her seat, bend her over my knee, spank her, and then fuck her over my desk with her hands tied behind her back. That would answer her ridiculous question. I take a deep calming breath. To my vindictive delight, she appears to be mortified by her own question.

"No, Anastasia, I'm not." I raise my eyebrows, but keep my expression impassive. *Anastasia.* It's a lovely name. I like the way my tongue rolls around it.

"I apologize. It's, um…written here." She's at it again with the hair behind the ear. Obviously it's a nervous habit.

Are these not her questions? I ask her, and she pales. Damn, she really is attractive, in an understated sort of way.

"Er…no. Kate—Miss Kavanagh—she compiled the questions."

"Are you colleagues on the student paper?"

"No. She's my roommate."

No wonder she's all over the place. I scratch my chin, debating whether or not to give her a really hard time.

"Did you volunteer to do this interview?" I ask, and I'm rewarded with her submissive look: she's nervous about my reaction. I like the effect I have on her.

"I was drafted. She's not well." Her voice is soft.

"That explains a great deal."

There's a knock at the door, and Andrea appears.

"Mr. Grey, forgive me for interrupting, but your next meeting is in two minutes."

"We're not finished here, Andrea. Please cancel my next meeting."

Andrea gapes at me, looking confused. I stare at her. *Out! Now!* I'm busy with Miss Steele.

"Very well, Mr. Grey," she says, recovering quickly, and turning on her heel, she leaves us.

I turn my attention back to the intriguing, frustrating creature on my couch. "Where were we, Miss Steele?"

"Please, don't let me keep you from anything."

Oh no, baby. It's my turn now. I want to know if there are any secrets to uncover behind that lovely face.

"I want to know about you. I think that's only fair." As I lean back and press my fingers to my lips, her eyes flick to my mouth and she swallows. *Oh yes—the usual effect.* And it is gratifying to know she isn't completely oblivious of my charms.

"There's not much to know," she says, her blush returning.

I'm intimidating her. "What are your plans after you graduate?"

"I haven't made any plans, Mr. Grey. I just need to get through my final exams."

"We run an excellent internship program here."

What possessed me to say that? It's against the rules, Grey. Never fuck the staff… But you're not fucking this girl.

She looks surprised, and her teeth sink into that lip again. Why is that so arousing?

"Oh. I'll bear that in mind," she replies. "Though I'm not sure I'd fit in here."

"Why do you say that?" I ask. *What's wrong with my company?*

"It's obvious, isn't it?"

"Not to me." I'm confounded by her response.

She's flustered again as she reaches for the recorder.

Shit, she's going. Mentally I run through my schedule for that afternoon—there is nothing that won't keep. "Would you like me to show you around?"

"I'm sure you're far too busy, Mr. Grey, and I do have a long drive."

"You're driving back to Vancouver?" I glance out the window. It's one hell of a drive, and it's raining. She shouldn't be driving in this weather, but I can't forbid her. The thought irritates me. "Well, you'd better drive carefully." My voice is sterner than I intend.

She fumbles with the recorder. She wants out of my office, and to my surprise, I don't want her to go.

"Did you get everything you need?" I ask in a transparent effort to prolong her stay.

"Yes, sir," she says quietly. Her response floors me—the way those words sound, coming out of that smart mouth—and I briefly imagine that mouth at my beck and call.

"Thank you for the interview, Mr. Grey."

"The pleasure's been all mine," I respond—truthfully, because I haven't been this fascinated by anyone for a while. The thought is unsettling. She stands and I extend my hand, eager to touch her.

"Until we meet again, Miss Steele." My voice is low as she places her hand in mine. Yes, I want to flog and fuck this girl in my playroom. Have her bound and wanting…needing me, trusting me. I swallow.

It ain't going to happen, Grey.

"Mr. Grey." She nods and withdraws her hand quickly, too quickly.

I can't let her go like this. It's obvious she's desperate to leave. It's irritating, but inspiration hits me as I open my office door.

"Just ensuring you make it through the door," I quip.

Her lips form a hard line. "That's very considerate, Mr. Grey," she snaps.

Miss Steele bites back! I grin behind her as she exits and follow her out. Both Andrea and Olivia look up in shock. *Yeah, yeah. I'm just seeing the girl out.*

"Did you have a coat?" I ask.

"A jacket."

I give Olivia a pointed look and she immediately leaps up to retrieve a navy jacket, passing it to me with her usual simpering expression. Christ, Olivia is annoying—mooning over me all the time.

Hmm. The jacket is worn and cheap. Miss Anastasia Steele should be better dressed. I hold it up for her, and as I pull it over her slim shoulders, I touch the skin at the base of her neck. She stills at the contact and pales.

Yes! She is affected by me. The knowledge is immensely pleasing. Strolling over to the elevator, I press the call button while she stands fidgeting beside me.

Oh, I could stop your fidgeting, baby.

The doors open and she scurries in, then turns to face me. She's more than attractive. I would go as far as to say she's beautiful.

"Anastasia," I say in farewell.

"Christian," she answers, her voice soft. And the elevator doors close, leaving my name hanging in the air between us, sounding odd and unfamiliar, but sexy as hell.

I need to know more about this girl.

"Andrea," I bark as I return to my office. "Get me Welch on the line, now."

As I sit at my desk and wait for the call, I look at the paintings on the wall of my office, and Miss Steele's words drift back to me. "*Raising the ordinary to extraordinary.*" She could so easily have been describing herself.

My phone buzzes. "I have Mr. Welch on the line for you."

"Put him through."

"Yes, sir."

"Welch, I need a background check."

SATURDAY, MAY 14, 2011

ANASTASIA ROSE STEELE

DOB:	Sept. 10, 1989, Montesano, WA
Address:	1114 SW Green Street, Apartment 7, Haven Heights, Vancouver, WA 98888
Mobile No:	360-959-4352
Social Security No:	987-65-4320
Bank:	Wells Fargo Bank, Vancouver, WA: Acct. No.: 309361 $683.16 balance
Occupation:	Undergraduate Student WSU Vancouver College of Arts and Sciences English Major
GPA:	4.0
Prior Education:	Montesano Jr. Sr. High School
SAT Score:	2150
Employment:	Clayton's Hardware Store, NW Vancouver Drive, Portland, OR (part-time)
Father:	Franklin A. Lambert, DOB: Sept. 1, 1969 Deceased Sept. 11, 1989
Mother:	Carla May Wilks Adams DOB: July 18, 1970 m. Frank Lambert March 1, 1989 widowed Sept. 11, 1989 m. Raymond Steele June 6, 1990 divorced July 12, 2006 m. Stephen M. Morton Aug. 16, 2006 divorced Jan. 31, 2007 m. Bob Adams April 6, 2009
Political Affiliations:	None Found
Religious Affiliations:	None Found
Sexual Orientation:	Not Known
Relationships:	None Indicated at Present

I pore over the executive summary for the hundredth time since I received it two days ago, looking for some insight into the enigmatic Miss Anastasia Rose Steele. I cannot get the damned woman out of my mind, and it's seriously beginning to piss me off. This past week, during particularly dull meetings, I've found myself replaying the interview in my head. Her fumbling fingers on the recorder, the way she tucked her hair behind her ear, the lip biting. Yes. The lip biting gets me every time.

And now here I am, parked outside Clayton's, a mom-and-pop hardware store on the outskirts of Portland where she works.

You're a fool, Grey. Why are you here?

I knew it would lead to this. All week…I knew I'd have to see her again. I'd known it since she uttered my name in the elevator. I'd tried to resist. I'd waited five days, five tedious days, to see if I'd forget about her.

And I don't do waiting. I hate waiting…for anything.

I've never pursued a woman before. The women I've had understood what I expected of them. My fear now is that Miss Steele is just too young and that she won't be interested in what I have to offer. *Will she*? Will she even make a good submissive? I shake my head. So here I am, an ass, sitting in a suburban parking lot in a dreary part of Portland.

Her background check has produced nothing remarkable—except the last fact, which has been at the forefront of my mind. It's the reason I'm here. *Why no boyfriend, Miss Steele?* Sexual orientation unknown—perhaps she's gay. I snort, thinking that unlikely. I recall the question she asked during the interview, her acute embarrassment, the way her skin flushed a pale rose… I've been suffering from these lascivious thoughts since I met her.

That's why you're here.

I'm itching to see her again—those blue eyes have haunted me, even in my dreams. I haven't mentioned her to Flynn, and I'm glad because I'm now behaving like a stalker. *Perhaps I should let him know.* No. I don't want him hounding me about his latest solution-based-therapy shit. I just need a distraction, and right now the only distraction I want is the one working as a salesclerk in a hardware store.

You've come all this way. Let's see if Miss Steele is as appealing as you remember.

Showtime, Grey.

A bell chimes a flat electronic note as I walk into the store. It's much bigger than it looks from the outside, and although it's almost lunchtime the place is quiet for a Saturday. There are aisles and aisles of the usual junk you'd expect. I'd forgotten the possibilities that a hardware store could present to someone like me. I mainly shop online for my needs, but while I'm here, maybe I'll stock up on a few items: Velcro, split rings. *Yeah.* I'll find the delectable Miss Steele and have some fun.

It takes me all of three seconds to spot her. She's hunched over the counter, staring intently at a computer screen and picking at her lunch—a bagel. Absentmindedly, she wipes a crumb from the corner of her lips into her mouth and sucks on her finger. My cock twitches in response.

What am I, fourteen?

My body's reaction is irritating. Maybe this will stop if I fetter, fuck, and flog her…and not necessarily in that order. *Yeah. That's what I need.*

She is thoroughly absorbed by her task, and it gives me an opportunity to study her. Salacious thoughts aside, she's attractive, seriously attractive. I've remembered her well.

She looks up and freezes. It's as unnerving as the first time I met her. She pins me with a discerning stare—shocked, I think—and I don't know if this is a good response or a bad one.

"Miss Steele. What a pleasant surprise."

"Mr. Grey," she says, breathy and flustered. *Ah, a good response.*

"I was in the area. I need to stock up on a few things. It's a pleasure to see you again." A *real pleasure.* She's dressed in a tight T-shirt and jeans, not the shapeless shit she was wearing earlier this week. She's all long legs, narrow waist, and perfect tits. Her lips are still parted in surprise, and I have to resist the urge to tip her chin up and close her mouth. I've flown from Seattle just to see you, and the way you look right now, it was really worth the journey.

"Ana. My name's Ana. What can I help you with, Mr. Grey?" She takes a deep breath, squares her shoulders like she did in the interview, and gives me a fake smile that I'm sure she reserves for customers.

Game on, Miss Steele.

"There are a few items I need. To start with, I'd like some cable ties."

My request catches her off guard; she looks stunned.

Oh, this is going to be fun. You'd be amazed what I can do with a few cable ties, baby.

"We stock various lengths. Shall I show you?" she says, finding her voice.

"Please. Lead the way."

She steps out from behind the counter and gestures toward one of the aisles. She's wearing chucks. Idly I wonder what she'd look like in skyscraper heels. Louboutins…nothing but Louboutins.

"They're with the electrical goods, aisle eight." Her voice wavers and she blushes…

She *is* affected by me. Hope blooms in my chest.

She's not gay, then. I smirk.

"After you." I hold my hand out for her to lead the way. Letting her walk ahead gives me the space and time to admire her fantastic ass. Her long, thick ponytail keeps time like a metronome to the gentle sway of her hips. She really is the whole package: sweet, polite, and beautiful, with all the physical attributes I value in a submissive. But the million-dollar question is, could she be a submissive? She probably knows nothing of the lifestyle—my lifestyle—but I very much want to introduce her to it. *You are getting way ahead of yourself on this deal, Grey.*

"Are you in Portland on business?" she asks, interrupting my thoughts. Her voice is high; she's feigning disinterest. It makes me want to laugh. Women rarely make me laugh.

"I was visiting the WSU farming division. It's based in Vancouver," I lie. *Actually, I'm here to see you, Miss Steele.*

Her face falls, and I feel like a shit.

"I'm currently funding some research there in crop rotation and soil science." That, at least, is true.

"All part of your feed-the-world plan?" She arches a brow, amused.

"Something like that," I mutter. *Is she laughing at me?* Oh, I'd love to put a stop to that if she is. But how to start? Maybe with dinner, rather than the usual interview… Now, that would be novel: taking a prospect out to dinner.

We arrive at the cable ties, which are arranged in an assortment of lengths and colors. Absentmindedly, my fingers trace over the packets. *I could just ask her out to dinner.* Like on a date? Would she accept? When I glance at her she's examining her knotted fingers. She can't look at me; this is promising. I select the longer ties. They are more flexible, after all, as they can accommodate two ankles and two wrists at once.

"These will do."

"Is there anything else?" she says quickly—either she's being super-attentive or she wants to get me out of the store. I don't know which.

"I'd like some masking tape."

"Are you redecorating?"

"No, not redecorating." *Oh, if you only knew…*

"This way," she says. "Masking tape is in the decorating aisle."

Come on, Grey. You don't have much time. Engage her in some conversation. "Have you worked here long?" Of course, I already know the answer. Unlike some people, I do my research. For some reason she's embarrassed. Christ, this girl is shy. I don't have a hope in hell.

She turns quickly and walks down the aisle toward the section labeled *Decorating.* I follow her eagerly, like a puppy.

"Four years," she mumbles as we reach the masking tape. She bends down and grasps two rolls, each a different width.

"I'll take that one." The wider tape is much more effective as a gag. As she passes it to me, the tips of our fingers touch, briefly. It resonates in my groin. *Damn!*

She pales. "Anything else?" Her voice is soft and husky.

Christ, I'm having the same effect on her that she has on me. Maybe...

"Some rope, I think."

"This way." She scoots up the aisle, giving me another chance to appreciate her fine ass.

"What sort were you after? We have synthetic and natural filament rope...twine...cable cord..."

Shit—stop. I groan inwardly, trying to chase away the image of her suspended from the ceiling in my playroom.

"I'll take five yards of the natural filament rope, please." It's coarser and chafes more if you struggle against it—my rope of choice.

A tremor runs through her fingers, but she measures out five yards like a pro. Pulling a utility knife from her right pocket, she cuts the rope in one swift gesture, coils it neatly, and ties it off with a slipknot. Impressive.

"Were you a Girl Scout?"

"Organized group activities aren't really my thing, Mr. Grey."

"What is your thing, Anastasia?"

Her pupils dilate as I stare.

Yes!

"Books," she answers.

"What kind of books?"

"Oh, you know. The usual. The classics. British literature mainly."

British literature? The Brontës and Austen, I bet. All those romantic hearts-and-flowers types.

That's not good.

"Anything else you need?"

"I don't know. What else would you recommend?" I want to see her reaction.

"For a do-it-yourselfer?" she asks, surprised.

I want to hoot with laughter. *Oh, baby, DIY is not my thing.* I nod, stifling my mirth. Her eyes flick down my body and I tense. She's checking me out!

"Coveralls," she blurts out.

It's the most unexpected thing I've heard her say since the "Are you gay?" question.

"You wouldn't want to ruin your clothing." She gestures to my jeans.

I can't resist. "I could always take them off."

"Um." She flushes beet red and stares down.

I put her out of her misery. "I'll take some coveralls. Heaven forbid I should ruin any clothing." Without a word, she turns and walks briskly up the aisle, and I follow in her enticing wake.

"Do you need anything else?" she says, sounding breathless as she hands me a pair of blue coveralls. She's mortified, eyes still cast down. *Christ, she does things to me.*

"How's the article coming along?" I ask in the hope she might relax a little.

She looks up and gives me a brief relieved smile.

Finally.

"I'm not writing it, Katherine is. Miss Kavanagh. My roommate, she's the writer. She's very happy with it. She's the editor of the newspaper, and she was devastated that she couldn't do the interview in person."

It's the longest sentence she's uttered since we first met, and she's talking about someone else, not herself. *Interesting.*

Before I can comment, she adds, "Her only concern is that she doesn't have any original photographs of you."

The tenacious Miss Kavanagh wants photographs. Publicity stills, eh? I can do that. It will allow me to spend time with the delectable Miss Steele.

"What sort of photographs does she want?"

She gazes at me for a moment, then shakes her head, perplexed, not knowing what to say.

"Well, I'm around. Tomorrow, perhaps..." I can stay in Portland. Work from a hotel. A room at The Heathman, perhaps. I'll need Taylor to come down, bring my laptop and some clothes. Or Elliot—unless he's screwing around, which is his usual MO over the weekend.

"You'd be willing to do a photo shoot?" She cannot contain her surprise.

I give her a brief nod. *Yeah, I want to spend more time with you…*

Steady, Grey.

"Kate will be delighted—if we can find a photographer." She smiles and her face lights up like a cloudless dawn. She's breathtaking.

"Let me know about tomorrow." I pull my wallet from my jeans. "My card. It has my cell number on it. You'll need to call before ten in the morning." And if she doesn't, I'll head on back to Seattle and forget about this stupid venture.

The thought depresses me.

"Okay." She continues to grin.

"Ana!" We both turn as a young man dressed in casual designer gear appears at the far end of the aisle. His eyes are all over Miss Anastasia Steele. *Who the hell is this prick?*

"Er, excuse me for a moment, Mr. Grey." She walks toward him, and the asshole engulfs her in a gorilla-like hug. My blood runs cold. It's a primal response.

Get your fucking paws off her.

I fist my hands and am only slightly mollified when she doesn't return his hug.

They fall into a whispered conversation. Maybe Welch's facts were wrong. Maybe this guy is her boyfriend. He looks the right age, and he can't take his greedy little eyes off her. He holds her for a moment at arm's length, examining her, then stands with his arm resting on her shoulder. It seems like a casual gesture, but I know he's staking a claim and telling me to back off. She seems embarrassed, shifting from foot to foot.

Shit. I should go. I've overplayed my hand. She's with this guy. Then she says something else to him and moves out of his reach, touching his arm, not his hand, shrugging him off. It's clear they aren't close.

Good.

"Er…Paul, this is Christian Grey. Mr. Grey, this is Paul

Clayton. His brother owns the place." She gives me an odd look that I don't understand and continues, "I've known Paul ever since I've worked here, though we don't see each other that often. He's back from Princeton, where he's studying business administration." She's babbling, giving me a long explanation and telling me they're not together, I think. The boss's brother, not a boyfriend. I'm relieved, but the extent of the relief I feel is unexpected, and it makes me frown. *This woman has really gotten under my skin.*

"Mr. Clayton." My tone is deliberately clipped.

"Mr. Grey." His handshake is limp, like his hair. *Asshole.* "Wait up—not *the* Christian Grey? Of Grey Enterprises Holdings?"

Yeah, that's me, you prick.

I watch him morph from territorial to obsequious in a heartbeat.

"Wow—is there anything I can get you?"

"Anastasia has it covered, Mr. Clayton. She's been very attentive." *Now fuck off.*

"Cool," he gushes, all white teeth and deferential. "Catch you later, Ana."

"Sure, Paul," she says, and he ambles off to the back of the store. I watch him disappear.

"Anything else, Mr. Grey?"

"Just these items," I mutter. *Shit,* I'm out of time, and I still don't know if I'm going to see her again. I have to know whether there's a hope in hell she might consider what I have in mind. How can I ask her? Am I ready to take on a submissive who knows nothing? She's going to need substantial training. Closing my eyes, I imagine the interesting possibilities this presents…getting there is going to be half the fun. Will she even be up for this? Or do I have it all wrong?

She walks back to the cashier's counter and rings up my purchases, all the while keeping her eyes on the register.

Look at me, damn it! I want to see her face again and gauge what she's thinking.

Finally she raises her head. "That will be forty-three dollars, please."

Is that all?

"Would you like a bag?" she asks as I pass her my AmEx.

"Please, Anastasia." Her name—a beautiful name for a beautiful girl—flows smoothly over my tongue.

She packs the items briskly. This is it. I have to go.

"You'll call me if you want me to do the photo shoot?"

She nods as she hands back my charge card.

"Good. Until tomorrow, perhaps." I can't just leave. I have to let her know I'm interested. "Oh—and Anastasia, I'm glad Miss Kavanagh couldn't do the interview." She looks surprised and flattered.

This is good.

I sling the bag over my shoulder and exit the store.

Yes, against my better judgment, I want her. Now I have to wait…fucking wait…again. Utilizing willpower that would make Elena proud, I keep my eyes ahead as I take my cell out of my pocket and climb into the rental car. I'm deliberately not looking back at her. I'm not. I'm not. My eyes flick to the rearview mirror, where I can see the shop door, but all I see is the quaint storefront. She's not in the window, staring out at me.

It's disappointing.

I press 1 on speed dial and Taylor answers before the phone has a chance to ring.

"Mr. Grey," he says.

"Make reservations at The Heathman; I'm staying in Portland this weekend, and can you bring down the SUV, my computer and the paperwork beneath it, and a change or two of clothes?"

"Yes, sir. And *Charlie Tango*?"

"Have Joe move her to PDX."

"Will do, sir. I'll be with you in about three and a half hours."

I hang up and start the car. So I have a few hours in Portland while I wait to see if this girl is interested in me. What to do? Time for a hike, I think. Maybe I can walk this strange hunger out of my system.

IT'S BEEN FIVE HOURS with no phone call from the delectable Miss Steele. What the hell was I thinking? I watch the street from the window of my suite at The Heathman. I loathe waiting. I always have. The weather, now cloudy, held for my hike through Forest Park, but the walk has done nothing to cure my agitation. I'm annoyed at her for not phoning, but mostly I'm angry with myself. I'm a fool for being here. What a waste of time it's been chasing this woman. When have I ever chased a woman?

Grey, get a grip.

Sighing, I check my phone once again in the hope that I've just missed her call, but there's nothing. At least Taylor has arrived and I have all my shit. I have Barney's report on his department's graphene tests to read and I can work in peace.

Peace? I haven't known peace since Miss Steele fell into my office.

WHEN I GLANCE UP, dusk has shrouded my suite in gray shadows. The prospect of a night alone again is depressing. While I contemplate what to do my phone vibrates against the polished wood of the desk and an unknown but vaguely familiar number with a Washington area code flashes on the screen. My heart is suddenly pumping as if I've run ten miles.

Is it her?

I answer.

"Er…Mr. Grey? It's Anastasia Steele."

My face erupts in a shit-eating grin. *Well, well.* A breathy, nervous, soft-spoken Miss Steele. My evening is looking up.

"Miss Steele. How nice to hear from you." I hear her breath hitch and the sound travels directly to my groin.

Great. I'm affecting her. Like she's affecting me.

"Um, we'd like to go ahead with the photo shoot for the article. Tomorrow, if that's okay. Where would be convenient for you, sir?"

In my room. Just you, me, and the cable ties.

"I'm staying at The Heathman in Portland. Shall we say nine thirty tomorrow morning?"

"Okay, we'll see you there," she gushes, unable to hide the relief and delight in her voice.

"I look forward to it, Miss Steele." I hang up before she senses my excitement and how pleased I am. Leaning back in my chair, I gaze at the darkening skyline and run both my hands through my hair.

How the hell am I going to close this deal?

SUNDAY, MAY 15, 2011

With Moby blasting in my ears I run down Southwest Salmon Street toward the Willamette River. It's 6:30 in the morning and I'm trying to clear my head. Last night I dreamed of her. Blue eyes, breathy voice…her sentences ending with "sir" as she knelt before me. Since I've met her, my dreams have been a welcome change from the occasional nightmare. I wonder what Flynn would make of that. The thought is disconcerting, so I ignore it and concentrate on pushing my body to its limits along the bank of the Willamette. As my feet pound the walkway, sunshine breaks through the clouds and it gives me hope.

TWO HOURS LATER AS I jog back to the hotel I pass a coffee shop. Maybe I should take her for coffee.

Like a date?

Well. No. Not a date. I laugh at the ridiculous thought. Just a chat—an interview of sorts. Then I can find out a little more about this enigmatic woman and if she's interested, or if I'm on a wild-goose chase. I'm alone in the elevator as I stretch out. Finishing my stretches in my hotel suite, I'm centered and calm for the first time since I arrived in Portland. Breakfast has been delivered and I'm famished. It's not a feeling I tolerate—ever. Sitting down to breakfast in my sweats, I decide to eat before I shower.

THERE'S A BRISK KNOCK on the door. I open it and Taylor stands on the threshold.

"Good morning, Mr. Grey."

"Morning. They ready for me?"

"Yes, sir. They're set up in room 601."

"I'll be right down." I close the door and tuck my shirt into my gray pants. My hair is wet from my shower, but I don't give a shit. One glance at the louche fucker in the mirror and I exit to follow Taylor to the elevator.

Room 601 is crowded with people, lights, and camera boxes, but I spot her immediately. She's standing to the side. Her hair is loose: a lush, glossy mane that falls beneath her breasts. She's wearing tight jeans and Chucks with a short-sleeved navy jacket and a white T-shirt beneath. Are jeans and Chucks her signature look? While not very convenient, they do flatter her shapely legs. Her eyes, disarming as ever, widen as I approach.

"Miss Steele, we meet again." She takes my extended hand and for a moment I want to squeeze hers and raise it to my lips.

Don't be absurd, Grey.

She turns her delicious pink and waves in the direction of her friend, who is standing too close, waiting for my attention.

"Mr. Grey, this is Katherine Kavanagh," she says.

With reluctance I release her and turn to the persistent Miss Kavanagh. She's tall, striking, and well groomed, like her father, but she has her mother's eyes, and I have her to thank for my introduction to the delightful Miss Steele. That thought makes me feel a little more benevolent toward her.

"The tenacious Miss Kavanagh. How do you do? I trust you're feeling better? Anastasia said you were unwell last week."

"I'm fine, thank you, Mr. Grey."

She has a firm, confident handshake, and I doubt she's ever faced a day of hardship in her privileged life. I wonder why these women are friends. They have nothing in common.

"Thank you for taking the time to do this," Katherine says.

"It's a pleasure," I reply and glance at Anastasia, who rewards me with her telltale flush.

Is it just me who makes her blush? The thought pleases me.

"This is José Rodriguez, our photographer," Anastasia says, and her face lights up as she introduces him.

Shit. Is this the boyfriend?

Rodriguez blooms under Ana's sweet smile.

Are they fucking?

"Mr. Grey." Rodriguez gives me a dark look as we shake hands. It's a warning. He's telling me to back off. He likes her. He likes her a lot.

Well, game on, kid.

"Mr. Rodriguez, where would you like me?" My tone is a challenge, and he hears it, but Katherine intervenes and waves me toward a chair. Ah. She likes to be in charge. The thought amuses me as I sit. Another young man who appears to be working with Rodriguez switches on the lights, and momentarily I'm blinded.

Hell!

As the glare recedes I search out the lovely Miss Steele. She's standing at the back of the room, observing the proceedings. Does she always shy away like this? Maybe that's why she and Kavanagh are friends; she's content to be in the background and let Katherine take center stage.

Hmm…a natural submissive.

The photographer appears professional enough and absorbed in the job he's been assigned to do. I regard Miss Steele as she watches both of us. Our eyes meet; hers are honest and innocent, and for a moment I reconsider my plan. But then she bites her lip and my breath catches in my throat.

Back down, Anastasia. I will her to stop staring, and as if she can hear me, she's the first to look away.

Good girl.

Katherine asks me to stand as Rodriguez continues to take snaps. Then we're done and this is my chance.

"Thank you again, Mr. Grey." Katherine surges forward and shakes my hand, followed by the photographer, who regards me with ill-concealed disapproval. His antagonism makes me smile.

Oh, man…you have no idea.

"I look forward to reading the article, Miss Kavanagh," I say, giving her a brief polite nod. It's Ana I want to talk to. "Will you walk with me, Miss Steele?" I ask when I reach her by the door.

"Sure," she says with surprise.

Seize the day, Grey.

I mutter some platitude to those still in the room and usher her out the door, wanting to put some distance between her and Rodriguez. In the corridor she stands fiddling with her hair, then her fingers, as Taylor follows me out.

"I'll call you, Taylor," I say, and when he's almost out of earshot I ask Ana to join me for coffee, my breath held for her response.

Her long lashes flicker over her eyes. "I have to drive everyone home," she says with dismay.

"Taylor," I call after him, making her jump. I must make her nervous and I don't know if this is good or bad. And she can't stop fidgeting. Thinking about all the ways I could make her stop is distracting. "Are they based at the university?"

She nods and I ask Taylor to take her friends home.

"There. Now can you join me for coffee?"

"Um, Mr. Grey… Er… This really…" She stops.

Shit. It's a "no." I'm going to lose this deal. She looks directly at me, eyes bright. "Look, Taylor doesn't have to drive them home. I'll swap vehicles with Kate, if you give me a moment."

My relief is tangible and I grin.

I have a date!

Opening the door, I let her back into the room as Taylor conceals his puzzled look.

"Can you grab my jacket, Taylor?"

"Certainly, sir."

He turns on his heel, his lips twitching as he heads up the corridor. I watch him with narrowed eyes as he disappears into the elevator while I lean against the wall and wait for Miss Steele.

What the hell am I going to say to her?

"How would you like to be my submissive?"

No. Steady, Grey. Let's take this one stage at a time.

Taylor is back within a couple of minutes, holding my jacket.

"Will that be all, sir?"

"Yes. Thanks."

He gives it to me and leaves me standing like an idiot in the corridor.

How long is Anastasia going to be? I check my watch. She must be negotiating the car swap with Katherine. Or she's talking to Rodriguez, explaining that she's just going for coffee to placate me and keep me sweet for the article. My thoughts darken. Maybe she's kissing him goodbye.

Damn.

She emerges a moment later, and I'm pleased. She doesn't look like she's just been kissed.

"Okay," she says with resolve. "Let's do coffee." But her reddening cheeks somewhat undermine her effort to look confident.

"After you, Miss Steele." I conceal my delight as she falls into step ahead of me. As I catch up with her my curiosity is piqued about her relationship with Katherine, specifically their compatibility. I ask her how long they've known each other.

"Since our freshman year. She's a good friend." Her voice is full of warmth. Ana is clearly devoted. She came all the way to Seattle to interview me when Katherine was ill, and I find myself hoping that Miss Kavanagh treats her with the same loyalty and respect.

At the elevators I press the call button and almost immediately the doors open. A couple in a passionate embrace spring apart, embarrassed to be caught. Ignoring them, we step into the elevator, but I catch Anastasia's impish smile.

As we travel to the first floor the atmosphere is thick with unfulfilled desire. And I don't know if it's emanating from the couple behind us or from me.

Yes. I want her. Will she want what I have to offer?

I'm relieved when the doors open again and I take her hand, which is cool and not clammy as expected. Perhaps I don't affect her as much as I'd like. The thought is disheartening.

In our wake we hear embarrassed giggling from the couple.

"What is it about elevators?" I mutter. And I have to admit there's something wholesome and naive about their giggling that's totally charming. Miss Steele seems that innocent, just like them, and as we walk onto the street I question my motives again.

She's too young. She's too inexperienced, but, damn, I like the feel of her hand in mine.

In the coffee shop I direct her to find a table and ask what she wants to drink. She stutters through her order: English Breakfast tea—hot water, bag on the side. That's a new one to me.

"No coffee?"

"I'm not keen on coffee."

"Okay, bag-out tea. Sugar?"

"No thanks," she says, staring down at her fingers.

"Anything to eat?"

"No thank you." She shakes her head and tosses her hair over her shoulder, highlighting glints of auburn.

I have to wait in line while the two matronly women behind the counter exchange inane pleasantries with *all* their customers. It's frustrating and keeping me from my objective: Anastasia.

"Hey, handsome, what can I get you?" the older woman asks with a twinkle in her eye. *It's just a pretty face, sweetheart.*

"I'll have a coffee with steamed milk. English Breakfast tea. Tea bag on the side. And a blueberry muffin."

Anastasia might change her mind and eat.

"You visiting Portland?"

"Yes."

"The weekend?"

"Yes."

"The weather sure has picked up today."

"Yes."

"I hope you get out to enjoy some sunshine."

Please stop talking to me and hurry the fuck up.

"Yes," I hiss through my teeth and glance over at Ana, who quickly looks away.

She's watching me. Is she checking me out?

A bubble of hope swells in my chest.

"There you go." The woman winks and places the drinks on my tray. "Pay at the register, honey, and you have a nice day, now."

I manage a cordial response. "Thank you."

At the table Anastasia is staring at her fingers, reflecting on heaven knows what.

Me?

"Penny for your thoughts?" I ask.

She jumps and turns red as I set out her tea and my coffee. She sits mute and mortified. Why? Does she really not want to be here?

"Your thoughts?" I ask again, and she fidgets with the tea bag.

"This is my favorite tea," she says, and I revise my mental note that it's Twinings English Breakfast tea she likes. I watch her dunk the tea bag in the teapot. It's an elaborate and messy spectacle. She fishes it out almost immediately and places the used teabag on her saucer. My mouth is twitching with my amusement. When she tells me she likes her tea weak and black, I wonder if it can be classed as tea at all.

Enough of this preamble; it's time for some due diligence in this deal. "Is he your boyfriend?"

Her brows knit together, forming a small *v* above her nose.

"Who?"

This is a good response.

"The photographer. José Rodriguez."

She laughs. At me.

At me!

And I don't know if it's from relief or if she thinks I'm funny. It's annoying. I can't get her measure. Does she like me or not? She tells me he's just a friend.

Oh, sweetheart, he wants to be more than a friend.

"Why did you think he was my boyfriend?" she asks.

"The way you smiled at him, and he at you." *You have no idea, do you?* The boy is smitten.

"He's more like family," she says.

Okay, so the lust is one-sided, and for a moment I wonder if she realizes how lovely she is. She eyes the blueberry muffin as I peel back the paper, and for a moment I imagine her on her knees beside me as I feed her, a morsel at a time. The thought is diverting—and arousing. "Do you want some?" I ask.

She shakes her head. "No thanks." Her voice is hesitant and she stares once more at her hands. Why is she so jittery? Maybe because of me?

"And the boy I met yesterday, at the store. He's not your boyfriend?"

"No. Paul's just a friend. I told you yesterday." She frowns again as if she's confused and crosses her arms in defense. She doesn't like being asked about these boys. I remember how uncomfortable she seemed when the kid at the store put his arm around her, staking his claim. "Why do you ask?" she adds.

"You seem nervous around men."

Her eyes widen. They really are beautiful, the color of the ocean at Cabo, the bluest of blue seas. I should take her there.

What? Where did that come from?

"I find you intimidating," she says and looks down, fidgeting once more with her fingers. On the one hand she's so submissive, but on the other she's…challenging.

"You should find me intimidating."

Yeah. She should. There aren't many people brave enough to tell me that I intimidate them. She's honest, and I tell her so—but when she averts her eyes, I don't know what she's thinking. It's frustrating. Does she like me? Or is she tolerating this meeting to keep Kavanagh's interview on track? Which is it?

"You're a mystery, Miss Steele."

"There's nothing mysterious about me."

"I think you're very self-contained." Like any good submissive. "Except when you blush, of course, which is often. I just wish I knew what you were blushing about." *There.* That will goad her into a response. Popping a small piece of the blueberry muffin into my mouth, I await her reply.

"Do you always make such personal observations?"

That's not that personal, is it? "I hadn't realized I was. Have I offended you?"

"No."

"Good."

"But you're very high-handed."

"I'm used to getting my own way, Anastasia. In all things."

"I don't doubt it," she mutters and then wants to know why I haven't asked her to call me by my first name.

What?

And I remember her leaving my office in the elevator—and

how my name sounded coming out of her smart mouth. Has she seen through me? Is she deliberately antagonizing me? I tell her that no one calls me Christian, except my family…

I don't even know if it's my real name.

Don't go there, Grey.

I change the subject. I want to know about her.

"Are you an only child?"

Her eyelashes flutter several times before she answers that she is.

"Tell me about your parents."

She rolls her eyes and I have to fight the compulsion to scold her.

"My mom lives in Georgia with her new husband, Bob. My stepdad lives in Montesano."

Of course I know all this from Welch's background check, but it's important to hear it from her. Her lips soften with a fond smile when she mentions her stepdad.

"Your father?" I ask.

"My father died when I was a baby."

"I'm sorry," I mutter automatically, and for a moment I'm catapulted into my nightmares, looking at a prostrate body on a grimy floor.

"I don't remember him," she says, dragging me back to the now. Her expression is clear and bright, and I know Raymond Steele has been a good father to this girl. Her mother's relationship with her, on the other hand—that remains to be seen.

"And your mother remarried?"

Her laugh is bitter. "You could say that." But she doesn't elaborate. She's one of the few women I've met who can sit in silence. Which is great, but not what I want at the moment.

"You're not giving much away, are you?"

"Neither are you," she parries.

Oh, Miss Steele. Game on.

And it's with great pleasure and a smirk that I remind her that she's interviewed me already. "I can recollect some quite probing questions."

Yes. You asked me if I was gay.

My statement has the desired effect and she's embarrassed. She starts babbling about herself and a few details hit home. Her mother is an incurable romantic. I suppose someone on her fourth marriage is embracing hope over experience. Is she like her mother? I can't bring myself to ask her. If she says she is, then I have no hope. But I don't want this interview to end. I'm enjoying myself too much.

I ask about her stepfather and she confirms my hunch. It's obvious she loves him. Her face is luminous when she talks about him: his job (he's a carpenter), his hobbies (he likes European soccer and fishing). She preferred to live with him when her mom married the third time.

Interesting.

She straightens her shoulders. "Tell me about *your* parents," she demands in an attempt to divert the conversation from her family.

I don't like talking about mine, so I give her the bare details. "My dad's a lawyer; my mom is a pediatrician. They live in Seattle."

"What do your siblings do?"

She wants to go there? I give her the short answer that Elliot works in construction and Mia is at cookery school in Paris.

She listens, rapt. "I hear Paris is lovely," she says with a dreamy expression.

"It's beautiful. Have you been?"

"I've never left mainland USA." The cadence in her voice falls, tinged with regret. I could take her there.

"Would you like to go?"

First Cabo, now Paris? Get a grip, Grey.

"To Paris? Of course. But it's England that I'd really like to visit."

Her face brightens with excitement. Miss Steele wants to travel. But why England? I ask her.

"It's the home of Shakespeare, Austen, the Brontë sisters, Thomas Hardy. I'd like to see the places that inspired those people to write such wonderful books." It's obvious this is her first love.

Books.

She said as much in Clayton's yesterday. That means I'm competing with Darcy, Rochester, and Angel Clare: impossible romantic heroes. Here's the proof I needed. She's an incurable romantic, like her mother—and this isn't going to work. To add insult to injury, she looks at her watch. She's done.

I've blown this deal.

"I'd better go. I have to study," she says.

I offer to walk her back to her friend's car, which means I'll have the walk back to the hotel to make my case.

But should I?

"Thank you for the tea, Mr. Grey," she says.

"You're welcome, Anastasia. It's my pleasure." As I say the words I realize the last twenty minutes have been…enjoyable. Giving her my most dazzling smile, guaranteed to disarm, I offer her my hand. "Come," I say.

She takes my hand, and as we walk back to The Heathman I can't shake how agreeable her hand feels in mine.

Maybe this could work.

"Do you always wear jeans?" I ask.

"Mostly," she says, and it's two strikes against her: incurable romantic who only wears jeans… I like my women in skirts. I like them accessible.

"Do you have a girlfriend?" she asks out of the blue, and it's the third strike. I'm out of this fledgling deal. She wants romance, and I can't offer her that.

"No, Anastasia. I don't do the girlfriend thing."

Stricken with a frown, she turns abruptly and stumbles into the road.

"Shit, Ana!" I shout, tugging her toward me to stop her from falling in the path of an idiot cyclist who's flying the wrong way up the street. All of a sudden she's in my arms clutching my biceps, staring up at me. Her eyes are startled, and for the first time I notice a darker ring of blue circling her irises; they're beautiful, more beautiful this close. Her pupils dilate and I know I could fall into her gaze and never return. She takes a deep breath.

"Are you okay?" My voice sounds alien and distant, and I realize she's touching me and I don't care. My fingers caress her cheek. Her skin is soft and smooth, and as I brush my thumb against her lower lip, my breath catches in my throat. Her body is pressed against mine, and the feel of her breasts and her heat through my shirt is arousing. She has a fresh, wholesome fragrance that reminds me of my grandfather's apple orchard. Closing my eyes, I inhale, committing her scent to memory. When I open them she's still staring at me, entreating me, begging me, her eyes on my mouth.

Shit. She wants me to kiss her.

And I want to. Just once. Her lips are parted, ready, waiting. Her mouth felt welcoming beneath my thumb.

No. No. No. Don't do this, Grey.

She's not the girl for you.

She wants hearts and flowers, and you don't do that shit.

I close my eyes to blot her out and fight the temptation, and when I open them again, my decision is made. "Anastasia," I whisper, "you should steer clear of me. I'm not the man for you."

The little *v* forms between her brows, and I think she's stopped breathing.

"Breathe, Anastasia, breathe." I have to let her go before I do something stupid, but I'm surprised at my reluctance. I want to hold her for a moment longer. "I'm going to stand you up and let you go." I step back and she releases her hold on me, yet weirdly, I don't feel any relief. I slide my hands to her shoulders to ensure she can stand. Her expression clouds with humiliation. She's mortified by my rebuff.

Hell. I didn't mean to hurt you.

"I've got this," she says, disappointment ringing in her clipped tone. She's formal and distant, but she doesn't move out of my hold. "Thank you," she adds.

"For what?"

"For saving me."

And I want to tell her that I'm saving her from me…that it's a noble gesture, but that's not what she wants to hear. "That idiot was riding the wrong way. I'm glad I was here. I shudder to think what could have happened to you." Now it's me who's babbling, and I still can't let her go. I offer to sit with her in the hotel, knowing it's a ploy to prolong my time with her, and only then do I release her.

She shakes her head, her back ramrod stiff, and wraps her arms around herself in a protective gesture. A moment later she bolts across the street and I have to hurry to keep up with her.

When we reach the hotel, she turns and faces me once more, composed. "Thanks for the tea and doing the photo shoot." She regards me dispassionately and regret flares in my gut.

"Anastasia… I…" I can't think what to say, except that I'm sorry.

"What, Christian?" she snaps.

Whoa. She's mad at me, pouring all the contempt she can into each syllable of my name. It's novel. And she's leaving. And I don't want her to go. "Good luck with your exams."

Her eyes flash with hurt and indignation. "Thanks," she mutters, disdain in her tone. "Goodbye, Mr. Grey." She turns away and strides up the street toward the underground garage.

I watch her go, hoping that she'll give me a second look, but she doesn't. She disappears into the building, leaving in her wake a trace of regret, the memory of her beautiful blue eyes, and the scent of an apple orchard in the fall.

THURSDAY, MAY 19, 2011

No! My scream bounces off the bedroom walls and wakes me from my nightmare. I'm drenched in sweat, with the stench of stale beer, cigarettes, and poverty in my nostrils and a lingering dread of drunken violence. Sitting up, I put my head in my hands as I try to calm my escalated heart rate and erratic breathing. It's been the same for the last four nights. Glancing at the clock, I see it's 3:00 a.m.

I have two major meetings tomorrow…today…and I need a clear head and some sleep. *Damn it, what I'd give for a good night's sleep.* And I have a round of fucking golf with Bastille. I should cancel the golf; the thought of playing and losing darkens my already bleak mood.

Clambering out of bed, I wander down the corridor and into the kitchen. There, I fill a glass with water and catch sight of myself, dressed only in pajama pants, reflected in the glass wall at the other side of the room. I turn away in disgust.

You turned her down.

She wanted you.

And you turned her down.

It was for her own good.

This has needled me for days now. Her beautiful face appears in my mind without warning, taunting me. If my shrink was back from his vacation in England I could call him. His psychobabble shit would stop me feeling this lousy.

Grey, she was just a pretty girl.

Perhaps I need a distraction; a new sub, maybe. It's been too long since Susannah. I contemplate calling Elena in the morning.

She always finds suitable candidates for me. But the truth is, I don't want anyone new.

I want Ana.

Her disappointment, her wounded indignation, and her contempt remain with me. She walked away without a backward glance. Perhaps I raised her hopes by asking her out for coffee, only to disappoint her.

Maybe I should find some way to apologize, then I can forget about this whole sorry episode and get the girl out of my head. Leaving the glass in the sink for my housekeeper to wash, I trudge back to bed.

THE RADIO ALARM JOLTS to life at 5:45 as I'm staring at the ceiling. I haven't slept and I'm exhausted.

Fuck! This is ridiculous.

The program on the radio is a welcome distraction until the second news item. It's about the sale of a rare manuscript: an unfinished novel by Jane Austen called *The Watsons* that will be auctioned soon in London.

"Books," she said.

Christ. Even the news reminds me of little Miss Bookworm.

She's an incurable romantic who loves the English classics. But then so do I, but for different reasons. I don't have any Jane Austen first editions, or Brontës, for that matter…but I do have two Thomas Hardys.

Of course! This is it! This is what I can do.

Moments later I'm in my library with *Jude the Obscure* and a boxed set of *Tess of the d'Urbervilles* in its three volumes laid out on the billiard table in front of me. Both are bleak books, with tragic themes. Hardy had a dark, twisted soul.

Like me.

I shake off the thought and examine the books. Even though *Jude* is in better condition, it's no contest. In *Jude* there is no redemption, so I'll send her *Tess*, with a suitable quote. I know it's not the most romantic book, considering the evils that befall the heroine, but she has a brief taste of romantic love in the bucolic idyll that is the English countryside. And Tess does exact revenge on the man who wronged her.

But that's not the point. Ana mentioned Hardy as a favorite and I'm sure she's never seen, let alone owned, a first edition.

"You sound like the ultimate consumer." Her judgmental retort from the interview comes back to haunt me. Yes. I like to possess things, things that will rise in value, like first editions.

Feeling calmer and more composed, and a little pleased with myself, I head back into my closet and change into my running gear.

IN THE BACK OF the car I leaf through book one of the *Tess* first edition, looking for a quote, and at the same time wonder when Ana's last exam will take place. I read the book years ago and have a hazy recollection of the plot. Fiction was my sanctuary when I was a teenager. My mother always marveled that I read; Elliot not so much. I craved the escape that fiction provided. He didn't need an escape.

"Mr. Grey," Taylor interrupts. "We're here, sir." He climbs out of the car and opens my door. "I'll be outside at two o'clock to take you to your golf game."

I nod and head into Grey House, the books tucked under my arm. The young receptionist greets me with a flirtatious wave.

Every day… Like a cheesy tune on repeat.

Ignoring her, I make my way to the elevator that will take me straight to my floor.

"Good morning, Mr. Grey," Barry on security greets me as he presses the button to summon the elevator.

"How's your son, Barry?"

"Better, sir."

"I'm glad to hear it."

I step into the elevator and it shoots up to the twentieth floor. Andrea is on hand to greet me.

"Good morning, Mr. Grey. Ros wants to see you to discuss the Darfur project. Barney would like a few minutes—"

I hold my hand up to silence her. "Forget those for now. Get me

Welch on the line and find out when Flynn is back from vacation. Once I've spoken to Welch we can pick up the day's schedule."

"Yes, sir."

"And I need a double espresso. Get Olivia to make it for me."

But looking around I notice Olivia is absent. It's a relief. The girl is always mooning over me and it's fucking irritating.

"Would you like milk, sir?" Andrea asks.

Good girl. I give her a smile.

"Not today." I do like to keep them guessing how I take my coffee.

"Very good, Mr. Grey." She looks pleased with herself, which she should be. She's the best PA I've had.

Three minutes later she has Welch on the line.

"Welch?"

"Mr. Grey."

"The background check you did for me last week. Anastasia Steele. Studying at WSU."

"Yes, sir. I remember."

"I'd like you to find out when her last final exam takes place and let me know as a matter of priority."

"Very good, sir, Anything else?"

"No, that will be all." I hang up and stare at the books on my desk. I need to find a quote.

ROS, MY NUMBER TWO and my chief operating officer, is in full flow. "We're getting clearance from the Sudanese authorities to put the shipments into Port Sudan. But our contacts on the ground are hesitant about the road journey to Darfur. They're doing a risk assessment to see how viable it is." Logistics must be tough; her normal sunny disposition is absent.

"We could always air-drop."

"Christian, the expense of an airdrop—"

"I know. Let's see what our NGO friends come back with."

"Okay," she says and sighs. "I'm also waiting for the all-clear from the State Department."

I roll my eyes. Fucking red tape. "If we have to grease some palms—or get Senator Blandino to intervene—let me know."

"So the next topic is where to site the new plant. You know the tax breaks in Detroit are huge. I sent you a summary."

"I know. But God, does it have to be Detroit?"

"I don't know what you have against the place. It meets our criteria."

"Okay, get Bill to check out potential brownfield sites. And let's do one more site search to see if any other municipality would offer more favorable terms."

"Bill has already sent Ruth out there to meet with the Detroit Brownfield Redevelopment Authority, who couldn't be more accommodating, but I'll ask Bill to do a final check."

My phone buzzes.

"Yes," I growl at Andrea—she knows I hate being interrupted in a meeting.

"I have Welch for you."

My watch says 11:30. That was quick. "Put him through."

I signal for Ros to stay.

"Mr. Grey?"

"Welch. What news?"

"Miss Steele's last exam is tomorrow, May 20."

Damn. I don't have long.

"Great. That's all I need to know." I hang up.

"Ros, bear with me one moment."

I pick up the phone. Andrea answers immediately.

"Andrea, I need a blank notecard to write a message within the next hour," I say and hang up. "Right, Ros, where were we?"

AT 12:30 OLIVIA SHUFFLES into my office with lunch. She's a tall, willowy girl with a pretty face. Sadly, it's always misdirected at me with longing. She's carrying a tray with what I hope is something edible. After a busy morning, I'm starving. She trembles as she puts it on my desk.

Tuna salad. Okay. She hasn't fucked this up for once.

She also places three different white cards, all different sizes, with corresponding envelopes on my desk.

"Great," I mutter. *Now go.* She scuttles out.

I take one bite of tuna to assuage my hunger, then reach for my pen. I've chosen a quote. A warning. I made the correct choice, walking away from her. Not all men are romantic heroes. I'll take the word "men-folk" out. She'll understand.

Why didn't you tell me there was danger? Why didn't you warn me? Ladies know what to guard against, because they read novels that tell them of these tricks...

I slip the card into the envelope provided and on it write Ana's address, which is ingrained in my memory from Welch's background check. I buzz Andrea.

"Yes, Mr. Grey."

"Can you come in, please?"

"Yes, sir."

She appears at my door a moment later. "Mr. Grey?"

"Take these, package them, and courier them to Anastasia Steele, the girl who interviewed me last week. Here's her address."

"Right away, Mr. Grey."

"They have to arrive by tomorrow at the latest."

"Yes, sir. Will that be all?"

"No. Find me a set of replacements."

"For these books?"

"Yes. First editions. Get Olivia on it."

"What books are these?"

"*Tess of the d'Urbervilles.*"

"Yes, sir." She gives me a rare smile and leaves my office.

Why is she smiling?

She never smiles. Dismissing the thought, I wonder if that will be the last I see of the books, and I have to acknowledge that deep down I hope not.

FRIDAY, MAY 20, 2011

I've slept well for the first time in five days. Maybe I'm feeling the closure I had hoped for, now that I've sent those books to Anastasia. As I shave, the asshole in the mirror stares back at me with cool, gray eyes.

Liar.

Fuck.

Okay. Okay. I'm hoping she'll call. She has my number.

Mrs. Jones looks up when I walk into the kitchen.

"Good morning, Mr. Grey."

"Morning, Gail."

"What would you like for breakfast?"

"I'll have an omelet. Thank you." I sit at the kitchen counter as she prepares my food and leaf through *The Wall Street Journal* and *The New York Times,* then I pore over *The Seattle Times.* While I'm lost in the papers my phone buzzes.

It's Elliot. What the hell does my big brother want?

"Elliot?"

"Dude. I need to get out of Seattle this weekend. This chick is all over my junk and I've got to get away."

"Your junk?"

"Yeah. You would know if you had any."

I ignore his jibe, and then a devious thought occurs to me. "How about hiking around Portland? We could go this afternoon. Stay down there. Come home Sunday."

"Sounds cool. In the chopper, or do you want to drive?"

"It's a helicopter, Elliot, and I'll drive us down. Come by the office at lunchtime and we'll head out."

"Thanks, bro. I owe you." Elliot hangs up.

Elliot has always had a problem containing himself. As do the women he associates with: whoever the unfortunate girl is, she's just another in a long, long line of his casual liaisons.

"Mr. Grey. What would you like to do for food this weekend?"

"Just prepare something light and leave it in the fridge. I may be back on Saturday."

Or I may not.

She didn't give you a second glance, Grey.

Having spent a great deal of my working life managing others' expectations, I should be better at managing my own.

ELLIOT SLEEPS MOST OF the way to Portland. Poor fucker must be fried. Working and fucking: that's Elliot's raison d'être. He sprawls out in the passenger seat and snores.

Some company he's going to be.

It'll be after three when we arrive in Portland, so I call Andrea on the hands-free.

"Mr. Grey," she answers in two rings.

"Can you have two mountain bikes delivered to The Heathman?"

"For what time, sir?"

"Three."

"The bikes are for you and your brother?"

"Yes."

"Your brother is about six two?"

"Yes."

"I'll get on it right away."

"Great." I hang up, then call Taylor.

"Mr. Grey," he answers on one ring.

"What time will you be here?"

"I'll check in around nine o'clock tonight."

"Will you bring the R8?"

"With pleasure, sir." Taylor is a car fanatic, too.

"Good." I end the call and turn up the music. Let's see if Elliot can sleep through The Verve.

As we cruise down I-5 my excitement mounts.

Have the books been delivered yet? I'm tempted to call Andrea again, but I know I've left her with a ton of work. Besides, I don't want to give my staff an excuse to gossip. I don't normally do this kind of shit.

Why did you send them in the first place?

Because I want to see her again.

We pass the exit for Vancouver and I wonder if she's finished her exam.

"Hey, man, where we at?" Elliot blurts.

"Behold, he wakes," I mutter. "We're nearly there. We're going mountain biking."

"We are?"

"Yes."

"Cool. Remember when Dad used to take us?"

"Yep." I shake my head at the memory. My father is a polymath, a real renaissance man: academic, sporting, at ease in the city, more at ease in the great outdoors. He'd embraced three adopted kids…and I'm the one who didn't live up to his expectations.

But before I hit adolescence we had a bond. He'd been my hero. He used to love taking us camping and doing all the outdoor pursuits I now enjoy: sailing, kayaking, biking—we did it all.

Puberty ruined all that for me.

"I figured if we were arriving midafternoon, we wouldn't have time for a hike."

"Good thinking."

"So who are you running from?"

"Man, I'm a love-'em-and-leave-'em type. You know that. No strings. I don't know, chicks find out you run your own business and they start getting crazy ideas." He gives me a sideways look. "You've got the right idea keeping your dick to yourself."

"I don't think we're discussing my dick; we're discussing yours and who's been on the sharp end of it recently."

Elliot snickers. "I've lost count. Anyway, enough of me. How's the stimulating world of commerce and high finance?"

"You really want to know?" I shoot him a glance.

"Nah," he bleats and I laugh at his apathy and lack of eloquence.

"How's the business?" I ask.

"You checking on your investment?"

"Always." It's my job.

"Well, we broke ground on the Spokani Eden project last week and it's on schedule, but then it's only been a week." He shrugs. Beneath his somewhat casual exterior my brother is an eco-warrior. His passion for sustainable living makes for some heated Sunday dinner conversations with the family, and his latest project is an eco-friendly development of low-cost housing north of Seattle.

"I'm hoping to install that new gray-water system I was telling you about. It will mean all the homes will reduce their water usage and their bills by twenty-five percent."

"Impressive."

"I hope so."

We drive in silence into downtown Portland and just as we're pulling into the underground garage at The Heathman—the last place I saw her—Elliot mutters, "You know we're missing the Mariners game this evening."

"Maybe you can have a night in front of the TV. Give your dick a rest and watch baseball."

"Sounds like a plan."

KEEPING UP WITH ELLIOT is a challenge. He tears down the trail with the same devil-may-fucking-care attitude he applies to most situations. Elliot knows no fear—it's why I admire him. But riding at this pace I have no chance to appreciate our surroundings. I'm vaguely aware of the lush greenery flashing past me, but my eyes are on the trail, trying to avoid the potholes.

By the end of the ride we're both filthy and exhausted.

"That was the most fun I've had with my clothes on in a while," Elliot says as we hand the bikes over to the bellboy at The Heathman.

"Yeah," I mutter, and then recall holding Anastasia when I saved her from the cyclist. Her warmth, her breasts pressed against me, her scent invading my senses.

I had my clothes on then… "Yeah," I murmur again.

We check our phones in the elevator as we head up to the top floor.

I have emails, a couple of texts from Elena asking what I'm doing this weekend, but no missed calls from Anastasia. It's just before 7:00—she must have received the books by now. The thought depresses me: I've come all the way to Portland on a wild-goose chase again.

"Man, that chick has called me five times and sent me four texts. Doesn't she know how desperate she comes across?" Elliot whines.

"Maybe she's pregnant."

Elliot pales and I laugh.

"Not funny, hotshot," he grumbles. "Besides, I haven't known her that long. Or that often."

AFTER A QUICK SHOWER I join Elliot in his suite and we sit down to watch the rest of the Mariners game against the San Diego Padres. We order up steak, salad, fries, and a couple of beers, and I sit back to enjoy the game in Elliot's easy company. I've resigned myself to the fact that Anastasia's not going to call. The Mariners are in the lead and it looks like it might be a blowout.

Disappointingly it isn't, though the Mariners win 4–1.

Go Mariners! Elliot and I clink beer bottles.

As the postgame analysis drones on, my phone buzzes and Miss Steele's number flashes on the screen.

It's her.

"Anastasia?" I don't hide my surprise or my pleasure. The background is noisy and it sounds like she's at a party or in a bar. Elliot glances at me, so I get up from the sofa and out of his earshot.

"Why did you send me the books?" She's slurring her words, and a wave of apprehension ripples down my spine.

"Anastasia, are you okay? You sound strange."

"I'm not the strange one, you are." Her tone is accusatory.

"Anastasia, have you been drinking?"

Hell. Who is she with? The photographer? Where's her friend Kate?

"What's it to you?" She sounds surly and belligerent, and I know she's drunk, but I also need to know she's okay.

"I'm...curious. Where are you?"

"In a bar."

"Which bar?" *Tell me.* Anxiety blooms in my gut. She's a young woman, drunk, somewhere in Portland. She's not safe.

"A bar in Portland."

"How are you getting home?" I pinch the bridge of my nose in the vain hope that the action will distract me from my fraying temper.

"I'll find a way."

What the hell? Will she drive? I ask her again which bar she's in and she ignores my question.

"Why did you send me the books, Christian?"

"Anastasia, where are you? Tell me now."

How will she get home?

"You're so...domineering." She giggles. In any other situation I would find this charming. But right now, I want to show her how domineering I can be. She's driving me crazy.

"Ana, so help me, where the fuck are you?"

She giggles again. *Shit, she's laughing at me!*

Again!

"I'm in Portland...'s a long way from Seattle."

"Where in Portland?"

"Good night, Christian." The line goes dead.

"Ana!"

She hung up on me! I stare at the phone in disbelief. No one has ever hung up on me. *What the fuck!*

"What's the problem?" Elliot calls over from the sofa.

"I've just been drunk-dialed." I peer at him and his mouth drops open in surprise.

"You?"

"Yep." I press the callback button, trying to contain my temper, and my anxiety.

"Hi," she says, all breathy and timid, and she's in quieter surroundings.

“I’m coming to get you.” My voice is arctic as I wrestle with my anger and snap my phone shut.

“I’ve got to go get this girl and take her home. Do you want to come?”

Elliot is staring at me as if I’ve grown three heads.

“You? With a chick? This I have to see.” Elliot grabs his sneakers and starts putting them on.

“I just have to make a call.” I wander into his bedroom while I decide if I should call Barney or Welch. Barney is the most senior engineer in the telecommunications division of my company. He’s a tech genius. But what I want is not strictly legal.

Best to keep this away from my company.

I speed-dial Welch and within seconds his rasping voice answers.

“Mr. Grey?”

“I’d really like to know where Anastasia Steele is right now.”

“I see.” He pauses for a moment. “Leave it to me, Mr. Grey.”

I know this is outside the law, but she could be getting herself into trouble.

“Thank you.”

“I’ll get back to you in a couple of minutes.”

Elliot is rubbing his hands in glee with a stupid smirk on his face when I return to the living room.

Oh, for fuck’s sake.

“I wouldn’t miss this for the world,” he says, gloating.

“I’m just going to get the car keys. I’ll meet you in the garage in five,” I growl, ignoring his smug face.

THE BAR IS CROWDED, full of students determined to have a good time. There’s some indie crap thumping over the sound system and the dance floor is crowded with heaving bodies.

It makes me feel old.

She’s here somewhere.

Elliot has followed me in through the front door. “Do you see her?” he shouts over the noise. Scanning the room, I spot Katherine Kavanagh. She’s with a group of friends, all of them men, sitting in a booth. There's no sign of Ana, but the table is littered with shot glasses and tumblers of beer.

Well, let's see if Miss Kavanagh is as loyal to her friend as Ana is to her.

She looks at me in surprise when we arrive at her table.

"Katherine," I say by way of greeting, and she interrupts me before I can ask her Ana's whereabouts.

"Christian, what a surprise to see you here," she shouts above the noise. The three guys at the table regard Elliot and me with hostile wariness.

"I was in the neighborhood."

"And who's this?" She smiles rather too brightly at Elliot, interrupting me again. What an exasperating woman.

"This is my brother Elliot. Elliot, Katherine Kavanagh. Where's Ana?"

Her smile broadens at Elliot, and I'm surprised by his answering grin.

"I think she went outside for some fresh air," Kavanagh responds, but she doesn't look at me. She has eyes only for Mr. Love 'Em and Leave 'Em. Well, it's her funeral.

"Outside? Where?" I shout.

"Oh. That way." She points to double doors at the far end of the bar.

Pushing through the throng, I make my way to the door, leaving the three disgruntled men and Kavanagh and Elliot engaged in a grin-off.

Through the double doors there is a line for the ladies' washroom, and beyond that a door that's open to the outside. It's at the back of the bar. Ironically, it leads to the parking lot where Elliot and I have just been.

Walking outside, I find myself in a gathering space adjacent to the parking lot—a hangout flanked by raised flower beds, where a few people are smoking, drinking, chatting. Making out. I spot her.

Hell! She's with the photographer, I think, though it's difficult to tell in the dim light. She's in his arms, but she seems to be twisting away from him. He mutters something to her, which I don't hear, and kisses her, along her jaw.

"José, no," she says, and then it's clear. She's trying to push him off.

She doesn't want this.

For a moment I want to rip his head off. With my hands fisted at my side I march up to them. "I think the lady said no." My voice carries, cold and sinister, in the relative quiet while I struggle to contain my anger.

He releases Ana and she squints at me with a dazed, drunken expression.

"Grey," he says, his voice terse, and it takes every ounce of my self-control not to smash the disappointment off his face.

Ana heaves, then buckles over and vomits on the ground.

Oh shit!

"Ugh! *Dios mío*, Ana!" José leaps out of the way in disgust.

Fucking idiot.

Ignoring him, I grab her hair and hold it out of the way as she continues to throw up everything she's had this evening. It's with some annoyance that I note she doesn't appear to have eaten much. With my arm around her shoulders I lead her away from the curious onlookers toward one of the flower beds. "If you're going to throw up again, do it here. I'll hold you." It's darker here. She can puke in peace. She vomits again and again, her hands on the brick. It's pitiful. Once her stomach is empty, she continues to retch, long dry heaves.

Boy, she's got it bad.

Finally her body relaxes and I think she's finished. Releasing her, I give her my handkerchief, which by some miracle I have in the inside pocket of my jacket.

Thank you, Mrs. Jones.

Wiping her mouth, she turns and rests against the bricks, avoiding eye contact because she's ashamed and embarrassed. And yet I'm so pleased to see her. Gone is my fury at the photographer. I'm delighted to be standing in the parking lot of a student bar in Portland with Miss Anastasia Steele.

She puts her head in her hands, cringes, then peeks up at me, still mortified. Turning to the door, she glares over my shoulder. I assume it's at her "friend."

"I'll, um, see you inside," José says, but I don't turn to stare him down, and to my delight, she ignores him, too, returning her eyes to mine.

"I'm sorry," she says finally while her fingers twist the soft linen.

Okay, let's have some fun.

"What are you sorry for, Anastasia?"

"The phone call, mainly. Being sick. Oh, the list is endless," she mumbles.

"We've all been here, perhaps not quite as dramatically as you." Why is it such fun to tease this young woman? "It's about knowing your limits, Anastasia. I mean, I'm all for pushing limits, but really this is beyond the pale. Do you make a habit of this kind of behavior?"

Perhaps she has a problem with alcohol. The thought is worrying, and I consider whether I should call my mother for a referral to a detox clinic.

Ana frowns for a moment, as if angry, that little *v* forming between her brows, and I suppress the urge to kiss it. But when she speaks she sounds contrite.

"No," she says. "I've never been drunk before and right now I have no desire to ever be again." She looks up at me, her eyes unfocused, and she sways a little. She might pass out, so without giving it a thought I scoop her up into my arms.

She's surprisingly light. Too light. The thought irks me. No wonder she's drunk.

"Come on, I'll take you home."

"I need to tell Kate," she says as her head rests on my shoulder.

"My brother can tell her."

"What?"

"My brother Elliot is talking to Miss Kavanagh."

"Oh?"

"He was with me when you called."

"In Seattle?"

"No, I'm staying at The Heathman."

And my wild-goose chase has paid off.

"How did you find me?"

"I tracked your cell phone, Anastasia." I head toward the car. I want to drive her home. "Do you have a jacket or a purse?"

"Er...yes, I came with both. Christian, please, I need to tell Kate. She'll worry."

I stop and bite my tongue. Kavanagh wasn't worried about her being out here with the overamorous photographer. *Rodriguez.* That's his name. What kind of *friend* is she? The lights from the bar illuminate her anxious face.

As much as it pains me, I put her down and agree to take her inside. Holding hands, we walk back into the bar, stopping at Kate's table. One of the young men is still sitting there, looking annoyed and abandoned.

"Where's Kate?" Ana shouts above the noise.

"Dancing," the guy says, his dark eyes staring at the dance floor.

Ana collects her jacket and purse, and reaching out, she unexpectedly clutches my arm.

I freeze.

Shit.

My heart rate catapults into overdrive as the darkness surfaces, stretching and tightening its claws around my throat.

"She's on the dance floor," she shouts, her words tickling my ear, distracting me from my fear. And suddenly the darkness disappears and the pounding in my heart ceases.

What?

I roll my eyes to hide my confusion and take her to the bar, order a large glass of water, and pass it to her.

"Drink."

Eyeing me over the glass, she takes a tentative sip.

"All of it," I command. I'm hoping this will be enough damage control to avoid one hell of a hangover tomorrow.

What might have happened to her if I hadn't intervened? My mood sinks.

And I think of what just happened to me.

Her touch. My reaction.

My mood plummets further.

Ana sways a little as she's drinking, so I steady her with a hand on her shoulder. I like the connection—me touching her. She's oil on my troubled, deep, dark waters.

Hmm...flowery, Grey.

She finishes her drink, and retrieving the glass, I place it on the bar.

Okay. She wants to talk to her so-called friend. I survey the crowded dance floor, uneasy at the thought of all those bodies pressing in on me as we fight our way through.

Steeling myself, I grab her hand and lead her toward the dance floor. She hesitates, but if she wants to talk to her friend, there's only one way; she's going to have to dance with me. Once Elliot gets his groove on, there's no stopping him. So much for his quiet night in.

With a tug, she's in my arms.

This I can handle. When I know she's going to touch me, it's okay. I can deal, especially since I'm wearing my jacket. I weave us through the crowd to where Elliot and Kate are making a spectacle of themselves.

Still dancing, Elliot leans toward me in mid-strut when we're beside him and sizes us up with a look of incredulity.

"I'm taking Ana home. Tell Kate," I shout in his ear.

He nods and pulls Kavanagh into his arms.

Right. Let me take Miss Drunk Bookworm home, but for some reason she seems reluctant to go. She's watching Kavanagh with concern. When we're off the dance floor she looks back at Kate, then at me, swaying and a little dazed.

"Fuck—" By some miracle I catch her as she passes out in the middle of the bar. I'm tempted to haul her over my shoulder, but we'd be too conspicuous, so I pick her up once more, cradling her against my chest, and take her outside to the car.

"Christ," I mutter as I fish the key out of my jeans and hold her at the same time. Amazingly, I manage to get her into the front seat and strap her in.

"Ana." I give her a little shake, because she's worryingly quiet. "Ana!"

She mumbles something incoherent and I know she's still conscious. I know I should take her home, but it's a long drive to Vancouver, and I don't know if she'll be sick again. I don't relish the idea of my Audi reeking of vomit. The smell emanating from her clothes is already noticeable.

I head to The Heathman, telling myself I'm doing this for her sake.

Yeah, tell yourself that, Grey.

SHE SLEEPS IN MY arms as we travel up in the elevator from the garage. I need to get her out of her jeans and her shoes. The stale stench of vomit pervades the space. I'd really like to give her a bath, but that would be stepping beyond the bounds of propriety.

And this isn't?

In my suite, I drop her purse on the sofa, then carry her into the bedroom and lay her down on the bed. She mumbles once more but doesn't wake.

Briskly I remove her shoes and socks and put them in the plastic laundry bag provided by the hotel. Then I unzip her jeans and pull them off, checking the pockets before stuffing the jeans in the laundry bag. She's splayed out like a starfish, all pale arms and legs, and for a moment I picture those legs wrapped around my waist as her wrists are bound to my Saint Andrew's cross. There's a fading bruise on her knee and I wonder if that's from the fall she took in my office.

She's been marked since then…like me.

I sit her up and she opens her eyes.

"Hello, Ana," I whisper as I remove her jacket and without her cooperation.

"Grey. Lips," she mutters.

"Yes, sweetheart." I ease her back down onto the bed.

She closes her eyes again and rolls onto her side but this time huddles into a ball, looking small and vulnerable. I pull the covers over her and plant a kiss in her hair. Now that her filthy clothes have gone, a trace of her scent has reappeared. Apples, fall, fresh, delicious…Ana. Her lips are parted, eyelashes fanning out over pale cheeks, and her skin looks flawless. One more touch is all I allow myself as I stroke her cheek with the back of my index finger.

"Sleep well," I murmur, then head into the living room to complete the laundry list. When it's done, I place the offending bag outside my suite so the contents will be collected and laundered.

Before I check my emails I text Welch, asking him to see if José Rodriguez has any police records. I'm curious. I want to know if he preys on drunk young women. Then I address the issue of clothes for Miss Steele: I send a quick email to Taylor.

From: Christian Grey
Re: Miss Anastasia Steele
Date: May 20, 2011 23:46
To: J B Taylor

Good morning,
Can you please find the following items for Miss Steele and have them delivered to my usual room before 10:00.
Jeans: Blue Denim Size 4
Blouse: Blue. Pretty. Size 4
Converse: Black Size 7
Socks: Size 7
Lingerie: Underwear—Size Small. Bra—Estimate 34C.

Thank you.

Christian Grey
CEO, Grey Enterprises Holdings, Inc.

Once it's disappeared from my outbox, I text Elliot.

> Ana is with me.
> If you're still with Kate, tell her.

He texts me back.

Will do.
Hope you get laid.
You soooo need it. ;)

His response makes me snort.

I so do, Elliot. I so do.

I open my work email and begin to read.

SATURDAY, MAY 21, 2011

Nearly two hours later, I go to bed. It's just after 1:45. She's fast asleep and hasn't moved from where I left her. I strip, pull on my PJ pants and a T-shirt, and climb in beside her. She's comatose; it's unlikely she's going to thrash around and touch me. I hesitate for a moment as the darkness swells within me, but it doesn't surface and I know it's because I'm watching the hypnotic rise and fall of her chest and I'm breathing in sync with her. In. Out. In. Out. In. Out. For seconds, minutes, hours, I don't know, I watch her. And while she sleeps I survey every beautiful inch of her lovely face. Her dark lashes fluttering while she sleeps, her lips slightly parted so I glimpse her even white teeth. She mutters something unintelligible and her tongue darts out and licks her lips. It's arousing, very arousing. Finally I fall into a deep and dreamless slumber.

IT'S QUIET WHEN I open my eyes, and I'm momentarily disoriented. Oh yes. I'm at The Heathman. The clock at my bedside says 7:43.

When was the last time I slept this late?

Ana.

Gradually I turn my head, and she's fast asleep, facing me. Her beautiful face is soft in repose.

I have never slept with a woman. I've fucked many, but to wake up beside an alluring young woman is a new and stimulating experience. My cock agrees.

This will not do.

Reluctantly, I climb out of bed and change into my running gear. I need to burn off this…excess energy. As I change into my sweats I can't remember the last time I've slept so well.

In the living room, I fire up my laptop, check my email, and respond to two from Ros and one from Andrea. It takes me a little longer than usual, as I'm distracted knowing that Ana is asleep in the next room. I wonder how she'll feel when she wakes.

Hungover. *Ah.*

In the minibar I find a bottle of orange juice and empty it into a glass. She's still asleep when I enter, her hair a riot of mahogany spread across her pillow, and the covers have slipped below her waist. Her T-shirt has ridden up, exposing her belly and her navel. The sight stirs my body once more.

Stop standing here ogling the girl, for fuck's sake, Grey.

I have to get out of here before I do something I'll regret. Placing the glass on the bedside table, I duck into the bathroom, find two Advil in my travel kit, and deposit them beside the glass of orange juice.

With one last lingering look at Anastasia Steele—the first woman I've ever slept with—I head out for my run.

WHEN I RETURN FROM my exercise, there's a bag in the living room from a store I don't recognize. I take a peek and see it contains clothes for Ana. From what I can see, Taylor has done well—and all before 9:00.

The man is a marvel.

Her purse is on the sofa where I dropped it last night and the door to the bedroom is closed, so I assume she's not left and that she's still asleep.

It's a relief. Poring over the room-service menu, I decide to order some food. She'll be hungry when she wakes, but I have no idea what she'll eat, so in a rare moment of indulgence I order a selection from the breakfast menu. I'm informed it will take half an hour.

Time to wake the delectable Miss Steele; she's slept enough.

Grabbing my workout towel and the shopping bag, I knock on the door and enter. To my delight, she's sitting up in bed. The tablets are gone and so is the juice.

Good girl.

She pales as I saunter into the room.

Keep it casual, Grey. You don't want to be charged with kidnapping.

She closes her eyes, and I assume it's because she's embarrassed.

"Good morning, Anastasia. How are you feeling?"

"Better than I deserve," she mutters as I place the bag on the chair. When she turns her gaze to me her eyes are impossibly big and blue, and though her hair is a tangled mess…she looks stunning.

"How did I get here?" she asks as though she's afraid of the answer.

Reassure her, Grey.

I sit down on the edge of the bed and stick to the facts. "After you passed out, I didn't want to risk the leather upholstery in my car, taking you all the way to your apartment. So I brought you here."

"Did you put me to bed?"

"Yes."

"Did I throw up again?"

"No." Thank God.

"Did you undress me?"

"Yes." *Who else would have undressed you?*

She blushes, and at last she has some color in her cheeks. Perfect teeth bite down on her lip. I suppress a groan.

"We didn't…?" she whispers, staring at her hands.

Christ, what kind of animal does she think I am?

"Anastasia, you were comatose. Necrophilia is not my thing." My tone is dry. "I like my women sentient and receptive." She sags with relief, which makes me wonder if this has happened to her before, that she's passed out and woken up in a stranger's bed and found out he's fucked her without her consent. Maybe that's the photographer's modus operandi. The thought is disturbing. But I recall her confession last night—that she'd never been drunk before. Thank God she hasn't made a habit of this.

"I'm so sorry," she says, her voice full of shame.

Hell. Maybe I should go easy on her.

"It was a very diverting evening. Not one that I'll forget in a while." I hope that sounds conciliatory, but her brow creases.

"You didn't have to track me down with whatever James Bond gadgetry you're developing for the highest bidder."

Whoa! Now she's pissed. Why?

"First, the technology to track cell phones is available over the internet."

Well, the Deep Net…

"Second, my company does not invest or manufacture any kind of surveillance devices."

My temper is fraying, but I'm on a roll. "And third, if I hadn't come to get you, you'd probably be waking up in the photographer's bed, and from what I can remember, you weren't overly enthused about him pressing his suit."

She blinks a couple of times, then starts giggling.

She's laughing at me again.

"Which medieval chronicle did you escape from? You sound like a courtly knight."

She's beguiling. She's calling me out…again, and her irreverence is refreshing, really refreshing. However, I'm under no illusion that I'm a knight in shining armor. Boy, has she got the wrong idea. And though it may not be to my advantage, I'm compelled to warn her that there's nothing chivalrous or courtly about me. "Anastasia, I don't think so. Dark knight, maybe." If only she knew—and why are we discussing me? I change the subject. "Did you eat last night?"

She shakes her head.

I knew it!

"You need to eat. That's why you were so ill. Honestly, it's drinking rule number one."

"Are you going to continue to scold me?"

"Is that what I'm doing?"

"I think so."

"You're lucky I'm just scolding you."

"What do you mean?"

"Well, if you were mine, you wouldn't be able to sit down for a week after the stunt you pulled yesterday. You didn't eat, you got drunk, you put yourself at risk." The fear in my gut surprises me—such irresponsible, risk-taking behavior. "I hate to think what could have happened to you."

She scowls. "I would have been fine. I was with Kate."

Some help she was!

"And the photographer?" I retort.

"José just got out of line," she says, dismissing my concern and tossing her tangled hair over her shoulder.

"Well, the next time he gets out of line, maybe someone should teach him some manners."

"You're quite the disciplinarian," she snaps.

"Oh, Anastasia, you have no idea."

An image of her shackled to my bench, peeled gingerroot inserted in her ass so she can't clench her buttocks, comes to mind, followed by judicious use of a belt or strap. *Yeah*... That would teach her not to be so irresponsible. The thought is hugely appealing.

She's staring at me wide-eyed and dazed, and it makes me uncomfortable. *Can she read my mind? Or is she just looking at a pretty face?*

"I'm going to have a shower. Unless you'd like to shower first?" I tell her, but she continues to gape. Even with her mouth open she's quite lovely. She's hard to resist, and I grant myself permission to touch her, tracing the line of her cheek with my thumb. Her breath catches in her throat as I stroke her soft bottom lip.

"Breathe, Anastasia," I murmur before I stand and inform her that breakfast will be here in fifteen minutes. She says nothing, her smart mouth silent for once.

Once in the bathroom I take a deep breath, strip, and climb into the shower. I'm half tempted to jerk off, but the familiar fear of discovery and disclosure, from an earlier time in my life, stops me.

Elena would not be pleased.

Old habits.

As the water cascades over my head I reflect on my latest interaction with the challenging Miss Steele. She's still here, in my bed, so she cannot find me completely repulsive. I noticed the way her breath caught in her throat, and how her gaze followed me around the room.

Yeah. There's hope.

But would she make a good submissive?

It's obvious she knows nothing of the lifestyle. She couldn't even say "fuck" or "sex" or whatever bookish college students use as a euphemism for fucking these days. She's quite the innocent. She's probably been subjected to a few fumbling encounters with boys like the photographer.

The thought of her fumbling with anyone irks me.

I could just ask her if she's interested.

No. I'd have to show her what she'd be taking on if she agreed to a relationship with me.

Let's see how we both fare over breakfast.

Rinsing off the soap, I stand beneath the hot stream and gather my wits for round two with Anastasia Steele. I switch off the water and, stepping out of the shower, grab a towel. A quick check in the steamed-up mirror and I decide to skip shaving today. Breakfast will be here shortly, and I'm hungry. Quickly I brush my teeth.

When I open the bathroom door she's out of bed and searching for her jeans. She looks up like the archetypal startled fawn, all long legs and big eyes.

"If you're looking for your jeans, I've sent them to the laundry." She really has great legs. She shouldn't hide them in pants. Her eyes narrow, and I think she's going to argue with me, so I tell her why. "They were spattered with your vomit."

"Oh," she says.

Yes. "Oh." Now, what do you have to say to that, Miss Steele?

"I sent Taylor out for another pair and some shoes. They're in the bag on the chair." I nod at the shopping bag.

She raises her eyebrows—in surprise, I think. "Um. I'll have a shower," she mutters, and then as an afterthought she adds, "Thanks."

Grabbing the bag, she dodges around me, darts into the bathroom, and locks the door.

Hmm… She couldn't get into the bathroom quick enough.

Away from me.

Perhaps I'm being too optimistic.

Disheartened, I briskly dry off and get dressed. In the living room I check my email, but there's nothing urgent. I'm interrupted by a knock on the door. Two young women have arrived from room service.

"Where would you like breakfast, sir?"

"Set it up on the dining table."

Walking back toward the bedroom, I catch their furtive looks, but I ignore them and suppress the guilt I feel over how much food I've ordered. We'll never eat it all.

"Breakfast is here," I call, and rap on the bathroom door.

"O-okay." Ana's voice sounds a little muted.

Back in the living room, our breakfast is on the table. One of the women, who has dark, dark eyes, hands me the check to sign, and I pull a couple of twenties for them from my wallet.

"Thank you, ladies."

"Just call room service when you want the table cleared, sir," Miss Dark Eyes says with a coquettish look, as if she's offering more.

My chilly smile warns her off.

Sitting down at the table with the newspaper, I pour myself a coffee and make a start on my omelet. My phone buzzes—a text from Elliot.

Kate wants to know if Ana is still alive.

I chuckle, somewhat mollified that Ana's so-called friend is thinking about her. It's obvious that Elliot hasn't given his dick a rest after all his protestations yesterday. I text back.

Alive and kicking ;)

Ana appears a few moments later: hair wet, in the pretty blue blouse that matches her eyes. Taylor has done well; she looks lovely. Scanning the room, she spots her purse.

"Crap, Kate!" she blurts.

"She knows you're here and still alive. I texted Elliot."

She gives me an uncertain smile as she walks toward the table.

"Sit," I say, pointing to the place that's been set for her.

She frowns at the amount of food on the table, which only accentuates my guilt.

"I didn't know what you liked, so I ordered a selection from the breakfast menu," I mutter by way of an apology.

"That's very profligate of you," she says.

"Yes, it is." My guilt blooms. But as she opts for the pancakes, scrambled eggs, and bacon with maple syrup and tucks in, I forgive myself. It's good to see her eat. "Tea?" I ask.

"Yes, please," she says between mouthfuls. She's obviously famished.

I pass her the small teapot of water. She gives me a sweet smile when she notices the Twinings English Breakfast tea, and I have to catch my breath at her expression. And it makes me uneasy.

It gives me hope.

"Your hair's very damp," I observe.

"I couldn't find the hair dryer," she says, embarrassed.

She'll get sick.

"Thank you for the clothes," she adds.

"It's a pleasure, Anastasia. That color suits you."

She stares down at her fingers.

"You know, you really should learn to take a compliment."

Perhaps she doesn't get many…but why? She's gorgeous in an understated way.

"I should give you some money for these clothes."

What?

I glare at her, and she continues quickly, "You've already given me the books, which, of course, I can't accept. But these, please let me pay you back."

Sweetheart.

"Anastasia, trust me, I can afford it."

"That's not the point. Why should you buy these for me?"

"Because I can." *I'm a very rich man, Ana.*

"Just because you can doesn't mean that you should." Her voice is soft, but suddenly I'm wondering if she's looked through me and seen my darkest desires. "Why did you send me the books, Christian?"

Because I wanted to see you again, and here you are…

"Well, when you were nearly run over by the cyclist—and I was holding you and you were looking up at me—all 'kiss me, kiss me, Christian'—" I stop, recalling that moment, her body pressed against mine. *Shit.* Quickly I shrug off the memory. "I felt I owed you an apology and a warning. Anastasia, I'm not a hearts-and-flowers kind of man. I don't do romance. My tastes are very singular. You should steer clear of me. There's something about you, though, and I'm finding it impossible to stay away. But I think you've figured that out already."

"Then don't," she whispers.

What?

"You don't know what you're saying."

"Enlighten me, then."

Her words travel straight to my cock.

Fuck.

"You're not celibate?" she asks.

"No, Anastasia, I'm not celibate." And if you'd let me tie you up I'd prove it to you right now.

Her eyes widen and her cheeks pink.

Oh, Ana.

I have to show her. It's the only way I'll know. "What are your plans for the next few days?" I ask.

"I'm working today, from midday. What time is it?" she exclaims in panic.

"It's just after ten; you've plenty of time. What about tomorrow?"

"Kate and I are going to start packing. We're moving to Seattle next weekend, and I'm working at Clayton's all this week."

"You have a place in Seattle already?"

"Yes."

"Where?"

"I can't remember the address. It's in the Pike Market District."

"Not far from me." *Good!* "So what are you going to do for work in Seattle?"

“I’ve applied for some internships. I’m waiting to hear.”

“Have you applied to my company, as I suggested?”

“Um…no.”

“And what’s wrong with my company?”

“Your company or your *company*?” She arches an eyebrow.

“Are you smirking at me, Miss Steele?” I can’t hide my amusement.

Oh, she’d be a joy to train…challenging, maddening woman.

She examines her plate, chewing at her lip.

“I’d like to bite that lip,” I whisper, because it’s true.

Her face flies to mine and she shuffles in her seat. She tilts her chin toward me, her eyes full of confidence. “Why don’t you?” she says quietly.

Oh. Don’t tempt me, baby. I can’t. Not yet.

“Because I’m not going to touch you, Anastasia—not until I have your written consent to do so.”

“What does that mean?” she asks.

“Exactly what I say. I need to show you, Anastasia.” So you know what you’re getting yourself into. “What time do you finish work this evening?”

“About eight.”

“Well, we could go to Seattle this evening or next Saturday for dinner at my place, and I’ll acquaint you with the facts then. The choice is yours.”

“Why can’t you tell me now?”

“Because I’m enjoying my breakfast and your company. Once you’re enlightened, you probably won’t want to see me again.”

She frowns as she processes what I’ve said. “Tonight,” she says.

Whoa. That didn’t take long.

“Like Eve, you’re so quick to eat from the tree of knowledge,” I taunt her.

“Are you smirking at me, Mr. Grey?” she asks.

I look at her through narrowed eyes.

Okay, baby, you asked for this.

I pick up my phone and call Taylor on speed dial. He answers almost immediately.

"Mr. Grey."

"Taylor. I'm going to need *Charlie Tango.*"

She watches me closely as I make arrangements to bring my EC135 to Portland.

I'll show her what I have in mind…and the rest will be up to her. She may want to come home once she knows. I'll need Stephan, my pilot, to be on standby so he can bring her back to Portland if she decides to have nothing more to do with me. I hope that's not the case.

And it dawns on me that I'm thrilled that I can take her to Seattle in *Charlie Tango.*

It'll be a first.

"Standby pilot from 22:30," I confirm with Taylor and hang up.

"Do people always do what you tell them?" she asks, and the disapproval in her voice is obvious. Is she scolding me now? Her challenge is annoying.

"Usually, if they want to keep their jobs." *Don't question how I treat my staff.*

"And if they don't work for you?" she adds.

"Oh, I can be very persuasive, Anastasia. You should finish your breakfast. And then I'll drop you off at home. I'll pick you up at Clayton's at eight when you finish. We'll fly up to Seattle."

"Fly?"

"Yes. I have a helicopter."

Her mouth drops open, forming a small *o.* It's a pleasing moment.

"We'll go by helicopter to Seattle?" she whispers.

"Yes."

"Why?"

"Because I can." I grin. Sometimes it's just fucking great to be me. "Finish your breakfast."

She seems stunned.

"Eat!" My voice is more forceful. "Anastasia, I have an issue with wasted food. Eat."

"I can't eat all this." She studies all the food on the table and I feel guilty once more. Yes, there is too much food here.

"Eat what's on your plate. If you'd eaten properly yesterday, you wouldn't be here, and I wouldn't be declaring my hand so soon."

Hell. This could be a huge mistake.

She gives me a sideways look as she chases her food around on the plate with a fork, and her mouth twitches.

"What's so funny?"

She shakes her head and pops the last piece of pancake into her mouth, and I try not to laugh. As ever, she surprises me. She's awkward, unexpected, and disarming. She really makes me want to laugh, and what's more, it's at myself.

"Good girl," I mutter. "I'll take you home when you've dried your hair. I don't want you getting ill."

You'll need all your strength for tonight, for what I have to show you.

Suddenly, she gets up from the table and I have to stop myself from telling her that she doesn't have permission.

She's not your submissive...yet, Grey.

On the way back to the bedroom, she pauses by the sofa.

"Where did you sleep last night?" she asks.

"In my bed." *With you.*

"Oh."

"Yes, it was quite a novelty for me, too."

"Not having...sex."

She said the *s*-word...and the telltale pink cheeks appear.

"No."

How can I tell her this without it sounding weird?

Just tell her, Grey.

"Sleeping with someone." Nonchalantly, I turn my attention back to the sports section and the write-up on last night's game, then watch as she disappears into the bedroom.

No, that didn't sound weird at all.

Well, I have another date with Miss Steele. No, not a date. She needs to know about me. I let out a long breath and drink what's left of my orange juice. This is shaping up to be a very interesting day. I'm pleased when I hear the buzz of the hair dryer and surprised that she's doing what she's been told.

While I'm waiting for her, I phone the valet to bring my car up from the garage and check her address once more on Google Maps. Next, I text Andrea to send me an NDA via email; if Ana wants enlightenment, she'll need to keep her mouth shut. My phone buzzes. It's Ros.

As I'm on the phone, Ana emerges from the bedroom and picks up her purse. Ros is talking about Darfur, but my attention is on Miss Steele. She rummages around in her purse and she's pleased when she finds a hair tie.

Her hair is beautiful. Lush. Long. Thick. Idly, I wonder what it would be like to braid. She ties it back and puts on her jacket, then sits down on the sofa, waiting for me to finish my call.

"Okay, let's do it. Keep me abreast of progress." I conclude my conversation with Ros. She's been working miracles and it looks like our food shipment to Darfur is happening.

"Ready to go?" I ask Ana. She nods. I grab my jacket and car keys and follow her out the door. She peeks at me through long lashes as we walk toward the elevator, and her lips curl into a shy smile. My lips twitch in response.

What the hell is she doing to me?

The elevator arrives, and I allow her to step in first. I press the first-floor button and the doors close. In the confines of the elevator, I'm completely aware of her. A trace of her sweet fragrance invades my senses... Her breathing alters, hitching a little, and she peeks up at me with a bright come-hither look.

Shit.

She bites her lip.

She's doing this on purpose. And for a split second I'm lost in her sensual, mesmerizing stare. She doesn't back down.

I'm hard.

Instantly.

I want her.

Here.

Now.

In the elevator.

"Oh, fuck the paperwork." The words come from nowhere and

on instinct I grab her and push her against the wall. Clasping both her hands, I pin them above her head so she can't touch me, and once she's secure, I twist my other hand in her hair while my lips seek and find hers.

She moans into my mouth, the call of a siren, and finally I can sample her: mint and tea and an orchard of mellow fruitfulness. She tastes every bit as good as she looks. Reminding me of a time of plenty. *Good Lord.* I'm yearning for her. I grasp her chin, deepening the kiss, and her tongue tentatively touches mine. Exploring. Considering. Feeling. Kissing me back.

Oh God in heaven.

"You. Are. So. Sweet," I murmur against her lips, completely intoxicated, punch-drunk with her scent and taste.

The elevator stops and the doors begin to open.

Get a fucking grip, Grey.

I push myself off her and stand beyond her reach.

She's breathing hard.

As am I.

When was the last time I lost control?

Three men in business suits give us knowing looks as they join us.

And I stare at the poster above the buttons in the elevator advertising a sensual weekend at The Heathman. I glance at Ana and exhale.

She grins.

And my lips twitch once more.

What the fuck has she done to me?

The elevator stops at the second floor and the guys get out, leaving me alone with Miss Steele.

"You've brushed your teeth," I observe with wry amusement.

"I used your toothbrush," she says, eyes shining.

Of course she has...and for some reason, I find this pleasing, too pleasing. I stifle my smile. "Oh, Anastasia Steele, what am I going to do with you?" I take her hand as the elevator doors open on the ground floor, and I mutter under my breath, "What is it about elevators?"

She gives me a knowing look as we stroll across the polished marble of the lobby.

The car is waiting in one of the bays in front of the hotel; the valet is pacing impatiently. I give him an obscene tip and open the passenger door for Ana, who is quiet and introspective.

But she hasn't run.

Even though I jumped her in the elevator.

I should say something about what happened in there—but what?

Sorry?

How was that for you?

What the hell are you doing to me?

I start the car and decide that the less said, the better. The soothing sound of Delibes's "Flower Duet" fills the car and I begin to relax.

"What are we listening to?" Ana inquires as I turn onto Southwest Jefferson Street. I tell her and ask her if she likes it.

"Christian, it's wonderful."

To hear my name on her lips is a strange delight. She's said it about half a dozen times now, and each time it's different. Today, it's with wonder—at the music. It's great that she likes this piece: it's one of my favorites. I find myself beaming; she's obviously excused me for the elevator outburst.

"Can I hear that again?"

"Of course." I tap the touch screen to replay the music.

"You like classical music?" she asks as we cross the Fremont Bridge, and we fall into an easy conversation about my taste in music. While we're talking, I get a call on the hands-free.

"Grey," I answer.

"Mr. Grey, it's Welch here. I have the information you require." Oh yes, details about the photographer.

"Good. Email it to me. Anything to add?"

"No, sir."

I press the button and the music is back. We both listen, now lost in the raw sound of the Kings of Leon. But it doesn't last long—our listening pleasure is disturbed once more by the hands-free.

What the hell?

"Grey," I snap.

"The NDA has been emailed to you, Mr. Grey."

"Good. That's all, Andrea."

"Good day, sir."

I sneak a look at Ana to see if she's picked up on that conversation, but she's studying the Portland scenery. I suspect she's being polite. It's difficult to keep my eyes on the road. I want to stare at her. For all her maladroitness, she has a beautiful neckline, one that I'd like to kiss from the bottom of her ear right down to her shoulder.

Hell. I shuffle in my seat. I hope she agrees to sign the NDA and to take what I have to offer.

When we join I-5 I get another call.

It's Elliot.

"Hi, Christian, d'you get laid?"

Oh…smooth, dude, smooth.

"Hello, Elliot. I'm on speakerphone, and I'm not alone in the car."

"Who's with you?"

"Anastasia Steele."

"Hi, Ana!"

"Hello, Elliot," she says, animated.

"Heard a lot about you," Elliot says.

Shit. What has he heard?

"Don't believe a word Kate says," she responds good-naturedly.

Elliot laughs.

"I'm dropping Anastasia off now. Shall I pick you up?" I interject.

There's no doubt Elliot will want to make a quick getaway.

"Sure."

"See you shortly." I hang up.

"Why do you insist on calling me Anastasia?" she asks.

"Because it's your name."

"I prefer Ana."

"Do you, now?"

"Ana" is too everyday and ordinary for her. And too familiar. Those three letters have the power to wound…

And in that moment I know that her rejection, when it comes, will be hard to take. It's happened before, but I've never felt this… invested. I don't even know this girl, but I want to know her, all of her. Maybe it's because I've never chased a woman.

Grey, get control of yourself and follow the rules; otherwise this will all go to shit.

"Anastasia," I say, ignoring her disapproving look. "What happened in the elevator—it won't happen again. Well, not unless it's premeditated."

That keeps her quiet as I park outside her apartment. Before she can answer me I climb out of the car, walk around and open her door.

As she steps onto the sidewalk, she gives me a fleeting glance. "I liked what happened in the elevator," she says.

You did? Her confession halts me in my tracks. I'm pleasantly surprised again by Miss Steele. As she walks up the steps to the front door, I have to scramble to keep up with her.

Elliot and Kate look up when we enter. They're sitting at a dining table in a sparsely furnished room, befitting a couple of students. There are a few packing boxes beside a bookshelf. Elliot looks relaxed and not in a hurry to leave, which surprises me.

Kavanagh jumps up and gives me a critical once-over as she hugs Ana.

What did she think I was going to do to the girl?

I know what I'd like to do to her…

As Kavanagh holds her at arm's length I'm reassured; maybe she does care for Ana, too.

"Good morning, Christian," she says, her tone cool and condescending.

"Miss Kavanagh." And what I want to say is something sarcastic about how she's finally showing some interest in her friend, but I hold my tongue.

"Christian, her name is Kate," Elliot says with mild irritation.

"Kate," I mutter, to be polite.

Elliot hugs Ana, holding her for a moment too long. "Hi, Ana," he says, all fucking smiles.

"Hi, Elliot." She beams.

Okay, this is becoming unbearable. "Elliot, we'd better go." *And take your hands off her.*

"Sure," he says, releasing Ana, but grabbing Kavanagh and making an unseemly show of kissing her.

Oh, for fuck's sake.

Ana's uncomfortable watching them. I don't blame her. But when she turns to me it's with a speculative look through narrowed eyes.

What is she thinking?

"Laters, baby," Elliot mutters, slobbering over Kavanagh.

Dude, show some dignity, for heaven's sake.

Ana's reproachful eyes are on me, and for a moment I don't know if it's because of Elliot and Kate's lascivious display or—

Hell! This is what she wants. To be courted and wooed.

I don't do romance, sweetheart.

A lock of her hair has broken free, and without thinking, I tuck it behind her ear. She leans her face into my fingers, the tender gesture surprising me. My thumb strays to her soft bottom lip, which I'd like to kiss again. But I can't. Not until I have her consent.

"Laters, baby," I whisper, and her face softens with a smile. "I'll pick you up at eight." Reluctantly, I turn away and open the front door, Elliot behind me.

"Man, I need some sleep," Elliot says as soon as we're in the car. "That woman is voracious."

"Really…" My voice drips with sarcasm. The last thing I want is a blow-by-blow account of his assignation.

"How about you, hotshot? Did she pop your cherry?"

I give him a sideways "fuck off" glare.

Elliot laughs. "Man, you are one uptight son of a bitch." He pulls his Sounders cap over his face and nestles down in his seat for a nap.

I turn up the volume of the music.

Sleep through that, Lelliot!

Yeah. I envy my brother: his ease with women, his ability to sleep…and the fact that he's not the son of a bitch.

JOSÉ LUIS RODRIGUEZ'S BACKGROUND check reveals a ticket for possession of marijuana. There is nothing in his police records for sexual harassment. Maybe last night would have been a first if I hadn't intervened. And the little prick smokes weed? I hope he doesn't smoke around Ana—and I hope she doesn't smoke, period.

Opening Andrea's email, I send the NDA to the printer in my study at home in Escala. Ana will need to sign it before I show her my playroom. And in a moment of weakness, or hubris, or perhaps unprecedented optimism—I don't know which—I fill in her name and address on my standard Dom/sub contract and send that to print, too.

There's a knock at the door.

"Hey, hotshot. Let's go hiking," Elliot says through the door.

Ah... The child has woken from his nap.

THE SCENT OF PINE, fresh damp earth, and late spring is a balm to my senses. The smell reminds me of those heady days of my childhood, running through a forest with Elliot and my sister Mia under the watchful eyes of our adoptive parents. The quiet, the space, the freedom...the scrunch of dry pine needles underfoot.

Here in the great outdoors I could forget.

Here was a refuge from my nightmares.

Elliot chatters away, needing only the occasional grunt from me to keep talking. As we make our way along the pebbled shore of the Willamette my mind strays to Anastasia. For the first time in a long time, I have a sweet sense of anticipation. I'm excited.

Will she say yes to my proposal?

I picture her sleeping beside me, soft and small...and my cock twitches with expectation. I could have woken her and fucked her then—what a novelty that would have been.

I'll fuck her in time.

I'll fuck her bound and with her smart mouth gagged.

CLAYTON'S IS QUIET. The last customer left five minutes ago. And I'm waiting—again—drumming my fingers on my thighs.

Patience is not my forte. Even the long hike with Elliot today has not dampened my restlessness. He's having dinner with Kate this evening at The Heathman. Two dates on consecutive nights is not his usual style.

Suddenly the fluorescent lights inside the store flicker off, the front door opens, and Ana steps out into a mild Portland evening. My heart begins to hammer. This is it: either the beginning of a new relationship or the beginning of the end.

She waves goodbye to a young man who's followed her out. It's not the same man I met the last time I was here—it's someone new. He watches her walk toward the car, his eyes on her ass. Taylor distracts me by making a move to climb out of the car, but I stop him. This is my call.

When I'm out of the car holding the door open for her, the new guy is locking up the store and no longer ogling Miss Steele.

Her lips curve into a shy smile as she approaches, her hair in a jaunty ponytail swinging in the evening breeze.

"Good evening, Miss Steele."

"Mr. Grey," she says. She's dressed in black jeans…*Jeans again.* She greets Taylor as she climbs into the back seat of the car.

Once I'm beside her I clasp her hand while Taylor pulls out onto the empty road and heads to the Portland helipad. "How was work?" I ask, enjoying the feel of her hand in mine.

"Very long," she says, her voice husky.

"Yes, it's been a long day for me, too."

It's been hell waiting for the past couple of hours!

"What did you do?" she asks.

"I went hiking with Elliot."

Her hand is warm and soft. She glances down at our joined fingers and I brush her knuckles with my thumb over and over. Her breath catches and her eyes meet mine. In them I see her longing and desire…and her sense of anticipation. I just hope she accepts my proposition.

Mercifully, the drive to the helipad is short. When we're out of the car I take her hand again. She looks a little perplexed.

Ah. She's wondering where the helicopter might be.

"Ready?" I ask. She nods, and I lead her into the building toward the elevator. She gives me a quick knowing look.

She's remembering the kiss from this morning, but then…so am I.

"It's only three floors," I mutter.

As we stand inside I make a mental note to fuck her in an elevator one day. That's if she agrees to my deal.

On the roof *Charlie Tango*, newly arrived from Boeing Field, is prepped and ready to fly, though there's no sign of Stephan, who's brought her down here. But Joe, who runs the helipad in Portland, is in the small office. He salutes when I see him. He's older than my grandpa, and what he doesn't know about flying is not worth knowing; he flew Sikorskys in Korea for casualty evacuation, and boy, does he have some hair-raising stories.

"Here's your flight plan, Mr. Grey," Joe says, his gravelly voice betraying his age. "All external checks are done. She's ready and waiting, sir. You're good to go."

"Thank you, Joe."

A quick glance at Ana tells me she's excited…and so am I. This is a first.

"Let's go." With her hand in mine once more, I lead Ana over the helipad to *Charlie Tango*. The safest Eurocopter in her class and a delight to fly. She's my pride and joy. I hold the door open for Ana; she scrambles inside and I climb in behind her.

"Over there," I order, pointing to the front passenger seat. "Sit. Don't touch anything." I'm amazed when she does as she's told.

Once in her seat, she examines the array of instruments with a mixture of awe and enthusiasm. Crouching down beside her, I strap her into the seat harness, trying not to imagine her naked as I do it. I take a little longer than is necessary because this might be my last chance to be this close to her, my last chance to inhale her sweet, evocative scent. Once she knows about my predilections she may flee. On the other hand, she may embrace the lifestyle. The possibilities this conjures in my mind are almost overwhelming. She's watching me intently, she's so close…so lovely. I tighten the last strap. She's not going anywhere. Not for an hour at least.

Suppressing my excitement, I whisper, "You're secure. No escaping." She inhales sharply. "Breathe, Anastasia," I add and caress her cheek. Holding her chin, I lean down and kiss her quickly. "I like this harness," I mutter. I want to tell her I have others, in leather, in which I'd like to see her trussed and suspended from the ceiling. But I behave, sit down, and buckle up.

"Put your cans on." I point to the headset in front of Ana. "I'm just going through all the preflight checks." All instruments look good. I press the throttle to 1500 rpm, transponder to stand-by, and position beacon on. Everything is set and ready to go.

"Do you know what you're doing?" she asks with wonder. I inform her I've been a fully qualified pilot for four years. Her smile is infectious.

"You're safe with me," I reassure her, and add, "Well, while we're flying." I give her a wink, she beams, and I'm dazzled. "Are you ready?" I ask—and I can't quite believe how excited I am to have her here beside me.

She nods.

I talk to the tower—they're awake—and increase the throttle to 2000 rpm. Once they've given us clearance I do my final checks. Oil temperature is at 104. *Good.* I increase the manifold pressure to 14, the engine to 2500 rpm, and pull back on the throttle. And like the elegant bird she is, *Charlie Tango* rises into the air.

Anastasia gasps as the ground disappears below us, but she holds her tongue, entranced by the waning lights of Portland. Soon we are shrouded in darkness; the only light emanates from the instruments before us. Ana's face is illuminated by the red and green glow as she stares into the night.

"Eerie, isn't it?"

Though I don't find it so. To me this is a comfort. Nothing can harm me here.

I'm safe and hidden in the dark.

"How do you know you're going the right way?" Ana asks.

"Here." I point to the panel. I don't want to bore her talking about instrument flight rules, but the fact is it's *all* the equipment in front of me that guides us to our destination:

the attitude indicator, the altimeter, the VSI, and of course the GPS. I tell her about *Charlie Tango* and how she's equipped for night flight.

Ana looks at me, amazed.

"There's a helipad on top of the building I live in. That's where we're heading."

I look back at the panel, checking all the data. This is what I love: the control, my safety and well-being reliant on my mastery of the technology in front of me. "When you fly at night, you fly blind. You have to trust the instrumentation," I tell her.

"How long will the flight be?" she asks, a little breathless.

"Less than an hour—the wind is in our favor." I glance at her again. "You okay, Anastasia?"

"Yes," she says, her voice oddly abrupt.

Is she nervous? Or maybe she's regretting her decision to be here with me. The thought is unsettling. She hasn't given me a chance. I'm distracted by air-traffic control for a moment. Then, as we clear cloud cover, I see Seattle in the distance, a beacon blazing in the dark.

"Look, over there." I direct Ana's attention to the bright lights.

"Do you always impress women this way? 'Come fly in my helicopter'?"

"I've never brought a girl up here, Anastasia. It's another first for me. Are you impressed?"

"I'm awed, Christian," she whispers.

"Awed?" My smile is spontaneous. And I remember Grace, my mother, stroking my hair as I read out loud from *The Once and Future King.*

"*Christian, that was wonderful. I'm awed, darling boy.*"

I was seven and had only recently started speaking.

"You're just so…competent," Ana continues.

"Why, thank you, Miss Steele." My face warms with pleasure at her unexpected praise. I hope she doesn't notice.

"You obviously enjoy this," she says a little later.

"What?"

"Flying."

"It requires control and concentration." Two qualities I most enjoy. "How could I not love it? Though my favorite is soaring."

"Soaring?"

"Yes. Gliding, to the layperson. Gliders and helicopters—I fly them both."

Perhaps I should take her soaring?

Getting ahead of yourself, Grey.

And since when do you take anyone soaring?

Since when do I bring anyone in *Charlie Tango*?

ATC refocuses me on the flight path, halting my rogue thoughts as we approach the outskirts of Seattle. We're close. And I'm closer to knowing whether this is a pipe dream or not. Ana is staring out the window, entranced.

I can't keep my eyes off her.

Please say yes.

"Looks good, doesn't it?" I ask so she'll turn and I can see her face. She does, with a huge cock-tightening grin. "We'll be there in a few minutes," I add.

Suddenly the atmosphere in the cabin shifts and I have a more heightened awareness of her. Breathing deeply, I inhale her scent and sense the anticipation. Ana's. Mine.

As we descend I take *Charlie Tango* through the downtown area toward Escala, my home, and my heart rate increases. Ana starts fidgeting. She's nervous, too. I hope she doesn't flee.

As the helipad comes into view, I take another deep breath.

This is it.

We land smoothly and I power down, watching the rotor blades slow and come to a stop. All I can hear is the hiss of white noise over our headphones as we sit in silence. I remove my cans, then remove Ana's, too. "We're here," I say quietly. Her face is pale in the glow of the landing lights, her eyes luminous.

Sweet Lord, she's beautiful.

I unbuckle my harness and reach over to undo hers.

She peers up at me. Trusting. Young. Sweet. Her delicious scent is almost my undoing.

Can I do this with her?

She's an adult.

She can make her own decisions.

And I want her to look at me this way once she knows me… knows what I'm capable of. "You don't have to do anything you don't want to do. You know that, don't you?" She needs to understand this. I want her submission, but more than that I want her consent.

"I'd never do anything I didn't want to do, Christian." She sounds sincere and I want to believe her. With those pacifying words ringing in my head, I climb out of my seat and open the door, then jump down onto the helipad. I take her hand as she exits the aircraft. The wind whips her hair around her face, and she looks anxious. I don't know if it's because she's here with me, alone, or if it's because we're thirty stories high. I know it's a giddy feeling being up here.

"Come." Wrapping my arm around her to shield her from the wind, I guide her to the elevator.

We are both quiet as we make the short journey to the penthouse. She's wearing a pale-green shirt beneath her black jacket. It suits her. I make a mental note to include blues and greens in the clothes I'll provide if she agrees to my terms. She should be better dressed. Her eyes meet mine in the elevator's mirrors as the doors open to my apartment.

She follows me through the foyer, across the corridor, and into the living room. "Can I take your jacket?" I ask.

Ana shakes her head and clutches the lapels to emphasize that she wants to keep her jacket on.

Okay.

"Would you like a drink?" I try a different approach and decide I need a drink to steady my nerves.

Why am I so nervous?

Because I want her…

"I'm going to have a glass of white wine. Would you like to join me?"

"Yes, please," she says.

In the kitchen I slip off my jacket and open the wine fridge. A sauvignon blanc would be a good icebreaker. Pulling out a serviceable Pouilly-Fumé, I watch Ana peer through the balcony doors at the view. When she turns and walks back toward the kitchen I ask if she'd be happy with the wine I've selected.

"I know nothing about wine, Christian. I'm sure it will be fine." She sounds subdued.

Shit. This isn't going well. Is she overwhelmed? Is that it?

I pour two glasses and walk to where she stands in the middle of my living room, looking every bit the sacrificial lamb. Gone is the disarming woman. She looks lost.

Like me…

"Here." I hand her the glass, and she immediately takes a sip, closing her eyes in obvious appreciation of the wine. When she lowers the glass her lips are moist.

Good choice, Grey.

"You're very quiet, and you're not even blushing. In fact, I think this is the palest I've ever seen you, Anastasia. Are you hungry?"

She shakes her head and takes another sip. Maybe she's in need of some liquid courage, too. "It's a very big place you have here," she says, her voice timid.

"Big?"

"Big."

"It's big." There's no arguing with that; it is more than ten thousand square feet.

She looks at the piano. "Do you play?"

"Yes."

"Well?"

"Yes."

"Of course you do. Is there anything you can't do well?"

"Yes…a few things."

Cook.

Tell jokes.

Make free and easy conversation with a woman I'm attracted to.

Be touched…

"Do you want to sit?" I gesture toward the sofa. A brisk nod tells me that she does. Taking her hand, I lead her there, and she sits down, giving me an impish look. "What's so amusing?" I ask as I take a seat beside her.

"Why did you give me *Tess of the d'Urbervilles* specifically?"

Oh. Where is this going? "Well, you said you liked Thomas Hardy."

"Is that the only reason?"

I don't want to tell her that she has *my* first edition and that it was a better choice than *Jude the Obscure.* "It seemed appropriate. I could hold you to some impossibly high ideal like Angel Clare or debase you completely like Alec d'Urberville." My answer is truthful enough and has a certain irony to it. What I'm about to propose I suspect will be very far from her expectations.

"If there are only two choices, I'll take the debasement," she whispers.

Damn. Isn't that what you want, Grey?

"Anastasia, stop biting your lip, please. It's very distracting. You don't know what you're saying."

"That's why I'm here," she says, her teeth leaving little indentations on a bottom lip moist with wine.

And there she is: disarming once more, surprising me at every turn. My cock concurs.

We are cutting to the chase on this deal, but before we explore the details, I need her to sign the NDA. I excuse myself and head into my study. The contract and NDA are ready on the printer. Leaving the contract on my desk—I don't know if we'll ever get to it—I staple the NDA together and take it back to Ana.

"This is a nondisclosure agreement." I place it on the coffee table in front of her. She looks confused and surprised. "My lawyer insists on it," I add. "If you're going for option two, debasement, you'll need to sign this."

"And if I don't want to sign anything?"

"Then it's Angel Clare high ideals, well, for most of the book anyway." And I won't be able to touch you. I'll send you home with Stephan, and I will try my very best to forget you. My anxiety mushrooms; this deal could all go to shit.

"What does this agreement mean?"

"It means you cannot disclose anything about us. Anything, to anyone."

She searches my face and I don't know if she's confused or displeased.

This could go either way.

"Okay. I'll sign," she says.

Well, that was easy. I hand her my Mont Blanc and she places the pen at the signature line.

"Aren't you even going to read it?" I ask, suddenly annoyed.

"No."

"Anastasia, you should always read anything you sign." *How could she be so foolish?* Have her parents taught her nothing?

"Christian, what you fail to understand is that I wouldn't talk about us to anyone anyway. Even Kate. So it's immaterial whether I sign an agreement. If it means so much to you, or your lawyer, whom *you* obviously talk to, then fine. I'll sign."

She has an answer for everything. It's refreshing. "Fair point well made, Miss Steele," I note dryly.

With a quick, disapproving glance, she signs.

And before I can begin my pitch, she asks, "Does this mean you're going to make love to me tonight, Christian?"

What?

Me?

Make love?

Oh, Grey, let's disabuse her of this straightaway. "No, Anastasia, it doesn't. First, I don't make love. I fuck, hard."

She gasps. That's made her think.

"Second, there's a lot more paperwork to do. And third, you don't yet know what you're in for. You could still run from here screaming! Come, I want to show you my playroom."

She's nonplussed, the little *v* forming between her brows. "You want to play on your Xbox?"

I laugh out loud.

Oh, baby.

"No, Anastasia, no Xbox, no PlayStation. Come." Standing, I offer her my hand, which she takes willingly. I lead her to the hallway and upstairs, where I stop outside the door to my playroom, my heart hammering in my chest.

This is it. Pay or play. Have I ever been this nervous? Realizing my desires depend on the turn of this key, I unlock the door, and in that moment I need to reassure her. "You can leave anytime. The helicopter is on standby to take you whenever you want to go; you can stay the night and go home in the morning. It's fine, whatever you decide."

"Just open the damn door, Christian," she says with a mulish expression and her arms crossed.

This is the crossroads. I don't want her to run. But I've never felt this exposed. Even in Elena's hands...and I know it's because she knows nothing about the lifestyle.

I open the door and follow her into my playroom.

My safe place.

The only place where I'm truly myself.

Ana stands in the middle of the room, studying all the paraphernalia that is so much a part of my life: the floggers, the canes, the bed, the bench... She's silent, drinking it in, and all I hear is the deafening pounding of my heart as the blood rushes past my eardrums.

Now you know.

This is me.

She turns and gives me a piercing stare as I wait for her to say something, but she prolongs my agony and walks farther into the room, forcing me to follow her.

Her fingers trail over a suede flogger, one of my favorites. I tell her what it's called, but she doesn't respond. She walks over to the bed, her hands exploring, her fingers running over one of the carved pillars.

"Say something," I ask. Her silence is unbearable. I need to know if she's going to run.

"Do you do this to people or do they do it to you?"

Finally!

"People?" I want to snort. "I do this to women who want me to."

She's willing to have a dialogue. There's hope.

She frowns. "If you have willing volunteers, why am I here?"

"Because I want to do this with you, very much." Visions of

her tied up in various positions around the room overwhelm my imagination; on the cross, on the bed, over the bench…

"Oh," she says and wanders to the bench. My eyes are drawn to her inquisitive fingers stroking the leather. Her touch is curious, slow, and sensual—is she even aware?

"You're a sadist?" she says, startling me.

Fuck. She sees me.

"I'm a Dominant," I say quickly, hoping to move the conversation on.

"What does that mean?" she inquires, shocked, I think.

"It means I want you to willingly surrender yourself to me, in all things."

"Why would I do that?"

"To please me," I whisper. *This is what I need from you.* "In very simple terms, I want you to want to please me."

"How do I do that?" she breathes.

"I have rules, and I want you to comply with them. They are for your benefit and for my pleasure. If you follow these rules to my satisfaction, I shall reward you. If you don't, I shall punish you, and you will learn."

And I can't wait to train you. In every way.

She stares at the canes behind the bench. "And where does all this fit in?" She waves at her surroundings.

"It's all part of the incentive package. Both reward and punishment."

"So you'll get your kicks by exerting your will over me."

Spot on, Miss Steele.

"It's about gaining your trust and your respect, so you'll let me exert my will over you." *I need your permission, baby.* "I will gain a great deal of pleasure, joy even, in your submission. The more you submit, the greater my joy—it's a very simple equation."

"Okay, and what do I get out of this?"

"Me." I shrug. *That's it, baby. Just me. All of me. And you'll find pleasure, too…*

Her eyes widen fractionally as she stares at me, saying nothing. It's exasperating. "You're not giving anything away, Anastasia.

Let's go back downstairs where I can concentrate better. It's very distracting having you in here."

I hold out my hand to her and for the first time she looks from my hand to my face, undecided.

Shit.

I've frightened her. "I'm not going to hurt you, Anastasia."

Tentatively she puts her hand in mine. I'm elated. She hasn't run.

Relieved, I decide to show her the submissive's bedroom.

"If you do this, let me show you." I lead her down the corridor. "This will be your room. You can decorate it how you like, have whatever you like in here."

"My room? You're expecting me to move in?" she squeaks in disbelief.

Okay. Maybe I should have left this until later.

"Not full-time," I reassure her. "Just, say, Friday evening through Sunday. We have to talk about all that. Negotiate. If you want to do this."

"I'll sleep here?"

"Yes."

"Not with you."

"No. I told you, I don't sleep with anyone, except you when you're stupefied with drink."

"Where do you sleep?"

"My room is downstairs. Come, you must be hungry."

"Weirdly, I seem to have lost my appetite," she declares with her familiar stubborn expression.

"You must eat, Anastasia."

Her eating habits will be one of the first issues I'll work on if she agrees to be mine…that, and her fidgeting.

Stop getting ahead of yourself, Grey!

"I'm fully aware that this is a dark path I'm leading you down, Anastasia, which is why I really want you to think about this."

She follows me downstairs into the living room once more. "You must have some questions. You've signed your NDA; you can ask me anything you want and I'll answer."

If this is going to work, she's going to have to communicate. In the kitchen I open the fridge and find a large plate of cheese and some grapes. Gail wasn't expecting me to have company, and this is not enough… I wonder if I should order some takeout. Or perhaps take her out?

Like a date.

Another date.

I don't want to raise expectations like that.

I don't do dates.

Only with her…

The thought is irritating. There's a fresh baguette in the bread basket. Bread and cheese will have to do. Besides, she says she's not hungry.

"Sit." I point to one of the barstools and Ana sits down, giving me a level gaze.

"You mentioned paperwork," she says.

"Yes."

"What paperwork?"

"Well, apart from the NDA, a contract saying what we will and won't do. I need to know your limits, and you need to know mine. This is consensual, Anastasia."

"And if I don't want to do this?"

Shit.

"That's fine," I lie.

"But we won't have any sort of relationship?"

"No."

"Why?"

"This is the only sort of relationship I'm interested in."

"Why?"

"It's the way I am."

"How did you become this way?"

"Why is anyone the way they are? That's kind of hard to answer. Why do some people like cheese and other people hate it? Do you like cheese? Mrs. Jones—my housekeeper—has left this for a late supper." I place the plate in front of her.

"What are your rules that I have to follow?"

"I have them written down. We'll go through them once we've eaten."

"I'm really not hungry," she whispers.

"You will eat."

The look she gives me is defiant.

"Would you like another glass of wine?" I ask as a peace offering.

"Yes, please."

I pour wine into her glass and sit down beside her. "Help yourself to food, Anastasia."

She takes a few grapes.

That's it? That's all you're eating?

"Have you been like this for a while?" she asks.

"Yes."

"Is it easy to find women who want to do this?"

Oh, if you only knew. "You'd be amazed." My tone is wry.

"Then why me? I really don't understand." She's utterly bemused.

Baby, you're beautiful. Why wouldn't I want to do this with you?

"Anastasia, I've told you. There's something about you. I can't leave you alone. I'm like a moth to a flame. I want you very badly, especially now, when you're biting your lip again."

"I think you have that cliché the wrong way around," she says softly, and it's a disturbing confession.

"Eat!" I order to change the subject.

"No. I haven't signed anything yet, so I think I'll hang on to my free will for a bit longer, if that's okay with you."

Oh... Her smart mouth.

"As you wish, Miss Steele." And I hide my smirk.

"How many women?" she asks, and she pops a grape into that mouth.

"Fifteen." I have to look away.

"For long periods of time?"

"Some of them, yes."

"Have you ever hurt anyone?"

"Yes."

"Badly?"

"No." Dawn was fine, if a little shaken by the experience. And if I'm honest, so was I.

"Will you hurt me?"

"What do you mean?"

"Physically, will you hurt me?"

Only what you can take.

"I will punish you when you require it, and it will be painful."

For example, when you get drunk and put yourself at risk.

"Have you ever been beaten?" she asks.

"Yes."

Many, many times. Elena was devilishly handy with a cane. It's the only touch I could tolerate.

Her eyes widen and she puts the uneaten grapes on her plate and takes another sip of wine. Her lack of appetite is irritating and is affecting mine. Perhaps I should just bite the bullet and show her the rules.

"Let's discuss this in my study. I want to show you something."

She follows me and sits in the leather chair in front of my desk as I lean against it, arms folded.

This is what she wants to know. It's a blessing that she's curious—she hasn't run yet. From the contract laid out on my desk I take one of the pages and hand it to her. "These are the rules. They may be subject to change. They form part of the contract, which you can also have. Read these rules and let's discuss."

Her eyes scan the page. "Hard limits?" she asks.

"Yes. What you won't do, what I won't do, we need to specify in our agreement."

"I'm not sure about accepting money for clothes. It feels wrong."

"I want to lavish money on you. Let me buy you some clothes. I may need you to accompany me to functions."

Grey, what are you saying? This would be a first. "And I want you dressed well. I'm sure your salary, when you do get a job, won't cover the kind of clothes I'd like you to wear."

"I don't have to wear them when I'm not with you?"

"No."

"Okay. I don't want to exercise four times a week."

"Anastasia, I need you supple, strong, and with stamina. Trust me, you need to exercise."

"But surely not four times a week. How about three?"

"I want you to do four."

"I thought this was a negotiation?"

Again, she's disarming, calling me out on my shit. "Okay, Miss Steele, another point well made. How about an hour on three days and one day half an hour?"

"Three days, three hours. I get the impression you're going to keep me exercised when I'm here."

Oh, I hope so.

"Yes, I am. Okay, agreed. Are you sure you don't want to intern at my company? You're a good negotiator."

"No, I don't think that's a good idea."

Of course she's right. And it's my number one rule: never fuck the staff.

"So, limits. These are mine." I hand her the list.

This is it, shit-or-bust time. I know my limits by heart and mentally tick off the list as I watch her read through. Her face grows paler and paler as she nears the end.

Fuck, I hope this isn't frightening her off.

I want her. I want her submission...badly. She swallows, glancing nervously up at me. *How can I persuade her to give this a try?* I should reassure her, show her that I'm capable of caring.

"Is there anything you'd like to add?"

Deep down I hope she won't add anything. I want carte blanche with her. She stares at me, still at a loss for words. It's irritating. I'm not used to waiting for answers. "Is there anything you won't do?" I prompt.

"I don't know."

Not the response I was expecting.

"What do you mean you don't know?"

She shifts in her seat, looking uncomfortable, her teeth toying with her bottom lip. *Again.* "I've never done anything like this."

Hell, of course she hasn't.

Patience, Grey. For fuck's sake. You've thrown a great deal of information at her. I continue my gentle approach. It's novel.

"Well, when you've had sex, was there anything you didn't like doing?" And I'm reminded of the photographer fumbling all over her yesterday.

She flushes and my interest is piqued. What has she done that she didn't like? Is she adventurous in bed? She seems so…innocent. Normally I don't find that attractive.

"You can tell me, Anastasia. We have to be honest with each other or this isn't going to work." I really have to encourage her to loosen up—she won't even talk about sex. She's squirming again and staring at her fingers.

Come on, Ana.

"Tell me," I order. *Sweet Lord, she's frustrating.*

"Well, I've not had sex before, so I don't know," she whispers.

The earth stops spinning.

I don't fucking believe it.

How?

Why?

Fuck!

"Never?" I'm incredulous.

She shakes her head, eyes wide.

"You're a virgin?" I don't believe it.

She nods, embarrassed.

I close my eyes. I can't look at her.

How the hell did I get this so wrong?

Anger lances through me. *What can I do with a virgin?* I glare at her as fury surges through my body. "Why the fuck didn't you tell me?" I growl and start pacing my study.

What do I want with a virgin?

She shrugs apologetically, at a loss for words.

"I don't understand why you didn't tell me." The exasperation is clear in my voice.

"The subject never came up," she says. "I'm not in the habit of revealing my sexual status to everyone I meet. I mean, we hardly know each other."

As ever, it's a fair point. I can't believe I've given her the bus tour of my playroom—thank heavens for the NDA.

"Well, you know a lot more about me now," I snarl. "I knew you were inexperienced, but a *virgin*! Hell, Ana, I just showed you..."

Not only the playroom: my rules, hard limits. She knows nothing. How could I do this? "May God forgive me," I mutter under my breath. I'm at a loss.

A startling thought occurs to me. Our one kiss in the elevator, where I could have fucked her there and then—was that her first kiss?

"Have you ever been kissed, apart from by me?" Please say yes.

"Of course I have." She looks offended. Yeah, she's been kissed, but not often. And for some reason the thought is...pleasing.

"And a nice young man hasn't swept you off your feet? I just don't understand. You're twenty-one, nearly twenty-two. You're beautiful." Why hasn't some guy taken her to bed?

Shit, maybe she's religious. No, Welch would have uncovered that.

She gazes down at her fingers, and I think she's smiling. She thinks this is funny? I could kick myself. "And you're seriously discussing what I want to do, when you have no experience."

Words fail me. How can this be?

"How have you avoided sex? Tell me, please." Because I don't get it. She's in college—and from what I remember of college all the kids were fucking like rabbits.

All of them. Except me.

The thought is a dark one, but I push it aside for the moment.

Ana shrugs, her small shoulders lifting slightly. "No one's really, you know..." She trails off.

No one has what? Seen how attractive you are? No one's lived up to your expectations—and I do?

Me?

She really knows nothing. How could she ever be a submissive if she has no idea about sex? This is not going to fly...and all the groundwork I've done has been for nothing. I can't close this deal.

"Why are you so angry with me?" she whispers.

Of course she would think that. *Make this right, Grey.*

"I'm not angry with you, I'm angry at myself. I just assumed—" *Why the hell would I be angry with you?* What a mess this is. I run my hands through my hair, trying to rein in my temper. "Do you want to go?" I ask, concerned.

"No, unless you want me to go," she says softly, her voice tinged with regret.

"Of course not. I like having you here." The statement surprises me as I say it. I *do* like having her here. Being with her. She's so...different. And I want to fuck her, and spank her, and watch her alabaster skin pink beneath my hands. That's out of the question now—isn't it? Perhaps not the fucking...perhaps I could. The thought is a revelation. I could take her to bed. Break her in. It would be a novel experience for both of us. Would she want to? She asked me earlier if I was going to make love to her. I could try, without tying her up.

But she might touch me.

Fuck. I glance down at my watch and note the time. It's late. When I look back at her the sight of her toying with her bottom lip arouses me.

I still want her, in spite of her innocence. Could I take her to bed? Would she want to, knowing what she knows about me now? *Hell,* I have no idea. Do I just ask her? But she's turning me on, biting her lip again. I point it out and she apologizes.

"Don't apologize. It's just that I want to bite it, too, hard."

Her breath hitches.

Oh. Maybe she's interested. *Yes. Let's do this.* My decision is made.

"Come," I offer, holding out my hand.

"What?"

"We're going to rectify the situation right now."

"What do you mean? What situation?"

"Your situation. Ana, I'm going to make love to you, now."

"Oh."

"That's if you want to. I mean, I don't want to push my luck."

"I thought you didn't make love. I thought you fucked hard," she says, her voice husky and so damned seductive, her eyes wide, pupils dilating. She's flushed with desire—she wants this, too.

And a wholly unexpected thrill unfurls inside me. "I can make an exception, or maybe combine the two, we'll see. I really want to make love to you. Please, come to bed with me. I want our arrangement to work, but you really need to have some idea what you're getting yourself into. We can start your training tonight—with the basics. This doesn't mean I've come over all hearts and flowers—it's a means to an end, but one that I want, and hopefully you do, too." The words rush out in a torrent.

Grey! Get ahold of yourself.

Her cheeks pink.

Come on, Ana, yes or no. I'm dying here.

"But I haven't done all the things you require from your list of rules." Her voice is timid. Is she afraid? I hope not. I don't want her to be afraid.

"Forget about the rules. Forget about all those details for tonight. I want you. I've wanted you since you fell into my office, and I know you want me. You wouldn't be sitting here calmly discussing punishment and hard limits if you didn't. Please, Ana, spend the night with me."

I offer her my hand again, and this time she takes it, and I pull her into my arms, holding her flush against my body. She gasps with surprise and I feel her against me. The darkness is quiet, perhaps subdued by my libido. I want her. She's so alluring. This girl confounds me, every step of the way. I've revealed my dark secret, yet she's still here; she hasn't run.

My fingers tug at her hair, pulling her face up to mine, and I gaze into captivating eyes.

"You are one brave young woman," I breathe. "I am in awe of you." I lean down and gently kiss her, then tease her lower lip with my teeth. "I want to bite this lip." I tug harder and she whimpers. My cock hardens in response.

"Please, Ana, let me make love to you," I whisper against her mouth.

"Yes," she responds—and my body lights up like the Fourth of July.

Get a grip, Grey. We have no arrangement in place, no limits set, she's not mine to do with as I please—and yet I'm excited. Aroused. It's an unfamiliar but exhilarating feeling, desire for this woman coursing through me. I'm at the tipping edge of a giant roller coaster.

Vanilla sex?

Can I do this?

Without another word I lead her out of my study, through the living room, and down the corridor to my bedroom. She follows, her hand tightly holding mine.

Shit. Contraception. I'm sure she's not on the pill… Fortunately, I have condoms for backup. At least I don't have to worry about every dick she's slept with. I release her by the bed, walk over to my chest of drawers, and remove my watch, shoes, and socks.

"I assume you're not on the pill."

She shakes her head.

"I didn't think so." From the drawer I take out a packet of condoms, letting her know I'm prepared. She studies me, her eyes impossibly large in her beautiful face, and I have a moment's hesitation. This is supposed to be a big deal for her, isn't it? I remember my first time with Elena, how embarrassing it was…but what a heaven-sent relief. Deep down I know I should send her home. But the simple truth is, I don't want her to go, and I want her. What's more, I can see my desire reflected in her expression, in her darkening eyes.

"Do you want the blinds drawn?" I ask.

"I don't mind," she says. "I thought you didn't let anyone sleep in your bed."

"Who says we're going to sleep?"

"Oh." Her lips form a perfect small *o*. My cock hardens further. Yes, I'd like to fuck that mouth, that *o*. I stalk toward her like she's my prey. *Oh, baby, I want to bury myself in you.* Her breathing is shallow and quick. Her cheeks are rosy…she's wary, but excited. She's at my mercy, and knowing that makes me feel powerful. She has no idea what I'm going to do to her.

"Let's get this jacket off, shall we?" Reaching up, I gently push her jacket off her shoulders, fold it, and place it on my chair.

"Do you have any idea how much I want you, Ana Steele?"

Her lips part as she inhales, and I reach up to touch her cheek. Her skin is petal-soft beneath my fingertips as they glide down to her chin. She's entranced—lost—under my spell. She's already mine. It's intoxicating.

"Do you have any idea what I'm going to do to you?" I murmur and hold her chin between my thumb and forefinger. Leaning down, I kiss her firmly, molding her lips to mine. Returning my kiss, she's soft and sweet and willing, and I have an overwhelming need to see her, all of her. I make quick work of her buttons, slowly peeling off her blouse and letting it fall to the floor. I stand back to look at her. She's wearing the pale-blue bra that Taylor bought.

She's stunning.

"Oh, Ana. You have the most beautiful skin, pale and flawless. I want to kiss every single inch of it." There's not a mark on her. The thought is unsettling. I want to see her marked—pink—with tiny, thin welts from a crop maybe.

She colors a delicious rose—embarrassed, no doubt. If I do nothing else, I will teach her not to be shy of her body. Reaching up, I pull her hair tie, freeing her hair. It tumbles lush and chestnut around her face, down to her breasts.

"Mmm, I like brunettes." She's lovely, exceptional, a jewel.

Holding her head, I run my fingers through her hair and pull her to me, kissing her. She moans against me and parts her lips, allowing me access to her warm, wet mouth. The sweet appreciative noise echoes through me—to the end of my cock. Her tongue shyly meets mine, tentatively probing my mouth, and for some reason, her fumbling inexperience is...hot.

She tastes luscious. Wine, grapes, and innocence—a potent, heady mix of flavors. I fold my arms tightly around her, relieved that she grips only my upper arms. With one hand in her hair, holding her in place, I run my other hand down her spine to her ass and push her against me, against my erection. She moans again. I continue to kiss her, coaxing her unschooled tongue to explore my mouth as I explore hers. My body tenses when she moves her hands up my arms—and for a moment I worry where she'll touch me next. She caresses my cheek, then strokes my hair. It's a little unnerving. But when she twists her fingers in my hair, pulling gently…

Damn, that feels good.

I groan in response but can't let her continue. Before she can touch me again, I push her against the bed and drop to my knees. I want her out of these jeans—I want to strip her, arouse her some more, and…keep her hands off me.

Grasping her hips, I run my tongue just north of the waistband up to her navel. She tenses and inhales sharply. Fuck, does she smell and taste good, an orchard in springtime, and I want my fill. Her hands fist in my hair once more; this I don't mind—in fact, I like it. I nip her hipbone and her grip tightens in my hair. Her eyes are closed, her mouth slack, and she's panting. As I reach up and undo the button on her jeans, she opens her eyes and we study each other. Lazily I ease down the zipper and move my hands around her ass. Slipping my hands inside the waistband, my palms against the soft cheeks of her behind, I slide her jeans off.

I can't stop myself. I want to shock her…test her boundaries right now. Not taking my eyes off hers, I deliberately lick my lips, then lean forward and run my nose up the center of her panties, inhaling her arousal. Closing my eyes, I savor her.

Lord, she's enticing.

"You smell so good." My voice is husky with want and my jeans are becoming extremely uncomfortable. I need to take them off. Gently, I push her onto the bed and, grasping her right foot, I make quick work of removing her sneaker and sock. To tease her I run my thumbnail along her instep and she writhes gratifyingly on the bed, her mouth open, watching me, fascinated. Leaning down, I trace my tongue along her instep, and my teeth graze the little line that my thumbnail has left in its wake. She lies back on the bed, eyes closed, groaning. She's so responsive, it's delightful.

"Oh, Ana, what I could do to you," I whisper as images of her writhing beneath me in my playroom flash through my mind:

shackled to my four-poster bed, bent over the table—suspended from the cross. I could tease and torture her until she begged for release… The images make my jeans even tighter.

Hell.

Quickly I remove her other shoe and sock, and pull off her jeans. She's almost naked on my bed, her hair framing her face perfectly, her long, pale legs stretched out in invitation before me. I have to make allowances for her inexperience. But she's panting. Wanting. Her eyes fixed on me.

I've never fucked anyone in my bed before. *Another first with Miss Steele.*

"You're very beautiful, Anastasia Steele. I can't wait to be inside you." My voice is gentle; I want to tease her some more, find out what she does know. "Show me how you pleasure yourself," I ask, gazing intently down at her.

She frowns.

"Don't be coy, Ana, show me." Part of me wants to spank the shyness out of her.

She shakes her head. "I don't know what you mean."

Is she playing games?

"How do you make yourself come? I want to see."

She remains mute. Clearly I've shocked her again. "I don't," she mutters finally, her voice breathless. I gaze at her in disbelief. Even I used to masturbate, before Elena sunk her claws into me.

She's probably never had an orgasm—though I find this hard to believe. *Whoa.* I'm responsible for her first fuck and her first orgasm. I'd better make this good.

"Well, we'll have to see what we can do about that." *I'm going to make you come like a freight train, baby.*

Hell—she's probably never seen a naked man, either. Not taking my eyes off hers, I undo the top button on my jeans and ease them onto the floor, though I can't risk taking my shirt off, because she might touch me.

But if she did…it wouldn't be so bad…would it? Being touched?

I banish the thought before the darkness surfaces, and grasping her ankles, I spread her legs. Her eyes widen and her hands clench my sheets.

Yes. Keep your hands there, baby.

I crawl slowly up the bed, between her legs. She squirms beneath me.

"Keep still," I tell her and lean down to kiss the delicate skin of her inner thigh. I trail kisses up her thighs, over her panties, across her belly, nipping and sucking as I go. She writhes beneath me.

"We're going to have to work on keeping you still, baby."

If you'll let me.

I'll teach her to just absorb the pleasure and not move, intensifying every touch, every kiss, every nip. The thought alone is enough to make me want to bury myself in her, but before I do, I want to know how responsive she is. So far she hasn't held back. She's allowing me free rein over her body. She's not hesitant at all. She wants this...she really wants this. I dip my tongue into her navel and continue my leisurely journey north, savoring her. I shift, lying beside her, one leg still between hers. My hand ghosts up her body, over her hip, up her waist, onto her breast. Gently I cup her breast, trying to gauge her reaction. She doesn't stiffen. She doesn't stop me...she trusts me. Can I extend her trust to letting me have complete dominion over her body...over her? The thought is exhilarating.

"You fit my hand perfectly, Anastasia." Dipping my finger into her bra cup, I jerk it down, freeing her breast. The nipple is small, rose pink, and it's already hard. I drag the cup down so the fabric and underwire rest under her breast, forcing it upward. I repeat the process with the other cup and watch, fascinated, as her nipples grow under my steady gaze. *Whoa*...I haven't even touched her yet.

"Very nice," I whisper in awed appreciation and blow gently on the nearest nipple, watching in delight as it hardens and extends.

Anastasia closes her eyes and arches her back.

Keep still, baby. Just absorb the pleasure. It will feel so much more intense.

Blowing on one nipple, I roll the other gently between my

thumb and forefinger. She grasps the sheets tightly as I lean down and suck—hard. Her body bows again and she cries out.

"Let's see if we can make you come like this," I whisper, and I don't stop. She starts to whimper.

Oh, yes, baby...feel this. Her nipples extend farther and she starts grinding her hips, around and around. *Keep still, baby. I will teach you to keep still.*

"Oh, please," she begs. Her legs stiffen. It's working. She's close.

I continue my lascivious assault. Concentrating on each nipple, watching her response, sensing her pleasure, is driving me to distraction. Lord, I want her.

"Let go, baby," I murmur and pull her nipple with my teeth. She cries out as she climaxes.

Yes! I move quickly to kiss her, capturing her cries in my mouth. She's breathless and panting, lost in her pleasure...

Mine.

I own her first orgasm, and I'm ridiculously pleased by the thought.

"You're very responsive. You're going to have to learn to control that, and it's going to be so much fun teaching you how." I can't wait...but right now, I want her. All of her. I kiss her once more and let my hand travel down her body, down to her vulva. I hold her, feeling her heat. Slipping my index finger through the lace of her panties, I slowly circle around inside her... *Fuck, she's soaking.*

"You're so deliciously wet. God, I want you." I thrust my finger inside her, and she cries out. She's hot and tight and wet, and I want her. I thrust into her again, taking her cries into my mouth. I press my palm to her clitoris...pushing down...pushing around. She cries out and writhes beneath me. *Fuck*, I want her—now. She's ready.

Sitting up, I drag her panties off, then my boxers, and reach for a condom. I kneel up between her legs, pushing them farther apart. Anastasia watches me with...what? Trepidation? She's probably never seen an erect penis before.

"Don't worry. You expand, too," I mutter. Stretching out over her, I put my hands on either side of her head, taking my weight on my elbows. God, I want her…but I check she's still eager. "You really want to do this?" I ask.

For fuck's sake, please don't say no.

"Please," she begs.

"Pull your knees up," I instruct her. This'll be easier. Have I ever been so aroused? I can barely contain myself. I don't get it… it must be her.

Why?

Grey, focus!

I position myself so I can take her at my whim. Her eyes are open wide, imploring me. She really wants this…as much as I do. Should I be gentle and prolong the agony, or do I go for it?

I go for it. I need to possess her.

"I'm going to fuck you now, Miss Steele. Hard."

One thrust and I'm inside her.

F. U. C. K.

She's so fucking tight. She cries out.

Shit! I've hurt her. I want to move, to lose myself in her, and it takes all my restraint to stop. "You're so tight. You okay?" I ask, my voice a hoarse, anxious whisper, and she nods, eyes wider. She's like heaven on earth, so tight around me. And even though her hands are on my forearms, I don't care. The darkness is slumbering, perhaps because I've wanted her for so long. I've never felt this desire, this…*hunger* before. It's a new feeling, new and shiny. I want so much from her: her trust, her obedience, her submission. I want her to be mine, but right now…I'm hers.

"I'm going to move, baby." My voice is strained as I ease back gradually. It's such an extraordinary, exquisite feeling: her body cradling my cock. I push into her again and claim her, knowing no one has before. She whimpers.

I stop. "More?"

"Yes," she breathes after a moment.

This time I thrust into her more deeply.

"Again?" I plead as sweat beads on my body.

"Yes."

Her trust in me—it's suddenly overwhelming, and I start

to move, really move. I want her to come. I will not stop until she comes. I want to own this woman, body and soul. I want her clenching around me.

Fuck—she starts meeting every thrust, matching my rhythm. *See how well we fit together, Ana?* I grasp her head, holding her in place while I claim her body and kiss her hard, claiming her mouth. She stiffens beneath me…*fuck yes.* Her orgasm is close.

"Come for me, Ana," I demand, and she cries out as she's consumed, tipping her head back, her mouth open, her eyes closed… and just the sight of her ecstasy is enough. I explode in her, losing all sense and reason, as I call out her name and come violently inside her.

When I open my eyes I'm panting, trying to catch my breath, and we're forehead to forehead and she's staring up at me.

Fuck. I'm undone.

I plant a swift kiss on her forehead, pull out of her, and lie down beside her.

She winces as I withdraw, but other than that she looks okay.

"Did I hurt you?" I ask, and I tuck her hair behind her ear, because I don't want to stop touching her.

Ana beams with incredulity. "You are asking me if you hurt me?"

And for a moment I don't know why she's grinning.

Oh. My playroom.

"The irony is not lost on me," I mutter. Even now she confounds me. "Seriously, are you okay?"

She stretches out beside me, testing her body and teasing me with an amused but sated expression.

"You haven't answered me," I growl. I need to know if she found that enjoyable. All the evidence points to a "yes"—but I need to hear it from her. While I'm waiting for her reply I remove the condom. Lord, I hate these things. I discard it discreetly on the floor.

She peers up at me. "I'd like to do that again," she says with a shy giggle.

What?

Again?

Already?

"Would you now, Miss Steele?" I kiss the corner of her mouth. "Demanding little thing, aren't you? Turn on your front."

That way I know you won't touch me.

She gives me a brief sweet smile, then rolls onto her stomach. My cock stirs with approval. I unhook her bra and run my hand down her back to her pert behind. "You really have the most beautiful skin," I say as I brush her hair off her face and push her legs apart. Gently I plant soft kisses on her shoulder.

"Why are you wearing your shirt?" she asks.

She's so damn inquisitive. While she's on her front I know she can't touch me, so I lean back and pull my shirt over my head, letting it drop to the floor. Fully naked, I lie on top of her. Her skin is warm and melts against mine.

Hmm…I could get used to this.

"So you want me to fuck you again?" I whisper in her ear, kissing her. She squirms deliciously against me.

Oh, this will never do. Keep still, baby.

I skim my hand down her body to the back of her knee, then hitch it up high, parting her legs wide so that she's spread beneath me. Her breath catches and I hope it's with anticipation. She stills beneath me.

Finally!

I palm her ass as I ease my weight onto her. "I'm going to take you from behind, Anastasia." With my other hand I grab her hair at the nape and tug gently, holding her in place. She cannot move. Her hands are helpless and splayed against the sheets, out of harm's way.

"You are mine," I whisper. "Only mine. Don't forget it."

With my free hand I move from her ass to her clitoris and begin circling slowly.

Her muscles flex beneath me as she tries to move, but my weight keeps her in place. I run my teeth along her jawline. Her sweet fragrance lingers over the scent of our coupling. "You smell divine," I whisper as I nuzzle behind her ear.

She starts to circle her hips against my moving hand.

"Keep still," I warn.

Or I might stop…

Tentatively, I insert my thumb inside her and circle it around and around, taking particular care to stroke the front wall of her vagina.

She groans and tenses beneath me, trying to move again.

"You like this?" I tease, and my teeth trace her outer ear. I don't stop my fingers from tormenting her clitoris, but I begin to ease my thumb in and out of her. She stiffens but can't move.

She groans loudly, her eyes scrunched up tight.

"You're so wet, so quickly. So responsive. Oh, Anastasia, I like that. I like that a lot."

Right. Let's see how far you'll go.

I withdraw my thumb from her vagina. "Open your mouth," I order, and when she does I thrust my thumb between her lips. "See how you taste. Suck me, baby."

She sucks my thumb…hard.

Fuck.

And for a moment I imagine it's my cock in her mouth.

"I want to fuck your mouth, Anastasia, and I will soon." I'm breathless.

She closes her teeth around me, biting me hard.

Ow! Fuck.

I grip her hair tightly and she loosens her mouth. "Naughty, sweet girl." My mind flits through a number of punishments worthy of such a bold move that, if she were my submissive, I could inflict on her. My cock expands to bursting at the thought. I release her and sit back on my knees.

"Stay still, don't move." I grab another condom from my bedside table, rip open the foil, and roll the latex over my erection.

Watching her, I see she's still, except for the rise and fall of her back as she pants in anticipation.

She's gorgeous.

Leaning over her again, I grasp her hair and hold her so she can't move her head.

"We're going to go real slow this time, Anastasia."

She gasps, and I gently ease into her until I can go no farther.

Fuck. She feels good.

As I ease out I circle my hips and slowly slip into her again. She whimpers and her limbs tense beneath me as she tries to move.

Oh no, baby.

I want you still.

I want you to feel this.

Take all the pleasure.

"You feel so good," I tell her and repeat the move again, circling my hips as I go. Unhurried. In. Out. In. Out. Her insides start to tremble.

"Oh no, baby, not yet."

No way am I letting you come.

Not when I'm enjoying this so much.

"Oh, please," she cries.

"I want you sore, baby." I pull out and sink into her again. "Every time you move tomorrow, I want you to be reminded that I've been here. Only me. You are mine."

"Please, Christian," she begs.

"What do you want, Anastasia? Tell me." I continue the slow torture. "Tell me."

"You, please." She's desperate.

She wants me.

Good girl.

I increase the pace and her insides begin to quiver, responding immediately.

Between each thrust I utter one word. "You. Are. So. Sweet. I. Want. You. So. Much. You. Are. Mine." Her limbs tremble with the strain of keeping still. She's on the edge. "Come for me, baby," I growl.

And on command she shudders around me as her orgasm rips through her and she screams my name into the mattress.

My name on her lips is my undoing, and I climax and collapse on top of her.

"Fuck. Ana," I whisper, drained yet elated. I pull out of her almost immediately and roll onto my back. She curls up at my side, and as I pull off the condom, she closes her eyes and falls asleep.

SUNDAY, MAY 22, 2011

I wake with a start and a pervading sense of guilt, as if I've committed a terrible sin.

Is it because I've fucked Anastasia Steele? Virgin?

She's snuggled up fast asleep beside me. I check the radio alarm: it's after three in the morning. Ana sleeps the sound sleep of an innocent. Well, not so innocent now. My body stirs as I watch her.

I could wake her.

Fuck her again.

There are definitely some advantages to having her in my bed.

Grey. Stop this nonsense.

Fucking her was merely a means to an end and a pleasant diversion.

Yes. Very pleasant.

More like incredible.

It was just sex, for fuck's sake.

I close my eyes in what will probably be a futile attempt to sleep. But the room is too full of Ana: her scent, the sound of her soft breathing, and the memory of my first vanilla fuck. Visions of her head thrown back in passion, of her crying out a barely recognizable version of my name, and her unbridled enthusiasm for sexual congress overwhelm me.

Miss Steele is a carnal creature.

She will be a joy to train.

My cock twitches in agreement.

Shit.

I can't sleep, though tonight it's not nightmares that keep me awake; it's Miss Steele. Climbing out of bed, I collect the used condoms from the floor, knot them, and dispose of them in the wastepaper basket. From the chest of drawers I pull out a pair of PJ pants and drag them on. With a lingering look at the enticing woman in my bed, I venture into the kitchen. I'm thirsty.

Once I've had a glass of water, I do what I always do when I can't sleep—I check my email in my study. Taylor has returned and is asking if he can stand *Charlie Tango* down. Stephan must be asleep upstairs. I email him back with a yes, though at this time of night it's a given.

Back in the living room I sit down at my piano. This is my solace, where I can lose myself for hours. I've been able to play well since I was nine, but it wasn't until I had my own piano, in my own place, that it really became a passion. When I want to forget everything, this is what I do. And right now I don't want to think about having propositioned a virgin, fucked her, or revealed my lifestyle to someone with no experience. With my hands on the keys, I begin to play and lose myself in the solitude of Bach.

A movement distracts me from the music, and when I look up Ana's standing by the piano. Wrapped in a comforter, her hair wild and curling down her back, eyes luminous, she looks stunning.

"Sorry," she says. "I didn't mean to disturb you."

Why is she apologizing? "Surely I should be saying that to you." I play the last notes and stand. "You should be in bed," I chide.

"That was a beautiful piece. Bach?"

"Transcription by Bach, but it's originally an oboe concerto by Alessandro Marcello."

"It was exquisite, but very sad, such a melancholy melody."

Melancholy? It wouldn't be the first time someone has used that word to describe me.

"May I speak freely? Sir." Leila is kneeling beside me while I work.

"You may."

"Sir, you are most melancholy today."

"Am I?"

"Yes, Sir. Is there something that you would like me to do…?"

I shake off the memory. Ana should be in bed. I tell her so again.

"I woke and you weren't there."

"I find it difficult to sleep, and I'm not used to sleeping with anyone." I've told her this—and why am I justifying myself? I wrap my arm around her naked shoulders, enjoying the feel of her skin, and guide her back to the bedroom.

"How long have you been playing? You play beautifully."

"Since I was six." I'm abrupt.

"Oh," she says. I think she's taken the hint—I don't want to talk about my childhood.

"How are you feeling?" I ask as I switch on the bedside light.

"I'm good."

There's blood on my sheets. Her blood. Evidence of her now-absent virginity. Her eyes dart from the stains to me and she looks away, embarrassed.

"Well, that's going to give Mrs. Jones something to think about."

She looks mortified.

It's just your body, sweetheart. I grasp her chin and tip her head back so I can see her expression. I'm about to give her a short lecture on how not to be ashamed of her body when she reaches out to touch my chest.

Fuck.

I step out of her reach as the darkness surfaces.

No. Don't touch me.

"Get into bed," I order, rather more sharply than I'd intended, but I hope she doesn't detect my fear. Her eyes widen with confusion and maybe hurt.

Damn.

"I'll come and lie down with you," I add as a peace offering, and from the chest of drawers I pull out a T-shirt and quickly slip it on, for protection.

She's still standing, staring at me. "Bed," I command more forcefully.

She scrambles into my bed and lies down and I climb in behind her, folding her in my arms. I bury my face in her hair and inhale her sweet scent: autumn and apple trees. Facing away, she can't touch me, and while I lie there I resolve to spoon with her until she's asleep. Then I'll get up and do some work.

"Sleep, sweet Anastasia." I kiss her hair and close my eyes. Her scent fills my nostrils, reminding me of a happy time and leaving me replete…content, even…

Mommy is happy today. She is singing.

Singing about what love has to do with it.

And cooking. And singing.

My tummy gurgles. She is cooking bacon and waffles.

They smell good. My tummy likes bacon and waffles.

They smell so good.

Opening my eyes, light is flooding through the windows and there's a mouthwatering aroma coming from the kitchen. Bacon. Momentarily I'm confused. Is Gail back from her sister's?

Then I remember.

Ana.

A look at the clock tells me it's late. I bounce out of bed and follow my nose to the kitchen.

There's Ana. She's wearing my shirt, her hair in braids, dancing around to some music. Only I can't hear it. She's wearing earbuds. Unobserved, I take a seat at the kitchen counter and watch the show. She's whisking eggs, making breakfast, her braids bouncing as she jiggles from foot to foot, and I realize she's not wearing underwear.

Good girl.

She has to be one of the most uncoordinated females I've ever seen. It's amusing, charming, and strangely arousing at the same time; I think of all the ways I can improve her coordination. When she turns and spots me, she freezes.

"Good morning, Miss Steele. You're very…energetic this morning." She looks even younger in her braids.

"I–I slept well," she stammers.

"I can't imagine why," I quip, admitting to myself that I did, too. It's after nine. When did I last sleep past six thirty?

Yesterday.

After I'd slept with her.

"Are you hungry?" she asks.

"Very." And I'm not sure if it's for breakfast or for her.

"Pancakes, bacon, and eggs?" she says.

"Sounds great."

"I don't know where you keep your place mats," she says, seeming at a loss, and I think she's embarrassed, because I caught her dancing.

Taking pity on her, I offer to set places for breakfast and add, "Would you like me to put some music on so you can continue your…er…dancing?"

Her cheeks pink and she looks down at the floor.

Damn. I've upset her. "Please, don't stop on my account. It's very entertaining."

With a pout she turns her back on me and continues to whisk the eggs with gusto. I wonder if she has any idea how disrespectful this is to someone like me…but of course she doesn't, and for some unfathomable reason it makes me smile. Sidling up to her, I gently tug one of her braids. "I love these. They won't protect you."

Not from me. Not now that I've had you.

"How would you like your eggs?" Her tone is unexpectedly haughty. And I want to laugh out loud, but I resist.

"Thoroughly whisked and beaten," I reply, trying and failing to sound deadpan. She attempts to hide her amusement, too, and continues her task.

Her smile is bewitching.

Hastily, I set up the place mats, wondering when I last did this for someone else.

Never.

Normally over the weekend my submissive would take care of all domestic tasks.

Not today, Grey, because she's not your submissive…yet.

I pour us both orange juice and put the coffee on. She doesn't drink coffee, only tea. "Would you like some tea?"

"Yes, please. If you have some."

In the cupboard I find the Twinings tea bags I'd asked Gail to buy.

Well, well, who would have thought I'd ever get to use them?

She frowns when she sees them. "Bit of a foregone conclusion, wasn't I?"

"Are you? I'm not sure we've concluded anything yet, Miss Steele," I answer with a stern look.

And don't talk about yourself like that.

I add her self-deprecation to the list of behaviors that will need modifying.

She avoids my gaze, busy with serving up breakfast. Two plates are placed on the place mats, then she fetches the maple syrup out of the fridge.

When she looks up at me I'm waiting for her to sit down. "Miss Steele." I indicate where she should sit.

"Mr. Grey," she replies with contrived formality and winces as she sits.

"Just how sore are you?" I'm surprised by an uneasy sense of guilt. I want to fuck her again, preferably after breakfast, but if she's too sore that will be out of the question. Perhaps I could use her mouth this time.

The color in her face rises. "Well, to be truthful, I have nothing to compare this to," she says tartly. "Did you wish to offer your commiserations?" Her sarcastic tone takes me by surprise. If she were mine, it would earn her a spanking at least, maybe over the kitchen counter.

"No. I wondered if we should continue your basic training."

"Oh." She startles.

Yes, Ana, we can have sex during the day, too. And I'd like to fill that smart mouth of yours.

I take a bite of my breakfast and close my eyes in appreciation. It tastes mighty fine. When I swallow she's still staring at me. "Eat, Anastasia," I order. "This is delicious, incidentally."

She can cook, and well.

Ana takes one bite of her food, then pushes her breakfast around on her plate.

I ask her to stop biting her lip. "It's very distracting, and I happen to know you're not wearing anything under my shirt."

She fidgets with her tea bag and the teapot, ignoring my irritation. "What sort of basic training did you have in mind?" she asks.

She's ever-curious—let's see how far she'll go.

"Well, as you're sore, I thought we could stick to oral skills."

She splutters into her teacup.

Hell. I don't want to choke the girl. Gently, I pat her on the back and hand her a glass of orange juice. "That's if you want to stay." I shouldn't push my luck.

"I'd like to stay for today. If that's okay. I have to work tomorrow."

"What time do you have to be at work tomorrow?"

"Nine."

"I'll get you to work by nine tomorrow."

What? I want her to stay?

It's a surprise to me.

Yes, I want her to stay.

"I'll need to go home tonight. I need clean clothes."

"We can get you some here."

She flips her hair and gnaws nervously at her lip…again.

"What is it?" I ask.

"I need to be home this evening."

Boy, she's stubborn. I don't want her to go, but at this stage, with no agreement, I can't insist that she stay. "Okay, this evening. Now eat your breakfast."

She examines her food.

"Eat, Anastasia. You didn't eat last night."

"I'm really not hungry," she says.

Well, this is frustrating. "I would really like you to finish your breakfast." My voice is low.

"What is it with you and food?" she snaps.

Oh, baby, you really don't want to know. "I told you, I have issues with wasted food. Eat." I glare at her. *Don't push me on this, Ana.* She gives me a mulish look and starts to eat.

As I watch her place a forkful of eggs in her mouth, I relax.

She's quite challenging in her own way. And it's unique. I've never dealt with this. *Yes.* That's it. She's a novelty. That's the fascination…isn't it?

When she finishes her food I take her plate.

"You cooked, I'll clear."

"That's very democratic," she says, arching an eyebrow.

"Yes. Not my usual style. After I've done this, we'll take a bath."

And I can test her oral skills. I take a swift breath to control my instant arousal at the thought.

Hell.

Her phone rings and she wanders to the end of the room, deep in conversation. I pause by the sink and watch her. As she stands against the glass wall, the morning light silhouettes her body in my white shirt. My mouth dries. She's slim, with long legs, perfect breasts, and a perfect ass.

Still on her call, she turns toward me and I pretend my attention is elsewhere. For some reason I don't want her to catch me ogling.

Who is it on the phone?

I hear Kavanagh's name mentioned and I tense. *What is she saying?* Our eyes lock.

What are you saying, Ana?

She turns away and a moment later hangs up, then walks back toward me, her hips swaying in a soft, seductive rhythm beneath my shirt. *Should I tell her what I can see?*

"The NDA, does it cover everything?" she asks, halting me in my tracks as I shut the pantry cupboard.

"Why?" *Where's she going with this? What has she said to Kavanagh?*

She takes a deep breath. "Well, I have a few questions, you know, about sex. And I'd like to ask Kate."

"You can ask me."

"Christian, with all due respect—" She stops.

She's embarrassed?

"It's just about mechanics. I won't mention the Red Room of Pain," she says in a rush.

"Red Room of Pain?"

What the hell?

"It's mostly about pleasure, Anastasia. Believe me. Besides, your roommate is making the beast with two backs with my brother. I'd really rather you didn't."

I don't want Elliot to know anything about my sex life. He'd never let me live it down.

"Does your family know about your…um, predilection?"

"No. It's none of their business."

She's burning to ask something.

"What do you want to know?" I ask, standing in front of her, scrutinizing her face.

What is it, Ana?

"Nothing specific at the moment," she whispers.

"Well, we can start with: How was last night for you?" My breathing shallows as I wait for her answer. Our whole deal could hang on her response.

"Good," she says and gives me a soft, sexy smile.

It's what I want to hear.

"For me, too. I've never had vanilla sex before. There's a lot to be said for it. But then, maybe it's because it's with you."

Her surprise and pleasure at my words are obvious. I brush her plump lower lip with my thumb. I'm itching to touch her… again. "Come, let's have a bath." I kiss her and take her into my bathroom.

"Stay there," I order, turning the faucet, then add scented oil to the steaming water. The tub fills quickly as she watches me. Normally, I would expect any woman I was about to bathe with to have her eyes cast down in modesty.

But not Ana.

She doesn't drop her gaze, and her eyes glow with anticipation and curiosity. But she has her arms wrapped around herself; she's shy.

It's arousing.

And to think she's never bathed with a man.

I can claim another first.

When the bath is full I peel off my T-shirt and hold out my hand. "Miss Steele."

She accepts my invitation and steps into the bath.

"Turn around, face me," I instruct. "I know that lip is delicious, I can attest to that, but will you stop biting it? Your chewing it makes me want to fuck you, and you're sore, okay?"

She inhales sharply, releasing her lip.

"Yeah. Get the picture?"

Still standing, she gives me an emphatic nod.

"Good." She's still wearing my shirt and I take the iPod from the breast pocket and place it by the sink. "Water and iPods—not a clever combination." I grab the hem and pull it off her. Immediately she hangs her head when I step back to admire her.

"Hey." My voice is gentle and encourages her to peek up at me. "Anastasia, you're a very beautiful woman, the whole package. Don't hang your head like you're ashamed. You have nothing to be ashamed of, and it's a real joy to stand here and look at you." Holding her chin, I tip her head back.

Don't hide from me, baby.

"You can sit down now."

She sits down with indecent haste and winces as her sore body hits the water.

Okay...

She screws her eyes shut as she lies back, but when she opens them, she looks more relaxed. "Why don't you join me?" she asks with a coy smile.

"I think I will. Move forward." Stripping, I climb in behind her, pull her to my chest, and place my legs around hers, my feet over her ankles, and then I pull her legs apart.

She wriggles against me, but I ignore her motion and bury my nose in her hair. "You smell so good, Anastasia," I whisper.

She settles and I grab the body wash from the shelf beside us. Squeezing some into my hand, I work the soap into a lather and start massaging her neck and shoulders. She moans as her head lolls to one side under my tender ministration.

"You like that?" I ask.

"Hmm," she hums in contentment.

I wash her arms and her underarms, then reach my first goal: her breasts.

Lord, the feel of her.

She has perfect breasts. I knead and tease them. She groans and flexes her hips and her breathing accelerates. She's aroused. My body responds in kind, growing beneath her.

My hands skim over her torso and her belly toward my second goal. Before I reach her pubic hair I stop and grab a washcloth. Squirting some soap onto the cloth, I begin the slow process of washing between her legs. Gentle, slow but sure, rubbing, washing, cleaning, stimulating. She starts to pant and her hips move in synchronization with my hand. Her head rests against my shoulder, her eyes closed, her mouth open in a silent moan as she surrenders to my relentless fingers.

"Feel it, baby." I run my teeth along her earlobe. "Feel it for me."

"Oh, please," she whines, and she tries to straighten her legs, but I have them pinioned under mine.

Enough.

Now that she's all worked up into a lather I'm ready to proceed.

"I think you're clean enough now," I announce and take my hands off her.

"Why are you stopping?" she protests, her eyes fluttering open, revealing frustration and disappointment.

"Because I have other plans for you, Anastasia."

She's panting and, if I'm not mistaken, pouting.

Good.

"Turn around. I need washing, too."

She does, her face rosy, her eyes bright, pupils large.

Lifting my hips, I grab my cock. "I want you to become well acquainted—on first-name terms, if you will—with my favorite and most cherished part of my body. I'm very attached to this."

Her mouth drops open as she looks from my penis to my face… and back again. I can't help my wicked grin. Her face is a picture of maidenly outrage.

But as she stares, her expression changes. First thoughtful, then assessing, and when her eyes meet mine, the challenge in them is clear.

Oh, bring it on, Miss Steele.

Her smile is one of delight as she reaches for the body wash. Taking her sweet time, she drizzles some of the soap into her palm and, without taking her eyes off mine, rubs her hands together. Her lips part and she bites her bottom lip, running her tongue across the little indentations left by her teeth.

Ana Steele, seductress!

My cock responds in appreciation, hardening further. Reaching forward, she grabs me, her hand fisting around me. My breath hisses out through clenched teeth and I close my eyes, savoring the moment.

Here, I don't mind being touched.

No, I don't mind at all... Placing my hand over hers, I show her what to do. "Like this." My voice is hoarse as I guide her. She tightens her hold around me and her hand moves up and down beneath mine.

Oh yes.

"That's right, baby."

I release her and let her continue, closing my eyes and surrendering to the rhythm she's set.

Oh God.

What is it about her inexperience that is so arousing? Is it that I'm enjoying all her firsts?

Suddenly she draws me into her mouth, sucking hard, her tongue torturing me.

Fuck.

"Whoa...Ana."

She sucks harder; her eyes are alight with feminine cunning. This is her revenge, her tit for tat. She looks stunning.

"Christ," I growl and close my eyes so I don't come immediately. She continues her sweet torture, and as her confidence grows I flex my hips, pushing myself farther into her mouth.

How far can I go, baby?

Watching her is stimulating, so stimulating. I grab her hair and start to work her mouth as she supports herself with her hands on my thighs.

"Oh. Baby. That. Feels. Good."

She confines her teeth behind her lips and pulls me into her mouth once more.

"Ah!" I groan and wonder how deep she'll allow me. Her mouth torments me, her shielded teeth squeezing hard. And I want more. "Jesus. How far can you go?"

Her eyes meet mine and she frowns. Then, with a look of determination, she slides down on me until I hit the back of her throat.

Fuck.

"Anastasia, I'm going to come in your mouth," I warn her, breathless. "If you don't want me to, stop now." I thrust into her again and again, watching my cock disappear and reappear from her mouth. It's beyond erotic. I'm so close. Suddenly she bares her teeth, gently squeezing me, and I'm undone, ejaculating into the back of her throat, crying out my pleasure.

Fuck.

My breathing is labored. She's completely disarmed me… again!

When I open my eyes she's glowing with pride.

As she should be. That was one hell of a blow job.

"Don't you have a gag reflex?" I marvel at her as I catch my breath. "Christ, Ana…that was…good, really good. Unexpected, though. You know, you never cease to amaze me." Praise for a job well done.

Wait, that was so good, perhaps she has some experience after all. "Have you done that before?" I ask, and I'm not sure I want to know.

"No," she says with obvious pride.

"Good." I hope my relief is not too obvious. "Yet another first, Miss Steele. Well, you get an A in oral skills. Come, let's go to bed. I owe you an orgasm."

I climb out of the bath a little dazed and wrap a towel around my waist. Grabbing another, I hold it up and help her out of the bath, swathing her in it so she's trapped. I hold her against me, kissing her, really kissing her. Exploring her mouth with my tongue.

I taste my ejaculate in her mouth. Grasping her head, I deepen the kiss.

I want her.

All of her.

Her body and soul.

I want her to be mine.

Staring down into bemused eyes, I implore her. "Say yes."

"To what?" she whispers.

"Yes to our arrangement. To being mine. Please, Ana." And it's the closest I've come to begging in a long time. I kiss her again, pouring my fervor into my kiss. When I take her hand, she looks dazed.

Dazzle her further, Grey.

In my bedroom, I release her. "Trust me?" I ask.

She nods.

"Good girl."

Good. Beautiful. Girl.

I head into my closet to select one of my ties. When I'm back in front of her, I take her towel and drop it on the floor. "Hold your hands together in front of you."

She licks her lips in what I think is a moment of uncertainty, then holds out her hands. Swiftly I bind her wrists together with the tie. I test the knot. *Yes.* It's secure.

Time for more training, Miss Steele.

Her lips part as she inhales. She's excited.

Gently I tug both her braids. "You look so young with these." But they're not going to stop me. I drop my towel. "Oh, Anastasia, what shall I do to you?" I grasp her upper arms and ease her back on the bed, keeping hold of her so she doesn't fall. Once she's prostrate, I lie down beside her, grab her fists, and raise them above her head. "Keep your hands up here. Don't move them. Understand?"

She swallows.

"Answer me."

"I won't move my hands," she says, her voice husky.

"Good girl." I can't help my smile. She lies beside me, wrists bound, helpless. *Mine.*

Not quite to do with as I wish—yet—but getting there.

Leaning down, I kiss her lightly and let her know that I'll kiss her all over.

She sighs as my lips move from the base of her ear down to the hollow at the bottom of her neck. I'm rewarded with her appreciative moan. Abruptly she lowers her arms so they circle my neck.

No. No. No. This will not do, Miss Steele.

Glaring down at her, I place them firmly back above her head. "Don't move your hands, or we just have to start all over again."

"I want to touch you," she whispers.

"I know." *But you can't.* "Keep your hands above your head."

Her lips are parted and her chest is heaving with each rapid breath. She's turned on.

Good.

Cupping her chin, I start kissing my way down her body. My hand travels over her breasts, my lips in hot pursuit. With one hand on her belly, holding her in place, I pay homage to each of her nipples, sucking and nipping gently, delighting in their hardening response.

She mewls and her hips start to move.

"Keep still," I warn against her skin. I plant kisses across her belly, where my tongue explores the taste and depth of her navel.

"Ah," she moans and squirms.

I will have to teach her to keep still…

My teeth graze her skin. "Hmm. You are so sweet, Miss Steele." I gently nip between her navel and pubic hair, then sit up between her legs. Grabbing both her ankles, I spread her legs wide. Like this, naked, vulnerable, she is a glorious sight to behold. Holding her left foot, I bend her knee and raise her toes to my lips, watching her face as I do. I kiss each toe, then bite the soft pad on each.

Her eyes are wide and her mouth is open, moving alternately from a small to a capital O. When I bite the pad on her little toe a little harder, her pelvis flexes and she whimpers. I run my tongue over her instep to her ankle. She scrunches her eyes closed, her head twisting from side to side, as I continue to torment her.

"Oh, please," she begs when I suck and bite her little toe.

"All good things, Miss Steele," I tease.

When I get to her knee, I don't stop but continue, licking, sucking, and biting up the inside of her thigh, spreading her legs wide as I do.

She trembles, in shock, anticipating my tongue at the apex of her thighs.

Oh no…not yet, Miss Steele.

I return my attentions to her left leg, kissing and nipping from her knee up the inside of her thigh.

She tenses when I finally lie between her legs. But she keeps her arms raised.

Good girl.

Gently, I run my nose up and down her vulva.

She writhes beneath me.

I stop. She has to learn to keep still.

She raises her head to look at me.

"Do you know how intoxicating you smell, Miss Steele?" Holding her stare with my own, I push my nose into her pubic hair and breathe deeply.

Her head flops back in the bed and she groans.

I blow gently up and down over her pubic hair. "I like this," I mutter. It's been a long time since I've seen pubic hair up close and personal like this. I tug it gently. "Perhaps we'll keep this."

Though it's no good for wax play…

"Oh, please," she pleads.

"Hmm, I like it when you beg me, Anastasia."

She moans.

"Tit for tat is not my usual style, Miss Steele," I whisper against her flesh. "But you've pleased me today, and you should be rewarded." And I hold down her thighs, opening her up to my tongue, and slowly start circling her clitoris.

She cries out, her body rising off the bed.

But I don't stop. My tongue is ruthless. Her legs stiffen, her toes pointed.

Ah, she's close, and carefully I slip my middle finger inside her.

She's wet.

Wet and waiting.

"Oh, baby. I love that you're so wet for me." I start to move my finger clockwise, stretching her. My tongue continues to torment her clitoris, over and over. She stiffens beneath me and finally cries out as her orgasm crashes through her.

Yes!

I kneel up and grab a condom. Once it's on, slowly I ease myself into her.

Fuck, she feels good.

"How's this?" I check.

"Fine. Good." Her voice is hoarse.

Oh… I start to move, reveling in the feel of her around me, beneath me. Again and again, faster and faster, losing myself in this woman. I want her to come again.

I want her sated.

I want her happy.

Finally, she stiffens once more and whimpers.

"Come for me, baby," I utter through clenched teeth, and she detonates around me.

"Thank fuck," I cry and let go, finding my own sweet release. Briefly I collapse on her, glorying in her softness. She moves her hands so they are around my neck, but because she's tied she can't touch me.

Taking a deep breath, I rest my weight on my arms and stare down at her in wonder.

"See how good we are together? If you give yourself to me, it will be so much better. Trust me, Anastasia, I can take you places you don't even know exist." Our foreheads touch and I close my eyes.

Please say yes.

We hear voices outside the door.

What the hell?

It's Taylor and Grace.

"Shit! It's my mother."

Ana cringes as I pull out of her.

Leaping out of bed, I throw the condom in the wastepaper basket.

What the hell is my mother doing here?

Taylor has diverted her, thank heaven. Well, she's about to get a surprise.

Ana is still prostrate on the bed. "Come on, we need to get dressed—that's if you want to meet my mother." I smile at Ana as I pull on my jeans. She looks adorable.

"Christian—I can't move," she protests, but she's grinning, too.

Leaning down, I undo the tie and kiss her forehead.

My mother is going to be thrilled.

"Another first," I whisper, unable to shift my grin.

"I have no clean clothes in here."

I slip on a white T-shirt, and when I turn around she's sitting up, hugging her knees. "Perhaps I should stay here."

"Oh no you don't," I warn. "You can wear something of mine."

I like her wearing my clothes.

Her face falls.

"Anastasia, you could be wearing a sack and you'd look lovely. Please don't worry. I'd like you to meet my mother. Get dressed. I'll just go and calm her down. I'll expect you in that room in five minutes; otherwise I'll come and drag you out of here myself in whatever you're wearing. My T-shirts are in this drawer. My shirts are in the closet. Help yourself."

Her eyes widen.

Yes. I'm serious, baby.

Cautioning her with a pointed look, I open the door and exit to find my mother.

Grace is standing in the corridor opposite the foyer door, and Taylor is talking to her. Her face lights up when she sees me. "Darling, I had no idea you might have company," she exclaims, and she looks a little embarrassed.

"Hello, Mother." I kiss her proffered cheek. "I'll deal with her from here," I say to Taylor.

"Yes, Mr. Grey." He nods, looking exasperated, and heads back into his office.

"Thank you, Taylor," Grace calls after him, then turns her full attention to me. "Deal with me?" she says in rebuke. "I was shopping downtown and I thought I might pop in for coffee." She stops.

"If I'd known you weren't alone..." She shrugs in an awkward, girlish way.

She has often stopped by for coffee and there *was* a woman here...she just never knew.

"She'll join us in a moment," I admit, putting her out of her misery. "Do you want to sit down?" I wave in the direction of the sofa.

"She?"

"Yes, Mother. She." My tone is dry as I try not to laugh. And for once she's silent as she wanders through the living room.

"I see you've had breakfast," she observes, eyeing the unwashed pans.

"Would you like some coffee?"

"No. Thank you, darling." She sits down. "I'll meet your... friend and then I'll go. I don't want to interrupt you. I had a feeling you'd be slaving away in your study. You work too hard, darling. I thought I might drag you away." She looks almost apologetic when I join her on the sofa.

"Don't worry." I'm thoroughly amused by her reaction. "Why aren't you at church this morning?"

"Carrick had to work, so we thought we'd go to evening Mass. I suppose it's too much to hope that you'll come with us."

I raise an eyebrow in cynical contempt. "Mother, you know that's not for me."

God and I turned our backs on each other a long time ago.

She sighs, but then Ana appears—dressed in her own clothes, standing shyly in the doorway. The tension between mother and son is averted, and I stand in relief. "Here she is."

Grace turns and gets to her feet.

"Mother, this is Anastasia Steele. Anastasia, this is Grace Trevelyan-Grey."

They shake hands.

"What a pleasure to meet you," Grace says with a little too much enthusiasm for my liking.

"Dr. Trevelyan-Grey," Ana says politely.

"Call me Grace," she says, all at once amiable and informal.

What? Already?

Grace continues, "I'm usually Dr. Trevelyan, and Mrs. Grey is my mother-in-law." She winks at Ana and sits down.

I motion to Ana and pat the cushion beside me, and she takes a seat.

"So how did you two meet?" Grace asks.

"Anastasia interviewed me for the student paper at WSU because I'm conferring the degrees there this week."

"So you're graduating this week?" Grace beams at Ana.

"Yes."

Ana's cell phone starts ringing and she excuses herself to answer it.

"And I'll be giving the commencement address," I say to Grace, but my attention is on Ana.

Who is it?

"Look, José, now's not a good time," I hear her say.

That fucking photographer. What does he want?

"I left a message for Elliot, then found out he was in Portland. I haven't seen him since last week..." Grace is saying.

Ana hangs up.

Grace continues as Ana approaches us again. "...and Elliot called to say you were around—I haven't seen you for two weeks, darling."

"Did he now?" I remark.

What does the photographer want?

"I thought we might have lunch together, but I can see you have other plans, and I don't want to interrupt your day." Grace stands, and for once I'm grateful that she's intuitive and can read a situation. She offers me her cheek again.

I kiss her goodbye.

"I have to drive Anastasia back to Portland."

"Of course, darling." Grace turns her bright—and if I'm not mistaken, grateful—smile on Ana.

It's irritating.

"Anastasia, it's been such a pleasure." Grace beams and takes Ana's hand. "I do hope we meet again."

"Mrs. Grey?" Taylor appears on the threshold of the room.

“Thank you, Taylor,” Grace responds, and he escorts her from the room and through the double doors to the foyer.

Well, that was interesting.

My mother’s always thought I was gay. But as she’s always respected my boundaries, she’s never asked me.

Well, now she knows.

Ana is worrying her bottom lip, radiating anxiety…as she should be.

“So the photographer called?” I sound gruff.

“Yes.”

“What did he want?”

“Just to apologize, you know—for Friday.”

“I see.” Maybe he wants another shot at her. The thought is displeasing.

Taylor clears his throat. “Mr. Grey, there’s an issue with the Darfur shipment.”

Shit. This is what I get for not checking my email this morning. I’ve been too preoccupied with Ana.

“*Charlie Tango* back at Boeing Field?” I ask Taylor.

“Yes, sir.”

Taylor acknowledges Ana with a nod. “Miss Steele.”

She gives him a broad smile and he leaves.

“Does he live here? Taylor?” Ana asks.

“Yes.”

Heading into the kitchen, I pick up my phone and quickly check my email. There’s a flagged message from Ros and a couple of texts. I call her immediately.

“Ros, what’s the issue?”

“Christian, hi. The report back from Darfur is not good. They can’t guarantee the safety of the shipments or road crew, and the State Department isn’t willing to sanction the relief without the NGO’s backing.”

Fuck this.

“I’m not having either crew put at risk.” Ros knows this.

“We could try to pull in mercenaries,” she says.

“No, cancel—”

"But the cost," she protests.

"We'll air-drop instead."

"I knew that's what you'd say, Christian. I have a plan in the works. It will be costly. In the meantime, the containers can go to Rotterdam out of Philly and we can take it from there. That's it."

"Good." I hang up. More support from the State Department would be helpful. I resolve to call Blandino to discuss this further.

My attention reverts to Miss Steele, who's standing in my living room, regarding me warily. I need to get us back on track.

Yes. The contract. That's the next step in our negotiation.

In my study, I gather the papers on my desk and stuff them into a manila envelope.

Ana's not moved from where I left her in the living room. Perhaps she's been thinking about the photographer… My mood takes a nosedive.

"This is the contract." I hold up the envelope. "Read it, and we'll discuss it next weekend. May I suggest you do some research so you know what's involved?" She looks from the manila envelope to me, her face pale. "That's if you agree, and I really hope you do," I add.

"Research?"

"You'll be amazed what you can find on the internet."

She frowns.

"What is it?" I ask.

"I don't have a computer. I usually use the computers at school. I'll see if I can use Kate's laptop."

No computer? How can a student not have a computer? Is she that broke? I hand her the envelope. "I'm sure I can, um…lend you one. Get your things. We'll drive back to Portland and grab some lunch on the way. I need to dress."

"I'll just make a call," she says, her voice soft and hesitant.

"The photographer?" I snap.

She looks guilty.

What the hell? "I don't like to share, Miss Steele. Remember that." I storm out of the room before I say anything else.

Is she hung up on him?

Was she just using me to break her in?

Fuck.

Maybe it's the money. That's a depressing thought…though she doesn't strike me as a gold digger. She was quite vehement about me not buying her any clothing. I remove my jeans and put on a pair of boxer briefs. My Brioni tie is on the floor. I stoop to pick it up.

She took to being tied up well… *There's hope, Grey. Hope.*

I stuff the tie and two others into a messenger bag along with socks, underwear, and condoms.

What am I doing?

Deep down I know I'm going to stay at The Heathman all next week…to be near her. I gather a couple of suits and shirts that Taylor can bring down later in the week. I'll need one for the graduation ceremony.

I slip on some clean jeans and grab a leather jacket, and my phone buzzes. It's a text from Elliot.

I'm driving back today in your car.
Hope that doesn't screw up your plans.

I text back.

No. I'm coming back to Portland now.
Let Taylor know when you arrive.

I buzz Taylor through the internal phone system.

"Mr. Grey?"

"Elliot is bringing the SUV back sometime this afternoon. Bring it down to Portland tomorrow. I'm going to stay at The Heathman until the graduation ceremony. I've left some clothes that I'd like you to bring down as well."

"Yes, sir."

"And call Audi. I may need the A3 sooner than I thought."

"It's ready, Mr. Grey."

"Oh. Good. Thanks."

So that's the car taken care of; now it's the computer. I call Barney, assuming he'll be in his office, and knowing he'll have a state-of-the-art laptop lying around.

"Mr. Grey?" he answers.

"What are you doing in the office, Barney? It's Sunday."

"I'm working on the tablet design. The solar-cell issue is bugging me."

"You need a home life."

Barney has the grace to laugh. "What can I do for you, Mr. Grey?"

"Do you have any new laptops?"

"I have two right here from Apple."

"Great. I need one."

"Sure thing."

"Can you set it up with an email account for Anastasia Steele? She'll be the owner."

"How are you spelling 'Steal'?"

"S-T-E-E-L-E."

"Cool."

"Great. Andrea will be in touch today to arrange delivery."

"Sure thing, sir."

"Thanks, Barney—and go home."

"Yes, sir."

I text Andrea with instructions to send the laptop to Ana's home address, then return to the living room. Ana is sitting on the sofa, fidgeting with her fingers. She gives me a cautious look and rises.

"Ready?" I ask.

She nods.

Taylor appears from his office. "Tomorrow, then," I tell him.

"Yes, sir. Which car are you taking, sir?"

"The R8."

"Safe trip, Mr. Grey. Miss Steele," Taylor says as he opens the foyer doors for us.

Ana fidgets beside me as we wait for the elevator, her teeth on her plump lower lip.

It reminds me of her teeth on my cock.

"What is it, Anastasia?" I ask as I reach out and pluck her chin. "Stop biting your lip, or I will fuck you in the elevator, and I don't care who gets in with us," I growl.

She's shocked, I think—though why would she be after all we've done… My mood softens.

"Christian, I have a problem," she says.

"Oh?"

In the elevator I press the button for the garage.

"W-well," she stutters, uncertain. Then she squares her shoulders. "I need to talk to Kate. I've so many questions about sex, and you're too involved. If you want me to do all these things, how do I know—?" She stops, as if weighing her words. "I just don't have any terms of reference."

Not this again. We've been over this. I don't want her talking to anyone. She's signed an NDA. But she's asked, again. So it must be important to her. "Talk to her if you must. Make sure she doesn't mention anything to Elliot."

"She wouldn't do that, and I wouldn't tell you anything she tells me about Elliot—if she were to tell me anything," she insists.

I remind her I'm not interested in Elliot's sex life but agree she can talk about what we've done so far. Her roommate would have my balls if she knew my real intentions.

"Okay," Ana says and gives me a bright smile.

"The sooner I have your submission the better, and we can stop all this."

"Stop all what?"

"You, defying me." I kiss her quickly and her lips on mine immediately make me feel better.

"Nice car," she says as we approach the R8 in the underground garage.

"I know." I flash her a quick grin, and I'm rewarded with another smile—before she rolls her eyes. I open the door for her, wondering if I should comment about the eye rolling.

"So what sort of car is this?" she asks when I'm behind the wheel.

"It's an Audi R8 Spyder. It's a lovely day; we can take the top down. There's a baseball cap in there. In fact there should be two."

I start the ignition and retract the roof, and the Boss fills the car. "Gotta love Bruce." I grin at Ana and steer the R8 out of her safe place in the garage.

Weaving in and out of traffic on I-5, we head toward Portland. Ana is quiet, listening to the music and staring out the window. It's difficult to see her expression, behind oversize Wayfarers and under my Mariners cap. The wind whistles over us as we speed past Boeing Field.

So far, this weekend has been unexpected. But what did I expect? I thought we'd have dinner, discuss the contract, and then what…? Perhaps fucking her was inevitable.

I glance across at her.

Yes… And I want to fuck her again.

I wish I knew what she was thinking. She gives little away, but I've learned some things about Ana. In spite of her inexperience, she's willing to learn. Who would have thought that under that shy exterior she has the soul of a siren? An image of her lips around my dick comes to mind and I suppress a moan.

Yeah…she's more than willing.

The thought is arousing.

I hope I can see her before next weekend.

Even now I'm itching to touch her again. Reaching across, I put my hand on her knee.

"Hungry?"

"Not particularly," she responds, subdued.

This is getting old.

"You must eat, Anastasia. I know a great place near Olympia. We'll stop there."

CUISINE SAUVAGE IS SMALL and crowded with couples and families enjoying Sunday brunch. With Ana's hand in mine, we follow the hostess to our table. The last time I came here was with Elena. I wonder what she'd make of Anastasia.

"I've not been here for a while. We don't get a choice—they cook whatever they've caught or gathered," I say, grimacing, feigning my horror.

Ana laughs.

Why do I feel ten feet tall when I make her laugh?

"Two glasses of the pinot grigio," I order from the waitress, who's making eyes at me from beneath blond bangs. It's annoying.

Ana scowls.

"What?" I ask, wondering if the waitress is annoying her, too.

"I wanted a Diet Coke."

Why didn't you say so? I frown. "The pinot grigio here is a decent wine. It will go well with the meal, whatever we get."

"Whatever we get?" she asks, her eyes round with alarm.

"Yes." And I give her my megawatt smile to make amends for not letting her order her own drink. I'm just not used to asking… "My mother liked you," I add, hoping this will please her and remembering Grace's reaction to Ana.

"Really?" she says, looking flattered.

"Oh yes. She's always thought I was gay."

"Why?"

"Because she's never seen me with a girl."

"Oh, not even one of the fifteen?"

"You remembered. No, none of the fifteen."

"Oh."

Yes…only you, baby. The thought is unsettling.

"You know, Anastasia, it's been a weekend of firsts for me, too."

"It has?"

"I've never slept with anyone, never had sex in my bed, never flown a girl in *Charlie Tango*, never introduced a woman to my mother. What are you doing to me?"

Yeah. What the hell are you doing to me? This isn't me.

The waitress brings us our chilled wine, and Ana immediately takes a quick sip, her bright eyes on me. "I've really enjoyed this weekend," she says with bashful delight in her voice.

I have, too, and I realize I haven't enjoyed a weekend for a while…since Susannah and I parted ways. I tell her so.

"What's vanilla sex?" she asks.

I laugh at her unexpected question and complete change of topic.

"Just straightforward sex, Anastasia. No toys, no add-ons." I shrug. "You know—well, actually you don't, but that's what it means."

"Oh," she says, and she looks a little crestfallen.

What now?

The waitress diverts us, putting down two soup bowls full of greenery. "Nettle soup," she announces and struts back into the kitchen.

We glance at each other, then back at the soup. A quick taste informs us both that it's delicious. Ana giggles at my exaggerated expression of relief.

"That's a lovely sound," I say softly.

"Why have you never had vanilla sex before? Have you always done…what you've done?" She's as inquisitive as ever.

"Sort of." And then I wonder if I should expand on this. More than anything, I want her to be forthcoming with me; I want her to trust me. I'm never this candid, but I think I can trust her so I choose my words carefully.

"One of my mother's friends seduced me when I was fifteen."

"Oh." Ana's spoon pauses midway from the bowl to her mouth.

"She had very particular tastes. I was her submissive for six years."

"Oh," she breathes.

"So I do know what it involves, Anastasia." *More than you know.* "I didn't really have a run-of-the-mill introduction to sex." I couldn't be touched. I still can't.

I wait for her reaction but she continues with her soup, mulling over this tidbit of information. "So you never dated anyone in college?" she asks when she's finished her last spoonful.

"No."

The waitress interrupts us to clear our empty bowls. Ana waits for her to leave. "Why?"

"Do you really want to know?"

"Yes."

"I didn't want to. She was all I wanted, needed. And besides, she'd have beaten the shit out of me."

She blinks a couple of times as she absorbs this news. "So if she was a friend of your mother's, how old was she?"

"Old enough to know better."

"Do you still see her?" She sounds shocked.

"Yes."

"Do you still…er…" She blushes crimson, her mouth turned down.

"No," I say quickly. I don't want her to have the wrong idea about my relationship with Elena. "She's a very good friend," I reassure her.

"Oh. Does your mother know?"

"Of course not."

My mother would kill me—and Elena, too.

The waitress returns with the main entrée: venison. Ana takes a long sip of her wine. "But it can't have been full-time?" She's ignoring her food.

"Well, it was, though I didn't see her all the time. It was… difficult. After all, I was still at school and then at college. Eat up, Anastasia."

"I'm really not hungry, Christian," she says.

I narrow my eyes. "Eat." I keep my voice low as I try to check my temper.

"Give me a moment," she says, her tone as quiet as mine.

What's her problem? Elena?

"Okay," I agree, wondering if I've told her too much, and I take a bite of my venison.

Finally, she picks up her cutlery and starts eating.

Good.

"Is this what our, um…relationship will be like?" she asks. "You ordering me around?" She scrutinizes the plate of food in front of her.

"Yes."

"I see." She tosses her ponytail over her shoulder.

"And what's more, you'll want me to."

"It's a big step," she says.

"It is." I close my eyes. I want to do this with her, now more than ever. What can I say to convince her to give our arrangement a try?

"Anastasia, you have to go with your gut. Do the research, read the contract. I'm happy to discuss any aspect. I'll be in Portland until Friday if you want to talk about it before then. Call me. Maybe we can have dinner—say, Wednesday? I really want to make this work. In fact, I've never wanted anything as much as I want this."

Whoa. Big speech, Grey. Did you just ask her on a date?

"What happened to the fifteen?" she asks.

"Various things, but it boils down to incompatibility."

"And you think that I might be compatible with you?"

"Yes."

I hope so…

"So you're not seeing any of them anymore?"

"No, Anastasia, I'm not. I am monogamous in my relationships."

"I see."

"Do the research, Anastasia."

She puts her knife and fork down, signaling she's finished her meal.

"That's it? That's all you're going to eat?"

She nods, placing her hands in her lap, and her mouth sets in that mulish way she has…and I know it will be a fight to persuade her to clean her plate. No wonder she's so slim. Her eating issues will be something to work on, if she agrees to be mine. As I continue to eat, her eyes dart to me every few seconds and a slow flush stains her cheeks.

Oh, what's this?

"I'd give anything to know what you're thinking right at this moment." She's clearly thinking about sex. "I can guess," I tease.

"I'm glad you can't read my mind."

"Your mind, no, Anastasia, but your body—*that* I've gotten to know quite well since yesterday." I give her a wolfish grin and ask for the check.

When we leave, her hand is firmly in mine. She's quiet—deep in thought, it seems—and remains so all the way to Vancouver. I've given her a great deal to think about.

But she's also given me a great deal to think about.

Will she want to do this with me?

Damn, I hope so.

It's still light when we arrive at her home, but the sun is sinking to the horizon and shining pink and pearl light on Mount St. Helens. Ana and Kate live in a scenic spot with an amazing view.

"Do you want to come in?" she asks after I've switched off the engine.

"No. I have work to do." I know that if I accept her invitation I'll be crossing a line I'm not prepared to cross. I'm not boyfriend material—and I don't want to give her any false expectations of the kind of relationship she'll have with me.

Her face falls, and deflated, she looks away.

She doesn't want me to go.

It's humbling. Reaching across, I grasp her hand and kiss her knuckles, hoping to take the sting out of my rejection.

"Thank you for this weekend, Anastasia. It's been…the best." She turns shining eyes to me. "Wednesday?" I continue. "I'll pick you up from work, from wherever?"

"Wednesday," she says, and the hope in her voice is disconcerting.

Shit. It's not a date.

I kiss her hand again and climb out of the car to open her door. I have to get out of here before I do something I'll regret.

When she gets out of the car, she brightens, at odds with how she looked a moment ago. She marches up to her front door but before reaching the steps she turns suddenly. "Oh, by the way, I'm wearing your underwear," she says in triumph, and she yanks the waistband up so I can see the words *Polo* and *Ralph* peeking over her jeans.

She's stolen my underwear!

I'm stunned. And in that instant I want nothing more than to see her in my boxer briefs…and only them.

She tosses back her hair and swaggers into her apartment, leaving me standing on the curb, staring like a fool.

Shaking my head, I climb back into the car, and as I start the engine I cannot help my shit-eating grin.

I hope she says yes.

I FINISH MY WORK and take a sip of the fine Sancerre, delivered from room service by the woman with dark, dark eyes. Trawling through my emails and answering where required has been a welcome distraction from thoughts of Anastasia. And now I'm pleasantly tired. Is it the five hours of work? Or all the sexual activity last night and this morning? Memories of the delectable Miss Steele invade my mind: in *Charlie Tango*, in my bed, in my bath, dancing around my kitchen. And to think it all started here on Friday…and now she's considering my proposal.

Has she read the contract? Is she doing her homework?

I check my phone once again for a text or a missed call but, of course, there's nothing.

Will she agree?

I hope so…

Andrea has sent me Ana's new email address and assured me the laptop will be delivered tomorrow morning. With that in mind, I type out an email.

From: Christian Grey
Subject: Your New Computer
Date: May 22 2011 23:15
To: Anastasia Steele

Dear Miss Steele,
I trust you slept well. I hope that you put this laptop to good use, as discussed.

I look forward to dinner Wednesday.

Happy to answer any questions before then, via email, should you so desire.

Christian Grey
CEO, Grey Enterprises Holdings, Inc.

The email doesn't bounce, so the address is live. I wonder how Ana will react in the morning when she reads it. I hope she likes the laptop. Guess I'll know tomorrow. Picking up my latest read, I settle onto the sofa. It's a book by two renowned economists who examine why the poor think and behave the way they do. An image of a young woman brushing out her long, dark hair comes to mind; her hair shines in the light from the cracked, yellowed window, and the air is filled with dancing dust motes. She's singing softly, like a child.

I shudder.

Don't go there, Grey.

I open the book and start to read.

MONDAY, MAY 23, 2011

It's after one in the morning when I go to bed. Staring at the ceiling, I'm tired, relaxed, but also excited, anticipating what the week will bring. I hope to have a new project: Miss Anastasia Steele.

MY FEET POUND THE sidewalk on Main Street as I run toward the river. It's 6:35 a.m., and the sun's rays are shimmering through the high-rise buildings. The sidewalk trees are newly green with spring leaves; the air is clean, the traffic quiet. I've slept well. "O Fortuna" from Orff's *Carmina Burana* is blaring in my ears. Today the streets are paved with possibility.

Will she respond to my email?

It's too early, far too early for any response, but feeling lighter than I have for weeks, I run past the statue of the elk and toward the Willamette.

BY 7:45 I'M IN front of my laptop, having showered and ordered breakfast. I email Andrea to let her know I'll be working from Portland for the week and to ask her to reschedule any meetings so they can take place by phone or videoconference. I email Gail to let her know I won't be home until Thursday evening at the earliest. I work through my inbox and find among other things a proposal for a joint venture with a shipyard in Taiwan. I forward it to Ros to add to the agenda of items we need to discuss.

Then I turn to my other outstanding matter: Elena. She's texted me a couple of times over the weekend and I've not replied.

From: Christian Grey
Subject: The Weekend
Date: May 23 2011 08:15
To: Elena Lincoln

Good morning, Elena.
Sorry not to get back to you. I've been busy all weekend, and I'll be in Portland all this week. I don't know about next weekend, either, but if I'm free, I'll let you know.

Latest results for the beauty business look promising.

Good going, Ma'am…

Best
C

Christian Grey
CEO, Grey Enterprises Holdings, Inc.

I press send, wondering again what Elena would make of Ana… and vice versa. There's a ping from my laptop as a new email arrives.

It's from Ana.

From: Anastasia Steele
Subject: Your New Computer (on loan)
Date: May 23 2011 08:20
To: Christian Grey

I slept very well, thank you—for some strange reason—*Sir.*
I understood that this computer was on loan, ergo not mine.

Ana

"Sir" with a capital S; the girl has been reading, and possibly researching. And she's still talking to me. I grin stupidly at the email. This is good news. Though she is also telling me she doesn't want the computer.

Well, that's frustrating.

I shake my head, amused.

From: Christian Grey
Subject: Your New Computer (on loan)
Date: May 23 2011 08:22
To: Anastasia Steele

The computer is on loan. Indefinitely, Miss Steele.

I note from your tone that you have read the documentation I gave you.

Do you have any questions so far?

Christian Grey
CEO, Grey Enterprises Holdings, Inc.

I hit send. How long will it be before she responds? I resume reading my email as a distraction while I wait for her reply. There's an executive summary from Fred, the head of my telecom division, about the development of our solar-powered tablet—one of my pet projects. It's ambitious but few of my business ventures matter more than this one and I'm excited about it. Bringing affordable technology to developing nations is something I'm determined to do.

There's a ping from my computer.

Another email from Miss Steele.

From: Anastasia Steele
Subject: Inquiring Minds
Date: May 23 2011 08:25
To: Christian Grey

I have many questions, but not suitable for email, and some of us have to work for a living.
I do not want or need a computer indefinitely.
Until later, good day. *Sir.*

Ana

The tone of her email makes me smile, but it seems she's off to work, so this might be the last one for a while. Her reluctance to accept the damned computer is annoying. But I suppose it shows she's not acquisitive. She's no gold digger—rare among the women I've known…yet Leila was the same.

"Sir, I am not deserving of this beautiful dress."

"You are. Take it. And I'll not hear another word on this. Understand?"

"Yes, Master."

"Good. And the style will suit you."

Ah, Leila. She was a good submissive, but she became too attached and I was the wrong man. Fortunately, that wasn't for long. She's married now and happy. I turn my attention back to Ana's email and reread.

"Some of us have to work for a living."

The sassy wench is implying I don't do any work.

Well to hell with that!

I spy Fred's rather dry summary report open on my desktop and decide to set the record straight with Ana.

From: Christian Grey
Subject: Your New Computer (again on loan)
Date: May 23 2011 08:26
To: Anastasia Steele

Laters, baby.

P.S. I work for a living, too.

Christian Grey
CEO, Grey Enterprises Holdings, Inc.

I find it impossible to concentrate on my work, waiting for the telltale ping to announce a new email from Ana. When it comes, I look up immediately—but it's from Elena. And I'm surprised by my disappointment.

From: Elena Lincoln
Subject: The Weekend
Date: May 23 2011 08:33
To: Christian Grey

Christian, you work too hard. What's in Portland? Work?
Ex

ELENA LINCOLN
ESCLAVA
For The Beauty That Is You™

Do I tell her? If I do, she'll call immediately with questions, and I'm not ready to divulge my weekend experiences yet. I type her a quick email saying it's work and get back to my reading.

Andrea calls me at nine and we run through my schedule. As I'm in Portland, I ask her to set up a meeting with the president and the assistant vice president of economic development at WSU to discuss the soil science project we've set up and their need for additional funding in the next fiscal year. She agrees to cancel all my social engagements this week and then connects me through to my first videoconference of the day.

AT 3:00 I'M PORING over some tablet design schematics that Barney has sent me when I'm disturbed by a knock at my door. The interruption is annoying but for a moment I hope it's Miss Steele. It's Taylor.

"Hello." I hope my voice doesn't reveal my disappointment.

"I have your clothes, Mr. Grey," he says politely.

"Come in. Can you hang them in the closet? I'm expecting my next conference call."

"Certainly, sir." He hurries into the bedroom, carrying a couple of suit bags and a duffel.

When he returns I'm still waiting for my call.

"Taylor, I don't think I'm going to need you for the next couple of days. Why don't you take the time to see your daughter?"

"That's very good of you, sir, but her mother and I—" He stops, embarrassed.

"Ah. Like that, is it?" I ask.

He nods. "Yes, sir. It will take some negotiating."

"Okay. Would Wednesday be better?"

"I'll ask. Thank you, sir."

"Anything I can do to help?"

"You do enough, sir."

He doesn't want to talk about this. "Okay. I think I'm going to need a printer. Can you arrange it?"

"Yes, sir." He nods. As he leaves, closing the door softly behind him, I frown. I hope his ex-wife isn't giving him grief. I pay for his daughter's schooling as another incentive for him to stay in my employment; he's a good man, and I don't want to lose him. The phone rings—it's my conference call with Ros and Senator Blandino.

MY LAST CALL WRAPS up at 5:20. Stretching in my chair, I think about how productive I've been today. It's amazing how much more I get done when I'm not in the office. Only a couple of reports to read and I'm finished for the day. As I look out the window at the early evening sky, my mind strays to a certain potential submissive.

I wonder how her day at Clayton's has been, pricing cable ties and measuring out lengths of rope. I hope one day I'll get to use them on her. The thought conjures images of her tethered in my playroom. I dwell on this for a moment…then quickly send her an email. All this waiting, working, and emailing is making me restless. I know how I'd like to release this pent-up energy, but I have to settle for a run.

From: Christian Grey
Subject: Working for a Living
Date: May 23 2011 17:24
To: Anastasia Steele

Dear Miss Steele,
I do hope you had a good day at work.

Christian Grey
CEO, Grey Enterprises Holdings, Inc.

I change back into my running gear. Taylor has brought me two more pairs of sweatpants. I'm sure that's Gail's doing. As I head toward the door I check my email. She's replied.

From: Anastasia Steele
Subject: Working for a Living
Date: May 23 2011 17:48
To: Christian Grey

Sir... I had a very good day at work.
Thank you.

Ana

But she hasn't done her homework. I email her back.

From: Christian Grey
Subject: Do the Work!
Date: May 23 2011 17:50
To: Anastasia Steele

Miss Steele,
Delighted you had a good day.

While you are emailing, you are not researching.

Christian Grey
CEO, Grey Enterprises Holdings, Inc.

And rather than leave the room, I wait for her reply. She doesn't keep me waiting long.

From: Anastasia Steele
Subject: Nuisance
Date: May 23 2011 17:53
To: Christian Grey

Mr. Grey, stop emailing me, and I can start my assignment.
I'd like another A.

Ana

I laugh out loud. *Yes.* That A was something else. Closing my eyes, I see and feel her mouth around my cock once more.

Fuck.

Bringing my errant body to heel, I press send on my reply and wait.

From: Christian Grey
Subject: Impatient
Date: May 23 2011 17:55
To: Anastasia Steele

Miss Steele,
Stop emailing *me*—and do your assignment.

I'd like to award another A.

The first one was so well deserved. ;)

Christian Grey
CEO, Grey Enterprises Holdings, Inc.

Her response is not as immediate, and feeling a little crest-fallen, I turn away and decide to go on my run. But as I open the door the ping from my inbox pulls me back.

From: Anastasia Steele
Subject: Internet Research
Date: May 23 2011 17:59
To: Christian Grey

Mr. Grey,
What would you suggest I put into a search engine?

Ana

Shit! Why didn't I think about this? I could have given her some books. Numerous websites spring to mind—but I don't want to frighten her off.

Perhaps she should start with the most vanilla…

From: Christian Grey
Subject: Internet Research
Date: May 23 2011 18:02
To: Anastasia Steele

Miss Steele,
Always start with Wikipedia.

No more emails unless you have questions.

Understood?

Christian Grey
CEO, Grey Enterprises Holdings, Inc.

I get up from my desk, thinking she won't respond, but as usual she surprises me and does. I can't resist.

From: Anastasia Steele
Subject: Bossy!
Date: May 23 2011 18:04
To: Christian Grey

Yes…*Sir.*
You are so bossy.

Ana

Damned right, baby.

From: Christian Grey
Subject: In Control
Date: May 23 2011 18:06
To: Anastasia Steele

Anastasia, you have no idea.

Well, maybe an inkling now.

Do the work.

Christian Grey
CEO, Grey Enterprises Holdings, Inc.

Show some restraint, Grey. Before she can distract me again, I'm out the door. With the Foo Fighters blaring in my ears I run to the river. I've seen the Willamette at dawn; now I want to see it at dusk. It's a fine evening: couples are walking by the riverside, some sitting on the grass, and a few tourists are cycling up and down the concourse. I avoid them, the music blasting in my ears.

Miss Steele has questions. She is still in the game—this is not a no. Our email exchange has given me hope.

As I run under the Hawthorne Bridge I reflect on how at ease she is with the written word, more so than when she's speaking. Maybe this is her preferred medium of expression. Well, she has been studying English literature. I'm hoping by the time I get back there'll be another email, maybe with questions, maybe with some more of her sassy banter.

Yeah. That's something to look forward to.

As I sprint down Main Street I dare to hope that she'll accept my proposition. The thought is exciting, invigorating even, and I pick up my pace, sprinting back to The Heathman.

IT'S 8:15 WHEN I sit back in my dining chair. I've eaten the wild Oregon salmon for dinner, courtesy of Miss Dark, Dark Eyes again, and I still have half a glass of Sancerre to finish. My laptop is open and powered up, should any important emails arrive. I pick up the report on the brownfield sites in Detroit that I've printed out. "It would have to be Detroit," I grumble out loud and start to read.

A few minutes later, I hear a ping.

It's an email with "Shocked of WSUV" written in the subject line. The heading makes me sit up.

From: Anastasia Steele
Subject: Shocked of WSUV
Date: May 23 2011 20:33
To: Christian Grey

Okay, I've seen enough.
It was nice knowing you.

Ana

Shit!

I read it again.

Fuck.

It's a no. I stare at the screen in disbelief.

That's it?

No discussion?

Nothing.

Just "It was nice knowing you"?

What. The. Fuck.

I sit back in my chair, dumbfounded.

Nice?

Nice.

NICE.

She thought it was more than nice when her head was thrown back as she came.

Don't be so hasty, Grey.

Maybe it's a joke?

Some joke!

I pull my laptop toward me to write a reply.

From: Christian Grey
Subject: NICE?
Date: May 23 2011
To: Anastasia Steele

But as I stare at the screen, my fingers hovering over the keys, I can't think of what to say.

How could she dismiss me so easily?

Her first fuck.

Get it together, Grey. What are your options? Maybe I should pay her a visit, just to make sure it's a no. Maybe I can persuade her otherwise. I certainly don't know what to say to this email. Perhaps she's looked at some particularly hardcore sites. Why didn't I give her a few books? I don't believe this. She needs to look me in the eye and say no.

Yep. I rub my chin as I formulate a plan, and moments later I'm in my closet, retrieving my tie.

That tie.

This deal isn't dead yet. From my messenger bag I take some condoms and slide them into the back pocket of my pants, then grab my jacket and a bottle of white wine from the minibar. Damn, it's a chardonnay—but it will have to do. Snatching my room key, I close the door and head toward the elevator to collect my car from the valet.

AS I PULL UP in the R8 outside the apartment she shares with Kavanagh, I wonder if this is a wise move. I've never visited any of my previous submissives at their homes—they always came to me. I'm pushing all the boundaries I've set for myself.

Opening the door of the car and climbing out, I'm uneasy; it's reckless and too presumptuous of me to come here. Then again, I've already been here twice, though for only a few minutes. If she does agree, I'll have to manage her expectations. This won't happen again.

Getting ahead of yourself, Grey.

You're here because you think it's a no.

Kavanagh answers when I knock at the door. She's surprised to see me. "Hi, Christian. Ana didn't say you were coming over." She stands aside to let me enter. "She's in her room. I'll call her."

"No. I'd like to surprise her." I give her my most earnest and endearing look and in response she blinks a couple of times. *Whoa. That was easy. Who would have thought?* How gratifying. "Where's her room?"

"Through there, the first door." She points to a door off the empty living room.

"Thanks."

Leaving my jacket and the chilled wine on one of the packing crates, I open the door to find a small hallway with a couple of rooms off it. I assume one is a bathroom, so I knock on the other door. After a beat, I open it and there's Ana, sitting at a small desk, reading what looks like the contract. She has her earbuds in as she idly drums her fingers to an unheard beat. Standing there for a moment, I watch her. Her face is scrunched in concentration; her hair is braided and she's wearing sweats. Perhaps she's been for a run this evening...perhaps she's suffering from excess energy, too. The thought is pleasing. Her room is small, neat, and girlish: all whites, creams, and baby blues, and bathed in the soft glow of her bedside lamp. It's also a little empty, but I spy a closed packing crate with *Ana's room* scrawled on the top. At least she has a double bed—with a white wrought-iron bedstead. *Yes.* That has possibilities.

Ana suddenly jumps, startled by my presence.

Yes: I'm here because of your email.

She pulls out her earbuds and the sound of tinny music fills the silence between us.

"Good evening, Anastasia."

She stares at me dumbfounded, her eyes widening.

"I felt that your email warranted a reply in person." I try to keep my voice neutral.

Her mouth opens and closes, but she remains mute.

Miss Steele is speechless. This I like. "May I sit?"

She nods, continuing to stare in disbelief as I perch on her bed.

"I wondered what your bedroom would look like," I offer as an icebreaker, though chitchat is not my area of expertise. She scans her room as if seeing it for the first time. "It's very serene and peaceful in here," I add, though I feel anything but serene or peaceful right now. I want to know why she's said no to my proposal with no discussion whatsoever.

"How…?" she whispers, but she stops, her disbelief still evident in her quiet tone.

"I'm still at The Heathman." She knows this.

"Would you like a drink?" she squeaks.

"No thank you, Anastasia." *Good.* She's found her manners. But I want to get on with the business at hand: her alarming email. "So, it was *nice* knowing me?" I emphasize the word that offends me most in that sentence.

Nice? Really?

She examines her hands in her lap, her fingers nervously tapping against her thighs. "I thought you'd reply by email," she says, her voice as small as her room.

"Are you biting your lower lip deliberately?" I inquire, my voice sterner than I'd intended.

"I wasn't aware I was biting my lip," she whispers, her face pale.

We gaze at each other.

And the air almost crackles between us.

Fuck.

Can't you feel this, Ana? This tension. This attraction. My breathing shallows as I watch her pupils dilate. Slowly, deliberately,

I reach for her hair and gently tug on the elastic, freeing one of her braids. She watches me, captivated, her eyes never leaving mine. I loosen her second braid.

"So you decided on some exercise?" My fingers trace the soft shell of her ear. With great care, I tug and squeeze the plump skin of her earlobe. She's not wearing earrings, though she does have pierced ears. I wonder what a diamond would look like twinkling there. I ask her why she's been exercising, keeping my voice low. Her breathing quickens.

"I needed time to think," she says.

"Think about what, Anastasia?"

"You."

"And you decided that it was nice knowing me? Do you mean knowing me in the biblical sense?"

Her cheeks pink. "I didn't think you were familiar with the Bible."

"I went to Sunday school, Anastasia. It taught me a great deal."

Catechism. Guilt. And that God abandoned me long ago.

"I don't remember reading about nipple clamps in the Bible. Perhaps you were taught from a modern translation," she goads me, her eyes shining and provocative.

Oh, that smart mouth.

"Well, I thought I should come and remind you how *nice* it was knowing me." The challenge is there in my voice and now between us. Her mouth drops open in surprise, but I glide my fingers to her chin and coax it closed. "What do you say to that, Miss Steele?" I whisper as we stare at each other.

Suddenly she launches herself at me.

Shit.

Somehow I grab her arms before she can touch me and twist so she lands on the bed, beneath me, and I have her arms stretched out above her head. Turning her face to mine, I kiss her, hard, my tongue exploring and reclaiming her. Her body rises in response as she kisses me back with equal ardor.

Oh, Ana. What you do to me.

Once she's squirming for more, I stop and gaze down at her. It's time for plan B.

"Trust me?" I ask when her eyelids flutter open.

She nods enthusiastically. From the back pocket of my pants I extract the tie so she can see it, then sit astride her and, taking both of her offered wrists, bind her to one of the iron spindles of her bedstead.

She wriggles beneath me, testing her bindings, but the tie holds fast. She's not escaping. "That's better." I smile with relief because I have her where I want her. Now to undress her.

Grabbing her right foot, I start to undo her sneakers.

"No," she grumbles with embarrassment, trying to withdraw her foot, and I know it's because she's been running and she doesn't want me to remove her shoes. Does she think perspiration would put me off?

Sweetheart!

"If you struggle, I'll tie your feet, too. If you make a noise, Anastasia, I will gag you. Keep quiet. Katherine is probably outside listening right now."

She stops. And I know that my instincts are right. She's worried about her feet. When will she understand that none of that stuff bothers me?

Quickly I remove her shoes, socks, and sweatpants. Then shift her so she's stretched out and lying on her sheets, not that dainty, homemade quilt. We're going to make a mess.

Stop biting that fucking lip.

I brush my finger over her mouth as a carnal warning. She purses her lips in the semblance of a kiss, prompting my smile. She's a beautiful, sensual creature.

Now that she's where I want her, I take my shoes and socks off, undo the top button of my pants, and remove my shirt. She doesn't take her eyes off me.

"I think you've seen too much." I want to keep her guessing, not knowing what's coming next. It will be a carnal treat. I've not blindfolded her before, so this will count toward her training. *That's if she says yes...*

Sitting astride her once more, I grab the hem of her T-shirt and roll it up her body. But rather than taking it off, I leave it rolled over her eyes: an effective blindfold.

She looks fantastic, laid out and bound. "Mmm, this just gets better and better. I'm going to get a drink," I whisper and kiss her. She gasps as I climb off the bed. Outside her room, I leave her door slightly ajar and enter the living room to retrieve the bottle of wine.

Kavanagh looks up from where she's sitting on the sofa, reading, and her eyebrows rise in surprise. *Don't tell me you've never seen a shirtless man, Kavanagh, because I won't believe you.* "Kate, where would I find glasses, ice, and a corkscrew?" I ask, ignoring her scandalized expression.

"Um. In the kitchen. I'll get them for you. Where's Ana?"

Ah, some concern for her friend. Good.

"She's a little tied up at the moment, but she wants a drink." I grab the bottle of chardonnay.

"Oh, I see," Kavanagh says, and I follow her into the kitchen, where she points to some glasses on the counter. All the glasses are out, I assume to be packed for their move. She hands me a corkscrew and from the fridge she removes a tray of ice and breaks out the ice cubes.

"We still have to pack in here. You know Elliot is helping us move." Her tone is critical.

"Is he?" I sound uninterested as I open the wine. "Just put the ice in the glasses." With my chin I indicate two glasses. "It's a chardonnay. It'll be more drinkable with the ice."

"I figured you for a red-wine kind of guy," she says when I pour the wine. "Are you going to come help Ana with the move?" Her eyes flash. She's challenging me.

Shut her down now, Grey.

"No. I can't." My voice is clipped, because she's pissing me off, trying to make me feel guilty. Her lips thin, and I turn around to leave the kitchen, but not before I catch the disapproval in her face.

Fuck off, Kavanagh.

No way am I going to help. Ana and I don't have that kind of relationship. Besides, I can't spare the time.

I return to Ana's room and shut the door behind me, blotting out Kavanagh and her disdain. Immediately I'm appeased by the sight of the enchanting Ana Steele, breathless and waiting, on her bed. Setting the wine down on her bedside table, I take the foil packet out of my pants and place it beside the wine, then drop my pants and underwear on the floor, freeing my erection.

I take a sip of wine—surprisingly, it's not bad—and gaze down at Ana. She hasn't said a word. Her face is turned toward me, her lips parted with anticipation. Taking the glass, I sit astride her once more. "Are you thirsty, Anastasia?"

"Yes," she whispers.

Taking a sip of wine, I lean down and kiss her, pouring the wine into her mouth. She laps it up, and deep in her throat I hear a faint hum of appreciation.

"More?" I ask.

She nods, smiling, and I oblige.

"Let's not go too far; we know your capacity for alcohol is limited, Anastasia," I tease, and her mouth splits in the widest of grins. Leaning down, I let her have another drink from my mouth, and she wriggles beneath me.

"Is this *nice*?" I ask as I lay down beside her.

She stills, all seriousness now, but her lips part as she inhales sharply.

I take another swig of wine, this time with two ice cubes. When I kiss her, I push a small shard of ice between her lips, then lay a trail of icy kisses down her sweet-smelling skin from her throat to her navel. There, I place the other shard, and a little wine.

She sucks in a breath.

"Now you have to keep still. If you move, Anastasia, you'll get wine all over the bed." My voice is low, and I kiss her again just above her navel. Her hips shift. "Oh no. If you spill the wine, I will punish you, Miss Steele."

She moans in response and pulls at the tie.

All good things, Ana…

I release each of her breasts from her bra so they're supported by the underwire cups; her breasts are pert and vulnerable, just how I like them. Slowly I tease them both with my lips.

"How *nice* is this?" I whisper and blow gently on one nipple. Her mouth slackens in a silent "Ah." Taking another piece of ice in my mouth, I trace a leisurely line down her sternum to her nipple and circle it couple of times with the ice. She moans beneath me. Transferring the ice to my fingers, I continue to torture each nipple with cool lips and the remaining ice cube that's melting in my fingers.

Whining and panting beneath me, she's tensing but managing to stay still. "If you spill the wine, I won't let you come," I warn.

"Oh. Please. Christian. Sir. Please," she begs.

Oh, to hear her use those words.

There's hope.

This is not a no.

I skim my fingers over her body toward her panties, teasing her soft skin. Suddenly her pelvis flexes, spilling the wine and the now-melted ice from her navel. I move quickly to lap it up, kissing and sucking it off her body.

"Oh dear, Anastasia, you moved. What am I going to do to you?" I slip my fingers into her panties and brush her clitoris as I do.

"Ah!" she whines.

"Oh, baby," I whisper with reverence. She's wet. Very wet.

See. See how nice *this is?*

I push my index and middle finger inside her and she trembles.

"Ready for me so soon," I murmur and push my fingers slowly in and out of her, eliciting a long sweet moan. Her pelvis starts lifting to meet my fingers.

Oh, she wants this.

"You are a greedy girl." My voice is still low and she matches the pace I'm setting as I begin to circle her clitoris with my thumb, teasing and tormenting her.

She cries out, her body bucking beneath me. I want to see her expression, and reaching up with my other hand, I slip her T-shirt off her head. She opens her eyes, blinking in the soft light.

"I want to touch you," she says, her voice husky and full of need.

"I know," I breathe against her lips and kiss her, all the while keeping up the relentless rhythm with my fingers and thumb. She tastes of wine and need and Ana. And she kisses me back with a hunger I've not felt in her before. I cradle the top of her head, keeping her in place, and continue to kiss and finger-fuck her. As her legs stiffen, I drop the pace of my hand.

Oh, no, baby. You're not coming yet.

I do this three more times while kissing her warm, sweet mouth. The fifth time I still my fingers inside her, and I hum soft and slow in her ear, "This is your punishment, so close and yet so far. Is this *nice*?"

"Please," she whimpers.

God, I love to hear her beg.

"How shall I fuck you, Anastasia?"

My fingers start again and her legs begin to quiver, and I gentle my hand once more.

"Please," she breathes again, the word so low I barely hear her.

"What do you want, Anastasia?"

"You…now," she pleads.

"Shall I fuck you this way, or this way, or this way? There's an endless choice," I murmur. Withdrawing my hand, I snatch the condom from the bedside table and kneel up between her legs. Keeping my eyes on hers, I pull her panties off and discard them on the floor. Her eyes are dark, full of promise and longing. They widen as I roll the condom on.

"How *nice* is this?" I ask as I wrap my fist around my erection.

"I meant it as a joke," she whimpers.

Joke?

Thank. The. Lord.

All is not lost.

"A joke?" I query as my fist slides up and down my cock.

"Yes. Please, Christian," she begs.

"Are you laughing now?"

"No." Her voice is barely audible, but the little shake of her head tells me all I need to know.

Watching her needing me…I could explode in my hand just looking at her. Grabbing her, I flip her over, keeping her fine, fine ass in the air. It's too tempting. I slap her cheek, hard, then plunge inside her.

Oh fuck. She's so ready.

She tightens around me and cries out as she comes.

Fuck. That's too quick.

Holding her hips in place, I fuck her, hard, riding through her orgasm. Gritting my teeth, I grind into her, again and again, as she begins to build once more.

Come on, Ana. Again, I will her, pounding on.

She moans and whimpers beneath me, a sheen of sweat appearing on her back.

Her legs begin to quiver.

She's close.

"Come on, Anastasia, again," I growl, and by some miracle her orgasm spirals through her body and into mine. *Thank fuck.* Wordlessly I come, pouring myself into her.

Sweet Lord. I collapse on top of her. That was exhausting.

"How *nice* was that?" I hiss against her ear as I draw air into my lungs.

As she lies flat on the bed, panting, I pull out of her and remove the wretched condom. I get off the bed and quickly get dressed. When I'm done, I reach down and unfasten my tie, freeing her. Turning over, she stretches her hands and fingers and readjusts her bra. Once I cover her with the comforter I lie down beside her, propped up on my elbow.

"That was really nice," she says with a mischievous smile.

"There's that word again." I smirk at her.

"You don't like that word?"

"No. It doesn't do it for me at all."

"Oh—I don't know…it seems to have a very beneficial effect on you."

"I'm a beneficial effect now, am I? Could you wound my ego any further, Miss Steele?"

"I don't think there's anything wrong with your ego." Her frown is fleeting.

"You think?"

Dr. Flynn would have plenty to say about that.

"Why don't you like to be touched?" she asks, her voice sweet and soft.

"I just don't." I kiss her forehead to distract her from this line of questioning. "So, that email was your idea of a joke?"

She gives me a coy look and an apologetic shrug.

"I see. So you are still considering my proposition?"

"Your indecent proposal...yes, I am."

Well, thank fuck for that.

Our deal is still in play. My relief is palpable; I can almost taste it.

"I have issues, though," she adds.

"I'd be disappointed if you didn't."

"I was going to email them to you, but you kind of interrupted me."

"Coitus interruptus."

"See? I knew you had a sense of humor somewhere in there." The light in her eyes dances with mirth.

"Only certain things are funny, Anastasia. I thought you were saying no—no discussion at all."

"I don't know yet. I haven't made up my mind. Will you collar me?"

Her question surprises me. "You have been doing your research. I don't know, Anastasia. I've never collared anyone."

"Were you collared?" she asks.

"Yes."

"By Mrs. Robinson?"

"Mrs. Robinson?" I laugh out loud. Anne Bancroft in *The Graduate*. "I'll tell her you said that; she'll love it."

"You still talk to her regularly?" Her voice is high-pitched with shock and indignation.

"Yes." Why's that such a big deal?

"I see." Now her voice is clipped. She's mad? Why? I don't

understand. "So you have someone you can discuss your alternative lifestyle with, but I'm not allowed." Her tone is petulant, but once again she's calling me out on my shit.

"I don't think I've ever thought about it like that. Mrs. Robinson is part of that lifestyle. I told you, she's a good friend now. If you'd like, I can introduce you to one of my former subs. You could talk to her."

"Is this *your* idea of a joke?" she demands.

"No, Anastasia." I'm surprised by her vehemence and shake my head to reinforce my denial. It's perfectly normal for a submissive to check with exes that their new Dominant knows what he's doing.

"No—I'll do this on my own, thank you very much," she insists and reaches for her comforter and quilt, pulling them up to her chin.

What? She's upset?

"Anastasia, I…I didn't mean to offend you."

"I'm not offended. I'm appalled."

"Appalled?"

"I don't want to talk to one of your ex-girlfriends, slaves, subs, whatever you call them."

Oh.

"Anastasia Steele, are you jealous?" I sound bewildered… because I am. She flushes beet red, and I know I've found the root of her problem. How the hell can she be jealous?

Sweetheart, I had a life before you.

A very active life.

"Are you staying?" she snaps.

What? Of course not. "I have a breakfast meeting tomorrow at The Heathman. Besides, I told you, I don't sleep with girlfriends, slaves, subs, or anyone. Friday and Saturday were exceptions. It won't happen again."

She presses her lips together with her stubborn expression. "Well, I'm tired now," she says.

Fuck.

"Are you kicking me out?"

This is not how this is supposed to go.

"Yes."

What the hell?

Disarmed again, by Miss Steele. "Well, that's another first," I mutter.

Kicked out. I can't believe it.

"So nothing you want to discuss now? About the contract?" I ask as an excuse to prolong my stay.

"No," she grunts. Her petulance is irritating, and were she truly mine, it would not be tolerated.

"God, I'd like to give you a good hiding. You'd feel a lot better, and so would I," I tell her.

"You can't say things like that. I haven't signed anything yet." Her eyes flash with defiance.

Oh, baby, I can say it. I just can't do it. Not until you let me. "A man can dream, Anastasia. Wednesday?" I still want this. Why, though, I don't know; she's so difficult. I give her a brief kiss.

"Wednesday," she agrees, and I'm relieved once again. "I'll see you out," she adds, her tone softer. "If you give me a minute." She pushes me off the bed and pulls on her T-shirt. "Please pass me my sweatpants," she orders, pointing to them.

Wow. Miss Steele can be a bossy little thing.

"Yes, ma'am," I quip, knowing she won't get the reference. But she narrows her eyes. She knows I'm making fun of her, but she says nothing as she slips her pants on.

Feeling a little bemused at the prospect of being tossed out onto the street, I follow her through the living room to the front door.

When was the last time this happened?

Never.

She opens the door, but she's staring down at her hands.

What is going on here?

"You okay?" I ask and brush her lower lip with my thumb. Perhaps she doesn't want me to go—or perhaps she can't wait for me to leave?

"Yes," she says, her tone soft and subdued. I'm not sure I believe her.

"Wednesday," I remind her. I'll see her then. Bending down, I kiss her, and she closes her eyes. And I don't want to go. Not with her uncertainty on my mind. I hold her head and deepen the kiss and she responds, surrendering her mouth to me.

Oh, baby, don't give up on me. Give it a try.

She grasps my arms, kissing me back, and I don't want to stop. She's intoxicating and the darkness is quiet, calmed by the young woman in front of me.

Reluctantly, I pull back and lean my forehead against hers. She's breathless, like me. "Anastasia, what are you doing to me?"

"I could say the same to you," she whispers.

I know I have to leave. She has me in a tailspin, and I don't know why. I kiss her forehead and walk down the path toward the R8. She stands watching me from the doorway. She hasn't gone in. I smile, pleased she's still watching as I climb into the car.

When I look back, she's gone.

Shit. What just happened? No wave goodbye?

I start the car and begin the drive back to Portland, analyzing what's taken place between us.

She emailed me.

I went to her.

We fucked.

She threw me out before I was ready to leave.

For the first time—well, maybe not the first time—I feel a little used, for sex. It's a disturbing feeling that reminds me of my time with Elena.

Hell! Miss Steele is topping from the bottom, and she doesn't even know it. And fool that I am, I'm letting her.

I have to turn this around. This soft-sell approach is messing with my head.

But I want her. I need her to sign.

Is it just the chase? Is that what's turning me on? Or is it her?

Fuck, I don't know. But I hope to find out more on Wednesday. And on a positive note, that was one hell of a *nice* way to spend an evening. I smirk in the rearview mirror and pull into the garage at the hotel.

When I'm back in my room I sit down at my laptop.

Focus on what you want, where you want to be. Isn't that what Flynn is always harassing me about, his solution-based shit?

From: Christian Grey
Subject: This Evening
Date: May 23 2011 23:16
To: Anastasia Steele

Miss Steele,
I look forward to receiving your notes on the contract.

Until then, sleep well, baby.

Christian Grey
CEO, Grey Enterprises Holdings, Inc.

And I want to add *Thank you for another diverting evening*...but that seems a little over the top. Pushing my laptop aside because Ana will probably be asleep, I pick up the Detroit report and continue reading.

TUESDAY, MAY 24, 2011

The thought of siting the electronics plant in Detroit is depressing. I loathe Detroit; it holds nothing but bad memories for me. Memories I do my damnedest to forget. They surface, mainly at night, to remind me of what I am and where I came from.

But Michigan is offering excellent tax incentives. It's hard to ignore what they are proposing in this report. I toss it on the dining table and take a sip of my Sancerre. *Shit.* It's warm. It's late. I should sleep. As I stand and stretch, there's a ping on my computer. An email. It might be from Ros, so I have a quick look.

It's from Ana. Why is she still awake?

From: Anastasia Steele
Subject: Issues
Date: May 24 2011 00:02
To: Christian Grey

Dear Mr. Grey,
Here is my list of issues. I look forward to discussing them more fully at dinner on Wednesday.

The numbers refer to clauses:

She's referring to the clauses? Miss Steele has been thorough. I pull a copy up on screen for my reference.

CONTRACT
Made this day _____ of 2011 ("The Commencement Date")
BETWEEN
MR. CHRISTIAN GREY of 301 Escala, Seattle, WA 98889
("The Dominant")
MISS ANASTASIA STEELE of 1114 SW Green Street,
Apartment 7, Haven Heights, Vancouver, WA 98888
("The Submissive")
THE PARTIES AGREE AS FOLLOWS

1 The following are the terms of a binding contract between the Dominant and the Submissive.

FUNDAMENTAL TERMS

2 The fundamental purpose of this contract is to allow the Submissive to explore her sensuality and her limits safely, with due respect and regard for her needs, her limits, and her well-being.

3 The Dominant and the Submissive agree and acknowledge that all that occurs under the terms of this contract will be consensual, confidential, and subject to the agreed limits and safety procedures set out in this contract. Additional limits and safety procedures may be agreed to in writing.

4 The Dominant and the Submissive each warrant that they suffer from no sexual, serious, infectious, or life-threatening illnesses, including but not limited to HIV, herpes, and hepatitis. If during the Term (as defined below) or any extended term of this contract either party should be diagnosed with or become aware of any such illness, he or she undertakes to inform the other immediately and in any event prior to any form of physical contact between the parties.

5 Adherence to the above warranties, agreements, and undertakings (and any additional limits and safety procedures agreed under clause 3 above) are fundamental to this contract. Any breach shall render it void with immediate effect and each party agrees to be fully responsible to the other for the consequence of any breach.

6 Everything in this contract must be read and interpreted in the

light of the fundamental purpose and the fundamental terms set out in clauses 2–5 above.

ROLES

7 The Dominant shall take responsibility for the well-being and the proper training, guidance, and discipline of the Submissive. He shall decide the nature of such training, guidance, and discipline and the time and place of its administration, subject to the agreed terms, limitations, and safety procedures set out in this contract or agreed additionally under clause 3 above.

8 If at any time the Dominant should fail to keep to the agreed terms, limitations, and safety procedures set out in this contract or agreed additionally under clause 3 above, the Submissive is entitled to terminate this contract forthwith and to leave the service of the Dominant without notice.

9 Subject to that proviso and to clauses 2–5 above, the Submissive is to serve and obey the Dominant in all things. Subject to the agreed terms, limitations, and safety procedures set out in this contract or agreed additionally under clause 3 above, she shall without query or hesitation offer the Dominant such pleasure as he may require and she shall accept without query or hesitation his training, guidance, and discipline in whatever form it may take.

COMMENCEMENT AND TERM

10 The Dominant and Submissive enter into this contract on the Commencement Date fully aware of its nature and undertake to abide by its conditions without exception.

11 This contract shall be effective for a period of three calendar months from the Commencement Date ("the Term"). On the expiry of the Term the parties shall discuss whether this contract and the arrangements they have made under this contract are satisfactory and whether the needs of each party have been met. Either party may propose the extension of this contract subject to adjustments to its terms or to the arrangements they have made under it. In the absence of agreement to such extension this contract shall terminate and both parties shall be free to resume their lives separately.

AVAILABILITY

12 The Submissive will make herself available to the Dominant from Friday evenings through to Sunday afternoons each week during the Term at times to be specified by the Dominant ("the Allotted Times"). Further allocated time can be mutually agreed to on an ad hoc basis.

13 The Dominant reserves the right to dismiss the Submissive from his service at any time and for any reason. The Submissive may request her release at any time, such request to be granted at the discretion of the Dominant subject only to the Submissive's rights under clauses 2–5 and 8 above.

LOCATION

14 The Submissive will make herself available during the Allotted Times and agreed additional times at locations to be determined by the Dominant. The Dominant will ensure that all travel costs incurred by the Submissive for that purpose are met by the Dominant.

SERVICE PROVISIONS

15 The following service provisions have been discussed and agreed and will be adhered to by both parties during the Term. Both parties accept that certain matters may arise that are not covered by the terms of this contract or the service provisions, or that certain matters may be renegotiated. In such circumstances, further clauses may be proposed by way of amendment. Any further clauses or amendments must be agreed, documented, and signed by both parties and shall be subject to the fundamental terms set out under clauses 2–5 above.

DOMINANT

15.1 The Dominant shall make the Submissive's health and safety a priority at all times. The Dominant shall not at any time require, request, allow, or demand the Submissive to participate at the hands of the Dominant in the activities detailed in Appendix 2 or in any act that either party deems to be unsafe. The Dominant will not undertake or permit to be undertaken any action which could cause serious injury or any risk to the Submissive's life. The remaining subclauses of this clause 15 are to be read subject to this proviso and to the fundamental matters agreed in clauses 2–5 above.

15.2 The Dominant accepts the Submissive as his, to own, control, dominate, and discipline during the Term. The Dominant may use the Submissive's body at any time during the Allotted Times or any agreed additional times in any manner he deems fit, sexually or otherwise.

15.3 The Dominant shall provide the Submissive with all necessary training and guidance in how to properly serve the Dominant.

15.4 The Dominant shall maintain a stable and safe environment in which the Submissive may perform her duties in service of the Dominant.

15.5 The Dominant may discipline the Submissive as necessary to ensure the Submissive fully appreciates her role of subservience to the Dominant and to discourage unacceptable conduct. The Dominant may flog, spank, whip, or corporally punish the Submissive as he sees fit, for purposes of discipline, for his own personal enjoyment, or for any other reason, which he is not obliged to provide.

15.6 In training and in the administration of discipline the Dominant shall ensure that no permanent marks are made upon the Submissive's body nor any injuries incurred that may require medical attention.

15.7 In training and in the administration of discipline the Dominant shall ensure that the discipline and the instruments used for the purposes of discipline are safe, shall not be used in such a way as to cause serious harm, and shall not in any way exceed the limits defined and detailed in this contract.

15.8 In case of illness or injury the Dominant shall care for the Submissive, seeing to her health and safety, encouraging and, when necessary, ordering medical attention when it is judged necessary by the Dominant.

15.9 The Dominant shall maintain his own good health and seek medical attention when necessary in order to maintain a risk-free environment.

15.10 The Dominant shall not loan his Submissive to another Dominant.

15.11 The Dominant may restrain, handcuff, or bind the Submissive at any time during the Allotted Times or any agreed additional times for any reason and for extended periods of time, giving due regard to the health and safety of the Submissive.

15.12 The Dominant will ensure that all equipment used for the purposes of training and discipline shall be maintained in a clean, hygienic, and safe state at all times.

SUBMISSIVE

15.13 The Submissive accepts the Dominant as her master, with the understanding that she is now the property of the Dominant, to be dealt with as the Dominant pleases during the Term generally but specifically during the Allotted Times and any additional agreed allotted times.

15.14 The Submissive shall obey the rules ("the Rules") set out in Appendix 1 to this agreement.

15.15 The Submissive shall serve the Dominant in any way the Dominant sees fit and shall endeavor to please the Dominant at all times to the best of her ability.

15.16 The Submissive shall take all measures necessary to maintain her good health and shall request or seek medical attention whenever it is needed, keeping the Dominant informed at all times of any health issues that may arise.

15.17 The Submissive will ensure that she procures oral contraception and ensure that she takes it as and when prescribed to prevent any pregnancy.

15.18 The Submissive shall accept without question any and all disciplinary actions deemed necessary by the Dominant and remember her status and role in regard to the Dominant at all times.

15.19 The Submissive shall not touch or pleasure herself sexually without permission from the Dominant.
15.20 The Submissive shall submit to any sexual activity demanded by the Dominant and shall do so without hesitation or argument.
15.21 The Submissive shall accept whippings, floggings, spankings, canings, paddlings, or any other discipline the Dominant should decide to administer, without hesitation, inquiry, or complaint.
15.22 The Submissive shall not look directly into the eyes of the Dominant except when specifically instructed to do so. The Submissive shall keep her eyes cast down and maintain a quiet and respectful bearing in the presence of the Dominant.
15.23 The Submissive shall always conduct herself in a respectful manner to the Dominant and shall address him only as Sir, Mr. Grey, or such other title as the Dominant may direct.
15.24 The Submissive will not touch the Dominant without his express permission to do so.

ACTIVITIES

16 The Submissive shall not participate in activities or any sexual acts that either party deems to be unsafe or any activities detailed in Appendix 2.
17 The Dominant and the Submissive have discussed the activities set out in Appendix 3 and recorded in writing on Appendix 3 their agreement in respect of them.

SAFE WORDS

18 The Dominant and the Submissive recognize that the Dominant may make demands of the Submissive that cannot be met without incurring physical, mental, emotional, spiritual, or other harm at the time the demands are made to the Submissive. In such circumstances related to this, the Submissive may make use of a safe word ("the Safe Word[s]"). Two Safe Words will be invoked depending on the severity of the demands.
19 The Safe Word "Yellow" will be used to bring to the attention of the Dominant that the Submissive is close to her limit of endurance.
20 The Safe Word "Red" will be used to bring to the attention

of the Dominant that the Submissive cannot tolerate any further demands. When this word is said, the Dominant's action will cease completely with immediate effect.

CONCLUSION

21 We the undersigned have read and understood fully the provisions of this contract. We freely accept the terms of this contract and have acknowledged this by our signatures below.

____

The Dominant: Christian Grey

Date:

____

The Submissive: Anastasia Steele

Date:

APPENDIX 1

Rules

Obedience:

The Submissive will obey any instructions given by the Dominant immediately without hesitation or reservation and in an expeditious manner. The Submissive will agree to any sexual activity deemed fit and pleasurable by the Dominant excepting those activities that are outlined in hard limits (Appendix 2). She will do so eagerly and without hesitation.

Sleep:

The Submissive will ensure she achieves a minimum of eight hours' sleep a night when she is not with the Dominant.

Food:

The Submissive will eat regularly to maintain her health and well-being from a prescribed list of foods (Appendix 4). The Submissive will not snack between meals, with the exception of fruit.

Clothes:

During the Term the Submissive will wear only clothing approved by the Dominant. The Dominant will provide a clothing budget for the Submissive, which the Submissive shall utilize. The Dominant shall accompany the Submissive to purchase clothing on an ad hoc basis. If the Dominant so requires, the Submissive shall, during the Term, wear adornments the Dominant shall require, in the presence of the Dominant and at any other time the Dominant deems fit.

Exercise:

The Dominant shall provide the Submissive with a personal trainer four times a week in hour-long sessions at times to be mutually agreed between the personal trainer and the Submissive. The personal trainer will report to the Dominant on the Submissive's progress.

Personal Hygiene/Beauty:

The Submissive will keep herself clean and shaved and/or waxed at all times. The Submissive will visit a beauty salon of the Dominant's choosing at times to be decided by the Dominant and undergo whatever treatments the Dominant sees fit. All costs will be met by the Dominant.

Personal Safety:

The Submissive will not drink to excess, smoke, take recreational drugs, or put herself in any unnecessary danger.

Personal Qualities:

The Submissive will not enter into any sexual relations with anyone other than the Dominant. The Submissive will conduct herself in a respectful and modest manner at all times. She must recognize that her behavior is a direct reflection on the Dominant. She shall be held accountable for any misdeeds, wrongdoings, and misbehavior committed when not in the presence of the Dominant.

Failure to comply with any of the above will result in immediate punishment, the nature of which shall be determined by the Dominant.

APPENDIX 2

Hard Limits

No acts involving fire play.

No acts involving urination or defecation and the products thereof.

No acts involving needles, knives, cutting, piercing, or blood.

No acts involving gynecological medical instruments.

No acts involving children or animals.

No acts that will leave any permanent marks on the skin.

No acts involving breath control.

No activity that involves the direct contact of electric current (whether alternating or direct), fire, or flames to the body.

APPENDIX 3

Soft Limits

To be discussed and agreed between both parties:

Does the Submissive consent to:

- Masturbation
- Cunnilingus
- Fellatio
- Swallowing Semen
- Vaginal intercourse
- Vaginal fisting
- Anal intercourse
- Anal fisting

Does the Submissive consent to the use of:

- Vibrators
- Butt plugs
- Dildos
- Other vaginal/anal toys

Does the Submissive consent to:

- Bondage with rope
- Bondage with leather cuffs
- Bondage with handcuffs/ shackles/manacles
- Bondage with tape
- Bondage with other

Does the Submissive consent to be restrained with:

- Hands bound in front
- Ankles bound
- Elbows bound
- Hands bound behind back
- Knees bound
- Wrists bound to ankles
- Binding to fixed items, furniture, etc.
- Binding with spreader bar
- Suspension

Does the Submissive consent to be blindfolded?

Does the Submissive consent to be gagged?

How much pain is the Submissive willing to experience?

Where 1 is likes intensely and 5 is dislikes intensely:
1—2—3—4—5

Does the Submissive consent to accept the following forms of pain/punishment/discipline:

- Spanking
- Whipping
- Biting
- Genital clamps
- Hot wax
- Paddling
- Caning
- Nipple clamps
- Ice
- Other types/methods of pain

So, her points.

2: Not sure why this is solely for MY benefit—i.e., to explore MY sensuality and limits. I'm sure I wouldn't need a ten-page contract to do that! Surely this is for YOUR benefit.

Fair point well made, Miss Steele!

4: As you are aware, you are my only sexual partner. I don't take drugs, and I've not had any blood transfusions. I'm probably safe. What about you?

Another fair point! And it dawns on me that this is the first time I haven't had to consider the sexual history of a partner. Well, that's one advantage of screwing a virgin.

8: I can terminate at any time if I don't think you're sticking to the agreed limits. Okay—I like this.

I hope it won't come to that, but it wouldn't be the first time if it did.

9: Obey you in all things? Accept without hesitation your discipline? We need to talk about this.

11: One-month trial period. Not three.

Only a month? That's not long enough. How far can we go in a month?

12: I cannot commit every weekend. I do have a life, or will have. Perhaps three out of four?

And she'll have the opportunity to socialize with other men? She'll realize what she's missing. I'm not sure about this.

15.2: Using my body as you see fit sexually or otherwise—please define "or otherwise."

15.5: This whole discipline clause. I'm not sure I want to be whipped, flogged, or corporally punished. I am sure this would be in breach of clauses 2–5. And also "for any other reason." That's just mean—and you told me you weren't a sadist.

Shit! Read on, Grey.

15.10: Like loaning me out to someone else would ever be an option. But I'm glad it's here in black and white.

15.14: The Rules. More on those later.

15.19: Touching myself without your permission. What's the problem with this? You know I don't do it anyway.

15.21: Discipline—please see clause 15.5 above.

15.22: I can't look into your eyes? Why?

15.24: Why can't I touch you?

Rules:

Sleep—I'll agree to six hours.

Food—I am not eating food from a prescribed list. The food list goes or I do—deal breaker.

Well, this is going to be an issue!

Clothes—as long as I only have to wear your clothes when I'm with you...okay.

Exercise—We agreed on three hours, this still says four.

Soft Limits:

Can we go through all of these? No fisting of any kind. What is suspension? Genital clamps—you have got to be kidding me.

Can you please let me know the arrangements for Wednesday? I am working until five p.m. that day.

Good night.

Ana

Her response is a relief. Miss Steele has put some thought into this, more so than anyone else I've dealt with over this contract. She's really engaged. She seems to be taking it seriously and we'll have much to discuss on Wednesday. The uncertainty I felt when leaving her apartment this evening recedes. There's hope for our relationship, but first—she needs to sleep.

From: Christian Grey
Subject: Issues
Date: May 24 2011 00:07
To: Anastasia Steele

Miss Steele,
That's a long list. Why are you still up?

Christian Grey
CEO, Grey Enterprises Holdings, Inc.

A few minutes later her answer is in my inbox.

From: Anastasia Steele
Subject: Burning the Midnight Oil
Date: May 24 2011 00:10
To: Christian Grey

Sir,
If you recall, I was going through this list when I was distracted and bedded by a passing control freak.

Good night.

Ana

Her email makes me laugh out loud but it irritates me in equal measure. She's much more sassy in print and she has a great sense of humor, but the woman needs sleep.

From: Christian Grey
Subject: Stop Burning the Midnight Oil
Date: May 24 2011 00:12
To: Anastasia Steele

GO TO BED, ANASTASIA.

Christian Grey
CEO & Control Freak, Grey Enterprises Holdings, Inc.

A few minutes pass and once I'm convinced she's gone to bed, persuaded by my capital letters, I head into my bedroom. I take my laptop just in case she replies again.

Once in bed, I grab my book and read. After half an hour I give up. I can't concentrate; my mind keeps straying to Ana, how she was this evening, and her email.

I need to remind her of what I expect from our relationship. I don't want her getting the wrong idea. I've strayed too far from my goal.

"Are you going to come and help Ana with the move?" Kavanagh's words remind me that unrealistic expectations have been set.

Perhaps I could help them move?

No. Stop now, Grey.

Opening my laptop, I read through her "Issues" email again. I need to manage her expectations and try to find the right words to express how I feel.

Finally, I'm inspired.

From: Christian Grey
Subject: Your Issues
Date: May 24 2011 01:27
To: Anastasia Steele

Dear Miss Steele,
Following my more thorough examination of your issues, may I bring to your attention the definition of submissive.

submissive [*suh*b-mis-iv]—adjective

1. inclined or ready to submit; unresistingly or humbly obedient: *submissive servants.*

2. marked by or indicating submission: *a submissive reply.*

Origin: 1580–90; submiss + -ive

> *Synonyms: 1.* tractable, compliant, pliant, amenable.
> *2.* passive, resigned, patient, docile, tame, subdued.
> *Antonyms: 1.* rebellious, disobedient.
>
> Please bear this in mind for our meeting on Wednesday.
>
> Christian Grey
> CEO, Grey Enterprises Holdings, Inc.

That's it. I hope she'll find it amusing, but it gets my point across.

With that thought, I switch off my bedside light and fall asleep and dream.

> His name is Lelliot. He's bigger than me. He laughs. And smiles. And shouts. And talks all the time. He talks all the time to Mommy and Daddy. He is my brother. *Why don't you talk?* Lelliot says again and again and again. *Are you stupid?* Lelliot says again and again and again. I jump on him and smack his face again and again and again. He cries. He cries a lot. I don't cry. I never cry. Mommy is angry with me. I have to sit on the bottom stair. I have to sit for the longest time. But Lelliot never asks me why I don't talk ever again. If I make my hand into a fist he runs away. Lelliot is scared of me. He knows I'm a monster.

WHEN I RETURN FROM my run the next morning, I check my email before having a shower. Nothing from Miss Steele, but then it's only 7:30. Maybe it's a little early.

Grey, snap out of this. Get a grip.

I glare at the gray-eyed prick who stares back at me from the mirror as I shave. *No more. Forget about her for today.*

I have a job to do and a breakfast meeting to attend.

"FREDDIE WAS SAYING BARNEY may have a prototype of

the tablet for you in a couple of days," Ros tells me during our videoconference.

"I was studying the schematics yesterday. They were impressive, but I'm not sure we're there yet. If we get this right there's no telling where the technology could go, and what it could do in developing countries."

"Don't forget the home market," she interjects.

"As if."

"Christian, just how long are you going to be in Portland?" Ros sounds exasperated. "What's going on down there?" Eyeing the webcam, she then peers hard at her screen, looking for clues in my expression.

"A merger." I try to hide my smile.

"Does Marco know?"

I snort. Marco Inglis is the head of my mergers and acquisitions division. "No. It's not that kind of merger."

"Oh." Ros is silenced momentarily and, from her look, surprised.

Yeah. It's private.

"Well, I hope you're successful," she says, smirking.

"Me, too," I acknowledge with a smirk of my own. "Now, can we talk about Woods?"

Over the past year, we've acquired three tech companies. Two are booming, surpassing all targets, and one is struggling despite Marco's initial optimism. Lucas Woods heads it up; he's turned out to be an idiot—all show, no substance. The money has gone to his head and he's lost focus and squandered the lead his company once had in fiber optics. My gut says asset-strip the company, fire Woods, and merge their technology division into GEH.

But Ros thinks Lucas needs more time—and that we need time to plan if we're going to liquidate and rebrand his company. If we do, it will involve expensive redundancies.

"I think Woods has had enough time to turn this around. He just won't accept reality," I say emphatically. "We need him gone, and I'd like Marco to estimate the costs of liquidating."

"Marco wants to join us for this part of the call. I'll get him to log in."

AT 12:30 P.M. TAYLOR drives me out to WSU in Vancouver for lunch with the president, the head of the Environmental Sciences Department, and the vice president of economic development. As we approach the long driveway I can't help looking out at all the students to see if I can spy Miss Steele. Alas, I don't see her; she's probably holed up in the library reading a classic. The thought of her curled up somewhere with a book is comforting. There has been no reply to my last email, but then she's been working. Perhaps there'll be something after lunch.

As we pull up outside the administration building my phone buzzes. It's Grace. She never calls during the week.

"Mom?"

"Hello, darling. How are you?"

"Fine. I'm about to go into a meeting."

"Your PA said you were in Portland." Her voice is full of hope.

Damn. She thinks I'm with Ana.

"Yeah, on business."

"How's Anastasia?" *There it is!*

"Fine as far as I know, Grace. What do you want?"

Oh good Lord. My mother is someone else whose expectations I have to manage.

"Mia's coming home a week early, on Saturday. I'm on call that day and your father is away at a legal conference presenting a panel on philanthropy and aid," she says.

"You want me to meet her?"

"Will you?"

"Sure. Ask her to send me her flight details."

"Thank you, darling. Say hi to Anastasia for me."

"I have to go. Goodbye, Mom." I hang up before she can ask any more awkward questions.

Taylor opens the car door.

"I should be out of here by three."

"Yes, Mr. Grey."

"Will you be able to see your daughter tomorrow, Taylor?"

"Yes, sir." His expression is warm and full of paternal pride.

"Great."

"I'll be here at three," he confirms.

I head into the university's administration building… This is going to be a long lunch.

I HAVE MANAGED TO keep Anastasia Steele out of every waking thought today. Almost. During lunch there were times when I found myself imagining us in my playroom… What did she call it? *The Red Room of Pain.* I shake my head, smiling, and check my email. That woman has a way with words, but so far there are no words from her today.

I change from my suit to my sweats to get ready for the hotel gym. As I'm about to leave my room, I hear a ping. It's her.

From: Anastasia Steele
Subject: My Issues…What about Your Issues?
Date: May 24 2011 18:29
To: Christian Grey

Sir,
Please note the date of origin: 1580–90. I would respectfully remind Sir that the year is 2011. We have come a long way since then.

May I offer a definition for *you* to consider for our meeting:

compromise [kom-pruh-mahyz]—*noun*

1. a settlement of differences by mutual concessions; an agreement reached by adjustment of conflicting or opposing claims, principles, etc., by reciprocal modification of demands. 2. the result of such a settlement. 3. something intermediate between different things: *The split-level is a compromise between a ranch house and a*

multistoried house. 4. an endangering, esp. of reputation; exposure to danger, suspicion, etc.: *a compromise of one's integrity.*

Ana

What a surprise, a provocative email from Miss Steele, but our meeting is still happening. *Well, that's a relief.*

From: Christian Grey
Subject: What about My Issues?
Date: May 24 2011 18:32
To: Anastasia Steele

Good point, well made, as ever, Miss Steele. I will collect you from your apartment at 7:00 tomorrow.

Christian Grey
CEO, Grey Enterprises Holdings, Inc.

My phone buzzes. It's Elliot.

"Hey, hotshot. Kate's asked me to hassle you about the move."

"The move?"

"Kate and Ana, help moving, you dipshit."

I give him an exaggerated sigh. He really is a crude asshole. "I can't help. I'm meeting Mia at the airport."

"What? Can't Mom do that, or Dad?"

"No. Mom called me this morning."

"Then I guess that settles it. You never told me how you got on with Ana? Did you f—"

"Goodbye, Elliot." I hang up. It's none of his business and there's an email waiting for me.

From: Anastasia Steele
Subject: 2011—Women Can Drive
Date: May 24 2011 18:40
To: Christian Grey

Sir,
I have a car. I can drive.
I would prefer to meet you somewhere.
Where shall I meet you?
At your hotel at 7:00?

Ana

How irritating. I write back immediately.

From: Christian Grey
Subject: Stubborn Young Women
Date: May 24 2011 18:43
To: Anastasia Steele

Dear Miss Steele,
I refer to my email dated May 24, 2011, sent at 1:27, and the definition contained therein.

Do you ever think you'll be able to do what you're told?

Christian Grey
CEO, Grey Enterprises Holdings, Inc.

Her response is slow, which does nothing for my mood.

From: Anastasia Steele
Subject: Intractable Men
Date: May 24 2011 18:49
To: Christian Grey

Mr. Grey,
I would like to drive.
Please.

Ana

Intractable? Me? Fuck. If our meeting goes as planned, her contrary behavior will be a thing of the past. With that in mind, I agree.

From: Christian Grey
Subject: Exasperated Men
Date: May 24 2011 18:52
To: Anastasia Steele

Fine.
My hotel at 7:00.

I'll meet you in the Marble Bar.

Christian Grey
CEO, Grey Enterprises Holdings, Inc.

From: Anastasia Steele
Subject: Not So Intractable Men
Date: May 24 2011 18:55
To: Christian Grey

Thank you.

Ana x

And I'm rewarded with a kiss. Ignoring how that makes me feel, I let her know she's welcome. My mood has lifted as I head to the hotel gym.

She sent me a kiss…

WEDNESDAY, MAY 25, 2011

I order a glass of Sancerre and stand at the bar. I've been waiting for this moment all day and look repeatedly at my watch. This feels like a first date, and in a way it is. I've never taken a prospect out to dinner. I've sat through interminable meetings today, bought a business, and fired three people. Nothing I've done today—including running, twice, and a quick circuit in the gym—has dispelled the anxiety I've wrestled with all day. That power is in the hands of Anastasia Steele. I want her submission.

I hope she's not going to be late. I glance toward the entrance of the bar…and my mouth dries. She's standing on the threshold, and for a second I don't realize it's her. She looks exquisite: her hair falls in soft waves to her breast on one side, and on the other it's pinned back so it's easier to see her delicate jawline and the gentle curve of her slender neck. She's wearing high heels and a tight dark purple dress that accentuates her lithe, alluring figure.

Wow.

I step forward to meet her. "You look stunning," I whisper and kiss her cheek. Closing my eyes, I savor her scent; she smells heavenly. "A dress, Miss Steele. I approve." Diamonds in her ears would complete the ensemble; I must buy her a pair.

Taking her hand, I lead her to a booth. "What would you like to drink?"

I'm rewarded with a knowing smile as she sits down. "I'll have what you're having, please."

Ah, she's learning. "Another glass of the Sancerre," I tell the waiter, and I slide into the booth opposite her. "They have an excellent wine cellar here," I add and take a moment to look at her. She's wearing a little makeup. Not too much. And I remember when she first fell into my office how ordinary I thought she looked. She is anything but ordinary. With a little makeup and the right clothes, she's a goddess.

She shifts in her seat and her eyelashes flutter.

"Are you nervous?" I ask.

"Yes."

This is it, Grey.

Leaning forward, in a candid whisper, I tell her I'm nervous, too. She looks at me as if I've grown three heads.

Yeah, I'm human, too, baby…just.

The waiter places Ana's wine and two small plates of mixed nuts and olives between us.

Ana squares her shoulders, an indication that she means business, like she did when she first interviewed me. "So, how are we going to do this? Run through my points one by one?" she asks.

"Impatient as ever, Miss Steele."

"Well, I could ask you what you thought of the weather today," she retorts.

Oh, that smart mouth.

Let her stew for a moment, Grey.

Keeping my eyes on hers, I pop an olive into my mouth and lick my index finger. Her eyes grow wider and darker.

"I thought the weather was particularly unexceptional today." I try for nonchalance.

"Are you smirking at me, Mr. Grey?"

"I am, Miss Steele."

She purses her lips to stifle her smile. "You know this contract is legally unenforceable."

"I am fully aware of that, Miss Steele."

"Were you going to tell me that at any point?"

What? I didn't think I'd have to…and you've worked it out for yourself. "You'd think I'd coerce you into something you don't want to do, and then pretend that I have a legal hold over you?"

"Well, yes."

Whoa. "You don't think very highly of me, do you?"

"You haven't answered my question."

"Anastasia, it doesn't matter if it's legal or not. It represents an arrangement that I would like to make with you—what I would like from you and what you can expect from me. If you don't like it, then don't sign. If you do sign and then decide you don't like it, there are enough get-out clauses so you can walk away. Even if it were legally binding, do you think I'd drag you through the courts if you did decide to run?"

What does she take me for?

She considers me with her unfathomable blue eyes.

What I need her to understand is that this contract isn't about the law—it's about trust.

I want you to trust me, Ana.

As she takes a sip of her wine I rush on, endeavoring to explain. "Relationships like this are built on honesty and trust. If you don't trust me—trust me to know how I'm affecting you, how far I can go with you, how far I can take you—if you can't be honest with me, then we really can't do this."

She rubs her chin as she considers what I've said.

"So it's quite simple, Anastasia. Do you trust me or not?"

And if she thinks so little of me, then we shouldn't do this at all.

My gut is knotting with tension.

"Did you have similar discussions with…um…the fifteen?"

"No." *Why is she going off on this tangent?*

"Why not?" she asks.

"Because they were all established submissives. They knew what they wanted out of a relationship with me and generally what I expected. With them, it was just a question of fine-tuning the soft limits, details like that."

"Is there a store you go to? Submissives 'R' Us?" She arches an eyebrow and I laugh out loud. And like a magician's rabbit the tension in my body disappears. "Not exactly." My tone is wry.

"Then how?"

She's ever-curious, but I don't want to talk about Elena again. Last time I mentioned her Ana turned frosty. "Is that what you want to discuss? Or shall we get down to the nitty-gritty? Your issues, as you say."

She frowns.

"Are you hungry?" I ask.

She looks suspiciously at the olives. "No."

"Have you eaten today?"

She hesitates.

Shit.

"No," she says.

I try not to let her admission anger me. "You have to eat, Anastasia. We can eat down here or in my suite. Which would you prefer?"

She'll never go for this.

"I think we should stay in public, on neutral ground."

As predicted—sensible, Miss Steele.

"Do you think that would stop me?" My voice is husky.

She swallows. "I hope so."

Put the girl out of her misery, Grey.

"Come, I have a private dining room booked. No public." Rising, I hold out my hand to her.

Will she come with me?

She looks from my face to my hand.

"Bring your wine," I order.

And she picks up her glass and places her hand in mine.

As we leave the bar, I notice admiring glances from other guests and, in the case of one handsome, athletic guy, overt appreciation of my date. It's not something I've dealt with before...and I don't think I like it.

Upstairs on the mezzanine, the liveried young host dispatched by the maître d' leads us to the room I've booked. He only has eyes for Miss Steele, and I give him a withering look that sends him in retreat from the opulent dining room. An older waiter seats Ana and drapes a napkin on her lap.

"I've ordered already. I hope you don't mind."

"No, that's fine," she says with a gracious nod.

"It's good to know that you can be amenable." I smirk. "Now, where were we?"

"The nitty-gritty," she says, focused on the task at hand, but then she takes a large gulp of wine and her cheeks color. She must be looking for courage. I'll have to watch how much she's drinking, because she's driving.

She could always spend the night here…then I could peel her out of that enticing dress.

Regaining my focus, I return to business—Ana's issues. From the inside pocket of my jacket I retrieve her email. She squares her shoulders once more and gives me an expectant look, and I have to hide my amusement. "Clause two. Agreed. This is for the benefit of us both. I shall redraft."

She takes another sip.

"My sexual health? Well, all of my previous partners have had blood tests, and I have regular tests every six months for all the health risks you mention. All my recent tests are clear. I have never taken drugs. In fact, I'm vehemently antidrug. I have a strict no-tolerance policy with regards to drugs for all my employees, and I insist on random drug testing."

In fact, one of the people I fired today failed his drug test.

She's shocked, but I plow on. "I've never had any blood transfusions. Does that answer your question?"

She nods.

"Your next point I mentioned earlier. You can walk away anytime, Anastasia. I won't stop you. If you go, however, that's it. Just so you know."

No. Second. Chances. Ever.

"Okay," she replies, though she doesn't sound certain.

We both fall silent as the waiter enters with our appetizers. For a moment I wonder if I should have held this meeting at my office, then dismiss the thought as ridiculous. Only fools mix business with pleasure. I've kept my work and private life separate; it's one of my golden rules, and the only exception to that is my relationship with Elena…but then she helped me start my business.

"I hope you like oysters," I remark to Ana as the waiter leaves.

"I've never had one."

"Really? Well. All you do is tip and swallow. I think you can manage that." I stare pointedly at her mouth, remembering how well she can swallow. On cue she blushes and I squeeze lemon juice on the shellfish and tip it into my mouth. "Hmm, delicious. Tastes of the sea." I grin as she watches me, fascinated. "Go on," I encourage her, knowing she's not one to back down from a challenge.

"So, I don't chew it?"

"No, Anastasia, you don't." And I try not to think about her teeth toying with my favorite part of my anatomy.

She presses them into her bottom lip, leaving little indentation marks.

Damn. The sight stirs my body and I shift in my chair. She reaches for an oyster, squeezes the lemon, holds back her head, and opens wide. As she tips the oyster into her mouth my body hardens.

"Well?" I ask, and I sound a little hoarse.

"I'll have another," she says with wry humor.

"Good girl."

She asks me if I've chosen oysters deliberately, knowing their reputed aphrodisiac qualities. I surprise her when I tell her they were simply at the top of the menu. "I don't need an aphrodisiac near you."

Yeah, I could fuck you right now.

Behave, Grey. Get this negotiation back on track.

"So where were we?" I return to her email and concentrate on her outstanding issues. Clause nine. "Obey me in all things. Yes, I want you to do that." This is important to me. I need to know she's safe and will do *anything* for me. "I need you to do that. Think of it as role play, Anastasia."

"But I'm worried you'll hurt me."

"Hurt you how?"

"Physically."

"Do you really think I would do that? Go beyond any limit you can't take?"

"You've said you've hurt someone before."

"Yes, I have. It was a long time ago."

"How did you hurt her?"

"I suspended her from my playroom ceiling. In fact, that's one of your questions. Suspension—that's what the carabiners are for in the playroom. Rope play. One of the ropes was tied too tightly."

Appalled, she holds up her hand in a plea for me to stop.

Too much information.

"I don't need to know any more. So you won't suspend me, then?" she asks.

"Not if you really don't want to. You can make that a hard limit."

"Okay." She exhales, relieved.

Move on, Grey. "So, obeying—do you think you can manage that?"

She stares at me with those eyes that see through to my dark soul, and I don't know what she's going to say.

Shit. This could be the end.

"I could try," she says, her voice low.

It's my turn to exhale. *I'm still in the game.* "Good."

"Now term." Clause eleven. "One month instead of three is no time at all, especially if you want a weekend away from me each month." We'll get nowhere in that time. She needs training and I can't stay away from her for any length of time. I tell her as much. Maybe we can compromise, as she suggested. "How about one day over one weekend per month you get to yourself—but I get a midweek night that week?"

I watch her weighing the possibility. "Okay," she says eventually, her expression serious.

Good.

"And please, let's try it for three months. If it's not for you, then you can walk away anytime."

"Three months," she says. Is she agreeing? I'll take it as a yes.

Right. Here goes.

"The ownership thing, that's just terminology and goes back to the principle of obeying. It's to get you into the right frame of mind, to understand where I'm coming from. And I want you to know that as soon as you cross my threshold as my submissive, I will do what I like to you. You have to accept that, and willingly. That's why you have to trust me. I will fuck you, anytime, any way I want—anywhere I want. I will discipline you, because you will screw up. I will train you to please me.

"But I know you've not done this before. Initially, we'll take it slowly, and I will help you. We'll build up to various scenarios. I want you to trust me, but I know I have to earn your trust, and I will. The 'or otherwise'—again, it's to help you get into the mind-set; it means anything goes."

Some speech, Grey.

She sits back—overwhelmed, I think.

"Still with me?" I ask gently.

The waiter sneaks into the room, and with a nod I give him permission to clear our table.

"Would you like some more wine?" I ask her.

"I have to drive."

Good answer.

"Some water, then?"

She nods.

"Still or sparkling?"

"Sparkling, please."

The waiter leaves with our plates.

"You're very quiet," I whisper. She's barely said a word.

"You're very verbose," she shoots straight back at me.

Fair point, Miss Steele.

Now for the next item on her list of issues: clause fifteen. I take a deep breath. "Discipline. There's a very fine line between pleasure and pain, Anastasia. They are two sides of the same coin, one not existing without the other. I can show you how pleasurable pain can be. You don't believe me now, but this is what I mean about trust. There will be pain, but nothing that you can't handle." I cannot emphasize this enough. "Again, it comes down to trust. Do you trust me, Ana?"

"Yes, I do," she says immediately. Her response knocks me sideways: it's completely unexpected.

Again.

Have I gained her trust already?

"Well then, the rest of this stuff is just details." I feel ten feet tall.

"Important details."

She's right. *Concentrate, Grey.*

"Okay, let's talk through those."

The waiter reenters with our entrées.

"I hope you like fish," I say as he places our food before us. The black cod looks delicious.

Ana takes a bite.

Finally, she's eating!

"The rules," I continue. "Let's talk about them. The food is a deal breaker?"

"Yes."

"Can I modify to say that you will eat at least three meals a day?"

"No."

Suppressing an irritated sigh, I persist. "I need to know you're not hungry."

She frowns. "You'll have to trust me."

"Oh, touché, Miss Steele," I mutter to myself. These are battles I'm not going to win. "I concede the food and the sleep."

She gives me a small, relieved smile. "Why can't I look at you?" she asks.

"That's a Dom/sub thing. You'll get used to it."

She frowns once more but looks pained this time. "Why can't I touch you?" she asks.

"Because you can't."

Shut her down, Grey.

"Is it because of Mrs. Robinson?"

What? "Why would you think that? You think she traumatized me?"

She nods.

"No, Anastasia. She's not the reason. Besides, Mrs. Robinson wouldn't take any of that shit from me."

"So nothing to do with her," she asks, looking confused.

"No."

I can't bear to be touched. And, baby, you really don't want to know why.

"And I don't want you touching yourself, either," I add.

"Out of curiosity, why?"

"Because I want all your pleasure."

In fact, I want it now. I could fuck her here to see if she can be quiet. Real quiet, knowing we're within earshot of the hotel staff and guests. After all, that's why I've booked this room.

She opens her mouth as if to say something but closes it again and takes another bite of food from her largely untouched plate.

"I've given you a great deal to think about, haven't I?" I say, folding up her email and tucking it into my inside pocket.

"Yes."

"Do you want to go through the soft limits now, too?"

"Not over dinner."

"Squeamish?"

"Something like that."

"You've not eaten very much."

"I've had enough."

This is getting old. "Three oysters, four bites of cod, and one asparagus stalk, no potatoes, no nuts, no olives, and you've not eaten all day. You said I could trust you."

Her eyes widen.

Yeah. I've been keeping count, Ana.

"Christian, please, it's not every day I sit through conversations like this."

"I need you fit and healthy, Anastasia." My tone is adamant.

"I know."

"And right now, I want to peel you out of that dress."

"I don't think that's a good idea," she whispers. "We haven't had dessert."

"You want dessert?" *When you haven't eaten your main course?*

"Yes."

"You could be dessert."

"I'm not sure I'm sweet enough."

"Anastasia, you're deliciously sweet. I know."

"Christian. You use sex as a weapon. It really isn't fair." She looks down at her lap, and her voice is low and a little melancholy. She looks up again, pinning me with an intense stare, her powder-blue eyes unnerving…and arousing.

"You're right. I do," I admit. "In life you use what you know.

Doesn't change how much I want you. Here. Now." *And we could fuck here, right now.* I know you're interested, Ana. I hear how your breathing has changed. "I'd like to try something." I really want to know how quiet she can be, and if she can do this with the fear of discovery.

Her brow creases once more; she's confused.

"If you were my sub, you wouldn't have to think about this. It would be easy. All those decisions—all the wearying thought processes behind them. The 'Is this the right thing to do? Should this happen here? Can it happen now?' You wouldn't have to worry about any of that detail. That's what I'd do as your Dom. And right now, I know you want me, Anastasia."

She tosses her hair over her shoulder, and her frown intensifies as she licks her lips.

Oh yes. She wants me.

"I can tell because your body gives you away. You're pressing your thighs together, you're flushed, and your breathing has changed."

"How do you know about my thighs?" she asks, her voice high-pitched, shocked, I think.

"I felt the tablecloth move, and it's a calculated guess based on years of experience. I'm right, aren't I?"

She's quiet for a moment and looks away. "I haven't finished my cod," she says, evasive but still blushing.

"You'd prefer cold cod to me?"

Her eyes meet mine, and they're wide, pupils dark and large. "I thought you liked me to clear my plate."

"Right now, Miss Steele, I couldn't give a fuck about your food."

"Christian. You just don't fight fair."

"I know. I never have."

We stare at each other in a battle of wills, both aware of the sexual tension stretching between us across the table.

Please, would you just do as you're told? I implore her with a look. But her eyes glint with sensual disobedience and a smile lifts her lips. Still holding my stare, she picks up an asparagus spear and deliberately bites her lip.

What is she doing?

Carefully, she places the tip of the spear in her mouth and sucks it. Hard.

Fuck.

She's trifling with me—a dangerous tactic that will have me fucking her over this table.

Oh, bring it on, Miss Steele.

I watch, mesmerized, hardening by the second.

"Anastasia. What are you doing?" I warn.

"Eating my asparagus," she says with a coy smile.

"I think you're toying with me, Miss Steele."

"I'm just finishing my food, Mr. Grey." Her lips curl wider, slowly, carnal, and the heat between us rises several degrees. She really has no idea how sexy she is… I'm about to pounce when the waiter knocks and enters.

Damn it.

I let him clear the plates, then turn my attention back to Miss Steele. But her frown is back, and she's fidgeting with her fingers.

Hell.

"Would you like some dessert?" I ask.

"No thank you. I think I should go," she says, still staring at her hands.

"Go?" *She's leaving?*

The waiter exits quickly with our plates.

"Yes," Ana says, her voice firm with resolve. She gets to her feet to leave. And automatically I stand, too. "We both have the graduation ceremony tomorrow," she says.

This is not going according to plan at all.

"I don't want you to go," I state, because it's the truth.

"Please, I have to," she insists.

"Why?"

"Because you've given me so much to consider, and I need some distance." Her eyes are pleading with me to let her go.

But we've gotten so far in our negotiation. We've made compromises. We can make this work. *I have to make this work.*

"I could make you stay," I tell her, knowing I could seduce her right now, in this room.

"Yes, you could easily, but I don't want you to."

This is all going south—I've overplayed my hand. This isn't how I thought the night would end. I rake my hands through my hair in frustration.

"You know, when you fell into my office to interview me, you were all 'Yes, sir,' 'No, sir.' I thought you were a natural-born submissive. But quite frankly, Anastasia, I'm not sure you have a submissive bone in your delectable body." I walk the few steps that separate us and look down into eyes that shine with determination.

"You may be right," she says.

No. No. I don't want to be right.

"I want the chance to explore the possibility that you do." I caress her face and her lower lip with my thumb. "I don't know any other way, Anastasia. This is who I am."

"I know," she says.

Lowering my head so my lips hover over hers, I wait until she raises her mouth to mine and closes her eyes. I want to give her a brief, chaste kiss, but as our lips touch, she leans in to me, her hands suddenly fisting in my hair, her mouth opening to me, her tongue insistent. I press my hand to the base of her spine, holding her against me, and deepen the kiss, mirroring her fervor.

Christ, I want her.

"I can't persuade you to stay?" I whisper against the corner of her mouth as my body responds, hardening with desire.

"No."

"Spend the night with me."

"And not touch you? No."

Damn. The darkness uncoils in my guts, but I ignore it.

"You impossible girl," I mutter and pull back, examining her face and her tense, brooding expression.

"Why do I think you're telling me goodbye?"

"Because I'm leaving now."

"That's not what I mean, and you know it."

"Christian, I have to think about this. I don't know if I can have the kind of relationship you want."

I close my eyes and rest my forehead against hers.

What did you expect, Grey? She's not cut out for this.

I take a deep breath and kiss her forehead, then bury my nose in her hair, inhaling her sweet, autumnal scent and committing it to memory.

That's it. Enough.

Stepping back, I release her. "As you wish, Miss Steele. I'll escort you to the lobby." I hold out my hand for what could be the last time, and I'm surprised how painful this thought is.

She places her hand in mine, and in silence we head down to reception.

"Do you have your valet ticket?" I ask as we reach the lobby. I sound calm and collected, but inside I'm in knots.

From her purse she retrieves the ticket, which I hand to the doorman.

"Thank you for dinner," she says.

"It's a pleasure as always, Miss Steele."

This cannot be the end. I have to show her—demonstrate what this all means, what we can do together. Show her what we can do in the playroom. Then she'll know. This might be the only way to save this deal.

Quickly I turn to her. "You're moving this weekend to Seattle. If you make the right decision, can I see you on Sunday?" I ask.

"We'll see. Maybe," she says.

That's not a no.

I notice the goose bumps on her arms. "It's cooler now. Don't you have a jacket?" I ask.

"No."

This woman needs looking after. I take off my jacket. "Here. I don't want you catching cold." I slip it over her shoulders and she hugs it around herself, closes her eyes, and inhales deeply.

Is she drawn to my scent? Like I am to hers?

Perhaps all is not lost?

The valet pulls up in an ancient VW Beetle.

What the hell is that?

"That's what you drive?" This must be older than Grandpa Theodore. *Jesus!* The valet hands over the keys and I tip him generously. He deserves danger pay.

"Is this roadworthy?" I glare at Ana. How can she be safe in this rust bucket?

"Yes."

"Will it make it to Seattle?"

"Yes. She will."

"Safely?"

"Yes." She tries to reassure me. "Okay, she's old. But she's mine, and she's roadworthy. My stepdad bought it for me."

When I suggest we could do better than this she realizes what I'm offering and her expression changes immediately.

She's mad.

"You are *not* buying me a car," she says emphatically.

"We'll see," I mutter, trying to keep calm. I hold open the driver's door, and as she climbs in I wonder if I should ask Taylor to take her home. *Damn.* I remember he's off this evening.

Once I've shut the door, she rolls down the window…painfully slowly.

For Christ's sake!

"Drive safely," I growl.

"Goodbye, Christian," she says, and her voice falters, as if she's trying not to cry.

Shit. My whole mood shifts from irritation and concern for her well-being to helplessness as her car roars off up the street.

I don't know if I'll see her again.

I stand like a fool on the sidewalk until her rear lights disappear into the night.

Fuck. Why did that go so wrong?

I stalk back into the hotel, make for the bar, and order a bottle of the Sancerre. Taking it with me, I head up to my room. My laptop lies open on my desk, and before I uncork the wine, I sit down and start typing an email.

From: Christian Grey
Subject: Tonight
Date: May 25 2011 22:01
To: Anastasia Steele

I don't understand why you ran this evening. I sincerely hope I answered all your questions to your satisfaction. I know I have given you a great deal to contemplate, and I fervently hope that you will give my proposal your serious consideration. I really want to make this work. We will take it slow.

Trust me.

Christian Grey
CEO, Grey Enterprises Holdings, Inc.

I glance at my watch. It will take her at least twenty minutes to get home, probably longer in that death trap. I email Taylor.

From: Christian Grey
Subject: Audi A3
Date: May 25 2011 22:04
To: J B Taylor

I need that Audi delivered here tomorrow.
Thanks.

Christian Grey
CEO, Grey Enterprises Holdings, Inc.

Opening the Sancerre, I pour myself a glass, and picking up my book, I sit and read, trying hard to concentrate. My eyes keep straying to my laptop screen. When will she reply?

As the minutes tick by, my anxiety balloons. Why hasn't she returned my email?

At 11:00, I text her.

Are you home safe?

But I get nothing in response. Perhaps she's gone straight to bed. Before midnight I send another email.

From: Christian Grey
Subject: Tonight
Date: May 25 2011 23:58
To: Anastasia Steele

I hope you made it home in that car of yours.
Let me know if you're okay.

Christian Grey
CEO, Grey Enterprises Holdings, Inc.

I'll see her tomorrow at the graduation ceremony and I'll find out then if she's turning me down. With that depressing thought I strip, climb into bed, and stare at the ceiling.

You've really fucked up this deal, Grey.

THURSDAY, MAY 26, 2011

Mommy is gone. Sometimes she goes outside.
And it is only me. Me and my cars and my blankie.
When she comes home she sleeps on the couch. The couch is brown and sticky. She is tired. Sometimes I cover her with my blankie.
Or she comes home with something to eat. I like those days. We have bread and butter. And sometimes we have macrami and cheese. That is my favorite.
Today Mommy is gone. I play with my cars. They go fast on the floor. My mommy is gone. She will come back. She will.
When is Mommy coming home?
It is dark now, and my mommy is gone. I can reach the light when I stand on the stool.
On. Off. On. Off. On. Off.
Light. Dark. Light. Dark. Light.
I'm hungry. I eat the cheese. There is cheese in the fridge. Cheese with blue fur.
When is Mommy coming home?
Sometimes she comes home with him. I hate him. I hide when he comes. My favorite place is in my mommy's closet. It smells of Mommy. It smells of Mommy when she's happy.
When is Mommy coming home?
My bed is cold. And I am hungry. I have my blankie and my cars but not my mommy. When is Mommy coming home?

I wake with a start.
Fuck. Fuck. Fuck.
I hate my dreams. They're riddled with harrowing memories,

distorted reminders of a time I want to forget. My heart is pounding and I'm doused with sweat. But the worst consequence of these nightmares is dealing with the overwhelming anxiety when I wake.

My nightmares have recently become more frequent, and more vivid. I have no idea why. Damned Flynn—he's not back until sometime next week. I run both hands through my hair and check the time. It's 5:38, and the dawn light is seeping through the curtains. It's nearly time to get up.

Go for a run, Grey.

THERE IS STILL NO text or email from Ana. As my feet pound the sidewalk, my anxiety grows.

Leave it, Grey.

Just fucking leave it!

I know I'll see her at the graduation ceremony.

But I can't leave it.

Before my shower, I send her another text.

Call me.

I just need to know she's safe.

AFTER BREAKFAST THERE'S STILL no word from Ana. To get her out of my head I work for a couple of hours on my commencement speech. At the graduation ceremony later this morning I'll be honoring the extraordinary work of the Environmental Sciences Department and the progress they've made in partnership with GEH in arable technology for developing countries.

"All part of your feed-the-world plan?" Ana's shrewd words echo in my head, and they nudge at last night's nightmare.

I shrug it off as I rewrite. Sam, my VP for publicity, has sent a draft that is way too pretentious for me. It takes me an hour to rework his media-speak bullshit into something more human.

Nine thirty and still no word from Ana. Her radio silence is worrying—and frankly rude. I call, but her phone goes straight to a generic voice mail message.

I hang up.

Show some dignity, Grey.

There's a ping in my inbox, and my heartbeat spikes—but it's from Mia. In spite of my bad mood, I smile. I've missed that kid.

From: Mia G. Chef Extraordinaire
Subject: Flights
Date: May 26 2011 18:32 GMT-1
To: Christian Grey

Hey, Christian.
I can't wait to get out of here!
Rescue me. Please.
My flight number on Saturday is AF3622. It arrives at 12:22 p.m. and Dad is making me fly coach! *pouting!
I will have lots of luggage. Love. Love. Love Paris fashion.
Mom says you have a girlfriend.
Is this true?
What's she like?
I NEED TO KNOW!!!!!
See you Saturday. Missed you so much.
À bientôt mon frère.

Mxxxxxxxxx

Oh hell! My mother's big mouth. Ana is not my girlfriend! And come Saturday I'll have to fend off my sister's equally big mouth, her inherent optimism, and her prying questions. She can be exhausting. Making a mental note of the flight number and time, I send Mia a quick email to let her know I'll be there.

At 9:45 I get ready for the ceremony. Gray suit, white shirt, and of course *that* tie. It will be my subtle message to Ana that I haven't given up and a reminder of good times.

Yeah, real good times... Images of her bound and wanting come to mind. *Damn it. Why hasn't she called?* I press redial.

Shit.

Still no fucking answer!

At 10:00 precisely, there's a knock on my door. It's Taylor.

"Good morning," I say as he comes in.

"Mr. Grey."

"How was yesterday?"

"Good, sir." Taylor's demeanor shifts, and his expression warms. He must be thinking of his daughter.

"Sophie?"

"She's a doll, sir. And doing very well at school."

"That's great to hear."

"The A3 will be in Portland later this afternoon."

"Excellent. Let's go."

And though I'm loath to admit it, I'm anxious to see Miss Steele.

THE CHANCELLOR'S SECRETARY USHERS me into a small room adjacent to the WSU auditorium. She blushes, almost as much as a certain young woman I know intimately. There, in the greenroom, academics, administrative staff, and a few students are having pre-graduation coffee. Among them, to my surprise, is Katherine Kavanagh.

"Hi, Christian," she says, strutting toward me with the confidence of the well-heeled. She's in her graduation gown and appears cheerful enough. Surely she's seen Ana.

"Hi, Katherine. How are you?"

"You seem baffled to see me here," she says, ignoring my greeting and sounding a little affronted. "I'm valedictorian. Didn't Elliot tell you?"

"No, he didn't." *We're not in each other's pockets, for Christ's sake.* "Congratulations," I add as a courtesy.

"Thank you." Her tone is clipped.

"Is Ana here?"

"Soon. She's coming with her dad."

"You saw her this morning?"

"Yes. Why?"

"I wanted to know if she made it home in that death trap she calls a car."

"Wanda. She calls it Wanda. And yes, she did." She gazes at me with a quizzical expression.

"I'm glad to hear it."

At that point the chancellor joins us, and with a polite smile to Kavanagh, escorts me over to meet the other academics.

I'm relieved Ana is in one piece but pissed she hasn't replied to any of my messages.

It's not a good sign.

But I don't have long to dwell on this discouraging state of affairs—one of the faculty members announces it's time to begin and herds us out into the corridor.

In a moment of weakness I try Ana's phone once more. It goes straight to voice mail, and I'm interrupted by Kavanagh. "I'm looking forward to your commencement address," she says as we walk down the hallway.

When we reach the auditorium I notice it's larger than I expected, and packed. The audience, as one, rises and applauds as we file onto the stage. The clapping intensifies, then subsides to an expectant buzz as everyone takes their seats.

Once the chancellor begins his welcome address I'm able to scan the room. The front rows are filled with students, in identical black-and-red WSU robes. *Where is she?* Methodically I inspect each row.

There you are.

I find her huddled in the second row. She's alive. I feel foolish for expending so much anxiety and energy on her whereabouts last night and this morning. Her brilliant blue eyes are wide as they lock with mine, and she shifts in her seat, a slow flush coloring her cheeks.

Yes. I've found you. And you haven't replied to my messages. She's avoiding me and I'm pissed. Really pissed. Closing my eyes, I imagine dripping hot wax onto her breasts and her squirming beneath me. This has a radical effect on my body.

Shit.

Get it together, Grey.

Dismissing her from my mind, I marshal my lascivious thoughts and concentrate on the speeches.

Kavanagh gives an inspiring address about embracing opportunities—*yes, carpe diem, Kate*—and gets a rousing reception when she's finished. She's obviously smart and popular and confident. Not the shy and retiring wallflower that is the lovely Miss Steele. It really amazes me that these two are friends.

I hear my name announced; the chancellor has introduced me. I rise and approach the lectern. *Showtime, Grey.*

"I'm profoundly grateful and touched by the great compliment accorded to me by the authorities of WSU today. It offers me a rare opportunity to talk about the impressive work of the Environmental Sciences Department here at the university. Our aim is to develop viable and ecologically sustainable methods of farming for developing countries; our ultimate goal is to help eradicate hunger and poverty across the globe. Over a billion people, mainly in sub-Saharan Africa, South Asia, and Latin America, live in abject poverty. Agricultural dysfunction is rife within these parts of the world, and the result is ecological and social destruction. I have known what it's like to be profoundly hungry. This is a very personal journey for me.

"As partners, WSU and GEH have made tremendous progress in soil fertility and arable technology. We are pioneering low-input systems in developing countries, and our test sites have increased crop yields up to thirty percent per hectare. WSU has been instrumental in this fantastic achievement. And GEH is proud of those students who join us through internships to work at our test sites in Africa. The work they do there benefits the local communities and the students themselves. Together we can fight hunger and the abject poverty that blights these regions.

"But in this age of technological evolution, as the West races ahead, widening the gap between the haves and the have-nots, it's vital to remember that we must not squander the world's finite resources. These resources are for all humanity, and we need to harness them, find ways of renewing them, and develop new solutions to feed our overpopulated planet.

"As I've said, the work that GEH and WSU are doing together will provide solutions, and it's our job to get the message out there. It's through GEH's telecommunications division that we intend to supply information and education to the developing world. I'm proud to say that we're making impressive progress in solar technology, battery life, and wireless distribution that will bring the internet to the remotest parts of the world—and our goal is to make it free to users at the point of delivery. Access to education and information, which we take for granted here, is the crucial component for ending poverty in these developing regions.

"We're lucky. We're all privileged here. Some more than others, and I include myself in that category. We have a moral obligation to offer those less fortunate a decent life that's healthy, secure, and well nourished, with access to more of the resources that we all enjoy here.

"I'll leave you with a quote that has always resonated with me. And I'm paraphrasing a Native American saying: Only when the last leaf has fallen, the last tree has died, and the last fish been caught will we realize that we cannot eat money.

As I sit down to rousing applause, I resist looking at Ana and examine the WSU banner hanging at the back of the auditorium. If she wants to ignore me, fine. Two can play at that game.

The vice chancellor rises to commence handing out the degrees and I follow suit. And so begins the agonizing wait until we reach the S's and I can see her again.

After an eternity I hear her name called: "Anastasia Steele." A ripple of applause, and she's walking toward me looking pensive and worried.

Shit.

What is she thinking?

Hold it together, Grey.

"Congratulations, Miss Steele," I say as I give Ana her degree. We shake hands, but I don't let hers go. "Do you have a problem with your laptop?"

She looks perplexed. "No."

"Then you *are* ignoring my emails?" I release her.

"I only saw the mergers and acquisitions one."

What the hell does that mean?

Her frown deepens, but I have to let her go—there's a line forming behind her.

"Later." I let her know we're not finished with this conversation as she moves on.

I'm in purgatory by the time we've reached the end of the line. I've been ogled and had eyelashes batted at me, silly giggling girls squeezing my hand, and five notes with phone numbers pressed into my palm. I'm relieved as I exit the stage along with the faculty to the strains of some dreary processional music and applause.

In the corridor I grab Kavanagh's arm. "I need to speak to Ana. Can you find her? Now."

Kavanagh is taken aback, but before she can say anything I add, in as polite a tone as I can manage, "Please."

Her lips thin with disapproval, but she waits with me as the academics file past and then she returns to the auditorium. The chancellor stops to congratulate me on my speech.

"It was an honor to be asked," I respond, shaking his hand once again. Out the corner of my eye I spy Kate in the corridor—with Ana at her side. Excusing myself, I stride toward Ana.

"Thank you," I say to Kate, who gives Ana a worried glance. Ignoring her, I take Ana's elbow and lead her through the first door I find. It's a men's locker room, and from the fresh smell I can tell it's empty. Locking the door, I turn to face Miss Steele. "Why haven't you emailed me? Or texted me back?" I demand.

She blinks a couple of times, consternation writ large on her face. "I haven't looked at my computer today, or my phone." She seems genuinely bewildered by my outburst. "That was a great speech," she adds.

"Thank you," I mutter, derailed. How can she not have checked her phone or email?

"Explains your food issues to me," she says, her tone gentle—and if I'm not mistaken, pitying, too.

"Anastasia, I don't want to go there at the moment."

I don't need your pity.

I close my eyes. All this time I thought she didn't want to talk to me. "I've been worried about you."

"Worried, why?"

"Because you went home in that death trap you call a car."

And I thought I'd blown the deal between us.

Ana bristles. "What? It's not a death trap. It's fine. José regularly services it for me."

"José, the photographer?" This just gets better and fucking better.

"Yes, the Beetle used to belong to his mother."

"Yes, and probably her mother and her mother before her. It's not safe." I'm almost shouting.

"I've been driving it for over three years. I'm sorry you were worried. Why didn't you call?"

I called her cell phone. Does she not use her damned cell phone? Is she talking about the house phone? Running my hand through my hair in exasperation, I take a deep breath. This is not addressing the fucking elephant in the room.

"Anastasia, I need an answer from you. This waiting around is driving me crazy."

Her face falls.

Shit.

"Christian, I… Look, I've left my stepdad on his own."

"Tomorrow. I want an answer by tomorrow."

"Okay. Tomorrow. I'll tell you then," she says with an anxious look.

Well, it's still not a no. And once more, I'm surprised by my relief.

What the hell is it about this woman? She stares up at me with sincere blue eyes, her face etched in concern, and I resist the urge to touch her. "Are you staying for drinks?" I ask.

"I don't know what Ray wants to do." She looks uncertain.

"Your stepfather? I'd like to meet him."

Her uncertainty magnifies. "I'm not sure that's a good idea," she says darkly as I unlock the door.

What? Why? Is this because she now knows I was dirt-poor as a kid? Or because she knows how I like to fuck? That I'm a freak?

"Are you ashamed of me?"

"No!" she exclaims, and she rolls her eyes in frustration. "Introduce you to my dad as what?" She raises her hands in exasperation. "'This is the man who deflowered me and wants us to start a BDSM relationship'? You're not wearing running shoes."

Running shoes?

Her dad is going to come after me? And just like that she has injected a little humor between us. My mouth twitches in response and she returns my smile, her face lighting up like a summer dawn.

"Just so you know, I can run quite fast," I respond playfully. "Just tell him I'm your friend, Anastasia." I open the door and follow her out but stop when I reach the chancellor and his colleagues. As one they turn and stare at Miss Steele, but she's disappearing into the auditorium. They turn back to me.

Miss Steele and I are none of your business, people.

I give the chancellor a brief, polite nod and he asks if I'll come meet more of his colleagues and enjoy some canapés.

"Sure," I reply.

It takes me thirty minutes to escape from the faculty gathering, and as I make my way out of the crowded reception Kavanagh falls into step beside me. We head to the lawn where the graduates and their families are enjoying a post-graduation drink in a large tented pavilion.

"So have you asked Ana to dinner on Sunday?" she asks.

Sunday? Has Ana mentioned that we're seeing each other on Sunday?

"At your parents' house," Kavanagh explains.

My parents?

I spot Ana.

What the fuck?

A tall blond guy who looks as if he's walked off a beach in California has his hands all over her.

Who the hell is that? Is this why she didn't want me to come for a drink?

Ana looks up, catches my expression, and pales as her roommate stands beside that guy. "Hello, Ray," Kavanagh says, and she kisses a middle-aged man in an ill-fitting suit standing beside Ana.

This must be Raymond Steele.

"Have you met Ana's boyfriend?" Kavanagh asks him. "Christian Grey."

Boyfriend!

"Mr. Steele, it's a pleasure to meet you."

"Mr. Grey," he says, quietly surprised.

We shake hands; his grip is firm, and his fingers and palm are rough to the touch. This man works with his hands. Then I remember—he's a carpenter. His dark-brown eyes give nothing away.

"And this is my brother, Ethan Kavanagh," says Kate, introducing the beach bum who has his arm wrapped around Ana.

Ah. The Kavanagh offspring, together.

I mutter his name as we shake hands, noting that they are soft, unlike Ray Steele's.

Now stop pawing my girl, you fucker.

"Ana, baby," I whisper, holding out my hand, and like the good woman she is, she steps into my embrace. She's discarded her graduation robe and wears a pale-gray halter-neck dress, exposing her flawless shoulders and back.

Two dresses in two days. She's spoiling me.

"Ethan, Mom and Dad wanted a word." Kavanagh hauls her brother away, leaving me with Ana and her father.

"So how long have you kids known each other?" Mr. Steele asks.

As I reach up to grasp Ana's shoulder I gently trace my thumb across her naked back and she trembles in response. I tell him we've known each other for a couple of weeks. "We met when Anastasia came to interview me for the student newspaper."

"Didn't know you worked on the student newspaper, Ana," Mr. Steele says.

"Kate was ill," she says.

Ray Steele eyes his daughter and frowns. "Fine speech you gave, Mr. Grey," he says.

"Thank you, sir. I understand that you're an avid fisherman."

"Indeed I am. Annie tell you that?"

"She did."

"You fish?" There's a spark of curiosity in his brown eyes.

"Not as much as I'd like to. My dad used to take my brother and me when we were kids. For him it was all about the steelheads. Guess I caught the bug from him."

Ana listens for a moment, then excuses herself and moves off through the crowd to join the Kavanagh clan.

Damn, she looks sensational in that dress.

"Oh? Where d'you fish?" Ray Steele's question pulls me back into the conversation. I know it's a test.

"All over the Pacific Northwest."

"You grew up in Washington?"

"Yes, sir. My dad started us on the Wynoochee River."

A smile tugs at Steele's mouth. "Know it well."

"But his favorite is the Skagit. The U.S. side. He'd get us out of bed at some ungodly hour of the morning and we'd drive up there. He's caught some mighty fine fish in that river."

"That's some sweet water. Caught me some rod breakers in the Skagit. On the Canadian side, mind."

"It's one of the best stretches for wild steelheads. Give you a much better chase than those that are clipped," I say, my eyes on Ana.

"Couldn't agree more."

"My brother's caught a couple of wild monsters. Me, I'm still waiting for the big one."

"One day, huh?"

"I hope so."

Ana is deep in a passionate discussion with Kavanagh. *What are those two women talking about?*

"You still get out much to fish?" I refocus on Mr. Steele.

"Sure do. Annie's friend José, his father, and I sneak out as often as we can."

The fucking photographer! Again?

"He's the guy that looks after the Beetle?"

"Yeah, that's him."

"Great car, the Beetle. I'm a fan of German-made cars."

"Yeah? Annie loves that old car, but I guess it's getting past its sell-by date."

"Funny you should mention that. I was thinking of loaning her one of my company cars. Do you think she'd go for it?"

"I guess. That would be up to Annie, mind."

"Great. I take it Ana's not into fishing."

"No. That girl takes after her mother. She couldn't stomach seeing the fish suffer. Or the worms, for that matter. She's a gentle soul." He gives me a pointed look. *Oh.* A warning from Raymond Steele.

I turn it into a joke. "No wonder she wasn't keen on the cod we ate the other day."

Steele chuckles. "She's fine with eating them."

Ana has finished talking to the Kavanaghs and is heading our way. "Hi," she says, beaming at us.

"Annie, where are the restrooms?" Steele asks.

She directs him to go outside the pavilion and to the left.

"See you in a moment. You kids enjoy yourselves," he says.

She watches him go, then peers nervously up at me. But before she or I can say anything we're interrupted by a photographer. She snaps a quick still of us together before hurrying away.

"So you've charmed my father as well?" Ana says, her voice sweet and teasing.

"As well?" *Have I charmed you, Miss Steele?* With my fingers I trace the rosy flush that appears on her cheek. "Oh, I wish I knew what you were thinking, Anastasia." When my fingers reach her chin I tilt her head back so I can scrutinize her expression.

She stills and stares back at me, her pupils darkening. "Right now," she whispers, "I'm thinking 'Nice tie.'"

I was expecting some kind of declaration; her response makes me laugh. "It's recently become my favorite."

She smiles.

"You look lovely, Anastasia. This halter-neck dress suits you, and I get to stroke your back, feel your beautiful skin."

Her lips part and her breath hitches, and I can feel the pull of the attraction between us.

"You know it's going to be good, don't you, baby?" My voice is low, betraying my longing.

She closes her eyes, swallows, and takes a deep breath. When she opens them again, she's radiating anxiety. "But I want more," she says.

"More?"

Fuck. What is this?

She nods.

"More?" I whisper again. Her lip is pliant beneath my thumb. "You want hearts and flowers." *Fuck.* It will never work with her. How can it? I don't do romance. My hopes and dreams begin to crumble between us.

Her eyes are wide, innocent, and beseeching.

Damn. She's so beguiling. "Anastasia. It's not something I know."

"Me, neither."

Of course. She's never had a relationship before. "You don't know much."

"You know all the wrong things," she breathes.

"Wrong? Not to me. Try it," I plead.

Please. Try it my way.

Her gaze is intense as she searches my face, looking for clues. And for a moment I'm lost in blue eyes that see everything.

"Okay," she whispers.

"What?" Every hair on my body stands to attention.

"Okay. I'll try."

"You're agreeing?" I don't believe it.

"Subject to the soft limits, yes. I'll try."

Sweet. Lord. I pull her into my arms and wrap her in my embrace, burying my face in her hair, inhaling her seductive scent. And I don't care that we're in a crowded space. It's just her and me. "Jesus, Ana, you're so unexpected. You take my breath away."

A moment later I'm aware that Raymond Steele has returned and is examining his watch to cover his embarrassment. Reluctantly, I release her. I'm on top of the world.

Deal done, Grey!

"Annie, should we get some lunch?" Steele asks.

"Okay," she says with a shy smile directed at me.

"Would you like to join us, Christian?" For a moment I'm tempted, but Ana's anxious glance in my direction says *Please, no.* She wants alone time with her dad. I get it.

"Thank you, Mr. Steele, but I have plans. It's been great to meet you, sir."

Try to control your stupid grin, Grey.

"Likewise," Steele replies—sincerely, I think. "Look after my baby girl."

"Oh, I fully intend to," I respond, shaking his hand.

In ways you can't possibly imagine, Mr. Steele.

I take Ana's hand and bring her knuckles to my lips. "Later, Miss Steele," I murmur. *You've made me a happy, happy man.*

Steele gives me a brief nod, and taking his daughter's elbow, leads her out of the reception. I stand dazed but brimming with hope.

She's agreed.

"Christian Grey?" My joy is interrupted by Eamon Kavanagh, Katherine's father.

"Eamon, how are you?" We shake hands.

TAYLOR COLLECTS ME AT 3:30. "Good afternoon, sir," he says, opening my car door.

En route he informs me that the Audi A3 has been delivered to The Heathman. Now I just have to give it to Ana. No doubt this will involve a discussion, and deep down I know it will be more than just a discussion. Then again, she's agreed to be my submissive, so maybe she'll accept my gift without any fuss.

Who are you kidding, Grey?

A man can dream. I hope we can meet this evening; I'll give it to her as her graduation present.

I call Andrea and tell her to put a WebEx breakfast meeting into my schedule tomorrow with Eamon Kavanagh and his associates in New York. Kavanagh is interested in upgrading his fiber-optic network. I ask Andrea to have Ros and Fred on standby for the meeting, too. She relays some messages—nothing important—and reminds me I have to attend a charity function tomorrow evening in Seattle.

Tonight will be my last night in Portland. It's almost Ana's last night here, too… I contemplate calling her, but there's little point since she doesn't have her cell phone. And she's enjoying time with her dad.

Staring out the car window as we drive toward The Heathman, I watch the good people of Portland go about their afternoon. At a stoplight there's a young couple arguing on the sidewalk over a spilled bag of groceries. Another couple, even younger, walks hand in hand past them, eyes locked and giggling. The girl leans up and whispers something in the ear of her tattooed beau. He laughs, leans down, and kisses her quickly, then opens the door to a coffee shop and steps aside to let her enter.

Ana wants "more." I sigh heavily and plow my fingers through my hair. They always want more. All of them. What can I do about that? The hand-in-hand couple strolling to the coffee shop—Ana and I did that. We've eaten together at two restaurants, and it was…fun. Perhaps I could try. After all, she's giving me so much. I loosen my tie.

Could I do more?

BACK IN MY ROOM, I strip down, pull on my sweats, and head downstairs for a quick circuit in the gym. Enforced socializing has stretched the limits of my patience and I need to work off some excess energy.

And I need to think about *more.*

ONCE I'M SHOWERED AND dressed and back in front of my laptop, Ros calls via WebEx to check in and we talk for forty minutes. We cover all the items on her agenda, including the Taiwan proposal and Darfur. The cost of the airdrop is staggering, but it's safer for all involved. I give her the go-ahead. Now we have to wait for the shipment to arrive in Rotterdam.

"I'm up-to-date on Kavanagh Media. I think Barney should be in on the meeting, too," Ros says.

"If you think so. Let Andrea know."

"Will do. How was the graduation ceremony?" she asks.

"Good. Unexpected."

Ana agreed to be mine.

"Unexpected good?"

"Yes."

From the screen Ros peers at me, intrigued, but I say nothing more.

"Andrea tells me you're back in Seattle tomorrow."

"Yes. I have a function to attend in the evening."

"Well, I hope your 'merger' has been successful."

"I would say affirmative at this point, Ros."

She smirks. "Glad to hear it. I have another meeting, so if there's nothing else, I'll say goodbye for now."

"Goodbye." I log out of WebEx and into email, turning my attention to this evening.

From: Christian Grey
Subject: Soft Limits
Date: May 26 2011 17:22
To: Anastasia Steele

What can I say that I haven't already?
Happy to talk these through anytime.

You looked beautiful today.

Christian Grey
CEO, Grey Enterprises Holdings, Inc.

And to think this morning I was convinced it was all over between us.

Jesus, Grey. You need to get a grip. Flynn would have a field day.

Of course, part of the reason was she didn't have her phone. Perhaps she needs a more reliable form of communication.

From: Christian Grey
Subject: BlackBerry
Date: May 26 2011 17:36
To: J B Taylor
Cc: Andrea Ashton

Taylor
Please source a new BlackBerry for Anastasia Steele with her email preinstalled. Andrea can get the account details from Barney and get them to you.
Please deliver it tomorrow either to her home or to Clayton's.

Christian Grey
CEO, Grey Enterprises Holdings, Inc.

Once that's sent, I pick up the latest *Forbes* and start to read.

By 6:30 there's no response from Ana, so I assume she's still entertaining the quiet and unassuming Ray Steele. Given they aren't related, they're remarkably similar.

I order the seafood risotto from room service and while I wait I read more of my book.

GRACE CALLS WHILE I'M reading.

"Christian, darling."

"Hello, Mother."

"Did Mia get in touch?"

"Yes. I have her flight details. I'll pick her up."

"Great. Now, I hope you'll stay for dinner on Saturday."

"Sure."

"And then on Sunday Elliot is bringing his friend Kate to dinner. Would you like to come? You could bring Anastasia."

That's what Kavanagh was talking about today.

I play for time. "I'll have to see if she's free."

"Let me know. It will be lovely to have all the family together again."

I roll my eyes. "If you say so, Mother."

"I do, darling. See you Saturday."

She hangs up.

Take Ana to meet my parents? How the hell do I get out of that?

As I contemplate this predicament, an email arrives.

From: Anastasia Steele
Subject: Soft Limits
Date: May 26 2011 19:23
To: Christian Grey

I can come over this evening to discuss if you'd like.

Ana

No, no baby. Not in that car. And my plans fall into place.

From: Christian Grey
Subject: Soft Limits
Date: May 26 2011 19:27
To: Anastasia Steele

I'll come to you. I meant it when I said I wasn't happy about you driving that car.

I'll be with you shortly.

Christian Grey
CEO, Grey Enterprises Holdings, Inc.

I print out another copy of the Soft Limits from the contract and her Issues email because I've left my first copy in my jacket, which she still has in her possession. Then I call Taylor in his room.

"I'm going to deliver the car to Anastasia. Can you pick me up from her place—say, nine thirty?"

"Certainly, sir."

Before I leave I stuff two condoms into the back pocket of my jeans.

I might get lucky.

THE A3 IS FUN to drive, though it's got less torque than I'm used to. I pull up outside a liquor store on the outskirts of Portland to buy some celebratory champagne. I forgo the Cristal and the Dom Pérignon for a Bollinger, mostly because it's the 1999 vintage and chilled, but also because it's pink—symbolic, I think with a smirk, as I hand my AmEx to the cashier.

Ana is still wearing the stunning gray dress when she opens the door. I look forward to peeling it off her later.

"Hi," she says, her eyes large and luminous in her pale face.

"Hi."

"Come in." She seems shy and awkward. *Why? What's happened?*

"If I may." I hold up the bottle of champagne. "I thought we'd celebrate your graduation. Nothing beats a good Bollinger."

"Interesting choice of words." Her voice is sardonic.

"Oh, I like your ready wit, Anastasia." There she is…my girl.

"We only have teacups. We've packed all the glasses."

"Teacups? Sounds good to me."

I watch her wander into the kitchen. She's nervous and skittish. Perhaps because she's had a big day, or because she's agreed to my terms, or because she's here alone—I know Kavanagh is with her own family this evening; her father told me. I hope the champagne will help Ana relax…and talk.

The room is empty, except for packing crates, the sofa, and the table. There's a brown parcel on the table with a handwritten note attached.

"I agree to the conditions, Angel; because you know best what my punishment ought to be; only—only—don't make it more than I can bear!"

"Do you want saucers as well?" she calls.

"Teacups will be fine, Anastasia," I respond, distracted. She's wrapped up the books—the first editions I sent her. She's giving them back to me. She doesn't want them. This is why she's nervous.

How the hell will she react to the car?

Looking up, I see her standing there, watching me. And carefully she places the cups on the table.

"That's for you." Her voice is small and strained.

"Hmm, I figured as much," I mutter. "Very apt quote." I trace her handwriting with my finger. The letters are small and neat, and I wonder what a graphologist would make of them. "I thought I was d'Urberville, not Angel. You decided on the debasement." Of course it's the perfect quote. My smile is ironic. "Trust you to find something that resonates so appropriately."

"It's also a plea," she whispers.

"A plea? For me to go easy on you?"

She nods.

To me these books were an investment, but for her I thought they'd mean something.

"I bought these for you." It's a small white lie—as I've replaced them. "I'll go easier on you if you accept them." I keep my voice calm and quiet, masking my disappointment.

"Christian, I can't accept them; they're just too much."

Here we go, another battle of wills.

Plus ça change, plus c'est la même chose.

"You see, this is what I was talking about, you defying me. I want you to have them, and that's the end of the discussion. It's very simple. You don't have to think about this. As a submissive you would just be grateful for them. You just accept what I buy you because it pleases me for you to do so."

"I wasn't a submissive when you bought them for me," she says quietly.

As ever, she has an answer for everything.

"No...but you've agreed, Anastasia."

Is she reneging on our deal? God, this girl has me on a roller coaster.

"So they are mine to do with as I wish?"

"Yes." *I thought you loved Hardy?*

"In that case, I'd like to give them to a charity—one working in Darfur, since that seems to be close to your heart. They can auction them."

"If that's what you want to do." I'm not going to stop you.

You can burn them, for all I care...

Her pale face colors. "I'll think about it," she mutters.

"Don't think, Anastasia. Not about this." Keep them, please. They're for you, because your passion is books. You've told me more than once. Enjoy them.

Placing the champagne on the table, I stand in front of her and cup her chin, tipping her head back so my eyes are on hers. "I will buy you lots of things, Anastasia. Get used to it. I can afford it. I'm a very wealthy man." I kiss her quickly. "Please," I add and release her.

"It makes me feel cheap," she says.

"It shouldn't. You're overthinking it. Don't place some vague moral judgment on yourself based on what others might think. Don't waste your energy. It's only because you have reservations about our arrangement; that's perfectly natural. You don't know what you're getting yourself into."

Anxiety is etched all over her lovely face.

"Hey, stop this. There is nothing about you that is cheap, Anastasia. I won't have you thinking that. I just sent you some old books that I thought might mean something to you, that's all."

She blinks a couple of times and stares at the package, obviously conflicted.

Keep them, Ana—they're for you.

"Have some champagne," I whisper, and she rewards me with a small smile.

"That's better." I open the champagne and fill the dainty teacups she's placed in front of me.

"It's pink." She's surprised, and I haven't the heart to tell her why I chose pink.

"Bollinger La Grande Année Rosé 1999—an excellent vintage."

"In teacups." She grins. It's infectious.

"In teacups. Congratulations on your degree, Anastasia."

We touch cups, and I drink. It tastes good, as I knew it would.

"Thank you." She raises the cup to her lips and takes a quick sip. "Shall we go through the soft limits?"

"Always so eager." Taking her hand, I lead her to the sofa—one of the only remaining pieces of furniture in the living room—and we sit, surrounded by boxes.

"Your stepfather's a very taciturn man."

"You managed to get him eating out of your hand."

I chuckle. "Only because I know how to fish."

"How did you know he liked fishing?"

"You told me. When we went for coffee."

"Oh, did I?" She takes another sip and closes her eyes, savoring the taste. Opening them again, she asks, "Did you try the wine at the reception?"

I grimace. "Yes. It was foul."

"I thought of you when I tasted it. How did you get to be so knowledgeable about wine?"

"I'm not knowledgeable, Anastasia. I just know what I like." And I like you. "Some more?" I nod toward the bottle on the table.

"Please."

I fetch the champagne and refill her cup. She regards me suspiciously. She knows I'm plying her with alcohol.

"This place looks pretty bare. Are you ready for the move?" I ask to distract her.

"More or less."

"Are you working tomorrow?"

"Yes, my last day at Clayton's."

"I'd help you move, but I promised to meet my sister at the airport. Mia arrives from Paris early on Saturday. I'm heading back to Seattle tomorrow, but I hear Elliot is giving you two a hand."

"Yes, Kate is very excited about that."

I'm surprised Elliot is still interested in Ana's friend; it's not his usual MO. "Yes, Kate and Elliot, who would have thought?" Their liaison makes matters complicated. My mother's voice rings in my head: *"You could bring Anastasia."*

"So what are you doing about work in Seattle?" I ask.

"I have a couple of interviews for internships."

"You were going to tell me this when?"

"Um...I'm telling you now," she says.

"Where?" I ask, hiding my frustration.

"A couple of publishing houses."

"Is that what you want to do, something in publishing?"

She nods, but she's still not forthcoming.

"Well?" I prompt.

"Well, what?"

"Don't be obtuse, Anastasia. Which publishing houses?" I mentally run through all the publishing houses I know of in Seattle. There are four...I think.

"Just small ones," she says evasively.

"Why don't you want me to know?"

"Undue influence," she says.

What does that mean? I frown.

"Oh, now *you're* being obtuse," she says, her eyes twinkling with mirth.

"Obtuse?" I laugh. "Me? God, you're challenging. Drink up. Let's talk about these limits."

Her eyelashes flutter and she takes a shaky breath, then drains her cup. She's really nervous about this. I offer her more liquid courage.

"Please," she responds.

Bottle in hand, I pause. "Have you eaten anything?"

"Yes. I had a three-course meal with Ray," she says, exasperated, and rolls her eyes.

Oh, Ana. At last I can do something about this disrespectful habit.

Leaning forward, I take hold of her chin and glare at her. "Next time you roll your eyes at me, I will take you across my knee."

"Oh." She looks a little shocked, but a little intrigued, too.

"Oh. So it begins, Anastasia." With a wolfish grin I fill her teacup, and she takes a long sip.

"Got your attention now, haven't I?"

She nods.

"Answer me."

"Yes, you've got my attention," she says with a contrite smile.

"Good." I fish out her email and Appendix 3 of my contract from my jacket. "So, sexual acts. We've done most of this."

She shuffles closer to me and we read down the list.

APPENDIX 3

Soft Limits

To be discussed and agreed between both parties:

Does the Submissive consent to:

- Masturbation
- Cunnilingus
- Fellatio
- Swallowing semen
- Vaginal intercourse
- Vaginal fisting
- Anal intercourse
- Anal fisting

"No fisting, you say. Anything else you object to?" I ask.

She swallows. "Anal intercourse doesn't exactly float my boat."

"I'll agree to the fisting, but I'd really like to claim your ass, Anastasia."

She inhales sharply, gazing at me.

"But we'll wait for that. Besides, it's not something we can dive into." I can't help my smirk. "Your ass will need training."

"Training?" Her eyes widen.

"Oh yes. It'll need careful preparation. Anal intercourse can be very pleasurable, trust me. But if we try it and you don't like it, we don't have to do it again." I delight in her shocked expression.

"Have you done that?" she asks.

"Yes."

"With a man?"

"No. I've never had sex with a man. Not my scene."

"Mrs. Robinson?"

"Yes." And her large rubber strap-on.

Ana frowns and I move on quickly, before she can ask me any more questions about that.

"And...swallowing semen. Well, you get an A in that." I expect a smile from her, but she's studying me intently, as if seeing me in a new light. I think she's still reeling over Mrs. Robinson and anal intercourse.

Oh, baby, Elena had my submission.

She could do with me as she pleased. And I enjoyed it.

"So, swallowing semen okay?" I ask, trying to bring her back to the now.

She nods and finishes her champagne.

"More?" I ask.

Steady, Grey, you just want her tipsy, not drunk.

"More," she whispers.

I refill her cup and get back to the list. "Sex toys?"

> Does the Submissive consent to the use of:
>
> - Vibrators
> - Dildos
> - Butt plugs
> - Other vaginal/anal toys

"Butt plug? Does it do what it says on the box?" She grimaces.

"Yes. And I refer to anal intercourse above. Training."

"Oh. What's in 'other'?"

"Beads, eggs, that sort of stuff."

"Eggs?" Her hands shoot to her mouth in shock.

"Not real eggs." I laugh.

"I'm glad you find me funny." The hurt in her voice is sobering.

"I apologize. I'm sorry."

For fuck's sake, Grey. Go easy on her.

"Any problem with toys?"

"No," she snaps.

Shit. She's sulking.

"Anastasia, I'm sorry. Believe me. I don't mean to laugh. I've never had this conversation in so much detail. You're just so inexperienced. I'm sorry."

She pouts and takes another sip of champagne.

"Right—bondage," I say, and we return to the list.

Does the Submissive consent to:

- Bondage with rope
- Bondage with leather cuffs
- Bondage with handcuffs/shackles/manacles
- Bondage with tape
- Bondage with other

"Well?" I ask, gently this time.

"Fine," she whispers and continues reading.

Does the Submissive consent to be restrained with:

- Hands bound in front
- Ankles bound
- Elbows bound
- Hands bound behind back
- Knees bound
- Wrists bound to ankles
- Binding to fixed items, furniture, etc.
- Binding with spreader bar
- Suspension

Does the Submissive consent to be blindfolded?

Does the Submissive consent to be gagged?

"We've talked about suspension. And it's fine if you want to set that as a hard limit. It takes a great deal of time, and I only have you for short periods anyway. Anything else?"

"Don't laugh at me, but what's a spreader bar?"

"I promise not to laugh. I've apologized twice." *For Christ's sake.* "Don't make me do it again." My voice is sharper than I intended, and she leans away from me.

Shit.

Ignore her reaction, Grey. Get on with it. "A spreader is a bar with cuffs for ankles and/or wrists. They're fun."

"Okay. Well, gagging me. I'd be worried I wouldn't be able to breathe."

"*I'd* be worried if you couldn't breathe. I don't want to suffocate you." Breath play is not my scene at all.

"And how will I use safe words if I'm gagged?" she inquires.

"First of all, I hope you never have to use them. But if you're gagged, we'll use hand signals."

"I'm nervous about the gagging."

"Okay. I'll take note."

She studies me for a moment as if she's solved the riddle of the sphinx. "Do you like tying your submissives up so they can't touch you?" she asks.

"That's one of the reasons."

"Is that why you've tied my hands?"

"Yes."

"You don't like talking about that," she says.

"No, I don't."

I'm not going there with you, Ana. Give it up.

"Would you like another drink?" I ask. "It's making you brave, and I need to know how you feel about pain." I refill her cup and she takes a sip, wide-eyed and anxious. "So, what's your general attitude to receiving pain?"

She remains mute.

I suppress a sigh. "You're biting your lip." Fortunately, she stops, but now she's pensive and staring down at her hands. "Were you physically punished as a child?" I prompt her gently.

"No."

"So you have no sphere of reference at all?"

"No."

"It's not as bad as you think. Your imagination is your worst enemy in this." *Trust me on this, Ana. Please.*

"Do you have to do it?"

"Yes."

"Why?"

You really don't want to know.

"Goes with the territory, Anastasia. It's what I do. I can see you're nervous. Let's go through methods."

We read through the list:

- Spanking
- Whipping
- Biting
- Genital clamps
- Hot wax
- Paddling
- Caning
- Nipple clamps
- Ice
- Other types/methods of pain

"Well, you said no to genital clamps. That's fine. It's caning that hurts the most."

Ana pales.

"We can work up to that," I state quickly.

"Or not do it at all," she counters.

"This is part of the deal, baby, but we'll work up to all of this. Anastasia, I won't push you too far."

"This punishment thing, it worries me the most."

"Well, I'm glad you've told me. We'll keep caning off the list for now. And as you get more comfortable with everything else, we'll increase intensity. We'll take it slow."

She looks uncertain, so I lean forward and kiss her. "There, that wasn't so bad, was it?"

She shrugs, still doubtful.

"Look, I want to talk about one more thing, then I'm taking you to bed."

"Bed?" she exclaims and color flushes her cheeks.

"Come on, Anastasia, talking through all this, I want to fuck you into next week, right now. It must be having some effect on you, too."

She squirms beside me and takes a husky breath, her thighs pressing together.

"See? Besides, there's something I want to try."

"Something painful?"

"No—stop seeing pain everywhere. It's mainly pleasure. Have I hurt you yet?"

"No."

"Well then. Look, earlier today you were talking about wanting more." I stop.

Fuck. I'm on a precipice.

Okay, Grey, are you sure about this?

I have to try. I don't want to lose her before we start.

Jump.

I take her hand. "Outside of the time you're my sub, perhaps we could try. I don't know if it will work. I don't know about separating everything. It may not work. But I'm willing to try. Maybe one night a week. I don't know."

Her mouth drops open.

"I have one condition."

"What?" she asks, her breath hitching.

"You graciously accept my graduation present to you."

"Oh," she says, her eyes widening with uncertainty.

"Come." I pull her to her feet, slip off my leather jacket, and drape it over her shoulders. Taking a deep breath, I open the front door and reveal the Audi A3 parked at the curb. "It's for you. Happy graduation." I wrap my arms around her and kiss her hair.

When I release her she stares dumbfounded at the car.

Okay...this could go either way.

Taking her hand, I lead her down the steps and she follows as if in a trance.

"Anastasia, that Beetle of yours is old and, frankly, dangerous. I would never forgive myself if something happened to you when it's so easy for me to make it right."

She gapes at the car, speechless.

Shit.

"I mentioned it to your stepfather. He was all for it."

Perhaps I'm overstating this.

Her mouth is still open in dismay when she turns to glare at me.

"You mentioned this to Ray? How *could* you?" She's annoyed, really annoyed.

"It's a gift, Anastasia. Can't you just say thank you?"

"But you know it's too much."

"Not to me it isn't, not for my peace of mind."

Come on, Ana. You want more. This is the price.

Her shoulders sag, and she turns to me, resigned, I think. Not quite the reaction I was hoping for. The rosy glow from the champagne has disappeared and her face is pale once more. "I'm happy for you to loan this to me, like the laptop."

I shake my head. Why is she so difficult? I've never had this reaction to a car from any of my submissives. They're usually delighted.

"Okay. On loan. Indefinitely," I agree through gritted teeth.

"No, not indefinitely, but for now. Thank you," she says quietly, and leaning up, she kisses me on the cheek. "Thank you for the car, Sir."

That word. From her sweet, sweet mouth.

I grab her and press her body to mine, her hair pooling in my fingers. "You are one challenging woman, Ana Steele." I kiss her forcefully, coaxing her lips apart with my tongue, and a moment later she's responding, matching my ardor, her tongue caressing mine. My body reacts—I want her. Here. Now. In the open. "It's taking all my self-control not to fuck you on the hood of this car right now, just to show you that you are mine, and if I want to buy you a fucking car, I'll buy you a fucking car. Now let's get you inside and naked," I growl.

I kiss her once more, demanding and possessive. Taking her

hand, I stride back into the apartment, slamming the front door behind us and heading straight for her bedroom. There I release her and switch on her bedside light.

"Please don't be angry with me," she whispers.

Her words douse the fire of my anger.

"I'm sorry about the car and the books—" She halts and licks her lips. "You scare me when you're angry."

Shit. No one has ever said that to me before. I close my eyes. The last thing I want to do is frighten her.

Calm down, Grey.

She's here. She's safe. She's willing. Don't blow it, just because she doesn't understand how to behave.

Opening my eyes, I find Ana watching me, not in fear, but with anticipation.

"Turn around," I demand, my voice soft. "I want to get you out of that dress."

She obeys immediately.

Good girl.

I remove my jacket from her shoulders and discard it on the floor, then lift her hair off her neck. The feel of her soft skin beneath my index finger is soothing. Now that she's doing what she's told, I relax. With the tip of my finger I follow the line of her spine down her back to the start of the zipper bound in gray chiffon. "I like this dress. I like to see your flawless skin."

Hooking my finger into the back of her dress, I pull her close so she's flush against me. I bury my face in her hair and breathe in her scent.

"You smell so good, Anastasia. So sweet."

Like fall.

Her fragrance is comforting, reminding me of a time of plenty and happiness. Still inhaling her delicious scent, I skim my nose from her ear down her neck to her shoulder, kissing her as I go. Slowly I unzip her dress and kiss, and lick, and suck my way across her skin to her other shoulder.

She shivers beneath my touch.

Oh, baby. "You are going to have to learn to keep still," I whisper between kisses and unfasten her halter neck. The dress falls to her feet.

"No bra, Miss Steele. I like that."

Reaching forward, I cup her breasts and feel her nipples pebble against my palm.

"Lift your arms and put them around my head," I order, my lips brushing her neck.

She does as she's told and her breasts lift farther into my palms. She twists her fingers into my hair, the way I like, and she tugs.

Ah... That feels so good.

Her head lolls to the side, and I take advantage, kissing her where her pulse hammers beneath her skin.

"Mmm..." I murmur in appreciation, my fingers teasing and tugging at her nipples.

She groans, arching her back, pushing her perfect tits even farther into my hands. "Shall I make you come this way?"

Her body bows a little more.

"You like this, don't you, Miss Steele?"

"Mmm..."

"Tell me," I insist, continuing my sensual assault on her nipples.

"Yes," she breathes.

"Yes, what?"

"Yes...Sir."

"Good girl."

I gently pinch and twist with my fingers and her body bucks convulsively against me while she moans, her hands tugging harder at my hair.

"I don't think you're ready to come yet." And I still my hands, just holding her breasts, while my teeth tug at her earlobe. "Besides, you have displeased me. So perhaps I won't let you come after all."

I knead her breasts and my fingers return my attention to her nipples, twisting and tugging. She groans and grinds her ass against my erection. Shifting my hands to her hips, I hold her steady and glance down at her panties.

Cotton. White. Easy.

I hook my fingers into them and stretch them as far as they'll go, then push my thumbs through the seam at the back. They tear apart in my hands and I throw them at Ana's feet.

She gasps.

I trace my fingers around her ass and insert one into her vagina. She's wet. Very wet.

"Oh yes. My sweet girl is ready."

I spin her around and slip my finger into my mouth.

Mmm. Salty. "You taste so fine, Miss Steele."

Her lips part and her eyes darken with want. I think she's a little shocked.

"Undress me." I keep my eyes on hers.

She tilts her head, processing my command, but hesitates. "You can do it," I encourage her.

She lifts her hands and all of a sudden I think she's going to touch me, and I'm not ready. *Shit.*

Instinctively I grab her hands.

"Oh no. Not the T-shirt."

I want her on top. We've not done this yet, and she may lose her balance, so I'll need the T-shirt for protection. "You may need to touch me for what I have planned." I release one of her hands, but the other I place over my erection, which is fighting for space in my jeans.

"This is the effect you have on me, Miss Steele."

She inhales, gazing at her hand. Then her fingers tighten around my cock and she glances up at me with appreciation.

I grin. "I want to be inside you. Take my jeans off. You're in charge."

Her mouth drops open.

"What are you going to do with me?" My voice is husky.

Her face transforms, bright with delight, and before I can react she pushes me. I laugh as I fall onto the bed, mainly at her bravado, but also because she touched me and I didn't panic. She removes my shoes, then my socks, but she's all fingers and thumbs, reminding me of the interview and her attempts to set up the recorder.

I watch her. Amused. Aroused. Wondering what she'll do next.

It's going to be one hell of a task for her to remove my jeans while I'm lying down. Stepping out of her pumps, she crawls up the bed, sits astride the top of my thighs, and slips her fingers beneath the waistband of my jeans.

I close my eyes and flex my hips, enjoying shameless Ana.

"You'll have to learn to keep still," she castigates me and tugs at my pubic hair.

Ah! *So bold, ma'am.*

"Yes, Miss Steele," I tease through clenched teeth. "In my pocket, condom."

Her eyes flash with obvious delight and her fingers rifle through my pocket, diving deep, brushing my erection.

Ah…

She produces both foil packets and tosses them onto the bed beside me. Her fumbling fingers reach for the button on my waistband, and after two attempts she undoes it.

Her naivete is captivating. It's obvious she's never done this before. Another first…and it's fucking arousing.

"So eager, Miss Steele," I tease.

She yanks down my zipper and, pulling at my waistband, gives me a look of frustration.

I try hard not to laugh.

Yeah, baby, how are you going to get these off me now?

Shuffling down my legs, she tugs at my jeans, concentrating hard, looking adorable. And I decide to help her out. "I can't keep still if you're going to bite that lip," I say while arching my hips, lifting them off the bed.

Rising up on her knees, she pulls down my jeans and boxers and I kick them off, onto the floor. She sits across me, eyeing my cock and licking her lips.

Whoa.

She looks hot, her dark hair falling in soft waves around her breasts.

"Now what are you going to do?" I whisper.

Her eyes flick to my face and she reaches up and grasps me firmly, squeezing hard, her thumb brushing over the tip.

Jesus.

She leans down.

And I'm in her mouth.

Fuck.

She sucks hard. And my body flexes beneath her. "Jeez, Ana, steady," I hiss through my teeth. But she shows no mercy as she fellates me again and again. *Fuck.*

Her enthusiasm is disarming. Her tongue is up and down; I'm in and out of her mouth to the back of her throat, her lips tight around me. It's an overwhelming erotic vision. I could come just watching her.

"Stop, Ana, stop. I don't want to come."

She sits up, her mouth moist and her eyes two dark pools directed down at me.

"Your innocence and enthusiasm are very disarming." *But right now I want to fuck you so I can see you.* "You, on top, that's what we need to do. Here, put this on." I place a condom in her hand. She examines it with consternation, then rips the packet open with her teeth.

She's keen.

She removes the condom and looks to me for direction.

"Pinch the top and then roll it down. You don't want any air in the end of that sucker."

She nods and does exactly that, absorbed in her task, concentrating hard, her tongue peeking between her lips.

"Christ, you're killing me here," I exclaim through clenched teeth.

When she's done she sits back and admires her handiwork, or me—I'm not quite sure, but I don't care. "Now. I want to be buried inside you." I sit up suddenly so we're face-to-face, surprising her. "Like this," I whisper, and wrapping my arm around her, I lift her. With my other hand I position my cock and lower her slowly onto me.

My breath escapes from my body as her eyes close and pleasure thrums noisily in her throat.

"That's right, baby, feel me, all of me."

She. Feels. So. Good.

I hold her, letting her get used to the feel of me. Like this. Inside her. "It's deep this way." My voice is hoarse, as I flex and tilt my pelvis, pushing deeper into her.

Her head lolls as she moans. "Again," she breathes. And she opens her eyes and they blaze into mine. Wanton. Willing. I love that she loves this.

I do as I'm asked and she moans again, throwing back her head, her hair tumbling in a riot over her shoulders.

I recline onto the bed to watch the show. "You move, Anastasia, up and down, how you want. Take my hands." I hold them out and she grabs them, steadying herself on top of me. Hesitantly she eases herself up, then sinks back down onto me.

My breath is coming in short, sharp pants as I restrain myself. She lifts herself again and this time I raise my hips to meet her as she comes down.

Oh yes.

Closing my eyes, I savor every delicious inch of her. Together we find our rhythm as she rides me. Over and over and over. She looks fantastic: her breasts bouncing, her hair swinging, her mouth slack as she absorbs each stab of pleasure.

Her eyes meet mine, full of carnal need and wonder. God, she's beautiful.

She cries out as her body takes over. She's almost there, so I tighten my grip on her hands, and she ignites around me. I grab her hips, holding her as she shouts incoherently through her orgasm. Then I tighten my hold on her hips and silently lose myself as I explode inside her.

She flops down onto my chest, and I lie, panting, beneath her.

My God, she's a good fuck.

We lie together for a moment, her weight a comfort. She stirs and nuzzles me through my shirt, then splays her hand on top of my chest.

The darkness slithers, quick and strong, into my chest, into my throat, threatening to suffocate and choke me.

No. Don't touch me.

I grab her hand and bring her knuckles to my lips, and roll over on top of her so she's no longer able to touch me.

"Don't," I plead and kiss her lips as I dampen down my fear.

"Why don't you like to be touched?"

"Because I'm fifty shades of fucked up, Anastasia." After years and years of therapy, it's the one thing I know to be true.

Her eyes widen, inquisitive; she's thirsty for more information. But she doesn't need to know this shit.

"I had a very tough introduction to life. I don't want to burden you with the details. Just don't." I gently brush my nose against hers, and withdrawing from her, I sit up, remove the condom, and drop it by the bed. "I think that's all the very basics covered. How was that?"

For a moment she seems distracted, then she tilts her head to one side and smiles. "If you imagine for one minute that I think you ceded control to me, well, you haven't taken into account my GPA. But thank you for the illusion."

"Miss Steele, you are not just a pretty face. You've had six orgasms so far and all of them belong to me." Why does that mere fact make me glad?

Her eyes stray to the ceiling, and a fleeting guilty expression crosses her face.

What's this? "Do you have something to tell me?" I ask.

She hesitates. "I had a dream this morning."

"Oh?"

"I came in my sleep." She flings her arm over her face, hiding from me, embarrassed. I'm stunned by her confession but aroused and delighted, too.

Sensual creature.

She peeks over her arm. Does she expect me to be angry?

"In your sleep?" I clarify.

"Woke me up," she whispers.

"I'm sure it did." I'm fascinated. "What were you dreaming about?"

"You," she says in a small voice.

Me!

"What was I doing?"

She hides beneath her arm again.

"Anastasia, what was I doing? I won't ask you again." Why is she so embarrassed? Her dreaming about me is…endearing.

"You had a riding crop," she mumbles.

I move her arm so I can see her face. "Really?"

"Yes." Her face is bright red. The research must be affecting her, in a good way.

I smile down at her. "There's hope for you yet. I have several riding crops."

"Brown plaited leather?" Her voice is tinged with quiet optimism.

I laugh. "No, but I'm sure I could get one."

I give her a swift kiss and stand to dress. Ana does the same, pulling on sweatpants and a camisole. Collecting the condom off the floor, I knot it quickly. Now that she's agreed to be mine, she needs contraception.

Fully dressed, she sits cross-legged on the bed watching me as I grab my pants. "When is your period due?" I ask. "I hate wearing these things." I hold up the knotted condom and pull on my jeans.

She's taken aback.

"Well?" I prod.

"Next week," she answers, her cheeks pink.

"You need to sort out some contraception."

I sit on the bed to slip on my socks and shoes. She says nothing.

"Do you have a doctor?" I ask. She shakes her head. "I can have mine come see you at your apartment—Sunday morning, before you come see me. Or he can see you at my place. Which would you prefer?"

I'm sure Dr. Baxter will make a house call for me, although I haven't seen him for a while.

"Your place," she says.

"Okay. I'll let you know the time."

"Are you leaving?"

She seems surprised that I'm going. "Yes."

"How are you getting back?" she asks.

"Taylor will pick me up."

"I can drive you. I have a lovely new car."

That's better. She's accepted the car as she should, but after all that champagne she shouldn't be driving. "I think you've had too much to drink."

"Did you get me tipsy on purpose?"

"Yes."

"Why?"

"Because you overthink everything, and you're reticent, like your stepdad. A drop of wine in you and you start talking, and I need you to communicate honestly with me. Otherwise you clam up, and I have no idea what you're thinking. In vino veritas, Anastasia."

"And you think you're always honest with me?"

"I endeavor to be. This will only work if we're honest with each other."

"I'd like you to stay and use this." She grabs the other condom and waves it at me.

Manage her expectations, Grey.

"I have crossed so many lines here tonight. I have to go. I'll see you on Sunday." I stand up. "I'll have the revised contract ready for you, and then we can really start to play."

"Play?" she squeaks.

"I'd like to do a scene with you. But I won't until you've signed, so I know you're ready."

"Oh. So I could stretch this out if I don't sign?"

Shit. I hadn't thought of that.

Her chin tilts up in defiance.

Ah…topping from the bottom again. She always finds a way.

"Well, I suppose you could, but I may crack under the strain."

"Crack? How?" she queries, her eyes alive with curiosity.

"Could get really ugly," I tease, narrowing my eyes.

"Ugly, how?" Her grin matches mine.

"Oh, you know, explosions, car chases, kidnapping, incarceration."

"You'd kidnap me?"

"Oh yes."

"Hold me against my will?"

"Oh yes." *Now, that's an interesting idea.* "And then we're talking TPE 24/7."

"You've lost me," she says, perplexed and a little breathless.

"Total Power Exchange—around the clock." My mind whirls as I think of the possibilities. She's curious. "So you have no choice," I add with a playful tone.

"Clearly." Her tone is sarcastic and she rolls her eyes to the heavens, perhaps looking for divine inspiration to understand my sense of humor.

Oh, sweet joy.

"Anastasia Steele, did you just roll your eyes at me?"

"No!"

"I think you did. What did I say I'd do to you if you rolled your eyes at me again?" My words hang between us and I sit down again on the bed. "Come here."

For a moment she stares at me, blanching. "I haven't signed," she whispers.

"I told you what I'd do. I'm a man of my word. I'm going to spank you, and then I'm going to fuck you very quick and very hard. Looks like we'll need that condom after all."

Will she? Won't she? This is it. Proof of whether she can do this. I watch her, impassive, waiting for her to decide. If she says no, it means she's paying lip service to the idea of being my submissive.

And that will be it.

Make the right choice, Ana.

Her expression is grave, her eyes wide, and I think she's weighing up her decision.

"I'm waiting," I murmur. "I'm not a patient man."

Taking a deep breath, she unfurls her legs and crawls toward me, and I hide my relief.

"Good girl. Now stand up."

She does as she's told, and I offer her my hand. She lays the condom on my palm, and I grasp her hand and abruptly pull her over my left knee so her head, shoulders, and chest are resting on the bed. I drape my right leg over her legs, holding her in place.

I've wanted to do this since she asked me if I was gay. "Put your hands up on either side of your head," I order and she complies immediately. "Why am I doing this, Anastasia?"

"Because I rolled my eyes at you," she says in a hoarse whisper.

"Do you think that's polite?"

"No."

"Will you do it again?"

"No."

"I will spank you each time you do it, do you understand?"

I'm going to savor this moment. It's another first.

With great care—relishing the deed—I tug down her sweatpants. Her beautiful behind is naked and ready for me. As I place my hand on her backside, she tenses every muscle in her body… waiting. Her skin is soft to the touch and I sweep my palm across both cheeks, fondling each. She has a fine, fine ass. And I'm going to make it pink…like the champagne.

Lifting my palm, I smack her, hard, just above the junction of her thighs.

She gasps and tries to rise, but I hold her down with my other hand at the small of her back, and I soothe the area I've just hit with a slow, gentle caress.

She stays still.

Panting.

Anticipating.

Yes. I'm going to do that again.

I smack her once, twice, three times.

She grimaces at the pain, her eyes screwed shut. But she doesn't ask me to stop even though she's squirming beneath me.

"Keep still, or I'll spank you for longer," I warn.

I rub her sweet flesh and start again, taking turns: left cheek, right cheek, middle.

She cries out. But she doesn't move her arms, and she still doesn't ask me to stop.

"I'm just getting warmed up." My voice is husky. I smack her again and trace the pink handprint I've left on her skin. Her ass is pinking up nicely. It looks glorious.

I smack her once more.

And she cries out again.

"No one to hear you, baby, just me."

I spank her over and over—the same pattern, left cheek, right cheek, middle—and she yelps each time. When I reach eighteen I stop. I'm breathless, my palm is stinging, and my cock is rigid.

"Enough," I rasp, trying to catch my breath. "Well done, Anastasia. Now I'm going to fuck you."

I stroke her pink behind gently, round and round, moving down. She's wet.

And my body gets harder.

I insert two fingers into her vagina.

"Feel this. See how much your body likes this. You're soaking, just for me." I slide my fingers in and out, and she groans, her body curling around them with each push and her breathing accelerating.

I withdraw them.

I want her. Now.

"Next time, I will get you to count. Now, where's that condom?" Grabbing it from beside her head, I ease her gently off my lap and onto the bed, facedown. Unzipping my fly, I don't bother to remove my jeans, and I make short work of the foil packet, rolling the condom on quickly and efficiently. I lift her hips until she's kneeling and her ass in all its rosy glory is poised in the air as I stand behind her.

"I'm going to take you now. You can come," I growl, caressing her behind and grabbing my cock. With one swift thrust I'm inside her.

She moans as I move. In. Out. In. Out. I pound into her, watching my cock disappear beneath her pink backside.

Her mouth is open wide and she grunts and groans with each thrust, her cries getting higher and higher.

Come on, Ana.

She clenches around me and cries out as she comes, hard.

"Oh, Ana!" I follow her over the edge as I climax into her and lose all time and perspective.

I collapse at her side, pull her on top of me, and, wrapping my arms around her, I whisper into her hair, "Oh, baby, welcome to my world."

Her weight anchors me, and she makes no attempt to touch my chest. Her eyes are closed and her breathing is returning to normal. I stroke her hair. It's soft, a rich mahogany, shining in the glow of her bedside light. She smells of Ana and apples and sex. It's heady. "Well done, baby."

She's not in tears. She did as she was asked. She's faced every challenge I've thrown at her; she really is quite remarkable. I finger the thin strap of her cheap cotton camisole. "Is this what you sleep in?"

"Yes." She sounds drowsy.

"You should be in silks and satins, you beautiful girl. I'll take you shopping."

"I like my sweats," she argues.

Of course she does.

I kiss her hair. "We'll see."

Closing my eyes, I relax in our quiet moment, a strange contentment warming me, filling me up inside.

This feels right. *Too right.*

"I have to go," I murmur and kiss her forehead. "Are you okay?"

"I'm okay," she says, sounding a little subdued.

Gently I roll out from underneath her and get up. "Where's your bathroom?" I ask, taking off the used condom and zipping up my jeans.

"Down the hall to the left."

In the bathroom I discard the condoms in a trash bin and spy a bottle of baby oil on the shelf.

That's what I need.

She's dressed when I return, evading my gaze. *Why so shy suddenly?*

"I found some baby oil. Let me rub it on your behind."

"No. I'll be fine," she says, examining her fingers, still avoiding eye contact.

"Anastasia," I warn her.

Please just do as you're told.

I sit down behind her and tug down her sweatpants. Squirting some baby oil on my hand, I rub it tenderly onto her sore ass.

She puts her hands on her hips in an obstinate stance but stays silent.

"I like my hands on you," I admit out loud to myself. "There." I pull her sweatpants up. "I'm leaving now."

"I'll see you out," she says quietly, standing aside.

I take her hand and reluctantly let go when we reach the front door. Part of me doesn't want to leave.

"Don't you have to call Taylor?" she asks, her eyes fixed on the zipper of my leather jacket.

"Taylor's been here since nine. Look at me."

Large blue eyes peek up at me through long, dark lashes.

"You didn't cry." My voice is low.

And you let me spank you. You're amazing.

I grab her and kiss her, pouring my gratitude into the kiss and holding her close. "Sunday," I whisper, fevered, against her lips. I release her abruptly before I'm tempted to ask her if I can stay, and I head out to where Taylor is waiting in the SUV. Once I'm in the car I look back, but she's gone. She's probably tired…like me.

Pleasantly tired.

That has to have been the most pleasurable soft limits conversation I've ever had.

Damn, that woman is unexpected. Closing my eyes, I see her riding me, her head tipped back in ecstasy. Ana does not do things halfheartedly. She commits. And to think she had sex for the first time only a week ago.

With me. And no one else.

I grin as I stare out the car window, but all I see is my ghostly face reflected in the glass. So I close my eyes and allow myself to daydream.

Training her will be fun.

TAYLOR WAKES ME FROM my doze. "We're here, Mr. Grey."

"Thank you," I mumble. "I have a meeting in the morning."

"At the hotel?"

"Yes. Videoconference. I won't need to be driven anywhere. But I'd like to leave before lunch."

"What time would you like me to pack?"

"Ten thirty."

"Very good, sir. The BlackBerry you asked for will be delivered to Miss Steele tomorrow."

"Good. That reminds me. Can you collect her old Beetle tomorrow and dispose of it? I don't want her driving it."

"Of course. I have a friend who restores vintage cars. He might be interested. I'll deal with it. Will there be anything else?"

"No thank you. Good night."

"Good night."

I leave Taylor to park the SUV and make my way up to my suite.

Opening a bottle of sparkling water from the fridge, I sit down at the desk and switch on my laptop.

No urgent emails.

But my real purpose is to say good night to Ana.

From: Christian Grey
Subject: You
Date: May 26 2011 23:14
To: Anastasia Steele

Dear Miss Steele,
You are quite simply exquisite. The most beautiful, intelligent, witty, and brave woman I have ever met. Take some Advil—this is not a request. And don't drive your Beetle again. I will know.

Christian Grey
CEO, Grey Enterprises Holdings, Inc.

She'll probably be asleep, but I keep my laptop open just in case and check email. A few minutes later her response arrives.

From: Anastasia Steele
Subject: Flattery
Date: May 26 2011 23:20
To: Christian Grey

Dear Mr. Grey,
Flattery will get you nowhere, but since you've been *everywhere,* the point is moot.

I will need to drive my Beetle to a garage so I can sell it—so will not graciously accept any of your nonsense over that.
Red wine is always more preferable to Advil.

Ana

P.S. Caning is a HARD limit for me.

Her opening line makes me laugh out loud. *Oh, baby, I have not been everywhere I want to go with you.* Red wine on top of champagne? Not a clever mix, and caning is off the list. I wonder what else she'll object to as I compose my reply.

From: Christian Grey
Subject: Frustrating Women Who Can't Take Compliments
Date: May 26 2011 23:26
To: Anastasia Steele

Dear Miss Steele,
I am not flattering you. You should go to bed.

I accept your addition to the hard limits.

Don't drink too much.

Taylor will dispose of your car and get a good price for it, too.

Christian Grey
CEO, Grey Enterprises Holdings, Inc.

I hope she's in bed now.

From: Anastasia Steele
Subject: Taylor—Is He the Right Man for the Job?
Date: May 26 2011 23:40
To: Christian Grey

Dear Sir,
I am intrigued that you are happy to risk letting your right-hand man drive my car but not some woman you fuck occasionally. How can I be sure that Taylor is the man to get me the best deal for said car? I have, in the past, probably before I met you, been known to drive a hard bargain.

Ana

What the hell? Some woman I fuck occasionally?

I have to take a deep breath. Her response irks me...no, infuriates me. How *dare* she talk about herself like that? As my submissive she'll be so much more than that. I'll be devoted to her. Does she not realize this?

And she has driven a hard bargain with me. *Good God!* Look at all the concessions I've made with regard to the contract.

I count to ten, and to calm down, I visualize myself aboard *The Grace*, my catamaran, sailing on the Sound.

Flynn would be proud.

I respond.

From: Christian Grey
Subject: Careful!
Date: May 26 2011 23:44
To: Anastasia Steele

Dear Miss Steele,
I am assuming it is the RED WINE talking, and that you've had a very long day.

Though I am tempted to drive back over there to ensure that you don't sit down for a week, rather than an evening.

Taylor is ex-army and capable of driving anything from a motorcycle to a Sherman tank. Your car does not present a hazard to him.

Now please do not refer to yourself as "some woman I fuck occasionally" because, quite frankly, it makes me MAD, and you really wouldn't like me when I'm angry.

Christian Grey
CEO, Grey Enterprises Holdings, Inc.

I exhale slowly, steadying my heart rate. Who else on earth has the ability to get under my skin like this?

She doesn't write back immediately. Perhaps she's intimidated by my response. I pick up my book, but soon find I've read the same paragraph three times while awaiting her reply. I look up for the umpteenth time.

From: Anastasia Steele
Subject: Careful Yourself
Date: May 26 2011 23:57
To: Christian Grey

Dear Mr. Grey,
I'm not sure I like you anyway, especially at the moment.

Miss Steele

I stare at her reply, and all my anger withers and dies, to be replaced by a surge of anxiety.

Shit.

Is she saying that's it?

FRIDAY, MAY 27, 2011

From: Christian Grey
Subject: Careful Yourself
Date: May 27 2011 00:03
To: Anastasia Steele

Why don't you like me?

Christian Grey
CEO, Grey Enterprises Holdings, Inc.

I get up and open another bottle of sparkling water.
And wait.

From: Anastasia Steele
Subject: Careful Yourself
Date: May 27 2011 00:09
To: Christian Grey

Because you never stay with me.

Six words.
Six little words that make my scalp tingle.
I told her I didn't sleep with anyone.
But today was a big day.
She graduated from college.

She said yes.

We went through all those soft limits that she knew nothing about. We fucked. I spanked her. We fucked again.

Shit.

And before I can stop myself, I grab the garage ticket for my car, pick up a jacket, and I'm out the door.

THE ROADS ARE EMPTY and I'm at her place twenty-three minutes later.

I knock quietly, and Kavanagh opens the door.

"What the fuck do you think you're doing here?" she shouts, her eyes blazing with anger.

Whoa. Not the reception I was expecting.

"I've come to see Ana."

"Well, you can't!" Kavanagh stands with arms folded and legs braced in the doorway, like a gargoyle.

I try reasoning with her. "But I need to see her. She sent me an email." *Get out of my way!*

"What the fuck have you done to her now?"

I grit my teeth. "That's what I need to find out."

"Ever since she met you she cries all the time."

"What?" I can't deal with her shit anymore, and I barge past her.

"You can't come in here!" Kavanagh follows me, shrieking like a harpy, as I storm through the apartment to Ana's bedroom.

I open Ana's door and switch on the main light. She's huddled in her bed, wrapped in her comforter. Her eyes are red and puffy, and squinting in the overhead light. Her nose is swollen and blotchy.

I've seen women in this state many times, especially after I've punished them. But I'm surprised by the unease that grips my gut.

"Jesus, Ana." I flick the main light off so she doesn't have to squint and I sit on the bed beside her.

"What are you doing here?" She's sniffling.

I turn on her bedside light.

"Do you want me to throw this asshole out?" Kate barks from the doorway.

Fuck you, Kavanagh. Raising an eyebrow, I pretend to ignore her.

Ana shakes her head, but her watery eyes are on me.

"Just holler if you need me," Kate says to Ana as if she were a child. "Grey," she snaps, so I'm obliged to look at her. "You're on my shit list, and I'm watching you." She sounds shrill, her eyes glinting with fury, but I don't give a fuck.

Fortunately she leaves, pulling the door to but not shutting it. I check in my inside pocket, and once again Mrs. Jones has exceeded all expectations; I fish out the handkerchief and give it to Ana. "What's going on?"

"Why are you here?" Her voice is shaky.

I don't know.

You said you didn't like me.

"Part of my role is to look after your needs. You said you wanted me to stay, so here I am." *Nice save, Grey.* "And yet I find you like this." *You weren't like this when I left.* "I'm sure I'm responsible, but I have no idea why. Is it because I hit you?"

She struggles to sit up and flinches when she does.

"Did you take some Advil?" As instructed?

She shakes her head.

When will you do as you're told?

I go to find Kavanagh, who's on the sofa, seething.

"Ana has a headache. Do you have any Advil?"

She raises her eyebrows, surprised, I think, by my concern for her friend. Glowering, she gets up and stomps into the kitchen. After some rustling through boxes she hands me a couple of tablets and a teacup of water.

Back in the bedroom I offer them to Ana and sit on the bed. "Take these."

She does, her eyes clouded with apprehension.

"Talk to me. You told me you were okay. I'd never have left you if I thought you were like this." Distracted, she toys with a loose thread on her quilt. "I take it that when you said you were okay, you weren't."

"I thought I was fine," she admits.

"Anastasia, you can't tell me what you think I want to hear. That's not very honest. How can I trust anything you've said to me?" This will never work if she's not honest with me.

The thought is depressing.

Talk to me, Ana.

"How did you feel while I was hitting you, and after?"

"I didn't like it. I'd rather you didn't do it again."

"You weren't meant to like it."

"Why do you like it?" she asks, and her voice is stronger.

Shit. I can't tell her why.

"You really want to know?"

"Oh, trust me, I'm fascinated." Now she's being sarcastic.

"Careful," I warn her.

She pales at my expression. "Are you going to hit me again?"

"No, not tonight." *I think you've had enough.*

"So…?" She still wants an answer.

"I like the control it gives me, Anastasia. I want you to behave in a particular way, and if you don't, I shall punish you, and you will learn to behave the way I desire. I enjoy punishing you. I've wanted to spank you since you asked me if I was gay."

And I don't want you rolling your eyes at me, or being sarcastic.

"So you don't like the way I am." Her voice is small.

"I think you're lovely the way you are."

"So why are you trying to change me?"

"I don't want to change you." *God forbid. You're enchanting.* "I'd like you to be courteous and to follow the set of rules I've given you and not defy me. Simple." *I want you safe.*

"But you want to punish me?"

"Yes, I do."

"That's what I don't understand."

I sigh. "It's the way I'm made. I need to control you. I need you to behave in a certain way, and if you don't—" My mind drifts. *I find it arousing, Ana. You did, too. Can't you accept that? Bending you over my knee, feeling your ass beneath my palm…* "I love to watch your beautiful alabaster skin pink and warm up under my hands. It turns me on." Just thinking about it stirs my body.

"So it's not the pain you're putting me through?"

Hell.

"A bit, to see if you can take it." Actually, it's a lot, but I don't want to go there right now. If I tell her, she'll throw me out. "But that's not the whole reason. It's the fact that you are mine to do with as I see fit—ultimate control over someone else. And it turns me on. Big-time."

I must lend her a book or two on being a submissive.

"Look, I'm not explaining myself very well. I've never had to before. I've not really thought about this in any great depth. I've always been with like-minded people." I pause to check she's still with me. "And you haven't answered my question: How did you feel afterward?"

She blinks. "Confused."

"You were sexually aroused by it, Anastasia."

You have an inner freak, Ana. I know it.

Closing my eyes, I recall her wet and wanting around my fingers after I spanked her. When I open them, she's staring at me, pupils dilated, her lips parted…her tongue moistening her top lip. She wants it, too.

Shit. Not again, Grey. Not when she's like this.

"Don't look at me like that," I warn, my voice gruff.

Her eyebrows rise in surprise.

You know what I mean, Ana. "I don't have any condoms, and you know, you're upset. Contrary to what your roommate believes, I'm not a priapic monster. So, you felt confused?"

She remains mute.

Jesus.

"You have no problem being honest with me in print. Your emails always tell me exactly how you feel. Why can't you do that in conversation? Do I intimidate you that much?"

Her fingers fiddle with the quilt.

"You beguile me, Christian. Completely overwhelm me. I feel like Icarus, flying too close to the sun." Her voice is quiet but brimming with emotion.

Her confession floors me like a swift kick to the head.

"Well, I think you've got that the wrong way around," I whisper.

"What?"

"Oh, Anastasia, you've bewitched me. Isn't it obvious?"

That's why I'm here.

She's not convinced.

Ana. Believe me. "You've still not answered my question. Write me an email, please. But right now, I'd really like to sleep. Can I stay?"

"Do you want to stay?"

"You wanted me here."

"You haven't answered my question," she persists.

Impossible woman. I just drove like a maniac to get here after your fucking message. There's your answer.

I grumble that I'll respond by email. I'm not talking about this. This conversation is over.

Before I can change my mind and head back to The Heathman, I stand, empty my pockets, remove my shoes and socks, and strip off my pants. Slinging my jacket over her chair, I climb into her bed.

"Lie down," I growl. She complies, and I lean up on my elbow, looking at her. "If you are going to cry, cry in front of me. I need to know."

"Do you want me to cry?"

"Not particularly. I just want to know how you're feeling. I don't want you slipping through my fingers. Switch the light off. It's late, and we both have to work tomorrow."

She does.

"Lie on your side, facing away from me."

I don't want you to touch me.

The bed dips as she moves, and I wrap my arm around her and gently pull her against me.

"Sleep, baby," I murmur and breathe in the scent of her hair.

Damn, she smells good.

Lelliot is running through the grass.

He's laughing. Loud.

I am running after him. My face is smiling.

I am going to catch him.
There are small trees around us.
Baby trees covered in apples.
Mommy lets me pick the apples.
Mommy lets me eat the apples.
I put the apples in my pockets. Every pocket.
I hide them in my sweater.
Apples taste good.
Apples smell good.
Mommy makes apple pie.
Apple pie and ice cream.
They make my tummy smile.
I hide the apples in my shoes. I hide them under my pillow.
There is a man. Grandpa Trev-Trev-yan.
His name is hard. Hard to say in my head.
He has another name. Thee-o-door.
Theodore is a funny name.
The baby trees are his trees.
At his house. Where he lives.
He is Mommy's daddy.
He has a loud laugh. And big shoulders.
And happy eyes.
He runs to catch Lelliot and me.
You can't catch me.
Lelliot runs. He laughs.
I run. I catch him.
And we fall down in the grass.
He is laughing.
The apples sparkle in the sun.
And they taste so good.
Yummy.
And they smell so good.
So, so good.
The apples fall.
They fall on me.
I twist and they hit my back. Stinging me.

Ow.

But the scent is still there, sweet and crisp.

Ana.

When I open my eyes I'm wrapped around her, our limbs entwined. She's regarding me with a tender smile. Her face is no longer blotchy and puffy; she looks radiant. My cock agrees and stiffens in greeting.

"Good morning." I'm disoriented. "Jesus, even in my sleep I'm drawn to you." Stretching out, I disentangle myself from her and scan my surroundings. Of course, we're in her bedroom. Her eyes glow with eager curiosity as my cock presses against her. "Hmm, this has possibilities, but I think we should wait until Sunday." I nuzzle her just below her ear and lean up on my elbow.

She looks flushed. Warm.

"You're very hot," she scolds.

"You're not so bad yourself." I grin and flex my hips, teasing her with my favorite body part. She tries a disapproving look but fails miserably—she's highly amused. Leaning down, I kiss her.

"Sleep well?" I ask.

She nods.

"So did I."

I'm surprised. I did sleep really well. I tell her so. No nightmares. Only dreams…

"What's the time?" I ask.

"It's seven thirty."

"Seven thirty? Shit!" I leap out of bed and start dragging on my jeans. She watches me dress, trying to suppress her laughter.

"You are such a bad influence on me," I complain. "I have a meeting. I have to go—I have to be in Portland at eight. Are you smirking at me?"

"Yes," she admits.

"I'm late. I don't do late. Another first, Miss Steele." I tug on my jacket, reach down and take her head in both my hands.

"Sunday," I whisper and kiss her. I grab my watch, wallet, and money from her bedside table, pick up my shoes, and head for the door. "Taylor will come and sort your Beetle. I was serious. Don't drive it. I'll see you at my place on Sunday. I'll email you a time."

Leaving her a little dazed, I rush out of the apartment and to my car.

I put on my shoes while I'm driving. Once they're on I open up the throttle and weave in and out of traffic heading to Portland. I'll have to meet Eamon Kavanagh's associates in my jeans. Thankfully this meeting is via WebEx.

I burst into my room at The Heathman and switch on my laptop: 8:02. *Shit.* I haven't shaved, but I smooth my hair, straighten my jacket, and hope they don't notice I'm only wearing a T-shirt underneath.

Who gives a fuck anyway?

I open WebEx and Andrea is online, waiting for me. "Good morning, Mr. Grey. Mr. Kavanagh is delayed, but they're ready for you in New York and here in Seattle."

"Fred and Barney?" *My Flintstones.* I smirk at the thought.

"Yes, sir. And Ros, too."

"Great. Thanks." I'm breathless. I catch Andrea's fleeting puzzled look and choose to ignore it. "Can you order me a toasted bagel with cream cheese and smoked salmon and a coffee, black. Have it sent to my suite ASAP."

"Yes, Mr. Grey." She posts the link to the conference in the window. "Here you go, sir," she says.

I click the link—and I'm in. "Good morning." There are two executives seated at a conference table in New York, both gazing expectantly at the camera. Ros, Barney, and Fred are each in separate windows.

To business. Kavanagh says he wants to upgrade his media network to high-speed fiber-optic connections. GEH can do it for them, but are they serious about buying in? It's a big investment up front but a great payoff down the line.

While we're talking an email notification with an arresting

title from Ana floats onto the top right corner of my screen. As quietly as I can, I click on it.

From: Anastasia Steele
Subject: Assault and Battery: The After-Effects
Date: May 27 2011 08:05
To: Christian Grey

Dear Mr. Grey,
You wanted to know why I felt confused after you…which euphemism should we apply—spanked, punished, beat, assaulted me.

A tad overdramatic, Miss Steele. You could have said no.

Well, during the whole alarming process, I felt demeaned, debased, and abused.

If you felt that way, why didn't you stop me? You have safe words.

And much to my mortification, you're right, I was aroused, and that was unexpected.

I know. Good. You've finally acknowledged it.

As you are well aware, all things sexual are new to me—I only wish I were more experienced and therefore more prepared. I was shocked to feel aroused.

What really worried me was how I felt afterward. And that's more difficult to articulate. I was happy that you were happy. I felt relieved that it wasn't as painful as I thought it would be. And when I was lying in your arms, I felt…sated.

As did I, Ana, as did I…

But I feel very uncomfortable, guilty even, feeling that way. It doesn't sit well with me, and I'm confused as a result. Does that answer your question?

I hope the world of Mergers and Acquisitions is as stimulating as ever...and that you weren't too late.

Thank you for staying with me.

Ana

Kavanagh joins the conversation, apologizing for his tardiness. While the introductions are made and Fred talks about what GEH can offer, I type out my reply to Ana. I hope it looks like I'm taking notes to those on the other side of the computer screen.

From: Christian Grey
Subject: Free Your Mind
Date: May 27 2011 08:24
To: Anastasia Steele

Interesting...if slightly overstated title heading, Miss Steele.

To answer your points:

- I'll go with spanking—as that's what it was.

- So you felt demeaned, debased, abused, and assaulted—how very Tess Durbeyfield of you. I believe it was you who decided on the debasement, if I remember correctly. Do you really feel like this or do you think you ought to feel like this? Two very different things. If that *is* how you feel, do you think you could just try to embrace these feelings, deal with them, for me? That's what a submissive would do.

- I am grateful for your inexperience. I value it, and I'm only beginning to understand what it means. Simply put...it means that you are mine in every way.

- Yes, you were aroused, which in turn was very arousing, there's nothing wrong with that.

- Happy does not even begin to cover how I felt. Ecstatic joy comes close.

- Punishment spanking hurts far more than sensual spanking—so that's about as hard as it gets, unless, of course, you commit some major transgression, in which case I'll use some implement to punish you. My hand was very sore. But I like that.

- I felt sated, too—more so than you could ever know.

- Don't waste your energy on guilt, feelings of wrongdoing, etc. We are consenting adults and what we do behind closed doors is between ourselves. You need to free your mind and listen to your body.

- The world of M&A is not nearly as stimulating as you are, Miss Steele.

Christian Grey
CEO, Grey Enterprises Holdings, Inc.

Her response is almost immediate.

From: Anastasia Steele
Subject: Consenting Adults!
Date: May 27 2011 08:26
To: Christian Grey

Aren't you in a meeting?
I'm very glad your hand was sore.

And if I listened to my body, I'd be in Alaska by now.

Ana

P.S. I will think about embracing these feelings.

Alaska! Really, Miss Steele. I chuckle to myself and look like I'm engaged with the online conversation. There's a knock on my door, and I apologize for interrupting the conference while I let room service in with my breakfast. Miss Dark, Dark Eyes rewards me with a flirtatious smile as I sign the check.

Returning to the WebEx, I find Fred briefing Kavanagh and his associates on how successful this technology has been for another client company dealing in futures.

"Will the technology help me with the futures market?" Kavanagh asks with a sardonic smile. When I tell him that Barney's hard at work developing a crystal ball to predict prices, they all have the grace to laugh.

While Fred discusses a theoretical timeline for implementation and tech integration, I email Ana.

From: Christian Grey
Subject: You Didn't Call the Cops
Date: May 27 2011 08:35
To: Anastasia Steele

Miss Steele,
I am in a meeting discussing the futures market, if you're really interested.

For the record, you stood beside me knowing what I was going to do.

You didn't at any time ask me to stop—you didn't use either safe word.

You are an adult—you have choices.

Quite frankly, I'm looking forward to the next time my palm is ringing with pain.

You're obviously not listening to the right part of your body.

Alaska is very cold and no place to run. I would find you.

I can track your cell phone—remember?

Go to work.

Christian Grey
CEO, Grey Enterprises Holdings, Inc.

Fred is in full flow when I get Ana's response.

From: Anastasia Steele
Subject: Stalker
Date: May 27 2011 08:36
To: Christian Grey

Have you sought therapy for your stalker tendencies?

Ana

I smother my laugh. She's funny.

From: Christian Grey
Subject: Stalker? Me?
Date: May 27 2011 08:38
To: Anastasia Steele

I pay the eminent Dr. Flynn a small fortune with regard to my stalker and other tendencies.
Go to work.

Christian Grey
CEO, Grey Enterprises Holdings, Inc.

Why hasn't she gone to work? She'll be late.

From: Anastasia Steele
Subject: Expensive Charlatans
Date: May 27 2011 08:40
To: Christian Grey

May I humbly suggest you seek a second opinion?
I am not sure that Dr. Flynn is very effective.

Miss Steele

Damn, this woman is funny…and intuitive; Flynn charges me a small fortune for his advice. Surreptitiously, I type my response.

From: Christian Grey
Subject: Second Opinions
Date: May 27 2011 08:43
To: Anastasia Steele

Not that it's any of your business, humble or otherwise, but Dr. Flynn is the second opinion.

You will have to speed, in your new car, putting yourself at unnecessary risk—I think that's against the rules.

GO TO WORK.

Christian Grey
CEO, Grey Enterprises Holdings, Inc.

Kavanagh throws me a question about future-proofing. I let him know we've recently acquired a company that's an innovative, dynamic player in fiber optics. I don't let him know that I have doubts about the CEO, Lucas Woods. He'll be gone anyway. I'm definitely firing that idiot, no matter what Ros says.

From: Anastasia Steele
Subject: SHOUTY CAPITALS
Date: May 27 2011 08:47
To: Christian Grey

As the object of your stalker tendencies, I think it is my business, actually.

I haven't signed yet. So rules, schmules. And I don't start until 9:30.

Miss Steele

SHOUTY CAPITALS. I love it.

I respond.

From: Christian Grey
Subject: Descriptive Linguistics
Date: May 27 2011 08:49
To: Anastasia Steele

"Schmules"? Not sure where that appears in Webster's dictionary.

Christian Grey
CEO, Grey Enterprises Holdings, Inc.

"We can take this conversation offline," Ros says to Kavanagh. "Now that we have an idea of your needs and expectations, we'll prepare a detailed proposal for you and reconvene next week to discuss it."

"Great," I say, trying to look engaged.

There are nods of agreement all around, then goodbyes.

"Thanks for giving us the opportunity to quote for this, Eamon," I address Kavanagh.

"It sounds like you guys know what we need," he says. "Great to see you yesterday. Goodbye."

They all hang up except Ros, who's staring at me as if I've grown two heads.

Ana's email pings into my inbox.

"Hang on, Ros. I need a minute or two." I mute her.

And read.

And laugh out loud.

From: Anastasia Steele
Subject: Descriptive Linguistics
Date: May 27 2011 08:52
To: Christian Grey

It's between control freak and stalker.
And descriptive linguistics is a hard limit for me.

Will you stop bothering me now?

I'd like to go to work in my new car.

Ana

I type a quick reply.

From: Christian Grey
Subject: Challenging but Amusing Young Women
Date: May 27 2011 08:56
To: Anastasia Steele

My palm is twitching.
Drive safely, Miss Steele.

Christian Grey
CEO, Grey Enterprises Holdings, Inc.

Ros is glaring at me when I unmute her. "What the hell, Christian?"

"What?" I feign innocence.

"You know what. Don't hold a goddamn meeting when you're obviously not interested."

"Was it that obvious?"

"Yes."

"Fuck."

"Yes. Fuck. This could be a huge contract for us."

"I know. I know. I'm sorry." I grin.

"I don't know what's got into you lately." She shakes her head, but I can tell she's trying to mask her amusement with exasperation.

"It's the Portland air."

"Well, the sooner you're back here, the better."

"I'm heading back around lunchtime. In the meantime, ask Marco to investigate all the publishing houses in Seattle and see if any are ripe for a takeover."

"You want to go into publishing?" Ros splutters. "It's not a high-potential-growth sector."

She's probably right.

"Just investigate. That's all."

She sighs. "If you insist. Will you be in later this afternoon? We can have a proper catch-up."

"Depends on the traffic."

"I'll pencil in a catch-up with Andrea."

"Great. Bye for now."

I close WebEx, then phone Andrea.

"Mr. Grey."

"Call Dr. Baxter and have him come to my apartment Sunday, around midday. If he's not available, find a good gynecologist. Get the best."

"Yes, sir," she says. "Anything else?"

"Yes. What's the name of the personal shopper I use at Neiman Marcus at the Bravern center?"

"Caroline Acton."

"Text me her number."

"Will do."

"I'll see you later this afternoon."

"Yes, sir."

I hang up.

So far it's been one interesting morning. I can't recall any exchange of emails being that fun, ever. I glance at the laptop, but there's nothing new. Ana must be at work.

I run my hands through my hair.

Ros noticed how distracted I was during that conversation.

Shit, Grey. Get your act together.

I wolf down my breakfast, drink some cold coffee, and head into my bedroom to shower and change. Even when I'm washing my hair I can't get that woman out of my head. Ana.

Amazing Ana.

The image of her bouncing up and down on top of me comes to mind; of her lying over my knee, ass pink; of her tethered to the bed, mouth open in ecstasy. Lord, that woman is hot. And this morning, waking up next to her, it wasn't so bad, and I slept well... really well.

Shouty capitals. Her emails make me laugh. They're entertaining. She's funny. I never knew I liked that in a woman. I'll need to think about what we'll do on Sunday in my playroom...something fun, something new for her.

While shaving I have an idea, and as soon as I'm dressed I get back on my laptop to browse my favorite toy store. I need a riding crop—brown plaited leather. I smirk. I'm going to make Ana's dreams come true.

Order placed, I turn to work emails, energized and productive, until Taylor interrupts me. "Good morning, Taylor."

"Mr. Grey." He nods, looking at me with a puzzled expression, and I realize I'm grinning because I'm thinking about her emails again.

Descriptive linguistics is a hard limit for me.

"I've had a good morning," I find myself explaining.

"I'm pleased to hear it, sir. I have Miss Steele's laundry from last week."

"Pack it with my things."

"Will do."

"Thank you." I watch him walk into my bedroom. Even Taylor

is noticing the Anastasia Steele effect. My phone buzzes: it's a text from Elliot.

You still in Portland?

Yes. But I'm leaving soon.

I'll be there later. I'm gonna
help the girls move.
Shame you can't stay.
Our first DOUBLE DATE
since Ana popped your cherry.

Fuck off. I'm picking up Mia.

I need deets, bro. Kate tells me nothing.

Good. Fuck off. Again.

"Mr. Grey?" Taylor interrupts once more, my luggage in hand. "The courier has been dispatched with the BlackBerry."

"Thanks."

He nods, and as he leaves I type up another email to Miss Steele.

From: Christian Grey
Subject: BlackBerry ON LOAN
Date: May 27 2011 11:15
To: Anastasia Steele

I need to be able to contact you at all times, and since this is your most honest form of communication, I figured you needed a BlackBerry.

Christian Grey
CEO, Grey Enterprises Holdings, Inc.

And maybe you'll answer this phone when I call.

At 11:30 I have another conference call, with our director of finance, to discuss GEH's charitable giving for the next quarter. That takes the better part of an hour, and when it's over I finish a light lunch and read the rest of my *Forbes* magazine.

As I swallow the last forkful of salad, I realize I have no other reason to stay at the hotel. It's time to go, yet I'm reluctant. And deep down I have to acknowledge it's because I won't see Ana until Sunday, unless she changes her mind.

Fuck. I hope not.

Pushing that unpleasant thought aside, I start packing my papers into my messenger bag, and when I reach for my laptop to put it away, I see there's an email from Ana.

From: Anastasia Steele
Subject: Consumerism Gone Mad
Date: May 27 2011 13:22
To: Christian Grey

I think you need to call Dr. Flynn right now.
Your stalker tendencies are running wild.
I am at work. I will email you when I get home.
Thank you for yet another gadget.
I wasn't wrong when I said you were the ultimate consumer.
Why do you do this?

Ana

She's scolding me! I respond immediately.

From: Christian Grey
Subject: Sagacity from One So Young
Date: May 27 2011 13:24
To: Anastasia Steele

Fair point well made, as ever, Miss Steele.

Dr. Flynn is on vacation.

And I do this because I can.

Christian Grey
CEO, Grey Enterprises Holdings, Inc.

She doesn't answer straightaway, so I pack my laptop. Grabbing my bag, I head down to reception and check out. While I'm waiting for my car, Andrea calls to tell me she's found an ob-gyn to come to Escala on Sunday.

"Her name is Dr. Greene, and she comes highly recommended by your MD, sir."

"Good."

"She runs her practice out of Northwest."

"Okay." Where is Andrea going with this?

"There's one thing sir—she's expensive."

I dismiss her concern. "Andrea, whatever she wants is fine."

"In that case, she can be at your apartment at one thirty on Sunday."

"Great. Go ahead."

"Will do, Mr. Grey."

I hang up, and I'm tempted to call my mother to check Dr. Greene's credentials, as they work in the same hospital, but that might provoke too many questions from Grace.

Once in the car I send Ana an email with details about Sunday.

From: Christian Grey
Subject: Sunday
Date: May 27 2011 13:40
To: Anastasia Steele

Shall I see you at 1 p.m. Sunday?
The doctor will be at Escala to see you at 1:30.

I'm leaving for Seattle now.

I hope your move goes well, and I look forward to Sunday.

Christian Grey
CEO, Grey Enterprises Holdings, Inc.

Right. All done. I ease the R8 onto the road and roar toward I-5. As I pass the exit for Vancouver I'm inspired. I call Andrea on the hands-free and ask her to organize a housewarming present for Ana and Kate.

"What would you like to send?"

"Bollinger La Grande Année Rosé, 1999 vintage."

"Yes, sir. Anything else?"

"What do you mean, anything else?"

"Flowers? Chocolates? A balloon?"

"Balloon?"

"Yes."

"What sort of balloons?"

"Well…they have everything."

"Okay. Good idea—see if you can get a helicopter balloon."

"Yes, sir. And a message for the card?"

"'Ladies, good luck in your new home. Christian Grey.' Got that?"

"I have. What's the address?"

Shit. I don't know. "I'll text it to you either later today or tomorrow. Will that work?"

"Yes, sir. I can get it delivered tomorrow."

"Thanks, Andrea."

"You're welcome." She sounds surprised.

I hang up and floor my R8.

BY 6:30 I'M HOME and my earlier ebullient mood has soured—I still haven't heard from Ana. I select a pair of cuff links from the drawers in my closet and as I knot my bow tie for the night's event I wonder if she's okay. She said she would contact me when she got home; I've called her twice, but I've heard nothing and it's pissing me off. I try her once more and this time I leave a message.

"I think you need to learn to manage my expectations. I'm not a patient man. If you say you are going to contact me when you finish work, then you should have the decency to do so. Otherwise I worry, and it's not an emotion I'm familiar with, and I don't tolerate it very well. Call me."

If she doesn't call soon I am going to explode.

I'M SEATED AT A table with Whelan, my banker. I'm his guest at a charity function for a nonprofit that aims to raise awareness of global poverty.

"Glad you could make it," Whelan says.

"It's a good cause."

"And thank you for your generous contribution, Mr. Grey." His wife is cloying, thrusting her perfect, surgically enhanced breasts in my direction.

"Like I said, it's a good cause." I give her a patronizing smile.

Why hasn't Ana called me back?

I check my phone again.

Nothing.

I look around the table at all the middle-aged men with their second or third trophy wives. God forbid this should ever be me.

I'm bored. Seriously bored and seriously pissed.

What is she doing?

Could I have brought her here? I suspect she would have been bored stiff, too. When the conversation around the table moves to the state of the economy, I've had enough. Making my excuses, I leave the ballroom and exit the hotel. While the valet is retrieving my car, I call Ana again.

There's still no answer.

Perhaps now that I'm gone she wants nothing to do with me.

When I get home, I head straight to my study and switch on the iMac.

From: Christian Grey
Subject: Where Are You?
Date: May 27 2011 22:14
To: Anastasia Steele

"I am at work. I will email you when I get home."
Are you still at work or have you packed your phone, BlackBerry, and MacBook?

Call me, or I may be forced to call Elliot.

Christian Grey
CEO, Grey Enterprises Holdings, Inc.

I stare out my window toward the dark waters of the Sound. Why did I volunteer to collect Mia? I could be with Ana, helping her pack all her shit, then going out for pizza with her and Kate and Elliot—or whatever ordinary people do.

For God's sake, Grey.

That's not you. *Get a grip.*

I wander around my apartment, my footsteps echoing through the living room, and it seems achingly empty since I was last here. I undo my bow tie. Perhaps it's me that's empty. I pour myself an Armagnac and stare back out at the Seattle skyline toward the Sound.

Are you thinking about me, Anastasia Steele? The winking lights of Seattle have no answer.

My phone buzzes.

Thank. Fuck. *Finally*. It's her.

"Hi." I'm relieved she's called.

"Hi," she says.

"I was worried about you."

"I know. I'm sorry I didn't reply, but I'm fine."

Fine? I wish I were…

"Did you have a pleasant evening?" I ask, reining in my temper.

"Yes. We finished packing, and Kate and I had Chinese take-out with José."

Oh, this just gets better and better. The fucking photographer again. That's why she hasn't called.

"How about you?" she inquires when I don't respond, and there's a hint of desperation in her voice.

Why? What isn't she telling me?

Oh, stop overthinking this, Grey!

I sigh. "I went to a fundraising dinner. It was deathly dull. I left as soon as I could."

"I wish you were here," she whispers.

"Do you?"

"Yes," she says fervently.

Oh. Perhaps she's missed me.

"I'll see you Sunday?" I confirm, trying to keep the hope out of my voice.

"Yes, Sunday," she says, and I think she's smiling.

"Good night."

"Good night, Sir." Her voice is husky and it takes my breath away.

"Good luck with your move tomorrow, Anastasia."

She stays on the line, her breathing soft. Why doesn't she hang up? She doesn't want to?

"You hang up," she whispers.

She doesn't want to hang up and my mood lightens immediately. I grin out at the view of Seattle. "No, you hang up."

"I don't want to."

"Neither do I."

"Were you very angry with me?" she asks.

"Yes."

"Are you still?"

"No." *Now I know you're safe.*

"So you're not going to punish me?"

"No. I'm an in-the-moment kind of guy."

"I've noticed," she teases, and that makes me smile.

"You can hang up now, Miss Steele."

"Do you really want me to, Sir?"

"Go to bed, Anastasia."

"Yes, Sir."

She doesn't hang up, and I know she's grinning. It lifts my spirits higher. "Do you ever think you'll be able to do what you're told?" I ask.

"Maybe. We'll see after Sunday," she says, temptress that she is, and the line goes dead.

Anastasia Steele, what am I going to do with you?

Actually, I have a good idea, provided that riding crop turns up in time. And with that enticing thought I toss down the rest of the Armagnac and go to bed.

SATURDAY, MAY 28, 2011

"Christian!" Mia squeals with delight and runs toward me, abandoning her cartload of luggage. Throwing her arms around my neck, she hugs me tightly.

"I've missed you," she says.

"I've missed you, too." I give her a squeeze in return.

She leans back and examines me with intense dark eyes. "You look good," she gushes. "Tell me about this girl!"

"Let's get you and your luggage home first." I grab her cart, which weighs a ton, and together we head out of the airport terminal toward the parking lot. "So how was Paris? You appear to have brought most of it home with you."

"*C'est incroyable!*" she exclaims. "Floubert, on the other hand, was a bastard. *Jesus.* He was a horrible man. A crap teacher but a good chef."

"Does that mean you're cooking this evening?"

"Oh, I was hoping Mom would cook."

Mia proceeds to talk nonstop about Paris: her tiny room, the plumbing, Sacré-Coeur, Montmartre, Parisians, coffee, red wine, cheese, fashion, shopping. But mainly about fashion and shopping. And I thought she went to Paris to learn to cook.

I've missed her chatter; it's soothing and welcome. She is the only person I know who doesn't make me feel…different.

"This is your baby sister, Christian. Her name is Mia."

Mommy lets me hold her. She is very small. With black, black hair.

She smiles. She has no teeth. I stick out my tongue. She has a bubbly laugh.

Mommy lets me hold the baby again. Her name is Mia.

I make her laugh. I hold her and hold her. She is safe when I hold her.

Elliot is not interested in Mia. She dribbles and cries.

And he wrinkles his nose when she does a poop.

When Mia is crying Elliot ignores her. I hold her and hold her and she stops.

She falls asleep in my arms.

"Mee-a," I whisper.

"What did you say?" Mommy asks, and her face is white like chalk.

"Mee-a."

"Yes. Yes, darling boy. Mia. Her name is Mia."

And Mommy starts to cry with happy, happy tears.

I TURN INTO THE driveway, pull up outside Mom and Dad's front door, unload Mia's luggage, and carry it into the hall.

"Where is everyone?" Mia is in full pout.

The only person around is my parents' housekeeper—she's an exchange student, and I can't remember her name. "Welcome home," she says to Mia in her stilted English, though she's looking at me with big cow eyes.

Oh God. It's just a pretty face, sweetheart.

Ignoring the housekeeper, I address Mia's question. "I think Mom is on call and Dad is at a conference. You did come home a week early."

"I couldn't stand Floubert another minute. I had to get out while I could. Oh, I bought you a present." She grabs one of her cases, opens it in the hallway, and starts rummaging through it. "Ah!" She hands me a heavy square box. "Open it," she urges, beaming at me. She is an unstoppable force.

Warily I open the box, and inside I find a snow globe containing a black grand piano covered in glitter. It's the kitschiest thing I've ever seen.

"It's a music box. Here..." She takes it from me, gives it a good shake, and winds a small key on the bottom. A twinkly version of "La Marseillaise" starts to play in a cloud of colored glitter.

What am I going to do with this? I laugh, because it's so Mia. "That's great, Mia. Thank you." I give her a hug and she hugs me back.

"I knew it would make you laugh."

She's right. She knows me well.

"So tell me about this girl," she says.

But we're both distracted as Grace hurries through the door, allowing me a reprieve as mother and daughter embrace. "I'm so sorry I wasn't there to meet you, darling," Grace says. "I've been on call. You look so grown up. Christian, can you take Mia's bags upstairs? Gretchen will give you a hand."

Really? I'm a porter now?

"Yes, Mom." I roll my eyes. I don't need Gretchen mooning over me.

Once that's done, I tell them I have an appointment with my trainer. "I'll be back this evening." Quickly kissing them both, I leave before I'm pestered with more questions about Ana.

BASTILLE WORKS ME HARD. Today we're kickboxing at his gym.

"You've gone soft in Portland, boy," he sneers after I'm toppled onto the mat from his roundhouse kick. Bastille is from the hard-knocks school of physical training, which suits me fine.

I scramble to my feet. I want to take him down. But he's right—he's all over my shit today, and I get nowhere.

When we finish he asks, "What gives? You're distracted, man."

"Life. You know," I answer with an air of indifference.

"Sure. You're back in Seattle this week?"

"Yeah."

"Good. We'll straighten you out."

AS I JOG BACK to the apartment I remember the housewarming present for Ana. I text Elliot.

What's Ana and Kate's address?
I want to surprise them with a present.

He texts me back an address and I forward it to Andrea. As I'm riding in the elevator up to the penthouse, Andrea texts me back.

Champagne and balloon sent. A.

Taylor hands me a package when I arrive back at the apartment. "This came for you, Mr. Grey."

Oh yes. I recognize the anonymous wrapping: it's the riding crop.

"Thanks."

"Mrs. Jones said she'd be back tomorrow, late afternoon."

"Okay. I think that's all for today, Taylor."

"Very good, sir," he says with a polite smile and returns to his office. Taking the crop, I stroll into my bedroom. This will be the perfect introduction to my world: by her own admission Ana has no sphere of reference with regard to corporal punishment, except the spanking I gave her that night. And that turned her on. With the crop, I'll have to take it slow and make it pleasurable.

Really pleasurable. The riding crop is perfect. I'll prove to her that the fear is in her head. Once she gets comfortable with this, we can move on.

I hope we can move on…

We'll take it slow. And we'll only do what she can handle. If this is going to work we're going to have to go at her pace. Not mine.

I take one more look at the crop and put it in my closet for tomorrow.

AS I FLIP OPEN my laptop to start work my phone rings. I hope it's Ana, but, disappointingly, it's Elena.

Was I supposed to call her?

"Hello, Christian. How are you?"

"Good, thanks."

"You're back from Portland?"

"Yes."

"Fancy dinner tonight?"

"Not tonight. Mia's just in from Paris and I've been ordered home."

"Ah. By Mama Grey. How is she?"

"Mama Grey? She's good. I think. Why? What do you know that I don't?"

"I was just asking, Christian. Don't be so touchy."

"I'll call you next week. Maybe we can do dinner then."

"Good. You've been off the radar for a while. And I've met a woman who I think might meet your needs."

So have I.

I ignore her comment. "I'll see you next week. Goodbye."

As I shower I wonder if having to chase Ana has made her more interesting…or is it Ana herself?

DINNER HAS BEEN FUN. My sister is back, the princess she's always been, the rest of the family merely her minions, wrapped around her little finger. With all her children home, Grace is in her element; she's cooked Mia's favorite meal—buttermilk fried chicken with mashed potatoes and gravy.

I have to say, it's one of my favorites, too.

"Tell me about Anastasia," Mia demands as we sit around the kitchen table.

Elliot leans back in his chair and rests his hands behind his head. "This I have to hear. You know she popped his cherry?"

"Elliot!" Grace scolds and swats him with a dish towel.

"Ow!" He fends her off.

I roll my eyes at all of them. "I met a girl." I shrug. "End of story."

"You can't just say that!" Mia objects, pouting.

"Mia, I think he can. And he just did." Carrick gives her a reproving paternal stare over his glasses.

"You'll all meet her at dinner tomorrow, won't we, Christian?" Grace says with a pointed smile.

Oh fuck.

"Kate's coming," Elliot goads.

Fucking stirrer. I glare at him.

"I can't wait to meet her. She sounds awesome!" Mia bounces up and down in her chair.

"Yeah, yeah," I mumble, wondering if there's any way I can wriggle out of dinner tomorrow.

"Elena was asking after you, darling," Grace says.

"She was?" I affect an uninterested air, developed over years of practice.

"Yes. She says she hasn't seen you in a while."

"I've been in Portland on business. Speaking of which, I should get going—I have an important call tomorrow and I need to prepare."

"But you've not had dessert. And it's apple cobbler."

Hmm…tempting. But if I stay they'll quiz me about Ana. "I have to go. I have work to do."

"Darling, you work too hard," Grace says as she starts from her chair.

"Don't get up, Mom. I'm sure Elliot will help with the dishes after dinner."

"What?" Elliot scowls.

I wink at him, say my goodbyes, and turn to leave.

"But we'll see you tomorrow?" Grace asks, too much hope in her voice.

"We'll see."

Shit. It looks like Anastasia Steele is going to meet my family.

I don't know how I feel about this.

SUNDAY, MAY 29, 2011

With the Rolling Stones' "Shake Your Hips" blasting in my ears, I sprint down Fourth Avenue and turn right on Vine. It's 6:45 a.m., and it's downhill all the way...to her apartment. I'm drawn; I just want to see where she lives.

It's between control freak and stalker.

I chuckle to myself. I'm just running; it's a free country.

The apartment block is a nondescript redbrick, with dark-green painted window frames typical of the area. It's in a good location near the intersection of Vine Street and Western. I imagine Ana curled up in her bed under her comforter and her cream-and-blue quilt.

I run several blocks and turn down into the market; the vendors are setting up for business. I dodge between the fruit and vegetable trucks and the refrigerated vans delivering the catch of the day. This is the heart of the city—vibrant, even this early on a gray, cool morning. The water on the Sound is a glassy leaden color, matching the sky. But it does nothing to dampen my spirits.

Today's the day.

AFTER MY SHOWER I don jeans and a linen shirt, and from my chest of drawers I take out a hair tie. I slip it into my pocket and head into my study to email Ana.

From: Christian Grey
Subject: My Life in Numbers
Date: May 29 2011 08:04
To: Anastasia Steele

If you drive you'll need this access code for the underground garage at Escala: 146963.

Park in bay five—it's one of mine.

Code for the elevator: 1880.

Christian Grey
CEO, Grey Enterprises Holdings, Inc.

A moment or two later, there's a response.

From: Anastasia Steele
Subject: An Excellent Vintage
Date: May 29 2011 08:08
To: Christian Grey

Yes, Sir. Understood.
Thank you for the champagne and the blow-up *Charlie Tango*, which is now tied to my bed.

Ana

An image of Ana tethered to her bed with my tie comes to mind. I shift in my chair. I hope she's brought that bed to Seattle.

From: Christian Grey
Subject: Envy
Date: May 29 2011 08:11
To: Anastasia Steele

You're welcome.

Don't be late.

Lucky *Charlie Tango.*

Christian Grey
CEO, Grey Enterprises Holdings, Inc.

She doesn't respond, so I hunt through the refrigerator for some breakfast. Gail has left me some croissants and, for lunch, a Caesar salad with chicken, enough for two. I hope Ana will eat this; I don't mind having it two days in a row.

Taylor appears while I'm eating my breakfast.

"Good morning, Mr. Grey. Here are the Sunday papers."

"Thanks. Anastasia is coming over at one today, and a Dr. Greene at one thirty."

"Very good, sir. Anything else on the agenda today?"

"Yes. Ana and I will be going to my parents' for dinner this evening."

Taylor cocks his head, looking momentarily surprised, but he remembers himself and leaves the room. I return to my croissant and apricot jam.

Yeah. I'm taking her to meet my parents. What's the big deal?

I CAN'T SETTLE. I'M restless. It's 12:15 p.m. Time is crawling today. I give up on work and, grabbing the Sunday papers, wander back into the living room, where I switch on some music and read.

To my surprise there's a photograph of Ana and me on the local news page, taken at the graduation ceremony at WSU. She looks lovely, if a little startled.

I hear the double doors open, and there she is… Her hair is loose, a little wild and sexy, and she's wearing that purple dress she wore to dinner at The Heathman. She looks gorgeous.

Bravo, Miss Steele.

"Hmm, that dress." My voice is full of admiration as I saunter toward her. "Welcome back, Miss Steele," I whisper, and holding her chin, I give her a tender kiss on the lips.

"Hi," she says, her cheeks a little rosy.

"You're on time. I like punctual. Come." Taking her hand, I lead her to the sofa. "I wanted to show you something." We both sit, and I pass her *The Seattle Times.* The photograph makes her laugh. Not quite the reaction I was expecting.

"So I'm your 'friend' now," she teases.

"So it would appear. And it's in the newspaper, so it must be true."

I'm calmer now that she's here—probably *because* she's here. She hasn't run. I tuck her soft, silky hair behind her ear; my fingers are itching to braid it.

"So, Anastasia, you have a much better idea of what I'm about since you were last here."

"Yes." Her gaze is intense...knowing.

"And yet you've returned."

She nods, giving me a coy smile.

I can't believe my luck.

I knew you were a freak, Ana.

"Have you eaten?"

"No."

Not at all? Okay. We'll have to fix this. I drag my hand through my hair, and in as even a tone as I can manage I ask, "Are you hungry?"

"Not for food," she teases.

Whoa. She might as well be addressing my groin.

Leaning forward, I press my lips to her ear and catch her intoxicating scent. "You are as eager as ever, Miss Steele—and just to let you in on a little secret, so am I. But Dr. Greene is due here shortly." I lean against the sofa. "I wish you'd eat." It's a plea.

"What can you tell me about Dr. Greene?" She deftly changes the subject.

"She's the best ob-gyn in Seattle. What more can I say?"

That's what my doctor told my PA, anyway.

"I thought I was seeing *your* doctor? And don't tell me you're really a woman, because I won't believe you."

I suppress my snort. "I think it's more appropriate that you see a specialist. Don't you?"

She gives me a quizzical look, but she nods.

One more topic to tackle. "Anastasia, my mother would like you to come to dinner this evening. I believe Elliot is asking Kate, too. I don't know how you feel about that. It will be odd for me to introduce you to my family."

She takes a second to process the information, then tosses her hair over her shoulder in that way she does before a fight. But she looks hurt, not argumentative. "Are you ashamed of me?" She sounds choked.

Oh, for heaven's sake. "Of course not." *Of all the ridiculous things to say!* I glare at her, aggrieved. How could she think that about herself?

"Why is it odd?" she asks.

"Because I've never done it before." I sound irritable.

"Why are you allowed to roll your eyes and I'm not?"

"I wasn't aware that I was." *She's calling me out. Again.*

"Neither am I, usually," she snaps.

Shit. Are we arguing?

Taylor clears his throat. "Dr. Greene is here, sir," he says.

"Show her up to Miss Steele's room."

Ana turns and looks at me and I hold out my hand to her.

"You're not going to come as well, are you?" She's horrified and amused at once.

I laugh, and my body stirs. "I'd pay very good money to watch, believe me, Anastasia, but I don't think the good doctor would approve."

She places her hand in mine, and I pull her up into my arms and kiss her. Her mouth is soft and warm and inviting; my hands glide into her hair and I deepen the kiss. When I pull away, she looks dazed.

I press my forehead to hers. "I'm so glad you're here. I can't wait to get you naked." *I can't believe how much I missed you.* "Come on. I want to meet Dr. Greene, too."

"You don't know her?"

"No."

I take Ana's hand and we head upstairs, to what will be her bedroom.

Dr. Greene has one of those myopic stares; it's penetrating and that makes me a tad uncomfortable. "Mr. Grey," she says, shaking my outstretched hand with a firm, no-nonsense grip.

"Thank you for coming on such short notice." I flash her my most benign smile.

"Thank you for making it worth my while, Mr. Grey. Miss Steele," she says politely to Ana, and I know she's sizing up our relationship. I'm sure she thinks I should be twiddling a mustache like a silent-movie villain. She turns and gives me a pointed "leave now" kind of look.

Okay.

"I'll be downstairs," I acquiesce. Though I would like to watch. I'm sure the good doctor's reaction would be priceless if I made that request. I smirk at the thought and head downstairs to the living room.

Now that Ana's no longer with me, I'm restless again. As a distraction I set the counter with two place mats. It's the second time I've done this, and the first time was for Ana, too.

You're going soft, Grey.

I select a Chablis to have with lunch—one of the few chardonnays I like—and when I'm done I take a seat on the sofa and browse through the sports section of the paper. Turning up the volume via the remote for my iPod, I hope the music will help me focus on stats from last night's Mariners win against the Yankees, rather than what's happening upstairs between Ana and Dr. Greene.

Eventually their footsteps echo in the corridor, and I look up as they enter. "Are you done?" I ask and hit the remote for the iPod to quiet the aria.

"Yes, Mr. Grey. Look after her; she's a beautiful, bright young woman."

What has Ana told her?

"I fully intend to," I say with a quick what-the-fuck glance at Ana.

She bats her lashes, clueless. *Good.* It's nothing she's said, then.

"I'll send you my bill," says Dr. Greene. "Good day, and good luck to you, Ana." The edges of her eyes crinkle with a warm smile as we shake hands.

Taylor escorts her toward the elevator and wisely closes the double doors to the foyer.

"How was that?" I ask, a little bemused by Dr. Greene's words.

"Fine, thank you," Ana answers. "She said that I had to abstain from all sexual activity for the next four weeks."

What the hell? I gape at her in shock.

Ana's earnest expression dissolves into one of taunting triumph. "Gotcha!"

Well played, Miss Steele.

My eyes narrow and her grin vanishes.

"Gotcha!" I can't help my smirk. Reaching around her waist, I pull her against me, my body hungering for her. "You are incorrigible, Miss Steele." I weave my hands through her hair and kiss her hard, wondering if I should fuck her over the kitchen counter as a lesson.

All in good time, Grey.

"As much as I'd like to take you here and now, you need to eat and so do I. I don't want you passing out on me later," I whisper.

"Is that all you want me for—my body?" she asks.

"That and your smart mouth." I kiss her once more, thinking of what's to come… My kiss deepens and desire hardens my body. I want this woman. Before I fuck her on the floor, I release her, and we're both breathless.

"What's the music?" she says, her voice hoarse.

"Villa-Lobos, an aria from *Bachianas Brasileiras.* Good, isn't it?"

"Yes," she says, gazing at the breakfast bar.

I take the chicken Caesar out of the fridge, place it on the table between the place mats, and ask her if she's okay with salad.

"Yes, fine, thank you." She smiles.

From the wine fridge I take out the Chablis, feeling her eyes on me. I didn't know I could be so domestic. "What are you thinking?" I ask.

"I was just watching the way you move."

"And?" I ask, momentarily surprised.

"You're very graceful," she says quietly, her cheeks pink.

"Why, thank you, Miss Steele." I sit beside her, unsure how to respond to her sweet compliment. Nobody's called me graceful before. "Chablis?"

"Please."

"Help yourself to salad. Tell me—what method did you opt for?"

"Mini pill," she says.

"And will you remember to take it regularly, at the right time, every day?"

A blush steals across her surprised face. "I'm sure you'll remind me," she says with a hint of sarcasm, which I choose to ignore.

You should have had the shot.

"I'll put an alarm on my calendar. Eat." She takes a bite, then another...and another. She's eating!

"So I can put chicken Caesar on the list for Mrs. Jones?" I ask.

"I thought I'd be doing the cooking."

"Yes. You will."

She finishes before I do. She must have been starving.

"Eager as ever, Miss Steele?"

"Yes," she says, giving me a demure look from beneath her lashes.

Fuck. There it is.

The attraction.

As if under her spell, I get up and tug her into my arms.

"Do you want to do this?" I whisper, inwardly begging her to say yes.

"I haven't signed anything."

"I know—but I'm breaking all the rules these days."

"Are you going to hit me?"

"Yes, but it won't be to hurt you. I don't want to punish you right now. If you'd caught me yesterday evening, well, that would have been a different story."

Her face turns to shock.

Oh, baby. "Don't let anyone try to convince you otherwise, Anastasia. One of the reasons people like me do this is because we either like to give or receive pain. It's very simple. You don't, so I spent a great deal of time yesterday thinking about that."

I wrap my arms around her, holding her against my hardening erection.

"Did you reach any conclusions?" she whispers.

"No, and right now, I just want to tie you up and fuck you senseless. Are you ready for that?"

Her expression is darker, sensual, and full of carnal curiosity. "Yes," she says, the word as soft as a sigh.

Thank fuck.

"Good. Come." I lead her upstairs and into my playroom. My safe place. Where I can do what I wish with her. I close my eyes, briefly savoring the exhilaration.

Have I ever been this excited?

Pushing the door shut behind us, I release her hand and study her. Her lips are parted as she inhales; her breathing is quick and shallow. Her eyes are wide. Ready. Waiting.

"When you're in here, you are completely mine. To do with as I see fit. Do you understand?"

Her tongue quickly licks her upper lip, and she nods.

Good girl.

"Take your shoes off."

She swallows and proceeds to take off her high-heeled sandals.

I pick them up and put them neatly by the door. "Good. Don't hesitate when I ask you to do something. Now I'm going to peel you out of this dress. Something I've wanted to do for a few days, if I recall." I pause, checking she's still with me. "I want you to be comfortable with your body, Anastasia. You have a beautiful body, and I like to look at it. It is a joy to behold. In fact, I could gaze at you all day, and I want you unembarrassed and unashamed of your nakedness. Do you understand?"

"Yes."

"Yes what?" My tone is sharper.

"Yes, Sir."

"Do you mean that?" *I want you unashamed, Ana.*

"Yes, Sir."

"Good. Lift your arms over your head."

Slowly she raises her arms in the air. I grab the hem and gently pull the dress up her body, revealing it inch by inch, for my eyes only. When it's off I stand back so I can have my fill of her.

Legs, thighs, belly, ass, tits, shoulders, face, mouth…she's perfect. Folding her dress, I place it on the toy chest. Reaching up, I tug her chin. "You're biting your lip. You know what that does to me," I scold. "Turn around."

She complies and turns to face the door. I unfasten her bra and pull the straps down her arms, skimming her skin with my fingertips as I do and feeling her tremble beneath my touch. I take off her bra and toss it on top of her dress. I stand close, not quite touching her, listening to her rapid breathing and sensing the warmth radiating off her skin. She's excited and she's not the only one. I gather her hair in both of my hands so it falls down her back. It's oh so silky to touch. I wind it around one hand and tug, angling her head to one side and exposing her neck to my mouth.

I run my nose from her ear to her shoulder and back again, inhaling her heavenly scent.

Fuck, she smells good.

"You smell as divine as ever, Anastasia." I place a kiss beneath her ear just above her pulse.

She moans.

"Quiet. Don't make a sound."

From my jeans pocket I grab the hair tie, and taking her hair in my hands, I braid it, enjoying the pull and twist against her beautiful, flawless back. Deftly I fasten the end with the hair tie and give it a quick tug, forcing her to step back and press her body into mine. "I like your hair braided in here," I whisper. "Turn around."

She does so, immediately.

"When I tell you to come in here, this is how you will dress. Just in your panties. Do you understand?"

"Yes."

"Yes what?"

"Yes, Sir."

"Good girl." She's learning fast. Her arms are by her sides, her eyes trained on mine. Waiting.

"When I tell you to come in here, I expect you to kneel over there." I point to the corner of the room beside the door. "Do it now."

She blinks a couple of times, but before I have to tell her again, she turns and kneels, facing me and the room.

I give her permission to sit back on her heels and she obliges. "Place your hands and forearms flat on your thighs. Good. Now part your knees. Wider." *I want to see you, baby.* "Wider." *See your sex.* "Perfect. Look down at the floor."

Don't look at me or the room. You can sit there and let your thoughts run wild while you imagine what I'm going to do to you.

I walk over to her, and I'm pleased she keeps her head bowed. Reaching down, I tug her braid, tilting her head so our eyes meet. "Will you remember this position, Anastasia?"

"Yes, Sir."

"Good. Stay here, don't move."

Walking past her, I open the door and for a moment look back at her. Her head is bowed; her eyes stay fixed on the floor.

What a welcome sight. *Good girl.*

I want to run, but I contain my eagerness and walk purposefully downstairs to my bedroom.

Maintain some fucking dignity, Grey.

In my closet I strip off all my clothes and from a drawer pull out my favorite jeans. My DJs. Dom jeans.

I slip them on and fasten all the buttons except the top one. From the same drawer I retrieve the new riding crop and a gray waffle robe. As I leave I grab a few condoms and stuff them into my pocket.

Here goes.

Showtime, Grey.

When I get back she's in the same position: her head bowed, her braid hanging down her back, her hands on her knees. I close the door and hang the robe on its hook. I walk past her. "Good girl, Anastasia. You look lovely like that. Well done. Stand up."

She stands, keeping her head down.

"You may look at me."

Eager blue eyes peek up.

"I'm going to chain you now, Anastasia. Give me your right hand." I hold out mine and she places her hand in it. Without taking my eyes off hers I turn her hand palm up and from behind my back produce the riding crop. I quickly flick the end across her palm.

She startles and cups her hand, blinking at me in surprise.

"How does that feel?" I ask.

Her breathing accelerates, and she glances at me before looking back at her palm.

"Answer me."

"Okay." Her brows knit together.

"Don't frown," I warn. "Did that hurt?"

"No."

"This is not going to hurt. Do you understand?"

"Yes." Her voice is a little shaky.

"I mean it," I stress, and I show her the crop.

Brown plaited leather. See? I listen.

Her eyes meet mine, astonished.

My lips twitch in amusement. "We aim to please, Miss Steele. Come."

I lead her to the middle of the room, beneath the restraining system. "This grid is designed so the shackles move across the grid." She stares up at the intricate system, then back at me.

"We're going to start here, but I want to fuck you standing up. So we'll end up by the wall over there." I point to the Saint Andrew's cross. "Put your hands above your head."

She does, immediately. Taking the leather cuffs that hang on the grid, I fasten one to each of her wrists in turn. I'm methodical, but she's distracting. Being this close to her, sensing her excitement, her anxiety, touching her. I find it hard to concentrate. Once she's cuffed I step back and take a deep breath, relieved.

Finally I've got you where I want you, Ana Steele.

Casually I walk around her, admiring the view. Could she look hotter? "You look mighty fine trussed up like this, Miss Steele. And your smart mouth quiet for now. I like that." I stop, facing her, curl my fingers into her panties, and oh so slowly drag them down her long legs until I'm kneeling at her feet.

Worshipping her. She's glorious.

With my eyes locked on hers, I take her panties, crush them to my nose, and inhale deeply. Her mouth pops open and her eyes widen in amused shock.

Yes. I smirk. *Perfect reaction.*

I slip the panties into the back pocket of my jeans and stand, considering my next move. Holding out the crop, I run it over her belly and gently circle her navel with the keeper, the leather tongue. She sucks in her breath and tremors at the touch.

This will be good, Ana. Trust me.

Slowly I begin to circle her, drawing the crop across her skin, across her belly, her flank, her back. On my second circuit I flick the tongue at the base of her behind so it makes sharp contact with her vulva.

"Ah!" she cries, and she tugs against the shackles.

"Quiet," I warn and prowl around her once more. I flick the crop against her in the same sweet spot and she whines on contact, her eyes closed as she absorbs the sensation. With another twitch of my wrist, the crop snaps against her nipple. She throws her head back and moans. I aim again, and the crop licks her other nipple, and I watch it harden and lengthen beneath the bite of the leather keeper.

"Does that feel good?"

"Yes," she rasps, eyes closed, head back.

I smack her across her behind, harder this time.

"Yes what?"

"Yes, Sir," she cries.

With great care and precision, I lavish strokes, licks, and flicks over her stomach and her belly, down her body, toward my goal. With one flick, the leather tongue bites her clitoris and she shouts out in a gargled cry, "Oh, please!"

"Quiet," I command and reprimand her with a harder flick across her backside.

I skim the leather tongue down through her pubic hair, against her vulva to her vagina. The brown leather is glistening with her arousal when I pull it back. "See how wet you are for this, Anastasia. Open your eyes and your mouth."

She's breathing hard, but she parts her lips and stares at me, her eyes dazed and lost in the carnality of the moment. And I slip the keeper into her mouth. "See how you taste. Suck. Suck hard, baby."

Her lips close around the tip and it's like they're around my dick.

Fuck.

She's so fucking hot and I can't resist her.

Easing the crop from her mouth, I wrap my arms around her. She opens her mouth for me as I kiss her, my tongue exploring her, reveling in the taste of her lust.

"Oh, baby, you taste mighty fine," I whisper. "Shall I make you come?"

"Please," she pleads.

One flick of my wrist and the crop smacks her behind. "Please what?"

"Please, Sir," she whimpers.

Good girl. I step back. "With this?" I ask, holding up the crop so she can see it.

"Yes, Sir," she says, surprising me.

"Are you sure?" I can barely believe my luck.

"Yes, please, Sir."

Oh, Ana. You fucking goddess.

"Close your eyes."

She does as she's told. And with infinite care and not a little gratitude, I rain quick, stinging licks over her belly once more. Soon she's panting again, her arousal heightened. Moving south, I gently flick the leather tongue over her clitoris. Again. And again. And again.

She pulls at her restraints, moaning and moaning. Then she's quiet and I know she's close. Suddenly she throws her head back, mouth open, and she screams her orgasm as it shudders through her entire body. I drop the crop and grab her, supporting her as her body dissolves. She sags against me.

Oh. We're not done, Ana.

With my hands under her thighs, I lift her trembling body and carry her, still shackled to the grid, toward the Saint Andrew's cross. There I release her, holding her upright, pinned between the cross and my shoulders. I tug my jeans, undoing all the buttons, and freeing my cock. Yanking a condom from my pocket, I rip the foil packet with my teeth and with one hand roll it over my erection.

Gently I pick her up again and whisper, "Lift your legs, baby, wrap them around me." Supporting her back against the wood, I help her wrap her legs around my hips, her elbows resting on my shoulders.

You are mine, baby.

With one thrust I'm inside her.

Fuck. She's exquisite.

I take a moment to savor her. Then I start to move, relishing each thrust. Feeling her, on and on, my own breathing labored as I gasp for air and lose myself in this beautiful woman. My mouth is open at her neck, tasting her. Her scent fills my nostrils, fills me. *Ana. Ana. Ana.* I don't want to stop.

Suddenly she tenses, and her body convulses around me.

Yes. Again. And I let go. Filling her. Holding her. Revering her.

Yes. Yes. Yes.

She's so beautiful. And sweet hell, was that mind-blowing.

I pull out of her, and as she collapses against me I quickly unbuckle her wrists from the grid and support her as we both sink to the floor. I cradle her between my legs, wrapping my arms around her, and she sags against me, her eyes closed, breathing hard.

"Well done, baby. Did that hurt?"

"No." Her voice is barely audible.

"Did you expect it to?" I ask, and I push stray strands of her hair off her face so I can see her better.

"Yes."

"You see? Most of your fear is in your head, Anastasia." I caress her face. "Would you do it again?" I ask.

She doesn't answer immediately, and I think she's fallen asleep.

"Yes," she whispers a moment later.

Thank you, sweet Lord.

I wrap her in my arms. "Good. So would I." *Again and again.* Tenderly I kiss the top of her head and inhale. She smells of Ana and sweat and sex. "And I haven't finished with you yet," I assert. I'm so proud of her. She did it. She did everything I wanted.

She's everything I want.

And suddenly I'm overwhelmed by an unfamiliar emotion that rocks through me, slicing through sinew and bone, leaving unease and fear in its wake.

She turns her head and starts to nuzzle my chest.

The darkness swells, startling and familiar, replacing my unease with a sense of dread. Every muscle in my body tenses.

Ana blinks up at me with clear, unflinching eyes as I struggle to control my fear.

"Don't," I whisper. *Please.*

She leans back and peers at my chest.

Get control, Grey.

"Kneel by the door," I order, uncurling around her.

Go. Don't touch me.

Shakily she gets to her feet and stumbles over to the door, where she resumes her kneeling position.

I take a deep, centering breath.

What are you doing to me, Ana Steele?

I stand and stretch, calmer now.

As she kneels by the door, she looks every bit the ideal submissive. Her eyes are glazed; she's tired. I'm sure she's coming down from the adrenaline high. Her eyelids droop.

Oh, this will never do. You want her as a submissive, Grey. Show her what that means.

From my drawer of toys I fish out one of the cable ties I bought from Clayton's, and a pair of scissors. "Boring you, am I, Miss

Steele?" I ask, masking my sympathy. She startles awake and regards me guiltily. "Stand up," I order.

Shakily she gets to her feet.

"You're shattered, aren't you?"

She nods with a bashful smile.

Oh, baby, you've done so well.

"Stamina, Miss Steele. I haven't had my fill of you yet. Hold out your hands in front, as if you're praying."

A crease mars her forehead for a moment, but she presses her palms together and holds up her hands. I fasten the cable tie around her wrists. Her eyes flash to mine with recognition.

"Look familiar?" I give her a smile and run my finger around the plastic, checking there's enough room and it's not too tight. "I have scissors here." I bring them into her view. "I can cut you out of this in a moment." She looks reassured. "Come." Taking her clasped hands, I lead her to the far corner of the four-poster bed. "I want more—much, much more," I whisper in her ear as she stares down at the bed. "But I'll make this quick. You're tired. Hold on to the post."

Halting, she grasps the wooden pillar.

"Lower," I order. She moves her hands down to the base until she's bending over. "Good. Don't let go. If you do, I'll spank you. Understand?"

"Yes, Sir," she says.

"Good." I grab her hips and lift her toward me so she's properly positioned, her beautiful behind in the air and at my disposal. "Don't let go, Anastasia," I warn her. "I'm going to fuck you hard from behind. Hold the post to support your weight. Understand?"

"Yes."

I smack her hard across her backside.

"Yes, Sir," she says immediately.

"Part your legs." I push my right foot against hers, widening her stance. "That's better. After this, I'll let you sleep."

Her back is a perfect curve, each vertebra outlined from her nape to her fine, fine ass. I trace the line with my fingers. "You have such beautiful skin, Anastasia," I say to myself. Bending over her, I follow the path my fingers have taken with tender kisses down her spine. As I do, I palm her breasts, trapping her nipples between my fingers, and tug. She writhes beneath me, and I plant a soft kiss at her waist, then suck and gently nip her skin while working her nipples.

She whimpers. I stop and stand back to admire the view, growing harder just looking at her. Reaching for a second condom from my pocket, I quickly kick my jeans off and open the foil packet. Using both hands, I wrap it around my cock.

I'd like to claim her ass. Now. But it's too soon for that.

"You have such a captivating, sexy ass. What I'd like to do to it." I stroke my hands over each cheek, fondling her, then slide two fingers inside her, stretching her.

She whimpers again.

She's ready.

"So wet. You never disappoint, Miss Steele. Hold tight. This is going to be quick, baby."

Clutching her hips, I position myself at the entrance of her vagina, then reach up, grab her braid, wind it around my wrist, and hold it tightly. With one hand on my cock and the other around her hair, I slide into her.

She. Is. So. Fucking. Sweet.

Slowly I slide out of her, then grip her hip with my free hand and tighten my hold on her hair.

Submissive.

I slam into her, forcing her forward with a cry.

"Hold on, Anastasia!" I remind her. If she doesn't she might get hurt.

Breathless, she pushes back against me, bracing her legs.

Good girl.

Then I start pounding into her, eliciting small, strangled cries from her as she clings to the post. But she doesn't back down. She pushes back.

Bravo, Ana.

And then I feel it. Slowly. Her insides curling around me. Losing control, I slam into her and still. "Come on, Ana, give it to me," I growl as I come, hard, her release prolonging mine as I hold her up.

Gathering her in my arms, I lower us to the floor with Ana on top of me, both of us facing the ceiling. She's utterly relaxed, exhausted no doubt, her weight a welcome comfort. I stare up at the carabiners, wondering if she'll ever let me suspend her.

Probably not.

And I don't care.

Our first time together in here, and she's been a dream. I kiss her ear. "Hold up your hands." My voice is husky.

Slowly, she raises them as if they're weighted with concrete, and I slide the scissors beneath the cable tie.

"I declare this Ana open," I murmur and snip, freeing her.

She giggles, her body juddering against mine. It's a strange and not unwelcome feeling that makes me grin.

"That is such a lovely sound," I whisper as she rubs her wrists. I sit up so she's in my lap.

I love making her laugh. She doesn't laugh enough.

"That's my fault," I admit to myself as I rub some life back into her shoulders and arms. She turns her face to me with a weary, searching look. "That you don't giggle more often," I clarify.

"I'm not a great giggler," she says and yawns.

"Oh, but when it happens, 'tis a wonder and joy to behold."

"Very flowery, Mr. Grey," she says, teasing me.

I smile. "I'd say you're thoroughly fucked and in need of sleep."

"That wasn't flowery at all," she scoffs, scolding me.

Lifting her off my lap so I can stand, I reach for my jeans and slip them on. "Don't want to frighten Taylor—or Mrs. Jones, for that matter."

It wouldn't be the first time.

Ana sits in a sleepy daze on the floor. I clasp her upper arms, help her to her feet, and take her to the door. From the hook on the back of the door I grab the gray robe and dress her. She's no help whatsoever; she really is exhausted.

"Bed," I announce, kissing her quickly.

An alarmed expression crosses her drowsy face.

"For sleep," I reassure her. Bending, I gather her in my arms, cradle her against my chest, and carry her to the sub's room. There, I pull back the comforter and lay her down, and in a moment of weakness climb into the bed beside her. Covering us both with the duvet, I embrace her.

I'll just hold her until she's asleep.

"Sleep now, gorgeous girl." I kiss her hair feeling utterly sated… and grateful. We did it. This sweet, innocent woman let me loose on her. And I think she enjoyed it. I know I did…more than ever before.

Mommy sits looking at me in the mirror with the big crack.
I brush her hair. It's soft and smells of Mommy and flowers.
She takes the brush and winds her hair round and round.
So it's like a bumpy snake down her back.
There, she says.
And she turns around and smiles at me.
Today, she's happy.
I like when Mommy is happy.
I like it when she smiles at me.
She looks pretty when she smiles.
Let's bake a pie, Maggot.
Apple pie.
I like when Mommy bakes.

I wake suddenly with a sweet scent invading my mind. It's Ana. She's fast asleep beside me. I lie back and stare at the ceiling.

When have I ever slept in this room?

Never.

The thought is unnerving, and for some unfathomable reason it makes me uneasy.

What's going on, Grey?

I sit up carefully, not wanting to disturb her, and stare down at her sleeping form. I know what it is—I'm unsettled because I'm in here with her. I climb out of bed, leaving her to sleep, and head back to the playroom. There I collect the used cable tie and condoms and stash them in my pocket, where I find Ana's panties. With the crop, her clothes, and her shoes in hand, I leave and lock the door. Back in her room, I hang her dress on the closet door, place her shoes beneath the chair, and lay her bra on top. I take her panties from my pocket—and a wicked idea comes to mind.

I head for my bathroom. I need a shower before we head to dinner with my family. I'll let Ana sleep awhile longer.

The piping-hot water cascades over me, washing away all the anxiety and unease I'd felt earlier. As first times go, that was not bad, for either of us. And I'd thought that a relationship with Ana was impossible, but now the future now seems full of possibility. I make a mental note to call Caroline Acton in the morning to dress my girl.

After a productive hour in my study, catching up on my reading for work, I decide Ana has had enough sleep. It's dusk outside, and we have to leave in forty-five minutes for dinner at my parents'. It's been easier to concentrate on my work, knowing she's upstairs in her bedroom.

Weird.

Well, I know she's safe up there.

From the refrigerator I take a carton of cranberry juice and a bottle of sparkling water. I mix them in a glass and head upstairs.

She's still fast asleep, curled up where I left her. I don't think she's moved at all. Her lips are parted as she breathes softly. Her hair is tousled, tendrils escaping from her braid. I sit on the edge of the bed beside her, lean down, and kiss her temple. She mumbles a protest in her sleep.

"Anastasia, wake up." My voice is gentle as I coax her awake.

"No," she grumbles, hugging her pillow.

"We have to leave in half an hour for dinner at my parents'."

Her eyes flicker open and focus on me.

"Come on, sleepyhead. Get up." I kiss her temple again. "I've brought you a drink. I'll be downstairs. Don't go back to sleep, or you'll be in trouble," I warn as she stretches her arms. I kiss her once more and with a glance at the chair, where she won't find her panties, I saunter back downstairs, unable to suppress my grin.

Playtime, Grey.

While I'm waiting for Miss Steele I press a button on the iPod remote and the music springs to life on random shuffle. Restless, I wander over to the balcony doors and stare out at the early evening sky, listening to Talking Heads' "And She Was."

Taylor enters. "Mr. Grey. Shall I bring the car around?"

"Give us five minutes."

"Yes, sir," he says and disappears toward the service elevator.

Ana appears a few minutes later at the entrance to the living room. She looks luminous, stunning even…and amused. What's she going to say about her missing panties?

"Hi," she says with a cryptic smile.

"Hi. How are you feeling?"

Her smile broadens. "Good, thanks. You?" She feigns nonchalance.

"I feel mighty fine, Miss Steele." The suspense is tantalizing and I hope my anticipation is not written all over my face.

"Frank? I never figured you for a Sinatra fan," she says, cocking her head and giving me a curious look, as the rich tones of "Witchcraft" fill the room.

"Eclectic taste, Miss Steele." I step toward her until I'm standing right in front of her. *Will she crack?* I'm searching for an answer in her glittering blue eyes.

Ask me for your panties, baby.

I caress her cheek with my fingertips. She leans her face into my touch, and I'm completely seduced—by her sweet gesture, by her teasing expression, and by the music. I want her in my arms.

"Dance with me," I whisper as I remove the remote from my pocket and turn up the volume until Frank's crooning surrounds us. She gives me her hand. I circle her waist and pull her beautiful body against mine, and we start a slow, simple fox-trot. She grasps my shoulder, but I'm prepared for her touch, and together we whirl across the floor, her radiant face lighting up the room…and me.

She falls into step with my lead, and when the song comes to an end, she's giddy and breathless.

And so am I.

"There's no nicer witch than you." I plant a chaste kiss on her lips. "Well, that's brought some color to your cheeks. Thank you for the dance. Shall we go and meet my parents?"

"You're welcome, and yes, I can't wait to meet them," she replies, looking flushed and lovely.

"Do you have everything you need?"

"Oh yes," she says with easy confidence.

"Are you sure?"

She nods, her lips carved in a smirk.

God, she has guts.

I grin. "Okay." I can't hide my delight. "If that's the way you want to play it, Miss Steele." I grab my jacket and we head to the elevator.

She never fails to surprise, impress, and disarm me. Now I will have to sit through dinner with my parents, knowing my girl is not wearing any underwear. In fact, I'm traveling down in this elevator right now, knowing she's naked beneath her skirt.

She's turned the tables on you, Grey.

SHE'S QUIET AS TAYLOR drives us north on I-5. I catch a glimpse of Union Lake; the moon disappears behind a cloud, and the water darkens, like my mood. Why am I taking her to see my parents? If they meet her, they'll have certain expectations. And so will Ana. And I'm not sure if the relationship I want with Ana will live up to those expectations. And to make matters worse, I put all this in motion when I insisted she meet Grace. I'm the only one to blame. Me, and the fact that Elliot is fucking her roommate.

Who am I kidding? If I didn't want her to meet my folks, she wouldn't be here. I just wish I wasn't so anxious about it.

Yeah. That's the problem.

"Where did you learn to dance?" she asks, interrupting my chain of thoughts.

Oh, Ana. She's not going to want me to go there.

"Christian, hold me. There. Properly. Right. One step. Two. Good. Keep in time to the music. Sinatra is perfect for the fox-trot." Elena is in her element.

"Yes, Ma'am."

"Do you really want to know?" I answer.

"Yes," she replies, but her tone says otherwise.

You asked. I sigh in the darkness beside her. "Mrs. Robinson was fond of dancing."

"She must have been a good teacher." Her whisper is tinged with regret and reluctant admiration.

"She was."

"That's right. Again. One. Two. Three. Four. Baby, you've got this."

Elena and I glide across her basement.

"Again." She laughs, her head thrown back, and she looks like a woman half her age.

Ana nods and studies the landscape, no doubt concocting some theory about Elena. Or maybe she's thinking about meeting my parents. I wish I knew. Perhaps she's nervous. Like me. I've never taken a girl home.

When Ana starts fidgeting I sense something is worrying her. Is she concerned about what we did today?

"Don't," I say, my voice softer than I intend.

She turns to look at me, her expression unreadable in the dark. "Don't what?"

"Overthink things, Anastasia." Whatever you're thinking about. I reach over, take her hand, and kiss her knuckles. "I had a wonderful afternoon. Thank you."

I get a brief flash of white teeth and a timid smile.

"Why did you use a cable tie?" she asks.

Questions about this afternoon; this is good. "It's quick, it's easy, and it's something different for you to feel and experience. I know they're quite brutal, and I do like that in a restraining device." My voice is dry as I try to inject a little humor back into our conversation. "Very effective at keeping you in your place."

Her eyes dart toward Taylor in the front seat.

Sweetheart, don't worry about Taylor. He knows exactly what's going on, and he's done this for four years.

"All part of my world, Anastasia." I give her hand a reassuring squeeze before I release it. Ana returns to staring out the window; we're surrounded by water as we cross Lake Washington on the 520 bridge, my favorite part of this journey. She draws up her feet and, curled on the seat, coils her arms around her legs.

Something is up.

When she glances at me, I ask, "Penny for your thoughts?"

She sighs.

Shit. "That bad, huh?"

"I wish I knew what you were thinking," she says.

I smirk, relieved to hear this, and glad she doesn't know what's really on my mind.

"Ditto, baby," I reply.

TAYLOR PULLS UP OUTSIDE my parents' front door. "Are you ready for this?" I ask. Ana nods and I squeeze her hand. "First for me, too," I whisper. When Taylor's out the door I give her a wicked, salacious grin. "Bet you wish you were wearing your underwear right now."

Her breath hitches and she scowls, but I climb out of the car to greet my mother and father, who are waiting on the doorstep. Ana looks cool and calm as she walks around the car to us. "Anastasia, you've met my mother, Grace. This is my dad, Carrick."

"Mr. Grey, what a pleasure to meet you." She smiles and shakes his outstretched hand.

"The pleasure is all mine, Anastasia."

"Please, call me Ana."

"Ana, how lovely to see you again." Grace hugs her. "Come in, my dear." Taking Ana's arm, she leads her inside and I follow in her pantyless wake.

"Is she here?" Mia screams from somewhere inside the house.

Ana gives me a startled look.

"That would be Mia, my little sister."

We both turn in the direction of the high heels clattering through the hall. And there she is.

"Anastasia! I've heard so much about you!" Mia wraps her in a big hug. Though she's taller than Ana, I remember they're almost the same age. Mia takes her hand and drags her into the vestibule as my parents and I follow. "He's never brought a girl home before," Mia tells Ana in a shrill voice.

"Mia, calm down," Grace chides.

Yes, for fuck's sake, Mia. Stop making such a scene.

Ana catches me rolling my eyes and shoots me a withering look.

Grace greets me with a kiss on both cheeks. "Hello, darling." She's glowing, happy to have all her children home.

Carrick offers his hand. "Hello, son. Long time no see." We shake hands and follow the women into the living room.

"Dad, you saw me yesterday," I mutter. "Dad jokes"—my father excels at them.

Kavanagh and Elliot are cuddling on one of the sofas. But Kavanagh gets up to hug Ana when we enter.

"Christian." She gives me a polite nod.

"Kate."

And now Elliot has his big paws all over Ana.

Fuck, who knew my family was so touchy-feely all of a sudden? *Put her down.* I glare at Elliot and he grins—an I'm-just-showing-you-how-it's-done expression plastered all over his face. I slip my arm around Ana's waist and pull her to my side. All eyes are on us.

Hell. This feels like a freak show.

"Drinks?" Dad offers. "Prosecco?"

"Please," Ana and I reply together.

Mia bounces on the spot and claps her hands. "You're even saying the same things. I'll get them." She dashes out of the room.

What the hell is wrong with my family?

Ana frowns. She's probably finding them weird, too.

"Dinner's almost ready," Grace says as she follows Mia out of the room.

"Sit," I tell Ana, and I lead her over to one of the sofas. She does as she's told and I sit at her side, careful not to touch her. I need to set an example for my overly demonstrative family.

Maybe they've always been this way?

My father diverts me. "We were just talking about vacations, Ana. Elliot has decided to follow Kate and her family to Barbados for a week."

Dude! I stare at Elliot. *What the hell happened to Mr. Love 'Em and Leave 'Em?* Kavanagh must be good in the sack. She certainly looks smug enough.

"Are you taking a break now that you've finished your degree?" Carrick asks Ana.

"I'm thinking about going to Georgia for a few days," she answers.

"Georgia?" I exclaim, unable to hide my surprise.

"My mother lives there," she says, her voice wavering, "and I haven't seen her for a while."

"When were you thinking of going?" I snap.

"Tomorrow, late evening."

Tomorrow! What the fuck? And I'm only learning of this now?

Mia returns with pink prosecco for Ana and me.

"Your good health!" Dad raises his glass.

"For how long?" I persist, trying to keep my voice level.

"I don't know yet. It will depend how my interviews go tomorrow."

Interviews? Tomorrow?

"Ana deserves a break," Kavanagh interrupts, staring at me with ill-concealed antagonism. I want to tell her to mind her own fucking business, but for Ana's sake I hold my tongue.

"You have interviews?" Dad asks Ana.

"Yes, for internships at two publishers, tomorrow."

When was she going to tell me this? I'm here with her for two minutes and I'm finding out details of her life that I should know!

"I wish you the best of luck," Carrick says to her with a kind smile.

"Dinner is ready," Grace calls from across the hall.

I let the others exit the room but grab Ana's elbow before she can follow.

"When were you going to tell me you were leaving?" My temper is rapidly unraveling.

"I'm not leaving. I'm going to see my mother. And I was only thinking about it." Ana dismisses me, as if I'm a child.

"What about our arrangement?"

"We don't have an arrangement yet."

But…

I lead us through the living room door and into the hallway. "This conversation is not over," I warn as we enter the dining room.

Mom has gone all out—best china, best crystal—for Ana's and Kavanagh's benefits. I hold out a chair for Ana; she sits down and I take a seat beside her. Mia beams at both of us from across the table. "Where did you meet Ana?" Mia asks.

"She interviewed me for the WSU student newspaper."

"Which Kate edits," Ana interjects.

"I want to be a journalist," Kate tells Mia.

My father offers Ana some wine while Mia and Kate discuss journalism. Kavanagh has an internship at the *Seattle Times*, no doubt set up for her by her father.

From the corner of my eye I notice Ana's studying me.

"What?" I ask.

"Please don't be mad at me," she says, so low that only I can hear.

"I'm not mad at you," I lie.

Her eyes narrow, and it's obvious she doesn't believe me.

"Yes, I am mad at you," I confess. And now I feel like I'm overreacting. I close my eyes.

Get a grip, Grey.

"Palm-twitchingly mad?" she whispers.

"What are you two whispering about?" Kavanagh interrupts.

Good God! Is she always like this? So intrusive? How the hell does Elliot put up with her? I glower at her, and she has the sense to back off.

"Just about my trip to Georgia," Ana says with sweetness and charm.

Kate smirks. "How was José when you went to the bar with him on Friday?" she asks with a brash look in my direction.

What. The. Fuck. Is. This?

Ana tenses beside me.

"He was fine," she says quietly.

"Palm-twitchingly mad," I whisper to her. "Especially now."

So she went to a bar with the guy who was trying to ram his tongue down her throat the last time I saw him. *And* she'd already agreed to be mine. Sneaking off to a bar with another man? And without my permission…

She deserves to be punished.

Around me, dinner is being served.

I've agreed not to go too hard on her…maybe I should use a flogger. Or maybe I should administer a straightforward spanking, harder than the last one. Here, tonight.

Yes. That has possibilities.

Ana's looking down at her fingers. Kate, Elliot, and Mia are in a conversation about French cooking, and Dad returns to the table. Where's he been?

"Call for you, darling. It's the hospital," he says to Grace.

"Please start, everyone," Mom says, passing a plate of food to Ana.

Smells good.

Ana licks her lips and the action resonates in my groin. She must be starving. *Good.* That's something.

Mom has surpassed herself: chorizo, scallops, peppers. Nice. And I realize that I, too, am hungry. That can't be helping my mood. But I brighten watching Ana eat.

Grace returns, looking worried.

"Everything okay?" Dad asks, and we all look up at her.

"Another measles case." Grace sighs heavily.

"Oh no," Dad says.

"Yes, a child. The fourth case this month. If only people would get their kids vaccinated." Grace shakes her head. "I'm so glad our children never went through that. They never caught anything worse than chicken pox, thank goodness. Poor Elliot." We all look at Elliot, who stops eating, midchew, mouth stuffed full, bovine. He's uncomfortable being the center of attention.

Kavanagh gives Grace a questioning look.

"Christian and Mia were lucky," Grace explains. "They got it so mildly, only a spot to share between them."

Oh, give it a rest, Mom.

"So, did you catch the Mariners game, Dad?" Elliot's clearly eager to move the conversation on, as am I.

"I can't believe they beat the Yankees," Carrick says.

"Did you watch the game, hotshot?" Elliot asks me.

"No. But I read the sports column."

"The M's are going places. Nine games won out of the last eleven, gives me hope." Dad sounds excited.

"They're certainly having a better season than 2010," I add.

"Gutierrez in center field was awesome. That catch! Wow." Elliot throws up his arms, and Kavanagh fawns over him like a lovesick fool.

"How are you settling into your new apartment, dear?" Grace asks Ana.

"We've only been there one night and I still have to unpack, but I love that it's so central—and a short walk to Pike Place and near the water."

"Oh, so you're close to Christian, then," Grace remarks.

Mom's helper starts to clear the table. I still can't remember her name. She's Swiss or Austrian or something, and she doesn't stop simpering and batting eyelashes at me.

"Have you been to Paris, Ana?" Mia asks.

"No, but I'd love to go."

"We honeymooned in Paris," Mom says. She and Dad exchange a look across the table, which frankly I'd prefer not to see. They obviously had a good time.

"It's a beautiful city, in spite of the Parisians. Christian, you should take Ana to Paris!" Mia exclaims.

"I think Anastasia would prefer London," I respond to my sister's ridiculous suggestion. Placing my hand on Ana's knee, I explore her thigh at a leisurely pace, her dress riding up as my fingers follow. I want to touch her, stroke her where her panties should be. As my cock rouses in anticipation I suppress a groan and shuffle in my seat.

She jerks away from me as if to cross her legs, and I close my hand around her thigh.

Don't you dare!

Ana takes a sip of wine, not taking her eyes off my mother's housekeeper, who is serving our entrées.

"So what was wrong with the Parisians? Didn't they take to your winsome ways?" Elliot teases Mia.

"Ugh, no, they didn't. And Monsieur Floubert, the ogre I was working for, he was such a domineering tyrant."

Ana chokes on her wine.

"Anastasia, are you okay?" I ask and release her thigh.

She nods, her cheeks red, and I pat her back and gently caress her neck. Domineering tyrant? Am I? The thought amuses me. Mia shoots me a look of approval at my public display of affection.

Mom has cooked her signature dish, beef Wellington, a recipe she picked up in London. I have to say it ranks close to yesterday's buttermilk fried chicken.

In spite of her choking episode, Ana tucks into her meal and it's so good to see her eat. She's probably hungry after our energetic afternoon. I take a sip of my wine as I contemplate other ways to make her hungry.

Mia and Kavanagh are discussing the relative merits of St. Bart's vs. Barbados, where the Kavanagh family will be staying.

"Remember Elliot and the jellyfish?" Mia's eyes shine with mirth as she looks from Elliot to me.

I chuckle. "Screaming like a girl? Yeah."

"Hey, that could have been a Portuguese man-of-war! I hate jellyfish. They ruin everything." Elliot is emphatic. Mia and Kate burst into giggles, nodding in agreement.

Ana is eating heartily and listening to the banter. Everyone else has calmed down, and my family is being less weird. Why am I so tense? This happens every day all across the country, families gathering to enjoy good food and each other's company. Am I tense because I have Ana here? Am I worried they won't like her or that she won't like them? Or is it because she's fucking off to Georgia tomorrow and I knew nothing about that?

It's confusing.

Mia takes center stage as usual. Her tales of French life and French cooking are entertaining. "Oh, Mom, les pâtisseries sont tout simplement fabuleuses. La tarte aux pommes de M. Floubert est incroyable," she says.

"Mia, chérie, tu parles français," I interrupt her. "Nous parlons anglais ici. Eh bien, à l'exception bien sûr d'Elliot. Il parle idiote, couramment."

Mia throws her head back with a bellowing laugh, and it's impossible not to join her.

But by the end of dinner the tension is really wearing me down. I want to be alone with my girl. I've only so much tolerance for inane chatter, even if it's with my family, and I've reached my limit. I peer down at Ana, then reach over and tug her chin. "Don't bite your lip. I want to do that."

I also have to establish a few ground rules. We need to discuss her impromptu trip to Georgia and going out for drinks with men who are infatuated with her. I put my hand on Ana's knee again; I need to touch her. Besides, she should accept my touch whenever I want to touch her. I gauge her reaction as my fingers travel up her thigh toward her panty-free zone, teasing her skin. Her breath catches and she squeezes her thighs together, blocking my fingers, stopping me.

That's it.

I have to excuse us from the dinner table. "Shall I give you a tour of the grounds?" I ask Ana, and I don't give her a chance to answer.

Her eyes are luminous and serious as she places her hand in mine. "Excuse me," she says to Carrick, and I lead her out of the dining room.

In the kitchen Mia and Mom are clearing up. "I'm going to show Anastasia the backyard," I announce to my mother, pretending to be cheerful.

Outside, my mood plunges south as my anger surfaces.

Panties. The photographer. Georgia.

We cross the terrace and climb the steps to the lawn. Ana pauses for a moment to admire the view.

Yeah, yeah. Seattle. Lights. Moon. Water.

I continue across the vast lawn toward my parents' boathouse.

"Stop, please," Ana pleads.

I do and glare at her.

"My heels. I need to take my shoes off."

"Don't bother," I growl and lift her quickly over my shoulder.

She squeals in surprise.

Hell. I smack her ass, hard. "Keep your voice down!" I snap and stride across the lawn.

"Where are we going?" she wails as she bounces on my shoulder.

"Boathouse."

"Why?"

"I need to be alone with you."

"What for?"

"Because I'm going to spank and then fuck you."

"Why?" she whines.

"You know why," I snap.

"I thought you were an in-the-moment guy?"

"Anastasia, I'm in the moment, trust me."

Throwing open the boathouse door, I step inside and switch on the light. As the fluorescents ping to life I head upstairs to the snug. There I flip another switch, and halogens illuminate the room.

I slide Ana down my body, glorying in the feel of her, and I set her on her feet. Her hair is dark and untamed, her eyes shining in the glow of the lights, and I know she's not wearing her panties. I want her. Now.

"Please don't hit me," she whispers.

I don't understand. I stare down at her blankly.

"I don't want you to spank me, not here, not now. Please don't."

But... I gape at her, paralyzed. *That's why we're here.*

She lifts her hand, and for a moment I don't know what she's going to do. The darkness stirs and twists around my throat, threatening to choke me if she touches me. But she places her fingers on my cheek and gently skims them down to my chin. The darkness melts into oblivion and I close my eyes, feeling her gentle fingertips on me. With her other hand she ruffles my hair, running her fingers through it.

"Ah," I moan, and I don't know if it's from fear or longing. I'm breathless, standing on a precipice. When I open my eyes, she steps forward so her body is flush against mine. She fists both hands in my hair and tugs gently, raising her lips to mine. And I'm watching her do this, like a bystander, not present in my body. I'm a spectator. Our lips touch and I close my eyes as she forces her tongue into my mouth. And it's the sound of my groan that breaks the spell she's cast.

Ana.

I wrap my arms around her, kissing her back, releasing two hours of anxiety and tension into our kiss, my tongue possessing her, reconnecting with her. My hands grip her hair and I savor her taste, her tongue, her frame against mine as my body ignites like gasoline.

Fuck.

When I pull away we're both dragging air into our lungs, her hands clutching my arms. I'm confused. I wanted to spank her. But she's said no. Like she did at the dinner table. "What are you doing to me?" I ask.

"Kissing you."

"You said no."

"What?" She's bewildered, or maybe she's forgotten what happened.

"At the dinner table, with your legs."

"But we were at your parents' dining table."

"No one's ever said no to me before. And it's so…hot." And different. I slide my hand around her backside and jolt her against me, trying to regain control.

"You're mad and turned on because I said no?" Her voice is throaty.

"I'm mad because you never mentioned Georgia to me. I'm

mad because you went drinking with that guy who tried to seduce you when you were drunk, and who left you when you were ill with an almost complete stranger. What kind of friend does that? And I'm mad and aroused because you closed your legs on me."

And you're not wearing panties.

My fingers inch her dress up her legs. "I want you, and I want you now. And if you're not going to let me spank you, which you deserve, then I'm going to fuck you on the couch, this minute, quickly—for my pleasure, not yours."

Holding her against me, I see she's panting as I slip my hand through her pubic hair and slide my middle finger inside her. I hear a low, sexy hum of appreciation in her throat. She's so ready.

"This is mine. All mine. Do you understand?" I slip my finger in and out of her, holding her as her lips part with shock and desire.

"Yes, yours," she whispers.

Yes. Mine. And I won't let you forget it, Ana.

I push her down onto the couch, unzip my fly, and lie down on top of her, pinning her beneath me. "Hands on your head," I growl through clenched teeth. I kneel up and spread my knees, forcing her legs wider. From the inside pocket of my jacket I take out a condom, then discard my jacket on the floor. With my eyes on hers I open the packet and roll the latex down my eager dick. Ana places her hands on her head, watching me, her eyes glinting with need. As I crawl over her she's squirming beneath me, her hips rising to tease and greet me.

"We don't have long. This will be quick, and it's for me, not you. Do you understand? Don't come or I will spank you," I order, focusing on her dazed wide eyes, and with a swift, hard move I bury myself inside her. She calls out in a welcome and familiar cry of pleasure. I hold her down so she can't move, and I start to fuck her, consuming her. But greedily she tilts her pelvis, meeting me thrust for thrust, spurring me on.

Oh, Ana. Yes, baby.

She gives it back to me, matching my fervent pace, over and over.

Oh, the feel of her.

And I'm lost. In her. In this. In her scent. And I don't know if it's because I'm mad or tense or…

Yessss. I come quickly, losing all reason as I explode inside her. I still. Filling her. Owning her. Reminding her she's mine.

Fuck.

That was…

I pull out of her and kneel up.

"Don't touch yourself." My voice is hoarse and breathless. "I want you frustrated. That's what you do to me by not talking to me, by denying me what's mine."

She nods, sprawled out beneath me, her dress bunched up around her waist so I can see she's wide and wet and wanting, and looking every bit the goddess that she is. I stand up, remove the wretched condom and knot it, then dress, picking up my jacket from the floor.

I take a deep breath. I'm calmer now. Much calmer.

Fuck, that was good.

"We'd better get back to the house."

She sits up, staring at me with dark, inscrutable eyes.

Lord, she's lovely.

"Here. You may put these on." From my jacket pocket I fish out her lacy panties and pass them to her. I think she's trying not to laugh.

Yeah, yeah. Game, set, and match to you, Miss Steele.

"*Christian!*" Mia yells from the floor below.

Shit.

"Just in time. Christ, she can be really irritating." But that's my little sister. Alarmed, I glance at Ana as she slips on her underwear. She scowls at me as she stands to straighten her dress and fixes her hair with her fingers.

"Up here, Mia," I call. "Well, Miss Steele, I feel better for that—but I still want to spank you."

"I don't believe I deserve it, Mr. Grey, especially after tolerating your unprovoked attack." She is crisp and formal.

"Unprovoked? You kissed me."

"It was attack as the best form of defense."

"Defense against what?"

"You and your twitchy palm." She's trying to suppress a smile.

Mia's high heels rattle up the stairs.

"But it was tolerable?" I ask.

Ana smirks. "Barely."

"Oh, there you are!" Mia exclaims, beaming at the two of us. Two minutes earlier and this could have been really awkward.

"I was showing Anastasia around." I hold out my hand to Ana and she takes it. I want to kiss her knuckles, but I settle for a soft squeeze.

"Kate and Elliot are about to leave. Can you believe those two? They can't keep their hands off each other." Mia wrinkles her nose in distaste. "What have you been doing in here?"

"Showing Anastasia my rowing trophies." With my free hand I wave toward the faux-precious-metal statuettes from my sculling days at Harvard arranged on shelves at the end of the room. "Let's go say goodbye to Kate and Elliot."

Mia turns to go and I let Ana precede me, but before we get to the stairs I smack her behind.

She smothers her yelp.

"I will do it again, Anastasia, and soon," I whisper in her ear, and folding her into my arms, I kiss her hair.

We walk hand in hand across the lawn back to the house while Mia gabbles beside us. It's a beautiful evening; it's been a beautiful day. I'm glad Ana's met my family.

Why haven't I done this before?

Because I've never wanted to.

I squeeze Ana's hand, and she gives me a shy look and an oh-so-sweet smile. In my other hand I hold her shoes, and at the stone steps I bend down to fasten each of her sandals in turn.

"There," I announce when I'm done.

"Why, thank you, Mr. Grey," she says.

"The pleasure is, and was, all mine."

"I'm well aware of that, Sir," she teases.

"Oh, you two are sooo sweet!" Mia coos as we head into the kitchen.

Ana gives me a sideways look.

Back in the hallway, Kavanagh and Elliot are about to leave. Ana hugs Kate but then pulls her aside to have a quick heated conversation. *What the hell is that about?* Elliot takes Kavanagh's arm and my parents wave them off as they climb into Elliot's pickup.

"We should go, too—you have interviews tomorrow." We have to drive her back to her new apartment and it's nearly 11:00.

"We never thought he'd find anyone!" Mia gushes as she hugs Ana, hard.

Oh, for fuck's sake…

"Take care of yourself, Ana dear," Grace says, smiling warmly at my girl.

I pull Ana to my side. "Let's not frighten her away or spoil her with too much affection."

"Christian, stop teasing," Grace chastises me in her usual manner.

"Mom." I give her a quick peck. Thank you for inviting Ana. It's been a revelation.

Ana says goodbye to my dad, and we head to the Audi, where Taylor waits, holding the rear passenger door open for her.

"Well, it seems my family likes you, too," I observe when I've joined Ana in the back. Her eyes reflect the light from my parents' porch, but I can't tell what she's thinking. Shadows shroud her face as Taylor drives smoothly out onto the road.

I catch her staring at me under the flicker of a streetlamp. She's anxious. Something's wrong.

"What?" I ask.

She's quiet at first, and when she speaks there's an emptiness in her voice. "I think you felt trapped into bringing me to meet your parents. If Elliot hadn't asked Kate, you'd never have asked me."

Damn. She doesn't understand. It was a first for me. I was nervous. Surely she knows by now that if I didn't want her here, she wouldn't be here. As we pass from light to shadow under the streetlamps, she looks distant and upset.

Grey, this will not do.

"Anastasia, I'm delighted that you've met my parents. Why are you so filled with self-doubt? It never ceases to amaze me. You're such a strong, self-contained young woman, but you have such negative thoughts about yourself. If I hadn't wanted you to meet them, you wouldn't be here. Is that how you were feeling the whole time you were there?" I shake my head, reach for her hand, and give it another reassuring squeeze.

She glances nervously at Taylor.

"Don't worry about Taylor. Talk to me."

"Yes. I thought that," she says quietly. "And another thing: I only mentioned Georgia because Kate was talking about Barbados. I haven't made up my mind."

"Do you want to go see your mother?"

"Yes."

My anxiety surfaces. Does she want out? If she goes to Georgia, her mother might persuade her to find someone more…suitable, someone who, like her mother, believes in romance.

I have an idea. She's met my folks; I've met Ray. Perhaps I should meet her mother, the incurable romantic. Charm her.

"Can I come with you?" I ask, knowing she'll say no.

"Um, I don't think that's a good idea," she answers, surprised by my question.

"Why not?"

"I was hoping for a break from all this…intensity. To try to think things through."

Shit. She does want to leave me.

"I'm too intense?"

She laughs. "That's putting it mildly!"

Damn, I love making her laugh, even if it is at my expense, and I'm relieved she's kept her sense of humor. Perhaps she doesn't want to leave me after all. "Are you laughing at me, Miss Steele?" I tease.

"I wouldn't dare, Mr. Grey."

"I think you dare, and I think you do laugh at me, frequently."

"You are quite funny."

"Funny?"

"Oh yes."

She's making fun of me. It's novel. "Funny peculiar or funny ha-ha?"

"Oh, a lot of one and some of the other."

"Which way more?"

"I'll leave you to figure that out."

I sigh. "I'm not sure if I can figure anything out around you." My tone is dry. "What do you need to think about in Georgia?"

"Us."

Fuck. "You said you'd try," I gently remind her.

"I know."

"Are you having second thoughts?"

"Possibly."

It's worse than I feared. "Why?"

She stares at me in silence.

"Why, Anastasia?" I persist. She shrugs, her mouth turned down, and I hope she'll find her hand in mine reassuring. "Talk to me. I don't want to lose you. This last week—"

Has been the best in my life.

"I still want more," she breathes.

Oh no, not this again. What does she need me to say?

"I know. I'll try." I clasp her chin. "For you, Anastasia, I will try."

I've just taken you to meet my parents, for heaven's sake.

Suddenly she unbuckles her seat belt, and before I know it she's scrambled into my lap.

What the hell?

I sit immobile as her arms slip around my head, and her lips find mine and coax a kiss from me before the darkness has a chance to stir. My hands slide up her back until I'm cradling her head and returning her passion, exploring her sweet, sweet mouth, trying to find answers... Her unexpected affection is utterly disarming. And new. And confusing. I thought she wanted to leave, and now she's in my lap and turning me on, again.

I've never...never... *Don't go, Ana.*

"Stay with me tonight. If you go away, I won't see you all week. Please," I whisper.

"Yes," she murmurs. "And I'll try, too. I'll sign your contract."

Oh, baby.

"Sign after Georgia. Think about it. Think about it hard." I want her to do this willingly—I don't want to force this on her. Well, part of me doesn't. The rational part.

"I will," she says and nestles against me.

This woman has me tied up in knots.

Ironic, Grey.

And I want to laugh because I'm relieved and happy, but I hold her, breathing in her redolent and comforting scent.

"You really should wear your seat belt," I scold, but I don't want her to move. She stays wrapped in my embrace, her body slowly relaxing against mine. The darkness inside me is quiet, contained, and I'm confused by my warring emotions. What do I want out of her? What do I need out of her?

This is not how we should be progressing, but I like her in my arms; I like cradling her like this. I kiss her hair, lean back, and enjoy the ride into Seattle.

Taylor stops outside the entrance to Escala. "We're home," I whisper to Ana. I'm reluctant to release her, but I lift her onto her seat.

Taylor opens her door and she joins me at the entrance to the building. A shiver runs through her.

"Why don't you have a jacket?" I ask as I slip mine off and drape it over her shoulders.

"It's in my new car," she says, yawning.

"Tired, Miss Steele?"

"Yes, Mr. Grey. I've been prevailed upon in ways I never thought possible today."

"Well, if you're really unlucky, I may prevail upon you some more." *If I get lucky.*

She leans against the wall of the elevator as we travel up to the penthouse. Under my jacket she looks slim and small and sexy. If she wasn't wearing her underwear I could take her in here... I reach up and free her lip from her teeth. "One day I will fuck you in this elevator, Anastasia, but right now you're tired—so I think we should stick to a bed." I bend down and gently take her bottom lip in my teeth. Her breath catches and she returns the gesture with her teeth and my upper lip.

I feel it in my groin.

I want to take her to bed and lose myself in her. After our conversation in the car I just want to be sure she's mine. When we exit the elevator I offer her a drink, but she declines.

"Good. Let's go to bed."

She looks surprised. "You're going to settle for plain old vanilla?"

"Nothing plain or old about vanilla. It's a very intriguing flavor."

"Since when?"

"Since last Saturday. Why? Were you hoping for something more exotic?"

"Oh no. I've had enough exotic for one day."

"Sure? We cater for all tastes here—at least thirty-one flavors." I give her a lascivious look.

"I've noticed." She raises one fine eyebrow.

"Come on, Miss Steele, you have a big day tomorrow. Sooner you're in bed, sooner you'll be fucked and sooner you can sleep."

"Mr. Grey, you are a born romantic."

"Miss Steele, you have a smart mouth. I may have to subdue it some way. Come."

Yeah. I can think of one way.

Closing the door of my bedroom, I feel lighter than I did in the car. She's still here. "Hands in the air," I order, and she does as she's told. I grip the hem of her dress and in one smooth move pull it up and over her body to reveal the beautiful woman beneath.

"Ta-da!" I'm a magician. Ana giggles and gives me a round of applause. I bow, enjoying the game, before placing her dress on my chair.

"And for your next trick?" she asks, eyes glittering.

"Oh, my dear Miss Steele. Get into my bed, and I'll show you."

"Do you think that for once I should play hard to get?" she teases, tilting her head to one side so her hair tumbles over her shoulder.

A new game. This is interesting.

"Well, the door's closed. Not sure how you're going to avoid me. I think it's a done deal."

"But I'm a good negotiator," she says, her voice soft but determined.

"So am I."

Okay, what's going on here? Is she reluctant? Too tired? What? "Don't you want to fuck?" I ask, confused.

"No," she whispers.

"Oh." Well, that's disappointing.

She swallows, then says in a small voice, "I want you to make love to me."

I stare at her, bemused.

What exactly does she mean?

Make love? We do. We have. It's just another term for fucking.

She studies me, her expression grave. *Hell.* Is this her idea of more? All the hearts-and-flowers shit, is that what she means? But we're just talking semantics, surely? This is semantics. "Ana, I—" What does she want from me? "I thought we did."

"I want to touch you."

Fuck. No. I step back as the darkness closes around my ribs.

"Please," she whispers.

No. *No.* Haven't I made it clear?

I can't bear to be touched. I can't.

Ever.

"Oh no, Miss Steele, you've had enough concessions from me this evening. And I'm saying no."

"No?" she queries.

"No."

And for a moment I want to send her home, or upstairs—anywhere away from me. Not here.

Don't touch me.

She's watching me warily and I think about the fact that she's leaving tomorrow and I won't see her for a while. I sigh. I don't have the energy for this. "Look, you're tired, I'm tired. Let's just go to bed."

"So touching is a hard limit for you?"

"Yes. This is old news." I can't keep the exasperation out of my voice.

"Please tell me why."

I don't want to go there. This is not a conversation I want to have. Ever. "Oh, Anastasia, please. Just drop it for now."

Her face falls. "It's important to me," she says, a hesitant plea in her voice.

"Fuck this," I mutter to myself. At the chest of drawers I pull out a T-shirt and throw it to her. "Put that on and get into bed." Why am I even letting her sleep with me? But it's a rhetorical question: deep down I know the answer. It's because I sleep better with her.

She's my dream catcher.

She keeps my nightmares at bay.

She turns away from me and removes her bra, then slips on the T-shirt.

What did I say to her in the playroom this afternoon? She shouldn't hide her body from me.

"I need the bathroom," she says.

"Now you're asking permission?"

"Er…no."

"Anastasia, you know where the bathroom is. Today, at this point in our strange arrangement, you don't need my permission to use it." I unbutton my shirt and slip it off, and she dashes past me out of the bedroom as I try to contain my temper.

What's gotten into her?

One evening at my parents' and she's expecting serenades and sunsets and fucking walks in the rain. That's not what I'm about. I've told her this. I don't do romance. I sigh heavily as I remove my pants.

But she wants more. She wants all that romantic shit.

Fuck.

In my closet I throw my pants into the laundry basket and pull on my PJ bottoms, then wander back into my bedroom.

This isn't going to work, Grey.

But I want it to work.

You should let her go.

No. I can make this work. Somehow.

The radio alarm reads 11:46. Time for bed. I check my phone for any urgent emails. There's nothing. I give the bathroom door a brisk knock.

"Come in," Ana garbles. She's brushing her teeth, literally foaming at the mouth—with my toothbrush. She spits into the sink as I stand beside her, and we stare at each other in the mirror. Her eyes are bright with mischief and humor. She rinses off the toothbrush and without a word hands it to me. I put it in my mouth and she looks pleased with herself.

And just like that, all the tension from our previous exchange evaporates.

"Do feel free to borrow my toothbrush," I say sardonically.

"Thank you, Sir." She beams, and for a moment I think she's going to curtsey, but she leaves me to brush my teeth.

When I reenter the bedroom she's stretched out under the covers. She should be stretched out under me. "You know this is not how I saw tonight panning out." I sound sullen.

"Imagine if I said to you that you couldn't touch me," she says, as argumentative as ever.

She's not going to let this go. I sit down on the bed. "Anastasia, I've told you. Fifty shades. I had a rough start in life—you don't want that shit in your head. Why would you?"

No one should have this shit in their head!

"Because I want to know you better."

"You know me well enough."

"How can you say that?" She sits up and kneels facing me, earnest and eager.

Ana. Ana. Ana. Let it go. For fuck's sake.

"You're rolling your eyes," she says. "Last time I did that, I ended up over your knee."

"Oh, I'd like to put you there again." Right now.

Her face brightens. "Tell me and you can."

"What?"

"You heard me."

"You're bargaining with me?" My voice betrays my disbelief.

She nods. "Negotiating."

I frown. "It doesn't work that way, Anastasia."

"Okay. Tell me and I'll roll my eyes at you."

I laugh. Now she is being ridiculous, and cute in my T-shirt. Her face shines with longing.

"Always so keen and eager for information," I marvel. And a thought occurs to me: I could spank her. I've wanted to since dinner, but I could make it fun.

I get off the bed. "Don't go away," I warn and leave the room. From my study I pick up the key to the playroom and head upstairs. In the playroom chest I retrieve the toys I want and contemplate lube as well, but on reflection, and judging from recent experience, I don't think Ana will need any.

She's sitting on the bed when I get back, her expression bright with curiosity.

"When's your first interview tomorrow?" I ask.

"Two."

Excellent. No early morning.

"Good. Get off the bed. Stand over here." I point to a spot in front of me.

Ana scrambles off the bed with no hesitation, eager as ever. She's waiting.

"Trust me?"

She nods, and I hold out my hand, revealing two silver kegel balls. She frowns and looks from the balls to me.

"These are new. I am going to put these inside you and then I'm going to spank you, not for punishment, but for your pleasure and mine."

MONDAY, MAY 30, 2011

Her sharp intake of breath is music to my dick. "Then we'll fuck," I whisper. "And if you're still awake, I'll impart some information about my formative years. Agreed?"

She nods. Her breathing has accelerated, her pupils are larger, darker, with her need and her thirst for knowledge.

"Good girl. Open your mouth."

She hesitates for a moment, bewildered. But she does as she's told before I can reprimand her.

"Wider."

I insert both of the balls into her mouth. They're a little big and heavy but will keep her smart mouth occupied for a moment or two.

"They need lubrication. Suck."

She blinks and tries to suck, her stance changing subtly as she presses her thighs together and squirms.

Oh yes.

"Keep still, Anastasia," I caution, but I'm enjoying the show.

Enough.

"Stop," I order and tug them from her mouth. At the bed I throw the comforter aside and sit down. "Come here."

She sidles up to me, wanton and sexy.

Oh, Ana, my little freak.

"Now turn around, bend down, and grab your ankles." Her expression tells me it's not what she was expecting to hear. "Don't hesitate," I chide her, and I pop the balls into my mouth. She turns around, and with no effort bends over, presenting her long legs and her fine ass to me, my T-shirt slipping up her back toward her head and her mane of hair.

Well, I could look at this glorious sight for a while and imagine what I'd like to do to it. But right now I want to spank and fuck her. I lay my hand over her backside, enjoying her warmth under my palm as I caress her through her panties.

Oh, this ass is mine, so mine. And it's going to get warmer.

I slide her panties to one side, exposing her labia, and hold them in place with one hand. I resist the urge to run my tongue up and down the length of her sex; besides, my mouth is full. Instead, I trace the line down from her perineum to her clitoris and up again, before easing my finger inside her.

Deep in my throat I hum with approval and slowly circle my finger, stretching her. She moans and I harden. Instantly.

Miss Steele approves. She wants this.

With my finger I circle inside her once more, then withdraw and remove the balls from my mouth. Gently, I insert the first ball into her, then the second, leaving the tag outside, draped against her clitoris. I kiss her bare ass and slide her panties back into place.

"Stand up," I command and grasp her hips until I know she's steady on her feet. "You okay?"

"Yes." Her voice is rough.

"Turn around."

She complies immediately.

"How does that feel?" I ask.

"Strange."

"Strange good or strange bad?"

"Strange good," she answers.

"Good."

She'll need to get used to them. What better way than to stretch and reach for something?

"I want a glass of water. Go and fetch one for me, please. And when you come back, I shall put you across my knee. Think about that, Anastasia."

She's puzzled, but she turns and walks gingerly, with tentative steps, out of the room. While she's gone I collect a condom from my drawer. I'm running low; I'll need to stock up on these until her pill kicks in. Sitting back down on the bed, I wait with impatience.

When she reenters her walk is more confident, and she has my water.

"Thank you," I say, taking a quick sip and placing the glass on my bedside table. When I look up she's watching me with overt desire.

It's a good look on her.

"Come. Stand beside me. Like last time."

She does, and now her breathing is irregular…heavy. Boy, she's really turned on. So different from the last time I spanked her.

Let's rile her up some more, Grey.

"Ask me." My voice is firm.

A mystified look crosses her face.

"Ask me."

Come on, Ana.

Her brow furrows.

"Ask me, Anastasia. I won't say it again." My voice is sharper.

Finally, she realizes what I'm asking for and she blushes. "Spank me, please, Sir," she says quietly.

Those words… I close my eyes and let them ring through my head. Grasping her hand, I tug her over my knees so her torso lands on the bed. While stroking her behind with one hand, I smooth her hair off her face with the other and tuck it behind her ear. Then I grasp her hair at the nape of her neck to hold her in place.

"I want to see your face while I spank you." I caress her behind and push against her vulva, knowing that the action will push the balls deeper inside her.

She hums her approval.

"This is for pleasure, Anastasia, mine and yours."

I lift my hand, then smack her right there.

"Ah!" she mouths, screwing up her face, and I caress her sweet, sweet ass while she adjusts to the sensation. When she relaxes, I smack her again. She groans, and I suppress my response. I begin in earnest, right cheek, left cheek, then the junction of her thighs and ass. Between each smack I fondle and knead her backside, watching her skin turn a delicate shade of pink beneath her lacy underwear.

She moans, absorbing the pleasure, enjoying the experience.

I stop. I want to see her ass in all its rosy glory. Unhurriedly, teasing her, I tug down her panties, skimming my fingertips down her thighs, the backs of her knees, and her calves. She lifts her feet, and I discard her panties on the floor. She squirms but stops when I place my hand flat against her pink, glowing skin. Grabbing her hair again, I start anew. Gently first, then resuming the pattern.

She's wet; her arousal is on my palm.

I grip her hair harder and she moans, eyes closed, mouth open and slack.

Fuck, she's hot.

"Good girl." My voice is hoarse, my breathing erratic.

I spank her a couple more times until I can bear it no more.

I want her.

Now.

I wrap my fingers around the tab and draw the balls out of her. She cries out in pleasure.

Turning her over, I pause to yank my pants off and put on a wretched condom, then lie down beside her. I grab her hands, lift them over her head, and slowly ease myself onto her and into her as she mewls like a cat.

"Oh, baby." She feels incredible.

"*I want you to make love to me.*" Her words ring in my head.

And gently, oh so gently, I start to move, feeling every precious inch of her beneath and around me. I kiss her, appreciating her mouth and her body at once. She wraps her legs around mine, meeting each gentle thrust, rocking against me until she spirals up and up and up and lets go.

Her orgasm tips me over the edge. "Ana!" I call, pouring myself into her. Letting go. A welcome release that leaves me…wanting more. Needing more.

As my equilibrium returns, I push away the strange swell of emotion that gnaws at my insides. It's not like the darkness, but it's something to fear. Something I don't understand.

She flexes her fingers around mine, and I open my eyes and look down into her sleepy, sated gaze.

"I enjoyed that," I whisper and give her a lingering kiss.

She rewards me with a drowsy smile. I get up, cover her with the comforter, pick up my PJ pants, and pad into the bathroom, where I remove and dispose of the condom. I pull on my pants and find the arnica cream.

Back at the bed, Ana gives me a contented grin.

"Roll over," I order, and for a moment I think she's going to roll her eyes, but she indulges me and moves. "Your ass is a glorious color," I observe, pleased with the results. I squirt some cream on my palm and slowly massage it onto her behind.

"Spill the beans, Grey," she says with a yawn.

"Miss Steele, you know how to ruin a moment."

"We had a deal," she insists.

"How do you feel?"

"Shortchanged."

With a heavy sigh I place the arnica cream on the bedside table and slip into bed, pulling Ana into my arms. I kiss her ear. "The woman who brought me into this world was a crack whore, Anastasia. Go to sleep."

She tenses in my arms.

I still. I do not want her sympathy or her pity.

"Was?" she whispers.

"She's dead."

"How long?"

"She died when I was four. I don't really remember her. Carrick has given me some details. I only remember certain things. Please go to sleep."

After a while she relaxes against me. "Good night, Christian." Her voice is sleepy.

"Good night, Ana." I kiss her once more, inhaling her soothing scent and fighting off my memories.

"Don't just pick the apples and throw them away, asshole!"

"Fuck off, you righteous dweeb."

Elliot picks an apple, takes a bite, and throws it at me.

"Maggot," he taunts.

No! Don't call me that.

I jump him. Pounding my fists into his face.

"You fucking pig. This is food. You're just wasting it. Grandpa sells these. You pig. Pig. Pig."

"ELLIOT. CHRISTIAN."

Dad drags me off Elliot, who is cowering on the ground.

"What is this about?"

"He's insane."

"Elliot!"

"He's destroying the apples." Anger swells in my chest, in my throat. I think I might explode. "He's taking a bite and then throwing them away. Throwing them at me."

"Elliot, is this true?"

Elliot turns red under Dad's hard stare.

"I think you'd better come with me. Christian, pick up the apples. You can help Mom bake a pie."

She's fast asleep when I wake, my nose in her fragrant hair, my arms cocooning her. I've dreamed about romping through my grandfather's apple orchard with Elliot; those were happy, angry days.

It's nearly seven—another lie-in with Miss Steele. It's odd waking up beside her, but odd in a good way. I contemplate waking her with a morning fuck; my body is more than willing—but she's practically comatose and she might be sore. I should let her sleep. I climb out of bed, careful not to wake her, grab a T-shirt, gather her clothes from the floor, and wander into the living room.

"Good morning, Mr. Grey." Mrs. Jones is busy in the kitchen.

"Good morning, Gail." Stretching, I look out the windows at the remnants of a vivid dawn.

"You have some laundry there?" she asks.

"Yes. These are Anastasia's."

"Do you want me to wash and press them?"

"Do you have time?"

"I'll put them on the quick cycle."

"Excellent, thank you." I pass her Ana's clothes. "How was your sister?"

"Very well, thanks. The kids are growing. Boys can be rough."

"I know."

She smiles and offers to make me some coffee.

"Please. I'll be in my study." As she watches me her smile changes from pleasant to knowing…in the way that's feminine and secretive. Then she hurries out of the kitchen, I assume to the laundry room.

What's her problem?

Okay, this is the first Monday—the first time—in the four years she's worked for me that there's been a woman asleep in my bed. But it's not that big a deal. *Breakfast for two, Mrs. Jones. I think you can manage that.*

I shake my head and wander into my study to start work. I'll shower later…maybe with Ana.

I check my emails and send one to Andrea and Ros, saying I'll be in this afternoon, not this morning. Then I take a look at Barney's latest schematics.

GAIL KNOCKS AND BRINGS me a second cup of coffee, letting me know it's already 8:15.

That late?

"I'm not going into the office this morning."

"Taylor was asking."

"I'll go this afternoon."

"I'll tell him. I've hung Miss Steele's clothes in your closet."

"Thank you. That was quick. She still asleep?"

"I think so." And there's that little smile again. I arch my brows and her smile broadens as she turns to leave my study. I put my work aside and head off with my coffee to take a shower and have a shave.

ANA IS STILL OUT for the count when I finish dressing.

You've exhausted her, Grey. And it was pleasurable, more than pleasurable. She looks serene, as if she doesn't have a care in the world.

Good.

From the chest I take my watch and on an impulse open the top drawer and pocket my last condom.

You never know.

I amble back through the living room toward my study.

"Do you want your breakfast yet, sir?"

"I'll have breakfast with Ana. Thanks."

I pick up the phone and call Andrea from my desk. After we've exchanged a few words she puts me through to Ros.

"So when can we expect you?" Ros's tone is sarcastic.

"Good morning, Ros. How are you?" I say sweetly.

"Pissed."

"At me?"

"Yes, at you, and your hands-off work ethic."

"I'll be in later. The reason I'm calling is I've decided to liquidate Woods's company." I've told her this already, but she and Marco are taking too long. I want this done, now. I remind her this was going to happen if the company's P&L didn't improve. And it hasn't.

"He needs more time."

"I'm not interested, Ros. We're not carrying deadweight."

"Are you sure?"

"I don't want any more lame excuses." Enough already. I've made up my mind.

"Christian—"

"Have Marco call me. It's shit-or-bust time."

"Okay. Okay. If that's what you really want. Anything else?"

"Yes. Tell Barney that the prototype looks good, though I'm not sure about the interface."

"I thought the interface worked well, once I figured it out. Not that I'm an expert."

"No, it's just missing something."

"Talk to Barney."

"I want to meet him this afternoon to discuss."

"Face-to-face?"

Her sarcasm is irritating. But I ignore her tone and tell her that I want his whole team there to brainstorm.

"He'll be pleased. So I'll see you this afternoon?" She sounds hopeful.

"Okay," I reassure her. "Transfer me back to Andrea."

While I wait for her to pick up the phone I gaze out at the cloudless sky. It's the same shade as Ana's eyes.

Sappy, Grey.

"Andrea—"

A movement distracts me. Looking up, I'm pleased to see Ana standing in the doorway, dressed in nothing but my T-shirt. Her legs, long and shapely, are on display for my eyes only. She has great legs.

"Mr. Grey," Andrea answers.

My eyes lock with Ana's. They *are* the color of a summer sky and just as warm. Good Lord, I could bask in her warmth all day—every day.

Don't be absurd, Grey.

"Clear my schedule this morning, but get Bill to call me. I'll be in at two. I need to talk to Marco this afternoon; that will need at least half an hour."

A soft smile tugs at Ana's lips and I find myself mirroring her.

"Yes, sir," Andrea says.

"Schedule Barney and his team in after Marco or maybe tomorrow, and find time for me to see Claude every day this week."

"Sam wants to talk to you this morning."

"Tell him to wait."

"It's about Darfur."

"Oh?"

"Apparently he sees the aid convoy as a great personal PR opportunity."

Oh God. He would, wouldn't he?

"No, I don't want publicity for Darfur." My voice is gruff with exasperation.

"He says there's a journalist from *Forbes* who wants to talk to you about it."

How the hell do they know?

"Tell Sam to deal with it," I snap. That's what he's paid to do.

"Do you want to speak to him directly?" she asks.

"No."

"Will do. I also need to RSVP to the event on Saturday."

"Which event?"

"Chamber of Commerce Gala."

"That's next Saturday?" I ask as an idea pops into my head.

"Yes, sir."

"Hold on." I turn to Ana, who's jiggling her left foot but not taking her sky-blue eyes off me. "When will you be back from Georgia?"

"Friday," she says.

"I'll need an extra ticket, because I have a date," I inform Andrea.

"A date?" Andrea squeaks with incredulity.

I sigh. "Yes, Andrea, that's what I said. A date. Miss Anastasia Steele will accompany me."

"Yes, Mr. Grey." She sounds as if I've made her day.

For fuck's sake. What is it with my staff?

"That's all." I hang up. "Good morning, Miss Steele."

"Mr. Grey," Ana says in greeting.

I walk around my desk until I'm in front of her and caress her face. "I didn't want to wake you; you looked so peaceful. Did you sleep well?"

"I am very well rested, thank you. I just came to say hi before I had a shower." She's smiling and her eyes are shining with delight. It's a pleasure to see her like this.

Before I get back to work I lean down to give her a gentle kiss. Suddenly she wraps her arms around my neck, tangles her fingers in my hair, and presses her body along the length of mine.

Whoa.

Her lips are persistent, so I respond, kissing her back, surprised by the intensity of her ardor. With one hand I cup her head, with the other her naked, recently spanked ass, and my body ignites like dry tinder.

"Well, sleep seems to agree with you." My voice is laced with sudden lust. "I suggest you go have your shower, or shall I lay you across my desk now?"

"I choose the desk," she whispers at the corner of my mouth, grinding her sex against my erection.

Well, this is a surprise.

Her eyes are dark and greedy with want. "You've really got a taste for this, haven't you, Miss Steele? You're becoming insatiable."

"I've only got a taste for you."

"Damn right. *Only me!*" Her words are a siren's call to my libido. Losing all self-restraint, I sweep everything off my desk, sending my papers, phone, and pens all clattering or floating to the floor, but I don't give a damn. I lift Ana and lay her across my desk so her hair spills over the edge and onto the seat of my chair.

"You want it, you got it, baby," I growl, whipping out the condom and unzipping my pants. Making quick work of covering my cock, I stare down at the insatiable Miss Steele. "I sure hope you're ready," I warn her, grabbing hold of her wrists and keeping them at her sides. With one swift move I'm inside her.

"Ah… Christ, Ana. You're *so* ready." I give her a nanosecond to adjust to my presence. Then I start to push. Back and forth. Over and over. Harder and harder. She tips her head back, mouth open in a wordless plea, as her breasts rise and fall in rhythm with each jolt to her body. She wraps her legs around me while I stand, drilling into her.

This what you want, baby?

She meets every thrust, rocking against me and moaning as I possess her. Taking her—higher and higher and higher—until I feel her stiffening around me.

"Come on, baby, give it up for me," I grit through clenched teeth, and she does, spectacularly, crying out and sucking me into my own orgasm.

Fuck. I come as spectacularly as she does, and I slump down on top of her while her body tightens around me with aftershocks.

Damn. That was unexpected.

"What the hell are you doing to me?" I'm breathless, my lips skimming her neck. "You completely beguile me, Ana. You weave some powerful magic."

And you jumped me!

I release her wrists and move to stand, but she tightens her legs around me, her fingers tangling in my hair.

"I'm the one beguiled," she whispers. Our eyes are locked, her scrutiny intense, as if she's seeing through me. Seeing the darkness in my soul.

Shit. Let me go. This is too much.

I cup her face in my hands to kiss her quickly, but as I do the unwelcome thought of her being in this position with someone else pops into my mind. *No. She's not doing this with anyone else. Ever.*

"You. Are. Mine." My words crack between us. "Do you understand?"

"Yes, yours," she says, her expression heartfelt, her words full of conviction, and my irrational jealousy recedes.

"Are you sure you have to go to Georgia?" I ask, smoothing her hair from around her face.

She nods.

Damn.

I pull out of her and she winces.

"Are you sore?"

"A little," she says with a timid smile.

"I like you sore. Reminds you where I've been, and only me." I give her a rough, possessive kiss.

Because I don't want her to go to Georgia.

And no one's jumped me since…since Elena.

And even then, it was always calculated, part of a scene.

Standing, I hold out my hand and pull her to a sitting position. As I tug off the condom, she murmurs, "Always prepared."

I give her a confounded look as I fasten my fly. She holds up the empty foil packet by way of explanation.

"A man can hope, Anastasia, dream even, and sometimes his dreams come true." *I had no idea I'd get to use it so soon, and on her terms, not mine. Miss Steele, for such an innocent, you are, as ever, unexpected.*

"So…on your desk…that's been a dream?" she asks.

Sweetheart. I've had sex on this desk many, many times, but always at my instigation, never at a submissive's.

This is not how it works.

Her face falls as she reads my thoughts.

Shit. What can I say? Ana, unlike you, I have a past.

I run my hand through my hair in frustration; this morning is not going according to plan.

"I'd better go have a shower," she says, subdued. She stands and takes a few steps toward the door.

"I've got a couple more calls to make. I'll join you for breakfast once you're out of the shower." I gaze after her, wondering what to say to make this right. "I think Mrs. Jones has laundered your clothes from yesterday. They're in the closet."

She looks surprised and impressed. "Thank you," she says.

"You're most welcome."

Her brow creases as she studies me, baffled.

"What?" I ask.

"What's wrong?"

"What do you mean?"

"Well, you're being more weird than usual."

"You find me weird?" Ana, baby, *weird* is my middle name.

"Sometimes."

Tell her. Tell her no one's pounced on you for a long time.

"As ever, I'm surprised by you, Miss Steele."

"Surprised how?"

"Let's just say that was an unexpected treat."

"We aim to please, Mr. Grey," she teases, still scrutinizing me.

"And please me you do," I acknowledge. *But you disarm me, too.* "I thought you were going to have a shower?"

Her mouth turns down.

Shit.

"Yes, um, I'll see you in a moment." She turns and scampers out of my study, leaving me standing in a maze of confusion. I shake my head to clear it, then begin picking up my scattered belongings from the floor and arranging them on my desk.

How the hell can she just waltz into my study and seduce me? I'm supposed to be in control of this relationship. This is what I was thinking about last night: her unbridled enthusiasm and affection. How the hell am I supposed to deal with that? It's not something I know. I pause as I pick up my phone.

But it's nice.

Yeah.

More than nice.

I chuckle at the thought and remember her "nice" email. Damn, there's a missed call from Bill. He must have phoned during my tryst with Miss Steele. I sit down at my desk, master of my own universe once more—now that she's in the shower—and call him back. I need Bill to tell me about Detroit…and I need to get back on my game.

Bill doesn't pick up, so I call Andrea.

"Mr. Grey."

"Is the jet free today and tomorrow?"

"It's not scheduled for use until Thursday, sir."

"Great. Can you try Bill for me?"

"Sure."

My conversation with Bill is lengthy. Ruth has done an excellent job scouting all the available brownfield sites in Detroit. Two are viable for the tech plant we want to build, and Bill is certain that Detroit has the available labor force we require.

My heart sinks.

Does it have to be Detroit?

I have vague memories of the place: drunks, hobos, and crackheads shouting at us on the streets; the seedy dive we called home; and a young, broken woman, the crack whore I called Mommy, staring into space while she sat in a drab, grimy room filled with stale air and dust motes.

And him.

I shudder. *Don't think about him…or her.*

But I can't help it. Ana has said nothing about my nocturnal confession. I've never mentioned the crack whore to anyone. Perhaps that's why Ana attacked me this morning: she thinks I need some TLC.

Fuck that.

Baby. I'll take your body if you offer it up. I'm doing just fine. But even as the thought pops into my head I wonder if I'm "just fine." I ignore my unease; it's something to discuss with Flynn when he's back.

Right now, I'm hungry. I hope she's gotten her sweet butt out of that shower, because I need to eat.

ANA IS STANDING AT the kitchen counter talking to Mrs. Jones, who has set places for our breakfast.

"Would you like something to eat?" asks Mrs. Jones.

"No thank you," Ana says.

Oh no you don't.

"Of course you'll have something to eat," I growl at both of them. "She likes pancakes, bacon, and eggs, Mrs. Jones."

"Yes, Mr. Grey. What would you like, sir?" she replies without batting an eyelid.

"Omelet, please, and some fruit. Sit," I tell Ana, pointing to one of the barstools. She does, and I take a seat beside her while Mrs. Jones makes our breakfast.

"Have you bought your air ticket?" I ask.

"No, I'll buy it when I get home, over the internet."

"Do you have the money?"

"Yes," she says as if I'm five years old, and she tosses her hair over her shoulder, flattening her lips, peeved, I think.

I arch an eyebrow in censure. *I could always spank you again, sweetheart.*

"Yes, I do, thank you," she says quickly in a more subdued tone.

That's better.

"I have a jet. It's not scheduled to be used for three days; it's at your disposal." This will be a no. But at least I can offer.

Her lips part in shock and her expression transforms, from stunned to impressed and exasperated in equal measure. "We've already made serious misuse of your company's aviation fleet. I wouldn't want to do it again," she says nonchalantly.

"It's my company; it's my jet."

She shakes her head. "Thank you for the offer. But I'd be happier taking a scheduled flight."

Surely most women would jump at the opportunity of taking a private jet, but it seems material wealth really doesn't impress this girl—or she doesn't like to feel indebted to me. I'm not sure which. Either way, she's a stubborn creature.

"As you wish." I sigh. "Do you have much preparation to do for your interview?"

"No."

"Good." I ask but she still won't tell me which of the publishing houses she's seeing. Instead she gives me a sphinxlike smile. There's no way she's divulging this secret.

"I'm a man of means, Miss Steele."

"I'm fully aware of that, Mr. Grey. Are you going to track my phone?"

Trust her to remember that. "Actually, I'll be quite busy this afternoon, so I'll have to get someone else to do it," I answer, smirking.

"If you can spare someone to do that, you're obviously overstaffed."

Oh, she's sassy today.

"I'll send an email to the head of human resources and have her look into our head count." This is what I like: our banter. It's refreshing and fun, and unlike anything I've known before.

Mrs. Jones serves us breakfast, and I'm pleased to see Ana relishing her food. When Mrs. Jones leaves the kitchen Ana peers up at me.

"What is it, Anastasia?"

"You know, you never did tell me why you don't like to be touched."

Not this again!

"I've told you more than I've ever told anybody." My voice is low to conceal my frustration. Why does she persist with these questions?

She eats another couple of mouthfuls of her pancakes.

"Will you think about our arrangement while you're away?" I ask.

"Yes." She's earnest.

"Will you miss me?"

Grey!

She turns to face me, as surprised as I am by the question.

"Yes," she says after a moment, her expression open and honest. I was expecting a smart remark, yet I get the truth. And strangely, I find her admission comforting.

"I'll miss you, too," I mutter. "More than you know." My apartment will be a little quieter without her, and a little emptier. I stroke her cheek and kiss her.

She gives me a sweet smile before returning to her breakfast. "I'll brush my teeth, then I should go," she announces once she's finished.

"So soon. I thought you might stay longer."

She's taken aback. Did she think I'd kick her out?

"I've prevailed upon you and taken up your time for long enough, Mr. Grey. Besides, don't you have an empire to run?"

"I can play hooky." Hope swells in my chest and my voice. And I've just cleared my morning.

"I have to do a little prep for my interviews. And get changed." She eyes me warily.

"You look great."

"Why, thank you, Sir," she says graciously. But her cheeks are coloring their familiar rosy pink, like her ass last night. She's embarrassed. When will she learn to take a compliment?

Rising, she takes her plate to the sink.

"Leave that. Mrs. Jones will do it."

"Okay. I'm just going to brush my teeth."

"Please feel free to use my toothbrush," I offer with sarcasm.

"I had every intention of doing so," she says and sashays out of the room. That woman has an answer for everything.

She returns a few moments later with her purse.

"Don't forget to take your BlackBerry, your Mac, and your chargers to Georgia."

"Yes, Sir," she says obediently.

Good girl.

"Come." I lead her to the elevator and step in with her.

"You don't have to come down. I can see myself to my car."

"It's all part of the service," I quip ironically. "Besides, I can kiss you all the way down." I fold her into my arms and do just that, enjoying her taste and her tongue and giving her a proper goodbye.

We're both aroused and breathless by the time the doors open on the garage level. But she's leaving. I take her to her car and open the driver's door for her, ignoring my need.

"Goodbye for now, Sir," she whispers and kisses me once more.

"Drive safely, Anastasia. And safe travels." I close her door, stand back, and watch her leave. Then I head upstairs.

I knock on Taylor's study door and let him know I'd like to go to the office in ten minutes. "I'll have the car waiting, sir."

I CALL WELCH FROM the car.

"Mr. Grey," he rasps.

"Welch. Anastasia Steele is buying an airline ticket today, leaving Seattle tonight for Savannah. I'd like to know which flight she's on."

"Does she have an airline preference?"

"I'm afraid I don't know."

"I'll see what I can do."

I hang up. My cunning plan is falling into place.

"MR. GREY!" ANDREA IS startled at my appearance several hours early. I want to tell her that I do fucking work here, but I decide to behave.

"I thought I'd surprise you."

"Coffee?" she chirps.

"Please."

"With or without milk?"

Good girl.

"With. Steamed milk."

"Yes, Mr. Grey."

"Try Caroline Acton. I'd like to speak to her right away."

"Of course."

"And make an appointment for me to see Flynn, next week." She nods and sits down to work. At my desk, I switch on my computer.

The first email in my inbox is from Elena.

From: Elena Lincoln
Subject: The Weekend
Date: May 30 2011 10:15
To: Christian Grey

Christian, what gives?
Your mother told me you took a young woman to dinner yesterday.
I'm intrigued. It's so not your style.
You've found a new submissive?
Call me.
Ex

ELENA LINCOLN
ESCLAVA
For The Beauty That Is You™

That's all I need. I close her email, resolving to ignore it for now. Olivia knocks and enters with my coffee as Andrea buzzes my phone.

"I have Welch for you, and I've left a message for Ms. Acton," Andrea announces.

"Good. Put him through."

Olivia places the latte on my desk and exits flustered. I do my best to ignore her.

"Welch."

"No airline tickets purchased as yet, Mr. Grey. But I'll monitor the situation and inform you, should that change."

"Please do."

He hangs up. I take a sip of coffee and dial Ros.

JUST BEFORE LUNCH ANDREA puts Caroline Acton through. "Mr. Grey, how lovely to hear from you. What can I do for you?"

"Hello, Ms. Acton. I'd like the usual."

"The capsule wardrobe? Do you have a color palette in mind?"

"Blues and greens. Silver maybe, for a formal event." The Chamber of Commerce dinner springs to mind. "Gem colors, I think."

"Nice," Ms. Acton responds with her usual enthusiasm.

"And satin and silk underwear and nightwear. Something glamorous."

"Yes, sir. Do you have a budget in mind?"

"No budget. Go all-out. I want everything high-end."

"Shoes, too?"

"Please."

"Great. Sizes?"

"I'll email you. I have your address from last time."

"When would you like delivery?"

"This Friday."

"I'm sure I can do that. Would you like to see photographs of my choices?"

"Please."

"Great. I'll get on it."

"Thank you." I hang up and Andrea puts Welch through.

"Welch."

"Miss Steele is traveling on DL2610 to Atlanta, departing at 22:25 this evening."

I jot down all the details of her flights and connection into Savannah. I summon Andrea, who enters moments later, carrying her notebook.

"Andrea, Anastasia Steele is traveling on these flights. Upgrade her to first class, check her in, and pay for her to enter the first-class lounge. And buy the seat beside her on all flights, there and back. Use my personal credit card."

Andrea's puzzled look tells me she thinks I've taken leave of my senses, but she recovers quickly and accepts my hand-scribbled note. "Will do, Mr. Grey." She's trying her best to keep it professional, but I catch her smiling.

This is none of her business.

MY AFTERNOON IS SPENT in meetings. Marco has prepared preliminary reports on the four publishing houses based in Seattle. I set them aside to read later. He's also in agreement with me about Woods and his company. This is going to get ugly, but having looked at the synergies, the only way forward is to absorb Woods's tech division and liquidate the rest of his company. It's going to be expensive, but it's best for GEH.

In the late afternoon I manage to have a quick and strenuous workout with Bastille, so I'm calm and relaxed when I head home.

After a light supper I sit down to read at my desk. First order of the evening is to reply to Elena. But when I open my emails, there's one from Ana. She hasn't been far from my thoughts all day.

From: Anastasia Steele
Subject: Interviews
Date: May 30 2011 18:49
To: Christian Grey

Dear Sir,
My interviews went well today.

Thought you might be interested.

How was your day?

Ana

I type my response immediately.

From: Christian Grey
Subject: My Day
Date: May 30 2011 19:03
To: Anastasia Steele

Dear Miss Steele,
Everything you do interests me. You are the most fascinating woman I know.

I'm glad your interviews went well.

My morning was beyond all expectations.

My afternoon was very dull in comparison.

Christian Grey
CEO, Grey Enterprises Holdings, Inc.

I sit back and rub my chin, waiting.

From: Anastasia Steele
Subject: Fine Morning
Date: May 30 2011 19:05
To: Christian Grey

Dear Sir,
The morning was exemplary for me, too, in spite of you weirding out on me after the impeccable desk sex. Don't think I didn't notice.

Thank you for breakfast. Or thank Mrs. Jones.

I'd like to ask you questions about her—without you weirding out on me again.

Ana

Weirding? What on earth does she mean by that? Is she saying

I'm weird? Well, I am, I suppose. Maybe. Perhaps she's realized how surprised I was when she jumped me—and no one's done that for a long time.

"Impeccable…" I'll take that.

From: Christian Grey
Subject: Publishing and You?
Date: May 30 2011 19:10
To: Anastasia Steele

Anastasia,
"Weirding" is not a verb and should not be used by anyone who wants to go into publishing. Impeccable? Compared to what, pray tell? And what do you need to ask about Mrs. Jones? I'm intrigued.

Christian Grey
CEO, Grey Enterprises Holdings, Inc.

From: Anastasia Steele
Subject: You and Mrs. Jones
Date: May 30 2011 19:17
To: Christian Grey

Dear Sir,
Language evolves and moves on. It is an organic thing. It is not stuck in an ivory tower, hung with expensive works of art and overlooking most of Seattle with a helipad stuck on its roof.

Impeccable—compared to the other times we have…what's your word…oh yes…fucked. Actually, the fucking has been pretty impeccable, period, in my humble opinion—but then, as you know, I have very limited experience.

Is Mrs. Jones an ex-sub of yours?

Ana

Her response makes me laugh out loud, then shocks me.

Mrs. Jones! Submissive?

No way.

Ana. Are you jealous? And speaking of language…watch yours!

From: Christian Grey
Subject: Language. Watch Your Mouth!
Date: May 30 2011 19:22
To: Anastasia Steele

Anastasia,
Mrs. Jones is a valued employee. I have never had any relationship with her beyond our professional one. I do not employ anyone I've had any sexual relations with. I am shocked that you would think so. The only person I would make an exception to this rule is you—because you are a bright young woman with remarkable negotiating skills. Though, if you continue to use such language, I may have to reconsider taking you on here. I am glad you have limited experience. Your experience will continue to be limited—just to me. I shall take "impeccable" as a compliment—though with you, I'm never sure if that's what you mean or if your sense of irony is getting the better of you, as usual.

Christian Grey
CEO, Grey Enterprises Holdings, Inc.,
from His Ivory Tower

Though perhaps it might not be a good idea for Ana to work for me.

From: Anastasia Steele
Subject: Not for All the Tea in China
Date: May 30 2011 19:27
To: Christian Grey

Dear Mr. Grey,
I think I have already expressed my reservations about working for your company. My views on this have not changed, are not changing, and will not change, ever. I must leave you now, as Kate has returned with food. My sense of irony and I bid you good night.

I will contact you once I'm in Georgia.

Ana

For some reason I'm mildly irritated to hear that she wouldn't want to work for me. She has an impressive GPA. She's bright, charming, funny; she'd be an asset to any company. She's also wise to say no.

From: Christian Grey
Subject: Even Twinings English Breakfast Tea?
Date: May 30 2011 19:29
To: Anastasia Steele

Good night, Anastasia.
I hope you and your sense of irony have a safe flight.

Christian Grey
CEO, Grey Enterprises Holdings, Inc.

I put all thoughts of Miss Steele aside and start on a response to Elena.

From: Christian Grey
Subject: The Weekend
Date: May 30 2011 19:47
To: Elena Lincoln

Hello, Elena.
My mother has a big mouth. What can I say?
I met a girl. Brought her to dinner.
It's not a big deal.
How goes it with you?

Best,
Christian

Christian Grey
CEO, Grey Enterprises Holdings, Inc.

From: Elena Lincoln
Subject: The Weekend
Date: May 30 2011 19:50
To: Christian Grey

Christian, that's bullshit.
Let's do dinner.
Tomorrow?
Ex

ELENA LINCOLN
ESCLAVA
For The Beauty That Is You™

Fuck!

From: Christian Grey
Subject: The Weekend
Date: May 30 2011 20:01
To: Elena Lincoln

Sure.

Best,
Christian

Christian Grey
CEO, Grey Enterprises Holdings, Inc.

From: Elena Lincoln
Subject: The Weekend
Date: May 30 2011 20:05
To: Christian Grey

Do you want to meet the girl I mentioned?
Ex

ELENA LINCOLN
ESCLAVA
For The Beauty That Is You™

Not at the moment.

From: Christian Grey
Subject: The Weekend
Date: May 30 2011 20:11
To: Elena Lincoln

I think I'll let the arrangement I have now run its course.
See you tomorrow.

C.

Christian Grey
CEO, Grey Enterprises Holdings, Inc.

I sit down to read Fred's draft proposal for Eamon Kavanagh, then move on to Marco's summary of the publishing houses in Seattle.

JUST BEFORE 10:00 I'M distracted by a ping from my computer. It's late. I assume it's a message from Ana.

From: Anastasia Steele
Subject: Over-Extravagant Gestures
Date: May 30 2011 21:53
To: Christian Grey

Dear Mr. Grey,
What really alarms me is how you knew which flight I was on.

Your stalking knows no bounds. Let's hope that Dr. Flynn is back from vacation.

I have had a manicure, a back massage, and two glasses of champagne—a very nice start to my vacation.

Thank you.

Ana

She's been upgraded. Well done, Andrea.

From: Christian Grey
Subject: You're Most Welcome
Date: May 30 2011 21:59
To: Anastasia Steele

Dear Miss Steele,
Dr. Flynn is back, and I have an appointment next week.

Who was massaging your back?

Christian Grey
CEO with Friends in the Right Places,
Grey Enterprises Holdings, Inc.

I check the time of her email. She should be on board right now, if her plane is on time. I quickly open Google and check departures from Sea-Tac. Her flight is on schedule.

From: Anastasia Steele
Subject: Strong Able Hands
Date: May 30 2011 22:22
To: Christian Grey

Dear Sir,
A very pleasant young man massaged my back. Yes. Very pleasant indeed. I wouldn't have encountered Jean-Paul in

the ordinary departure lounge—so thank you again for that treat.

What the hell?

I'm not sure if I'll be allowed to email once we take off, and I need my beauty sleep since I've not been sleeping so well recently.

Pleasant dreams, Mr. Grey...thinking of you.

Ana

Is she trying to make me jealous? Does she have any idea how mad I can get? She's been gone for a few hours, and she's deliberately making me angry. Why does she do this to me?

From: Christian Grey
Subject: Enjoy It While You Can
Date: May 30 2011 22:25
To: Anastasia Steele

Dear Miss Steele,
I know what you're trying to do—and trust me, you've succeeded. Next time you'll be in the cargo hold, bound and gagged in a crate. Believe me when I say that attending to you in that state will give me so much more pleasure than merely upgrading your ticket.

I look forward to your return.

Christian Grey
Palm-Twitching CEO,
Grey Enterprises Holdings, Inc.

Her response is almost immediate.

From: Anastasia Steele
Subject: Joking?
Date: May 30 2011 22:30
To: Christian Grey

You see, I have no idea if you're joking—and if you're not, then I think I'll stay in Georgia. Crates are a hard limit for me. Sorry I made you mad. Tell me you forgive me.

A

Of course I'm joking...sort of. At least she knows I'm mad. Her plane should be taking off. How is she emailing?

From: Christian Grey
Subject: Joking
Date: May 30 2011 22:31
To: Anastasia Steele

How can you be emailing? Are you risking the life of everyone on board, including yourself, by using your BlackBerry? I think that contravenes one of the rules.

Christian Grey
Two-Palms-Twitching CEO,
Grey Enterprises Holdings, Inc.

And we know what happens if you contravene the rules, Miss Steele. I check the Sea-Tac website for flight departures; her plane has left. I won't be hearing from her for a while. That thought, as well as her little email stunt, has put me in a foul mood. Abandoning my work, I head into the kitchen and decide to pour myself a drink, tonight Armagnac.

Taylor pops his head around the entrance to the living room.

"Not now," I bark.

"Very good, sir," he says and heads back to wherever he came from.

Don't take your mood out on the staff, Grey.

Annoyed at myself, I walk toward the windows and stare out at the Seattle skyline. I wonder how she's gotten under my skin and why our relationship is not progressing in the direction I would like. I'm hoping that once she's had a chance to reflect in Georgia, she'll make the right decision. Won't she?

Anxiety blooms in my chest. I take another slug of my drink and sit down at my piano to play.

TUESDAY, MAY 31, 2011

Mommy is gone. I don't know where.
He's here. I hear his boots. They are loud boots.
They have silver buckles. They stomp. Loud.
He stomps. And he shouts.
I am in Mommy's closet.
Hiding.
He won't hear me.
I can be quiet. Very quiet.
Quiet because I'm not here.

"You fucking bitch!" he shouts.
He shouts a lot.
"You fucking bitch!"
He shouts at Mommy.
He shouts at me.
He hits Mommy.
He hits me.
I hear the door close. He's not here anymore.
And Mommy is gone, too.
I stay in the closet. In the dark. I'm very quiet.
I sit for a long time. A long, long, long time.
Where is Mommy?

There's a whisper of dawn in the sky when I open my eyes. The radio alarm says 5:23. I've slept fitfully, plagued by unpleasant dreams, and I'm exhausted, but I decide to go for a run to wake myself up. Once I'm in sweats, I pick up my phone. There's a text from Ana.

Arrived safely in Savannah. A :)

Good. She's there, and safe. The thought pleases me and I quickly scan my email. The subject of Ana's latest message leaps out at me: "Do you like to scare me?"

No fucking way.

My scalp prickles and I sit down on the bed, scrolling through her words. She must have sent this during her layover in Atlanta, before she sent her text.

From: Anastasia Steele
Subject: Do you like to scare me?
Date: May 31 2011 06:52 ET
To: Christian Grey

You know how much I dislike you spending money on me. Yes, you're very rich, but still it makes me uncomfortable, like you're paying me for sex. However, I like traveling first class, it's so much more civilized than coach. So thank you. I mean it—and I did enjoy the massage from Jean-Paul. He was very gay. I omitted that bit in my email to you to wind you up, because I was annoyed with you, and I'm sorry about that.

But as usual you overreact. You can't write things like that to me—bound and gagged in a crate. (Were you serious or was it a joke?) That scares me… You scare me… I am completely caught up in your spell, considering a lifestyle with you that I didn't even know existed until last week, and then you write something like that and I want to run screaming into the hills. I won't, of course, because I'd miss you. Really miss you. I want us to work, but I am terrified of the depth of feeling I have for you and the dark path you're leading me down. What you are offering is erotic and sexy, and I'm curious, but I'm also scared you'll hurt me—physically and emotionally.

After three months you could say goodbye, and where will that leave me if you do? But then I suppose that risk is there in any relationship. This just isn't the sort of relationship I ever envisaged having, especially as my first. It's a huge leap of faith for me.

You were right when you said I didn't have a submissive bone in my body...and I agree with you now. Having said that, I want to be with you, and if that's what I have to do, I would like to try, but I think I'll suck at it and end up black and blue—and I don't relish that idea at all.

I am so happy you have said you will try more. I just need to think about what "more" means to me, and that's one of the reasons why I wanted some distance. You dazzle me so much I find it very difficult to think clearly when we're together.

They are calling my flight. I have to go.

More later.

Your Ana

She's reprimanding me. Again. But she's stunned me with her honesty. It's illuminating. I read her email again and again, and each time I pause at "Your Ana."

My Ana.

She wants us to work.

She wants to be with me.

There's hope, Grey.

I place my phone on my bedside and decide I need that run, to clear my head so I can think about my response.

I take my usual route up Stewart to Westlake Avenue then around Denny Park a few times, Four Tet's "She Just Likes to Fight" ringing in my ears.

Ana's given me a great deal to process.

Paying her for sex?

Like a whore.

I've never thought of her that way. Just the idea makes me mad. Really fucking mad. I sprint once more around the park, my anger spurring me on. Why does she do this to herself? I'm rich. So what? She just needs to get used to that. I'm reminded of our conversation yesterday about the GEH jet. She wouldn't take that offer.

At least she doesn't want me for my money.

But does she want me at all?

She says I dazzle her. But boy, has she got that the wrong way around. She dazzles me in a way I've never experienced, yet she's flown across the country to get away from me.

How's that supposed to make me feel?

She's right. It is a dark path I'm leading her down, but one that is far more intimate than any vanilla relationship—or so I've seen. I only have to look at Elliot and his alarmingly casual approach to dating to see the difference.

And I'd never hurt her physically or emotionally—how can she think that? I just want to push her limits, see what she will and won't do. Punish her when she colors outside the lines... Yeah, it might hurt, but not beyond anything she can take. We can work up to what I'd like to do. We can take it slow.

And here's the rub.

If she's going to do what I want her to do, I'm going to have to reassure her and give her "more." What that might be...I don't yet know. I've taken her to meet my parents. That was more, surely. And that wasn't so hard.

I take a slower jog around the park to think about what disturbs me most about her email. It isn't her fear; it's that she's terrified of the depth of feeling she has for me.

What does that mean?

That unfamiliar feeling surfaces in my chest as my lungs burn for air. It scares me. Scares me so much that I push myself harder so all I feel is the pain of exertion in my legs and in my chest and the cold sweat that trickles down my back.

Yeah. Don't go there, Grey.

Stay in control.

BACK IN MY APARTMENT I have a quick shower and shave, then I dress. Gail is in the kitchen when I walk through on the way to my study.

"Good morning, Mr. Grey. Coffee?"

"Please," I say, not stopping. I'm on a mission.

At my desk I fire up my iMac and compose my response to Ana.

From: Christian Grey
Subject: Finally!
Date: May 31 2011 07:30
To: Anastasia Steele

Anastasia,

I am annoyed that as soon as you put some distance between us, you communicate openly and honestly with me. Why can't you do that when we're together?

Yes, I'm rich. Get used to it. Why shouldn't I spend money on you? We've told your father I'm your boyfriend, for heaven's sake. Isn't that what boyfriends do? As your Dom, I would expect you to accept whatever I spend on you with no argument. Incidentally, tell your mother, too.

I don't know how to answer your comment about feeling like a whore. I know that's not what you've written, but it's what you imply. I don't know what I can say or do to eradicate these feelings. I'd like you to have the best of everything. I work exceptionally hard so I can spend my money as I see fit. I could buy you your heart's desire, Anastasia, and I want to. Call it redistribution of wealth, if you will. Or simply know that I would not, could not *ever* think of you in the way you described, and I'm angry that's how you perceive yourself. For such a bright, witty, beautiful young woman, you have some real self-esteem issues, and I have half a mind to make an appointment for you with Dr. Flynn.

I apologize for frightening you. I find the thought of instilling fear in you abhorrent. Do you really think I'd let you travel in the hold? I offered you my private jet, for heaven's sake. Yes, it was a joke, a poor one obviously. However, the fact is the thought of you bound and gagged turns me on (this is not a joke—it's true). I can lose the crate—crates do nothing for me. I know you have issues with gagging—we've talked about that—and if/when I do gag you, we'll discuss it. What I think you fail to realize is that in Dom/sub relationships it is the sub who has all the power. That's you. I'll repeat this—you are the one with all the power. Not me. In the boathouse you said no. I can't touch you if you say no—that's why we have an agreement—what you will and won't do. If we try things and you don't like them, we can revise the agreement. It's up to you—not me. And if you don't want to be bound and gagged in a crate, then it won't happen.

I want to share my lifestyle with you. I have never wanted anything so much. Frankly, I'm in awe of you, that one so innocent would be willing to try. That says more to me than you could ever know. You fail to see I am caught in your spell, too, even though I have told you this countless times. I don't want to lose you. I am nervous that you've flown three thousand miles to get away from me for a few days, because you can't think clearly around me. It's the same for me, Anastasia. My reason vanishes when we're together—that's the depth of my feeling for you.

I understand your trepidation. I did try to stay away from you; I knew you were inexperienced, though I would never have pursued you if I had known exactly how innocent you were—and yet you still manage to disarm me completely in a way that nobody has before. Your email, for example: I have read and reread it countless times trying to understand your point of view. Three months is an arbitrary amount of time. We could make it six months, a year? How long do you want it to be? What would make you comfortable? Tell me.

I understand that this is a huge leap of faith for you. I have to earn your trust, but by the same token, you have to communicate with me when I am failing to do this. You seem so strong and self-contained, and then I read what you've written here and I see another side to you. We have to guide each other, Anastasia, and I can only take my cues from you. You have to be honest with me, and we have to both find a way to make this arrangement work.

You worry about not being submissive. Well, maybe that's true. Having said that, the only time you do assume the correct demeanor for a sub is in the playroom. It seems that's the one place where you let me exercise proper control over you and the only place you do as you're told. "Exemplary" is the term that comes to mind. And I'd never beat you black and blue. I aim for pink. Outside the playroom, I like that you challenge me. It's a very novel and refreshing experience, and I wouldn't want to change that. So, yes, tell me what you want in terms of more. I will endeavor to keep an open mind, and I shall try to give you the space you need and stay away from you while you are in Georgia. I look forward to your next email.

In the meantime, enjoy yourself. But not too much.

Christian Grey
CEO, Grey Enterprises Holdings, Inc.

I press send and take a sip of my cold coffee.

Now you have to wait, Grey. See what she says.

I stomp into the kitchen to see what Gail has prepared for breakfast.

TAYLOR IS WAITING IN the car to whisk me to work.

"What was it you wanted last night?" I ask him.

"It was nothing important, sir."

"Good," I respond and gaze out the window, trying to put Ana and Georgia out of my mind. I fail miserably, but an idea starts to take shape.

I call Andrea. "Morning."

"Good morning, Mr. Grey."

"I'm on my way in, but can you put me through to Bill?"

"Yes, sir."

A few moments later I have Bill on the line.

"Mr. Grey."

"Did your people look at Georgia as an option to site the tech plant? Savannah in particular?"

"I believe we did, sir. But I'll need to check."

"Check. Come back to me."

"Will do. Is that all?"

"For now. Thanks."

MY DAY IS FULL of meetings. I look at my email sporadically, but there's nothing from Ana. I wonder if she's daunted by the tone of my email or if she's busy doing other things.

What other things?

It's impossible to avoid thoughts of her. Throughout the day I exchange texts with Caroline Acton, approving and vetoing outfits she's chosen for Ana. I hope she likes them: she'll look stunning in all of them.

Bill has come back to me with a potential site near Savannah for our plant. Ruth is making inquiries.

At least it's not Detroit.

Elena calls, and we decide to have dinner at Columbia Tower.

"Christian, you're being so coy about this girl," she chides.

"I'll tell you everything this evening. Right now I'm busy."

"You're always busy." She laughs. "See you at eight."

"See you then."

Why are the women in my life so nosy? Elena. My mother. Ana… I wonder for the hundredth time what she's doing. And behold, there's a response from her, at last.

From: Anastasia Steele
Subject: Verbose?
Date: May 31 2011 19:08 ET
To: Christian Grey

Sir, you are quite the loquacious writer. I have to go to dinner at Bob's golf club, and just so you know, I am rolling my eyes at the thought. But you and your twitchy palm are a long way from me so my behind is safe, for now. I loved your email. Will respond when I can. I miss you already.
Enjoy your afternoon.

Your Ana

It's not a no, and she misses me. I'm relieved and amused at her tone. I respond.

From: Christian Grey
Subject: Your Behind
Date: May 31 2011 16:10
To: Anastasia Steele

Dear Miss Steele,
I am distracted by the title of this email. Needless to say it *is* safe—for now.

Enjoy your dinner, and I miss you, too, especially your behind and your smart mouth.

My afternoon will be dull, brightened only by thoughts of you and your eye rolling. I think it was you who so judiciously pointed out to me that I, too, suffer from that nasty habit.

Christian Grey
CEO & Eye Roller,
Grey Enterprises Holdings, Inc.

A few minutes later her reply pings into my inbox.

From: Anastasia Steele
Subject: Eye Rolling
Date: May 31 2011 19:14 ET
To: Christian Grey

Dear Mr. Grey,
Stop emailing me. I am trying to get ready for dinner. You are very distracting, even when you are on the other side of the continent. And yes—who spanks you when you roll your eyes?

Your Ana

Oh, Ana, you do.
All the time.

I remember her telling me to keep still and tugging my pubic hair while she was sitting astride me, naked. The thought is arousing.

From: Christian Grey
Subject: Your Behind
Date: May 31 2011 16:18
To: Anastasia Steele

Dear Miss Steele,
I still prefer my title to yours, in so many different ways. It is lucky that I am master of my own destiny and no one castigates me. Except my mother occasionally, and Dr. Flynn, of course. And you.

Christian Grey
CEO, Grey Enterprises Holdings, Inc.

I find myself drumming my fingers, waiting for her reply.

From: Anastasia Steele
Subject: Chastising...Me?
Date: May 31 2011 19:22 ET
To: Christian Grey

Dear Sir,
When have I ever plucked up the nerve to chastise you, Mr. Grey? I think you are mixing me up with someone else... which is very worrying. I really do have to get ready.

Your Ana

You. You chastise me via email at every opportunity—and how could I ever mix you up with anyone else?

From: Christian Grey
Subject: Your Behind
Date: May 31 2011 16:25
To: Anastasia Steele

Dear Miss Steele,
You do it all the time in print. Can I zip up your dress?

Christian Grey
CEO, Grey Enterprises Holdings, Inc.

From: Anastasia Steele
Subject: NC-17
Date: May 31 2011 19:28 ET
To: Christian Grey

I would rather you unzipped it.

Her words travel directly to my dick, passing Go on the way.
Fuck.
This calls for…what did she call them? SHOUTY CAPITALS.

From: Christian Grey
Subject: Careful what you wish for…
Date: May 31 2011 16:31
To: Anastasia Steele

SO WOULD I.

Christian Grey
CEO, Grey Enterprises Holdings, Inc.

From: Anastasia Steele
Subject: Panting
Date: May 31 2011 19:33 ET
To: Christian Grey

Slowly...

From: Christian Grey
Subject: Groaning
Date: May 31 2011 16:35
To: Anastasia Steele

Wish I were there.

Christian Grey
CEO, Grey Enterprises Holdings, Inc.

From: Anastasia Steele
Subject: Moaning
Date: May 31 2011 19:37 ET
To: Christian Grey

SO DO I.

Who else can turn me on via email?

From: Anastasia Steele
Subject: Moaning
Date: May 31 2011 19:39 ET
To: Christian Grey

Gotta go.

Laters, baby.

I smirk at her words.

From: Christian Grey
Subject: Plagiarism
Date: May 31 2011 16:41
To: Anastasia Steele

You stole my line.
And left me hanging.

Enjoy your dinner.

Christian Grey
CEO, Grey Enterprises Holdings, Inc.

Andrea knocks on the door with new schematics from Barney for the solar-power tablet we're developing. She's startled that I'm pleased to see her. "Thanks, Andrea."

"You're most welcome, Mr. Grey." She gives me a curious smile. "Would you like some coffee?"

"Please."

"Milk?"

"No thanks."

MY DAY HAS IMPROVED immensely. I have knocked Bastille on his ass twice in our two rounds of kickboxing. That never happens. As I slip on my jacket after my shower, I feel ready to face Elena and all her questions.

Taylor appears. "Would you like me to drive, sir?"

"No. I'll take the R8."

"Very good, sir."

Before I leave I check my email.

From: Anastasia Steele
Subject: Who are you to cry thief?
Date: May 31 2011 22:18 ET
To: Christian Grey

Sir, I think you'll find it was Elliot's line originally.

Hanging how?

Your Ana

Is she flirting with me? Again?

And she's my Ana. Again.

From: Christian Grey
Subject: Unfinished Business
Date: May 31 2011 19:22
To: Anastasia Steele

Miss Steele,
You're back. You left so suddenly—just when things were getting interesting.

Elliot's not very original. He must have stolen that line from someone.

How was dinner?

Christian Grey
CEO, Grey Enterprises Holdings, Inc.

I press send.

From: Anastasia Steele
Subject: Unfinished Business?
Date: May 31 2011 22:26 ET
To: Christian Grey

Dinner was filling—you'll be very pleased to hear I ate far too much.

Getting interesting? How?

I'm glad she's eating...

From: Christian Grey
Subject: Unfinished Business—Definitely
Date: May 31 2011 19:30
To: Anastasia Steele

Are you being deliberately obtuse? I think you'd just asked me to unzip your dress.

And I was looking forward to doing just that. I am also glad to hear you are eating.

Christian Grey
CEO, Grey Enterprises Holdings, Inc.

From: Anastasia Steele
Subject: Well...There's Always the Weekend
Date: May 31 2011 22:36 ET
To: Christian Grey

Of course I eat… It's only the uncertainty I feel around you that puts me off my food.

And I would never be unwittingly obtuse, Mr. Grey.

Surely you've worked that out by now. ;)

She loses appetite around me? That's not good. And she's making fun of me. *Again.*

From: Christian Grey
Subject: Can't Wait
Date: May 31 2011 19:40
To: Anastasia Steele

I shall remember that, Miss Steele, and no doubt use the knowledge to my advantage.

I'm sorry to hear that I put you off your food. I thought I had a more concupiscent effect on you. That has been my experience, and most pleasurable it has been, too.

I very much look forward to the next time.

Christian Grey
CEO, Grey Enterprises Holdings, Inc.

From: Anastasia Steele
Subject: Gymnastic Linguistics
Date: May 31 2011 22:46 ET
To: Christian Grey

Have you been playing with the thesaurus again?

I hoot with laughter.

From: Christian Grey
Subject: Rumbled
Date: May 31 2011 19:50
To: Anastasia Steele

You know me so well, Miss Steele.

I am having dinner with an old friend now so I will be driving.

Laters, baby.©

Christian Grey
CEO, Grey Enterprises Holdings, Inc.

As much as I'd like to keep up the banter with Ana, I don't want to be late for dinner. If I were, Elena would be displeased. I power down my computer, collect my wallet and phone, and take the elevator to the garage.

THE MILE HIGH CLUB is on the penthouse floor of Columbia Tower. The sun is sinking toward the peaks of Olympic National Park, coloring the sky with an impressive fusion of oranges, pinks and opals. It's stunning. Ana would love this view. I should bring her here.

Elena is seated at a corner table. She gives me a small wave and a big smile. The maître d' escorts me to her table, and she rises, presenting her cheek to me.

"Hello, Christian," she purrs.

"Good evening, Elena. You're looking great, as usual." I kiss her cheek.

She tosses her sleek platinum hair to one side, which she does when she's feeling playful. "Sit," she says. "What would you like to drink?" Her fingers and her trademark scarlet fingernails are wrapped around a champagne flute.

"I see you've started on the Cristal."

"Well, I think we've got something to celebrate, don't you?"

"We do?"

"Christian. This girl. Spill the beans."

"I'll have a glass of the Mendocino sauvignon blanc," I tell the hovering waiter. He nods and hurries off.

"So, not a cause for celebration?" Elena takes a sip of her champagne, eyebrows raised.

"I don't know why you're making such a big deal of this."

"I'm not making a big deal. I'm curious. How old is she? What does she do?"

"She's just graduated."

"Oh. A little young for you?"

I arch a brow. "Really? You're going to go there?"

Elena laughs.

"How is Isaac?" I ask with a smirk.

She laughs again. "Behaving." Her eyes sparkle with mischief.

"How boring for you." My voice is dry.

She smiles, resigned. "He's a good pet. Shall we order?"

HALFWAY THROUGH THE CRAB chowder I put Elena out of her misery.

"Her name is Anastasia, she studied literature at WSU, and I met her when she came to interview me for the student newspaper. I gave the commencement address this year."

"Is she in the lifestyle?"

"Not yet. But I'm hopeful."

"Wow."

"Yeah. She's escaped to Georgia to think it through."

"That's a long way to go."

"I know." I look down at my chowder, wondering how Ana is and what she's doing; sleeping, I hope…alone.

When I raise my head Elena is studying me. Intently. "I haven't seen you like this," she says.

"What do you mean?"

"You're distracted. That's not like you."

"Is it that obvious?"

She nods, her eyes softening. "Obvious to me. I think she's turned your world upside down."

I inhale sharply but hide the fact by raising my glass to my lips.

Perceptive, Mrs. Lincoln.

"You think?" I murmur after my sip.

"I think," she says, her eyes searching mine.

"She's very disarming."

"I'm sure that's novel. And I bet you're worrying about what she's doing in Georgia, what she's thinking. I know how you are."

"Yes. I want her to make the right decision."

"You should go see her."

"What?"

"Get on a plane."

"Really?"

"If she's undecided, go use your considerable charm."

My snort is derisive.

"Christian," she scolds, "when you want something badly enough, you go after it and you always win. You know that. You're so negative about yourself. Drives me crazy."

I sigh. "I'm not sure."

"The poor girl is probably bored to tears down there. Go. You'll get your answer. If it's no, you can move on; if it's yes, you can enjoy being yourself with her."

"She's back Friday."

"Seize the day, my dear."

"She did say she missed me."

"There you go." Her eyes flash with certainty.

"I'll think about it. More champagne?"

"Please," she says and gives me a girlish grin.

DRIVING BACK TO ESCALA, I contemplate Elena's advice. I *could* go to see Ana. She said she's missed me…the jet's available.

Back home, I read her latest email.

From: Anastasia Steele
Subject: Suitable Dinner Companions
Date: May 31 2011 23:58 ET
To: Christian Grey

I hope you and your friend had a very pleasant dinner.

Ana

P.S. Was it Mrs. Robinson?

Shit.

This is the perfect excuse. This is going to need an answer in person.

I buzz Taylor and tell him I'm going to need Stephan and the Gulfstream in the morning.

"Very good, Mr. Grey. Where are you going?"

"*We're* going to Savannah."

"Yes, sir." And there's a hint of amusement in his voice.

WEDNESDAY, JUNE 1, 2011

It's been an interesting morning. We left Boeing Field at 11:30 PT; Stephan is flying with his first officer, Jill Beighley, and we're due to arrive in Georgia about 19:30 ET.

Bill has managed to arrange a meeting with the Savannah Brownfield Redevelopment Authority tomorrow, and I might be meeting them for a drink this evening. So if Anastasia is otherwise occupied, or doesn't want to see me, the journey won't be a complete waste of time.

Yeah, yeah. Tell yourself that, Grey.

Taylor has joined me for a light lunch and is now sorting through some paperwork, and I have a whole lot of reading to do.

The only part of the equation I've yet to solve is arranging to see Ana. I'll see how that goes once I arrive in Savannah; I'm hoping some inspiration will come to me on the flight.

I run my hand through my hair, and for the first time in a long while I lie back and doze as the G550 cruises at thirty thousand feet, bound for Savannah/Hilton Head International. The drone of the engines is soothing, and I'm tired. So tired.

That would be the nightmares, Grey.

I don't know why they are worse at the moment. I close my eyes.

"This is how you will be with me. Do you understand?"

"Yes, Ma'am."

She runs a scarlet fingernail across my chest.

I flinch and pull against the restraints as the darkness surfaces, burning my skin in the wake of her touch. But I don't make a sound.

I don't dare.

"If you behave, I'll let you come. In my mouth."

Fuck.

"But not yet. We've got a long way to go before then."

Her fingernail blazes down my skin, from the top of my sternum to my navel.

I want to scream.

She grabs my face, squeezing open my mouth, and kisses me. Her tongue demanding and wet.

She brandishes the leather flogger.

And I know this will be tough to endure.

But I have my eye on the prize. Her fucking mouth.

As the first lash falls and blisters across my skin, I welcome the pain and the endorphin rush.

"Mr. Grey, we'll be landing in twenty minutes," Taylor informs me, startling me awake. "Are you okay, sir?"

"Yeah. Sure. Thanks."

"Would you like some water?"

"Please." I take a deep breath to bring my heart rate down, and Taylor passes me a glass of cold Evian. I take a welcome sip, glad it's just Taylor on board. It's not often I dream about my heady days with Mrs. Lincoln.

Out the window the sky is blue, the sparse clouds pinking with the early evening sun. The light up here is brilliant. Golden. Tranquil. The sinking sun reflecting off the cumulus clouds. For a moment I wish I were in my sailplane. I bet the thermals are fantastic up here.

Yes!

That's what I should do: take Ana soaring. That would be *more*, wouldn't it?

"Taylor."

"Yes, sir."

"I'd like to take Anastasia soaring in Georgia—at dawn tomorrow, if we can find somewhere to do that. But later would be fine, too." If it's later I'll have to move my meeting.

"I'll get on it."

"Never mind the cost."

"Okay, sir."

"Thanks."

Now I just have to tell Ana.

THERE ARE TWO CARS waiting for us when the G550 comes to a halt on the tarmac near the Signature Flight Support terminal at the airport. Taylor and I step out of the plane and into the suffocating heat.

Hell, it's sticky, even at this time.

The rep hands the keys for both cars to Taylor. I raise a brow at him. "Ford Mustang?"

"It's all I could find in Savannah at short notice." Taylor looks sheepish.

"At least it's a red convertible. Though in this heat I hope it has AC."

"It should have everything, sir."

"Good. Thanks." I take the keys from him and, grabbing my messenger bag, leave him to unload the rest of the luggage from the plane into his Suburban.

I shake hands with Stephan and Beighley and thank them for a smooth flight. In the Mustang, I cruise out of the airport and onward to downtown Savannah, listening to Bruce on my iPod through the car sound system.

ANDREA HAS BOOKED ME into a suite at the Bohemian Hotel, which looks out over the Savannah River. It's dusk and the view from the balcony is impressive: the river is luminous, reflecting the graduated colors of the sky and the lights on the suspension bridge and the docks. The sky is incandescent, the colors shaded from deep purple to a rosy pink.

It's almost as striking as twilight over the Sound.

But I don't have time to stand here and admire the view. I set up my laptop, crank the air-conditioning to full blast, and call Ros for an update.

"Why the sudden interest in Georgia, Christian?"

"It's personal."

She huffs down the phone. "Since when have you let your personal life interfere with business?"

Since I met Anastasia Steele.

"I don't like Detroit," I snap.

"Okay." She backs off.

"I might meet the Savannah Brownfield liaison for a drink later," I add, attempting to placate her.

"Whatever, Christian. There are a few other things we need to talk about. The aid has arrived in Rotterdam. Do you still want to go ahead?"

"Yes. Let's get it done. I made a commitment at the End Global Hunger launch. This needs to happen before I can face that committee again."

"Okay. Any further thoughts on the publishing acquisition?"

"I'm still undecided."

"I think SIP has some potential."

"Yeah. Maybe. Let me think about it for a while longer."

"I'm seeing Marco to discuss the Lucas Woods situation."

"Okay, let me know how that goes. Call me later."

"Will do. Bye for now."

I'm avoiding the inevitable. I know this. But I decide it would be better to tackle Miss Steele—via email or phone, I've yet to decide which—on a full stomach, so I order dinner. While I'm waiting there's a text from Andrea letting me know my drinks appointment is off. I'm fine with that. I'll see them tomorrow morning, provided I'm not soaring with Ana.

Before room service arrives, Taylor calls.

"Mr. Grey."

"Taylor. Are you checked in?"

"Yes, sir. Your luggage will be on its way up in a moment."

"Great."

"The Brunswick Soaring Association has a glider free. I've asked Andrea to fax through your flying credentials to them. Once the paperwork's signed, we're good to go."

"Great."

"They'll do anytime from six a.m."

"Even better. Have them ready from then. Send me the address."

"Will do."

There's a knock on the door. My luggage and room service have arrived simultaneously. The food smells delicious: fried green tomatoes and shrimp and grits. Well, I'm in the South.

While I eat I contemplate my strategy with Ana. I could pay a visit to her mom's tomorrow at breakfast. Bring bagels. Then take her soaring. That's probably the best plan. She hasn't been in touch all day, so I guess she's mad. I reread her last message once I've finished dinner.

What the hell has she got against Elena? She knows nothing about our relationship. What we had happened a long time ago and now we're just friends. What right does Ana have to be mad?

And if it wasn't for Elena, God knows what would have happened to me.

There's a knock on the door. It's Taylor.

"Good evening, sir. Happy with your room?"

"Yes, it's fine."

"I have the paperwork for the Brunswick Soaring Association here."

I scan the hire agreement. It looks fine. I sign it and give it back to him. "I'll drive myself tomorrow. I'll see you there?"

"Yes, sir. I'll be there from six."

"I'll let you know if anything changes."

"Shall I unpack for you, sir?"

"Please. Thanks."

He nods and takes my suitcase into the bedroom.

I'm restless, and I need to get what I'm going to say to Ana clear in my mind. I glance at my watch; it's nine twenty. I've left this really late. Perhaps I should have a quick drink first. I leave Taylor to unpack and decide to check out the hotel bar before I speak to Ros again and write to Ana.

The rooftop bar is crowded, but I find a seat at the end of the counter and order a beer. It's a hip, contemporary place, with moody lighting and a relaxed vibe. I scan the bar, avoiding eye contact with the two women sitting next to me...and a movement captures my attention: a frustrated flip of glossy mahogany hair that catches and refracts the light.

It's Ana. Fuck.

She's facing away from me, seated opposite a woman who could only be her mother. The resemblance is striking.

What are the fucking odds?

In all the gin joints... *Jesus.*

I watch them, transfixed. They're drinking cocktails—cosmopolitans, by the look of them. Her mother is stunning: like Ana, but older. She looks late thirties, with long, dark hair, and eyes that are Ana's shade of blue. She has a bohemian vibe about her...not someone I'd automatically associate with the golf club set. Perhaps she's dressed that way because she's out with her young, beautiful daughter.

This is priceless.

Seize the day, Grey.

I fish my phone out of my jeans pocket. It's time to email Ana. This should be interesting. I'll test her mood...and I get to watch.

From: Christian Grey
Subject: Dinner Companions
Date: June 1 2011 21:40 ET
To: Anastasia Steele

Yes, I had dinner with Mrs. Robinson. She is just an old friend, Anastasia.

Looking forward to seeing you again. I miss you.

Christian Grey
CEO, Grey Enterprises Holdings, Inc.

Her mother looks earnest; maybe she's concerned for her daughter, or maybe she's trying to extract information from her.

Good luck, Mrs. Adams.

And for a moment I wonder if they're discussing me. Her mother stands; it looks like she's visiting the restroom. Ana checks her purse and pulls out her BlackBerry.

Here we go…

She begins to read, her shoulders hunched over, her fingers flexing and drumming on the table. She starts tapping furiously at the keys. I can't see her face, which is frustrating, but I don't think she's impressed with what she's just read. A moment later she abandons the phone on the table in what appears to be disgust.

That's not good.

Her mother returns and signals one of the waiters for another round of drinks. I wonder how many they've had.

I check my phone, and sure enough, there's a response.

From: Anastasia Steele
Subject: OLD Dinner Companions
Date: June 1 2011 21:42 ET
To: Christian Grey

She's not just an old friend.

Has she found another adolescent boy to sink her teeth into?

Did you get too old for her?

Is that the reason your relationship finished?

What the hell? My temper simmers as I read.

Isaac is in his late twenties.

Like me.

How dare she?

Is it the drink talking?

Time to declare yourself, Grey.

From: Christian Grey
Subject: Careful...
Date: June 1 2011 21:45 ET
To: Anastasia Steele

This is not something I wish to discuss via email.

How many cosmopolitans are you going to drink?

Christian Grey
CEO, Grey Enterprises Holdings, Inc.

She studies her phone, sits up suddenly, and looks around the room.

Showtime, Grey.

I deposit ten bucks on the counter and saunter over to them.

Our eyes meet. She blanches—shocked, I think—and I don't know how she'll greet me, or how I'll contain my temper if she says anything else about Elena.

She tucks her hair behind her ears with restless fingers. A sure sign that she's nervous. "Hi," she says, her voice strained and high-pitched.

"Hi." I lean down and kiss her cheek. She smells amazing, even if she does tense as my lips brush her skin. She looks lovely; she's caught some sun, and she's not wearing a bra. Her breasts are straining against the silky material of her top but hidden by her long hair.

For my eyes only, I hope.

And even though she's mad, I'm glad to see her. I've missed her.

"Christian, this is my mother, Carla." Ana gestures to her mom.

"Mrs. Adams, I am delighted to meet you."

Her mom's eyes are all over me.

Shit! She's checking me out. *Best ignore it, Grey.*

After a longer-than-necessary pause, she reaches out to shake my hand. "Christian."

"What are you doing here?" Ana asks, her tone accusatory.

"I came to see you, of course. I'm staying in this hotel."

"You're staying here?" she squeaks.

Yes. I can't quite believe it, either. "Well, yesterday you said you wished I were here." I'm trying to gauge her reaction. So far there's been nervous fidgeting, tensing, an accusatory tone, and a strained voice. This is not going well. "We aim to please, Miss Steele," I add, deadpan, hoping to put her in a good mood.

"Won't you join us for a drink, Christian?" Mrs. Adams says graciously and catches the eye of the waiter.

I need something stronger than beer. "I'll have a gin and tonic," I tell the waiter. "Hendrick's, if you have it, or Bombay Sapphire. Cucumber with the Hendrick's, lime with the Bombay."

"And two more cosmos, please," Ana adds with an anxious look at me.

She's right to be anxious. I think she's had enough to drink already.

"Please pull up a chair, Christian."

"Thank you, Mrs. Adams."

I do as she asks and sit down beside Ana.

"So you just happen to be staying in the hotel where we're drinking?" Ana's tone is tense.

"Or you just happen to be drinking in the hotel where I'm staying. I just finished dinner, came in here, and saw you. I was distracted, thinking about your most recent email"—I give her a pointed look—"and I glance up and there you are. Quite a coincidence, eh?"

Ana looks flustered. "My mother and I were shopping this morning and on the beach this afternoon. We decided on a few cocktails this evening," she says hurriedly as if she has to justify drinking in a bar with her mother.

"Did you buy that top?" I ask. She really does look stunning. Her camisole is emerald green; I've made the right choices—gem colors—for the clothes Caroline Acton has selected for her. "The color suits you. And you've caught some sun. You look lovely." Her cheeks color and her lips lift at my compliment. "Well, I was going to pay you a visit tomorrow. But here you are." I take her hand, because I want to touch her, give it a gentle squeeze, and caress her knuckles with my thumb. Her breathing alters.

Yes, Ana. Feel it.

Don't be mad at me.

Her eyes meet mine, and I'm rewarded with her coy smile.

"I thought I'd surprise you. But as ever, Anastasia, you surprise me by being here. I don't want to interrupt the time you have with your mother. I'll have a quick drink and then retire. I have work to do." I resist kissing her knuckles. I don't know what she's said to her mother about us, if anything.

"Christian, it's lovely to meet you finally. Ana has spoken very fondly of you," Mrs. Adams says with a charming smile.

"Really?" I glance at Ana, who's blushing.

Fondly, eh?

This is good news.

The waiter places my gin and tonic in front of me.

"Hendrick's, sir."

"Thank you."

He serves Ana and her mother fresh cosmopolitans.

"How long are you in Georgia, Christian?" her mom asks.

"Until Friday, Mrs. Adams."

"Will you have dinner with us tomorrow evening? And please, call me Carla."

"I'd be delighted to, Carla."

"Excellent," she says. "If you two will excuse me, I need to visit the restroom."

Hasn't she just been to the restroom?

I stand as she leaves, then sit down again to face the wrath of Miss Steele. I take her hand once more. "So, you're mad at me for having dinner with an old friend." I kiss each knuckle.

"Yes." She's curt.

Is she jealous?

"Our sexual relationship was over long ago, Anastasia. I don't want anyone but you. Haven't you worked that out yet?"

"I think of her as a child molester, Christian."

My scalp tingles in shock. "That's very judgmental. It wasn't like that." I release her hand in frustration.

"Oh, how was it, then?" she snaps, sticking out her stubborn little chin.

Is this the drink talking?

She continues, "She took advantage of a vulnerable fifteen-year-old boy. If you had been a fifteen-year-old girl and Mrs. Robinson was a Mr. Robinson, tempting you into a BDSM lifestyle, that would have been okay? If it was Mia, say?"

Oh, now she's being ridiculous. "Ana, it wasn't like that."

Her eyes flash. She's really angry. Why? This has nothing to do with her. But I don't want a full-blown argument here in the bar. I moderate my voice. "Okay, it didn't feel like that to me. She was a force for good. What I needed." Good God, I'd probably be dead by now if it weren't for Elena. I'm struggling to control my temper.

Her brow furrows. "I don't understand."

Shut her down, Grey.

"Anastasia, your mother will be back shortly. I'm not comfortable talking about this now. Later, maybe. If you don't want me here, I have a plane on standby at Hilton Head. I can go."

Her expression changes to panic. "No—don't go. Please. I'm thrilled you're here," she adds quickly.

Thrilled? You could have fooled me.

"I'm just trying to make you understand," she says. "I'm angry that as soon as I left, you had dinner with her. Think about how you are when I get anywhere near José. José is a good friend. I have never had a sexual relationship with him. Whereas you and her—"

"You're jealous?"

How can I make her realize that Elena and I are friends? She has nothing to be jealous about.

Clearly, Miss Steele is possessive.

And it takes me a moment to realize that I like that.

"Yes, and angry about what she did to you," she continues.

"Anastasia, she helped me. That's all I'll say about that. And as for your jealousy, put yourself in my shoes. I haven't had to justify my actions to anyone in the past seven years. Not one person. I do as I wish, Anastasia. I like my autonomy. I didn't go to see Mrs. Robinson to upset you. I went because every now and then we have dinner. She's a friend and a business partner."

Her eyes widen.

Oh. Didn't I mention that?

Why would I mention that? It's nothing to do with her.

"Yes, we're business partners. The sex is over between us. It has been for years."

"Why did your relationship end?"

"Her husband found out. Can we talk about this some other time—somewhere more private?"

"I don't think you'll ever convince me that she's not some kind of pedophile."

Fucking hell, Ana! Enough is enough!

"I don't think of her that way. I never have. Now that's enough!" I growl.

"Did you love her?"

What?

"How are you two getting on?" Carla is back.

Ana forces a smile that makes my stomach churn. "Fine, Mom."

Did I love Elena?

I take a sip of my drink. I fucking worshipped her…but did I love her? What a ridiculous question. I know nothing about romantic love. That's the hearts-and-flowers shit she wants. The nineteenth-century novels she's read have filled her head with nonsense.

I've had enough.

"Well, ladies, I shall leave you to your evening. Please put these drinks on my tab, room 612. I'll call you in the morning, Anastasia. Until tomorrow, Carla."

"Oh, it's so nice to hear someone use your full name."

"Beautiful name for a beautiful girl." I shake Carla's hand, sincere about the compliment but not the smile on my face.

Ana is quiet, imploring me with a look I ignore. I kiss her cheek.

"Laters, baby," I murmur in her ear, then turn, walking through the bar and back down to my room.

That girl provokes me like no one has before.

And she's pissed at me; maybe she has PMS. She said her period was due this week.

I burst into my room, slam the door, and head straight for the balcony. It's warm outside, and I take a deep breath, inhaling the pungent salty scent of the river. Night has fallen, and the river is inky black, like the sky…like my mood. I didn't even get to discuss gliding tomorrow. I rest my hands on the balcony rail. The lights on the shore and the bridge improve the view…but not my temperament.

Why am I defending a relationship that began when Ana was still in fourth grade? It's none of her business. Yes, it was unconventional. But that's all.

I run both hands through my hair. This trip isn't working out how I expected at all. Perhaps it was a mistake to come down here. And to think it was Elena who encouraged me to make the trip.

My phone buzzes, and I hope it's Ana. It's Ros.

"Yes," I snap.

"Jeez, Christian. Am I interrupting something?"

"No. Sorry. What's up?" *Calm down, Grey.*

"I thought I'd update you on my conversation with Marco. But if now is a bad time, I'll call back in the morning."

"No, it's fine."

There's a knock on the door. "Hang on, Ros." I open it, expecting Taylor or someone from housekeeping to do turndown—but it's Ana, standing in the corridor, looking bashful and beautiful.

She's here.

Opening the door wider, I motion her in.

"All the redundancy packages concluded?" I ask Ros without taking my eyes off Ana.

"Yes."

Ana walks into the room, watching me warily, her lips parted and moist, her eyes darkening. *What's this? A change of heart?* I know that look. It's desire. She wants me. And I want her, too, especially after our spat in the bar.

Why else would she be here?

"And the cost?" I question Ros.

"Nearly two million."

I whistle through my teeth. "That was one expensive mistake."

"GEH gets to exploit the fiber-optic division." She's right. This was one of our goals.

"And Lucas?" I ask.

"He reacted badly."

I open the minibar and gesture to Ana to help herself. Leaving her there, I stroll into the bedroom.

"What did he do?"

"He threw a fit."

In the bathroom I turn on the faucet to run water into the huge sunken marble bath and add some scented bath oil. There's room for six people in here.

"The majority of that money is for him," I remind Ros as I check the water temperature. "And he has the buyout price for the company. He can always start again."

I turn to leave, but as an afterthought I decide to light the various candles that are artfully arranged on the stone bench. *Lit candles count as "more," don't they?*

"Well, he's threatening lawyers, though I don't understand why. We're bulletproof on this. Is that water I hear?" Ros asks.

"Yeah, I'm running a bath."

"Oh? Do you want me to go?"

"No. Anything else?"

"Yes, Fred wants to talk to you."

"Really?"

"He's gone over Barney's new design."

As I wander back into the living room, I acknowledge Barney's design solution for the tablet and ask her to have Andrea send me the revised schematics. Ana has retrieved a bottle of orange juice.

"Is this your new management style: not being here?" Ros asks.

I laugh out loud, but mainly at Ana's choice of beverage. *Wise woman.* And I tell Ros that I won't be back in the office until Friday.

"Are you seriously going to change your mind about Detroit?"

"There's a plot of land here that I'm interested in."

"Is Bill aware of this?" Ros is snippy.

"Yeah, get Bill to call."

"Will do. Did you get a drink with the Savannah people this evening?"

I tell her I'll be seeing them tomorrow. I'm more conciliatory and mindful of my tone, as this is a hot button for Ros. "I want to see what Georgia will offer if we move in." I take a glass off the shelf, hand it to Ana, and point to the ice bucket. "If their incentives are attractive enough," I continue, "I think we should consider it, though I'm not sure about the damned heat here."

Ana pours her drink.

"It's late to be changing your mind on this, Christian. But it might give us some leverage with Detroit," Ros muses.

"I agree, Detroit has its advantages, too, and it's cooler."

But there are too many ghosts there for me.

"Get Bill to call. Tomorrow." It's late now and I have a visitor. "Not too early," I warn. Ros says good night and I hang up.

Ana eyes me with reserve as I drink her in. Her lush hair falls over small shoulders, framing her lovely, pensive face. "You didn't answer my question," she murmurs.

"No. I didn't."

"No you didn't answer my question, or no you didn't love her?"

She's not going to let this go. I lean against the wall and fold my arms so I don't pull her into them. "What are you doing here, Anastasia?"

"I've just told you."

Put her out of her misery, Grey.

"No. I didn't love her."

Her shoulders relax and her face softens. It's what she wanted to hear.

"You're quite the green-eyed goddess, Anastasia. Who would have thought?"

But are you my *green-eyed goddess?*

"Are you making fun of me, Mr. Grey?"

"I wouldn't dare," I retort.

"Oh, I think you would, and I think you do—often." She smirks and sinks perfect teeth into her lip.

She's doing that on purpose.

"Please stop biting your lip. You're in my room, I haven't set eyes on you for nearly three days, and I've flown a long way to see you." I need to know we're okay, the only way I know how. I want to fuck her, hard.

My phone buzzes, but I switch it off without checking the caller. Whoever it is can wait.

I step toward her. "I want you, Anastasia. Now. And you want me. That's why you're here."

"I really did want to know," she says.

"Well, now that you do, are you coming or going?" I ask, standing in front of her.

"Coming," she says, her eyes on mine.

"Oh, I hope so." I stare down at her, marveling as her irises darken.

She wants me.

"You were so mad at me," I whisper.

It's still novel, dealing with her anger, taking her feelings into account.

"Yes."

"I don't remember anyone but my family ever being mad at me. I like it." Gently I touch her face with the tips of my fingers and run them down to her chin. She closes her eyes and angles her cheek to my touch. Leaning down, I run my nose along her naked shoulder, up to her ear, inhaling her sweet scent as desire floods my body. My fingers move to her nape and into her hair.

"We should talk," she whispers.

"Later."

"There's so much I want to say."

"Me, too." I kiss the spot beneath her ear and tug her hair, pulling back her head to expose her throat. My teeth and lips graze her chin and down her neck as my body hums with need. "I want you," I whisper as I kiss the spot where her pulse beats beneath her skin. She moans and holds my arms. I tense for a moment, but the darkness stays dormant.

"Are you bleeding?" I ask between kisses.

She stills. "Yes," she says.

"Do you have cramps?"

"No." Her voice is quiet yet vehement with embarrassment.

I stop kissing her and look down into her eyes. Why is she embarrassed? It's her body. "Did you take your pill?"

"Yes," she answers.

Good. "Let's go have a bath."

In the over-the-top bathroom I release Ana's hand. The atmosphere is hot and humid, steam gently rising above the foam. I'm overdressed in this heat, my linen shirt and jeans sticking to my skin.

Ana watches me, her skin dewy from the humidity.

"Do you have a hair tie?" I ask. Her hair will start clinging to her face.

She pulls out a hair elastic from her jeans pocket.

"Put your hair up," I tell her and watch as she follows my command with quick, efficient grace.

Good girl. No more arguing.

A few strands escape from her ponytail, but she looks lovely. I turn off the faucet and, taking her hand, guide her into the other part of the bathroom, where a large gilded mirror hangs over two sinks set in marble. My eyes on hers in the mirror, I stand behind her and ask her to take off her sandals. Hastily she removes them and lets them drop to the floor.

"Lift up your arms," I whisper. Grasping the hem of her pretty top, I peel it off and over her head, freeing her breasts. Reaching around, I undo the top button and the zipper of her jeans.

"I'm going to have you in the bathroom, Anastasia."

Her eyes stray to my mouth and she licks her lips. Under the soft light her pupils gleam with excitement.

Bending down, I drop tender kisses on her neck, hook my thumbs into the waistband of her jeans, and peel them down over her fine ass, catching her panties in my hands on the way down. Kneeling behind her, I ease them down her legs, to her feet. "Step out of your jeans," I order.

Grabbing the edge of the sink, she obliges; now she's naked and I'm face-to-face with her ass. I pop her jeans, panties, and top onto a white stool beneath the sink and contemplate all the things I could do to that ass. I notice a blue string between her legs; her tampon is still in place, so I settle for kissing and nipping her behind gently before standing up. Our eyes connect in the mirror once more and I splay my hand out over her smooth, flat belly.

"Look at you. You are so beautiful. See how you feel." Her breathing quickens as I take both her hands in mine and spread her fingers on her belly beneath my outstretched hands.

"Feel how soft your skin is," I whisper and guide her hands across her torso in a wide sweeping circle, then travel them up to her breasts. "Feel how full your breasts are." I hold her hands beneath her breasts so she's cupping them and tease her nipples with my thumbs. She moans and bows her back, pressing her breasts into our conjoined hands. Trapping her nipples between her thumbs and mine, I tug gently again and again and take pleasure watching them harden and lengthen in response.

Like a certain part of my anatomy.

She closes her eyes and wriggles against me, brushing her behind over my erection. She moans, her head against my shoulder.

"That's right, baby," I murmur against her neck, enjoying her body coming alive beneath her touch. I guide her hands down her front to her hips, then in toward her pubic hair. I push my leg between hers and with my foot widen her stance as I guide her hands over her vulva, one hand at a time, over and over, pressing her fingers over her clitoris again and again.

She groans and I watch her writhe against me in the mirror.

Lord, she's a goddess.

"Look at you glow, Anastasia." I kiss and nip her neck and her shoulder, then I let go, leaving her hanging, and she opens her eyes as I step back.

"Carry on," I tell her, wondering what she'll do.

She falters for a moment, then rubs herself with one hand, but not nearly as enthusiastically.

Oh, this will never do.

Quickly I strip off my sticky shirt, jeans, and underwear, freeing my erection.

"You'd rather I do this?" I ask, her eyes blazing at mine in the mirror.

"Oh yes, please," she says, a desperate, needy edge to her voice.

I wrap my arms around her, my front against her back, my cock resting in the cleft of her fine, fine ass. I take her hands in mine once more, guiding them over her clitoris, one at a time, again and again, pressing, stroking, and arousing her. She whimpers as I suck and nip at her nape. Her legs begin to tremble. Abruptly I spin her around so she's facing me. I grasp her wrists in one of my hands, holding them behind her back, while I tug on her ponytail with the other, bringing her lips up to mine. I kiss her, consuming her mouth, reveling in the taste of her: orange juice and sweet, sweet Ana. Her breathing is harsh, like mine.

"When did you start your period, Anastasia?"

I want to fuck you without a condom.

"Yesterday," she breathes.

"Good." I step back and spin her around again. "Hold on to the sink," I command. Grasping her hips, I lift her and pull her backward so she's bent over. My hand glides down her ass to the blue string, and I tug out the tampon, which I toss in the trash can. She gasps, shocked, I think, but I grab my cock and slide into her quickly.

My breath whistles between my teeth.

Fuck. She feels good. So good. Skin against skin.

I edge back, then sink into her once more, feeling every precious, slick inch of her. She groans and pushes against me.

Oh yes, Ana.

She tightens her grip on the marble as I pick up speed, and I grasp her hips, building…building, then hammering into her. Claiming her. Possessing her.

Don't be jealous, Ana. I want only you.

You.

You.

My fingers find her clitoris and I tease her, caress her, and stimulate her so her legs begin to tremble once more. "That's right, baby," I murmur, my voice hoarse as I pound into her with a punishing I-own-you rhythm.

Don't argue with me. Don't fight with me.

Her legs stiffen as I grind into her and her body starts to quiver. Suddenly she cries out as her orgasm seizes her, taking me with her.

"Oh, Ana," I breathe as I let go, the world blurring, and I come inside her.

Fuck.

"Oh, baby, will I ever get enough of you?" I whisper as I sink onto her.

Slowly I descend to the floor, bringing her with me and wrapping my arms around her. She sits, her head against my shoulder, still panting.

Sweet Lord.

Was it ever like this?

I kiss her hair and she calms, her eyes closed, her breathing gradually returning to normal as I hold her. We're both sweaty and hot in a humid bathroom, but I don't want to be anywhere else.

She shifts. "I'm bleeding," she says.

"Doesn't bother me." I don't want to let her go.

"I noticed." Her tone is dry.

"Does it bother you?" *It shouldn't. It's natural.* I've known only one woman who was squeamish about period sex, but I wouldn't take any of that crap from her.

"No, not at all." Ana peers up at me with clear blue eyes.

"Good. Let's have a bath." I free her and her brows knit for a moment while she stares at my chest. Her rosy face loses some of its color, and clouded eyes meet mine.

"What is it?" I ask, alarmed by her expression.

"Your scars. They're not from chicken pox."

"No, they're not." My tone is arctic.

I do not want to talk about this.

Standing, I hold my hand out to her and pull her to her feet. Her eyes are wide with horror.

It'll be pity next.

"Don't look at me like that," I warn and release her hand.

I don't want your fucking pity, Ana. Don't go there.

She studies her hand, suitably chastened, I hope. "Did she do that?" Her voice is almost inaudible.

I scowl at her, saying nothing, as I try to contain my sudden rage. My silence compels her to look at me. "She?" I snarl. "Mrs. Robinson?"

Ana pales at my tone.

"She's not an animal, Anastasia. Of course she didn't. I don't understand why you feel you have to demonize her."

She bows her head to avoid eye contact, walks briskly past me, and steps into the bath, sinking into the foam so I can no longer see her body. Looking up at me, her face contrite and open, she says, "I just wonder what you would be like if you hadn't met her. If she hadn't introduced you to your, um, lifestyle."

Damn it. We're back to Elena.

I stalk toward the tub, slip into the water, and sit on the underwater shelf out of her reach. She watches me, waiting for an answer. The silence between us swells until all I can hear is the blood pumping through my ears.

Fuck.

She doesn't take her eyes off mine.

Stand down, Ana!

Nope. It's not going to happen.

I shake my head. *Impossible woman.*

"I would probably have gone the way of my birth mother, had it not been for Mrs. Robinson."

She tucks a damp tendril behind her ear, staying quiet.

What can I say about Elena? I think about our relationship: Elena and me. Those heady years. The secrecy. The furtive couplings. The pain. The pleasure. The release… The order and calm she brought to my world. "She loved me in a way I found…acceptable," I muse, almost to myself.

"Acceptable?" Ana says in disbelief.

"Yes."

Ana's expression is expectant.

She wants more.

Shit.

"She distracted me from the destructive path I found myself following." My voice is low. "It's very hard to grow up in a perfect family when you're not perfect."

She inhales sharply.

Hell. I hate talking about this.

"Does she still love you?"

No! "I don't think so, not like that. I keep telling you, it was a long time ago. It's in the past. I couldn't change it even if I wanted to, which I don't. She saved me from myself. I've never discussed this with anyone.

"Except Dr. Flynn, of course. And the only reason I'm talking about this now, to you, is because I want you to trust me."

"I do trust you," she says, "but I do want to know you better, and whenever I try to talk to you, you distract me. There's so much I want to know."

"Oh, for pity's sake, Anastasia. What do you want to know? What do I have to do?"

She stares at her hands under the surface of the water. "I'm just trying to understand; you're such an enigma. Unlike anyone I've met before. I'm glad you're telling me what I want to know."

Abruptly filled with resolve, she moves through the water to sit beside me, leaning against me so my skin sticks to hers.

"Please don't be angry with me," she says.

"I am not angry with you, Anastasia. I'm just not used to this kind of talking—this probing. I only have this with Dr. Flynn and with—"

Damn.

"With her? Mrs. Robinson? You talk to her," she says, her voice breathy and quiet.

"Yes, I do."

"What about?"

I turn to face her so suddenly that water sloshes out of the bath and onto the floor. "Persistent, aren't you? Life, the universe—business. Anastasia, Mrs. R and I go way back. We can discuss anything."

"Me?" she asks.

"Yes."

"Why do you talk about me?" she asks, and now she sounds sullen.

"I've never met anyone like you, Anastasia."

"What does that mean? Anyone who didn't just automatically sign your paperwork, no questions asked?"

I shake my head. *No.* "I need advice."

"And you take advice from Mrs. Pedo?" she snaps.

"Anastasia—enough," I almost shout. "Or I'll put you across my knee. I have no sexual or romantic interest in her whatsoever. She's a dear, valued friend and a business partner. That's all. We have a past, a shared history, which was monumentally beneficial for me, though it fucked up her marriage—but that side of our relationship is over."

She squares her shoulders. "And your parents never found out?"

"No," I growl. "I've told you this."

She regards me warily, and I think she knows she's pushed me to my limit.

"Are you done?" I ask.

"For now."

Thank God for that. She wasn't lying when she told me there was much she wanted to say. But we're not talking about what I want to talk about. I need to know where I stand. If our arrangement has a chance.

Seize the day, Grey.

"Right—my turn. You haven't responded to my email."

She tucks her hair behind her ear, then shakes her head. "I was going to respond. But now you're here."

"You'd rather I wasn't?" I hold my breath.

"No, I'm pleased," she says.

"Good. I'm pleased I'm here, too—in spite of your interrogation. So, while it's acceptable to grill me, you think you can claim some kind of diplomatic immunity just because I've flown all this way to see you? I'm not buying it, Miss Steele. I want to know how you feel."

Her brows knit together. "I told you. I am pleased you're here. Thank you for coming all this way." She sounds sincere.

"It's my pleasure." I lean down and kiss her, and she opens like a flower, offering and wanting more. I pull back. "No. I think I want some answers first before we do any more."

She sighs, her wary look returning. "What do you want to know?"

"Well, how you feel about our would-be arrangement, for starters."

She makes a moue with her mouth, as if her response will be unpalatable.

Oh dear.

"I don't think I can do it for an extended period of time. A whole weekend being someone I'm not." She looks down, away from me.

That's not a no. What's more, I think she's right.

Grasping her chin, I tilt her head up so I can see her eyes.

"No, I don't think you could, either."

"Are you laughing at me?"

"Yes, but in a good way." I kiss her again. "You're not a great submissive."

Her mouth drops open. Is she feigning offense? And then she laughs, a sweet, infectious laugh, and I know she's not offended.

"Maybe I don't have a good teacher."

Good point well made, Miss Steele.

I laugh, too. "Maybe. Perhaps I should be stricter with you." I search her face. "Was it that bad when I spanked you the first time?"

"No, not really," she says, her cheeks flushing a little.

"It's more the idea of it?" I ask, pressing her further.

"I suppose. Feeling pleasure when one isn't supposed to."

"I remember feeling the same. Takes a while to get your head around it." We are finally having the discussion. "You can always use the safe word, Anastasia. Don't forget that. And, as long as you follow the rules, which fulfill a deep need in me for control and to keep you safe, then perhaps we can find a way forward."

"Why do you need to control me?"

"Because it satisfies a need in me that wasn't met in my formative years."

"So it's a form of therapy?"

"I've not thought of it like that, but yes, I suppose it is."

She nods. "But here's the thing—one moment you say 'don't defy me,' the next you say you like to be challenged. That's a very fine line to tread successfully."

"I can see that. But you seem to be doing fine so far."

"But at what personal cost? I'm tied up in knots here."

"I like you tied up in knots."

"That's not what I meant!" She dashes her hand through the water, soaking me.

"Did you just splash me?"

"Yes," she says.

"Oh, Miss Steele." I wrap my arm around her waist and tug her onto my lap, slopping water onto the floor once again. "I think we've done enough talking for now."

I hold her head between my hands and kiss her, my tongue teasing her lips apart, then delving into her mouth, dominating her. She runs her fingers through my hair, returning my kiss, twisting her tongue around mine. Angling her head with one hand, I shift her with the other so she's astride me.

I pull back to take a breath. Her eyes are dark and carnal, her lust plain to see. I pull her wrists behind her back and grasp them in one hand. "I'm going to have you now," I declare, and I lift her so my erection is poised beneath her. "Ready?"

"Yes," she breathes, and I lower her onto me, watching her expression as I fill her. She moans and closes her eyes, thrusting her breasts forward into my face.

Oh, sweet Jesus.

I flex my hips, lifting her, burying myself even deeper inside her, and lean forward so our foreheads are touching.

She feels so good.

"Please let my hands go," she whispers.

I open my eyes and see her mouth open as she drags air into her lungs.

"Don't touch me," I plead, and release her hands and grasp her hips. She grabs the edge of the bath and slowly starts to take me. Up. Then down. Oh so slowly. She opens her eyes to find mine on her face. Watching her. Riding me. Leaning down, she kisses me, her tongue invading my mouth. I close my eyes, reveling in the sensation.

Oh yes, Ana.

Her fingers are in my hair, tugging and pulling as she kisses me, her wet tongue entwining with mine as she moves. I hold her hips and start lifting her higher and faster, vaguely aware that water is cascading out of the bath.

But I don't care. I want her. Like this.

This beautiful woman who moans into my mouth.

Up. Down. Up. Down. Over and over.

Giving herself to me. Taking me.

"Ah." The pleasure catches in her throat.

"That's right, baby," I whisper as she quickens around me, then cries out as she explodes into her orgasm.

I wrap my arms around her, embracing her, holding her tightly as I lose myself and come inside her. "Ana, baby!" I cry, and I know I never want to let her go.

She kisses my ear.

"That was—" she breathes.

"Yeah." Holding her arms, I urge her back so I can study her. She looks sleepy and sated, and I imagine I must look the same. "Thank you," I whisper.

She looks confused.

"For not touching me," I clarify.

Her face softens and she raises her hand. I tense. But she shakes her head and traces my lips with her finger.

"You said it's a hard limit. I understand." And she leans forward and kisses me. The unfamiliar feeling surfaces, swelling in my chest, unnamed and dangerous.

"Let's get you to bed. Unless you have to go home?" I'm alarmed at where my emotions are going.

"No. I don't have to go."

"Good. Stay."

I stand her up and climb out of the bath to fetch us both towels, dismissing my unsettling feelings.

I wrap her in a towel, drape one around my waist, and drop another on the floor in a vain attempt to clean up the water sloshed on the floor. Ana wanders over to the sinks as I drain the bath.

Well. That was an interesting evening.

And she was right. It was good to talk, though I'm not sure we've resolved anything.

She's brushing her teeth with my toothbrush when I walk through the bathroom to the bedroom. It makes me smile. I pick up my phone and see that the missed call was from Taylor.

I text him.

> Everything okay?
> I'll be leaving to go gliding at 6 a.m.

He responds immediately.

> That's why I was calling.
> Weather looks good.
> I'll see you there.
> Good night, sir.

I'm taking Miss Steele soaring! My delight bubbles up into a broad grin that widens when she comes out of the bathroom wrapped in the towel.

"I need my purse," she says, looking a little shy.

"I think you left it in the living room."

She scampers off to fetch it, and I brush my teeth, knowing the toothbrush has just been in her mouth.

In the bedroom I discard the towel, pull back the sheets, and lie down, waiting for Ana. She's disappeared into the bathroom again and closed the door.

Moments later she returns. She drops her towel and lies down beside me, naked except for a shy smile. We lie in bed facing each other, hugging our pillows. "Do you want to sleep?" I ask. I know we have to get up early, and it's nearly eleven.

"No. I'm not tired," she says, her eyes shining.

"What do you want to do?" *More sex?*

"Talk."

More talking. Oh Lord. I smile, resigned. "About what?"

"Stuff."

"What stuff?"

"You."

"What about me?"

"What's your favorite film?"

I like her quick-fire questions. "Today, it's *The Piano*."

She beams back at me. "Of course. Silly me. Such a sad, exciting score, which no doubt you can play. So many accomplishments, Mr. Grey."

"And the greatest one is you, Miss Steele."

Her grin broadens. "So I am number seventeen."

"Seventeen?"

"Number of women you've, um…had sex with."

Oh shit. "Not exactly."

Her smile vanishes. "You said fifteen."

"I was referring to the number of women in my playroom. I thought that's what you meant. You didn't ask me how many women I'd had sex with."

"Oh." Her eyes widen. "Vanilla?" she asks.

"No. You are my one vanilla conquest." And for some strange reason, I feel insanely pleased with myself. "I can't give you a number. I didn't put notches in the bedpost or anything."

"What are we talking—tens, hundreds…thousands?"

"Tens. We're in the tens, for pity's sake." I feign outrage.

"All submissives?"

"Yes."

"Stop grinning at me," she says haughtily, trying and failing to stifle hers.

"I can't. You're funny." And I feel a little light-headed as we beam at each other.

"Funny peculiar or funny ha-ha?"

"A bit of both, I think."

"That's damned cheeky, coming from you," she says.

I kiss her nose to prepare her. "This will shock you, Anastasia. Ready?"

Her eyes are wide and eager, full of delight.

Tell her.

"All submissives in training, when I was training. There are places in and around Seattle that one can go and practice. Learn to do what I do."

"Oh," she exclaims.

"Yep, I've paid for sex, Anastasia."

"That's nothing to be proud of," she scolds me. "And you're right, I am deeply shocked. And cross that I can't shock you."

"You wore my underwear."

"Did that shock you?"

"Yes. You didn't wear your panties to meet my parents."

Her delight is restored. "Did that shock you?"

"Yes."

"It seems I can only shock you in the underwear department."

"You told me you were a virgin. That's the biggest shock I've ever had."

"Yes, your face was a picture, a Kodak moment." She giggles, and her face lights up.

"You let me work you over with a riding crop." I'm grinning like the fucking Cheshire cat. When have I ever stretched out naked beside a woman and just talked?

"Did that shock you?"

"Yep."

"Well, I may let you do it again."

"Oh, I do hope so, Miss Steele. This weekend?"

"Okay," she says.

"Okay?"

"Yes. I'll go to the Red Room of Pain again."

"You say my name."

"That shocks you?"

"The fact that I like it shocks me."

"Christian," she whispers, and the sound of my name from her lips spreads warmth through my body.

Ana.

"I want to do something tomorrow."

"What?"

"A surprise. For you."

She yawns.

Enough. She's tired.

"Am I boring you, Miss Steele?"

"Never," she confesses.

I lean across and give her a quick kiss. "Sleep," I order and switch off the bedside light.

And a few moments later I hear her even breathing; she's fast asleep. I pull a sheet over her, roll onto my back, and stare up at the whirring ceiling fan.

Well, talking isn't so bad.

Today worked out after all.

Thank you, Elena…

And with a sated smile, I close my eyes.

THURSDAY, JUNE 2, 2011

"No. Don't leave me." The whispered words penetrate my slumber, and I stir and wake.

What was that?

I look around the room. Where the hell am I?

Oh yes, Savannah.

"No. Please. Don't leave me."

What? It's Ana. "I'm not going anywhere," I mutter, bemused. Turning, I prop myself up on my elbow. She's huddled beside me and she looks like she's asleep.

"I won't leave you," she mumbles.

My scalp prickles. "I'm very glad to hear that."

She sighs.

"Ana?" I whisper. But she doesn't react. Her eyes are closed. She's fast asleep. She must be dreaming. What is she dreaming about?

"Christian," she says.

"Yes," I respond automatically.

But she says nothing; she's definitely asleep, but I've never heard her talk in her sleep before.

I watch her, fascinated. Her face is illuminated by ambient light from the living area. Her brow crinkles for a moment, as if an unpleasant thought is plaguing her, then it's smooth once more. With her lips parted as she breathes, her face soft in sleep, she's beautiful.

And she doesn't want me to go, and she won't leave me. The candor of her subconscious admission sweeps through me like a summer breeze, leaving warmth and hope in its wake.

She's not going to leave me.

Well, you have your answer, Grey.

I smile down at her. She seems to have settled and stopped talking. I check the time on the radio alarm: 4:57.

It's time to get up anyway, and I'm elated. I'm going soaring. *With Ana.* I love soaring. I place a quick kiss on her temple, rise, and head into the main room of the suite, where I order breakfast and check the local weather report.

Another hot day with high humidity. No rain.

I shower quickly, dry myself, then gather Ana's clothes from the bathroom and lay them out on a chair near the bed. As I pick up her panties I remember how my devious plan to confiscate her underwear backfired.

Oh, Miss Steele.

And after our first night together…

"Oh, by the way, I'm wearing your underwear." And she yanks the waistband up so I can see the words Polo *and* Ralph *peeking over her jeans.*

I shake my head, and from the armoire I take a pair of my boxer briefs and deposit them on the chair. I like it when she wears my clothes.

She mumbles again, and I think she said *cage,* but I'm not sure. *What the hell is that about?*

She doesn't stir but remains blissfully asleep while I dress. As I pull on my T-shirt there's a knock on the door. Breakfast has arrived: pastries, a coffee for me, and Twinings English Breakfast tea for Ana. Fortunately the hotel stocks her favorite blend.

It's time to wake Miss Steele.

"Strawberry," she mutters as I sit down beside her on the bed.

What's with the fruit?

"Anastasia," I summon her gently.

"I want more."

I know you do, and so do I. "Come on, baby." I continue to coax her awake.

She gripes. "No. I want to touch you."

Shit. "Wake up." I lean down and gently tug her earlobe with my teeth.

"No." She screws her eyes tight.

"Wake up, baby."

"Oh no," she protests.

"Time to get up, baby. I'm going to switch on the side light." I reach across and switch it on, bathing her in a pool of dim light. She squints.

"No," she whines. Her reluctance to wake is amusing and different. In my previous relationships a sleepy submissive could expect to be disciplined.

I nuzzle her ear and whisper, "I want to chase the dawn with you." I kiss her cheek, kiss each eyelid in turn, kiss the tip of her nose, and kiss her lips.

Her eyes flicker open.

"Good morning, beautiful."

And they close again. She grumbles, and I grin down at her. "You are not a morning person."

She opens one unfocused eye, studying me. "I thought you wanted sex," she says, her relief obvious.

I suppress my laugh. "Anastasia, I always want sex with you. It's heartwarming to know that you feel the same."

"Of course I do, just not when it's so late." She hugs her pillow.

"It's not late, it's early. Come on—up you go. We're going out. I'll take a rain check on the sex."

"I was having such a nice dream." She sighs, peering up at me.

"Dream about what?"

"You." Her face warms.

"What was I doing this time?"

"Trying to feed me strawberries," she says with a small voice.

That accounts for her babbling. "Dr. Flynn could have a field day with that. Up—get dressed. Don't bother to shower; we can do that later."

She protests but sits up, ignoring the sheet that slips down to her waist and exposes her body. My cock stirs. With her hair mussed, cascading over her shoulders and curling around her naked breasts, she looks gorgeous. Ignoring my arousal, I stand up to give her some room.

"What time is it?" she asks, her voice sleepy.

"Five thirty in the morning."

"Feels like three a.m."

"We don't have much time. I let you sleep as long as possible. Come." I want to drag her out of bed and dress her myself. I can't wait to get her airborne.

"Can't I have a shower?"

"If you have a shower, I'll want one with you, and you and I know what will happen then—the day will just go. Come."

She gives me a patient look. "What are we doing?"

"It's a surprise. I told you."

She shakes her head and beams, very much amused. "Okay." She climbs out of bed, oblivious to her nudity, and notices her clothes on the chair. I'm delighted she's not her usual shy self; maybe it's because she's sleepy. She slides on my underwear and gives me a broad smile.

"I'll give you some room now that you're up." Leaving her to dress, I wander back into the main room, sit down at the small dining table, and help myself to some coffee.

She joins me a few minutes later.

"Eat," I order, motioning for her to take a seat. She stares at me, transfixed, her eyes glazed. "Anastasia," I say, interrupting her daydream.

Her eyelashes flutter as she comes back from wherever she's been. "I'll have some tea. Can I take a croissant for later?" she asks hopefully.

She's not going to eat.

"Don't rain on my parade, Anastasia."

"I'll eat later, when my stomach's woken up. About seven thirty, okay?"

"Okay." I can't force her.

She looks defiant and stubborn. "I want to roll my eyes at you," she says.

Oh, Ana, bring it on.

"By all means, do, and you will make my day."

She looks up at the fire sprinkler on the ceiling. "Well, a

spanking would wake me up, I suppose," she says as if she's weighing the option.

She's considering it? It doesn't work that way, Anastasia!

"On the other hand, I don't want you to be all hot and bothered; the climate here is warm enough." She gives me a saccharine smile.

"You are, as ever, challenging, Miss Steele." My voice is droll. "Drink your tea."

She sits down and takes a couple of sips.

"Drink up. We should go." I'm keen to get on the road—it's quite a drive.

"Where are we going?"

"You'll see."

Stop with the grinning, Grey.

She pouts with frustration. Miss Steele, as ever, is curious. But all she's wearing is her camisole and jeans; she'll be cold once we're airborne.

"Finish your tea," I order and leave the table. In the bedroom I rifle through the armoire and pull out a sweatshirt. This should do. I call the valet and tell him to bring the car out front.

"I'm ready," she says as I return to the main room.

"You'll need this." I toss the sweatshirt to her as she gives me a bewildered look. "Trust me."

I plant a swift kiss on her lips. Taking her hand, I open the door to the suite and we head for the elevators. There's a hotel employee standing there—Brian, according to his name tag—also waiting for the elevator.

"Good morning," he says, giving us both a cheerful salute as the doors open. I glance at Ana and smirk as we enter.

No shenanigans in elevators this morning.

She hides her smile and peers at the floor, her cheeks coloring. She knows exactly what's going through my mind. Brian wishes us a good day as we exit.

Outside, the valet is waiting with the Mustang. Ana arches a brow, impressed by the GT500. Yeah, it's a fun drive, even if it's only a Mustang.

"You know, sometimes it's great being me," I tease her, and with a polite bow I open her door.

"Where are we going?"

"You'll see." I get behind the wheel and ease the car into drive. At the stoplight I quickly program the address of the airfield into the GPS. It directs us out of Savannah toward I-95. I switch on my iPod via the steering wheel, and the car is filled with a sublime melody.

"What's this?" Ana asks.

"It's from *La Traviata*. An opera by Verdi."

"*La Traviata*? I've heard of that. I can't think where. What does it mean?"

I give her a knowing look. "Well, literally, 'the woman led astray.' It's based on Alexandre Dumas's book *La Dame aux Camélias*."

"Ah. I've read it."

"I thought you might have."

"The doomed courtesan," she recounts, her voice tinged with melancholy. "Hmm, it's a depressing story," she says.

"Too depressing?" We can't have that, Miss Steele, especially when I'm in such a good mood. "Do you want to choose some music? This is on my iPod."

I tap the navigation screen and bring up the playlist.

"You choose," I offer, wondering if she'll like anything I have in iTunes.

She studies the list and scrolls through it, concentrating hard. She taps on a song, and Verdi's dulcet strings are replaced by a pounding beat and Britney Spears.

"'Toxic,' eh?" I observe with wry humor.

Is she trying to tell me something?

Is she referring to me?

"I don't know what you mean," she says innocently.

Does she think I should wear a warning?

Miss Steele wants to play games.

So be it.

I turn the music down a tad. It's a little early for this remix, and for the reminder.

"Sir, this submissive respectfully requests Master's iPod."

I glance away from the spreadsheet I'm reading and study her as she kneels beside me, her eyes cast down.

She's been exceptional this weekend. How can I refuse?

"Sure, Leila, take it. I think it's in the dock."

"Thank you, Master," she says and stands with her usual grace, without looking at me.

Good girl.

And wearing only red high heels, she teeters over to the iPod dock and collects her reward.

"I didn't put that song on my iPod," I tell Ana breezily and floor the gas, throwing us both into the back of our seats, but I hear her small, exasperated huff above the roar of the engine.

As Britney continues at her sultry best, Ana drums her fingers on her thigh, radiating disquiet as she stares out the car window. The Mustang eats up the miles on the freeway; there's no traffic, and dawn's first light is chasing us down I-95.

Ana sighs as Damien Rice begins.

Put her out of her misery, Grey.

And I don't know if it's my good mood, our talk last night, or the fact that I'm about to go soaring—but I want to tell her who put the song on the iPod. "It was Leila."

"Leila?"

"An ex, who put the song on my iPod."

"One of the fifteen?" She turns her full attention to me, hungry for information.

"Yes."

"What happened to her?"

"We finished."

"Why?"

"She wanted more."

"And you didn't?"

I glance at her and shake my head. "I've never wanted more, until I met you."

She rewards me with her bashful smile.

Yes, Ana. It's not just you who wants more.

"What happened to the other fourteen?" she asks.

"You want a list? Divorced, beheaded, died?"

"You're not Henry VIII," she scolds me.

"Okay. In no particular order, I've only had long-term relationships with four women, apart from Elena."

"Elena?"

"Mrs. Robinson to you."

She pauses for a moment, and I know she's scrutinizing me. I keep my eyes on the road.

"What happened to the four?" she asks.

"So inquisitive, so eager for information, Miss Steele," I tease.

"Oh, Mr. When Is Your Period Due?"

"Anastasia, a man needs to know these things."

"Does he?"

"I do."

"Why?"

"Because I don't want you to get pregnant."

"Neither do I. Well, not for a few years yet," she says a little wistfully.

Of course, that would be with someone else... The thought is disquieting. *She's mine.*

"So the other four, what happened?" she persists.

"One met someone else. The other three wanted...more. I wasn't in the market for more then." *Why did I open this can of worms?*

"And the others?"

"Just didn't work out."

She nods and stares out the window as Aaron Neville sings "Tell It Like It Is."

"Where are we headed?" she asks again.

We're close now. "An airfield."

"We're not going back to Seattle, are we?" She sounds panicked.

"No, Anastasia." I chuckle at her reaction. "We're going to indulge in my second favorite pastime."

"Second?"

"Yep. I told you my favorite this morning." Her expression tells me she's completely perplexed. "Indulging in you, Miss Steele. That's got to be top of my list. Any way I can get you."

She looks down at her lap, her lips twitching. "Well, that's quite high up on my list of diverting, kinky priorities, too," she says.

"I'm pleased to hear it."

"So, airfield?"

I beam at her. "Soaring. We're going to chase the dawn, Anastasia." I take a left into the airfield and drive up to the Brunswick Soaring Association hangar, where I stop the car.

"You up for this?" I ask.

"You're flying?"

"Yes."

Her face glows with excitement. "Yes please!"

I love how fearless and enthusiastic she is with any new experience. Leaning over, I kiss her quickly. "Another first, Miss Steele."

Outside it's cool but not cold, and the sky is lighter now, pearl and bright at the horizon. I walk around the car and open Ana's door. With her hand in mine we make our way to the front of the hangar.

Taylor is waiting there with a young bearded man in shorts and sandals.

"Mr. Grey, this is your tow pilot, Mr. Mark Benson," says Taylor. I release Ana so I can shake hands with Benson, who has a wild glint in his eye.

"You've got a great morning for it, Mr. Grey," Benson says. "The wind is at ten knots from the northeast, which means the convergence along the shore should keep you up for a wee while."

Benson is British, with a firm handshake.

"Sounds great," I answer and watch Ana as she shares a private joke with Taylor. "Anastasia. Come."

"See you later," she says to Taylor.

Ignoring her familiarity with my staff, I introduce her to Benson.

"Mr. Benson, this is my girlfriend, Anastasia Steele."

"Pleased to meet you," she says.

Benson gives her a bright smile as they shake hands. "Likewise," he says. "If you'd like to follow me."

"Lead the way." I take Ana's hand as we fall into step beside Benson.

"I have a Blaník L23 set up and ready. She's old school. But she handles well."

"Great. I learned to fly in a Blaník. An L13," I tell Benson.

"Can't go wrong with a Blaník. I'm a big fan." He gives me a thumbs-up. "Though I prefer the L23 for the aerobatics."

I nod in agreement.

"You're hooked up to my Piper Pawnee," he continues. "I'll take her up to three thousand feet, then set you guys free. That should give you some flying time."

"I hope so. The cloud cover looks promising."

"It's a bit early in the day for much lift. But you never know. Dave, my mate, will spot the wing. He's in the jakes."

"Okay." I think *jakes* means restroom. "You've been flying long?"

"Since my days in the RAF. But I've been flying these tail-draggers for five years now. We're on CTAF 122.3, so you know."

"Got it."

The L23 looks to be in fine shape, and I make a note of her FAA registration: November. Papa. Three. Alpha.

"First we need to strap on your parachute." Benson reaches into the cockpit and pulls out a parachute for Ana.

"I'll do that," I offer, taking the bundle from Benson before he has a chance to put it or his hands on Ana.

"I'll fetch some ballast," Benson says with a cheery smile, and he heads toward the plane.

"You like strapping me into things," Ana says with a raised brow.

"Miss Steele, you have no idea. Here, step into the straps." I hold open the leg fastenings for her. Leaning over, she puts her hand on my shoulder. I stiffen instinctively, expecting the darkness to wake and choke me, but it doesn't. It's weird. I don't know how I'm going to react where her touch is concerned. She lets go once the loops are around her thighs, and I hoist the shoulder straps up over her arms and fasten the parachute.

Boy, she looks good in a harness.

Briefly, I wonder how she'd look spread-eagled and hanging from the carabiners in the playroom, her mouth and her sex at my disposal. But alas, she's set suspension as a hard limit. "There, you'll do," I mutter, trying to banish the image from my mind. "Do you have your hair tie from yesterday?"

"You want me to put my hair up?" she asks.

"Yes."

She does as she's told. For a change.

"In you go." I steady her with my hand and she starts to climb into the back.

"No, front. The pilot sits in the back."

"But you won't be able to see."

"I'll see plenty." I'll see her enjoying herself, I hope.

She climbs in and I bend over into the cockpit to fasten her into her seat, locking the harness and tightening the straps. "Hmm, twice in one morning. I am a lucky man," I whisper and kiss her.

She beams up at me, her anticipation palpable.

"This won't take long—twenty, thirty minutes at most. Thermals aren't great this time of the morning, but it's so breathtaking up there at this hour. I hope you're not nervous."

"Excited," she says, still grinning.

"Good." I stroke her cheek with my index finger, then put on my own parachute and climb into the pilot seat.

Benson comes back carrying ballast for Ana, and he checks her straps.

"Yep, that's secure. First time?" he asks her.

"Yes."

"You'll love it."

"Thanks, Mr. Benson," Ana says.

"Call me Mark," he replies, *fucking twinkling* at her. I narrow my eyes at him. "Okay?" he asks me.

"Yep. Let's go," I say, impatient to be airborne and to get him away from my girl.

Benson nods, shuts the canopy, and ambles over to the Piper. Off to the right I notice Dave, Benson's mate, has appeared, propping up the wingtip. Quickly I test the equipment: pedals (I hear the rudder move behind me); control stick—side to side (a quick glance at the wings and I can see the ailerons moving); and control stick—front to back (I hear the elevator respond).

Right. We're ready.

Benson climbs into the Piper and almost immediately the single propeller starts up, loud and throaty in the morning quiet. A few moments later his plane is rolling forward, taking up the slack of the towrope, and we're off. I balance the ailerons and the rudder as the Piper picks up speed, then I ease back on the control stick, and we sail into the air before Benson does.

"Here we go, baby," I shout to Ana as we gain height.

"Brunswick Traffic, Delta Victor, heading two-seven-zero." It's Benson on the radio. I ignore him as we climb higher and higher. The L23 handles well, and I watch Ana; her head whips from side to side as she tries to take in the view. I wish I could see her smile.

We head west, the newborn sun behind us, and I note when we cross I-95. I love the serenity up here, away from everything and everyone, just me and the glider looking for lift…and to think I've never shared this experience with anyone before. The light is beautiful, lambent, all I had hoped it would be…for Ana and for me.

When I check the altimeter we're nearing three thousand feet and coasting at 105 knots. Benson's voice crackles over the radio, informing me that we're at three thousand feet and we can release.

"Affirmative. Release," I radio back and pull the release knob. The Piper disappears and I roll us into a slow dip, until we're heading southwest and riding the wind. Ana laughs out loud. Encouraged by her reaction, I continue to spiral, hoping we might find some convergence lift near the coastline or thermals beneath pale-pink clouds—the shallow cumulus might mean lift, even this early.

Suddenly filled with a heady combination of mischief and joy, I shout at Ana, "Hold on tight!" And I take us into a full roll. She squeals, her hands shooting up and bracing against the canopy. When I right us once more she's laughing. It is the most gratifying response a man could want, and it makes me laugh, too.

"I'm glad I didn't have breakfast!" she shouts.

"Yes, in hindsight it's good you didn't, because I'm going to do that again."

This time she holds on to the harness and stares directly down at the ground as she's suspended over it. She giggles, the noise mixing with the whistle of the wind.

"Beautiful, isn't it?" I shout.

"Yes."

I know we haven't got long, as there's not much lift out here—but I don't care. Ana is enjoying herself…and so am I.

"See the joystick in front of you? Grab hold."

She tries to turn her head, but she's buckled in too tight.

"Go on, Anastasia. Grab it," I urge her.

My joystick moves in my hands, and I know she's holding hers.

"Hold tight. Keep it steady. See the middle dial in front? Keep the needle dead center."

We continue to fly in a straight line, the yaw string staying perpendicular to the canopy.

"Good girl."

My Ana. Never backs down from a challenge. And for some bizarre reason I feel immensely proud of her.

"I am amazed you let me take control," she shouts.

"You'd be amazed what I'd let you do, Miss Steele. Back to me now."

In command of the joystick once more, I turn us in the direction of the airfield as we begin to lose altitude. I think I can land us there. I call over the radio to inform Benson and whoever might be listening that we're going to land, then I execute another circle to bring us closer to the ground.

"Hang on, baby. This can get bumpy."

I dip again and bring the L23 into line with the runway as we descend toward the grass. We land with a bump, and I manage to keep both wings up until we reach a teeth-jarring stop near the end of the runway. I unclip the canopy, open it, release my harness, and clamber out.

I stretch my limbs, undo my parachute, and smile down at the rosy-cheeked Miss Steele. "How was that?" I ask, reaching down to unbuckle her from the seat and the parachute.

"That was extraordinary. Thank you," she says, her eyes sparkling with joy.

"Was it more?" I pray she can't hear the hope in my voice.

"Much more." She beams, and I feel ten feet tall.

"Come." I hold out my hand and help her out of the cockpit. As she jumps down I fold her into my arms, pulling her against me. Filled with adrenaline, my body responds immediately to her softness. In a nanosecond my hands are in her hair, and I'm tipping her head back so I can kiss her. My hand skims down to the base of her spine, pressing her against my growing erection, and my mouth takes hers in a long, lingering, possessive kiss.

I want her.

Here.

Now.

On the grass.

She responds in kind, her fingers twisting in my hair, tugging, begging for more, as she opens up for me like a morning glory.

I break away for air and rationality.

Not in a field!

Benson and Taylor are nearby.

Her eyes are luminous, pleading for more.

Don't look at me like that, Ana.

"Breakfast," I whisper before I do something I'll regret. Turning, I clasp her hand and walk back toward the car.

"What about the glider?" she asks as she tries to keep up with me.

"Someone will take care of that." It's what I pay Taylor to do. "We'll eat now. Come."

She bounces along beside me, brimming with happiness; I don't know if I've ever seen her so buoyant. Her mood is infectious and I don't remember if I've ever felt this upbeat, either. I can't help my big, fat grin as I hold the car door open for her.

With Kings of Leon belting from the sound system I ease the Mustang out of the airfield toward I-95.

As we cruise along the freeway, Ana's BlackBerry starts beeping.

"What's that?" I ask.

"Alarm for my pill," she mutters.

"Good, well done. I hate condoms."

From the sideways look I give her, I think she's rolling her eyes, but I'm not sure.

"I like that you introduced me to Mark as your girlfriend," she says, changing the subject.

"Isn't that what you are?"

"Am I? I thought you wanted a submissive."

"So did I, Anastasia, and I do. But I've told you, I want more, too."

"I'm very happy you want more," she says.

"We aim to please, Miss Steele," I tease as I pull into the International House of Pancakes—my father's guilty pleasure.

"IHOP?" she says in disbelief.

The Mustang rumbles to a stop. "I hope you're hungry."

"I would never have pictured you here."

"My dad used to bring us to one of these whenever my mom went away to a medical conference." We shuffle into a booth, facing each other. "It was our secret." I pick up a menu, watching Ana as she tucks her hair behind her ears and examines what IHOP has to offer for breakfast. She licks her lips in anticipation. And I'm forced to suppress my physical reaction. "I know what I want," I whisper and wonder how she would feel visiting the restroom with me. Her eyes meet mine, and her pupils expand.

"I want what you want," she murmurs. As ever, Miss Steele does not back away from a challenge.

"Here?" *Are you sure, Ana?* Her eyes dart around the quiet restaurant, then come to rest on me, darkening and full of carnal promise.

"Don't bite your lip," I warn. Much as I'd like to, I'm not going to fuck her in the restroom at IHOP. She deserves better than that, and frankly, so do I. "Not here, not now. If I can't have you here, don't tempt me."

We're interrupted.

"Hi, my name's Leandra. What can I get for you…er…folks… er…today, this mornin'?"

Oh God. I ignore the redheaded server.

"Anastasia?" I prompt her.

"I told you, I want what you want."

Hell. She might as well be addressing my groin.

"Shall I give you folks another minute to decide?" the waitress asks.

"No. We know what we want." I cannot tear my gaze from Ana's. "We'll have two portions of the original buttermilk pancakes with maple syrup and bacon on the side, two glasses of orange juice, one black coffee with skim milk, and one English Breakfast tea, if you have it."

Ana smiles.

"Thank you, sir. Will that be all?" the waitress exclaims, all breathy and embarrassed.

Tearing my attention away from Ana, I dismiss the waitress with a look and she scurries away.

"You know, it's really not fair," Ana says, her voice quiet as her finger traces a figure eight on the table.

"What's not fair?"

"How you disarm people. Women. Me."

"Do I disarm you?" I'm stunned.

"All the time."

"It's just looks, Anastasia."

"No, Christian, it's much more than that."

She has this the wrong way around, and once again I tell her how disarming I find her.

Her brow furrows. "Is that why you've changed your mind?"

"Changed my mind?"

"Yes—about…er…us?"

Have I changed my mind? I think I've just relaxed my boundaries a little, that's all. "I don't think I've changed my mind per se. We just need to redefine our parameters, redraw our battle lines, if you will. We can make this work, I'm sure. I want you submissive in my playroom. I will punish you if you digress from the rules.

Other than that…well, I think it's all up for discussion. Those are my requirements, Miss Steele. What say you to that?"

"So I get to sleep with you? In your bed?"

"Is that what you want?"

"Yes."

"I agree, then. Besides, I sleep very well when you're in my bed. I had no idea."

"I was frightened you'd leave me if I didn't agree to all of it," she says, her face a little pale.

"I'm not going anywhere, Anastasia. Besides…" *How can she think that?* I need to reassure her. "We're following your advice, your definition: compromise. You emailed it to me. And so far, it's working for me."

"I love that you want more."

"I know." My tone is warm.

"How do you know?"

"Trust me. I just do." *You told me in your sleep.*

The waitress returns with our breakfast and I watch Ana devour it. "More" seems to be working for her.

"This is delicious," she says.

"I like that you're hungry."

"Must have been all the exercise last night and the thrill this morning."

"It was a thrill, wasn't it?"

"It was mighty fine, Mr. Grey," she says as she pops the final piece of pancake into her mouth. "Can I treat you?" she adds.

"Treat me how?"

"Pay for this meal."

I snort. "I don't think so."

"Please. I want to."

"Are you trying to completely emasculate me?" I raise an eyebrow in warning.

"This is probably the only place that I'll be able to afford to pay."

"Anastasia, I appreciate the thought. I do. But no."

She purses her lips with irritation when I ask the redhead for the check.

"Don't scowl," I warn and check the time: it's 8:30. I have a meeting at 11:15 with the Savannah Brownfield Redevelopment Authority, so unfortunately we have to get back to the city. I contemplate canceling the meeting, because I'd like to spend the day with Ana, but no, that's too much. I'm running after this girl when I should be concentrating on my business.

Priorities, Grey.

With her hand in mine, we head to the car looking like any other couple. She's swamped in my sweatshirt, looking casual, relaxed, beautiful—and yes, she's with me. Three guys strolling into IHOP check her out; she's oblivious even when I put my arm around her to stake my claim. She really has no idea how lovely she is. I open her car door and she gives me a sunny smile.

I could get used to this.

I program her mother's address into the GPS and we set off north on I-95, listening to the Foo Fighters. Ana's feet tap to the beat. This is the sort of music she likes—all-American rock. The traffic on the freeway is heavier now, with commuters heading into the city. But I don't care: I like being here with her, spending time. Holding her hand, touching her knee, watching her smile. She tells me about previous visits to Savannah; she's not big on the heat, either, but her eyes light up when she talks about her mother. It'll be interesting to see her interacting with her mother and stepfather this evening.

I pull up outside her mother's home with some regret. I wish we could play hooky all day; the last twelve hours have been…nice.

More than nice, Grey. Sublime.

"Do you want to come in?" she asks.

"I need to work, Anastasia, but I'll be back this evening. What time?"

She suggests seven, then looks from her hands to me, her eyes bright and joyful. "Thank you…for the more."

"My pleasure, Anastasia." I lean over and kiss her, inhaling her sweet, sweet scent.

"I'll see you later."

"Try to stop me," I whisper.

She climbs out of the car, still in my sweatshirt, and waves goodbye. I head back to the hotel, feeling a little emptier now that she's not with me.

IN MY ROOM, I call Taylor.

"Mr. Grey."

"Yeah…thanks for organizing this morning."

"You're most welcome, sir." He sounds surprised.

"I'll be ready to leave at ten forty-five for the meeting."

"I'll have the Suburban waiting outside."

"Thanks."

I change out of my jeans and into my suit but leave my favorite tie beside my laptop as I order up coffee from room service.

I work through my emails, drink coffee, and consider calling Ros; however, it's too early for her. I read through all the paperwork that Bill has sent: Savannah does make a good case for siting the plant here. I check my inbox, and there's a new message from Ana.

From: Anastasia Steele
Subject: Soaring as Opposed to Sore-ing
Date: June 2 2011 10:20 ET
To: Christian Grey

Sometimes, you really know how to show a girl a good time.

Thank you.

Ana x

The title makes me laugh and the kiss makes me feel ten feet tall. I type up my response.

From: Christian Grey
Subject: Soaring vs Sore-ing
Date: June 2 2011 10:24 ET
To: Anastasia Steele

I'll take either of those over your snoring. I had a good time, too.

But I always do when I'm with you.

Christian Grey
CEO, Grey Enterprises Holdings, Inc.

Her answer is almost immediate.

From: Anastasia Steele
Subject: SNORING
Date: June 2 2011 10:26 ET
To: Christian Grey

I DO NOT SNORE. And if I do, it's very ungallant of you to point it out.

You are no gentleman, Mr. Grey! And you are in the Deep South, too!

Ana

I chuckle.

From: Christian Grey
Subject: Somniloquy
Date: June 2 2011 10:28 ET
To: Anastasia Steele

I have never claimed to be a gentleman, Anastasia, and I think I have demonstrated that point to you on numerous occasions. I am not intimidated by your SHOUTY capitals. But I will confess to a small white lie: no—you don't snore, but you do talk. And it's fascinating.

What happened to my kiss?

Christian Grey
Cad & CEO, Grey Enterprises Holdings, Inc.

This will drive her crazy.

From: Anastasia Steele
Subject: Spill the Beans
Date: June 2 2011 10:32 ET
To: Christian Grey

You are a cad and a scoundrel—definitely no gentleman.

So, what did I say? No kisses for you until you talk!

Oh, this could run and run…

From: Christian Grey
Subject: Sleeping Talking Beauty
Date: June 2 2011 10:35 ET
To: Anastasia Steele

It would be most ungallant of me to say, and I have already been chastised for that.

But if you behave yourself, I may tell you this evening. I have to go into a meeting now.

Laters, baby.

Christian Grey
CEO, Cad & Scoundrel, Grey Enterprises Holdings, Inc.

With a broad grin I slip on my tie, grab my jacket, and head downstairs to find Taylor.

JUST OVER AN HOUR later, I'm winding up my meeting with the Savannah Brownfield Redevelopment Authority. Georgia has a great deal to offer, and the team has promised GEH some serious tax incentives.

There's a knock at the door and Taylor enters the small conference room. His face looks grim, but what's more worrying is that he never, ever interrupts my meetings. My scalp prickles.

Ana? Is she okay?

"Excuse me, ladies and gentlemen," he says to all of us.

"Yes, Taylor," I ask, and he approaches and speaks discreetly in my ear.

"We have a situation at home concerning Miss Leila Williams."

Leila? What the hell? And part of me is relieved it's not Ana.

"Would you excuse me please?" I ask the two men and two women from the SBRA.

In the hallway, Taylor's tone is grave as he apologizes once more for interrupting my meeting.

"Don't worry. Tell me what's happened."

"Miss Williams is in an ambulance on the way to the ER at Seattle Free Hope."

"Ambulance?"

"Yes, sir. She broke into the apartment and made a suicide attempt in front of Mrs. Jones."

Fuck. "Suicide?" *Leila? In my apartment?*

"She slashed her wrist. Gail went with her in the ambulance. She's informed me that the EMTs arrived in time and Miss Williams is not in any immediate danger."

"Why Escala? Why in front of Gail?" I'm shocked.

Taylor shakes his head. "I don't know, sir. Neither does Gail. She can't get any sense out of Miss Williams. Apparently, she only wants to talk to you."

"Fuck."

"Exactly, sir," Taylor says without judgment.

I scrape my hands through my hair, trying to grasp the magnitude of what Leila has done. What the hell am I supposed to do? Why did she come to me? Was she expecting to see me? Where's her husband? What's happened to him?

"How's Gail?"

"A little shaken."

"I'm not surprised."

"I thought you should know, sir."

"Yes. Sure. Thanks," I mumble, distracted. I can't believe it; Leila seemed happy when she last emailed…what, six or seven months ago. But there are no answers for me here in Georgia—I have to go back and talk to her. Find out why. "Tell Stephan to ready the jet. I need to go home."

"Will do."

"Let's leave as soon as we can."

"I'll be in the car."

"Thank you."

Taylor heads toward the exit, raising the phone to his ear.

I'm reeling.

Leila. What the hell?

She's been out of my life for a couple of years. We've shared the occasional email. She got married. She seemed happy. What's happened?

I head back into the boardroom and make my apologies before stepping outside into the stifling heat, where Taylor is waiting in the Suburban.

"The plane will be ready in forty-five minutes. We can head back to the hotel, pack, and go," he informs me.

"Good," I respond, grateful for the car's air-conditioning. "I should call Gail."

"I've tried, but her phone goes to voice mail. I think she's still at the hospital."

"Okay, I'll call her later." This is not what Gail needs on a Thursday morning. "How did Leila get into the apartment?"

"I don't know, sir." Taylor makes eye contact with me in the rearview mirror, his face apologetic and grim at once. "I'll make it a priority to find out."

OUR BAGS ARE PACKED and we're on our way to Savannah/Hilton Head International when I call Ana, but frustratingly, she doesn't answer. I brood, staring out the window as we cruise toward the airport. I don't have to wait long for her to return my call.

"Anastasia."

"Hi," she says, her voice breathy, and it's such a pleasure to hear her.

"I have to return to Seattle. Something's come up. I am on my way to the airport now. Please apologize to your mother—I can't make dinner."

"Nothing serious, I hope?"

"I have a situation I have to deal with. I'll see you tomorrow. I'll send Taylor to meet you at Sea-Tac if I can't come myself."

"Okay." She sighs. "I hope you sort out your situation. Have a safe flight."

I wish I didn't have to go.

"You, too, baby," I whisper and hang up before I change my mind and stay.

I CALL ROS AS we taxi toward the runway.

"Christian, how's Savannah?"

"I'm on the plane coming home. I have a problem I have to deal with."

"Something at GEH?" Ros asks, alarmed.

"No. It's personal."

"Anything I can do?"

"No. I'll see you tomorrow."

"How did your meeting go?"

"Positive. But I had to cut it short. Let's see what they put in writing. I might prefer Detroit just because it's cooler."

"The heat's that bad?"

"Suffocating. I've got to go. I'll call for an update later."

"Safe travels, Christian."

ON THE FLIGHT I throw myself into work to distract me from the problem waiting at home. By the time we've touched down I've read three reports and written fifteen emails. Our car is waiting, and Taylor drives through the pouring rain straight to Seattle Free Hope. I have to see Leila and find out what the hell is going on. As we near the hospital my anger surfaces.

Why would she do this to me?

The rain is lashing down as I climb out of the car; the day is as bleak as my mood. I take a deep breath to control my fury and head through the front doors. At the reception desk I ask for Leila Reed.

"Are you family?" The nurse on duty glowers at me, her mouth pinched and sour.

"No." I sigh. This is going to be difficult.

"Well, I'm sorry. I can't help you."

"She tried to open a vein in my apartment. I think I'm entitled to know where the hell she is," I hiss through my teeth.

"Don't take that tone with me!" she snaps.

I glare at her. I'm not going to get anywhere with this woman. "Where is your ER department?"

"Sir, there's nothing we can do if you're not family."

"Don't worry, I'll find it myself," I growl and storm over to the double doors. I know I could call my mother, who would expedite this for me, but then I'd have to explain what's happened.

The ER is bustling with doctors and nurses, and triage is full of patients. I accost a young nurse and give her my brightest smile. "Hello, I'm looking for Leila Reed—she was admitted earlier today. Can you tell me where she might be?"

"And you are?" she asks, a flush creeping over her face.

"I'm her brother," I lie smoothly, ignoring her reaction.

"This way, Mr. Reed." She bustles over to the nurses' station and checks her computer. "She's on the second floor, Behavioral Health ward. Take the elevators at the end of the corridor."

"Thanks." I reward her with a wink and she pushes a stray lock behind her ear, giving me a flirtatious smile that reminds me of a certain girl I left in Georgia.

As I step out of the elevator on the second floor I know something is wrong. On the other side of what look like locked doors, two security guards and a nurse are combing the corridor, checking each room. My scalp prickles, but I walk over to the reception area, pretending not to notice the commotion.

"Can I help you?" asks a young man with a ring through his nose.

"I'm looking for Leila Reed. I'm her brother."

He pales. "Oh. Mr. Reed. Can you come with me?"

I follow him to a waiting room and sit down on the plastic chair that he points to; I note it's bolted to the floor. "The doctor will be with you shortly."

"Why can't I see her?" I ask.

"The doctor will explain," he says, his expression guarded, and he exits before I can ask any further questions.

Shit. Perhaps I'm too late.

The thought nauseates me. I get up and pace the small room, contemplating a call to Gail, but I don't have to wait long. A young man with short dreads and dark, intelligent eyes enters. Is he her doctor?

"Mr. Reed?" he asks.

"Where's Leila?"

He assesses me for a moment, then sighs and steels himself. "I'm afraid I don't know," he says. "She's managed to give us the slip."

"What?"

"She's gone. How she got out I don't know."

"Got out?" I exclaim in disbelief and sink onto one of the chairs.

He sits down opposite me. "Yes. She's disappeared. We're doing a search for her now."

"She's still here?"

"We don't know."

"And who are you?" I ask.

"I'm Dr. Azikiwe, the on-call psychiatrist."

He looks too young to be a psychiatrist. "What can you tell me about Leila?" I ask.

"Well, she was admitted after a failed suicide attempt. She tried to slash one of her wrists at an ex-boyfriend's house. His housekeeper brought her here."

I feel the blood draining from my face. "And?" I ask. I need more information.

"That's about as much as we know. She said it was an error of judgment, that she was fine, but we wanted to keep her here under observation and ask her further questions."

"Did you talk to her?"

"I did."

"Why did she do this?"

"She said it was a cry for help. Nothing more. And, having made such a spectacle of herself, she was embarrassed and wanted to go home. She said she didn't want to kill herself. I believed her. I suspect it was just suicidal ideation on her part."

"How could you let her escape?" I run my hand through my hair, trying to contain my frustration.

"I don't know how she's gotten away. There'll be an internal investigation. If she contacts you, I suggest you urge her to come back. She needs help. Can I ask you some questions?"

"Sure," I agree, distracted.

"Is there any history of mental illness in your family?"

I frown, then remember that he's talking about Leila's family. "I don't know. My family is very private about such matters."

He looks concerned. "Do you know anything about this ex-boyfriend?"

"No," I state a little too quickly. "Have you contacted her husband?"

The doctor's eyes widen. "She's married?"

"Yes."

"That's not what she told us."

"Oh. Well, I'll call him. I won't waste any more of your time."

"But I have more questions for you—"

"I'd rather spend my time looking for her. She's obviously in a bad way." I rise.

"But this husband—"

"I'll get in touch with him." This is getting me nowhere.

"But we should do that—" Dr. Azikiwe stands.

"I can't help you. I need to find her." I head to the door.

"Mr. Reed—"

"Goodbye," I mutter, hurrying out of the waiting room and not bothering with the elevator. I take the fire escape stairs two at a time. I loathe hospitals. A memory from my childhood surfaces: I'm small and scared and mute, and the smell of disinfectant and blood clouds my nostrils.

I shudder.

As I step out of the hospital I stand for a moment and let the torrential rain wash that memory away. It's been a stressful afternoon, but at least the rain is a refreshing relief from the heat in Savannah. Taylor swings around to pick me up in the SUV.

"Home," I direct him as I get back in the car. Once I've buckled my seat belt I call Welch from my cell.

"Mr. Grey," he growls.

"Welch, I have a problem. I need you to locate Leila Reed, née Williams."

GAIL IS PALE AND quiet as she studies me with concern. "You're not going to finish, sir?" she asks.

I shake my head.

"Was the food okay?"

"Yes, of course." I give her a small smile. "After today's events, I'm not hungry. How are you bearing up?"

"I'm good, Mr. Grey. It was a total shock. I just want to keep busy."

"I hear you. Thanks for making dinner. If you remember anything, let me know."

"Of course. But like I said, she only wanted to speak to you."

Why? What is she expecting me to do?

"Thanks for not involving the police."

"The police are not what that girl needs. She needs help."

"She does. I wish I knew where she was."

"You'll find her," she says with quiet confidence, surprising me.

"Do you need anything?" I ask.

"No, Mr. Grey. I'm fine." She takes the plate with my half-eaten meal to the sink.

The news from Welch about Leila is frustrating. The trail has gone cold. She's not at the hospital, and they're still mystified as to how she escaped. A small part of me admires that; she was always resourceful. But what could have made her so unhappy? I rest my head in my hands. What a day—from the sublime to the ridiculous. Soaring with Ana, and now this mess to deal with. Taylor is at a loss as to how Leila got into the apartment, and Gail has no idea, either. Apparently, Leila marched into the kitchen demanding to know where I was. And when Gail said I wasn't there, she cried out "He's gone," then slashed her wrist with a box cutter. Fortunately, the cut wasn't deep.

I glance at Gail cleaning up in the kitchen. My blood runs cold. Leila could have hurt her. Perhaps Leila's objective was to hurt me. *But why?* I scrunch my eyes, trying to remember if anything in our last correspondence might give me a clue as to why she's gone off the rails. I draw a blank, exasperated, and with a sigh I head into my study.

As I sit down my phone buzzes with a text.

Ana?

It's Elliot.

Hey hotshot. Wanna shoot some pool?

Shooting pool with Elliot means him coming here and drinking all my beer. Frankly, I'm not in the mood.

Working. Next week?

Sure. Before I hit the beach.
I'll thrash you.
Laters.

I toss my phone onto the desk and pore over Leila's file, looking for anything that might give me a clue as to where she is. I find her parents' address and phone number, but nothing for her husband. Where is he? Why isn't she with him?

I don't want to call her parents and alarm them. I call Welch and give him their number; he can find out if she's been in touch with them.

When I switch on my iMac there's an email from Ana.

From: Anastasia Steele
Subject: Safe Arrival?
Date: June 2 2011 22:32 ET
To: Christian Grey

Dear Sir,
Please let me know that you have arrived safely. I am starting to worry. Thinking of you.

Your Ana x

Before I know it, my finger is on the little kiss she's sent me.

Ana.

Sappy, Grey. Sappy. Get a grip.

From: Christian Grey
Subject: Sorry
Date: June 2 2011 19:36
To: Anastasia Steele

Dear Miss Steele,
I have arrived safely, and please accept my apologies for not letting you know. I don't want to cause you any worry. It's heartwarming to know that you care for me. I am thinking of you, too, and as ever looking forward to seeing you tomorrow.

Christian Grey
CEO, Grey Enterprises Holdings, Inc.

I press send and wish she were here with me. She brightens up my home, my life…me. I shake my head at my fanciful thoughts and look through the rest of my emails.

A ping tells me there's a new one from Ana.

From: Anastasia Steele
Subject: The Situation
Date: June 2 2011 22:40 ET
To: Christian Grey

Dear Mr. Grey,
I think it is very evident that I care for you deeply. How could you doubt that?

I hope your "situation" is under control.

Your Ana x

P.S. Are you going to tell me what I said in my sleep?

She cares for me deeply? That's nice. All at once that foreign feeling, absent all day, stirs and expands in my chest. Beneath it is a well of pain I don't want to acknowledge or deal with. It tugs at a lost memory of a young woman brushing out her long, dark hair…

Fuck.

Don't go there, Grey.

I respond to Ana's email—and as a distraction decide to tease her.

From: Christian Grey
Subject: Pleading the Fifth
Date: June 2 2011 19:45
To: Anastasia Steele

Dear Miss Steele,
I like very much that you care for me. The "situation" here is not yet resolved.

With regard to your P.S., the answer is no.

Christian Grey
CEO, Grey Enterprises Holdings, Inc.

From: Anastasia Steele
Subject: Pleading Insanity
Date: June 2 2011 22:48 ET
To: Christian Grey

I hope it was amusing. But you should know I cannot accept any responsibility for what comes out of my mouth when I am unconscious. In fact—you probably misheard me.

A man of your advanced years is surely a little deaf.

For the first time since I got back to Seattle, I laugh. What a welcome distraction she is.

From: Christian Grey
Subject: Pleading Guilty
Date: June 2 2011 19:52
To: Anastasia Steele

Dear Miss Steele,
Sorry, could you speak up? I can't hear you.

Christian Grey
CEO, Grey Enterprises Holdings, Inc.

Her response is swift.

From: Anastasia Steele
Subject: Pleading Insanity Again
Date: June 2 2011 22:54 ET
To: Christian Grey

You are driving me crazy.

I like driving her crazy.

From: Christian Grey
Subject: I Hope So...
Date: June 2 2011 19:59
To: Anastasia Steele

Dear Miss Steele,
I intend to do exactly that on Friday evening. Looking forward to it.

;)

Christian Grey
CEO, Grey Enterprises Holdings, Inc.

I'll have to think of something extra-special for my little freak.

From: Anastasia Steele
Subject: Grrrrrr
Date: June 2 2011 23:02 ET
To: Christian Grey

I am officially pissed at you.

Good night.

Miss A. R. Steele

Whoa. Would I tolerate this from anyone else?

From: Christian Grey
Subject: Wild Cat
Date: June 2 2011 20:05
To: Anastasia Steele

Are you growling at me, Miss Steele?

I possess a cat of my own for growlers.

Christian Grey
CEO, Grey Enterprises Holdings, Inc.

She doesn't respond. Five minutes go by and nothing. Six… Seven.

Damn. She means it. How can I tell her that while she slept she said she wouldn't leave me? She'll think I'm crazy.

From: Christian Grey
Subject: What You Said in Your Sleep
Date: June 2 2011 20:20
To: Anastasia Steele

Anastasia,
I'd rather hear you say the words that you uttered in your sleep when you're conscious. That's why I won't tell you. Go to sleep. You'll need to be rested, with what I have in mind for you tomorrow.

Christian Grey
CEO, Grey Enterprises Holdings, Inc.

She doesn't respond; I hope for once she's doing what she's told and she's asleep. Briefly I think of what we could do tomorrow, but it's too arousing, so I push the thought aside and concentrate on my emails.

But I have to confess I feel a little lighter after some email banter with Miss Steele. She's good for my dark, dark soul.

FRIDAY, JUNE 3, 2011

I can't sleep. It's after two and I've been staring at the ceiling for an hour. It's not my sleeping nightmares that are keeping me awake tonight. It's a waking one.

Leila Williams.

The smoke detector on my ceiling is winking at me, its flashing green light mocking me.

Hell!

I close my eyes and let my thoughts run free.

Why was Leila suicidal? What possessed her? Her desperate unhappiness resonates with a younger, miserable me. I'm trying to quash my memories, but the anger and desolation of my solitary teen years resurfaces and it won't go away. It reminds me of my pain and of how I lashed out at everyone during my youth. Suicide crossed my mind often, but I always held back. I resisted for Grace. I knew she'd be devastated. I knew she would blame herself if I took my life, and she'd done so much for me—how could I hurt her like that? And after I met Elena…everything changed.

Rising from the bed, I push these disquieting thoughts to the back of my mind. I need the piano.

I need Ana.

If she'd signed the contract and everything had gone according to plan, she would be with me, upstairs, asleep. I could wake her and lose myself in her…or, under our new arrangement, she would be beside me, and I could fuck her and then watch her sleep.

What would she make of Leila?

As I sit down on the piano bench I know Ana will never meet

Leila, which is a good thing. I know how she feels about Elena. Lord knows how she'd feel about an ex...a wayward ex.

This is what I can't reconcile: Leila was happy, mischievous, and bright when I knew her. She was an excellent submissive; I thought she'd settled down and was happily married. Her emails never indicated that anything was awry. What went wrong?

I start to play...and my troubled thoughts recede until it's just the music and me.

Leila is servicing my cock with her mouth.

Her skilled mouth.

Her hands are tied behind her back.

Her hair braided.

She's on her knees.

Eyes cast down. Modest. Alluring.

Not seeing me.

And suddenly she's Ana.

Ana on her knees before me. Naked. Beautiful.

My cock in her mouth.

But Ana's eyes are on mine.

Her blazing blue eyes see everything.

See me. My soul.

She sees the darkness and the monster beneath.

Her eyes widen in horror and suddenly she disappears.

Shit! I wake with a start, and with a painful erection that wanes as soon as I recall Ana's wounded look in my dream.

What the hell?

I rarely have erotic dreams. *Why now?* I check my alarm; I've beaten it by a few minutes.

The morning sunlight is creeping between the buildings as I rise. Already I'm restless, no doubt as a result of my disturbing dream, so I decide to go for a run to burn off some energy. There are no new emails, no messages, no updates on Leila. The apartment is quiet as I leave. There's no sign of Gail yet. I hope she's recovered from yesterday's ordeal.

I open the glass doors in the lobby, step outside into a balmy, sunny morning, and carefully scan the street. As I start my run I check down the alleys and in the doorways I pass, and behind the parked cars, to see if Leila is there.

Where are you, Leila Williams?

I turn the volume up on the Foo Fighters and my feet pound the sidewalk.

OLIVIA IS EXCEPTIONALLY IRRITATING today. She's spilled my coffee, dropped an important call, and keeps mooning at me with her big brown eyes.

"Get Ros back on the line," I bark at her. "Better still, get her up here." I shut my office door and go back to my desk; I must try not to take my temper out on my staff.

Welch has no news, except that Leila's parents think their daughter is still in Portland with her husband. There's a knock on my door.

"Come in." I hope to God it's not Olivia.

Ros pokes her head around. "You wanted to see me?"

"Yes. Sure. Come in. Where are we with Woods?"

ROS EXITS JUST BEFORE ten. All is on track: Woods has decided to accept the deal, and the aid for Darfur will soon be on the road to Munich in preparation for the airlift. There's no news yet from Savannah about their offer.

I check my inbox and find a welcome email from Ana.

From: Anastasia Steele
Subject: Homeward Bound
Date: June 3 2011 12:53 ET
To: Christian Grey

Dear Mr. Grey,
I am once again ensconced in first class, for which I thank you. I am counting the minutes until I see you this evening

and perhaps torturing the truth out of you about my
nocturnal admissions.

Your Ana x

Torturing me? *Oh, Miss Steele, I think it will be the other way around.* As I have a great deal to do, I keep my reply short.

From: Christian Grey
Subject: Homeward Bound
Date: June 3 2011 09:58
To: Anastasia Steele

Anastasia, I look forward to seeing you.

Christian Grey
CEO, Grey Enterprises Holdings, Inc.

But Ana is not satisfied.

From: Anastasia Steele
Subject: Homeward Bound
Date: June 3 2011 13:01 ET
To: Christian Grey

Dearest Mr. Grey,
I hope everything is okay re "the situation." The tone of your email is worrying.

Ana x

At least I still earned a kiss. Surely she should be airborne by now?

From: Christian Grey
Subject: Homeward Bound
Date: June 3 2011 10:04
To: Anastasia Steele

Anastasia,
The situation could be better. Have you taken off yet? If so, you should not be emailing. You are putting yourself at risk, in direct contravention of the rule regarding your personal safety. I meant what I said about punishments.

Christian Grey
CEO, Grey Enterprises Holdings, Inc.

I'm about to call Welch for an update, but there's a ping—Ana again.

From: Anastasia Steele
Subject: Overreaction
Date: June 3 2011 13:06 ET
To: Christian Grey

Dear Mr. Grumpy,
The aircraft doors are still open. We are delayed but only by ten minutes. My welfare and that of the passengers around me is vouchsafed. You may stow your twitchy palm for now.

Miss Steele

A reluctant smile tugs at my lips. *Mr. Grumpy, eh?* And no kiss. *Oh dear.*

From: Christian Grey
Subject: Apologies—Twitchy Palm Stowed
Date: June 3 2011 10:08
To: Anastasia Steele

I miss you and your smart mouth, Miss Steele.

I want you safely home.

Christian Grey
CEO, Grey Enterprises Holdings, Inc.

From: Anastasia Steele
Subject: Apology Accepted
Date: June 3 2011 13:10 ET
To: Christian Grey

They are shutting the doors. You won't hear another peep from me, especially given your deafness.

Laters.

Ana x

My kiss is back. *Well, that's a relief.* Grudgingly, I drag myself away from the computer screen and pick up my phone to call Welch.

AT ONE O'CLOCK I decline Andrea's offer of lunch at my desk. I need to get out. The walls of my office are closing in on me, and I think it's because there's been no news about Leila.

I'm worried about her. *Hell, she came to see me.* She decided to use my home as her stage. How could I not take this personally? Why didn't she email me or phone? If she was in trouble, I could have helped. I would have helped—I've done it before.

I need some fresh air. I march past Olivia and Andrea, who both look busy, though I catch Andrea's puzzled look as I step into the elevator.

Outside, it's a bright, bustling afternoon. I take a deep breath and detect the soothing tang of salt water from the Sound. Perhaps I should take the rest of the day off? But I can't. I have a meeting with the mayor this afternoon. It's irritating—I'm seeing him tomorrow at the Chamber of Commerce gala.

The gala!

Suddenly I have an idea, and with a renewed sense of purpose I head toward a small store I know.

AFTER MY MEETING AT the mayor's office, I walk the ten or so blocks back to Escala; Taylor has gone to collect Ana from the airport. Gail is in the kitchen when I enter the living room.

"Good evening, Mr. Grey."

"Hi, Gail. How was your day?"

"Good, thank you, sir."

"Feeling better?"

"Yes, sir. The clothes arrived for Miss Steele. I unpacked them and hung them in the closet in her room."

"Great. No sign of Leila?" Dumb question: Gail would have called me.

"No, sir. This also arrived." She holds up a small red store bag.

"Good." I take the bag from her, ignoring the delighted twinkle in her eye.

"How many for supper this evening?"

"Two, thanks. And Gail—"

"Sir?"

"Can you put the satin sheets on the playroom bed?"

I really hope to get Ana in there at some point over the weekend. "Yes, Mr. Grey," she says, her tone a little surprised. She turns back to whatever she's conjuring in the kitchen, leaving me a little baffled by her behavior.

Maybe Gail doesn't approve, but it's what I want from Ana.

In my study I take the Cartier box from its bag. It's a present for Ana, which I'll give to her tomorrow in time for the gala: a pair of earrings. Simple. Elegant. Beautiful. Just like her. I smile. Even in her Chucks and jeans she has a certain gamine charm.

I hope she accepts my gift. As my submissive, she'd have no choice, but under our alternative arrangement, I don't know what her reaction will be. Whatever the outcome, it will be interesting. She always surprises me. As I put the box in my desk drawer a ping on my computer distracts me. Barney's latest tablet designs are in my inbox, and I'm eager to see them.

Five minutes later, Welch calls.

"Mr. Grey," he wheezes.

"Yes. What news?"

"I spoke with Russell Reed, Mrs. Reed's husband."

"And?" Immediately I'm agitated. I storm out of my study and across the living room to the windows.

"He says his wife is away visiting her parents," Welch reports.

"What?"

"Precisely." Welch sounds as pissed as I am.

Seeing Seattle at my feet, knowing Mrs. Reed a.k.a. Leila Williams is out there somewhere, increases my irritation.

I rake my fingers through my hair. "Maybe that's what she told him."

"Maybe," he says. "But we've found nothing so far."

"No trace?" I can't believe she could just disappear.

"Nothing. But if she so much as uses an ATM, cashes a check, or logs in to her social media, we'll find her."

"Okay."

"We'd like to scour the CCTV footage from around the hospital. It's going to cost money and take a little longer. Is that acceptable?"

"Yes." A tingle prickles my scalp—and not from the call. For some unknown reason I sense I'm being watched. Turning, I see

Ana standing on the threshold of the room, scrutinizing me, her brow furrowed and her lips pensive, and she's wearing a short, short skirt. She's all eyes and legs...especially legs. I imagine them wrapped around my waist.

Desire, raw and real, fires my blood as I stare.

"We'll get right on it," Welch says.

I finish up with him, my eyes fixed on Ana's, and I prowl toward her, stripping off my jacket and tie and tossing them onto the sofa.

Ana.

I wrap my arms around her, tugging at her ponytail, lifting her eager lips to mine. She tastes of heaven and home and fall and Ana. Her scent invades my nostrils as I take everything her warm, sweet mouth has to offer. My body hardens with expectation and hunger as our tongues entwine. I want to lose myself in her, to forget about the shitty end to my week, forget about everything but her.

My lips feverish against hers, I tug the hair tie from her ponytail as her fingers knot in mine. I'm suddenly overwhelmed by my need, desperate for her. And I pull away, staring down into a face that's dazed with passion.

I feel the same way. *What is she doing to me?*

"What's wrong?" she whispers.

And the answer is clear, ringing in my head.

I've missed you.

"I'm so glad you're back. Shower with me. Now."

"Yes," she responds, her voice hoarse.

I take her hand and we head to my bathroom. I turn on the shower, then face her. She's gorgeous, her eyes bright and gleaming with anticipation as she watches me. My gaze rakes down her body to her naked legs. I've never seen her in such a short skirt, with so much of her flesh on display, and I'm not sure I approve. *She's for my eyes only.*

"I like your skirt. It's very short." *Too short.* "You have great legs." Stepping out of my shoes, I take off my socks, and without breaking eye contact, she, too, slips off her shoes.

Fuck the shower. I want her now.

Stepping toward her, I clasp her head, and we step back so she's against the tiled wall, her lips parting as she inhales. Holding her face and lacing my fingers into her hair, I kiss her: her cheek, her throat, her mouth. She's nectar and I can't get enough. Her breath catches in her throat and she grasps my arms, but at her touch there's no protest from the darkness within. There's just Ana, in all her beauty and innocence, kissing me back with a fervor that matches mine.

My blood is thick with desire, my erection painful. "I want you now. Here…fast, hard," I murmur as my hand runs up her naked thigh beneath her skirt. "Are you still bleeding?"

"No."

"Good." I push her skirt up over her hips, hook both thumbs into her cotton panties and drop to the floor, kneeling, slipping the panties down her legs.

She gasps when I grab her hips and kiss the sweet junction beneath her pubic hair. Moving my hands to the backs of her thighs, I part her legs, exposing her clitoris to my tongue. When I start my sensual assault her fingers dive into my hair. My tongue torments her, and she moans and tips her head back against the wall.

She smells exquisite. She tastes better.

As she purrs she tilts her pelvis toward my invading, insistent tongue, and her legs begin to tremble.

Enough. I want to come inside her.

It will be my skin against her skin again, like in Savannah. Releasing her, I stand and grasp her face, capturing her surprised and disappointed mouth with mine, kissing her hard. I unzip my fly and lift her, clutching her under her thighs. "Wrap your legs around me, baby." My voice is rough and urgent. As soon as she does, I thrust forward, sliding into her.

She's mine. She's heaven.

Clinging to me, she whimpers as I plunge into her—slowly at first, then building as my body takes control, driving me forward, driving me into her, faster and faster, harder and harder, my face at her throat. She moans and I feel her quicken around me, and I'm lost, in her, in us, as she climaxes, crying out her release. The feel of her pulsing around me tips me over the edge and I come deep and hard inside her, growling out a garbled version of her name.

I kiss her throat, not wanting to withdraw, waiting for her to calm. We're in a cloud of steam from the shower, and my shirt and pants are sticking to my body, but I don't care.

Ana's breathing slows, and she feels weightier in my arms as she relaxes. Her expression is wanton and dazed as I pull out of her, so I hold her fast while she finds her feet. Her lips rise in a winsome smile. "You seem pleased to see me," she says.

"Yes, Miss Steele, I think my pleasure is pretty self-evident. Come—let me get you in the shower."

I undress quickly, and when I'm naked I begin undoing the buttons on Ana's blouse. Her eyes move from my fingers to my face.

"How was your journey?" I ask.

"Fine, thank you," she says, her voice a little throaty. "Thanks once again for first class. It really is a much nicer way to travel." She takes a quick breath, as if she's steeling herself. "I have some news," she says.

"Oh?" What now? I remove her blouse and deposit it on top of my clothes.

"I have a job." She sounds reticent.

Why? Did she think I'd be angry? Of course she's found a job. Pride swells in my chest. "Congratulations, Miss Steele. Now will you tell me where?" I ask with a smile.

"You don't know?"

"Why would I know?"

"With your stalking capabilities, I thought you might have—" She stops to study my face.

"Anastasia, I wouldn't dream of interfering in your career. Unless you ask me to, of course."

"So you have no idea which company?"

"No. I know there are four publishing companies in Seattle—so I am assuming it's one of them."

"SIP," she announces.

"Oh, the small one, good. Well done." It's the company that Ros identified as ripe for takeover. This will be easy.

I kiss Ana's forehead. "Clever girl. When do you start?"

"Monday."

"That soon, eh? I'd better take advantage of you while I still can. Turn around."

She obeys immediately. I remove her bra and skirt, then cup her behind and kiss her shoulder. Leaning against her, I nuzzle her hair. Her scent lingers in my nostrils, soothing, familiar, and uniquely Ana. The feel of her body against mine is both calming and enticing. She really is the whole package.

"You intoxicate me, Miss Steele, and you calm me. Such a heady combination." Grateful that she's here, I kiss her hair, then take her hand and pull her into the hot shower.

"Ow," she squeaks and closes her eyes, flinching under the steamy cascade.

"It's only a little hot water." I grin down at her.

Opening one eye, she lifts her chin and slowly surrenders to the heat.

"Turn around," I order. "I want to wash you."

She complies, and I squeeze some shower gel on my hand, work up a lather, and begin to massage her shoulders.

"I have something else to tell you," she says, her shoulders tensing.

"Oh yes?" I keep my voice mild. *Why is she tense?* My hands glide over her chest to her beautiful breasts.

"My friend José's photography show is opening Thursday in Portland."

"Yes, what about it?" The photographer again?

"I said I would go. Do you want to come with me?" The words come in a rush, as if she's anxious to get them out.

An invitation? I'm stunned. I only get invitations from my family, from work, and from Elena.

"What time?"

"The opening is at seven thirty."

This will count as *more*, surely. I kiss her ear and whisper, "Okay."

Her shoulders soften as she leans back against me. She seems relieved and I'm not sure whether to be amused or annoyed. Am I really that unapproachable?

"Were you nervous about asking me?"

"Yes. How can you tell?"

"Anastasia, your whole body's just relaxed." I mask my irritation.

"Well, you just seem to be, um…on the jealous side."

Yes. I'm jealous. The thought of Ana with anyone else is…unsettling. Very unsettling. "Yes, I am. And you'd do well to remember that. But thank you for asking. We'll take *Charlie Tango*."

She flashes me a quick grin as my hands slide down her body, the body she's given to me and no one else.

"Can I wash you?" she asks, diverting me.

"I don't think so." I kiss her neck as I rinse her back.

"Will you ever let me touch you?" Her voice is a gentle entreaty, but it doesn't stop the darkness that's swirling suddenly from nowhere and tightening around my throat.

No.

I will it away, cupping and concentrating on Ana's ass, her fucking glorious behind. My body responds on a primal level—at war with the darkness. I need her. I need her to chase my fear away.

"Put your hands on the wall, Anastasia. I'm going to take you again," I whisper, and with a startled glance at me, she splays her hands on the tiles. I grab her hips, pulling her back from the wall. "Hold fast, Anastasia," I warn as the water streams over her back.

She bends her head and braces herself as my hands sweep through her pubic hair. She squirms, her behind brushing my arousal.

Fuck! And like that, my residual fear melts away.

"Do you want this?" I ask as my fingers tease her. In answer she wiggles her butt against my erection, making me smile. "Tell me," I demand, my voice strained.

"Yes." Her agreement slices through the pouring water, keeping the darkness at bay.

Oh, baby.

She's still wet from earlier—from me, from her—I don't know. In the moment I give a silent word of thanks to Dr. Greene: no more condoms. I ease into Ana and slowly, deliberately make her mine again.

I WRAP HER IN a bathrobe and kiss her soundly. "Dry your hair," I order, handing her a hair dryer I never use. "Are you hungry?"

"Famished," she admits, and I don't know if she means it or if she's said it merely to please me. But pleased I am.

"Great. Me, too. I'll check where Mrs. Jones is with dinner. You have ten minutes. Don't get dressed." I kiss her once more and pad out to the kitchen.

Gail is washing something at the sink. She looks up as I peer over her shoulder.

"Clams, Mr. Grey," she says.

Delicious. Pasta alle Vongole, one of my favorites.

"Ten minutes?" I ask.

"Twelve," she says.

"Great."

She gives me a look as I head into my study. I ignore it. She's seen me in less than my bathrobe before. What the hell is her problem?

I check through some emails and my phone to see if there's any news about Leila. Nothing—but since Ana's arrival, I don't feel as hopeless as I did earlier.

Ana enters the kitchen at the same time I do, lured no doubt by the tantalizing smell of our dinner. When she sees Mrs. Jones she clutches the neck of her bathrobe.

"Just in time," Gail says, serving our meal in two large bowls at the place settings on the counter.

"Sit." I point to one of the barstools.

Ana's anxious eyes pass from me to Mrs. Jones.

She's self-conscious.

Baby, I have staff. Get over it.

"Wine?" I offer to distract her.

"Please," she says, sounding reserved as she takes her seat.

I open a bottle of Sancerre and pour two small glasses.

"There's cheese in the fridge if you'd like, sir," Gail says.

I nod, and she exits the room, much to Ana's relief. I take my seat. "Cheers." I raise my glass.

"Cheers," Ana replies, and the crystal glasses sing as we clink.

She takes a bite of her food and makes an appreciative noise in the back of her throat. Perhaps she *is* famished.

"Are you going to tell me?" she asks.

"Tell you what?" Mrs. Jones has outdone herself; the pasta tastes delicious.

"What I said in my sleep."

I shake my head. "Eat up. You know I like watching you eat."

She pouts with mock exasperation. "You are so pervy," she exclaims under her breath.

Oh, baby, you have no idea. And a thought springs to mind: maybe we should explore something new in the playroom tonight. Something fun.

"Tell me about this friend of yours," I ask.

"My friend?"

"The photographer." I keep my voice light, but she regards me with a fleeting frown.

"Well, we met the first day of college. He's an engineering major, but his passion is photography."

"And?"

"That's it." Her evasive answers are irritating.

"Nothing else?"

She tosses her hair over her shoulder. "We've become good friends. It turns out my dad and José's dad served together in the military before I was born. They've gotten back in touch, and they're now best buds."

Oh. "Your dad and his dad?"

"Yeah." She twirls more pasta around her fork.

"I see."

"This tastes delicious." She gives me a contented smile, and her robe gapes a little, revealing the swell of her breast. The sight stirs my cock.

"How are you feeling?" I ask.

"Fine," she says.

"Up for more?"

"More?"

"More wine?" *More sex? In the playroom?*

"A small glass, please."

I pour her a little more Sancerre. I don't want either of us to drink too much if we're going to play.

"How's the, um...situation that brought you to Seattle?"

Leila. Shit. This I do not want to discuss. "Out of hand. But nothing for you to worry about, Anastasia. I have plans for you this evening."

I want to see if we can play this so-called arrangement of ours both ways.

"Oh?"

"Yes. I want you ready and waiting in my playroom in fifteen minutes." I stand up, watching her closely to gauge her reaction. She takes a quick sip of her wine, her pupils widening. "You can get ready in your room. Incidentally, the walk-in closet is now full of clothes for you. I don't want any arguments about them."

Her mouth sets in a surprised *o*. And I give her a stern look, daring her to argue with me. Remarkably, she says nothing, and I head off to my study to send a quick email to Ros telling her I want to start the process to acquire SIP as soon as possible.

I scan a couple of work emails but see nothing in my inbox about Mrs. Reed. I put thoughts of Leila out of my mind; she's preoccupied me for the last twenty-four hours. Tonight I'm going to focus on Ana—and have some fun.

When I return to the kitchen Ana's disappeared; I presume she's getting ready upstairs.

In my closet I remove my robe and slip on my favorite jeans. As I do, images of Ana in my bathroom come to mind—her flawless back, then her hands pressed against the tiles while I fucked her.

Boy, the girl has stamina.

Let's see how much.

With a sense of exhilaration I collect my iPod from the living room and bolt upstairs to the playroom.

When I find Ana kneeling as she should be at the entrance facing the room—eyes down, legs parted, and wearing only her panties—my first feeling is one of relief.

She's still here; she's game.

My second is pride: she has followed my instructions to the letter. My smile is hard to hide.

Miss Steele does not back down from a challenge.

Closing the door behind me, I note that her bathrobe has been hung up on the peg. I walk past her barefoot and deposit my iPod on the chest. I've decided I'm going to deprive her of all her senses but touch and see how she fares with that. The bed has been made up with satin sheets.

And the leather shackles are in place.

At the chest I take out a hair tie, a blindfold, a fur glove, earbuds, and the handy transmitter that Barney designed for my iPod. I lay out the items in a neat row, plugging the transmitter into the top of the iPod, letting Ana wait. Anticipation is half the buildup to a scene. Once I'm satisfied I go and stand over her. Ana's head is bowed, the ambient light burnishing her hair. She looks modest and beautiful, the epitome of a submissive.

"You look lovely." I cup her face and tilt her head up until blue eyes meet gray. "You are one beautiful woman, Anastasia. And you're all mine," I whisper. "Stand up."

She's a little stiff as she gets to her feet. "Look at me," I order, and when I look into her eyes I know I could drown in her serious, rapt expression. I've got her full attention. "We don't have a signed contract, Anastasia. But we've discussed limits. And I want to reiterate we have safe words, okay?"

She blinks a couple of times but remains mute.

"What are they?" I demand.

She hesitates.

Oh, this will never do.

"What are the safe words, Anastasia?"

"Yellow."

"And?"

"Red."

"Remember those."

She raises an eyebrow in obvious scorn and is about to say something.

Oh no. Not in my playroom.

"Don't start with your smart mouth in here, Miss Steele. Or I will fuck it with you on your knees. Do you understand?"

As pleasing as that thought is, her obedience is what I want right now.

She swallows her chagrin.

"Well?"

"Yes, Sir," she says quickly.

"Good girl. My intention is not that you should use the safe word because you're in pain. What I intend to do to you will be intense. Very intense, and you have to guide me. Do you understand?"

Her face remains impassive, giving nothing away.

"This is about touch, Anastasia. You will not be able to see me or hear me. But you'll be able to feel me." Ignoring her confounded look, I turn to the audio player above the chest and switch it to auxiliary mode.

I just have to choose a song, and in that moment I recall our conversation in the car after she'd slept in my bed at The Heathman. Let's see if she likes some Tudor choral music.

"I am going to tie you to that bed, Anastasia. But I'm going to blindfold you first and"—I show her the iPod—"you will not be able to hear me. All you will hear is the music I'm going to play for you."

I think it's surprise I see registering on her face, but I'm not sure.

"Come." I lead her to the foot of the bed. "Stand here." Leaning down, I breathe in her sweet scent and whisper in her ear, "Wait here. Keep your eyes on the bed. Picture yourself lying here, bound and totally at my mercy."

She sucks in her breath.

Yes, baby. Think about it. I resist the temptation to plant a soft kiss on her shoulder. I need to braid her hair first and fetch a flogger. From the top of the chest I grab the hair tie, and from the rack I select my favorite flogger, which I stuff into the back pocket of my jeans.

When I return to stand behind her, I gently take her hair and braid it. "While I like your pigtails, Anastasia, I am impatient to have you right now. So one will have to do." I fasten and tug on the braid so she's forced to step back against me. Winding the end around my wrist, I pull to the right, bending her head to expose her neck. I run my nose from her earlobe to her shoulder, sucking and biting gently.

Hmm... She smells so good.

She shivers and hums deep in her throat.

"Hush, now," I caution, and taking the flogger from my pocket, I reach around her, my arms brushing hers, and show it to her.

I hear her catch her breath and see her fingers twitch.

"Touch it," I whisper, knowing that's what she wants. She raises her hand, pauses, then runs her fingers through the soft suede tails. It's arousing. "I will use this. It will not hurt, but it will bring your blood to the surface of your skin and make you very sensitive. What are the safe words, Anastasia?"

"Um...'yellow' and 'red,' Sir," she murmurs, transfixed by the flogger.

"Good girl. Remember, most of your fear is in your mind." I drop the flogger on the bed and brush my fingers down her sides, past the soft swell of her hips, and slip them into her panties. "You won't be needing these." I drag them down her legs and kneel behind her. She grabs hold of the pillar to shuffle awkwardly out of her underwear.

"Stand still," I command and kiss her behind, gently nipping each cheek. "Now lie down. Faceup." I spank her once, and she jumps, startled, and scurries onto the bed. She lies down facing me, her eyes on mine, glowing with excitement—and a little trepidation, I think.

"Hands above your head."

She does as she's told. I retrieve the earbuds, blindfold, iPod, and the remote from atop the chest of drawers. Sitting beside her on the bed, I show her the iPod with the transmitter. Her look darts from my face to the devices and back again.

"This sends what's playing on the iPod to the system in the room. I can hear what you're hearing, and I have a remote control unit for it."

Once she's seen everything, I insert the earbuds into her ears and place the iPod on the pillow. "Lift your head." She obeys, and I slip the blindfold over her eyes. Rising, I take her left hand and cuff her wrist to the leather shackle at the top corner of the bed. I let my fingers linger down her outstretched arm and she wriggles in response. As I walk slowly around the bed, her head follows the sound of my footsteps; I repeat the process with her right hand, cuffing her wrist.

Ana's breathing alters, becoming erratic and fast through parted lips. A flush creeps up her chest, and she squirms and lifts her hips in anticipation.

Good.

At the bottom of the bed I grab both of her ankles. "Lift your head again," I order. She does so immediately, and I drag her down the bed so that her arms are fully extended.

She lets out a quiet moan and lifts her hips once more.

I cuff each of her ankles to the corresponding corner of the bed so she's spread-eagled before me and I step back to admire the view.

Fuck.

Has she ever looked this hot?

She's totally and willingly at my mercy. The knowledge is intoxicating, and I stand for a moment to marvel at her generosity and courage.

I drag myself away from the spellbinding sight and from the chest of drawers collect the rabbit-fur glove. Before I put it on I press play on the remote; there's a brief hiss, and then the forty-part motet begins, the singer's angelic voice ringing through the playroom and over the delectable Miss Steele.

She stills as she listens.

And I walk around the bed, drinking her in.

Reaching out, I caress her neck with the glove. She inhales sharply and pulls at her shackles, but she doesn't cry out or tell me to stop. Slowly I run my gloved hand down her throat, over her sternum, then over her breasts, enjoying her restrained squirm. Circling her breasts, I gently tug on each of her nipples, and her moan of appreciation encourages me to head south. At a leisurely, deliberate pace I explore her body: her belly, her hips, the apex of her thighs, and down each leg. The music swells, more voices joining the choir in perfect counterpoint to my moving hand. I watch her mouth to determine how she's feeling; now she gapes in pleasure, now she bites her lip. When I run my hand over her sex she clenches her behind, pushing herself into my hand.

Though I normally like her to keep still, the movement pleases me.

Miss Steele is enjoying this. She's greedy.

When I brush her breasts again her nipples harden in the wake of the glove.

Yes.

Now that her skin is sensitized I remove the glove and pick up the flogger. With great care I trail the beaded ends over her skin, following the same pattern: over her chest, her breasts, her belly, through her pubic hair, and down her legs. As more choristers lend their voices to the motet I lift the handle of the flogger and flick the tresses across her belly. She cries out, I think in surprise, but she doesn't safe-word. I give her a moment to absorb the sensation, then do it again—a little harder this time.

She pulls at her shackles and calls out once more, a garbled cry—but it's not the safe word. I lash the flogger over her breasts, and she tilts her head back and lets out a soundless cry, her mouth slack as she writhes on the red satin.

Still no safe word. Ana is embracing her inner freak.

I feel giddy with delight as I rain the tails up and down her body, watching her skin warm under their bite. When the choristers pause, so do I.

Christ. She looks stunning.

I begin again as the music crescendoes, all the voices singing together; I flick the flogger over her, again and again, and she writhes beneath each blow.

When the last note rings through the room I stop, dropping the flogger on the floor. I'm breathless, panting with want and need.

Fuck.

She lays on the bed, helpless, her skin pretty in pink, and she's panting, too.

Oh, baby.

I climb onto the bed between her legs and crawl over her, holding myself above her. When the music starts again, the lone voice singing a sweet seraphic note, I follow the same pattern as the glove and the flogger—but this time with my mouth, kissing and sucking and worshipping every inch of her body. I tease each of her nipples until they are glistening with my saliva and standing at attention. She writhes as much as the restraints allow and groans beneath me. My tongue trails down to her belly, around her navel, laving her. Tasting her. Venerating her. Moving down, through her pubic hair to her sweet, exposed clitoris that's begging for the touch of my tongue. Around and around I swirl, drinking in her scent, drinking in her reaction, until I feel her tremble beneath me.

Oh no. Not yet, Ana. Not yet.

I stop and she huffs her voiceless disappointment.

I kneel up between her legs and pull open my fly, freeing my erection. Then, leaning over, I gently undo the left shackle around her ankle. She curls her leg around me in a long-limbed caress while I release her other ankle. Once she's free I massage and knead the life back into her legs, from her calves up to her thighs. She wriggles beneath me, raising her hips in perfect rhythm to the Tallis motet, as my thumbs work their way up her inner thighs, which are dewy from her arousal.

I stifle a growl and grasp her hips, lifting her from the bed, and in one swift, rough move I bury myself inside her.

Fuck.

She's slick and hot and wet and her body pulses around me, on the edge.

No. Too soon. Way too soon.

I stop, holding myself still over her and in her, while sweat beads on my brow.

"Please," she calls out, and I tighten my hold on her as I quell the urge to move and lose myself in her. Closing my eyes so I can't see her laid out beneath me in all her wonder, I concentrate on the music, and once I'm in control again, slowly I start to move. As the intensity of the choral piece builds I gradually increase my pace, matching the power and rhythm of the music, cherishing every tight inch inside her.

She fists her hands and tilts her head back and moans.

Yes.

"Please," she pleads between gritted teeth.

I hear you, baby.

Laying her back down on the bed, I stretch out over her, supporting my weight on my elbows, and I follow the rhythm, thrusting into her and losing myself in her and the music.

Sweet, brave Ana.

Sweat glides down my back.

Come on, baby.

Please.

And finally she explodes around me, shouting out her release and pushing me into an intense, draining climax where I lose all sense of self. I collapse on top of her as my world shifts and realigns, leaving that unfamiliar emotion swirling in my chest, consuming me.

I shake my head, trying to chase away the ominous and confusing feeling. Reaching up, I grab the remote and switch off the music.

No more Tallis.

The music definitely contributed to what was almost a religious experience. I frown, attempting but failing to get a handle on my feelings. I slide out of Ana and stretch to release her from each cuff.

She sighs as she flexes her fingers, and gently I remove the blindfold and the earbuds.

Big blue eyes blink up at me.

"Hi," I whisper.

"Hi yourself," she says, playful and bashful. Her response is delightful, and leaning down, I plant a tender kiss on her lips.

"Well done, you." My voice is filled with pride.

She did it. She took it. She took it all.

"Turn over."

Her eyes widen in alarm.

"I'm just going to rub your shoulders."

"Oh, okay."

She rolls over and flops down on the bed with her eyes closed. I sit astride her and massage her shoulders.

A pleasurable rumble resonates deep in her throat. "What was that music?" she asks.

"It's called *Spem in Alium*, a forty-part motet by Thomas Tallis."

"It was…overwhelming."

"I've always wanted to fuck to it."

"Not another first, Mr. Grey?"

I grin. "Indeed, Miss Steele."

"Well, it's the first time I've fucked to it, too," she says, her voice betraying her fatigue.

"You and I, we're giving each other many firsts."

"What did I say to you in my sleep, Chris—er, Sir?"

Not this again. *Put her out of her misery, Grey.*

"You said lots of things, Anastasia. You talked about cages and strawberries. That you wanted more, and that you missed me."

"Is that all?" She sounds relieved.

Why would she be relieved?

I stretch out beside her so I can see her face.

"What did you think you'd said?"

She opens her eyes for a brief moment and shuts them again quickly.

"That I thought you were ugly, conceited, and that you were hopeless in bed." One blue eye peeks open and watches me warily.

Oh…she's lying.

"Well, naturally I am all those things, and now you've got me really intrigued. What are you hiding from me, Miss Steele?"

"I'm not hiding anything."

"Anastasia, you're a hopeless liar."

"I thought you were going to make me giggle after sex; this isn't doing it for me."

Her answer is unexpected, and I give her a reluctant smile. "I can't tell jokes," I confess.

"Mr. Grey! Something you can't do?" She rewards me with a broad, infectious grin.

"No, hopeless joke teller," I say as if it's a badge of honor.

She giggles. "I'm a hopeless joke teller, too."

"That is such a lovely sound," I whisper and kiss her. But I still want to know why she's relieved. "And you are hiding something, Anastasia. I may have to torture it out of you."

"Ha!" The space between us is filled with her laughter. "I think you've done enough torturing."

Her response wipes the smile off my face, and her expression softens immediately. "Maybe I'll let you torture me like that again," she says coyly.

Relief sweeps through me. "I'd like that very much, Miss Steele."

"We aim to please, Mr. Grey."

"You're okay?" I ask, humbled and anxious at once.

"More than okay." She gives me her timid smile.

"You're amazing." I kiss her forehead, then climb off the bed as that ominous feeling ripples through me once more. Shaking it off, I button my fly and hold out my hand to help her off the bed. When she's standing I pull her into my arms and kiss her, savoring her taste.

"Bed," I mutter and lead her to the door. There I wrap her in the bathrobe she's left hanging on the peg, and before she can protest I pick her up and carry her downstairs to my bedroom.

"I'm so tired," she mumbles once she's in my bed.

"Sleep now," I whisper and wrap her in my arms. I close my eyes, fighting the disquieting sensation that surges and fills my chest once more. It's like homesickness and a homecoming rolled into one…and it's terrifying.

SATURDAY, JUNE 4, 2011

The summer breeze teases my hair, its caress the nimble fingers of a lover.

My lover.

Ana.

I wake suddenly, confused. My bedroom is shrouded in darkness, and beside me Ana sleeps, her breathing gentle and even. I prop myself up on one elbow and run my hand through my hair with the uncanny feeling that someone has just done exactly that. I glance around the room, peering into the shadowy corners, but Ana and I are alone.

Strange. I could swear someone was here. Someone touched me.

It was just a dream.

I shake off the disturbing thought and check the time. It's after four thirty in the morning. As I flop back down onto my pillow, Ana mumbles an incoherent word and turns over to face me, still fast asleep. She looks serene and beautiful.

I stare at the ceiling, the flashing light of the smoke alarm taunting me once more. We have no contract. Yet Ana's here. Beside me. *What does this mean?* How am I supposed to deal with her? Will she abide by my rules? I need to know she's safe. I rub my face. This is uncharted territory for me; it's out of my control, and it's unsettling.

Leila pops into my mind.

Shit.

My mind races: Leila, work, Ana...and I know I won't get back to sleep. Getting up, I pull on some PJ pants, close the bedroom door, and head into the living room to my piano.

Chopin is my solace; the somber notes match my mood and I play them over and over. A small movement at the edge of my vision catches my attention, and looking up, I see it's Ana coming toward me, her footsteps hesitant. "You should be asleep," I mutter but continue playing.

"So should you," she volleys back. Her face is firm with resolve, yet she looks small and vulnerable dressed only in my oversize bathrobe.

I hide my smile. "Are you scolding me, Miss Steele?"

"Yes, Mr. Grey, I am."

"Well, I can't sleep."

I have too much weighing on my mind, and I'd rather she went back to bed and slept. She must be tired from yesterday.

She disregards my mood and sits down beside me on the piano bench, leaning her head on my shoulder. It's such a tender and intimate gesture that for a moment I lose my place in the prelude, but I continue playing, feeling more at peace because she's with me.

"What was that?" she asks when I finish.

"Chopin. A prelude. Opus 28, number 4. In E minor, if you're interested."

"I'm always interested in what you do."

Sweet Ana. I kiss her hair. "I didn't mean to wake you."

"You didn't," she says, not moving her head. "Play the other one."

"Other one?"

"The Bach piece you played the first night I stayed."

"Oh, the Marcello."

I can't remember when I last played for someone upon request. For me the piano is a solitary instrument, for my ears only. My family hasn't heard me play for years. But since she's asked, I'll play for my sweet Ana. My fingers caress the keys and the haunting melody echoes through the living room.

"Why do you only play such sad music?" she asks.

Is it sad?

"So you were just six when you started to play?" She continues her questions, lifting her head and studying me. Her face is open and eager for information, as usual, and after last night, who am I to deny her anything?

"I threw myself into learning the piano to please my new mother."

"To fit into the perfect family?" My words from our candid night in Savannah echo in her soft voice.

"Yes, so to speak." I don't want to talk about this and I'm surprised how much of my personal information she's retained. "Why are you awake? Don't you need to recover from yesterday's exertions?"

"It's eight in the morning for me. And I need to take my pill."

"Well remembered," I muse. "Only you would start a course of time-specific birth control pills in a different time zone. Perhaps you should wait half an hour, and then another half hour tomorrow morning. So eventually you can take them at a reasonable time."

"Good plan," she says. "So what shall we do for half an hour?"

Well, I could fuck you over this piano.

"I can think of a few things." My voice is seductive.

"On the other hand, we could talk." She smiles, provocative.

I'm not in the mood for talking. "I prefer what I have in mind." I snake my arm around her waist, pull her into my lap, and nuzzle her hair.

"You'd always rather have sex than talk." She laughs.

"True. Especially with you." Her hands curl around my biceps, yet the darkness stays still and quiet. I trail kisses from the base of her ear to her throat. "Maybe on my piano," I murmur as my body responds to a mental image of her sprawled naked on the top, her hair spilling down over the side.

"I want to get something straight." She speaks quietly in my ear.

"Always so eager for information, Miss Steele. What needs straightening out?" Her skin is soft and warm against my lips as I nudge her bathrobe off her shoulder with my nose.

"Us," she says, and the simple word sounds like a prayer.

"Hmm. What about us?" I pause. *Where is she going with this?*

"The contract."

I stop and stare into her shrewd gaze. *Why is she doing this now?* My fingers glide down her cheek.

"Well, I think the contract is moot, don't you?"

"Moot?" she says, and her lips soften with the hint of a smile.

"Moot." I mirror her expression.

"But you were so keen." Uncertainty clouds Ana's eyes.

"Well, that was before. Anyway, the rules aren't moot; they still stand." I need to know you're safe.

"Before? Before what?"

"Before..." Before all this. Before you turned my world upside down, before you sleeping with me. Before you laid your head on my shoulder at the piano. It's all... "More," I murmur, driving away the now-familiar unease in my gut.

"Oh," she says, and I think she's pleased.

"Besides, we've been in the playroom twice now, and you haven't run screaming for the hills."

"Do you expect me to?"

"Nothing you do is expected, Anastasia."

The *v* between her brows is back. "So, let me be clear. You just want me to follow the rules element of the contract all the time, but not the rest of the contract?"

"Except in the playroom. I want you to follow the spirit of the contract in the playroom, and yes, I want you to follow the rules—all the time. Then I'll know you're safe. And I'll be able to have you anytime I wish," I add flippantly.

"And if I break one of the rules?" she asks.

"Then I'll punish you."

"But won't you need my permission?"

"Yes, I will."

"And if I say no?" she persists.

Why is she being so willful?

"If you say no, you'll say no. I'll have to find a way to persuade you." She should know this. She didn't let me spank her in the boathouse, and I wanted to. But I got to do it later that evening... with her approval.

She stands and walks toward the entrance of the living room, and for a moment I think she's storming off, but she turns, her expression perplexed. "So the punishment aspect remains."

"Yes, but only if you break the rules." This is clear to me. Why not to her?

"I'll need to reread them," she says, suddenly all businesslike.

She wants to do this now?

"I'll fetch them for you."

In my study I fire up my computer and print out the rules, wondering why we are discussing this at five in the morning.

She's at the sink, drinking a glass of water, when I return with the printout. I sit down on a stool and wait, watching her. Her back is stiff and tense; this does not bode well. When she turns around I slide the sheet of paper toward her across the kitchen island.

"Here you go."

She scans the rules quickly. "So the obedience thing still stands?"

"Oh yes."

She shakes her head, and an ironic smile tugs at the corner of her mouth as her eyes dart to the heavens.

Oh joy.

My spirits suddenly lift.

"Did you just roll your eyes at me, Anastasia?"

"Possibly. Depends what your reaction is." She looks wary and amused at once.

"Same as always." If she'll let me…

She swallows and her eyes widen with anticipation. "So…"

"Yes?"

"You want to spank me now?"

"Yes. And I will."

"Oh really, Mr. Grey?" She folds her arms, her chin thrust upward in a challenge.

"Are you going to stop me?"

"You're going to have to catch me first." She wears a coquettish smile, which addresses my dick directly.

She wants to play.

I ease myself off the stool, watching her carefully. "Oh really, Miss Steele?" The air almost crackles between us.

Which way will she run?

Her eyes are on mine, brimming with excitement. Her teeth tease her lower lip.

"And you're biting your lip." *Is she doing it on purpose?* I move slowly to my left.

"You wouldn't," she taunts. "After all, you roll your eyes." With her eyes fixed on me, she, too, moves to her left.

"Yes, but you've just raised the bar on the excitement stakes with this game."

"I'm quite fast, you know," she teases.

"So am I."

How does she make everything so thrilling?

"Are you going to come quietly?"

"Do I ever?" She grins, taking the bait.

"Miss Steele, what do you mean?" I stalk her around the kitchen island. "It'll be worse for you if I have to come get you."

"That's only if you catch me, Christian. And right now, I have no intention of letting you catch me."

Is she serious?

"Anastasia, you may fall and hurt yourself. Which will put you in direct contravention of rule number seven, now six."

"I have been in danger since I met you, Mr. Grey, rules or no rules."

"Yes, you have."

Perhaps this is not a game. Is she trying to tell me something? She hesitates, and I make a sudden lunge to grab her. She squeals and dashes around the island, to the relative safety of the opposite side of the dining table. With her lips parted, her expression both wary and daring at once, the bathrobe slips off one shoulder. She looks hot. Really fucking hot.

I prowl toward her, and she backs away.

"You certainly know how to distract a man, Anastasia."

"We aim to please, Mr. Grey. Distract you from what?"

"Life. The universe." *Ex-subs who've gone missing. Work. Our arrangement. Everything.*

"You did seem very preoccupied as you were playing."

She's not backing down. I stop and fold my arms, reassessing my strategy. "We can do this all day, baby, but I will get you, and it will just be worse for you when I do."

"No you won't," she says with absolute certainty.

I frown. "Anyone would think you didn't want me to catch you."

"I don't. That's the point. I feel about punishment the way you feel about me touching you."

And from nowhere the darkness crawls over me, shrouding my skin, leaving an icy trail of despair in its wake.

No. No. I can't bear to be touched. Ever.

"That's how you feel?" It's like she's touched me, her nails leaving white tracks over my chest.

She blinks several times, assessing my reaction, and when she speaks her voice is gentle. "No. It doesn't affect me quite as much as that, but it gives you an idea." Her expression is anxious.

Well, hell! This shines a whole different light on our relationship. "Oh," I mutter, because I can't think of anything else to say.

She takes a deep breath and approaches me, and when she's standing in front of me she looks up, her eyes burning with apprehension.

"You hate it that much?" I whisper.

This is it. We are really incompatible.

No. I don't want to believe that.

"Well…no," she says, and relief washes through me. "No," she continues. "I feel ambivalent about it. I don't like it, but I don't hate it."

"But last night, in the playroom, you—"

"I do it for you, Christian, because you need it. I don't. You didn't hurt me last night. That was in a different context, and I can rationalize that internally, and I trust you. But when you want to punish me, I worry that you'll hurt me."

Fuck. Tell her.

It's truth-or-dare time, Grey.

"I want to hurt you. But not beyond anything you couldn't take." I'd never go too far.

"Why?"

"I just need it," I whisper. "I can't tell you."

"Can't or won't?"

"Won't."

"So you know why?"

"Yes."

"But you won't tell me."

"If I do, you will run screaming from this room, and you'll never want to return. I can't risk that, Anastasia."

"You want me to stay."

"More than you know. I couldn't bear to lose you."

I can no longer stomach the distance between us. I grab her to stop her from running, and I pull her into my arms, my lips seeking hers. She answers my need, her mouth molding to mine, kissing me back with the same passion and hope and longing. The hovering darkness recedes and I find my solace.

"Don't leave me," I whisper against her lips. "You said you wouldn't leave me, and you begged me not to leave you in your sleep."

"I don't want to go," she says, but her eyes are searching mine, looking for answers. And I'm exposed—my ugly, torn soul on display.

"Show me," she says.

And I don't know what she means. "Show you?"

"Show me how much it can hurt."

"What?" I lean back and stare at her in disbelief.

"Punish me. I want to know how bad it can get."

Oh no. I release her and step out of her reach.

She gazes at me: open, honest, serious. She's offering herself to me once more, mine for the taking, to do with as I wish. I'm stunned. She'd fulfill this need for me? I can't believe it. "You would try?"

"Yes. I said I would." Her expression is full of resolve.

"Ana, you're so confusing."

"I'm confused, too. I'm trying to work this out. And you and I will know, once and for all, if I can do this. If I can handle this, then maybe you—"

She stops, and I take a further step back. She wants to touch me.

No.

But if we do this, then I'll know. She'll know.

We're here much sooner than I thought we'd be.

Can I do this?

And in that moment I know there's nothing I want more… There's nothing that will satisfy the monster within me more.

Before I can change my mind I grasp her arm and lead her upstairs to the playroom. At the door I stop. "I'll show you how bad it can be, and you can make up your own mind. Are you ready for this?"

She nods, her face set with the stubborn determination that I've come to know so well.

So be it.

I open the door, quickly grab a belt from the rack before she changes her mind, and lead her to the bench in the corner of the room.

"Bend over the bench," I order quietly.

She does as she's told, saying nothing.

"We're here because you said yes, Anastasia. And you ran from me. I am going to hit you six times, and you will count with me."

Still she says nothing.

I fold the hem of her bathrobe over her back, revealing her beautiful naked behind. I run my palm over her buttocks and the top of her thighs, and a frisson runs through me.

This is it. What I want. What I've been working toward.

"I am doing this so you remember not to run from me, and as exciting as it is, I never want you to run from me. And you rolled your eyes at me. You know how I feel about that." I take a deep breath, savoring this moment, trying to steady my thundering heartbeat.

I need this. This is what I do. And we're finally here.

She can do it.

She's never let me down yet.

Holding her in place with one hand at the small of her back, I shake out the belt. I take another deep breath, focusing on the task in hand.

She won't run. She's asked me.

Then I wield it, striking her across both cheeks, hard.

She cries out, in shock.

But she's not called out the number…or the safe word.

"Count, Anastasia!" I demand.

"One!" she shouts.

Okay…no safe word.

I hit her again.

"Two!" she screams.

That's right, let it out, baby.

I hit her once more.

"Three!" She winces.

There are three stripes across her backside.

I make it four.

She shouts the number, loud and clear.

There's no one to hear you, baby. Shout all you need.

I belt her again.

"Five," she sobs, and I pause, waiting for her to safe-word.

She doesn't.

And one for luck.

"Six," Ana whispers, her voice forced and hoarse.

I drop the belt, savoring my sweet, euphoric release. I'm punch-drunk, breathless, and finally replete. Oh, this beautiful girl, my beautiful girl. I want to kiss every inch of her body. We're here. Where I want to be. I reach for her, pulling her into my arms.

"Let go. No—" She struggles out of my grasp, scrambling away from me, pushing and shoving and finally turning on me like a seething wildcat. "Don't touch me!" she hisses. Her face is blotchy and smeared with tears, her nose is running, and her hair is a dark, tangled mess, but she has never looked so magnificent…and at the same time so angry.

Her anger crashes over me like a tidal wave.

She's mad. Really mad.

Okay, I hadn't figured on anger.

Give her a moment. Wait for the endorphins to kick in.

She dashes away her tears with the back of her hand. "This is what you really like? Me, like this?" She wipes her nose with the sleeve of the bathrobe.

My euphoria vanishes. I'm stunned, completely helpless and paralyzed by her anger. The crying I know and understand, but this rage…somewhere deep inside it resonates with me and I don't want to think about that.

Don't go there, Grey.

Why didn't she ask me to stop? She didn't safe-word. She deserved to be punished. She ran from me. She rolled her eyes. *This is what happens when you defy me, baby.*

She scowls. Blue eyes wide and bright, filled with hurt and rage and sudden, chilling insight.

Shit. What have I done?

It's sobering.

I'm unbalanced, teetering at the edge of a dangerous precipice, desperately searching for the words to make this right, but my mind is blank.

"Well, you are one fucked-up son of a bitch," she snarls.

All the breath leaves my body, and it's like she's whipped *me* with a belt… *Fuck!*

She's recognized me for what I am.

She's seen the monster.

"Ana," I whisper, pleading with her. I want her to stop. I want to hold her and make the pain go away. I want her to sob in my arms.

"Don't you dare Ana me! You need to sort your shit out, Grey!" she snaps and walks out of the playroom, quietly shutting the door behind her. Stunned, I stare at the closed door, her words ringing in my ears.

You are one fucked-up son of a bitch.

No one has ever walked out on me. *What the hell?* Mechanically, I run my hand through my hair, trying to rationalize her reaction, and mine. I just let her go. I'm not mad… *I'm…what?* I stoop to pick up the belt, walk to the wall, and hang it on its peg. That was, without doubt, one of the most satisfying moments of my life. A moment ago I felt lighter, the weight of uncertainty between us gone.

It's done. We're there.

Now that she knows what's involved, we can move on.

I told her. People like me like inflicting pain.

But only on women who like it.

My sense of unease grows.

Her reaction—the image of her injured, haunted look is back, unwelcome, in my mind's eye. It's unsettling. I am used to making women cry—it's what I do.

But Ana?

I sink to the floor and lean my head against the wall, my arms on my bent knees. Just let her cry. She'll feel better for crying. Women do, in my experience. Give her a moment, then go offer her aftercare. She didn't safe-word. She asked me. She wanted to know, curious as ever. It's just been a rude awakening, that's all.

You are one fucked-up son of a bitch.

Closing my eyes, I smile without humor. *Yes, Ana, yes I am, and now you know.* Now we can move forward with our relationship…arrangement. Whatever this is.

My thoughts don't comfort me and my sense of unease grows. Her wounded eyes glaring at me, outraged, accusatory, pitying… She can see me for what I am. A *monster.*

Flynn springs to mind: *Don't dwell on the negative, Christian.*

I close my eyes once more and see Ana's anguished face.

What a fool I am.

This was too soon.

Way, way too soon.

Fuck.

I'll reassure her.

Yes—let her cry, then reassure her.

I was angry with her for running from me. *Why did she do that?*

Hell. She's so different from any other woman I've known. Of course she wouldn't react in the same way.

I need to face her, hold her. We'll get through this. I wonder where she is.

Shit!

Panic seizes me. Suppose she's gone? No, she wouldn't do that. Not without saying goodbye. I stand and race out of the room and down the stairs. She's not in the living room—she must be in bed. I dash to my bedroom.

The bed is empty.

Full-blown anxiety erupts in the pit of my belly. No, she can't have gone! Upstairs—she must be in her room. I take the stairs three at a time and pause, breathless, outside her bedroom door. She's in there, crying.

Oh, thank God.

I lean my head against the door, overwhelmed by my relief.

Don't leave. The thought is awful.

Of course she just needs to cry.

Taking a steadying breath, I head to the bathroom beside the playroom to fetch some arnica cream, Advil, and a glass of water, and I return to her room.

Inside it's still dark, though dawn is a pale streak on the horizon, and it takes me a moment to find my beautiful girl. She's curled up in the middle of the bed, small and vulnerable, sobbing quietly. The sound of her grief rips through me, leaving me winded. My subs never affected me like this—even when they were bawling. I don't get it. Why do I feel so lost? Putting down the arnica, water, and tablets, I lift the comforter, slide in beside her, and reach for her. She stiffens, her whole body screaming, *Don't touch me!* The irony is not lost on me.

"Hush," I whisper in a vain attempt to halt her tears and calm her. She doesn't respond. She remains frozen, unyielding.

"Don't fight me, Ana, please."

She relaxes a fraction, allowing me to pull her into my arms, and I bury my nose in her wonderfully fragrant hair. She smells as sweet as ever, her scent a soothing balm to my nerves. And I plant a tender kiss on her neck.

"Don't hate me," I murmur as I press my lips to her throat, tasting her.

She says nothing, but slowly her crying dissipates into soft sniffling sobs. At last she's quiet. I think she might have fallen asleep, but I cannot bring myself to check, in case I disturb her. At least she's calmer now.

Dawn comes and goes, and the ambient light gets brighter, intruding into the room as morning moves on. And still we lie quietly. My mind drifts as I hold my girl in my arms, and I observe the changing quality of the light. I can't remember an instance when I just lay down and let time creep by and my thoughts wander. It's relaxing, imagining what we could do for the rest of the day. Maybe I should take her to see *The Grace.*

Yes. We could go sailing this afternoon.

If she's still talking to you, Grey.

She moves, a slight twitch in her foot, and I know she's awake.

"I brought you some Advil and some arnica cream."

Finally she responds, slowly turning in my arms to face me. Pain-riven eyes focus on mine, her look intense, questioning. She takes her time to scrutinize me, as if seeing me for the first time. It's unnerving because, as usual, I have no idea what she's thinking, what she's seeing. But she's definitely calmer, and I welcome the small spark of relief this brings. Today might be a good day after all.

She caresses my cheek and runs her fingers along my jaw, tickling my stubble. I close my eyes, savoring her touch. It's still so new, this sensation, being touched and enjoying her innocent fingers gently stroking my face, the darkness quiet. I don't mind her touching my face…or her fingers in my hair.

"I'm sorry," she says.

Her soft-spoken words are a surprise. She's apologizing to me?

"What for?"

"What I said."

Relief courses unchecked through my body. She's forgiven me. Besides, what she said in anger was right—I am a fucked-up son of a bitch.

"You didn't tell me anything I didn't know." And for the first time in so many years I find myself apologizing. "I'm sorry I hurt you."

Her shoulders lift a little and she gives me a slight smile. I've won a reprieve. We're safe. We're okay. I'm relieved.

"I asked for it," she says.

You sure did, baby.

She swallows nervously. "I don't think I can be everything you want me to be," she concedes, her eyes wide with heartfelt sincerity.

The world stops.

Fuck.

We're not safe at all.

Grey, make this right.

"You are everything I want you to be."

She frowns. Her eyes are red-rimmed and she's so pale, the palest I've ever seen her. It's oddly stirring. "I don't understand," she says. "I'm not obedient, and you can be as sure as hell I'm not going to let you do *that* to me again. And that's what you need—you said so."

And there it is—her coup de grace. I pushed too far. Now she knows—and all the arguments I had with myself before I embarked on the pursuit of this girl flood back to me. She's not into the lifestyle. How can I corrupt her this way? She's too young, too innocent—too...*Ana.*

My dreams are just that...dreams. This isn't going to work.

I close my eyes; I can't bear to look at her. It's true, she would be better off without me. Now that she's seen the monster, she knows she can't contend with him. I have to free her—let her go her own way. This won't work between us.

Focus, Grey.

"You're right. I should let you go. I'm no good for you."

Her eyes widen. "I don't want to go," she whispers. Tears pool in her eyes, glistening on long dark lashes.

"I don't want you to go, either," I answer, because it's the truth, and that feeling—that ominous, frightening feeling—is back, overwhelming me. The tears trickle down her cheeks once more. Gently I wipe away a falling tear with my thumb, and before I know it the words tumble out. "I've come alive since I met you." I trace my thumb along her bottom lip. I want to kiss her, hard. Make her forget. Dazzle her. Arouse her—I know I can. But something holds me back—her wary, injured look. Why would she want to be kissed by a monster? She might push me away, and I don't know if I could deal with any more rejection. Her words haunt me, pulling at some dark, repressed memory.

You are one fucked-up son of a bitch.

"Me, too," she whispers. "I've fallen in love with you, Christian."

I remember Carrick teaching me to dive. My toes gripping the pool edge as I fell arching into the water—and now I'm falling once more, into the abyss, in slow motion.

There's no way she can feel that about me.

Not me. *No!*

And I'm choking for air, strangled by her words pressing their momentous weight on my chest. I plunge down and down, the darkness welcoming me. I can't hear them. I can't deal with them. She doesn't know what she's saying, who she's dealing with—*what* she's dealing with.

"No." My voice is raw with pained disbelief. "You can't love me, Ana. No. That's wrong."

I need to set her right on this. She cannot love a monster. She cannot love a fucked-up son of a bitch. She needs to go. She needs out—and in an instant, everything becomes crystal clear. This is my eureka moment; I can't make her happy. I can't be what she needs. I can't let this go on. This has to finish. It should never have started.

"Wrong? Why's it wrong?"

"Well, look at you. I can't make you happy." The anguish is plain in my voice as I sink deeper and deeper into the abyss, shrouded in despair.

No one can love me.

"But you do make me happy," she says, not comprehending.

Anastasia Steele, look at yourself. I have to be honest with her. "Not at the moment. Not doing what I want to do."

She blinks, her lashes fluttering over her large, wounded eyes, studying me intently as she searches for the truth. "We'll never get past that, will we?"

I shake my head, because I can't think of anything to say. It comes down to incompatibility, again. She closes her eyes, as if in pain, and when she reopens them, they are clearer, full of resolve. Her tears have stopped. And the blood starts pounding through my head as my heart hammers. I know what she's going to say. I dread what she's going to say.

"Well, I'd better go, then." She winces as she sits up.

Now? She can't go now.

"No, don't go." I'm free-falling, deeper and deeper. Her leaving feels like a monumental mistake. My mistake. But she can't stay if she feels this way about me; she just can't.

"There's no point in me staying," she says and gingerly climbs out of the bed still wrapped in her bathrobe.

She's really leaving. I can't believe it. I scramble out of bed to stop her, but her look pins me to the floor—her expression so bleak, so cold, so distant—not my Ana at all.

"I'm going to get dressed. I'd like some privacy," she says. How flat and empty her voice sounds as she turns and leaves, closing the door behind her. I stare at the closed door.

This is the second time in one day that she's walked out on me.

I sit up and cradle my head in my hands, trying to calm down, trying to rationalize my feelings.

She loves me?

How did this happen? How?

Grey, you fucking fool.

Wasn't this always a risk, with someone like her? Someone good and innocent and courageous. A risk that she'd not see the real me until it was too late. That I would make her suffer like this?

Why is this so painful? I feel like I've punctured a lung. I follow her out of the room. She might want privacy, but if she's leaving me I need clothes.

When I reach my bedroom, she's showering, so I quickly change into jeans and a T-shirt. I've chosen black—suitable for my mood. Grabbing my phone, I wander through the apartment, tempted to sit at the piano and hammer out some woeful lament. But instead I stand in the middle of the room, feeling nothing.

Vacant.

Focus, Grey! This is the right decision. Let her go.

My phone buzzes. It's Welch. Has he found Leila?

"Welch."

"Mr. Grey, I have news." His voice grates over the phone. This guy should stop smoking. He sounds like Deep Throat.

"You found her?" My spirits lift a little.

"No, sir."

"What is it, then?" *Why the hell have you called?*

"Leila left her husband. He finally admitted it to me. He's washed his hands of her."

This is news.

"I see."

"He has an idea where she might be, but he wants his palm greased. Wants to know who's so interested in his wife. Though that's not what he called her."

I fight my surging anger. "How much does he want?"

"He said two thousand."

"He said what?" I shout, losing it. Why didn't he just admit earlier that Leila had walked out on him? "Well, he could have told us the fucking truth. What's his number? I need to call him. Welch, this is a real fuckup."

I glance up, and Ana is standing awkwardly at the entrance to the living room, dressed in jeans and an ugly sweatshirt. She's all big eyes and tight, pinched face, her suitcase beside her.

"Find her," I snap, hanging up. I'll deal with Welch later.

Ana walks over to the sofa and from her backpack removes the Mac, her phone, and the key to her car. Taking a deep breath, she marches to the kitchen and lays all three items on the counter.

What the hell? She's returning her things?

She turns to face me, determination clear on her small ashen face. It's her stubborn look, the one I know so well.

"I need the money that Taylor got for my Beetle." Her voice is calm but monotone.

"Ana, I don't want those things—they're yours." She can't do this to me. "Please, take them."

"No, Christian. I only accepted them under sufferance, and I don't want them anymore."

"Ana, be reasonable!"

"I don't want anything that will remind me of you. I just need the money that Taylor got for my car." Her voice is devoid of emotion.

She wants to forget me.

"Are you really trying to wound me?"

"No, I'm not. I'm trying to protect myself."

Of course—she's trying to protect herself from the monster.

"Please Ana, take that stuff."

Her lips are so pale.

"Christian, I don't want to fight—I just need that money."

Money. It always comes down to the fucking money.

"Will you take a check?" I snarl.

"Yes. I think you're good for it."

She wants money, I'll give her money. I storm into my study, barely holding on to my temper. Sitting at my desk I call Taylor.

"Good morning, Mr. Grey."

I ignore his greeting. "How much did you get for Ana's VW?"

"Twelve thousand dollars, sir."

"That much?" In spite of my bleak mood, I'm surprised.

"It's a classic," he says by way of explanation.

"Thanks. Can you take Miss Steele home now?"

"Of course. I'll be right down."

I hang up and take out my checkbook from my desk drawer. As I do, I remember my conversation with Welch about Leila's fucking asshole of a husband.

It's always about fucking money!

In my anger I double the amount Taylor got for the death trap and stuff the check into an envelope.

When I return she's still standing by the kitchen island, lost, almost childlike. I hand her the envelope, my anger evaporating at the sight of her.

"Taylor got a good price...it's a classic car," I mumble in apology. "You can ask him. He'll take you home." I nod to where Taylor is waiting at the entrance of the living room.

"That's fine. I can get myself home, thank you."

No! Accept the ride, Ana. Why does she do this?

"Are you going to defy me at every turn?"

"Why change a habit of a lifetime?" She gives me a blank look.

That's it in a nutshell—why our arrangement was doomed from the start. She's just not cut out for this, and deep down, I always knew it. I close my eyes.

I am such a fool.

I try a softer approach, pleading with her.

"Please, Ana. Let Taylor take you home."

"I'll get the car, Miss Steele," Taylor announces with quiet authority and leaves. Maybe she'll listen to him. She glances around, but he's already gone down to the basement to fetch the car.

She turns back to me, her eyes wider all of a sudden. And I hold my breath. I really can't believe she's going. This is the last time I'll see her, and she looks so sad. It cuts deep that I'm the one responsible for that look. I take a hesitant step forward; I want to hold her one more time and beg her to stay.

She steps back, and it's a move that signals all too clearly that she doesn't want me. I've driven her away.

I freeze. "I don't want you to go."

"I can't stay. I know what I want, and you can't give it to me, and I can't give you what you need."

Oh, please, Ana—let me hold you one more time. Smell your sweet, sweet scent. Feel you in my arms. I step toward her again, but she holds up her hands, halting me.

"Don't—please." She recoils, panic etched on her face. "I can't do this." And she grabs her suitcase and backpack and heads for the foyer. I follow, meek and helpless in her wake, my eyes fixed on her small frame.

In the foyer I call the elevator. I can't take my eyes off her…her delicate, elfin face, those lips, the way her dark lashes fan out and cast a shadow over her pale, pale cheeks. Words fail me as I try to memorize every detail. I have no dazzling lines, no quick wit, no arrogant commands. I have nothing—nothing but a yawning void inside my chest.

The elevator doors open and Ana heads straight in. She looks around at me—and for a moment her mask slips, and there it is: my pain reflected on her beautiful face.

No…Ana. Don't go.

"Goodbye, Christian."

"Ana…goodbye."

The doors close, and she's gone.

I sink slowly to the floor and put my head in my hands. The void is now cavernous and aching, overwhelming me.

Grey, what the hell have you done?

WHEN I LOOK UP again, the paintings in my foyer, my Madonnas, bring a mirthless smile to my lips. The idealization of motherhood. All of them gazing at their infants, or staring inauspiciously down at me.

They're right to look at me that way. She's gone. She's really gone. The best thing that ever happened to me. After she said she'd never leave. She promised me she'd never leave. I close my eyes, shutting out those lifeless, pitying stares, and tip my head back against the wall. Okay, she said it in her sleep—and like the fool I am, I believed her. I've always known deep down I was no good for her, and she was too good for me. This is how it should be.

Then why do I feel like shit? Why is this so painful?

The chime announcing the arrival of the elevator forces my eyes open again, and my heart leaps into my mouth. She's back. I sit paralyzed, waiting, and the doors pull back—and Taylor steps out and momentarily freezes.

Hell. How long have I been sitting here?

"Miss Steele is home, Mr. Grey," he says as if he addresses me while I'm prostrate on the floor every day.

"How was she?" I ask as dispassionately as I can, though I really want to know.

"Upset, sir," he says, showing no emotion whatsoever.

I nod, dismissing him. But he doesn't leave.

"Can I get you anything, sir?" he asks, much too kindly for my liking.

"No." *Go. Leave me alone.*

"Sir," he says, and he exits, leaving me slouched on the foyer floor.

Much as I'd like to sit here all day and wallow in my despair, I can't. I want an update from Welch, and I need to call Leila's poor excuse for a husband.

And I need a shower. Perhaps this agony will wash away in the shower.

As I stand I touch the wooden table that dominates the foyer, my fingers absentmindedly tracing its delicate marquetry. I'd have liked to fuck Miss Steele over this. I close my eyes, imagining her sprawled across this table, her head held back, chin up, mouth open in ecstasy, and her luscious hair pooling over the edge. Shit, it makes me hard just thinking about it.

Fuck.

The pain in my gut twists and tightens.

She's gone, Grey. Get used to it.

And drawing on years of enforced control, I bring my body to heel.

THE SHOWER IS BLISTERING, the temperature just a notch below painful, the way I like it. I stand beneath the cascade, trying to forget her, hoping this heat will scorch her out of my head and wash her scent off my body.

If she's going to leave, there's no coming back.

Never.

I scrub my hair with grim determination.

Good riddance.

And I suck in a breath.

No. Not good riddance.

I raise my face to the streaming water. It's not good riddance at all—I am going to miss her. I lean my forehead against the tiles. Just last night she was in here with me. I stare at my hands, my fingers caressing the line of grout in the tiles where only yesterday her hands were braced against the wall.

Fuck this.

Switching off the water, I step out of the shower cubicle. As I wrap a towel around my waist, it sinks in: each day will be darker and emptier, because she's no longer in it.

No more facetious, witty emails.

No more of her smart mouth.

No more curiosity.

Her bright, blue eyes will no longer regard me in thinly veiled amusement...or shock...or lust. I stare at the brooding morose jerk staring back at me in the bathroom mirror.

"What the hell have you done, asshole?" I sneer at him. He mouths the words back at me with vitriolic contempt. And the bastard blinks at me, big gray eyes raw with misery.

"She's better off without you. You can't be what she wants. You can't give her what she needs. She wants hearts and flowers. She deserves better than you, you fucked-up prick." Repulsed by the image glowering back at me, I turn away from the mirror.

To hell with shaving for today.

I dry off at my chest of drawers and grab some underwear and a clean T-shirt. As I turn I notice a small box on my pillow. The rug is pulled from under me again, revealing once more the abyss beneath, its jaws open, waiting for me, and my anger turns to fear.

It's something from her. What would she give me? I drop my clothes and, taking a deep breath, sit on the bed and pick up the box.

It's a glider. A model-making kit for a Blaník L23. A scribbled note falls from the top of the box and wafts onto the bed.

This reminded me of a happy time.
Thank you.

Ana

It's the perfect present from the perfect girl.
Pain lances through me.
Why is this so painful? *Why?*
Some ugly, long-lost memory stirs, trying to sink its teeth into the here and now. No. That is not a place I want my mind to return to. I get up, tossing the box onto the bed, and dress hurriedly. When I'm finished I grab the box and the note and head for my study. I will handle this better from my seat of power.

MY CONVERSATION WITH WELCH is brief. My conversation with Russell Reed—the miserable lying bastard who married Leila—is briefer. I didn't know they'd wed during one drunken weekend in Vegas. No wonder their marriage failed after just eighteen months. She left him twelve weeks ago. *So where are you now, Leila Williams? What have you been doing?*

I focus my mind on Leila, trying to think of some clue from our past that might tell me where she is. I need to know. I need to know she's safe. And why she came here. Why me?

She wanted more and I didn't, but that was long ago. It was easy when she left—our arrangement was terminated by mutual consent. In fact, our whole arrangement had been exemplary: just how it should be. She was mischievous when she was with me, deliberately so, and not the broken creature that Gail described.

I recall how much she enjoyed our sessions in the playroom. Leila loved the kink. A memory surfaces—I'm tying her big toes together, turning her feet in so she can't clench her backside and avoid the pain. Yeah, she loved all that shit, and so did I. She was a great submissive. But she never captured my attention like Anastasia Steele.

She never drove me to distraction like Ana.

I gaze at the glider kit on my desk and trace the edges of the box with my finger, knowing Ana's fingers have touched it.

My sweet Anastasia.

What a contrast you are to all the women I've known. The only woman I've ever chased, and the one woman who can't give me what I want.

I don't understand.

I've come alive since I've known her. These last few weeks have been the most exciting, the most unpredictable, the most fascinating in my life. I've been enticed from my monochrome world into one rich with color—and yet she can't be what I need.

I put my head in my hands. She will never like what I do. I tried to convince myself that we could work up to the rougher shit, but that's not going to happen, ever. She's better off without me. What would she want with a fucked-up monster who can't bear to be touched?

And yet she bought me this thoughtful gift. Who does that for me, apart from my family? I study the box once more and open it. All the plastic parts of the craft are stuck on one grid, swathed in cellophane. Memories of her squealing in the glider during the wingover come to mind—her hands up, braced against the Perspex canopy. I can't help but smile.

Lord, that was so much fun—the equivalent of pulling her pigtails in the playground. Ana in pigtails... I shut down that thought immediately. I don't want to go there, our first bath. And all I'm left with is the thought that I won't see her again.

The abyss yawns open.

No. Not again.

I need to make this plane. It will be a distraction. Ripping open the cellophane, I scan the instructions. I need glue, modeling glue. I search through my desk drawers.

Shit. Nestled at the back of one drawer I find the red leather box containing the Cartier earrings. I never got the chance to give them to her—and now I never will.

I call Andrea and leave a message on her cell, asking her to cancel tonight. I can't face the gala, not without my date.

I open the red leather box and examine the earrings. They

are beautiful: simple yet elegant, just like the enchanting Miss Steele…who left me this morning because I punished her… because I pushed her too hard. I cradle my head once again. But she let me. She didn't stop me. She let me because she *loves* me. The thought is horrifying, and I dismiss it immediately. She can't. It's simple: no one can feel like that about me. Not if they know me.

Move on, Grey. Focus.

Where's the damned glue? I stash the earrings back in the drawer and continue my search. Nothing.

I buzz Taylor.

"Mr. Grey?"

"I need some modeling glue."

He pauses for a moment. "For what sort of model, sir?"

"A model glider."

"Balsa wood or plastic?"

"Plastic."

"I have some. I'll bring it down now, sir."

I thank him, a little stunned that he has modeling glue. Moments later he knocks on the door.

"Come in."

He paces into my study and places the small plastic container on my desk. He doesn't leave and I have to ask.

"Why do you have this?"

"I build the odd plane." His face reddens.

"Oh?" My curiosity is piqued.

"Flying was my first love, sir."

I don't understand.

"Color-blind," he explains flatly.

"So you became a Marine?"

"Yes, sir."

"Thank you for this."

"No problem, Mr. Grey. Have you eaten?"

His question takes me by surprise.

"I'm not hungry, Taylor. Please, go, enjoy the afternoon with your daughter, and I'll see you tomorrow. I won't bother you again."

He pauses for a moment, and my irritation builds. *Go.*

"I'm good." *Hell,* my voice is choked.

"Sir." He nods. "I'll return tomorrow evening."

I give him a quick dismissive nod, and he's gone.

When was the last time Taylor offered me anything to eat? I must look more fucked up than I thought. Sulking, I grab the glue.

THE GLIDER IS IN the palm of my hand. I marvel at it with a sense of achievement, memories of that flight nudging my consciousness. Anastasia was impossible to wake—I smile as I recall—and once up she was difficult, disarming and beautiful, and funny.

Christ, that was fun: her girlish excitement during the flight, the squealing, and afterward, our kiss.

It was my first attempt at *more*. It's extraordinary that over such a short time I have collected so many happy memories.

The pain surfaces once more—nagging, aching, reminding me of all I've lost.

Focus on the glider, Grey.

Now I have to stick the transfers in place; they're fiddly little suckers.

FINALLY THE LAST ONE is on and drying. My glider has its own FAA registration. November. Nine. Five. Two. Echo. Charlie.

Echo Charlie.

I look up and the light is fading. It's late. My first thought is that I can show this to Ana.

No more Ana.

I clench my teeth and stretch my stiff shoulders. Standing slowly, I realize I haven't eaten all day or had anything to drink, and my head is throbbing.

I feel like shit.

I check my phone in the hope that she's called, but there's only a text from Andrea.

CC Gala canx.

Hope all is well.

A

While I'm reading Andrea's message the phone buzzes. My heart rate immediately spikes, then falls when I recognize it's Elena.

"Hello." I don't bother to disguise my disappointment.

"Christian, is that any way to say hi? What's eating you?" she scolds, but her voice is full of humor.

I stare out the window. It's dusk over Seattle. I wonder briefly what Ana is doing. I don't want to tell Elena what's happened; I don't want to say the words out loud and make them a reality.

"Christian? What gives? Tell me." Her tone shifts to brusque and annoyed.

"She left me," I mutter, sounding morose.

"Oh." Elena sounds surprised. "Want me to come over?"

"No."

She takes a deep breath. "This life isn't for everyone."

"I know."

"Hell, Christian, you sound like shit. Do you want to go out to dinner?"

"No."

"I'm coming over."

"No, Elena. I'm not good company. I'm tired and I want to be alone. I'll call you during the week."

"Christian…it's for the best."

"I know. Goodbye."

I hang up. I don't want to talk to her. She encouraged me to fly down to Savannah. Perhaps she knew this day would come. I scowl at the phone, toss it onto my desk, and go in search of something to drink and eat.

I EXAMINE THE CONTENTS of my fridge.

Nothing appeals.

In the cupboard I find a bag of pretzels. I open them and eat one after the other as I walk to the window. Outside, night has fallen; lights twinkle and wink through the pouring rain. The world moves on.

Move on, Grey.

Move on.

SUNDAY, JUNE 5, 2011

I gaze up at the bedroom ceiling. Sleep eludes me. I'm tormented by Ana's fragrance, which still clings to my bedsheets. I pull her pillow over my face to breathe in her scent. It's torture, it's heaven, and for a moment I contemplate death by suffocation.

Get a grip, Grey.

I rerun the morning's events in my head. Could they have unfolded any differently? As a rule I never do this, because it's a waste of energy, but today I'm looking for clues as to where I went wrong. And no matter how I play it out, I know in my bones we would have reached this impasse, whether it was yesterday morning, or in a week, or a month, or a year. Better that it happened now, before I inflicted any further pain on Anastasia.

I think of her huddled in her little white bed. I can't picture her in the new apartment—I've not been there—but I imagine her in that room in Vancouver where I once slept with her. I shake my head; that was the best night's sleep I'd had in years. The radio alarm reads 2:00 a.m. I have lain here for two hours, my mind churning. I take a deep breath, inhaling her scent once more, and I close my eyes.

Mommy can't see me. I stand in front of her. She can't see me. She's asleep with her eyes open. Or sick.

I hear a rattle. His keys. He's back.

I run and hide and make myself small under the table in the kitchen. My cars are here with me.

Bang. The door slams shut, making me jump.

Through my fingers I see Mommy. She turns her head to see him. Then she's asleep on the couch. He's wearing his big boots with the shiny buckles and standing over Mommy shouting. He hits Mommy with a belt. *Get up! Get up!*

You are one fucked-up bitch. You are one fucked-up bitch.

Mommy makes a noise. A wailing noise.

Stop. Stop hitting Mommy. Stop hitting Mommy.

I run at him and hit him and I hit him and I hit him.

But he laughs and smacks me across the face.

No! Mommy shouts.

You are one fucked-up bitch.

Mommy makes herself small. Small like me. And then she's quiet. *You are one fucked-up bitch. You are one fucked-up bitch. You are one fucked-up bitch.*

I am under the table. I have my fingers in my ears and I close my eyes. The sound stops. He turns and I can see his boots as he stomps into the kitchen. He carries the belt, slapping it against his leg. He is trying to find me. He stoops down and grins. He smells nasty. Of smoking and drinking and bad smells. *There you are, you little shit.*

A chilling wail wakes me. I'm drenched in sweat and my heart is pounding. I sit bolt upright in bed.

Fuck.

The eerie noise was from me.

I take a deep steadying breath, trying to rid my memory of the smell of body odor and cheap bourbon and stale Camel cigarettes.

You are one fucked-up son of a bitch.

Ana's words ring in my head.

Like his.

Fuck.

I couldn't help the crack whore.

I tried. Good God, I tried.

There you are, you little shit.

But I could help Ana.

I let her go.

I had to let her go.

She didn't need all this shit.

I glance at the clock: it's 3:30. I head into the kitchen and after drinking a large glass of water I make my way to the piano.

I WAKE AGAIN WITH a jolt and it's light—early morning sunshine fills the room. I was dreaming of Ana: Ana kissing me, her tongue in my mouth, my fingers in her hair, pressing her delectable body against me, her hands tethered above her head.

Where is she?

For one sweet moment I forget all that transpired yesterday—then it floods back.

She's gone.

Fuck.

The evidence of my desire presses into the mattress—but the memory of her bright eyes, clouded with hurt and humiliation as she left, soon solves that problem.

Feeling like shit, I lie on my back and stare at the ceiling, arms behind my head. The day stretches out before me, and for the first time in years, I don't know what to do with myself. I check the time again: 5:58.

Hell, I might as well go for a run.

PROKOFIEV'S "ARRIVAL OF THE Montagues and Capulets" blares in my ears as I pound the sidewalk through the early morning quiet of Fourth Avenue. I ache everywhere—my lungs are bursting, my head is throbbing, and the yawning, dull ache of loss eats away at my insides. I cannot run from this pain, though I'm trying. I stop to change the music and drag precious air into my lungs. I want something…violent. "Pump It" by the Black Eyed Peas, yeah. I pick up the pace.

I find myself running down Vine Street, and I know it's insane, but I hope to see her. As I near her street my heart races still harder and my anxiety escalates. I'm not desperate to see her—I just want to check that she's okay. No, that's not true. I want to see her. Finally on her street, I pace past her apartment building.

All is quiet—an Oldsmobile trundles up the road, two dog walkers are out—but there's no sign of life from inside her apartment.

Crossing the street, I pause on the sidewalk opposite, then duck into the doorway of an apartment building to catch my breath.

The curtains of one room are closed, the others open. Perhaps that's her room. Maybe she's still asleep—if she's there at all. A nightmare scenario forms in my mind: she went out last night, got drunk, met someone…

No.

Bile rises in my throat. The thought of her body in someone else's hands, some asshole basking in the warmth of her smile, making her giggle, making her laugh—making her come. It takes all my self-control not to go barging through the front door of her apartment to check that she's there and on her own.

You brought this on yourself, Grey.

Forget her. She's not for you.

I tug my Seahawks cap low over my face and sprint on down Western Avenue.

My jealousy is raw and angry; it fills the gaping hole. I hate it—it stirs something deep in my psyche that I really don't want to examine. I run harder, away from that memory, away from the pain, away from Anastasia Steele.

IT'S DUSK OVER SEATTLE. I stand up and stretch. I've been at my desk in my study all day, and it's been productive. Ros has worked hard, too. She's prepared and sent me a first draft business plan and letter of intent for SIP.

At least I'll be able to keep an eye on Ana.

The thought is painful and appealing in equal measure.

I've read and commented on two patent applications, a few contracts, and a new design spec, and while lost in the detail of those, I have not thought about her. The little glider is still on my desk, taunting me, reminding me of happier times, like she said. I picture her standing in the doorway of my study, wearing one of my T-shirts, all long legs and blue eyes, just before she seduced me.

Another first.

I miss her.

There—I admit it. I check my phone, hoping in vain, and there's a text from Elliot.

Beer, hotshot?

I respond:

No. Busy.

Elliot's response is immediate.

Fuck you, then.

Yeah. Fuck me.

Nothing from Ana. No missed call. No email. The nagging pain in my gut intensifies. She's not going to call. She wanted out. She wanted to get away from me, and I can't blame her.

It's for the best.

I head to the kitchen for a change of scenery.

Gail is back. The kitchen has been cleaned, and there's a pot bubbling on the stove. Smells good…but I'm not hungry. She walks in while I'm eyeing what's cooking.

"Good evening, sir."

"Gail."

She pauses—surprised by something. Surprised by me? *Shit, I must look bad.*

"Chicken Chasseur?" she asks, her voice uncertain.

"Sure," I mutter.

"For two?" she asks.

I stare at her, and she looks embarrassed.

"For one."

"Ten minutes?" she says, her voice wavering.

"Fine." My voice is frigid.

I turn to leave.

"Mr. Grey?" She stops me.

"What, Gail?"

"It's nothing. Sorry to disturb you." She turns to the stove to stir the chicken, and I head off to have another shower.

Christ, even my staff have noticed that something's rotten in the state of fucking Denmark.

MONDAY, JUNE 6, 2011

I dread going to bed. It's after midnight, and I'm tired, but I sit at my piano, playing the Bach Marcello piece over and over again. Remembering her head resting on my shoulder, I can almost smell her sweet fragrance.

For fuck's sake, she said she'd try!

I stop playing and clutch my head in both hands, my elbows hammering out two discordant chords as I lean on the keys. She said she'd try, but she fell at the first hurdle.

Then she ran.

Why did I hit her so hard?

Deep inside I know the answer—because she asked me to, and I was too impetuous and selfish to resist the temptation. Seduced by her challenge, I seized the opportunity to move us on to where I wanted us to be. And she didn't safe-word, and I hurt her more than she could take—when I promised her I'd never do that.

What a fucking fool I am.

How could she trust me after that? It's right that she's gone.

Why the hell would she want to be with me, anyway?

I contemplate getting drunk. I have not been drunk since I was fifteen—well, once, when I was twenty-one. I loathe the loss of control: I know what alcohol can do to a man. I shudder and snap my mind shut to those memories, deciding to call it a night.

Lying in my bed, I pray for a dreamless sleep...but if I am to dream, I want to dream of her.

Mommy is pretty today. She sits down and lets me brush her hair. She looks at me in the mirror and she smiles her special smile. Her special smile for me. There is a loud

> noise. A crash. He's back. No! *Where the fuck are you, bitch? Got a friend in need here. A friend with dough.* Mommy stands and takes my hand and pushes me into her closet. I sit on her shoes and try to be quiet and cover my ears and close my eyes tight. The clothes smell of Mommy. I like the smell. I like being here. Away from him. He is shouting. *Where is the little fucking runt?* He has my hair and he pulls me out of the closet. *Don't want you spoiling the party, you little shit.* He slaps Mommy hard on her face. *Make it good for my friend and you get your fix, bitch.* Mommy looks at me and she has tears. Don't cry, Mommy. Another man comes into the room. A big man with dirty hair. The big man smiles at Mommy. I am pulled into the other room. He pushes me onto the floor and I hurt my knees. *Now, what am I going to do with you, you piece of shit?* He smells nasty. He smells of beer and he is smoking a cigarette.

I wake. My heart is hammering like I've run forty blocks chased by the hounds of hell. I vault out of bed, pushing the nightmare back into the recesses of my consciousness, and hurry to the kitchen to fetch a glass of water.

I need to see Flynn. The nightmares are worse than ever. I didn't have nightmares when I slept with Ana beside me.

Hell.

It never occurred to me to sleep with any of my subs. Well, I never felt the inclination. Was I worried that they might touch me in the night? I don't know. It took an inebriated innocent to show me how restful it could be.

I'd watched my subs sleep before, but it was always as a prelude to waking them for some sexual relief.

I remember gazing at Ana for hours when she slept at The Heathman. The longer I watched her the more beautiful she became: her flawless skin luminous in the soft light, her dark hair fanning out on the white pillow, and her eyelashes fluttering while she slept. Her lips were parted, and I could see her teeth, and her tongue when she licked her lips. It was a most arousing experience—just watching her. And when I finally went to sleep beside her, listening to her even breathing, watching her breasts rise and fall with each breath, I slept well…so well.

I wander into my study and pick up the glider. The sight of it elicits a fond smile and comforts me. I feel both proud to have made it and ridiculous for what I am about to do. It was her last gift to me. Her first gift being…what?

Of course. *Herself.*

She sacrificed herself to my need. My greed. My lust. My ego… my fucking damaged ego.

Damn, will this pain ever just stop?

Feeling a little foolish, I take the glider with me to bed.

"WHAT WOULD YOU LIKE for breakfast, sir?"

"Just coffee, Gail."

She hesitates. "Sir, you didn't eat your dinner."

"And?"

"Maybe you're coming down with something."

"Gail, just coffee. Please." I shut her down—this is none of her business. Her lips thin, but she nods and turns to the Gaggia. I head into the study to collect my papers for the office and look for a padded envelope.

I CALL ROS FROM the car.

"Great work on the SIP material, but the business plan needs some revision. Let's offer."

"Christian, this is fast."

"I want to move quickly. I've emailed you my thoughts on the offering price. I'll be in the office from seven thirty. Let's meet."

"If you're sure."

"I'm sure."

"Okay. I'll call Andrea to schedule. I have the stats on Detroit versus Savannah."

"Bottom line?"

"Detroit."

"I see."

Shit…not Savannah.

"Let's talk later." I hang up.

I sit, brooding in the back of the Audi, as Taylor speeds through traffic. I wonder how Anastasia will be getting to work this morning. Perhaps she bought a car yesterday, though somehow I doubt it. I wonder if she feels as miserable as I do… I hope not. Maybe she's realized that I was a ridiculous infatuation.

She can't love me.

And certainly not now—not after all I've done to her. No one's ever said they loved me, except Mom and Dad, of course, but even then it was out of their sense of duty. Flynn's nagging words about unconditional parental love—even for kids who are adopted—ring in my head. But I've never been convinced; I've been nothing but a disappointment to them.

"Mr. Grey?"

"Sorry, what is it?" Taylor has caught me unawares. He's holding the car door open, waiting for me with a look of concern.

"We're here, sir."

Shit…how long have we been here? "Thanks. I'll let you know what time this evening."

Focus, Grey.

ANDREA AND OLIVIA BOTH look up as I come out of the elevator. Olivia flutters her eyelashes and tucks a strand of hair behind her ear. *Christ—I'm done with this silly girl.* I need HR to move her to another department.

"Coffee, please, Olivia—and get me a croissant."

She leaps up to follow my orders.

"Andrea—get me Welch, Barney, then Flynn, then Claude Bastille on the phone. I don't want to be disturbed at all, not even by my mother…unless…unless Anastasia Steele calls. Okay?"

"Yes, sir. Do you want to go through your schedule now?"

"No. I need coffee and something to eat first." I scowl at Olivia, who is moving at a snail's pace toward the elevator.

"Yes, Mr. Grey," Andrea calls after me as I open the door to my office.

From my briefcase I take the padded envelope that holds my most precious possession—the glider. I place it on my desk, and my mind drifts to Miss Steele.

She'll be starting her new job this morning, meeting new people…new men. The thought is depressing. She'll forget me.

No, she won't forget me. Women always remember the first man they fucked, don't they? I'll always hold a place in her memory, for that alone. But I don't want to be a memory: I want to stay in her mind. I need to stay in her mind. What can I do?

There's a knock at the door and Andrea appears. "Coffee and croissants for you, Mr. Grey."

"Come in."

As she scurries over to my desk her eyes dart to the glider, but wisely she holds her tongue. She places breakfast on my desk.

Black coffee. *Well done, Olivia.* "Thanks."

"I've left messages for Welch, Barney, and Bastille. Flynn is calling back in five."

"Good. I want you to cancel any social engagements I have this week. No lunches, nothing in the evening. Get Barney on the phone and find me the number of a good florist."

She scribbles furiously on her notepad.

"Sir, we use Arcadia's Roses. Would you like me to send flowers for you?"

"No, give me the number. I'll do it myself. That's all."

She nods and leaves promptly, as if she can't get out of my office fast enough. A few moments later the phone buzzes. It's Barney.

"Barney, I need you to make me a stand for a model glider."

BETWEEN MEETINGS I CALL the florist and order two dozen white roses for Ana, to be delivered to her home this evening. That way she won't be embarrassed or inconvenienced at work.

And she won't be able to forget me.

"Would you like a message with the flowers, sir?" the florist asks.

A message for Ana?

What to say?

Come back. I'm sorry. I won't hit you again.

The words pop unbidden into my head, making me frown.

"Um…something like 'Congratulations on your first day at work. I hope it went well.'" I spy the glider on my desk. "'And thank you for the glider. That was very thoughtful. It has pride of place on my desk. Christian.'"

The florist reads it back to me.

Damn, it doesn't express what I want to say to her at all.

"Will that be all, Mr. Grey?"

"Yes. Thank you."

"You're welcome, sir, and have a nice day."

I look daggers at the phone. *Nice day my ass.*

"HEY, MAN, WHAT'S EATING you?" Claude gets up from the floor, where I've just knocked him flat on his lean, mean rear end. "You're on fire this afternoon, Grey." He rises slowly, with the grace of a big cat reassessing its prey. We are sparring alone in the basement gym at Grey House.

"I'm pissed off," I hiss.

His expression is cool as we circle each other.

"Not a good idea to enter the ring if your thoughts are elsewhere," Claude says, amused, but not taking his eyes off me.

"I'm finding it helps."

"More on your left. Protect your right. Hand up, Grey."

He swings and hits me on my shoulder, almost knocking me off balance.

"Concentrate, Grey. None of your boardroom bullshit in here. Or is it a girl? Some fine piece of ass finally cramping your cool?" he sneers, goading me. It works: I middle-kick to his side and drop-punch once, then twice, and he staggers back, dreadlocks flying.

"Mind your own fucking business, Bastille."

"Whoa, we have found the source of the pain," Claude crows in triumph. He swings suddenly, but I anticipate his action and block him, thrusting up with a punch and a swift kick. He jumps back this time, impressed.

"Whatever shit's happening in your privileged little world, Grey, it's working. Bring it on."

Oh, he is going down. I lunge at him.

THE TRAFFIC IS LIGHT on the way home.

"Taylor, can we make a detour?"

"Where to, sir?"

"Can you drive past Miss Steele's apartment?"

"Yes, sir."

I've gotten used to this ache. It seems to be ever-present, like tinnitus. In meetings it's muted and less obtrusive; it's only when I'm alone with my thoughts that it flares up and rages inside me. How long does this last?

As we approach her apartment, my heartbeat spikes.

Perhaps I'll see her.

The possibility is thrilling and unsettling. And I realize that I have thought of nothing but her since she left. Her absence is my constant companion.

"Drive slow," I instruct Taylor as we near her building.

The lights are on.

She's home!

I hope she's alone, and missing me.

Has she received my flowers?

I want to check my phone to see if she's sent me a message, but I can't drag my gaze away from her apartment; I don't want to miss seeing her. Is she well? Is she thinking about me? I wonder how her first day at work went.

"Again, sir?" Taylor asks as we slowly cruise past, and the apartment disappears from view.

"No." I exhale. I hadn't realized I'd stopped breathing. As we head back to Escala I sift through my emails and texts, hoping for something from her…but there's nothing. There's a text from Elena.

> You okay?

I ignore it.

IT'S QUIET IN MY apartment; I hadn't really noticed before. Anastasia's absence has accentuated the silence.

Taking a sip of cognac, I wander listlessly into my library. It's ironic I never showed her this room, given her love of literature. I expect to find some solace in here because the room holds no memories of us. I survey all my books, neatly shelved and cataloged, and my eyes stray to the billiard table. Does she play billiards? I don't suppose she does.

An image of her spread-eagled over the green baize springs to my mind. There may not be any memories in here, but my mind is more than capable, and more than willing, to create vivid erotic images of the lovely Miss Steele.

I can't bear it.

I take another swig of cognac and head out of the room.

TUESDAY, JUNE 7, 2011

We're fucking. Fucking hard. Against the bathroom door. She's mine. I bury myself in her, again and again. Glorying in her: the feel of her, her smell, her taste. Fisting my hand in her hair, holding her in place. Holding her ass. Her legs wrapped around my waist. She can't move; she's pinioned by me. Wrapped around me like silk. Her hands pulling my hair. Oh yes. I'm home, she's home. This is the place I want to be…inside her…

She. Is. Mine. Her muscles are tightening as she comes, clenching around me, her head back. Come for me!

She cries out and I follow… Oh yes, my sweet, sweet Anastasia. She smiles, sleepy, sated—and oh so sexy.

She stands and gazes at me, that playful smile on her lips, then pushes me away and walks backward, saying nothing. I grab her and we're in the playroom. I'm holding her down over the bench. I raise my arm to punish her, belt in hand…and she disappears. She's by the door. Her face white, shocked and sad, and she's silently drifting away… The door has disappeared, and she won't stop. She holds out her hands in entreaty. *Join me*, she whispers, but she's moving backward, getting fainter…disappearing before my eyes…vanishing…

She's gone. *No!* I shout. *No!* But I have no voice. I have nothing. I'm mute. Mute…again.

I wake, confused.

Shit—it's a dream. Another vivid dream.

Different, though.

Hell! I'm a sticky mess. Briefly I feel that long-forgotten but familiar sense of fear and exhilaration—but Elena doesn't own me now.

Jesus H. Christ, I've come for Team USA. This hasn't happened to me since I was, what? Fifteen, sixteen?

I lie back in the darkness, disgusted with myself. I drag my T-shirt off and wipe myself down. There's semen everywhere. I find myself smirking in the darkness, despite the dull ache of loss. The erotic dream was worth it. The rest of it…fucking hell. I turn over and go back to sleep.

He is gone. Mommy is sitting on the couch. She is quiet. She looks at the wall and blinks sometimes. I stand in front of her, but she doesn't see me. I wave and she sees me, but she waves me away. No, Maggot, not now. He hurts Mommy. He hurts me. I hate him. He makes me so mad. It's best when it's just Mommy and me. She is mine then. My Mommy. My tummy hurts. It is hungry again. I am in the kitchen, looking for cookies. I pull the chair to the cupboard and climb up. I find a box of crackers. It is the only thing in the cupboard. I sit down on the chair and open the box. There are two left. I eat them. They taste good. I hear him. He's back. I jump down and I run to my bedroom and climb into bed. I pretend to be asleep. He pokes me with his finger. *Stay here, you little shit. I'm going to fuck your bitch of a mother. I don't want to see your fuck-ugly face for the rest of the evening. Understand?* He slaps my face when I don't reply. *Or you get the burn, you little prick.* No. No. I don't like that. I don't like the burn. It hurts. *Got it, retard?* I know he wants me to cry. But it's hard. I can't make the noise. He hits me with his fist—

Startled awake again, I lie panting in the pale dawn light, waiting for my heart rate to slow, trying to lose the acrid taste of fear in my mouth.

She saved you from this shit, Grey.

You didn't relive the pain of these memories when she was with you. Why did you let her leave?

I glance at the clock: 5:15. Time for a run.

HER BUILDING LOOKS GLOOMY; it's still in shadow, untouched by the early morning sun. Fitting. It reflects my mood. Her apartment is dark inside, yet the curtains to the room I watched before are drawn. It must be her room.

I hope to God she's sleeping alone up there. I envisage her curled up on her white iron bed, a small ball of Ana. Is she dreaming of me? Do I give her nightmares? Has she forgotten me?

I've never felt this miserable, not even as a teenager. Maybe before I was a Grey… My memory spirals back. No, no—not awake as well. This is too much. Pulling my hood up and leaning against the granite wall, I'm hidden in the doorway of the building opposite. The awful thought crosses my mind that I might be standing here in a week, a month…a year? Watching, waiting, just to catch a glimpse of the girl who used to be mine. It's painful. I've become what she's always accused me of being—her stalker.

I can't go on like this. I have to see her. See that she's okay. I need to erase the last image I have of her: hurt, humiliated, defeated…and leaving me.

I have to think of a way.

BACK AT ESCALA, GAIL watches me impassively.

"I didn't ask for this." I stare at the omelet she's placed in front of me.

"I'll throw it away, then, Mr. Grey," she says and reaches for the plate. She knows I hate waste, but she doesn't quail at my hard stare.

"You did this on purpose, Mrs. Jones." Interfering woman.

And she smiles, a small victorious smile. I scowl, but she's unfazed, and with the memory of last night's nightmare lingering, I devour my breakfast.

COULD I JUST CALL Ana and say hi? Would she take my call? My eyes wander to the glider on my desk. She asked for a clean break. I should honor that and leave her alone. But I want to hear her voice. For a moment I contemplate calling her and hanging up, just to hear her speak.

"Christian? Christian, are you okay?"

"Sorry, Ros, what was that?"

"You're so distracted. I've never seen you like this."

"I'm fine," I snap. *Shit—concentrate, Grey.* "What were you saying?"

Ros eyes me suspiciously. "I was saying that SIP is in more financial difficulty than we thought. Are you sure you want to go ahead?"

"Yes." My voice is vehement. "I am."

"Their team will be here this afternoon to sign the heads of agreement."

"Good. Now, what's the latest on our proposal for Eamon Kavanagh?"

I STAND BROODING, STARING down through the slatted wooden blinds at Taylor, who is parked outside Flynn's office. It's late afternoon and I'm still thinking about Ana.

"Christian, I'm more than happy to take your money and watch you stare out the window, but I don't think the view is the reason you're here," Flynn says.

When I turn to face him he's regarding me with an air of polite anticipation. I sigh and make my way to his couch.

"The nightmares are back. Like never before."

Flynn lifts a brow. "The same ones?"

"Yes."

"What's changed?" He cocks his head to one side, waiting for my response. When I remain mute, he adds, "Christian, you look as miserable as sin. Something's happened."

I feel like I did with Elena; part of me doesn't want to tell him, because then it's real.

"I met a girl."

"And?"

"She left me."

He looks surprised. "Women have left you before. Why is this different?"

I stare at him blankly.

Why is it different? *Because Ana was different.*

My thoughts blur together in a colorful tangled tapestry: she wasn't a submissive. We had no contract. She was sexually inexperienced. She was the first woman I wanted more from than just sex. Christ—all the firsts I experienced with her: the first girl I'd slept beside, the first virgin, the first to meet my family, the first to fly in *Charlie Tango*, the first I took soaring.

Yeah… Different.

Flynn interrupts my thoughts. "It's a simple question, Christian."

"I miss her."

His face remains kind and concerned, but he gives nothing away.

"You've never missed any of the women you were involved with previously?"

"No."

"So there was something different about her," he prompts.

I shrug, but he persists.

"Did you have a contractual relationship with her? Was she a submissive?"

"I'd hoped she would be. But it wasn't for her."

Flynn frowns. "I don't understand."

"I broke one of my rules. I chased this girl, thinking she'd be interested, and it turned out it wasn't for her."

"Tell me what happened."

The floodgates open and I recount the past month's events, from the moment Ana fell into my office to when she left last Saturday morning.

"I see. You've certainly packed a lot in since we last spoke." He rubs his chin as he studies me. "There are many issues here, Christian. But right now the one I want to focus on is how you felt when she said she loved you."

I inhale sharply, my gut tightening with fear.

"Horrified," I whisper.

"Of course you did." He shakes his head. "You're not the monster you think you are. You're more than worthy of affection, Christian. You know that. I've told you often enough. It's only in your mind that you're not."

I give him a level gaze, ignoring his platitude.

"And how do you feel now?" he asks.

Lost. I feel lost.

"I miss her. I want to see her." I'm in the confessional once more, owning up to my sins: the dark, dark need that I have for her, as if she were an addiction.

"So in spite of the fact that, as you perceive it, she couldn't fulfill your needs, you miss her?"

"Yes. It's not just my perception, John. She can't be what I want her to be, and I can't be what she wants me to be."

"Are you sure?"

"She walked out."

"She walked out because you belted her. If she doesn't share your tastes, can you blame her?"

"No."

"Have you thought about trying a relationship her way?"

What? I stare at him, shocked.

He continues, "Did you find sexual relations with her satisfying?"

"Yes, of course," I snap, irritated.

He ignores my tone. "Did you find beating her satisfying?"

"Very."

"Would you like to do it again?"

Do that to her again? And watch her walk out—again?

"No."

"And why's that?"

"Because it's not her scene. I hurt her. Really hurt her…and she can't… She won't…" I pause. "She doesn't enjoy it. She was angry. Really fucking angry." Her expression, her wounded eyes, will haunt me for a long time…and I never want to be the cause of that look again.

"Are you surprised?"

I shake my head. "She was mad," I whisper. "I'd never seen her so angry."

"How did that make you feel?"

"Helpless."

"And that's a familiar feeling," he prompts.

"Familiar how?" *What does he mean?*

"Don't you recognize yourself at all? Your past?" His question knocks me off balance.

Fuck, we've been over and over this.

"No, I don't. It's different. The relationship I had with Mrs. Lincoln was completely different."

"I wasn't referring to Mrs. Lincoln."

"What were you referring to?" My voice is pin-drop quiet, because suddenly I see where he's going with this.

"You know."

I gulp for air, swamped by the impotence and rage of a defenseless child. Yes. The rage. The deep infuriating rage…and fear. The darkness swirls angrily inside me.

"It's not the same," I hiss through gritted teeth as I strain to hold my temper.

"No, it's not," Flynn concedes.

But the image of her rage comes unwelcome to my mind.

"This is what you really like? Me, like this?"

It dampens my anger.

"I know what you're trying to do here, Doctor, but it's an unfair comparison. She asked me to show her. She's a consenting adult, for fuck's sake. She could have safe-worded. She could have told me to stop. She didn't."

"I know. I know." He holds his hand up. "I'm just callously illustrating a point, Christian. You're an angry man, and you have every reason to be. I'm not going to rehash all that right now—you're obviously suffering, and the whole point of these sessions is to move you to a place where you are more accepting and comfortable with yourself." He pauses. "This girl…"

"Anastasia," I mutter petulantly.

"Anastasia. She's obviously had a profound effect on you. Her leaving has triggered your abandonment issues and your PTSD. She clearly means much more to you than you're willing to admit to yourself."

I take a sharp breath. *Is that why this is so painful? Because she means more, so much more?*

"You need to focus on where you want to be," Flynn continues. "And it sounds to me like you want to be with this girl. You miss her. Do you want to be with her?"

Be with Ana?

"Yes," I whisper.

"Then you have to focus on that goal. This goes back to what I've been banging on about for our last few sessions—the SFBT. If she's in love with you, as she told you she is, she must be suffering, too. So I repeat my question: Have you considered a more conventional relationship with this girl?"

"No, I haven't."

"Why not?"

"Because it's never occurred to me that I could."

"Well if she's not prepared to be your submissive, you can't play the role of Dominant."

I glare at him. It's not a role—it's who I am.

And from nowhere, I recall an earlier email to Anastasia. My words: *What I think you fail to realize is that in Dom/sub relationships it is the sub who has all the power. That's you. I'll repeat this—you are the one with all the power. Not me.*

If she doesn't want to do this…then neither can I.

Hope stirs in my chest.

Could I?

Could I have a vanilla relationship with Anastasia?

My scalp prickles.

Fuck. Possibly.

If I could, would she want me back?

"Christian, you have demonstrated that you are an extraordinarily capable person, in spite of your problems. You're a rare individual. Once you focus on a goal, you drive ahead and achieve it—usually surpassing all your own expectations. Listening to you today, it's clear you were focused on getting Anastasia to where you wanted her to be, but you didn't take into account her inexperience or her feelings. It seems to me that you've been so focused on reaching your goal that you missed the journey that you were taking together."

The last month flashes before me: her tripping into my office, her acute embarrassment at Clayton's, her witty, snarky emails, her smart mouth…her giggle…her quiet fortitude and defiance, her courage—and it occurs to me that I have enjoyed every single minute. Every infuriating, distracting, humorous, sensual, carnal second of her—yes, I have. We've been on an extraordinary journey, both of us. Well, I certainly have.

My thoughts take a darker turn.

She doesn't know the depths of my depravity, the darkness in my soul, the monster beneath—maybe I should leave her alone.

I'm not worthy of her. She can't love me.

But even as I think the words, I know I don't have the strength to stay away from her…if she'll have me.

Flynn summons my attention. "Christian, think about it. Our time is up now. I want to see you in a few days and talk through some of the other issues you mentioned. I'll have Janet call Andrea to arrange an appointment." He stands, and I know it's time to leave.

"You've given me a lot to think about," I tell him.

"I wouldn't be doing my job if I didn't. Just a few days, Christian. We have so much more to talk about." He shakes my hand and gives me a reassuring smile, and I leave with a small blossom of hope.

STANDING ON THE BALCONY, I survey Seattle at night. Up here I'm at one remove, away from it all. What did she call it?

My ivory tower.

Normally I find it peaceful—but lately my peace of mind has been shattered by a certain blue-eyed young woman.

"Have you thought about trying a relationship her way?" Flynn's words taunt me, suggesting so many possibilities.

Could I win her back? The thought terrifies me.

I take a sip of my cognac. Why would she want me back? Could I ever be what she wants me to be? I won't let go of my hope. I need to find a way.

I need her.

Something startles me—a movement, a shadow at the periphery of my vision. I frown. What the…?

I turn toward the shadow but find nothing. I'm seeing things now. I slug the cognac and head back into the living room.

WEDNESDAY, JUNE 8, 2011

Mommy! Mommy! Mommy is asleep on the floor. She has been asleep for a long time. I shake her. She doesn't wake up. I call her. She doesn't wake up. He isn't here and still Mommy doesn't wake up.

I am thirsty. In the kitchen I pull a chair to the sink and I have a drink. The water splashes over my sweater. My sweater is dirty. Mommy is still asleep. Mommy, wake up! She lies still. She is cold. I fetch my blankie and I cover Mommy and I lie down on the sticky green rug beside her.

My tummy hurts. It is hungry, but Mommy is still asleep. I have two toy cars. One red. One yellow. My green car is gone. They race by the floor where Mommy is sleeping. I think Mommy is sick. I search for something to eat. In the icebox I find peas. They are cold. I eat them slowly. They make my tummy hurt. I sleep beside Mommy. The peas are gone. In the icebox is something. It smells funny. I lick it and my tongue sticks. I eat it slowly. It tastes nasty. I drink some water. I play with my cars and I sleep beside Mommy. Mommy is so cold and she won't wake up. The door crashes open. I cover Mommy with my blankie. *Fuck. What the fuck happened here? Oh, the crazy fucked-up bitch. Shit. Fuck. Get out of my way, you little shit.* He kicks me and I hit my head on the floor. My head hurts. He calls somebody and he goes. He locks the door. I lay down beside Mommy. My head hurts. The lady policeman is here. No. No. No. Don't touch me. Don't touch me. Don't touch me. I stay by Mommy. No. Stay away from me. The lady policeman has my blankie and she grabs me. I scream.

Mommy! Mommy! The words are gone. I can't say the words. Mommy can't hear me. I have no words.

I wake breathing hard, taking huge gulps of air, checking my surroundings. Oh, thank God—I'm in my bed. Slowly the fear recedes. I'm twenty-seven, not four. This shit has to stop.

I used to have my nightmares under control. Maybe one every couple of weeks, but nothing like this—night after night.

Since she left.

I turn over and lie flat on my back, staring at the ceiling. When she slept beside me, I slept well. I need her in my life, in my bed. She was the day to my night. I'm going to get her back.

How?

"Have you thought about trying a relationship her way?"

She wants hearts and flowers. Can I give her that? I frown, trying to recall the romantic moments in my life...and there's nothing. Except with Ana. The "more." The gliding, and IHOP, and taking her up in *Charlie Tango.*

Maybe I *can* do this. I drift back to sleep, the mantra in my head: *She's mine. She's mine...*and I smell her, feel her soft skin, taste her lips, and hear her moans. Exhausted, I fall into an erotic, Ana-filled dream.

I wake suddenly. My scalp tingles, and for a moment I think whatever's disturbed me is external rather than internal. I sit up, rub my head, and slowly scan the room.

In spite of the carnal dream, my body has behaved. Elena would be pleased. She texted yesterday, but Elena's the last person I want to talk to—there's only one thing I want to do right now. I get up and pull on my running gear.

I'm going to check on Ana.

HER STREET IS QUIET except for the rumble of a delivery truck and the out-of-tune whistling of a solitary dog walker. Her apartment is in darkness, the curtains to her room closed. I keep a silent vigil from my stalker's hide, staring up at the windows and thinking. I need a plan—a plan to win her back.

As dawn's light brightens her window, I turn my iPod up loud, and with Moby blaring in my ears I run back to Escala.

"I'LL HAVE A CROISSANT, Mrs. Jones."

She stills in surprise and I raise a brow.

"Apricot preserves?" she asks, recovering.

"Please."

"I'll heat up a couple for you, Mr. Grey. Here's your coffee."

"Thank you, Gail."

She smiles. Is it just because I'm having croissants? If it makes her that happy, I should have them more often.

IN THE BACK OF the Audi, I plot. I need to get up close and personal with Ana Steele, to begin my campaign to win her back.

I call Andrea, knowing that at 7:15 she won't be at her desk yet, and I leave a voice mail. "Andrea, as soon as you're in, I want to run through my schedule for the next few days."

There—step one in my offensive is to make time in my schedule for Ana. What the hell am I supposed to be doing this week? Currently, I don't have a clue. Normally I'm on this shit, but lately I've been all over the place. Now I have a mission to focus on. *You can do this, Grey.*

But deep down I wish I had the courage of my convictions. Anxiety unfurls in my gut. Can I convince Ana to take me back? Will she listen? I hope so. This has to work. I miss her.

"MR. GREY, I CANCELED all your social events this week, apart from the one for tomorrow—I don't know what the occasion is. Your calendar says Portland, that's it."

Yes! The fucking photographer!

I beam at Andrea, and her eyebrows shoot up in surprise. "Thanks, Andrea. That's all for now. Send in Sam."

"Sure, Mr. Grey. Would you like some more coffee?"

"Please."

"With milk?"

"Yes. Latte. Thank you."

She smiles politely and leaves.

This is it! My in! The photographer! Now…what to do?

MY MORNING HAS BEEN back-to-back meetings, and my staff has been watching me nervously, waiting for me to explode. Okay, that's been my modus operandi for the last few days—but today I feel clearer, calmer, and present, able to deal with everything.

It's now lunchtime; my workout with Claude has gone well. The only fly in the ointment is that there's no more news about Leila. All we know is that she's split up with her husband and she could be anywhere. If she surfaces, Welch will find her.

I'm famished. Olivia sets a plate down on my desk.

"Your sandwich, Mr. Grey."

"Chicken and mayonnaise?"

"Um…"

I stare at her. She just doesn't get it.

Olivia offers an inept apology.

"I said chicken *with mayonnaise*, Olivia. It's not that hard."

"I'm sorry, Mr. Grey."

"It's fine. Just go."

She looks relieved but scrambles to leave the room.

I buzz Andrea.

"Sir?"

"Come in here."

Andrea appears at the doorway, looking calm and efficient.

"Get rid of that girl."

Andrea pulls herself up straight.

"Sir, Olivia is Senator Blandino's daughter."

"I don't care if she's the queen of fucking England. Get her out of my office."

"Yes, sir." Andrea flushes.

"Get someone else to help you," I offer in a gentler tone. I don't want to alienate Andrea.

"Yes, Mr. Grey."

"Thank you. That's all."

She smiles and I know she's back on board. She's a good PA; I don't want her to quit because I'm being an asshole. She exits, leaving me to my chicken sandwich—no mayo—and my campaign plan.

Portland.

I know the form of email address for employees at SIP. I think Anastasia will respond better in writing; she always has. How to begin?

~~Dear Ana~~

No.

~~Dear Anastasia~~

No.

~~Dear Miss Steele~~

Shit!

HALF AN HOUR LATER I'm still staring at a blank computer screen. What the hell do I say?

Come back…please?

~~Forgive me.~~

No.

~~I miss you.~~

No.

~~Let's try it your way.~~

No.

I put my head in my hands. Why is this so difficult?

Keep it simple, Grey. Just cut the crap.

I take a deep breath and tap out an email. *Yes…this will do.*

Andrea buzzes me. "Ms. Bailey is here to see you, sir."

"Tell her to wait."

I hang up and take a moment, and with my heart pounding, I press send.

From: Christian Grey
Subject: Tomorrow
Date: June 8 2011 14:05
To: Anastasia Steele

Dear Anastasia

Forgive this intrusion at work. I hope that it's going well. Did you get my flowers?

I note that tomorrow is the gallery opening for your friend's show, and I'm sure you've not had time to purchase a car, and it's a long drive. I would be more than happy to take you—should you wish.

Let me know.

Christian Grey
CEO, Grey Enterprises Holdings, Inc.

I watch my inbox.

And watch.

And watch…my anxiety growing with every second that crawls by.

Getting up, I pace the office—but that takes me away from my computer. Back at my desk, I check my email yet again.

Nothing.

To distract myself, I trace my finger along the wings of my glider.

For fuck's sake, Grey, get a grip.

Come on, Anastasia, answer me. She's always been so prompt. I check my watch: 2:09.

Four minutes!

Still nothing.

Getting up, I pace around my office once more, peering at my watch every three seconds, or so it feels.

By 2:20 I'm in despair. She's not going to reply. She really does hate me... Who could blame her?

Then I hear the ping of an email. My heart leaps into my throat.

Hell! It's from Ros, telling me she's gone back to her office.

And then it's there, in my inbox, the magical line:

From: Anastasia Steele.

From: Anastasia Steele
Subject: Tomorrow
Date: June 8 2011 14:25
To: Christian Grey

Hi Christian

Thank you for the flowers; they are lovely.

Yes, I would appreciate a lift.

Thank you.

Anastasia Steele
Assistant to Jack Hyde, Editor, SI.

Relief floods through me. I close my eyes, savoring the feeling.

YES!

I pore over her email looking for clues, but as usual I have no idea what the thoughts are behind her words. The tone is friendly enough, but that's it. Just friendly.

Carpe diem, Grey.

From: Christian Grey
Subject: Tomorrow
Date: June 8 2011 14:27
To: Anastasia Steele

Dear Anastasia

What time shall I pick you up?

Christian Grey
CEO, Grey Enterprises Holdings, Inc.

I don't have to wait quite so long.

From: Anastasia Steele
Subject: Tomorrow
Date: June 8 2011 14:32
To: Christian Grey

José's show starts at 7:30. What time would you suggest?

Anastasia Steele
Assistant to Jack Hyde, Editor, SIP

We can take *Charlie Tango.*

From: Christian Grey
Subject: Tomorrow
Date: June 8 2011 14:34
To: Anastasia Steele

Dear Anastasia

Portland is some distance away. I shall pick you up at 5:45.

I look forward to seeing you.

Christian Grey
CEO, Grey Enterprises Holdings, Inc.

From: Anastasia Steele
Subject: Tomorrow
Date: June 8 2011 14:38
To: Christian Grey

See you then.

Anastasia Steele
Assistant to Jack Hyde, Editor, SIP

My campaign to win her back is under way. I feel elated; the small blossom of hope is now a Japanese flowering cherry.

I buzz Andrea.

"Miss Bailey went back to her office, Mr. Grey."

"I know, she emailed me. I need Taylor here in an hour."

"Yes, sir."

I hang up. Anastasia is working for a guy named Jack Hyde. I want to know more about him. I call Ros.

"Christian." She sounds pissed. *Tough.*

"Do we have access to the employee files from SIP?"

"Not yet. But I can get them."

"Please. Today if you can. I want everything they have on Jack Hyde and anyone who's worked for him."

"Can I ask why?"

"No."

She's silent for a moment.

"Christian, I don't know what's gotten into you recently."

"Ros, just do it, okay?"

She sighs. "Okay. Now can we have our meeting about the Taiwan shipyard proposal?"

"Yes. I had an important call to make. It took longer than I thought."

"I'll be right up."

WHEN ROS LEAVES I follow her out of the office.

"WSU next Friday," I tell Andrea, who scribbles a reminder in her notebook.

"And I get to fly in the company chopper?" Ros bubbles with enthusiasm.

"Helicopter," I correct her.

"Whatever, Christian." She rolls her eyes as she enters the elevator, and it makes me smile.

Andrea watches Ros leave, then gives me an expectant look.

"Call Stephan—I'll be flying *Charlie Tango* to Portland tomorrow evening, and I'll need him to fly her back to Boeing Field," I tell Andrea.

"Yes, Mr. Grey."

I see no sign of Olivia. "Has she gone?"

"Olivia?" Andrea asks.

I nod.

"Yes." She seems relieved.

"Where to?"

"Finance."

"Good thinking. It'll keep Senator Blandino off my back."

Andrea looks pleased at the compliment.

"You're getting someone else to help out here?" I ask.

"Yes, sir. I'm seeing three candidates tomorrow morning."

"Good. Is Taylor here?"

"Yes, sir."

"Cancel the rest of my meetings today. I'm going out."

"Out?" she squeaks in surprise.

"Yes." I grin. "Out."

"WHERE TO, SIR?" TAYLOR asks as I stretch out in the back of the SUV.

"The Mac store."

"On Northeast Forty-Fifth?"

"Yes."

I'm going to buy Ana an iPad. Leaning back in my seat, I close my eyes and contemplate which apps and songs I'm going to download and install for her. I could choose "Toxic." I smirk at the thought. No, I don't think that would be popular with her. She'd be mad as hell—and for the first time in a while the thought of her mad makes me smile. Mad like she was in Georgia, not like last Saturday. I shift in my seat; I don't want to be reminded of that. I turn my thoughts back to potential song choices, feeling more buoyant than I have in days. My phone buzzes, and my heart rate spikes.

Dare I hope?

Hey, asshole. Beer?

Hell. A text from my brother.

No. Busy.

You're always busy.
Going to Barbados tomorrow.
To, you know, RELAX.
See you when I get back.
And we will have that beer!!!

Laters, Lelliot. Safe travels.

IT'S BEEN A DIVERTING evening, filled with music—a nostalgic journey through my iTunes, making a playlist for Anastasia.

I remember her dancing in my kitchen; I wish I knew what she'd been listening to. She looked totally ridiculous, and utterly adorable. That was after I fucked her for the first time.

No. After I made love to her the first time?

Neither term feels right.

I recall her impassioned plea the night I introduced her to my parents. *"I want you to make love to me."* How shocked I was by her simple statement—and yet all she wanted was to touch me. I shudder at the thought. I have to make her understand that this is a hard limit for me—I cannot tolerate being touched.

I shake my head. *You're getting way ahead of yourself, Grey*—you have to close this deal first. I check the inscription on the iPad.

Anastasia—this is for you.
I know what you want to hear.
This music on here says it for me.
Christian

Perhaps this will do it. She wants hearts and flowers; perhaps this will come close. But I shake my head, because I have no idea. There's so much I want to say to her, if she'll listen. And if she won't, the songs will say it for me. I just hope she allows me the opportunity to give them to her.

But if she doesn't like my proposition, if she doesn't like the thought of being with me—what will I do? I might just be a convenient ride to Portland. The thought depresses me, as I head toward my bedroom for some much-needed sleep.

Do I dare to hope?

Damn it. Yes, I do.

THURSDAY, JUNE 9, 2011

The doctor holds up her hands. *I'm not going to hurt you. I need to check your tummy. Here.* She gives me a cold, round sucky thing and she lets me play with it. *You put it on your tummy, and I won't touch you and I can hear your tummy.* The doctor is good...the doctor is Mommy.

My new mommy is pretty. She's like an angel. A doctor angel. She strokes my hair. I like it when she strokes my hair. She lets me eat ice cream and cake. She doesn't shout when she finds the bread and apples hidden in my shoes. Or under my bed. Or under my pillow. *Darling, the food is in the kitchen. Just find me or Daddy when you're hungry. Point with your finger. Can you do that?* There is another boy. Lelliot. He is mean. So I punch him. But my new mommy doesn't like the fighting. There is a piano. I like the noise. I stand at the piano and press the white and the black. The noise from the black is strange. Miss Kathie sits at the piano with me. She teaches the black and the white notes. She has long brown hair and she looks like someone I know. She smells of flowers and apple pie baking. She smells of good. She makes the piano sound pretty. She is kind to me. She smiles and I play. She smiles and I am happy. She smiles and she's Ana. Beautiful Ana, sitting with me as I play a fugue, a prelude, an adagio, a sonata. She sighs, resting her head on my shoulder, and she smiles. *I love listening to you play, Christian. I love you, Christian.*

Ana. Stay with me. You're mine. I love you, too.

I wake with a start.

Today, I win her back.

EXCERPT FROM *Darker*

THURSDAY, JUNE 9, 2011

I sit. Waiting. My heart is thumping. It's 5:36 and I stare through the privacy glass of my Audi at the front door of her building. I know I'm early, but I've been looking forward to this moment all day.

I'm going to see her.

I shift in my seat in the rear of the car. The atmosphere feels stifling, and though I'm trying to remain calm, the anticipation and anxiety are knotting my stomach and pressing down on my chest. Taylor sits in the driver's seat, staring straight ahead, wordless, looking his usual composed self, while I can barely breathe. It's irritating.

Damn it. Where is she?

She's inside—inside Seattle Independent Publishing. Set back beyond a wide, open sidewalk, the building is shabby and in need of renovation; the company's name is etched haphazardly in the glass, and the frosted effect on the window is peeling. The business behind those closed doors could be an insurance company or an accounting firm—they're not displaying their wares. Well, that's something I can rectify when I take control. SIP is mine. Almost. I've signed the revised heads of agreement.

Taylor clears his throat and his eyes dart to mine in the rearview mirror. "I'll wait outside, sir," he says, surprising me, and he climbs out of the car before I can stop him.

Maybe he's more affected by my tension than I thought. Am I that obvious? Maybe *he's* tense. But why? Maybe it's because he's had to deal with my ever-changing moods this past week, and I know I've not been easy.

But today has been different. Hopeful. It's the first productive day I've had since she left me, or so it feels. My optimism has driven me through my meetings with enthusiasm. Ten hours until I see her. Nine. Eight. Seven... My patience has been tested by the clock as it ticks closer to my reunion with Miss Anastasia Steele.

And now that I'm sitting here, alone and waiting, the determination and confidence I've enjoyed all day are evaporating.

Perhaps she's changed her mind.

Will it be a reunion? Or am I just the free ride to Portland?

I check my watch again.

5:38.

Shit. Why does time move so slowly?

I contemplate sending her an email to let her know I'm outside, but as I fumble for my phone, I realize I don't want to take my eyes off the front door. Leaning back, I run through her recent emails in my mind. I know them by heart, all of them friendly and concise but without a hint that she's been missing me.

Maybe I *am* the free ride.

I dismiss the thought and stare at the doorway, willing her to appear.

Anastasia Steele, I'm waiting.

The door opens and my heart soars into overdrive but then quickly stutters with disappointment. It's not her.

Damn.

She has always kept me waiting. A humorless smile tugs at my lips: waiting at Clayton's, at The Heathman after the photo shoot, and again when I sent her the Thomas Hardy books.

Tess...

I wonder if she still has them. She wanted to give them back to me; she wanted to give them to a charity.

I don't want anything that will remind me of you.

The image of Ana leaving surfaces in my mind's eye: her sad, ashen face stricken with hurt and confusion. The memory is unwelcome. Painful.

I made her that miserable. I took everything too far, too quickly. And it fills me with a despair that has become all too familiar since she left. Closing my eyes, I try to center myself, but I'm confronted by my deepest, darkest fear: she's met someone else. She's sharing her little white bed and her beautiful body with some fucking stranger.

Damn it, Grey. Stay positive.

Don't go there. All is not lost. You'll be seeing her shortly. Your plans are in place. You are going to win her back. Opening my eyes, I stare at the front door through the window, my mood now as dark as the Audi's tinted glass. More people leave the building, but still no Ana.

Where is she?

Taylor is pacing outside and glancing toward the front door. Christ, he looks as nervous as I feel. *What the hell is it to him?*

My watch says 5:43. She'll be out in a moment. I take a deep breath and tug at my cuffs, then try to straighten my tie, only to find I'm not wearing one. *Hell.* Raking my hand through my hair, I try to dismiss my doubts, but they continue to plague me. *Am I just a free ride to her? Will she have missed me? Will she want me back? Is there someone else?* I have no idea. This is worse than waiting for her in the Marble Bar, and the irony is not lost on me. I thought that was the biggest deal I'd ever negotiate with her and that didn't turn out the way I expected. Nothing turns out as I expect with Miss Anastasia Steele. Panic knots my stomach once more. Today, I have to negotiate a bigger deal.

I want her back.

She said she loved me…

My heart rate spikes in response to the adrenaline that floods my body.

No. No. Don't think about that. She can't feel that way about me.

Calm down, Grey. Focus.

I glance once more at the entrance to Seattle Independent Publishing and she's there, walking toward me.

Fuck.

Ana.

Shock sucks the breath from my body like a kick to the solar plexus. Beneath a black jacket she's wearing one of my favorite dresses, the purple one, and black high-heeled boots. Her hair, burnished by the early-evening sun, sways in the breeze as she moves. But it's not her clothing or her hair that holds my attention. Her face is pale, almost translucent. There are dark circles beneath her eyes, and she's thinner.

Thinner.

Guilt lances through me.

Christ.

She's suffered, too.

My concern at her appearance turns to anger.

No. Fury.

She hasn't been eating. She's lost, what, five or six pounds in the last few days? She glances at some random guy behind her and he gives her a broad smile. He's a good-looking son of a bitch, full of himself. *Asshole.* Their carefree exchange only fuels my rage. He watches her with blatant male appreciation as she walks toward the car, and my wrath increases with each of her steps.

Taylor opens the door and offers her his hand to help her climb inside. And suddenly she is sitting beside me.

"When did you last eat?" I snap, struggling to keep my composure.

Her blue eyes peer up at me, stripping me bare and leaving me as raw as they did the first time I met her. "Hello, Christian. Yes, it's nice to see you, too," she says.

What. The. Fuck.

"I don't want your smart mouth now. Answer me."

She stares at her hands in her lap so I've no idea what she's thinking, then trots out some lame excuse about eating a yogurt and a banana.

That's not eating!

I try, really try, to keep a rein on my temper.

"When did you last have a real meal?" I press her, but she ignores me, looking out the window. Taylor pulls away from the curb, and Ana waves to the prick who followed her out of the building. "Who's that?"

"My boss."

So that's Jack Hyde. I recall the employee details I flipped through this morning: from Detroit, scholarship to Princeton, worked his way up at a publishing firm in New York but has moved on every few years, working his way across the country. He never retains an assistant—they don't last more than three months. He's on my watch list, and I'll have my security adviser Welch find out more.

Focus on the matter at hand, Grey.

"Well? Your last meal?"

"Christian, that really is none of your concern," she whispers.

Shit, I'm the free ride.

"Whatever you do concerns me. Tell me." Don't write me off, Anastasia. *Please.*

I'm the free ride.

She sighs in frustration and rolls her eyes to piss me off. And I see it—a soft smile pulling at the corner of her mouth. She's trying not to laugh. She's trying not to laugh *at me*. After all the heartache I've suffered, it's so refreshing that it cracks through my anger. It's so Ana. I find myself mirroring her, and I try to mask my smile.

"Well?" My tone is much gentler.

"Pasta alla Vongole, last Friday," she answers, her voice subdued.

Jesus H. Christ, she's not eaten since our last meal together! I want to pull her across my knee, right now, here in the back of the SUV—but I know I can't ever touch her like that again.

What do I do with her?

She looks down, examining her hands, her face paler and sadder than it was before. And I drink her in, trying to fathom what to do. An unwelcome emotion blooms in my chest, threatening to overwhelm me but I push it aside. As I study her it becomes achingly clear that my biggest fear is unfounded. I know she didn't get drunk and meet someone. Looking at how she is now, I know she's been on her own, tucked up in her bed, weeping her heart out. The thought is at once comforting and distressing. I'm responsible for her misery.

Me.

I'm the monster. I did this to her. How can I ever win her back?

"I see." The words feel inadequate. My task suddenly feels too daunting. She will never want me back.

Get a grip, Grey.

I damp down my fear and make a plea. "You look like you've lost at least five pounds, possibly more since then. Please eat, Anastasia." I'm helpless. What else can I say?

She sits still, lost in her own thoughts, staring straight ahead, and I have time to study her profile. She's as elfin and sweet and as beautiful as I remember. I want to reach out and stroke her cheek. Feel how soft her skin is… check that she's real. I turn my body toward her, itching to touch her.

"How are you?" I ask, because I want to hear her voice.

"If I told you I was fine, I'd be lying."

Damn. I'm right. She's been suffering—and it's all my fault. But her words give me a modicum of hope. Perhaps she's missed me. Maybe? Encouraged, I cling to that thought. "Me, too. I miss you." I reach for her hand because I can't live another minute without touching her. Her hand feels small and ice-cold engulfed in the warmth of mine.

"Christian. I—" She stops, her voice cracking, but she doesn't pull her hand from mine.

"Ana, please. We need to talk."

"Christian. I… Please. I've cried so much," she whispers, and her words, and the sight of her fighting back tears, pierce what's left of my heart.

"Oh, baby, no." I tug her hand and before she can protest I lift her into my lap, circling her with my arms.

Oh, the feel of her.

"I've missed you so much, Anastasia." She's too light, too fragile, and I want to shout in frustration, but instead I bury my nose in her hair, overwhelmed by her intoxicating scent. It's reminiscent of happier times: An orchard in the fall. Laughter at home. Bright eyes, full of humor and mischief…and desire. My sweet, sweet Ana.

Mine.

At first, she's stiff with resistance, but after a beat she relaxes against me, her head resting on my shoulder. Emboldened, I take a risk and, closing my eyes, I kiss her hair. She doesn't struggle out of my hold, and it's a relief. I've yearned for this woman. But I must be careful. I don't want her to bolt again. I hold her, enjoying the feel of her in my arms and this simple moment of tranquility.

But it's a brief interlude—Taylor reaches the Seattle downtown helipad in record time.

"Come." With reluctance, I lift her off my lap. "We're here."

Perplexed eyes search mine.

"Helipad—on the top of this building." How did she think we were getting to Portland? It would take at least three hours to drive. Taylor opens her door and I climb out on my side.

"I should give you back your handkerchief," she says to Taylor with a coy smile.

"Keep it, Miss Steele, with my best wishes."

What the hell is going on between them?

"Nine?" I interrupt, not just to remind him what time he'll pick us up in Portland, but to stop him from talking to Ana.

"Yes, sir," he says quietly.

Damn right. She's my girl. Handkerchiefs are my business, not his.

Flashes of her vomiting on the ground, me holding back her hair, run through my head. I gave her my handkerchief then. I never got it back. And later that night I watched her sleep beside me. Perhaps she still has it. Perhaps she still uses it.

Stop. Now. Grey.

Taking her hand—the chill has gone, but her hand is still cool—I lead her into the building. As we reach the elevator, I recall our encounter at The Heathman. That first kiss.

Yeah. That first kiss.

The thought wakes my body.

But the doors open, distracting me, and reluctantly I release her to usher her inside.

The elevator is small, and we're no longer touching. But I sense her.

All of her.

Here. Now.

Shit. I swallow.

Is it because she's so near? Darkening eyes look up at mine.

Oh, Ana.

Her proximity is arousing. She inhales sharply and looks at the floor.

"I feel it, too." I reach for her hand again and caress her knuckles with my thumb. She looks up at me, her fathomless eyes clouding with desire.

Fuck. I want her.

She bites her lip.

"Please don't bite your lip, Anastasia." My voice is low, full of longing. Will I always want her like this? I want to kiss her, press her into the elevator wall like I did during our first kiss. I want to fuck her here and make her mine again. She blinks, her lips gently parted, and I suppress a groan. How does she do this? Derail me with a look? I am used to control—and I'm practically drooling over her because her teeth are pressing into her lip. "You know what it does to me." And right now, baby, I want to take you in this elevator, but I don't think you'll let me.

The doors slide open and the rush of cold air brings me back to the now. We're on the roof, and although the day has been warm, the wind has picked up. Anastasia shivers beside me. I wrap my arm around her and she huddles into my side. She feels too slight, but her petite frame fits perfectly under my arm.

See? We fit together so well, Ana.

We head out onto the helipad toward *Charlie Tango*. The rotors are slowly spinning—she's ready for liftoff. Stephan, my pilot, runs toward us. We shake hands, and I keep Anastasia tucked under my arm.

"Ready to go, sir. She's all yours!" he roars above the sound of the helicopter engines.

"All checks done?"

"Yes, sir."

"You'll collect her around eight thirty?"

"Yes, sir."

"Taylor's waiting for you out front."

"Thank you, Mr. Grey. Safe flight to Portland. Ma'am." He

salutes Anastasia and heads to the waiting elevator. We duck down under the rotors and I open the door, taking her hand to help her climb aboard.

As I strap her into the seat, her breath hitches. The sound travels straight to my groin. I cinch the straps extra-tight, trying to ignore my body's reaction to her.

"This should keep you in your place." The thought runs through my head, and I realize I've said it out loud. "I must say, I like this harness on you. Don't touch anything."

She flushes. Finally, some color stains her face—and I can't resist. I run the back of my index finger down her cheek, tracing the line of her blush.

Lord, I want this woman.

She scowls, and I know it's because she can't move. I hand her some headphones, take my seat, and buckle up.

I run through my preflight checks. All instruments are in the green with no advisory lights. I roll the throttles to "fly," set the transponder code, and confirm that the anticollision light is on. It all looks good. I don my headphones, switch on the radios, and check the rotor rpm.

When I turn to Ana, she's watching me intently. "Ready, baby?"

"Yes." She's wide-eyed and excited. I can't help my wolfish grin as I radio the tower to make sure they're awake and listening.

Once I have permission to take off, I check the oil temperature and the rest of the gauges. They're all in normal operating range, so I increase the collective, and *Charlie Tango*, elegant bird that she is, rises smoothly into the sky.

Oh, I love this.

Feeling a little more confident as we gain altitude, I glance at Miss Steele beside me.

Time to dazzle her.

Showtime, Grey.

"We've chased the dawn, Anastasia. Now the dusk." I smile, and I'm rewarded with a shy smile that illuminates her face. Hope stirs in my chest. I have her here when I thought all was lost and she seems happier now than when she walked out of her office. I might just be the free ride, but I'm going to try to enjoy every damn minute of this flight with her.

Dr. Flynn would be proud.

I'm in the moment. And I'm optimistic.

I can do this. I can win her back.

Baby steps, Grey. Don't get ahead of yourself.

"As well as the evening sun, there's more to see this time," I say, interrupting the silence. "Escala's over there. Boeing there—and you can just see the Space Needle."

Curious as ever, she cranes her slim neck to look. "I've never been," she says.

"I'll take you. We can eat there."

"Christian, we broke up." I hear the dismay in her voice.

That is not what I want to hear, but I try not to overreact. "I know. I can still take you there. And feed you." I give her a pointed look and she blushes a lovely pale rose.

"It's very beautiful up here. Thank you." She changes the subject.

"Impressive, isn't it?" I play along—and she's right, I never get tired of the view from up here.

"Impressive that you can do this."

Her compliment surprises me. "Flattery from you, Miss Steele? But I'm a man of many talents."

"I'm fully aware of that, Mr. Grey," she responds tartly, and I suppress a smirk imagining what she's referring to. This is what I've missed: her impertinence, disarming me at every turn.

Keep her talking, Grey. "How's the new job?"

"Good, thank you. Interesting."

"What's your boss like?"

"Oh. He's okay." She sounds less than enthusiastic about Jack Hyde. Has he tried anything with her?

"What's wrong?" I want to know—has that prick done anything inappropriate? I will fire his ass if he has.

"Aside from the obvious, nothing."

"The obvious?"

"Oh, Christian, you really are very obtuse sometimes," she says with playful disdain.

"Obtuse? Me? I'm not sure I appreciate your tone, Miss Steele."

"Well, don't, then," she quips, pleased with herself. I like that she mocks and teases me. She has the ability to make me feel two feet tall or ten feet tall with just a look or a smile—it's refreshing, and unlike anything I've known before.

"I've missed your smart mouth, Anastasia." An image of her on her knees in front of me pops into my mind and I shift in my seat.

Shit. Concentrate, Grey. She looks away, concealing her smile, and stares down at the suburbs passing beneath us while I check the heading. All is well; we're on track for Portland.

She's quiet, and I steal the occasional glance at her. Her face is lit with curiosity and wonder as she gazes out at the landscape below and the opal sky. Her cheeks are soft and glowing in the evening light. And in spite of her pallor and the dark circles beneath her eyes—evidence of the suffering I've caused her—she's stunning. How could I have let her walk out of my life?

What was I thinking?

While we race above the clouds in our bubble, high in the sky, my optimism grows and the turmoil of the last week recedes. Slowly, I begin to relax, enjoying a serenity I've not felt since she left. I could get used to this. I'd forgotten how content I feel in her company. And it's refreshing to see my world through her eyes.

But as we near our destination my confidence falters. I hope to God that my plan works. I need to take her somewhere private. To dinner maybe. *Damn it.* I should have booked a table somewhere. She needs feeding. If I get her to dinner, I'll just need to find the right words. These last few days have shown me that I need someone—I need her. I want her, but will she have me? Can I convince her to give me a second chance?

Time will tell, Grey—just take it easy. Don't frighten her off again.

We land on Portland's downtown helipad fifteen minutes later. As I bring *Charlie Tango*'s engines to idle and switch off the transponder, fuel, and radios, the uncertainty I've felt since I resolved to win her back resurfaces. I need to tell her how I feel, and that's going to be hard—because I don't understand my feelings toward her. I know that I've missed her, that I've been miserable without her, and that I'm willing to try a relationship her way. But will it be enough for her? Will it be enough for me?

Talk to her, Grey.

Once I've unbuckled my harness I lean across to undo hers and catch a trace of her sweet fragrance. As ever, she smells good. Her eyes meet mine in a furtive glance—revealing an inappropriate thought? What exactly is she thinking? As usual I'd love to know but have no idea.

"Good trip, Miss Steele?"

"Yes, thank you, Mr. Grey."

"Well, let's go see the boy's photos." I open the door, jump down, and hold my hand out for her.

Joe, the manager of the helipad, is waiting to greet us. He's an antique: a veteran of the Korean War, but still as spry and acute as a man in his fifties. Nothing escapes his notice. His eyes light up as he gives me a craggy smile.

"Joe, keep her safe for Stephan. He'll be along around eight or nine."

"Will do, Mr. Grey. Ma'am. Your car's waiting downstairs, sir. Oh, and the elevator's out of order. You'll need to use the stairs."

"Thank you, Joe."

As we head for the emergency stairwell, I eye Anastasia's high-heeled boots and remember her less-than-dignified fall into my office.

"Good thing for you this is only three floors—in those heels." I hide my smile.

"Don't you like the boots?" she asks, looking down at her feet. A pleasing vision of them hooked over my shoulders springs to mind.

"I like them very much, Anastasia." I hope my expression doesn't betray my lascivious thoughts. "Come. We'll take it slow. I don't want you falling and breaking your neck." I'm thankful that the elevator is out of order—it gives me a plausible excuse to hold her. Putting my arm around her waist, I pull her to my side and we descend the stairs.

In the car on the way to the gallery my anxiety doubles; we're attending the opening of an exhibition by her so-called friend. The man who, last time I saw him, was trying to push his tongue into her mouth. Perhaps over the last few days they've talked. Perhaps this is a long-anticipated rendezvous between them.

Hell, I hadn't considered that before. I sure hope it's not.

"José is just a friend," Ana explains.

What? She knows what I'm thinking? Am I that obvious? Since when?

Since she stripped me of all my armor and I discovered that I needed her.

She stares at me and my stomach tightens. "Those beautiful eyes look too large in your face, Anastasia. Please tell me you'll eat."

"Yes, Christian, I'll eat." She sounds less than sincere.

"I mean it."

"Do you, now?" Her voice is laced with sarcasm, and I almost have to sit on my hands.

Fuck this.

It's time to declare myself.

"I don't want to fight with you, Anastasia. I want you back, and I want you healthy." I'm honored with her shocked, all-eyes look.

"But nothing's changed." Her expression shifts to a frown.

Oh, Ana, it has—there's been a seismic shift in me.

We pull up at the gallery and I have no time to explain before the show. "Let's talk on the way back. We're here."

Before she can say she's not interested, I exit the car, walk around to her side, and open the door. She looks mad as she climbs out.

"Why do you do that?" she exclaims, exasperated.

"Do what?" *Shit—what's this?*

"Say something like that and then just stop."

That's it—that's why you're mad?

"Anastasia, we're here. Where you want to be. Let's do this and then talk. I don't particularly want a scene in the street."

She presses her lips together in a petulant pout, then gives me a begrudging "Okay."

Taking her hand, I move swiftly into the gallery, and she scrambles behind me.

The space is brightly lit and airy. It's one of those converted warehouses that are fashionable at the moment—all wood floors and brick walls. Portland's cognoscenti sip cheap wine and chat in hushed tones while they admire the exhibition.

A young woman greets us. "Good evening and welcome to José Rodriguez's show." She stares at me.

It's only skin deep, sweetheart. Look elsewhere.

She's flustered but seems to recover when she spies Anastasia. "Oh, it's you, Ana. We'll want your take on all this, too." She hands her a brochure and points us toward the makeshift bar. Ana's brow furrows, and that little *v* that I love forms above her nose. I want to kiss it, like I've done before.

"You know her?" I ask. She shakes her head and her frown deepens. I shrug. *Well, this is Portland.* "What would you like to drink?"

"I'll have a glass of white wine, thank you."

As I head for the bar I hear an exuberant shout. "Ana!"

Turning, I see that *that boy* has his arms wrapped around my girl.

Hell.

I can't hear what they're saying, but Ana closes her eyes, and for one horrible moment I think she's going to burst into tears. But she remains composed as he holds her at arm's length, appraising her.

Yeah, she's that thin because of me.

I fight back my guilt—though it seems she's trying to reassure him. For his part, he looks really fucking interested in her. Too interested. Anger flares in my chest. She says he's just a friend, but it's obvious he doesn't feel that way. He wants more.

Back off, buddy, she's mine.

"The work here is impressive, don't you think?" A balding young man in a loud shirt sidetracks me.

"I've not looked around yet," I answer and turn to the barman. "Is this all you have?"

"Yep. Red or white?" he says, sounding disinterested.

"Two glasses of white wine," I grunt.

"I think you'll be impressed. Rodriguez has a unique eye," the irritating prick with the irritating shirt tells me. Tuning him out, I glance at Ana. She's staring at me, her eyes large and luminous. My blood thickens and it's impossible to look away. She's a beacon in the crowd and I'm lost in her gaze. She looks sensational. Her hair frames her face and falls in a lush cascade to curl at her breasts. Her dress, looser than I remember, still hugs her curves. She might have worn it deliberately. She knows it's my favorite. Doesn't she? Hot dress, hot boots…

Fuck—control yourself, Grey.

Rodriguez asks Ana a question and she's forced to break eye contact with me. I sense she's reluctant to do so, which is pleasing. But damn it, that boy's all perfect teeth, broad shoulders, and sharp suit. He's a good-looking son of a bitch, for a dope smoker, I'll give him that. She nods at something he says and gives him a warm, carefree smile.

I'd like her to smile like that at me. He leans down and kisses her cheek. *Fucker.*

I glare at the bartender.

Hurry up, man. He's taking an eternity to pour the wine, incompetent fool.

Finally, he's finished. I grab the glasses, cold-shoulder the young man beside me who's talking about another photographer or some such crap, and head back to Ana.

At least Rodriguez has left her alone. She's lost in thought, contemplating one of his photographs. It's a landscape, a lake, and not without merit, I suppose. She glances up at me with a guarded expression as I hand her a glass. I take a quick sip from mine. Christ, it's disgusting, a warm over-oaked chardonnay.

"Does it come up to scratch?" She sounds amused, but I have no idea what she's referring to—the exhibition, the building? "The wine," she clarifies.

"No. Rarely does at these kinds of events." I change the subject. "The boy's quite talented, isn't he?"

"Why else do you think I asked him to take your portrait?" Her pride in his work is obvious. It irks me. She admires him and takes an interest in his success because she cares about him. She cares about him too much. An ugly emotion with a bitter sting rises in my chest. It's jealousy, a new feeling, one that I've only ever felt around her—and I don't like it.

"Christian Grey?" A guy dressed like a vagrant thrusts a camera in my face, interrupting my dark thoughts. "Can I have a picture, sir?"

Damned paparazzi. I want to tell him to fuck off but decide to be polite. I don't want Sam, my publicity guy, dealing with a press complaint.

"Sure." I reach out and pull Ana to my side. I want everyone to know she's mine—if she'll have me.

Don't get ahead of yourself, Grey.

The photographer takes a few snaps. "Mr. Grey, thank you." At least he sounds appreciative. "Miss… ?" he asks, wanting to know her name.

"Ana Steele," she answers shyly.

"Thank you, Miss Steele." He slithers off and Anastasia steps out of my grasp. I'm disappointed to let her go and fist my hands to resist the urge to touch her again.

She peers at me. "I looked for pictures of you with dates on the internet. There aren't any. That's why Kate thought you were gay."

"That explains your inappropriate question." I can't help smiling as I remember her awkwardness at our first meeting: her lack of interview skills, her questions. *Are you gay, Mr. Grey?* And my annoyance.

That seems so long ago. I shake my head and continue. "No—I don't do dates, Anastasia, only with you. But you know that."

And I'd like many, many more.

"So you never took your"—she lowers her voice and glances over her shoulder to check that no one's listening—"subs out?" She blanches at the word, embarrassed.

"Sometimes. Not on dates. Shopping, you know." Those occasional trips were just a distraction, maybe a reward for good submissive behavior. The one woman I've wanted to share more with… is Ana. "Just you, Anastasia," I whisper, and I want to plead my case, ask her about my proposition, see how she feels, and if she'll take me back.

However, the gallery is too public a setting. Her cheeks turn that delicious pink that I love, and she stares down at her hands. I hope it's because she likes what I'm saying, but I can't be sure. I need to get her out of here and on her own. Then we can talk seriously and eat. The sooner we've seen the boy's work, the sooner we can leave.

"Your friend here seems more of a landscape man, not portraits. Let's look around." I hold out my hand, and to my delight, she takes it.

We stroll through the gallery, stopping briefly at each photograph. Though I resent the boy and the feelings he inspires in Ana, I have to admit he's quite good. We turn the corner—and stop.

There she is. Seven full-blown portraits of Anastasia Steele. She looks jaw-droppingly beautiful, natural, and relaxed—laughing, scowling, pouting, pensive, amused, and in one of them, wistful and sad. As I scrutinize the detail in each photograph, I know, without a shadow of a doubt, that *he* wants to be much more than her friend. "Seems I'm not the only one," I mutter. The photographs are his homage to her—his love letters—and they're all over the gallery walls for any random asshole to ogle.

Ana is staring at them in stunned silence, as surprised as I am to see them. Well, there's no way anyone else is having these. I want the pictures. I hope they're for sale.

"Excuse me." I abandon Ana for a moment and head to the reception desk.

"May I help you?" asks the woman who greeted us when we arrived.

Ignoring her fluttering eyelashes and provocative, overly red smile, I inquire, "The seven portraits you have hanging at the back, are they for sale?"

A look of disappointment flits across her face but resolves into a broad smile. "The Anastasia collection? Stunning work."

Stunning model.

"Of course they're for sale. Let me check the prices," she gushes.

"I want them all." And I reach for my wallet.

"All of them?" She sounds surprised.

"Yes." *Irritating woman.*

"The collection is fourteen thousand dollars."

"I'd like them delivered as soon as possible."

"But they're due to hang for the duration of the exhibition," she says.

Unacceptable.

I give her my full-kilowatt smile, and she adds, flustered, "But I'm sure we can arrange something." She fumbles with my credit card as she swipes it.

When I return to Ana, I find a blond dude chatting with her, trying his luck. "These photographs are terrific," he says. I place a territorial hand on her elbow and give him my best fuck-off-now glare. "You're a lucky guy," he adds, taking a step back.

"That I am," I answer, dismissing him as I usher Ana over to the wall.

"Did you just buy one of these?" Ana nods toward the portraits.

"One of these?" I scoff. *One? Are you serious?*

"You bought more than one?"

"I bought them all, Anastasia." And I know I sound condescending, but the thought of someone else owning and enjoying these photographs is out of the question. Her lips part in astonishment, and I try not to let it distract me. "I don't want some stranger ogling you in the privacy of their home."

"You'd rather it was you?" she counters.

Her response, though unexpected, is entertaining; she's admonishing me. "Frankly, yes," I respond in kind.

"Pervert," she mouths and bites her lip, I suspect to suppress a laugh.

Lord, she's challenging and funny and right. "Can't argue with that assessment, Anastasia."

"I'd discuss it further with you, but I've signed an NDA." With a haughty look, she turns to study the pictures once more.

And she's doing it again: laughing at me and trivializing my lifestyle. Christ, I'd like to put her in her place—preferably under me or on her knees. I lean in closer and whisper in her ear, "What I'd like to do to your smart mouth."

"You're very rude." She's scandalized, her expression prim, while the tips of her ears turn a fetching pink.

Oh, baby, that's old news.

I glance back at the pictures. "You look very relaxed in these photographs, Anastasia. I don't see you like that very often."

She examines her fingers once more, hesitating as if she's contemplating what to say. I don't know what she's thinking, so, reaching forward, I tilt her head up. She gasps as my fingers make contact with her chin.

Again, that sound; I feel it in my groin.

"I want you that relaxed with me." I sound hopeful.

Damn it. Too hopeful.

"You have to stop intimidating me if you want that," she retorts, surprising me with her depth of feeling.

"You have to learn to communicate and tell me how you feel!" I snap back.

Shit, are we doing this here, now? I want to do this in private. She clears her throat and draws herself up to full height.

"Christian, you wanted me as a submissive," she says, keeping her voice down. "That's where the problem lies. It's in the definition of a submissive—you emailed it to me once." She pauses, glaring at me. "I think the synonyms were, and I quote, 'compliant, pliant, amenable, passive, tractable, resigned, patient, docile, tame, subdued.' I wasn't supposed to look at you. Not talk to you, unless you gave me permission to do so. What do you expect?"

We need to discuss this in private! Why is she doing this here?

"It's very confusing being with you," she continues, in full flow. "You don't want me to defy you, but then you like my 'smart mouth.' You want obedience except when you don't so that you can punish me. I just don't know which way is up when I'm with you."

Okay, I can see how that could be confusing—however, I do not want to discuss it here. We need to leave.

"Good point well made, as usual, Miss Steele." My tone is arctic. "Come, let's go eat."

"We've only been here for half an hour."

"You've seen the photos. You've spoken to the boy."

"His name is José," she asserts, louder this time.

"You've spoken to *José*—the man who, if I am not mistaken, was trying to push his tongue into your mouth the last time I met him, while you were drunk and ill." I grit my teeth.

"He's never hit me," she retaliates with fury in her eyes.

What the hell? She *does* want to do this now.

I can't believe it. *She fucking asked me how bad it could get!* Anger erupts like Mount St. Helens deep in my chest. "That's a low blow, Anastasia." I'm seething. Her face reddens, and I don't know if it's from embarrassment or anger. I run my hands through my hair to prevent myself from grabbing her and dragging her outside so we can continue this discussion in private. I take a deep breath.

"I'm taking you for something to eat. You're fading away in front of me. Find the boy, say goodbye." My tone is clipped as I struggle to control my temper, but she doesn't move.

"Please, can we stay longer?"

"No. Go. Now. Say goodbye." I manage not to shout. I recognize that stubborn, mulish set to her mouth. She's mad as hell, and in spite of all I've been through over the last few days, I don't give a shit. We are leaving if I have to pick her up and carry her. She gives me a withering look and turns with a sharp spin, her hair flying so that it hits my shoulder. She stalks off to find him.

As she moves away I struggle to recover my equilibrium. What is it about her that presses all my buttons? I want to scold her, spank her, and fuck her. Here. Now. And in that order.

I scan the room. The boy—no, Rodriguez—is standing with a flock of female admirers. He notices Ana, and forgetting his fans, he greets her like she's the center of his whole goddamn universe. He listens intently to everything she has to say, then sweeps her into his arms, spinning her around.

Get your fat paws off my girl.

She glances at me, then weaves her hands into his hair and presses her cheek to his and whispers something in his ear. They continue talking. Close. His arms around her. And he's basking in her fucking light.

Before I'm even aware that I'm doing it, I'm striding over, ready to rip him limb from limb. Fortunately for him, he releases her as I approach.

"Don't be a stranger, Ana. Oh, Mr. Grey, good evening," the boy mumbles, sheepish and a little intimidated.

"Mr. Rodriguez, very impressive. I'm sorry *we* can't stay longer, but *we* need to head back to Seattle. Anastasia?" I take her hand.

"Bye, José. Congratulations again." She leans away from me, gives Rodriguez a tender kiss on his reddening cheek, and I'm going to have a coronary. It takes all my self-control not to haul her over my shoulder. Instead I drag her by the hand to the front door and out onto the street. She's stumbling behind me, trying to keep up, but I don't care.

Right now. I just want to—

There's an alley. I hurry us into it, and before I know what I'm doing I've pressed her against the wall. I grab her face between my hands, pinning her body with mine as rage and desire mix in a heady, explosive cocktail. I capture her lips with mine and our teeth clash, but then my tongue is in her mouth. She tastes of cheap wine and delicious, sweet, sweet Ana.

Oh, this mouth.

I have missed this mouth.

She ignites around me. Her fingers are in my hair, pulling hard. She moans into my mouth, giving me more access, and she's kissing me back, her passion unleashed, her tongue entwined with mine. Tasting. Taking. Giving.

Her hunger is unexpected. Desire bursts through my body, like a forest fire licking through dry tinder. I'm so aroused—I want her now, here, in this alley. And what I'd intended as a punishing I-own-you kiss becomes something else.

She wants this, too.

She's missed this, too.

And it's more than arousing.

I groan in response, undone.

With one hand, I hold her at the nape of her neck as we kiss. My free hand travels down her body, and I reacquaint myself with her curves: her breast, her waist, her ass, her thigh. She moans as my fingers find the hem of her dress and start tugging it higher. My goal is to pull it up, fuck her here. Make her mine, again.

The feel of her.

It's intoxicating, and I want her like I've never wanted her before.

In the distance and through the fog of my lust, I hear a police siren wail.

No! No! Grey!

Not like this. Get a grip.

I pull back, gazing down at her, and I'm panting and mad as hell.

"You. Are. Mine!" I growl and push myself away from her as my reason returns. "For the love of God, Ana." I bend over, hands on my knees, trying to catch my breath and calm my raging body. I'm painfully hard for her right now.

Has anyone ever affected me like this? Ever?

Christ! I nearly fucked her in a back alley.

This is jealousy. This is what it feels like: my insides gutted and raw, my self-control absent. I don't like it. I don't like it one bit.

"I'm sorry," she says, hoarse.

"You should be. I know what you're doing. Do you want the photographer, Anastasia? He obviously has feelings for you."

"No." Her voice is soft and breathless. "He's just a friend." At least she sounds contrite, and it goes some way toward pacifying me.

"I have spent all my adult life trying to avoid any extreme emotion. Yet you… you bring out feelings in me that are completely alien. It's very…" Words fail me. I cannot find the vocabulary to describe how I feel. I'm out of control and at a loss. "Unsettling" is the best I can manage. "I like control, Ana, and around you, that just"—I stand and look down at her—"evaporates."

Her eyes are wide with carnal promise, and her hair is mussed and sexy, falling to her breasts. I rub the back of my neck, thankful that I've recovered some semblance of self-control.

See how I am around you, Ana? See?

I run my hand through my hair, taking deep, thought-clearing breaths. I grab her hand. "Come, we need to talk." *Before I fuck you.* "And you need to eat."

There's a restaurant close to the alley. It's not what I would have chosen for a reunion, if that's what this is, but it will suffice. I don't have long, as Taylor will be arriving soon.

I open the door for her. "This place will have to do. We don't have much time." The restaurant looks like it caters to the gallery crowd, and maybe students. It's ironic that the walls are painted the same color as my playroom, but I don't dwell on the thought.

An obsequious waiter leads us to a secluded table; he's all smiles for Anastasia. I glance at the chalkboard menu on the wall and decide to order before the waiter retreats, letting him know we're tight for time. "So we'll each have sirloin steak cooked medium, béarnaise sauce if you have it, fries, and green vegetables, whatever the chef has—and bring me the wine list."

"Certainly, sir," he says and rushes off.

Ana purses her lips, annoyed.

What now?

"And if I don't like steak?"

"Don't start, Anastasia."

"I am not a child, Christian."

"Well, stop acting like one."

"I'm a child because I don't like steak?" She doesn't hide her petulance.

No!

"For deliberately making me jealous. It's a childish thing to do. Have you no regard for your friend's feelings, leading him on like that?"

Her cheeks pink and she examines her hands.

Yes. You should be embarrassed. You're confusing him. Even I can see that.

Is that what she's doing to me? Leading me on?

In the time we've been apart, maybe she's finally recognized that she has power. Power over me.

The waiter returns with the wine list, giving me a chance to regain my cool. The selection is average: only one drinkable wine on the menu. I glance at Anastasia, who looks like she's sulking. I know that look. Perhaps she wanted to select her own meal. And I can't resist toying with her, aware that she has little knowledge of wine. "Would you like to choose the wine?" I ask and I know I sound sarcastic.

"You choose." She presses her lips together.

Yeah. Don't play games with me, baby.

"Two glasses of the Barossa Valley Shiraz, please," I say to the waiter, who's hovering.

"Er, we only sell that wine by the bottle, sir."

"A bottle, then." *You stupid prick.*

"Sir." He retreats.

"You're very grumpy," she says, no doubt feeling sorry for the waiter.

"I wonder why that is?" I keep my expression neutral, but even to my own ears *I'm* now sounding childish.

"Well, it's good to set the right tone for an intimate and honest discussion about the future, wouldn't you say?" She gives me a saccharine smile.

Oh, tit for tat, Miss Steele. She's called me out again and I have to admire her nerve. I realize our bickering will get us nowhere.

And I'm being an ass.

Don't blow this deal, Grey.

"I'm sorry," I say, because she's right.

"Apology accepted. And I'm pleased to inform you I haven't decided to become a vegetarian since we last ate."

"Since that *was* the last time you ate, I think that's a moot point."

"There's that word again, 'moot.'"

"Moot," I mouth. *That word, indeed.* I remember I last used it while discussing our arrangement on Saturday morning. The day my world fell apart.

Fuck. Don't think about that.

Man up, Grey. Tell her what you want.

"Ana, the last time we spoke, you left me. I'm a little nervous. I've told you I want you back, and you've said… nothing."

She bites her lip as the color drains from her face.

Oh no.

"I've missed you… really missed you, Christian," she says, quietly. "The past few days have been… difficult."

Difficult is an understatement.

She swallows and takes a steadying breath. This doesn't sound good. Perhaps my behavior over the last hour has finally driven her away. I tense. Where's she going with this?

"Nothing's changed. I can't be what you want me to be." Her expression is bleak.

No. No. No.

"You are what I want you to be." You are everything I want you to be.

"No, Christian, I'm not."

Oh, baby, please believe me. "You're upset because of what happened last time. I behaved stupidly, and you—so did you. Why didn't you safe-word, Anastasia?"

She looks surprised, as if this isn't something she's considered.

"Answer me," I urge.

This has haunted me. *Why didn't you safe-word, Ana?*

She wilts in her seat. Sad. Defeated.

"I don't know," she whispers.

What?

WHAT?

I'm rendered speechless. I've been in hell because she didn't safe-word. But before I recover, words tumble from her mouth. Soft, quiet, as if she's in a confessional, as if she's ashamed.

"I was overwhelmed. I was trying to be what you wanted me to be, trying to deal with the pain, and it went out of my mind." Her look is raw, her shrug small and apologetic. "You know… I forgot."

What the hell?

"You forgot!" I'm dismayed. We've been through all this shit because she *forgot*?

I can't believe it. I clutch the table for something to anchor me to the now as I let this alarming information register.

Did I remind her of her safe words? *Christ.* I can't remember.

The email she sent me the first time I spanked her comes to mind.

She didn't stop me then.

I'm an idiot.

I should have reminded her.

Wait. She knows she has safe words. I remember telling her more than once.

"We don't have a signed contract, Anastasia. But we've discussed limits. And I want to reiterate we have safe words, okay?"

She blinks a couple times but remains mute.

"What are they?" I demand.

She hesitates.

"What are the safe words, Anastasia?"

"Yellow."

"And?"

"Red."

"Remember those."

She raises an eyebrow in obvious scorn and is about to say something.

"Don't start with your smart mouth in here, Miss Steele. Or I will fuck it with you on your knees. Do you understand?"

"How can I trust you? Ever?" If she can't be honest with me, what hope do we have? She can't tell me what she thinks I want to hear. What kind of relationship is that? My spirits sink. This is the problem in dealing with someone who isn't in the lifestyle. She doesn't get it.

I should never have chased her.

The waiter arrives with the wine as we stare with incredulity at each other.

Maybe I should have done a better job of explaining it to her.

Damn it, Grey. Eliminate the negative.

Yes. It's irrelevant now. I'm going to try a relationship her way, if she'll let me.

The irritating prick takes too much time opening the bottle. Jesus. Is he trying to entertain us? Or is it just Ana he wants to impress? He finally pops the cork and pours a taste for me. I take a quick sip. It needs to breathe, but it's passable.

"That's fine." *Now go. Please.* He fills our glasses and leaves.

Ana and I haven't taken our eyes off each other. Each trying to discern what the other is thinking. She's the first to look away, and she takes a sip of wine, closing her eyes as if seeking inspiration. When she opens them, I see her despair. "I'm sorry," she whispers.

"Sorry for what?" *Hell.* Is she done with me? Is there no hope?

"Not using the safe word," she says.

Oh, thank God. I thought it was over.

"We might have avoided all this suffering," I mutter in response, and also in an attempt to hide my relief.

"You look fine." There's a tremor in her voice.

"Appearances can be deceptive. I'm not fine. I feel like the sun has set and not risen for five days, Ana. I'm in perpetual night here."

Her gasp is just audible.

How did she think I'd feel? She left me when I'd almost begged her to stay. "You said you'd never leave, yet the going gets tough and you're out the door."

"When did I say I'd never leave?"

"In your sleep." Before we went soaring. "It was the most comforting thing I'd heard in so long, Anastasia. It made me relax."

She inhales sharply. Her open and honest compassion is written all over her lovely face as she reaches for her wine. This is my chance.

Ask her, Grey.

Ask her the one question I haven't allowed myself to think about because I know I'll dread her answer, whatever it is. But I'm curious. I need to know.

"You said you loved me," I whisper, almost choking on the words. She can't feel that way about me still. Can she? "Is that now in the past tense?"

"No, Christian, it's not," she says, as if in the confessional again.

I'm unprepared for the relief that rushes through me. But it's relief mixed with fear. It's a confounding combination because I know she shouldn't love a monster.

"Good," I mumble, confused. I want to stop thinking about that right now, and with impeccable timing, the waiter returns with our meal.

"Eat," I demand. The woman needs feeding.

She examines the contents of her plate with distaste.

"So help me God, Anastasia, if you don't eat, I will take you across my knee here in this restaurant. And it will have nothing to do with my sexual gratification. Eat!"

"Okay. I'll eat. Stow your twitching palm, please." She's trying for humor—but I'm not laughing. She's wasting away. She picks up her cutlery with stubborn reluctance but she takes one bite, closes her eyes, and licks her lips in satisfaction. The sight of her tongue is enough to provoke a response from my body—already in a heightened state from our kiss in the alley.

Hell, not again! I stop my response in its tracks. There'll be time for that later, *if* she says yes. She takes another bite and another and I know she'll continue eating. I'm grateful for the diversion that our food has provided. Slicing into my steak, I take a bite. It's not bad.

We continue to eat, watching each other but saying nothing.

She hasn't told me to fuck off. This is good. And as I study her I realize how much I'm enjoying just being in her company. Okay, so I'm tied up in all kinds of conflicting emotions… but she's here. She's with me and she's eating. I'm hopeful we can make my proposition work. Her reaction to the kiss in the alley was… visceral. She still wants me. I know I could have fucked her there and she wouldn't have stopped me.

She interrupts my reverie. "Do you know who's singing?" Over the restaurant sound system, a young woman with a soft lyrical voice can be heard. I don't know who she is, but we both agree she's good.

Listening to this singer reminds me that I have the iPad for Ana. I hope she lets me give it to her, and that she likes it. In addition to the music I uploaded yesterday, I spent some time this morning adding more features—photographs of the glider on my desk and of the two of us at her graduation ceremony and a few apps, too. It's my apology, and I'm optimistic that the simple message I've had engraved on the back conveys my sentiment. I hope she doesn't think it's too cheesy. I just need to give it to her first, but I don't know if we'll get to that point. I suppress my sigh because she's always been difficult about accepting gifts from me.

"What?" she asks. She knows I'm up to something, and not for the first time I wonder if she can read my mind.

I shake my head. "Eat up."

Bright, blue eyes regard me. "I can't manage any more. Have I eaten enough for Sir?"

Is she deliberately trying to goad me? I scrutinize her face, but she seems genuine, and she's eaten more than half of what was on her plate. If she hasn't eaten anything over the last few days she's probably had enough to eat this evening.

"I'm really full," she reiterates.

As if on cue, my phone vibrates in my jacket pocket, signaling a message. It will be from Taylor. He's probably close to the gallery by now.

I glance at my watch. "We have to go shortly. Taylor's here, and you have to be up for work in the morning." I hadn't considered that before. She's working now—she needs sleep. I may have to revise my plans and my body's expectations. The thought of deferring my desire displeases me.

Ana reminds me that I need to be up for work, too.

"I function on a lot less sleep than you do, Anastasia. At least you've eaten something."

"Aren't we going back via *Charlie Tango*?"

"No, I thought I might have a drink—Taylor will pick us up. Besides, this way I have you in the car all to myself—for a few hours, at least. What can we do but talk?" And I can put my proposition to her.

I shift uncomfortably in my chair. Stage three of the campaign has not gone as smoothly as I anticipated.

She's made me jealous.

I've lost control.

Yes. As usual, she's derailed me. But I can turn this around and close the deal in the car.

Don't give up, Grey.

Summoning the waiter, I ask for the check, then call Taylor. He answers on the second ring.

"Mr. Grey."

"We're at Le Picotin, Southwest Third Avenue," I inform him and hang up.

"You're very brusque with Taylor… In fact, with most people."

"I just get to the point quickly, Anastasia."

"You haven't gotten to the point this evening. Nothing's changed, Christian."

Touché, Miss Steele.

Tell her. Tell her now, Grey.

"I have a proposition for you."

"This started with a proposition."

"A different proposition," I clarify.

She's a little skeptical, I think, but maybe she's curious, too. The waiter returns and I give him my card, but I keep my attention on Ana. Well, at least she's intrigued.

Good.

My heart rate accelerates. I hope she goes for this… or I really will be lost. The waiter hands me the credit card slip to sign. I enter an obscene tip and sign my name with a flourish. The waiter seems excessively grateful. And it's still irritating.

My phone buzzes and I scan the text. Taylor's arrived. The waiter gives me my card back and disappears.

"Come. Taylor's outside."

We both stand and I take her hand. "I don't want to lose you, Anastasia," I murmur and raise her hand and brush my lips against her knuckles. Her breathing accelerates.

Oh, that sound.

I glance at her face. Her lips are parted, cheeks pink and eyes wide. The sight fills me with hope and desire. I stifle my impulses and lead her through the restaurant and outside, where Taylor is waiting at the curb in the Q7. It occurs to me that Ana might be reluctant to talk if he's in front.

I have an idea. Opening the rear door, I usher her in and

walk around to the driver's side. Taylor gets out to open the door for me.

"Good evening, Taylor. Do you have your iPod and headphones?"

"Yes, sir, never leave home without them."

"Great. Use them on the way home."

"Of course, sir."

"What will you listen to?"

"Puccini, sir."

"*Tosca?*"

"*La Bohème.*"

"Good choice." I smile. As ever, he surprises me. I'd always assumed his musical tastes leaned toward country and rock. Taking a deep breath, I climb into the car. I'm about to negotiate the deal of my life.

I want her back.

Taylor presses play on the car's sound system and the stirring notes from Rachmaninov swell quietly in the background. He regards me for a second in the mirror and pulls out into the light evening traffic.

Anastasia is watching me when I turn to face her. "As I was saying, Anastasia, I have a proposition for you."

She looks anxiously at Taylor, as I knew she would.

"Taylor can't hear you."

"What?" She looks perplexed.

"Taylor," I call. Taylor doesn't respond. I call him again, then lean over and tap his shoulder. He removes an earbud.

"Yes, sir?"

"Thank you, Taylor. It's okay—resume your listening."

"Sir."

"Happy now? He's listening to his iPod. Puccini. Forget he's here. I do."

"Did you deliberately ask him to do that?"

"Yes."

She blinks in surprise. "Okay… your proposition," she says, hesitant and apprehensive.

I'm nervous, too, baby. Here goes. *Don't blow this, Grey.*

How to begin?

I take a deep breath. "Let me ask you something first. Do you want a regular vanilla relationship, with no kinky fuckery at all?"

"Kinky fuckery?" she squeaks in disbelief.

"Kinky fuckery."

"I can't believe you said that." She looks anxiously at Taylor again.

"Well, I did. Answer me."

"I like your kinky fuckery," she whispers.

Oh, baby, so do I.

I'm relieved. Step one… okay. *Keep cool, Grey.*

"That's what I thought. So what don't you like?"

She's silent for a moment, and I know she's scrutinizing me in the light and shadows of the intermittent streetlamps. "The threat of cruel and unusual punishment," she says.

"What does that mean?"

"Well, you have all those"—she stops, glancing at Taylor once more, and her voice lowers—"things in your playroom, the canes and whips, and they frighten the living daylights out of me. I don't want you to use them on me."

This I have worked out for myself.

"Okay, so no whips or canes. Or belts, for that matter," I add, unable to keep the irony out of my voice.

"Are you attempting to redefine the hard limits?" she asks.

"Not as such. I'm just trying to understand you—get a clearer picture of what you do and don't like."

"Fundamentally, Christian, it's your joy in inflicting pain that's difficult for me to handle. And the idea that you'll do it because I have crossed some arbitrary line."

Hell. She knows me. She has seen the monster. I'm not going there or I will blow this deal. I ignore her first comment and concentrate on her second point. "But it's not arbitrary—the rules are written down."

"I don't want a set of rules."

"None at all?"

Fuck—she might touch me. How can I protect myself from that? And suppose she does something stupid that puts herself at risk?

"No rules," she states, shaking her head for emphasis.

Okay, million-dollar question.

"But you don't mind if I spank you?"

"Spank me with what?"

"This." I hold up my hand.

She shifts in her seat, and a silent, sweet joy unfurls deep in my gut. *Oh, baby, I love it when you squirm.*

"No, not really. Especially with those silver balls..."

My cock stirs at the thought. *Damn.* I cross my legs. "Yes, that was fun."

"More than fun," she adds.

"So you can deal with some pain." I can't keep the hope out of my voice.

"Yes, I suppose." She shrugs.

Okay. So we may be able to structure a relationship around this.

Deep breath, Grey. Give her the terms.

"Anastasia, I want to start again. Do the vanilla thing and then maybe, once you trust me more—and I trust you to be honest and to communicate with me—we could move on and do some of the things that I like to do."

That's it.

Fuck. My heart rate escalates; blood thrums through my body, pounding past my eardrums as I wait for her reaction. My well-being hangs in the balance. And she says... nothing! She stares at me as we pass under a streetlight and I see her clearly. She's assessing me. Her eyes still impossibly large in her beautiful, thinner, sadder face.

Oh, Ana.

"But what about punishments?" she says finally.

I close my eyes. It's not a no. "No punishments. None."

"And the rules?"

"No rules."

"None at all? But you have needs..." Her voice trails off.

"I need you more, Anastasia. These last few days have been

hell. All my instincts tell me to let you go, tell me I don't deserve you. Those photos the boy took—I can see how he sees you. You look untroubled and beautiful, not that you're not beautiful now, but here you sit. I see your pain. It's so hard knowing that I'm the one who has made you feel this way."

It's killing me, Ana.

"But I'm a selfish man. I've wanted you since you fell into my office. You are exquisite, honest, warm, strong, witty, beguilingly innocent; the list is endless. I am in awe of you. I want you, and the thought of anyone else having you is like a knife twisting in my dark soul."

Fuck. Flowery, Grey! Real flowery.

I'm like a man possessed. I'm going to scare her off.

"Christian, why do you think you have a dark soul?" she cries out, totally surprising me. "I would never say that. Sad maybe, but you're a good man. I can see that—you're generous, you're kind, and you've never lied to me. And I haven't tried very hard. Last Saturday was such a shock to my system. It was my wake-up call. I realized that you'd been easy on me and that I couldn't be the person you wanted me to be. Then, after I left, it dawned on me that the physical pain you inflicted was not as bad as the pain of losing you. I do want to please you, but it's hard."

"You please me all the time." When will she understand this? "How often do I have to tell you that?"

"I never know what you're thinking."

She doesn't? Baby, you read me like one of your books, except I'm not the hero. I'll never be the hero.

"Sometimes you're so closed off, like an island state," she continues. "You intimidate me. That's why I keep quiet. I don't know which way your mood is going to go. It swings from north to south and back again in a nanosecond. It's confusing and you won't let me touch you and I want so much to show you how much I love you."

Anxiety bursts in my chest and my heart starts hammering. She said it again, the three potent words I cannot bear. And touching. No. No. *No.* She can't touch me. But before I can respond, before the darkness takes hold, she unfastens her seat belt and crawls across the seat and into my lap, ambushing me. She places her hands on either side of my head, staring into my eyes, and I stop breathing.

"I love you, Christian Grey," she says. "And you're prepared to do all this for me. I'm the one who is undeserving. And I'm just sorry that I can't do all those things for you. Maybe with time—I don't know—but yes, I accept your proposition. Where do I sign?" She curls her arms around my neck and hugs me, her warm cheek against mine.

I can't believe what I'm hearing.

Anxiety turns to joy. It expands in my chest, lighting me up from head to toe, spreading warmth in its wake. She's going to try. I get her back. I don't deserve her, but I get her back. I wrap my arms around her and hold her tightly, burying my nose in her fragrant hair, as relief and a kaleidoscope of colorful emotions fill the void that I've carried inside me since she left.

"Oh, Ana," I whisper, and I hold her, too dazed and too… replete to say anything else. She snuggles into my arms, her head on my shoulder, and we listen to the Rachmaninov. I go over her words.

She loves me.

I test the phrase in my head and what's left of my heart and swallow the knot of fear that forms in my throat as those words ring through me.

I can do this.

I can live with this.

I must. I need to protect her and her vulnerable heart.

I take a deep breath.

I can do this.

Except the touching. I can't do that. I have to make her understand—manage her expectations. Gently I stroke her back. "Touching is a hard limit for me, Anastasia."

"I know. I wish I understood why." Her breath tickles my neck.

Shall I tell her? Why would she want to know this shit? My shit? Maybe I can hint at it, give her a clue.

"I had a horrific childhood. One of the crack whore's pimps…"

"There you are, you little shit."

No. No. No. Not the burn.

"Mommy! Mommy!"

"She can't hear you, you fucking maggot." He grabs my hair and pulls me out from under the kitchen table.

"Ow. Ow. Ow."

He's smoking. The smell. Cigarettes. It's a dirty smell. Like old and nasty. He's dirty. Like trash. Like drains. He drinks brown licker. From a bottle.

"And even if she could, she doesn't give a fuck," he shouts. He always shouts.

His hand hits me across my face. And again. And again. No. No.

I fight him. But he laughs. And takes a puff. The end of the cigarette shines bright red and orange.

"The burn," he says.

No. No.

The pain. The pain. The pain. The smell.

Burn. Burn. Burn.

Pain. No. No. No.

I howl.

Howl.

"Mommy! Mommy!"

He laughs and laughs. He has two teeth gone.

I shudder as my memories and nightmares float together like smoke from his discarded cigarette, fogging my brain, dragging me back to a time of fear and impotence.

I tell Ana I remember it all and she tightens her hold on me. Her cheek on my neck. Her soft, warm skin against mine, bringing me back to the now.

"Was she abusive? Your mother?" Ana's voice is hoarse.

"Not that I remember. She was neglectful. She didn't protect me from her pimp."

She was a sad excuse and he was a sick fuck.

"I think it was me who looked after her. When she finally killed herself, it took four days for someone to raise the alarm and find us. I remember that." I close my eyes and see vague, muted images of my mother slumped on the floor, me covering her with my blanket and curling up beside her.

Anastasia gasps. "That's pretty fucked up."

"Fifty shades."

She kisses my neck, a soft, tender press of her lips onto my skin. And I know it's not pity she's offering. It's comfort, maybe even understanding. My sweet, compassionate Ana.

I tighten my hold on her and kiss her hair as she nestles in my arms.

Baby, it was a long time ago.

My exhaustion catches up with me. Several sleepless nights plagued with nightmares have taken their toll. I'm tired. I want to stop thinking. She's my dream catcher. I never had nightmares when she was sleeping at my side. Leaning back, I close my eyes, saying nothing, because I have nothing more to say. I listen to the music, and when it's finished, to her soft, even breathing. She's asleep. She's weary. Like me. I realize I can't spend the night with her. She'll get no sleep if I do. I hold her, enjoying her weight on me, honored that she can sleep on me. I can't help my self-satisfied grin. I've done it. I've won her back. Now all I have to do is keep her, which will be challenging enough.

My first vanilla relationship—who would have thought? Closing my eyes, I imagine the look on Elena's face when I tell her. She'll have plenty to say. She always has…

I can tell by the way you're standing that you have something to tell me.

I dare a quick peek at Elena as her scarlet lips curl into a smile and she crosses her arms, flogger in hand.

Yes, Ma'am.

You may speak.

I have a place at Harvard.

Her eyes flash.

Ma'am, I add quickly and stare down at my toes.

I see. She walks around me as I stand naked in her basement. The chill spring air caresses my skin, but it's the anticipation of what's to come that makes each of my hair follicles stand on end. That, and the smell of her expensive perfume. My body begins to respond.

She laughs. *Control!* she snaps, and the flogger bites across my thighs. And I try, really try, to bring my body to heel.

Though perhaps you should be rewarded for good behavior, she purrs. And she hits me again, across my chest this time, but soft, more playful. *It's quite the achievement to get into Harvard, my dear, dear pet.* The flogger flies again, stinging my ass, and my legs quiver in response.

Hold still, she warns. And I stand straight, waiting for the next blow. *So you'll leave me,* she whispers, and the flogger strikes my back.

My eyes spring open and I glance at her in alarm.

No. Never.

Eyes down, she commands.

And I stare at my feet as panic overwhelms me.

You'll leave me and find some young college girl.

No. No.

She grabs my face, her nails biting into my skin.

You will. Her ice-blue eyes burn into mine, scarlet lips twisted in a snarl.

Never, Ma'am.

She laughs and pushes me away and raises her hand.

But the blow never comes.

When I open my eyes, Ana stands before me. She caresses my cheek and smiles. *I love you,* she says.

I wake, momentarily disoriented, my heart thudding like a klaxon, and I don't know if it's fear or excitement. I'm in the back of the Q7 and Ana is curled up asleep in my lap.

Ana.

She's mine once more. And for a moment I feel giddy. A stupid grin splits my face and I shake my head. Have I ever felt like this?

I'm excited for the future. I'm excited to see where our relationship will go. What new things we'll try. There are so many possibilities.

I kiss her hair and rest my chin on her head. When I glance out of the window I notice that we've reached Seattle.

Taylor's eyes meet mine in the rearview mirror. "Are we heading to Escala, sir?"

"No, Miss Steele's."

The corners of his eyes crinkle. "We'll be there in five minutes," he says.

Whoa. We're nearly home.

"Thank you, Taylor." I've slept longer than I thought possible in the back of a car. I wonder what time it is, but I don't want to move my arm to check my watch as I'm holding her. I gaze down at my sleeping beauty. Her lips are gently parted, her dark lashes fanned out, shadowing her face. And I remember watching her sleep at The Heathman, that first time. She looked so peaceful then; she looks peaceful now. I'm reluctant to disturb her.

"Wake up, baby." I kiss her hair. Her eyelashes flutter and she opens her eyes. "Hey," I murmur in greeting.

"Sorry," she mumbles as she sits up.

"I could watch you sleep forever, Ana." No need to apologize.

"Did I say anything?" She looks worried.

"No," I reassure her. "We're nearly at your place."

"We're not going to yours?" She sounds surprised.

"No."

She sits up straight and glares at me. "Why not?"

"Because you have work tomorrow."

"Oh." Her pout says all I need to know about her disappointment. I want to laugh out loud.

"Why, did you have something in mind?" I tease her.

She squirms in my lap.

Ow.

I still her with my hands.

"Well, maybe," she says, looking anywhere but at me and sounding a little shy. I can't help my laugh. She's courageous in so many ways, yet still so coy in others. And as I watch her, I realize

I've got to get her to open up about sex. If we're going to be honest with each other, she has to tell me how she feels. Tell me what she needs. I want her to be confident enough to express her desires. All of them.

"Anastasia, I am not going to touch you again, not until you beg me to."

"What!" She sounds a little upset.

"So that you'll start communicating with me. Next time we make love, you're going to have to tell me exactly what you want in fine detail."

That will give you something to think about, Miss Steele.

I lift her off my lap when Taylor pulls up at the curb beside her apartment. I climb out of the car, walk to her door, and open it for her. She looks sleepy and adorable as she struggles out of the car.

"I have something for you."

This is it. Will she accept my gift? This is the final stage of my campaign to win her back. Opening the trunk, I grab the gift box that contains her Mac, her phone, and an iPad. She looks from the box to me with suspicion. "Open it when you get inside."

"You're not coming in?"

"No, Anastasia." As much as I'd like to. We both need to sleep.

"So when will I see you?"

"Tomorrow?"

"My boss wants me to go for a drink with him tomorrow."

What the hell does that fucker want? I must chase Welch for his report on Hyde. There's something off about him that isn't reflected in his employee records. I don't trust him one bit. "Does he, now?" I try to sound nonchalant.

"To celebrate my first week," she says quickly.

"Where?"

"I don't know."

"I could pick you up from there."

"Okay. I'll email or text you."

"Good."

We walk to the lobby door together and I watch, amused, as

she rummages around in her purse for her keys. She unlocks the door and turns to say goodbye—and I can't resist her any longer. Leaning down, I cup her chin in my fingers. I want to kiss her hard, but I hold back and trace soft kisses from her temple to her mouth. She moans and the sweet sound travels straight to my cock.

"Until tomorrow," I say, failing to keep the desire out of my voice.

"Good night, Christian," she whispers, and her longing echoes my own.

Oh, baby. Tomorrow. Not now.

"In you go," I order, and it's one of the hardest things I've ever done: letting her leave knowing that she's mine for the taking. My body ignores my noble gesture and stiffens in anticipation. I shake my head, amazed as ever by my lust for Ana.

"Laters, baby," I call after her, and turning toward the street I head to the car, determined not to look back. Once I'm inside the car, I allow myself to look. She's still there, standing on the doorstep, watching me.

Good.

Go to bed, Ana, I will her. As if she hears me, she closes the door, and Taylor starts the car to head home to Escala.

I lean back in my seat.

What a difference a day makes.

I grin. She's mine once more.

I imagine her in her apartment, opening the box. Will she be pissed? Or will she be delighted?

She'll be pissed.

She never took kindly to gifts.

Shit. Was it a step too far?

Taylor heads into the garage at Escala and we pull into the vacant parking space next to Ana's A3. "Taylor, will you deliver Miss Steele's Audi to her place tomorrow?" I hope she will accept the car, too.

"Yes, Mr. Grey."

I leave him in the garage, doing whatever he does, and head for the elevator. Once inside, I check my phone to see if she has anything to say about the gifts. Just as the elevator doors open and I step into my apartment, there's an email.

From: Anastasia Steele
Subject: iPad
Date: June 9 2011 23:56
To: Christian Grey

You've made me cry again.
I love the iPad.
I love the songs.
I love the British Library app.
I love you.
Thank you.
Good night.

Ana xx

I grin at the screen. *Happy tears, great!*
She loves it.
She loves me.

FRIDAY, JUNE 10, 2011

She loves me.

It's taken a three-hour car ride for me not to flinch at this thought. But then again, she doesn't really know me. She doesn't know what I'm capable of, or why I do what I do. No one can love a monster, no matter how compassionate they are.

I put the thought out of my mind because I don't want to dwell on the negative.

Flynn would be proud.

Quickly, I type a response to her email.

From: Christian Grey
Subject: iPad
Date: June 10 2011 00:03
To: Anastasia Steele

I'm glad you like it. I bought one for myself.

Now, if I were there, I would kiss away your tears.

But I'm not—so go to sleep.

Christian Grey
CEO, Grey Enterprises Holdings, Inc.

I want her well rested for tomorrow. I stretch, feeling a contentment that's entirely unfamiliar, and wander into my bedroom.

Looking forward to collapsing into bed, I put my phone on the nightstand and notice there's another email from her.

From: Anastasia Steele
Subject: Mr. Grumpy
Date: June 10 2011 00:07
To: Christian Grey

You sound your usual bossy and possibly tense, possibly grumpy self, Mr. Grey.

I know something that could ease that. But then, you're not here—you wouldn't let me stay, and you expect me to beg…

Dream on, Sir.
Ana xx

P.S. I also note that you included the Stalker's Anthem, "Every Breath You Take." I do enjoy your sense of humor, but does Dr. Flynn know?

And there it is. The Anastasia Steele wit. I have missed it. I sit down on the edge of the bed and compose my reply.

From: Christian Grey
Subject: Zen-Like Calm
Date: June 10 2011 00:10
To: Anastasia Steele

My Dearest Miss Steele

Spanking occurs in vanilla relationships, too, you know.

Usually consensually and in a sexual context... but I am more than happy to make an exception.

You'll be relieved to know that Dr. Flynn also enjoys my sense of humor.

Now, please go to sleep, as you won't get much tomorrow.

Incidentally—you will beg, trust me. And I look forward to it.

Christian Grey
Tense CEO, Grey Enterprises Holdings, Inc.

I watch my phone, waiting for her reply. I know she won't let this go. And, sure enough, her response appears.

From: Anastasia Steele
Subject: Good Night, Sweet Dreams
Date: June 10 2011 00:12
To: Christian Grey

Well, since you ask so nicely, and I like your delicious threat, I shall curl up with the iPad that you have so kindly given me and fall asleep browsing in the British Library, listening to the music that says it for you.

A xxx

She likes my threat? Lord, she's confusing. Then I remember her squirming in the car while we talked of spanking.

Oh, baby, it's not a threat. It's a promise.

I get up and wander into my closet to take off my jacket while I think of something to say.

She wants a softer approach; surely I can think of something. And then it comes to me.

From: Christian Grey
Subject: One more request
Date: June 10 2011 00:15
To: Anastasia Steele

Dream of me.

x

Christian Grey
CEO, Grey Enterprises Holdings, Inc.

Yes. Dream of me. I want to be the only one in her head. Not that photographer. Not her boss. Just me. I change quickly into PJ bottoms and brush my teeth.

As I slip into bed, I check my phone once more, but there's nothing from Miss Steele. She must be asleep. When I close my eyes it occurs to me that I've not thought about Leila all evening. Anastasia has been so diverting, beautiful, funny…

The radio alarm wakes me for the first time since she left me. I've slept a soundless and dreamless sleep and I awake refreshed. My first thought is of Ana. How is she this morning? Has she changed her mind?

No. Stay positive.

Okay.

I wonder what her morning routine is?

Better.

And I get to see her this evening. I bound out of bed and into my sweats. My run will take me on my usual route to check on her building. But this time, I won't linger. I'm a stalker no more.

My feet pound the pavement. The sun is peeping through the buildings as I make my way to Ana's street. It's still quiet, but I have the Foo Fighters turned up loud and proud as I run. I wonder if I should be listening to something that's more in sync with my mood. Maybe "Feeling Good." Nina Simone's version.

Too sappy, Grey. Keep running.

I dash past Ana's building, and I don't have to stop. I'll see her later today. All of her. Feeling particularly pleased with myself, I wonder if perhaps we'll end up here tonight.

Whatever we do, it will be up to Ana. We're doing this her way.

I run up Wall Street, back home to begin my day.

"Good morning, Gail." Even to my own ears I sound unusually hearty. Gail stops in her tracks in front of the stove and stares at me as if I've grown three heads. "I'll have scrambled eggs and toast this morning," I add and wink at her as I head toward my study. Her chin drops, but she says nothing.

Ah, speechless Mrs. Jones. This is novel.

In my study, I check emails on my computer and there's nothing that can't wait until I get into the office. My thoughts stray to Ana and I wonder if she's had breakfast.

From: Christian Grey
Subject: So Help Me...
Date: June 10 2011 08:05
To: Anastasia Steele

I do hope you've had breakfast.

I missed you last night.

Christian Grey
CEO, Grey Enterprises Holdings, Inc.

In the car, on the way to the office, I get a response.

From: Anastasia Steele
Subject: Old books...
Date: June 10 2011 08:33
To: Christian Grey

I am eating a banana as I type. I have not had breakfast for several days, so it is a step forward. I love the British Library app—I started rereading *Robinson Crusoe*... and, of course, I love you.

Now leave me alone—I am trying to work.

Anastasia Steele
Assistant to Jack Hyde, Editor, SIP

Robinson Crusoe? A man alone, stranded on a deserted island. Is she trying to tell me something?

And she loves me.

Loves. Me. And I'm surprised that those words are getting easier to hear... but not *that* easy.

So I shift my focus to what irritates me most about her email.

From: Christian Grey
Subject: Is that all you've eaten?
Date: June 10 2011 08:36
To: Anastasia Steele

You can do better than that. You're going to need your energy for begging.

Christian Grey
CEO, Grey Enterprises Holdings, Inc.

Taylor pulls up at the curb in front of Grey House.

"Sir, I'll take the Audi to Miss Steele's this morning."

"Great. Until later, Taylor. Thank you."

"Good day, sir."

In the elevator at Grey House, I read her response.

From: Anastasia Steele
Subject: Pest
Date: June 10 2011 08:39
To: Christian Grey

Mr. Grey—I am trying to work for a living—and it's you who will be begging.

Anastasia Steele
Assistant to Jack Hyde, Editor, SIP

Ha! I don't think so.

"Good morning, Andrea." I give her a friendly nod as I stride past her desk.

"Um," she stalls, but recovers quickly, because she's ever the adept PA. "Good morning, Mr. Grey. Coffee?"

"Please. Black." I close my office door and when seated at my desk respond to Ana.

From: Christian Grey
Subject: Bring It On!
Date: June 10 2011 08:42
To: Anastasia Steele

Why, Miss Steele, I love a challenge…

Christian Grey
CEO, Grey Enterprises Holdings, Inc.

I love that she's so feisty over email. Life is never boring with Ana. I lean back in my chair with my hands behind my head, trying to understand my effervescent mood. When have I ever felt this cheerful? It's frightening. She has the power to give me hope, and the power to make me despair. I know which I prefer. There's a blank space on my office wall; perhaps one of her portraits should fill the void. Before I can brood on this further, there's a knock on the door.

Andrea enters, carrying my coffee. "Mr. Grey, may I have a word?"

"Of course."

She perches on the chair opposite me, looking nervous. "Do you remember I'm not here this afternoon and I'm not in on Monday?"

I stare at her, completely blank. *What the hell?* I don't remember this. I hate it when she's not here.

"I thought I should remind you," she adds.

"Do you have someone covering for you?"

"Yes. HR is sending someone from another department. Her name is Montana Brooks."

"Okay."

"It's only a day and a half, sir."

I laugh. "Do I look that worried?"

Andrea gives me a rare smile. "Yes, Mr. Grey, you do."

"Well, whatever you're up to, I hope it's fun."

She stands. "Thank you, sir."

"Do I have anything scheduled for this weekend?"

"You have golf tomorrow with Mr. Bastille."

"Cancel it." I'd rather have fun with Ana.

"Will do. You also have the masquerade ball at your parents' place for Coping Together," Andrea reminds me.

"Oh. Damn."

"It's been in the schedule for months."

"Yes. I know. Leave that."

I wonder if Ana will come as my date?

"Okay, sir."

"Did you find someone to replace Senator Blandino's daughter?"

"Yes, sir. Her name is Sarah Hunter. She starts on Tuesday when I'm back."

"Good."

"You have a nine o'clock with Miss Bailey."

"Thanks, Andrea. Get me Welch on the line."

"Yes, Mr. Grey."

Ros is concluding her report on the Darfur airdrop. "Everything has gone as scheduled and early reports from the NGOs on the ground are that it's come at the right time and to the right place," Ros says. "Frankly, it's been a huge success. We're going to help so many people."

"Great. Perhaps we should do it every year where it's needed."

"It's expensive, Christian."

"I know. But it's the right thing to do. And it's only money."

She gives me a slightly exasperated look.

"Are we done?" I ask.

"For now, yes."

"Good."

She continues to regard me with curiosity.

What?

"I'm glad you're back with us," she says.

"What do you mean?"

"You know what I mean." She gets up and gathers her papers. "You've been absent, Christian." Her eyes narrow.

"I was here."

"No, you weren't. But I'm glad you're back and focused, and you seem happier." She gives me a broad smile and heads for the door.

Is it that obvious?

"I saw the photo in the paper this morning."

"Photo?"

"Yes. You and a young woman at a photo exhibition."

"Oh, yes." I can't hide my smile.

Ros nods. "I'll see you later this afternoon for the meeting with Marco."

"Sure."

She leaves, and I'm left wondering how the rest of my staff will react to me today.

Barney, my tech wizard and senior engineer, has produced three prototypes of the solar tablet. It's a product I hope we'll sell at a premium globally and also underwrite philanthropically in the developing world. Democratizing technology is one of my passions—making it cheap, functional, and available in the poorest nations to help bring these countries out of poverty.

Later that morning we're gathered in the lab discussing the prototypes that are scattered over the workbench. Fred, the VP of our telecom division, is making a pitch to incorporate the solar cells into the rear casing of each device.

"Why can't we incorporate them into the entire casing of the tablet, even into the screen?" I ask.

Seven heads turn my way in unison.

"Not the screen, but a cover...maybe?" says Fred.

"Expense?" Barney pipes up at the same time.

"This is blue sky, people. Don't concern yourselves with the economics," I answer. "We'll sell it as a premium brand here and practically give it away in the third world. That's the point."

The room erupts in creativity and two hours later we have three ideas about how to cover the device in solar cells.

"Of course we'll make it WiMAX-enabled for the home market," Fred states.

"And incorporate the capability for satellite internet access for Africa and India," Barney adds. "Provided we can get access." He looks quizzically toward me.

"That's a little down the line. I'm hoping we can piggyback on the EU GPS system Galileo." I know this will take a while to negotiate, but we have time. "Marco's team is looking into it."

"Tomorrow's technology today," Barney states proudly.

"Excellent." I nod in approval. I turn to my VP of procurement.

"Vanessa, where are we with the conflict mineral issue? How are you dealing with it?"

Later, we're sitting around the table in my boardroom and Marco is running through the modified business plan for SIP and their contract stipulations following the signing of our revised heads of agreement yesterday.

"They want to embargo the acquisition news for a month," he says. "Something about not freaking out their authors."

"Really? Will their authors care?" I ask.

"This is a creative industry," Ros says gently.

"Whatever." And I want to roll my eyes.

"You and I have a call scheduled with Jeremy Roach, the owner, at four thirty today."

"Good. We can hash out remaining details then." My mind drifts to Anastasia. How is her day going? Has she rolled her eyes at anyone today? What are her work colleagues like? Her boss? I've asked Welch to investigate Jack Hyde; just reading Hyde's employee file, I know there's something odd about his career trajectory. He started in New York, and now he's here. Something doesn't add up. I need to know more about him, especially if Ana is working for him.

I'm also waiting for an update on Leila. Welch has nothing new to report on her whereabouts. It's like she's disappeared completely. I can only hope that wherever she is, she's in a better place.

"Their email monitoring is almost as stringent as ours," Ros says, interrupting my reverie.

"So?" I ask. "Any company worth its equity has a rigorous email policy."

"It surprises me for such a small operation. All emails are checked by the HR function."

I shrug. "I don't have an issue with that." Though I should warn Ana. "Let's go through their liabilities."

Once we've dealt with SIP, we move to the next item on the agenda. "We're going to make a tentative inquiry about the shipyard in Taiwan," Marco says.

"I don't see what we've got to lose," Ros agrees.

"My shirt and the goodwill of our workforce?"

"Christian, we don't have to do it," Ros says with a sigh.

"It makes financial sense. You know it. I know it. Let's see how far we can run with this."

My phone flashes, announcing an email from Ana.

At last!

I've been so busy I haven't managed to contact her since this morning, but she's been hovering at the edge of my consciousness all day, like a guardian angel. My guardian angel. Ever present but not intrusive.

Mine.

Grey, get a grip.

As Ros lists next steps for the Taiwan project, I read Ana's email.

From: Anastasia Steele
Subject: Bored...
Date: June 10 2011 16:05
To: Christian Grey

Twiddling my thumbs.
How are you?
What are you doing?

Anastasia Steele
Assistant to Jack Hyde, Editor, SIP

Twiddling her thumbs? The thought makes me smile as I recall her fumbling with the tape recorder when she came to interview me.

Are you gay, Mr. Grey?

Ah, sweet, innocent Ana.

No. Not gay.

I love that she's thinking about me and has taken time out of her day to make contact. It's… distracting. An unfamiliar warmth seeps into my bones. It makes me uneasy. Really uneasy. Ignoring it, I quickly type a response.

From: Christian Grey
Subject: Your thumbs
Date: June 10 2011 16:15
To: Anastasia Steele

You should have come to work for me.

You wouldn't be twiddling your thumbs.

I am sure I could put them to better use.

In fact, I can think of a number of options…

Fuck. Not now, Grey.

My eyes meet Ros's, and I sense her disapproval.

"Urgent response required," I tell her. She shares a look with Marco.

I am doing the usual humdrum mergers and acquisitions.

It's all very dry.

Your emails at SIP are monitored.

Christian Grey
Distracted CEO, Grey Enterprises Holdings, Inc.

I can't wait to see her this evening, and she's yet to email where we'll meet. It's frustrating. But we've agreed to try our relationship her way, so I put my phone down and turn my attention back to my meeting.

Patience, Grey. Patience.

We've moved on to discuss the mayor of Seattle's visit to Grey House next week, an appointment I set up when I met him earlier this month.

"Is Sam on this?" Ros asks.

"Like a rash," I respond. Sam never misses a PR opportunity.

"Okay. If you're ready I'll get Jeremy Roach on the line from SIP to go through those final details."

"Let's do it."

Back in my outer office, Andrea's replacement is applying yet more lipstick to her scarlet mouth. I don't like it. And the color reminds me of Elena. One of the things I love about Ana is that she doesn't cake herself in lipstick, or any other makeup for that matter. Hiding my disgust, and ignoring the new girl, I head into my office. I can't even remember her name.

Fred's revised proposal for Kavanagh Media is open on my desktop, but I'm preoccupied and finding it hard to concentrate. Time is moving on and I've not heard from Anastasia; as ever, I'm waiting for Miss Steele. I check my email once more.

Nothing.

I check my phone for texts.

Nothing.

What's keeping her? I hope it's not her boss.

There's a knock on my door.

What now?

"Come in."

Andrea's replacement pokes her head around the door and, *ping*, there's an email, but it's not from Ana.

"What?" I bark, trying to remember the woman's name.

She's unfazed. "I'm just about to leave, Mr. Grey. Mr. Taylor left this for you." She holds up an envelope.

"Just leave it on the console there."

"Do you need me for anything else?"

"No. Go. Thanks." I give her a thin smile.

"Have a good weekend then, sir," she offers, simpering.

Oh, I fully intend to.

I dismiss her, but she doesn't leave. She pauses for a moment, and I realize she's expecting something from me.

What?

"I'll see you Monday," she says with an annoying, nervous giggle.

"Yes. Monday. Shut the door behind you."

Looking a little crestfallen, she does as she's told.

What was that about?

I pick up the envelope from the console. It's the key to Ana's Audi, and written in Taylor's tidy hand are the words: *Parked in allocated parking space at rear of apartment building.*

Back at my desk, I turn my attention to my emails, and finally there's one from Ana. I grin like the Cheshire Cat.

From: Anastasia Steele
Subject: You'll Fit Right In
Date: June 10 2011 17:36
To: Christian Grey

We are going to a bar called Fifty's.
The rich seam of humor that I could mine from this is endless.
I look forward to seeing you there, Mr. Grey.

A. x

Is this a reference to fifty shades?

Weird. Is she making fun of me?

Okay. Let's have some fun with this.

From: Christian Grey
Subject: Hazards
Date: June 10 2011 17:38
To: Anastasia Steele

Mining is a very, very dangerous occupation.

Christian Grey
CEO, Grey Enterprises Holdings, Inc.

Let's see what she makes of that.

From: Anastasia Steele
Subject: Hazards?
Date: June 10 2011 17:40
To: Christian Grey

And your point is?

So obtuse, Anastasia? That's not like you. But I don't want to fight.

From: Christian Grey
Subject: Merely...
Date: June 10 2011 17:42
To: Anastasia Steele

Making an observation, Miss Steele.

I'll see you shortly.

Sooners rather than laters, baby.

Christian Grey
CEO, Grey Enterprises Holdings, Inc.

Now that she's been in contact, I relax and concentrate on the Kavanagh proposal. It's good. I send it back to Fred and tell him to send it on to Kavanagh. Idly I speculate whether Kavanagh Media might be ripe for a takeover. It's a thought. I wonder what Ros and Marco would say. I shelve the idea for now and head down to the lobby, texting Taylor to let him know where I'm meeting Ana.

50's is a sports bar. It's vaguely familiar, and I realize I've been here before with Elliot. But then Elliot is a jock, a real guy's guy, who's the life and soul of any party. This is his type of place, a shrine to team sports. I was too hotheaded to play on a team at any of my schools. I preferred more solitary pursuits like sculling and full-contact sports like kickboxing, where I could kick the shit out of someone… or have the shit kicked out of me.

Inside, it's crowded with young office workers starting their weekends with a quick drink or five, and it takes me only two seconds to spot her by the bar.

Ana.

And he's there. *Hyde.* Crowding her.

Asshole.

Her shoulders are tense. She's obviously uncomfortable.

Fuck him.

With great effort I keep my walk casual, trying to maintain my cool. When I'm by her side, I drape my arm over her shoulder and pull her toward me, freeing her from his unwanted advances.

I kiss her, just behind her ear. "Hello, baby," I whisper into her hair. She melts against me as the asshole stands taller, appraising me. I want to rip the "fuck you" expression off his rugged, smug face, but I deliberately ignore him to focus on my girl.

Hey, baby. Is this guy bothering you?

She beams at me. Eyes shining, lips moist, her hair cascading over her shoulders. She's wearing the blue blouse that Taylor bought her, and it complements her eyes and skin. Leaning in, I kiss her. Her cheeks color, but she turns to the asshole who's taken the hint and stepped back a little.

"Jack, this is Christian. Christian, Jack," she says, waving between us.

"I'm the boyfriend," I state, so there's no confusion, and hold out my hand to Hyde.

See. I can play nice.

"I'm the boss," he responds as we shake. His grip is tight, so I tighten mine.

Keep your hands off my girl.

"Ana did mention an ex-boyfriend," he says with a patronizing drawl.

"Well, no longer ex." I give him a slight fuck-off smile. "Come on, baby, time to go."

"Please, stay and join us for a drink," Hyde says, emphasizing the word "us."

"We have plans. Another time, perhaps."

Like. Never.

I don't trust him, and I want Ana far away from him. "Come," I say when I take her hand.

"See you Monday," she says as she tightens her fingers around mine. She's addressing Hyde and an attractive woman, who must be one of her colleagues. At least Ana wasn't on her own with him. The woman gives Ana a warm smile while Hyde scowls at us both. I sense his eyes boring into my back as we leave. But I don't give a fuck.

Outside, Taylor is waiting in the Q7. I open the rear door for Ana.

"Why did that feel like a pissing contest?" she asks as she gets in.

Perceptive as ever, Miss Steele.

"Because it was," I confirm and close her door.

When I'm in the car, I reach for her hand because I want to touch her and raise it to my lips. "Hi," I whisper. She looks so good. The dark circles beneath her eyes have disappeared. She's slept. She's eaten. Her healthy glow has returned. From her bright smile, I'd say she's brimming with happiness, and it washes over me.

"Hi," she says, all breathy and suggestive. Damn, I want to jump her now—though I'm sure Taylor wouldn't appreciate it if I did. I glance at him and his eyes dart to mine in the rearview mirror. He's waiting for instruction.

Well, we're doing this Ana's way.

"What would you like to do this evening?" I ask.

"I thought you said we had plans."

"Oh, I know what I'd like to do, Anastasia. I'm asking you what you want to do."

Her smile widens into a salacious grin that speaks directly to my cock.

Hot damn.

"I see. So… begging it is, then. Do you want to beg at my place or yours?" I tease.

Her face shines with humor. "I think you're being very presumptuous, Mr. Grey. But by way of a change, we could go to my apartment." She bites down on her plump lower lip and peers at me through her dark lashes.

Fuck.

"Taylor, Miss Steele's please." *And hurry!*

"Sir," Taylor acknowledges, and he pulls out into traffic.

"So how has your day been?" I ask and brush my thumb across her knuckles.

Her breath hitches. "Good. Yours?"

"Good, thank you." Yes. Really good. I've done more work today than I've done all week. I kiss her hand, because I have her to thank for that. "You look lovely."

"As do you."

Oh, baby, it's just a pretty face.

Speaking of pretty faces… "Your boss, Jack Hyde. Is he good at his job?"

She frowns and the *v* I like to kiss forms above her nose. "Why? This isn't about your pissing contest?"

"That man wants into your panties, Anastasia," I warn her,

trying to sound as neutral as possible. She looks shocked. Jesus, she's so innocent. It was obvious to me and anyone who was paying attention at the bar.

"Well, he can want all he likes," she says, her tone prim. "Why are we even having this conversation? You know I have no interest in him whatsoever. He's just my boss."

"That's the point. He wants what's mine. I need to know if he's good at his job." Because if not, I'll fire his sorry ass.

She shrugs but looks down at her lap.

What? Has he tried something already?

She tells me she thinks he's good at what he does, but she sounds like she's trying to convince herself.

"Well, he'd better leave you alone, or he'll find himself on his ass on the sidewalk."

"Oh, Christian, what are you talking about? He hasn't done anything wrong."

Why is she frowning? Does he make her uncomfortable? Talk to me, Ana. Please. "He makes one move, you tell me. It's called gross moral turpitude—or sexual harassment."

"It was just a drink after work."

"I mean it. One move and he's out."

"You don't have that kind of power," she scoffs, amused. But her smile fades and she regards me with skepticism. "Do you, Christian?"

I do, actually. I smile at her.

"You're buying the company?" she whispers, and she looks appalled.

"Not exactly." This is not the reaction I was expecting, nor is the conversation going the way I thought it would.

"You've bought it. SIP. Already." Her face pales.

Christ! She's pissed.

"Possibly," I answer cautiously.

"You have or you haven't?" she demands.

Showtime, Grey. Tell her.

"Have."

"Why?" Her voice is shrill.

"Because I can, Anastasia. I need you safe."

"But you said you wouldn't interfere in my career!"

"And I won't."

She snatches her hand back. "Christian!"

Shit. "Are you mad at me?"

"Yes. Of course I'm mad at you," she yells. "I mean, what kind of responsible business executive makes decisions based on who he is currently fucking?" She glances nervously at Taylor, then glares at me, her expression full of recrimination.

And I want to admonish her for her foul mouth and for overreacting. I start to tell her so, then decide that it might not be a good idea. Her lips are set in the mulish Steele pout that I know so well… I have missed that, too.

She folds her arms in disgust.

Fuck.

She's really mad.

I glare back at her, wanting nothing more than to drag her across my knee—but, sadly, that's not an option.

Hell, I was only doing what I thought was best.

Taylor parks outside her apartment, and before he's stopped, it seems, she's out of the car.

Shit! "I think you'd better wait here," I say to Taylor, and I scramble after her. My evening may be about to take a radically different course than the one I'd planned. I may have blown it already.

When I reach her at the lobby door, she's rummaging around in her purse for keys while I stand behind her, helpless.

What to do?

"Anastasia," I entreat her as I try to remain calm.

She lets out an exaggerated sigh and turns to face me, her mouth pressed in a hard line.

Following up what she said in the car, I try for humor. "First, I haven't fucked you for a while—a long while, it feels—and second, I wanted to get into publishing. Of the four companies in Seattle, SIP is the most profitable." I keep talking about the company but what I really want to say is… *Please don't fight with me.*

"So you're my boss now?" she snaps.

"Technically, I'm your boss's boss's boss."

"And technically, it's gross moral turpitude—the fact that I am fucking my boss's boss's boss."

"At the moment, you're arguing with him." My voice is beginning to rise.

"That's because he's such an ass."

Ass. Ass!

She's calling me names! The only people who do that are Mia and Elliot.

"An ass?" Yes. Maybe I am. And suddenly I want to laugh. Anastasia called me an ass—Elliot would approve.

"Yes." She's trying to stay mad at me, but her mouth is lifting at the corners.

"An ass?" I repeat, and I cannot help my smile.

"Don't make me laugh when I'm mad at you!" she shouts, trying and failing to stay serious. I give her my best one-thousand-watt smile and she unleashes an uninhibited, spontaneous laugh that makes me feel ten feet tall.

Success!

"Just because I have a stupid damn grin on my face doesn't mean I am not mad as hell at you," she claims between giggles.

Leaning forward, I nuzzle her hair and inhale deeply. Her scent and her proximity stir my libido. I want her. "As ever, Miss Steele, you are unexpected." I gaze down, treasuring her flushed face and shining eyes. She's beautiful. "So are you going to invite me in, or am I to be sent packing for exercising my democratic right as an American citizen, entrepreneur, and consumer to purchase whatever I damn well please?"

"Have you spoken to Dr. Flynn about this?"

I laugh. Not yet. It will be a mindfuck when I do.

"Are you going to let me in or not, Anastasia?"

For a moment she looks undecided, making my heartbeat spike. But she bites her lip, then smiles and opens the door for me. I wave Taylor off and follow Ana upstairs, enjoying the fantastic view of her ass. The gentle sway of her hips as she climbs each step is beyond seductive—more so, I think, because she has no idea she's so alluring. Her innate sensuality stems from her innocence: her willingness to experiment, and her ability to trust.

Damn. I hope I still have her trust. After all, I drove her away. I will have to work hard to rebuild it. I don't want to lose her again.

Her apartment is neat and tidy, as I would expect, but it has an unused, uninhabited vibe about it. It reminds me of the gallery: it's all old brick and wood. The concrete kitchen island is a stark and novel design statement. I like it.

"Nice place," I remark with approval.

"Kate's parents bought it for her."

Eamon Kavanagh has indulged his daughter. It's a stylish place—he's chosen well. I hope Katherine appreciates it. I turn and stare at Ana as she stands by the island. I wonder how she feels living with such a well-off friend. I'm sure she pays her way… but it must be tough to play second fiddle to Katherine Kavanagh. Maybe she likes it, or maybe she finds it a struggle. She certainly doesn't squander her money on clothes. But I've remedied that; I have a closetful for her at Escala. I wonder what she'll think about that? She'll likely give me a hard time.

Don't think about that now, Grey.

Ana's studying me, her eyes dark. She licks her bottom lip, and my body lights up like a firework.

"Er… would you like a drink?" she asks.

"No thank you, Anastasia." I want you.

She clasps her hands together, seemingly at a loss and looking a little apprehensive. Do I still make her nervous? This woman can bring me to my knees, and she's the one who's nervous?

"What would you like to do, Anastasia?" I ask and move closer to her, my eyes not leaving hers. "I know what I want to do."

And we can do it here, or in your bedroom, or your bathroom. I don't care—I just want you. Now.

Her lips part as her breath hitches and her breathing quickens.

Oh, that sound is beguiling.

You want me, too, baby.

I know it.

I feel it.

She backs up against the kitchen island with nowhere else to go.

"I'm still mad at you," she asserts, but her voice is tremulous and soft. She doesn't sound mad at all. Wanton, maybe. But not mad.

"I know." I give her a wolfish grin.

Her eyes widen.

Oh, baby.

"Would you like something to eat?" she whispers.

I nod slowly. "Yes. You."

Standing over her, staring into eyes that are dark with desire, I feel the heat from her body. It's searing me. I want to be wrapped in it. Bathed in it. I want to make her scream and moan and call out my name. I want to reclaim her and wipe the memory of our breakup from her mind.

I want to make her mine. Again.

But first things first.

"Have you eaten today?" I need to know.

"I had a sandwich at lunch."

That will do. "You need to eat," I chide her.

"I'm really not hungry right now…for food."

"What are you hungry for, Miss Steele?" I lower my face so our lips are almost touching.

"I think you know, Mr. Grey."

She's not wrong. I stifle my groan and it takes all my self-control not to grab her and toss her onto the concrete counter. But I was serious when I said she'd have to beg. She has to tell me what she wants. She has to vocalize her feelings, her needs, and her desires. I want to learn what makes her happy. I lean down as if to kiss her, fooling her, and whisper in her ear instead.

"Do you want me to kiss you, Anastasia?"

She inhales sharply. "Yes."

"Where?"

"Everywhere."

"You're going to have to be a bit more specific than that. I told you I'm not going to touch you until you beg me and tell me what to do."

"Please," she pleads.

Oh no, baby. I'm not going to make this easy on you. "Please what?"

"Touch me."

"Where, baby?"

She reaches for me.

No.

The darkness erupts inside me and grips my throat with its claws. Instinctively, I step back, my heart pounding as fear courses through my body.

Don't touch me. Don't touch me.

Fuck.

"No. No," I mutter.

This is why I have rules.

"What?" She's confused.

"No." I shake my head. She knows this. I told her yesterday. I have to make her understand she can't touch me.

"Not at all?" She steps toward me and I don't know what she intends. The darkness stabs at my insides, so I take another step back and hold up my hands to ward her off.

With a smile, I beseech her, "Look. Ana…" But I can't find the right words.

Please. Don't touch me. I can't handle it.

Damn, it's frustrating.

"Sometimes you don't mind," she protests. "Perhaps I should find a marker pen, and we could map out the no-go areas."

Well, that's an approach I've not considered before. "That's not a bad idea. Where's your bedroom?" I need to move her on from this subject.

She nods to the left.

"Have you been taking your pill?"

Her face falls. "No."

What!

After all the trouble we went through to get her on the fucking pill! I can't believe she just stopped taking it.

"I see."

This is a disaster. What the hell am I going to do with her? Damn it. I need condoms. “Come, let’s have something to eat,” I say, thinking we can go out and I can replenish my supply.

“I thought we were going to bed. I want to go to bed with you.” She sounds sullen.

“I know, baby.”

But with us it’s two steps forward and one step back.

This evening is not going as planned. Maybe it was too much to hope. How can she be with a fucked-up asshole who can’t bear to be touched? And how can I be with someone who forgets to take their damned pill? I hate condoms.

Christ. Maybe we are incompatible.

ACKNOWLEDGMENTS

Thanks to:

Anne Messitte for her guidance, good humor, and belief in me. For her generosity with her time and for her unstinting effort to untangle my prose, I am forever indebted.

Tony Chirico and Russell Perreault for always looking out for me, and the fabulous production editorial and design team who saw this book across the finish line: Amy Brosey, Lydia Buechler, Katherine Hourigan, Andy Hughes, Claudia Martinez, and Megan Wilson.

Niall Leonard for his love, support, and guidance, and for being the only man who can really, really make me laugh.

Valerie Hoskins, my agent, without whom I'd still be working in TV. Thank you for everything.

Kathleen Blandino, Ruth Clampett, and Belinda Willis: thanks for the pre-read.

The Lost Girls for their precious friendship and the therapy.

The Bunker Babes for their constant wit, wisdom, support, and friendship.

The FP ladies for help with my Americanisms.

Peter Branston for his help with SFBT.

Brian Brunetti for his guidance in flying a helicopter.

Professor Dawn Carusi for help in navigating the U.S. higher education system.

Professor Chris Collins for an education in soil science.

Dr. Raina Sluder for her insights into behavioral health.

And last but by no means least, my children. I love you more than words can ever say. You bring such joy to my life and to those around you. You are beautiful, funny, bright, compassionate young men, and I could not be more proud of you.

E L James

GREY

E L James is an incurable romantic and a self-confessed fangirl. After twenty-five years of working in television, she decided to pursue a childhood dream and write stories that readers could take to their hearts. The result was the controversial and sensuous romance *Fifty Shades of Grey* and its two sequels, *Fifty Shades Darker* and *Fifty Shades Freed*. In 2015, she published the #1 bestseller *Grey*, the story of *Fifty Shades of Grey* from the perspective of Christian Grey, and in 2017, the chart-topping *Darker*, the second part of the Fifty Shades story from Christian's point of view. She followed with the #1 *New York Times* bestseller *The Mister* in 2019. In 2021, she released the #1 *New York Times, USA Today, Wall Street Journal*, and international bestseller *Freed*, the third novel in the "As Told by Christian" trilogy. Her books have been published in fifty languages and have sold more than 165 million copies worldwide.

E L James has been recognized as one of *Time* magazine's Most Influential People in the World and *Publishers Weekly*'s Person of the Year. *Fifty Shades of Grey* stayed on the *New York Times* bestseller list for 133 consecutive weeks. *Fifty Shades Freed* won the Goodreads Choice Award (2012), and *Fifty Shades of Grey* was selected as one of the 100 Great Reads, as voted by readers, in PBS's The Great American Read (2018). Darker was longlisted for the 2019 International DUBLIN Literary Award.

She was a producer on each of the three Fifty Shades movies, which made more than a billion dollars at the box office. The third installment, *Fifty Shades Freed*, won the People's Choice Award for Drama in 2018. E L James is blessed with two wonderful sons and lives with her husband, the novelist and screenwriter Niall Leonard, and their West Highland terriers in the leafy suburbs of West London.

"Passion APLENTY."

—*People* magazine

Fall in love with ***The Mister***, the thrilling romance from #1 *New York Times* bestselling author **E L James**, author of the phenomenal bestselling Fifty Shades trilogy.

From the heart of London through wild, rural Cornwall to the bleak, forbidding beauty of the Balkans, ***THE MISTER*** is a roller-coaster ride of danger and desire that leaves the reader breathless to the very last page.

Available wherever books are sold.

Bloom books

READ MORE FROM

E L JAMES

Provocative Romance

THE FIFTY SHADES TRILOGY

Erotic, amusing, and deeply moving, the Fifty Shades trilogy is a tale that will *obsess you, possess you, and stay with you forever.*

Available wherever books are sold.

Bloom books

See the world of
FIFTY SHADES OF GREY anew
through the eyes of
CHRISTIAN GREY

A fresh perspective on the love story that has enthralled millions of readers around the world.

Collect the other books in the
Fifty Shades of Grey as Told by Christian trilogy

Available wherever books are sold.

Bloom books

See yourself
in
Bloom
every story is a
celebration.
Visit bloombooks.com
for more information about
E L JAMES
and more of your favorite authors!
bloombooks
@read_bloom
@read_bloom
read_bloom
Bloom books